The Random House Publishing Group

Ballantine Books · Del Rey · Modern Library · One World · Presidio Press · Random House · Random House Trade Paperbacks · Villard

D0028362

Kate Medina
EXECUTIVE VICE PRESIDENT
EXECUTIVE EDITORIAL DIRECTOR
ASSOCIATE PUBLISHER
RANDOM HOUSE

Dear Reader:,

David Ebershoff's *The 19th Wife* is a magnificent, spellbinding novel of literary suspense, set against the background of the history of the Mormon Church, and combining historical fiction with an enthralling modern mystery. When David Ebershoff was publishing director of the Modern Library, he heard about Ann Eliza Young, the nineteenth wife of Brigham Young, and he began to think: What would it be like to be someone's nineteenth wife? Or to be the child of a man's nineteenth wife? And so began this wonderful novel, in which Ebershoff explores polygamy, love, and the mysteries of faith, family, and history even as he tells us a can't-put-it-down fictional story. I hope you will read David Ebershoff's superb *The 19th Wife* and help us tell others about it.

Sincerely,

Kate Medina

1745 Broadway, New York, New York 10019 TEL: (212) 572-2812 FAX: (212) 572-4949 E-MAIL: kmedina@randomhouse.com

ALSO BY THE AUTHOR

Pasadena

The Rose City

The Danish Girl

THE
19TH
WIFE

THE
19TH
WIFE

A NOVEL

———

DAVID
EBERSHOFF

RANDOM HOUSE
NEW YORK

This is a work of historical fiction. Apart from the well-known actual people, events, and locales that figure in the narrative, all names, characters, places, and incidents are the products of the author's imagination or are used fictitiously. Any resemblance to current events or locales, or to living persons, is entirely coincidental.

Copyright © 2008 by David Ebershoff

All rights reserved.

Published in the United States by Random House, an imprint of The Random House Publishing Group, a division of Random House, Inc., New York.

RANDOM HOUSE and colophon are registered trademarks of Random House, Inc.

The illustration on page ███, based on the original by Stanley Fox, is copyright © 2008 by Catherine Hamilton and is used with her permission.

LIBRARY OF CONGRESS CATALOGING-IN-PUBLICATION DATA

Ebershoff, David.
The 19th wife : a novel / David Ebershoff.
p.   cm.
ISBN 978-1-4000-6397-0
1. Mormons—Fiction.   2. Utah—Fiction.   3. Young, Ann Eliza,
b. 1844—Fiction.   4. Polygamy—Utah—Fiction.
I. Title.   II. Nineteenth wife.
PS3555.B4824A615 2008
813'.54—dc22   2008000074

Printed in the United States of America on acid-free paper

www.atrandom.com

2 4 6 8 9 7 5 3 1

FIRST EDITION

Book design by Simon M. Sullivan

for my parents
DAVE *and* BECKY EBERSHOFF
and for
DAVID BROWNSTEIN

Faith is to believe what you do not see; the reward of this faith is to see what you believe.

—ST. AUGUSTINE

Like all the other arts, the Science of Deduction and Analysis is one which can only be acquired by long and patient study, nor is life long enough to allow any mortal to attain the highest possible perfection in it.

—ARTHUR CONAN DOYLE

And now, if there are faults they are the mistakes of men.
—The Book of Mormon, translated by JOSEPH SMITH, JUN.

CONTENTS

Contents

I

TWO WIVES

THE 19TH WIFE

PRESENTING,

ONE LADY'S ACCOUNT OF

Plural Marriage and Its Woes

AND,

A True History of Polygamy in America

FEATURING,

THE CHRONICLE OF PERSONAL EXPERIENCE

OF

ANN ELIZA YOUNG—

19TH AND REBEL WIFE OF THE

LEADER OF THE UTAH SAINTS AND

PROPHET OF THE MORMON CHURCH,

BRIGHAM YOUNG

WRITTEN BY HERSELF

WITH AN INTRODUCTION BY

MRS. HARRIET BEECHER STOWE

AND INCLUDING STEEL-PLATE ILLUSTRATIONS

EASTON & CO.

NEW YORK

1875

THE 19TH WIFE

PREFACE TO THE FIRST EDITION

In the one year since I renounced my Mormon faith, and set out to tell the nation the truth about American polygamy, many people have wondered why I ever agreed to become a plural wife. Everyone I meet, whether farmer, miner, railman, professor, cleric, or the long-faced Senator, and most especially the wives of these—everyone wants to know why I would submit to a marital practice so filled with subjugation and sorrow. When I tell them my father has five wives, and I was raised to believe plural marriage is the will of God, these sincere people often ask, *But Mrs. Young—how could you believe such a claim?*

Faith, I tell them, is a mystery, elusive to many, and never easy to explain.

Now, with the publication of this autobiography, my enemies will no doubt suspect my motives. Having survived attempts on both my life and character, however, I now stand unconcerned by their assaults. I have chosen to commit my memories to the page neither for fame, the trough from which I have drunk and would be happy never to return to, nor fortune, although it is true I am without home and have two small boys to care for. Simply, I wish to expose the tragic state of polygamy's women, who must live in a bondage not seen in this country since the abolishment of slavery a decade ago; and to reveal the lamentable situation of its children, lonely as they are.

I promise my Dear Reader I shall recount my story truthfully, even when it distresses me to do so. In these pages you will come to know my mother, who by religious duty welcomed four wives into her husband's bed. You will encounter the old woman forced to share her husband with a girl one-fifth her age. And you shall meet the gentleman with so many wives that when one approaches him on the street, he answers, "Madame, do I know you?"

I can, and will, go on.

Under what circumstances does such outrage thrive? The Territory of Utah, glorious as it may be, spiked by granite peaks and red jasper rocks, cut by echoing canyons and ravines, spread upon a wide basin of gamma grass and wandering streams, this land of blowing snow and sand, of iron, copper, and the great salten sea— Utah, whose scarlet-golden beauty marks the best of God's handiwork—the Territory of Utah stands defiant as a Theocracy within the borders of our beloved Democracy, *imperium in imperio.*

I write not for sensation, but for Truth. I leave judgment to the hearts of my good Readers everywhere. I am but one, yet to this day countless others lead lives even more destitute and enslaved than mine ever was. Perhaps my story is the exception because I escaped, at great risk, polygamy's conjugal chains; and that my husband is the Mormon Church's Prophet and Leader, Brigham Young, and I am his 19th, and final, wife.

Sincerely Yours,
ANN ELIZA YOUNG
Summer, 1874

WIFE #19:

A DESERT MYSTERY

By Jordan Scott

––––

PROLOGUE
Her Golden Boy

According to the *St. George Register,* on a clear night last June, at some time between eleven and half-past, my mom—who isn't anything like this—tiptoed down to the basement of the house I grew up in with a Golden Boy .22 in her hands. At the foot of the stairs she knocked on the door to my dad's den. From inside he called who is it? She answered me, BeckyLyn. He said—or must've said—come in. What happened next? Nearly everyone in southwest Utah can tell you. She needed one ace shot to blew his heart clean from his chest. The paper says he was in his computer chair, and from the way the blood splattered the drywall they're pretty sure the blast spun him three times around.

At the time of his death my dad was online playing Texas hold em and chatting with three people, including someone named DesertMissy. He spent the final seconds of his life in this exchange:

Manofthehouse2004: hang on
DesertMissy: phone?
Manofthehouse2004: no my wife
DesertMissy: which one?
Manofthehouse2004: #19

Sometime later—a few seconds? minutes?—DesertMissy wrote: u there??

Later she tried again: u there????

Eventually she gave up. They always do.

When my mom pulled the trigger my dad had a full house, three fives and a pair of ducks. He was all in. The paper says although dead he ended up winning seven grand.

I once heard someone on tv say we die as we lived. That sounds about right. After my dad was shot the blood seeped across his gunsandammo.com t-shirt in a heavy stain. He was sixty-seven, his face precancerously red. Everything about him was thick and worn from a life boiled by the sun. When I was a kid I used to dream he was a cowboy. I would imagine him out in the barn saddling his roan with the white socks, readying himself for a ride of justice. But my dad never rode anywhere for justice. He was a religious con man, a higher-up in a church of lies, the kind of schemer who goes around saying God meant for man to have many women and children and that they shall be judged on how they obey. I know people don't really talk like that, but he did and so do a lot of the men where I come from, which is—let's just say—way the fuck out in the desert. You might've heard of us. The First Latter-day Saints, but everyone knows us as the Firsts. I should tell you right off we weren't Mormons. We were something else—a cult, a cowboy theocracy, a little slice of Saudi America. We've been called everything. I know all that because I left six years ago. That was the last time I saw my dad. My mom too. I know you know this but just in case: she was wife #19.

His first wife was more than willing to put the rap on my mom. For someone who wasn't supposed to talk to nonbelievers, Sister Rita had no trouble telling the *Register* everything. "I was up in the keeping room with the girls' hose," she blabbed to the paper. "That's when I saw her come upstairs. She had one of those faces—it looked funny, all squished up and *red,* like she'd seen something. I thought about asking but I didn't, I don't know why. I found him about twenty minutes after that when I went down myself. I should've gone down the minute I saw that face of hers, but how was I supposed to know? When I saw him in his chair like that, with his head, you know, just hanging in his chest like that, and all that blood—it was everywhere, I mean all over him, everything so, so *wet*, and *red*—well I started calling, just calling out to anyone for help. That's when they came running down, all of them, the women I mean, one after the next, the kids too, they kept coming. The house shook, there were so many running down the stairs. The first to get there was Sister Sherry, I think. When I told her what happened, and then she saw for herself, she started crying, screaming really, and the next one, she started crying too, and then the next after her, and so on. I never heard anything like it. The shrieks spread up the line, like fire, catching and spreading, one after the next and pretty soon it seemed the whole house was on fire with screams, if you know what I mean. You see, we all loved him just the same."

The next morning the Lincoln County sheriff handcuffed my mom. "You'll have to come with me, Sister." I don't know who called him in, he usually didn't get out to Mesadale. There's a picture of her being guided into the backseat of the cruiser—the rope of her braid flat against her back as she ducks in. The paper says she didn't resist. Tell me about it. She didn't resist when her husband married her fifteen-year-old niece. She didn't resist when the Prophet told her to throw me out. "No point in making a fuss"— she used to say that all the time. For years she was obedient, believing it part of her salvation. Then one day I guess she went *pop!* That's how these things go, you hear about it all the time. Except because of the suppressor it was probably more like a *phump!* than a *pop!*

Did Sister Rita do her in? Actually, it was the chat session. The *Register* loved the irony: VICTIM NAMES HIS MURDERER BEFORE SHE PULLS THE TRIGGER. Technically he didn't name her, he numbered her. But really, Rita's statement didn't help either. It gave the sheriff enough. The next day my mom was booked and that picture was up on the *Register*'s home page, my mom sliding into the cruiser, her hair a heavy chain.

That's how I found out. I was at the library with my friend Roland. We were tooling around the web, checking out nothing in particular, then all of a sudden there it was, the story about my mom:

WIFE #19 KILLS HUSBAND

———

SIGN OF STRIFE IN RENEGADE SECT?

In the picture she's shackled at the wrists. Her forehead is white and glossy, reflecting a camera's flash in the dawn, and she has a look in her eyes. How to describe it? Should I say her eyes were dark and damp, the eyes of a small snouted animal? Or will you know what I mean if I say she had the scared-shitless look of a woman busted for murder and about to spend the rest of her life in the can?

II

———

WIFE #19

THE RED IN THE DESERT

WELCOME TO FLIPPIN' UTAH

———

Before I go any further there are a few things you should know. I'm twenty years old but a lot of people say I look younger. In the last six years I've lived almost everywhere between southern Utah and LA, five of them with Elektra. For two years we lived in and around Vegas out of a beat-up florist's van with a bunch of hydrangeas stenciled on the side. I still have the van but now Elektra and I live in Pasadena, in a studio apartment above a garage.

I probably should tell you a little something about Elektra, because she's the only reason I made it, given the circumstances. She's got rich brown hair that turns red in the sun, yellow-gold nearly electric eyes—you'd swear there were bulbs behind them—and the kind of long long legs that make people turn around and whistle. Roland likes to say she's got the legs of a supermodel, but that's just him. I found her in a parking lot off Industrial about a year after I was kicked out. Her snout was in a Taco Bell bag, which is pretty much what I was doing too. I don't know what she is exactly— some sort of hound/birddog mix with a few drops of pit. That gives her cred with some people but I'm not into things like that. All I care is she's my girl. For the record she came with that name tattooed to the underside of her left ear. It looks like this:

ELEKTRA
BITE ME!

If you want to know what I look like I should tell you what a customer once said: *You got a face like a fucking doll.* That old guy, as he was paying me fifty bucks, he said, *Kid, you got some fucking roses in your cheeks. I like that.* In addition to the roses, I've got a high kinda girlish voice I used to wish was lower but I don't bother worrying about anymore. A priest I once went to (mistake) said my eyes reminded him of the blue sea glass he found on the Jersey shore when he was a boy. I left before he could look into them any deeper. Someone else, a loser with a wife and twins, said they were like two little sapphires, little gemstones he said, then paid me to put my arm somewhere it should never go. But I don't do that anymore. Those were my lean & teen years. Now I make a living in construction, which I'm actually pretty good at. It's the only thing I can thank the Prophet for. I'm especially good at framing and roofing, which means I work outside a lot. Roland likes to say, "Another year in the sun, Jo-Jo, and you'll be old like the rest of us." He's the only person who calls me Jo-Jo. I don't know why he does it. My name's Jordan. Jordan Scott.

I'm telling you all this because people always get me wrong. I know what they see—hustler, twink, whatever. But I'm not some precious stone or some fucking doll. I'm just a guy who got totally screwed when he was fourteen and by all odds should be in jail or dead or both but actually is managing just fine. That's it. That's all you need to know.

Oh, and this: once I was at the library in line checking out a book on the history of God and this finger tapped me on the shoulder: "What is someone like *you* doing with a book like *that*?" That's how Roland and I met. We don't have much in common except we hang out at the library a lot. It's a nice library, the Pasadena Public, I've never seen them bother anyone who doesn't have a place to go. Once the librarian, Sue, once she even let Elektra into the children's room to meet the kids. She liked that—Elektra, I mean. But this story isn't about Sue and it's not about Roland or Elektra and it isn't even really about me. It's about my mom, and I guess my dad, and about this bullshit Prophet who I used to believe could speak to God. I know, can you believe it? Unfortunately it's all true.

I was at the library when I saw that picture on the *Register*'s home page. "Oh my God, Roland," I said. "That's my mom." He was too busy studying last month's *Vogue* to hear me. "Roland, look." I had to kick him to get his attention. "My mom."

"Who? What?" Then he looked up. "Oh my God. Your *mom*? Really? How'd she get on the home page?"

"It says she killed my dad."

"She *what*?" He leaned into the screen for a closer look and his eyebrows shot up. "Oh honey, you told me it was bad out there, but you didn't mention that awful braid." He said something about my mom's Little House on the Prairie dress, but I stopped listening. That picture—I can't explain it. I couldn't look away.

"Jo-Jo. . . . Jordan? You all right?"

"Where do you think they're taking her?"

"Well let's find out." Roland scooted over and began googling. "What's the name of the county out there in Utah?"

"Lincoln. Why?"

"Lincoln County . . . Utah . . . corrections . . ." He typed gently, as if protecting a manicure. "Uh-huh, this looks right. . . . OK, Jo-Jo, I think we're going to find her. Give it a sec." He clicked the mouse. "Yep, this is it: inmate inquiry. Her name?"

"BeckyLyn, capital B, capital L, no space."

He pursed his lips, like he'd seen something tacky. "All righty, let's see what we can find. Capital B"—click click click—"capital L. Scott, like the tissue. OK, just give it a second: There she is!"

And there she was, not her picture, but her name on a list of inmates:

BOOKING NO.	INMATE ID	LAST NAME	FIRST NAME
066001825	207334	Scott	BeckyLyn

He clicked her booking number and an hourglass turned on the screen. Then it came up: Inmate Information for BeckyLyn Scott. "Remember, Jordan, no one looks good in a mug shot. I'm speaking only from experience."

He was right. She was in a mustard jumpsuit, standing before a board that measured her height in inches (62) and centimeters (157). Her complexion was gray and cloudy. Her eyes pleaded from their sockets. "It's her," I said.

"Let's see her profile." Roland clicked the screen. Her right profile showed the hard tendons in her throat, her left revealed an ear as small as a shell. But it was the first shot that did me. That's how she looked the last time I saw her. Like she was in a trance.

"I don't want you to take this the wrong way," said Roland, "but I see a resemblance."

I hope you know what I'm talking about when I say every once in a while, not very often, we know exactly what we're supposed to do with our lives, even if we can't explain why. Where does that come from? I can't tell you that but the trick is to tune in for it, like scanning the radio for a favorite song.

"I'm going to Utah," I said.

You should've seen Roland's face: "You're going to Utah? *Now?*"

"She's my mom."

"I thought you said you'd never go back there."

"I need to see her."

"After what she did to you?"

Right before we looked at the *Register*'s home page, Roland had been checking out this diet website with a banner that kept flashing LATER IS NOW! So cheesy, I know, but I couldn't get it out of my head. It was Sunday afternoon, I just got paid, I had a lame job installing a vanity on Monday I could get out of, and Elektra was always up for a road trip. "Later is now," I said.

"Oh please, later is later. Besides, I thought we were going to celebrate your birthday."

"Next year."

"Jo-Jo, what's gotten into you?"

"Look at her—her eyes I mean. I need to see her. I'll be gone a day, two max."

"Sweetie, before you get in that van of yours and drive all the way to Utah, can I remind you of two small but highly relevant facts? One—and I'm sorry to put it like this—your mom dumped you on the highway in the middle of the night when you were—what?—fourteen. Not a nice thing. And two, she just popped off your dad. Are you really sure a family reunion's such a good idea?"

"I don't know, but I'm going." And then, "Want to come?"

"Oh no thanks, honey, I'm going to hell in my next life. I see no point in dropping in early."

Outside of Barstow I called the jail. Turns out there's a twenty-four-hour rule, so I couldn't see my mom until the next afternoon. I tried to talk the officer into a morning visit, but she cut me off: "It's not going to happen, all right?" She went over the rules, no interaction with other inmates, that sort of stuff, and how I couldn't bring anything into the jail except my clothes. "That means no jewelry, earrings, or body rings of *any* kind. If you weren't born with it, don't bring it."

"What about my dog?"

I don't know why I said that but it's a good thing I did, because by chance she was a dog person. She asked me what I had and I told her about Elektra. "Sounds like a beauty," she said, then went on to describe her own pair of corgis. "If you have any questions, you can call me back, I'll give you my direct. But I have to warn you: your mom has the right to refuse your visit but she doesn't have to give a reason. If that happens, I'll give you a ring."

I kept driving east on 15, looking at my phone to see if Officer Cunningham had called while I was out of signal. Somewhere past Vegas, Elektra became anxious, trembling and whimpering in my ear. I let her out to pee but that wasn't it. She's really good at picking up how I feel even before I know how I feel. She climbed into my lap and draped her head over my shoulder and I stroked her with one hand while steering with the other.

When I reached the Utah Welcome Center there was a message on my phone. I feared it might be Officer Cunningham, but it was

Roland checking in. "Honey, if it gets bad out there, promise me you'll come home."

The next day at the county jail I handed over my ID to Officer Cunningham. "Where's Elektra?"

Quick version of a long story: I met this goth girl at an internet café who agreed to watch her, and right about now she was probably eating cookies on a couch. I could tell the officer thought less of me for leaving my dog with a stranger, but it was 115 outside and around here you need to look hard for a scrap of shade.

Officer Cunningham passed me through the metal detector, punched something into her terminal, frowned, punched something else. "OK, here's the drill," she said. "Your mom's still on secure visits, which is never any fun. Go on through the door to the left, you're in the cubicle at the end. Officer Kane will bring her out in a few."

The cubicles looked like a row of phone booths, the kind you sit in. A small stool with a round red plastic seat. A yellow phone receiver mounted to the left partition. The room was pretty crowded, several women waving pacifiers and squeaky toys in a vain effort to keep their babies from exploding into tears. Visits were limited to two people but babies under one didn't count. It seemed everyone had brought as many infants as they could carry. A sign on the wall said, MOTHERS: KEEP YOUR CHILDREN UNDER CONTROL! As if.

I waited on my stool, staring through the thick glass screen. In my reflection I saw the red patches in my cheek. My eyes looked small and dark—my mom's eyes, anyone could see that.

After I was kicked out (they call it excommunicated, but whatever), I honestly thought I'd never see her again, and I have to say I didn't really care. I was mad, starting with God, then the Prophet, but my mom was next up on the list. I'm still mad at him—God I mean—because my mom tossed me on the highway at two a.m. in his name. Trust me: that can mess you up. Instead of bawling about

it, I vowed never to think about any of them again. You have to remember I was fourteen. I'd never left Mesadale. I knew jack about
the world. In my backpack I had a sweatshirt, some sacred underwear (don't ask), and seventeen bucks. In my pockets: nada. In all
fairness my mom took a risk slipping me the money, but it didn't
feel like much at the time. I was real lucky that trucker hauling
bedding picked me up after about an hour. He could've wanted a
blow job or something, but really all he wanted was to talk about
his wife. She had recently died in a fire and he couldn't keep the
memories to himself. I rode with him to St. George. Together we
watched the sunrise behind us in the sideviews. You ever see the
sun come up over the Utah desert? Imagine the coals of hell burning in the clouds. "Man, check that out," the driver said at one
point. "It's like God took a torch to the whole fucking sky."

On the other side of the glass, a corrections officer escorted my
mom to the stool. Our eyes met, and it was like following your gaze
in a mirror. Wherever I looked she looked. At the stool, at the wall
clock, at the phone.

    She looked more or less the same—the tough jaw, the small
snout of a nose—but they'd cut her hair into a dense ugly shrub. I'd
never seen her with a haircut. She could tell I was staring at it because she touched it, as if she were wearing a wig about to slip off.
What else can I tell you about her? She was fourteen when she
married my dad, which means she's now thirty-five. Her voice is
small and girlish, kinda like mine. She has those same roses in her
cheeks. What else? For the record, she's my dad's niece *and* his first
cousin. Which makes me . . . oh, you figure it out.

    "Jordan? Can you hear me?"

    "Yes."

    "My goodness, look at you: you're all grown up."

    "I heard about Dad."

    "It's a tragedy."

"It sounds like a mess."

"I knew you'd come to see me. I've been praying for it."

"Mom. Don't take this the wrong way, but that's not why I'm here."

"Yes, Jordan. Yes, it is." She was leaning in very close to the glass, her face done up in the pink and blue of irrational excitement.

"Look, Mom, can you tell me how this happened?"

She sat back, the color wiped from her face. "I have no idea."

In the next cubicle a baby was gagging on sobs and tears. The baby's mom or aunt or whoever kept saying it's all right, everything's going to be all right—which in this case was a total lie.

"Was it how Sister Rita described it?"

"Why, what'd she say?"

As I recapped Rita's statement, my mom's eyes filled with tears. "It wasn't like that," she said.

"Then what happened?"

She hesitated, as if gathering up the memory. "You've never seen so much blood. I saw them take him out on the stretcher. That's when I knew—" But a sob got the better of her, and she couldn't finish the thought. "Jordan, I know everything's been hard on you. Us saying good-bye like that. And now you seeing me like this. I never thought it would be like this. I always thought, well, I just thought—" Her voice cut off and she pressed her eyes with the heels of her hands.

When she calmed herself down she said, "Tell me what you've been doing all this time, where you've been, where you live. Are you married? Maybe you're a father yourself? I want to know if your life's at all like I imagined."

Call me crazy, but it seems if you throw out your son because some con man Prophet told you to, well, it just seems to me you really don't have a right to know what comes after. "It's a long story," I said. "I live in California and everything's fine."

"Are you on your own?"

I told her about Elektra, and that seemed to brighten her up.

"But Mom, that's not why I'm here. Can you tell me what's going on?"

"All I know is there was some sort of hearing this morning. It only lasted a few minutes. I told Mr. Heber—"

"Who's Mr. Heber?"

"The lawyer they gave me. I told him I wanted to speak to the judge, but he said it wasn't the right time, just tell him your name. They were talking about bail, the judge didn't want to set any and Mr. Heber said that wasn't fair and he won, but it doesn't matter. Where am I going to come up with a million dollars? Then they brought me back here."

"At least you're out of Mesadale."

She switched the receiver from her left ear to her right. "It was your birthday yesterday, wasn't it? I kept thinking of you all day. Isn't it amazing how God works? I was thinking of you and you were thinking of me."

You know what, maybe Roland was right: I shouldn't be here. Maybe later was later. Maybe later was never. If I left now, I could be back in Pasadena before midnight. He and I could meet for a late night coffee and a doughnut at Winchell's.

"Remember how you used to love the birthday parties?" she went on. "I can picture you when you were just a little guy, waiting in line with a paper plate for a slice of cake. You were always such a good boy, Jordan, always so patient and good."

"To be perfectly honest, those are some of the worst memories of my life."

"What? Why?"

"Those parties were for the Prophet."

"I know, but that's what made it so much fun."

"Fun? Mom, they made us celebrate our birthdays on his. You realize how screwed up that is?"

"I don't know, I think it's nice, everyone celebrating together like that."

I caught myself. "OK, Mom, let's not do this."

"Do what?"

"Go over the past."

"I'm sorry, I didn't mean to upset you."

"Look, Mom, before I go, is there anything I can get you?"

"You're going?"

"It's a long drive home."

"Jordan, you can't go now. I need your help."

"What kind of help?"

"I need you to talk to Mr. Heber."

"About what?"

"About when I can get out of here."

"You should probably do that yourself."

"I did. And he said he couldn't say, which is unacceptable as far as I'm concerned."

You know how when you're away from your mom you miss her, and the minute you see her she starts driving you crazy? Multiply that feeling by a million.

"Mom, why now?"

"Why now what?"

"I mean after all this time? Something must've happened. You always seemed so sure of everything. When you said good-bye to me that night, you told me you had to do whatever God said."

"That's right. Of course I didn't want to leave you like that, I told you that. But I knew it was God testing me. That's what the Prophet said: BeckyLyn, this is your test, your test from God. It's not that I didn't love you, it's just what God wanted for you, and for me. I thought you'd understand that."

"You know what I understand: it's all bullshit. Everything about that place, starting with God, then the Prophet, then Dad. So when I read what happened with Dad, what you did, I was like thank God, she's finally woken up."

"What I *did*? Wait a minute . . . Do you honestly think—do you really believe I killed your father? Oh Jordan, no. No no no no no. How could you believe such a thing?"

"How could I believe such a thing? Mom, you're in jail."

"I can understand the authorities getting it wrong, but *you?*"

"Sister Rita spelled it out pretty clearly."

"Sister Rita?" She balled up her fist. "Just so you know: I did not kill your father. He was my husband. I was his wife. Why in heaven's name would I kill him?"

I could think of a million reasons. It hadn't crossed my mind that she was innocent.

"On the Prophet's life, I did not kill your father."

It's a little weird to admit but I was disappointed by her denial. And I didn't believe her, not for a second. "Then who did?"

"I don't know. One of the wives. But it wasn't me."

"What'd your lawyer say?"

"I don't think he believes me. He said he had to review a lot of evidence before he could come up with a strategy. I told him, I didn't do it, that's your strategy. I keep telling myself this isn't happening." She said that again: "This isn't happening." She dropped her forehead into her hand to bolster herself, then looked up. "Oh Jordan, isn't it wonderful, you being here, coming here like this."

"I guess."

"It's a miracle."

"Mom."

"I prayed to our heavenly father to bring you to me and he did."

Here we go again. "I seriously doubt that."

"Jordan, don't you see? There was a reason he made me send you away. So you could come back to help me when I needed you. We couldn't know it at the time, but now I understand. Look: there you were in California leading I'm sure a real busy life, and you happen to read about me on the, on the, is it the web or is it the net, because I've heard people call it both?"

"The web. The net. It doesn't matter."

"OK, the web. And something *told* you to come help me. Don't you see: if you were still in Mesadale you wouldn't be able to help me. It was God's plan all along. If that isn't proof, then I don't know what is."

"I'm not even going to respond to that."

"Then tell me: why were you looking up the local paper on that day of all days?"

"I don't know, every once in a while I read it online, just to see what's going on out here, but every time I do I get depressed."

"See!" She pressed her fingers against the glass, the tips going flat and white. "God told you to read the web yesterday. If it hadn't been for God—"

"Jesus, Mom, cut the God crap. That's not why I was online, I spend like half my life online. When are you going to be free of all of this?"

"Free?"

"Mom, I'm sorry, I just don't believe any of that." My throat was clamping up. "Not any more." I set down the receiver and wiped my eyes. Goddammit, I wasn't supposed to crack up. That night, years ago, when the trucker dropped me off, I promised myself I would never cry again over any of it. And I didn't, not once, until now. Now my eyes were wet and there weren't any tissues in here, there wasn't anything in this place, just a red plastic stool and a yellow plastic phone and a wall of glass and a dozen crying babies. Fuck me.

"I should be going."

"Jordan, no. I need your help."

I took a second to think about what that might mean. "I'll see if I can make an appointment with your lawyer." Then I hung up. Through the glass I saw her mouth, *One more thing.* I picked up the receiver. "Yeah?"

"I'm very sorry for doing that. I didn't have a choice. I only hope you can understand that now."

"You don't need to say anything else."

"You need to know it's the only reason I would've done that to you."

"Mom, look, fine. It was a long time ago."

"I like to think you could hear my prayers. I guess you don't like talking about things like that anymore, but it's true. The only way I could sleep at night was knowing you could hear me pray for you." Her mouth darkened and puckered and she set down the receiver to cry. The officer behind her offered a packet of tissues. I could see my mom say thanks and Officer Kane say no problem, you take your time. She was on the heavy side, her uniform tight on her thighs, and was about as threatening as the senior citizen who greets you at Wal-Mart.

My mom picked up the phone again. "You'll help me, right? I know you'll help me."

I told her I'd see what I could do. She nodded. Then we hung up. For a while I didn't move and she didn't move, except for her hands, they trembled on the counter. Then they settled down, lying there small and white behind the glass, like a tiny pair of unclaimed gloves.

THE 19TH WIFE

AN INTRODUCTORY ESSAY

MRS. HARRIET BEECHER STOWE

When I first heard of the enslaved state of the women of Utah, I, like many Americans, questioned the veracity of these tales. Surely the profane stories, the recollections of abuse and neglect, and the rage of the apostates speaking out against their Church and its leaders were exaggerations; or at least aberrations from the norm. In my years, I have met and corresponded with several members of the Church of Jesus Christ of Latter-day Saints, or Mormons—for many have stood forthright and firm in their opposition to slavery. My Mormon friends have impressed me as straightforward and sincere, rational and informed, a people who value education and industry as much as religious duty. Their greatest passion, it seemed, was their desire to pursue their religion in liberty. In my mind, the tales of conjugal debasement could not be reconciled with the Saints I knew, both by face and in the letter. The enmity the Mormons have engendered among so many, it seemed to me, came from a general ignorance of their customs, and a public fear of their private rites. I, for one, have long felt that we, as Americans, should let the Mormons practice their faith in peace.

Yet for some time now the stories have continued to blow forth from that desert region, like the livid Sirocco, from one plural wife after the next, and many gentlemen too, each reinforcing a prevailing impression of marital bondage for so many women of Deseret. Was it possible some of these stories were true?

I first encountered Mrs. Brigham Young in February of this year, 1874, when she lectured at Boston's Tremont Temple. Her simple presentation, and her natural appeal, convinced me that she had little to gain, and much to suffer, by speaking of polygamy so frankly. It became clear that she would have much preferred a private life with her sons to the one she was leading as crusader, informer, and, now with this volume, author. Her life as a daughter of polygamy, and a wife of polygamy, had exposed her to many variations of this cruel institution, and she felt compelled to reveal it for what it was. It was also clear to me that she had no choice in the matter. Her opposition to polygamy had become her new faith, its abolition her salvation.

By the conclusion of our first meeting, and now upon reading her memoirs, I have become convinced that polygamy must meet the same final defeat slavery met a decade ago. Both are relics of barbarism. We were right to conquer slavery first, but now with its eradication, we must set our sights on its twin. Many people call this the Mormon Question, just as, for many years, slavery was called the Southern Question. In fact it is a question concerning all of us, as a nation and a people. Our response to the moral and spiritual enslavement of Utah's women and children will define us in the years to come. Should you possess any doubts about the true debasement of the plural wife, or her child, I recommend the story that follows herein.

—Hartford, September 1874

THE CHURCH, YOUR DAD, THE HOUSE, THE WIVES

I found Mr. Heber's name on a door between a dermatologist and a podiatrist. Inside I discovered a blue blur bustling around watering the ferns. "You must be Jordan. I'm Maureen. Mr. Heber's a little backlogged this afternoon—you have no idea what our afternoons are like when he's been in court—but I know he's really glad you called." Then she stopped. "Wait a minute! Who. Is. This?"

"Elektra. I hope you don't mind. It's too hot to leave her in the van."

"Of course it is!" She squatted with the agility of a gymnast to kiss Elektra.

My first impression of Maureen was Mormon Grandma. This was not an especially fond thought. It's not that I actively dislike Mormons, it's just that they actively dislike me. Maureen was tall and sturdy, definitely some pioneer stock in her big-boneness. She wore her hair up in an airy mass of curls, the effect of a once-a-week beauty parlor visit. Her outfit was all royal blue, slacks, matching blouse, and a cape of a sweater buttoned at the throat.

"Mr. Heber shouldn't be long, he's just finishing a call, I'll let you know the minute he gets off." She hurried back to her desk while I flipped through a copy of *Ensign*. It took about a second to find the article on, and I'm quoting here, defeating same-gender attraction. Eye roll, please. I swapped the magazine for *Us Weekly*. While I read about Hollywood bumps, Maureen typed up five letters, took seven messages, and worked her way to the bottom of a to-file basket. "Oh me," she said a bit wearily. Then a light on the phone console went out and she started back up again. "Ooops, he's off. Come on, let's get in there before he gets back on."

As she led me down a corridor, I said her hair looked nice. "Thank you! Just got it set this morning." From her smile I could tell it'd been a while since anyone had paid her a compliment. Roland says every woman needs a gay guy in her life: "Honey, we're the only ones who bother to notice a perm."

At the end of the hall Maureen hipped open an office door. "Here we are."

I know it's not fair, but my first impression of Mr. Heber was Mormon Asshole. His first impression of me probably was Beyond Redemption, so we were even. He was about seventy-five, a drift of snowy hair, and watery, untrustable eyes. On the wall several pictures showed him teeing off on golf courses around the world.

"Jordan Scott, it's a pleasure. I can't tell you how pleased I was when you called. Surprised, yes, but pleased even so." I apologized for bringing Elektra into his office. "Too hot to leave her in the car. Believe me, I understand. My wife won't leave our Yorkie in the wagon for five minutes. Now, Jordan, first I want to tell you how sorry I am about your mom. And your dad. And all of this. If there's ever anything I can do—for you, I mean—I hope you'll let me know." I'm going to spare you my mental commentary that was sidebarring this conversation, but you can probably guess I was liking this guy less and less.

"Can you tell me what's going to happen to my mom?" I said.

"My goodness, straight to business, a man after my own heart. All righty, have a seat. Now I understand you were just out at the jail. Tell me, how'd you find her?"

"Pretty upset. And confused. She doesn't seem to understand what's going on."

"I'm doing my best to figure that out myself."

"Did the paper get the story right?"

"As far as I can tell. Here, look at this, it just came in." He waved a file folder. "It's the ballistics report. Her latent prints showed up on the Golden Boy. They found others, but they found a lot of hers."

"In other words, she's in deep shit."

"Your words, not mine. But yes." He came around from behind the desk to sit on the corner near me. "It's pretty screwed up out there in Mesadale, isn't it?"

"Look, Mr. Heber, I don't really feel like going into all that. Just tell me what's going to happen to her. And you don't need to sugarcoat it. She and I—we're not very close."

"I got that impression. I understand you left a while back. A lost boy, is that right?"

I hate that name, but that's what they call us, the boys the Prophet kicks out. "Yeah, something like that."

"I'm sure these past few years haven't been easy."

"Yeah, they pretty much sucked, but you know what, things are fine now."

"Do you mind telling me what happened? When you were excommunicated?"

"I don't really know what that has to do with my mom being in jail."

"I understand if it's hard to talk about."

"It's not hard, it's just it doesn't seem to be relevant to why I'm here."

Mr. Heber squeezed my knee. "Jordan, we're on the same team here, OK? We're going to have to trust each other. Eventually this will come up. A prosecutor's going to ask if your mom could leave you like that, when you were just a boy, then perhaps she's also capable of killing your dad."

"It's a lot more complicated than that."

"I'm sure it is."

And that's how Mr. Heber got me to tell him the story of my mom dragging me out of bed and driving me down the highway and telling me to get out. "The Prophet made her do it."

"Your dad didn't try to stop her?"

"My dad. He was probably in the basement getting high."

"What prompted this?"

"It was pretty lame." I couldn't believe I was telling Heber all this—I almost never talk about it—but there I went. "I was holding hands with one of my stepsisters, this girl named Queenie. That wasn't her real name, but that's what I called her. We weren't doing anything, but out there boys and girls aren't supposed to hang out like that. We were just talking one day and I don't know why, I just took her hand. My dad saw us and he reported it to the Prophet. And that was it. I mean it's true, yeah, my mom left me there and everything, but in Mesadale they tell you all this stuff, like you'll go to hell if you don't do what the Prophet wants. And they believe it, *she* believes it. Fuck—excuse me—frick, I used to believe it. So one night, boom, she dumps me on the road, fast-forward six years, and here I am."

Mr. Heber and Maureen were silent. It's hard to know what to say after you hear a story like that. Then they figured it out. They both said how sorry they were. That's what people always say, *Gee, I'm awfully sorry.* I hate that. Look at Heber and Maureen: their eyes were full of the one thing I didn't want. How did this turn into a pity party?

"Just your regular run-of-the-mill polygamist boo-hoo tragedy," I said. Most people assume I was kicked out because I was gay. But I was fourteen, a late bloomer. I didn't know what gay was. Roland likes to read the columns in the women's magazines. He says I was holding Queenie's hand for reverse psychology reasons. I don't think so. I took her hand because she was my friend and I felt alone.

"Listen, the only reason I'm here is to find out what's going to happen to my mom. She's on her own and she needs someone to explain to her the truth. So go ahead and tell me what she's looking at. It's life, isn't it? Maybe a little less with parole?"

Mr. Heber said nothing.

"OK, no parole."

Still silent.

"If that's it, tell me. I can handle it. I'm really not surprised. I don't know, maybe it's what she deserves."

"I like you, Jordan. You're honest and you know a fact is a fact. I can tell you really want the truth—not all people do, you know. They say they do, but when it comes down to it, they don't. That's why I'm going to tell you everything I know. I'm afraid things don't look good for your mother. I'm very concerned she'll be found guilty." He hesitated, but only for a second. "And face execution."

"Execution?"

"I wish I could be more optimistic. But my job is to be realistic."

"You're sure?"

"I'm rarely sure."

Mr. Heber returned to the other side of his desk. "I'm hoping to get her trial pushed out a bit. Give us some time to figure out what's really going on out there. She didn't kill him in a vacuum—that's the only thing I do know for sure. This wasn't a simple domestic dispute. I want to put the crime into some context. And meanwhile maybe the feds will finally get off their rear ends and do something about that so-called Prophet. As far as I'm concerned, it's that cult that should be put on trial, not your mom. And that's why I'm really glad you called. I could use your help."

"Me?"

"I'd like you to tell me everything you know about Mesadale, walk me through what it's like out there, what life was like for you, and the Prophet, what's he like, the church, your dad, the house, the wives, everything about the Firsts you can tell me."

"I haven't been there in six years."

"You know a lot more than I do."

I guess I could do that. It might help tweezer out the splinter of guilt I'd been feeling since I left my mom behind that slab of glass. "OK, so what do you want to know?"

"Whatever you think is most important. But I'm afraid not right now."

"Not right now?"

"I want to do this carefully, sit down, go over everything, make sure we cover all the bases. Maureen's going to take you back to her desk and find a few hours when we can really talk." He fished a gold-plated golf tee out of a tray and began rolling it around his palm.

"Are you kidding me?" Elektra stood up and shook out her ears. She needed to pee.

"I wish I had more time today, but I didn't know you were in town until a half hour ago. Maureen, take him up front and arrange something, all right? Squeeze him in as soon as possible."

In a flash she was on her feet. "Come on, let's have a look at the old calendar."

"Wait a minute," I said. "I can't just hang in St. George forever. I've got a job in California. A good job"—lie—"and an apartment. We're living out of the back of my van."

Elektra yawned, as if she'd heard it before. Maureen stood in the open door. Mr. Heber flipped some pages on a legal pad. This meeting was so over. "Jordan, you're going to have to trust me. We both want the same thing."

Just one problem: I've never been too good in the trust department.

HELL HATH NO FURY

The news out of Salt Lake's seraglio has caught even our attention. At last Mrs. Young—or should we say, *a* Mrs. Young—has told her husband enough is enough. This one—Number 19, if the numbers can be believed—has filed suit against the Prophet, Supreme Leader, etc. etc. of the Saints. All we can say is: It's about time. While husband and wife ensnare one another in accusation and counter-accusation, we would like to add two observations to the fracas. One, Brigham Young is a Confidence Man in the grand tradition of the hoodwinkers of the West. A message from Heaven has told him he should possess 19 wives? A message from Heaven has told us we should possess a finer house, a larger income, and at least one day each year free from this esteemed publication, but those minor miracles have yet to transpire. As for Mrs. Young, Number 19, we most respectfully inquire: What did she expect? At the gate of the slaughterhouse, even the squealing pig understands his fate. Could she not smell the blood in the air? Under some Divine plan, it seems Destiny intended these two noble creatures to be united in either matrimony or warfare, if there is a difference. As the battle begins, we shall mount our hill with somber hearts to watch out over the carnage.

THE BIG HOUSE

———

That night I couldn't sleep. Same with Elektra. She kept shifting on the futon and growling at every sound at the Welcome Center—car doors, motorcycles, eighteen-wheelers gasping in their sleep. At one point a t-ball team dashed from a minivan for the men's room, calling one another pussy and dick. It was one of those nights when I never really shut my eyes.

Around four I started driving. Elektra sat alert in the passenger seat, the fur buckled on her brow. It was like she understood where we were going and didn't think it was a good idea.

Outside St. George, past the oxy-cotton dens of Hurricane, there's a long county highway to nowhere. It rises up, crossing an empty desert plateau. Out in the distance are the red mesas and the stony mountains and the stands of piñon. On the road there's nothing for fifty miles except a gas station, a lunch counter, and a wire cross marking the site of a fatal crash. If you keep going, eventually you'll hit the turnoff for Mesadale. Theoretically this highway leads to Kanab, then the Grand Canyon, but there are better routes to both, and there really isn't any reason to drive down this highway unless you're headed to Mesadale or you're lost. It's got to be the loneliest road in America. Somewhere along here my mom dumped me. I remember there was a dead cottonwood beside the road. I remember wishing it would come to life and hold me in its limbs.

Ten miles before Mesadale I pulled over. With the engine off, everything was quiet, just a few early birds rustling in the sagebrush. After fifteen minutes a semi came along. I could hear it before I saw it, its thunder mounting, consuming the desert. When it passed, the van shook and Elektra barked once. The roar subsided and after a long time everything was silent again and the truck's taillights were lost to the night.

Finally there was pink in the eastern sky and I let Elektra out to pee. She ran twenty feet into the desert and started barking at a bitterbrush. Probably a jackrabbit or gila monster. I called her back to the van but she ignored me and I had to drag her in.

I was parked by the sign telling you how far to Mesadale, but buckshot had chewed it up so bad you couldn't read it. Every time the sign went up the Prophet sent out an apostle to shoot it up. My dad did that once. I remember him boasting about it at breakfast. "Took out Satan's marker," he said, stuffing his mouth with fried ham.

I should probably make it clear why the Firsts aren't Mormon. Not like the Mormons you see on tv singing in the Tabernacle or cheering at a BYU game or the hottie missionaries chatting up strangers on the street. The guys who run the Mormon Church— those old dudes in out-of-date eyeglasses up in Salt Lake—they hate the Prophet almost as much as I do. They call him a heretic, a blasphemer, and a whole bunch of other things like rapist, pedophile, and tax cheat. The point of contention between the Firsts and the Mormons—you probably figured this out—is polygamy. The Prophet says when the Mormon Church gave it up in 1890, they sold out. That's when the Firsts broke away. It's why the Prophet—our Prophet, I mean—used to always say on Sundays, Brothers and Sisters, *you* are the first and true Saints. You are the descendants of Joseph and Brigham. You will be first in line when Judgment comes and man hopes to be saved.

As you can imagine, the Mormons have another opinion on that. Can you spell rift? That book I was reading, the one about the history of God, it says this sort of split happens all the time. The Jews and the Christians. The Catholics and the Protestants. The Mormons and the Firsts. It's been going on forever and the only thing I know for sure is it messes up a lot of shit for the rest of us.

Over in the foothills I could see Mesadale waking up to the dawn. From here it was a cluster of white and yellow lights beneath the mountain. I knew exactly what was going on at each of those lights. I knew it the way you know a dvd you've watched a hundred times. A sister wife was flicking on a lamp to brush out her hair. Another was striking a match to light the stove. A third wife was pulling the string on the pantry bulb, hauling out a giant box of corn mush. Ten, fifteen, twenty more lights in a house—each was a sister wife rising to perform her chores.

And the kids. About now the kids would be climbing out of bed, rubbing the sand from their eyes. They'd be forming a line at the sink to wash. The boys would be searching the boxes for a shirt. The girls would be helping one another pin up their hair. You don't talk much at that hour. You just want to dress fast so you can get to the kitchen in time for your plop of mush. Sometimes there was toast and canned peaches, but not always. Whatever there was, there was never enough. Only a fool would waste time taking a piss before getting something to eat.

As I drove closer I could see Mesadale had grown. There were a few hundred houses now, warehouses for a family of seventy-five. No one knows how many people live out there but I'm going to guess twelve thousand, maybe fifteen. Counting is complicated. The numbers are part of the mystery. The less you know, the less you know.

The turnoff is hidden behind a stand of cottonwoods. It looks like a dry river wash, and even if you're looking for it, it's hard to spot. No one stumbles across Mesadale and that's the point. Roland likes to call the Firsts the Greta Garbo of cults. "Oh honey, that Prophet of yours, he just wants to be left alone."

As I left the asphalt, the van began to rattle. Elektra sat up and growled. No matter how slowly you drive, the road kicks up a cloud of red dust that can be seen from almost anywhere in town. The journalists who sometimes snoop around don't realize it alerts the Prophet's militia. I'm totally serious. You'll see.

About halfway up the road I passed a pickup headed out. Five wives squeezed into the cab, four across and one perched awkwardly in a lap. They were older, probably barren, which was why the Prophet would let them leave town like this. He never lets the girls out, but women like these, he didn't care. They stared ahead, their eyes vacant. They looked familiar. It was perfectly possible they were my aunts, cousins, or half-sisters, or all three. Elektra shoved her head out the window to bark at them, which is her way of being friendly. The women remained expressionless. It was as if they didn't see me and we were passing in two parallel worlds.

A couple of miles up the road you see the first houses. Eight, ten, twelve thousand square feet. Often two or three side by side in a compound. They're not mansions, more like barracks or barns, built cheaply from plywood, plastic sheeting, tar paper, aluminum, and sheetrock. Many are unfinished—an exposed side wall, a wing with a plastic roof, a front door made from pressed wood. When I was a kid my dad told me he couldn't afford proper siding for our house. That made me feel sad for him—I sensed the shame in his voice. But that wasn't the reason. It was to avoid property taxes. Some loophole I never understood.

One thing was different since I left: a lot of houses were now surrounded by walls. Or instead of a wall, a ring of trailers, circled like pioneer wagons. I guess the Prophet was getting paranoid. Of what, exactly? It's not like the government hasn't had a hundred years to shut this place down.

I turned on Field Avenue and halfway down there it was, our place—three houses and a couple of outbuildings on five acres of useless scrubby land. From the street it looked like nothing had changed. The dozen picnic tables where the kids ate except on the coldest days. The laundry lines with fifty little shirts flapping in the wind. The vegetable garden, the barnyard, the cornfield—all of it parched and pathetic. The property backed up to scrub and when I was little that's where I'd hide when I wanted to be alone. The main house was a large rectangle of plywood stained dark green. Twenty bedrooms, a vast kitchen with pots the size of oil drums, and my dad's basement. The kids weren't allowed down there, just the wives, one after the next, each getting her piece. You know what's weird? A week earlier and he would've been down there right now, doing who knows what nasty shit online.

Here's something: I have no idea how many brothers and sisters I have. There isn't a good way to count. There's full, half, step, and foster. Who goes into the tally and who doesn't? I'd like to tell you I loved each of my siblings, but that's pretty much impossible. And what about the ones you've never met—the children a sister wife left behind somewhere to marry your dad? Do you count them? Oh, and your sister who's now married and no longer allowed to talk to you because you're a guy and she's a girl and around here brothers and sisters do it all the time? Do you count her? And what about me—I've been gone six years, the Prophet told everyone I was banished to the bleak pits of damnation. Do they count me? I wouldn't. I'm going to guess I have a hundred siblings, maybe one-ten. That's about as accurate as I can be. My dad used to say he never went to bed at night without thanking God for his children. And the crazy part is: I believed him.

Mind if I tell you some more? We slept in triple-decker bunks; or five to a bed, head to foot; or on the couch, four boys elbowing over three cushions; or on the living room floor, on blankets and pillows, twenty kids laid down like tiles. Shirts and sweaters in plastic garbage bins labeled by size. Shoes handed down. Tennis balls and kickballs stolen from one kid to the next. The only thing in that house that was all my own, that I never had to share with anyone, was a drawer in a dresser, twelve inches wide by fifteen inches deep. I measured it a million times. If you're bad at math, that's 1.25 square feet, which was really more than I needed because I didn't have anything to keep inside.

Saturdays were washing days: a pair of sister wives would fill a zinc tub with cold water, throw two boys in at a time, scrub their backsides with a brush on a stick, then fling them out. They changed the water every tenth boy. It would take all morning. But at least I wasn't a girl. The girls used the bathroom according to a schedule that kept the plumbing on this side of chaos. On Saturdays they washed their hair in special sinks. The Prophet didn't let them cut it, he said they'd need it when they got to heaven to wash their husbands' feet. Some of the girls got nosebleeds from the weight of all that hair. A few complained about it hurting their backs or getting headaches, but most said nothing, at least not to me. When the girls washed their hair it sounded like a mop in a bucket. You can imagine the clogs in the drain. It took hours to dry—they'd lie on the picnic tables and spread their hair out around them. I loved to watch them from the window in my mom's room. The girls looked beautiful like that, their clean hair fanned out like angels' wings.

Roland once asked if there was anything good about growing up in Mesadale, if I had one fond memory among all the bad. "One thing's for sure," I said. "You're never alone."

I stood outside the house, looking up at my mom's window. A roller shade was drawn halfway but I could see the aloe plant she grew on the sill. She used to break open its leaves and massage the clear liquid into her hands and throat. Sometimes I'd sit on her bed and watch her while I told her about school. Sometimes she'd squeeze a drop from the broken leaf into my palm and I'd stay with her until it was gone.

I saw someone in my mom's window, a dark shape pulling down the shade. They were all in the house, everyone, my brothers and sisters and all the wives, but I guess no one was coming out to say hello. Then Virginia shot out from the barn, running right for me and rolling over at my feet. She was thin and hot under her thick coat. A belly rub was all it took to make her love me.

That's when someone said, "What do you want?"

I looked up. It was Sister Rita. "I don't know if you remember me," I said.

"I remember you. You shouldn't be here."

To be perfectly honest, Rita was never one of my favorites. She used her position as first wife to boss everyone around. You can't marry a new wife without the first wife's permission. So every time my dad wanted a fresh bride he went groveling back to Rita. I don't even want to think about what he had to do to get her to say yes.

"I'd like to see my mom's room."

"No."

"Please. Just for a few minutes."

"No. God sent you away. The Prophet revealed it. I can't go against his will."

I know it's hard to believe people really talk like that, but consider this: if you didn't know anything else, if your only source of information was the Prophet, if you spent seven hours in church on Sunday listening to a man who claimed to have a direct line to God, who your father and mother swore was a Prophet, and your brothers and sisters, and your teachers, and your friends, and everyone else too assured you, promised you, his word was the word of God, and those that he damned were damned for all of eternity, you'd probably believe it too. You wouldn't know how to form a doubt. The Prophet told us all sorts of shit and we believed it, all of it, just ate it up.

Like once he told us that Europe had been destroyed in a battle of good and evil. He said it didn't exist anymore. France—no longer on the map. He described the fires of Paris, the bodies in the Seine, the cathedrals reduced to rubble, the wolves that had returned to the Champs-Élysées. I had no reason—no ability—to doubt any of it. Everyone around me said it was true. We didn't have tv, there was no internet when I was a kid, everything we knew came from the Prophet. The first time I met a Frenchman in Vegas, I was shocked. I actually said, "How did you survive?" That's the level of brainwashing I'm talking about. When I first told Roland all this, he said, "Oh honey, you've *got* to be kidding? You should go on *Oprah* or something." But I'm not kidding.

"I'm sorry about my dad," I said. "I'm sure this is really difficult for you."

"Go on, the Prophet doesn't want you here. You're scaring the kids. Turn around and go." The windows had started to fill with little kids, eight or ten faces coming to look down at the stranger in the yard. Did any recognize me? Did any wonder how I fit into all the lies? I imagined one child, at least one, whispering, *Take me with you.* I imagined a tiny finger tapping on the glass.

Rita was now standing before me. I could smell the summer peaches on her breath. I'll try to be nice, but let's just say she was the complete opposite of sexy in her prairie dress and drooping hair bun. The sun had puckered her skin into a gray hide and the grim line of her mouth suggested she hadn't had a good laugh, or fuck, in fifty years.

"Jordan, my duty is to protect them. You know that. Now please go."

"Protect them from what?"

"Please. Before I have to call the police."

The Mesadale police. You don't want to run into them. I said good-bye to Rita and Virginia and walked back to the van. Before I got in I looked back to the house. There were two kids in every window now, noses fogging the glass. As I drove down Field Avenue I thought about them. Who were they? Did even Rita know their names? I started thinking about the fate of my siblings: Jamie would be eighteen now, so probably kicked out. Charlotte would be seventeen, most likely married. And Queenie—she'd be twenty. No chance she still lived in the house. It was just a matter of how many sister wives she had by now. And the younger kids? I never got close to them. They were mostly anonymous to me—dozens of girls and boys I passed in the hall, all of them blond and freckled and thin. When you're one of a hundred, you look up to the older kids because they might offer a bit of love, and you hate the younger kids for taking up room.

I got so lost thinking through the parade of nameless children I didn't notice the police cruiser tailing me. Suddenly he was in my rearview mirror, dark glasses on top of an eat-you-alive grin. His left palm was flat on the steering wheel, his right arm draped across the seat back. I turned down a side street and he followed. I turned again and he turned too. We passed three women working in a small barnyard. They looked up, hoes in hand, their faces washed in sunshine.

I wanted to visit the post office but it no longer seemed like a good idea. Out here the police are the bad guys. Every member of the Mesadale Police Department is a polygamist. Once one of my stepsisters walked into the police station and said my dad was cuddling her. (Out here, if your dad says he wants to cuddle, get ready to be raped.) The cop at the front desk took some notes, then called my dad. "I'd watch out for this one," he said. "She came in here hot as a nymph." He drove her home and my dad took her down to his basement for an hour. I remember waiting for her to come back upstairs. When she did she had a hollow look to her, like her eyes had been replaced with glass.

People say, *Oh come on, it can't be that bad.*

Actually, it's worse.

People say, *Why don't the authorities step in and do something?*

I don't know, ask them. But there are a few theories floating around. Some people say the Mormons, who more or less own Utah, are embarrassed by the Firsts because of our connected past. They prefer us tucked away in the desert, where no one can see us. I guess they're still touchy when it comes to polygamy. Others say the Mormons secretly want to return to polygamy one day, so they let it slide. I don't know about that one. Another theory: some say it's a case of religious freedom—you know, people have a right to believe what they want and the authorities need to be careful about trampling on that. Maybe. Then I've heard a really good one: it's actually hard to prove polygamy in court. Think about it: it's not illegal for a man and a bunch of women to live together. And if the state doesn't recognize the marriages, how can they be breaking the law?

I have my own theory about why all this has gone down in Mesadale for so long: no one cares. They don't give a fuck about a bunch of God goons fifty miles from the nearest cell tower. It's funny, they call us the lost boys when we get kicked out, but really, we were lost the day we were born. When I lived out there I often wondered if anyone other than my mom knew I was alive.

I turned back to the highway. The cruiser stayed behind me just enough to avoid my wake of dust. He escorted me all the way, descending the gradual hill, kicking up his own red cloud. At one point he picked up his radio to call something in. If this were a cop movie, the camera'd cut to the interior of his cruiser. But this wasn't a cop movie, and I can't tell you what he was radioing. *All clear? He's gone? It's him?*

I reached the highway and the van stopped rattling. Behind me, the cruiser idled at the asphalt's bank as if it were a river too deep to enter. The cop watched me drive off, making sure I was gone. In my rearview he grew smaller and smaller, then made a three-point turn and drove back up the long road into town. At the end of the day he'd file a report, lock up his firearm, and head home to a macaroni supper with his dozen lonesome wives.

III

EARLY HISTORY

THE 19TH WIFE

———

CHAPTER ONE:
The Convert

Among the many questions I have encountered since my apostasy from the Mormon Church, none arises with more confusion, or mystification, than as to why I ever joined the Latter-day Saints. The American public recognizes the Mormon Missionary devoutly traveling the road, the young man knocking upon well-locked doors, toiling through sun and snow to spread his word. Many people, I now understand, mistake me for the Missionary's recent convert and wonder why a woman of reason would succumb to such persuasions. Once, at a lecture in Denver, a minister's wife scolded me, "That's where you went wrong, Mrs. Young! You should never have let those Missionaries through your door!"

In fact, I was born a Mormon, the daughter of early converts, two devout Saints who reared me on the Book of Mormon and the epic story of the birth of that faith—just as another pair might raise their daughter on the grand stories of the Old Testament. I knew of the angel Moroni before Gabriel; the first and second Books of Nephi before the Gospel of John. As a small child I joined the Saints' exodus from Nauvoo into Zion, and always understood it to be as miraculous as the Israelites' brave flight from Egypt.

Even so, the curious public, long wary of the roaming Missionary, often doubts the origins of my parents' faith, and thus my own. This bewilderment, and a general skepticism over sudden religious conversion, makes it necessary for me to describe my mother's entry into the Church, and that of my father, too, and how together they first encountered the doctrine of celestial marriage, or polygamy.

My mother was born Elizabeth Churchill in 1817 in Cayuga County, New York; and for the sake of this narrative I shall call her by her given name. When she was four, her mother, a Methodist of wavering conviction, died of cholera. At the time they lived in a one-room cottage of no distinction, the only decoration being a St. Louis fiddle pegged to the wall. The seizures came around midnight. Elizabeth's mother sat up in bed, cried out once, "My Lord!" and twenty hours later she was dead. Although only four, Elizabeth understood that when her mother had asked for God's mercy, it failed to come.

Her father, a penniless son of the Enlightenment, a musician by training, and a Doubting Thomas by temperament, found himself incapable of caring for his daughter. Two days after her mother's death, he deposited Elizabeth behind the iron gate of a house belonging to Mr. and Mrs. Brown, a childless, indifferent couple who took her in as their born girl. Elizabeth's father promised he would return for her as soon as he could. She clung to that promise until she was sixteen.

Twelve years later Elizabeth left the Browns with a firm, but inexplicable desire to travel to St. Louis. She could not articulate the impulse. True, it was the only city she recalled her father speak of. Yet she was not so naïve to believe she would find him there. I will venture to say her desire was like that of the pilgrim—he does not expect to find Jesus in the orchards of Gethsemane, but even so he longs to visit Jerusalem.

Having made it as far as Pittsburgh by the grace of a family traveling west, Elizabeth resorted to the sole possession of a young woman with an empty purse. A passenger agent wrote her a ticket for passage down the Ohio in exchange for an interlude in his booth, the shade drawn. The agent was a gentle man with a chin dimpled like the bottom of a pear. Afterward, he drew up a ticket to St. Louis just as he had promised. The two parted, as clerk and customer part at the end of an exchange.

The following winter in St. Louis, Elizabeth gave birth in the Catholic women's home to a baby with a chin imprinted like the bottom of an unripe piece of fruit. "The Sisters and I will bring him into the arms of God," declared the nursemaid. This had been Elizabeth's intention as well, but once she held Gilbert she could not bear to leave him. The next day she tied her bonnet's pearl ribbon beneath her chin and stepped into the streets of St. Louis with her baby babbling in her arms. She was all of seventeen.

I will not be the first to report there is little work for a girl in such a situation. Elizabeth was quick to recognize her only option. She accepted a position with Mrs. Harmony in her mansarded mansion with an ebony piano in the parlor. Her role could best be described as Girl No. 8.

This is how Elizabeth came to meet Captain Zucker, a trim Slav who wore his ginger mustache waxed to a point. Quickly he adopted her as his favorite among Mrs. Harmony's harem, visiting her *salle* each time his paddle-wheel, *The Lucy*, called in St. Louis. Eventually he proposed, "Elizabeth, my beauty, why don't you quit this by-the-dozen work and come live with me?" She moved out of Mrs. Harmony's house that day. Captain Zucker established Elizabeth and Gilbert in a cabin with walls flocked in velvet and a palm standing alert in a Cantonese urn. She had never known such luxury.

Aboard *The Lucy* Elizabeth encountered a new kind of dignity. The sailors removed their caps when she passed, as if she were the mistress of the ship, and the musicians liked to show Gilbert their shiny horns. For his part, every day Captain Zucker gave Gilbert a new toy—cloth balls, jackstraws, and a quoits set with a bright red hob. Captain Zucker spoiled Elizabeth with expensive gifts, including a pair of half-boots of Turkish satin and a parasol trimmed in peony, which she has since bequeathed to me.

The lone exception to this kindness emanated from the Reverend Rice, *The Lucy*'s man of cloth. He was a Baptist of a variety I am not familiar with and cannot say for certain still exists. The only greeting he could muster was a curt "Madame." He refused to acknowledge Gilbert, declining Captain Zucker's invitation to baptize him. "That damn reverend wouldn't know God from a flea," the Captain would say. He often talked about expelling the Reverend from his ship but never summoned the courage. It left Elizabeth discouraged in many ways, but most especially in God.

Eventually Captain Zucker paid Reverend Rice a large enough tithing that he agreed to baptize Gilbert. The Sunday before the rite—this was July 1834—they were up river in Hannibal, Missouri. Captain Zucker sent Elizabeth into town to purchase embroidering cotton for Gilbert's gown and four buttons at a store with a sheepdog guarding its door. With her purchases, and Gilbert, in her arms, Elizabeth stepped over the dog into the sunlight, touched by an unfamiliar, open joy.

The Lucy was not sailing until nightfall. Curious about this stretch of the Mississippi, Elizabeth followed a path to the flatland between the cliffs and the river. The summer grass was damp and warm, and the sun was hot on the baby's brow. She walked about a quarter of a mile when she came across a crowd of twenty or twenty-five gathered in the shade of a buttonwood tree. A man of about thirty was speaking from atop a shipping crate, projecting as if two hundred were in his audience, or two thousand. Before this, many times Elizabeth had encountered a man calling out from atop a box, for at this time in our national history, prophet-preachers roamed the backwoods like bears. But this man, she has said at least a thousand times since, was unlike any of them. "All of you," he said. "Please come closer. I have a story to tell."

What first struck her was the quality of the man's voice—the hand-bell clarity and the force it achieved without the spectacle of bulging eyes and throbbing throat. "You won't believe what I tell you, not because you lack wits, or knowledge, but because it is not easy to believe. But if you can believe this tale, you will know the truth of all things, and your presence in the life after this one will be secure."

In those days few had heard of Joseph Smith or his Church of Latter-day Saints, which was four years old at the time. To Elizabeth, and the others gathered, he was a stranger without reputation or institution. His only tools for persuasion were his person and his fantastical tale of God's plan for man. Yet I must note the manner in which Joseph appeared atop the shipping crate that afternoon. He was a good head taller than most men and carried himself like a general or other such commander of a large force. I sometimes wonder if he shared the same physique as General George Washington—they were both taller than six feet, I understand, and strongly built. I often think he had the face a sculptor would use when cutting statues of the Great Men.

"I'm a farmer's son," Joseph began. "Originally from Vermont, but we settled in Palmyra—Palmyra, New York. If any of you have been there you'll know it as a bustling town of four thousand, surrounded by peaceful country, with many farms and brooks, and in the distance the gentle rolling drumlins and other hills. Yet in my youth, and even today, there was little peace in our village. There, at the crossroads, where almost every day I passed, four churches stood off in competition, each claiming to offer the true interpretation of God's will. I was an average boy in many ways, certainly of no higher intelligence than most, and my physical appearance, well, I'll leave it to you to judge my form. There was no reason to think that I, Joseph Smith, Junior—heir to a hundred acres and a stand of sugar-maples, and a cake-shop where my mother sold gingerbread and beer—that such a common lad would one day become a Prophet of God.

"But I was a curious boy, doubtful with many questions, most especially—which Church, among the many competing voices, was best for me? Should I become a Catholic, a Baptist, a Methodist, a Shaker, an Episcopal? Was there another sect I was yet to know? Although only fourteen, I had enough of a logical mind to understand that when ten preachers claim to be the rightful interpreter of God, at least nine may be in the wrong.

"Torn by this question, and eager for an answer as only a young man can be, one fine day—it was early spring—I walked into the woodland and fell to my knees. I asked the Heavenly Father to lead me to the door of His preferred Church, for I wanted to worship rightly. The day was clear, and the sun had washed the woods in its light, and the new, feathery leaves atop the trees were burnished like flakes of gold. For some time I prayed, searching for my answer, when to my great astonishment—and fear! for above all I was afraid—a glorious light, unlike anything I had ever seen appeared before me. At first I thought it must be the light of the day coming through the trees. But it was not a beam of light but a shell, and inside this shell of light were two people, I saw, two men, Father and Son.

"Now, Friends, I know what you're thinking—I can see it in your eyes! You're saying to yourself, Pshaw! This is where the man's tale becomes fantasy. I can see such thoughts flickering—there!—across your brows. You don't believe me, but that's fine, you're experiencing the same questions I did on that day. For surely what was before me was not before me. Surely I was imagining it, or the sunlight was playing a trick! I was prepared to believe any explanation but the most plain—which was, as it always is, the Truth. Father and Son, God and Christ, had descended from Heaven to bring a message. They said, Do not join any Church, for none is the true Church of God. Since the time of Christ, the men who claim to be His rightful interpreters—the Apostles, the priests, the Popes, the ministers, the reverends, the fathers, all of them, and each—these men have led the world away from the true words and deeds of Jesus Christ. Joseph, they said, you are living in an era of Great Apostasy. Man on Earth has wandered from the Truth. But the time has come for its Restoration, and you will be its messenger.

"With this news, the Heavenly Father and His Son departed, leaving me prone in the mud. Now, what does a boy do with such news? How did I react upon learning I was to be a Prophet?

Friends, I assure you I did my best to ignore all that I had heard and seen. You see, I was like yourself here today—my inclination was to disbelieve all that I could not understand. Yet ponder that, will you? If you cannot understand something, does that mean it is not true? Who here speaks French? Or Russian? None of you. Yet, were a man to say the sky is blue and the sun is hot in Russian or French, would that mean his words are not true?

"Three years passed. I was not seventeen. I still pondered the question that had originally taken me into the woods, but I had acted not at all on the knowledge God had provided me. Then one night—it was eleven years ago this September—a second miracle occurred. In my room an angel by the name of Moroni appeared at my bedside. He told me, as I'm here telling you now, that buried in a hill outside Palmyra was a set of golden plates. Yes, plates, and on them was a book written in an ancient language. This angel told me one day I would go to this hill and find the plates in a stone box. It was my duty, the angel said, to deliver this book to Man.

"What did I do? What would you have done? Yes, I think I know. Again, I did not believe it; or I did not want to believe it. Although I knew I had seen this angel, and talked with him, and knew the angel as something real, I did not want to believe the Truth: that I was a Prophet, here to communicate to all of Man. I waited. And a year later the angel returned with the same message. And so it passed each year for four years, until my time had come to dig up the golden plates. With my beloved wife Emma, I journeyed to the Hill Cumorah and dug in the spot as the angel had described it. There, in the stone box, were the golden plates, along with a tool for translating, which looked much like a large pair of spectacles. If any doubt remained in my heart, it was now driven off by the fact of these items. I held them. I knew they existed, as I know now that you exist, and as you know, or at least I hope, that I exist. Carefully I brought the plates home and began the task of translating them, transcribing this miraculous book so all could read it. And here it is, the Book of Mormon, named such because it was brought to you and me by Mormon's son, the angel Moroni. Here it is. Here it is." Joseph lifted his personal copy to his heart and closed his eyes.

Now might be a good time to point out a singular truth of all Prophets, from Jesus through Muhammid to Joseph Smith. They do not come in unappealing form. A Prophet usually possesses beauty, in his heart, of course, but in his physical being as well. His refined features and powerful stature are among his most potent natural gifts. To deny this is to deny the truth of the Human and how We, both man and woman, function. I intend not to belittle the Prophet's achievements nor the import of his message. Yet ask yourself—Would you stand in a hot field for hours with flies buzzing about your head to listen to a man with a disagreeable presence? Although this fact hints at Man's animal nature, it is the truth and therefore worth recording. There, I have said enough on this particular subject.

"When I go forth," Joseph continued before the crowd beneath the buttonwood tree, "and spread the news of this new Gospel, often I am asked, Brother Joseph, what is your message? Indeed, what is my message? What is the message of our new Church? What have the other men forgotten, and what am I here to restore? Friends, my message is clear, for it came to me from our God. We are here, all of us, we are here on Earth for but one reason, and that is to love. What was Christ's message? To love. The Truth is simple, as it always is. I am here to restore that message to all of Man while we live through these last days.

"Now if you do not believe my story, nor have any interest in reading this Book, then peace to you, my Friend, for I wish you no ill. But take one thing from our meeting today. Take my love and share it with all that you meet for the rest of your time."

Joseph jumped down to greet the assembled, and there was much fuss made over him, people reaching to touch his coat. Enraptured, Elizabeth asked one of his companions for a copy of the miraculous book. When at last Joseph made his way to her he said,

"Tell me, Sister, where are you going?"

"Up the river and down."

"No final destination?"

"I live on a paddle-wheel."

"Then why not come with us? We've been to Independence de-fending our brothers. Now it's time to go home to Kirtland. It's a long walk to Ohio, but I promise you'll find a kind people there."

"And my son?"

"If you join us, I promise you both will be loved."

At the time, of course, Elizabeth could not know she had met Joseph and his Zion's Camp in retreat from their failed attempt to establish a new Zion in Missouri. Joseph, Brigham, Heber Kimball, and the other Apostles had been recently tested by a growing enemy. They lost fourteen men along the way to cholera, but their faith had strengthened in their long march home. On that damp day in July Elizabeth had followed a path through the summer grass and come upon a moment in history. Dear Reader, consider it! A stranger beneath a buttonwood tree promising love! Imagine the power this has over the lonely heart!

Elizabeth never returned to *The Lucy*. Joseph introduced her to Brigham Young, my future husband, who at the time was a humble carpenter from Vermont and only thirty-three. "This woman is joining us," Joseph said. "Look after her and her child." Brother Brigham followed these orders, never letting Elizabeth and Gilbert out of sight for the six-hundred-mile walk to Kirtland. We know Brigham now as Joseph's successor, a man of wealth and power, but then he was a woodworker, a glazier, a furniture maker. One could see his trade in his scuffed hands.

Brigham carried Gilbert for much of the journey and revealed himself to be a friend to my mother. The next day they stopped at a creek. He set Gilbert upon a bed of leaves, then guided Elizabeth into the water, across the mossy stones, until the current reached her breast. He gently pushed her head beneath the surface and blessed her. When she emerged she was a Latter-day Saint, and would always be.

After many days of walking they passed through a dark wood that opened onto a hilly clearing beside a river. Here the Saints' new city of Kirtland gleamed. Brigham gave Elizabeth a room in the small house he shared with his new bride, Mary Ann Angell, a recent convert from New York. "Gather yourself and rest," he said. "You are tired and your boy needs sleep. My wife will give you some land where you can grow some cabbage. She'll invite you into her kitchen to bake bread. Her barn is your barn, and you may feed our pig, and when the time comes part of that pig will be yours. These are your duties now. Only when you are settled should you turn your mind to spiritual devotion. Now you must simply live."

On her first morning in Kirtland, Elizabeth set out to see the busy milling town. With Gilbert in her arms she went down to the bank of the Chagrin. While watching the quick current, and pondering the movement of her life, and seeing an imprint of her fate in the rippled water, a far-away voice cawed in her ear: "Must be the whore."

"I heard they picked her up in a Missouri brothel," hissed a second voice.

"Makes you wonder what they were doing there."

"And to think she brought her bastard here."

Elizabeth looked up river. Far off two young women stood upon a fishing dock. Their voices had traveled down with the current, farther than they would have ever thought possible. Elizabeth pulled the bonnet over Gilbert's head and returned to Brigham's house. She never said a thing.

The next day at Sunday Services, following Joseph's sermon, Brigham rose to bear testimony. He paused, his throat darkening. "Before word of the Restoration came to Brother Joseph," he began, "and we knew of its Glory, we were destitute and depraved. Now, through His love and wisdom, we know we live in these latter days, these days leading up to Judgment and Redemption. We await them with our hearts full." Brigham looked to the collected souls cramped in a neighbor's parlor, some on the floor, many along the wall, others standing outside leaning through the open windows. "But if anyone here, or anywhere, believes himself, or herself, to be no less destitute or depraved than we were before our knowledge, if anyone here, or anywhere, believes he has already achieved Salvation, I ask him, or I ask her, to come forth now, and show yourself. If any of you think yourself purer, fairer, or closer to the foot of God than the rest of us, show yourself now, for I should like to know you. If any of you, because you come from a proud family, or your husband earns a fine income, or you possess a fine complexion and a multitude of bonnets, believes you are of a better kind than any of the rest of us, then step forward now and show yourself, for we all should like to know you. But beware, for although you may think yourself as such, He shall be the judge of all things and will not withhold His judgment. Who here thinks himself better than the rest? . . . Anyone? . . . No one at all? . . . I did not think so. Now go forth and prove to Him you are His Latter-day Saints."

After the services, the women of Kirtland overwhelmed my mother with gifts, clothing, cooking pans, jars of preserves. A widow named Graeve offered a permanent room. A drive was called for cotton, toys, seeds, and a vegetable plot. New friends invited Elizabeth for supper, others for singing. Sisters brought their babies to see Gilbert and everyone kissed his head when they met him on the street. Never again did someone speak cruelly of her past. The Saints knew of it, and understood it. They never pitied her, never shamed her, never again questioned her place.

So it was, through love and kindness, Brigham joined Joseph Smith in welcoming Elizabeth Churchill as his newest Saint; and so she was when soon thereafter met another fresh convert, a blacksmith from New York, the man who would become my father, Chauncey Webb.

IV

—

THE ORIGINS
OF LOVE

LDS CHURCH ARCHIVES

SPECIAL COLLECTIONS

Pioneer Biographies & Autobiographies

Salt Lake City

Access to the Special Collections is restricted to Latter-day Saints in possession of a current temple recommend. Those unable to visit the Collections themselves may send a relative or friend on their behalf, provided he or she has a temple recommend. You may also engage an ancestral researcher or scholar, provided that he or she also has a temple recommend.

Updated by Deb Savidhoffer, Church Archivist, 9/3/2004

THE AUTOBIOGRAPHY
OF CHAUNCEY G. WEBB

——

PART I

Since the publication of *The 19th Wife* last year, I have been left with many questions about the nature of my life. In my daughter's book, she recounts a version of our family history in which I do not recognize myself. According to Ann Eliza, I have become a ghost of a man, my corporeal presence consumed by my many wives. In those pages, now read by hundreds of thousands of Americans across this land, she calls me "a man who wanders about the desert without soul"—a charge I find painful to read even now. With her words cold upon my heart, I have come to believe it would serve some purpose—whether personal or historical I cannot say—if I were to set down in my own words the story of how I came to be a Saint and marry five wives. In her Preface Ann Eliza writes, "I leave judgment to the hearts of my good Readers everywhere." Yet in truth, only two can judge a man: himself and God.

My mother first heard Brigham preach in 1833, while he prose-lytized in our village of Hanover, N.Y. She attended a meeting on a September afternoon and returned home agitated by religious fervor. "I'll be departing with Brother Brigham in the morning," she announced. "I have but a few years left on this earth. I want to spend them with one who loves me." Underestimating the power of the new Gospel, at first I scoffed at her sudden conversion, yet the next day she left with Brigham to join Joseph in Kirtland, O.H. I was twenty-one and for the first time in my life I found myself alone.

I was an apprentice in a blacksmith's shop then, with a bright fu-ture as a wheelwright, and I spent those lonely days, and often my nights, toiling before my forge. Often I think back on this time— more than forty years ago—and I ponder my future wife, Eliza-beth, and her ordeals. About the same time my mother left me, Elizabeth was making her way through the streets of St. Louis, ex-pecting a child. Of course I could not know this at the time; I could not even imagine such a woman. Yet in my musings about the past, I like to think each of us had set down on a path to find one an-other. Now I shall describe the road I chose.

Although I was still an apprentice to Mr. Fletcher, men came to me by name to repair their carriage wheels, for the reputation of my work had traveled as far as Buffalo. Although I had very little money, it was clear to me, especially now with my mother departed, that with hard work and good fortune, and the blessing of that mysterious being known as God, I might one day become a wealthy man.

I must admit—for my hope in recounting my long journey into polygamy is to reveal the truth, if only to myself—that I was not altogether sad when my mother left for Kirtland. Since the tragic and early death of my father, her great effort in life had been to preserve the dignity and grandeur of her widowhood. She wore her voluminous mourning gown the day she met Brigham; for Kirtland, she packed a small trunk containing blackcloth and somber lace. Tending to her had become a burden of minor proportions, for I was a young man in pursuit of those items which young men are known to pursue. There were many evenings I would have preferred to stay at the forge, with my apron heavy around my neck and the fire warm in my face, than return home for a silent supper of winter stew, followed by the long hours providing her wordless company while she worked her sewing hoop.

This, therefore, is why no one found greater surprise than I in the depths of my loneliness after my mother's departure. Or the heights of my elation when her first letter arrived two months later. "My good son—I have settled in Kirtland," she wrote. "The Prophet Joseph Smith baptized me in our river, the Chagrin. Do not scorn your mother. I am an old woman. I was afraid of death until I met the Latter-day Saints. They have promised me Glory in the Afterlife. I shall meet you there."

I responded to her letter, declaring the emptiness of my evenings and my general longing to see her again. She replied that if I were to accept Joseph Smith as a Prophet, I should come to Kirtland and be near her.

I was not yet prepared to do so. I knew very little about this new Church except what my mother had relayed and the gossip already surrounding it. Even then there were rumors of unusual marriage customs. I wrote my mother, asking her to explain why I should devote myself to a man who was no more than any other man. "You do not know him," she replied. "Although he is a man, he is the man on Earth chosen by God." With each letter my mother's fa-

naticism expanded until she wrote freely describing angels and divine revelations and the miraculous golden plates. The letters confirmed that I could not abandon my future in Hanover for a small
city in the Ohio swampland run by a man who promised that
which only the Lord Himself can deliver.

Then my mother wrote with a different sort of news: "Kirtland
is growing by the day. Newly converted Saints from New York and
Pennsylvania and even Vermont, New Hampshire, and Maine, add
to our census weekly. With each passing month, the City expands
into the forest. Any man with an axe can make a fine living clearing the woods. Here, in this growing Metropolis, one must think of
Rome at her birth to imagine it properly. There is an urgent need
for a second blacksmith and wheelwright. I told the Prophet my
son is the best in Chautauqua County. He has invited you, my dear
son Chauncey. The Prophet has invited you to join us."

Not long after this, Mr. Fletcher came to see me at my station.
He explained that his business was suffering—which I knew it was
not—and told me he would have to cut my take on each wheel I repaired. I complained, knowing my work brought him his most
profits, but he dismissed my outrage. "Your wheels are no better
than the rest," he said.

With that, I hung my apron on its peg and left Mr. Fletcher's
service for good. He expected me back in the morning, I am sure,
but by then I was on my way to Kirtland, tying my fortune forever
to the Latter-day Saints. The coincidence between the arrival of
my mother's letter and Mr. Fletcher's duplicity has consumed many
of my pondering hours over the years. Was it the hand of my
beloved mother? Or the hand of God? Or is it possible one event
can ensnare itself upon another, as a tripwire entraps the ankle,
without reason, plan, or meaning? I cannot say.

The journey from New York to Ohio was relatively easy even
back then. Wagons and carriages filled the road with travelers and
journeymen—settlers and trappers and wandering preachers—yet
none of these gave me as lasting an impression as the girl I met

twenty miles beyond Erie while resting at a roadside inn. I supped in a small room lit by the hearth and, as I completed my meal, the innkeeper, a durable woman with full-blown gray-blue cheeks, asked if I needed anything more. "A bit of sweet? A hot-tot for bed? No? Then how about a nice girl?"

I understood the meaning of her offer. Rather than claim I resisted and voiced my offense, I must describe my reaction in honest terms. I was twenty-one years of age. I was eager to know a woman in such a manner. For most of my life I had assumed this would be my wife, but recently I came to realize that I might not have to wait until matrimony. In Hanover fear for my reputation kept me from visiting the brothel I knew existed above the printing shop. But on the road, in this dark forested limbo between my old home and my new, where nearly everyone I met seemed to be testing the pliability of Christian morals, I felt suddenly free of past and future restraint. "Mrs. Mack," I said, "who do you know?"

"I know a handful of right pretty ladies. How do you like 'em? Fat or thin? Dark or fair? The older ones know the best tricks, but the younger ones ain't got much in the way of fur. What will it be, Mr. Webb?"

I asked Mrs. Mack if she knew of a woman who was old enough to know her way through the activities she was proposing and yet not too old. "Right, you ain't looking for your mother, are you? Wait right here. Have yourself another whiskey. If you take the girl, the cup's on me." She scurried out the front door; her movement was low on the ground and slow but with enough agility that she reminded me, as the door closed behind her wide, hobbling rear-side, of a gopher disappearing down its hole.

A quarter of an hour later she returned with a young woman. "This here's Jenetta. Pretty, isn't she? Originally from New York, ain't that right, dear? Came up this way to be near her gramps."

I bowed and the young woman said, with surprising boldness, "Which way's your room? You mind if I go first to fix myself up?"

This comment was so exotic—the notion of a woman working

on herself, whatever that might mean, for me—that I could not speak and merely pointed to the stairs. Mrs. Mack said, "Second room at the top. Be fast, deary. God made you beautiful enough."

I sat for a bit, stunned, I believe, not only by Jenetta's beauty but by Mrs. Mack's frankness; I had never seen femininity in such full and assertive relief. Other than my mother, I realized, I knew few women except to nod hello on the streets of Hanover. Up until this point I believed that women came in but few varieties: the delicate virgin, the industrious wife, the declining widow, and of course the black-hearted whore. Certainly I had met others who fit into none of these categories, but the world presented them to me, or perhaps more accurately, I saw them, in rather simple terms. In short, I was fast becoming overwhelmed by woman's great complexity.

When I entered my room, Jenetta stood at the mirror regarding herself. She wore a sort of sleeping gown that looked neither comfortable nor practical to sleep in. I asked if she wasn't cold. She wrapped her long, lovely arms around my neck and said, "I won't be." What ensued was of the usual sort for this kind of encounter, but I must note for these efforts that Jenetta led the way, initiating me to more pleasure than I had ever imagined possible on earth. She stayed with me for the night, a cost that left my limited traveling funds worrisomely depleted, but I had decided everything in my earthly possession was worth making these joys last until the dawn. By sunrise I could not face saying good-bye, and proposed that she join me on my journey.

"To Ohio?" she laughed. "Oh critters, no. I got my husband right here with me."

"But Mrs. Mack said you lived with your gramps?"

"That's what I call my husband, he's so old. He'll be wanting his breakfast about now." She sprang from the bed, dressed, and departed as efficiently as she had arrived; and I buried my face into the pillow to inhale her sweet odor; and, I am afraid, to weep.

"Mrs. Mack," I wailed, "the most horrible and wonderful thing has happened. I have fallen in love. I must see Jenetta again."

"That's real nice, but I've heard it a thousand times before. Afraid you'll never find it again, but you will, I promise, you will. Now shouldn't you be on your way, Mr. Webb? Didn't you say your mother's waiting in Ohio? Thank you very much, dear, but get on, there you go, right now, good-bye!"

She swept me over her threshold into her garden and shut the door. I stood in the sunlight, confused by and desperate.

Because I am an engineer and possess a mostly logical mind, eventually I talked myself to pass through Mrs. Mack's garden gate and never once look over my shoulder. Yet the head does not need to turn and the eyes need not gaze back for the heart to remain behind.

It was with such longing that I arrived in Kirtland. On that first night my mother served a feast of ham hocks followed by angel pie. "In the morning, I'll take you down to meet the Prophet and he'll get you work in one of the manufactories. Why didn't you eat all your pie? Go on, finish up. I baked it for you."

There is comfort in knowing that people remain the same.

As it turns out, my mother had overstated the case. Indeed there was opportunity for a wheelwright, but Joseph had invited dozens of men to meet the demand. I took a job in one of his wagon manufactories as a junior apprentice, earning less than I had in Hanover. "At least you're near me," my mother said.

On Sundays, with little else to do, I accompanied her to services led by the Prophet, although I was still not a member of the Latter-day Saints. Joseph had a presence unlike most men, with eyes wide and blue, and the stature of a man who knows his place in history. I did not have to attend more than one Sunday meeting to know the command he possessed over his followers. If he were not a Christian, he might very well have been a sorcerer—so capable of casting a spell he was.

"Look around!" he said one Sunday. "Look around and tell me

what you see. Do you see gambling, drinking, swindling, the whoring that goes on throughout our country? Do you see the sin that walks down the street dressed as proud gentleman in top hat and dear sweet lady in her flimsy dress? Do you? Because that is not what I see. No, I see on those dirty streets those things that are missing—compassion, caring, love. When I look around I see neighbor ignoring neighbor, man snubbing wife, child abandoning parent. This is the Great Apostasy. For Christ taught us to love and so it has come to pass that He has returned in Revelation to restore love to our earth. Such is the truth as I know it, as He has revealed it to me."

I had lived in Kirtland about four months when I came to accept that my future lay with Joseph and his Church. Despite my mother's high standing among the ladies who organized Kirtland society and its circles, I was but a Gentile laborer. They would employ me as long as there was work that would otherwise go undone, but I could see a time in the future when there would be enough Saints to meet their wagonry needs. Joseph ruled Kirtland like a theocracy, and there was a firm strata of citizenship based on faith. The very best of the Gentiles were owed less than the very worst of the Saints. Thus my resistance to Joseph Smith's teachings began to erode. I respected his call to love; I responded more urgently to his call for able men.

It was about this time, on a late summer afternoon in 1834, at a picnic on the bank of the Chagrin, that I met Elizabeth. She was running in a woman's race with her leg tied to another girl's. The prize was a plaque engraved with the winner's name, the metalwork to be done by me. I stood at the end of the course, waiting for the winner to lean her breast triumphantly across the finishing ribbon, when I saw her for the first time. Elizabeth was adjusting the rope that bound her leg to her partner—a plump, indelicate girl sweating in the heat.

At the crack of the pistol Elizabeth and Martha began to run like a strange, hobbled animal, their eyes shining through the summer haze. When Elizabeth looked ahead to the finish line our eyes met—and it was then that I knew. Everyone was jumping up and down in excitement, but not I. I stood very still, observing her. Just then, the two young women ran ahead of the others, breaking through the finishing ribbon with such propulsion they fell into my arms. After unmooring the girls, I found myself alone at Elizabeth's side, unable to find any words. It was she who suggested we walk.

We strolled into a field beyond the picnic. Along the way I found the courage to squeeze her arm. I led her to a felled tree carved with initials, brushing away the dirt. I wished I had a large house to welcome her into, a drawing-room with a winged chair and extra bedrooms waiting to be filled; in time I knew—perhaps with her help. I told her so. As afternoon gave way to dusk, and the mosquitoes rose from the grass, I held her. As the blue evening fluttered down upon the field, I kissed her. I did not intend to kiss her a second time, but I lost my way. I would like to say it was the force of Christ and Joseph Smith that brought us together, or some other mysterious, celestial reason, but, to follow my established rule of honesty, nothing more noble than desire, and the early, vibrant shoots of love, pushed us into the grass. Lying atop her, my heart pounding in motion with hers, I knew we would marry; I knew this one would not abandon me in the morn.

We lay in the grass for some time. For a brief moment her expression became unknowable; it was as if she had left me, her mind off and away. "Tell me your thoughts," I said.

"You know nothing of me."

I said to her, "You know nothing of me."

Then we talked about the future, as if what had preceded us need not matter; as if, through the compounding force of our union, we could determine all that lay ahead. We shared our dreams—a loving marriage, children, lots of children, a large framed house, and a family name that only rose in the community of Saints.

Elizabeth spoke of eternal salvation. She declared her love for Joseph Smith. As she spoke, the lantern of her face illuminated. "I've never loved anyone like Joseph. But there's something you must know." She recounted her life before conversion, her voice clear of shame. When she finished her tale she asked if it troubled me. "Really," I said, "your past is no different than mine."

"That's not true. For you the past is past. For me, my past is with me, in my son, Gilbert."

"I want to meet him." She set her cheek upon my breast, and I promised her I would love her child. "When can we marry?" I said.

"I'm afraid I can't."

I felt crushed, in the way Jenetta had crushed me. Desperately I asked why.

"You're not a Saint." For Elizabeth, it was a simple matter. Yet I would do anything to possess her. I wanted her for myself, every night, for the rest of my days. Forgive my effusion—if a man is honest, he will understand.

The next day Joseph baptized me at a bend in the Chagrin. As he held me beneath the current I cannot tell you that I felt something pass from him to me, as others have described it. They compare it to a bolt of lightning traveling through their frames—it is that sudden and powerful, a fury that can come only from God. For me, I felt nothing but the cold water and fingers of river grass upon my neck. That is all. The sensation was entirely of the earth. In name, I was now a Saint. My motivations too were of the earth—I wanted to marry; and I wanted to succeed. I believed in God and Christian goodness; of everything else I was less than sure. I am even less certain now, when I think back to all that has passed and the mistakes I have made. When I read again and again the outcome of my life, as my daughter has described it in *The 19th Wife*, I become unsure of almost everything—most especially of myself and my faith.

Joseph and I returned to the river bank wet and shivering.

Awaiting me were my mother, whose life, I could not know then, was about to end, and Elizabeth, golden in the sunlight. We would marry the next day, and she would be my sole wife for a dozen years. Had I been told that day I would take another wife in the future, and others still, I would have sworn it not true. I would have insisted it was an impossible fate. Like most men, I believed my heart lay beyond corrosion and decay.

NOTA BENE

The Autobiography of Chauncey G. Webb, Part II, has been archived under restricted access in the Special Collections. For further information, please see a Church Archivist.

—Church Archives, January 16, 1940

V

———

WIFE #19

AN EYE IN THE DARK

THAT'S THE THING

———

"Officer Cunningham? It's me, Jordan Scott. Listen, I know the rules." I was driving back from Mesadale with Elektra in my lap. "But this is urgent. Any chance of seeing my mom? Like today?"

The line went silent. Then, "You know the rules."

I tried again and she turned me down. I went a different way, going on about not having a place to leave Elektra tomorrow. Officer Cunningham sighed, "Please don't do this to me." I apologized. Then I begged. Soon we both knew she was about to cave. "This is a onetime event, you understand?"

After leaving Elektra with the goth girl at the internet café, I passed through the jail's metal detector. Officer Cunningham didn't look pleased. "Let's not talk about this, all right?" she said.

Ten minutes later Officer Kane was settling my mom onto the stool on the opposite side of the glass. We stared at each other for some time and it was like we were playing a game of who's going to go first. She picked up the receiver and said, "I feel like we ended on a bad note last time."

"Don't worry about it."

"I didn't know if you'd be back."

"Me neither."

"I was hoping we'd come to some sort of understanding."

"First I need to tell you what's going on. I went to see Mr. Heber."

I started to describe the meeting, but I hesitated when I got to the meat. "He said some pretty difficult things. About what might happen. You sure you want to hear this?" She nodded. "In a nutshell, it's not looking good. How should I put this? He thinks . . . you might . . . well, there's a chance—" But I chickened out. How do you tell your mom she will be executed?

"Jordan, you can tell me."

"You know what, he really should tell you all this." She urged me on. I resisted, but she kept asking, and no matter what, moms are pretty good at wearing down their kids. "It's just that there's a lot of evidence," I said. "I mean, a lot of facts, that, well, kinda indicate you did it."

She was looking into my eyes as only a mom can. "You don't believe me," she said.

"Mom, it's hard to know what's true. I mean, everything out there is so messed up."

"You have to believe me." This wasn't a plea, it was a statement. I told her about my trip to Mesadale. "I went to the house," I said. "I saw Sister Rita."

"Is she still blaming all this on me?"

"Yes, but she wouldn't really talk to me. I wanted to go up to your room, but she wouldn't let me in."

My mom set the receiver on the counter to say something to Officer Kane. She seemed agitated, her finger moving through the air to make some point. She picked up the receiver again. "Jordan, I only get three visits a week. You can't come back until Friday. We don't have a lot of time. How can I convince you I didn't do it? You need to help me."

"I know," I said. "That's why I came today: to say good-bye. I'm going to have another meeting with Mr. Heber, help him with some basic info about Mesadale, then I'm headed back to California."

She stared at me calmly, her nostrils flickering. "Please don't go until I'm out of here."

"That could be a long time." I balled up my courage. "That might not happen. Ever."

For a long time she didn't say anything. Finally, "He thinks I'll be put to death, doesn't he?" The amazing thing was she seemed settled and certain, her eyes sharp and clear.

"Yes."

"And you're giving up."

"It's not like that."

"I guess you're right. You don't owe me anything."

"Mom, I just don't think I can help you."

"You should probably go."

"Mom, if there's something I can do, tell me."

"Please go."

"Is there anything else I can—"

She hung up. Officer Kane helped her from the stool. She looked at me once—Officer Kane, I mean. A face that said, *She's your* mother. They left, and I was on my own.

"Look who's back." Maureen was at her desk, typing. "We weren't expecting you till tomorrow."

"I need to see Mr. Heber."

"I'm afraid he's all booked this afternoon."

I wasn't going to wait. Elektra and I walked down the hall, right into Mr. Heber's office. He was on the phone, working on a legal document. "Uh, Jim, I'm going to have to call you back."

"I'm sorry, Mr. Heber," said Maureen. "I tried to stop him."

"I need to see you," I said.

"Apparently. But first, calm down."

"I am calm, but this can't wait."

"All right, all right. Maureen, take some notes."

I unleashed Elektra and after a lot of coaxing got her to lie down. "I know this is going to sound crazy," I said, "but she didn't do it." Saying it out loud made it seem even more true.

"Tell me why you think that."

"It doesn't add up."

"How do you mean?"

"She still believes in all that stuff. The Prophet, the church, polygamy as salvation, the whole thing. She wants to go back."

Mr. Heber removed his glasses to rub his eyes. "Is it possible she says she still believes in all that even though she doesn't?"

"Nope, absolutely not. It would give her an excuse. She didn't kill my dad."

"I'm still not with you."

"She had no reason to kill him. This is the crazy part: she actually liked her life."

"All right, let's go back to the basic evidence that led to her arrest. There's a chat session in which your dad says your mom just entered the room, which happens to be right before he was shot. We've got an eyewitness saying your mom came up from the basement around the time of his death. And we've got your mom's prints on the murder weapon. Right now I have no good explanation for any of those."

"Let's find them."

"I need you to see this from my point of view. The way things stand it won't take a prosecutor much imagination to come up with a dozen hypothetical reasons why your mom would want to kill your dad."

"Hypotheticals don't matter. She didn't do it."

"We're a long way from proving that."

You know all that business about being on the same team? Suddenly it didn't feel that way. I had to ask myself why was this Mormon lawyer working for someone like my mom? His religion and my ex-religion have been at a standoff for more than a hundred years. "Why are you helping her?" I said. "Why'd you take this case?"

"I take lots of pro bono cases."

"But why hers?"

"Jordan, you want to tell me what's going on? You were here yesterday, and you and I were pretty much on the same page. Now you're doubting everything. Did something happen?"

"I went back to Mesadale—that's what happened. When you're

there and see how screwed up it is, you realize nothing is what it seems."

"Jordan, settle down. I understand."

"You don't understand."

Mr. Heber snapped open a bottle of water. "Look, I don't blame you for being upset. I know you want something to happen right away, but that's really not the best thing for your mom."

"Then what is?"

"I don't like what's going on out there any more than you do. That guy, that phony Prophet, he's ruined a lot of lives, and along the way he's distorted my religion. And it's been going on for way too long. Jordan, things are changing. Almost every week there's another call to the FBI or the attorney general or the media about this. We need to let it play itself out. I don't want your mom to go on trial. I want the Prophet and his church to go on trial. So let's give it a little time, all right?"

"How much?"

"I'd like to stall this for several months, maybe a year."

"A year?"

"I know that sounds like a long time, but it isn't, not really. There's a lot of stuff going on that you and I don't know about. Rival factions, people running away, some challenges to the Prophet's authority. The Prophet's under a lot of pressure right now, both from the outside and within. Your mom's going to be a whole lot better off if she's part of that bigger story."

"I don't know who you're talking to, but I'm sorry, I was just in Mesadale and nothing's changed, it never has and it never will. Before the Prophet there was his father. And before him, his uncle. Con man after con man, for more than a hundred years, all the way back to 1890 and Aaron fucking Webb." I stood up, tugged Elektra's leash, and we left.

Maureen followed us down the hall, quick on high-heel sandals.

"How do I get a new lawyer?" I said.

"Your mother has to request one."

"Fine, I'll tell her to."

"She'll end up with someone worse."

"Why doesn't he want to save her?"

"He wants to save her."

"Why isn't he outraged?"

"He wouldn't be a very good lawyer if he was always outraged."

I was so pissed I was about to start yelling, but then Maureen touched me, her fingers soft on my arm, and I lost it. The tears fell and they kept falling. "I don't know what to do," I said.

She sat me down in the chair with a box of tissues. "Take your time." I kept saying I was sorry and she kept saying it was all right. She wrote her cell number on a sticky and folded it into my palm, just in case. Sensing a group hug, Elektra worked her way between us, shoving her nose into Maureen's crotch.

"Do you want to talk about it?" Maureen said.

I did, but I didn't.

"Was it strange going back?"

"Yes and no. No, because everything was the same. But yes, because I felt like a kid again and I kept expecting to see my mom. And my dad."

"Can I ask you something?" She scooted closer. "Why do all those people believe in him like that?"

"They don't know anything else."

"I know, but in this day and age." She clucked her tongue.

"I know it sounds crazy, but our whole world began and ended in Mesadale. That was it. And you know what, for most of them—for most of us—it was enough."

She shook her head, as if she'd been told the most preposterous thing in the world. "Do you mind if I ask what he's like?" she said. "The Prophet?"

"He's . . . I don't know—I mean, I never really knew him. He was just always there, but I never really spoke to him or anything. I actually only saw him in church on Sundays. He'd stand very still as he gave his sermon, he wasn't a pacer or anything like that, just his feet planted in one place, and it was like he was part of the altar. The more I think about it, the harder it is to describe him. It's like trying to describe the wind."

"Is he old or young? Fat or thin?"

"He's old, but I don't even really know how old. You know how you know God's old, but you don't know how old. It's like that. I guess more than anything, I remember his voice. He wasn't a yeller, his voice was actually kinda soft and high, with the slightest lisp. I remember it being very gentle, very lulling, just pulling you in. When I was little I would sit in my mom's lap in church and she'd kiss my head and whisper, Listen, it's the voice of God."

"I just don't think it's fair to tell children things like that."

"That's nothing. At school the teacher would pop in a cassette and we'd listen to the Prophet for hours. For the boys he often talked about priesthood history. Queenie told me for the girls he talked about home economics, the role of being a good wife, obedience, that kind of stuff. But most of the time, for everyone, he talked about the end of time, which was always coming soon. He told us how one day we'd have to slit the throats of our enemies, just like Nephi." I looked at Maureen. "You sure you want to hear all this?"

"If you want to tell me."

"They taught us how to do that in school, cutting throats, I mean. We had to practice on rabbits and chickens in the schoolyard. You must pray for the spirit while doing it—that's what the Prophet would say on his tape, and then he went on to describe how a human throat will look when the head's pulled back and how to slice it from ear to ear and how the blood will look when it pours out thick and how not to be afraid. When we got older, we had to slaughter dogs and sheep. But I refused to do it, I could never kill a dog. I think those were my first inklings of doubt because I knew— I don't know how, but I just knew—those animals didn't have to die. It was all in preparation for the day when our enemies would come to slaughter us—that's what he told us. And we'd sit there for hours and listen to his voice coming out of the cassette player, and then there'd be a test. It seemed like the most natural thing in the world—to go to school and learn stuff like that from a voice on a cassette." I stopped and laughed. "I mean, it all sounds so cheesy now, but when I was a kid it really felt like God was in the room."

"What'd your mom tell you about all of this?"

"She always told me to listen to the Prophet and everything would be fine."

Maureen shook her head. "It's such a shame. If only she'd known the truth."

"But that's the thing," I said. "People are always going to believe what they believe."

HAUN'S MILL MASSACRE

From Wikipedia, the free encyclopedia

MORMONS IN MISSOURI

In the mid-1830s, the **Latter-day Saints** (also known as the **Mormons**), facing religious persecution in their home of **Kirtland, Ohio,** began moving to western **Missouri.** The majority settled in a community known as Far West, but some 75 families settled beside Shoal Creek in Caldwell County, establishing a milling town known as **Haun's Mill.** By 1838, **Joseph Smith, Brigham Young,** and other Church leaders, as well as most of the Mormons, had relocated to Missouri.

Their hope to find a peaceful home faded quickly. By the summer of 1838 tensions were high between the Mormons and the surrounding non-Mormon communities. The non-Mormons feared the Mormons for three reasons:

1) The Mormons voted in block and thus had quickly become a powerful political force in their new land.
2) The Mormons had swiftly, and some say surreptitiously, bought up large tracts of land.
3) Most controversially, rumors of polygamy had followed the Mormons from Ohio. Joseph and Brigham repeatedly denied the accusations, but many Missourians were suspicious of their new neighbors' marital customs.

MASSACRE

On October 27, 1838, Missouri governor **Lilburn W. Boggs** signed the notorious Extermination Order, which told the Mormons to leave the state or face extermination. The Mormons took the order seriously, but rather than fleeing they chose to fight, making plans for a military defense. Three days later, around four o'-clock in the afternoon of October 30, between 200 and 250 members of the Missouri Militia rode into Haun's Mill. The women and children escaped across the shallow creek into the forest, fleeing with naked babies and frying pans. The men and a number of boys who refused to leave their fathers took up a defensive position in the blacksmith. The militia surrounded the building and shot at the huddled Mormons at close range through the loose chinking. Seventeen Mormons were killed, along with one sympathetic non-Mormon, who had been there on business. Among those in the blacksmith, only one survived, the wainwright **Chauncey G. Webb.** Chauncey's wife, Elizabeth, and stepson, Gilbert, heard the nearly one hundred rifle shots from behind the mill's water wheel, where they were hiding in shoulder-high water. During the battle, Elizabeth prayed for her husband's survival. When he was found alive, she, and many others, deemed it a miracle and long after spoke of it as one.

The close-range murders were particularly gruesome. Simon Cox was shot in the side, bits of his kidney splattering his fellow Mormons. Using a corn knife, one member of the militia chopped seventy-eight-year-old Thomas McBride into pieces. Another shot the top off the head of ten-year-old **Sardius Smith,** who was discovered beneath the bellows. But most offensive to the Mormons, and many non-Mormons, too, when word of the massacre got out, was that the governor had sanctioned the murders and thus they were legitimate in the eyes of the state's law.

CONSEQUENCES

After the Haun's Mill massacre, the Mormons began to flee Missouri, eventually settling on the Illinois side of the Mississippi at a swampy outpost then known as Commerce. Here they built the proud city of **Nauvoo,** which in five years would become the second largest in Illinois. Chauncey Webb, the massacre's lone survivor, moved his family to Nauvoo around 1840 or 1841, becoming the city's leading wagon builder. In Nauvoo, also known as Beautiful City, Joseph Smith and the Saints would experience their golden age.

The murders were never officially investigated, and no one was ever brought to justice. The massacre remains an important turning point in LDS history and is remembered annually through memorials, reenactments, and special prayers. The mill's original red mill stone has been erected as a memorial to the victims. For many Mormons in the 19th century, Chauncey Webb's survival came to symbolize their resolve. Records show, however, that Chauncey Webb was a reluctant hero and disagreed with his wife's assessment that he had survived because of divine intervention.

REFERENCES

1. History of the Church, Vol. III
2. Mormon Polygamy: A Historical Perspective by Charles Green
3. "The Women of Haun's Mill" by Mary P. Sprague
4. *The 19th Wife* by Ann Eliza Young

I'M NOT AN EXPERT OR ANYTHING

The next morning I drove out to the Mesadale Post Office. Mailing labels, a poster of wildflower stamps, the FBI's Most Wanted—you might forget you were in an outlaw town until you met the postmistress, Sister Karen, in her Utah burka (think Laura Ingalls) and forty years of hair.

"I know I know you," she said. "Give me a second and I'll figure it out. I never forget a face." She tapped her temple with a pencil. "Jordan Scott! My goodness, what brings you back here?"

"I'm looking for someone."

"You came to the right place."

"One of my sisters. Stepsister, really. Her name's Elizabeth the Second. Blond hair, blue gray eyes. You know her?"

"You'll have to be more specific than that." Sister Karen wasn't being flip. In Mesadale there the limited gene pool produced a common look—white gold hair and fair, almost translucent skin that doesn't do well in the sun.

"She's pretty tall," I said. "Originally from Idaho."

"Originally from Idaho," Sister Karen said to herself. She was sorting the welfare checks waiting for delivery. The Prophet used to preach about welfare, claiming it was our religious duty to cheat the government. "The Devil's people are meant to support God's people," he'd say. The sister wives passed around a cassette of him teaching how to lie on a single-mother form. The checks arrived so frequently you had to wonder who in Salt Lake and Washington had been paid off.

"I don't know if this will help," I said, "but I used to call her Queenie."

"Queenie! Why didn't you say so? Brother Hiram's wife."

"So she's married?"

"Of course. To Brother Caleb's son, Hiram. Real nice man. A police officer. They live up Red Creek, across from the canyon."

In a flash I imagined my old friend's life: the big barn of a house, the chicken-scratched yard, the softball team of wives. I saw Queenie mending her husband's night-blue uniform, letting out the waist. I heard the stampede of children on the stairs. "How many wives?" I said.

"Actually, it's just Queenie. He really loves that girl. The Prophet keeps pressing him to take another and he keeps telling the Prophet he doesn't want anyone else."

I thanked Sister Karen for her help. "I know you're not supposed to talk to me."

"I love the Prophet, but honest to goodness you can't go around in life not *talking* to people. You going to Queenie's now? Do me a favor and tell her she's got a package."

I drove up the road next to Red Creek. It was midmorning and the streets were quiet. You might think, well, that's normal: the kids at school, the men at work, the women either at home or out at a job. Except that's not exactly how it was. Any kid older than eight was in school. The younger kids, I'm talking like five to seven, were looking after the babies or doing housework. Most of the wives were working, on the farms or in the few shops. Many worked in the church's sewing plant, making eyeglass cords. Some upholstered chairs and sofas in a furniture shop. A lot worked as secretaries over in church headquarters—doing who knows what, but I guess there's a ton of paperwork when you're planning for the end of time. Some women were nurses or midwives in St. George or Cedar City, usually the ones who couldn't have children. My mom worked part-time at the co-op as a cashier. When I was little sometimes I'd go to work with her, standing at her side as she rung up the groceries. The only customers were other Firsts, usually three or four sister wives out doing the marketing. They'd fill five or six baskets with cartons of cereal and sides of bacon and cases of fruit cocktail. Sometimes they'd fight over apple or grape juice, and sometimes they never even spoke. I remember once a guy came in who obviously wasn't a First. He was in a pair of jeans and a t-shirt with a pack of cigarettes rolled up into the sleeve. He walked up and down the aisles like he didn't know what he was looking for. When he passed a cluster of sister wives, they stepped aside and looked the other way. The guy chose my mom's aisle to buy a chocolate bar. He was staring at us, and my mom drew me close to her side. "Is there a restaurant or a café around here?" the guy said. My mom shook her head. She rang up his candy and handed him his change. I watched the guy walk back to his car. I watched the car back out of the lot. I watched my mom reassure herself that she'd done nothing wrong in taking the guy's money and touching his flesh when she gave him his two dimes.

And the men? What do they do in Mesadale? Some worked construction out on jobs in Kanab and St. George, where the wages were good. The boys did a lot of the construction in town, putting up more houses for wives and kids and more and more church admin. buildings. During my last year in Mesadale I helped reroof the church. I spent like half a year nailing down shingles. You know what Roland said when I told him that? "Oh honey, talk about an angel on the roof!"

But a lot of the men in the church didn't work at all. Especially the Apostles, the band of loyalists who kept an eye on everything for the Prophet. My dad was an Apostle, and in exchange he got to marry as many women as he wanted. At this hour in the morning a lot of these guys were passed out, sleeping off a hangover or a high. I'll guesstimate half the men had a whiskey and/or meth problem, and maybe half of those played with vicodin and oxy cotton, which is easy to score in Hurricane and St. George. There's no point in telling you the Prophet officially bans alcohol and drugs, or that I'm pretty sure he deals.

Queenie's house was easy to spot: a small stucco ranch, probably two bedrooms and a bath. The other thing that gave it away: her husband's patrol car parked at an angle in the drive.

Across the street I turned up a dry gulley and drove into the canyon. The van picked its way up the wash, the tires grinding in the sand, until we were behind a bend where no one could see us. The canyon walls cast a long shadow that would keep Elektra cool. I poured a bowl of water and cracked the windows. I told her she was a good girl, but she knew what was coming: her tail fell limp off her ass. When I got out she started barking, howling like I'd eaten her young. It echoed up the canyon. When I shhhhhed her, that echoed too.

"Oh come on," I said, leashing her up. "You big baby." Her tail flicked back to life.

The canyon walls were cold and gritty and almost blue from the shadow. At the mouth of the canyon we stepped into a world of white sunlight. The difference in temperatures must have been thirty degrees. We ran across the road to Queenie's door. It opened before I could knock.

"What are you doing here?"

"Good to see you, too."

"Shhh, Hiram's sleeping. Come on, let's go out to the garage." She led Elektra and me across a dark living room, down a path worn in the carpet. In the garage she turned on a painter's lamp. A thick beery light illuminated a workbench and a gun rack mounted with rifles and shotguns. "What are you up to?" she said.

"I guess you heard about my mom."

"Of course I did."

"Well, I'm looking into a few things."

"Like what?"

"Like what really happened."

In this light Queenie's face looked yellow and cold. She hadn't changed much, still beautiful, still a rebel gleam in her eyes. Her mother married my father not long before I was kicked out. She was his 23rd or 24th wife, I think, a bucktoothed woman who ate her nails. They met through this polygamy personals website (www.2wives.com; check it out). She showed up at the house with her thirteen-year-old daughter, Elizabeth. My father started calling the girl Elizabeth the Second to avoid confusion with another stepdaughter. I remember how shocked she looked those first few weeks in the house: the livid brow, the sense of betrayal in her eyes when her mother called her Elizabeth the Second. She knew she had landed in a very strange place. I took to her because she seemed, well, kinda fabulous, although this was of course before I had ever used that word. One night she told me she hated everyone calling her Elizabeth the Second. "It makes me feel like the fucking queen," she said. The what? She gave me a brief tutorial on British royalty. At first I didn't believe her. The Prophet had said on one of his tapes that although England had managed to avoid total destruction in the last war, there was nothing there now other than a ruined people living in huts and sheds. "He's lying," she said. I told her she was the one who was lying, but this wasn't long after I had refused to slaughter the dogs and the sheep. These two events rubbed together, shaping a baby pearl of doubt. Six weeks later my dad caught us holding hands. You know the rest.

In the garage I asked Queenie what had happened after I left. "It was no big deal," she said. "Your punishment was excommunication. Mine was marriage. The Prophet chose Hiram for me. Or I guess I should say he chose me for Hiram. Hiram was twenty at the time, so not really that old. We were sealed the next day. You know how it goes, you've heard the story a million times. But you know what—and this is the insane part—we fell in love. He's a good man. He loves me. He loves our little girl. Jordan—stop making that face."

"What face?"

"You think I'm out of my mind."

"No, no, it's great," I lied. "He sounds great."

Was she kidding? Love? In Mesadale? "I'm just surprised," I

said. "Monogamy is sort of a no-no out here."

"I know. Lately the Prophet's been putting pressure on Hiram. But so far we've resisted."

I asked how her mom was. She looked down to Elektra, then back up. A gray storm had moved across her eyes. "She's dead."

"What? How?"

"She got sick a few years ago. Her kidneys."

I told her I was sorry.

"But that wasn't it," she said. "About six months ago she started having doubts about everything. She wanted to leave your dad. She wanted out of here. So they murdered her."

"Excuse me?"

"They put salt in her dialysis machine. It crystallized her heart. She went into the clinic for a treatment and never came home."

OK, let me stop for a second. I know what you're thinking. And I'd be thinking it too. But in Mesadale it's not as unlikely as it sounds.

"Who was it?"

"The Prophet. Well, not him himself, but a couple of his men. He wanted to show everyone what happens if you try to leave."

"You know this for a fact?"

"No, but I know it's true."

I think one of the reasons Mesadale's been ignored for so long are the stories like these. When they seep out, when people outside hear them, they think, Oh please. Salt in the dialysis machine? A crystallized heart? It sounds like a bad movie. And so the stories are dismissed, and the Prophet and his disciples have been left alone. Mr. Heber was totally wrong to think anything out here had changed.

"Anyway," said Queenie. "So you're like what, snooping around?"

"Yeah, something like that."

"You don't think your mom did it?"

"I don't know."

"That doesn't surprise me. There isn't anyone more devout than your mom."

"I know, that's why I want to find out a little more."

"Did you talk to his latest wives? If I were you, I'd start with them."

"Why?"

"I don't know, it's just a feeling I have. Everything started to change with the last couple of wives."

"What are their names?"

"Let's see, Sister Kimberly is the newest. She lives behind the big house in a log cabin your dad built. Maybe start with her."

Then a little girl started crying on the other side of the house. "That's Angela, I need to go. You really have to get out of here before anyone sees you."

"Queenie, can I come back?"

"I don't think that's such a good idea." But then she softened up. "If you have to, yes, of course. Jordan, I don't want to turn all mushy on you, but after you were gone I never stopped thinking about you. I prayed a lot that you were OK."

"Me too. But I guess we're both doing fine, given the circumstances."

"I guess," she said. "You should go. And be careful." She pressed a button and the garage door opened to a wall of blinding light.

"I almost forgot," I said. "Sister Karen has a package for you."

"Oh really? I wonder what."

But the sunlight made it impossible to read her eyes.

From there I drove out to Kanab, a high-desert town that's one part granola-hiker-eco-tourist, two parts LDS. It's about forty miles beyond Mesadale, and arriving there is like time travel, *whoosh*ing in from the nineteenth century and landing in the twenty-first. I stopped at a sandwich shop called the Mega Bite and ordered a tuna fish from a girl whose name tag said "5."

"This is so weird," she said when she brought me the sandwich.

"I know you."

"You do?"

"You're only like my brother."

I was less astonished by this statement than you might think. The only remarkable part of this encounter was that she was a pretty teenage girl who had managed to escape Mesadale. The pretty ones never got out.

"My mom married your dad after you left. He used to talk about you. He said you fucked your sister. That chick, what's her name."

"I didn't fuck her."

"I figured that much, but that's what he said. He was just trying to scare us into never messing around with the boys. By the way, I'm Sarah Five."

"For the record, I was holding her hand. That's all."

"Oh, was that it? I used to wonder." She shrugged. "Anyway, I recognize you from your picture."

"What picture?"

"The one your mom kept in her room beside her bed. You were probably eleven or twelve in it, I don't know. It was at one of those birthday parties and you're standing in line with a paper plate, waiting for a piece of cake. Your mom showed it to me once."

"I don't even remember that picture being taken."

"You know what she said when she showed it to me? She said she was going to see you again in heaven. I don't mean to pick on your mom, but give me a fucking break."

"So who's your mom?"

"Kimberly."

"His last wife?"

"Yeah. I think she had something on your dad, because he'd do whatever she wanted. Like she said she wasn't going to live in that house with all those wives. The next day he started building her a log cabin. He made all the boys work on it, which pissed them off because they knew their moms were getting it worse. Anyway, that's where we lived, my mom and me. But they booby-trapped the place. It was always falling apart on us, a floor plank caving in, stuff like that. Once a window popped out on my mom. Nearly shredded her alive."

"So, Sarah. When'd you leave?"

"Five."

"What?"

"I call myself Five. Fuck the Sarah part. I left about eight months ago. My mom has no clue I'm living so nearby. I told her I was leaving Utah and never coming back. Guess that didn't happen. So anyway, what's going on with your mom?"

"I don't know. That's why I'm here."

"She's like in jail, right? It was all over the papers. Man, when I heard she shot him I was like, Lady, you beat me to it."

"That's what I thought until I got here."

"What was she, number fifteen or something?"

"Nineteen."

"The numbers are so screwed up. I doubt he really knew how many he had. It was all about pussy anyway. He was just counting cunts."

"Isn't it a little dangerous for you to be hanging out here?"

"I know," she said. "I probably shoulda gone to Vegas or Phoenix or something."

"They come into town pretty often, don't they?"

"Some of them, yeah. But you know what, those old guys have no idea who's who. No one but my mom remembers me. Here's the thing, I want to get my mom outta there."

"How you going to do that?"

"Same way I got out. There's this agency in Salt Lake that helps women like her."

"Really?"

"It's how I escaped. No one knows this, but there's a system to get messages in and out, you know, to people who want to leave. For a while they used the dairy fridge at the co-op to pass notes. Bet you didn't know that. Anyway, I heard about it and started communicating with them, and then they sent me a message telling me to meet them on the highway. So one night around three I sneak out of the house and run like crazy down to the highway. I had no idea if they'd actually be there, or even who they were. It all could've been a setup. It could've been the Prophet himself looking to screw me over. Literally. But I get there and this van pulls up with a man and a woman inside. I climb in and pray they're on my side. I know, can you believe it, me praying?

"Anyway, they drove me here to Kanab that first night and the next morning they were going to take me to Salt Lake, to this house for kids like me, but I was like, Thanks, I'll stop right here. They tried to talk me out of it, but when I make up my mind, forget it. I've been hanging around here trying to figure out how to get my mom out. When I heard your dad was dead, I went back to see her. I was like, Mom, let's get the fuck out of here. You know what she said? She tells me she doesn't want to go. She wants to hang around and play widow. She said she loved the old bastard. Is that fucked up or what?"

"It's pretty fucked up."

Elektra was growing impatient in the sun. 5 poured some water into her palm and Elektra licked it out. "You know what happens next, don't you? The Prophet's going to get some guy to marry all of them in one fell swoop. You know, keep the family together. And they'll all end up belonging to another man. Probably some young asshole who'll live another sixty years. No one would believe this goes on today. They're still looking for the Taliban, right? Well, hello? They're right here."

"Want to hear something crazy?" I said. "My mom says she didn't kill him."

"No shit. You think she's telling the truth?"

"I think so. That's why I'm looking around."

"For what?"

"That's the problem. I don't really know."

"Well, let me know if you find anything out."

A customer came in with a large order of veggie wraps. 5 took her place behind the counter. She pulled on a pair of plastic gloves and began laying out a row of tortillas. By the time she was done another large order came in, then another. But she kept her eye on me the whole time. When I stood to leave she waved from behind the counter, a plastic baggie on her hand.

I called Roland. "Kanab? Sounds Kanasty. Oh honey, where on earth?" Then I called the contractor who gives me most of my work. He wasn't pissed about my skipping out on the bathroom vanity job. I was still on for next Monday, a job in San Marino re-doing a nursery. "This lady's about to have triplets," he said. "Expect madness." Then I called my mom. Excluding calls from Mr. Heber, she's allowed only two calls a week. It took a while to get her on the phone. When I heard her voice, I told her I was going to see Kimberly.

"Is there anything I should know?" I said. The line crackled the way it does in a creepy old movie.

"I don't think she knew who I was before all this happened," she said. "The new wives pretty much ignore the old ones."

"Mom, I want to go up and look around your old room. Do you think I'll find anything there?"

"I doubt it. I wouldn't be surprised if one of the wives has already dumped my things."

After that I drove to a park and lay down on the futon in the back of the van. Elektra curled up next to me. I started reading that book about God. I was at the part about religion and war. I've been trying to get through it for a while now, but I always fall asleep after a few pages.

When I woke the sun was balling up and getting ready to set. It was time to go back to Mesadale. The closer I got, the redder the desert burned. Not red and orange and pink and yellow. Just red. Everything. Red and red and red. By the time I reached the turnoff, it was dark. I drove up the road with my headlights out.

Kimberly's cottage looked like one of those houses that comes as a kit in the mail. The windows were full of soft pinkish light. I heard water running in a sink. The front door was open and I could look through the screen door into the living room. A shotgun hung on two brackets above the mantel. I know my guns: it was a Golden Boy .22. But they weren't all that rare.

I called hello.

The water stopped. "Who's that?"

"Sister Kimberly?"

A young woman appeared on the other side of the screen, her hair up in an airy roll. She looked like one of those actors, if that's the right word, who works in a frontier-town theme park. "Can I come in?"

She knew who I was. "I don't think that's a good idea."

"It won't take long." I put my hand on the door.

"Please, stay out there." She locked the latch from inside. A shove would've yanked the door off its frame, but it seemed far-fetched. Me? Breaking down a (screen) door?

"Can you tell me what happened?"

"I don't know any more than you do. Besides, I can't talk to you. You know that."

"You can if you want to."

"Jordan, please."

"Five minutes. Give me five minutes."

I asked where she was when my dad was killed, and she said, "I was right here, of course."

I asked what she heard. "Nothing. Not until all the sister wives started screaming."

"Who was here that night?"

"I don't know, everyone, I suppose, but I never go in the main house."

"Did anyone leave right before he was killed? Anything suspicious like that?"

Through the screen, with the pinkish light behind her, she looked like a saint in an old painting, everything glowing around her beautiful round face. "No, nothing like that. Jordan, what are you up to? You really shouldn't be here."

"Are you all alone?" I said.

"Yes, of course."

"Don't you have a daughter?"

"Had."

"Had?"

"They took her."

"Who took her?"

Her eyes narrowed. "I don't know why I'm even talking to you."

"Because your husband was my dad. Where do you think your daughter is?"

"They've been coming for our young girls lately. Telling them all sorts of lies."

"Who?"

"The casinos."

"The casinos?" If it weren't so sad, I would've laughed.

"From Mesquite, and some from Las Vegas. They come over and take our girls."

"You're saying a casino kidnapped your daughter?"

"Yes, it just happened, right after he was killed. And I know what they do: They brainwash them, the pretty ones at least. The Prophet warned us to be on the lookout for people claiming to help our girls. They're the casinos." Tears came to her golden eyes.

"Here," I said. "Take this."

She hesitated, then unlatched the screen, opening it enough to take my bandanna. Quickly she set the hook back in its eye and dabbed her eyes. "The Prophet says I've got to forget all about her. She's gone into the world of sin and I can no longer love her, that's what he says." She let out a small cry. "But it's hard."

Those tears were real, that much I knew. We were standing close together, separated only by the screen. She said, "You should probably leave."

"Can I come another time?"

"What for?"

"To talk. To tell you if I find anything."

"I don't know." She shivered, and I left her, a silhouette in the screen.

I walked quickly around the side of the big house. I could hear the chatter of girls getting ready for bed. How many were still inside? No one knew: that was the thing. I felt sorry for them, everyone in my dad's house, even if one of them had put the rap on my mom.

A PROPHET ON THE MISSISSIPPI:
An Interview with Joseph Smith

Special to the *New York Herald*

July 28, 1843

Nauvoo, Illinois—Yesterday, in this beautiful city situated on a horseshoe bend in the Mississippi River, Howard Greenly of the *Herald* interviewed Joseph Smith, Jr., Prophet to the Latter-day Saints. Our correspondent met with Smith in the second-story offices above his Red Brick Store, sitting at the wood table where Smith regularly confers with the Quorum of the Twelve Apostles, his council of religious and political advisors. In the interview Smith would speak to the thus-called Gentile press more openly than he ever had before.

Smith is thirty-nine, equipped with a tall, lithely powerful frame, vivid in everything he does. Up and down the Mississippi he is famous for the flash in his blue gemstone eyes. His tenor voice carries far, with a natural clarity to it that attracts the ear. Since establishing his Church in 1830, this son of Vermont farmers has led his followers through a number of arduous relocations in search of a home where they could worship undisturbed, including colonies in Kirtland, Ohio, and Far West, Missouri, before settling in Nauvoo. Over the years Smith has been denounced as a charlatan, a plagiarist, and a speculator in fraud. He has been tarred-and-feathered, arrested for treason, chased across state lines, thrown in a Missouri jail cell, and faced orders of execution. He has seen his most faithful adherents slaughtered in pitiless battles such as the one at Haun's Mill. Yet each blow of adversity has only increased his position in the eyes of his devout. The Mormons, or Saints as they call themselves, revere him in a fervid manner unfamiliar to modern times. Nearly everyone in this bustling city of 12,000 speaks of him with the same reverence others reserve elsewhere for Jesus Christ, Son of God.

Smith's counselor and friend, Brigham Young, attended the interview. He is a quiet, thoughtful carpenter and glazier, with a stolid presence and fast, flinty eyes. This silent giant spoke but once, as the reader shall see.

H.G.—Can you tell us, are you a Christian?

J.S.—Yes. We believe in the Lord Jesus Christ fully. He is our Savior. We pray to him. We know he suffered on our behalf. He is at the center of all we believe.

H.G.—Then who are you?

J.S.—I am Joseph Smith Junior, son of Joseph Smith Senior and Lucy Mack Smith, and husband to Emma Hale Smith.

H.G.—Theologically speaking, who are you to this religion?

J.S.—I am the Prophet. The Lord has revealed many truths for man through me.

H.G.—What truths?

J.S.—He has restored the Gospel.

H.G.—The Book of Mormon?

J.S.—That's correct.

H.G.—Many people say it's a feeble imitation of the Bible.

J.S.—Have you read it?

H.G.—I must confess, I've given it a go a few times and couldn't make heads or tails.

J.S.—You didn't finish it, then?

H.G.—I did not.

J.S.—You strike me as a just man, so may I ask that you refrain from dismissing it before you've read it all the way through?

H.G.—Fair enough. What do you say to people who don't believe we live in a time of Prophets and revelations? That the days of mystical events belonged to the ancients?

J.S.—I say, Look around. Tell me why the Lord should stop communicating with man now? Aren't we in need of His word more so than ever? Why would He reserve His right to speak to man solely in ancient times?

H.G.—For some it's difficult, even impossible, to believe the stories of an angel in the woods, and the golden plates buried in the hills, and the other myths of your creed's origins.

J.S.—If they can believe Christ rose from His grave, I do not understand why they can't believe the fact of plates of gold.

H.G.—Very well. You are also the political leader of Nauvoo. Is this perhaps an instance of Church and State being one?

J.S.—It is.

H.G.—And yet we have a tradition of separating the two. Christ himself called upon separating that which was Caesar's from all things spiritual. Why should Americans accept your arrangement here?

J.S.—If the people of Nauvoo can accept it, the American people should do so as well. Show me the harm it is to them.

H.G.—What is your position on slavery?

J.S.—We believe slavery even more morally corrosive to the owner than to the enslaved.

H.G.—There is a group called the Danites, also called Destroying Angels, which is known as a militia, violent in its mission, and commanded by you, similar to Rome's Praetorian Guard. Can you tell the American people who they are and what they do?

J.S.—You astound me with your vivid tales. I have never heard of this group, nor do I lead any private bands. Tell me, where do these stories come from?

H.G.—Your enemies have depicted the Danites as a secret police authorized to destroy those who speak out against you.

J.S.—Think of your source: My enemies can be expected to depict such things.

H.G.—Not only your enemies, independent observers, too.

J.S.—Show me an independent observer. I would like to meet such a rare creature.

H.G.—You're denying such group exists?

J.S.—I ask you this: Nearly five years ago, a group of Saints was massacred at Haun's Mill by government sanction. A ten-year-old boy lost the top of his head to the Governor's militia. What was our response? Fury? Destruction? Revenge? No, we responded with grief and mercy, as Christ has taught us. If I employed a secret militia, shouldn't I have called them out to avenge that boy's death?

[At this point, the interview was interrupted by Chauncey Webb, a leading wainwright in Nauvoo. His business pulled Smith away for some ten minutes. Upon his return, Smith apologized and explained the interruption.]

J.S.—Brother Chauncey, my good friend who was just here, has brought news of the arrival of a caravan of Saints. Their wagons have pulled in from the coast of Maine.

H.G.—Fresh converts?

J.S.—Yes, and new friends.

H.G.—Your Church is expanding rather rapidly.

J.S.—If it does so, it is thanks to the power of God and the Truth of His word.

H.G.—Yet isn't there another reason? For nearly as long as your Church has existed, rumors of polygamy have surrounded it. Can you tell us once and for all, do you practice polygamy?

J.S.—We do not.

H.G.—Are there exceptions?

J.S.—Our enemies create the exceptions in the mind of the public. That does not make them true.

H.G.—Do you have any idea why these rumors persist?

J.S.—We seek to practice our religion freely. In the history of man, those who have sought religious freedom have been persecuted, maligned, and, if they are not careful, destroyed. We are no different than the early Christians in the Emperors' Rome. And yet, this country was founded on religious tolerance. And so it should be.

H.G.—I have been told you have at least twenty wives.

J.S.—Sir, my house is just up the street. You are free to search it. Let's go there now! If you find these twenty wives, please inform me.

H.G.—Sir, can you assure the general public that the Latter-day Saints do not practice plural marriage, never have practiced it, and never will practice it?

J.S.—I can assure you.

B.Y.—If I may interrupt.

J.S.—Of course.

B.Y.—Sir, why not ask our wives? Mrs. Smith, or my Mrs. Young, will gladly tell you about their households.

H.G.—Thank you, I wouldn't want to disturb them.

J.S.—I would think my Emma would have something to say if I came home with twenty women.

H.G.—Yes, I should say. So let's leave it at that, shall we? One last question: What is in your future?

J.S.—Peace, I should hope, to pursue our beliefs. In my heart I believe our countrymen deem this our right.

AN EYE IN THE DARK

———

When I got back to St. George I bought a ticket for whatever was playing in the cineplex's theater 8. I walked down the aisle to the front of the theater, folding a piece of paper into a little wedge. I opened the fire door and propped the lock with the wedge of paper. After fetching Elektra from the van, we slipped back into the theater. She seemed to know something was up because she came along silently, staying close. I sat in the second row against the wall, and Elektra curled up at my feet. The movie was about a pair of detectives, one black and one white. They're not supposed to get along, but they actually like each other and they go on to catch a jewelry thief who has some connection to international terrorism, and then it turns out the black guy's Muslim and the white guy's a Jew. I know: What? Then I fell asleep.

I woke up, slowly remembering where I was. Elektra was asleep on my feet. The movie was ending, the credits rolling up the screen. But the theater looked emptier than before.

"Wow," a voice said from behind. "You must've been wiped."

When I turned around I couldn't see anything but an eye gleaming in the dark.

"You slept through the movie twice."

"What time is it?" And then, "Who are you?"

"Johnny Barlow." He said it like we knew each other.

"How long've you been here?"

"A lot longer than you." The house lights were coming up, and now I could see the guy. He looked like every kid in Utah: blondish, blue, a splash of freckles. "This place is closing," he said.

"Closing?"

"Dude, it's almost one in the morning."

I turned on my phone. The kid was right.

"Do you have a dog with you?"

"Look, I have to go."

"Me too!"

The kid followed me up the aisle. Now that we were standing, I could see he really was a kid, twelve or thirteen, a late bloomer, just this side of puberty. His turquoise muscle T showed wiry but strong kid-arms. The lobby was empty except for a heavy girl in a black-and-buff cineplex uniform vacuuming popcorn from the carpet. "Can't have a dog in here," she said, but you could tell she didn't care.

Outside it was still hot in the parking lot, the asphalt throwing back the heat. "Look, I'm leaving," I said.

"Yeah, same here." He had one of those kid voices that goes high and low and back again in one sentence. "How about a lift?"

"Where do you live?"

"Well, you see, right now I'm sort of in between places." He said it so smoothly, I figured he'd picked up that line from someone else. He followed me to the van, staying real close. He came up to about my chest, and I bet he didn't weigh more than a hundred pounds. "Nice van," he said, touching the pom-pom on the side. The truth is, it's a piece of shit and no one ever says anything about it except, *That thing really run?*

"I can drop you on St. George Avenue, but that's it."

"Awesome." He didn't wait for me: he crawled across the driver's seat to the passenger side and started bouncing in the seat. "This is the phattest van I've ever seen."

"Put your seat belt on."

"Where'd you say you were going?" he said.

"Just tell me where on St. George you want me to drop you."

"Here's the thing." He forced his voice down an octave. "I wouldn't mind staying with you for the night. Just one night. That's all." He was talking in a voice he must've picked up from the movie. "But no funny business, you know what I'm saying?" He thought this was especially funny, slapping his thigh and throwing his head back in laughter, like a little kid watching a cartoon.

But this was my van and I wasn't going to be insulted by a kid. "No, I don't know what you're saying."

"You know. I'm no fag." More of the cartoon laugh.

"I am."

The kid stopped. He looked at me with big, no-shit eyes. Then he smiled. "I get it. Very funny. You had me for a second. Ha-ha." He stopped. "Wait a minute, you telling me you're a homo?"

"Only because you brought it up."

He whipped a three-inch kitchen knife out of his pants and pointed it at my chest. "You touch me and I kill you."

I took the knife from the kid. "What're you doing with that?"

"Protecting myself from pervos like you."

"Get out of my van."

"Fucking faggot." He unclicked his seat belt and pushed open the door and slid a leg out. He was so small his foot dangled several feet above the asphalt. But he didn't jump.

"Get out."

"Fuck you." The thing is, he said this almost tenderly. He stayed in the seat, his face all broken up. "I thought you were cool."

"You're the one who's not being cool."

He moved a little closer to the edge of the seat but still didn't jump. "Look, I'll stay with you tonight, but you got to promise you won't touch me."

"Kid, get out of my van."

"But why?"

"Because you asked for a ride and now you're calling me all sorts of names. I don't put up with stuff like that anymore. I blew off this place a long time ago."

The kid slid his leg back into the van. "Wait a minute, you don't live here?"

"Nope."

"What're you doing here, then?"

"Long story."

"You run away or something like that?" He closed the door and the overhead light went out.

"Are you from where I think you're from?" I said.

"Yup." He pulled his knees into his chest. "Was it hard making it on your own? I mean, look at you. You got a phone and a van. You're rich."

"I'm not rich."

"To me you are."

"You said your name's Johnny."

He nodded eagerly.

"Want to get something to eat?"

"Totally. But first, can I have my knife back?"

Twenty minutes later we were outside the Chevron, eating a sack of microwaved burritos. "Now I know who you are," said Johnny. "But remind me: why'd you get kicked out?"

"I was caught alone with one of my stepsisters. What about you?"

"I was listening to the Killers. It wasn't even my disc, it was my brother's. But they caught me. I don't even like the Killers."

That wasn't the real reason. They get rid of the boys to take away the competition. With no boys around, the old men have the girls to themselves. I handed Johnny the last burrito. "How'd you end up here?"

"Two of the Apostles drove me in. Worst night of my life. I was crying my eyes out and they just sat up front and pretended like I wasn't there. I kept asking why're you doing this? I'm just a kid. How'm I going to live? But they wouldn't even talk to me. I had to stare at their necks the whole way. I wanted to cut off their heads. If I had a better knife, I would've. You saw my blade, it's pretty lame. Then they left me in the parking lot of the Pioneer Lodge."

"When was that?"

"Six months ago."

"What've you been up to since?"

"Hanging out. I stayed in one of the Butt Huts for a while, and then I went down to Vegas, but I didn't really like it so I came back here."

"And the knife?"

"It's my mom's. I took it from the kitchen. It's the only thing of hers I got. See, she wrote her name on a piece of paper and taped it to the handle." He showed it to me proudly. *Tina,* in a bad blue cursive. His mom probably wasn't yet thirty.

"Do me a favor and be careful with that."

After that we watched the cars pull in for gas and the people running inside for cigarettes and visine. "Isn't your mom like in jail?"

"How do you know about that?"

"Everyone knows about that."

"She didn't do it. Everyone thinks she did, but she didn't."

Johnny was eating a bag of potato chips, tipping the remnants down his throat. "When I heard about what happened," he said, "I wasn't all that surprised. Things are weird out there right now. Something's happening. There were all these rumors going around before I left."

"What kind of rumors?"

"Like we were all moving to Texas or Mexico or something. And there was stuff about your dad."

"What stuff?"

"I don't know. Just stuff like he was trying to take over from the Prophet. I don't really know everything, but I just heard stuff like that. Other stuff, too. That's why I wasn't surprised when I heard he was killed."

I said nothing. Was the kid full of shit or did he know something? We hung around the Chevron for about a half hour until the manager told us we couldn't loiter. He was nice about it, just said the cops watch the parking lot and we had to leave.

I turned to Johnny. "Where to?"

"You tell me."

"Let's go out to Snow Canyon. I know this place we can park overnight. It should be cool there."

"OK, but no funny business."

"Get out."

"Kidding! I thought you gay guys were supposed to have a sense of humor."

We drove out on Highway 18. The road was dark, the only light from the moon and the stars. Johnny fell asleep, his head against the window and his mouth open. When I parked the van he rolled his head around, murmured, then went back to sleep. Like this, he really looked like a kid. It was hard to imagine anyone with a thump in his heart abandoning Johnny. I picked him up and laid him on the futon. I pulled a sheet over him and rolled up my sweat-shirt for a pillow. I lay down behind him on my back with my arm behind my head. Elektra was curled up between us. I wasn't tired, and for a long time I looked at the ceiling of the van. Johnny was snoring. Nothing loud, just a soft little chug. Kids don't really make a racket when they sleep. I thought about what I would do in the morning. What did he know? I pondered it for a long time, then fell off into a shallow sleep.

VI

CELESTIAL MARRIAGE

THE 19TH WIFE

———

CHAPTER THREE:

The Doctrine of Celestial Marriage and the Death of Joseph Smith

Now, having described the religious conversions of my mother, Elizabeth, and my father, Chauncey, and their unyielding allegiance to Joseph Smith; having depicted the horror of the massacre at Haun's Mill and the long migration out of Missouri; having spilled perhaps too much ink describing the rise of Nauvoo, Illinois, and the peace the Saints found therein; having established all this for you, my Patient Reader, I shall move forward to the subject that no doubt first drew you to these pages: the doctrine of celestial marriage, otherwise known as polygamy.

On the evening of June 6, 1844, Joseph visited my parents' home in Nauvoo. He came bearing news. The Prophet stood before them in the keeping room, clearing his throat several times, making the Ah-hem sound familiar to anyone who knew him. (The skeptical Reader will ask, How does Mrs. Young know all this? To him I say, My mother has spoken of the Prophet's visit to her home at least once a month for the past thirty years.)

"I have received another Revelation," Joseph began.

Elizabeth could not contain the excitement in her heart. For her, hearing a Revelation was all but the same as hearing the words of God.

"The Lord has commanded us to expand the Kingdom," Joseph explained.

Chauncey asked, "Do you mean we're leaving Nauvoo?" He did not want to abandon his wagonry yet again. He had done so twice before, in Ohio and Missouri; often he said he would not move a third time.

"We're here to stay," said Joseph. "Nauvoo is our Zion. The Kingdom is to grow here."

It occurred to Elizabeth that Joseph had not heard her news. Hence she told him in September there would be a child. "If it's a girl I'll name her Ann Eliza," she announced.

"It's a blessing," said Joseph. "And now I must tell you the words of our Heavenly Father. He has commanded us to fill the earth with Saints, to replenish the lands with the devout." As Joseph spoke, a high whistling sound mingled with his words. The source was a missing tooth, an injury from a mob attack in Ohio many years before. The whistling rang out like a tiny, tiny bell.

"What more can we do?" said Chauncey. He reminded Joseph of their two newborns lost in infancy and Elizabeth's poor health thereafter.

"I asked our Heavenly Father the same question," said Joseph. "What else can I do? Tell me, Dear Lord, what must I do expand the Kingdom? Over time, the Revelation has made itself clear. Now I must share it with the most faithful, Saints like you."

"I'll have my child," said Elizabeth. "And if the Lord wants another I'll have another. And yet another, until He decides I can't bear more."

"You're a good woman, among the best of the Saints. That's why I've come to tell you what I know."

Joseph looked to the ceiling in a moment that suggested he was peering up at the feet of God.

"Do you recall my words about Abraham and Sarah?" he began. "God ordered Abraham to take another wife. This was not Abraham's wish, it was not Sarah's wish, but it was God's command. And so Sarah told Abraham to take Hagar as his wife, although she was his wife. Was Abraham wrong to do it? Did he commit adultery? No, because it had been commanded of him by God." Joseph stopped, then turned to Elizabeth. "Sister, do you understand me?"

Many times before this night, Elizabeth had heard the rumors of Joseph's marital relations. Faithless people permitted their tongues to flap, going on about a bounty of wives—a dozen, two dozen, some said more. Elizabeth never listened to such talk. It is true, once she witnessed the Prophet driving intimately with a woman who was not Mrs. Smith. Another time she spotted him calling at the door of the widow Mrs. Martin. Yet Elizabeth never permitted such evidence to dent her belief. Now Joseph had come to reveal the rumors were true. The incidents she had witnessed were indeed indiscretions. That she had defended the Prophet when he was indefensible. Even more startling, Joseph was telling her these acts of passion were divined by God!

For a long time the room was silent, the evening sun burning low outside. Elizabeth looked up to find her boys, Gilbert and Aaron, outside peering through the window. Their noses were pink and had the look of two fresh buds beneath a glass.

"As you know," said Joseph, "we must accept God's will."

The idea of sharing her husband, in the manner of lustful animals sharing a lair, was abhorrent to Elizabeth. She could not accept it as true. She turned in her chair. She could no longer look at Joseph Smith.

"Sister Elizabeth, tell me, what do you say?"

"My husband has a wife," she said. "Me."

The hour was dusk. The room had filled with the dull silver of the gloaming. Joseph's face was now obscure, except the blue stones of his eyes. "I'll tell you, I first resisted this Revelation as well. My dear sweet Emma, she turned against it. She wanted nothing of it. For a long time we denied it. Many nights we prayed over it. Now the time has come to embrace it, for it is the truth. Consider why the Lord would want us to accept it. Think of what He has planned for the Latter-day Saints. He has chosen us to populate the Earth in preparation for Judgment. To fill the lands with the faithful. To ready His people for—"

"Stop!" cried Chauncey. "For God's sake, stop. We don't want any part of it."

For some time thereafter they were silent, staring at the fire dying on the stone. After many sad minutes, Joseph said it was time to leave. Before he departed, he made a final attempt.

"I said the same thing. I begged the Lord to change this truth. This was the one Revelation I pleaded to be not so. Do you think this is what I wanted? He has commanded it, as with all else. Your regret does not surprise me. I expected no other response. Before I leave I must ask one thing."

"My wife has said no," said Chauncey. "Even if she were to say yes, I would never agree."

The quality of his resolve placed him even closer to Elizabeth's heart.

"I understand," said Joseph. "And I ask you to pray over the meaning of God's love."

When Joseph was gone, Elizabeth and Chauncey fell to their knees. They prayed for knowledge, but it did not come, for their hatred of the Revelation would not relent. Chauncey took Elizabeth's hand. In his fingers she felt his fury. It nearly crushed her bones.

"Tomorrow I'll go see him," he said. "Even if I have to wait all day I'll tell him we can't follow this order. The other Revelations guide us to lead a good life, but this one?"

"But it's the Lord's will."

"No, this time Joseph is wrong. He's using his authority to cover his personal sins."

"If Joseph is wrong about this," said Elizabeth. Yet she could not finish. The meaning was too heavy to bear.

"I'll go tomorrow," said Chauncey. "And tell him you refuse."

"What if he says I'm unfaithful?"

"Do you believe you are?"

Yet the next day the events of history preceded Chauncey's defiance. On June 7 the *Nauvoo Expositor* published its maiden issue, every inch of its newsprint determined to reveal the truth about Joseph Smith. The newspaper accused him of "abominations and whoredoms." Most damning of all was the fact that former Saints were printing these stories, men who had once believed in Joseph and yet had come to recognize him as a liar and scoundrel. Each of the newspaper's two principal editors, William Law and Robert D. Foster, had a particularly damning story to tell. Law, a leading economic advisor to Smith, had learned that Smith had asked his wife—and by this I mean William Law's wife!—to become a spiritual wife. That is, quite simply, a theologically cloaked manner of inviting a woman to commit adultery. Robert Foster, a contractor, returned home one evening to discover his wife dining alone with the Prophet. She admitted the Prophet was trying to convince her to become his spiritual wife. The Prophet was, as they say, seducing women all over town.

There is no fiercer wrath than that of the cornered animal's. Joseph was wounded by the *Expositor*'s revelations. For years his loyal Saints had ignored the rumors of adultery, polygamy, and a Prophet driven by lust, but now it was impossible, for the accusations came from friends. Law and Foster were leaders of Nauvoo, known for their honesty and devotion. On that day in June 1844, in the beautiful city of Nauvoo, beneath the high summer sky, there was not a Saint who did not have a cloud of doubt in his heart about Joseph Smith.

Joseph responded by denouncing the *Expositor* and the men behind it. This time, however, his denials were not enough. It seems he never considered telling the truth. Instead he gathered his city council, declared the *Expositor* a civic nuisance, and sent his men to destroy it. A squadron from Joseph's private militia, the Nauvoo Legion, cousins of the infamous Danites, marched over to the newspaper's offices, tore apart the press, and burned every copy of the *Expositor*.

It must be noted at this time Joseph's enemies beyond Nauvoo were taking aim. His theocratic rule in Nauvoo had long piqued the political elite throughout the country, stirring up profound animosity and suspicion. Clerical leaders all over Illinois denounced the Mormons and their leader as impure. With the *Expositor*'s unconstitutional destruction, Joseph's outside enemies had reason to pounce.

Long piqued by Joseph's accumulation of power, the Governor of Illinois could no longer tolerate a Prophet of God as a rival. The Governor charged Joseph with riot and treason.

The news of these events came as great confusion to Elizabeth. She prayed for understanding—is it a whoredom and abomination if it is commanded by God? *Heavenly Father, tell me.*

Before his arrest Joseph addressed his followers outside the new Temple. Chauncey and Elizabeth stood in the crowd, listening to Joseph defend himself. "The newspaper lies," he cried. "The legislature lies. The Governor lies. Next, I tell you, the President of the United States will lie to you. Show me where in all Nauvoo are these supposed abominations and whoredoms? Where, I ask you? Where? If they are here, I should like to see them for myself and judge them for myself, as should you!"

These were the last words Elizabeth was to hear from the Prophet. She struggled to understand their meaning. In her struggle she reached a pitiful conclusion—she was no longer faithful, for now, during Joseph's time of need, she had abandoned him to doubt.

The order came for Joseph to submit to the jailhouse at Carthage. At midday on June 24 Joseph and his loyal brother, Hyrum, and several others departed Nauvoo, riding through the Flats. They knew the dangers awaiting them. The hatred for the Saints, and Joseph especially, had grown in recent days. At night, packs of invisible men slit the throats of oxen and burned crops. They pulled men from their horses and threatened their wives. They poisoned Mormon dogs. That bright June, the mood in Nauvoo was dark.

Joseph rode to Carthage without force. Emma has since reported he said to her, "I am going like a lamb to slaughter." At Carthage he spent two nights. The jailer, Mr. Stigall, moved him and the others from the suffocating dungeon, to the debtor's cell on the first floor, which exposed them to assassins, and finally to his own bedroom atop the stairs.

It was evident to all that the prisoners' lives were in danger. I do not believe we will ever know if Mr. Stigall, who lived in the jailhouse with wife and daughters, played a role in the murder, although it is unlikely, for his daughters were present at the time of the attack. He was away from his post when the mob arrived on June 27 in the afternoon. There were between 150 and 200 men, many with faces blackened by coal soot. They stormed the jailhouse, mounted the stairs, and fired through the door into the bedroom. A ball hit Hyrum beside the nose. Joseph lunged to aid his brother, but he was already dead. Soon the attackers broke through the door. Joseph ran to the window—his only escape. It was twenty feet to the ground. He hesitated at the sill. Shots rang out and he took two balls to the back. A rifleman stationed at the water well below shot him through the heart. Joseph plunged out the window to the ground. Willard Richards, a witness and friend, claims his final words were, "Oh Lord, my God!"

The agony of martyrdom is almost too much to bear. In the early hours, when the loss is fresh, there is no comfort in knowing Glory will live on. We speak of the martyrs of History but we cannot know the actual pain they suffered in their final living hours. They enter the realm of the mythic, but we must never forget these were men like ourselves. When their flesh is torn, they cry out. They suffer as you and I would suffer, although more bravely. Remember Christ. Although I am now an enemy to Joseph's legacy, I shudder when recalling his suffering.

After Joseph's murder, his enemies across the county and the state believed the Saints would rise up in revenge. They fled or hid their families and livestock, fearful of Mormon wrath. Yet the Saints did not return violence with violence. Instead they withstood their grief. Joseph's body was set out in the dining room of the Mansion House. Elizabeth, along with her two sons, waited hours to pass by his open coffin to see his historic face one last time. When she saw him, and the depth of his sleep, and truly understood she would not see him again until the Last Day, she wept.

Three years later, upon departing Nauvoo for the Utah Territory, my mother wrote a Testimony of Faith. She sealed it in a granite box that was buried at the Temple's foundation, there to be found by a new generation of Saints. Yet before she did so, she crosshatched a draft of her Testimony into a Book of Mormon, which she has since given me. I will quote from it here to describe, in her words, her reaction to the Prophet's death.

"I could not summon, neither then nor now, the words to depict the complexities of my grief. My Prophet was gone; but his death had freed me from his loathsome request. Had he spoke the truth throughout his life, erring only in his final days? Was this why he had succumbed to the enemy's ball? Or were his final words also true and devout? Upon seeing his body laid out, I prayed to God, frightened I had caused Joseph's fall. Was his murder, I asked, punishment for my doubt? Was I to blame? I feared the truth."

Thereafter, throughout the summer, the Apostles fought over who would lead the Church of Latter-day Saints. At the time of Joseph's death, several, including Brigham, were away on mission, and the matter was not settled until the 8th of August of that year. On that day, at ten in the morning, Brother Sidney Rigdon gathered the community of Saints in a hollow east of the Temple. The day was warm and damp, the flies buzzing in the boughs. The grove could not provide enough shade, and many stood in the shadow of their horses. Brother Rigdon hoped to lead the Saints and asked for their support. At length he preached with honest remorse in his voice. Yet his performance had not convinced the Saints he was their leader. Brigham followed Rigdon, and to describe his appearance I must quote my mother's Testimony again, for it is in this passage she is at her most eloquent on the mysteries of belief.

"When Brigham took the stand to describe his grief and his hope for our Church, he inspired our hearts. He began to speak as Joseph had once spoken, adopting his voice and mannerisms, often clearing his throat with the familiar Ah-hem and creating his peculiar whistle. As time passed, Brigham began to appear even more like Joseph, until it no longer seemed he was adopting the voice and expressions of our beloved Prophet—the familiar gestures of his right hand, the movement of body—but in fact the mantle of Joseph had passed to Brigham, and Brigham was now Joseph! In the limp summer haze, there before me, a miracle occurred. I saw Brigham transform into Joseph himself. Upon the stand, where Brigham had stood, stood now our beloved Joseph! As clear as the page before me now, and the lines of ink, our Prophet appeared.

"Some say it was a trick of the sunlight, or the ghostly way Brigham's voice traveled through the hollow. Others claim the heat had tampered with our minds; or fresh grief had overcome our reasoning. I understand why they might say such things, yet I write this now to say—I know what I saw. Before me, and the community of Saints, in the dappled light, for one brief moment in Time, Joseph returned, entering Brigham's powerful body, the two united by the force of God. Chauncey did not see this. My Husband becomes discouraged when I speak of it. Yet I know the fact of it as well as I know anything, for I understand why. Joseph had returned to clear the dark doubt from my heart. And so it came to pass."*

By the end of the day the succession was settled. Brigham Young was proclaimed the new leader of the Latter-day Saints. He was forty-three years old, and about to become one of the most influ-

---

* The authoress would like to assert that many eyewitnesses have left similar accounts of an inexplicable vision and that was not unique in seeing that which could not be seen. Even some thirty years later, my mother still claims she experienced the supernatural on that summer day in Nauvoo.

ential men in the United States. Elizabeth rejoiced, for her experience told her it was meant to be. A month later, on September 13,
1844, she bore a tiny daughter who came into this world with the
voice of a howling angel, I am told. That child, of course, was me.

VII

—

WOMEN'S STUDIES

Women's Research Institute
Brigham Young University
WS 492—Women's Studies Senior Research Seminar
Professor Mary P. Sprague
April 23, 2005

THE FIRST WIFE

By Kelly Dee

1.

The subject of this paper, Elizabeth Churchill Webb (1817–1884), is not familiar to many. She was an early convert to the Church and the first wife of wainwright Chauncey Webb (1812–1903), whose Nauvoo wagonry played a crucial role in the Exodus (1846–1847). Brigham Young personally chose Chauncey to lead the wagon manufacturing for the Pioneers in their trek to Zion.

My interest in Elizabeth Webb, however, has less to do with her role in supporting her husband during this historic period. Instead, I am more curious about her relationship to her daughter, Ann Eliza, who would go on to become Brigham Young's infamous 19th wife. In the 1870s and 1880s, Ann Eliza (1844–date unknown) became a leading crusader in the fight to end polygamy in the United States. In her battle against plural marriage she became a vocal enemy of both the Church and Brigham, writing a bestselling memoir of her experiences, *The 19th Wife* (1875). Her book, and especially her attacks against Brigham, continue to divide people today. Given that she was born into the Church, and her parents were faithful members, her deep hatred of Mormonism has surprised and confused many. It is therefore worth investigating her early family life, especially her mother's attitude to plural marriage. This is why I have chosen Elizabeth Churchill Webb as the subject of my seminar paper. Specifically, I will use two key texts to depict this historic period in her life: 1) Elizabeth's recently discovered Testimony of Faith[1] to narrate the period in her life when she first accepted the doctrine of celestial marriage; and 2) her Exodus Diary, written on her journey to Zion in 1848, an insightful document that has sat ignored in the Church archives for more than one hundred years.

2.

One day in the fall of 1845, Brigham Young walked to Elizabeth and Chauncey Webb's small but prominent brick house on the corner of Parley and Granger streets in the central district of Nauvoo known as the Flats.[2] The spiritual and political leader of the Latter-day Saints, and successor to Joseph Smith's title of Prophet, came alone. Such a private visit by Brigham Young, unannounced

---

[1] In 1999, not long after the rebuilding of the Nauvoo Temple began, Church historians were excited to discover a time capsule buried in the original Temple's foundation. The capsule itself is a granite box, measuring three feet long and two feet wide and one and a half feet tall. An inscription on its stone lid describes the contents to be the Testimonies of Faith, or personal statements of belief, written by a number of Saints departing Nauvoo for Salt Lake in 1846. When Church historians and leaders opened the time capsule at the rededication of the Nauvoo Temple on June 27, 2002, they were disappointed to discover that water had destroyed, or partially damaged, a number of Testimonies, including an estimated twelve pages of the Testimony written by Elizabeth Churchill Webb. While frustratingly truncated, the surviving fragments of Elizabeth's Testimony provide many insightful glimpses into her outlook during this historic period (1844–1846). Today the document is held in the Family Research Center in Nauvoo.

[2] Unless otherwise stated, my source is Elizabeth Churchill Webb's Testimony. General information about early Mormon history and Nauvoo comes from personal research conducted during my recent spring break trip there.

and unattended by aide, was an unusual event. No doubt Chauncey and Elizabeth were surprised to see him at their door.

The mood in Nauvoo at this time was anxious. Since Joseph's martyrdom in June 1844, the Saints had been fearful of a massacre similar to the one at Haun's Mill. There were signs that a major raid was about to come. At night haystacks were burned in open fields. Dogs were beheaded and livestock poisoned. Carriages on the road to Quincy were ambushed. Illinois governor Thomas Ford warned Brigham to lead his followers out of the state; if he did not, the governor could not promise their safety. The Saints' future was altogether uncertain to everyone except Brigham, who was busy making secret plans for the Exodus that would lead his followers to what was still an unknown destination.

Brigham and Chauncey met in the keeping room at the front of the house. Elizabeth remained in the kitchen at the back of the house while her sons, Gilbert, age eleven, and Aaron, age seven, played outside in the orchard. Ann Eliza, now one year old, lay restless in her cradle beside the fire. The Webbs' house girl, Lydia Taft,[3] came and went through the back door, minding the boys in the orchard. They had invented a game of looking for the faces of Jesus, Mary, and Joseph Smith in the rotten apples littering the orchard yard this time of year. Lydia and the boys fed the apples to the billy goat, a spotted animal christened (ironically, it must be assumed) Mr. Pope.[4]

After half an hour Brigham asked Elizabeth to join them in the keeping room. With baby Ann Eliza in her arms, she went to see her husband and her Prophet. Elizabeth thought she knew the topic of the conversation: "I was certain he had come to remind me of the Revelation I feared most," Elizabeth writes in one fragment, referring to celestial marriage, or polygamy. "I know now I feared it

---

[3] Her real name was Elizabeth Taft, but they called her Lydia to avoid confusion.

[4] See Taft, Lydia, Letters (Family History Library).

because it was true."

First, Brigham had other business, however. He told her about the wagon order he had just placed with Chauncey. Soon he would announce an Exodus from Nauvoo, he said, commencing the following spring. "Our destination is Zion," Brigham explained. "Soon God will reveal its location to me."

Chauncey would lead the crucial effort to build the necessary wagons for the journey. Elizabeth took understandable pride in her husband's selection as chief wainwright. "He is a necessary man," she writes.

They discussed in detail the requirements.[5] Each wagon would need to haul two thousand pounds of supplies. Every fifth wagon would carry a spare front wheel, every tenth wagon a spare rear wheel. Every twentieth required a slot for a beehive. Brigham's meticulous orders displayed his considerable skills at planning and organizing. Before he was to lead nearly twenty thousand people across the plains and the Rockies, he was to think through every possible requirement and contingency. Between 1847 and 1869, some seventy thousand Pioneers would owe their lives to Brigham's painstaking planning, staging, and organization. This is why George Bernard Shaw called him an American Moses. This is why his statue stands in the Capitol in Washington, D.C., today, alongside other national heroes such as George Washington and Dwight D. Eisenhower.[6]

It is important to remember that at this time Brigham was still a relatively young man. Our image of him today is based on the later portraits made long after the establishment of the Utah Territory and he had entered late middle age. In 1845, however, he was a vig-

---

[5] Chauncey would end up building between 1,000 and 1,500 wagons used at various stages of the Exodus.

[6] Much of my general information about Brigham comes from *Brigham Young: American Moses* by Leonard J. Arrington (Knopf, 1985).

orous man of forty-four. One immigrant described his face as "that of a sea captain"—firm, a bit square, with iron-colored eyes. He had wide cheeks, a small mouth, and an altogether determined look.[7]

"It was no relief to know that he had come with a request for wagons, and not another," Elizabeth writes in her Testimony. "For I knew one day he would ask what I dreaded most." Understandably, she was frightened. Section 132 of the Doctrine & Covenants—the Revelation Joseph Smith had personally revealed to Elizabeth and Chauncey the day before his arrest—says that those who fail to meet the requirements of plural marriage cannot achieve Salvation. It is a point worth emphasizing: The Church—that is, the men Elizabeth believed and trusted most—was telling her that she would be condemned eternally if she did not submit fully to this hated custom.

"And yet, there is another matter," said Brigham. With those few words, the mood in the room had changed. The baby began to simper. Even as she minded her daughter, Elizabeth knew her fear had been warranted: He had in fact come to discuss plural marriage.

"I know Brother Joseph discussed the covenant of celestial marriage with you shortly before his martyrdom. I know he shared the revelation of plural marriage."

"Is it really the will of the Lord?" Elizabeth asked.

"It is."

As much as she loathed the idea, she then knew that this time she could not deny her Lord or her Prophet. She thought back to the meeting with Joseph. We cannot know how many times she blamed herself for his fate by refusing to comply, but such a sentiment appears forcefully in her Testimony.

"Tell me, Sister," said Brigham, "what do you say?"

"I will do as He asks."

It was done. Brigham blessed her. Elizabeth wept softly in her

---

[7] To me, this younger Brigham looks a lot like Russell Crowe.

husband's arms.

A decade later, in a letter to one of his sons, Brigham describes how he had to "console the astonished hearers of this news. I told them that I too heard of it and hated it immediately. Yet if we are to listen to our God, and follow His command, we cannot choose those orders which most please us, and ignore those that cause us pain. For verily, it has been revealed, this is our way to Heaven, and to ignore the path is to ignore Salvation altogether. I remember telling a Brother and a Sister of the Revelation in Nauvoo. Together we fell to our knees and prayed. It was all I could offer, for the truth comes as such."[8]

Next Brigham explained to Elizabeth and Chauncey that the approval of the second wife belonged to the first. "Brother Chauncey must come to you for your consent. The choice of wife, who she shall be, lies with you."

A "small fury" burned within Elizabeth as Brigham explained the process. If she must submit to plural marriage, she wanted nothing to do with the selection of the wife. Although it is doubtful she thought of it in such terms, Elizabeth resented the complicity the institution was forcing upon her.

When Brigham was gone, Chauncey and Elizabeth discussed the matter. Chauncey probably hated the idea even more than his wife did. Unlike Elizabeth, there seemed to be a bottom to his faith. He said he would tell Brigham they could not follow his orders. "He cannot force us."

Yet for Elizabeth, it was too late. She had searched her soul and reached a truth. "We must obey," she said. For her, apostasy was not an option. She remembered what had happened the last time she had defied her Prophet.

---

[8] Brigham to Brigham Jr., November 3, 1855.

3.

Lydia Taft was seventeen when she left her family in Saint Clair County, Michigan, in the summer of 1844. A few months before, a missionary had come to preach from the Book of Mormon in a neighbor's parlor, electrifying Lydia with his news of the Restoration and his depiction of Nauvoo, the shining city on the hill. She left the meeting with a copy of the Book of Mormon, determined to read it. By the time she turned the last page, her faith was secure. "I knew. Mother, I knew!" she would later write in one of her three surviving letters.

When news of Joseph Smith's martyrdom reached her, she decided to travel to Nauvoo to live among the Saints. "The time is now. That's what Joseph Smith in death has taught me. Now! Oh my dear Mother. Please read this Book! And then come be with me in Nauvoo! It's a city that gleams upon the river bank, and men can see the white Temple from all directions, and every day the faithful arrive from all over the world."

After landing in Nauvoo, Lydia found work in the Webb household. At the time, Elizabeth was pregnant with Ann Eliza. It was a difficult pregnancy and she needed the help. When she hired Lydia, Elizabeth could not have imagined that a little more than a year later the girl would become her rival wife.

The only known picture of Lydia was taken many years later in Salt Lake. It shows a thin, tired woman with buried eyes. But in 1845, when she was seventeen, she was "pale and lovely," according to Elizabeth, "with a quick soft mouth and flecks of gold in her eyes."

There is conflicting evidence over who first suggested Lydia to become Chauncey's second wife. In the surviving fragments of her Testimony, Elizabeth writes, "Lydia no doubt loved my children. I had grown accustomed to her presence and the sound of her feet." In *The 19th Wife* Ann Eliza says she recalls her father looking at Lydia "in a manner a husband reserves for his wife." Perhaps he did so, but Ann Eliza's memory of it is doubtful (she was one year old at the time). We may not know whose idea it was, but by late 1845 Chauncey and Elizabeth had decided to enter a plural marriage with Lydia. Now they only needed her to agree.

At some point, Elizabeth writes, Lydia began to eat with the family at the supper table. "She ceased being our servant in many ways." We don't know if this was after the idea was broached or before. We have Lydia's account of the actual conversation preserved in a letter to her mother. It took place late on a blizzardy night, the children already in bed. The snow was blowing hard, and the drifts were mounting past the windowsills. To Lydia, it seemed like the type of storm that would trap them in the house for a week. Chauncey invited Lydia and Elizabeth into the keeping room to pray.

After fifteen minutes on their knees, Chauncey rose and began to throw more wood on the fire. His back was to the women as he poked the coals. Without turning around, he described the Revelation, as told first by Joseph then Brigham.

"I know." Lydia shrugged. "I've heard of it, too. Girls can talk."

Chauncey asked her opinion of the Revelation.

"I see it only one way. I will do what the Lord asks to achieve Salvation and to carry forth His Kingdom." This is what Lydia says she said. There is no way to confirm whether or not she truly showed such resolve at such a young age. In reading through a number of letters and diaries by the early Saints, I have noted a pattern of speech that sounds more like religious text than actual dialogue. It is difficult to know if the early Saints truly used such language and diction, or if they recorded their conversations in a way that exalted their words. Even so, there is little reason to doubt that Lydia embraced the idea swiftly.

In *The 19th Wife* Ann Eliza says her mother thanked Lydia but privately fumed. I have tried to confirm this particular detail, but there seems to be little record of exactly how Elizabeth felt that night. Given what we know, Elizabeth most likely felt a sense of deliverance, accomplishment, and submission mixed with regret, betrayal, confusion, and jealousy. She writes of comparing her own hands ("worn, raw, scraped on the knuckle") to Lydia's ("white as a petal, and just as soft"). There's a hint that she was surprised—and perhaps apalled—by Lydia's quick consent. Most painfully, Lydia claims that Chauncey, as he finally turned from the mantel, looked as if he might devour the teenage girl. "I could see he was so over-come with desire for me," Lydia writes to her mother. "He could not speak. Men, for the most part, reveal their true thoughts in their shallow faces. Concealment will always remain the female art. I thought, if he could he would wed me that night."

In the surviving scraps of Elizabeth's testimony there is one line that stands out. I cannot identify the event that caused it, but it very well could be her description of how she felt after this conver-sation. "I cried through the night," she writes. "Until the dawn, and beyond." There is no reason to think these were tears of joy.

4.

On the clear, frozen morning of January 21, 1846, they gathered at the Nauvoo Temple. Although still under construction, the Temple had been used by Brigham for several months for services and seal-ing and Endowment Ceremonies. At the time the Temple was one of the largest buildings in the western United States. Built of white limestone cubes, it was like a beacon to the river traffic going north and south.[9]

Much of what we know about the sealing and the wedding cer-emony comes from *The 19th Wife*. Chauncey wore a high collar that irritated his beard. Elizabeth was in a plain dark dress with

---

[9] Although the Saints were preparing to abandon Nauvoo, hundreds of laborers con-tinued to erect the Temple until their last days in Illinois. This effort always strikes me as a profound symbol of their faith in both their Church and Brigham.

narrow silk cuffs. Lydia had draped a new lace shawl across her shoulders. Her iron hairpins caught the winter sun. According to Ann Eliza, Chauncey and Elizabeth appeared solemn, while Lydia seemed giddy.[10]

Brigham began the ceremony by sealing Chauncey and Elizabeth. The sealing ceremony varies little from most Christian wedding ceremonies. The difference, of course, is that instead of "until death do us part" the couple is united through eternity. Although this is typically one of the happiest moments in the life of a member of the LDS Church, we cannot assume it was so for Elizabeth. "She believed she would be with her husband forever—no doubt a comforting thought—but at what price?" asks Ann Eliza. "My mother stood in the Temple and the sunlight came down upon her. I believe if my mother ever had a moment of doubt, it was now." Elizabeth's account of this day was all but destroyed. Yet among the fragments one curious line leaps out: "oh my faith!"

With Chauncey and Elizabeth now sealed, Brigham instructed Elizabeth to step aside. He guided her to his left, replacing her with Lydia, who "was bouncing on her toes."[11] Quickly he united Chauncey and Lydia in marriage. Their vows were also similar to those used at most Christian weddings. Here, at death, their marriage would cease. In the afterlife, Chauncey would have one wife, the woman who had just been ushered aside. How did Elizabeth feel as she stood by and listened to her husband devote himself to a girl almost half her age? How did she feel, knowing they would all return home, share in a wedding feast, and followed by her husband withdrawing to Lydia's bedroom to consummate the mar-

---

[10] In *The 19th Wife*, Ann Eliza writes about many events in her parents' lives that took place either before she was born or when she was too young to remember them. According to her public lectures, she wrote about her parents by interviewing her mother and her half-brother, Gilbert, while preparing her manuscript.

[11] *The 19th Wife.*

riage?

We must rely on her children, and our imaginations, for the answer. Ann Eliza writes: "After supper, the newlyweds retired to Lydia's room off the kitchen. My father had purchased a new brass-post bed. The lamplight reflected off the brass exotically, casting the room in a golden glow. My mother saw Lydia go in first, sit upon the bed, and remove the pins from her hair. Her hair fell to her shoulders in a flaxen wave. She brushed it out and it shone around her head like a halo. When my father came to Lydia's door she held her hand out and said, 'Come.' He closed the door behind him, leaving my mother to the dirty dishes in the pan."

Gilbert, Elizabeth's illegitimate son, witnessed the same scene, recording it in his diary.[12] "Lydia seemed eager for the night to come to an end. Her foot tapped as we ate and she said she was too tired for singing. After supper she disappeared into her room. Soon my father followed. I helped my mother with the dishes and the pots. I went outside to fetch water from the well. I had to pass by Lydia's window. I would be a liar if I said I did not look in. I witnessed what I expected—a mound of flesh. I didn't like the idea that they were doing this because of God. It's terrible to see your own Pa in such a manner."

It is worth noting that we have diaries and letters from many women who praised the day a second (or third, fourth, or even fifth wife) entered her house. A sister wife meant a woman was fulfilling her religious obligations. It meant she was that much closer to Heaven. More practically, a sister wife also meant help with the household chores and, typically, some relief from conjugal relations. Many women found joy in the institution. But many did not. The evidence suggests Elizabeth was among those who mourned

---

[12] See Webb, Gilbert, Diary (Family History Library). Gilbert Webb, Ann Eliza's half-brother, was an eloquent but infrequent diarist. He is best remembered for his written deposition provided in Ann Eliza's divorce against Brigham Young in 1873.

the night she passed her husband to another woman. As one Pioneer woman described it a decade later, "A piece of my soul chipped off that night and fell away."[13]

A curious postscript to Chauncey's first plural marriage: Brigham himself may have entered into up to eleven plural marriages the same month. The numbers have been a source of debate for more than 150 years. I have little hope of settling the matter here. According to some accounts, on January 21, 1846, the same day he sealed Lydia to Chauncey, Brigham took two wives himself, Martha Bowker (1822–1890) and Ellen Rockwood (1829–1866). The evidence for these weddings is far from ideal: mostly secondhand testimonies or statements made long after the fact. Yet given the secretive and illegal nature of plural marriage in general, and especially those of the leader of the Latter-day Saints, it is understandable that there is little paper trail.[14]

5.

According to Ann Eliza, the wedding night was an extended affair. Like many homes in Nauvoo, the Webb house, although comfortable, was not large. It is easy to imagine noise traveling from one room to the next, across the floorboards or through the space where a door meets its jamb. "My father tried to quiet the girl," Ann Eliza writes in *The 19th Wife*. "But she did not care. Lydia squealed like a pig at the docking of its tail. Someone less forgiving might say she wanted my mother to hear." This is the kind of secondhand reporting and passive-aggressive tone that Ann Eliza uses through-

---

[13] "The Other Wife in Pioneer Homes: Recollections of Joy & Sorrow," edited by the Daughters of the Utah Pioneers (1947).

[14] The most conservative estimate of Brigham's total number of wives at the time of his death (August 29, 1877) is nineteen. The most liberal estimates are about fifty-six. Many LDS historians have settled on the number twenty-seven.

out her memoir; it's why many have dismissed it as unreliable. No doubt Ann Eliza is taking sides here; her bias is hardly veiled. But when compared with Gilbert's version of events, one can see that she was more or less reporting the truth, even if her tone is sharpened: "That first night," Gilbert writes in his diary, "Lydia made herself known to my father and the rest of us too. I went to the barn to sleep, knowing the horses to be more quiet and always preferring their company."

"People change." That's Ann Eliza's assessment of Lydia following her marriage to Chauncey. The former house girl now expected to be treated as the woman of the house. Almost at once she refused to participate in the household work, demanding that Chauncey hire a girl to take over her former chores. She wanted a replica of every finery in Elizabeth's wardrobe: hat, pin, and glove. There was a nasty spat over a piece of jewelry Chauncey had given his wife when Ann Eliza was born, a pearl on a gold stick. Ann Eliza reports a fight between the two women. "Lydia scratched my mother until there was blood," she writes in her memoir. Elizabeth responded with a slap and pulling Lydia's hair. Ann Eliza analyzes this particular episode astutely: "So often plural marriage reduces a thoughtful, generous, mature woman to a sniveling, selfish little girl. Perhaps it is the cruelest outcome: the removal, and destruction, of a woman's dignity. I have seen it too many times to count. I forgive the men who have done this to womankind, but I never forget."

"In conjugal matters," Ann Eliza writes frankly, "[Lydia's] demands were even greater." It was common in a plural marriage for the newest wife to resent sharing her husband's affections with the previous spouses. According to Ann Eliza, "In the first two weeks of marriage, my father spent each night with his new bride. He offered little attention to his original wife. When it was time to retire he would kiss my mother on the tip of the nose, and slip into Lydia's room. I know my mother wondered if she would ever see her husband again."

Even so, Lydia complained to Chauncey that he was spending too much time with the first Mrs. Webb. Gilbert recalls the young bride sighing, "And what am I supposed to do while you're with *her?*"

As monstrous as these recollections make Lydia out to be, we should remember that she was still a teenager, naive, and devout. She was cast into a situation that even the savviest courtesan might not know how to maneuver. She feared that the secretive nature of her marriage meant it could be quickly abandoned, annulled, or even denied. During the first month of marriage, Lydia wrote her mother: "You were right, Mother. The meaning of marriage can be unknowable. I try to keep him happy, but sometimes I do not know what will please him, and what will cause a wrinkled look of displeasure. I do not cry in front of him, or before the children, and certainly not Mrs. Webb. When I feel the need, I go outside with the animals. My faith comforts me more than ever, for I know that God and His Son will now welcome me, when the time comes, for I have fulfilled my duty. I am now Wife." We must bear this in mind before we condemn Lydia: Her spiritual leaders had told her this was her only path to salvation.

Elizabeth put up with Lydia's selfish behavior for only so long. One evening she spoke with her husband. "I have drawn up a chart," she said. "On Mondays, Wednesdays, and Fridays, you will spend the evening with her."

Chauncey relented immediately. "You're right. Tuesdays, Thursdays, and Saturdays will be yours. I'll spend Sunday night alone, here in the keeping room. That'll even it out."

"On Sundays," Elizabeth said firmly, "you'll be with me."

6.

Such disharmony in the Webb household took place while the Saints were preparing for their greatest test yet. The Exodus was scheduled to begin with the spring weather, but new threats of massacre compelled Brigham to declare Nauvoo no longer safe. On February 4, 1846, in the dark heart of winter, the first Saints crossed the Mississippi to Sugar Creek, Iowa. Brigham did not make the treacherous crossing for another eleven days, staying behind in Nauvoo to perform several Endowment Ceremonies to Saints anxious to be blessed before abandoning their beloved Temple. By March 1, some two thousand Saints huddled in wagons and tents in Sugar Creek. Their journey had begun, yet their destination was still unknown. From here Brigham led the Saints roughly 350 miles, at a rate of approximately 6 miles per day, to what would become a yearlong waystation on the Nebraska side of the Missouri River, Winter Quarters, an encampment six miles upriver from present-day Omaha.

Chauncey and his family remained in Nauvoo until early April 1846. He was too busy building wagons to join the early emigrants. Eventually they too packed up, leaving behind nearly all their possessions and wealth. The Webbs—Chauncey, his two rival wives, and three children—joined the Exodus, crossing the Mississippi in two bonneted wagons pulled by three yoke of oxen. They carried a year's supply of provisions, their clothing, and their faith. They reached Winter Quarters in midsummer. By September, some twenty thousand Saints had gathered there, each having placed his or her life into the hands of Brigham Young. Once a city rivaling Chicago, Nauvoo was now a ghost town. The wondrous Temple— the pride and handiwork of thousands of Saints—was abandoned. In a few years it would be in ruins, resembling a pile of ancient rubble in Rome or Greece, with animals sleeping among its stones.[15] The Nauvoo Temple would not rise again until 2002.

For Elizabeth Churchill Webb, this event would prove momentous. This is the moment she buried her Testimony in the time cap-

---

[15] At the end of *The 19th Wife*, Ann Eliza poignantly describes returning to Nauvoo to see the Temple ruins.

sule, leaving for us an eloquent, if incomplete, record of her faith.

7.

As every LDS member knows, the Saints would end up staying in Winter Quarters for almost a year. Under Brigham's direction, they laid out blocks of tents, dugouts, and simple log sheds, building a temporary city to survive the winter of 1846–1847. Brigham called it the Camp of Israel. The settlement included community facilities such as a gristmill, a school, and several workshops to produce basic goods. Among these was Chauncey's wainwright. Here, with help from his stepson, Gilbert, he built and repaired the wagons that would carry the Saints on their upcoming journey.

In January 1847, in a Revelation, God instructed Brigham to lead the Saints to the Rocky Mountains. The Heavenly Father assured His Prophet he would know the exact place to build their new Zion when he saw it. Word spread through Winter Quarters that a long journey would begin soon; everyone busied themselves with final preparations. For the Webbs, however, this meant their own departure would have to be delayed. Once again Chauncey's wainwright was needed to support the departing Saints, the majority of whom left Winter Quarters in the spring and summer of 1847. By the time Chauncey's work was done, it was too late for the Webbs to depart for Zion; the autumn snows would catch them. The Webbs would have to wait through the winter of 1847–1848 before they could join the new settlement in Utah.

According to Ann Eliza, during this time Chauncey was under the misperception that his plural marriage remained a secret. "Sometimes a husband is wrong about very much," Ann Eliza observes. In every society—from the forums of ancient Rome to the dorms of BYU—the romantic life of others has always been subject to gossip. The early Saints were no exception. Everyone knew that Lydia was now the second Mrs. Webb. As Ann Eliza puts it, "The girl made sure of that."

Elizabeth's pain from sharing her husband with Lydia was renewed when, in November 1847, Lydia announced she would have
a child. Gilbert's record of how Lydia told Elizabeth she was pregnant is worth quoting at length.

My mother set out a stew and didn't say much, minding her own
business in the way that she had since Lydia became her rival. The
wind was fierce, blowing through the chinks in the logs. My mother
never sat to join us, she ran from the table to the hearth and back
with the biscuits and the drippings and everything else. Anyone
would see the difference now, what with my mother in her apron
with the gravy stain above her heart while Lydia sat at the head of
the table in a Summertime dress too thin for November. Her complexion was as white as the frost on the water in the well. "Children,
your father and I have something important to tell you," Lydia said.
"Soon you'll have a baby brother or sister." She took my father's fist
and held it up like she had won a relay race.

My Ma is the most generous woman I know. She never thinks of
herself if there is someone else to think of. That's why she didn't
speak. When she heard the news she took a step backward. One
step followed by another, and again another. It was like a moment
in a fairy tale because she seemed to be disappearing. I know it
doesn't make any sense and it isn't possible and all the rest, but that's
what happened before my eyes—my mother was swallowed up by
Lydia's news. If the Lord can send an angel to Joseph Smith, then a
woman learning the news of her husband's baby with his other wife
can disappear. And that's what happened. She was gone. For a moment we didn't know where she was. I had to go out into the cold
night to bring her in. She was shivering. Several times she said—
not loud but soft in a whisper—"Please. No." I led her to her bed
beside the hearth and removed her shoes, and by now my mother
stopped talking altogether. I set her down and under the blankets.
"Lay quiet," I said. It's a hard feeling for a boy to put his mother to
bed like she were the child.

8.

Thankfully, Elizabeth's impulse to document her life did not end with the Testimony of Faith. In *The 19th Wife*, Ann Eliza describes her mother writing in her travel diary during the Exodus. Many Saints, especially the women, kept detailed records of their journeys. These documents, many now archived by the Church, have been central to our understanding of the arduous trek from Nauvoo to Winter Quarters and ultimately to Zion. I have relied on Elizabeth's Pioneer diary, written between May 1848 and September 1848, to narrate her story during this transformative period.

The Webbs left for Zion on May 4, 1848, in a company of 1,229 Saints. The column of 397 wagons driving westward carried every imaginable provision: stoves, bureaus, rockers, farm tools, a piano. The livestock roped to the rear of the wagons included cattle, horses, mules, and pigs. Elizabeth notes in her diary the sounds of the other animals: "dogs barking, cats mewing, thousands of bees buzzing in their hives, and a brown squirrel flitting about its cage."

The Webbs and their fellow travelers were following in the footsteps of the Saints who had traveled a year earlier along the old Oregon Trail. Brigham had established a system of roadside mailboxes at ten-mile markers—typically the skull of an antelope or a bison—to leave information about the trail, crossings, conditions, and so forth. In 1847, the journey for Brigham and his Saints had been treacherous and uncertain. By 1848, the trip, while arduous, was no longer a mystery. Ann Eliza was almost four years old at the time. Her earliest memories, she tells us in *The 19th Wife*, come from this trip. For her, the journey was a period of great adventure and joy. As the wagons rolled through the prairie grass, she would skip along, picking flowers and singing hymns. The sound of more than a thousand Saints singing "The Spirit of God Like a Fire Is Burning!" must have fortified them through their long days.

The itinerary was almost always the same: Every day for four and a half months the Saints rose at five, ate a hot breakfast in the

dawn, and pushed forward until dusk. They rested only on the Sab-
bath. In her Exodus diary, Elizabeth writes of ending a day and
"circling the wagons, lighting the supper fire, and watering the animals. When the chores were done, and the children fed, the blue
night sky had turned black and was lit by stars. The moonlight
shined upon the hides of the sleeping oxen, on their moist noses,
and on the white brow of Ann Eliza, who always sleeps like an
angel, whether sun or storm."

The hopeful quality of their journey changed dramatically when
in early June Lydia gave birth. The baby—to be named Diantha—
was born with complications. Already on the journey Elizabeth
had witnessed in her company three newborns die, two followed by
their mothers to their prairie graves. What exactly happened to
Lydia and her baby we will never know. That the situation was serious is, however, entirely clear.[16]

Elizabeth immediately recognized that the lives of both mother
and child were in danger. "Lydia lay upon the tickings in the
wagon-bed unable to open her eyes," Elizabeth writes. "When I
called her name she did not respond. The child Diantha was even
more lifeless, tiny and still at her mother's side. I did not know
what to do."

At this time it was common for Saints facing illness to resort to
prayer and the healing powers of priests. Elizabeth describes an
Elder (I cannot determine who) sitting with Lydia in the wagon-
bed. "He came at night when we had stopped beside a creek. He
was an old man, so worn by the journey I doubted whether he
would ever see the Zion we sung about. I worried over what he was

---

[16] According to a University of Chicago study by Professor Kwang-Sun Lee, infant
mortality rates in the nineteenth century were in the range of 130 to 230 for every
1,000 births. The main causes were diarrhea, respiratory illness, and infectious dis-
eases such as scarlet fever, measles, whooping cough, smallpox, diphtheria, and
croup. For the mid-nineteenth-century mother, parturition in any situation could be
dangerous; on the wagon trail it was particularly hazardous.

capable of."

The Elder gathered the family around Lydia in the wagon. He set his hands upon her head and prayed for her recovery. He did the same with the baby. "If the Lord so pleases, then He will save them. Now you must pray," he told the Webbs.

"What if they don't improve?"

"Then the Lord must have a reason to leave your prayers unanswered."

This struck Elizabeth in the heart. Since the wedding more than two years before, many times she had wished Lydia out of her house. She admits to having prayed for the Lord to take her away. "Many times, when I am alone at night, I must listen to my husband visiting my rival in the manner he no longer visits me. How many times have I begged the Lord to end this humiliation?" she admits in her diary. "Yet again and again I find myself alone."

Before the Elder departed he said to Elizabeth, "Look after this girl and her child. Do not let them suffer. Do what you can."

Did Elizabeth hesitate? Did she think: This is my chance to be free of my competition and return my husband to me? We do not know. If she did, the selfish impulse soon passed. For two weeks Elizabeth devoted herself to Lydia's and Diantha's recovery, refusing to leave their side. During the daily trek across the summer plains, Elizabeth applied compresses and spoon-fed water and gruel. "Above all," she writes, "I prayed."

The following passage from her diary is a remarkable articulation of her faith. It provides important insight into how many early LDS women came to terms, both practical and spiritual, with plural marriage:

I came to see the test the Lord had set before me. Previously I had allowed myself to hate my Sister Wife. I resented each breath she pulled from the air. I resented each morsel she plucked from the plate. I resented the dent in the cushion she left when she stood from the chair. I resented the tendril of hair left on the brush. I resented her voice rising to greet me. I resented her lips on the brows of my children. I resented the very qualities that made her a fellow creature of God. My dark hatred, too, had spilled over to her un- born child. Verily I came to see that the Lord Jesus Christ had set before me a test. Do I love? He asked, Or do I hate? He had heard the cries from my wicked heart and He took pity on me. Had He answered my prayers, and removed Lydia from our family, and de- stroyed her child, He would not have truly loved me. No! He loved me by testing me. When I first met Brother Joseph all those years before he said, "Let us pour forth love—show forth our kindness unto all mankind, for love begets love." I await my Day of Judgment with a heart bursting open with love. Yet I had forgotten all that I believed. Kneeling beside Lydia in the wagon-bed, my faith re- turned. The love the Saints had shown me returned. When it did, Lydia rose and the baby howled and their health was restored. Their recovery coincided with the restoration of my faith. I can never for- get this! Its meaning is clear and shall always be.

By September 1848, the Webbs and their party had reached the red mudstone canyon of the Weber River, only a few days out from the Salt Lake Valley. At some point, Brigham had driven from Salt Lake to meet them. At night, around the campfire, he described the Mormon Canaan they would soon find. After only a year in the Valley, the Saints had built up a small city of one-room log homes, roads on a grid, an imposing defensive fort, several gristmills and granaries, and some five thousand acres of thriving crops irrigated by a sophisticated system of channels and dams. "Brigham told us," Elizabeth writes in her final diary entry, "of our Promised Land. God had revealed it to Brigham, and now Brigham was revealing it to us. I held my sister wife's hand as we listened to Brigham de- scribe the world that awaited over the pass."

On September 13, 1844, Ann Eliza celebrated her fourth birth- day. "Brigham held me and touched me," she writes in *The 19th Wife*, "and smiled such that I knew I was his favorite child. On my birthday he kissed me and declared, 'This beautiful child is the future of the Saints of Deseret!' " We will never know whether or not Ann Eliza, at the age of four, could remember this scene with such clarity. Even so, when she writes of it years later in her memoir, she notes, "I was happy because I saw my mother and father happy, and my Prophet happy too. I remember his fingers on my arm and the wool of his beard on my cheek. In no way could I have known many years later this man would marry me and then try to destroy me. There were no clouds on the horizon that September. The vista was clear."

When Chauncey Webb, his two wives, and now four children arrived in Salt Lake on September 20, 1848, they were, by all accounts, a happy family. Plural marriage, once so loathsome to Elizabeth in concept, had become a part of her daily existence. Elizabeth recorded this thought in her diary: "Brigham used to say: We make room for what the Lord gives us. Always." She had accommodated Lydia into her household; and the second Mrs. Webb had come to appreciate Elizabeth's companionship. Each woman felt for the other's children the way an aunt might feel for a niece or nephew. In the next few years, as the Webbs worked to establish themselves in Salt Lake, Elizabeth came to accept the second wife. "Lydia is of our family, no more or less. So says God," she often told Ann Eliza.

As Elizabeth set up a new household and participated in the settling of the Utah Territory, she would have little time to linger over the insults of polygamy again until 1855—when in one feverish, indulgent month Chauncey, who must have been suffering from what we would now call a midlife crisis, married three women, each under the age of seventeen. But that, as they say, is another story.

9.

I wrote this paper for three reasons. One, to show the effects of plural marriage on one woman's life. Her story is neither representative nor unusual. It is simply that: one woman's story. There are many other narratives, written or waiting to be told, that shed further light on the practice of polygamy in early Church history. Anyone familiar with even a few of these will know that many women despised the institution, while others rejoiced in it for practical and/or spiritual reasons. Among the practical reasons were the sharing of housework, child care, and the relief from sexual obligations to one's husband. The spiritual reasons were of the highest order: The happiest plural wives believed their entrance into Heaven was secure.

The secondary purpose of this paper has been to raise up the subject of polygamy as a legitimate and unfinished topic of inquiry for LDS scholars and writers. The Church, of course, banned the practice in 1890. Since then our leaders have spoken out forcefully and consistently against it. Any honest observer would have to concede that there has been no official connection between the Church of Jesus Christ of Latter-day Saints and polygamy for more than one hundred years.

Even so, there is no denying plural marriage was an important part of early Church culture. As scholars we must look at it rigorously, understand it honestly, and place it correctly in our heritage. Some present-day Church leaders have dismissed polygamy as a "noncentral" issue, a peripheral "sideshow" to the larger issues of accepting the Restoration of the Gospel, understanding the Revelations, knowing the Lord Christ, and preparing for salvation. Yet for some nineteenth-century Saints, such as Elizabeth Churchill Webb, plural marriage was so very much a part of their daily lives, of their terrestrial existence, that to label it as "minor" or "noncentral" is to, in effect, cast aside their very earthly experiences as "minor" and "noncentral." The fact of the matter is many of the men who laid the foundations of today's Church, including our beloved Prophets Joseph and Brigham, participated in polygamy with astonishing vigor. They sanctioned it, promoted it, spread it, and exalted it. They also lied about it. This is not a criticism, but a fact. Its sting can be lessened by facing it for what it is.

Just as a long and sustained critical inquiry into slavery has helped fortify the national psyche and shore up our nation's moral standing, so too would an examination of our founders' role in this deplorable practice help clear, at last, the misperception that Mormonism and polygamy remain somehow entwined.

Make no mistake, our detractors continue to use the issue against us today. Best-selling books, influential newspapers and magazines, and popular television programs investigate present-day polygamy and inevitably connect it back to the LDS Church. We rightly protest such misrepresentation; we reasonably decry the unfairness of the coverage; over and over we try to correct the errors. Yet I believe that our strident denial of any connection has in fact hurt our image in the larger public rather than helped it. The LDS Church has been so intent on distancing itself from polygamy, on letting the world know that we stand adamantly and unequivocally opposed to the institution, that we have ignored its actual role in our own history. By repeating the message "That has nothing to do with us!" we inadvertently minimized the effects it played on our early members, especially its women. This strategy of putting a distance between the Church today and the polygamous acts of our forefathers—while understandable—has been misconstrued by some as whitewashing or even denial. Hence the suspicion and the constant repetition of old stories and rumors. Hence the continuous and harmful misperception that polygamous sects such as the Firsts in Mesadale and the LDS Church are one and the same.

As scholars we can change this.

My last reason is more personal. I am the great-great-great-granddaughter of Ann Eliza Young. Although my family has always taken pride in having roots that go back to the Church's founding, we have also felt shame at being the offspring of such a hurtful apostate. When I was growing up, many in my family would refer to Ann Eliza as "that woman" or simply "her." They despised her as if they had known her personally. Few had actually read *The 19th Wife*. "Nothing but a pack of lies," my grandmother used to say.[17]

Despite this, Ann Eliza and her contradictions have long fascinated me. I decided to start my inquiry into her life with her mother, my great-great-great-great-grandmother Elizabeth Churchill Webb. This seemed the best place to begin an effort to unravel Ann Eliza's true history and legacy. I plan to continue my inquiry into Ann Eliza's life itself in my graduate studies next year. The research I conducted for this paper is an important foundation for that inquiry. This summer, when I'm in Salt Lake,[18] I hope to study a wide range of documents in the Church archives, some of which scholars have never had access to. I hope these texts will provide a fuller portrait of this complex woman and her complicated place in the history of the Church of Jesus Christ of Latter-day Saints.

Lastly, through my research, I hope to determine the fate of Ann Eliza Young. After a second edition of *The 19th Wife* was published in 1908, there is no further record of her. No one knows when she died, or where, or under what circumstances. There are no obituaries, no estate records, not even a death certificate. At some point after 1908 she simply disappeared. She was once one of the most

---

[17] For years LDS scholars have noted Ann Eliza's obvious bias and political agenda in *The 19th Wife*. Yet for this paper, whenever I could check her version of events against another source I found general agreement. To my surprise, I have come to the opinion that Ann Eliza's memoir, at least in the depiction of her mother's life and her family's years in Nauvoo and journey to Zion, is for the most part factually reliable, although her emphasis on certain matters, while skipping over others, can at times leave the reader with a distorted impression of early Church history. Whether or not the entire memoir is factually correct, especially the passages concerning her relationship with Brigham Young, will be part of my future research.

[18] I would like to thank the Department, especially Professor Sprague, for the generous work-study grant supporting my upcoming internship at the Ann Eliza Young House, which I'm really excited about.

famous women in America. She changed the lives of thousands of women by fighting to end polygamy, nearly bringing down the Mormon Church in doing so. And yet she has been lost from history without a trace. We simply have no idea what happened to her. Ann Eliza's death remains a mystery. But mysteries, by their very nature, are meant to be solved.

VIII

—

WIFE #19:

THE GUN ON THE SCREEN

I WAS LIKE WOW

"Johnny, wake up."

"What the—?"

"I need you to get up."

"Where are we?"

We were in Mr. Heber's parking lot. The bank sign across the street said it was eight in the morning and already ninety degrees. The kid sat up, his face creased from the futon. "You got anything for breakfast?"

I threw him a packet of powdered doughnuts. Ten minutes later Maureen arrived in a yellow Honda with a family of stuffed penguins in the back window. She sat for a minute, listening to the morning talk station, flicking a plastic comb through her hair. I knocked on her window.

"Jordan," she gasped. "Shoot, you scared me."

"Sorry, but I just realized you never gave me a copy of the police report."

"All right, just give me a second to land." Something caught her attention over my shoulder. "Who's that?"

Johnny and Elektra were running straight for me, each panting like, well, like a dog. "This is Johnny. I'm looking after him for a friend." I sent Johnny and Elektra back to the van, but they didn't want to go. I had to give them each a little shove.

"You dick," he said over his shoulder.

Inside the office it was dark and warm. Maureen went around turning on the lights and the a/c and her computer while talking about how busy Mr. Heber was lately. Finally she went to the wall of file cabinets and started riffling through the S drawer. "Here it is, let me make a copy. But first I want you to be honest—who's Johnny?"

"He doesn't have a place to go right now."

"If he's a runaway, you should call the police."

"He's not a runaway."

"I see," she sighed. "Another lost boy. It just breaks my heart. Did you try Jim Hooke? He runs a shelter. The man's a saint. Let me give you his number." She pecked at her keyboard and brought up the guy's deets.

Maureen put the police report in a file folder for me. "It's pretty basic," she said, "but here you are."

It described the murder scene pretty much the same as the *Register* did. Whoever filled it out had been meticulous, measuring the distance between the door and the chair, the height of the blood splatters on the wall, that sort of thing. There was a diagram of a human body, and the investigator had marked it where the bullet entered my dad and a second diagram of the backside, showing the exit wound. At the bottom of the last page, the investigator signed his name: Hiram Alton.

Queenie's husband.

Well there you go.

More interesting were two little questions next to his signature: *Were photographs taken?* A little yes box was checked. *Is the investigation complete?* No.

"Maureen? Do you have the photographs?"

"What photographs?" I showed her the report. "Let me check." But there weren't any photos in the file.

"Would you ask Mr. Heber?"

"Ask me what?" Mr. Heber stood in the front door, his wraparound sunglasses making it impossible to tell if he was pissed. "Maureen, what's going on?"

"Jordan wanted the police report."

"I see." He moved in the direction of his office, then turned around. "What did you want to ask me about?"

"The pictures. The report says they took pictures."

"I realize that. I made a request, but they haven't turned up yet."

"When will they be here?"

"Should be soon. We'll call you when they arrive. Maureen has your cell?" He might as well have been wearing a sign that said I don't have time for this.

"Before I go, I need to tell you something." I blurted out the whole business about Sister Kimberly and 5, about one of them lying about where 5 was the night my dad was killed.

Mr. Heber removed his sunglasses. He said, "Hmm." Just hmm. Nothing more.

"Isn't that fishy?"

"Yes, I'll agree those stories don't add up."

"What do you think it means?"

"I don't know."

"You don't know?" I'm not sure why I thought he would be able to take this info, drop it into some sort of thinking machine, and come up with the answer that would pop my mom free from jail, but I guess deep down that's what I expected.

"Unfortunately, there could be a hundred reasons why one of them or both are lying. Now we need to figure out what they are."

"I know, I want to go back and ask them."

"Before you go any further, let me give you three bits of advice. One: most people lie. Two: the reason they lie usually has nothing to do with your case. And three: unless you're careful, their more or less innocent lies can really throw you off."

The thing about Heber was I never could quite tell what he wanted—my mom out of jail or me out of his office. "Come on. Not everyone goes around lying."

"No, not everyone, but you'd be amazed how many liars are always buzzing around a crime."

Maureen shrugged. "I'm afraid he's right."

About fifteen miles outside St. George, Johnny finished eating everything in the van. He wiped his sugary fingers on his thighs, burped, then thought to say, "Where we going?"

"Mesadale Police Department. I want to try to get those pictures myself."

"Are you out of your fucking mind?"

"Calm down."

"They'll kill me."

"They won't kill you."

"Dude, I know that place a whole lot better than you. Everyone's like freaking out." He punched the dash. "Stop this van!"

"Johnny, relax. When we get there, you can help me."

"If you don't stop right now, I'm going to jump out."

"Johnny, I know what I'm doing."

"So do I." He pulled his bag into his lap, opened the door, said, "You're so full of shit," and leaped out. It happened so quickly, I drove another fifty yards before I could stop. In my rearview Johnny rolled down the embankment with his bag tight to his chest. When he came to a stop he stood and slapped the sand out of his hair. Tough little kid. Stupid too. I backed up along the road until I was next to him.

"Get in."

"Fuck you."

"I'll make sure nothing happens to you."

"You know what they said when they kicked me out? They said if I ever came back, my mom would end up dead. So fuck you for taking me back there, and fuck your fucking van, and fuck your mom, I don't give a shit about her."

He started walking in the direction of St. George, hugging his little bag, but there was no way he could walk back to town. I backed up some more until I was next to him again, but he kept walking and I kept driving in reverse. "I didn't mean to scare you. Come on, get in."

"I'm not going anywhere with you."

"Fine. What do you want to do?"

"None of your fucking business."

"Look, all right, don't come. But let me take you back to St. George. I'll drop you wherever you want."

He kept walking but eventually said, "I'm not talking to you."

"Johnny, you're acting like a baby."

"What do you expect?" He wiped his nose with his shoulder. "I thought you were cool." We went backward like that another twenty yards.

"Hey, Maureen told me about this place, maybe we should go there."

He stopped. "What place?"

"Some guy named Jim Hooke. He has this house."

Johnny started walking again, and I threw the van into reverse. "You know him?"

"You getting ready to dump me, too?"

"No, not at all." Heber was right: people lie all the time. "Tell you what," I said. "I'll drop you at the movies and go to Mesadale myself. When I get back I'll pick you up."

He stopped. "Only if you promise to come back."

"I promise."

He pondered the promise, turning it over like a bit of treasure found in the sand. "Deal. But I'm going to need some cash for candy." I told him no problem. "And popcorn."

"I'll give you five bucks." I stopped the van and Johnny climbed in. Elektra welcomed him back with a lick. "Put your seat belt on."

"Whatever."

We didn't say anything for ten miles. As we approached St. George, my cell picked up reception again. There was a message. "Yeah, hi, Jordan, it's me, Maureen. Guess what. Those pictures came right after you left. You can pick them up anytime."

A PLURALITY OF WIVES:[1]
A DISCOURSE

———

DELIVERED BY BRIGHAM YOUNG IN THE TABERNACLE,
Great Salt Lake City, August 29, 1852

Now, following the words of Elder Pratt, I will tell you, in plain
language, why we believe in the sanctity of plural marriage and
shall always do so. Going forth you will meet those who question
your right to this belief, and who shall tell you you are acting outside the law. Yet I shall tell you it is they who do not understand the
law, and most certainly it is they who do not understand the will of
God.

We believe in plural marriage because God has commanded it.
He has spoken, first to Joseph and now to me. I cannot change the
word of God to suit my needs, nor can I change His word to suit
the politics of today. His word is the word of Eternity, and shall always be. A man who disagrees with our practice of plural wifery is
disagreeing with God. His disagreement is not with us, but with
his Maker.

We look to the authority of Scripture, for there, in the Old Testament, are many examples of man with many wives. If we accept
Scripture as God's Truth, then we must accept it as unchanging
and constant through Time. The Latter-day Saints are here to restore the Truth of God as he intended it for man. The entire Chris-

---

[1] This was Brigham Young's first public acknowledgment of polygamy. In laying out
these arguments, he provided the Latter-day Saints with the spiritual/political armament to defend the practice for the next forty years.

tian world, from Popedom to her many rebellious children, has run amok on the Truth of God. With Joseph as His Prophet, and myself after, God has set out to restore his Truths, and we are doing so.

Further, in taking many wives we are expanding the Kingdom. We are performing the works of Abraham. A man who marries many wives and a woman who joins a plural family—they are doing the work of God and will be exalted for doing so. They are closer to Glory than the man who refuses this doctrine, or the woman who refuses it. This is how it shall be.

Let it be known I am a son of Vermont's Green Mountains. I was raised with a deep awareness of the rights afforded to all by our nation's Constitution. The right to religious freedom is a right guaranteed to all. This includes the Saints of Deseret. If you encounter an antagonist who believes none of what I have just said to you, who believes neither in the Truth of God, or the Authority of the Scripture, or my position as His Prophet, then you should remind your enemy of our Constitution. There is no doubt it plainly protects our right to pursue our faith as we so believe.

A WOMAN SCONED

———

"You stink," said Johnny.

"*I* stink?" But he was right. I turned in the direction of the pool. The envelope of pictures was in my lap but I didn't want to open it right away. I guess I was afraid of them. Not the gore, I could handle that. I just wasn't ready for what they might say.

The municipal pool attracts all sorts. Old ladies with achy knees, stoned teenagers, homeless guys avoiding the heat. I guess technically Johnny and I fell into that last lot.

"That's a dollar seventy-five for you," said the girl at the registration. "And a dollar twenty-five for your brother."

I didn't correct her, thinking it might hurt Johnny's feelings, but he piped up, "He's so not my brother." I gave him a don't be a dick look. "What? You're not."

We threw down our towels on a quiet strip of concrete. Johnny took off, leaping feet first into the pool. He swam over to four boys hanging on to the lane dividers. It took him about ten seconds to become part of their group. They started a game of underwater tag and Johnny wiggled across the pool, looking happy. And clean. He was laughing with his new friends, karate-chopping water in their faces, oblivious of me.

There were twenty pictures in the envelope, xeroxes but clear enough. They documented the scene pretty much as I imagined it. There was the door to his basement den with the NO TRESPASSING decal. Inside, the painted concrete floor, the ripped corduroy sofa, the broken swamp cooler in the corner. His cot was unmade. Even in the low res of xerox the sheets looked filthy. Then his desk: a door over two filing cabinets, a computer, and a plastic margarine tub filled with rounds of ammo. The next photos were more graphic: his computer chair with a hole chewed through the mesh and wet with blood. The blood on the drywall, splattered like mud on a flap. A picture of the computer screen showed his poker hand and the chat session the bullet so rudely interrupted. Actually there were three chat sessions—so there's something the *Register* didn't report. The one that nailed my mother, between Manofthehouse2004 and DesertMissy, and two others that looked pretty average, I mean given the circumstances.

Manofthehouse2004: where in st george?
ALBIL: u no the Malibu Inn?
Manofthehouse2004: yup
ALBIL: not far from there
Manofthehouse2004: live alone?

That's where the chat ended. You ever stop to imagine things differently? What if my father had been sitting there waiting in such overheated anticipation for the answer to his question—*all alone* or *my husband's gone till morning* or *with my girlfriend*—and his heart got so worked up with stupid male hope that it broke. Imagine it. His head lolling on his neck. His body going cold in the basement. Sister Rita would've found him like that, dead from a stupid old heart. Imagine if that's how he had died. Or if he'd gotten in his truck and driven over to ALBIL's place near the Malibu Inn. Everything would be different now.

The second chat went like this:

SweetieNVAZUT: how old?
Manofthehouse2004: 47 but look 39-42.
(Please.)
SweetieNVAZUT: married?
Manofthehouse2004: yes
SweetieNVAZUT: go fuck your wife

Manofthehouse2004: rather watch u fuck her

SweetieNVAZUT: she got a hot pussy?

Manofthehouse2004: depends

SweetieNVAZUT: you nasty prick

They could've put it on his tombstone.

Johnny plopped down on my towel. "Let me see." I turned the pictures over. "Hey, if I'm your sidekick, how'm I going to help you get your mom out of jail if you don't tell me everything?"

"You're not my sidekick."

"Love you, too, bro." He flipped over on his back and turned his head. "Did I mention I knew your dad?"

"So?"

"I'm just saying he taught my Sunday school."

"Big deal."

"Yeah, you're probably right. I'm sure it was nothing."

"What was nothing?"

"Nope, it's not worth going into."

"What are you talking about?"

"You going in the pool or what?"

"First tell me what you're talking about."

"First go swimming. You reek."

I swam a few laps past a trio of teenage girls, each in a bikini smaller than the other. "You're such a slut!" one shouted to her friend. Clearly this was a good thing.

When I got back to my towel, Johnny was leafing through the photos. "What're you doing?"

"You see this one?" He was holding out the last picture in the pile.

"I've seen it. Now give them back to me."

"Man, look at him." It was the only picture of my dad. Manofthehouse2004 slumped in his computer chair, feeble and arthritic, the blood wet on his T-shirt. Eyes rolled back in his head, mouth open, one hand turned at a funny angle like a claw. He looked ancient—the flesh hanging off his bones. Just a diabetic, swollen-ankled, old man. Why were we so afraid of him?

"Dude, that sucks. I know he was an ass and everything, but he was still your dad."

"What were you going to tell me?"

"Just that he used to teach us about the end of time. He kept saying it was coming soon. He used to bring his gun to church and show us how he'd fight the enemy until the end. It was kinda cheesy."

"That's it?"

"Yeah, like I said, it was nothing."

I lay on my back and threw my arm over my eyes. Do you ever wonder how you got where you are?

Then I sat back up.

"What kind of gun was it?"

"I think a Golden Boy. Why? Is that important?"

"I don't know."

We went over to the internet café where I'd been leaving Elektra. The place was pretty sleepy, a couple of kids nursing lattes on saggy couches. It was called A Woman Sconed, and the goth girl who worked there was in love with my dog. "Who's my girl?" she said the minute we walked in, and she wasn't talking about me.

I started drafting an email. After a few rewrites I had a note that sounded friendly but serious. I sent it first to SweetieNVAZUT.

Hey, I know you once chatted with someone named Manofthehouse2004. Can I ask you a few questions? I'm his son and I'm just trying to find a few things out. He died the night you talked, actually he was murdered. There are a lot of things we don't know, and I'm trying to figure them out. I know this is weird, but it's true.

Johnny sat down, read my note on the screen, his lips moving, and about halfway through his brow squiggled up.

"What?" I said.

"Nothing. I'm not saying a word."

"You think it's too creepy? I was trying to make it sound sincere."

"This is your show, bro."

He was probably right. I wrote up an email that didn't say much—just a *hey, want to chat?*—and sent it off to ALBIL and DesertMissy.

The goth girl asked if she could give Elektra a cupcake. "On the house," she said. She reminded me of 5, which reminded me I needed to talk to her again.

"Holy shit!" said Johnny. "You've got mail!" He shoved my shoulder.

It was from ALBIL, and she went straight to the point: *You sound nice. Got a pic?*

"Score!"

"Johnny, sit down."

"Hey, wait a minute, let me see that pic you're sending her." He looked at the picture I pulled down from my myspace profile. "Not bad. But you look gay."

"I am gay."

"I guess just send it anyway. See what happens."

About thirty seconds later she wrote back: *Nice, wanna meet?*

"Dude, for a gay guy, you sure know how to work the ladies. Tell her to meet us here."

"Us?"

"Well, yeah. Besides, I'm just a kid. She'll take one look at me and know you're a decent guy."

He was right. About an hour later a woman walked through the door. She had that pale and plump look that made her seem both young and middle-aged. "You can have her," Johnny whispered.

"Be nice." I called out, "ALBIL?"

She looked a little startled when she saw Johnny. "You must be Jordan. Wow. You look just like your picture. Most guys don't, you know."

"I know. Sit down. You want something to drink?"

She was nibbling the stem of her sunglasses and looking at Johnny. "I didn't realize you were bringing your son."

"He's a friend. I'm just looking after him for a little while."

"Since moron's not going to introduce me, I'm Johnny." He offered his hand. It was at moments like this—when his hand hung out there, so small and clearly belonging to a boy—that I remembered how young he was.

"Johnny, you want to—"

"Yup, give me some quarters and I'll go play Ms. Pac-Man." I gave him the change in my pocket and he hopped across the café.

"I guess that means you like kids."

"I never really thought about it until he came around."

"How long're you looking after him?"

"Only a couple of days. Listen, ALBIL—"

"Alexandra."

"Alexandra?"

"ALBIL's my screen name. Alexandra Likes Being In Love. I'm a romantic. I probably shouldn't put that out there in the first five minutes, but there you are."

"That's all right." Now I really felt bad. "I have to tell you something. I asked you here because, well, I wanted to ask you some questions."

"Stop. I should say up front, you can ask me *any*thing. I'm just that kind of person. Nothing to hide. So just to get it out of the way, I'll start: I'm thirty-six, divorced, have two kids but they live with my wasband in Kingman, and you see these extra fifteen pounds, they're not going anywhere. I'm so glad you like kids. I mean, that's a relief because that would be a real problem."

"Um, that's not exactly what I meant."

"You know what? I like you."

"Here's the real reason I emailed you."

As I explained everything, her eyes opened to the size of poker chips. "Oh my God. Killed?" She pulled a napkin from the dispenser and held it to her mouth. "Wait a minute. You lied to me."

"I didn't want to. You gotta understand. She's my mom." Alexandra looked like she couldn't decide whether to stay or go. "Do you remember chatting with him?"

"I don't know, I'm still in shock." She fanned herself with the napkin. Johnny was absorbed in his video game, his little hands bonded to the joystick. "I don't know what's worse, you lying or your dad being murdered."

"The thing is, he was a real prick. I bet he didn't tell you he had more than twenty wives."

"Oh my God, it gets worse?"

"Yup. He lived in Mesadale. So, do you think you remember him?"

"There must be some mistake. I never chat with married men. I've been down that road. Twice."

"He probably lied to you about that. Do you remember anything?"

"I don't know. I mean, I do like to play some poker every now and then as practice. Two or three times a year the girls and I go to Vegas for the weekend, and I don't want to show up rusty. When did you say this was? Saturday? What time?"

"Around eleven."

"Yeah, that sounds right, I think I was online. But I don't know if I remember your dad specifically. I tend to strike up a chat with whoever's at the table. You know, to be friendly."

"He might have said he was pretty religious."

"Around here they all say that."

"Maybe he talked about trucks? He loved trucks."

"Ditto."

"He's a big hunter."

"Who isn't? Wait a minute! Was he the Gulf War vet with that strange disease?"

"No." We ended up doing this—the misfired question, the off-the-mark response—for another few minutes, but eventually we both realized their chat had been too insignificant to leave an impression. "I don't want you to think I spend a lot of time chatting online," she said, "but I guess I do."

"If you think of something, you have my email."

"Give me your number, too, just in case." She wrote it down in a blank appointment book. Turns out Johnny had kept his eye on us the whole time because he raced away from the video game. "Could you help him?"

"Not really." She sounded like she had taken this personally. The bell on the door tinkled for a few long seconds after she said good-bye.

BROTHER GILBERT WEBB
Great Salt Lake

My Dear Brother Gilbert,

You ask a fair question, and I shall attempt to answer it fairly. Your facts are correct. Indeed there were instances when I publicly discussed our unique institution in a manner I knew to be not wholly forthright. If I am to be judged solely on this one indiscretion, without regard to other struggles and achievements, so be it.

Without seeming to evade your accusation, I should like to establish the context for my withholding. I need not remind you, I am sure, the persecution the Saints once faced. Lawless mobs, antagonistic governors and sheriffs, 100 foes to every friend—we were, and remain, a feared people. Shall we recall the dead from the Zion Brigade, Haun's Mill, and Far West? Is there a Saint anywhere who does not weep when he hears the name Carthage? We will forever hear the shot that took our beloved Joseph.

Above all, I see that here on Earth I have been charged with two duties. First I must do whatever I can to guide the faithful to Heavenly Glory. It is a humble task. Second I must protect the tens of thousands of Saints who risk their well-being because they believe in the Restoration. Had I openly acknowledged the institution before reaching the security of Zion, I would have risked the lives of all our Saints—yours too.

I appreciate very much your letter and invite you, Young Friend, to call on me at the Beehive House. I admire most among our

youth he who can set forth with an open heart and a probing mind.
Now go forth and share the Truth, for that is what it is.

Please send my greetings to your parents, your brother, Aaron,
and your sister, Ann Eliza, angelic child that she is.

I am,
Most Sincerely,
Your Prophet

BRIGHAM YOUNG

THE HARDLY BOYS

———

"Where to, Nancy Drew?"

Johnny and I were on our way to Kanab. It was at that point late in the afternoon when it's so hot you think the car will spontaneously ignite. As we got closer to Mesadale we passed a truck with three old Firsts in the cab, guys with yellow white hair greased back and one eye squinted up. Between them they probably had forty or fifty wives and a hundred and fifty kids, maybe two hundred. The truck was worth fifty thousand bucks, pimped with smoked windows and a roof rack. If you got twenty wives at home but the government recognizes only one as your legal spouse, the other nineteen can receive assistance. The more wives and kids, the more welfare checks. That's how a man with seventy mouths to feed and no job can afford a truck like that. And kickbacks from the church for pledging your life to defend the Prophet when the whole thing blows up.

We passed a billboard that said, ON YOUR OWN? NEED HELP? It showed a blond girl walking down a lonely road that didn't look like anywhere near here. An 800 number and an address in Salt Lake. I have a sister who got screwed by that sign. The number only works during the day. But no one can make a call during the day. My sister, she was the daughter of my dad's 12th wife (I think). One night she woke up at about three or four and slipped downstairs and called that number, believing they'd come rescue her. She even had a little bag packed. She was ready. But you know where her call was forwarded to? Straight to the Mesadale Police Department. Who called my dad. He drove her to his brother, who married her. I remember he told her, "You're sixteen, it's time."

We passed the turnoff to Mesadale and looked at the big houses in the distance. I thought of all the kids—the rashy infants, the scabby toddlers, the hungry boys and girls, the lonely teens, each desperate for love. I thought of my mom.

"Thank God we're out of there," said Johnny.

"I just wish I could help all the kids."

"A lot more girls are escaping. At night, they just disappear."

"That must piss off the Prophet."

"There was this one girl, totally hot, maybe like fifteen, he was about to marry her but then she took off."

"Where are they going?"

"Anywhere but here."

In Kanab I parked about a block from the Mega Bite. Johnny was going to try to talk to 5. "Act like you recognize her from Mesadale. Tell her you ran away too. Then ask her when she left. I want to find out if she's lying. Here's two dollars."

"Two dollars?"

I gave him another three bucks and he rolled his eyes. "Give me a half hour." He hopped down from the van. He looked so sure of himself, so pleased to be able to help, that for the first time I worried how I'd get rid of him. While I waited I opened my map of California. In the folds I keep my cash. I had $192 and a credit card with something like $280 left on it. Gas was killing me. After four days in Utah, the only thing I knew for sure was I needed to get back to Pasadena in time for that nursery job. I called Roland but got voice mail. "I won't be here much longer," I said.

"Here's the deal," said Johnny. "She lied to you."

"How do you know?"

"I went in, ordered a ham and cheese—thanks for the money, by the way—and said, 'You look familiar.' She sort of looked at me like, *Do I know you?* So I said, 'You're from Mesadale.' See, the good thing about being a kid is I wasn't going to freak her out. She said, 'Yeah,' and I said, 'Me too.' So I go, 'Wait a minute, I recognize you. You're one of Brother Scott's daughters, right? I recognize you from church.' She just nodded and got a little uneasy, like maybe someone had sent me, which of course someone did send me, but she didn't know that, and so I go, 'Don't worry, I'm on the run, too.' Then I go, 'So were you there when he was killed?' You know what she said? She goes, 'Yeah, I was trying to get my mom to leave, I knew something bad was about to happen, but she wouldn't come with me. Now I have no idea what's going to happen to her.' " Johnny stopped. "So how about that for a lead!"

"You've seen too many bad cop movies."

"Just doing what you couldn't."

"Let's go."

"Where we headed now?"

"Put your seat belt on."

"What? Now you're my mom?"

We stopped at a taco stand and then drove out to an empty trailhead to eat. While we ate the sun set, and the desert went from pink to red to blue to black. The moon wasn't up yet and it was very dark in the van, and the white taco bags were the only thing I could see. Elektra was asleep on the futon, and everything was very quiet except for the wind. I thought Johnny had fallen asleep when he said, "I've done it."

"Done what?"

"You know. With a guy, I mean."

"What?"

"In Vegas. A couple of times. I was down to my last buck." It was too dark to see his face. "I didn't like it."

"That's OK."

"I don't think I'm a homo."

"I don't think so either."

"But if I was, I think I'd like you."

"Thanks. I guess."

"Jordan?"

"Yeah?"

"I don't want to do that anymore."

"You won't have to."

"Promise?"

"I promise."

"Because I'd really rather be nailing a chick."

"You're the crudest person I know."

"Thank you."

Then we talked about all the stuff we had lived through. "Remember how the Prophet would say you could get a girl pregnant by just looking at her when you were horny?" Johnny threw back his head like it was the funniest thing he'd ever heard. "The best part is," he said, "I totally believed him. Man, I thought I'd knocked up every chick in town." We laughed and laughed about all the wacky crap we once believed. What else is there to do?

"Johnny?"

"Yeah?"

"We're going back tonight."

He stopped laughing.

"You up for it?"

He hesitated. And then, "If you are."

IN OUR HOUSE
A Poem
By Lydia Taft Webb[1]

In our house, Thou will find
Loving Sisters, true and kind.
Spouses living righteously
United by the words of Thee.
Numbers two, three, four, or five
The more souls gathered, the more alive!
We pray together, hand-in-hand,
Loving Thou and our husband,
For 'tis Thy will and Thy Command,
Together we shall enter Thy Holy Land!

—1853

---

[1] Lydia Taft Webb, loyal second wife of Chauncey Webb, wrote this poem as an expression of her belief in celestial marriage. Two decades later, when the Saints began to face outside pressure to abandon polygamy, the verse was set to music and sung defiantly by plural wives throughout Deseret. The song remains a popular hymn among the Firsts and other twenty-first-century polygamists.

THE GUN ON THE SCREEN

As we drove into Mesadale, Johnny kept scanning the road. "So far so good. I don't think anyone's noticed us." On one of the side roads we passed a house roofed in plywood and tarp, with two horses hitched to a post out front. "I used to live there," he said. "Such a shithole."

"Do you miss it?"

"What do you think?"

"It's weird, isn't it?"

"What?"

"Being this close to home."

"Except it's not my home anymore," he said. "And it's definitely not yours."

Queenie's house was quiet, and the patrol car—just as I'd hoped—was gone. "Wow," said Johnny. "How'd you know?"

"Total guess."

We were walking up the driveway when the garage door began to roll up, revealing a pair of feet. "Get in here!"

We ducked in, and the door started rolling back down.

Queenie's nightdress cut off at the knee, and she obviously wasn't wearing her sacred underwear. She could get publicly flogged for looking like that. Or raped. Or excommunicated. Or all three.

"I need your help," I said.

"Who's this?"

"He's a friend."

"A friend?" Then she figured it out. "Oh shit, Jordan, you're going to ruin everything."

"Calm down. Hiram's out, right?"

"Yes, but his new wife's in there."

"New wife?"

"They were sealed yesterday. The Prophet had had enough of his monogamy. He said it sent the wrong signal. Hiram had no choice."

"Romantic," I said. "How old is she?"

"Old. Like nineteen."

"Barely legal."

"Dude, you've seen those dvds?"

"Not now, Johnny."

"You're going to have to leave," said Queenie.

"I need you to find something out from your husband."

"Shhhh. Be quiet. She's a hawk. She already hates me."

I wished Q would just say fuck this and climb in the van with me and take off, but in real life people don't do that as often as you think.

"Don't look at me like that," she said.

"Like what?"

"Like you think I'm crazy. I'm not like you, I can't just leave."

"I didn't just leave."

"You know what I mean. Besides, now's not a good time."

"Why not?"

Then it hit me: damn, I can be slow. She was pregnant. "How far along?"

"Three months. I'm sure I'll be on bedrest soon. Last time I was on my back for six months."

"Listen, that's real nice and everything," said Johnny, "but you got anything to eat?"

"You guys need to go."

"I know, but I'm like starving."

"Wait right here," she said. "And don't make any noise."

While we waited Johnny checked out Alton's guns. Flintlock pistols, a couple of snipers, a pump-action shotgun, a boy's rifle, and an antique revolver with a gold cylinder. "If things get bad," said Johnny, "at least I've got my knife."

"You and your knife."

Queenie returned with a muffin and a glass of milk and Johnny downed them like he hadn't eaten in a week.

"Queenie, I need to ask you a question," I said. "Do you know anything about the police report?"

"Hiram doesn't talk to me about things like that."

"Can you ask him why the investigation isn't complete?"

"He'll wonder why I'm asking. And with her around, it's going to be even harder."

"Try."

"What should I tell him when he asks why I want to know?"

"Tell him a lot of people are talking about it, like the sister wives down at the co-op. They're wondering and they asked you."

She was thinking about it. "Even if he does tell me, how am I going to tell you?"

"Can you call my cell?"

"He'll know."

"Do you have email?" She and Johnny looked at me like, what a stupid question.

"Then leave a note at the post office with Sister Karen," I said. Queenie was very still. I knew she'd do it. "How much time do you need?" I said.

"Till tomorrow. Now you better go. She's going to wonder why I'm out here. And be careful." I told her I would. "And do me a favor, don't come back. Jordan, I love you, but you're about to cause a lot of trouble."

The road back to the highway was deserted. The houses were lit up, but there was no one in sight. "I don't think anyone's seen us."

Johnny turned to look back at the town retreating behind us. "I wonder why we came up with the bad, bad luck to be born here. Do you think God was playing a joke on us or something?"

"I don't know."

"You know what my mom said when we said good-bye?"

"What?"

"See you in heaven." He snorted. "Heaven my ass."

"You know what my mom said? One day you'll understand."

That's when a jacked pickup pulled out from the brush and started following us. It sped in close, and a row of lights on the roof rack came on, filling the van with silver blue light. "Shit," said Johnny. Elektra started barking at the window in the back door.

"Can you see who it is?" I said.

"Not with those lights."

The truck revved closer, then pulled back, then drove up on my rear again. Everything around us was black except for the hard lights on the roof rack. "I guess someone saw us," I said.

"Man, we are so screwed."

"Hang on." I swerved around on the road, throwing up a cloud of red dust. The truck slowed, giving me some space. "He's just playing with us," I said.

"You sure?"

"No."

"Who do you think it is?"

"Could be anyone."

"You think it's the Prophet?"

"No. I don't know." I slammed on the brakes. Elektra flew off the futon, and the truck swerved off the road into the sagebrush. The lights were on the desert now, and it was like the brightest moon had risen over the scrub and the sand. "Can you see anyone now?"

"Just one guy."

"What does he look like?"

"An asshole."

In my rearview I watched the truck back out of the sagebrush. Its monster wheels turned in the sand, spitting it out behind. The truck pushed itself over a ridge of sand at the side of the road and righted itself back into place. The lights were now pointing ahead on the road again, but we were out of their range. When we reached the highway I said, "We're OK."

"What if he follows us?" said Johnny.

"He won't. He can only pull that shit in Mesadale."

"I hope he doesn't take it out on my mom."

"He wasn't looking for you."

Driving back to St. George, I was trying to think things through, but Johnny kept yakking on about his mom and stepdad, how they'd screwed up his whole life.

"You want to know how my mom ended up with my stepdad?"

"Not really."

"We were living up near Brigham City, my mom and me, I mean. All of a sudden one day when I was five she just throws my crap in the car and drives me down here. I was like, 'Is this a vacation?' And she goes, 'You'll get used to it.' We moved right in with my stepdad. I'm not sure how they met, but I guess it was through the mail or the internet or something. I remember the first time I saw him I was thinking, Is that someone's grandpa? He was old even then. Skinny, with all that old-man skin and that old-man smell. He said, 'I think you'll like it here.' I just looked up at him and said, 'I doubt it.' You know what he did? He smacked my ear. It was the first time anyone ever hit me, and I just looked over at my mom like, 'Are you going to let him do that?' I mean, I was so certain she'd drive us home that very minute, but she only said, 'Johnny, you got to listen to your dad.' That was when I knew she was a goner, except when you're five you don't really know what that means. All I knew was my mom wasn't my mom anymore, something had happened to her, and they told me if I did anything to piss the old guy off, God would take it out on her."

"It's the same story," I said. "Over and over."

"Man, I wish my mom would go and blow his fucking heart out, too."

"My mom didn't kill my dad."

"Yeah, well, you know what I mean."

By the time we got back to St. George almost everything was

closed. The lights were still on at A Woman Sconed. The goth girl was leaning on the bagel bar, watching TV. "Finally a customer I actually like," she said. She looked like she'd had the dullest night of her life. While Elektra and Johnny begged for cookies, I jumped on the computer to check email.

"Any word from the chicks?" said Johnny.

I clicked the mouse. "Looks like there's something from Alexandra."

"Dude, she wants you. Open it."

It was real nice to meet you Jordan. Im sorry about your dad. But guess what. I found his pic in my computer. We only chatted for a little bit so even if I did remember more of it Im sure it wouldn't be of much use. But here's the pic he sent me. I thought you might want it.

I opened the attached picture and slowly, from top to bottom, it appeared on the screen. There he was, with this message: *As you can see I like my guns!*

"Shit," said Johnny. "He used *that* to pick up chicks?"

My dad was standing in the basement in a cheap wine-colored tie, his arm around a woman whose face had been scratched out so lazily you could tell it was my mom. They were holding a rifle between them, the way a couple of fishermen would pose with their catch. There's one good thing about growing up off the grid: I know my guns. The gun on the screen was the Golden Boy. And fitted to its muzzle was a suppressor as fat as a can of Mountain Dew.

IX

ZION

CHAPTER FIVE:
My Youth in Deseret

Now, with your permission, I will tell the stories of my youth in Utah and how those years, the 1850s, led me to my fate as Brigham's final wife. In the autumn of 1848, when I was four years old, we settled in Great Salt Lake City, a new city overlooking a silver saline sea. When my family arrived in this forsaken land, we were a wretched lot in possession of little more than our wagons and oxen, a milking cow, and the clothes encrusted to our backs. No doubt you have seen many daguerreotypes of the Westward-ho family: the bearded father in suspenders, the mother in an apron (she always thinner than her brood), the children with dark half-moons of exhaustion beneath their eyes. This is who we were, any American family waging everything on the West. Except, to this historic image, you must add Sister Lydia and her child, Diantha. To the untrained eye she would look like a widowed aunt, but by now my Dear Reader knows the secrets of the Mormon clan.

In our first year in Deseret, we were so busy digging, clearing, building, and sowing there was little time for misery. In order to represent the fullest form of honesty, I must confess that those early years in Zion were among the happiest my family has known. We, each newly arrived Saint, were set upon a purpose: to build a home while establishing a colony where we could be free in our beliefs. This is a noble cause, one that can inspire even the tiniest of hearts, such as mine was at the time, and return doubting minds to course. My father, ever industrious, set up a new wagonry and very soon his forges blazed. My mother, who never spent a day in school, was asked by the Prophet himself to teach one day a week in the Zion school house. (I won't expend ink by digressing into Brother Brigham's curious effort to establish the Deseret Alphabet, made up of thirty-eight mostly new characters which gave the Saints a secretive method of writing English. This alphabet was briefly forced upon the children of Zion, including myself. For a short time my mother, in obeying her spiritual leaders, had to teach it at the blackboard, all the while knowing it was useless back-slang.)

Anyone who has embarked on a great adventure, started a new phase of his life, or begun life freshly in an unfamiliar land will understand the general excitement and sense of possibility of those early years in Utah. We were concerned less by what we lacked and more by what we one day might possess. This is a healthy vision of life, and for this we all owe Brigham Young. From his pulpit in the Tabernacle he set the tone of each day in the Territory. He demanded the laying out of orderly streets and set to building Temple Square on a scale so large he said it was not for any of us alive but for the Saints of the next century, and the century thereafter. He commanded the digging of artesian wells, which delivered water along a pebbly bed to our door. He organized the city into wards and set up a bishop in each to lead the local population through times of duress and spiritual weakness. He tapped his most industrious men to open a tannery, a curriery, a crockery, warehouses for paint and whip, stores for shoes, cloth, soap, and candles, and quite nearly everything else. In no time there was a city where previously there had been a moonscape of sand, sage-brush, aloe, and the dusty cottonwood. All this sprang out of nothing—as the giddy wildflowers appear in the desert after the April downpour, each a tiny colored miracle aloft on the stalk; all evidence of God's might. Although Brigham Young would one day become my enemy, I must acknowledge all that which he created for his Saints. The "go-a-headitiveness" for which the Mormons have become known comes from, I believe, the leadership of their Prophet at this time. In less than ten years he transformed a basin so arid and inhospitable that even the most intrepid and resourceful Indian nations had avoided it for thousands of years, into the City of the Saints, a metropolis of some twenty thousand souls and a thriving theocracy for him to rule with, he assured us, Divine legitimacy.

This, then, is what I called home.

In the late fall of 1854, not long after my tenth birthday, our idyll was interrupted by Brigham's selection of my father, Chauncey, and my half-brother Gilbert, to journey to England to serve on a Mission. One might suspect that we would receive this news as an honor—an opportunity to carry forth the new Gospel to our distant cousins. Yet in those early days of the Territory, nothing was as it seemed.

Brigham Young, as President of the Church of Jesus Christ of Latter-day Saints, Lord's Prophet, Governor of the Utah Territory, and general owner of the largest businesses and industries in the land, had become a ruler of absolute authority. He controlled the Church, the civic government, the police, the press, the major economic institutions, including the busiest stores, mills, and warehouses, and owned much of the Territory's land, and other things, too. His holdings were so vast some claimed even he could not know all that he possessed.

By 1854 my father had become a wealthy man again in his own right. His wagonry was the most productive in the Territory. Because the railroad would not arrive for another fifteen years, Utah's isolation, and the great distances between its stakes, made wagon manufacturing one of the most valuable industries. He who controlled the manufacturing of wagons could control much else. Enter the Mission.

With my father abroad, Brother Brigham could run the manufactory himself, for a fee, of course. My father understood the arrangement immediately. "You'll have to cut back," he told his two wives. "The next two years will be long. Look out for each other." Saying good-bye to his family, my father kissed each wife, then his children. He told Aaron he was now the man of the house. The boy, all pimple and whisker, declared himself ready for the task. My father lifted Diantha in the air, twirling her around. She was of that age (six) and made of that peculiar demeanor that compels an otherwise modest girl to lift her hems upward anytime given the chance (I imagine the showgirl has some of the same fiber in her). When my father approached me, I bit down hard on a trembling lip. "How do I know you'll come back?" I said. He promised he would, but already I had my doubts.

The concept of a Mission is not easy for a ten-year-old to grasp. My father had always been a quietly religious man. I had a difficult time envisioning him—and tongue-tied Gilbert even less so!—standing before strangers and speaking of the Lord. The journey was long, the seas rough, and the climate in England, my mother said, damp and disagreeable. Floating through the schoolyards of Zion were stories of Missionaries who never returned: "A bloody Catholic put blew a ball through his head!" Speaking on behalf of Christ is a dangerous task, especially when the faith you carry forth is tainted by rumors of the harem.

"What if I don't recognize you after two years," I complained.

"In two years," my father laughed, "I might not recognize you."

Thus my father and Gilbert departed, their hearts dense with faith and fear. Of course I did not accompany them on their Mission, and therefore will leave his years abroad to my Dear Reader's imagination, which I trust is fertile and capable of filling in.

In his absence, the household of harmony and happiness crumbled. Very soon the payments from the manufactory upon which my mother and Lydia survived ceased. Distressed by her circumstances, my mother visited the wagonry to inquire after its affairs. Brother Brigham had appointed Mr. Morley to serve as general manager and foreman. He kept my mother and me waiting nearly three-quarters of an hour, despite this being our property. When at last he agreed to see my mother (he made no acknowledgment of me), the man said, "I have but a minute, Madame."

"My husband's been gone three weeks," my mother began, "and it's taken three weeks for our income to dry up. If you were me, wouldn't you come down here to ask? I have a household, Mr. Morley, and little ones. I need to know what I can expect for the next two years."

Mr. Morley was a thickly set pale man with a beard that grew in so darkly against his pallid skin, it appeared blue. "My first obligation is to the Prophet," he said.

"So is mine."

"Your husband and many others are over there in Europe converting Saints. Well, when these foreign Saints reach our shores they'll need wagons to cross the plains. Brother Brigham's placed an order for two hundred wagons. I need to cover the cost of the materials and pay the men and heat up the forge. That leaves very little at the end of the day. I can't go raising the prices on the Church, can I?"

"Of course not, but what about that little extra? When can I expect to see it?"

"Mrs. Webb, I'm very sorry if your husband didn't explain this to you. This wagonry doesn't throw off much. Your husband hardly paid himself. The little bit of profit is now going to me. I can assure you it's hardly a fair fee. I'm sacrificing, too."

None of this sounded true to my mother, but she had no recourse.

"May I make a suggestion," said Mr. Morley. "You and the second Mrs. Webb might want to turn some of your house work into something you can sell. Are you any good with the butter churn? Making cakes of soap? I bet you make a fine hat. But really, Mrs. Webb, this isn't my realm. I know the women's organizations are good about helping women such as yourself."

Later that night, after we children had gone to bed, I overheard my mother and Lydia discuss the situation. Lydia, ever resourceful and bright, said, "I could bake batches of bishop squares and sell them to the hotel dining room."

"That's not enough."

"I'll knit socks and you can raise laying hens."

"Socks and eggs won't be enough."

"We could always rent out a room."

My mother reminded Lydia there wasn't a spare room to let out.

"I could move into your room," Lydia suggested, "or you could move into mine and we could fix up the empty one for a widow who needs a roof and if she's got little ones we can bring them in, too."

I imagine that the thought of another woman under her roof convinced my mother to find another path to financial stability. In the morning she applied to the Prophet's office for an appointment as teacher in one of the distant stakes. At this time Brigham was busy colonizing the vast Utah Territory, mapping it into a system of wards and stakes. (A stake is similar to a county, and each stake is made up of several wards; apparently these are biblical terms.) Some wards were so remote and forsaken that few Saints wanted to move there. Teachers especially were in demand, for how could the Prophet encourage multiple wives and the voluminous offspring they produced if he did not provide schools for all those beautiful little heads? Within a week of her request, Brother Brigham dispatched my mother, Aaron, and me to Payson, sixty miles south of Great Salt Lake.

By January 1855 we had settled, as best we could, in a one-room adobe hut with a dirt floor and two beds flanking the hearth. Known for its high sun and desert climes, Deseret, I should remind the Reader, is equally familiar with winter's bitterness. The wind whips, the snow blows, the temperature plummets, the ice collects. So it did this January in Payson, where wood was scarce, forcing us to fuel our fire by buffalo dung. Aaron, who at seventeen was of ample frame, took more than his share of the bedclothes. Each night was a difficult but eventually victorious battle of retaking the woolly territory my shivering body had lost to him, so that by dawn, after an exhaustive but committed effort, I finally had gained enough warmth to sleep an hour. I do not know which is worse: the rancid nighttime odors produced by a boy caught in the throes of early manhood or the stench of burning buffalo dirt. Needless to say, I had yet to become accustomed to our new lot.

Not long after our arrival, our new neighbor, Mrs. Myton, appeared in a flutter at our door. "Have you heard?" she gasped. "There's an Elder coming to speak in the Meeting House!" She was excited in a fluffed-up way, her arms flapping about. A Mormon Elder speaking to his people is a common event in every ward and so my mother inquired for further detail. Mrs. Myton handed over a broadside that appeared ripped from its post. "He's coming to Payson to discuss our sins!"

So it had been arranged that a Saint by the name of Elder James Beckwith would preach in the evening to the sinners of Payson. How or why Elder Beckwith selected Payson I will never know, for I doubt it was any more, or less, sinful than the other communities of Zion.

Before his arrival, the town stirred with anticipation. Sister wives donned their finest scarves and swatted at their husbands until they had washed properly. Children scraped mud from their boots. Everyone wanted to appear clean at the meeting. My mother and I were no less susceptible. She hurried about our little hut in search of something to wear, while I rinsed out my stockings. Aaron, however, had recently acquired the dour, resentful air of his age. He had begun putting up a fuss on Sunday mornings, turning out for Church in an untidy manner that was all too deliberate and designed to provoke the sharpest of irritation in my mother.

"You cannot wear that," my mother advised when he put on a dirty shirt. Aaron shrugged that she could not tell him what to do. The women among my Dear Readers will recognize this confrontation between mother and son. After several repetitions of these seemingly irreconcilable positions, my mother relented, as every mother learns to do. "Go as you please," she sighed.

She turned to find me plaiting my hair. Since my apostasy from the Mormon Church I have been accused of many things, most of them wholly untrue. However, the accusations that I have always appreciated a pretty dress and other womanly finery, and have been known to spend a minute too long at the looking glass, is, I must confess, deserved and true. So be it: I am guilty!

The Meeting House was hot and unpleasant from all the people crowded into it. Many I had never seen before. Judging by the plainness of cloth and the dirt in their seams, they were settlers who had journeyed a day or more to hear the preacher. Such a setting, I will note, is a valuable scene to record the demographic peculiarities of plural marriage. Allow me to take one bench as an example: Near where my mother and I stood along the wall (while Aaron fidgeted with his pocket knife!) was a long bench that in most Christian congregations could hold two or three families. But here, on this portentous evening, I shall describe who sat there: First the father (always the father first!), a farmer in his patched shirt; then his lovely young wife, slender in her bodice; then the next wife, older than the first, yellowish hair with worrisome streaks of gray; in her lap was a boy of seven or eight in need of wiping his nose and his three little brothers and sisters squeezed in at her side; next to them, an older woman even still, her hair a dull drained buff, and a general emaciation that suggests the difficulty of her days; next to her were two lads about Aaron's age, their Adam's apples the size of rocks. And, because this is the way, next to her, an older woman even still, hair too wiry to hold neatly in a bun; her head sat upright with dignity and grace upon a thick, tired neck. She had one daughter, full grown, portly, and unmarried; I can only presume they shared a bed in this man's house. I will make the presumptuous leap to state that the father at the opposite end of the bench had not visited his first wife's bed in a decade. So I present your average Payson family, in its full relief.

Finally, at a quarter past eight, Elder Beckwith stood before the gathered lot. "Brothers and Sisters, I'm here to tell you that each of you, both man and woman, child and parent, is a sinner. Yet you have taken the first step toward redemption by being here tonight." The man carried on like this for nearly twenty minutes, accusing everyone gathered of sin. He assured us we were damned eternally unless we cleansed our souls through confession. "Now who will confess his thievery, his deception, his lustful heart, his treachery and fraud, his hypocrisy, his perfidy, and his lack of fervor in his religion?"

The man was in possession of a fair, angelic complexion set off by dark, wavy hair. His touching, boyish appearance contrasted with his bullying sermon in a way that made his audience listen even more intently.

"Do you believe I am up here merely for the sake of rhetoric? Do you think I ask this question as a speaker's gesture? These are not the preacher's questions, left to be answered in the privacy of your heart. These are the questions of the reformer and savior of the soul. I ask you here and now: Who is prepared to repent? There is but one path to salvation: Repent, reveal your sins and allow yourself to be baptized anew! And so it has come to pass that now is the time for you to repent!"

He stared out at his audience, making each of us feel as if he were glaring into our individual souls and could see the lies and deceit. My heart was racing, so terrified was I of his power to know my most secret truths. I began to feel the urge to speak. I sensed that he wanted me, among the hundreds of people gathered, to confess as example. But what would I confess? True, I had coveted Missy Horman's velvet-trimmed cloak. I had prayed my father would return early from his Mission, even if it meant leaving souls unsaved. Once, I called Brother Brigham plump as a pig (not to his face, of course). Was this what Elder Beckwith wanted to hear?

Upon the stage he paced back and forth repeating his calls until finally Mrs. Myton, our neighbor, shot up in her seat. "I can't stay quiet any longer."

"Sister, what have you done?"

"I have sinned." Gasps and clucks filled the hall.

"Tell us, what are your transgressions?"

"It's difficult to say."

"Yet you've already stood. We know for certain you're guilty. Now you must tell us your errors and we shall help you atone."

"I can't. They'll hate me for it."

"Who?"

Mrs. Myton wrung her handkerchief. She was a widow and had come to the Meeting House alone but for her spinster daughter, Connie, who had trouble seeing at night. Elder Beckwith prodded Mrs. Myton: "Have you lied?"

"Well—"

"Have you stolen?"

"Well—"

"Speak, Sister. Hundreds are waiting for you."

"All right. I'll say it. I took her hen."

"Whose hen?"

"My neighbor's, Mrs. Webb's. When she moved in, her hen wandered into my yard and it was Connie's twentieth birthday and I just picked it up and before I'd known what I'd done it was boiling in my pot. I'll replace the bird, I promise."

The crowd twittered with shock. Many turned to look at my mother in order to offer pity and compassion, although a few, it seemed, appeared to suggest that she was somehow equal to blame. My mother had long wondered about that hen, which, truth be told, had never been much of a layer. Now, made aware of her status as victim of a larceny, she held me tight, uncertain of how to react. Was this a test of her as well?

"Was it one hen, Sister?" asked the Elder.

"Just one," said Mrs. Myton. "And I haven't slept well since." (This I would label a half truth, for just the day before I passed

Mrs. Myton's window and heard a snoring equal to the clatter of picks in the quarry.)

"Mrs. Webb, tell us, can you forgive this wretched soul?"

"If the Lord can," said my mother, "then so can I."

"Very good," said the Elder. He stood contentedly before us, as a school master stands while his students await the next question in an oral exam. "Now who's next?"

Mrs. Myton had been the chink in the dam. What followed was a flood of confession. Brothers and Sisters raced each other to stand before their community and confess their sins: a stolen fence; a ladder borrowed but not returned; a hand-saw pilfered from the mill. One dear woman, whose husband was up in Great Salt Lake with his second and third wives, pressed hard against her conscience to find a moral error in her past; all she could produce was this: "I once stole a rose from a bush that was not mine," she admitted in minor triumph. "To make matters worse, I pressed it in my Bible and have it to this day."

The admissions of thievery and deceit continued for three hours, reaching such fervor that it became almost a contest of who could admit to the greater sin. When one Brother stood and confessed mere doubt in his heart, he was nearly booed from the Meeting House. "What else have you done!" someone called. "Tell the truth!"

Then something unexpected occurred. Aaron stood up. "I've got something to say."

Elder Beckwith stopped. "Tell me, Brother, what have you done?"

"I've been wrong to a girl."

"Go on." Clearly this was the type of confession Elder Beckwith had been fishing for all night. Now that the topic had moved from larceny to true impropriety, the crowd of Saints was freshly enraptured.

"I promised I would marry her and I haven't."

"What will you do about it?"

"I'll marry her, if she'll have me."

Aaron had been such an undistinguished boy his entire life that many who knew my family did not know of his existence. He was average in every way: a plain appearance, a plain mind, a plain and guileless sense of purpose in life. I do not write this with judgment but simply as a matter of recording the truth—and in effort for the Reader to understand how exceptional his confession was.

"Is she here tonight?" asked Elder Beckwith.

"She is."

"Will you make amends to her now? In front of your gathered Brothers and Sisters and before God?"

Every eye was on Aaron. He stepped forward, moving around the crowded pews. There was a great anticipation as he walked, everyone wondering at whose feet he would stop. When he had to step over a family seated on the floor, people stirred as if one of these girls—freckled like the leopard, all of them—had submitted to his will. But no, he was only passing. He paused before a black-laced widow whose husband had been lost in Missouri. Had she had her way with my brother? No, he was only hesitating before moving to, of all people, Connie, our dear, dull neighbor, who had celebrated her twentieth birthday unknowingly feasting on my mother's hen.

Imagine the stir when my brother took Connie's plump hand and asked her to become Mrs. Aaron Webb! His voice was so soft and timid that two older Sisters squawked, "What'd he say?" People began stomping their feet and a small section broke into a spontaneous hymn about atonement and the path to Heaven.

"And so this fine couple shall be sealed," announced Elder Beckwith. "With their confessions, we can now forgive."

If Mrs. Myton had let loose a flood of stories of theft, my brother released a tidal wave of perversion too graphic to print. Suffice it to say: at least half the population of Saintly Brothers had a confession of the heart or loins. The revelations continued for more than an hour, men rising to admit relations with women who were not their wives. The only resolution was marriage, even if the men were already wed. Elder Beckwith asked several women on the spot, "Will you forgive your husband and permit him to marry the woman he has wronged in order to prevent his eternal damnation and hers?" Tell me, does a woman put to such a question have any option in her reply?

It will be noted that in this litany of intercoursal relations there were no confessions of liaisons between a man and a previously married woman. No man was stupid enough to admit to that. It is not for me to say whether such sins had been committed but not confessed, or if Payson was somehow spared from such unforgivable acts. In any event, after five hours of confession, we had heard enough. We left exhausted, my mother and Mrs. Myton forced to walk home amicably, newly united by crime.

———

CHAPTER SIX:
The Utah Reformation

The subsequent weeks brought great change and confusion to my depleted little family in Payson. The confessional meeting was followed by several more, some lasting all day, wherein every last sin imaginable and many never before deemed possible were confessed. There was never a more devout Saint than my mother, but she worried over the upheaval these meetings caused. "I don't understand it. People are lying about lying," she observed. "You can't impress the Lord with extra sins."

She was under a new duress, for Aaron had kept his promise and was sealed to Connie Myton in the Endowment House. It was a joyless ceremony, attended by but a few, myself excluded for I was too young to enter. Afterward, my mother served a custard cake to her new daughter and Mrs. Myton, who ate more than her share and left my mother with but a spoonful. (Why this sticks in my memory, I cannot say, but there it is once again: the truth!) After supper Aaron set about hanging a blanket along a wire run across the hut. Connie was to replace me in his bed, and I would sleep next to my mother. It was only that first night, as I tossed uncomfortably and plugged my ears against the strange noises from the other side of the blanket, that I learned that my mother's ticking was no more comfortable or soft than a dry river bed. She had given her children the finer mattress without once complaining of her sacrifice. This is the sort of woman my mother has always been, I shall note plainly here.

Newly married, and awakened to the omnipresence of sin in our community, Aaron joined up with the gang of men who had taken it upon themselves to enforce atonement. These were frightening days in Payson. Although distracted by the vagaries of girlhood, I took full notice of the change of climate, and I am not referring to winter's end and the arrival of spring. During the first months of 1855, the confessions continued. Those who refused to confess, or confessed they had nothing to confess, were dragged to meetings by gangs of young men, my brother included, and put before a hall of peers and shouted at to repent. "You're no better than the rest of us!" It did not occur to these mobs that a man or woman could in fact live righteously and therefore have no sins to offer up. The Church had been guiding all of us for years, long before Elder Beckwith's arrival, to live sinlessly. I shall not bother to point out the broken logic herein.

In the evenings Aaron took down my father's rifle and went out to round up sinners. Connie, I am sorry to report, was a meek, twitching-nosed creature who squeaked from the corner of our hut. "When will you be back?" seemed to be her favorite phrase. When Aaron was out, I invited her to sit with my mother and me at the fire, but she preferred to stay on her side of the blanket, passing her time I do not know how, although every now and then a small little sniffle would emerge from her and my mother and I would lift our eyes from our needlework.

Once I asked Aaron, when he came through the door flushed and excited, where he had gone off to. He hung up his gun like a hunter home from the kill and said, "Making sure all are saved." A noble endeavor, I am sure, but coming from a boy of seventeen who only a few months before feigned fever on Sunday mornings, it sounded, to my youthful and inexperienced ears, at least, insincere.

It does not take long, I do not need to tell you, for such an environment of confession to turn on itself. Soon not only were souls being cleansed, but neighbors were realizing they lived next to adulterers and thieves. Nearly everyone in Payson was told at some point he had been a victim by he who was previously deemed friend. This was enough to cast a long cloud of suspicion over the village. While the sinners were being re-baptized in the creek their minds were preoccupied with their belongings left on the shore.

"It isn't right," my mother concluded in her admirably succinct way.

She wrote the Prophet, alerting Brigham to the hypocrisy Elder Beckwith had unleashed in Payson. She was certain her old friend and counselor would not approve of such behavior, for where in the Book of Mormon were the tales of mass confession and repentance? (Well, maybe they are in there somewhere, because I might as well admit, as a child I tried to read the book a dozen times but always failed. If you find hypocrisy in this confession, so be it, but I ask you, Dear Reader, pick up a copy yourself and tell me how long you last.)

Brother Brigham replied to my mother from Fillmore, where he was busy with the legislature. "If they are sinful," he replied coldly, "then they should admit to their sins." It would be incorrect to state this callous reply did not wound my mother. She could have dismissed its blow from any other Saint but Brigham, the man who had personally saved her with baptism in that cold creek all those years before. At the time she of course did not reveal the Prophet's response to me directly, yet in reconstructing these events for this publication more than one person has assured me that these words were his.

Had the events in Payson remained in Payson, this would be but a quaint story of provincial religious fervor. Yet, as History now knows, the mood of inquisition that struck our village was but a precursor for what would become known as the Utah Reformation. By the following winter of 1856, Brother Brigham and the other Church leaders instituted a likeminded reform throughout the Utah Territory. "All are guilty! None is clean until he has been cleansed!" So the charge went against Saints everywhere, even those who never transgressed. The Utah Reformation showed far better organization than the little version originated in Payson. Brigham ran it like a General leading a War, commanding his Bishops, Elders, and others as if they were foot soldiers in a fierce battle for the soul. Among his many tactics in the campaign, Brigham created a secret police disguised as local proselytizers called the Home Missionaries. Their function was to spy on his followers and carry out his will.

One afternoon my brother returned to the hut in such a somber mood, I feared he was bearing fateful news about our father. "I've been named a Home Missionary," he announced.

"What's that?" I asked in that way only an eleven-year-old can.

"We go around visiting people in their homes, ensuring everyone's living righteously." Next he told my mother and me, and his wife in her corner, that he must put us each through a catechism. "That's how I'll know if your souls are pure."

"Child, sit down," my mother said. "You sound like a fool."

"Anyone who refuses the catechism must be reported to the Bishop." My mother told Aaron to stop his nonsense.

"I'll do it," squeaked Connie.

"You see," said Aaron. "My wife has nothing to hide."

He shooed my mother and me out the door into the garden. It was a fine spring day with a breeze rippling the grass. We waited upon a log beneath the cottonwood. Mrs. Myton spotted us from her window. "He promised he'd come over and do me when he's through with you!" she called.

"It didn't used to be like this," said my mother.

"It's all Brigham's fault," I said.

"No, it's the men around him. They tell him lies. There is no finer man on Earth than Brigham Young."

Imagine, if you will, the effect such a declaration can have on a young girl's heart. I was on the threshold of maturity, and acutely sensitive to how women responded to men. I loved no one more in this world than my mother. If she could love Brigham, even as his words and deeds created animosity in her own house, then my heart naturally followed course.

After nearly an hour, Aaron and Connie appeared in the kitchen yard. She had a confused, far-off expression, as if recovering from a sharp but temporary pain. "Is she all right?"

"She'll wait at her mother's while we continue. All right, Ann Eliza, you're next."

My mother told Aaron he could not interview me unless she was present. Aaron whined, an impetuous noise that reminded us he was not far from boyhood. "The Elders insist that each catechism be performed alone. Those are the rules."

"I won't let you talk to her without me." My mother folded her arms across her breasts—the universal maternal gesture that tells all children everywhere, This matter is settled.

Aaron relented with a huff and a stomp. We followed him into the hut. He had set two chairs opposite each other and he nervously indicated us to sit down while he perched on the bed. "Now I must ask you some very important questions. You must swear to the Lord you will answer honestly and truthfully."

I told him I would.

"All right, let's begin." He flipped through a pamphlet provided to him by our Bishop. "The first question is, Have you ever killed a man, woman, or child?"

"This is crazy," my mother snapped. "I know I've never thought about killing anyone until this very moment."

"Ma, I need to ask the questions in the order they're printed. Ann Eliza, yes or no?"

I could not help myself from laughing. "Who would I kill?"

"Answer the question straightforward and truthfully."

"No."

And so the inquisition continued. My brother, in earnest voice, asked the most ridiculous questions I have ever encountered, at least until my lawsuit against Brigham Young. He inquired if I had committed adultery. (This to an eleven-year-old!) He asked if I had drunk ale, whiskey, or wine.

"Are you finished?" said my mother.

"One more question. Do you accept plural marriage as true?"

"Are you asking me or Ann Eliza?"

"Both."

"My husband has a second wife. I think that clarifies my belief."

"Ann Eliza? What about you?"

"I think so." Oh, if I could take back that response!

The interview ended, as Aaron had been taught to do so, with instruction to observe the wishes of my mother and father (though absent) and to rightfully enter a plural marriage when I was of the age. "There," he said, reverting to his more accustomed role of son and brother. "How'd I do?"

"You'll be real good at this miserable task," my mother said.

Aaron, never exceedingly swift, took this as a compliment until he felt its underlying sting.

From thence Aaron, and many others like him, visited the houses of neighbor and friend, subjecting good men and women to a humiliating volley of questions. Most were afraid to turn the Home Missionaries away, for doing so would set off suspicion of being guilty of some great and yet unknown sin. During this time every Saint in the Territory underwent a re-baptismal, shivering in the fonts while their sins, no matter how trivial, were supposedly washed away. Within a few months, the people of Utah believed themselves the cleanest body of souls ever to grace the Earth. Despite my mother's denial, in truth all of this was done at the behest of Brigham Young.

THE 19TH WIFE

CHAPTER SEVEN:
Blood Atonement

Every now and then my mother and I journeyed to Great Salt Lake City to shop in the well-stocked outlets of Main Street. These were not frivolous trips—not as you, my young ladies of the East, might think of a shopping journey—but, rather, necessary excursions for survival. The stores in Payson, if you were to call them such, carried such crude supplies that in some ways it might have been more convenient were they not in business at all.

On one such trip we—my mother and I, accompanied by Aaron and Connie—stayed overnight to hear the Prophet preach in the Tabernacle in the morning. For those who have not visited the City of the Saints, the Tabernacle is an enormous hall with a low, rounded roof that will remind you of nothing so much as a giant tortoise. It is one of the Great Buildings of the World, and, God willing, shall survive centuries of man's folly to show itself to future ages. Unfortunately, the world-famous turtle-roofed Tabernacle would not be built for another ten years. No, on this particular trip in 1856, as the Utah Reformation was boiling over into violence, the Tabernacle was a more modest affair (although it was a vast improvement over the first Tabernacle in the Territory, which was nothing more than a shady spot beneath a bowery). Yet, no matter the edifice, the Saints would always turn up by the thousands to hear their Prophet, Brigham Young.

By now I was of the age to form a mature and reasoned opinion of the great man. He loomed over my childhood as a beloved grandfather might: omnipresent and seemingly limitless in his influence over our lives; loving but also somewhat frightening; and as constant as the sun and moon combined. Before we moved to Payson, I would see him on Sundays or on occasion in Temple Square, and he would nod hello, for he was always friendly with children. Every child in the Territory knew where he lived, in the Beehive House behind a high stone wall. Many others have depicted him accurately, at least in visage, so there is little point in my expanding upon previous efforts. Except I shall note the appropriate metallic color of his eyes and the generally square and solid shape of his entire personage. In my youthful imagination I could not render a more apt representative of God.

On this particular Sunday the Old Tabernacle was full of expectancy. The Reformation had been sweeping the Territory for several weeks, fomenting a fervor of introspection, admission, and re-baptism. Twenty-five hundred Saints had come to hear their Prophet on how they could further atone. Surely some, though how many we can never be certain, were also looking for counsel on how to help their neighbors atone more effectively. Brother Brigham provided ample advice, for when he took the speaker's stand, his subject was atonement. I can assure you, nothing ignites an audience's heart like the discussion of someone else's penitence! Working himself into a magnificent outrage, Brigham Young announced, "There are sins that can be atoned for by an offering on an altar, as in ancient days; and there are sins that the blood of a lamb or calf, or of turtle-doves, cannot remit, but they must be atoned for by the blood of the man."

As if his point were not clear, the Prophet continued, "The time is coming when justice will be laid to the line and righteousness to the plummet; when we shall take the old broadsword, and ask, 'Are you for God?' and if you are not heartily on the Lord's side, you will be hewn down."

He also said, although I cannot be certain if it was on this particular day, "Will you love your brothers and sisters likewise, when they have a sin that cannot be atoned for without the shedding of their blood? Will you love that man or that woman well enough to shed their blood? That is what Jesus meant. This is loving our neighbor as our self; if he needs help, help him; if he wants salvation, and it is necessary to spill his blood upon the earth in order that he may be saved, spill it." (To my doubting Reader, I assure you these words are correct quotations and not mere paraphrasings. Brigham's words from the pulpit have always been dutifully recorded and distributed. You may search any archive in Deseret to learn that here I am transcribing his words verbatim without any enhancement or coloring.)

This was the doctrine of Blood Atonement—any man, woman, or child who did not believe in the doctrines of the Church, or the words of its leaders, could rightfully be destroyed by the sword. The Saints, already hot with religious fever, received the Prophet's words as Wisdom and Truth. Brigham had established his new doctrine and sent the Saints on their way to kill in the name of faith.

Terrified, I broke into tears. Although I was young, Brigham's meaning was clear to me.

After the services we walked over to Main Street, where a restaurant sold ice-cream for twenty-five cents a glass, a high luxury well beyond my mother's crimped budget. Yet she knew I needed a distraction. As I probed the ball of ice-cream I asked, "Why does Brother Brigham want to kill some men?"

"He didn't mean it," my mother said. "Not like that."

"He meant it," said Aaron. He had finished his ice-cream and was digging into his wife's. "Brigham means what he says."

"Generally, yes," said my mother. "But this time he was speaking in metaphor."

Aaron looked confused, while Connie fidgeted with her curls. I thought, No doubt God had carefully selected them to be together.

Perhaps my mother's assessment was correct. Even so, the Prophet's tirade had a profound effect on me, and on many others.

Here was the leader of our Church, the Governor of our land, a man in control of nearly every institution that made up our Saintly civilization, announcing from the pulpit that murder was justified in order to save souls. There, before my own eyes and ears, he asked men to murder! If he did not mean it, he should have said so.

Since then, I have heard the arguments against my interpretation of events: Brigham's words have been taken out of their original context (true, he often preached mercy and compassion, but so does the crack preacher on the crossroads); he was speaking in metaphor (perhaps, for it is true no one rushed out of the Tabernacle that day and lifted his sword like Laban); Blood Atonement was a product of its time, for the fiercely independent Saints were on the verge of war with the United States of America (could be, but does that justify it?). Excuses—that is all these are.

Those who disavow my testimony as merely (*merely!*) the tirade of a spurned wife, to them I say: You were not there! You did not hear the hatred in the Prophet's words. You did not see his fury.

I am neither theologian nor philosopher nor historian. I can only repeat that which I heard or which I know with near certainty others heard. The above quotes, as far as I know, are not in dispute. The dispute lies in their interpretation. Placing my full trust in my Dear Reader, I shall cease with interpretation now and leave that important task to you.

Yet I ask: Even if Brigham Young was calling for Blood Atonement merely for rhetorical effect, as some have argued, one cannot believe such vicious words would have no consequence. Make no mistake, there is no doubt that he dropped these appeals into this world. As poison enters a well, contamination must follow.

Word travels as swift as the horse. We returned to our hut in Payson to discover that Mrs. Myton had already heard of the Prophet's sermon.

"If Brigham declares this to be true, then it must be." Such was the analysis Aaron offered to his mother-in-law.

Connie, my dear sister-in-law, managed to peep, "Are we in danger?"

Aaron ignored her. "There's a lot of work in keeping souls clean."

"If Brigham's really so interested in cleanliness, he wouldn't have sent us to this dusty old town!" That was my contribution to the debate; you can imagine its reception.

There followed more general discussion of what the Prophet had meant. My mother genuinely believed that the Prophet, although susceptible to extremes, did not mean to incite murder. My brother, on the other hand, said there was little doubt about what should be done should we encounter an unrepentant sinner. This argument was repeated in households throughout the Territory in the subsequent days. It seemed wrong, even to my underdeveloped mind, for the Prophet, no matter his meaning, to have left his followers with such violent but unclear instructions of how to proceed.

Well, a minority of men found the instructions clear enough to act upon them. It was but a week later that rumors began to spread that a certain Mrs. Jones and her son, Jacob, had gone flabby in their faith. I did not know Mrs. Jones personally, although I could recognize her on the street, for she was tall for the female species and often wore elaborately feathered bonnets. (During the Reformation, some Sisters were known to condemn others for the mortal sin of overly fine millinery.) Mrs. Jones was a widow, her husband was lost at Winter Quarters, yet she had long resisted offers to enter a plural marriage. Enough men had felt the slap of her rejection that she was already, at the outset of the Reformation, a woman whom many suspected of disloyalty to the doctrine of spiritual wifery. Her son, Jacob, was Aaron's age but in many ways more of a man, and capable of growing a full brushy beard. Jacob held an unusual interest in the Indians, collecting headdresses and necklaces of beads. Outcast is too strong a word for Mrs. Jones and her son, yet this pair was never one with the provincial Payson.

They fought the onslaught of the Reformation as best they

could. Although they attended Church meetings and paid their tithings, they resisted the public confessions and turned the Home Missionaries away from their door (Aaron happily supplied this bit of information). With Blood Atonement officially in the air, and the Prophet's words ringing in the ears of men inclined to violence, it took but seven days for the mob to settle on its prey.

Late one night, while sleeping in our hut, we awoke to voices rising down the road, a scream, a plea, the sound of something heavy falling on something soft but thick, like a mallet to a sack of flour.

Connie flung the blanket along its wire, crying, "Aaron isn't here!" In the moonlight stood the most pitiful creature I've ever seen: She was trembling and tears dripped like wax down her face. "He told me to stay in bed no matter what."

My mother's face crumpled upon itself. "He's out there with them," she said. It is painful for me to recall, but my mother began to weep. Although my enemies have many times questioned my memory in accounting certain events, I will never let anyone accuse me of lying about my mother's tears that night.

Then two pistol shots cracked in the night, and each of us froze with genuine fear.

In the morning, word came that Mrs. Jones and her son were dead, their bodies disfigured and defaced. Officially, the stated cause was slaughter by the Indians. Aaron, who came home before dawn and went to bed without speaking, said in the morning, "Jacob was always meeting up with the Indians. Figures they'd go kill him one day. I heard he was stealing their feathers, or something like that."

"You can't lie to me," my mother said.

"Ma, I'm not lying. Go ask the Bishop. Go ask the chief of police."

Aaron made his point: He was only repeating the official account. Justice would not come, not here. In the afternoon, the grave-digger drove the bodies to the cemetery. The wagon passed by our hut, but my mother refused to let me look out, holding me to her breast. Connie was crying too and made Aaron hold her as she wept.

The wagon made its way up the street. Many doors opened and the residents inside spat at their fallen Sister and Brother. "Apostates!" they cried. "Burn forever!" I hear, but cannot verify, that some threw rotten fruit at the bodies and that by the time the wagon reached the open graves, it rattled with old apples and gourds. One item about this terrible day has been reported as entirely true: Mrs. Jones was baking bread when the mob arrived at her door, and the white, floury dough remained on her fingers, and some in her hair, as the grave-digger drove her through Payson on her last ride before eternal sleep.

X

———

THE MISSION

LDS CHURCH ARCHIVES

SPECIAL COLLECTIONS

Biographies & Autobiographies

Salt Lake City

RESTRICTED ACCESS

RECORD OF PETITION FOR ACCESS

NAME: Professor Charles Green
DATE: Jan. 17, 1940
DOCUMENT NAME: Autobiography of C. G. Webb
PURPOSE OF RESEARCH: Scholarly book on the end of plural marriage
PETITION OUTCOME: Declined, by C. Bock, Archivist

NAME: Kelly Dee
DATE: July 10, 2005
DOCUMENT NAME: Autobiography of Chauncey G. Webb, The
PURPOSE OF RESEARCH: Master's Thesis on Ann Eliza Webb Young and the legacy of polygamy
PETITION OUTCOME: Approved by D. Savidhoffer, Archivist

THE AUTOBIOGRAPHY OF
CHAUNCEY G. WEBB

PART II

As Ann Eliza notes in *The 19th Wife*, our family's first years in Utah
were marked by harmony and unified purpose. My two wives, once
rivals, became companions—or at least it seemed so to me. If one
of my wives nursed a deep wound in her heart, I never knew of it,
for neither woman spoke of such injury during this time. In her
book, Ann Eliza accuses me of "blithe unawareness" for failing to
notice her mother's suffering. Yet when I look back on those first
years in Deseret, I believe our family, even in its unique configura-
tion, had achieved a happiness most can only pray for. At least I
hope this was the case.

This interlude of domestic contentment ended abruptly when
Brother Brigham ordered Gilbert and me to England on a Mission. We departed in the winter of 1855, journeying via Saint Louis,
reaching Liverpool's damp shores in the early days of a limp gray
spring. We rented a room from a young, talkative widow called
Mrs. Cox, who shared a narrow house with her small daughter,
Virginie, whose likeness to Ann Eliza made me miss my family
even more.

That first day in Liverpool, and the early days thereafter, we
were quick to learn what type of man will not greet a plain stranger
speaking of God on the refined streets of St. James and Great
George. The gentleman strolling with his family and nurse; the nobleman nibbling toffees in his coach; the lady ornamented in satin
and jewel; the sisters preoccupied with society and fashion—these

busy people had no time, or disposition, to respond to our "Good day" or "Afternoon." Before them I felt like a ghost, for they had no awareness I was alive.

In Liverpool, God's most wretched souls congregated along the streets near Prince's Dock, for it was here they could rake through the piles of rubbish tossed over the shipyard's masonry walls. The one-armed sailor, the toothless hag, the skimpy orphan smeared with a lifetime of grime—here the saddest allotment of humankind sifted through the dirt with picking-irons in hopes of finding bread crusts, fruit rinds, and strips of filthy cotton that could be rinsed and sold for a penny. Every day at noon the sailors from the many ships from all over the world disembarked to dine at taverns such as the Baltimore Clipper and the Unicorn. This throng of salty men, with their odor of sea mist, and their ribald, foreign talk, poured past the beleaguered souls. Occasionally a sailor would toss a spare copper to a beggar, and a commotion would erupt in the chase for it. What pity it engendered in my heart and Gilbert's—a dozen hopeless men fighting one another for the smallest of coins.

On our first visit to the deprived neighborhood we passed a legless maiden perched on a wood platform with four small iron wheels. Her skirt was a cheap green calico, dirty and patched, yet she had fluffed it up and spread it about her with a touching amount of purpose and hope, so that she appeared, despite her missing limbs, almost as a lass sitting atop a picnic blanket. Propped before this stalwart girl was a panel on which a clear, strong hand had written out the brief narrative of her fate: *Sucked in by the harvesting machine.* At her side squatted a classically handsome young man, with silken black locks and Roman nose. His misery rested in his eyes, which had milked over with disease. Next to him crouched a skeletal woman with a starving babe latched to her shriveled blue breast. Beside her huddled a desperate young pair, brother and sister, I presume. They called out, "Please, we ain't eaten in four days."

"May we speak to you," I said, "about the Lord?"

"Please, do you have some bread?"

Gilbert broke off half of the butter sandwich Mrs. Cox had packed. He was offering it to the girl when the hag with the babe stole it, devouring it before our eyes.

"That was for the girl and her brother," I complained.

"It might as well've been for me and my child." The woman sat beatifically, as if she bore no remorse for her theft.

Gilbert offered the girl the second half, careful it landed in the intended hands. She shared it with her brother, while others all around shouted and cried for a morsel of their own.

"Now," I said to the pair of siblings. "May we have a word about Jesus Christ?"

"I'm sorry," replied the girl. "But I don't believe any of it. Not any more."

I could not fault her. If I had been handed her fate, I cannot say for certain my faith would hold firm. Such misery is too profound to suppose we can know its meaning.

My son and I tried the young man on the wooden cart. "May we have a word, kind sir?"

"I don't want your pity, I want work."

"May we talk to you about Jesus Christ?"

"I don't need salvation, I need work."

We approached the man with the clouded eyes. "Sir, do you have a moment to spare?"

"If you have a copper to spare."

"I don't."

"Then neither do I."

Thus our efforts passed, with no success for nearly a year.

Each night we would return to a coal fire lit by Mrs. Cox. In our room we would fall to our knees and pray for success and fortitude. By the glow of the candle I would write two letters, one to each Mrs. Webb. Often I struggled to offer each woman a unique account of my day, for I feared they might share the letters and find I had copied my sentiments from one to the next. If I signed my letters to Elizabeth *Your true husband,* then I carefully signed those to Lydia *Your husband most sincere.* As time passed, my longing for both women grew, and often I stayed up late, with Gilbert asleep beside me, writing out my desire to see each; and imagining the day I would. Any man who has endured a long separation from his wife will understand.

One night, while on our knees, Gilbert said, "Father, I'm not sure how much longer I can do this."

It had been a difficult day at the end of a lonely week. The weather was damp, the city's mood foul, and a frivolous young woman done up in fox fur had passed us on the street, giggling to her companion, "What a waste of a man!"

"Father," said Gilbert, "I'm not sure we're doing any good."

There, before Mrs. Cox's glowing grate, I promised my son the next day would bring success. "I can't tell you how, or who, but you'll see your efforts rewarded." There is but one explanation for why I promised what I should not have—desperation to tamp down my son's kindling doubt. He was an unknowable young man, distant in every way. Sometimes I suspected he privately accused me of vanity, hypocrisy, and the other sins of the wealthy and well-stationed. No doubt his questions about faith and the Church itself had deepened during our stay abroad; and I worried he might rashly choose to defy, or even depart, the creed that had saved his mother and brought them to me. I worried over his future, as all fathers do. It was this worry that kept me from sensing my own doubt unfolding within. In *The 19th Wife* my daughter accuses of me of blind faith, "a blindfold woven from mammon tied across my eyes," she says. Her assault is cruel, I know, but I often wonder if her assassin's blade has been forged from an unalloyed truth.

The next day was bright with sun, as clear as the previous day had been gray. We spent nearly twelve hours in the quadrangle of the Merchant's Exchange near the statue of Lord Nelson. Everywhere windows were open to the breeze. Benign weather can add difficulty to the Missionary's work, for the general hopefulness of the world helps Man forget his woes. The day was no different than all the previous, except one woman, done up in jelly-colored silk, wrongly accused us of stealing a bundle of lace which later turned up on a bench.

We returned to Mrs. Cox's little house dispossessed and weary. I carried a heavy shame for attempting prophecy. I could hardly muster a greeting to our landlady and her child.

"Right, 'ave a nice day, did you?" said Mrs. Cox. "Virginie, dear, leave the gentlemen alone, they've been out working for the Lord. Now I set your fire the way you like it, and I've just put the kettle on. Go and settle yourselves in and I'll fetch some biscuits, or if you like I can bring a plate of swipes."

Always loquacious, with very little to say but many words at her disposal, Mrs. Cox seemed particularly eager to hold us at the foot of her staircase longer than usual. "May I 'ave a word? If you're not too tired"—and when she saw we had failed to understand her intent she continued—"about your Church and your Book? I was born into the Anglican Church, of course. But ever since Mr. Cox's passing I 'ave to say I've 'ad me doubts."

It was then I understood. I moved to begin to speak, but Gilbert interrupted. "Father, can I try?"

His sudden eagerness to proselytize surprised me, and left me proud. We passed the evening in Mrs. Cox's parlor, Gilbert, for the most part, leading our discussion. Virginie lay upon the carpet, dressing and undressing her doll. Gilbert recounted the story of Joseph's Revelations, and the Latter-day Saints, a few times forgetting an important point which I added delicately, careful not to insult his capabilities. Mrs. Cox listened patiently, providing delightful commentary to the events of the Church's early history: "And 'e found the plates of gold in the earth, did 'e? Right lucky no one else came along. Most men would boil 'em down, they would."

"Would you like to read our Book?" said Gilbert. It was after midnight, and the street outside Mrs. Cox's window had fallen silent long ago. Virginie lay asleep in my lap.

She accepted it, holding it close to her breast. "Now then, I've got a lot of questions, but it's getting late so maybe I'll ask just the one that's been at me for some time."

I urged Mrs. Cox to ask whatever she needed to know.

"There's some who go round saying a Mormon man takes a dozen wives, maybe more. When I 'ear this, I tell whoever it is speaking it can't be true. I got two Mormons living right 'ere in me 'ouse and I'd know, wouldn't I, if they kept a 'arem back 'ome."

Before our departure, Brigham had instructed us to deny the truth of plural marriage. "Far away, across the oceans," he said, "you will find the stranger cannot imagine the reds of Zion, nor the snowy heights of our peaks, nor the vastness of our great basin. Just as these ignorant men and women cannot see the beauty of our land, they cannot understand the uniqueness of our families. Speak not of the plural wife until our foreign brothers and sisters have arrived in Deseret and can see for themselves how red our sand blows."

For most men, myself included, the lie comes quickly and more naturally than we want to admit. Thus I denied the truth of polygamy to Mrs. Cox, and forever after regretted doing so.

"That's what I wanted to 'ear," she said. "Right, I've kept you up late, 'aven't I?" She lifted her daughter while expressing such genuine gratitude and love that I knew for certain we had converted our first soul.

Joseph Young, Brigham's son, was stationed in London on his own Mission. I wrote to him about our first convert, and he journeyed the eight hours to baptize Mrs. Cox. We met in a field dotted with sheep, beside a fast-running stream. He led Mrs. Cox into the water and submerged her. With that, we had brought forth our first Saint!

When Mrs. Cox emerged from the stream, her wet robe permitted the rosy color of her flesh to come through. To ignore her beauty would be to ignore God's mastery. To look at it would be to commit a sin. I must confess I could not help but stare. Mrs. Cox stood in a sunbeam that gave her the look of a statue carved by the hand of an artist from classical Greece—a sheer marble gown draped over her form in such a manner that every curve was apparent to the morn.

Later that night, after a celebration in the parlor, Gilbert and I lay upon our bed studying the Book. I sensed an agitation in my son—his foot was kicking the bedpost irritably. When I asked him to stop, for it was disturbing my concentration, he did so sullenly. I asked if there was a matter he wished to discuss, but he said he had nothing to share.

I have seen the gloomy air visit Gilbert many times. Aware of the stifled energies of the unmarried young man, I never pressed him on the matter. I decided the next day I would speak to him about marriage. There was a great possibility of meeting a young woman in Liverpool—a pretty soul eager for conversion and deliverance to Zion. My boy needed something to look forward to, I concluded, and having solved, or so I believed, my son's anxiety, I raked the coals for a final time, turned down the lamp, and settled beneath the bedclothes with a fine sense of accomplishment. It was still early, and the streets threw up the lamentable noise of urban sin—the singing drunk, the wench twirling on the sailor's arm, the gang of orphans scurrying across the cobblestones in broken shoes. It took some time for my mind to clear of the wretchedness below our warm, cloistered room and permit me to enter a peaceful sleep.

Late that night, after the clamor from the street had died, a foreign noise woke me. I turned on my side and discovered Gilbert missing from the bed. The moon cast a silver glow upon the room, illuminating the pink nosegays in the paper on the wall. I opened the door with such precision that its hinge brought no attention to my movements—a stealth which enabled me to witness, at the opposite end of the corridor, my son positioned near Mrs. Cox at her chamber's door. Their persons stood so close together a Bible would not pass between them. The window beside them was cracked and a night breeze wound its way into the hall, billowing their sleeping gowns in a way that unified them like a double cumulus cloud.

I cleared my throat. "Gilbert."

In unison they peered down the hallway in my direction. "Father—"

"Evening, Mr. Webb. Need some milk, do you? I'll fetch the pail."

"Father, I was on my way outside when I ran into Mrs. Cox. She asked me a question about the Afterlife."

"That's right. I was lying in me bed awake as the rooster, thinking about what will 'appen when it's time to go on. What I want to know is, will I meet Mr. Cox in 'eaven? It's what I was thinking when I 'eard 'is footsteps out 'ere, so I opened the door and asked. 'E was explaining 'ow things work when you came along."

"Mrs. Cox would like us to baptize by proxy her husband," Gilbert explained. "I'm willing to stand in his place."

I felt a great shame for my accusations and retreated to our room. My ear remained pricked, taking in the click of Mrs. Cox's door and the fall of my boy's step as he made his way down the crickety stairs and outside. The privy door squealed with its recognizable glee. I was still awake when he entered the room. He climbed over me and turned to face the wall. In the moonlight I watched him pick at the seam in the paper until at last sleep transported me, for a few hours, at least, home to my two loving wives.

In March of 1856, almost a year before I had anticipated a return voyage home, Brigham sent word that he had selected me to organize a new plan to increase the rate of immigration. Up until then it cost on average $55 in gold for one Saint to journey from Europe to Great Salt Lake, via New York and Iowa City, or Saint Louis— a reasonable sum for a voyage consisting of many thousands of miles via ship, train, and wagon. Yet Brigham had come to believe, for what reason I cannot be sure, that the Church needed a more economical method of importing its Saints. His advisors had convinced him of a plan they called Divine. In *The 19th Wife* Ann Eliza correctly labels it a scheme.

The largest expense of the voyage are the teams of oxen that pulled the wagons from Iowa City into Utah, more than one thousand miles, and therefore Brigham and his advisors had concluded the oxen should be removed from the trip. The immigrant Saints, all of them, would pull their belongings across the plains and the mountains in hand-carts.

I complained to Brigham's son, Joseph, but he dismissed my concerns. "The Prophet has chosen you. It's the will of the Lord. Now prepare to leave England."

A few days before departing, I came to a decision about my future. I wanted to take Mrs. Cox as my wife. If I were another man, with a different set of values, I suspect I might have had the opportunity to embrace her in her boardinghouse; and I suspect she might have accepted my kiss. But I am not such a man. I have made a vow to my wives never to stray, and I have not and will not.

"Will you and Virginie return to Zion with us?" I proposed one evening shortly before our farewell. I told her she could live in my household in Great Salt Lake and become a part of it.

For a long while Mrs. Cox did not speak. My meaning was not to deceive this woman by importing her to Utah and then, once she was an ocean and continent away from home, demand she become my wife. I have known Saints to do so to foreign women and even young girls. It is an abhorrence I was always sorry Brigham never set out to fix. This was not my intention with Mrs. Cox, but I could not outright discuss marriage with Mrs. Cox until I had first discussed it with my beloved Elizabeth.

"'Ere's what I'll do. I'll give it a think tonight and tell you in the morning."

It is unsettling, even for me, to look back at myself and recount here the impetuous feelings early love can inspire in a full-grown man. Yet because I promised myself this to be a full and true account, I will commit to paper how my heart pounded in my chest! I wanted to run through the front door and shout in the street! I knew then she would come to Utah, and I knew she would marry me once Mrs. Webb had agreed, and I will admit my mind raced months ahead to our wedding night, when at last I could touch this lovely creature and she would be mine.

Our farewell was an awkward moment. A carriage came for our trunks. The horses idled in the mud while we managed to part Mrs. Cox's company. Gilbert, Mrs. Cox, and myself stood at her door, each with a crooked smile that bore extended meaning. When Gilbert and I were in the carriage, Mrs. Cox pressed her face through the door. "'Tisn't good-bye. We'll be right behind you in another month."

"The Saints will greet you when you arrive," I promised.

"I'll make sure of it," said Gilbert.

The carriage pulled away. We, father and son, turned to admire Mrs. Cox standing beside the rose climbing her gate. In the wind the early red leaves trembled on the stem, brushing her throat and cheek.

When she was out of sight Gilbert declared, "Father, I'm going to marry her."

I was so startled by my son's announcement that I had to struggle to suppress my jealousy. "Marry Mrs. Cox? My boy, what are you talking about?"

"When she lands in Utah, I'll marry her."

"Have you discussed this with Mrs. Cox?"

"No, but I know she'll have me."

"Are you sure?"

"I've never been so sure of anything."

The leonine pride which resides in the cage of my heart had been stirred. I wanted to lash out and defend the woman who, in only a matter of time, would be mine. But I would not challenge my son in such a manner. I loved him too much. I had no doubt Mrs. Cox would become Mrs. Webb, my Mrs. Webb, that is, but to state the fact so baldly would leave him, I feared, irreparably harmed and, perhaps, weakened in the eyes of other women. The boy would need to marry soon, and I would help him, but he would not marry the woman I had already settled upon. Somewhere in *The 19th Wife* Ann Eliza asks, "Did my father not think himself selfish, claiming one woman when he already had two?"

Her question devastates me, even today.

Upon our arrival in Iowa City, we found no materials for the construction of the hand-carts, no process of assembly, no leader with the temperament or skill to enact the Prophet's plan. Even worse, only a few days behind us was the first arrival of Saints—anxious souls from London, Glasgow, Copenhagen, and Stockholm spilling from the train with their belongings strapped to their backs. They wanted nothing more than shelter and food, and yet Brigham's agents had not prepared any. They had failed to establish a camp of any sort or stores of nourishment and water. These European souls—by early summer there were several thousand—were left to unroll their tickings in a field. When it rained, they propped coats and tarpaulins upon sticks. The kind people of Iowa City opened their larders to the emigrants, passing out bread, potatoes, and waxy wheels of cheese. There was no meat unless a pig was donated, or stolen. Water came from a single well.

Such conditions led to immediate squalor—the stench of the refugee camp is one that no man shall ever forget. Often I walked among them, looking for Mrs. Cox, grateful to never find her encamped in such suffering.

Always I saw the same question burning in the emigrants' dispossessed eyes: Why? Why had the Church that promised them Salvation and taken their money for the journey left them in a prairie, a thousand miles from Zion? The Apostles sent from Salt

Lake—men whose names I shall refrain from presenting here—
told the hungry and disenchanted souls that any impatience would
be interpreted as distrust of God. "You have been given a Divine
challenge. Only the faithful will pass." I cannot know whether the
immigrants believed these men or were too weary to defy them.

By June the first carts were ready. They were a crude vehicle of
poor craftsmanship and material in which I could take little pride.
One cart could haul a family's personal belongings, no more than
seventeen pounds of garments and bedclothes per person. The Divine plan conceived of a man pulling the cart, while his wife and
children walked alongside. In reality, there were a large number of
young girls traveling alone and widows with babes, or the elderly.
These fair creatures were never meant to drag their earthly possessions across the plains and over the Rocky Mountains.

Given the disorganization of the mission, and the slowness of
the building supplies, I advised Brigham's agents that the last party
could leave no later than the end of June. The others would need to
remain in Iowa City until the following spring. But these men, who
were religious zealots, not organizational leaders, refused to adhere
my counsel. The last party of hand-carts left in the middle of August, walking toward their own death, I was quite sure. These foreign immigrants knew nothing of our climate or the mountains
awaiting them. To make matters more precarious, these men, who
promised to look over the immigrants like angels, sent them on
their journey with criminally small rations—ten ounces of flour,
and a little rice, per day for each man and woman, and five ounces
of flour, and no rice, for the young Saints under eight. Many of the
immigrants were from Northern Europe and the cold harbors of
Sweden and Norway and thus spoke little English, certainly not
enough to complain about these insufficient supplies. Along the
trail, at infrequent posts, the weary Saints would find supplements
of brown sugar, cured pork, and weak coffee dispersed by the fat,
careless Elders assigned to the task. It takes little forethought to
know this is not enough food to walk a thousand miles while

pulling one's belongings. I advised the agents present that not only would the Saints freeze, they would also starve. One Apostle replied, "This is the will of Brigham himself. Take your complaints to him." Were he there and not one thousand miles away, I would have appealed directly to the Prophet. Instead, I was forced to argue in the ears of his men, who proved themselves wholly ordinary. There are many to blame for the tragedy that ensued. I include myself in that wretched lot.

With the last party departed, we prepared for the journey ourselves. We formed a party of two dozen men, mostly Missionaries on return voyage from their work in European lands. The party included Joseph Young, who I must admit had grown from boy to man during his years abroad. He too had seen the risk facing the emigrants and had complained about it. But not even the Prophet's son could affect the men who worked under the standard of Brigham Young. We left Iowa City well-prepared, with teams of oxen and mules, our wagons stocked with flour and rice, coffee and sugar, dried beef and pork, chickens, a pig for every five men, and a milking cow. This is how it should be done, and great pangs of regret overcame me, and Gilbert, too, as we overtook that last party of hand-carts on the trail. They saw us comfortable on the wagon seat, or nudging along the cow with a reed, and heard the chickens cluck from the cage, and certainly they must have wondered why they were not so well-equipped.

On the Platte River's North Fork we joined an encampment of emigrants. They were flung around several pits of fire, men and women and children alike, collapsed upon bundles of clothing and sacks of flour, too tired to set up camp properly. Many wore shoes held together by rawhide string. "What will they do when winter comes?" Gilbert asked. I could not answer him.

Gilbert and I, and the other men in our party, offered as much food as we could spare and handed over a pair of asses for the sick who were too enfeebled to walk. We promised we would send help once we reached the Salt Lake Valley. In the morning, with no more than a strip of sunlight in the east, we continued on our journey. Each man was determined to reach Zion as soon as possible. It was our only chance of saving these souls.

Upon reaching Great Salt Lake, our hearts broke open with relief. The city had grown in our absence, and had we not been arriving with urgent news, we would have stopped to marvel at Zion's progress. But there was no time. Gilbert and I traveled to Payson, while Joseph Young went directly to speak to his father.

On the matter of the hand-cart expedition, this is where my account differs from that of my daughter's in her published memories. When Brigham heard of the danger awaiting these innocent emigrants, he shook with anger. He scolded the men, his apparent agents, who had misinterpreted his words. Certainly the Prophet wanted the expedition performed economically, but he had never meant to risk a life. Ann Eliza doubts the Prophet's sincerity, claiming Brigham had known all along the dangers and misery facing the emigrants. This is not true, for I witnessed the Prophet preach in the Tabernacle that every Saint in Zion must contribute to the rescue effort. He denounced the men who had made such reckless decisions in his name. He denied that the perils facing the emigrants were a test of God but, rather, a sign of man's incompetence and indifference. As he orated, blood filled his throat. His voice reached across, or so it seemed, the entire Salt Lake Valley. It is impossible to deny the sincerity of his rage.

I should stop my account of the hand-cart emigrants to describe my return home. There were, of course, two homes to return to. Lydia lived in Great Salt Lake with Diantha; Elizabeth lived in Payson with Ann Eliza and Aaron, who had since wed the neighboring girl. Because I arrived in Great Salt Lake first, I stayed with my second wife on my first night back in Zion. Lydia welcomed me with caresses and boiled beef, a clean house, a warm bed. Any man who has sustained himself through long intervals separated from his wife knows how welcome her initial touch is upon return.

I wanted to linger with her all day, all autumn and winter, in fact, but I knew I must ride to Payson. Word travels quickly in the territory. There was little doubt the first Mrs. Webb had news of my arrival. The separation is no easier on the man than it is on the woman, and I know Lydia felt it her right to keep her husband a few more hours. "Let me pretend a little longer you're all mine," she said. It was not a selfish statement, merely the honest expression of a lonely heart. It pained me to deny her. I kissed my wife good-bye and rode off to see my wife.

My homecoming in Payson was less joyous. Our separation had tried Mrs. Webb. I attempted to soothe her with an embrace, yet when I kissed her, I felt the subtle manifestation of suffering in her brittle lip. "How I missed you," I said.

Gilbert and I explained the plight of the emigrants and our need to return at once to their rescue. Here my old affection for Mrs. Webb rose, for she became overwhelmed with concern for her fellow man. "The poor souls," she said. "Take them food and blankets and anything they need." I found reassurance in her compassion. I slept well that night at her side.

In the morning I prepared to return to Great Salt Lake to assist in the relief effort. My good wife declared, "I'll be baking bread till the last of them arrive." Her selfless outlook perhaps explains my distress at Ann Eliza's sudden outburst.

"You promised you'd stay!"

I tried to hold the girl, but she shrugged herself away. By now Ann Eliza was twelve. The mysterious veil that falls upon a girl at the outset of maturity had descended. Her tears were those of a child. Her rage was that of a woman. I must admit, I was uncertain of what comfort I should offer.

"I have to help these people," I said. "They'll die if we don't. When I return, it'll be for good. I promise."

This was my mistake, one that I continue to rue. I was promising one type of return, while Ann Eliza was looking for another.

When it was time to depart I asked Elizabeth to follow me to my wagon. Across the kitchen yard Ann Eliza stood in the door frame, watching. I did not believe she could hear us, but in her book she records the words of our conversation accurately.

"There's one thing I'd like to discuss before I go," I said.

"Tell me."

"On the subject of marriage."

Elizabeth winced—almost imperceptibly. "What is it?"

"There is a woman, from Liverpool, who might be among the emigrants."

"What is it about this woman I need to know?"

"If I find her, I would like—"

Are there any more difficult words for a husband to express than these?

"If she makes it, we might want to—"

"Yes?"

Then she understood. "Oh, Chauncey. You just got home."

"I know, but this woman will need a home. Tell you what, if I find her, I'll bring her here and you two can—"

Elizabeth lifted her hand to stop me. "You may have her."

"Elizabeth, please."

"You want her, and you'll have her. There's nothing more to say."

"I want you to know her, to approve of her."

"I don't want to know her."

"Then I can't marry her."

"You can, and you will."

"She might not even arrive. I might never see her again. I only wanted to raise the possibility. Elizabeth, are you all right?"

"I'm fine," she said. "I'll be fine."

I returned to Great Salt Lake with a miserable heart. I was there no more than half a day when the first hand-cart company arrived. These were the pioneering souls who had departed Iowa City in

June, and now, at the end of September, they limped into Zion. Even outside Liverpool's docks I had never seen such a broken lot. Men with the skin blistered off their palms. Women with hair falling out from lack of nourishment. Babes suckling air, their mouths dry and blue. Goblin-eyed children floating about. The emigrants had walked more than one thousand miles, waded every river between the Mississippi and the Wasatch Range, pulled their belongings, and resorted to eating long grass when their flour ran out.

They stumbled through the city until they arrived at the gates of Temple Square. A crowd had gathered to witness their arrival. Thinking they had come to enjoy a triumphant parade, many people wore colorful clothing. They carried baskets of rose petals to shower upon the travelers. The shock on their faces said they could not understand how God—or Brigham—would let this happen to His chosen people.

Brigham emerged from his offices at the Beehive House. "Take them into your homes!" he instructed the Saints. "Bathe them! Feed them! Clothe them! Welcome them to Zion!"

At once the Saints descended upon the emigrants. Generosity to the stranger is one of our long traditions. Witnessing it still can cause a rise in my throat. I joined the effort, wading into the crowd, looking for a soul or two whom I could take back to Lydia's cottage for a meal.

"Excuse me, sir," a voice called. "My sister's not well."

A hand petted on my sleeve. I turned to find a girl of fifteen standing beside a hand-cart. She pointed at another girl, perhaps a year older, lying in the cart at an angle that made her look all but dead.

"My sister was strong until a week back. She wanted to give up, but I told her I'd pull her along. We ate all our flour. There was nothing left. Then we ate our shoes."

Their feet were black as coal.

"Come with me." I pulled the hand-cart myself across the city to

Lydia's cottage.

"My name is Margaret. My sister's Eleanor. Margaret and Eleanor Oakes."

"Where are you from?"

"London. We were house-girls for Lady Wellingham when we heard the Prophet's son speak. I said to my sister, 'Let's go to America.' She didn't want to, not at first. Then our situation changed and we no longer worked for Lady Wellingham. We didn't have a home when we encountered Mr. Joseph Young a second time. I said to Eleanor, 'Lightning doesn't strike twice.' "

When my wife saw the anguished sisters, she set to work laying out dresses and preparing a meal of ham hocks and lima beans. She assured Margaret and Eleanor they could stay as long as they needed. "I'll help you plant your feet," Lydia said. I thanked my good wife for welcoming the girls. Lydia's cottage was small, her allowance almost nothing, yet she offered Margaret and Eleanor everything she could, and more. "Maybe you're too good for me," I told Lydia in private.

"Probably," she replied.

I left the household to return to organizing the relief effort. When I returned that evening I found two sparkling young women, their complexions polished to the yellow-rosy hue for which the English are known. They sat on the rag-rug playing with Diantha, showing the child how to dress her doll. I could see Diantha already loved Margaret and Eleanor like sisters. She kissed each on the peachy cheek.

With food and water, Eleanor had been restored to such vigor that when she saw me, she leapt to her feet to embrace me. "Thank you, Mr. Webb! You saved my life." Her form in my arms was both soft and firm.

Margaret followed, kissing my forehead. I was aware of the wet impression lingering on my brow for some time.

This was a great deal of female attention for any one man, and I struggled to maintain my composure. If I were not wearing a beard, no doubt the girls would have seen the deep blush in my cheek. "We should thank you for putting your trust in us," I managed.

Margaret and Eleanor returned to the rug, helping Diantha assemble a puzzle. Lydia took up her sewing in her rocker, and I joined them in my chair with my mother's Bible. Yet I found, with such female splendor before me, I could not concentrate on the words. It was as if I were trying to read without my spectacles. My mind wandered elsewhere: to Mrs. Cox, wherever she may be. To my sweet Lydia in her rocker—how much she had transformed from girl to woman since she came into our house in Nauvoo. To Mrs. Webb in Payson. I loved her as no other, but that love, over the years, had evolved from romantic to respectful—an evolution that might be expected in relations between man and woman.

I thought of all this, but foremost in my mind were the two girls on the carpet, their slim legs folded beneath them. Eleanor had a slightly longer throat, I noticed. Margaret, although younger, was fuller in the breast. I had divined, through careful questioning, that she had come into trouble in London. It was for this reason Lady Wellingham had dismissed them from her household. Pondering her fate, I became overwhelmed with desire. I wish I could write that I looked upon these girls as a father looks upon his children. That had been my intention when I led them to my wife's cottage. But my intention had exploded into a terrible passion, one that I immediately recognized.

"I think I shall go to bed," I announced.

"But Webby!" cried Eleanor. "So soon?"

The sisters unfolded their legs, like colts lifting themselves from a bed of straw, kissed me, a pair of lips on each whiskery side. The sensation was so great that I felt bolted into my chair. Many minutes passed before I could unlatch myself. I was slow to see the anger in Lydia's narrowed eyes. "I thought you said you were retiring," she finally said.

Yet I could not sleep. My ears remained pricked to the sounds of the sisters—their cheering when the puzzle was complete; their feet upon the floorboards; the water of their ablutions; their whispers when they were in bed and believed no one could hear. What were they discussing? Was it possible they were speaking of me?

In the morning, I rode to Payson. I ran into Mrs. Webb's house, my old heart thumping in my throat, prepared to make my speech—when she stopped me. My Elizabeth! Her face is only honest and good! She never masks her intentions! Disguises her heart! And yet I had descended upon her with a request that would require she deceive herself.

"Did the woman from England arrive?" she said.

"Yes! Or I should say no. No sight of Mrs. Cox. I'm frightened for her. Oh Elizabeth, you should see the poor creatures who arrived yesterday. Barely alive. And behind them on the trail are the bodies of who knows how many dead. It was a terrible day."

Pity appeared in her eyes. "You shouldn't be here with me," she said. "You should go and help as many as you can."

"I will, shortly, but first, there's something I need to tell you. Ask you, that is."

She peered into my eyes, searched about, and located the lust and greed. As she recognized it, her face broke apart into shards of woe. "Another wife?"

"No, not another. Or I should say, instead. Instead of Mrs. Cox."

"Chauncey, listen to yourself."

"I know. I can hardly believe I'm saying these things. But something's happened. And I know that this is what I must do."

"Who is she?"

"You should have seen her. She was a waif! She has no one."

"Chauncey. How many is it going to be?" My wife turned away from me. She wept into her own shoulder. "I never thought you were this kind of man."

"She needs me. She needs a home."

"Where will this end?"

"Elizabeth, we both know this is our duty to God."

I had probed Mrs. Webb's most tender spot. She could not deny that the Prophet had made this clear. Her faith was always pure, while I layered mine with expediency. I am ashamed of many things, but none so much as when I excused my passions in the name of God.

"What's her name?"

"Her name?"

"You don't know?"

"Miss Oakes."

"Miss Oakes? You might want to ask her given name before you marry her."

Elizabeth returned to her kitchen chores. Her restraint of tongue deepened my already profound respect for her. Were I not blinded by my desire, her noble actions would have caused me to reconsider my next step.

I should note that I was not aware that Ann Eliza was behind the curtain during this conversation. Later she told me she had overheard it, but I never believed her, for more than once she had resorted to fabrication in order to manipulate my feelings. In her book she repeats this encounter with a recollection that all but matches my own. She describes Elizabeth's pain as a spade of sorrow sharp enough to hollow out the soul.

The question remained: Which Miss Oakes would I marry? Would it be Eleanor, with her affectionate habit of calling me Webby? Or Margaret, with her calming voice that suggested, to me, at least, the sensibility of a young woman who knows much about the world? Each had her unique merits and appeal.

I invited Eleanor on a stroll through Temple Square. She appeared for our assignation in Lydia's finest walking dress, the scalloped neckline revealing a swath of flesh I found impossible to ignore. To think God had nearly permitted this creature to perish!

"Tell me, have you heard anything about celestial marriage?"

"Do you mean polygamy?"

I nodded.

"Same as in the Bible?"

"That's right. No different than the forefathers."

"Back in England, Brother Young was asked about it at one of his meetings. He denied it, he did. Told a hundred people nothing of the sort existed, not in his father's Church. Most people believed him. Not me. I said to Margaret, 'I know they go around marrying this girl and that, it's what they believe.' Margaret said, 'Is that right?' And I said, 'It is. I've heard some women speak of it. They say it's not so bad. In the kitchen four hands are better than two. That's what they said.' Margaret said, 'Ellie, don't be silly.' But I said, 'It's not silly if it's true.' "

"So you understand it?"

"I suppose I do. A man takes a wife, and then another. That's all there is to it, right?"

"Yes, and we call it celestial marriage."

"Do you? Quite a fancy name for buggering all over the place."

I was having trouble discerning her opinion on the matter and ventured forth with the necessary delicacy. "The Lord revealed this truth to Joseph Smith."

"Did He? Then it must be true. How many have you got, Webby?"

"I have two wives."

"Sister Lydia here, she's what? The first or the second?"

"She's my second wife."

"Where's the first?"

"South of here."

"Does she mind sharing you like that?"

"She knows it's part of her salvation. My first wife, Sister Elizabeth, is the most devout woman I know."

"She isn't jealous?"

"Not that I know of."

"Are there any others?"

"At the moment, no."

Eleanor chuckled and poked my breast. "Webby! Do you plan on taking another? Is that what this is all about? You want me for your third wife? Is that why you asked me out for a stroll? Why, Webby, you're quite the sneak, aren't you?"

I cannot think of a time when a woman had reduced me so swiftly to a quivering mass of nerves. If I were a young man, I would wax rhapsodic over the beauty before me—the eyes, the lips, the small upturned nose! Yet I am no Romeo and shall leave the wordplay to the poets.

"Is it?" she pressed. "Don't be shy. Tell me what's on your mind." She was teasing me, and I could not speak. "Why, Webby! You're as red as the rose."

A thought entered Eleanor's head, and her own countenance darkened. "Or is it Margaret? Have you led me all the way here to ask me about my sister?"

"I hardly know where to begin," I said.

Up until that point I had managed to hide my true feelings from myself. Now I understood I desired both.

Both! I cannot explain what had overcome me. Perhaps the long months of Missionary work had pent up an uncontrollable longing. Perhaps something within had been starved in Liverpool, and now I was inhaling a certain kind of nourishment just as the weary emigrants devoured loaf after loaf.

I tried my best to tamp down my yearnings. "I want to marry you," I said.

Eleanor took my arm, bringing it close to her breast. "I'll do it," she said. "I want to have my place in this Church."

I deposited her at Lydia's gate and went to speak with the Bishop. As with all government, there is a certain amount of bureaucratic lethargy encrusted around the Church's administrators, but not so when the issue is celestial marriage. It took only a few hours to arrange. Brigham himself conducted the ceremony that afternoon.

Eleanor and I spent our wedding night at Brigham's hotel. She had been my wife no more than twelve hours before she summoned the dressmaker and the milliner. She wasted no time drawing up a list of items she would need in her future home: a stained-glass window, a visitor's settee, a chandelier. The list lengthened by the hour. One day as Mrs. Webb, and she had nearly bankrupted me.

Yet I worried not about the expense of maintaining three houses or the envy Eleanor's demands would install in the hearts of Elizabeth and Lydia. Instead, my worries were those of the vain young man—did Eleanor find me appealing? Did she mind my odors? How did I appear to her when I stepped outside my clothes? I am not proud of this regression to boyish idleness. Yet there it is.

My follies continued. If only they ceased here.

The day after our nuptials Margaret visited us at the hotel. Eleanor showed her sister the embroidered ribbon that, when yanked, brought the butler to the door. She laid out on the sofa the swatches of material the dressmaker had left behind. The sisters turned to the list of household items. With Margaret's help it doubled in length.

"You'll live with us, won't you?" asked Eleanor.

"I don't want to intrude on Mr. Webb."

Eleanor leapt across the room, attaching herself to my arm. "Mind? Don't be silly! Webby doesn't mind a thing!"

It was now apparent I had married a frivolous girl who would drain my accounts and ignore my orders. My mistake was clear: I had chosen the wrong sister. I had only myself to blame. Soon Elizabeth and Lydia would learn of the promised cut-glass chandelier, and each would rightfully demand her own. I would spend the rest of my life devoted to the wagon manufactory to support my domestic situations. What had I done? For what cause? I left the sisters to unwrap a bundle of packages delivered from the shops. The packing paper crackled so loudly, they did not hear me depart.

Elizabeth froze in shock. "Another wife?"

"It's not like that. They're sisters. They'll live together."

I had found her busy beating her rugs on the line. It was a fine day in Payson. Ann Eliza twirled on the swing hanging from the nearby cottonwood. "I won't do it unless you consent."

"You don't care what I think."

"You're mistaken."

She continued beating her rugs. "This isn't what the Lord had in mind. He didn't mean it to be like this."

"What do you want me to do? Tell me, and I'll follow your command. You're the first Mrs. Webb, you'll always be the first."

"I want you to leave my house."

"May I marry this girl?"

"I don't care what you do." Her beater came down hard on the rug, bursting a cloud of dust in my face. Ann Eliza laughed at her ridiculous father.

"Are you withholding your consent? Because if you are, then I'll drop this right now."

"Stop," she said. She leaned against the side of the house, exhausted. The dust had settled on her skin, and she appeared worn and gray. "It's your choice, we both know that."

"The Prophet says it's your decision."

"The Prophet."

It was the first time I had heard her speak of him bitterly.

"Elizabeth, what should I do?"

"Marry the girl, I don't care."

"Elizabeth."

"Go. Please go."

When I left, Ann Eliza followed me to my wagon. "Are you trying to replace Mother?"

"No, no, no, no, nothing like that at all."

"Then what are you doing?"

I tried to explain but failed. "One day you'll understand."

"I doubt it." Her rejection continues to sting. Perhaps that has been the most troubling aspect of reading Ann Eliza's book—learning of the hatred I had inspired.

Margaret accepted my proposal. Only after I had her consent did I inform Eleanor. She absorbed the news sourly, claiming I had deceived her. "If you think this gets you out of buying me that chandelier, you should think again," she said. "And I mean the large one with the three tiers." I assured her she would get her chandelier.

That evening the Prophet married Margaret and myself. Our wedding night was spent in a room down the hall from Eleanor's suite. She was now mine, but at what cost? In the morning Margaret moved into Eleanor's suite. They were now sister wives in all senses, and I was their fool.

What occurred next, and how this conjugal folly ends, might be taken as proof that the Lord punishes those who misinterpret His words. In less than a week I had gone from two wives to four. Almost any Saint will tell you this was not what the Lord intended in His Revelation. Even I was surprised by my conduct. As Ann Eliza reports in her book, neighbors and acquaintances commented. Although four wives is a small number compared to the dozen or more among the Apostles and the most powerful Elders, and the countless Brigham himself has amassed in the Lion House, the swiftness of my third and fourth matrimonies caused more than a few tongues to flap.

During my week of matrimonial indulgence, other men more selfless than myself continued to rescue the emigrants stranded on the trail. Day after day teams left Great Salt Lake loaded with supplies. Brigham himself headed the organizational planning. I understand a large map was posted in his office, marked with red dots between Utah and Iowa where he believed emigrant parties waited for assistance. He led the campaign like a commander in battle, and the swiftness of his decisions would go on to save many lives. At an encampment on the Sweetwater, near the Rocky Ridges, despair had already descended on dozens of emigrants. Food was gone, and death took one emigrant after the next. The survivors, weakened themselves, exerted their final energy to dig a mass grave. But with the arrival of nourishment, the survivors' ordeal had come to an end. Brigham's efforts were at last saving lives.

Such a scene repeated itself across the trail. Rescuers led the hand-cart expeditions over the mountains and into the Great Salt Lake Valley. Some arrived grateful for salvation. Others arrived angry for what they perceived as treachery. Some joined the community of Saints. Others, once restored to health, left for California, abandoning the leader who had brought them so far. Throughout the autumn the emigrant parties arrived. Once or twice a week they appeared at the mouth of what became known as Emigration Canyon. They would descend from the mountains in a weary column, arriving at Temple Square, just as the party that brought Eleanor and Margaret to me had done so a month before.

By November, the last party arrived. They were the most miserable of all. Noses, ears, and fingers blackened by frostbite. Mothers of dead children wandered with their arms cupped around the ghost of their babes. Broken men wept. It was a terrible sight, but at least it was the last of the hand-cart fiasco.

Standing on Temple Street, I witnessed these final emigrants stagger into Zion. With me was my most recent wife, Margaret, who thankfully never showed as much interest in her tailor as her sister did. She cried for her fellow journeymen, her own ordeal still fresh, and showered them with white chrysanthemums. It was startling to see how starvation and deprivation had removed their individuality. Each now appeared similar—eyes sunk into their skulls, cheeks carved out, lips the color of ash. I held my new wife as we watched the last of the souls pass before us. The creak of the cart-wheels will remain in my ear until my final day. As will the shout that rose up from the mass of starving souls. "Virginie, look! It's Mr. Webb!"

At once Mrs. Cox and Virginie ran from the parade of misery into my arms. She was as much an image of wretchedness as the other souls, but in truth even more so, for I had known her previous beauty. "Mrs. Cox, I didn't know," I said. "I didn't know."

I led Mrs. Cox and the girl to Lydia's cottage. Once again my second wife welcomed strangers into her home. As Lydia worked through the evening, satisfying her visitors' needs, on occasion she shot me a glance that said all too clearly: Another wife-to-be? I took Lydia outside. "It's not what you think," I said.

"What do I think?"

"You think I've brought her here as a future wife. Well, I haven't."

"I hope four is enough."

I assured Lydia four women could meet my needs. "I have another plan for Mrs. Cox. You'll see."

Despite my previous affection for Mrs. Cox, I had come to realize that the feelings generated by her in Liverpool had been supplanted by my present conjugal duties. My plan was this: I would reunite Mrs. Cox with Gilbert in Payson. I would be more than happy to see my son take over as her betrothed. After all, this is what he wanted. Even Elizabeth would respect this arrangement. "You'll like Payson very much," I told Mrs. Cox on the journey south. "I know Gilbert will be glad to see you."

I deposited Mrs. Cox and Virginie at Elizabeth's house. If Lydia had restrained her displeasure, Elizabeth did not hesitate to unload hers. She pulled me into the barn, where Ann Eliza was watering the horse. "Don't tell me she's another one of your brides."

"No, no, no—you don't understand. Gilbert's the one who wants to marry her. He's long had his heart set upon Mrs. Cox. True, she's a widow, but she isn't a year or two past thirty. And although she comes with a child, she also comes, I believe, with an income that should help our boy establish himself beyond our purse."

Elizabeth softened. "Does he know she's here?"

"I was just about to set out to find him."

I left my wife with the feeling one has after a narrow escape from danger and located my son at the manufactory. "She's arrived," I reported.

"Who?"

"Mrs. Cox."

Gilbert dropped his mallet. "Mrs. Cox? And she's well? Virginie, too?"

"Weary but well. The child, too. Very much the same indeed. She's waiting for you at your mother's house."

I was not privy to his first conversation with Mrs. Cox, but I know its outcome. Later that evening I found my son in a tavern, drunk on whiskey. I lifted him by the collar to carry him home when he said, "It's you."

"Of course it's me. I'm here to take you home."

The boy swatted me away, stumbling, trying to right himself by gripping the bar. "That's not what I mean," he said. "It's you she wants."

"You're drunk."

"Not drunk enough to know that she came all this way to marry you."

Although intoxicated by the quart, he spoke the truth. Mrs. Cox had journeyed to be my wife. I had given her enough signal to ensure, in her mind, my intentions.

"She will be the last," I begged of Elizabeth. "But I must go through with it."

"Three in one month," she said. "Three!"

"There'll be no more. You have my word."

"Your word."

"I promise."

"If you marry her, you'll never live with me again."

I married Mrs. Cox in Salt Lake and settled her in a cottage between Lydia's and the one shared by Margaret and Eleanor. I have spent the years since shuttling between their beds. I do not believe I have ever in my life behaved more like a beast than during this period, for this is how a dog acts, not man. Three wedding nights in three weeks—alas, all excessive pleasures must be repaid.

Yet to say I regret my marriages would imply I regret knowing these women. Only with Eleanor is this the case. Among the others, each is a kind-hearted woman who has been asked to bear more than she should. I have vowed to them all never to marry again. I shall keep this promise. Already I had more than my share. I tried to apologize to Elizabeth. She waved me off. "What's done is done," she said. I tried again, but she shut her door in my face. On the third attempt she said with quiet resignation, "I forgave you long ago."

The noteworthy sorrow had reached its climax and was now in retreat. My life has continued on for many successful years. I only wish I could say the same for Ann Eliza. Often I wonder if it was I who set her on her path of antipathy to our faith. How else to explain the root of her rage?

Here, beside my writing table lays open her book. How many people across the country hold *The 19th Wife* in their hands? How many are meeting me through its pages? And yet now that I have recounted my own memories, and peered into the well of my soul, I can see that my daughter has been right. Her words have destroyed me because they are true. She concludes her long assessment by writing, "In the end, I suppose my greatest disappointment has been in realizing my father, like Joseph and Brigham before him, tried to shroud his passions in the mantle of religion. He used God to defend his adultery. I have yet to hear him acknowledge his lies."

She is correct. My deceit has separated us.

Yet some truths come too late.

I am, I realize, but a man.

XI

WIFE #19:
THE CON OF THE WEST

BACK AT THE MOTEL GRAYBAR

———

"There it is," I told Mr. Heber. "Proof of how my mom's prints got on the Golden Boy."

He leaned across his desk to look at the picture again. "Tell me where you got this."

I walked him through my meeting with Alexandra.

"Oh, for crying out loud." He pressed a button on his phone. "Maureen, can you come in here? Listen, Jordan, these date stamps are thrown out of court all the time. Everyone knows they're usually wrong." The door cracked open. "Maureen, would you make a copy of this?"

She looked at the picture. "This your dad?"

"So what if the date stamp's wrong," I said. "We have someone who says she received the picture just before he was shot, and that's a big deal." He didn't say anything. "Isn't it?" Still didn't say anything. "Mr. Heber, am I totally clueless, or what?"

"I'm just thinking of all the ways a prosecutor could tear this apart. We're going to have do better."

"But right now it's all I've got."

All this, everything I've been telling you, it was happening too fast. I stared into Heber's face—the slick, Aqua Velva complexion, the eyes blue as dawn—but it was like seeing a set of meaningless colors and shapes. I couldn't pick up anything from this guy. You know when your mind's off, just wandering anywhere but where it should be, and you open a book and you see the letters but they don't make any sense? Might as well be Chinese? It was like that. Maybe reading this is like that for you. I don't know. I thought of my mom in her cell. Did she understand any of this better than me?

"Jordan, let me give you a little advice. When you find a lead, you've got to turn it over and over, again and again, look at it from every angle before you decide what it is. That's how things work around here. Think of every reason this photo might not help your mom. If it's still got some value after you've done that, then you're on to something. Ask Maureen, she's the best."

"Not the best," she said.

"Look, I've been back in Utah for—what?—five days, and at least I've figured one thing out: there's no such thing as perfect evidence, Mr. Heber. Or the complete truth, or whatever you want to call it."

Heber and Maureen stared at me, working hard not to roll their eyes. So much for my little speech.

"I went out to see your mom yesterday," Mr. Heber said.

"And?"

"And she's not telling me some things she really should be."

"Like what?"

"Her story about what she was doing that night is still a little fuzzy. That's not going to work. I keep getting the sense there's something she doesn't want to tell me."

"Maybe she'll tell Maureen?"

"No, I think she'll tell you. Go back and see her, Jordan. Find out what you can."

"I thought you were leaving Utah." My mom was cradling the yellow receiver between her shoulder and her chin.

"I decided to stay." And then, "I believe you."

She looked up, the glass partition magnifying her eyes.

"I know there's all this evidence against you," I said. "But I believe you."

Everything was the same at the jail today: Officer Kane, the ammonia covering the smell of piss, the row of women weeping into yellow handsets, baby-talking to their children who were growing up without them. I used to tell Roland Mesadale was like living in jail. But it wasn't. Jail was like living in jail.

I held the picture up to the glass. "Do you remember taking this?"

"Of course. That was just last week. It was our anniversary."

"Your anniversary?"

"Yes, I wanted to take a picture with your father. I got dressed up and asked him to put on a tie, and we went down to his den and shot that picture."

"Who took it?"

"No one. We used the automatic button thingy." I told her how I got the picture. It upset her to hear her husband was sending it out to strange women, but she understood why this was a break.

"But we need more," I said. "I need to figure out why Rita said she saw you coming up from the basement."

"Because she did. Your father had asked me to see him, and we talked for some time and I was on my way upstairs when I passed Rita."

"What'd you talk about?"

"It was a husband-and-wife conversation."

"Mom, the more I know, the more I can help you."

"Let's just say we had a conversation about the time he was spending with me. Or lack thereof." Some facts are less good than others. And this was one of those facts. It was a potential motive— jealous wife.

"Did you have an argument?"

"I wouldn't say an argument, your father and I never argued. But we discussed the matter, and I told him how I felt."

"Which was?"

"He's my husband, and I expected to see him from time to time. That's all. And that's when I went upstairs. And then—" She looked down at nothing in particular, just away. "And then I never saw him again. That's the hardest part. I always thought I'd spend the rest of my life as his wife." She took her time to collect herself.

"You know what Office Kane said after you left the last time? She said you'd be back. I told her I didn't think so, but she said she could see it in your eyes." A few feet behind my mom, Office Kane stared out into nothing. Clearly she wasn't supposed to get involved.

Isn't it interesting what a stranger can offer? A little wisdom, a little mercy, a little love. That's what I was thinking as I drove off from the jail. And this: unless I came up with better proof, twelve strangers in a box would decide my mom's fate. It's crazy to think it could come to that, but I guess it happens all the time.

My father brings home his fifth wife, Mrs. Cox,
while I greet her warily from behind the door.

WOMEN AND CHILDREN FIRST

——

I called Maureen. "I have a big favor to ask."

"Shoot."

"No, a really big favor. I need you to drive Johnny and me to Mesadale. Right now. I wouldn't be asking if you hadn't—" That's all I had to say. She agreed to meet me at A Woman Sconed in half an hour.

When I got to the café, the goth girl and Johnny were playing Ms. Pac-Man and Elektra was sleeping on the couch. "How'd it go?" said Johnny.

"I need to get some info out of the house."

"Like what?"

"I'm not sure exactly."

"How you going to get in there?"

"I'm working on it."

"Sounds like an awesome plan you got going there." Johnny went behind the counter to get me a cupcake. You'd think he owned the place. "Here. Maybe this will help you think."

That's when I had an idea.

When Maureen pulled in, Johnny said, "What's she doing here?"

"Come on. It's all part of my plan."

As we drove out to Mesadale, I was still thinking things through. Johnny kept saying you sure you know what you're doing and I kept saying yeah. He was up front and I was in back with Elektra. Some dry cleaning was hanging back there and every time Johnny cracked the window, the plastic wrapper would blow in my face. Elektra thought Maureen's stuffed penguins were dog toys and she kept knocking them over with her snout. I'd tell her no and she'd do it again, which is pretty much how things go between us.

As we passed the shot-up sign on the highway, Johnny said, "Get ready to enter another universe."

"What do you want me to do when we get there?" said Maureen.

"I'm still thinking."

"You better hurry up," said Johnny.

"These your husband's clothes?"

"No, Mr. Heber's. He likes me to fetch his laundry. I know I shouldn't have to, but some things just aren't worth fighting over." In the plastic wrapper was a pair of gray slacks and a couple of white dress shirts.

"You think he'd mind if I borrowed them?" I said.

"What for?"

"I need to dress a little less, I don't know, a little less—"

"A little less gay?" said Johnny.

"A little less LA was what I was thinking."

"Go ahead. I'll take them back to the cleaners. He'll never know the difference."

"Pardon me while I change." Tucked in the backseat, I took off my clothes and put on Mr. Heber's, which felt really weird. Other than the pants, they fit.

"Here," said Maureen. "I have some safety pins." She handed me a small plastic box of gold safety pins and I quickly hemmed the pants.

"How do I look?"

"Pretty blah," said Johnny.

"Good, that's exactly what I was going for. OK, we're getting close. Johnny, can you tell Maureen where the turnoff is?"

"Sure, why?"

I lay down on my side on the backseat. Elektra thought this meant it was cuddle time, and she curled up in the crook of my arm. "Because I want to drive into town without anyone seeing me. And you too. Once you spot the turnoff, Johnny, I want you to slide down in your seat."

"It's coming up."

"Maureen, you see it?"

"Yup"

"OK, turn there. Johnny, you get down. And Maureen, all you need to do is follow this road about four miles until you see the post office on the left. Tell me when you see it and I'll tell you what to do."

I heard Maureen's turn signal, and Johnny was crouching down in the well in front of the passenger seat. He kept giving me a thumbs-up sign and whispering, "This is so cool!" When the car left the asphalt everything started rattling hard. "Just keep going up this road," I told Maureen. From the way I was lying, I could see her profile. She looked very confident, her mouth set firm, and I could tell she was doing this not because she was a nice person or a good secretary, but because it was right.

"I see the post office."

"Turn into the lot. Park in the last spot on the right."

"It's full."

"Then park next to it."

The car slowed, turned, and came to a halt.

"Now everyone stay still while I tell you what's going to happen. Maureen, you're going to go inside. The postmistress's name is Sister Karen. I'm pretty sure we can trust her. Tell her you're waiting for me there. She'll let you hang out. Maybe she'll let you into the back so no one sees you. But even if someone sees you, it'll be fine, they'll have no idea why you're in town."

"What about us?"

"When she's been inside for five minutes, we're sneaking out and walking up to the house."

"What about Elektra?"

Dammit. I forgot to include her in the plan.

"We should've left her with the goth girl," said Johnny.

"Never mind. Maureen, you're going to have to take her."

"If we really can trust Sister Karen," she said, "then wait a second, I'll be right back."

A few minutes later, the driver's-side door opened. It was Sister Karen. "I'm going to slip Elektra in through the loading door. No one will see her." Then they were gone, and Johnny and I were left alone.

"What now?"

"We're walking. Slip out of the car, stay low, run to the far side of the post office. I'll follow you." He did everything I said, and a minute later we were standing against the hot concrete bricks of the post office's western wall, hidden from the street. "Now we'll just walk up one of the side roads. If we play it cool, no one should notice us."

We started walking. It was probably 110 and I could feel the sun on my neck. Maybe that's another reason the Firsts have been left more or less alone for so long. It was hot as Mars out here. No one wanted this land.

"So far so good," I said. This side road was quiet, some big houses, some empty lots. Not a lot of traffic. Anyone who saw us would assume we were two kids walking back from the co-op.

"So what's the plan?" said Johnny.

"You're going to think I'm crazy."

"Too late."

"You got your knife?"

"Yeah, why?"

"Here, give it to me."

At the back of the lot, I began cutting branches from the scrub. "Start breaking off some twigs and make them small and very thin, like toothpicks. We're going to start a fire."

"We are?"

"Actually, you are."

He screwed up his eyes. "Dude, you're a total nut job."

"Just break off some twigs, we need kindling. I never thought I'd say this, but thank God we're out in the middle of the desert. This wood is bone dry."

When we had a good pile I said, "Now we need tinder. Do you have any lint in your pockets?" He pulled out a few wads and set them delicately atop the pile of kindling.

I checked the pockets of Mr. Heber's pants. In one I found a couple of wads of white lint, in the other two dry-cleaned bucks. "Here, shred these up."

"You're going to burn money?"

"Just do it." I found a stick about a foot long and hacked a notch in each end. I bent down to unlace one of my shoes.

"What are you doing?"

"I'm making a bow." I gave him a quick lesson on the bow-drill method of starting a fire.

"Where'd you learn this shit?"

"You forget, I was on my own for a long time." I got the pieces ready for him and told him he'd have to keep at it for a long time. "The trick is to catch the coals and get them onto the tinder. It's going to take a while, but if you keep doing it, it should work."

"Why am I doing this?"

"Because I'm going to sneak through the cornfield, then behind Sister Kimberly's cabin. That's where I'll wait. When you get the fire going, throw as much wood on it as you can, then go back to the post office. Don't run, just walk calmly like you belong here. That's the good thing about Mesadale: there are so many kids, no one will notice one more."

"What about you?"

"When the fire starts, hopefully everyone will come out of the houses, and I can slip inside."

"You really are out of your mind."

"I know. But it might work."

I waited behind Sister Kimberly's cottage for almost an hour before I saw the white smoke. The smoke darkened, first gray, then black, then I saw a flame. From the big house I heard a scream, then another, and another after that, and they spread until all the women were calling out. The commotion began, people spilling out of the houses, babies crying, women and children running to the back of the lot with pots of water. Pretty soon there were at least seventy-five people at the back of the lot, the women in their prairie dresses and the kids in their hand-me-downs.

I didn't run. I walked straight to the side door and went inside. No one was in the hall, but I heard two women talking in a panic at the top of the stairs. If they were to look down, they would've seen me, but they were distracted by the fire out the window. I made it to the door that led to the basement stairs but found a tiny padlock, like a luggage lock, on an eye and hook.

The wives at the top of the stairs were deciding whether they too should go outside. One was saying we should go out and the other was saying someone needs to stay with the babies. Just then a baby started wailing, and one of the wives said you go check on him, I'll look on the others.

The lock was so delicate, it looked like it belonged to a doll. I jammed the lock with Johnny's knife. A couple of shoves and it broke apart. One of the wives upstairs said you hear that? But the other said it was Timmy, he threw his paci across the room.

I tiptoed down the stairs. At the bottom was the door with the NO TRESPASSING decal. I slowly pushed it open. It was the first time I'd ever been down here. My dad called it his sanctuary. Ever since I left Mesadale, I thought of it as his grave.

It didn't look like a death scene or anything. The blood had been mopped up, and everything looked like he'd just left and would be back any minute. Even the hole in the chair seemed harmless. But the truth is, you can tell when you're where someone's died. I could feel it, like a bad vibe, like you don't even want to know what shit went down here. I stood there feeling that feeling for a while. That's when I figured out where to look: up on the shelf above the gun rack, where the Golden Boy used to hang. I rolled the computer chair over and climbed up to get it. It was a Book of Mormon turned over on its side. But inside wasn't the Book of Mormon.

The text looked like a log a foreman would use to keep track of times and outputs on an assembly line. There was a long column of initials—R, K, S, S1, P3, etc.—and a row that showed the days of the week. I climbed back down and rolled the chair back to the desk. Outside I heard the fire brigade, men yelling, trucks idling, a diesel pump.

I rolled the chair over to the window well. I opened the window and climbed up into it. The well was one of those steel half tubes you put around a basement window to hold back the soil. That's when it happened, the thing I never thought would happen. I heard a couple of cars screech in, doors slamming, then that voice I'll never forget: "Sisters, be not afraid."

The well was big enough to crouch in. Its lip projected four inches above the ground, and if I was very careful, I could peer over it. I was on the side of the house and everyone was in the back, but I could see the Prophet's suburban with the smoked windows and bulletproof plating. One of his bodyguards circled the car, checking things out. He looked like a weird cross between a missionary and a mercenary—formal slacks, a short-sleeved dress shirt, a soldier's buzz cut, and a nine-millimeter semiautomatic tucked into his belt.

While the men worked to put out the fire, the Prophet gathered the women and children around. "There's nothing to worry about," he said. "The Brothers will have the fire out in no time. Sisters, come closer, and I will explain what's happened, for I want you to know what I know; and I can see from the fear in your eyes you want to know what I know. There are two explanations for this sudden fire here today. First, some will tell you it's a heat fire, nothing more. We are in the middle of the summer in the middle of a drought in the middle of a desert. And so that is what it is, a heat fire, and there is no mystery to it all. If that is what you believe, then so be it. Yet others will tell you, it's a message from God just as the burning bush was God's message to Moses. I will let you decide which it is. I won't even tell you which I believe it to be. Yet think wisely, Sisters, for you will be judged on what you believe, both now and ever after, when you meet our Heavenly Father at his gate."

A lot of the sister wives and the kids were crying and the Prophet said, "Why are you afraid? The Lord will protect you if you've been obedient. For it is obedience upon which you'll be judged. If you loved your husband and obeyed him, and you, children, if you loved your father and obeyed him, if all of you have loved God and obeyed him, then you will be taken care of, both in this world and beyond. Do not be afraid." He was as close to shouting as he ever got: "Do not be afraid."

There were a lot of other people around too, neighbors, Apostles, whoever coming to see the fire and the Prophet, everyone in the back. Now was a good time to run for it. I started climbing out of the well when I heard the Prophet say, "I know many of you are wondering what will happen to you, and to this house, who will lead it, you ask, how can you now be a wife when you no longer have a husband? I know you fear living out your days without a husband, and you worry how you will be admitted to heaven having left earth without a husband. But I do not want you to worry, for tomorrow I will come to you and I will marry you myself, each of you, and this house will become my house, and you my wives, so that when you rise to heaven and are asked by God himself whether or not you are a wife, you can tell him you are his Prophet's wife, and with this news I promise he shall let you in."

The women started cheering, and crying too, and dogs were barking and babies howling. The bodyguard made a sweep around the suburban again. When he was gone, I climbed out of the well. I moved slowly down the drive to the street and then away from the house. With all the other people around, I was just another kid carrying his Book of Mormon. I looked over my shoulder once. The fire was smoldering, the smoke dying. The men were hauling their equipment to their truck, the women and children were returning to the house, and the Prophet was nowhere to be found.

September 12, 2005

Prophet and President Gordon Hinckley
The Church of Jesus Christ of Latter-day Saints
50 East North Temple
Salt Lake City, UT 84111

Dear President Hinckley,

I want to introduce you to a promising young scholar from BYU named Kelly Dee.

Kelly is working on her master's thesis, a project I know will enhance our understanding of Church history. She is honest, hardworking, and devout. Yet despite these qualities, she has run into various roadblocks gaining access to certain documents in our Archives. Why? Because her subject is Ann Eliza Young, Brigham's infamous 19th wife. In the late 1930s an LDS scholar named Charles Green tried to write an authoritative account of Ann Eliza but was thwarted by the Church at nearly every turn. I sincerely hope Kelly does not meet the same fate.

I am writing to you personally because I believe in the importance of her scholarship. Although Ann Eliza Young is no hero of mine, and there is no doubt her faulty memoir has caused considerable harm to the Latter-day Saints in general, and Brigham's reputation in particular, nonetheless honest inquiry and critical scholarship should always be encouraged and valued. It's central to everything we do, as members and as God's children.

I hope you will encourage your colleagues throughout the

Church to further assist Kelly with her scholarly requests. Her search for the truth can only benefit us, today and always.

Sincerely Yours,
DEB SAVIDHOFFER
Church Archivist

CONFIDENCE, MAN

I knocked on the post office delivery door. I knocked again. "Sister Karen, it's me."

Maureen and Johnny were playing a hand of Texas hold em. Elektra was curled up on an empty mail bag. They looked surprised to see me, like they hadn't expected me to ever return.

"What?" I said.

"A fire?" said Maureen. "Honestly."

"They put it out."

"How big was it?" said Johnny.

"It doesn't matter," said Maureen. "We need to get going." She stood up, swatting the dust from her ass. The back room was filled with bins of WIC checks—I could see the marbled pink paper through the envelopes' windows. It was always a big day in Mesadale when the WIC checks arrived.

Sister Karen asked if everything was all right up at the house. I told her the Prophet had come by and what he had said to the sister wives. She frowned. "He's not going to marry all of them."

"That's what he said."

"I know, but he's going to cherry-pick, so to speak. He'll take the pretty ones, the young girls, and he'll farm out the rest. It makes me sick."

"Boys," said Maureen, "I need to get on the road."

"What the Prophet doesn't seem to understand," said Sister Karen, "is the wives talk. And they've been talking a whole lot lately."

"Boys."

"Wait a minute, Maureen." To Sister Karen: "Talking about

what?"

"Ever since your dad was killed, they've been splitting off into rival packs. Sister Rita's leading some of them, and a lot of the other women are following Sister Kimberly. I can guarantee you the Prophet's not going to marry Sister Rita. So she's got to have all these women on her side. If she forms a group of ten or twelve, that's ten or twelve welfare checks, and it's hard to ignore that. But there's no doubt the Prophet wants to marry Sister Kimberly, so a lot of the other wives are aligning themselves with her."

"You've got to be kidding me," said Maureen. "This is just crazy."

"No crazier than some of the stuff you believe."

Maureen flinched, like someone had touched her inappropriately.

"I'm sorry," I said. "That didn't come out right."

"Dude, your mouth and foot have to stop meeting like that."

Maureen threw her purse strap over her shoulder. "I'm going out to the car. Don't be long, I need to get home."

"Johnny, would you go after her? Tell her I'll be there in a sec. And stay down low in the car." He left, and I was feeling awfully alone on this mission. But I wasn't finished. I asked Sister Karen what she thought would happen at the house tomorrow.

"Oh, he'll definitely marry some of them, but the question is what will happen to the others. Already one's disappeared."

"Who?"

"Sister Sherry. You probably don't know her. She was recently reassigned to your dad. She was married to Brother Eric, but he was excommunicated for challenging the Prophet on some matters. He had four wives; the Prophet took the youngest and split up the others. That's how Sherry landed with your dad. But she's been missing for a few days now."

"What do you think happened to her?"

"I don't know. She could've run off, but I don't know." She looked at me, deciding something. "I shouldn't be doing this." She opened a drawer, lifted out an organizing tray, and held it above her head. An envelope was taped to the bottom of the tray. "After Brother Eric was excommunicated, Sister Sherry came in here and gave me this. She said if anything ever happened to her, I should contact this address." She removed the envelope from the bottom of the tray and opened it. On a piece of paper was an address in Denver. No name, no phone, just 43 Atwood Street, Denver.

"You think Sherry went there?"

"She might have. I don't know, Jordan, but I just have a feeling she might know something about what's going on. Why don't I write her address down for you."

"Never mind, I got it memorized. I should be going."

Sister Karen stuck her head out the delivery door to scan for trouble. "It's clear." Elektra and I ran to the car and lay down on the backseat. I told Maureen to drive out the way we came. "Just play it cool." Johnny wanted to chat but I told him to shut up until we were on the highway. Maureen drove down the red dirt road and I could see the dust rise behind us. The car shook and rocks shot up and clinked against the underside of the car.

When we got to the highway, the car stilled and the only sound was the lull of the wheels turning against the pavement. "Do you see any cars?" I said.

"No one."

"Ahead or behind you?"

"No one."

"Johnny, it's OK." And we both sat up.

"Man, that was awesome."

I changed out of Mr. Heber's clothes. "I'll get these cleaned," I said.

"I'll take care of it." We argued over that, but Maureen said, "Jordan, it's fine."

I told them about what Sister Karen had said, about Sister Sherry disappearing to Denver.

"Denver," said Johnny. "I was there a few months ago. Not bad."

"She thinks this wife might know something."

"Why would she think that?" said Johnny.

"That's just it: she doesn't think that. She wants me to drive all the way to Denver to talk to someone who isn't there."

"Dude, what're you talking about?"

"We can't trust her."

"Sister Karen? But she just helped us like big-time."

"I know, but she wants us out of town. Something's about to happen and she doesn't want me anywhere near Mesadale when it does."

"You're sounding paranoid."

"I don't care."

"Dude, have you been watching *Twenty-four*?"

It was late afternoon and the sun was hitting the car at a low angle. Everything ahead of us was yellow and gold. Sometimes when you're driving down a back road in Utah, you think if there is a God, then he probably had something to do with all of this. It's just that fucking beautiful.

"Maureen," I said, "who's that?"

"Who?"

I pointed at the souvenir hanging from her rearview mirror. On one side it said Zion, 2006, and on the other was a picture of two young women standing in front of the famous lone tree, the pine bending atop a mesa of stacked red sandstone. I'm sure you've seen it. One of the most famous trees in the world.

"That's my granddaughter Jess and her best friend."

"They look nice," said Johnny. "How old are they?"

"Twenty-three?"

"They married?" said Johnny.

"Oh no, they're up in grad school. They take their educations very seriously." I asked what they were studying. "Jess is getting her master's in nutrition," she said. "And Kelly—Kelly, she's studying history, I think it is."

"History?"

"Snooze," said Johnny.

"So what'd you find up at the house?" said Maureen.

"My dad's fuck chart."

"His what?"

"Oh, my God," said Johnny. "You found his fuck chart? Let me see." He grabbed it and started flipping through it. "Yup, that's what this is."

"Jordan," said Maureen, "what is that?"

"I guess the more polite term is a marriage management note-book. He used it to keep track of the time he spent with each wife, when he ate with whom, how much time he spent talking with each, that sort of thing."

"Yeah, and who he fucked and when."

"Johnny."

"Dude, am I telling the truth or what?"

He was. That's why all the boys called them fuck charts. Almost every man kept one and there was nothing the boys of Mesadale liked to do more than find one and read it. On my dad's chart there were a lot of indecipherable notations, letters and numbers and squiggly marks.

"That's code, dude. Code for what the women like under the sheets. You can't expect a man to remember all that."

"Oh please," I said. "As if he cared."

"I'm telling you. My dad had one just like this, and we cracked the code."

"Jordan," said Maureen, "you realize it's stolen. We can't use stolen evidence."

"I know," I said. But I actually didn't know that. "Even if there's some important information in it?"

"It gets automatically thrown out."

"No exceptions? Because this has something really useful."

"No exceptions."

Well, that sucked, because on the last page my dad had made a note that on the night he was killed he spent an hour alone with Sister Rita in her room.

Maureen dropped us in the parking lot of A Woman Sconed. When I said good-bye, she simply held up her hand. I guess she was still hurt by what I had said.

It was Friday evening, and by Monday morning I needed to be back in Pasadena. I didn't know when I'd see Maureen next. I tried to thank her for all her help, but she stopped me. "I'll tell Mr. Heber you'll be in touch with him about the notebook." She pulled out, the stuffed penguins swaying as she turned out of the lot.

"You really messed that up," said Johnny.

"Would you shut up for once?"

He climbed into the van. "Don't blame this one on me."

I sat on my rear bumper and called Roland. I listened to his line ring and ring. Voice mail. "Yeah, hey, it's me. Things have been a little intense lately. Anyway, I'll be home soon, maybe even tomorrow. Anyway, if you get—" But I lost the signal and left the rest of my message on a dead line.

I left Elektra with the goth girl, and Johnny and I drove over to the swimming pool. We both needed a bath, and I needed to think about where I was. After jumping in the water, Johnny sidled up to two teenage girls catching the last rays of sun on a patch of grass. "You let me know if you ladies need some help applying that suntan lotion, all right?"

"Fuck off."

"Asshole."

"Nice to meet you, too, ladies."

"Loser." The girl who said this was lying on her back in a strawberry bikini. Her downy thighs glistened in oil. It was apparent why Johnny wasn't ready to give up.

"Let me start over. I'm Johnny, and despite my first impression, I'm actually a nice guy."

It was enough to get the second girl to smile. She set down her paperback mystery and said, "I'm Jen. And this is Laura."

Johnny seized the opening: he sat on a tiny corner of Jen's towel. Fifteen minutes later, he was sharing half of it. They were laughing, and once Johnny pointed in my direction and the girls looked over at me with profound curiosity. The wind had shifted and their voices were no longer clear, but I caught a few scraps of conversation, including, "He's pretty OK." And then, "But I love his dog."

And so that's where I was: sitting on the lip of a public pool, my legs hanging in the water. My mom was still in jail, Maureen was pissed, Johnny was ignoring me, Elektra was off getting a sugar high, and who knows what Roland was up to. And my dad was still dead. It was Friday evening. If I was going to make that nursery job, I needed to wrap things up.

"Yo, Jordan! Get over here!"

Johnny introduced me to the girls as "the dude I was telling you about." And then, his voice dropping: "Listen, dude. We're going to head back to Jen's house. I'll catch you later."

"What do you mean, *later*?"

"As in, later. As in, not now. Dude, chill."

"Where will I catch you?"

"Man, what's your problem today?"

The low sun speckled on the water. All around kids were running and dive-bombing into the pool. A gang of teenage boys was sharing a pack of Marlboros. Two old ladies were wading in the shallow end. "Nothing's my problem."

"So I'll give you a call." He rolled over, exposing his narrow back. He was thin and strong, and his shoulder blades sharpened as he reached for a sip from Jen's Coke. In another life, Johnny would've been a high school wrestler with a so-so GPA. Now he was just a sweet little con.

XII

———

THE ACTRESS

THE 19TH WIFE

CHAPTER NINE:
Secrets of the Faith

Not long after I turned sixteen, I fell ill with a malady that remains unexplained to this day. I took to bed with a sodden chest and fever. After three days my mother sent word to my father about my condition. They had lived separately since my father's conjugal spree four years before, he in Salt Lake switching beds among his wives, and my mother and I alone on a small farm in South Cottonwood, about ten miles outside the city.

When my father saw how my true condition, he accused my mother of neglect for not having called a doctor. They argued at the foot of my bed over how to improve my health. Finally she conceded her prayers were no longer adequate and sent for the one man she believed could restore my condition—Brigham Young. Brigham decided I should receive my Endowments—a sacred honor bestowed on few youths outside his immediate family. For the first time since I fell ill, my mother's face sparkled with joy. For a woman with a faith as deep as hers, this was as high an honor as one can hope for while on Earth.

The Endowment Ceremony is a ritual so secret that a Saint risks expulsion from the Church, and even death, should he reveal its contents; it is so esteemed that Saints speak of it as second in glory only to their promised ascent to Heaven. Up until this point, I had never spent much time pondering theological truths. I accepted everything I was told about God, Christ, and Joseph and his Revelations, for everyone I loved told me they were true. If you were to ask me at this age if I considered myself devout, I would have enthusiastically replied, Yes! I prayed, attended services, sung the hymns with full lungs, and tried to live by the Articles of Faith and all the other wisdom Brigham imparted in his sermons on Sundays. Yet I had never wrestled with any metaphysical questions for myself, for Brigham's churchly system, all-inclusive as it was, left no open territory in the theological landscape to mull over. I believed my Endowment Ceremony would be the highlight of my young spiritual life; yet now, so many years later, I understand I believed all this simply because I had been told it was so.

The next morning at seven o'clock, still under the spell of a fever, I entered the Endowment House. In those days it was the most sacred site in all of Great Salt Lake, and the most secretive. Those who had been inside were forbidden to speak of it. Such secrecy encouraged every kind of rumor; some described the interior as a simulacrum of Heaven itself; while others suggested it was as dark and dank as a crypt. The Endowment House is said to share architectural traits with the Freemason's Temple. As a young man Joseph encountered Freemasonry, and perhaps joined a Lodge, and thus some of his detractors have declared the Endowment Ceremony a derivative of Freemasonry's ritualized meetings. Both utilize secret grips and pass-words, a structured order of personal development based on degrees, and other symbolic gestures and signs. Yet having little personal knowledge of the Freemason's organization, I cannot verify these claims. However, I can reveal to my Dear Reader that the only exoticism inside the Mormons' Endowment House is the unusual number of bathing tubs.

Once through the doors I was met by Sister Eliza R. Snow, one of Joseph's many widows whom Brigham had married shortly after his martyrdom. Sister Snow led me into a large bath-room with a row of tubs and a long green curtain. I was not the only one present—five other women, all unknown to me, had come for their Endowments as well. In addition to them a dozen women, most years past sixty, stood around, for what purpose I did not know.

The old women, buttoned up in blackcloth, stared at me intently, and when it came time for me to strip my clothes, they chose not to avert their eyes.

"First we must cleanse you," Sister Snow said, helping me out of my dress. In a matter of seconds she had me crouching in a steaming bath. Sister Snow had a heavy, downward appearance. The skin of her cheek looked as if it might slide off the bone. The old woman bathed me from foot to ear and everywhere in between, scrubbing as if sudsing the flank of a horse. There is an indignity to such submission, especially with others looking on. Yet, given the circumstances, it was difficult not to hope—not to believe, I should say—that this ancient woman, with her raw red hands, could scrub away my mysterious malady.

Next Sister Snow raised a horn above me, declaring it to represent the horn of plenty. Olive oil filled the horn, and in a swift motion similar to how a butcher slaughters a pig, she pulled my head back, exposed my throat, and dribbled the oil across my brow. "Sister, I prepare thy head for glory's crown." The oil ran into my eyes and ears, and yet I did not fidget or break the solemnity of the moment despite feeling like a slab of meat being dressed for the broiler. "Sister, I anoint your mouth." She poured the oil across my lips. "Sister, I anoint your breast." The oil was slimy upon my chest and flowed down the flesh in between.

Sister Snow continued: My stomach, my thighs, my loins! Soon I glistened in oil. I was miserable, and yet this was supposed to be the greatest day of my life. I wanted to ask: Did Jesus intend this? But I dared not. Sister Snow was so certain in everything she did, I knew my doubts had to be wrong. And so I stood naked, golden and slick, while the line of old women ogled and prayed. I glanced to my oiled companions in this ritual, but each woman, as naked as I, had shut her eyes.

I had deduced what was transpiring on the other side of the green curtain: several Brothers were receiving their anointments. I could hear them sloshing in their baths and the slurping oil trick-

ling into their unthinkable regions. Reader, recall I was sixteen:
Find me the girl of this age who does not giggle when imagining
fat old men greased up like pigs!

Cleansed and anointed, I was ready to dress for my Endowment.
Sister Snow handed me two undergarments, each made of plain
muslin. The first was similar to a sleeping-robe, the shirt and drawers of one piece, and covered every inch of flesh between my head
and feet, save my hands. Sister Snow explained that I must always
wear it until I entered my grave. "It will keep you safe," she said.
"And protect you from the assassin's bullet and the enemy's sword.
If only Joseph had been wearing his at Carthage."

The second garment was identical to the first and was its replacement. When I needed to wash one, I would remove half of the
first and cover myself up again with the second before removing
the rest of the first. This way I would never be naked again. If Mormondom's young men rebel against the Church's restrictions
against alcohol and tobacco, the young women rebel against the sacred undergarment. I have known many girls to secretly trim theirs
with lace, satin ribbons, and other frippery. Oh, were to Brigham
Young discover this concealed truth, would he be angry or pleased?

Atop this unpleasant item, I was dressed in a white dress and a
secondary skirt, bleached stockings that bunched at my ankles, and
soft linen slippers. Over this I wore my Temple robe—a baggy item
that fell to my feet. A strip of linen belted it in place. For a hat, Sister Eliza tied a small flag of Swiss muslin to my head, the extra material hanging behind like a strange plume. I looked like nothing so
much as how a schoolmistress would dress a child in a pageant of
angels. I felt silly and very much like a little girl; and yet none of the
women around me seemed to share my sentiments. They held out
their arms, letting the Sisters pull on their clothing as if they were
a corpse being prepared for burial. (In fact, these were the garments
we would be buried in, whenever that grim day came.) These
women were older than I, certainly more knowledgeable, and I was
ashamed of my own levity of spirit in comparison to theirs. I told

myself I must stop thinking the way I was. I prayed to God to reveal the magnitude of the moment.

Next the curtain dividing the bath-room was pulled back in a
dramatic fashion, similar to how a theater's curtain swiftly reveals a
new scene. Standing opposite were six men dressed in their own
white robes and caps. Men are generally less capable of tolerating
discomfort, and for the most part they fidgeted and looked to their
feet. Anyone could see they were embarrassed to stand before their
friends and neighbors in an outfit suitable for a doll.

We were ushered into an empty interior room. Two male voices
from above interrupted the silence. At first I could not understand
what they were saying, but then, as if they had moved in closer,
their words became clear. Elohim was talking to Jehovah, who was
growing more elaborate and excited in his chronicle of the world's
creation and Adam's need for a companion. I thought I recognized
Jehovah's voice as Brother Allan's: An Apostle, he is the barber
Gilbert visits and possesses a grand baritone's voice. I knew I
should surrender to the fantasy, as the others were doing. I told myself to concentrate and to believe. And yet, as you no doubt know,
no one can force belief. Even so, for the next two hours, I tried and
tried, draining off the last of my energy in the effort.

Brother Allan, or, I should say, Jehovah recounted how God created the Earth and the seas, the beasts and the trees. Behind us, a
curtain opened to a stage. The scenes of Genesis appeared in cutout and costume, as they might in an earnest but budget theatrical
production. Adam, or a young man I did not quite recognize playing Adam, took center stage, followed by Eve, played by Mary Jane
Cobb. Some said she had recently married Brigham Young. The
Prophet never claimed her as one of his own, although many years
later, she and I would become acquainted, and she shared with me
a detail of Brigham's personage that only a wife would know.

Before us, Adam and Eve acted out their own familiar drama.
Somehow, the unsurprising and long-known denouement terrified
the audience. Everyone was enraptured, and two women actually

gasped with fear when the serpent—a man in black mask and tail, knee breeches, and hands dusted with coal—slithered onto the stage. Once again I felt alone in my suspicions and blamed myself. Only a weak mind and soul could not share in the terror of Man's downfall. But the whole event left me numb. I have heard an esteemed medical doctor say that illness is the loneliest state. I would argue that doubt deserves that claim.

Next a second, recessed curtain drew back to reveal Satan. I do not know who played him, but he was a slim, athletic man in a tight black suit with strips of pink and black stockings. He wore a mask meant to be frightening, with two soft little horns, like the fuzzy knobs atop the head of a lamb. More than anything, this Satan resembled the many Mephistopheles one has no doubt seen in playhouses around the country. I was disappointed that the Church, with its celestial insight, could not conceive the Devil with more originality. Satan danced around, tormenting Adam and Eve, neither of whom was gifted with the art of Tragedy, and then ran among the men and women in the audience. Everyone loves a devil, and this audience was no exception. They made noises like people watching a fireworks display. Meanwhile, I felt I might faint from exhaustion and looked for a bench to sit down.

"Up, up, up, up!" Sister Snow tooted, pulling me back to my feet. This hard little woman supported me in her arms. From whence does such might come?

Thereafter, we filed onto the stage, all the while Satan prancing about. Whoever was beneath that mask possessed a long pent-up desire to dance and flit about like the happiest of bumblebees. Next came a series of visitors, each representing Christianity's many sects—the Quaker, the Methodist, the Baptist, the Catholic. Each representative claimed his was the way of Christ. They surrounded us, shouting their positions, until a great cacophony overtook us and several members pressed their hands to their ears. For dramatic effect, I will admit, this was the pageant's highlight, for I came to understand, almost instantly, that for two thousand years men have been claiming there is but one way to God: Mine!

Satan chuckled over this war of opinion. "You see, Man has fallen into my trap!" Although I am not a writer, and this memoir is my only attempt to capture life in words, despite this lack of skill and experience, even I would suggest a revision to Satan's script.

Thereafter the Apostles instructed us on a number of passwords to be used as we graduated through the degrees of the Order of the Melchisedec Priesthood; and a set of tickling grips or handshakes that would revel ourselves as true Saints in the hereafter. Next Sister Snow leaned into my ear, cupping her hand around her mouth, and whispered, "As you enter the Celestial Kingdom, call yourself Sarah, for this is your secret name and shall guarantee your entry. You must never reveal this name to anyone other than your husband on the day of your sealing. Otherwise, take it to your grave. Do you understand?" In my mind I turned over this new name—Sarah!—many times, taking pride in its Biblical symbolism. I promised myself I would protect it throughout my life, as if it were my child and its very life depended on my care.

The woman beside me was a shriveled, bent-over creature; it was clear to all that she would require her secret name sometime soon. Sister Snow leaned into her ear.

"Can't hear you, child," yawped the old woman.

Sister Snow attempted a second delivery in a slightly louder voice.

I thought I heard her say Sarah as well, but this would have been impossible. I told myself I had not understood Sister Snow correctly; and that I should not worry. Yet I have always wondered if Sister Snow named the old lady Sarah, and the other women, too; and if in the Endowment House each woman is given the same secret name, its celestial qualities tarnished by much abuse. Once, after my marriage to Brigham, I asked him about this. He reddened in the face and laughed, "You know what I love about you? Your fertile mind. My goodness, Ann Eliza—why are you always prone to the conspiracy?"

What followed was a nearly two-hour depiction of Joseph Smith's life, the angel Moroni's visit to his bedroom, the discovery of the golden plates, &etc. The final scene showed Smith's murder in the Carthage jailhouse and the Mormon people wandering without Prophet or leader. But just when all seemed lost, the Apostles appeared on the stage, banished Satan to his rightful fiery hole, and pronounced Brigham Young Prophet and President. Brigham Young would lead his Saints to Zion and redemption. In the red deserts of America, Salvation would be achieved.

The end.

Or so I thought. The Apostles, playing themselves, told us to kneel in a circle. The Apostles led us in promises and declarations. We raised our arms into the air. The women vowed total submission to their husbands. The men vowed never to marry a wife without permission from the Church. Together we promised to obey the Church's authority fully. We swore to take retribution for Joseph Smith's murder and to defend the life of Brigham Young, even if it meant shedding blood. Finally we swore never to reveal the secrets of the Endowment Ceremony. Punishment for doing so would be disembowelment, followed by one's tongue and heart knifed out of the body and burned. The Apostles informed us of this penance with such menace and certainty that each of us shook with fear.

At last at three o'clock in the afternoon the ceremony was over. While the others wept, I simply sat on the bench, exhausted and empty, but not in the way I had anticipated. Of my illness, I was certain I had never been closer to the grave.

That night my mother and I slept at Lydia's cottage. I lay awake upon the bed, unable to fall off, while she slumbered beside me. With each breath she emitted a small purr and her eyelids fluttered with dreams. I envied her peace of mind and the certainty of her faith. I longed to know what she knew; and to take comfort in it. I thought about the long day at the Endowment House. Why was I different from the other Saints—all good souls with open hearts.

From where did my skepticism come? I tried to fall asleep, but my mind ran with the images from the ceremony. Each time I recalled a detail—Eve, with her beautiful hair; or Satan, hopping on one foot—something inside me provided commentary that was neither sincere nor serious. *Why is Eve wearing a horse-hair wig? I didn't realize Satan knew the Scottish jig.* I became convinced I possessed a wicked soul, and that I was alone in my wretchedness. I would die soon, I concluded, and I was to blame.

After a while I could hear my father and Lydia above in her bedroom. They were talking about Diantha's performance in school. "She can recite the Articles of Faith all the way through." Their voices softened, then went silent altogether, and I heard the familiar creak of the bed, the sigh of the mattress as it absorbed two people embraced as one. Then nothing—the effortful silence that was so familiar in a house of many wives.

I got up and went outside. It was a clear night and the smoke tree was in silhouette along the fence. The smoke from the chimney was thick in the crisp air. The mountains rose blackly over the valley and the three-quarter moon cast a silver net over everything. I sat on the stump by the water pump, looking back at Lydia's little house. A candle burned in her room, and after some time my father appeared in her window. He looked out over his land and the houses beyond. I am sure he did not see me, even though the moonlight caused my robe to glow. He stood for a long time, as if something grave were on his mind. Then with his tongue he wetted his finger and his thumb and, in a gesture I could not see, snuffed out the candle. The window went black. The house was now dark and after a little while the smoke from the chimney thinned and died out. A poet might have thought the world had come to an end but for the wind turning the tree's early leaves.

In the morning I woke to find my illness in retreat. There was no way to explain it, although many people tried.

THE 19TH WIFE

CHAPTER TEN:
The Prophet Enters My Life

Sometime after my recovery, I acquired my first beau. Frederick Free was a sensitive, artistic young man who liked to sketch me in my mother's garden. By chance he was the younger brother of one of Brigham's favorite wives, Emmeline, who by most accounts was Number 10, although, in truth, I believe that number discounts the existence of a few wives Brigham married and quickly abandoned for reasons we shall never know.

Our friendship was still in its early days when Brigham summoned my mother to his office at the Beehive House. As President and Prophet of the Church, and leader of the Utah Territory, he was indeed a busy man. My mother could only presume that the matter to be discussed was of grave concern. Yet when she sat opposite his desk, Brigham, in a serious voice more suitable for lawyering than meddling, advised my mother to break off the relationship between myself and Frederick.

My mother came to my defense. "All he does is sketch her sitting on the fence."

"Sister, trust me. The boy is weak in the soul."

Brigham's interference was so unusual, and delivered in such dire tone, that my mother had no reason but to believe it was based on informed opinion. When she relayed it to me, I was equally puzzled, for I knew Brigham to be many things, but one was not a liar.

The next day I met three friends at Goddard's Confectionery on Main Street. Although Katherine, Lucinda, and I had gathered for cake and conversation only three days prior, enough had passed in the interval to fill several hours with the important details of our lives. My news of course concerned the Prophet.

"I always liked Frederick," said Katherine, a talented friend known for her skill in hair-art. Her interest in hair started with her own yellow locks, which she was always stroking and plaiting and otherwise playing with. "Why would Brigham want to protect you from him?"

"It's perfectly obvious," said Lucinda. "He's jealous."

"Jealous?" cried Katherine. "Of Ann Eliza?"

"Don't be daft. Of Frederick." Lucinda was a quick girl with a perfect memory. She could recall every Sunday outfit I had worn since I was twelve.

"Why would the Prophet be jealous of Frederick Free? Does he want to draw?"

"Katherine, you know I love you, but sometimes I wonder what goes on in that head of yours. Ann Eliza, explain it." Lucinda turned in my direction and flipped over her hand in a gesture that said—*Tell her.*

"The only thing I can think of is he somehow learned that the Endowment Ceremony has left me with quite a few questions."

"Ladies, when will you open your eyes?" Lucinda looked to me and Katherine and back. Her grayish eyes had the silver sheen of a looking glass, and I could see something of my own reflection in them. "He doesn't want some boy flipping around your yard."

"Why not?"

"Honestly, do I have to do all the thinking around here? He wants to marry you himself."

"*Marry* me?"

"I'm afraid so."

An extended clatter of female speculation followed—of how Brigham would propose, what number wife I would become, of whether or not he would establish me in my own house, as he does with his favorite wives, or encamp me in the Lion House.

"This is silly. If he were to ask me, which he won't, but if he were, I would say thank you very much but no. I'm going to marry a man who wants one wife."

"Good luck," said Lucinda.

Katherine proved equally supportive. "No one says no to Brigham Young."

Only a few days thereafter, while I was walking home in the afternoon, the Presidential Carriage appeared out of nowhere, pulling up alongside me on the road. I was so surprised by its appearance, I almost did not recognize Brigham in the driver's seat. "Quite a walk for you, Sister. May I drive you home?"

It was unusual to find the President driving alone, for typically his revered coachman, Isaac, a former servant to Joseph Smith, drove him about the city. I wish I could report that I declined the invitation and continued on my way, but I accepted his extended hand and settled in next to him on the leather bench.

Once on the road he said, "Now I understand you've been going around telling people you would never marry me. I'm sure you don't know how much that wounds me."

If it surprises my Reader that a man as preoccupied as Brigham Young would have the time or the inclination to gather information on girlish gossip, then I have not skillfully portrayed the complete control with which he ruled the Territory. He employed a network of spies who wandered through public gatherings, listening in for opinions of heresy and apostasy. No doubt one had been nearby at Goddard's, dispatching an urgent report to the Beehive House.

"Tell me: is it true?"

In most tales, this would be the opportunity for the hero to act bravely. Yet I was not prepared to defy Brigham Young. "It's not true," I lied.

"Ann Eliza? Are you blushing?"

"Yes."

"Is that color because of me?"

Brigham smiled, believing the red in my cheek had exposed an affection for him. Why is it the most brilliant men can be the least perceptive? For the rest of the journey he was as pleasant as the most humble and sincere gentleman, calling upon the delights of the fair weather. He spoke of the flowers in the gardens we passed and his love of the rose. He never pressed himself upon me, show-ing such deference and delight at my company that it was as if I were riding with a man who was wholly different from he who had just attacked me with my own words. When we arrived at my gate, he leapt to the ground to help me down. "I'll see you Sunday." He tipped his hat and bowed.

"Sunday," I sputtered. "Yes, Sunday."

The carriage threw up a cloud of dust as it coursed down the street, and heads poked from windows to get a glimpse of the Prophet. When he was gone my mother and Connie descended upon me, asking if I had really come home with Brigham Young.

After the incident in the carriage, Brigham disappeared from my life. He made no attempt to call, send word, or greet me at the Tabernacle on Sundays. I became, once again, one of some fifty thousand Saints under his command. My mother accused me of having offended him. "You must've said something. Brigham doesn't turn up like that, then disappear."

During this interval, my interest in Frederick Free diminished. I became tired of the afternoons perched on the fence rail. "You only want to sketch me," I complained. "Don't you like to talk?" He set down his stick of charcoal, took my hand, and together we discov-ered he had nothing to say. We struggled to make a connection of intimacy, but his eye was on his artistic pursuits, and mine was on—well, at that age, everything around me.

"I'll tell you why you lost interest," said Lucinda. "It's because you've got Brigham on your mind."

"Don't be cruel," I said. Yet I remained curious why Brigham had not called since our drive.

"Maybe he knows you're no longer close to Frederick," suggested Katherine.

"Poor Katherine," said Lucinda. "How long have you lived in Utah?"

"As long as I can remember."

"And yet you still don't see. I pity you, I really do. At least Ann Eliza understands."

I pretended that I did, but in truth, I did not. I had no idea what would befall me.

Then one day an invitation arrived to visit Brigham in his office. My mother and I arrived at the Prophet's compound a half hour early and waited outside the wall. I turned my attention to the Lion House, which sits across a small courtyard from Brigham's home. Many of his wives lived there, and his children too, in small rooms and apartments similar to those one might find in a depot hotel. I saw some women coming and going from the front door above which the famous stone lion perches. Some of these were girls about my age, dressed gaily in plum and blueberry silks, as was the fashion that season. They chatted in hushed voices and giggled as I would giggle with Lucinda and Katherine. Were they Brigham's wives or daughters? Or both? (He was known to marry more than one step-daughter.) A severe woman walked up the street, passing those of us in line to see Brigham. Her collar appeared to strangle her and her mouth twitched violently, as if she were busy nibbling away on the inside of her cheek. She passed through the gate and entered the Lion House. No doubt she was one of Brigham's early wives. A plump, overheated woman in front of us said to her companion, "I'll bet you he hasn't visited her since Nauvoo."

"Nauvoo?" said the companion. "I'd say it's been since Kirtland. If he ever did."

My mother stood stalwart in their ribald breeze.

At exactly four o'clock Brigham greeted us at the door to his office. Although it was autumn, the weather had been especially hot, and Brigham was wearing his summer costume familiar to all in Deseret: the prunella suit, a vivid white shirt kept pristine by his laundress daughter, Claire, and a neck cloth. His Panama hat hung from the hat-tree beside the door. He was now around sixty and looked very much like a man who had accomplished much in his day. His wide brow was creased and thick, his jowls heavy and tufted with white whisker. His girth was large enough to fill the chair, and then some, behind his desk. Yet he was not altogether unappealing. His flinty eyes sparkled as they must have when he was a young man.

"I've got a proposal for you," he said.

My mother sat up and began a speech I had not known she had prepared. "Brigham, you know quite well I love you as much as anyone. But be kind to my daughter. She's now barely a woman and sometimes she doesn't know what she's after. Please consider her happiness as well, not merely yours."

"Sister Elizabeth, it's her happiness I have in mind. Now let me make my proposition, then you'll see for yourself. As you know, our theater had a successful opening this past March. Our second season begins on Christmas Day. I would like your daughter to join the company. As an actress."

His gaze lingered upon me in such a mysterious fashion that I was at a loss to interpret his meaning. "I'm not an actress," I said.

"I don't want my daughter on the stage."

"Of course not. You shouldn't. Not just any stage. But this is my stage. We would never put up anything wicked. I can't think of a more perfect setting for Ann Eliza's talents."

Since my apostasy, Brigham has publicly accused me of always loving an audience. Many newspapers have reported him as saying I all but begged him to put me on his stage. This could not be further from the truth! I pondered his proposal for several days, coming close to turning him down. But I sensed my mother wanted me to follow Brigham's command; and I will admit I was at the age when any young woman has a mild curiosity about standing on the boards with the clam-shell lamps upon her. Thus, I reluctantly accepted Brigham's proposal and joined his theatrical company.

I made my debut on Christmas Day 1862 in the Irish farce *Paddy Miles' Boy* in the minor role of Jane Fidge. Because my talents were new and untrained, I refrained from complaining about my limited time on stage. Two nights later I appeared as Caroline Leslie in *The Two Polts*. Four nights thereafter I played the young Blanche Howard in *Old Phil's Birthday*—a role more suitable for my physical attributes and instincts. In one week I had gone from novice to veteran. In one month I was a player the critics, some from as far as California, mentioned in their columns. If I am to believe them, my dramatic gifts were effortless and well-disposed. One wrote, "Miss Webb possesses the most natural beauty to be seen on the Utah stage this season." Why I remember that particular line of criticism I cannot say.

By January I had become such a part of the company, and so enfolded in the weekly repertory, that the long drive to and from my mother's house in South Cottonwood was no longer practical. It was decided the most practical thing would be for me to move into the Lion House.

At the time, the Lion House was one of the most infamous private homes in all of America. Many speculated about the activities taking place inside; and every Gentile visitor to Salt Lake, on his way to California, made certain to see it, standing before its wall, gazing up at its cream plaster and green shutters, hoping to witness a salacious endeavor within. Newspapers whose editors disliked Brigham ran cartoons of him, plumped up in bed in the Lion House, twenty wives about him, ten on each side. They called it by many names—Brigham's harem, his seraglio, and the hen house. Brigham's supporters, on the other hand, often referred to it as "the Mount Vernon of the West." Even in the Territory, were you to ask the most loyal Saint how many wives lived inside, he would not know. The mysteries of its hallways, and what transpired beyond its notorious dormer windows, kept tongues busy with speculation. I know this, for since my apostasy, everyone, it seems, wants to hear about the inner workings of the Lion House.

I arrived one afternoon just before dinner, greeted in the glassed-in vestibule by Sister Snow, my old friend from the Endowment Ceremony. She led me up the stairs to a hallway bisecting the length of the top floor, ten doors on each side. Along the way we passed half a dozen children and several women I did not recognize. The children ran past me as if I did not exist—excited, straining creatures accustomed to many women and few men. The women were Brigham's wives, although they called one another "Aunt." Each took me in with a silent glare.

At the end of the hall Sister Snow opened a door to a small room with a sunflower paper that was dirty where pictures used to hang. There was a bed, dresser, and a tiny stove. "I hope I didn't drive someone out of her room."

"You didn't, so don't let it trouble you. Dinner's at four-thirty. See you downstairs." Sister Snow has always given me the impression of a woman ready to die but will outlive everyone she knows.

Dinner was an affair for fifty, overseen by childless Aunt Twiss. She had been a young widow in Nauvoo when Brigham discovered her notable domestic skills. So industrious was she that other women gossiped about her as if she had committed a crime against them personally. Once a week Aunt Twiss stayed up through the night to scour down her hearth, so that it might gleam in the morning light—an effort that caused some women to boil red with envy. Others chittered on about her method of sweeping: on her knees with a hand-broom, from one corner of a room to the opposite, and back. If her thoroughness in keeping house angered some women, it pleased Brigham, who had been employing her many useful skills since their marriage a few days before departing Nauvoo in 1846.

The large dining room was in the western part of the basement.

When I entered for the first time, Aunt Twiss sat me at the end of a table with a group of girls called the Big Ten—Brigham's elder daughters, ten young women known all over the Valley for their interest in fine clothing and attachment to the curling iron. Aunt Twiss pointed out my chair and said, "I hope you like eggs." She was neither hostile nor friendly, merely overwhelmed by a compulsive desire for efficiency. She wore a heavy, burdened brow and a complexion overheated from her work. I would soon learn, from four separate sources, that Brigham had never visited her conjugally and never would. "Yet every night, she props herself up in bed, in a fancy sleeping bonnet no less, as if he might come!" one of the Big Ten would go on to laugh in my ear.

The room was loud with women and children, but at precisely four-thirty Brigham arrived. Immediately everyone fell silent except for a few restless children, who were promptly pinched behind the ear. Brigham blessed our food, and afterward we ate a light supper of eggs and spinach, followed by composition tea. Brigham sat at the head of the table, with Sister Snow at his right and Aunt Twiss at his left. I quickly noticed that they dined on pigeon and gravy, with bread, butter, peach jam, and a bowl of strawberries and blackcaps.

Throughout the meal women approached Brigham to discuss their business, and for some, I would later learn, this was their only chance to consult their husband on matters typically discussed between man and wife at the table. Brigham hardly had a chance to eat while advising his wives, although it would not take a sleuth to deduce he must have taken a second (or third?) meal elsewhere. The wives formed a line behind him. When her time came, which was limited to a minute or two, each wife had to leap into her topic while everyone, including her rivals, listened in.

"I need a new kettle."

"I found my hand-glass in Sister Clara's room."

"Susannah isn't reading properly."

"There'll be another next June."

No matter how serious, or petty, the situation, this was the only opportunity most wives had to discuss their business with their husband.

Often a child—one of fifty-seven—climbed his leg and swung from his arm while he conversed with his wives. He was always playful with them, singing "too-roo-loo-rool-lool-or-lool" or producing a raisin from his pocket. It must be said that Brigham loved his children, was interested in their well-being, and guided his wives on discipline and other matters to their proper rearing. Yet even his sincerity could not compensate for the fact that fifty-seven children shared his fatherly heart.

During this the Big Ten huddled in the corner to discuss the topics all girls of this age find most urgent. I felt alone in this foreign world and assumed I would be excluded for it.

My brooding was interrupted by a touch to the wrist. "Aren't you the actress?"

I turned to find a slender woman a few years older than myself extending a gentle hand in greeting. Pinned to her breast was a brooch of glass grapes as green as her eyes. "I'm Maeve Cooper."

"Are you one of his daughters?"

"Step-daughter. My mother is Amelia Cooper." She pointed across the room. "Number thirty-four."

"Thirty-four what?"

Maeve laughed brightly, throwing back her chin. "You are new here, aren't you?"

"Do you mean his thirty-fourth wife?"

"Don't worry, lately he's slowed down." She cocked her chin and thought about something for a moment. "I'd say approximately fifty."

"Fifty what?"

"Weren't you about to ask me how many he has in total?"

I liked Maeve immediately and embraced her as an ally in the Lion House. She told me she had been a small child when her mother married the Prophet. "But I might as well be a stranger to him," she said. "I'm convinced he doesn't know my name." And then, "Not that I care." She was a sly, dangerous girl and our bond was cemented that first evening.

"Here's what you need to know. Never be late for supper, never be the last one in at night, the ironing is done from dusk to dawn, and don't bother trying to speak with Brigham directly. Anything you need you can get from making friends with Aunt Twiss or Harriet Cook. Twiss is somewhere between number twenty-five and forty, I don't really know. And Harriet, I'm pretty sure she's down around number four or five, so I don't need to tell you how long she's been around. Anyway, they might look a bit grim, but they're really sweet old girls."

After supper we moved upstairs to the front parlor, also called the prayer room, where the women gathered in circles to knit, sing, and talk in the evenings. It was Sunday night and the theater was dark. There were some eight or ten wives present, plus daughters and friends. I felt as if each wife had a careful eye on me. "I won't let it bother me," I told my new friend. "At the end of the season, you and all these women will see me pack my trunk and move out. They have no reason to be jealous."

"That's what Elsa said."

"Elsa?"

"Never mind. Tell me about the theater. What's on tomorrow night?"

"No, Maeve, tell me. Who's Elsa?"

It took no more pleading for Maeve to recount the story of what she called "wife number forty-seven or forty-eight, I think." A coloratura soprano imported from Wadowice, where the beautiful girls are dark and cold. According to Maeve, she was a shapely creature with a mane of red-black hair who sang with one arm draped across an alabaster pedestal. Brigham hired her to entertain at his private occasions, commanding her to sing his favorite bel canto roles from the Italian repertory. "She lived in the room across from yours," Maeve said. "Then he married her. She didn't want to, but what choice did she have? She was all alone. Her money came from him. She barely spoke English. How could she leave Utah? The wives made her life miserable."

"What happened?"

"She disappeared. Ran away, probably. But it's not an easy crossing to California. I should know. Some say Brigham's Danites went after her and murdered her in the desert. Forty miles out there's a pile of white bones by the road and the girls say that's Elsa. The way the wind whistles through the sockets in the skull, it sounds like her singing, practicing her scales."

"That's not true. I don't believe it."

"Neither did I. Not at first. But the truth is she was here one night, and gone the next. If you mention her to Brigham—and I'm warning you not to—he'll turn red as a pepper and huff out of the room. A few wives, when they knew she was really gone, they raided her room and fought over her silk."

"It can't be true."

"Maybe not. But no one's come up with a better explanation."

The next night at the theater my mind was preoccupied. I fear I gave one of my lesser performances, but the audience forgave me. Looking out into the theater, with thousands of eyes glowing in the dark, it was impossible not to wonder: What would become of me?

———

CHAPTER ELEVEN:
Marriage and Its Aftermath

For the next three months, I turned my attention to the theater. The more time I spent on stage, the more comfortable I became and, perhaps, the more my talent took root. I was cast as the little sister or ingénue in a number of slight plays no longer remembered, including *That Blessed Baby* and *The Good-for-Nothing*. The players, myself included, launched a movement to offer more serious fare, but Brigham re-enforced his ban on tragedy. "I won't have our women and children coming here to be frightened so they can't sleep at night." (He would later revise this policy, when he discovered he could not attract a beautiful Gentile actress to play in *Macbeth* rewritten with a happy ending.) There was also a prohibition against sentimental romances that glorified monogamous love. I remember one evening when a Saint of about seventy stood up in his seat and hollered, "I ain't sitting through no play where a man makes such a cussed fuss over *one* woman." He turned to his twenty-four wives: "Git up!" They filed out of the theater, all twenty-five, in a noisy column. For any actor pursuing his art, Brigham's theater was not always a venue of ideals.

Despite these restrictions, the theater became my refuge from the Lion House. I spent most of my time there, arriving early in the morning and staying until long after the curtain fell. The Lion House served as nothing more than a way-station, and I had little time to consider the plight of the women stranded there. For several weeks, the only time I saw Brigham was when I was on stage and looked into the Presidential box. He was often with six or seven wives and a number of children, watching raptly from his velvet-padded rocker.

After each performance, I would sit at my dressing table, my heart anxious whenever a knock fell on my door. Yet always it would turn out to be one of my new company friends coming to share in the triumph of our evening, or my director, with notes to improve my technique. One night—it was during my run as Emily Wilton in *The Artful Dodger*—I sensed Brigham's gaze upon me with even more intent as he leaned forward on his cane. The director had placed me upon the stage so close to Brigham's box I could nearly feel his eyes upon my flesh. It seemed his mind was sorting out the details of some plan, one that most likely involved me. In the final act, I stumbled on my lines. For a long moment—one of the longest in my life—I could not think of what to say. I looked about me, but my co-actor offered no assistance, for my stumble had thrown off his presence of mind as well. I turned and found myself looking into the Presidential box. Brigham mouthed the words *I shall be . . .* and it was as if an invisible hand had reached down and turned a crank to revive my memory and I carried on to the end with a particular intensity that brought the audience, Prophet included, to its feet.

Afterward, sitting at my table, I waited for the inevitable knock. I knew Brigham would come tonight, and I would have to thank him for his assistance. Up until then I had tried to deny the grasp he had about me, but this incident had made everything clear. I worked in his theater, I lived in his house, he was my spiritual leader, now he even told me what to say!

Then it came: the knock on my door. "Brother Brigham—"

Yet I opened the door to find a stranger greeting me with a box of sugar-stick jaw. "Will you permit an admirer to commend you on your performance?" The man spoke with an English accent, had a rugged complexion, and wore boots caked in plaster. His name, I soon learned, was James Dee. We spoke for what turned into an hour about the theater, his passion for Shakespeare, and Brigham's silly ban on tragedy. "What a lovely Ophelia you would make!" he said. Dee plastered log cabins for a living, a more lucrative practice than I might have realized, for he owned a fine six-room house not far from Temple Square. "I might be revealing too much in telling you I have been following your career."

"It's hardly a career, Mr. Dee. I've only been on the stage two months."

"Yes, but already your talent outshines your peers."

I scolded him for his flattery and decided this was a good time to open the box of candy. We sampled the sweets, then, alas, parted company. "Farewell!" he cried. "Thou art too dear for my possessing."

There might be no greater cause for caution than a suitor who quotes the Bard on the threshold. Yet, Dear Reader, please recall at the time I was eighteen. I had been standing guard against Brigham's inscrutable affections for so long that Mr. Dee's slipped unnoticed under the gate. He promised he would return the following night, and he did. He said he would bring me a yellow rose and there it appeared, on my dressing table, a tight bud upon a long red-green stem. He said he would read *Twelfth Night* aloud to me, and he did so. In the first week of our acquaintance he kept each promise he made. He offered to help my mother with a crack in her ceiling, arriving at the promised hour. He balanced atop his ladder while my mother and her visiting sister wives looked on with interest. "Who's this one, then?" Eleanor asked. "Wish I had someone bringing me a box of sugar-stick jaw."

Mr. Dee made his presence felt so quickly and with such command that I could not help but grow feelings for him. By the seventh day of our friendship, we were in love and engaged.

"Engaged?" cried my mother. "You hardly know the man."

I reminded her she hardly knew my father when they married.

"Even so, I have to tell you something: I don't like him."

"How can you say that? After he plastered your ceiling!"

"I used to know men like James Dee."

At the Lion House I sought an ally in Maeve. "Tell me you're happy for me," I begged.

"I wish I could."

"You too? But why?"

"Because I know Mr. Dee. In reputation." We were in the parlor, gathered for the evening in a corner where the other women and girls could not overhear. Maeve whispered, "He's known to know many women."

"Again, I don't believe you." We argued for as long as we could before our voices disturbed the wives from their knitting. They looked our way with desperate interest. I knew at least one of them would not stop until she had learned the subject of our debate. Polygamy inspires this in otherwise thoughtful women—the relentless need to know another's business. And yet what did I have to hide? Soon Mr. Dee would move me out of the Lion House and I would never have to suffer another night with the eyes of a dozen lonely wives dismantling me with their glares.

I could see that my new friend Maeve was not really as close to my heart as I had believed. The root of her displeasure, I assumed, was jealousy. I blamed this not so much on Maeve herself but on the warping effects of polygamy. Even its children can't escape its distortions of the heart.

For comfort, I turned to my old friends Lucinda and Katherine.

"Tell me what he looks like again?" inquired Lucinda.

"Is he kind?" asked Katherine.

There is great comfort in knowing that old friends, even after a gap of time, remain the same. Neither knew anything of Mr. Dee. Neither had a reason to doubt my judgment, although Lucinda said, as we left Goddard's, "I wonder why your mother doesn't like him."

I could look back and examine why I ignored the counsel of

those I loved most. A number of reasons might explain it, but none more so than my desire to escape the clutches of Brigham Young.

"Tell me," I said one evening to my betrothed. "What do you think of plural marriage?"

"Horrid institution."

"Even if it's the surest way into Heaven?"

"If you ask me, it's our Church's one great stain. I sometimes worry it'll be our undoing."

I nearly collapsed with relief. With this declaration locked in my heart, James Dee and I were married on April 4, 1863, in the Endowment House. Brigham sealed us before a small group, including my mother, whose rumpled face told me she could not enjoy the day. For a bridal dress I wore a bulky robe and ugly green apron. Beneath this, the sacred undergarments embroidered with cabalistic designs at the breast, navel, and knee. Brigham invited Maeve to attend the ceremony, and although she was no longer my closest friend, an old and gentle affection for her renewed itself on that special day.

I was scheduled to perform in *The Artful Dodger* on my wedding night. Brigham asked if I would prefer to hand the role over to my understudy. "Never!" I was a professional and I would meet my obligations. And so as a fresh bride, I took the stage. Word had spread that I had been wed earlier that day. When I made my entrance the audience erupted in congratulatory cheers. The applause repeated itself each time I entered from the wings and again at the end of the evening. By the time my husband and I returned to our rented room at Brigham's hotel, I was afloat on the triumph of the day. It was the greatest moment of my marriage. Rare joy would follow that eve.

The first trouble came swiftly, when Dee suggested we move in with my mother. "What about your house?" I said.

"It's rented. I thought they'd be gone by now, but their plans changed. Lovely family of Saints. A wig-maker, he is. You should see what he can do with a horse's tail. Only one wife, a nice girl from Sweden. They asked for an extension. They've a child who's not been well. What could I possibly say?"

Reader, what could *I* say? Temporary financial trouble had recently forced my father to retreat from supporting four separate households. A few months before my marriage, Sister Lydia and Diantha had returned to my mother's house, as well as Mrs. Cox and Virginie. I told my husband her house was full and he would not be comfortable.

"It's only for a month or two."

"I don't want to live in a house full of wives."

"Darling, I don't know what to tell you. It's that, or a tent."

My mother accepted us without any complaint or I-told-you-so's. She was also grateful for Dee's plastering skills, for a number of chinks and hairline cracks in her walls had been preoccupying her. Dee, skillful in the art of pleasing a mother-in-law, fixed whatever she asked of him, whether of plaster or not. He even plugged the mouse hole behind the stove with a stopper he whittled down to size. "It's good of you to help her like that," I told him after we had been living with her for a month.

"Do I have a choice?"

"If that's how you feel, next time tell her no."

"Oh, Ann Eliza, aren't you sweet. Life isn't so simple. I can't say no to your mother."

"Of course you can, if there's a reason."

"You are a child, aren't you?"

"Don't speak to me like that."

"You really don't understand. Your mother, she's been dying to have a man to boss around. What with your father living anywhere but here, she's had all her wifely energy bottled up."

"You don't know a thing about my mother."

"When I agreed to move in here, I thought you would side with your husband, but that was my mistake."

"Agreed to move in here!"

Oh, you can imagine the words that ensued. When our argument had worn itself out, I went to bed but found myself too agitated to sleep. I lay awake through the night, waiting for dawn when I could ask Dee his true feelings about our marriage. But I didn't have to. The next day I met an even clearer version of my husband, and I cared not for him in the least. We were strolling on Main Street when we happened upon Maeve. A delicate veil framed her lovely if overlong face. I introduced my former friend to my present husband. The exchange was brief and un-noteworthy until, after our departure, Dee said, "Who is she?"

To my Dear Female Readers, I ask—is there a question more devastating to the heart? These three simple words, when put together on a husband's lip, are constructed of nothing but betrayal and deceit. Or at least in Mormondom, where a man's whim can bring him another wife. "You met her at our wedding," I said.

"That's right, now I remember. She was in blue, with some sort of large broach—a bunch of grapes, wasn't it? Yes, it's all coming back. The blue, the grapes, the position on the breast. Indeed."

"She's one of my friends who warned me against you."

"Don't be coy, darling. Tell me exactly what you mean."

Repeating the rumors back to my husband would bring me no happiness. It would only make me look the fool. I therefore fibbed my way around the truth. "There have been a few words spoken that your faith is less than full." Oh, what a mistake to be dishonest!

"My faith! Is that it? She doesn't know me from Adam, does she? She doesn't know anything about my good family I left behind in England for my faith. She doesn't know anything about the hardship of my journey here, it's a big ocean, the Atlantic is, and rather rough in December. I arrived with no friends, no contacts, nothing more than my plastering trowel and my faith. My good faith. Now why would this girl go on about the sincerity of my belief? Because I haven't fifteen wives, is that it? Does everyone around here think a man's got to have his own harem to be a true Mormon? If that's it, if that's the reason my good reputation's been tarnished, then I'm quite sure something can be done about it." If only that were the end of his speech, but I shall spare the Reader the second phase of his rant. My husband's monologue ended with: "I love my Church, and I'll prove it if I have to."

As you no doubt know, the best way to incite outrage is to attack false piety. When provoked, the insincere man must certify his earnestness. It is the animal in him—the scratching, the grunting, the marking of territory. This is how I account for Dee's subsequent actions. A few days later he announced, "I saw Sister Maeve. By chance we happened to be visiting the tinsmith at the same time. She asked after you."

"Please don't do this to me."

"Do what? By the way, you said Maeve lives in the Lion House?"

"That's right, upstairs, the seventh door on the left, tell her I say hello. And while you're there, why not call on Brigham's daughters? I'm sure the whole of the Big Ten will appeal to you."

"No need to get prickly, my love. Maeve's a lovely girl—what with those enchanting green eyes—but not a beauty in the classical sense, wouldn't you say? . . . Love, what's wrong? Where are you going?"

I abandoned my husband on the curb.

After a few months of marriage, Dee and I were in steady battle. He knew how to torture me and never once passed up the opportunity to turn the knife. "I was thinking of taking a second wife," he would say, igniting me with rage. No doubt he took pleasure in seeing me degrade myself in fury. Even the threat of a plural marriage reduced my composure and self-containment; its ugly promise reverted me to childish dismay. During these days, I was in rehearsals for the upcoming season at Brigham's theater, set to open in October. As my marriage collapsed, I became more and more disengaged. The disruptions of home-life consumed me. By the time we went into dress rehearsals for the season premiere, I withdrew from the company, never to return to the stage.

Reader, do you not see! *This* is polygamy! Not the family portraits of forty, bursting with clean, smiling children and simple, proud wives. Before I married Dee I was a reasonable and assured woman. A man's word could not destroy my self-regard. I was but eighteen and I had already defied Brigham Young! Now, in a few short months, I had become one of those pitiable creatures—the woman who begs for her husband's attention and weeps when she is alone. Those who know me today would not recognize me during this period. I take no pride in my former self, but my mission in writing this book would not be served were I to portray myself as always strong, always defiant, always certain of her path. Polygamy undermines even the most resolute.

Such was the pathetic state my husband had reduced me to when I discovered I was carrying my first child.

THE 19TH WIFE

———

CHAPTER TWELVE:
Brigham Rescues Me

I shall refrain from detailing our marital discontent, which went on for the next two years. Our arguments were always of the same variety—Dee noting a young girl, speaking incessantly of her beauty, followed by reports of the two strolling downtown. If only the unfaithful heart could act with originality! Every so often he would mention spending time with Maeve, and my greatest fear was that she would become my sister wife. I endured this for two years, my sole comfort, aside from my mother, coming from my boys, first James Edward and, in 1865, Lorenzo Leonard.

During my recent travels, as I have discussed my personal history from the lectern, many times a woman in the audience has inquired, *Mrs. Young, why did you ever put up with that horrid Mr. Dee?*

Why, indeed? I can offer many reasons, although none is inspiring or that which we expect from our heroines. I was young. I had two small children. I knew no women who had divorced their husbands, and so this option was all but foreign to me. Lastly, I did not wish to admit I had been wrong. These "excuses" are not exceptional, but they reflect my truth, familiar as it may be. Honest Reader, if you peer into your own heart, I know you will understand.

I shall jump forward, then, to an evening in the autumn of 1865, when Dee interrupted a quiet hour in my mother's sitting room by saying, "Ann Eliza, dear, did I mention I passed your old friend

Maeve?"

The boys were playing with wooden blocks on the carpet at my feet. I watched their glossy heads bent over the house they were erecting. James, the elder, was showing his brother the different sizes. They were so pure and free of matrimonial agony!—and I became mournful that they would not remain so forever. They would grow up in Deseret, and suddenly I had a vision of my boys as young men, marrying women one after the next, consuming them with gluttonous speed, inflicting their own version of conjugal tyranny upon undeserving hearts. My boys would become their father.

"Ann Eliza? Did you hear me? I saw Maeve."

"I heard you."

"Now I don't want you to get upset, but I went ahead and asked her to marry me."

"What did she say?"

"To be perfectly honest, it wasn't the first time I asked. I've been in pursuit for many months. But I'm telling you now because this time, ah, yes, this time, she said, 'Let me speak with Brigham.'"

"I see. And if he grants her permission?"

"We'll marry as soon as possible."

"Where will she live? Because she won't be moving in here."

"Yes, you see. The timing could not be better. My tenants have decamped. Gone down to St. George, God bless them. My little house is free. It's not very big, and the stove is old and you have to duck when you climb the stairs, but Maeve doesn't strike me as the kind of girl who cares about those things."

"Not at all."

"Please don't be like that. Maeve has never said a bad word about you. She loves you like a sister."

"Why are you telling me all this?"

"Always in a rush, aren't you? All right, then. We both know I can't marry again without your approval. So I'm asking for it. There you are. After this, I won't ask for another thing."

The next day I called at the Lion House. More than two years had passed since I had been there, but little appeared different. True, there was a new rotation of wives and visitors, along with the attendant children and widowed mothers &etc. Yet the mood was as I had left it: the dim halls, the constant patter of feet on the stairs, the girls whispering behind open books. On my way to Maeve's room I passed Aunt Twiss. "We've missed you," she said, weighed down with a basket of wash.

I confronted Maeve immediately. "You've seen Dee," I said.

"Yes, he's been plastering downstairs for a month. Did he tell you I sent my good word?"

But I would not be deceived by her innocent demeanor. "What did Brigham say?"

"About what?"

"About Dee's proposal?"

"Proposal for what?" Then she understood and her eyes widened into little pools. "Oh, Ann Eliza. You don't think—" She rose to close the door. "It's not what you think."

"Did my husband propose to you, or did he not?"

"I'm telling you, you don't understand. He's proposed to me six or seven times now, and each time I tell him I can't marry him. But he persists."

"Maybe he persists because you encourage him."

"He persists because that's the sort of man he is. His head's thick as his plaster."

"Why did you tell him you would discuss it with Brigham?"

"Because I was tired of his attentions and I knew Brigham would shoo him off. Ann Eliza, can you keep a secret?" It was a clear morning and the early light from the window framed her in a shimmer of white sun. "You mustn't tell anyone, but I'm Brigham's wife."

"What?"

"Number fifty-something or other. For the past six years."

"Why would you marry him?"

"Because I loved him, or thought I did. Now I hate him."

"Then why not leave?"

"Oh, that's why I've missed you." She kissed me. "Yes, why not leave? There are a thousand reasons. I have no money. I know no one outside Mormondom. Leaving would mean leaving my mother as well. Where would I go? How would I get there? What's between here and California? A desert white with bones."

"There must be a way."

"Maybe there is, but what then? And what about later, when I die?"

We both knew such defiance would mean exclusion from Glory. I'd be a reckless friend to advise her to risk her Salvation. "I can't take that chance," said Maeve.

"What did your mother say when he told her he married her daughter?"

"It broke her heart three times. Together her husband, her Church, and her daughter had betrayed her."

I held Maeve, and our old friendship repaired itself with this intimacy. I stayed with her for an hour, then kissed her good-bye. That evening Dee and I were in the parlor of my mother's house. He was busy with the newspaper while I worked my needle. The boys were on the carpet with a yellow ball.

"James," said Dee, folding down his newspaper, "be a big boy and climb up and get your father the dictionary." I told my husband I would do it. "No, let the boy."

"It's too high."

"Let him stand on a chair."

"He'll fall."

"Not if he's careful."

James was so eager to please his father that he dragged a chair to the bookshelf and struggled to stand upon its seat. "James," I said, "get down." But the boy was determined to please his father. "Dee, he's going to fall."

"Let him try. You're bringing him up soft."

We argued some more until little James, not even two years old, was wobbling upon the chair, struggling to reach the dictionary that was higher than his head. It was absurd! I leapt to my feet and pulled the boy from the chair. Dee flew to grab the boy from me. "Let him be!" Our beautiful child was caught in a tug-of-war. Dee yanked on his legs so roughly that the boy began to cry.

My father happened to be visiting that night, discussing financial matters with my mother in the next room. "What's this?" he said, rushing in—my mother half a step behind. He shoved Dee in the shoulder, sending him reeling against the carpet. He landed so hard he popped the air out of the yellow ball, which caused Lorenzo to burst into a fit of laughter. "You don't go around roughing up children," shouted my father. "Not in my house."

After two and a half years, I could no longer hide the true state of my marriage. I told my parents the full and miserable account, and within an hour they asked him to leave. Dee protested, claiming his various rights, but my father dragged him to the wagon and drove him to Salt Lake, depositing him in the street.

In the morning, my father and I went to see Brigham. I maintained my composure as I told the Prophet the intimate details of my marriage. Throughout my story, Brigham maintained a sympathetic gaze. His brow buckled at the most painful parts, and his lip ruffled with true and deep empathy. "You have been treated worse than an animal," he said. "You must divorce him."

"But how?"

"I shall tell you." Brigham proceeded to lay out a legal strategy for me to be rid of Dee. In his power as leader of the Church, he dissolved the marriage at once. But for purposes of custody, he advised me to file for a divorce in the Probate Court of Great Salt Lake County. "I will do whatever I can to facilitate this. I'll write the judge personally. I'll serve as witness. I promise you"—and here he touched me, or so it seemed, with his iron eyes—"that you will be free from this man before Christmas."

On December 23 I gave testimony before the court. Dee failed to appear, and in short order I was divorced from my husband with full custody of my boys. Brigham had honored his promise with such resolution that on Christmas Day I gave thanks to God for the birth of His son and the wise guidance of our Prophet. On that glorious day there was no Saint in all of Mormondom than I who owed more to Brigham Young.

XIII

CONTRACT OF FAITH

WRITTEN DEPOSITION
IN THE CASE OF

———

Ann Eliza Webb Dee Young
Versus
Brigham Young

No. 71189

On this 3rd day of October, 1873, in Salt Lake, in the Territory of Utah, Gilbert Webb personally appeared before me, Judge Albert Hagan, counsel to the plaintiff, Ann Eliza Webb Dee Young, to enter into the record of this Special Examination a written deposition consisting of his Testimony in the matter between the plaintiff and Brigham Young.

I am Gilbert Webb, thirty-nine years old, son of Elizabeth and Chauncey Webb. I received my ordinances in the Nauvoo Temple in January 1846, in the state of Illinois. I presently live in South Cottonwood on my father's land. I work as a shepherd, rancher, and wagon manufacturer. I have two wives, Kate and Annabelle, and eighteen children. My statement, as written here, is limited to my knowledge of, and direct experience with, Brigham Young, President, between the periods of May 1866 and March 1868, leading to my indebtedness to him, and the engagement of my sister, Ann Eliza, to become his 19th wife. With our Heavenly Father watching over, I swear everything I write here is true as far as I know it and I know no other version of these events.

It started on a Sunday in May 1866. My wives and I stopped on the Salt Lake Road under the nine o'clock sun. The Prophet wasn't due for another hour. By my count more than a thousand people had come and a thousand more would come before ten. The valley was green from the grass and out to the East the mountains were blue with morning shade and white on the cap with old snow.

My wives had stitched a welcome banner saying "The Daughters of Zion—Virtue" and held it above our heads on two sticks. Under the locust we could feel the spring chill on our necks but when in the sun it was hot as June and my wives fanned themselves with the leaflets announcing the Prophet's visit to South Cottonwood.

Up the road I could see my ma and pa, along with his wives. Sisters Lydia and Lucinda held a banner that said "Mothers in Israel." Ann Eliza was with them, along with her boys, James and Lorenzo. It looked as if she was holding a banner that read "Hail to the Prophet," but the woman next to her was carrying it. There were so many people it was hard to tell.

After an hour a brass band led Brigham into town, followed by a brigade of children waving sticks with ribbons on the ends, then the hundred carriages in his party escorted by fifty horsemen. People stood three deep along the road and everyone cheered and waved. "Do you see him?" cried Kate, bouncing on her toes. "All I see is a hat in a window." Annabelle set her hand on my shoulder and jumped a foot off the ground. "That's him all right," she said. "I recognize the brim."

I picked up one child after the next, set him on my shoulders, gave him a glimpse of the Prophet, then set him back down and picked up the next. There were twelve then. The oldest was eleven. By the time I hoisted the baby, Brigham was down the road.

We followed Brigham over to the bowery. It was an open-air structure, with a roof of branches held up by columns of white pine. My wives and children filled two benches, leaving no room for me. I stood next to them in the aisle, leaning against one of the columns. Two of the boys were fidgeting, pinching each other on the knee. One of the boys belonged to Kate, the other to Annabelle, but both were mine—I could see my chin on them, dimpled underneath.

When Brigham took the pulpit everyone went silent, even the children. As soon as he started speaking I admit I started thinking about my lambs and how the high the grass was this year and how much they'd bring when they went to slaughter. I must've been day-dreaming for a long time because Brigham was deep in sermon before I heard anything he had to say. On this morning two themes interested him above the rest—the fashion of the women and the drinking habits of the men. When he gets going on something it's hard to know if he'll ever stop.

"My goodness, Sisters, if another one of you comes to me to discuss the fashions of the Gentiles, I shall tell you, Go, dress like the Gentile woman, appear as the whore, if that is what you want. You tell me about the hoops and the heart-shaped collars and the silks that cling and reveal the shapes of all of you; you ask why you cannot wear what the women of Paris wear, what the women of New York wear. By all means, you may wear the fashions of New York, the couture of Paris. If that is what you want. And if it is what you want, than you shall understand why I must assume you also want to be known as the whore. So be it. Sister-whores, order as you like from the Eastern catalogs! Dress as you if you were walking up Broadway! But in doing so, know that you are not a Sister to me, and you are not a Latter-day Saint. So ponder your choice in garment, Sisters. For the cloth on your back reveals much more than your lovely shape."

Hearing the Prophet talk of women's hoops got one of my boys snickering. The wives tried to settle him, but the boy was worked up. He laughed until Brigham called him out: "Young man, why is this funny?" Brigham was sixty-six, fat and vigorous, with a large head that went red and dark when he condemned his people. His chins and mustaches quivered when he cried my boy's name. The boy didn't peep again all day.

"Brothers, you laugh when I talk about our Sisters' interest in frippery? You nod in agreement that our women are choosing satin over Saintliness? But what about you? You, Brothers, your sins are worse, far worse. For although our women debase their bodies when they don a dress that enhances their tother ends, you, Brothers, you debase your souls when you drown your days in whiskey and rye. If the Sisters worship at the altar of the catalog, you, Brothers, kneel before the bottle and the barrel. Each drink shall be remembered. Each sip shall be tallied. Each swallow shall swallow you!"

I looked to survey my brood. Kate's eyes had glazed over. I gathered she was pondering the rolls of Boston wallpaper Dalby's had put out for sale. Annabelle was upright and alert with envy for Mrs. Ball's quail-feathered bonnet bobbing across the aisle. I looked forward to hearing all about it at the supper table. My twelve children were asleep, propped against one another or slumped over in their mothers' laps. Little Gilbert lay like a pup on the ground. Sometimes I could not believe they were mine. Certainly twelve is not a record. In Deseret twelve children causes no comment. Sometime soon Annabelle or Kate would announce a thirteenth. The fourteenth could not be far behind.

For a while now I sensed Brigham was looking down in my direction. True I enjoyed whiskey as much as the next man, but no more so, not enough for Brigham to call me out. In the last year only once did Jamison have to dump me at the door too drunk to walk. I've never lifted my hand to either wife and by God never to my children. So why was Brigham gazing my way? His eyes shone the way the sun catches a scar on a plow's blade. Perhaps a false rumor had spread and reached his ear. I'd seen it happen—stories passing as if they were fact and men condemned because of it. I try not to ask too much of my wives but if I hear them sharing out tittle-tattle I tell them to stop and go back and clean up their debris. I once heard my pa say, Live by rumor, die by it too. And so it be.

Now, with Brigham's stare on me, I figured someone I didn't know to count as my enemy had gone about twisting up my name.

Yet I came to see he wasn't looking at me but admiring my sister standing near-by. Ann Eliza was twenty-one now and more beautiful than ever. I am no poet and can't depict beauty and won't try. Since divorcing Dee she had turned down half a dozen marriage proposals. More than a few men had come to tell me of their desire to take my sister's hand.

After the services, we all walked home to my ma's house for supper. Along the way, the Presidential Carriage pulled up. Brigham stepped down and asked Ann Eliza if he might walk with her.

My brood and I were twenty paces behind this scene. We could see them plainly but the wind was wrong for us to hear. My wives galloped forward, dragging the children and me, stopping ten paces from their target, where we were close enough to pick up their words.

"You've never looked finer," Brigham remarked.

"You've never sounded angrier," said my sister. "When you return to Salt Lake, please send my best to Mrs. Young."

If Brigham grimaced or winced, I could not see it. "They ask after you. They remember you fondly from your stay."

"I remember some of them quite fondly as well." Each time my sister jabbed the Prophet with her words, my wives looked at each other with quick-moving eyes that spoke a language all their own.

"Do you think you'll ever remarry?" Brigham asked.

"I hope not."

"What if it were your duty to marry again?"

"Thankfully it isn't."

Brigham took Lorenzo in his arms. As he continued to walk with my sister, more and more people speculated on the nature of his interest. Kate whispered her theory: "I guess it's time for a new wife. It's been nearly a year."

"He's chasing the wrong hoop," said Annabelle. "He's the last man in Utah she'd ever marry."

"She *says* that. But look at her!"

Without my wives I would have been at a loss for interpretation. My ma's house was near and I could tell you exactly what was on my wives' minds: Would Ann Eliza invite the Prophet in for supper? Before a decision had to be made, my ma swooped in to invite him to supper.

Following the meal Brigham asked my pa and me to meet him in my ma's house for a discussion. After some talk about the May grasses and the water levels, Brigham tore into his purpose. "Chauncey, Friend, I've known your daughter since she was a babe. I've watched her grow from child to woman. When she met Dee I tried to warn her but she wouldn't listen. I would've married her myself, but I'd just only recently taken Amelia as my wife. Washington was after me just then, going on about my wives. It wasn't the right time for another marriage. I can't tell you how it strained me to watch that man abuse her. And those boys. I shall make those boys mine." Brigham implored my pa for some time. He didn't think to address me. It didn't matter, I didn't want to be a part of it. Brigham finished his appeal with a promise. "I'll treat her well."

"How will your wives treat her?" said my pa.

"They love her. When she stayed with them, they took her in."

"That's not what she says," I said. "She was lonely."

"Lonely?" said Brigham. "In the Lion House?"

"That's what she said."

"Did she?" asked my pa.

"She was very young," said Brigham. "It was her first time away from her mother. Of course she'd be lonely. But this time, no, she'll have me, and the boys, and Mrs. Webb, if she wants, she can come live with us. You know how much I love Sister Elizabeth."

My pa thought about all this. "Maybe you should ask her now."

"No," said Brigham. "First I need you to agree. If she doesn't care for the Lion House, I'll set her up in a fine home of her own, furnished as she likes, and provide her with five hundred dollars a year.

Each boy will have a room. I have a house in mind—it's not far from mine. There's a tree out back with an elbow where the boys can build a tree house. I'll help them. Think of it—your daughter will have a husband. Your grandsons will have a father."

"You should ask her," said my pa.

"Yes, but how does it sound to you?"

"I can't talk about it anymore without consulting her."

"Let's say seven hundred and fifty dollars. Will that be enough?"

"I don't know."

"One thousand? How's that?"

"Brother Brigham, I can't speak for my daughter."

"Yes, but will you recommend it?"

"I can only present it," said my pa.

Our meeting lasted an hour. "Walk me to my carriage," he said to me upon conclusion. At the road, the Prophet asked about my family. "How many children are there now? Ten, eleven?"

"Twelve."

"That's a lot of mouths. It can strain a man. I see you still live on your pa's land and tend his sheep."

"That's right."

"You need a little fortune to come your way."

"Doesn't everyone?"

"How much do I pay you for your sheep?" I told him my deal with the Church's butchery. "Let's improve it, shall we? Another dollar?"

"I'd appreciate that."

The Prophet rested his hand on my arm. "Now I need your help. Will you tell your sister to take my offer?"

"It's a good offer," I said. "But that doesn't mean it's good for her."

When I returned to the house my pa was already telling Ann Eliza about the Prophet's proposal. "I'm afraid he loves you," he said.

"Did he say that?"

"In his own way."

"His own way is to love one woman, then the next, then the next again."

My ma entered the fray. "Ann Eliza, settle down. You act like he's come to lock you up."

"Hasn't he? Isn't that what he wants—for me to be one of a hundred wives?"

"He doesn't have a hundred wives," said my ma.

"No? Then how many?"

"That's enough," said my ma. "All Brigham's done is propose."

Ann Eliza cooled her fury. "Mother, I know you love him. And I love him too, but as my Prophet, not my husband."

"You think you're smarter than everyone," my ma said. "But you're not. I'm not blind. I know Brigham has his weaknesses, but do they erase everything good he's ever done?"

I went out into the kitchen yard. I had no more desire to be with my wives than I had to be back in that argument. My only place it seemed was outside in the night. The moon was up and lit the path to my cottage. The cattle were lowing and the sheep were bleating and the night was empty but noisy too. I could smell the rye in the paddock and last year's hay in the barn. It was cold, and the cold gathered in the stones of the path.

When my wives greeted me at the door, I stopped them before they could begin. "Not tonight," I said. "Not tonight."

They offered milk and cake but I was not hungry and asked the women to let me alone. They retreated to their bedrooms, one door latching, then the next. Upstairs the children slept, four boys across the Mormon sofa, two babes bundled in the cradle, the rest divided between two beds. I had a vision of myself in the future, five or six years along, gone silver in the beard, another six or eight children under my roof. And if I were foolish enough, maybe another wife. What was to stop it—this terrible vision of my future days? When I thought of happiness I thought of my horse bending to drink from a stream. I thought of a meadow where the only chatter came from the jays and the squirrels. I thought of a bedroll under the stars. I thought of stretching out beneath the night, falling asleep alone.

I drifted off in my chair but woke at midnight. Sunday was my night of rest from my women and typically I slept in the bed behind the kitchen, but I didn't want to lie down there tonight. I went outside. The wind had kicked up, throwing around the cold. There was a dew that'd go to frost by dawn. Inside the barn my sorrel greeted me with a sneeze. The barn smelled of hay and manure and cold water in the metal trough. I climbed up into the hay loft, disturbing a hen. I lay down and propped my head in a saddle and threw a striped saddle blanket over my chest. A barn cat with a bend in its tail tiptoed through the straw and climbed on top of me. His paws delicately dented my belly and his bent tail flapped my face. A stranger might think I had argued with my wives, sleeping in the loft like that, but I hadn't argued with anyone. I was very tired and the cat curled up and pulled his tail up alongside him. He was very small and in need of milk and he didn't weigh anything at all on my chest where he slept, going up and down, up and down.

Over the next two years my wives gave me three more children. First Annabelle, then Kate, then Annabelle again. A boy and two girls. I loved them as much as a man can divide up his heart among fifteen. It's a queer feeling, slicing up affection like a wheel of cheese. I've heard them say the heart's bottomless but I don't agree. I love my boys and girls but when my mind is clear I have to admit I wish I could give out more love. There's another queer feeling to it too. A man isn't meant to greet a new baby at the rate of more than one a year. But the men of Deseret got to adjust. Sometimes you get two a year. If you've got three wives, that might mean three. It goes on from there. I felt myself moving on in years faster than I should. I was already hard in the bone and tired, like a man who's winding down too soon.

Course the more children my wives gave me, the more I needed my pa to fish me out. I relied mostly on him for my land, my house, my wagons and teams, my sheep and the hands I hired, and my accounts at the store and the granary. Even my horse was his, a nice little sorrel with front socks and heavy feet. When money went tight, I borrowed from a neighbor or took credit at the hardware. I always meant to pay down my own debts but it never worked out. My pa would hear about my holes and fill them in.

That's how it went for a long time and that was how it was going to be. I knew this as a fact when the latest baby was born. She was a dense little thing with a carrot swirl of hair. Holding my fifteenth child for the first time I became sick with a feeling that I'd failed. When I was a young man on Mission with my pa, I'd lie awake in our bed and picture myself as a husband. As I pictured it, I owned a small board house in a meadow with a tin chimney. It was so clear in my mind I could even picture the white smoke puffing from the chimney in the cold spring air. I saw the mountains big and shiny above the house and my wife working the vegetable patch while I plowed the field. I saw a babe in a basket napping in the sunlight. I imagined a supper table set for two with the plates turned down. Those were my dreams.

Soon after the baby's arrival I went to see Kate in her room. It was her night. I found her waiting on the bed in her nightdress and the bonnet with the braided ribbon. "Shut the door," she said. "We need to talk."

Yet she had said enough—another baby was coming. It was clear.

I looked out the window. It was early spring and the final winter storm was coming. You could see it from the way the moon burned behind the clouds. My wife came to my side. Her fingers played with my sleeve. "You're supposed to be happy."

I don't know how much longer I stood at the window. Might've been an hour. I don't know. The mountains were black and hidden but even when you can't see them you know they're there. For a long time I was ashamed to look at my wife. When I turned around I couldn't see anything but the white bonnet crumpled in her hands.

It snowed nearly a foot that night, but by daybreak the sun was up and already melting the pack on the southern roof. When I went out the path to my pa's house was hidden, but from the way the wind was blowing soon it would clear. I waved to Ann Eliza out on her porch. She was in a green dress and the green was strong against the house's white boards and the snow. She had done it. I reminded myself of that. She had escaped a life she did not want.

I rode out to Lark's Meadow, my horse chopping through the snow. Lark's is a long narrow meadow with a timber of white pine on one side and the foothills on the other. The mountains stand tall over it, and half the meadow can go marshy in the spring. It was a good spot for sheep because of the grass and the water and the shade.

When I reached the meadow I pulled up for a look. The sun was just then clearing the mountains and the snow hadn't begun to melt. Everything looked hard and cold like in January and the white pines bent with the snow on the bough and the creek ran with ice. The log cabin at the far end was white with snow and it looked like no one had been to the meadow in some time and that wasn't right.

I rode down to the cabin and tied my horse. "Harkness?" I called.

"It's about time!" Harkness yelled from inside the cabin.

When I opened the door I found him roped to a chair. "What happened here?"

"First get me out of these damn ropes." They'd worked the rope around Harkness a dozen times. The knot was tight and the cold made it stiff and unworkable and I had to cut the rope. When Harkness was free he jumped around the room getting the blood back to his legs. "Thought I'd freeze to my death in that damn chair."

"How many?" I said.

"Two."

"That's all?"

"The wind was picking up and I didn't hear them ride in. They were carrying, each with a Winchester and a pistol."

"What time was it?"

"About an hour before the snow."

"Local," I said.

"How do you know?"

"They were waiting for a storm to cover their tracks. They seem familiar?"

"Not really. But they knew what they were doing. They had them all rounded up and out the gate in a couple of minutes. Had a few dogs with them showing the way."

"Meanwhile you sat in that chair."

"Waiting for you, Sister."

"It's not funny. I just lost a hundred sheep."

"And I nearly lost my legs tied down in this cold."

"Here's my handkerchief. Go have a cry and come back when you can tell me who they were."

"They were two rustlers just like you imagine them. Quick in their dealings and good on a horse and real comfortable holding a gun."

I built a fire in the stove. I boiled some coffee and fried a pair of sausages and we ate without talking. Outside the sky was clear and the sun was strong. When I left the meadow was green again and springy under foot. You could smell the pine resin burning off the wet trees in the sun.

Eventually Harkness found my sheep out on Van Etten's land, up in a high pasture a mile off the road. Their brands had been burned over but if you looked you could see what had come first. Van Etten had been suspected of rustling a couple of times before. No one trusted him much, he was known for reporting false crimes to Brigham's office. When I went to see Van Etten he denied knowing anything. He puffed up his chest but I told him I knew my sheep. "If you don't stop accusing me," he said, "I'll go to the Prophet." He was wearing his rifle but I was madder than I could remember. "I'll go to him myself," I said, and that's what I did.

I rode up to Salt Lake and took my place on line outside the Beehive House. When it was my turn I told Brigham my business.

"If you're certain," he said, "then I'll speak to the man." A clerk in armbands interrupted Brigham to sign some papers. As he went about scratching off his name, he asked after my family. "I understand you've had more children. No one can accuse you of not doing your part. I hope you're managing." I told him I was. "Glad to know it. Now you'll send my regards to your sister?"

I told him I would and got up to leave.

"In a hurry?" He laughed, his flesh pressing against the buttons of his coat. "Sit down and tell me your plans. You've lost a hundred sheep. That must be difficult for a man in your position."

"It'd be difficult for any man."

He went quiet. Anyone could see his mind turning behind his eyes. "What do you know about telegraph poles?"

"They go in the ground."

"That's about all you need to know. How many teams do you have?"

"Ten wagons and sixty mules."

"That might not be enough."

"For what?"

"I need a man to deliver poles to the line my son's running down to Denver."

"I can do it."

"They're moving fast, making twenty-five miles a week."

"I can do it."

"How does two dollars and fifty cents a pole sound? Cut, shaped, and delivered."

This was the type of deal a man waits most of his life for. There was good timber at Lark's Meadow. If I hired enough men and bought a few more teams it would work out all right. Brigham and

I went over the details but it was all pretty clear. I'd set up a mill in the meadow to debark them and plane them and dry them in the sun, then treat them with the creosote. The teams would deliver them to the line. I knew I could do as fine a job as any man in Utah. We shook on the deal.

Cutting and curing a telegraph pole is a simple process. Most any man with a good team and strong timber and quick saws can do it. The only special requirement is capital. For the men and the extra wagons and provisions I needed $11,000. I borrowed half the money from a Gentile banker named Walter Karr and the other half from a Mormon banker named Alfred Eagleton, at 5 percent a month. The job would be complete by mid-summer. After paying back the loan I'd have plenty to build out my house and keep my wives happy a few more years. I got ahead of myself and for one night thought about taking another wife. The truth is I'm as weak as the next man, maybe more.

My wives were happy with the news. "We'll help out by making your men their meals," said Kate. She was showing under her apron, and for the first time the sight of her belly made me glad. "I'll fix up the food in the morning, and Annabelle will drive it out to Lark's."

"And I'll give 'em each half a peach a day," said Annabelle. "Nothing like my peaches to make a man want to work."

It didn't take long for us to reach twenty-five miles a week. The men laying the poles weren't my men but we liked working together. With each delivery they said my poles were good, well-planed poles with a base as wide as it should be. They knew what was coming, which means they could dig their holes better and faster and stand the poles the right way. The job ran easy and smooth for everyone and I think everyone working on that line felt the way you do when you know well-earned money's coming your way.

By July we were nearing Denver. That's when Brigham called me to his office. I thought he was going to pay off the job in advance because my work was quality work and everyone said so. "You've done such a fine job," he said. "I want you to take over the line running to Montana. They're in real trouble and might not finish this year. I'll give you three dollars for every pole delivered, and a dollar for standing it in the ground."

A man who's recently made real money has but one inclination, and that's to make more. That same day I drove a load of poles north myself. I spent about two weeks straightening out the job and pulling up the bad poles and filling in old holes and digging new ones. On the Denver line the Prophet's office paid me twice a month. But once I started driving north the payments stopped. I needed those deposits to pay my men. After three weeks I was low and could barely pay them out. After four weeks I spent everything I had to keep the men on the roll and the line extending north.

When I went to see Brigham about the dried-up payments, his secretary kept me waiting for a long time and then told me to come back the next day. The next day it was the same. I couldn't wait another day in Salt Lake. I needed to ride back up to the job. Even though I wasn't being paid I knew I couldn't stop driving the line. In summer winter feels far away, but not if you've got a line of poles to get in the ground before frost. That's what I was thinking as I left Salt Lake, and that's all. I never thought I'd never see my money. I've seen swindling up close. I've heard all about it and always shook my head, wondering how a man could be so foolish to hand out his money to a crook, because a crook looks like a crook and talks like one too. And that's how I thought about swindling. I don't have the kind of mind to imagine the Prophet cheating, and I'm both sorry and glad I don't.

It took a month to see the Prophet. By then I couldn't hold down my anger. My men were chewing me up and some had walked off and the job was behind. They accused me of swindling and some talked of stealing my teams. When I finally got to see Brigham, I blew apart. "I've got thirty men laying your poles and I haven't seen a penny from you since I sent them north."

"From what I hear, your poles are rotting. On top of that you're behind schedule. Now why would you expect me to pay for that?"

That's when I lost my head. I leapt across his desk and fisted his lapels, shaking him hard. "Give me my money!"

"Get off me." He shoved at me but I held on.

"You're cheating me," I said, "and you know you're cheating me, and there's nothing worse than a cheat who knows he's doing it."

Brigham put together enough force to throw me down. I was on the carpet with my hat bent beneath me. He looked as fresh as he does on Sunday morning. "What about our deal?" I muttered.

"Produce a contract, and I'll honor it."

"You never offered one."

"That's because one isn't necessary among old friends. Brother Gilbert, I will pay you as soon as you've earned it."

Two clerks appeared to escort me from the Beehive House. They dumped me on the curb at the head of the line. Everyone on the street was looking at me. It's not every day a man gets thrown out of the Beehive House. "He's a liar!" I yelled, warning anyone who could hear. "He's a cheat and a liar!" The men on line pretended not to listen and I know for certain each of them couldn't wait to get home to repeat the story at the supper table. I'm sure the story moved up and down Deseret faster than if it had been sent on our telegraph.

The next day I rode up to the job to explain everything to my men. When I got there my foreman pulled me aside. "Thank God you're here." I asked him the trouble. "The poles, they're rotting off at the ends." We walked a line of poles. At each one he pointed up and it was true, indeed the top was black and soft. I asked my man what was wrong. "One of two things. Either the curing didn't take . . ."

"Or?"

"Or sabotage."

I didn't know what to think, not then or now. I gathered my men up and told them the job was done. I explained as best I could the circumstances, but I no longer understood them as well as I'd thought. The men didn't care about my troubles, whether my timber hadn't cured or Brigham wasn't paying or anything. "I'm a pole layer," said one, "and I've laid your damn poles." They spoke angrily, cursing my name and this damn job. They were rough men of the West, used to settling debts by any means. They surrounded me—maybe thirty at once—and they demanded to know what I was going to do. "Give me two days," I told them. One man, a con from Nevada, said he wouldn't wait a third.

To pay my men I sold my teams and my gear and the little bit of land my pa had given me. I sold everything I could to clear up my men enough so they would never call me a cheat and a liar. I asked my bankers for a deal to pay off the debt. Karr agreed to forgive the remaining money if I paid half. But Eagleton wanted all his money and interest and penalties too. I can't blame him for it, but I didn't have it. When Brigham heard, he was angry I favored the Gentile banker over Eagleton. He spoke about it in a sermon. "There's a brother here who feels he owes more to a Gentile than a Saint. I ask you: Would you trust him?" I didn't favor anyone but that's how Brigham saw it and how most people saw it, too.

By the spring of '68 I was bankrupt and facing legal suits. Eagleton, with the Prophet's blessing, was coming after me. Debt's a cruel hole. The more you try to climb out of it, the more it caves in on you. That's what I learned. And don't go into business with the Church. There's no way to wind up on the right side.

So with all this behind me, was I surprised to see the Presidential Carriage in my ma's yard that day in April? I'd been expecting it for some time. I heard it from the barn—the wheels squealing, the leather reins twisting, the horses clopping to a stop. The door swung open and the Prophet eased himself out with one hand on the roof. The carriage swayed with him as he stepped down and the springs groaned and the horses flicked and twitched. My ma came out of her house and I came out of the barn and we met the Prophet on the path. "Sister Elizabeth, I've come to warn you about your son," he said. "He owes a good Saint money. He's wrongfully accused a close friend of rustling sheep. He's cheated me with a bad job. Something's got in him, Sister. I'll have to take steps."

"I'm paying out what I can," I said. "And those sheep were mine."

"Brother, you're not acting like a Saint."

"Brigham," my ma said, "neither are you." My ma says she's never been angrier in her life. You might wonder why she didn't quit the Church then, but she's not like that. She's always saying she lives in the middle, where everything has two meanings, and the shades are gray. Besides, she had witnessed too much to give up now.

"Consider yourself warned." Brigham climbed into his carriage and it tipped with his weight. He shouted to his driver and the team bucked and lunged forward and the carriage swung around and drove up the white dirt road to Salt Lake.

"He's not the same," said my ma. She was white with anger. "He used to be another man." I told her not to worry, but we both knew there was plenty to worry over.

Two days the letter arrived.

Sir—

Let it be known that in consideration of your recent actions, and your refusal to acknowledge outstanding debts and false claims of slander and libel, your challenges against fellow Saints and honest men stand, from this day forward, as challenges to the Church itself and therefore as apostasy. A board, chaired by myself, shall gather to determine your future participation in our beloved Church, both today and in the Everafter. Any appeal should be made to me directly; otherwise you shall receive notice of the date and time of your trial.

I remain most respectfully &c. your Prophet—
BRIGHAM YOUNG

I rode up to Salt Lake. By now the rains were mostly gone and on both sides of the road the grasses were high. Most of the time I go along, doing what comes up next, but this time I knew I had to go a particular way. At the Beehive House I told the secretary my name. He was a thin old man with a long blue nose and old yellow hair. If you threw him on a scale I bet he didn't weigh a hundred pounds. There was a long list of men waiting to see the Prophet but the man told me to wait in the hall, Brigham would see me right away.

The hall was decorated with a red and blue runner and a glass lamp hanging from the ceiling on three little chains. How many times had I been there in the last year? Six or eight or more. Most men don't have any business with the Prophet except listening to him on Sundays and reading the proclamations and every now and then making an appeal for a plural wife. I thought of that dream I once had: the house in the meadow, the smoke in the chimney, the wife, and the child. It all felt far away.

When I met Brigham he said, "I haven't yet set your trial date."

"What do I need to do?"

Brigham perched on the corner of his desk. He wasn't going to say any more until I broke down. He wanted me in a puddle on his carpet, and there I went: "I don't want to leave. I've got my family, my wives, my children. Where will I go?"

I'm ashamed to say I wept in his office. He stood by, letting me crack up like a woman. When my face was streaked and bent up, he passed me a handkerchief with his monogram in gold. "What do you want?" he said.

"I want to be a good man."

"I can help you."

A few minutes passed with Brigham pacing and going to his window and looking out at the front garden and returning to his desk to review the paper at the top of the pile. The whole time I sat in a heap in his visitor's chair, wiping up my face.

"Ever since your sister was a child," he began, "I've seen her as my own. I've protected her, watched out for her, made sure your family was tended to. I invited her to live next door to be near me. I asked her to join my theater so I could look at her every night. All of your troubles will be gone if you can convince her to marry me. I'm sure it's impossible for her brother to see her beauty as I do: but she's the most splendid woman who's ever set foot in Deseret. Her eyes, her throat, her skin."

There's something to see in a grown man gushing like a boy. If I hadn't been in so much trouble myself, I'd have been disgusted by it and told him so.

"Go to your sister, tell her of my qualities, convince her that she will never want for anything. I'll give her a house, I'll care for her children, she'll have an allowance and freedom. Anything she wants will be hers, but she must be mine."

"She doesn't listen to anyone."

"Make her." He shook his mouth out like a twitching horse. "You know women: they can be brought home and tamed."

"I'm not sure that's true."

"Trust me, it is, I should know."

"And my debts?"

"Forgiven. Your position in the Church: restored. Your name: exalted. Your financial situation: vastly improved. I'll pay you an allowance to help you meet your family needs. What do you need? A thousand a year? Two? I'll give it to you. You tell me what you need, but bring me your sister."

"I can't force her."

"That's not what I want. I want her to see for herself what I can give. I think she fears marriage will somehow restrict her. In fact, it will be just the opposite. Make her see this. That's all I ask."

He stood in his window. His beard appeared pink in the sunlight and his cheeks were full and red. "Gilbert, have you thought about taking another wife?"

"Not much."

"In this scenario, you can if you like. If you find a woman to join your household, you'll be able to invite her in." He was so overcome by anticipation, I thought he might kiss me. "You'll speak to her?"

"I'll try."

"Go now." He led me to the door. He didn't open it until he'd made his final plea. "Go now, and when you've succeeded come to me."

"And if I can't?"

"You will. I know you, and I know her."

He showed me into the waiting hall and thanked me. Outside I stood on the steps of Brigham's house for some time. I could see into the window of his office. He was behind his desk, conducting business and negotiating something or other with his next visitor. Might've been a railroad deal or a building contract or might've been a bargain concerning a man's soul. It was always from one to the next with Brigham Young.

I went to Ann Eliza's house. I found her in the kitchen, feeding the boys. They were fussing over the food and throwing peas about, and my sister looked harried. "What is it?" she said. I told her I'd come back later. I went to the barn and lay down in the hay loft and lay there for some time thinking. The barn cat came over and curled up on my chest and went to sleep.

In the evening I went back to Ann Eliza. "You look upset about something," she said. I told her I'd come from the Beehive House. I described my conversation with Brigham, and as she came to understand it she became very still and sad.

"I'm leaving tonight," I said.

"Leaving?"

"Before he can kick me out."

"What about Kate and Annabelle? What about the children?"

"They'll get on. Pa will look after them. I can't stay. Brigham's made that clear."

"What will happen to you after?"

"I don't know." My sister wasn't asking about after I left the Utah Territory and the Church. She meant after death in the beyond.

We understood eternity to be a welcoming place only for the Saints. This is what we believed. It's all we believed to be true.

"You can't," she said.

"I don't have a choice."

"I do," she said.

"I won't let you."

"I've made up my mind."

"Ann Eliza, please—" I pleaded with my sister for an hour or more but she had made her decision. I didn't want her to, I never wanted her to, but I'm an honest man and I will admit here down in the deepest crevice of my heart I felt a throb of relief. I dislike myself for feeling it, but it's true.

The next day Ann Eliza accepted Brigham's proposal and soon they married and that's how my sister became the 19th wife. If it weren't for me it would never have been so, and this is the truth as far as I know it and I swear by it, and for this I've never felt more ashamed.

XIV

———

WIFE #19:

OFF THE STRIP

AND I SHOULD HELP YOU BECAUSE—?

So Johnny was gone and Elektra and I were on our own. No big deal, we were used to it. And I'm not just saying that. In the morning we drove out to Kanab. It was nice enough—the hot wind and the am radio playing *redneck woman* and the quiet that comes when you're alone. I got to thinking about things. Like what I was hoping for.

The Mega Bite wasn't open yet but 5 was behind the counter laying out the cold cuts. The ceiling lights cast a sickly green on everything. She was pale and green and the slices of ham and turkey looked green too. Eventually she saw me in the window and came to unlock the door. I told her I wanted a turkey club but she said, "You didn't drive all the way out here for a fucking sandwich."

"Maybe not."

"How's the sleuthing going? Find your killer?"

I told her not yet but in a way that didn't reveal much.

"Got it," she said. "You don't want to share any clues with a girl who's got a fishy story."

"Maybe."

"Save yourself the time, I had nothing to do with it." She stopped. "You know what they say: follow the pussy."

"Isn't it follow the money?"

"Same thing." She finished making the sandwich and pulled a long knife to slice it in half. "You talk to my mom yet?"

"Yes," I said. "Did you talk to her?"

"Not in a while. How is she?"

"Shaken up."

"I know, it's crazy. I think she actually loved the guy." After a moment 5 set her elbow on the counter and planted her chin into the heel of her palm. "While you're out nosing around, I wish you could answer the real mystery."

"What's that?"

"Why?"

"Why what?"

"Why do they keep on believing all this crap? Where's the skepticism? Why don't they ask themselves—just once, that's all it would take—why none of it makes sense?"

"If it's the only thing you know—"

"No, that's not it. I mean, sure, yeah, if it's all you know it's hard to imagine anything else. But I'm talking about something different. I'm talking about why they never once have any suspicion that something's not right. You don't need to know anything to have a doubt. You just need to listen. To yourself. Why are so many people lousy at listening to themselves?"

"Maybe they're scared."

"Of what?"

"Of death. Of what comes after."

"And I'm not?" The more we talked, the less certain I was of where she fit into all this. "That reminds me, there's this website you might want to check out: 19thwife.com. It's some antipolygamy group. I guess they help women escape and do legal work and stuff like that. Maybe they can help your mom. But for all I know it could be a trap. Anyway, check it out. Oops, time to open up. Morning rush." She unlocked the door to let in a man and his college-age son. The boy was all arm and leg, with an Adam's apple the size of a rock. The boy inhaled his muffin the way you or I would eat a nut. When they were gone, 5 said, "You liked him."

"He was cute, so what?"

"You need to get laid."

"Tell me about it. But first I need to get my mom out of jail."

"I wish I could help you."

"Then tell me what you know about that night."

"I already told you: nothing. I wasn't there." I know I blush bad, but 5 went as red as the peppers in the prep tray. "I can't help you," she said. "I don't know anything about what happened to your dad."

"He was your dad, too."

"Stepdad. Look, I got to get to work. See you around." She shouldered her way through the swinging doors, into the kitchen with the canned tomatoes and a fresh delivery of presliced ham.

On my way back to St. George, a cop pulled me over. I was going eight, maybe ten miles above the limit, but that's not what this was about. We both knew it, each of us sitting behind our wheels at the side of the road. The cop stayed in his cruiser for a long time doing paperwork. His lightbars were spinning blue and red, and they got Elektra jumping around barking at the rear window and the fur on her back was up like a brush.

The brim of the cop's hat hid his face and the late morning sun made it hard to see anything. When he stepped out of the cruiser the sun was behind him and all I could see was a black cutout coming toward me. Elektra lost it, showing her teeth and howling like she was ready to sacrifice herself in my defense. I tried to calm her but she sensed I was scared. "It's all right," I said, but you can't lie to dogs.

"I'm sure you know why I'm pulling you over."

"Why don't you tell me."

Elektra shoved her snout out the window and began licking the cop's hand. "Hello, puppy." I handed him my license. He cupped it in his hand almost like it was something delicate that might blow away, then handed it back. "Here you go, Jordan."

"My registration's in here somewhere," I said.

"That's all right. Why don't you step out of the van."

"Why?"

"Just step out of the van."

"OK."

"Now let's go back to the station."

"Why? What's back there?"

"C'mon, leash up the dog and let's go."

"I'm not going anywhere."

"Jordan." The guy touched my arm. He looked familiar, but almost everyone in Mesadale looks familiar. He was about thirty, a regular guy in decent shape, like a JCPenney underwear model. "I think it's time you and I had a talk."

When I got out of the van, I saw who I was dealing with. Shield number 714, Mesadale Police Department, Alton. Well, there you go.

"Is something wrong with Queenie?"

"She's fine. Everything's fine. You and I just need to have a little chat."

"Can't we talk right here?"

"C'mon, let's go." I got Elektra on her leash and we followed Alton back to the cruiser. The lightbars were still spinning and Elektra was tugging at the leash. She didn't like any of this and she didn't want to get in the car. The highway was empty and it was eleven in the morning and I'd bet a buck it was already 110 out on the asphalt. The poor girl, her paws must've been burning up.

Elektra and I rode in back, watching the road through the grill. This was my first time in the back of a police cruiser, and you know what—it sucks. There's something about looking out at the world through a steel grill. Even if you haven't done anything, you feel guilty. A voice came across the police radio and Alton spoke into his mike, saying something about home.

"Am I under arrest?" I asked.

Officer Alton laughed. "You're not under arrest."

"I know, silly mistake, crazy me. It's just that I'm in the back of a cruiser talking to you through a cage."

He didn't say anything else until we pulled into the police station lot. "Just follow me."

"What about Elektra?"

"Bring her in."

I walked with her close at my side while Alton kept me close to his. His hand was at my elbow, but it was a weird proximity. It wasn't like I was being apprehended, but it wasn't like I was free to go.

"Do you want to tell me what's going on?" I said.

"In a minute."

In the station we passed a desk manned by a cop who looked like Alton, only redder in the face. "I'm going into three," Alton said.

"What do you got?"

"POI."

"I'll tell the captain."

Officer Alton shook his head. "Not yet. Let me figure out what he is."

"Want me to take the dog?"

Alton shook his head. "We'll keep her." He led me down a hall and into a small room with a table and two plastic chairs. "Have a seat."

"I get it," I said. "Interrogation room number three."

"This isn't an interrogation."

"What's that—a two-way mirror?"

"It is."

"Who's on the other side? The whole police force?"

"No."

"Maybe the Prophet himself?"

Alton dragged a chair around so it was next to the other and sat down. He set his hat on the table and his forehead was dented with a red band. "Fine, don't sit. But I thought it would be more comfortable for you. Jordan, would you stop looking at the mirror. No one's on the other side."

"I'm not quite ready to believe you."

"Maybe you should."

"Why don't you first tell me what this is all about."

"I know you've been to see my wife."

I once saw a movie about this guy accused of killing his girl-friend. When they hauled him in he kept saying to himself, Don't say anything, don't say anything. He thought it so hard that those words appeared on the two-way mirror and for the rest of the in-terrogation he kept looking at those words. In the end, the cops got nothing and they had to let him go. The thing was, the guy actually killed his girlfriend, strangled her with her sweater, and that's how it ended, the guy being released into the world.

"Jordan?"

"Yeah."

"Queenie told me you wanted to know why the investigation's still open."

"You checked the no box."

"Can I talk to you not as a member of law enforcement, but as a"—he searched for the word—"as a friend. The Prophet, he wanted me to talk to you."

"Me?"

"He thinks you're right."

"Right about what?"

"He thinks someone else killed your dad."

This was either going really well or I was totally fucked. "Why does he think that?"

"Because it doesn't make sense to him either. Your mom, she never liked making a fuss. Why would she start now? The Prophet knows you've been snooping around. Turns out he's got the same questions as you."

"So why'd you bring me here?"

"You look like you could use something to drink. I'll be right back."

When he left I looked at myself in the mirror. My eyes were what I saw—not my hair or my nose or my skinny arms. Just my eyes. They seemed to float on the smoked glass.

Alton came back with two waxed paper cups of apple juice. He set the cups on the table and I took mine. It was a small cup, like what you use at a water cooler. The juice was golden pink and clear. Alton gulped his down and swiped his mouth with the back of his hand. "Man, I love apple juice." And then, "You're not drinking yours?"

Now might be a good time to tell you about the vitamins. Sometimes at school they would pass out vitamins. Each kid got a waxed paper cup with a pink vitamin rolling around the bottom. Once I remember they passed out cups with a pink powder in it. The room monitor filled each cup with apple juice and made us drink it. He said it was fluoride for our teeth, but it tasted like baking soda. The vitamins made you feel groggy and you'd go kinda blank for a couple of hours. Not exactly passed out, but not really there either. I still don't know why they did that to us. Maybe they played more of the Prophet's tapes while we were drugged, with him talking about murder and stuff like that. Maybe they raped the girls. I really don't know. Once I saw a kid refuse to take his vitamin. They hauled him out into the school courtyard and lashed him with a horsewhip. He still refused. That night he was kicked out. The chance of that kid still being alive is slim to none.

I pushed the cup away. "No thanks."

"You sure?"

"So the Prophet thinks I might be right about my mom?"

"That's right, and that leaves him concerned."

"I have a hard time believing he's concerned about my mom rotting in jail."

"Well, that too, but what I was referring to is, if she didn't do it, the killer's still out there."

"And he's scared he might be next on the list."

"In a nutshell, yes." Alton leaned forward, his face close to mine. I could smell his sweat and the white-bar soap he used to wash his hands. "He thought maybe you and he could help each other."

"Let me get this straight: the guy excommunicates me and now he wants my help?"

"You might want his as well."

"I doubt it."

"He knows everything about this town, where everyone is, who's doing what, everything."

"Everything except who killed my dad."

"Look, you both want the same thing. You want your mom out of jail and the Prophet wants the killer. It's a win-win."

"No such thing. Give me one good reason why I should make a deal with the guy who ruined my life."

"Because he could save your mom."

He handed me a slip of paper with a phone number on it. The handwriting was so bad you'd think a six-year-old had scrawled it out. I pushed it back to him. "Keep it," he said, but I already had it memorized.

"You'll take me back to my van?"

Elektra and I followed him down the hall and out the station door. Overhead the sun blazed, reflecting against the white concrete, and for a second everything flashed white and I couldn't see. I lost my way and had to reach for Alton.

"Here," he said. "Take this," and the cop offered his big stone of a hand.

Welcome to 19thwife.com! We're the only online community (as far as we know!) of ex-plural wives (and their children) telling THE TRUTH about polygamy in America today! We take our name from Ann Eliza Young, who fought to end polygamy in the US in the 19th century. She was a totally bad-ass chick! To join, click here. To read, scroll down.

Posted by GirlNumber5 (July 2)

Can someone please explain to me how the LDS guys go around saying all the Doctrine & Covenants are the word of God and that Joseph Smith heard them through revelation but put an asterisk on that because it turns out Joseph was all wrong about the one that deals with polygamy. Huh? So if that one's a mistake, what's to say all the others are true? I mean, isn't that why the Firsts, as much as I hate them, in some ways don't they actually make more sense than the Mormons? They believe in all the D&Cs, they don't pick and choose. How can the Mormons go around *editing* God? If you ask me, it proves the whole thing, whether LDS or Firsts or whatever, is a piece of crap. But I'm open to persuasion (doubtful).

(11 responses)

Posted by KADeeBYU (July 6)

There's a big difference in what you're talking about. First of all you're taking everything out of context. Second the D&C you're referring to, Section 132, was revised and repudiated by President Woodruff, when he released his Manifesto on October 6, 1890. What you're not understanding is that our theology is not static. It's an evolving, changing entity, which is wholly consistent with the way things work in life. Why should religious doctrine be static when nothing in the natural world, including Man, is static? Throughout time, in every culture, religions and theologies of all sects and creeds have always evolved. They have to. Those that don't inevitably die out. Please don't make the mistake of equating the Latter-day Saints of today with the Firsts. Although our faiths originate from the same doctrines, long ago we chose separate paths, which is why we now stand so far apart.

Posted by GirlNumber5 (July 7)

Huh? Either the D&Cs are the word of God or they aren't. You can't have it both ways Baby.

A FRIEND IN THE NIGHT

———

As soon as my cell picked up a signal, I called Maureen. "Why would the Prophet want my help?"

No response.

"Maureen, what do you think?"

"I'm sorry, my granddaughter and her roommate are here visiting. We're out on the patio and it's hard to hear."

"I know I probably shouldn't call you on a Saturday. I just felt like telling someone about this."

"And I'm glad you did. I know Mr. Heber will want to hear all about it on Monday. Or will you be back in California by then?"

"I don't know."

"Either way, let him know." I heard a splash, like someone jumping in a pool. "I should go now."

"Maureen, is everything all right?" She said everything was fine, but I could tell it wasn't, not really.

When Elektra and I walked into A Woman Sconed, the goth girl barely looked up from her manga. "The computer's down," she said. "You can try the lobby of the Malibu Inn, they have a computer for guests. Just go in and pretend you're staying there. They won't say anything if you act cool. The day manager's chill. Hey, where's your brother?"

"He's not my brother."

"I know the feeling," and she flipped a page.

It was that time of day when few people are around a place like the Malibu Inn. Last night's guests had checked out and tonight's were still on the road. The guy behind the desk said, "Can I help you?"

"I'm just going to use the computer for a second."

"Are you staying with us?"

"Not really."

"The computer's for guests only."

"Since no one's around would you mind if I hopped on for a few minutes? I need to check my email."

He was a neat guy, his polo tucked snugly into ironed khakis. Maybe twenty-five, yellow hair flicked up into little gelled spikes— nothing too punk, but just a tiny bit cool. "Oh, all right," he said. "But if a guest needs to use it, you'll have to get off."

"Fair enough."

The way the computer was set up, my back was to him. It was an old machine and it took a while to get a connection. I could feel the guy's eyes on me, and just when I felt like I needed to turn around he said, "By the way, my name's Tom. In case you need anything."

"Thanks. Jordan here."

At last I got into my email box. A message from Alexandra with lots of chatter about her cats and kids and a guarantee: "I make a mean macaroni." Tons of spam, but my program filters most of it out. That's how I ended up deleting the email from DesertMissy. I only know about it now. Had I opened it, I would've saved myself a lot of trouble and close to five hundred credit card bucks in gas. But let's put that on hold.

"I thought you might want a coke." I was so startled by the gesture, I didn't respond. "Or a diet coke?"

"If you have one, yeah."

"Sure, that's what I drink, too." The guy dropped two tokens into the coke machine. "So where's home for you?"

"California."

"Nice. Me, I'm originally from Provo, but I've been down here a while."

He seemed to want to talk about his life and I didn't want to talk about mine, so I let him go. "I started out in room service at the property in Cedar City. That was five years ago. Then I became a night clerk and eventually assistant manager, and then the owner transferred me down here. He set me up pretty well. You know what the crazy part is?" I couldn't imagine. "I was planning on leaving Utah. Probably for California. Like you."

"Maybe one day."

"I mean, St. George isn't exactly the dream location for a single gay guy."

Was I being hit on in the lobby of the Malibu Inn?

"LDS?" he said.

"Sort of," I said. "But not anymore."

"Yeah, me too. I was kicked out when I was twenty. What about you? Did they kick you out or did you quit before they could do it?"

"I was definitely kicked out."

"I know, I was so shocked because I wasn't even really out to myself." The guy stopped, as if all the thoughts about his past were pressing inside his head. Then his eyes came back to life. "What're you doing later on? Want to get together or something? I'm off at six." I tried to make an excuse, but I came up blank. "Meet me here around seven. Room 112. We'll go out."

"You live here?"

"Yeah, they put me up. It's not as nice as it sounds." Tom appeared so cleanhearted and gentle that I felt something stir in my chest, and I was shocked by the sentiment. I'm definitely not a romantic kind of guy. The last time I had a date was never.

"Awesome. I'm really looking forward to it. Now I should get back to work. They start rolling in about now." On cue, a dusty motor home pulled into the Malibu's portico.

I was headed over to the pool when I saw Mr. Heber's Lexus in his office lot. I had to ring twice before he came to the door. He looked surprised to see me. Surprised to see anyone. He was in a pair of golf shorts and bare feet, and his reading glasses were up on his head. "I'm sorry to disturb you on Saturday," I said, "but I saw your car."

"That's all right. I try to sneak in here for a few hours on the weekend to get ahead." While he led me back to his office, I told him about Alton and the Prophet. "What do you think?"

"I want you to be careful, Jordan."

"Do you think I should talk to him?"

"That might be hard to do."

"Why's that?"

"I was going to tell you this on Monday. The Prophet's now officially a wanted man. The feds finally got off their duffs and put out a warrant for his arrest. He's wanted on sexual assault on a minor, conspiracy to commit sexual assault on a minor, and racketeering. They went out to Mesadale last night."

"He's in jail?"

"They couldn't find him."

"Couldn't find him? He was right there yesterday afternoon."

"I'm sure he was, but no one's talking. Here, let me show you." Mr. Heber turned his monitor and got onto the FBI's site. On the Wanted by the FBI page, there was a grainy picture of the Prophet. He wasn't on the Most Wanted list, but he was a Featured Fugitive, and his picture was right beneath Osama bin Laden's.

"That's an old picture," I said.

"It's all they got." He clicked on it and brought up the Prophet's rap sheet.

DESCRIPTION

DATE OF BIRTH USED: August 19 1936 or December 25 1941 or December 25 1946

PLACE OF BIRTH: Unknown

HEIGHT: 5'7" or 5'9"

WEIGHT: 145–155 pounds

OCCUPATION: Unknown

SCARS OR MARKS: None known

HAIR: Brown/light brown or gray

EYES: Blue or gray

SEX: Male

RACE: White

REMARKS: Suspect may be residing in or around Mesadale, Utah; also has ties to Arizona, Nevada, Texas, Idaho, and northern Mexico

SHOULD BE CONSIDERED ARMED AND DANGEROUS

"Why now?" I said.

"I told you, things've been heating up. Your dad's murder was probably the catalyst. I think they finally realized this is about a lot more than a man sleeping with a bunch of women. Anyway, Jordan, it could all be very good news for your mom."

This seemed like as good a time as any to tell Heber about my visit to the house. I didn't go into details like the fire. "But I managed to get down to his den, and I found this."

I handed him the fuck chart disguised as the Book of Mormon. Mr. Heber fanned through it, stopped to read something, fanned some more. "I already have it. They found it during the search on his hard drive." He dug around a file and pulled a sheet of papers to compare the two copies, flipping between the pages.

"You mean I went through all that to get something you already have?"

"You really should've talked to me first." He kept on flipping between the two charts, matching up the tables and the notations. Then something caught his attention. "Wait a minute, you might have the latest version. Let me make a copy."

We leaned against the copier, waiting for it to warm up. "There's something that's been bugging me about all this," he said.

"What's that?"

"How many wives did your dad actually have?"

"I don't know, twenty-five-ish. But they never tell you that. I think it's a way to keep everything confused. You know, the more confused you are, the less likely you are to realize you're being screwed."

"What's interesting about this marriage management notebook is, if we can believe it—and I think we can—it looks like he had twenty-seven wives." The copier was ready, and he lifted the lid.

"I know this is going to sound screwy," I said, "but if the law doesn't recognize these marriages, then how can it be polygamy in the eyes of the law? It's sort of a chicken-egg situation."

"It's an old dilemma. Goes back to the nineteenth century and Brigham. It's probably why the feds left Mesadale alone for so long. You can see why they're going after the Prophet for racketeering and the stuff with the underage girls. They can get him on that."

"If they catch him."

"The thing about men like the Prophet is they need a stage. They need to tell people what to do. That kind of man can't stay in hiding forever. When he's all alone in a basement or an attic or wherever, he can't run from the truth about himself. He'll come out," said Mr. Heber. "They always do. And when he does, they'll catch him and then it's welcome to the clink."

"And my mom?"

"I'm working on it."

"Any luck?"

"To tell the truth, I'm afraid not."

Tom opened the door to Room 112 and a snowy-faced golden retriever lumbered off the bed. He was a gentle old guy with a white muzzle and a plumed tail. He lifted his paw to scratch my thigh. "That means he likes you," said Tom.

"What's his name?"

"Gosling's Joseph Manna from Heaven."

"What?"

"But everyone calls him Joey."

"He looks like a good boy."

"He is. When I got kicked out I took Joey with me. He's literally the only thing I have from home. I'm lucky Mr. Saluja lets me keep him here, I mean I've had him since I was eleven. Oh, my gosh, I just realized: I don't even know if you like dogs."

"If I like dogs? Hang on a sec." I went out to fetch Elektra from the van. She sensed something was up and switched into a higher gear of spaz, straining on her leash and barking, preparing for a big entrance. She dog-sledded me across the parking lot and exploded into Room 112 in a whirl of canine chaos. You know how dogs get so excited they can't decide what to do? Elektra jumped on the bed, off the bed, back on the bed, slurped out of Joey's water bowl, ran over to Tom with water running out of her jowls, leapt into the air to kiss him, then back to the bowl, back to the bed, and back to Tom's feet, back to the bed, and so on. "Sorry, she's a little nuts at first."

"I never met a dog I didn't love." Joey, on the other hand, wasn't so interested in Elektra. He scooted over to the far side of the bed and lay down with his snout on his paws. "What do you feel like doing tonight? Want to catch a movie?"

Tom was still getting dressed, tucking his shirt into his pants and looping his belt. It was weird to think he lived in a motel room, but I guess no weirder than living out of a van. He started looking up the movie times on his laptop. He was sitting and I leaned over from behind. Turns out he's the kind of guy who wears cologne, which I usually hate, but on him it was sorta nice. Cinnamon and cedar. Maybe some lemon and smoke.

"Don't hate me if it's lame," he said, "but I kinda want to see that movie about the retarded kid and the missing dad."

We got ready to leave, filling the dog bowls with water and telling them to be good, and there was a tiny moment when we looked at each other. We were thinking the same thing, we could kiss and fuck right now and skip the movie. But I don't know, it didn't seem like the right thing to do, which totally isn't like me. Anyway, outside in the parking lot there was a little tussle over who should drive—he thought my van looked cool, but I didn't want

him in my van because, well, I was living out of it and that's probably not the best information to reveal on a first date. In the end I
won and we drove to the cineplex in his tidy toyota.

"So what happened with you and the church?" he said.

"It's a little complicated."

"It always is." He was fiddling with the radio and stopped when
he found a song by the Killers. "For me it happened my sophomore
year. I was at BYU, and you know what that place can be like. I was
up in Salt Lake with my soccer team and one night I just kind of
gave in and went to a gay bar. It was my first time ever in a place
like that. I mean, I hadn't even kissed a guy or anything, but I knew,
and I wanted to go. And guess what: someone saw me. I'm still not
sure who, but they sent an anonymous letter to my bishop outing
me. The bishop sent a really scary letter to my parents and pretty
soon it was all over. What a flippin' mess."

"That sucks."

"What about you? Did you have a trial?"

"Not exactly."

"I did. I mean, the works. I had to go before this committee who
were all these guys I've known my whole life like my baseball coach
and the guy who used to drive my carpool. And they were all sitting behind this table and I was sitting on this metal folding chair
and they just came out and asked me—was I a homosexual? On my
way into the trial I thought I was going to lie. It never occurred to
me to confess, because I knew what that would mean. Good-bye
life as you know it. But when they asked the question like that, and
it really did feel like a trial and everything, it just hit me: I can't lie,
not if it's true. So I said, Yes. My coach said, Do you know what
this means? And again I said, Yes. Nothing more. And so he goes,
Do you realize with this confession you'll lose many things, but
none more important than the salvation of your soul? And so you
know what I said? I said, What do you want me to do about it?
And that was it. Excommunicated. My parents cut me off. And
that's how I ended up at the Malibu Inn. The owner's from India,

and he doesn't care about anything except how I do my job."

"That's messed up."

"Tell me about it. But it had to happen. There are a lot of things I don't know, but one thing I know for sure is those men weren't speaking for God. They say they were, but they weren't. God isn't like that, not my God, anyway." He turned into the cineplex parking lot. "Now what about you?"

"The thing is," I said, "I'm not LDS. I'm a First. Or was. I'm from Mesadale."

"A First? No kidding. That's crazy. You mean like a gazillion wives and everything?"

"Yep, a gazillion wives and everything."

Almost anyone will tell you if your mom's in jail for killing your dad, it's probably a bad idea to talk about it on the first date. Which is probably why I told Tom everything right there in the cineplex lot. When I finished he said, "Shoot, that's a lot to deal with." And then, "There's no way this movie's going to be more interesting than our own lives."

He was right, the movie wasn't any good—a retarded kid, an absent father, a bitter reunion, a reconciliation. None of it true. Halfway through I took Tom's hand. It felt like the hand of a gentle, capable man. I was pretty surprised that such a hand belonging to such a man was warming up in my clutch, but there it was and here we were and some things sour only if you think about them too much. During the credits, just before the lights came up, Tom leaned over to kiss me.

"I think I like you," he said.

And that's when I heard Johnny say, "No PDA, dude."

I turned around. Two rows back, Johnny's eyes shined in the dark. He was alone, his T-shirt filthy with popcorn lint. He heaved with the pure enthusiasm of a lost dog returning to his master. Slowly the house lights came up on his jackass smile and he said, "Aren't you going to introduce me to your man?"

LDS ARCHIVES

THE LION HOUSE COLLECTION
Restricted Access—Access Must Be Approved
by the First Presidency

Some of Brigham's wives developed a system of private communication within the Lion House. Two sister wives, or sometimes more, would circulate a copy of the Book of Mormon, into which they would crosshatch a private conversation about topics such as their children, the other wives, and domestic business like cooking, keeping house, and social gossip heard at Brigham's store. Most often, however, the subject was their mutual husband, Brigham. On file here is an approximate transcript of a private dialogue between two of Brigham's wives written in a kind of shorthand across the pages of the Book of Alma. From the events discussed we know it dates to the spring of 1868, shortly before Brigham's marriage to Ann Eliza Webb. Due to the cramped, unnatural style of handwriting, we cannot identify with any certainty which of Brigham's wives wrote these words.

—He's after another.
—It was only a matter of time. Does Amelia know?
—I doubt it. He'll tell her only when it's too late.
—I'd like to see her face when she finds out she has a new rival. So much for everlasting beauty.
—Guess who the new one is.
—I'm not familiar with the girls of Salt Lake.
—Remember the actress?
—Say it isn't so. She thinks she's the queen of something.
—I hope she enjoys her position at Number 19.

—I thought he tried to reel her in before, but the fish fought him on the line.

—I heard he set a trap for her.

—She'll make a fine counterpoint to Amelia.

—That's the only consolation. He was always longing for her, wasn't he? Even when she lived here, his eyes always followed her around the room.

—He never knows when his eyes are popping out of his head.

—If only it were his eyes sticking out from his person.

—I'd scold you if it wasn't true.

—Although I see a silver lining in arrival of the 19th.

—What?

—He's less likely to come knocking on my door.

—He hasn't knocked at mine in eight years.

—See, Brigham is correct—God does indeed hear our prayers!

OFF THE STRIP

———

"Every Sunday?"

"Every Sunday," said Tom. "Ten a.m."

It was eight in the morning and we were on our way to Vegas for—you're not going to believe this—church.

"What if you're tired?"

"I drag my ass out of bed and I go. That's what it means to make a commitment."

"But Vegas? For church?"

"What's a two-hour drive when it's something you believe in? Besides, what else am I going to do on a Sunday morning?"

"I don't know, lie in bed and fuck?"

"You know what I mean." He rocked my shoulder the way you do when someone's told a good joke. "Besides, I love this drive. Look at those mountains. You know God's been hard at work when you see those."

OK, so we weren't a perfect match. I didn't expect this to last long anyway. They never do. But we'd had a good time last night. I stayed over at the Malibu and Tom put Johnny up in a room next door and, well, we got up early for church.

"So this church," I said. "It's for gay Mormons?"

"It's actually for anyone, but that's generally who comes."

"Isn't a gay Mormon like an oxymoron?"

"Do I look like an oxymoron to you?"

"An oxymormon."

"I think you'll find it's a really nice place."

"I don't get it. If the Mormons don't want you in their church, why do you want to be in their church?"

"I don't want to be in their church. I want my faith. That's all. I don't need to go to their temples to have my faith."

Out on East Sahara Boulevard, two miles off the strip, we pulled into a third-rate shopping center. The church shared a parking lot with an insurance agent, a massage parlor, and a head shop. Tom turned off the engine and kissed me. "Happy fifteen-hour anniversary."

"This is by far the longest relationship I've ever had."

"Are you always this romantic?"

"Usually."

"Come on, let's go inside. And try to enjoy yourself."

"I'll try, but church and I have some bad blood."

"That wasn't a church, that was a cult. You can't let one con man with a thing for teenage girls go and ruin all the love Christ put in your life."

Should I go home now? I didn't say that, it'd be too cruel. Tom was too good for that sort of ridicule. Besides, he didn't talk about Jesus all the time. Just often enough to make me wonder if we'd last another fifteen hours.

"Look, I know you're always internally rolling your eyes when I talk about Christ—I can see it, Jordan—but I'm sorry, that's just who I am." He kissed me again. "Besides, I know that's what you like about me, deep down, I can see it behind your sneer."

Who was this guy? I could go over his physical inventory, his green eyes and how they changed to gray at night, his Matt Damon smile, a mouth literally crammed with teeth, his slim waist and grabable ass. Is that why I spent the night with him in 112? Or was it an even more basic need: he had a bed and a shower and a tv, and he liked kids and dogs, especially Elektra, who right now was curled up on a wide motel mattress in front of the a/c with the tv on and kibble in her bowl? Or was it something else?

Tom leaned into the backseat and shook Johnny's arm. "Time to get up, big boy, we're here."

Johnny yawned. "Where?"

"Church, chop-chop."

"You can't be serious?" Johnny sat up halfway and rubbed his eye with a fist. "I thought you were kidding."

"Why else would we drive to Vegas on a Sunday morning?"

"I don't know, hookers?"

"Not today. Now get up."

Johnny flopped back down onto the seat and pulled his Raiders ski cap over his eyes. "Dude, wake me when it's over."

"Tom," I said, "Forget it. He'll be fine out here."

"No, no, no. I didn't drive all this way just so you could sleep in the car."

"What difference does it make?"

"Why don't you go in and find out."

"Dude," said Johnny. "You sure you're into this guy?"

"Tell him to get up," said Tom.

They were both looking at me as if I had some control over the situation. "He doesn't listen to me. Let him sleep."

"He's just putting on a show. He wants to go in, he just won't admit it."

Tom got out of the car and opened the back door. He plucked the cap off Johnny's head. The kid's hair shot up with static. "What the fuck?"

"Tom, this is crazy," I said. "We're not his parents. He can do what he wants."

Tom looked a little defeated. "Jordan, it's not going to hurt him to sit there for an hour."

"I don't want to be the only kid," said Johnny.

"You won't be."

"I thought this was a gay church."

"Gays can have kids."

"Tom, man, I hate to break it to you, but you and Jordan aren't having kids, I don't care how hard you try."

"Tom, let's just go inside. He's fine out here." I got out of the car and started walking.

"Then why'd he want to come with us, anyway?"

"Because he didn't want to be alone."

We walked through the door. A man in a leather vest and a bushy mustache descended upon us. "Tom! Who is *this*?"

"This is Jordan. He's my—"

His what?

"My new best friend."

"Jordan, welcome to our church." The man hugged me, which wasn't so unusual because other people were greeting and hugging, but this guy whispered into my ear, "I hope you find the peace and love God wants you to have," while squeezing my ass.

When the guy was gone I said, "He felt me up."

"He did not."

"I'm telling you, he did."

The church looked like a bingo hall or a senior citizens' center. A blank space with a dropped ceiling, bad lighting, and coffee stains in the carpet. The color scheme reminded me of the lobby of the Malibu Inn, purple on beige with hunter green accents. Some queen had stenciled a garland of grapes around the walls. The whole thing depressed me. I know, how does a guy who's been living out of his van get off calling anything tacky? But it was.

Tom waved at a lot of people and they came over to hug him and shake my hand. "You have a lot of friends," I said.

"And what could possibly be wrong with that?"

It's pointless to argue with someone so logical. Still, he seemed to know everyone—the chatty dyke in Hello Kitty suspenders, the diabetic guy on the mobility cart, the kid with the safety pin in his eyebrow who wasn't much older than Johnny. His name was Lawrence; two weeks ago this little church helped him off the streets. "Thanks in part to Tom," he said shyly. Tom denied doing anything out of the ordinary. "All I did was make a phone call. You got the job yourself." Lawrence's patchy, anxious face was an assortment of pimples and whiskers and lingering hurt. He pressed together his courage to tell me, "You're real lucky, man."

When the service started the pastor asked if there were any special visitors who needed an introduction. "Tom. Please don't."

But it was too late. Tom was on his feet saying he was here with me. The congregation—there were about seventy-five people—said "Hi Jordan" or "Welcome Jordan" or "Amen."

"Jordan," Tom said through his teeth "stand up."

I rose and lifted my hand for a little wave. Everyone waved back and several people applauded as if I'd actually accomplished something. Am I a hater for cringing?

There were a few other guests there—a mother visiting from Fresno; a friend in from Albuquerque. Everyone waved and called out hello and it was no big deal. Really, what was the point of getting embarrassed? As Tom likes to say, It's just life.

"Before we start," said Pastor Wayne, "does anyone have a praise they want to share?"

A slight woman in heavy denim jumped to her feet. "Yes, thanks." She wore a big, out-of-date phone clipped to her belt, a buckle that said, "Kick Ass!" and a pair of hearing aids. "As many of you know, Tiger had his operation this week and thanks to God everything went just fine. He was home the next day and I was able to take the drain out after only four days, even though the vet told me it would take a week." She went on a little longer about Tiger's condition and a lot of people said "Amen" and several people raised their arms as if invisible wires were pulling them from above.

A couple of other people shared their praises—a medical test that came back all right, the return of an estranged child, a new job: the usual stuff that is so common that you sometimes forget these events define our lives. It made me think of something I once read on a billboard: How we spend our days is, of course, how we spend our lives. Is that religion or wisdom? Because I don't go around quoting religion, at least not that I know of.

"Let us now each take a few moments to think about our blessings." That's when Tom put his arm around me. The pastor concluded the moment of silence by declaring, "I personally want to thank God for our new second bathroom! Brothers and Sisters, it's finally finished!" More applause and a lot of amens. "No more sharing a single toilet with a hundred people!"

If you haven't been to church in a while, you might forget how much chatter there is about day-to-day business—the newsletter, the board elections, the day care. I guess it makes sense. It's probably why a lot of people bother: the organization, the community, the belonging, the having something to do. A lot of the people here looked like they'd had a hard time fitting in—the blind dyke; the six-foot-four-inch tranny; the hairy bear ravaged by HIV; this kid Lawrence. As if he were reading my mind, the pastor said, "Most of all, I want to thank God for our sanctuary where everyone is welcome, and where everyone is loved."

The pastor spoke with a curious accent I couldn't quite place, southern regal, something like that. He wore his longish hair oiled back so that it bunched up in little curls at the nape, sort of a gay male version of the do worn by the Queen. He was about forty-five, might've had some eye work, and clearly had the admiration of his congregation.

There's no point in my recounting the service. Except for the lesbian couple passing the offering trays and the ushers in leather chaps and the pretty tranny giving communion, it was more or less familiar. If it had a theological point of view, it was that Christ loves everyone and that Joseph Smith was right—the churches of the world had moved away from Christ's true message of universal love. Look at these people here—they were proof of it. "This is why I still believe," Tom whispered. "This is why I don't need their temples."

He pointed out a quotation in the bulletin:

The one who comes to me, I will certainly not cast out (John 6:37).

(Under that it said, "Please note: All communion stations use grape juice.")

Next the deacon stood up to give the sermon. "Today I want to talk about love," she said. Her name was Irene, and she was a sincere person with limp, practical face. Soon her voice turned to noise in my ear because she was saying what you'd expect: love is the greatest gift, and God's greatest gift to man was Jesus, and that shows how much he loves us, blog, blog, blog.

"But instead of me telling you what I think love is, I decided to ask my students. So here's how a few first, second, and third graders define love." She flipped nervously through some papers.

"The first one's from Christie, who's only seven: 'Last year when my grandma fell and broke her hip she couldn't paint her toenails anymore. So my grandpa started doing it for her, even after he fell and broke his hand. For me, that's love.' " Everyone laughed and it was so ridiculous I chuckled too.

"And Benjamin, who's just six, describes it like this: 'I know someone loves me from how they say my name. Like with my mom and dad, when they say "Benjamin" it's like my name is safe in their mouth.' " More laughter, and a couple of sentimental aaahs.

"This one's from Kevin, age five: 'You know a girl loves a boy and a boy loves a girl when she sprays herself with perfume and he sprays himself with cologne and they go outside and smell each other all over.' "

"Or two girls or two boys," someone in the front row said.

"Absolutely," said Irene. "And Catherine, age six, came up with this definition: 'For the people I love, I'll always give them the last bite of my ice cream without asking for the last bite of theirs.' "

"And Nancy, who's only seven but already a wise soul, says, 'I think the best way to learn how to love is starting with someone you hate.' "

And then Irene said the one that caused me—forgive me—to go to mush inside: "Melanie, who's just four years old, says, 'When my doggy licks my face, even after I've left her outside all day—I know that's love.' "

I couldn't take it anymore. Not because they were so corn-dog, which they were, but because they were true. Kids. They always call it as it is. I hated feeling this way. The combo of love and God was supposed to make me puke—so why were my eyes going misty?

Two things happened that morning in the Vegas LGBT-friendly ex–Mormon church two miles off the strip (try saying that real fast). First, I got to sit through a sermon holding Tom's hand. Big fucking deal, I know, but where in the world do you get to do that? Not many places that call themselves houses of the Lord.

Tom leaned over. "Isn't this nice?"

The second thing was this: halfway through the sermon, the back door opened. Irene stopped and waved. "Come in, don't be shy." It was Johnny, his Raiders cap pulled low on his brow. He climbed over a woman to sit between Tom and me.

"You're such a player," I whispered.

"You know it, dude."

Then he listened as Irene read even more definitions of love.

"Oh, and I really like this one from Justine, who just turned eight: 'You should be careful about saying "I love you" too much. If you don't really mean it the words will lose their value. But if you do mean it, then you can go ahead and say it all the time.'"

"There," said Tom when we were back in the car. "That wasn't so bad."

"Do they always have doughnuts?" Johnny was laying out four apple fritters on the backseat, taking inventory the way a dog hoards his bones.

"They like people to stick around after. They're really into being a community. So what'd you think?"

"I don't know," I said.

"Is that a good 'I don't know' or a bad 'I don't know'?"

"It's an 'I don't know' I don't know. I mean, I'm still not sure it's for me."

"That's OK, as long as you understand that it's for me." He was pulling onto the freeway, maneuvering into the fast lane. For such a clean guy, he was a bit of a maniac driver. "Utah, here we come."

He started fiddling with the radio, searching for NPR. "Boy, do I love Sundays. So what do you want to do when we get back? We could go for a hike when it cools down."

"I'm not really much of a hiker. I don't really like the desert."

"Around here," said Johnny, "that's like a fucking problem."

"Want to catch a movie?"

"I might have some things to do," I said.

"Jordan, is anything wrong?"

I don't know about you, but I hate the phrase *nicest guy in the world. I just met the nicest guy in the world.* As if. But now it seemed true. So why was I being such an ass?

"I was just thinking about my mom," I said.

"When can you see her next?"

"Tuesday. That is, if I'm still around. I have a job that starts tomorrow."

Tom didn't say anything but a man doesn't have to speak to reveal his wound. After a while he pulled over at a parking area. He got out and walked several yards into the desert. Johnny ran after him and unzipped a few yards from Tom. He was talking over his shoulder, yapping about something or other, then a gust of wind came along, billowing the arc of his piss. Johnny laughed and kept on talking and shook off and hopped over to Tom's side for the walk back to the car. He was very small next to Tom, a pipsqueak of a kid looking way up into the eyes of a man. Tom rubbed Johnny's head. When he pulled his hand away, the spring of Johnny's cowlick popped back up.

Johnny fell asleep for the rest of the drive and Tom stayed quiet. Ten minutes before St. George, we cut through the Virgin River Gorge, and Tom said, "I want you to stay."

I didn't say anything. Not a word. When we pulled into the Malibu, Tom said, "I see."

He and Johnny went swimming. I stayed in Room 112 with the dogs and went online to check out that site 5 was talking about. It was a community/resource page for people dealing with polygamy one way or another. I clicked the tab that said, If You Need Help. Tom had left the History Channel on, and while I read the website a navy crew was preparing to launch a missile from the deck of a battleship. When the missile was fired, a white yellow plume of fire shot out of its tail. That's when Tom came back to the room, dripping in his suit. The missile's fire flashed in his face. He watched it until the missile hit its target, blowing up a warehouse in the desert. "I was going to enlist," he said. "After college. Wanted to be an admiral."

"Really? Why?"

"I wanted to serve my country. So much for making plans." He changed into dry clothes, then lay down on the bed. "What're your plans?"

"I'm going back," I said.

"To California?"

"To Mesadale."

"All right."

"I mean now."

"I'll go with you."

"No, you stay with Johnny."

"We'll all go."

"I should go by myself."

"Should, or want to?"

"I don't know." You know what's the craziest part of living in a house with a hundred people? It trains you to be alone.

"You sure it's safe?"

"No."

"Let me go with you."

"No, you stay here."

"Jordan?"

"What?"

"What are you looking for?" I tried to answer, but the words didn't come. Lying on his side, his head resting on his elbow, he looked like an ad for packs of t-shirts and tube socks. "I know what you're thinking," he said. "You're thinking we hardly know each other. And that's true. But everybody has to start somewhere."

I got up and opened the curtains. They were gold and backed by a heavy sheet of plastic. Johnny was lying on the concrete rim of the pool, his eyes closed, one foot tapping along to Tom's ipod.

"Jordan, don't overthink everything. You'll talk yourself out of a life."

"This isn't about you, Tom."

"I want you to make it about me."

Later, driving out of St. George, I called the number Alton gave me. "It's Jordan Scott."

There was a pause. Then, "Come to the house." He hung up. That was it. The Prophet and I had a date.

The sun was going down before I reached Mesadale, a livid ball plunging from the sky. The desert was burning, everything shot through with reds. In the last twenty miles I didn't see another car. That's what the desert's about: solitude. It's a test. A test to see if you can stand yourself.

I reached the turnoff. The last of the light was gone now, and the desert cried under the yellow moon. My headlights swept the hard dirt and behind the van the dust coughed up into the black. Up the road the big houses were lit up, gold and white lights in the windows and above the doors. How many did the feds knock on before they gave up? One more and would they have found their man? Taken the Prophet in? Booked him? Put him on secure visits like my mom? Why can't the FBI find this guy, while he's inviting me to his house? Is that fucked up or what?

Questions lead to questions. Answers aren't really answers. Mysteries don't get solved. Isn't that what it's all about? Knowing almost nothing. Accepting the unknowable as the end of the story? The end of life?

Maybe.

But if so, then why did I believe in the bottom of my heart I was this close to finding out who shot my dad and stuck the rap on my mom?

XV

———

THE PROPHET'S WIFE

THE 19TH WIFE

CHAPTER SIXTEEN:
My Wedding Day

On April 6, 1868, I married Brigham Young in a secret ceremony in the Endowment House. The only witness was the old-timer Bishop who performed the rites. In a matter of minutes, I had become a Mrs. Brigham Young.

My first task as the Prophet's wife was to accompany him to a small community across the Valley that had found itself torn apart by tragedy. A few days before, two boys, brothers no less, had drowned in a swollen creek. The boys' mother had begged her local Bishop for an explanation, but the man had failed to console the woman in her time of grief. His inadequacy set off a public meeting of complaints about the Church, Brigham, and the unreliability of God. "What will you say to these people?" I asked Brigham.

"I'll tell them what I know," he said. "And what I don't know, which is a lot. It's all I can do."

Our marriage was one hour old, and I found myself touched by Brigham's willingness to reveal his modesty to me. Brigham pushed his face out the carriage window to take in the breeze. The day was clear and cold, and the afternoon light colored the snow on the western mountains blue and on the eastern front the snow was pink and gold. Watching him, I must confess to a certain fondness, in the way one might feel toward an old, not especially close acquaintance who has maneuvered a place into the heart simply through the longevity of his presence.

As we approached our destination, the shadows off the mountains darkened great patches of the valley and Brigham became somber. "I read the report," he said, staring at the empty space before him. "The two boys struggled for some time. The mother watched them cling to a branch. She wanted to jump in herself, but her sister wife held her down. Was she right to do so? Was there any chance of saving the boys? I can't blame them for wanting answers."

At the village nearly fifty agitated Saints awaited us. There was not a proper Meeting House, so Brigham stood before the community in the home of a local farmer. "If I could give you the answer that would heal your grief," he said, "and alleviate your sorrow—if I could explain the role of your boys' lives and deaths in the context of all things, then I would not be a man standing before you, then I would be our Heavenly Father Himself. But I am not He, nor is any man He, and therefore I cannot tell you what you so desperately want to know. But over time, with prayer and faith, you will come to understand, and your heart will know, even if your mind cannot, that these boys lived and died with purpose, and now await you in the Kingdom above."

When it was time to depart, the sorrowful mother kissed Brigham's fingers. As our carriage left the little hamlet, she ran behind it as far as she could, crying, "God bless you, Brigham, God bless!" Her transparent voice echoed across the blushing land.

For some time the carriage groaned along the rutted road, the wheels creaking, the leather snapping, the driver clicking and calling at his team. We were deep in the basin, surrounded by young scrub and new grass and the lonely cattle bent in search for early leaf. I interrupted our quiet by saying, "May I ask a question?"

"Of course, anything."

"What number am I?"

Brigham reached for my hand to warm it between his. "Number?"

"Which wife?"

"It's distasteful to me to put a number next to you, or any

woman."

"I appreciate that. But I'd like to know."

"In that case, you are number nineteen."

"Nineteen? What about the others?"

"Others?"

"At the Lion House?"

"They're friends, but not wives."

"But I've heard—"

"Ann Eliza, you'll hear many things now that you're my wife."

"Nineteen, really? That's all?"

"Nineteen. Really. That's all."

As we drove on, dusk poured into the valley and I fell asleep. When I woke it was dark. "You're a beautiful creature when you sleep," said Brigham, stroking my arm. The carriage curtains had been drawn, and I moved away from my husband to reopen them. The night was without a moon, and the Valley was black and empty. Other than the driver we were alone.

"You don't like me?" said Brigham.

"It's not that."

"Then what?" He shifted toward me, the great bulk of him tilting the carriage on its groaning springs. The horseman slowed his team, adjusting for the shifting cargo. I suspect he was used to this sort of situation. Lurching closer, Brigham attempted to kiss me. Soon he was on me, struggling with my garments, crying, "Tell me you've always wanted me as I've wanted you!" He pressed me into the corner of the carriage. "Knock, knock, I'm at your door!"

"Brigham, please—" But his animal had been set free from its cage. I turned my head, pressed my cheek to the curtain, and prayed.

Dear Reader!

I speak the truth when I tell you it was at this moment my dress ripped. The bodice tore, exposing my sacred undergarments. According to Brigham himself, a woman must never reveal them to a man, even her husband. Eliza Snow had penned a letter to the women of Zion on the subject: "At the time of connubiality, the wife must open a slot in her sacred garments no bigger than necessary to permit the husband his entry. At no time should she preen before him in anything less than what she might wear on the street, nor reveal to neither his eyes nor hands what lay beneath."

Married half a day, I had already violated my husband's doctrines. "Turn the other way," I demanded. "Please don't look at me."

Brigham was stunned, apologizing, "I don't know what happened." He tried to fig-leaf my breast with the torn cloth.

"Turn around!"

"Yes, yes, of course."

His animal had retreated to its lair, and Brigham sat beside me, deflated. "I should drive you home," he said. He rang a bell, his signal, I would later learn, to the horseman to stop circling and head onward to his destination.

When we arrived at my mother's house Brigham said, "I'll send my man in, have your mother come out here, and you can ask her to bring you another garment." He leapt from the carriage. I could hear him speak to the driver, who then trotted to the front door. I could see my mother at her threshold, peering around the man to the carriage. They spoke briefly and she walked with some hesitation to the car.

"Ann Eliza? What is it?"

I explained my predicament. "I see," she said. She went into the house, returning with an old dress. When she entered the carriage she looked around at the velvet and the lamps and the mother-of-pearl inlay. I could not tell if she was impressed or appalled. After helping me change, she said, "That should get you from the street to the door."

Brigham tapped the carriage with his walking stick. "Almost ready?"

Through the glass I said, "First I want a word with you." He climbed into the carriage. "Shut the door." He obeyed my command and settled into the seat with an obvious shame. "What has gotten into you?" I demanded.

"I'm sorry, I was overcome. I didn't mean to alarm you, but you can't know how beautiful you are."

"Thank you, but you're not fifteen."

I saw his anger rise, his color deepen, and the eruption begin. Yet he managed to check his passions and the color washed off his face. "I don't mean to offend you."

"It's too late."

"In that case, you'll have to forgive me. That's all I can ask." Brigham Young, the Great Man of the West, had the hurt look of a scolded boy. He stepped down from the carriage and crossed the street, waiting beneath a poplar. An old couple out for a night walk greeted him. They were astonished to see the Prophet in their path. Brigham spoke with them warmly, as if they were old friends, and the couple flattered him, babbling about the quality of his recent sermon.

My mother helped me out of the carriage, but I refused to go inside. I stood at her gate, waiting for my husband's return. "Come on," she said. "Let's go in." Slowly I realized my husband would not say good-bye to me on the street. He stayed with the couple until I was behind the closed door. From inside I watched him run back to the carriage, hopping on his fat tapered legs. The driver snapped his reins. The horses stamped and flicked and lunged. The carriage tore off before Brigham's foot was inside. His arm came out and closed the door behind him, and thus alone I spent my wedding night.

THE 19TH WIFE

———

CHAPTER SEVENTEEN:
The Lonely Wife

I had not seen my husband for three weeks when he came around for a second drive. I tried engaging him in discourse, but he seemed preoccupied in thought. Gradually I came to understand he had not come to engage his new wife in conversation. Once the carriage drew beyond the city limits, Brigham sprang to life, listing across the seat. "Oh, my pet," he moaned, shrugging off his green cape and emitting an odor of the lemon drops he kept in a bowl on his secretary's desk.

Such was our marriage.

For three months our marriage remained a secret affair. Even my boys knew nothing of their mother's new status. I had wanted to tell them, but I could not bring myself to explain the peculiar circumstances. Often I thought of my mother, who had passed through her youth without shame. Yet in my case, whenever I left my husband after an assignation in the carriage, I carried the humiliation of a second-choice whore. Years later, during our divorce, Brigham would accuse me of demanding money at the end of our interludes, but there is no truth to this claim. I received nothing except a rumpled dress, a dented bonnet, and an urgent need to bathe.

During this time, what for most couples is known as the honeymoon, every Sunday I attended services pretending I had no more relation to Brigham than before. Sunday services in Deseret is a time for society to assert itself, and there is a great fuss put into where one sits and with whom. As a divorced woman, my status was lower than that of a widow or virgin. My secret wedding had changed none of this in the eyes of the community of Saints. I would sit with my mother and the boys on a bench at the back, while Brigham preached to his thousands of followers. Up in front, filling a dozen rows, was the brigade of his family—the wives, the daughters, the sons, their wives, and so on. To them, I was nothing more than one more eager disciple in a land filled with some fifty thousand. They paid me no mind.

Each Sunday, invariably, Brigham's sermon turned to the subject of Truth. Nothing winds Brigham up more than this, and he could spin out an hour's worth on the notion without so much as coming up for breath. As he did so each week, I would stew in a juice of shame and worry. If Truth was the key to Glory, as Brigham proclaimed, what did this mean for me? I took a great disliking to myself during this time, and in my thoughts referred to myself as simply No. 19. There were many times I could not look my boys in the face.

Finally, after months of ignominy, Brigham said he was ready to announce me as his 19th wife. "The first thing to do is establish you in a home suited to your position." He drove me to a sad little cottage of uncoated plank where he hoped I would reside happily, waiting for his call. It was furnished with left-overs—I recognized the worn parlor rug from the Lion House, the black-stained lamp from the theater's dressing room, and the chipped crockery from Brigham's bakery. (An acquaintance I made in Washington after my divorce advised me not to dwell on such household matters when recounting my tale. "They're petty," he said. "And you sound petty when you do so." To this I told the esteemed gentleman, "You have, I'm quite certain, never attempted a compote in a leaky pan.")

Sensing my disappointment, my husband said, "You don't like it?" The truth was, I was not upset about the house, if that is the correct word for such a lean-to. Walking about the tiny half-furnished parlor, hearing the echo of my step, I came to understand that I would lead a lonely existence here. True, I would have my boys, but I knew as the Prophet's wife my activities would be monitored and restricted. I could no longer expect to visit with friends as I once did, or stroll down the street alone, or do any of the daily activities that bring a basic kind of enjoyment to the day. I was now a married woman, and would be expected to behave as such, yet unlike most wives I did not have a husband in any sense of the word. I was neither maiden, widow, nor even divorcee. I was a plural wife, and this little house, with the cheap runner on the stairs, represented my conjugal purgatory in such fine relief that I felt a piercing to my heart.

To improve my spirits, Brigham moved my mother into the cottage with my boys. We tried to colonize it as best we could, but it had come with such few supplies that everything about our existence there would be best described as bare.

As one of Brigham's wives I was entitled to monthly rations to be collected at Brigham's Family Store. The store sits behind the Beehive House, and when my mother and I went for the first time there was a long line of women and children running out the door and down the street. Many had brought empty pushcarts and miner's sacks, and the children, proudly aware of their purpose, held hand-baskets with caution and care. A number of Indian women had also come to barter large lidded baskets and other weavings for soap and candles.

At the counter I gave my name to an efficient, wide-bosomed woman who ran her finger down a list. "There you are," she said, and disappeared into the storeroom. She was most likely one of my sister wives, yet our relationship was wholly transactional. She returned with a five-pound sack of beet sugar, a pound of oily candles, a cake of chalky soap, a spool of mending thread, and a small box of white-phosphorous matches.

"What I really need is some cambric," I said.

"So do I, Sister. Anything else?"

Now might be a good time to confess to my Dear Reader that

which, at the time, I was unable to confess to myself. During the
early stages of my marriage I had—I can see now—suppressed my
skepticism. Despite the mounting evidence, I wanted to believe my
marriage to Brigham Young, unorthodox as it was, had some measure of truth to it. I knew he did not love me as a young girl imagines a husband will love his wife. I knew I did not love him in any
profound or cosmic way. Yet marriage has many purposes beyond
the romantic, including the practical and the spiritual. I had hoped
Brigham would be a surrogate father to my boys. I had hoped my
mother's move to my cottage would free her from her rivals. Perhaps more important, I had hoped my proximity to the Church
would blow fresh winds into the sagging sails of my faith. I was still
a daughter of Mormondom, and at night, when I was alone, and
the wind tapped the almond branch against my pane, I continued
to pray.

After many months of marriage Brigham invited me to sup at the
Lion House as his wife. "How will the others greet me?" I asked.

"Frankly, I gave up trying to predict my wives long ago."

On the day of my debut, Brigham asked me to meet him in the
gardens behind his house. Brigham's gardens, it should be said, are
like the estate of a king. Behind a nine-foot wall are acres and acres
of flower beds and walking paths, as well as fruit and nut orchards,
vegetable plots, racks of beehives, and a pigeon house. As I approached the garden at the time of my meeting with my husband,
I saw ten paces before me Sister Amelia, whom I knew only by
face—her youthful beauty cannot be denied—and reputation,
which was so unpleasant, I willed myself not to think of it.

When first planning this memoir, I had no intention of dipping
into the histories of my fellow wives. For one, such digression
would divert my reader for too many pages. For another, each arrived at Brigham's bed in such a unique manner, through individual and sometimes mysterious circumstances, that I could not

accurately represent all their paths. Yet in the case of Amelia Folsom, a diversion seems warranted. I hope my Reader will agree.

She had become the Prophet's 17th wife in 1863, taking, and holding quite firmly, the undisputed position of his favorite. He provided her a private carriage with her initials stenciled in gold on the door, although the other wives walked about the city in the dust. Amelia ordered her silk from France, while Brigham's silkworms spun tirelessly for the rest of us. And most frustrating to her rival wives (I exclude myself from this jealous lot), she visited her husband whenever she desired. She was known to arrive at his office and expel his present guests so that she could be alone with her mate. Most scandalously, I have been told she once demanded a diamond necklace before she would allow Brigham to return to her boudoir. Although this particular anecdote is second-hand, I trust its source, for were you to greet Amelia today you very well might find the diamonds gleaming around her throat.

I also know that she intended to be Brigham's final wife. It was a condition of their marriage. We must give Brigham some credit. He kept his word for two years.

In 1865, not long before he began his campaign for me, Brigham broke his vow to Amelia to wed Mary Van Cott, a fair, strong-minded Saint from a devout family. Mary, who would become a friend, was always kind-hearted and selfless. She knew her presence would hurt Amelia and asked Brigham what she could do to assuage her. "Respect her," Brigham advised. Upon arrival in the Lion House, Mary sent a kitten named Honey to Amelia's room in a gesture of peace. Amelia set the poor creature loose in the city creek and returned the empty box to her rival's door. Honey was never seen again.

Mary was saddened by the cat's loss, yet she could not bring herself to blame Amelia. "I understand her devastation even more," she told Brigham, who later told me. (My detractors have often accused me of knowing things I could not possibly know. "She wasn't there!" they shout. Oh, but this shows their naiveté about plural marriage. In the Saints' troubled institution, a wife's confession to her husband hops from one pillow to the next with the determination of a bed bug.)

The standoff between Amelia and Mary continued until my arrival. They say nothing heals a wound better than time. In plural marriage, nothing dulls the pain of a new wife better than the next one after. There is a cruel logic in a polygamous household. A wife generally ignores the women who preceded her but loathes the first woman to follow. When that woman gets replaced herself, the previous wife takes an un-Christian pleasure in seeing her pained as she had been. This is not always the case. Many women are too noble in heart to nurture such feelings. But they are the exception. Amelia's rage was the rule.

Thus, my Reader, this is the household I entered that day.

As I went to enter Brigham's garden, I found the gate purposely locked by Amelia. Leggett, Brigham's gardener, saw me fumbling to enter. "Be right there," he said, hobbling over. "There you are, ma'am. Sister Amelia's in quite a blow, isn't she?"

As much as I wanted to, I was not about to gossip about another wife.

"It's always a fine day around here, until she blows through," the man continued. "I should hire a militia to protect my flowers. Look at her." Indeed, Amelia was swiping a brush of cosmos with her parasol, destroying the blooms. But I would not take Leggett's line, and commented on the beauty of his lavender rose.

"I'm lucky to have it. Amelia took her shears to my butter rose the other day."

"Mr. Leggett," I said, "please remember her business is not mine."

"Of course," he said. "Until she makes it."

"I'm sorry she treats you so poorly."

"That's nothing. You should see how she cuts through Brigham. I'll tell you this much: it makes me love the man more. He stands up there on Sundays giving wisdom and all the such, and that's all right and fine, but I never trust a man until I've seen him weak. That's how I know he's honest. Everyone has his chinks!"

Later, at dinner, I found myself seated across from Amelia. She ignored me, spoke to no one, and never once touched her food. At the end of the meal, as the cake basket was passed, she shoved it under my nose. "You look like you enjoy your sweets," she said. It was the only time we spoke in the five years we shared a husband.

I never became a regular wife at the Lion House, and after a few months I stopped going altogether. I remember one afternoon Brigham was visiting me in the cottage. He thought to ask, "When did you stop supping with us?"

"Months ago."

"Has it been that long? I miss seeing my wife."

"I'm not your wife," I said.

He rose from the bed and began to assemble himself, buttoning up and refastening his cuffs. He said nothing more, grunting incomprehensibly as he bent to pull on his boots. He left my room without another word, as if wounded and retreating to his lair. Yet the space where he had stood did not empty. It was as if he had left the spirit of himself behind, a black ghost, large and shaped to his form. This apparition watched me as I dressed. It penetrated my thoughts as I worried if I had somehow destroyed my soul's redemption, and that of my boys. I do not believe in phantasmagorical events, but this presence was so formidable, and real, I must describe it as it seemed to me.

On the stairs I heard Brigham greet my mother. I heard the door open and the Prophet's heavy boots on the porch. I went to my window and watched him walk down the path. Outside the boys were throwing rocks at a lizard. "Lorenzo! James!" the Prophet called. "How would you like it if some great big thing was throwing stones at you?" Brigham lowered himself heavily to one knee and pried open the boys' hands. He took their armament of rocks and gently set them upon the ground. He whispered something to the boys, who listened carefully, then smiled and laughed, throwing their arms around him. At the same time, the apparition up in my room spoke. *Everything is for them.* The voice was Brigham's. *Everything you do is for your boys.*

———

CHAPTER EIGHTEEN:
Faith in Marriage

On our first anniversary Brigham transferred me, along with my mother and my boys, to Forest Farm, his agricultural compound south of the city. "I know you don't care much for your little cottage," he said. "But many people say Forest Farm is one of the prettiest places in all of Utah. I think you'll find the land a good place for the boys. As for you—I spent twenty-five thousand dollars on the farm house. It has two stories, not including the cellar. If this doesn't suit, my goodness, I don't know what will." In this he was truthful: the house was a gabled, Gothic-style home laid out in the shape of a double cross. It sat upon a fine flat parcel of rich soil, with a black walnut orchard and open views to the mountains. It seemed as fine a place in all of Deseret to raise my sons.

What I did not know, nor did Brigham inform me until my arrival, was that most of the farm's operations were now my responsibility. Forest Farm served as Brigham's larder. Each day it delivered fresh milk, eggs, butter, vegetables, and meats to his scores of wives and children throughout Salt Lake. Every day in the black of morning I rose to begin my chores in the barn, finishing long after the sun had set. My mother did the same, looking after the house and cooking for the thirty farm hands who tended Brigham's field of beets and alfalfa, his cocoonery, and his thousand head of registered cattle. When one chore was complete, five others waited. The end of each day simply brought the beginning of the next.

"I've never worked so hard in my life," I said to my mother.

"You don't know the meaning of the word." My mother had the common outlook of the Pioneer—that the ordeal of the early Saints would never be surpassed. In terms of toil and hardship, I am certain she is right. Even so, the farm work wore away at my spirits. "Do you ever wonder why we're doing all of this?" I asked my mother.

My mother buttoned up her expression in a manner that meant, *No point in asking about the will of God.* My mother is an intelligent, experienced woman. She has known many kinds of man. When people ask me now, why is it that I continued to believe in the teachings of the Mormon Church for so long, I speak of her. Dear Reader, let me tell you this: Love and trust are Siamese twins, as conjoined as Chang and Eng. I loved my mother and trusted her judgment, even more than I trusted my own. Every time doubt formed hard in my heart, my mother broke it apart with her love.

From time to time Brigham drove out to the farm to inspect his operation and visit with me. While engaged with my husband upstairs, I could hear the boys playing on the rope that hung from the locust tree. They played more loudly when Brigham was present, shouting in a way they never did when we were alone. As I lay with my husband, I imagined they were calling to me: *Mother! I have not forgotten you!* It was the thought I held to through Brigham's visits. This was how I put him out of my mind, even while he was there.

Each Sunday we rode into Salt Lake for services to renew our faith. Church lasted several hours, and with the afternoon meetings it took most of the day. For some it was also a social affair, with a few female Saints flaunting their garments as if they were sewn from the shrouds of Christ. Some men, though certainly not all, would boast of business transactions and successful crops and their latest wives. This kind of vanity is not exclusive to the Saints on Sunday, I know. Anywhere the devout gather to worship, there will always be a parade.

During this period I began to form new questions. I thought of the men around the country, indeed across the Globe—from the high-hatted Pope in Rome to the turbaned Caliph among the Turks—who stood before their people and proclaimed, each in his own language, a set of infallible truths, many similar to those Brigham offered. How can so many men claim the key to Divine Truth? At the time, I could not articulate this question or others, not in the manner I have just now on the page. Yet they were forming, in the manner of the pearl, I suppose, grinding into a truth. It was an all but imperceptible feeling, but on Sundays I sensed it, rubbing against me, deep within. It would be years before I would fully recognize this gem.

Above all, one sermon imprinted itself upon my mind. Many weeks had passed since I had received word from my husband. My daily life involved such a variety of tasks that many days would come and go without his name or image entering my mind. Over time Brigham became a distant figure, such as the men of Washington are distant to us. Certainly we know they exist, for we read of their declarations and pronouncements. Yet to many they do not feel alive, no more than a Roman statesman depicted in the History book feels alive to the student today. This was my benign opinion of my husband when one Sunday he opened up on the topic of his wives.

Shall I tell you now the question most men and women concern themselves over? The truth most Brothers and Sisters seek? Shall I reveal to you the inquiry that most preoccupies your minds? I know this because often I meet you on the street, or you call upon me at the Beehive House, or when I travel round the Territory, driving to the most remote Stakes to greet the Faithful—no matter where this is, it is always the same question brought to me. And so now I shall share it with you. Brother Brigham—the sincere man or the sincere Sister, and even sometimes the sincere child; Brother Brigham, tell me how many Mrs. Youngs do you possess? How many women sleep at night in the Lion House? How many times have you been sealed? My goodness, is this your most profound question for me? You are at liberty to bring me all inquiries, any unsettling of the mind, and yet this is always the first off your tongues. How I wish you asked me something else. Brother Brigham—how do I know if I am living righteously? If I am serving the Kingdom? If I love my wife, if I love my husband, if I love my daughter or my son? Brother Brigham, what does our Heavenly Father want of me? How shall I know if I am His child? Brothers, Sisters, Saints everywhere—why not these questions, and many like them? Why not the enlightened questions about service and humility and devotion, and evil everywhere conquered by peace? Why no examinations of the Gospel? Of the Revelations? Why do I never hear the question—Brother Brigham, tell me how I can be a true Saint? Instead, always, tell me of your bed! Listen to your words—for in them are all truths of the spirit, and thus they shall be.

This sermon, long remembered by many, and reprinted before, had good effect in quieting Brigham's critics. It armed his defenders with rhetoric to respond to the many questions about polygamy. It caused many people, whose curiosity was natural, to feel profane for wondering about such things. It transferred the misdeed from Brigham to his opponents. By the end of the sermon, these powerful words had erased the question—*Brother Brigham, indeed, how many wives do you have?*—from the minds of thousands of Saints.

As for me, these fine words would have done much to buttress my eroding faith—were half of them true.

THE 19TH WIFE

———

CHAPTER NINETEEN:
My Awakening

After more than three years at Forest Farm, an agent from the Church rode out one day to notify my mother and me our services were no longer needed and a wagon would come for our belongings in the morning. I did not know this man. He was one of the many polished, eager youths who worked for the Church administration. He told me I was being transferred to a new house in the city, while my mother was being sent home.

"Home?" said my mother. "What home?"

The boy read through a letter but could not come up with an answer. "Your home, I presume."

"Don't presume anything, my boy."

The boy's face shone with the youthful dew that no one misses until it is gone. I did not know what he was thinking, what his ambitions were, how deep his faith, but I could imagine he hoped for wealth and a large enough house for many wives. Why should he not? Certainly many men in Deseret remained true and loyal to their first and only wife. The average man's family life was no different from that of the average man's in Babylon. But among the leaders of the Church and the leaders of the Territory, who were one and the same, among the men who controlled industry and land resources and deeds to water, who ranked in the militia and the police services, who managed the supply of goods and protected the routes between settlements, among the men who administered the post and the judges who ruled from the bench—among these men, plural marriage was common and ad-mired. Of course this boy, who was already serving Brigham in such intimate capacity, would want the same for himself. I told him I would be ready in the morning.

The boys and I settled into a cozy house with a stained-glass window depicting an Alpine scene that cast a brightly colored light on the landing on the stairs. In fairness to Brigham, the house was appealing and clean, and, most important, it was mine. I would not complain about the house but for its two inadequacies. One, my mother was not permitted to live there. Brigham claimed he could no longer afford supporting her, which had hardly amounted to anything at all.

The second inadequacy was a lack of a well, forcing me to draw water from my neighbors. I tried to distribute my borrowings equally among them. I would take James and Lorenzo with me, so we could draw as much water at one time. I was always ashamed when I knocked on the doors, pail in hand, humiliated by every force that had brought me to this moment of begging before my boys.

When Brigham visited the cottage for the first time, he an-nounced he was bearing bad news. "I'm afraid my revenues are no longer what they were," he said. "We're all scaling back. I'm going to have to cut your allowance."

"Cut it? By how much?"

"I'm afraid we're cutting your allowance entirely."

"You're giving me nothing?"

"Not nothing. You'll live in this house without rent and you can still collect your rations at the store."

Here I must honor the promise I made at the outset of this book. I swore that I would not withhold the details the Reader is most keenly interested in. In my experiences as lecturess, no matter the venue, no matter who sits in the audience before me, always the same questions arise. They are difficult questions to pose before your peers, but eventually a brave soul, typically a woman, ventures forth. Then there is great relief in the hall as everyone's mutual curiosity is satisfied. Never have I told my story without someone inquiring about the conjugal relations between Brigham and myself. I will sate your curiosity now by telling you those relations ceased between me and Brigham sometime in my third year at Forest Farm.

I now realized a great cost attached itself to this revised arrangement. Once Brigham had removed me from the farm I was merely, like so many plural wives no longer on the schedule, a financial burden.

"How am I to feed my boys?" I asked.

"Start a garden. Hire out your needle. Take in some laundry."

"Take in some laundry! I have to walk up and down the street with bucket in hand begging for water. You don't know—no, you can't know—what it's like for me to have to ask for water. These people, these kind people, don't have the heart to turn me away. But they work hard too. The well is only so deep. Why should they have to share their water with me?"

"Because they are Saints and they would do well to remember who brought them here." His hideous anger spilled over. It squeezed out of him in perspiration and ire and a dire loathing of everything before him. The Prophet was reduced to a bilious, fat, old man. He blew out of the cottage. I could not know then he would never visit again.

To ease my financial duress, I decided to take in boarders. Ever since the completion of the railroad a few years earlier, Gentiles had been arriving in Deseret in numbers never seen before. There was an inadequate number of hotels to house them, and quickly there became a custom of Saints renting out rooms to these new visitors and residents. It was an odd evolution for our isolated Territory—Saints who had never known the outside world suddenly were sharing a home with Babylonian strangers. Of course, every

Saint in Deseret had been raised on stories of depravity among the Gentiles: They worship falsely, they fornicate loosely, they eat their young! Although I did not believe every tale, they had left me with a general impression that I could never trust a Gentile. In the end, my empty purse over-ruled my superstitions and I placed an advertisement in the *Daily Tribune*.

The first person to reply was Major James Burton Pond, formerly of the Third Wisconsin Cavalry, ally of John Brown, and now a reporter for the *Tribune* itself. He arrived at my house in full uniform, with a silver-handled sword. "Is the room still free?"

"It's three dollars a week," I said. "Board included. Washing is extra. You must like children. I have two boys, James, who's nine, and Lorenzo, who's eight. They're good boys, but they are boys and can make noise. You're free to congregate here or on the porch, but not in the kitchen or the dining room. Visitors should be out by ten, and if you—"

I stopped talking, for Major Pond was regarding me queerly. "Is something wrong?"

"Are you really a Mrs. Young?"

I told him his information was correct.

"Why on earth are you letting out your rooms?"

"Because I have spare rooms and no income. I'd rather take in boarders than deprive my sons."

"What about your husband?"

"Would you like to see the room or not, Major Pond?"

Judge Albert Hagan, the old Confederate colonel and mineral attorney, and Mrs. Hagan became my next boarders. Their arrival was more expected, preceded with a card announcing their intention to let. Judge Hagan lived mostly in California, but his expertise in mining law brought him to Salt Lake for extended periods. He seemed to me, at least at first, a gentle, fluffy-haired soul, with a cautious mouth buried in a cottony beard. Mrs. Hagan was, in my estimation, the most suitable creature for her husband: She was ample in every sense, including a plentiful bosom atop an abundant heart. The nature of their relationship was a revelation. Judge Hagan never once failed to thank his wife, praise her intelligence, or appreciate her presence. Ten times a day he said, "I'm the luckiest man in the world," and lay his hand upon her soft behind.

Thus my house was transformed in less than a week. It was by coincidence and circumstances of the time, but in no part by design, that my three boarders were Gentiles.

In the evenings Judge Hagan and his wife, along with Major Pond, liked to gather on my porch for conversation. They invited friends and acquaintances, intelligent, lively men—lawyers, journalists, historians, and other reasoned Gentiles—who typically brought their equally bright and lively wives. These women, most of them wearing their hair in the loose (and prohibited) waterfall style, knew as much about any topic as their husbands. Almost every night outside my parlor window, a seminar of ideas and philosophy was conducted. "Have you any thoughts on the Modocs?" Judge Hagan would begin, initiating a long engagement of opinion, agreements, and disagreements. Everyone would participate, the women's estimation of all matters listened to with equivalent respect.

Each night I worked in the kitchen while listening in. I have always hated washing dishes, but never more so during these evenings when the water and the clinking cutlery obscured an important word in the dialogue. I took to propping the window with a block of wood so that the ideas could travel to the kitchen more clearly. I longed to join my boarders but knew I could not.

One night Judge Hagan said, "The more I learn of polygamy, the more I despise it. I admire Brigham a good deal, but he's got to be careful with this thing. Everyone knows it's the wild wick that burns down the house."

"More than anything," said Mrs. Hagan, "I think about the children."

"Has anyone," asked Judge Hagan, "ever met a partner in a polygamatic marriage, man or woman, who was happy? I mean truly happy?"

"What do you mean by happy?" said Major Pond.

"What does he mean by happy?" said Mrs. Hagan. "He means happy. Happy: cheerful, glad, fortunate, hopeful. Happy."

"I'm only asking, Mrs. Hagan. I'm not supporting. They of course believe this is their ticket to Heaven. Now if you believed that, I mean truly believed that, I mean believed it as much as you believed the sun will rise tomorrow and the sky will be blue, then wouldn't you be happy, even if a few extra wives caused some inconvenience or indignity in this present life?"

"I have an idea," said Mrs. Hagan. "Let's not speculate, not when we have Mrs. Young as an expert witness."

In a matter of seconds she was in the kitchen, begging me to join the conversation. I told her there were dishes and a late loaf in the oven, but Mrs. Hagan would not relent.

In addition to the Judge and his wife and Major Pond, that evening there was the Rev. Mr. Stratton, a Methodist. He was the first representative of a foreign religion I had ever known. All my life Brigham, the Apostles, the Bishops, the Elders—everyone in a position to know—had told me that I must mind my purse and person around Gentiles. "But a reverend, a preacher, a man of their cloth, he is the devil in our land," I had been warned since I was a child.

And now the Rev. Stratton was rising from his rocker to shake my hand. "Will you join us, Mrs. Young?" The group regarded me with gentle curiosity. I longed to open up, to tell them all I had seen. At the same time, I felt a lingering duty to defend my faith. "It's all rather complicated," I said. "There are many sides to the debate."

"Don't feel obliged," said Mrs. Hagan.

"It's quite rude of us," said Rev. Stratton. "Why, it's none of our business at all."

"I'm sorry," said Mrs. Hagan. "We didn't mean to make a specimen of you."

I accepted their apologies and left their company, although I longed to tell them all I knew.

The next day the Rev. Stratton sent his card and an invitation to call upon him and Mrs. Stratton any time. For two weeks I kept the card in my pocket, fingering it as I went about my work, rubbing the embossing so many times that it had begun to wear away by the time I decided to pay them a visit.

The Strattons lived several blocks away, in a new neighborhood where Gentiles clustered, a foreign land I had never visited before. I left the boys with Mrs. Hagan and walked to the Strattons, taking a circuitous route, careful to note anyone who might be spying on me. My relations with Brigham had deteriorated to such a state it was possible to imagine him trying to blackmail me with evidence of betrayal. A walk that should take no more than twenty minutes took nearly an hour, as I zigzagged through the neighborhood and finally arrived at the Strattons' gate.

Mrs. Stratton shared her husband's dual nature of seeming both youthful and wise. Her posture was so erect I never once saw her sit back in her chair. This was remarkable given that my visit, originally planned for twenty minutes, lasted almost four hours. I had not intended to unload all my grief to these strangers, but the Rev. Mr. Stratton broke away my reserve when he said, "Mrs. Young, you should know, my wife and I, we already consider ourselves your friend."

There was no reason for the Strattons to make such a declaration—Except, is this not how Man is meant to treat his fellow creature? I was too weary to be skeptical, too raw to protect myself further, and too depleted, in every sense, to lose anything more. "I don't know where to begin," I said. Rev. and Mrs. Stratton said nothing further. They were not going to pry, nor even, as some do, pretend they were satisfied with nothing said when in fact they craved every detail. "I hardly know what's happened."

"Everything in time," said Mrs. Stratton.

Thus I began to tell my story. It was the first time I had pieced it together even for myself. The afternoon slipped into evening. The plate of cookies turned into a platter of strips of ham and beef. It grew dark and I continued talking. Mrs. Stratton brought the lamp from the hall. A yellow radiance reached out just far enough to encircle us, and I carried on until the end of my tale.

THE 19TH WIFE

―――――

CHAPTER TWENTY:
The Battle of the Stove

Emboldened by my new friends, sometime in June 1873 I went to
see Brigham. I had to wait on line outside the Beehive House along
with all the curious travelers, the men conducting business with the
Church, and the hundreds of pilgrims. I considered running up and
down the line and telling the faithful the truth about my husband.
What would the pilgrims think if they knew how Brigham's wives
lived behind this very wall they leaned against now? Would they
crave to rub the hem of his coat, or take home a sheet of paper from
his wastebasket as a relic, if they understood the truth?

Yet I had a more practical matter to discuss with Brigham. I
wanted a new stove.

"A new what?"

"A stove."

"What's wrong with the one you have?"

"It's fine for one or two people, but I'm now running a boarding
house. I need to cook for twice as many as the kitchen's meant for,
and I need a new stove. These people pay three dollars a week for
room and board and what can I tell them when their supper isn't
ready?"

"I don't care what you tell them, but I'll tell you, I can't afford a
new stove. Do you have any idea how much they cost?"

"I do. I've picked one out. It can be delivered in four weeks."

Our argument continued for some time until Brigham said, "All
right. I'll think about it."

"You won't think about it. You will give me a check now so I can place the order."

"Madame, you are not the treasurer of this household."

"Sir, I am your wife and you will provide for my most basic needs."

Brigham opened an accounting book and in a great show of irritation scratched out a check. "I always thought you of all people would understand what it meant to be my wife."

I left the Beehive House for the last time. Outside, one of Brigham's aides announced to the expectant pilgrims, "The President will meet no more visitors today." At least a hundred stood on the veranda and down the steps into the street. They cried about waiting for hours and needing the Prophet's advice. "Go home," said the aide. "Come back tomorrow, but go home." The man retreated into the Beehive and shut the door.

Even after the pilgrims were gone, I remained outside my husband's house. A pair of Brigham's daughters, two of the Big Ten in fashionable mushroom hats, passed me on their way to the Lion House. I had shared several meals with these girls, and sat with them in the parlor on Sunday nights. Now they did not recognize me.

Dusk arrived, and still I remained at Brigham's gate. I do not know why I lingered, but I felt an urgent need to witness his household one final time. As dusk descended, one of Brigham's wives, I do not know who, moved through the Beehive House illuminating the lamps, the golden light filling one window and then the next. I saw Brigham pass from his office to his upstairs parlor, where Amelia was waiting with two of his sons. The parlor's large window allowed me to view a portion of their evening. Amelia leaned against the piano in a low silver gown, the famous diamonds around her throat. Brigham kissed her neck, then moved to look out the window as if to examine the night sky. For some time he stood motionless behind the glass. His eyes looked tired in their pouches of flesh. His beard was white and frayed. He looked, to me, like an old man worried about his fate. He gazed out, with an aurora of lamplight behind him, not at me but into his future, I believe. At one point he winced, a small shock of something running through him, his thick body flinching almost imperceptibly. It was a tiny jolt; no one in the parlor perceived it. Then it passed and Brigham returned to his family. Although I have no more evidence than this, I am certain that night I witnessed my husband looking into his heart and regretting what he found.

Shortly after my victory of the stove, I took to bed with a mysterious illness similar to the one that befell me all those years ago. My boarders urged me to consult a doctor. When I refused, I know they believed I was doing so because of my faith. The truth was I could not afford the call. For two weeks, I was unable to look after them, and I feared they would rightly demand a refund on their rent. Instead they became my nurses and closest friends. They tended to me, not only Mrs. Hagan but her husband and the Major as well. They took over the house, cooking and cleaning and polishing the lovely stained-glass window, and looking after James and Lorenzo.

One day during my convalescence my boarders and the Rev. and Mrs. Stratton came to speak with me. "Mrs. Young, can we have an honest word?"

I was sure they were going to fairly complain that they were paying three dollars a week to serve me. "I know what you're going to say."

"It's none of our business," said Mrs. Hagan, "but it's impossible not to notice that your husband has abandoned you."

Judge Hagan continued, "If you were so inclined, you might consider bringing suit against him."

"Suit for what?"

"For divorce," advised the Judge.

"You have no idea what that means."

"I think I do," said the Judge. "Let me be your guide. You have legal rights. Any court of law will see that your husband has abandoned you and you're entitled to be set free."

"It'll be a test case," Mrs. Hagan said. "For polygamous women everywhere."

I did not know how to perceive what they were saying. My new friends were emphasizing my legal rights while I remained concerned with my spiritual fate. "My whole life," I said, "everyone I have ever known, everyone has told me that this is the way to Salvation. How can I leave it all behind?" I asked the Reverend Stratton for his advice.

"I'm afraid," he said, "no one—not me, not Brigham, no one at all—can tell you what your heart has to say."

"If I may," said Mrs. Hagan, "with all due respect to the Reverend's wise words, I should like to ask you a simple question: Is this what you really believe? Even now?"

To you, reasoned Reader, the answer might appear obvious, yet doubt is not the same as knowledge. On my journeys I have met people who have forsworn any belief in God and Christ, and yet they are married in a church and plan to be buried beneath a stone cross. At the great moment of death, with the eternal future undecided, few are truly prepared to defy everything they have been told to be true.

"What about my boys?"

"They're the reason we've come to you like this," said Mrs. Hagan. "Do you really want them to see their mother so abused? Do you want them thinking this is how a man treats his wife?"

It was a terrible vision—ten or fifteen years into the future, my boys as young men, greedily acquiring women. There was no reason to think they would be any different from my father, brother, and husband. Unless something changed, their fate was sealed, as was mine.

After my health had improved, and I could take up again my duties in the house, two Ward Teachers paid me a visit. They were young men of twenty or twenty-one, one thick with fatty muscle while his companion wore a dense black beard. They sat in my parlor, perched at the edge of their chairs, their air an admixture of compassion and distaste. "Sister, we've been sent out to evaluate the quality of your faith," the bearded one began.

"We have a few questions," said other.

"First," I said, "I have a question for you: What makes you capable of evaluating my faith?"

"Sister, don't you understand? We're teachers of the ward. We've received our ordinances."

"Yes, I know that, but what makes you capable of knowing my heart better than myself?"

They smiled weakly. I could read the mind of the thicker one: He could not wait to leave my house and discuss with anyone he met my infidelity.

The bearded one cleared his throat. "If I may begin the evaluation. Now, first of all, do you remain faithful to the Revelations of Joseph and the Prophecy of Brigham Young?"

"No."

The men looked at each other. I doubt anyone had ever answered as such. The thicker one appeared astonished; his companion seemed pleased to meet a challenge. "I'm sure you don't know what you're saying," he said. "Brother Broadhead was asking if you hold the Prophets in your heart."

"I understand, and I do not."

The young men looked at each other once again. Their expressions changed from surprise to irritation.

"Listen, Sister," the fat one began. "What you're saying could get you in a lot of trouble, not just with God and in Heaven, but with Brigham and everyone else. You need to be more careful. I'm going to have to report everything you say to the Bishop."

"Gentlemen, I'll do it myself, thank you." I told the men that their religion had betrayed me, their Prophet had abandoned me, their system of conjugality all but destroyed my family. "Tell me then, yes, please tell me, how I'm supposed to love this religion? Perhaps it has brought you personally nothing but joy, and perhaps you, too, and your families and everyone you know. Perhaps you've profited under this system, found yourself nourished and enriched both physically and spiritually. In that case, I can understand your fervor and your desire to share it. But, Brothers, please try, for a moment *try* and see what it has done to me. If you do, you might understand why my faith is crumbling, even as we speak here now."

The heavy man's expression lifted, as if he had just arrived at a very good idea. "I know what you need. You need your faith restored. Here's what we'll do. We'll get you re-baptized. You'll go through the ceremony again and your heart will be cleansed and your disbelief will be washed away."

I argued for some time that I did not care for any more ceremonies, but the men would not relent. They warned me of my lonely fate and the chill of an eternity without the love of God. "On your deathbed, Sister, you will regret this day. On your deathbed, I guarantee it, you will hear my voice."

"I have no idea what will happen after I die," I said, "yet I know one thing for sure: Neither do you."

After this, I never again tried to believe in the Latter-day Saints. My faith had been emptied out like a can. When I told my mother, she said, "You don't know what you're saying."

"Mother, I do."

"You'll lose everything."

"I already have."

THE 19TH WIFE

CHAPTER TWENTY-ONE:
The Apostate Wife

My escape from Mormondom began with six men and a moving van. They dismantled my house and hauled the load to auction. One man asked if he should pry the stained-glass window from its casement. I told him to leave it for the next wife, and the one after her.

When the house was empty I sat on the porch with my boys to tell them about the great adventure we were embarking on.

"Like the Pioneers?" said James.

"Yes, something like that. And like all adventures, there will be difficult times. And now is going to be one of those. I need both of you to be brave and not cry even if you feel like crying." I was sending James, my eldest, to live with my father and his wives until I was settled. When I told him this, his eyes flickered with sorrow. He fought back his tears as best he could, but then the brave boy broke down.

"I promise we'll be together again very soon."

"Why does Lorenzo get to stay with you and I don't?"

The truth was I could not face my coming ordeal alone. I needed one of my boys with me, yet even one was probably more than I would be able to care for over the coming days. James begged me not to leave him. He wept on my breast until Judge and Mrs. Hagan drove him away.

I was so distressed by his departure that I considered canceling my scheme. Then little Lorenzo squeezed my hand. "Where are we going?" he asked. His warm fingers reminded me why I had chosen this path to freedom, and why I could not turn back.

When it was dark Lorenzo and I set out for a walk through the neighborhood, pretending to be on a stroll, nodding at the neighbors. I carried nothing extraordinary with me, giving no one any reason to believe I was fleeing. While walking we met up with the Reverend and Mrs. Stratton. Lorenzo jumped up and down at the sight of them, for he loved them like a fond uncle and aunt. They fell in with us in a most natural way, and we moved about at a casual pace, noticing the summer vines on a trellis and the yellow pom-poms in a bed of marigolds. With little effort, and no apparent intention, we meandered downtown, then wandered about until we were standing before the Walker House, the Gentile hotel. I told Lorenzo we would spend the night inside.

"Why can't we sleep in our house?"

"You saw the men take away the furniture."

"Why can't they bring it back?"

Sometimes with children it is impossible to catch up with their clear logic. Their questions are always sharp and full of perception, exposing the twisted thinking of the mature man's world. "They can't bring it back because I've sold it. We have left that house for good. One day we'll have a new house, but for now we'll live here."

On our first night in the Walker House I warned Lorenzo to remain silent. "No one is to know we're here."

"The bellman knows we're here."

"Yes, but he doesn't know our actual names. We are in hiding, do you understand what that means?"

He nodded. "It means you don't want Brigham to know where you are."

Since beginning my preparations to flee, I had been too preoccupied to ponder my fate. Now the fullness of it seemed to be pressing at the door of Suite No. 412. In abandoning my husband, I had given up almost everything I had ever known. I was sleepless that night, alert to every sound in the hall. Several times I heard footsteps pass my door, my heart quickening until they retreated down the corridor. Once, around three in the morning, I heard the sound of a man moving carefully down the hall. Whoever he was, he walked deliberately as if he wanted to go undetected. They were big feet, I could tell, in clumsy country boots. Soon they were standing at my door.

I lay still, holding Lorenzo so firmly I still cannot believe he did not awaken in my arms. I heard the man breathing on the other side of our door. He stood there for some time. His breath was the sound of a man hesitating, or praying, before committing a dangerous act. I became certain it was one of Brigham's Danites, come to assassinate me. I imagined the cold animal black in his eyes. I was too frightened to move. I awaited the rattle of the knob and the turn of the stolen key.

Then at some point the man was gone.

I cannot tell you if I imagined an assassin at my door; or if in fact a killer had not been able to carry out his religious duty. I recalled Brigham's black ghost, the presence he left in a room he did not inhabit. Was that what I had perceived? Had he come for me? Oh, sober-minded Reader! Never sneer at such fantasies. In the quiet of your mind, when the deep night is at its blackest, are you always so certain of what is real?

"Mrs. Young? . . . Mrs. Young? Are you in there?"

I sat up in bed. The mantel clock said it was a little past ten. Next to me Lorenzo stared up from the pillow. Two small, dark crescents of fatigue had appeared beneath his eyes.

"It's me, Mrs. Hagan."

When I admitted her, she had a hurried, anxious look, yet before stating the purpose of her visit she gave Lorenzo a steaming sweet bun. The boy took the treat to the corner and sat with it between his crossed legs. I could tell he wanted to pretend he was not listening, yet his ears, I know, were always pricked.

"It's out," said Mrs. Hagan. "Your apostasy. Everyone knows."

Mrs. Hagan handed over the *Daily Tribune,* the Territory's lead-ing Gentile paper, where Major Pond worked. Immediately I saw that its editors, all strangers, had become my friends. The lead ed-itorial praised my fortitude and chastised Brigham for his indiffer-ence and hypocrisy. There were a number of items about my apostasy, including a satirical cartoon with the caption "Brother Brigham is forlorn—his last rib has deserted his bed and board."

"Did Brigham's papers learn of it?" I asked.

Mrs. Hagan hesitated, and I wrested the Mormon papers from her. I was not surprised to see my name denounced in his press, but I could not have anticipated the lies and false accusations. If you were to gather all your news exclusively from Brigham's papers, as most Saints do, you would believe I was woven of such dishonest fabric I might try to convince you to dig up your mother's coffin to hand over her wedding band.

To this day I do not know how my story got out, but the dissem-ination was so thorough and in such detail that Americans every-where woke up to my tale. I would later learn I was on the front page of the papers in San Francisco, Saint Louis, and New York. The farther from Mormondom, the more lurid and scandal-loving was the reporting.

"Momma, look."

"Lorenzo, please. Get away from the window."

But the boy would not listen. He was peeling back the shade to look outside. I went to pull him away, but then I saw the crowd below. Some five hundred had gathered, jostling and shoving and trying to enter the hotel. The manager held his arms up, trying to bring order to the street.

"They're here for you," said Mrs. Hagan.

"Who are they?"

"Reporters, sympathizers, denouncers, everyone."

The truth comes both instantly and in a slow, steady seep. I was feeling it creep through me—a profound understanding of what I would be facing for some time to come. I could hardly move, and Mrs. Hagan had to help me dress.

Not a minute after I was clothed, and my hair prepared in a beaded net, did a knock come to the door. "Mrs. Young, it's me, Judge Hagan." At once the Judge's presence helped settle me. "Now that the cat's out of the bag," he reported, "I want you to know I'll be filing the divorce papers very soon."

"When can we leave Utah?"

"There's a mood out there," he said. "I'm not sure it's safe. You're best staying here for the time being. Here, I brought you this." The Judge handed me an envelope. I recognized the writing at once. There was no one I wanted to hear from more than my mother.

> My Dear Child:
>
> I would have come to deliver this message in person, but I cannot enter the Gentile Hotel which you now call home. I know you have suffered in your marriage, and that your husband has failed in many ways. It has pained me to witness this. I too know the hardships of our unique institution; often I have prayed for a relief to its strains. Yet I am certain, as certain as I am of anything, that plural marriage will open the door to Heaven, and that my sufferings here on Earth are my path to Glory. My child, ponder your words and deeds, for they shall last far longer than your physical self. Be certain, my child, that I cannot know you in your present state.
>
> Your Mother,
> ELIZABETH C. WEBB

"Mother?" Lorenzo set his little hand on my knee, reviving me from the letter. "Mother, what's wrong?" He climbed into my arms, his breath warm from the sweet bun. I held him for some time, an hour, perhaps, pitying myself. I wish I could claim I faced my first day of apostasy with courage and certainty. Yet in truth, I had never felt more afraid.

XVI

MY MOTHER'S FLIGHT

From the Desk of
Lorenzo Dee, Eng.
Baden-Baden-by-the-Sea
Calif.

August 2, 1939
Professor Charles Green
Brigham Young University
Joseph Smith Building
Provo

Dear Professor Green,

How on earth did you find me? It's been a long time since I've had contact with Utah, so hats off to you, Professor. Yet I'm afraid I can't answer your questions about my mother. I'm not invoking my right to privacy, although I cherish it. No, I'm simply too poorly equipped to tell you what you'd like to know. For example, when you ask, did Ann Eliza ever discuss her divorce with any of Brigham's other wives? My answer is, I have no idea. I understand why you ask—what a nugget such a conversation would be for your proposed narrative. But please remember, in 1873 I was eight years old. The events you are asking about took place when I was so young I do not trust my memory of them; or at the very best my memories are more like someone else's memories; or, at least, memories that time, skillful decorator that she is, has embroidered into something beautiful yet not wholly true. For your purposes, this simply will not do.

I should apologize for not writing sooner, but over the past few weeks a number of matters have kept me from my desk, including the white-sided dolphins which have taken to appearing in the cove in the afternoons. It seems that every time I sit down to answer the mail I look out and see their pewter-tipped snouts in the surf. It's such a sight of uncomplicated joy, as you can imagine, that I hurry outside and down the path. Several years ago I built a viewing bench on the bluff. I conceived of it as a reading spot, but I can never get any reading done, what with the ocean and the sun and the dolphins in the waves. I go down there for twenty minutes and find I've lost the afternoon.

For some time I considered ignoring your letter. You are asking about so many events which have been recorded before. Newspaper accounts, the documents from the trial, the Church's repudiations, and of course my mother's book. The stories about her marriage to Brigham have been told and retold and disputed and dismissed by so many interested parties, I cannot imagine there's anything left to say. I'm sorry to be so discouraging.

I must admit I was shocked when you pointed out that September next will be the 50th anniversary of President Woodruff's manifesto renouncing polygamy. It feels even longer ago—almost ancient in its distance from us today; and, at the same time, it feels like last night's dream. My mother, I know, took great pride in the Church's change of mind, perhaps too much. I'll leave it to you and the other historians to determine her role in bringing about its reversal. Certainly she played some. Certainly she cannot accept full credit. The truth lies somewhere in between, but isn't that always the case?

I'll tell you—in the years leading up to the Church's about-face, what with the Edmunds Act in '82 and Edmunds-Tucker five years later and all the other drum-beating out of Washington, I was convinced the federal government and the Saints would have a showdown of biblical proportions, one that would leave the Mormons destroyed. Look at Brigham—he was willing to go to jail over the issue! (That reminds me, I don't recall any talk of a letter or a diary or what have you from his time in prison, but I really wouldn't know.) In the years leading up to 1890 I imagined a great battle of wills—the Saints fighting the U.S. Army to their deaths. But in the end the Mormons relented. They gave up polygamy in a simple policy shift. In doing so, they chose the future. And look at them now! (I suppose I should say, look at you!) How many are you? How many millions more to come? If the Church had clung to plural marriage, it's safe to say it would have withered into a fringe.

Let me say, I appreciate your understanding the irony of all this. If your letter had failed to acknowledge it, I would have quickly filed it away. But, as you say, time changes our point of view. This notion has been on my mind lately. Frankly, it's been a trying summer. I lost my wife a year ago July. About nine months after her departure I managed to back my grief into its cage, but the anniversary opened the door and let the beast out again. There has been no solace. Her name was Rosemary. Her eyes were the blue of a winter ocean. We were married forty-three years. It's been difficult, more difficult than I could have known.

My goodness, I've just looked back at my opening paragraphs to you. I cannot believe how far from your questions I've already strayed. First let me acknowledge that your questions are fair and they show that you are an honest historian. You might know (or you might not) I was an engineer. I invented a small but useful device used to lay macadam accurately upon the roads. My point is, I like things orderly and as they are. And so I will say directly, in response to your questions, I cannot answer them for I was not there. I have no interpretation to add, no analysis to offer, no hearsay to pass along, no old family stories to share. If I did not witness it, I am not your source.

Except, you correctly state that I was with my mother during the period July–November 1873, while we lived in the Walker House. As you must know, she sketches this period in *The 19th Wife*. Of course, some of what she writes can be dismissed as grandstanding. The same can be true of the stories Brigham published about her in his periodicals. They were engaged in battle. Manipulation of the truth has always been part of the warrior's arsenal. Neither

Brigham nor my mother is more culpable, or less.

As I wrote that last sentence, the dolphins returned. I hurried down the path to my viewing bench. Can I describe the joy of a spouting blow hole? The white blaze of sea foam is, to me, at least, one of the purest expressions of life itself. Will you forgive my lack of critical reasoning when I say I see God in that frothy column of water? I know nothing about you, Professor, but I trust you have seen the ocean. If you have, then you have witnessed the divine. How barren the ground is in comparison! If I could count the hours I have spent staring out at it! And yet those hours never feel lost. I cannot imagine how else I could refill them were I given a second chance.

As you know, on July 15, 1873, my mother and I moved into the Walker House. In Brigham's mind, and the minds of his followers, this was her act of apostasy, not the lawsuit she filed against him ten days later or the charges she laid out in the newspapers over the next many months. The Walker House was known throughout the Territory as a Gentile den. The rumors about it included orgiastic gatherings in the parlor, a Satanic altar in a linen closet, and murderous rituals practiced in the root cellar. It's laughable now, but such stories were told again and again in the Territory. No one questioned them. We believed every word.

I don't know if our lives were truly in danger that first night in the hotel. Indeed, my mother's statements in *The 19th Wife* have come to seem overwrought. I can tell you this, however: She was genuinely afraid. Imagine, if you will, departing the only world you have ever known—your family, your landscape, your customs, your neighbors, your faith, even if that faith has been shaken. Ponder it: saying good-bye without knowing where you are headed. It would be something like decamping for the moon.

I can tell you this about our first hours at the Walker House: I was frightened, too. At that age it is hard to know the root of one's fear, but I gather it was because I saw my mother in distress. There is nothing more alarming to a boy than seeing a mother, or a father, buckling. It says to him that all will not be well. The boy does not know this, but he senses it, as a dog senses his master's true state of mind.

I remember the hotel bed as quite high and laid out with bolsters and pillows faced in blue damask. Although it was summer I recall being cold and burying myself beneath the bedclothes in my mother's arms. We lay very still, never falling asleep. Whenever we heard a noise downstairs or in the corridor our bodies went rigid. At one point, I remember vividly, there was the sound of a man standing outside our door. I am sure it was a butler realizing he had gone to the wrong suite. But he stood there for what seemed eternity, breathing, waiting, hovering. We held each other, my mother and I. Yes, in fact I did fear for my life at that moment. I know she did, too. My mother had said nothing to me of the possibility of assassination by the Danites, but she didn't have to. You know how boys talk: in the schoolyard I had heard all about Brigham's secret police. The rumor was they cut the hearts out of anyone who abandoned their faith. There were stories of apostates driven into the desert and scalped to make it look as though the Indians had murdered them. I recall the tale of a man who one morning declared to his wife he no longer believed in Brigham's word. By afternoon he had simply disappeared. No trace, not a footprint in the sand, nor a glove fallen in the path. I don't know why, but that always frightened me the most—a person simply disappearing, poof! These of course were schoolyard tales, which tend to be among the tallest. There is no way to verify them, not now. Even so, think of the impression they would leave on an eight-year-old whose mother has checked into a notorious Gentile refuge. And so, whether or not our lives were truly at risk, it seemed that way and our fear was as real as the white moon burning in the sky.

The next morning a number of visitors came to the room. One brought me a warm bun topped with walnuts and honey—a distraction, I realize. It was clear something significant had taken place. I did not know what, of course, but all day people continued to visit our suite—not just the Strattons and the Hagans and Major Pond, but others, men I did not know. During these visits my mother sat in a mahogany chair with a cluster of cherries carved into the frame. Her visitor sat opposite her, asking questions and writing things down. These interviewers reminded me of the Ward Teachers. I knew these men were not Ward Teachers, but I assumed they shared some sort of purpose. I did not connect these interviews with the newspaper stories about my mother that appeared the next day.

I am not going to recap for you how the feud between my mother and Brigham played out in the press. Suffice it to say Brigham's papers, especially the *Herald*, waged a robust campaign against her. I'm sure you have read the accounts in the archives. He laid upon her every accusation short of murder.

All of this was to be expected. I recall Major Pond, whose uniform always impressed me, coming to the room and telling my mother and the others (who was it? Judge Hagan? I never cared for him, I will add) that Brigham had manipulated the Western Telegraph Office and the Associated Press's man in Utah. False stories about her were appearing outside Utah. Major Pond was red-faced, perspiration glistening in the branches of his mustache. "I'll fix that damn *Chronicle*!" he bellowed. I remember it distinctly—the way his brass buttons shook on his chest.

Of course, I was for the most part unaware of the daily items about my mother's apostasy. How could a little boy locked in a fourth-floor hotel room in Salt Lake know that editorial writers in San Francisco and New York took lurid interest in his mother? I knew that many people wanted to meet her. Often a crowd collected outside the Walker House, pointing up to our window. The hotel became another stop on the polygamy tour—the Beehive House, the infamous Lion House, and now the Walker House. Who on their way to California could resist viewing these sites? I remember I liked to peel back the shade to see them. It was clear they were not from Utah. I don't know how I knew this, but perhaps it was their impatience or their brightly colored clothes or the way they spoke casually of Joe Smith and Brig Young—the way you and I might refer to a character from a film or a novel. There was no reverence or awe or fear. Yes, that's what it was—that was their difference. They were indifferent to the profundity of belief. Faith was just one more hullabaloo on a long list. I remember one fellow saying to his companion in the lobby, "These people have lost their minds. Imbeciles, all of them, including Mrs. 19."

I'm sorry to say I don't have the letter from my grandmother. My mother's transcription of it in *The 19th Wife* will have to be accepted as true. It was the only time, I believe, my mother considered reversing her course of action. By then, of course, it was too late; and, no less important, she had surrounded herself by many whose interests lay in her pressing ahead in her defiance of the Church.

On the second day of our confinement, my uncle Gilbert came to visit. Until that point I had little contact with the man. He spent much of his time at South Cottonwood with his two wives and eighteen children—my first cousins, but I could spend the rest of my days trying to remember their names. I remember Gilbert's first words when he entered the suite: "This is all my fault." I remember the tender woe in his voice.

Of course, I did not know he was on his way out of the Church at this time. He promised my mother full support. I understand Gilbert helped my mother financially in this period. It could have been he who paid our hotel bill, yet I cannot tell you for certain. If it was, most likely his funds came from the payments Brigham gave him for his help in arranging his marriage to my mother. What do the Easterners call this? Karma? I suppose I'm asking the wrong man.

Before leaving the suite that day, Gilbert knelt down beside me. He set his thumb beneath my chin, tilting my head up so I was looking into his eye. "You'll look after your mother?" He fished two gold coins from his pocket and thumbed them, one after the next, into in my palm. I will tell you, Professor Green, I have those coins today. They are mounted in a felt display atop the desk I write you from.

Before I continue, I feel I must say a few words about memory. It is full of holes. If you were to lay it out upon a table, it would resemble a scrap of lace. I am a lover of history, Professor Green. I can nibble my way through the sagas and biographies of the great men and the most tumultuous days. Napoleon, Jefferson, Elizabeth, Alexander! Herodotus, Thucydides, Gibbon, Carlyle! You should see my shelves. They sag under their tomes. I have the highest respect for your trade. The master historians have been my friends, never more so since Rosemary's departure. Even so, history has one flaw. It is a subjective art, no less so than poetry or music. The true historian has two sources: the written record and the witness's testimony. This is as it should be. Yet one is memory and the other is written, quite often, from memory. There is nothing to be done about this defect except acknowledge it for what it is. This is your field's Achilles' heel. You say in your letter the historian writes the truth. Forgive me, I must disagree. The historian writes a truth. The memoirist writes a truth. The novelist writes a truth. And so on. My mother, we both know, wrote a truth in *The 19th Wife*—a truth that corresponded to her memory and desires. It is not *the* truth, certainly not. But *a* truth, yes. Your Church has exerted admirable effort in destroying her credibility. No one can deny she got many details wrong. But the elders and others responsible for dismissing her from the record have failed. Her book is a fact. It remains so, even if it is snowflaked with holes.

I am sorry. After that I had to take a walk. I meant to return to the typewriter in a few minutes, but I went down to my bench. The dolphins did not come today. Just as glorious as their arrival is the swiftness with which they disappear. The mystery of it! If I did not record my impressions of them in my letters and shamefully spotty diary, even I would wonder if they existed at all. They are creatures of the dream. There are times when I miss her terribly. My mother, I mean. She was a brave fool. I love her for that, and so much else.

I see no reason to recount for you the legal wrangling that took place between July and November of that year. It is all rather dull, isn't it: the back-and-forths, the petitions, the claims, the what-have-yous, the lawyers' verbiage as thick as sludge. When I discussed it with Rosemary I told her it was like any divorce case, only grimier by a magnitude of 1,000. One other difference, of course: although the case was about money (when are they not?), it was cloaked in the language of God. (Can I share a sacrilegious thought? When I think about such things—a husband declaring, in deposition, that his wife will be turned away from Heaven—I wish the dolphins were given the responsibility of turning our minds to God, not the clergy. Strike me down, but they have meant more to me than any man of cloth.)

Two things I recall from my child's vantage. Brigham sent, via an agent, an offer to my mother. This was a few days after we arrived at the Walker House. He must have realized she was determined to carry out as public a divorce as possible. He offered—I believe it was—$20,000, to, as they say, disappear. In *The 19th Wife* my mother insists she was indignant at the offer and dismissed it at once. That is not my recollection. Tempted by the large sum, she lingered over it, consulting with her advisers. Both Judge Hagan and Major Pond told her it was not enough. "Twenty thousand dollars is enough to take care of my boys," my mother said. She looked to me as she said this. My memory of it is as clear as if it occurred this morning. Or right now.

Not long after this (it could have been the same afternoon), my mother and Judge Hagan had a disagreement. We were alone in the suite, and they behaved as if I were not present or did not understand them. As payment for his legal services, Judge Hagan wanted 50% of my mother's future settlement. My mother rightly objected. "You're robbing me," she said. "I need every penny for James and Lorenzo."

They settled on 20%, but I know thereafter my mother never fully trusted Judge Hagan again. As time passed, it became clear he was more interested in his own gain and notoriety than saving my mother from Brigham's wrath.

By the end of July, my mother had formally filed suit against the Prophet of the Latter-day Saints. To them—the Saints, I mean—it was no less an affront than serving papers to Christ. (I once read in the newspaper of a man from West Texas who, disappointed that his patch of dirt was not an oil field, filed suit against the Lord. Bureaucracy pondered the case for eleven days.)

On the subject of irony, Brigham responded with an unexpected legal maneuver. Via his lawyers he claimed my mother was not his legal wife for the simple reason that he was already married. At the time there was a dual justice system in Utah—Brigham's and the American code of law. They lay atop one another in a not always natural fit. Some matters were brought before the Church, others before the courts. Brigham chose to use the federal laws for his counterattack. The courts, of course, did not (and do not) recognize polygamy. Therefore my mother was not married to Brigham, never had been his wife, and hence had no valid claims to his property. (Do you ever consider, Professor Green, how the law can be both magnificent and idiotic?) In essence, he made legal claim that he had never married my mother.

I don't know what my mother thought when she learned of Brigham's tactics. I know that would provide fresh detail for your book, but I'm afraid she never spoke to me directly about it. Was she "mad as Hades"? Professor Green, are you married? If you are, then you have learned the futility of guessing a woman's mind. And isn't that one of woman's 1,001 delights? She is not predictable. The moment you believe you can anticipate her, she will prove you wrong. Rosemary was like that. She used to say, "Don't tell me what's on my mind." If there is any constancy, it's that men are fools.

That's where I stopped yesterday. It was afternoon. No sign of the dolphins. Have they already moved south? They do not migrate as regularly as the whales. You cannot turn your calendar by them.

Although they are gone, I will not be surprised if they return to-morrow or next week. Then again, if I were not to see them for many months, that too would not surprise me. Do you know what I miss most about Rosemary? Simply knowing she was there.

I'm afraid even your question about myself—was I ever excommunicated from the Church?—I am unable to answer. You probably have the resources to research that. In any event, whether or not through clerical error or grand scheme I am technically still a member of the Latter-day Saints matters none to me. I do not say that to offend you. I should think I would offend you more if I did not write in full honesty, especially on the subject of faith. In my adulthood I flirted with the Episcopals. Rosemary was a Catholic, although she disagreed with nearly everything they proclaimed. What do I consider myself now? A man attempting to be good. In this endeavor I have no use for church and steeple. If another man does, I only wish he finds what he needs.

I have just now reread your letter. Did Brigham really treat my mother as she describes in *The 19th Wife*? Did she truly want to end polygamy or was she more interested in destroying Brigham? What was her final fate? I wish I could tell you where to turn to answer these questions, but I'm in the dark like you. On the last one—what happened to her?—I suppose in writing this letter, I am subconsciously encouraging you to dig around her story so that one day you may come to me and explain the mystery of her disappearance. How I wish I had even a clue to guide you in your search.

I think at this juncture it would be best if I jumped to November 1873. (I can hear Rosemary now, reminding me to get to the point.) My memories of the flight are clear and sure. I doubt I have given you any insight thus far, but concerning that long night I might be able to pull up a few fresh scraps. But first let me tell you how my mother's career as a public lecturer formed. During our confinement at the Walker House, while Judge Hagan and the others worked up my mother's legal strategy, Major Pond began to plot a different sort of path for her. At the time she was in a precarious financial position. Although future income seemed likely, at the present moment her purse was empty. Gilbert supplemented, but my mother had legitimate concern over how she would house and feed my brother and me. She never expressed this in my presence, but any child of an impoverished household can tell you when the coins are few. I offered her my two gold coins, but she told me to keep them, folding them up in my palm.

My mother's national notoriety was such that a number of promoters telegraphed with offers of representation. These men believed there was such interest in my mother's account that she would be a viable member on the lecture circuit. For the most part my mother ignored the appeals. She was truly interested in her legal situation and restoring her family, not in expanding her fortune. When Barnum wrote offering a substantial sum, her attention sat up for the first time. "Is it for real?" she asked Major Pond. "All this money?" (I never learned the sum, but I understand that a few years before he offered to send Brigham on the road for a fee of $100,000. One can assume Barnum's number for the 19th wife was in this range.)

In rapid response Major Pond, former Confederate, irritable reporter, conferred upon himself a new profession: lecture agent. "I can get you more," he said. He realized my mother's story was gold. He instructed her to prepare some lectures concerning her experiences. In her writings and commentary she has shrilly denied she began to speak publicly of her ordeals for profit. She claims she solely took to the lecture podium in her crusade to demolish polygamy from the United States. On the subject of mammon, she said repeatedly she simply was trying to ensure a roof and food for her boys. As they say: True, but. I loved my mother, but God bless her—she loved her jewels.

I remember the days in early November when she worked at the writing table near the stove. Typically my mother was restless with energy, unable to sit for long. She was always moving about a room, rearranging her skirts and cuffs, turning her rings, patting down her hair. She spoke quickly, sometimes, I fear, without thinking over her words. She was not a born writer. For nearly a week she agonized at the writing table, drafting a sentence or two, standing up, moving to the window, pulling back the shade, sighing with exasperation, and returning to her chair. It was a melodramatic reenactment of what the writer endures to produce a page. (I should know: three days have passed since I began this letter, Professor Green!)

Eventually she wrote three lectures concerning her experiences married to the Prophet and an insider's view of Brigham's harem; the general conditions of polygamy; and the politics of the Mormon Church. Do I need to tell you which became her most popular?

In a trial run, the Major arranged a lecture in the parlors of the Walker House, inviting nearly every Gentile in the Territory. Hundreds, perhaps even 1,000, showed up. I was not allowed to attend the event, but from the suite's window I watched the river of people flow into the hotel. I waited alone in our rooms while my mother spoke downstairs. For more than an hour there wasn't a sound in the hotel other than my mother's clear soprano. I will confess I felt abandoned that night. I do not share this with you to wallow in an old hurt but simply to relay the feelings of a child. Eventually a great roar overtook the hotel. They were applauding my mother, cheering her name, pleading for more. Thereafter Major Pond began to plan my mother's triumph on America's stage.

He arranged her debut in Denver. But there was still the risk of traveling out of Utah. Judge Hagan worried Brigham might not let her depart the Territory; or worse, might send a pack of Danites after her carriage. I do not know on what basis this opinion was formed, but everyone believed it, and suddenly the mood in the suite had changed. (I'm sure you will recall that the investigation of the Mountain Meadows massacre had resumed at this time, and there was much speculation in Brigham's role in those terrible murders. I'm not telling you anything you don't already know when I say many people believed he ordered the killings, or at least condoned them. This speculation no doubt colored her perception of the dangers she faced.)

An air of busy planning overtook the suite. Allies came and went, secret methods of escape were proposed and dismissed. After a few days, a plan was settled on. My mother, Major Pond, Judge Hagan, and the Strattons swore themselves to secrecy. At the time I had no idea what the secret was, but soon it went into implementation. Whenever a guest came to visit, my mother sent him off with one or two items concealed in his coat: a pair of shoes, a hat, a notebook, her hair oil. Item by item, my mother decamped.

Once I realized my mother was planning to depart, I burst into tears. "I don't want you to leave me," I told her. I expected her to say, "I'm taking you with me." She did not. She rubbed my back while saying, "I have to go."

Again I expected her to add, "I'll return for you." But she did not offer any assurances over our future. I cannot tell you why she behaved as she did at this moment. I like to think she was not so indifferent to my feelings. Yet I doubt there has been a moment in my life when I felt so uncertain of my place in the world as then. I lay awake at night with a sickened heart.

In the morning she said, "If I tell you a secret you have to promise to keep it. Tonight I will leave here for dinner with the Strattons. Later, your uncle Gilbert will come for you. You must do whatever he says. If he tells you to be quiet, you mustn't make a noise. If he tells you to hide in a box, you must fold yourself up like a cat."

In the evening she dressed for dinner as she might on any evening. Gilbert arrived, but he acted as if something were wrong. He gave me a peppermint stick, but became annoyed with my questions. "Lorenzo," said my mother, "remember what we discussed?"

When the Strattons called I began to cry. My mother had become preoccupied with her escape, and thus no longer had the capacity to comfort me. It was Gilbert who held me as she departed the suite. In *The 19th Wife* she writes there was no time for kisses and good-byes. "I was already a fugitive, there wasn't a minute to spare!" No time for love? My goodness, I hope there's never such a time on my clock.

For about an hour my uncle and I looked at each other. He was never comfortable around children. He asked about my toy horse, but when I told him its name I sensed his interest was not real. Children can tell. I do not fault Gilbert for this. His life in plural marriage—two wives and eighteen children—had eaten away at the love in his soul. Gilbert was a good man; he tried to love his family. Whoever said love is a pie was correct, at least in the polygamous family; there is a finite number of slices to pass out. Eventually I lay down on a blanket and fell asleep.

I do not know what time he woke me, perhaps ten o'clock. The room was dark and I was very tired. Gilbert helped me into my coat and shoes and led me down the servants' stairs into the Walker House kitchen. A very large woman in a wide apron was plunging her arms into a sink of hot soapy water. She barely looked up as we passed. At the door there was a tall round basket of the kind I once saw an Indian woman use to haul maize from a field. Gilbert told me to climb in. "I'm going to carry you out to the carriage. Once we're inside you can get out. It will only be a minute. But you can't be seen leaving."

I climbed into the basket, crouching with my knees to my chest. Gilbert set the lid on top. Light came through the basket and my vision was like that of a medieval knight peeping out through his mail. I could see the woman at the sink. She never once stopped washing the dishes. Gilbert heaved me up, and I felt a sway in the pit of my stomach. I wanted to cry out and beg to be released, but I told myself to stay still for the sake of my mother. The driver helped Gilbert set the basket on the carriage floor. When the door was closed, he lifted the lid.

We drove for several blocks, stopping in front of a large shrub that had turned skeletal with autumn. "You must be very still," Gilbert warned. We sat in the carriage for over an hour, the only sound was my heart in my ears. Then I heard footsteps. Gilbert pulled back the curtain. "It's them." He opened the door. My mother climbed in and the Strattons closed the door behind her. She took me into her arms. "I know, my child," she said. "I know. But we're not there yet."

The driver pulled away. With the curtains drawn it was difficult to know our destination. I dared not ask, for both my mother and uncle had looks of grave concern. When the road roughened I could tell we had left the city's limits. The carriage rocked and creaked and the night was filled with the sound of the crying springs and the horse leather. Eventually my mother released my hand from her grasp, and I assumed we were safe.

I climbed over to the window and pulled back the curtain. From the mountains I could tell we were driving up the Valley, headed north. We drove through bare orchards silvered by the moon. The patches of alkali shone in the night. In the fens geese were calling to one another. Across a meadow a herd of cattle was standing in the dark.

We turned off the road into a canyon. I saw the canyon walls narrow around us. Because I had no idea where we were going, I did not think to alert my mother. Eventually we were driving alongside a frozen creek. Everywhere neat mounds of early snow sat upon the ice. The moonlight, reflecting off the ice, illuminated the canyon. I pulled back the curtain farther to show my mother the ghostly effect.

She began to panic. "Where are we? What's happening?"

Gilbert banged on the carriage roof and leapt out to talk to the man. I heard the driver say he must have made the wrong turn. "I was certain this was the way to Uintah," he said.

"What if he's working for Brigham?" my mother said when Gilbert was back in the carriage. "What if we've been had by our own plan?"

As we drove out of the canyon, the walls retreated. Eventually the valley opened before us and the cattle were standing where we left them across the meadow.

It was forty miles to Uintah. We arrived just before daybreak, pulling up to the tiny station. We were waiting for the eastward Union Pacific. As you probably know, Brigham owned the line between Salt Lake and Ogden. That's where you used to catch the U.P.—probably still do, I don't know. Anyhow, I'm sure you understand my mother's plan: anyone tracking my mother would have expected her in Ogden. By driving across the desert in the night, she bypassed their trap.

As the cold day took hold, and the sun revealed the tiny town encased in ice, we heard the air brakes from down the track. I could see the smoke puffing out of the engine. Shortly thereafter the train pulled into the depot, blowing snow all about.

Gilbert embraced my mother. To me he said, "Look after her."

My mother took my hand and we ran to the platform. A porter in white coat and gloves led us to our compartment in the Pullman, where our belongings waited. When the train lurched forward, leaving the station behind, my mother collapsed onto the bench.

"May I speak?" I asked.

She was looking out the window and did not respond. Her profile was very beautiful and still. The morning light had turned yellow and it poured forth upon her, giving her a golden quality. She looked like a woman in a painting in a foreign museum. She studied the landscape as it passed—the high meadows white and yellow in late fall, the sparkling wool of the frost-covered sheep, the mountaintops padded with ancient snow that will never melt. I climbed into her lap and together we watched the world go by.

Three hours later the air brakes screamed and the conductor called, "Wyoming! Evanston, Wyoming!"

Having crossed the Utah border, she said, "Now you can speak."

And there, Professor Green, in that little border town, my

mother achieved her freedom. I could not understand the importance of the moment, of course. But I recall while we idled in the station how a cloud drifted before the sun, darkening my mother's face, and how seconds later it passed and her face seemed to burst open with the clearest of light.

Oh look! The dolphins have returned. Explain it! The coincidence, I mean. We can't. We simply have to take note of it and love it for its mystery. As you go about your research about my mother, I ask you to forgive her errors and vainglory. Is she any more guilty than you or I? When you publish your research, will you send a copy? I should like to know what you have learned, most especially how she spent her last days. Sometimes I can hardly believe I don't know my own mother's fate. It seems like a dismal twist at the end of an epic tale. But so it is, and the unknowable keeps me up. With Rosemary gone, the nights are lonely. I lie awake burdened by my mother's disappearance. I trust you'll share with me whatever you discover, even if the news is grim. It's the uncertainty I cannot bear. The not knowing. The endless speculation of where she was on her last day. A chill dashes up my spine when I think of it—there, just now, as if my mother's loving hand were stroking my nape. She's with me. She will always be with me. Remember this as you analyze her life and deeds.

I am, Most Sincerely Yours,

LORENZO DEE

XVII

———

WIFE #19:

THE GIRL IN SLC

A LITTLE SOMETHING SOMETHING

———

I parked across the street from the Prophet's house. Alton was in his cruiser by the gate, one arm thrown across the seat back, looking down the road, waiting for me. "You have a good memory," he said.

"You thought I'd forget the number?"

"I would've."

"She's not your mom."

"Go talk to Brother Luke." He pointed to a guard standing at the gatepost. "He'll let you in."

"I heard about the FBI. What's happening out here?"

"We don't know."

"How's Queenie?"

"Anxious, like everyone. But OK."

I looked over to the guard. He had his eye on me. I could tell he didn't like that I was here. "Am I going to be all right?"

"Jordan, you have to trust me. Now go inside."

I introduced myself to the guard. "I know," he said. He brought a two-way radio to his mouth: "He's here." The guard led me through a door in the gate and locked it behind us.

Few people get to see inside the Prophet's compound. My dad used to come here for meetings but he never talked about it. The house was by far the biggest in town, which makes sense because he had the most wives. Exactly how many was anyone's guess but definitely more than a hundred. Maybe 150. I don't know. I bet he doesn't either.

"We'll go through the kitchen," the guard said. He was in dark pants and a white dress shirt and a short red tie. If you ignored the

Glock 17 in his belt holster, you'd think he was on his way to church.

Three wives were baking in the kitchen. One was looking up a recipe when she saw me. She froze with her finger on the page. The other two pressed themselves against the counter to step out of my way. "Evening, Sisters," the guard said. The women nodded and looked at their feet. We walked down a hall, past a large reception room with a white marble floor. Across the hall, a dining room with a U-shaped table for fifty. I saw a steel-plate door leading to, what—a vault? a safe room? an armory?

"Is he here?" I said.

The guard led me up three flights of stairs. Along the way we passed four more wives. They were young, younger than me. Here they were—the reason the boys get kicked out. The Prophet wanted the prettiest girls for himself. The pervy thing was, they all looked the same.

On the top floor, at the end of the hall, the guard knocked on a door. "Sister?" He knocked again. "Sister, he's here."

The door cracked, then opened wider, then wider still. It was the Prophet's first wife, Sister Drusilla. She waved us in. Her room was bare to the point of heartbreaking—a narrow bed shrouded by a dingy summer spread. A writing table with a goose-neck lamp. Two wood chairs. She poured a glass of water from a spiderwebbed ceramic pitcher.

"Is the Prophet here?" I said.

"You haven't heard?" she said. "They came for him." Drusilla's soft old mouth sank in on itself.

"I heard they couldn't find him."

"That's because he's gone," she said.

"Where is he?"

"I don't know. He could be dead."

"He isn't dead. I spoke to him a little while ago."

"I'm not so sure."

The best way to describe Drusilla is something like a cross between the First Lady and the Virgin Mary. In the springtime there was a pageant in her honor. All the girls in town would put on yellow dresses and dance and sing Pioneer hymns like "In Our House" while Sister Drusilla viewed the festivities from a platform. Other than that and Sunday services, we never saw her. Everyone loved her, but no one really knew a thing about her.

"I suppose you know I'm trying to find out what really happened to my dad."

"Yes, he told me."

"My mom's just not the murderer type."

"No one is until they are."

"How well do you know Rita?"

"My whole life."

"I think she had something to do with this."

"Jordan, there's something you need to know. About Rita." Drusilla's right, livered hand trembled in her lap. Was she frightened? Early Parkinson's? Or was she putting on a show to freak me out? "Rita's also gone. Disappeared. I don't know when exactly. Sometime in the last twenty-four hours. I think they kidnapped her."

"Is it possible she ran away?"

Drusilla shook her head and sighed. "I know what's coming next. We've lived through this before."

"Through what?"

"The Siege."

The Siege. Every kid in Mesadale grows up learning about the Siege. We had to read about it, listen to the Prophet sermonize on it, in Sunday school reenact it, chirp songs exalting it, and the girls needlepointed scenes from it. Since breaking off from the Mormons in 1890, the Firsts managed to live in the desert for sixty years pretty much undisturbed. They started off as a cluster of renegades, led by Aaron Webb. Over time this minor outpost grew into a full-blown town, a polygamous theocracy tucked into the sands of the American Southwest. By the early 1950s, the feds could no longer look the other way. Cut to July 26, 1953. Agents drove into town in unmarked cars, backed up by one hundred state troopers. Quickly they had Mesadale surrounded. You know this kind of scene: the troopers taking position behind car doors; the first-ins standing ready with rammer and shield; an agent in wingtips calling for surrender through a megaphone.

The Siege was about one man. The Prophet. Not the Prophet I've been telling you about, but his father. If he surrendered peacefully, the feds promised to withdraw. That's what the agent shouted through the megaphone: "If you come with us, this can all be over now."

At sunset the Siege began. The shoot-out lasted seven hours. By dawn seventeen Firsts were dead, including nine kids. Hoping to show the country the truth about American polygamy, the feds brought a news photographer. But one picture told the wrong story—that's all it took for the plan to blow up in the feds' clean, Barbasol faces. If you google it, you can find the picture: a little girl lying in a bean field, a neat bullet wound above her left eye. If you didn't know what you were looking at, you'd think it was a drop of a jam. That picture ran in the evening papers. By the next morning the feds were caving. The Siege was over. The feds left town, trench coats between their legs.

But the feds got what they wanted. In the last hour a sniper nailed the Prophet. One shot through the neck. That's all it takes. That's how the current Prophet came into power. He was seventeen at the time. The day after the Siege, the new Prophet did two things: he buried his father, and he married his dad's youngest wife, a pretty soft-chinned girl named Drusilla. A year later, on the first anniversary, the new Prophet renamed the town Mesadale. It used to be called Red Creek. He wanted America to forget all about the Firsts. And America obliged. Until now.

Sister Drusilla gathered up her skirts to sit beside me on the bed. "This time they want us all dead."

"I don't think so," I said.

"Your dad's dead. How do we know Rita isn't dead? And your mom—we all know what's going to happen to her. Maybe they'll say it's her punishment, but it doesn't matter, dead is dead. And now the Prophet. They want us all gone. But I'm not going anywhere."

"You don't have to."

"This isn't some story in the newspaper. This is my life. This is my family. This is what I believe."

"I know, but all I'm really trying to do is get my mom out of jail."

"They're afraid of us, Jordan."

"Afraid?"

"Afraid of the Prophet, because they know he's right." Her shaky hand balled up into a blue white fist. "After the Siege, the Prophet always said they'd be back. He always said, Just you wait. And now here they are."

Seeing Drusilla sitting there, with her collar reaching high on her neck, I figured out one thing: some people don't want your help. No point in throwing them a line, they'll swim right past it.

"The Prophet thinks you're looking in the wrong place."

"Wrong place? What's that supposed to mean?"

"We have so many enemies. In Washington, in Salt Lake City. Everyone wants us gone. Your father and the Prophet were very close. It makes sense they'd start with him. They want everyone to think we're falling apart from within when in truth, someone's standing outside and picking us off, one by one."

You know that feeling when you think you're almost at the end of a road, and you turn the corner and see only more road ahead?

"If I were you," said Drusilla, "I'd find that girl. Sister Kimberly's daughter, you know the one I'm talking about—Sarah Five? She's been working with organizations trying to stop us."

"She didn't kill him."

"How do you know?"

"She told me."

"And you believe her?"

"I do."

Sister Drusilla's worn face hardened into a mask. "Interesting." I asked her what she was talking about. When she told me, I couldn't believe it.

"Are you sure?"

"A hundred percent."

"Why didn't she tell me?"

"She's hiding something."

"I can't believe it."

"Believe it, it's true."

Turns out 5 was hiding a little something something: about twelve hours before he was killed, my dad took her as his latest bride.

ANOTHER REVELATION
FROM GREAT SALT LAKE

Yesterday, in the Territory of Utah's Third District Court, the war between our friends, Brigham and Mrs. XIX, took a turn that even we could not have anticipated. At six o'clock in the evening, Brigham, via his imaginative lawyers, Mssrs. Hempstead and Kirkpatrick, filed a formal answer to his wife's bill of complaint against the Great Almighty Prophet of the West.

In a quick review of Brigham's legal papers we have determined his novel strategy for victory. His adamant reply contends that he and Ann Eliza were never married on April 6, 1868, as her suit originally claims. According to Brigham, whose sense of veracity and candor make him well-suited for our distinguished publication, Ann Eliza is not and has never been his legal wife. He makes this claim from a heartfelt and honorable position. Brigham touchingly claims his undying devotion to his first and only wife, the aptly named Mary Angell, who has been his rib since the tenth day of January, 1834, when they were happily betrothed in old Kirtland. Thus already married, Brigham could not enter into a second, let alone nineteenth union of the heart. That would by polygamy!

So you see, Your Honor, this woman's suit is without merit. She is—and here we must adopt the Prophet's unique words as our own—"merely a social harlot." What of Brigham's long-promoted custom of celestial marriage? Simply a hedonistic religious rite with no more legal standing than adultery, admitted the Prophet. Who are the women sleeping beneath the dormers of the infamous Lion House? Concubines, all of them, God bless them each.

Next, Brigham confessed to a disloyal liaison with Madame 19. Thus he respectfully asked the court, in its wisdom, to dismiss the matter so that he may return in peace to his only wife, the previously mentioned Angell, to make the kind of restitution we are all too familiar with.

THIS CAN'T GO ON

———

Tom was on the phone freaking out. "It's Johnny. He disappeared. I was doing some work at the front desk, I told him to stay with the dogs, and when I came back he was gone."

"When was this?"

"Almost two hours ago. I went driving around looking for him, but I didn't even know where to start. I just drove up and down St. George Ave. Jordan, where are you? I've been calling."

"There's no reception in Mesadale. Right now I'm in Kanab."

"I need you to come home, now. It's just that—" Tom stopped. "Johnny could be anywhere."

"Don't worry. He's like this."

"I'm going out of my mind here. What if something's happened to him?"

"Don't start thinking like that."

"I called the cops. They thought I was nuts. They said, 'Let me get this straight. You're reporting a runaway runaway?' They said they couldn't do anything for at least twenty-four hours. Jordan, I didn't even know his last name."

Part of me wanted to say: Tom, get a grip. The kid's a flake. He's gone and there's nothing you can do. Another part of me wanted to say: I know, I know, and turn this into a conversation between the sob sisters. But neither seemed right and all I could come up with was, "I'll be there as soon as I can."

When I got to the sandwich shop, 5 was closing up, her hair under a plastic beret. "Why the fuck didn't you tell me you married my dad?"

She went behind the counter for a cup of coffee. She took her time, pouring the cream and the sugar, stirring it, rinsing the spoon. Her eyes had a cold gleam, like chips of soda machine ice. "Why would I want to tell you about the worst day of my life?"

"Because my mom's in jail for something she didn't do."

"That has nothing to do with me."

"You were his wife."

She sipped her coffee slowly, cautiously putting together her words. "If you think holding a knife to your stepdaughter's throat while you rape her is a wedding ceremony, then I guess I am his wife. Or his widow or whatever. But if you don't think like that—and for some reason I thought you of all people wouldn't—then you'd realize I'm no more his wife than you are, asshole." She started cleaning up the sandwich counter and throwing the prep trays into the sink, and they made a terrible clang, stainless steel on stainless steel. "You think your life sucks so much? Well, guess what? My life sucks worse."

"Jesus, I had no idea."

"Yeah, well, you have no idea about a lot of shit. Now go sit down."

I sat in a booth by the window, and she carried over two sodas and two wax-paper cups. "Don't say anything. Just let me tell you what's going on."

"OK, but first—"

"No, stop. When I'm done, then you can speak. All right? First, let me start by saying this whole thing sucks. Like big-time. OK, let's begin. Like I said, I ran away a couple of months ago. I just split, caught a ride over here, and got this job. I knew it was crazy to stop here. I should've left Utah, but you know what, I love my mom. Or I used to, or I still do, I don't know. Anyway, like I told you, I couldn't leave her back there so I thought I'd go back and res- cue her. Except, how the fuck was I going to do that? I didn't have a car or any money or anything. But I kept thinking it was possible.

You know Sister Karen?"

"The postmistress?"

"She's been really helpful in all this. She got my letters to my mom without him seeing them. I kept writing her telling her I was OK and not far away and to hold tight, I was coming for her."

"And?"

"Jordan, let me finish. So that went on for a few months and I was kinda at a standstill. Then my mom writes me this letter saying she's sick, real sick, maybe even dying. Says she's had a heart attack or something, she was real vague about it, but she said the Prophet told her she didn't have much time. When I got the letter I totally flipped. I walked down to the end of town and caught a ride back to Mesadale. When I got to my mom's cabin, she was really happy to see me and started crying, but I was like, Mom, I thought you were sick? So she goes, Oh that? I'm all better now. The important thing is you're back. I know your stepfather will be real glad to see you. Then she walked over to the big house to get him. When they came back I was totally scared to see him, but he just said, I'm glad you're back. Please stay as long as you like.

"And that was it until the next day. I woke up and everything was really peaceful, you know how quiet the desert is in the morning before everyone gets up, and I was lying in bed just thinking about that when my mom came and sat down. Sarah, honey, there's something I want to talk about. That's when she sprang it on me. She wanted me to marry him, her own husband—I know, right? But she had it all planned out, or he did, or someone did. Obviously it was time for me to go, but when I opened the door there he was on the porch. He was in a bolo tie and his hair was greased back and he was wearing some sort of cologne, like old leather, and he wasn't alone."

"The Prophet?"

"You guessed it. He had this creepy smile, his lips curled up on his teeth, and it was so obvious what was coming next I started screaming my head off, yelling, There's no fucking way! My mom, she took me into her room, told me to calm down, and when I didn't she slapped me, not hard, but just hard enough to show the Prophet whose side she was on. Then you aren't going to believe what she did, I mean no one's ever going to believe this, but it's true: She got out her wedding dress and said, real calm and everything, Now, honey, put this on.

"I was fighting her, kicking her, telling her to go fuck herself. Then there was a knock on the door. It was the Prophet. Sister Kimberly, let me have a word. When we were alone he came real close and squeezed the back of my neck the way you grab a dog. If you don't shut the fuck up, I'm going to kill your mother and then you. I swear to God that's exactly what he said, not that I believe in God, but you know what I mean. He goes, I'll kill you, you little slut. Not now. Not tomorrow. But I'll be coming for you and you'll be scared the rest of your life because you'll know one night I'll be at your door and when you open it you're going to find your mother's head in a fucking bag."

She stopped. Her eyes looked like they'd seen the worst the world could offer.

Then she laughed.

"And so I married him. That night—the night he was killed—I took off from Mesadale. I heard all the screams in the house, I didn't know what was happening, but it was my chance to get out of there and so I ran down the road into the night."

"And here you are."

"Here I am. You know what the fucked-up part is? I still love my mom. Jordan, I'm only fifteen. I want her back. Am I insane or what?"

"You're not insane."

After that, 5 and I talked about the Prophet and Mesadale and all sorts of other shit too. If you drove by the sandwich shop that night, you would've seen the silver green lights burning through the plate glass and two kids at a booth in the window, eating corn chips and drinking soda and shredding their wax-paper cups on the table and talking for hours, just like two kids anywhere who'd rather stay out than go home.

"Just one question," I said. "Why would Sister Karen help you like that?"

"You haven't figured that out by now?"

"Figured out what?"

"You really don't know, do you? Sister Karen's the conductor."

"The conductor?"

"Of our underground railroad. She's the one who helps the girls get out."

REDPATH'S LYCEUM

Under the Directorship of

JAMES REDPATH

PRESENTS

Mrs. Ann Eliza Young

The Notorious 19th Wife!

Apostate & Crusader!

LECTURING ON THE SUBJECTS OF:

MORMON POLYGAMY!

INSIDE BRIGHAM'S HAREM!

THE LIFE OF THE PLURAL WIFE!

&

OTHER TRUTHS ABOUT

MULTIPLE MARRIAGE!

THE TREMONT TEMPLE

BOSTON

• ONE NIGHT ONLY •

FEBRUARY 19, 1874

Admission—Only Fifty Cents!

Inside Room 112, I found Tom holding a bag of ice to Johnny's eye. "What happened here?"

"Not much, dude. And you?"

"He's high," said Tom. "And he has a black eye. And I found this on him." He pointed to a cheap gold watch on the credenza.

"Where'd you get that?"

"This guy. It was weird, he just gave it to me. Isn't that weird?"

"Plus he's scaring the dogs." They were watching the scene from the bed. Elektra was agitated and shaking, and Joey was panting hard.

"Johnny, where were you?"

"With the ladies."

"There's no point in talking to him," said Tom. "He's totally looped. Thank goodness you're home."

Technically it wasn't my home, but it didn't seem like a good time to point that out. "What can I do?"

"Get him ready for bed. He should sleep in here tonight."

"Anyone got anything to eat?" said Johnny. "Krispy Kremes, maybe?"

"Bedtime, big guy." I pulled Johnny out of his jeans, dumped him on the bed, and threw a blanket over him. "Now go to sleep."

"I'd kill for a Whopper," he said. "Or some McNuggets." He was stumbling into sleep, his words slowing down. He smacked his lips, let out a soft moan, and pushed out a final thought for the night: "You think they got a Snickers in the vending machine?" Then he was out. He'd sleep till dawn.

Tom was on the edge of the other bed, stroking Joey. He had to be pissed at me for bringing this mess into his life. "I was really worried," he said. "About both of you. What do you think got into him? Maybe he freaked out because you weren't around?"

"I'm afraid this wasn't a onetime event. Johnny's got a lot of issues."

Tom shrugged. "I don't care. He can stay as long as he wants." And then, "You too."

He went into the bathroom to get ready for bed. I opened his laptop and went online to that website 19thwife.com. Under the If You Need Help tab, there was information about a place in Salt Lake called the Ann Eliza Young House. There was a picture of an old Victorian house with a stained-glass window. At the top of the page it said, We're always here.

Tom came out of the bathroom stripped to his sacred underwear. That's another thing I love about the Mormons: that crazy holy underwear is actually kinda sexy. Roland calls it God's lingerie. Which reminded me: I hadn't talked to him in days. He still thought I was coming back for the nursery job tomorrow morning. Isn't that how it works sometimes—the big decisions, I mean. You don't actually make them, you just roll into them once they've become inevitable. Sometime between meeting Tom in the lobby of the Malibu Inn and now, I had decided to stay in Utah to see this thing through.

"Question," I said.

"Shoot."

"Why do you still wear that?"

"What? You don't like it?"

"It's not that. I mean, don't you have to be a Mormon to wear that underwear?"

"Technically, but it's not about the church anymore. It's about me. Besides, it's actually pretty comfortable. You know what my mom used to say when I was a kid? She used to say, wearing these was like wearing a hug. I know that's cheesy but it's kinda true. The only problem now is you have to have a temple recommend to buy them. But I found this site online where I can get new ones." He sat on the bed. "What about you? Do you always sleep in your clothes?"

I hadn't even noticed that I had crawled into bed in my jeans. "I don't know, I guess. Does that bother you?"

"It makes me feel like you're ready to bolt."

"Don't think of it like that."

"Tomorrow I'm going to buy you some PJs."

"I wish you wouldn't."

We pulled up the blanket, and Elektra dug under and curled up between us. Joey found a spot at the foot of the bed. The room went quiet except for the sighs of the dogs. "Jordan?"

"Yeah?"

"Can I ask you a question about your mom?"

"OK."

"What was she like?"

"What do you mean?"

"What kind of mom was she?"

"I don't know, pretty average, I mean considering."

"Did you get to spend a lot of time with her?"

"Sure."

"What would you do?"

"I don't know, the usual stuff."

"Like what?"

"We'd hang out, I guess."

"Did she bake you cookies and things like that?"

"Not really."

"No?"

"It was kind of hard to do any baking. The kitchen had all these rules."

"What else would you do?"

"I'd hang out in her room sometimes."

"And talk?"

"Yeah."

"About what?"

"All sorts of stuff."

"Like what?"

"God and the church and things like that, but other things, too."

"Like what?"

"I don't know. Like the sun, and how different it was in the summer from the winter. And the mountains and how pretty they looked when there was snow. And Virginia."

"Who's that?"

"Our old dog."

"What happened to her?"

"She's still alive."

"You must miss her."

"Virginia? Yeah, sometimes."

"I meant your mom."

"Sure, I guess."

Tom dented his pillow and turned on his side. "Jordan?"

"Yeah."

"What do you think's going to happen?"

"She'll either get out or she won't."

"When are you going to see her?"

"Soon." And then, "Real soon."

In the morning I told Tom about the place in SLC. "I'm taking Johnny there."

"Maybe there's someplace closer." He was getting ready to go to the front desk, pinning his name tag to his shirt. He had a bright polished look, his cheeks shining with morning cheer.

"There's noplace else," I said. "I don't want him to put you through another night like last night. I'll be back tomorrow."

"Wait till Saturday and I'll go with you."

"This can't wait. A lot can happen in a week."

"I'll miss you."

"C'mon, it's only been two days."

"Two days are enough for me." And then, "But I guess not for you."

I decided to leave Elektra with Joey in the room. She didn't like that idea and ran out to the van and tried to jump through the window. I had to drag her back inside. As I pulled out of the lot her brown snout was in the window, leaving prints on the glass. Tom was in the lobby behind the front desk, keeping his eye on my van, watching me as I drove off. He waved as I pulled out but I don't think he saw me wave back.

Johnny slept most of the way on the futon, still hung over from last night. Every once in a while he woke up to announce he needed to piss, but other than that he was more or less passed out. It was nearly five hours to SLC, which gave me way too much time to think.

I first saw the temple from the freeway. I guess you'd say it's beautiful, what with all that white granite and the forest of spires and the gold angel playing his trumpet on top of that gold ball. I shook Johnny's foot and told him to wake up. "There it is," I said. "The mother ship."

Johnny stared out at the temple. "You ever been here before?" he said.

"Nope."

"Me neither. It's not really what I expected."

"What'd you expect?"

"I don't know, for some reason I thought it would look like heaven."

"Maybe it does."

"Where's this famous lake?"

"Out there somewhere."

"I don't see it."

"I'm sure it's there."

"So tell me, Mr. International Poster Boy for Gay Marriage, what brings us to Salt Lake?"

"What are you talking about now?"

"You and Tom, pretty serious, right, right?" He started whistling *here comes the bride.* "No, seriously, why'd we drive all the way up here?"

"I've got an appointment."

"Is it one of our chat session ladies? I've been dying to meet the others."

"I never heard back from them. This is someone else."

We were off the freeway now, driving toward Temple Square along an eight-lane road pumping traffic into the city. Except there wasn't much traffic and no one was walking around. I stopped at a red light for a tram to cross. I was the only car waiting and there wasn't anyone on the tram.

"I'm going to drop you somewhere and I'll go have my meeting and then come back for you. I'll probably be gone a little more than an hour."

"Whoa whoa whoa, wait a minute, you want me to do what?"

"Just hang out somewhere."

"Why are you giving me the heave-ho all of a sudden?"

"Because you look like shit and smell like pot. I can't take you to a meeting."

"No way, dude, you don't haul my ass to SLC and then leave me in the van."

"I won't leave you in the van. We'll find a park somewhere."

"I'm not sitting in a boiling ass park where all the repressed Mormon fags can chase me."

"Johnny. You know how I feel about that word."

He mimicked me: "*You know how I feel about that word.*"

"Here. Right here." I pulled over, cutting off the guy behind me. "Here's a mall right here. You go in there and hang out. Give me two hours. Here's ten dollars. Buy yourself a hot dog and go fuck yourself."

"Someone didn't get laid last night and is now taking it out on me."

"Why are you always so nasty?"

"Because I'm from Mesadale, you mother."

"That excuse is getting old."

"Look in the mirror, buddy."

"And none of your running-off shit, either. If you aren't here in exactly two hours, I'm driving back to St. George and you can have a really nice life."

"You're a total motherfucker, you know that?" He popped the door and ran off, the black soles of his sneakers flashing until he was gone.

I recognized the Ann Eliza Young House by the stained-glass window. The place looked nice enough, fresh paint on the porch and yellow daisies along the path. I rang the bell and a girl a few years older than me opened up. I told her I'd seen the website and wanted to know if it was true.

"If what's true?" she said.

"If you're really here to help."

She laughed like I'd made a joke or something, and then she saw I was totally serious and led me inside to a back office. There were a couple of pictures of the girl on her desk, shots of her with her arms around other blond girls. One picture showed the girl in her missionary outfit, with the black-and-white name tag and the long dark skirt, standing in front of the lurid lights of Times Square.

"Have a seat. Our director's out for about an hour," she said, "but you're welcome to wait right here."

"I only need a little information."

"I'm happy to tell you about our program, get you oriented and everything, but only the director can formally admit you. If you want, I can show you the boys' room and you can take a shower and put on some—"

She stopped. "What's wrong? Are you hungry? We have some veggie lasagna left over."

I told the girl I wasn't hungry. I told the girl I wasn't there for me. "I've got a kid. I mean, he's not mine, he just started hanging out with me down in St. George." I told her the whole story. Well, not the whole story, just the part about Johnny. I didn't bother going into all the stuff about me and my mom.

"I am so sorry," the girl said. "I thought—"

"I know."

"You look so young."

"I wanted to check this place out. But I don't want to leave Johnny just anywhere."

"Of course not. You want to leave him someplace where he's going to have a chance."

She was an attractive girl, pert, maybe twenty-four, her banged hair well conditioned and full of shine. Her features were small and precise, almost a little hard and cold, a shard of a nose, and she gave off a fresh, antibacterial soap odor. "The Ann Eliza Young House is a really special place," she said, her voice a little formal and practiced. "There's nothing like it in Utah, or the country, for that matter. With all this debate about polygamy and the Firsts, sometimes we lose sight of the fact that there are kids out there who need a place to sleep. Tonight. That's why we're here, for those kids who don't have anywhere to go and can't wait for the policy debates to get sorted out. You want a quick tour?"

Leading me down the hall, she said, "I don't know how much you know about what's going on with polygamy these days."

"A little."

"Then you know how much help these kids need. What we do is give them a place to live and begin the process of letting them be kids again. What was happening before was they'd go from a house with eight or ten wives and thirty or forty kids—"

"Sometimes more."

"Yes, sometimes more, and then they'd get dropped into a foster family and the kids would be sent off to school, and everyone would say, OK they're fine. Well, they weren't fine. These kids have some unique issues, and we're here to help them adjust. By the way, what's your name?"

I told her. "And yours?"

"Kelly. Kelly Dee."

She showed me around upstairs, the boys' bunk room, the community bathroom, a lounge with a box of DVDs and a rack of worn-out paperbacks. She was leading me down the staircase when she stopped on the landing to point out the stained-glass window. The sun was hitting it, illuminating a mountain scene, and the pieces of glass were thick and smooth and green and white. "Isn't that beautiful?" she said. "That's original to the house, from the 1870s. Stained glass was very rare at the time around here. That window's sort of famous. Do you know who Ann Eliza Young was?"

"No idea."

"She was one of Brigham's wives. She lived here for a while, before she divorced him. She always said he put in this window so his spies could find her house, but there's no proof that's true, but that's what makes it pretty well-known today. Anyway, she went on to become a crusader in the fight to end polygamy."

"I guess she failed."

"No, not at all. She played a big part in forcing the church to give it up."

The tour was over and we were back in the office, sitting around waiting for the director to show up. "You like working here?"

"Actually, I'm just a volunteer. I'm here full-time in the summer, and two days a week during school. I'm getting my master's at BYU. In history. Women's studies." She said it with a touch of pride, or rebellion. "It's how I got involved with this place. I'm writing my thesis on Ann Eliza Young. That's how I first heard about what was going on with polygamy today. I had no idea—I mean, I heard the stories about places like Mesadale and everything, but I never really thought it was as bad as everyone said. At the time I was really immersed in my research. Because I'm writing about the nineteenth century, it's all old documents and texts, you know—rummaging around the archives. I was learning a lot, but one thing I was having a hard time understanding was her rage—Ann Eliza's, I mean. She was really mad at Brigham and the Mormons over polygamy. Not mad like pissed off, but mad like she was waging spiritual battle. Over the years a lot of Saints, they've just kind of dismissed her as the angry ex-wife, but this was more than that. This was a woman on a mission, so to speak. It had become her faith, which was a really interesting idea to me, you know, to give up one faith for another, one that's so opposite to what you used to believe.

"Then I thought—you know, the best way to understand what she was feeling, to actually understand why she was so outraged, was maybe to truly comprehend what polygamy was like for her. At first I just couldn't wrap my head around it—I mean, I'm just your average LDS girl with a mother and a father and an older brother and a younger sister and a dog named Lilly. Sure I saw the world when I was on my mission—here, that's me in New York, which I totally loved. Maybe it was my time on mission that helped me realize that the only way to understand people is to listen to them. So anyway, I decided I had to meet someone who had come from that world, someone who could help me get what she'd gone through. Eventually I found the website 19thwife.com and arranged an interview with a plural wife."

"You should've called me."

"What?"

"Nothing. It's a joke. Not funny. You were saying—"

"I met this woman in a coffee shop not far from here. I took my tape recorder, my notepad, and I felt, you know, almost like a detective. It was very exciting because usually historians, we only meet people through documents, never in person. Then this woman walks in and she was very thin and very frightened, and very young, younger than me by a couple of years. Her eyes were red—I'll never forget how red they were—but she wasn't crying. That's when it hit me: This isn't a research subject, these are people's lives, people's lives ruined by this doctrine that is a by-product of *my* church. Of course I knew that before, but it's one thing to know something intellectually, it's another to meet it face-to-face. This woman, she sat opposite me in the booth and her back was very rigid and she just began to tell me about her husband and her twelve sister wives, very quietly, very methodically, as if she had practiced it over and over. Eventually she ran away, eventually she decided that if this life was what God wanted for her, then she didn't want God, but what was killing her, the reason she wanted to talk to me in the first place, was she had to leave her kids behind, a boy and a girl. You should've seen her—she just kind of crumpled as she said she decided the only way to save her kids was to leave them and come back for them later, but you could just tell it was one of those terrible decisions a mother shouldn't have to make, but she made it, and there she was. Now she wanted to get them out, but she really didn't have any way of doing that. I mean, they talk about the disenfranchised, but this woman had nothing, not even a faith. Eventually she took my hand and said, 'Can you help me?' I'll never forget how cold her hand was, like a claw of ice.

"It was then I knew I had to do something. I couldn't just sit in my library carrel and read through all my texts and take my seminars and write a master's thesis that was full of ideas but empty on people. Of course, that's what the department wanted me to do, but I couldn't, and fortunately my adviser, Professor Sprague, she totally understood what I was talking about and sort of sponsored me. So I got an internship here and that was two years ago. And now I just try to help out women like that, and the kids. This whole experience has changed my life."

Kelly looked at the clock. "The director should be back soon."

"So this lady you were talking about?"

"The lady I interviewed?"

"No, the lady this place is named after. What'd you say she did?"

"She really helped bring an end to polygamy. She went around giving lectures, telling everyone what it was really like. People all over the country went to see her, and for a while there she was as famous as, I don't know, a rock star or someone on TV, but this was in the 1870s. Eventually she went to Congress and described polygamy and met President Grant and told him all about it. After her visit to Washington the government finally started putting some teeth into the antipolygamy laws. She got the ball rolling, and eventually the church had to give it up. She called us on it, and she won."

"How do you know so much about her?"

"I've spent the last two years of my life reading everything I can about Ann Eliza Young. There's a lot out there, she wrote this really famous book called *The 19th Wife*, and there are diaries and letters and all these records by people who knew her and the more I read, the more I want to know. You know what's funny, even today a lot of members don't like her. She fought Brigham pretty hard in their divorce, and she said lots of nasty things about the church in her book, some of which were misleading and completely biased, but she also made us see the truth about something very important. She saved the church, in her own way, you know, by forcing us to give up polygamy. There's no way I could believe in a church that supported that, especially now that I've seen it for myself. I feel like I owe her so much—my faith, it's the most important thing I have, along with my family, of course, but I love my church as much as I can love anything. I'm just really glad she put us through that, and flushed it out of our system.

"To some she was a real hero. But a lot of Saints, even today, they're angry at her. Some people, like some of Brigham's descendants, won't even say her name. A few years ago they put out a book of remembrances about Brigham, you know, collecting old letters and other papers by Brigham's children and grandchildren describing Brigham at home, what kind of father he was, and in the back there's a list of his wives. They completely left her off. Edited out of history! Thankfully not everyone's like that. This house, it's run by a group of LDS members who felt the need to do something about polygamy today. It wasn't very hard to raise the money to buy it and fix it up. A lot of people wanted to help. They see it as I do, as our duty, you know, because in some ways it's part of our legacy."

"I know I need to talk to the director," I said, "but can you tell me how this whole thing is going to work for Johnny?"

"Sure, first she has to meet him and make sure he'll fit in. This is a community, and we can't have someone destructive or violent or what have you."

"He's not like that."

"Of course there are rules, which we're real strict about. Among the many things these kids need is discipline. No drinking and drugs, no stealing, no weapons of any kind—any signs of those and you're immediately out. It's a no-tolerance zone. Before he's admitted Johnny will have to sign a statement saying he won't break the rules. It's an important step, making a commitment and keeping it. Last but definitely not least, there's a lot of paperwork, filing with the various agencies, but that can happen after he checks in. We try to spare the kids from the bureaucracy. How do you think he'll feel about all that?"

"He's a bit, I don't know, unpredictable."

"Usually the longer they've been on their own, the less they want to stay. They're scared they're going to be kicked out again. It's perfectly natural. Whenever I think about what these kids have gone through"—she looked up and her face darkened, as if it had been slapped—"it makes me really mad. You see, I finally understand what Ann Eliza was so outraged about. It's the kids. These men, in their search for an unlimited supply of women, they end up destroying a lot of kids."

"Tell me about it."

"You know what makes me the angriest? That someone has put them through this in the name of God. That's the saddest part, these kids come out and they've been robbed of everything. Their childhoods, their families, but, worst of all, they've been robbed of

God. And most of them never find him again."

"That's not the worst part," I said. "The worst part is you come out of there and it's pretty much impossible to ever love anyone again."

"You're right," she said. "But I think we're talking about the same thing."

I told Kelly it was fine if she had something to do, she didn't have to wait with me, but she said she didn't have anything else to do. "So this lady," I said, "Ann Eliza Young? She was like wife number what?"

"It depends."

"On?"

"Who's counting."

"I'm asking you."

"Then I don't know. She was commonly known as his nineteenth wife, but everyone agrees that she was at least his twenty-seventh. But there's a lot of evidence that suggests Brigham married more women than that. With all the secret weddings, the numbers get pretty screwy."

"They always are."

"That's one of the things I'm researching. Not what number she was, because to tell the truth I don't think we'll ever know for sure. I'm more interested in what it meant to a woman to not even know her position in her family. It's one of those things that gets brushed over and a lot of scholars say, Well, what difference does it make? But I think it must've had a huge psychological impact on these women to not know their number."

"My mom. She's a nineteenth wife."

"Come again?"

And so I told her. Everything. It just came out, and it took a long time, but I told her like I've just told you.

At the end of it Kelly said, "I wish there was something I could do."

"You can help Johnny. He won't make it if he stays with me."

We stopped talking. There was so much to think about. I can't tell you what she was thinking, but I was thinking, Look at this girl. LDS through and through, BYU rah rah rah, *Rise, all loyal Cougars and hurl your challenge to the foe,* no coffee, no tea, no Diet Coke, never a drink or a smoke or a hit, temple garments as white as Wasatch snow, Relief Society chick, missionary missy—where was it she went in New York? Times Square? Blond, banged, sharp-nosed Kelly Dee bringing the word of the restoration to the street, bringing the news of the Prophet to 42nd Street? Two years with her companion, Sister Kimmie probably, or Sister Connie or Sister Meg or someone, the two of them always together, never apart, smiling, talking, chatting, helping, maybe handing out a book, maybe not, Sister Kelly never tiring, never giving up, never getting angry or disappointed or dispirited when someone says I'd like to fuck your tight Mormon cunt or Joseph Smith can suck my dick, just continuing firm in her belief, never once thinking, I'm better than this, never once thinking, I'm better than *you.* Here she was, Kelly Dee, of hearty Pioneer stock, always well loved, always loving, three years from marriage, four from motherhood, Sister Kelly, who probably plans for weeks in advance when it's her turn to stand up in church and bear witness, Sister Kelly, who probably keeps a to-do list clipped to her fridge, who probably spends Sunday nights shampooing those waves of blond hair, so clean, so hardworking, a human honeybee, she of the chosen people, of the desert kingdom, of the Saints. Yes, here she was, sitting in a crappy office chair helping kids like me. And not just helping, because there are people who are like, *Oh, you poor thing,* and cluck their tongues, and maybe give you a dollar, but they don't understand and don't want to understand. And then there are people who are like, *Oh, you poor thing, now come and meet my God, He is the only way.* But not Kelly—she wasn't just helping, assisting, offering a hand. No, she was researching, reading, learning, talking, understanding. Working hard to understand, wanting to understand, telling herself that's the most important thing she can do: understand. And it meant more to me than anything else. She got it. I could see it in her blue-as-a-Deseret-morn eyes. She got me. She knew I had been completely totally royally screwed. She knew religion had fucked me, like that nasty john who paid me fifty bucks to shove his arm up my ass. And she also understood there's a point when you have no choice but to get up and move on. And oh boy, here I went, more of those goddamn tears. "I'm sorry," I sobbed. "I didn't come here for this."

Kelly handed me a tissue. "It's all right," she said. "I understand. I completely understand."

XVIII

RESTORATION
OF ALL THINGS

THE 19TH WIFE

CHAPTER TWENTY-SIX:
The Stones of Nauvoo

After a brief stop at the border between Utah and Wyoming, Lorenzo and I rode on to Laramie. It was my first time in a Gentile city, and I expected the highest form of civilization. Surely any metropolis ruled by law and reason, rather than superstition and tyranny, would have organized itself into a Great City. Yet in Laramie, this proved not to be the case. We exited the station to find a frozen town of dirt, cows, and pigs. The wind whipped from all ends and the livestock used much of downtown as its huddling shed. The ranchers and cowhands walked around in the caliper-legged manner of the man molded on horseback. The women, it seemed, were as rough as the men. I asked one the direction to my hotel. She was corseted up in red and black, with a velvet ribbon about her throat. She eyed me warily. "Why? You working there too?"

I must confess my disappointment. Brigham's city outranked this town in every way but one. Walking down the street, dodging the hogs and the sheep, I counted six steeples, spires, and bell towers. At one crossroads, Baptist and Methodist Churches faced one another in seeming harmony. Despite the rustic quality of my environs, I was grateful to be free of Orthodoxy.

Lorenzo and I had sequestered ourselves in a hotel room for two days when Major Pond arrived from Salt Lake, carrying the newspapers. The *Tribune* had run an article on my escape entitled, "Godspeed, Mrs. Young!" He was very excited and worn from his trip, and I urged him to rest before we got on to business. But he would not hear of it. "Everyone wants to hear from you," he said. "Look at this telegram, they want you to speak here in Laramie." I told him I wanted to rest for a few days and spend time with Lorenzo, who had suffered much during our flight.

"I understand, but you'll need to be in your finest form in Denver," the Major advised. "We'll need money for the trip, the hotels, a new dress for you." With my consent, he wanted to rent a lecture hall at the Wyoming Institute. "We'll charge a dollar fifty a head, and the hall can hold four hundred."

Reader, I was not practicing false modesty when I said, "Surely there can't be four hundred people in all of Wyoming who want to hear from me."

But there were! My first night of lecturing in a free land was a success. Every seat was sold, and Major Pond regretfully turned many dozen away. I have been advised by my wise editor, to whom I owe a certain amount, that a personal story such as mine will inevitably lose the reader's attention if I go on too long about triumphs and success. ("The reader wants challenges, obstacles, and despair!" he has suggested.) Although I do not wholly agree with this fine man's opinion, on this and other matters, I will spare my Reader any further description of my lecturing triumphs in Laramie, and move onward with my tale.*

After my evening at the Wyoming Institute, more invitations arrived. Major Pond convinced me that en route to Denver we should stop in Cheyenne and Fort Russell. I tried to decline, worried that I had already spoken to everyone in the Teton Range who might take interest in my tale. Major Pond assured me many more would be found. Again I will spare you the details of those events,

---

* The authoress wishes to point the more serious reader to the archives of the *Laramie Union* should he care to read their substantial review of my appearance. The same is true of the local newspapers of all the cities I appeared in as I journeyed to Washington (with, of course, the exception of New York).

but I can assure you (and the newspapers will attest) that my success at the lectern continued in Cheyenne and Fort Russell. Interest in the harem, it seems, runs deep.

In Denver, a newspaper out of Central City greeted me with my first blast of skepticism: "We can only hope Mrs. Young does not expect the citizenry of Denver to be as easily astonished as she has become accustomed to. Our ladies and gentlemen have listened to the greatest speakers of our day, company by no means which we include her in."

"Ignore them," advised the Major. "You will be loved."

As I took the lectern of Denver's New Baptist Church, a heavy anxiety overtook me, burdening me with the sensation of walking through deep sand. Looking out into the mass of faces and the lights upon me, I recalled my days on Brigham's stage. But how easy that job was in comparison—simply spilling out someone else's words. That evening I gave my well-practiced lecture, "My Life in Bondage." I began nervously, I know. For many minutes I stirred no response in my audience. There is no greater silence than that of an auditorium waiting anxiously for something to happen. In the front row two young girls, each no older than ten, stared up at me. One was dark in the brow, with wide-set wondrous eyes. Her sister wore her red hair down in ringlets. They regarded me sincerely. If I had any doubt about my purpose, their lovely gaze blew it away. By the time I began recounting my mother's conversion, I lost myself in my tale. The feeling was such that I was no longer lecturing, but re-living my ordeal. The Reformation, the hand-cart fiasco, Mr. Dee! Were someone to tap me on the shoulder and ask, Do you have the date and time? I would have regarded him blankly, unaware of where I was. My story possessed me, as that black ghost of Brigham had once possessed me. It controlled the words forming on my tongue. I have gone on to meet many great writers in my time. It was Mrs. Stowe who described the act of composition similar to this. "I become, quite simply, the vessel for the muse," she said to me. For those of you who wonder how

Joseph could put his face in a hat and dictate his Book: I offer this alternative explanation. Imagination can take command of the body. Ask the artist, the actress, the poet feverishly producing line after line of his Epic! Is it God speaking, or the mysterious mind?

Now it seemed my life's adventure was in possession of my audience, too. Anyone who has stood before a gathering knows when he has captivated his audience, or when he has failed to do so. There is a spirit in the hall for each scenario, and they are as opposite in nature as the bright angel and the dark demon. Tonight the angel visited Denver, shining its light upon me. As I concluded my story, describing my escape through the night, my audience exploded with applause. When I left the lectern at least a hundred rushed the stage to meet me.

The lecture was such a success, even the skeptics out of Central City commended me: "There is no doubt her story, if true, holds a certain amount of interest for many." Major Pond showed me a telegram from James Redpath, whose Lyceum Agency in Boston represented the talents of Susan B. Anthony and Frederick Douglass, personas whose names I recognized but whose reputations, at the time, I little understood. He proposed a contract of fifty lectures for $10,000. "We can get more," said Major Pond.

Major Pond concocted a plan for us to travel to Boston, where Mr. Redpath could listen to me in person. "I'm convinced once he has sat at your feet, and heard your tale, he'll sign you on as his biggest attraction for whatever fee we demand."

"As long as we get to Washington."

"We will," Pond promised. "Washington is our last stop. But tonight you're the toast of the Rockies, the Queen of the Eastern Slopes."

Despite my local triumphs, I felt little pleasure. My mission was not to entertain, nor to haul in high-grossing receipts, nor to serve as top-billing for Mr. Redpath, as much as Pond admired his roster. I took little reward from the thunder of twelve hundred hands beating in applause, or as many feet tramping upon the floorboards. The columns of newsprint praising my bravery and my orating skills, my sense of timing, and my gentle comic touch—these could not embolden me. None of this mattered except as a weapon in my larger Crusade. I had left Utah with a single purpose, and I would not rest, or find comfort, or take pleasure, or measure pride, until at last I had presented my story to the men of Congress, and President Grant, too, forcing upon them, and our nation, the Truth of so many women like myself, and the plight of our children. I had but one hope—to witness the rewriting of our laws.

From Denver we toured the middle of the country—Topeka, Lawrence, Leavenworth, St. Louis, Peoria, Quincy, Chicago. In some cities the halls were full, in others only partially so, but each night I achieved my objective of informing the world of this relic of Barbarism. Wherever I went many good men and women greeted me with sympathy, the newspapers reported on me understandingly, and the editorials acknowledged my purpose. Even the more prurient columns, as undignified as they were, supported my cause, for there was hardly a soul in the vast middle of our great Land who was not shocked by Mormondom's peculiar institution. "How can this go on in America?" asked many. No one denounced, contradicted, or maligned me. I should have taken comfort in this general warm reception. Instead, my enemies' silence concerned me.

"Nonsense," said Major Pond. "In Utah, you might have enemies, but the rest of America loves you!" If ever there was a man meant for promotion and salesmanship, it was Major Pond. In a futile effort to console, he showed me Brigham's Salt Lake papers. Only occasionally did they report on my crusade. By now, they mostly ignored me.

In the frozen days after the New Year of 1874, I visited Burlington, Iowa, a red-brick metropolis approximately thirty miles up the Mississippi from my birthplace, Nauvoo. It was here that I encountered my first competition on the lecture circuit. On the same night I was to speak, by coincidence a second, somewhat smaller venue had booked Mrs. Victoria Woodhull, the suffragist, spiritualist, newspaper editoress, Wall Street broker, and unsuccessful candidate for President. Of course I did not know Mrs. Woodhull in person, but her character had long before made my acquaintance— for Brigham often invoked her as an example of Gentile depravity. Among her many beliefs, for which she was paid handsomely to discuss, Mrs. Woodhull held a deep conviction in the open sensuality of women and the female's "right" to amorous satisfaction. Her other accomplishments included the exposure of Reverend Beecher's compromising interlude with the wife of his dear friend, thus destroying his repute; and, I am told, a sojourn in Manhattan's squalid Ludlow Street Jail. To call Mrs. Woodhull's reputation notorious is to label the lion timid or the buffalo delicate on the foot.

Having become familiar with the public's interest in the lurid, I worried that she would draw away my natural audience. Major Pond assured me not to concern myself, and set out from our hotel, with its fine view of the icy river, to gather information on my competitor's numbers.

I was in the room reading to Lorenzo when a clerk announced Mrs. Woodhull was downstairs, calling to pay her respects.

"Tell her I'm not in," I said.

"But, Mrs. Young, you are in." The boy was young, with waves of corn-colored hair, and hobbled by a limited understanding of the ways of women. I told him I was busy with my son, this was my only time to spend with him, and that he should inform Mrs. Woodhull that I was not present. The boy persisted. "She knows you're here. She said she saw you return an hour ago."

"Then tell her I cannot see but I'll accept her card." I closed the door, dropping the woman's card into the stove. From the window I saw Mrs. Woodhull move down the street, her sturdy comportment making way, the plum ribbon of her hat fluttering with the snow flurries. Suddenly she stopped and turned around. Her eyes quickly found me in the window, and I shall always remember how they acknowledged me and dismissed me in one succinct glare.

That evening, at my lecture, I expected some sort of return of favor from Mrs. Woodhull, but none came. At the end of the night my audience embraced me for sharing with them my story. The lecture was a success, but I went to bed needled by concern.

In the morning, we crossed the Mississippi by sleigh and drove down to Nauvoo. We approached from the North, our hired team stamping happily in the crisp snow. It was a clear day, the sun high and cold, the sky a thin, brittle blue. Lorenzo kept peering from beneath the blanket, anxious to see the city he had heard so much about from his grandmother. Major Pond was in a fouler mood. "It's another fifty miles to Quincy," he said repeatedly. "We won't have much time."

My memories of Nauvoo were both distinct and limited, the miniature portraits of the young child's mind. They came to me with a warm bathing sensation, as memories of early childhood often do. I recalled the orderly streets where we lived, our tidy brick house facing its opposite across the way. Thinking of my father's wainwright churned up other memories I had not conjured for years. I recalled the bitter smell of the thick smoke in the black-smith's chimney, the glowing red of iron in the flame, and the sparks spraying from Gilbert's shodding hammer. From there, I thought of the fetid, almost animal smell of the river in summer, the way the stench climbed slowly up the bank; and the dry, lifeless scent of winter's wind running down the Temple's hill. I recalled my mother as a young woman, her pure devotion, her simple manner. And my father, quick and hard-working, his complexion yet to toughen and brown. Brigham's younger self came to mind, sturdy but not yet fat, with his boyish grin. How I remember him walking down the streets of Nauvoo, touching his followers, inviting them in, feeding them, helping them, praying with them, lending them a hand in building a house, a barn, or planting a field. He had a sense of humor in those days, for I recalled the day he visited our barn and named our buckling, with his unusual high-hat of white hair, Mr. Pope.

Above all, I remembered the Temple on the hill. When I was little, no matter where I was in town, I would look for its tower topped by the golden statue of Moroni. The sun on the gold was as comforting as my mother's hand upon my head. I thought of the limestone blocks, like enormous cubes of ice, and how my father and brothers, along with all the men and boys of Nauvoo, worked to put them in place with rope, pulley, and mule. And how the sun cut through the panes in the elliptical windows; and how the bronze bell rang. Perhaps most vividly, I recalled the Temple high above the Mississippi, standing firmly as we retreated across the river in our journey to Zion. For many miles I watched it as it became smaller and smaller, throwing back the sunlight, gleaming on the horizon, until it fell from sight.

"Are you sure this is the right way?" I asked our driver.

"Nauvoo. Straight ahead."

I said there must be something wrong, I could not see the tower.

"What tower?"

As we entered town, and mounted the hill, the driver said, "You mean that?" He was pointing at a set of ruins, broken stones lying haphazardly atop one another. All that remained of the famous Temple was an end wall with two supporting columns, its edge jagged as if the rest of the building had been torn from it. The decay was similar to what you might encounter, I understand, in Rome or Greece.

Opposite us were a pair of pilgrims, an old couple, looking out over the destruction. They were small creatures, bent with age, their complexion an everlasting gray. They surveyed their lost sanctuary with dying eyes. They stood separate from us, yet the winter day was so clear I could peer across the distance to see the tears frozen to their cheeks.

There is a great shock to seeing a building you've known since childhood destroyed. There are certain structures in our lives—our first home, our first school, our first house of worship—which we naively believe will stand forever. To see these toppled bluntly delivers life's coldest lesson: Time will take all.

We drove down the hill to the Flats. Where houses once stood, I found nothing but an empty lot or a pile of bricks. At the corner of Parley and Kimball Streets, I saw the outline of a foundation in the snow. The snow lay upon it higher than the rest of the ground. Other than that, there was nothing but a lonely fence post leaning in a drift. I told Lorenzo I once lived here.

"But there's nothing here."

"There used to be." And I told the driver to head on. On our way out of Nauvoo we passed the site I knew to be Joseph Smith's grave. There was no marker, only a neat mound of blue snow.

As much as I now opposed the Latter-day Saints, I took no joy in seeing such total destruction. I do not believe the mythologies of the Ancients, with their bickering gods and thunderbolts, yet even so I feel a loss when I see etchings of their ruins. Who cannot pity the lonely Doric column standing in a field of rubble? Or the severed marble torso of a precious youth? Seeing Nauvoo destroyed was like learning an acquaintance from long ago has been dead for years. Such news comes with an awkward guilt—how is it I did not know? As we drove on to Quincy, a difficult question formed in my mind—was my mission not to destroy the Saints in similar fashion? How would I feel if one day I found Great Salt Lake ruined to a pile of stone?

THE 19TH WIFE

CHAPTER TWENTY-SEVEN
Distant Enemies

In Boston the lion roared. After a successful tour of the country's middle parts, including a diversion into Wisconsin's warm embrace, Major Pond, Lorenzo, and I traveled East. The journey was, above all, unpleasant to the nose. The railway car smelled of nothing but decay—the sloshing spittoon, the stale sandwiches, the unbathed travelers, and the sour latrine. As much as we could Lorenzo and I sat beside the window, preferring the cold blast to the stench. We spent hours looking out, surveying the winter flatlands of Indiana, then Ohio and beyond. The fields banked with snow, the brown cornstalks standing valiantly in the drifts, the farmhouses huddled against the gales—the train sped by these, and then they appeared again, on a different farm, all but the same. In the distance the land stretched flatly, nothing rising from it but a stand of chestnuts, skeletal in the winter light, or a silo, as solitary as a minaret. No mountains, no ravines, no vast valleys! Already I missed the majesty of the West.

On February 18 at last we arrived in our nation's cultural capital. Outside the station, while orienting ourselves to this busy metropolis, I found my name shrieking out from an advertising bill. Under sponsorship of Redpath's Lyceum came an announcement of my lecture the following evening in Tremont Temple. I was grateful for such promotion, yet I felt uneasy. I assigned the feeling to fatigue and the anxiety over meeting Mr. Redpath for the first time. My lecture in Boston would determine whether I would join his roster, or if he would send me on my way. Under his sponsorship I could travel on to New York and Washington. Without it, it was doubtful we could arrange any more engagements in the world-weary East.

We met Mr. Redpath in his Lyceum Bureau on Bromfield Street. "Here she is," he said, "Brigham's headache!" This little man, who weighed no more than 150 pounds, hustled about his office waving letters and telegrams concerning me. He had followed my progress across the country, sending for the local news accounts and gauging my appeal through a string of contacts. "You might be the most popular woman in America," he said. Excited, he told us about the advance ticket sales and the general anticipation for my appearance. He had arranged a series of interviews with the Boston newspapers in the afternoon, with a precise plan for the stories to run in the morning. "Once they hit, we'll be sold out. Now let me give you one piece of advice: Keep telling the truth."

I assured him I had no other weapons in my arsenal.

"And another thing: Don't shy away from the more—how should I put it?—difficult aspects of your ordeal. People are fascinated. Absolutely fascinated. You can't tell them too much." I came to see how such a small man, with his wispy side whiskers and rather high, feminine voice, had overwhelmed the nation with his speakers. He had made his name promoting John Brown, which was the connection to Major Pond, and had earned a specialty of putting talented women such as Anna E. Dickinson and Mrs. Stanton on the boards. I told him ultimately I had one goal: to speak to the highest levels of Government. "If everything goes according to my plan," he said, "that will happen." The meeting concluded with this little lively man calling me his future star and giving Lorenzo a yellow and green cup and ball.

We hurried to our rooms at the Parker House to begin the newspaper interviews. Major Pond organized the men outside the room, while I sat with each individually by the fire. Lorenzo played with the cup and ball all afternoon, challenging himself to catch the ball in the cup one hundred times consecutively. As I answered the reporters' questions, which were of such a standard variety I had answered them a hundred times before, I kept a fond eye on my son at the bench by the window as he tossed the yellow ball and caught it in its green cup. He counted in his soft, careful voice, nine, ten, eleven. . . . When he missed, he said to himself, "Shooty shoot."

Long after dusk Major Pond admitted the final reporter, a Miss Christine Lee representing the *Sun* of New York. "I hear you're on your way to New York," she began.

"If all goes well here."

"I have to say, Utah feels very far away to most New Yorkers. Tell me why we should care about the Brighamites?"

I explained my purpose was to speak more about polygamy than the Saints themselves, but of course to do so I needed to provide some information on the religion and territory that introduced the practice to the United States. "As I see it," I said, "it's a relic of Barbarism, and I believe most Americans, especially New Yorkers, should be interested in banishing Barbarism from the land."

"I see," said Miss Lee, writing something down. She was not yet twenty-five, wore her yellow hair loose about her polished face, and had a small jagged smile. I had no doubt there was a dangerous quality to her beauty.

The interview began routinely. She asked the general questions about my experiences, and I answered them as I have always done. For thirty minutes we spoke in a straightforward manner and I sensed she was responding to my biography. When I described my early months of marriage and the indignities of my cottage, she clicked her tongue and said, "It must've been terrible." When I depicted Brigham's mistreatment of my mother, her reply was, "Such a shame." When I described my flight, and my son's fear, she said, "Unbelievable."

I concluded by describing my lectures and the general response.

"Let me ask you this," said Miss Lee. "I still don't understand why you married him."

"I had no choice."

"Yes, you said that, but what I don't understand is why you went through with it. You disliked him already, or at least you said you did. You did not trust him. You had seen with your own eyes how his wives lived. If you knew all that, why on earth would you agree to marry such a man?"

I had encountered this skepticism before and clipped at it without concern. "You must remember, I was born into this system. It was all I knew. I did not know a Gentile until I was an adult woman. I had been told the world beyond Deseret was Babylon and Sodom combined. I had been raised to believe Brigham delivered messages from God. And above all, I was told this was my spiritual duty, and that if I wanted to enter Heaven—and who among us, Miss Lee, does not?—then I would need to submit to Brigham's command and become a plural wife."

"Yes, you've said that, but I still don't understand."

"What don't you understand?"

"You despised this man, yet you married him. Is it possible, Mrs. Young, you didn't despise him as much as you say? Is it possible, even a little bit, that you were enticed into his arms by thoughts of becoming the Queen of Utah?"

"Not at all."

"I must tell you, Mrs. Young, before I came here, I spent some time following certain aspects of your story. Did you know I've been to Utah? I was in California. On my way home I stopped by. I happened to be at the Walker House the night you departed, and I read about your exit in the *Tribune*. It caught my eye. So I stayed a few extra days, then a week, to look around. I had the opportunity to visit the Lion House, in fact."

"Good. Then you saw it for yourself."

"Yes indeed. And it is as you described it."

"I'm glad that's not in dispute."

"Except in one manner."

"What's that?"

"I didn't see the misery."

I would be dishonest if I withheld from my Reader my true feeling at this moment: I wanted to swat this woman with my handbag.

"Miss Lee," I said, "sometimes, in my experience, at least, misery is not always apparent to the casual visitor."

"Very true, but I had a chance to speak to a number of his wives, and no one gave me a report that was at all similar to yours."

"I cannot tell you about anyone else's experience but my own."

"Of course, but it makes me wonder if yours is maybe, perhaps exaggerated?"

"It isn't."

"Or if not exaggerated, then perhaps unique to you? That you and President Young were simply not compatible and so you fought, as all incompatible couples do, and it's this reason you have stories to tell from an unhappy marriage?"

"I wish that were true. I wish my experience was wholly alien to the women of Utah. If that were the case, I could go home to my other son today and settle into a house somewhere with my boys, and live out the rest of my life in privacy. My mission would be done. But this is not the case. And until it is the case, I intend to speak about what I know."

"Do you know what people say about you?"

"I've heard many things."

"You know the expression 'The lady doth protest too much'?"

"I can't say I do."

"What? How can't you know that? It's Shakespeare. *Hamlet.* Surely you're familiar with *Hamlet,* being a former actress."

"In fact, no, I'm not. Do you know why I'm not familiar with *Hamlet*? Because Brigham banned Shakespeare from the stages of Deseret, unless the scripts were revised to suit his theology. So in my days on the stage I never encountered *Hamlet,* nor in my schooling, nor upon the shelves of my parents, or in the homes of friends, because, Miss Lee, anything or anyone who contradicts Brigham's doctrine is edited, banished, or destroyed."

"May I read a quote to you? This is one of President Young's wives answering some of your charges. 'She is a liar of considerable skill. She uses her dramatic training to bring her inventions to life. If half the things she speaks of were true, this Church, and family, would have been devoured already by its own rotten soul. I'm here to tell you this is a happy household, with sister wives loving one another and our children, and nothing brings us greater joy than knowing we have set out on the path to Heaven.' Do you have a reply to that, Mrs. Young?"

"Miss Lee, do you plan to marry?"

"Yes, in fact I'm engaged. How did you know?"

"I had a sense. That's wonderful for you. Tell me: Who's your groom?"

"I'd rather not say."

"All right. But tell me one thing about him, so I might begin to form an image of him in my mind."

"One thing? He's a printer."

"Very nice. A man of your trade. Then imagine this man, this printer, with his inky fingers, and, I'll venture to say, handsome appearance, and a way with words—for knowing you now a little, Miss Lee, any man you've settled on must have a way with words. So think of the day your printer first told you he loved you, that he hoped to marry you, to spend his life with you, to begin a family with you. Think of that day. Yes, it's a fond memory, is it not, Miss Lee? Of course it is, as it should be. A man, an attractive printer, he must be strong—for those plates are heavy, aren't they? This printer wants to be with you all his life. It is the definition of love, of Christian love, I will add. It's a wonderful thought, even the hardest cynic would have to agree. Where is this printer now? While you're on your journeys?"

"He's in New York. He prints seven days a week."

"Of course. He's industrious, isn't he? Like yourself. But he can't work day and night. What does he do when he puts the press to bed? He has a meal, he talks with his friends, they drink whiskey? He talks about you, perhaps? And why not? Now imagine he spent his free time, what little of it there is, not with his friends from the print-shop, but with eighteen other women. So that when he's not at his letter press, not slaving over those boxes of letters and all those tiny dingbats, he is slicing his time and affection and money and everything else into nineteenths. You will get your share, and your future children will get their share. One-nineteenth. What is rightfully yours will be yours, but no more and no less. Now, Miss Lee, will such a situation bring you happiness or misery? And if someone were to tell you it brought her happiness, could it possibly be true? Isn't it possible she's been told to lie? Or, isn't it also possible she's deceived herself into believing she's happy when in fact she's anything but? And why shouldn't she lie? Either way, she's been told her marital suffering will be rewarded in the Afterlife. She's been told she must defend the system to death. She's been told that Gentiles will be left on Earth at the time of the Resurrection. Now if you've never known anything else, anything other than these statements which sound so impossibly untrue to your keen New York ears, isn't it perfectly possible you would claim to a reporter from the East that you were happy? Even if you were not? Miss Lee, do not present me with your cold, skeptical questions. Not when I'm describing a world founded on fear, intimidation, and anti-reason."

The woman sat back, all courage and puffery eliminated from her soul. "I have one final question."

"Please."

"If polygamy is a religious practice, if it's part of the Mormons' eternal beliefs, why should you, or anyone, stop them from pursuing their faith? Don't the Mormons have the right to practice their religion as they please under the Constitution?"

"And if someone were to say, I believe in slavery because it appears in the Bible, would you say, Go then, and be free to practice it. I believe this country has answered that question rather firmly. Anything else, Miss Lee?"

Soon thereafter Miss Lee departed, leaving me to worry over the story that would await me in New York City.

Later that night I sat restlessly by the window. It was very late and Lorenzo was snoring lightly in the bed. Outside it was sleeting, the street lamps burning a thick ugly yellow upon the fog. Although I had won my spar with Miss Lee, the encounter had left me uncertain of my path. I returned to the image of the ruined Temple in Nauvoo—the piles of stone, the column holding up nothing, the chipped piece of the baptismal font. Did any sect or creed, any group of man, deserve such a fate? I believed in everything I said at the lectern, I knew it was true. Surely Brigham, when he stands before his people, would say the same. He believes everything he says, and he knows it is true. How to reconcile our competing truths? By obliterating one? Is it the only way? I turned the question this way and that, doing my best to look at it from each end, pressing upon its points, and I began to feel anxious. Perhaps the Temple ruins were not a symbol of the Mormons' fate, but my own. If one side must be right, and the other wrong, how could I be so certain of everything I knew? Inevitably we were both right, and both wrong, or was this not true? It was a circular question, like an iron hoop, and I could trace my finger along it, around and around, and never reach its end. I fumbled with this idea for a long time, losing my grasp on my beliefs, until the early sun came through the fog, and the streets illuminated with the goodness of day.

It was time to dress, and just as I went to wake Lorenzo, Major Pond knocked on my door. "Mrs. Young? . . . Mrs. Young?"

"What is it?"

"I'm sorry to disturb you so early, but there's something you must see."

The situation was written out in the Major's eyes. He handed me a newspaper. The story came from the *Chicago Times*. The author was identified simply as Special Correspondent. It began with a benign description of my lectures through Illinois and Iowa and a general appreciation of my appearance. Yet soon enough the secretive writer began his assault:

> Now I shall turn to the portion of this report that will no doubt most interest the reader. Mrs. 19, like other lecturesses, employs an agent who arranges her schedule and travels along her side. In most cases these are wise old gentlemen, blunt in manner but also efficient, capable of settling whatever matter that might arise on the road. Mrs. 19, however, has chosen as her business partner a debonair and suave military gentleman by the name of Major Pond. Pond's reputation begins with his features—his good square jaw, a fine nose, and teeth as white as china. He speaks elegantly, with all the powers of persuasion, and there are rumors of his physicality, which can be previewed through his snug uniform, that have caused more than one woman to swoon—as far as this Correspondent knows. While the pair visited Bloomington, Iowa, residing in its most luxurious hotel, several guests and maids noted an unusual closeness between Mrs. 19 and the Major, an intimacy that needs no further explanation to be understood.

I did not need to read any more. I was as aware as anyone that the people who came to my lectures, those who rewarded me with their applause and approval, the newspaper editors who spent ink on my cause, did so because they sensed I was a modest woman. Were they to think I was an adulteress just as my husband was an adulterer, my message would be lost in the haze of scandal.

How to describe the day? Even now, after writing so many pages, I feel incapable of depicting those first lonely hours after this attack. I forced myself to dress and traveled to Mr. Redpath's office. Had my new sponsor seen the news? Of course, as had most of Boston, by his estimation. A few inquiries supported my larger fear: the telegraphs had carried the story to news outlets across the country. Anyone interested in my tale, or the plight of Utah's women, knew of it by noon. I imagined Brigham in his office at the Beehive House, cloistered by his account books and maps, settling into his armchair and reviewing the reports. His assistants would come and go, bringing him accounts from the East and the West, each more devastating to me than the previous. The effect was like a shovelful of dirt into a grave, slowly the hole fills in and the body is buried. I imagined the thin smirk upon Brigham's lips, imperceptible even to the clerks. I was certain one word was running through his mind—Success.

I asked Mr. Redpath if I should cancel my appearance.

"I'll tell you in an hour." He set about gauging the effect of the scandal on my repute, sending half a dozen nimble assistants and clerks about the city to listen in on the morning talk. He trotted over to the Tremont Temple himself. Were tickets being returned? Were people gathering to denounce me? "I'll find out," he said, and out he went, like a red fox.

He returned an hour later with good news. "We've sold out. It seems there was a stampede for tickets when the box office opened."

The afternoon brought more hostile news. A second report, also from our nameless friend at the *Chicago Times,* had run across the telegraph lines. Now Mrs. Woodhull was claiming she too had encountered evidence of my indiscretions while in Burlington. Yet this great lady, friend to the female race, wanted Americans everywhere to know she was not denouncing me. In fact, she fully supported my "right" to amorous liberty. "Now she is truly free," the woman said of me.

"What time's the next train?" I said. "I don't care where it's headed, but I need to leave right away."

"Mrs. Young," said Mr. Redpath, "you need to steady yourself."

But I could not—I hurried about his office, gathering my hat and bag, my gloves, and the purple coat that had brought me so much luck since Denver. I called for Lorenzo. The boy, at one corner of Mr. Redpath's desk, was preoccupied with a drawing he was making. When I told him it was time to go, he held up his artwork. "It's you." And it was—a kind, loving portrait on the very newspaper that maligned me. The black ink of his art had all but covered over the lies.

It was the betrayal of strangers that most alarmed me. Who was the Special Correspondent so intent on destroying me? And Mrs. Woodhull—had she punished me for ignoring her call? For some time that afternoon I could not speak. I sat anxiously in Mr. Redpath's office, looking about at the framed telegrams from Presidents and Generals, and the memorabilia from the stage, the engraved swords, the autographed playbills, and a dusty ostrich plume. I felt something slip out from beneath me. The Temple ruins returned to mind—the piles of rubble, the winter sun bright on the worn white stones.

Since the news that morning, a feeling had been taking shape in my heart. At first I could not identify it, but now it was there, as solid as a stone. "It's Brigham," I said.

"What's that, Mrs. Young?"

"Brigham did this. He bought that story in the press."

Historians speak of the unintended consequences of planned events. The consequences of Brigham's attack was a mob on the steps of Tremont Temple. Nearly one thousand people had to be turned away. Behind the curtain, waiting to take the stage, I heard the commotion, the shouts and calls, the irate voices claiming they had been promised a seat. "I could fill this place twice over," said Redpath. "Ninety-five percent of them are on your side."

My lecture in Boston was standard, but its reception was not. I was received with the greatest wave of enthusiasm I had yet to encounter. I concluded the discussion with a rebuttal of the charges and a challenge: "I do not know how, or by what means, but I know in my heart, just as surely as I know the faces of my sons, that Brigham's Church was involved in this assault on my character. In time I will prove it, and if anyone here tonight remains skeptical of my ordeal, of the truthfulness of my life, you shall see, with this lie exposed, the extent to which Brigham Young can deceive."

The triumph in Boston was followed by failure in New York, for Miss Lee's pointed story preceded me. The editors of her newspaper buttressed her opinion by a handful of essays questioning the veracity of my life. The reports out of Boston failed to impress the doubting Thomases of New York. More than half the seats of Association Hall stared back at me empty. My declaration of innocence was met with a phlegmatic yawn.

I asked Mr. Redpath if the scandal had wounded my appeal.

He stroked his whiskers. "New York is a funny place. I suspect the scandal hasn't hurt you as much as your response to it. This town loves a sinner more than a saint."

While in New York, I met with editors from the publishing houses to discuss my memoirs. Mr. E—— of Easton & Co. impressed me the most. He is a lean, subtle, Prussian-looking man, with a full nose like a small turnip. He spoke intelligently, if nervously, about my plight, his brittle, alabaster fingers fluttering about. "The important thing," he said, "is to show everyone what it's like for the women of Utah. You'll need to make it clear how bad polygamy is, how it's not only disagreeable, but how it destroys the soul. You need to show it's not only a conjugal issue, but a moral one. That's how to draw readers to your side. It's a travesty, and it seems to me Brigham's making a mockery of the rest of us and the very foundations of this country." For a man who has never taken a wife, and of whom I suspect deep theological skepticism, he showed unusual sympathy for my topic. I agreed to pen a summary of my life for this young, feline editor. A contract was produced, a date agreed upon, and we signed on our respective lines.

(Since then many critics have wrongly accused me of walking out of the offices of Easton & Co. with bags of money. One newspaper even ran an illustration of me dragging a large sack of gold with Brigham's head on the side. This is another distortion. I received nothing for my efforts, not until Easton's salesmen began to canvass the nation, selling subscriptions to the volume you are now reading. Mr. E—— sent a telegram announcing advance orders comparable to Mrs. Stowe's and, only then, my first remuneration. Is it wrong for an authoress to earn a penny for her toil? For the record, Mr. E—— urged me not to include this paragraph. The parentheses are a concession to his concern.)

We continued on to Rochester, Buffalo, and Baltimore. During this time, Major Pond and I spent many hours, and much money, investigating Brigham's libel. With Mr. Redpath's help, we collected a list of every newspaper in the country that had reprinted the falsehoods. I personally wrote a letter to the editor of each. Major Pond did the same. My story was widely known, but his was not. He was a widower when he arrived in Salt Lake, having lost his wife only recently. There was not a day in our relationship when he did not speak of her, and how he longed for the peal of her laugh.

We hired a detective out of Chicago to investigate the story's origins. The man's fees totaled nearly half of what I had earned at the lectern, but I was happy to turn over every cent when he delivered his findings. After two weeks of sleuthing, he unearthed a check in the amount of $20,000 made out to the editor of the *Chicago Times*. The signature on the check was a man named George Reef. I knew nothing of Mr. Reef. It took the detective another week to locate him in Provo. Rich from mining, devout to Brigham, married to two dozen women, perhaps more, Mr. Reef was prepared, he later confessed, to wage war for his right to an infinity of wives. Upon the exposure of his bribery, it is reported he said, "I should have paid more."

Brigham denied any relationship with Mr. Reef. A statement bellowed out of the Beehive House: "This man, whoever he may be, has acted without my authority or consent, and his actions should be punished, as the law sees fit." Our detective never could produce the evidence to make the connection between Brigham and Mr. Reef. It seems only fair, then, to give him the last word on the matter. But first I must make a point—even if Brigham did not coordinate this attack, is there not something foul in his Church that would inspire a believer to launch such an assault? Is the leader responsible in any way? To you, Friend, I leave this question to ponder.

Within two weeks of the scandal's debut, reports began to appear declaring my innocence. Editorials cleared my name and restored my relationship with Major Pond to propriety. More followed, and soon nearly every paper that had printed the rumor was forced to correct its error. Yet when the fire burns itself out, ash and the stench of smoke remain. When we are told a woman is an adulteress, and then this description is revised, the untruth will continue to linger in the mind. It is a ghost-thought—an idea proven unreal yet present even so. Such is the subtle shaping of reputation and legacy; and such was the perception I had to contend with. Wherever I went I recognized the look in the eyes of men with profane imaginations. They assessed me as they might a whore. In Rochester, on the street, a young man outside a foundry called out, "I live around the corner, Mrs. Young!" In Baltimore, a man as old as my father hollered, "Go get another one of those wives and meet me upstairs!" When this happened, I held Lorenzo close to me, continued on, and sealed my eyes to fight away the tears. He understood my distress, for every time I was assaulted with insults, the boy squeezed my hand within the mitt of his.

Out of this interlude of slander, libel, and the clearing of my name, I found my purpose even more defined. I had learned something I had heretofore failed to see—in fact, I was not Mormondom's destroying angel, as so many claimed me to be, intent on reducing the creed to a pile of lonely, winterblown stones. In truth, it was plural marriage itself, with all its inherent corruptions, that would destroy the religion, razing its temples and tabernacles, and poisoning its way of life. This cruel practice would end the Saints' legitimate right to their faith. The day would come when the religion would collapse upon itself—a future implosion now so very clear to me, I was distressed that I had not perceived it before. I came to understand that were I to succeed in my mission, and eradicate celestial marriage from Deseret, I would also be saving the Latter-day Saints from themselves.

With this awareness came another. A few days later, after the libelous episode had seemed to blow clear from the fields, our detective in Chicago wrote with news of his investigation's final clue.

> Dear Mrs. Young—
> Although I have failed to find any connection between Mr. Reef and Brigham Young, and now do not expect to do so, there is one link of another sort that has recently come to light. I do not know the meaning of it, yet it stands out among the many clues and therefore I bring it to you. Mr. Reef is an associate of your brother Aaron Webb. The two share a title to a small, not especially productive copper mine in Southwestern Utah, near a settlement called Red Creek. Your brother's first wife, Connie (my records show he has taken an even dozen in total)—she is the sister to Mr. Reef's seventh wife. I have yet to turn up evidence connecting your brother to Mr. Reef's actions pertaining to you, but the coincidence of association is noteworthy. Before I investigate any further, is there any reason to suspect your brother might have had a hand in this libelous plot?
> I await your instructions.
>
> Yours sincerely,
> CARL CUMMINGS, INVEST., CHICAGO

Although no betrayal is as painful as that inflicted by a family member, Mr. Cummings's revelation, distressing as it was, did not come wholly as a surprise. Ever since his involvement in the Reformation, Aaron had become a blind defender of polygamy. He reveled in his right to acquire women, blithely bringing a fresh bride into his bed whenever he desired a conjugal change. He embodied the hypocrisy of the Mormon polygamist so well that even before my apostasy I had done my best to limit my boys' interaction with their uncle. For his part, I am sure Aaron recognized my skepticism even before I did; although brother and sister, it was obvious we were enemies.

At this point, after having endured so much, I chose to ignore Mr. Cummings's ominous but circumstantial evidence. What good would come from it? I looked to my conscience for counsel and never responded to Mr. Cummings's letter. The truth would have to lie privately in Aaron's heart and mine, where God would judge it.

Sadder still was the silence from others. My dear father, so regretful over his own multiple marriages, never found the courage to speak out on my behalf. My half-sister Diantha, whom I loved, went missing from the debate. And most painfully, my mother's farewell letter always burned in my pocket, where I protected it, hoping another would come to revise its contents, to change her view of me.

On the eve of my arrival in Washington, where I would meet my most important audience, a letter from my beloved brother Gilbert was delivered to my door.

Sister—

I know the news about you is untrue. Anyone who knows you will say the same. Anyone who believes in your crusade knows it too. Don't worry about your friends. We remain steadfast and true. Yet you have enemies. They repeat these tales, adding to them and puffing them up. I hear them in town, at the mill, in church. Whenever I can I tell the speaker to shut his mouth but there are too many mouths in Deseret for me to finish the job.

Since your departure I've been planning my own. By the time you read this, I should be half way to California. I'll have to leave my wives behind, and my children too—an abandonment I know I'll feel painful about for the rest of my days. But I have no choice.

I no longer believe in anything this Church has to say. When I see Brigham, it's like looking at the face of a criminal. I know he feels the same. If I were to stay, I'd be dead soon enough, so either way my family will be left without husband and father. If I make any money in California, I'll send it to my wives. But I won't promise anything I don't know for sure I'll have. When I settle on the coast, I'll write with my news. Until then, you should know I believe you, and only you.

Before closing, I want to tell you our Ma's sick. Not of body but in heart. She's twisted up about how Brigham's been talking about you. She can't stand it, I know, because she knows he's telling lies. If I were a wagerer, I'd put a dollar down on her apostasy too. It's a pitiful sight—watching someone so devout lose her faith. If you can, you might write her. Right now, only words from you might soothe. I can't tell the future, but I suspect one day soon you and she will reunite. I know she wants to bring James to you. She's in South Cottonwood, but how long she'll last I can't say.

Your Brother—
GILBERT WEBB

Immediately I wrote my mother, posting the letter in Baltimore.

My Dear Mother—
On this journey of mine, of which I know you are aware, each night, kneeling before the stiff hotel bed, I pray twice. Once for a swift return to James. And once for a reunion with you. If these prayers are not answered, I will live out my days burdened with doubt about the value of my Crusade. If I succeed in my mission, and eradicate polygamy from our land, and yet remain separated from you or my son, then I will ask myself, At what cost? Indeed, at what cost has all this been? These are my most private thoughts, shared with only you and my God.

—Your Daughter

THE 19TH WIFE

CHAPTER TWENTY-EIGHT
Defeating Polygamy

In Washington we drove up a muddy street, past a row of one-story private houses, narrow, crowding structures displaying squalor in their windows. Here and there were patches of springtime grass, ready to be trampled by the pigs who seemed to outnumber the Capital's citizens. The street led to a wide avenue, grandly laid out, yet its buildings were no more elegant, or noble, in design than the huts we had previously passed. Had the Capitol's dome not beckoned us, flashing in the April sun, I would have been sure we were on a highway to nowhere. On that drive it was impossible not to compare Washington to Great Salt Lake. The former had a fifty-year advantage on the latter, and yet any fair observer would crown the capital of Zion the more colonized metropolis.

We were a party of four—Lorenzo, Major Pond, Mr. Redpath, and myself—who entered the Capitol building, through a dim hall known as the Crypt. A clerk in epaulette informed us we were standing directly beneath the famous dome. The room was held up by forty brown columns, the veins in the stone coursing with force, as if revealing their strain as they worked to hold aloft the building above.

The clerk, a birdy fellow with clipped, flapping arms, led us to the House chamber. I was shown to the Ladies Waiting Area, a cordoned section of chairs, while the Major and Mr. Redpath were invited to sit with the gentlemen. The clerk wanted to seat Lorenzo with them, but I insisted he remain with me.

Mr. James Blaine, the House Speaker, is a quick-minded, flinty man, trained and fortified in the cold blasts of Maine. He has the inscrutable eyes of a newspaper editor, which he once was in Portland. When I arrived he was orating from his chair of authority, the famous gavel in his grasp, filling the chamber with, by chance, a lecture on the subject of the separation of Church and State. The clerk delivered to him my card and letter of introduction.

To my surprise, the Speaker set down his gavel, left his chair, and invited me into the elegant Speaker's Room. By the warmth of a fire, and beneath the gentle glow of a French chandelier, Mr. Blaine invited me to tell my story. I began, and not far into it, he sent the clerk back to the chamber with the instruction of having another member replace him in the Speaker's chair. I continued with my story, and some twenty minutes later, the person responsible for filling in for the Speaker gave up that position to come listen to me as well. For two hours I spoke; every few minutes another member of the great Chamber quit the floor to join me in the Speaker's Room. Before I had finished the room was full and more members stood on toes in the hall.

I told them everything I have disclosed here, Dear Reader, from the early glories of Joseph Smith to the story of my parents' conversion. I described my first meetings with Brigham, my unhappy marriage to Dee, and Brigham's friendship at the time of my divorce. I discussed my mother's sorrow as one wife, then the next entered her house, and my sense that I had lost my father to polygamy, so demanding upon his moral soul was it. I portrayed for these Gentlemen the workings of the Lion House, and the authority of the Beehive House next door. I recounted Brigham's courtship, and my brother's legal troubles, and my eventual submission. I offered every honest detail of what it has been like for me to be the 19th wife—the few morsels of affection and support it afforded me. All of this I portrayed for the Gentlemen of Congress, those responsible for the laws of our miraculous land. I could perceive the effects of my tale in their wincing eyes, in their agitated lips, twitching behind mustaches and beards.

I urged them to pass the necessary laws to ban this relic of the barbarian. "What kind of country are we that we let this pass? That today, beside this warm fire, sitting in this fine furniture, under the roof of this great building, we should be here while thousands of women and even more children suffer under this system. The Mormons will appeal to you in the name of religious freedom. They will tell you—indeed have already told you—that to subject them to the laws of the land is to persecute them for their faith. If you are inclined to believe this, if you are hesitant to trample on the rights of the religious, then I beg you to consider the question this way: Let a man be with a woman and another and another after her if he so chooses, and if they so choose. Let this happen for the sake of freedom, which we all hold so dear. But as soon as there is a child, as soon as one boy or one girl enters the house, you can no longer look away or protect the situation for the sake of religious freedom. Doesn't every child deserve something better than neglect? Don't you, and we, and all of us, have the obligation to protect that child? And what of this child's rights—his right to be protected, her right to grow up to choose his or her own faith?

"Good Gentlemen, Sirs, I implore you, do not let doctrine ensnare you. Don't hesitate over questions of God and the Lord. You are lawmakers, and your laws have been circumvented. Make it a crime to neglect a wife. Make it a crime to neglect a child. Make it a crime to force one woman to accept another into her home. Make it a crime, for that is what it is. It is not a religious practice, it is not a declaration of faith, it is not a testament of freedom, it is a crime of cruelty and abandonment. And it is permitted today, in your borders, with your consent. Brigham has sanctioned adultery in the name of God, and you, in doing nothing, have condoned it. Your silence has allowed Brigham to claim it to be true. I of course cherish my freedom, but I shall never want my freedom to restrict the freedom of another. In that case then I am not truly free, and none of us is truly free.

"Gentlemen, here, let me introduce you to my son Lorenzo. He has traveled with me all this way. I selfishly took him with me, for I could not imagine the journey without him. I should have left him in school with his brother. But I could not, for he, ultimately, is the reason I wage this fight. I look at him and am reminded of my purpose. If my story has not impressed you, consider it from his eyes. Imagine what he has seen, and how it has affected him. If you owe me no protection, I at least ask you to give it to him."

When I concluded my speech, the Gentlemen of Congress rushed to meet me, offering their cards and promising their support. For some time a circle of men ten-deep surrounded me and there was a general noise of congratulation, like a party, with a hundred voices collecting to form a roar. At some point, something I could not see was taking place at the rim of this crowd, for many men fell silent, and urged others to do so too, and the men began to step aside. The quiet was sudden and complete and had an ominous quality to it. The men were making way for someone to pass through, I could tell, and at first I could not imagine who. Then, slowly, it became clear that somehow Brigham had followed me to the Capitol. He was here, but I did not know why. The Gentlemen continued to step aside, and I waited for my husband to appear from behind the shoulders and heads. I saw a presence, a form moving to me. I held on to Lorenzo, my fingers digging into his shoulders, and I loathed myself for not pushing him out of harm's way, but I could not let go of my child. As the crowd continued to part, the man stepping forward began to take shape, and when at last the final ring of men moved aside, letting the visitor pass—just at this moment I saw before me, as close as my hand is to my face when I hold it out, President Grant. Mrs. Grant was at his side, her eyes crossed with fury. "It will be an everlasting disgrace to this country," the President said, "if this Congress does not heed your call."

I thanked the President for his support. Next I introduced my son, and the great General knelt to discuss matters with my boy, including the quality of fishing in the Potomac. At the end of our interview, President Grant pledged his support.

The final word came from Mrs. Grant. "I want to assure you," she said, "I won't let him sleep until he gets this done."

A few weeks after my visit, Congress passed the anti-polygamy Poland Bill. I can claim only a fraction of the credit for it, for many others have taken part in this Crusade. Time will tell of the bill's effects, and its ability to dismantle what Brigham has so vigorously fought for, but my mission, as I saw it, was complete. I had brought to the nation's attention the suffering of Utah's women and children and forced the country to respond. How Brigham and the Church would react to this new onslaught would be up to them. Would they accept it, give up polygamy, and finally enter through our nation's gates? Or defy it, and invite a battle that would lead to Deseret's humiliation and defeat, along with the surrender of its leaders, like that of the South a decade before? I could not predict the next chapter in the Church's life, nor the future of Brigham's reign, or the prospect of his household, nor the final outcome of this tale of faith. At this point I was certain of only one thing—I had played my part and was ready to reunite my boys and find a home, wherever that may be.

THE END

XIX

―――

PRISON DIARY
OF BRIGHAM YOUNG

CLOSED ARCHIVE

BY ORDER OF

WILFORD WOODRUFF

Prophet & President

October 5, 1890

SEALED

———————

Access Shall Be Limited to

The Prophet & Leader of the Latter-day Saints,

Whoever He Shall Be.

Night has come. Outside the snow clouds have cleared, allowing the moon, my old friend, to burn through. I could look at it all night if I did not have this other task before me. The snow atop the Penitentiary walls reflects the moon in a glowing ring. Beyond the walls the valley basin lays dark. I can see nothing, although I know someone is out there.

They have given me the Warden's office. It is a bare room with a bare floor, and a simple, rectangular writing table where the Warden drafts the papers for the incoming and outgoing prisoners. Earlier Warden Paddock drafted my papers here. Out of deference to my age, I gather, he has decided to house me here with a guard outside the door. Upstairs the Warden's wife is looking after her children, including a newborn, a singing babe with a yellow forelock named Esther. Earlier Mrs. Paddock brought a plate of bread, spiced peaches, and a strip of apricot leather. She asked if I needed anything else. I requested a longer candle, an ink pot, and these pages. I will not sleep tonight.

The Warden's house stands outside the adobe walls, adjoining them at the gate. From the window, I can see into the prison yard, an acre of snowy mud, and the Penitentiary itself, a block-house better suited to corral sheep than to house men. I see the barred windows, the gate studded with iron buttons, and the chimney coughing white smoke. At least the men have a fire. The Warden has fourteen prisoners tonight, myself included, and two guards, not including himself. If there is a rebel among us, a riot could break out easily. I have not met the prisoners, although I saw them an hour before dusk running in a circle around the prison yard. The men wear black-and-white striped pajamas, the stripes running horizontally, and simple Chinese-style caps. They are mostly young men, imprisoned, the Warden tells me, for crimes as mundane as stealing flour and as heinous as ravishment and murder. Looking down at them, all thirteen, running about the yard, kicking their feet high to clear the mounds of snow, I, nor anyone, could tell who has committed the worst crime. Which man has stolen the sack of flour off the mill's wagon? Who ravished the maiden down by the creek? Which man among the thirteen slit his neighbor's throat with a deer knife, as the Warden tells it, from ear to ear? Each man is hungry, cold, and anxious to be free.

I too wear a prison uniform, although my stripes run vertically. I asked the Warden about this, but he did not have an explanation. I believe he is too thoughtful to attribute it to my girth, which has expanded in proportion to my years. My younger wives tease me about this. Mary calls me her water buffalo. Amelia, she likes to poke me in the middle until I laugh like a child. During the brief time we were fond of one another, Ann Eliza would fall off to sleep with her head on my belly. She was a good wife. I am only sorry it has come to this.

The events that led me to this writing table—with its short fourth leg and the rapidly burning candle—began with her apostasy. I knew our relations had soured; I am too familiar with the ways of marriage to expect them all to last. What surprised me, and continues to surprise me, is her tenacity. In truth, I expected her to quit my household, perhaps accept a small sum, and be gone. In all this noise about my 19th Wife, people have ignored the fact that Ann Eliza is not the first woman I have separated from. Mary Woodward, Mary Ann Clark Powers, Mary Ann Turley, Mary Jane Bigelow, Eliza Babcock, Elizabeth Fairchild—all fine Sisters who requested a release from our engagements. They were young, a few not yet twenty if I recall, and our time together was sweet but shallow, not unlike a pie. A pie on the table is always a marvelous sight, but soon it shall be gone, its tin nicked by fork and knife. In each case they requested a disunion and I agreed. In the case of Mary

Jane I paid her five hundred dollars and wished her joy and peace. Once outside my household, these good women proceeded with their lives. A few might have married again, I am not certain. Yet I know none ever spoke of our time as man and wife. My first mistake was assuming Ann Eliza would be the same.

Four weeks ago the subject of my sermon was "How Have I Come Here?" I spoke of our chosen paths, and the meaning of these. I invoked the Pioneers pushing across the plains in '47 and '48, and the thousands of emigrants since, sailing, riding, walking to Zion. Each man, woman, and child present has come to God, I said, and yet the course of each has been different, and so it must always be. I asked my followers to go forth and consider this question in their prayers. How have I come here? Indeed, ever since, when I meet Saints on the street, many have told me they have spent much time pondering the question for themselves.

And so I must do so as well.

After Ann Eliza's apostasy, a long legal battle ensued. At the time it seemed to me Ann Eliza, in her public statements, wanted both sides of a coin. She says in my bountiful household, with so many wives and children, she had truly never been a wife. If this is so, let the woman complain. Yet she also says I owed her a vast sum of alimony. If this is so, let the woman complain. Yet according to her logic, it cannot be both. Either she was my wife and I owe her a claim, or she was not my wife and I owe her nothing. My lawyers, good men, perhaps too eager to please, advised that under federal law she was never my wife. The civil courts, which so despise our marital customs, would never honor her request for alimony. Thus our strategy was set. Ann Eliza Young had never been my wife. My mistress and my confidant, yes—but not my wife. My lawyers were the first to publicly call her a social harlot—an unfortunate outburst of hostility yet benign compared to the charges she laid against me.

For many months the lawyers argued. The man she hired, Judge Hagan, never truly had her interests in mind. In truth, I did not pay close attention to the case, for so many other matters engaged me. I admit bewilderment then, when on February 25th of this year Judge McKean ordered me to pay Ann Eliza alimony in the sum of five hundred dollars a month by March 10th or be held in contempt of court. When I read the court order I remember thinking, It is a bluff. The United States government has ordered me to pay alimony to a 19th wife? It would mean they believed my wives to be legal in every sense. It would mean an acceptance of plural marriage. I knew this had not come to pass, and I shredded the court order, throwing the bits into the fire.

It was after nine o'clock this morning when the Deputy United States Marshal, A. K. Smith, a modest, dutiful man whose brass buttons shone like the sun, arrived at the Beehive with a warrant for my arrest. My loyal men—Brother Adam at the guardpost, Brother Caleb at the door, Brother Orson and Brother Herman in my office—each attempted to stop the Marshal from nearing me. The man had come armed with certified papers, and I told my men that we shall always respect the force of law, and its majesty. "A piece of paper written with legal will is a weapon more powerful than a rifle," I advised.

The morning was cold, blustery, the winds throwing fresh, fine-grained snow against the window panes. At the time of the Marshal's arrival I had been planning an emergency rescue for the citizens of Big Cottonwood. Yesterday's snows, and those from the day before, had caused snow slides from Canyon Flat to Porcupine Cabin, burying the canyon in near fifty feet of snow, blocking the creek and the road for one mile. We did not know how many pitiable souls lay under the snow, whether dead, frozen blue into the frost, or alive and awaiting rescue. Together my men and I were organizing the teams to be sent when the Marshal entered my office.

The Marshal said we were due in court but allowed me the time necessary to sign my morning letters and documents. His orders had been to bring me at once, but he is a good man and under-

stands that every man, whether crook or king, has business to finish before he can leave his house. I dressed in my cape and hat,
hung my watch from my shirtwaist, and said good-bye to my men.
I told them to continue with the rescue, and worry none for me. In
the hall, as I was leaving the Beehive, I met Sister Mary Ann. She
is nearly as old as I, fortified in her routine, suspicious of all Gentiles, Babylonians she names them, refusing to greet any outside
our faith, even President Grant, she often says, were he to call.
When she saw the Marshal, she looked as if she was about to reach
for her pistol and bucket and chase him from the house in the fearless manner she drives the rats from the orchard. I told my wife to
be still and pray.

At ten o'clock we entered the Third District Court Room and
the Marshal seated me in a chair on the east side. So many had
gathered for the spectacle, supporters and enemies alike, that mine
was the last vacant seat, with the exception of the chair awaiting
Judge McKean. My supporters included many of my sons and
sons-in-law, who sat in a row headed by Hiram Clawson; members
of the Nauvoo Legion, some of them now older than I, their shoulders bent under fond memories of the olden days; a variety of Bishops, Elders, and other well-wishers; and Captain Hooper from the
co-op's hat department, who, just before the proceedings began,
called out, "All of Zion rise up for our Prophet, Brigham Young!"

Judge McKean silenced the court room with his angry gavel.
With each bang of the mallet's head he looked at me with obvious
disgust. From whence his adversity to our Faith comes I know not.
True, the recent publication of Ann Eliza's memoir has soiled my
character in many parts of the nation. I am told it has sold more
than 100,000 copies, sending the publisher back to the printing
press three or four times. Are there 100,000 men and women interested in the Saints? If only they had read our Book, not hers. Now,
for many, knowledge of our Church, and of me, comes mostly from
her pen. I have not read *The 19th Wife,* but I have it here with me,
should I need the company. I hope it does not come to that.

My attorneys, Brother Hempstead and Brother Kirkpatrick, had prepared themselves with an armory of books and briefs. Their adversary, Judge Hagan, stood nearby, solid with confidence. In dealing with him, he is the kind of lawyer who grants you the sensation of victory, while in truth you have lost everything.

Hagan began by declaring I had shown disdain for the court's mandate by refusing to pay Ann Eliza's fee in the stated time. Judge McKean asked my attorneys if this was true. Kirkpatrick attempted first, claiming it was not. Hempstead fortified Kirkpatrick's position, saying, "While it's true Brother Brigham has not paid the fees, he has not shown disdain for the court or its mandate." Both men continued adequately for more than an hour, incorporating legal thinking derived from American and English courts, all in my support. While competent in legal history, they possess ordinary imaginations and therefore they could not create, as an artist would, a means for my escape. At 12:35, Judge McKean called an hour recess. When the court returned, I was found in contempt of court and ordered to the Penitentiary.

The cheers and whoops of hurrah drowned out the weeping of my supporters. The Marshal shackled me at the wrist, apologizing for having to do so. As he led me from the court room a voice cried out, "Remember Carthage!" A second echoed the first, "We'll always remember Carthage!"

I too was thinking of Carthage, of the stone jailhouse where the mob assassinated my dear Joseph and his brother, Hiram, nearly thirty-one years before. Joseph had submitted to the rule of law, giving himself up to the Gentile authorities, yet in the end the law could not protect him from the mob. I was away on mission that terrible day. I did not speak to him in his last hours. What were his thoughts? Those who witnessed him said he was pensive and in peace. Yet there is no greater mystery to me, at least among matters from here on Earth, than what occupied Joseph's mind on his last day on Earth. We have his letter to Emma, but how often I have wished he had kept a deeper record of his final hours. I know he was not afraid, yet there is much more I wish I could know.

If this candle burns out before dawn, I will have to write by moonlight. Perhaps the guard outside my door will ask Mrs. Paddock for a second, yet he must do so now, before she falls asleep. To do this he will have to leave his post and he will only do so if he can trust me. The guard, a Catholic boy named Christopher, he reminds me of Willard. They share the same supple smile and wave of chestnut hair. They could be the same age, I shall ask when I request the second candle. I think of Willard often, of how bravely my son withstood the slander when he arrived at West Point a few years ago. Many called for his removal from campus, writing Senators and Congressmen letters of disapproval, disparaging him as the son of whores. When I read this in the newspapers, I telegraphed Willard, inviting him to return home. His reply was swift and short: "Father, will stay." Now he's preparing to graduate from the Military Academy with a commission in the national Corps of Engineers.

There, I have spoken with the guard. His name is Officer O'-Conner, he is twenty-three—Willard's age by a month. He will fetch a second candle from Mrs. Paddock's cupboard. While waiting for him, I stood at the window for some time. The immense valley lay in blackness, yet the moon on the snow casts a revealing silver-blue light. While gazing at it, I sensed a movement out there. I could not perceive it with any precision. That is what it was to my eye—a movement in the dark. I do not know if it was a trick of the light, or a wolf pack crouching through the snow, or men gathering. Or perhaps there was no movement, perhaps all is still, and it is time for me to sleep.

When Officer O'Conner returned I asked if he worried I might try to escape. "No, Sir," he said. "You gave me your word." He handed me a long tapered candle barely burned at the top.

Now, with ample candle-power, I should have the friend of light to guide me through the night. When I think of all there is to do, I become anxious and walk in circles around this small room. I am not restless for lack of freedom. During my house arrest in the winter of '72, I could stay at my desk day and night, hacking away at my tasks at a pace even I had never before known. There is always much to do, matters to consider, works to accomplish. Next month I would like to return to St. George to review the progress of the Temple. The roof will rise soon—how I hope to witness that! When it is up, and the building stands secure, we can begin our many important rites, starting with the baptism of the dead. Then I must tend to the United Order, which has yet to take root. Later this summer I should like to reintroduce the New Alphabet. How much easier it will be on our emigrants when they arrive in Deseret, unfamiliar with English as they are. The last attempt failed, I know, because I did not lead the Saints to it. This time they will know its importance to me. And always so much more—the letters I owe my sons, including Willard, to whom I must describe the guard. The upcoming conference of the councils of the Priesthood. The audit of the statements of the Z.C.M.I. The meeting with the Board of Directors of the Deseret Bank, and of the Street Railroad Co. too, and that of the Deseret Telegraph Co., all of which shall be held very soon, and a review of the Utah Southern Railroad's future tracks, and the annual meeting of the Gas Co., &c. &c.—these are the matters, and many others, preoccupying my mind of late. The misperception among those who do not know me, or care not to know me, is that my spoiled marriage to Ann Eliza has consumed my days. Ann Eliza does not hold such a commanding position in my thoughts. She is perhaps 87th on a list of tasks and items requiring my attention. This no doubt has fueled her rage. I should have been more mindful of this. My rage for her, however, has never matched hers for me. I admire her, and always will. I remember the night she was born. There are no words to depict the joy she brought her mother, herself a true Saint. As a baby Ann Eliza was dark in the face, with two slits for eyes. How those eyes opened as she grew, blossoming into a beauty that, even tonight, can catch upon my old heart.

The Marshal led me from the courthouse to a carriage. Hundreds of Saints waited along the cordoned path, all somber and withdrawn, many weeping softly, a few Sisters wailing with grief. I walked as proudly as a man can with his hands manacled behind his back. "Pray for the wisdom of our Father," I called to them. "Pray for the mercy and justice of our Lord." But my words could not travel far, for pressing against the Saints were nearly a thousand enemies, their fists in the air and calling for their own interpretation of justice. How I longed for the days when we were alone in Deseret! I always knew we would rue the railroad.

Marshal Smith ushered me into the carriage. His orders were to deliver me directly to the Warden of the Penitentiary. Again, at my request, he disobeyed them, driving first to the Beehive. I sent my guardsman to bring me Mrs. Young. Sister Mary Ann approached the carriage, torn apart by tears. I explained to my wife the task I needed her to perform. She understood, pushing a small cloth at her damp nose, and ran inside. She returned with a pair of caramel leather boots. These were the boots Joseph had worn when he rode to Carthage to submit to the jailhouse. In the carriage I changed my shoes, donning Joseph's boots for the first time. Although our feet were not the same size, the boots fit as if they had been cobbled for me. I wear them now.

Admirers and enemies had gathered along the route to the Penitentiary. Several times a rifle was shot into the sky, sending fear and paranoia through the crowd. I cannot know the total number of people in the streets, yet I shall estimate it to be ten thousand. Most were my followers, yet the relative few who were there to oppose me controlled the argument. What astonished me, even more than the noise and the rancor, and the vicious shouts of slander— *American Sultan!* and *No More Harems!* and *Isn't 19 enough!*—was the piety my Saints maintained, for they understood what they were witnessing. Their Prophet, shackled, being led to punishment. At a crossroads near the city's limit, where the crowd was smaller and the shouting less, a small girl ran into the road, pelting my carriage with blue crocus. "Like Jesus before him," she cried, running back to her mother, who kissed her head.

By the time we reached the Penitentiary gate, four miles from the city, twenty carriages were following us. I realized my men, friends all, filled them, and they had come to protect me. Warden Paddock met us at the gate, while his guards, Officer O'Conner and his partner, held back the men in the carriages. As the Marshal led me from the carriage, my men cried out for my release. Many held rifles in the air, while others raised up axes, scythes, and other blades.

Warden Paddock welcomed me, leading me up the stairs to his office, where I now sit. He instructed the Marshal to release me from the cuffs. The papers were drafted and signed, and officially the Marshal transferred me into the custody of the Warden. I thanked the good man for his attendance and said good-bye. From the window I watched him return to his carriage. The pair of Penitentiary officers escorted him through the throng of my supporters onto the road.

The Warden looked out the window with concern, for no doubt the crowd appeared ready to boil over into a mob. I assured him they would not attack the penitentiary as long as they deemed I was safe. I asked to speak to them. The Warden considered this unusual request from his newest prisoner. I had never before met this man, yet surely he knew of me. I wondered with which portion of my public character he was familiar. I realize, more than anyone else, that for all the Saints who understand me as their Prophet, and trust me as their spiritual guide on Earth, and into the Afterlife, many more people believe me to be a scoundrel. I can accept this misperception if it means being constant in my faith.

"You have five minutes, Sir." The Warden led me to the gate. With the two guards stationed beside me, I spoke to my followers. "Do not worry for me tonight, for these are good men here, who understand the rule of law. I am safe, now you must disperse."

The men, however, did not want to disperse. Many called out,

"Carthage!"

"Please, Brethren, you must withdraw."

Still the men stayed in place. "Carthage!" the men cried again. "Carthage!"

I tried a third time. "My dear friends, you must listen to me and disperse now. You wonder why you should do so and I shall tell you. For we are a people of law, and rule, and Christian kindness. We do not attack because we fear being attacked. Even if you worry for my safety, you must now push back, go out, and disperse. Do so now, for that is what I want of you. I know you want to protect me, but understand, God protects me, as He protects you, and His will, whatever that may be, shall be borne out tonight, whether your rifle is drawn or not. Do not defy me, for in doing so you shall defy our Heavenly Father. You cry, Think of Carthage! Brethren, one day has not passed since June 27, 1844, when I have not thought of Carthage. I think of Carthage on days of joy and rest, on days of fear and toil, always I think of Carthage. At night, before sleep, I call Joseph's name, knowing he awaits me, as he awaits you, all of you! Joseph came to tell us the Latter-day Saints are the inheritors of Christ, and Christ has shown us that we do not take an eye for an eye. Friends, go now, leave the Warden in peace, and his guards in peace, and this Penitentiary in peace! Even if it is now my home, and I know not my future, you must leave in peace, for that is what we believe."

Silently the crowd broke, drifting out in all directions, to the factory and to the mill, and down the road to Salt Lake. Would an enemy mob replace them? From my window I have been anticipating it ever since.

It is late now. Half the night is gone. What will the darkness bring before the dawn? The prisoners are asleep. The Warden's family has retired. Outside my door I hear Officer O'Conner pacing to keep himself awake. When I look out into the dark, into the land beyond the Penitentiary, I see the movement again. Now they are black shapes shifting against other black shapes. I cannot tell what they are. Wagons? Buffalo? Men on horseback? A forming brigade? For a long time now I have stood at the window, with my new candle burning itself down, staring into the night, trying to perceive what moves out there. It occurs to me I should snuff out the candle, so that I may stand in the darkened window, but then I will have no light until daybreak. The longer I look out, the more certain I am that there are men out there. Friend or enemy? I look for a signal, but see none. The snow has muffled the sounds of the earth. An attack could come as a surprise. If it does, and they are assassins, I pray they spare Mrs. Paddock and her children. And Officer O'Conner—I should note he even speaks like Willard, slowly, with his tongue soft against the roof of his mouth. The similarity is perplexing. If it is a sign, I cannot interpret it. So I continue to stand alert at the window, considering so much.

Yesterday a reporter from the *San Francisco Examiner* came to see me. This man writes a daily unsigned column that has made him famous and, I am quite sure, rich. I would hold a grudge against him, for he has spared no venom in dissecting me and my divorce. But I cannot hold a grudge for he loathes everyone equally, and with good aim. Against the opinion of my advisors, I invited him to the Beehive. During our meeting he asked a question I am still pondering tonight. "What mistakes have you made?" I assured him there were many, but he pressed me for details.

First, I was wrong about Ann Eliza. Quite simply, I judged her incorrectly. I sensed she understood, or would come to understand, the arrangements of my household, and know that while I could not tend to her in every manner, I would always care for her. She is a selfish woman, by which I do not mean to condemn her, for most men and women are selfish, in that most often they think of themselves first. It is man's most natural instinct, an impulse that connects us with the animals. Yet some women are extraordinary in this regard, they can submerge their natural impulses for the sake of their belief. These are the women best suited to plural marriage. Ann Eliza, I have learned, is not this kind of woman. So be it. I only wish we could have settled our matters more kindly. For now, with our case on the public stage, all the world it seems has become curious about my wives. Every day the mail brings a hundred letters wanting to know how many I have. Yesterday, the man from the *Examiner* pressed me on that question. "Surely, you must know how many wives you keep?" he asked not once, but eight or ten times.

Each time I replied, "I do."

"Then why won't you tell me how many Mrs. Youngs there are? Why is it a secret?" He is an intelligent man, but not so intelligent to realize he is most likely the thousandth person to inquire on the matter. Why this never-ending speculation over how many wives? Why do visitors to Great Salt Lake stand outside the Lion House, and the Beehive House too, counting windows and doors, attempting to estimate the number of spouses therein. Surely they must know it is a futile exercise—one cannot know how many sleep inside a house by counting the dormers! Yet they do, I see them outside the wall every day. One, two, three, four, five, their moving lips say. Next they wonder if I keep two wives in one bed. Or perhaps three, a rude man suggests to his friend. They share a debased laugh, a putrid guffaw, one that degrades the very idea of woman and her dignity. Next they wonder how I can manage my conjugal duties with so many wives waiting her turn. Their interest in the number of wives is always prurient. If, on the other hand, it were spiritual and came as a true inquiry into the will of God, I would explain my household to them, count up the wives to show the abundance of our faith. Yet I see no point when it will only feed the imagination of the profane.

The good Saints know why I do not announce the number of wives. Wife is an inadequate term, for each woman plays a different role in my life, just as each person plays a different role in all our lives. For lack of a more precise term, we label them all wives, but they are not all wives. Indeed some are my mates and mothers of my children. Yet others are more like affectionate aunts. Others are

intellectual friends, with whom I can debate and discuss all matters. Others still are, indeed, the keepers of the house, the kitchen,
the children. Others remind me, in their distance, of neighbors to
whom one might wave across a wall. Others still are very old and
retired in their rocking chairs. They find comfort in knowing I shall
provide them with a bed and meals for the rest of their days. Only
a few are like a wife in the common sense, none more so than
Amelia. She is all of this, and more, but imagine the uproar—
among my women and the public at large—were I to so publicly
dissect the ranks within my household. I shall not subject these
good women to that, and therefore I do not answer the question
how many wives. I must admit to the smallest pleasure it gives
me—how this numerical mystery irritates the world!

Sometimes, also, I permit the hypocrisy to bemuse me. In the
evening, when I am with Amelia, or my sons, or other friends, and
the business of the day is done, and we can sit by a fire, and loosen
the laces in our shoes, I allow myself to chuckle, like when I have
been told a fine irony. These indignant Gentiles, lamenting the nature of my household, having never known it in person, tolerate in
their midst a broader range of crimes—drunkenness, infanticide,
neglect of the elderly, prostitution—crimes that are all but unknown in Deseret. Let's ponder the latter. I have seen the whore at
work—the painted lips, the exposed bosom, the voice darkened by
whiskey and tobacco. She is an unnatural sight, in defiance of
God's grace and the beauty of man given to us by Adam. Yet visit
any Gentile city at dusk, or thereafter, and stroll the streets. You
shall find one lady after the next vying for her spot on the corner.
Or enter a tavern, where drink is deified, and you will find a woman
prepared to spill her breasts onto the counter for a dollar, or less. In
my younger days, when I saw Gentile whores on the street, I
thought back in time. I imagined them as little girls in their Sunday dresses, with white collars and straw bonnets. I envisioned their
mothers brushing their flaxen hair, kissing their smooth brows, and
praying to our Father to protect them. Then I saw them now, be-

fore me, in the dim corners of the Gentile city—the whore with her nest of false curls permitting any man with a coin to paw her parts, to reach beneath her skirts in search of the desecrated hollow raked over by a thousand men. Where is the outrage among the Gentile crusaders? Why do they not demand an end to her whoredom? Only hypocrisy can explain it, and withered reasoning.

Each time my enemies attack me as America's foremost adulterer, they fail to admit an important matter to the debate. Their society is rife with adultery, yet among the Saints, this sin remains unknown. To my mind, adultery is worst among the sins, with the exception of murder, for the one act corrodes many souls. The practice of plural marriage has eliminated adultery from our society, freeing us of its ill effects. I look to King David with many sacred wives. He was a good and devout man, but when he stole Uriah's wife, snatching her from the heart of her husband, he became an adulterer, and in God's eyes he had committed sin. Worse still, his selfish act—prompted by the other sins of greed, vanity, and lust—forced her to become an adulteress. Thus the sinner created a second sinner. This is not right.

I wonder if Ann Eliza has illuminated this truth to her reader. Opening her book at random, I find this declaration: "Brigham leads the Church, and all of Utah, as a tyrant rules from his throne. He will not tolerate dissent or open opinion, for in his claim to be Prophet of God he believes there is no truth except that which he has spoken." My goodness, am I really such? I laugh over her depiction, for I've heard it before, and will do so again.

I must say, Ann Eliza always proved insightful. Behind her denunciation, she has illuminated one of the most troublesome aspects of my leadership. There is, and, to my mind, always will be, the problem of balancing the Truth, as I know it, with the rights of man, in which I believe. How to reconcile this problem? I know my faith to be the true faith of God, and Joseph His first Prophet since Christ, and myself after him, yet I cannot force belief upon others—or can I? Is this not my task, my mission? How to solve this quandary of religious duty? If we are right, and our faith is the true expression of God's will, to what extent should I enforce that will? This is not merely a practical question of conversion and missionary work, but a theological question concerning divine duty. I have pondered it for many years, without full resolution. In my heart I know we are right, and Joseph has brought us the Truth, and now I am to carry it forth. In my heart I know I am to bring it to all the lands with the force of God, and His wrath too, for Truth can never respect falsehoods and lies. But it is not always feasible to do so. Is it a failing when I tell my Brethren to respect the Methodist, the Episcopal, the Jew? Am I failing God? I cannot know. I must accept it as one of our Heavenly Father's many mysteries, its answer unknowable until our last day.

Just now I have returned from the window. I am certain men have gathered out there, for they are closer, maybe a hundred yards from the Warden's house. I can see the flash in their horses' eyes. I hear the hoofs stomping on the snow. I can see the orange embers of burning tobacco which tells me, then, these are not my men. When the mob attacked the jailhouse in Carthage, two hundred men had painted their faces black to mask their identities. The men out there—they are using the black of night as a mask. I respect them less, and fear them less—for a camouflaged enemy is a cowardly enemy. Stand in the daylight and fight for what you believe! I will grant Ann Eliza this—she has taken her shot at me from a stage where I can see her.

Often I think back to my old friend and enemy E. L. T. Harrison and his well-argued words against me in *The Utah Magazine*. Among men's mental powers, I have always had a special fondness for logic. I remember Harrison's words of dissent as if they were on a page before me now. "I believe in the right to discuss freely, provided I do it respectfully and moderately, any measure or principle that may be presented. I do not believe I have the right to be rabid in regard to my use of vindictive language, but provided I am temperate—provided I accord to others the same privilege I do myself,

I believe that men should be guided entirely by their own light and intelligence. I do not believe in the principle of implicit obedience, unconditional obedience without the judgment being convinced. If it is apostasy to differ with Brigham on some points, I am an apostate because I honestly differ with him. I do protest that I differ in a spirit of love and due regard for him." How to reconcile his views and mine, when I know mine to be the wisdom of our Father, and his to be the sincere but misguided inclinations of a good man? Liberty, I know, rests nowhere but in Truth. Freedom—always in Truth! Must I, then, for the sake of Liberty, respect Harrison's thoughtful but defiant judgments? Ignore them? Condemn them? How can I guide others in the principles of Truth if I do not condemn these opinions? Oh! were He to tell me with all certainty my course. Yet I have come to know that wrestling with this question shall be my fate while on Earth. I only pray that when I kneel before Him in the Heavenly Kingdom He shall tell me I have acted wisely.

I have faced such opposition since the Gladdenites, for there is no more ferocious enemy than he who comes from within. Apostasy is inevitable to holding firm to one's belief. That a few believers will fall away is the by-product of unbending faith. If this were not the case, if I never lost a follower, I would wonder if I had bent, unbeknownst to myself, to popular opinion. My duty, I know, is to lead. I cannot offer an array of options. I must offer a long but narrow path to Salvation, and guide the Saints down it. Were that path wide and varied, it would lead nowhere; and I will then have failed both God and man. I cannot go forth into the next life, with the knowledge I will meet Joseph there, without knowing I have made every effort to promote and preserve his wisdom on all matters, including plural marriage. How have I come here? It is by this.

Outside, beyond the adobe walls, the men are moving in. I see them—the last of the moonlight burns on their muzzles, it illuminates the hatred in their eyes. I see them, crouching, sneaking forward, preparing their siege. Is this my hour? Did Joseph see his enemies in the Illinois brush before they stormed the stone jail-house? Did he see the blue-white of their seething eyes? How have I come here indeed! If they are to take me, they are to take me while preoccupied with the work of God.

This, then, has been my second mistake, and its effects are more dangerous than the first. I was wrong to let my attorneys persuade me to claim I have only one wife. They convinced me that in declaring Ann Eliza and all my other wives social harlots, the matter would fall away. Their tactics are legal, with no concern for the theological or moral. I am to blame for accepting their counsel. This, I know, has been my gravest error, for in following their advice, I renounced my faith. I know the force of my leadership has come from always standing firm before friend and foe. What did the Saints everywhere think when they heard me, via the legal brief, dismiss our most sacred institution? Calling the good sisters of the Lion House social harlots? I am ashamed to think of the turmoil I have unleashed in their hearts. And what of God? He who has given me wisdom for many years? I turned to lawyers for answers, not Him! Consider it! The loss of faith! Oh, Joseph! Joseph! How great is the capacity to forgive?

"Officer O'Conner!" I rap upon the door. "Officer O'Conner!" My ear tells me the young man is asleep. The men outside the walls have anticipated this. Ambush relies on the element of surprise. The young guard, Willard's unknown twin, will awaken to a rifle in his face. He will unlock my door while the assassin presses his gun to his temple. The poor boy—he knew nothing of what it meant to protect me. "Officer O'Conner!" How he sleeps! His mind must be free of worry. For me, I have no resource but prayer.

I do not know how long I have been on my knees now. These words here I write from the floor, putting down the pen between prayers. The candle burns low, the soft wax folding over the candlestick. Just now I have looked out the window. I see the men. The siege is about to begin. In Carthage, Joseph had a six-shooter smuggled in by a friend to defend himself. He fired all his shots before succumbing to the assassin's ball. I have nothing but my pen and my prayers. With these, I will hold out as long as I can.

But, look, on the horizon! A sliver of light! Not yet pink. Silver and blue. A minute ago all was dark, now a crevice of light, and with each breath of man it expands. In the time it has taken to write those words, the light has grown. Now beyond the black mountains I see a wash of blue. With it I can see the horses and the men. There must be two hundred—no, three hundred out there on the roads. They have blockaded the road to the mill, and the other to the factory. When will they attack? Do they wish to see my face in the clear light of dawn? If so, they are not cowards. They are fearless—the most dangerous enemy. Come! I say. Attack! I shall stand before you and never relent!

I have returned to my knees to ask our Dear Heavenly Father for forgiveness, for I have turned away from Your wisdom. I am not afraid for my life, but I fear dying by the assassin's ball while having renounced You. Grant me another day on Earth to return to Your path. Bring me the wisdom to know the course I must take. I believe, as I have always believed, in the doctrine of plural marriage as You revealed it to Joseph, as You have confirmed it to me. Your word is the word of God, and always shall be. I will go forth and affirm its Truth, if only You will grant me another day.

Thus I prayed. I have been on my knees for so long they are sore from the boards. Outside, dawn's arrival is now irreversible. The colors fill the sky. The mountains are lit, the valley is lit, the river runs in its canyon, carrying chips of ice. If the assault is to come, it is to come now. Why do they wait? I will check the window. I will show them my face.

Dear Heavenly Father! The men on the roads! They are packing up! I can see them rolling blankets, saddling horses, storing guns. I can see them turning the carriages around. Who are they? Why did they not attack? How often does life prove itself unknowable? How many mysteries can the heart bear? I only know this is the mercy of the Lord! I know it, I recognize it, I feel the warmth on my skin.

"Officer O'Conner! Officer O'Conner! Tell the Warden I want to return to court! Call the Marshal! Call Judge McKean!" I shall inform Judge McKean I accept his orders. I will pay Ann Eliza's fees. I will grant her a rightful divorce. Her demands are just. She has been my wife. For five years she was my wife. How true she is, she has been my wife! The women of the Lion House—God has granted each to me as a full wife!

I will go forth and declare to the Saints everywhere, and the world too, this shall be our last battle, I know, for we will never relent. We will defy the authorities, the army, even the great General, President Grant! If we must, we will take up our arms to fight in the name of God. I can only hope my new resolve will inspire the Saints to fight for this principle until the end of time. He who abandons it is not a Saint, as I now understand, for God has spoken. His words are clear.

The desert sun now pours through the window, warm on the writing desk. How I long to be home among my women! The sacred practice of celestial marriage is not my will, or Joseph's will, but the will of God. And so the Truth has come to pass. It is as clear as the desert morn outside. Through Revelation, God has spoken, and we must obey. Saints of Zion—be not afraid! We know the wisdom of the Lord, and we shall defend it until our Last Day!

WIFE #19:
THE CONVICTION
OF JORDAN SCOTT

ENDING IT ALL

———

I checked the food court, the gadget store, the men's room. I spent more than an hour looking for Johnny in the mall. The last place to search was the LDS bookstore. I approached a clerk unloading a carton of books. The guy didn't recognize Johnny from my description but said he'd keep an eye out.

"Wait a minute," I said. "What's that?"

"What, this?" The clerk looked at the book in his hand. There was a modelly gay-looking guy on the jacket. Its title: *Triumphing over Same-Gender Attraction.* The clerk had already unloaded a dozen copies and there were another dozen in the box.

"Yeah, that. What is it?"

"It's, uh, I don't know." The guy flipped the book over and started reading the copy. "I guess it's something for parents who think their kid's gay or something."

"I know what it is."

The clerk looked at me like, Huh?

"You sell a lot of these?"

"Excuse me?" We were probably the same age, could've been born on the same day, two young men from opposite ends of the state, opposite ends of the world, really.

"Do you sell a lot of these?"

"That's not really, I mean, I can't really—" But he pulled his wits together, as if he'd been trained to deal with nut jobs. "Sir, is there something I can help you with?"

I started looking at the book myself. It was written by a couple whose son had noosed up his missionary necktie and let it all hang out because he was gay. And right there on the first page they wrote, "Although bereft, after Josh's death we were overcome by a certain peace because his anguish had come to an end."

Don't. Make. Me. Scream.

"You realize you're selling total and complete bullshit."

"Sir?"

"This book. It's a total lie."

"Sir, if there's nothing here you want, maybe you should leave."

"What? I'm not allowed to browse?"

"I really don't want to have to call security."

"Be my guest." I was bluffing. We both knew it. I threw the book on the table, turned around, and bumped right into Johnny.

"Dude, *what* has crawled up your ass today?"

Outside on the street I said, "You've got to stop disappearing like that."

"You're the one who dumped me on the curb."

"I told you I'd be back."

"That's what they all say." He punched me in the shoulder. "C'mon, I'm starving. There's this cool place across the street."

He led me over to an old gabled house with a stone lion above the door. "You want to eat here?" I said.

"There's this major buffet down in the basement. All you can eat for four ninety-nine."

I couldn't believe it. We were standing in front of the Lion House. It was now a museum and catering hall. I told him no way. I wasn't going to eat in Brigham's harem.

"Why not?"

"Why not? You know what this place represents?"

"Get over yourself. It's only fucking lunch."

There was nothing special about the place. A cafeteria in the basement, heaps of carby food in enamel pans. We filled our plates with limp turkey and macaroni and fake cheese and dinner rolls.

"So what was that all about?" said Johnny.

"I don't know. That book just struck a chord." I described the book and I didn't want to, but I let a tirade get the best of me. Off

I went, lamenting all the gay Mormon kids who are lied to, the *Ensign* articles warning them to deny who they are, eighteen-year-old Josh hanging from a necktie in his Ogden closet, those nasty parents finding peace—*peace!*—after his death. And then writing a book about it. I went on and on, flailing my hands, banging the table in the corner of the Lion House basement, preaching to a kid who listened with a give-me-a-break face while picking his nose.

When I was done he pushed a slab of turkey into his mouth and went back to the buffet for seconds. He returned to the table, saying, "Isn't this place awesome? All you can eat for five bucks. You gotta love the Mormons."

"Johnny, did you hear anything I just said?"

The kid was busy chewing, flashing gray blue bits of turkey on his tongue. "I heard."

"Well?"

"When are you going to realize you're not the only person in the world who's been fucked? I mean, crap, welcome to the club."

An hour later we parked in front of the Ann Eliza Young House. "Let's go in."

Johnny looked at the house, then me. "Where are we?"

"It's a home for kids."

"What kind of home?"

"There's someone I want you to meet."

His mouth bit into a hard line. "Are you fucking with me?"

"C'mon, let's go."

"Because if you are, at least have the guts to admit it to my face, you lying piece of shit."

I thought he might take off, run down the sidewalk, and disappear. I could imagine it—his little black-soled sneakers slapping the concrete, taking him around a corner, down an alley, through a lobby, anywhere. I'd go looking for him, but this time he wouldn't turn up. It seemed like the most obvious outcome to all this. There'd be the days of searching, the panicked calls to Tom, the sorry explanation to Kelly, the police report, the false hope, the dead ends, the giving up. It was as if it had already happened, like I'd already seen this movie and knew the ending line by line.

But he didn't run. He walked up the path with me to the door, silent and furious, picking a daisy along the way, shredding its petals, and hurling them at me. They hit the back of my head with the impact of a moth. "Who the fuck is Ann Eliza Young, anyway?"

"Some Mormon lady, it doesn't matter."

"Now I get it, it's all coming clear. Earth to Johnny, once again you're the last one to realize you've been screwed."

Kelly met us at the door. She looked very pretty and very calm. When she talked to Johnny she talked to him like a person, not like a messed-up booted-out kid. "Can I get you something to eat? Maybe an apple or a banana?"

"Next." His livid eyes were saying, *I'm going to kill you for this.*

"The director's here, she's looking forward to meeting you."

"And I'm looking forward to telling her she can suck my—"

"Johnny."

"Kidding!" The dimples ran up his cheeks like when you hold your finger on the)))))))))) key. He turned to Kelly. "All right, sweetheart. I suppose every outlaw has to eventually come in." He took her hand and they walked down the hall. The amber light from the old brass sconce silhouetted them, two figures retreating into a celestial glow, like lovers strolling into the sunset on a corn-dog greeting card. And that was it.

Or, almost.

"Johnny, wait!"

He turned around.

"Your knife!"

"What about it?"

"I'll keep it for you." I walked to him with my hand out. He hesitated, then pulled it out of his pants. We looked at it, at his mom's name taped to the handle.

"I'll be wanting that back," he said.

"One day," I said.

"I mean it, it's all I got from her." The kid shoved my shoulder and lurched forward for an awkward hug. "Now get out of here before we both start breaking up like a couple of girls."

PROMETHEUS UNBOUND

Even we do not know what to say. On Friday last, the Lord's Lion, fresh from a good night's sleep in the United States Penitentiary, emerged with a changed heart. He marched into Judge McKean's courtroom to declare, Sir, you are right! Brigham paid the fees, in doing so admitting Ann Eliza had been his wife and she was due a proper alimony.

Now, in any other part of the world, this would be an unremarkable event. Yet this is Deseret, and oh, how we enjoy its many ironies! In accepting Brigham's fees, and releasing him from custody, Judge McKean acknowledged Ann Eliza, and all the rest, numbers one through nineteen, and beyond—all of them to be lawful wives. Thus, for our slower readers, a federal judge, appointed by the President himself, had given legal claim to polygamy.

Oh, what we would have paid to be present when the news reached old Grant wheezing in his bed. How his mustaches must have fluttered from his bellows! The General fumed, orders were given, and in due time Judge McKean has been removed from the court, replaced by a jurist with a finer understanding of the case's subtleties. Summarily, Judge McKean's original decisions were reversed. Brigham Young was found to owe Ann Eliza nothing, for she never was, and never will be, his wife. The case was dismissed, the parties thrown out, and by God, the General screamed at poor Mrs. Grant, these Mormons are going to be the end of me!

This, as far as we can tell, is the end of the tale of the 19th Wife. To all, Godspeed!

WE MET ONLINE

———

It was past midnight when I pulled into the Malibu. Tom's alarm clock washed the room in digital green. He was asleep, a dog on each side. The dogs were snoring lightly, their snout lips fluttering, their breath filling the room with the castoff of sleep. Watching Tom and the dogs, I felt something I didn't quite recognize, something so tender I worried it would pop and disappear if I asked for its meaning. I unlaced my sneakers and dropped my jeans and pulled back the blanket.

Elektra stirred, lifting her head. Then Joey, and at last Tom. Each looked momentarily confused. Elektra was the first to recognize me, her tail thumping. Tom said, "Oh, hi," and Joey budged himself over for a lick.

"I think everything's going to be OK," I said.

"You mean you left him there?"

I kissed him—Tom, I mean.

"What are you going to do now?"

"Shhh," I said. "Go back to sleep. We'll figure it out tomorrow." I reached for Tom. His sacred underwear was so thin and diaphanous it was like touching his chest through an ethereal gauze. On the undershirt's belly there's a short line of stitching called a navel marker; it's there to remind you of God's nourishment, or something like that. It's just a little dash of thread, and as Tom and I fell toward sleep I rubbed it over and over, the way a finger returns impulsively to a scar.

In the morning I went to Heber's office. "I was just about to call you," Maureen said. "Mr. Heber wants to see you."

"Actually, I came to see you. I want to apologize for that stuff I said."

Her eyebrows locked in a line of contemplation. She was thinking about whether or not she believed me. Then she reached her conclusion. "I know you didn't. Now come on, let's go see the old man."

She led me down the hall. More than a week had passed since we'd first met, and she was fresh out of the beauty parlor again, her hair curled under at the nape. "It's going to be a real scorcher out there," she said. "I hope Elektra's someplace cool."

When we entered his office, Mr. Heber said, "Where's the dog?" I told him, but in that noncommittal way you tell something to someone who you know doesn't really care. "The Malibu Inn? Sounds like a good place to be on a day like today. So listen, I've got news, that's why I wanted you to come in. It's hit the radar."

"What has?"

"Everything. Mesadale, the Prophet, and most important your mom. A TV crew from New York is on its way. They land in Vegas in an hour, they should be in Mesadale by midafternoon."

"What for?"

"To report. And just as I thought, this is going to change everything. I spoke to the producer. They're real sympathetic to women like your mom, they want to tell the story from her side, they want to get this right. And so here's the thing: they want to talk to you."

"What for?"

"You're the guy who can tell America what it's really like out there."

"I don't think I can do that."

"Of course you can. They're setting up in the conference room tomorrow at two."

I know how TV works. They make you explain things that can't be explained. Some questions don't have answers. There's a mystery to all this—I mean, the reason why we do what we do. After a week it was the only Eureka! I'd had.

Mr. Heber gave me more details about the TV crew. The reporter was the cute guy with the silver hair you see all the time. "You might want to wear something other than a t-shirt," Mr. Heber advised. "Dress it up a bit, all right? And we'll need to work on what you're going to say. I want to write out some talking points."

Heber still didn't get it, or I guess what I really mean was Heber still didn't get me. I don't dress it up a bit. I don't have an interview outfit. I don't do talking points.

"I went back to Mesadale Sunday night," I said.

Heber looked up. "You need to be careful, Jordan."

"I heard something pretty interesting. About Rita."

"What's that?"

"She's disappeared." I told him what Drusilla had said. Heber was interested; the flesh on his face didn't move.

"Does this mean what I think it means?" I said.

He hesitated, as if he needed a moment to put it all together. "Yes, I think so."

"We're getting closer."

"But there's still that IM from your dad. He told us it was your mom."

"I know," I said. "That's the problem with the internet. Nothing ever disappears."

I decided not to tell Tom about the TV stuff. I still didn't believe they'd fly in from New York, spend all that money to help my mom. They'd probably flash that picture of her ducking into the cruiser, then air a story about a holy roller who dumped her son and shot her husband. Not only would it be wrong, I was pretty sure it would mess things up even more.

Tom was busy anyway. There was a problem with Room 208; the guests had trashed the place with lighters, burning brown skid marks into the furniture. "I sensed something was wrong the moment they got here," he kept telling the cop writing up the report. "I mean, I don't like to judge people, but I just had a feeling." What feeling was that? "Like they'd steal my dog."

I took this lull in my day to go online. An email from kadee@byu.edu looked ominous. Something must've gone wrong with Johnny.

> Hey Jordan—
> Just wanted to let you know Johnny's doing fine and I think everything's going to be all right. Call me if you have any questions or anything. He's lucky he found you.
> —Kelly

When I closed her e-mail I found a new message in my box. The subject line—"Might Be Important"—looked spammy, but I opened it anyway.

> i'm not sure if you got my last email or what so i thought i'd try again. i remember chatting with your dad, that wasn't the first time, we sort of had this on-line poker/flirting thing going on, it didn't mean anything never in a million years would i have ever met him or anything, it was just one of those internet things and I don't know if i know anything that might be useful but i might. maybe we should talk. by the way my name's not really desertmissy (obvi), it's albert but he didn't know that.

I wrote DesertMissy, asking what he knew, and he replied right away.

> first of all i'm sorry about your dad i read about him in the register and stuff i've been following the case and what's been going on out in mesadale and somehow i knew he was manofthehouse2004. we'd been chatting for several months and we talked about a lot of things not just poker and sex but all sorts of things

like life and he told me all about his wives and kids and was really
honest about it all about how hard it was on a lot of them and he
felt bad about that. he said sometimes it broke him up having to
see so many of his kids wanting him to be a normal dad and he
couldn't be that kind of dad because there were too many of them.
but he always said it was worth it because this is how god wanted
it. i'm not too sure about that myself i've never been much of a god
person but i admire a man who knows what he believes and sticks
to it. all great men are like that and who am i to say what he believes is any crazier than the rest of the shit everyone out there believes, including me. i was at that point of actually liking your dad
a lot and i could tell he liked me but there was this problem you
know of how do i tell him the truth, i mean about me, and i wasn't
sure how to bring it up then our chat session just stopped that
night and he never responded and i read about a plural wife killing
her husband out in mesadale and i knew it was him, i just knew,
you know how sometimes you just know? that's why i wasn't surprised when i got your email last week.

I asked Albert where he lived, if we could meet. We needed to
talk.

no that won't be possible this is the internet i don't meet people
over the internet.

What about a phone call?

no i'll talk to anyone online but i always want to remain anon
but i'll tell you this much i'm not like other people online i always
tell people the truth for me it's a place i can really tell people what
i think and feel it's so hard to do that in real life for me it's the
only place i can truly be myself. except the desertmissy thing
(obvi) but that's just a name.

I begged Albert for his help.

i'll tell you what i can but i can't tell you who i am.

"Hey, how's it going?"

I jumped. "Oh, Tom, shit. You scared me."

"Who you writing?"

"Just some lead on my dad. I don't know. How'd it go with the cops?"

"They'll trace the license plate and stuff, but I've been through this kind of thing before. The paperwork's crushing."

"Anything I can do?"

"Maybe check on the dogs. I've still got a lot of checkouts."

In Room 112, the dogs were sleeping butt to butt on the bed. I refilled their water ball and went back to the lobby. I was thinking about Albert. Could he possibly know anything? And even if he did, would it count—info from an anonymous online source? Can they subpoena a man named DesertMissy?

I sent Albert another email, asking if my dad ever talked about any of his wives.

all the time he really seemed to love them. i know he thought of some of them more like aunts or grandmas than wives, like sister what's her name the first wife i guess she's real old he always said she's a good woman. he loved the newer ones like sister kimberly to be perfectly honest we sometimes got a little graphic when we talked about them he was definitely still in love with kimberly she gave amazing head or at least that's what he said, sorry that's probably more than you want to know. he had just married a new girl Sarah and he was talking pretty macho about her and what he'd done to her after they were sealed. i know i should be outraged but you know he was my friend she wasn't so i always saw it from his point of view. but in general he loved all the wives in his own way, i know that much for sure

From this stranger, a binary voice flashing in from somewhere— was he nearby or around the globe?—I was learning more about my father than I had ever known.

damn it just occurred to me she might be your mom you never told me who your mom is. i hope i haven't insulted you.

So I told him who my mom was.

holy crap that's crazy. that was your mom? maybe i shouldn't say anything more i mean i really don't want to get involved.

Albert, I wrote. *You are involved. If you know which wives my dad liked to fuck, you're very much involved.*

i guess you're right. besides i have nothing to hide.

I asked him if he knew anything else about the wives, was there anything else going on? I told him about the fuck chart, but it still didn't mean anything to me.

i don't know about that but you know i guess there was shit going on in the wife department he was pretty excited about that. i don't know if you know but that night he talked to your mom about their relationship i guess i'm not really sure but he said that it'd been a long time since they you know had been together and there was no point in trying to pretend they were really man and wife. i don't know but that's what he said which is why when i read that she had killed him i was shocked but not really surprised.

"Hey, Jordan?" said Tom. "Isn't it time you got going?"

I looked at the clock on the computer. Shit. I was late for my visit to see my mom.

An Open Letter to President Woodruff
And Latter-day Saints Everywhere
October 23, 1890

———

I, the undersigned, stand in opposition to the recent manifesto of September 26, and approved October 6, regarding the doctrine of plural marriage. Section 132, as revealed to the Prophet Joseph Smith by our Heavenly Father, states plainly that anyone who shall not believe in this doctrine, and pursue it to his fullest extent, shall never attain Eternal Glory. I accept the truth of the Doctrine & Covenants, including Section 132, and refuse to edit God on this, or any, matter. As Brigham Young preached for more than thirty years, "To ignore it is to ignore His will." So said he until the last day of his life thirteen years ago.

I, the undersigned, challenge you to reverse this decision. Written in the spirit of political compromise and capitulation, rather than in the spirit of Truth and Glory, this manifesto shall send a fissure through the heart of our beloved Church, forcing Saints everywhere to choose between political expediency and Divine will.

I, the undersigned, demand a retraction of the manifesto, and all its meaning, or face a splintering of faith never before seen among Christians in the two thousand years since the days our Lord, Jesus Christ, walked the Earth, in the company of men.

I, the undersigned, declare openly that until the manifesto has been rescinded, and our natural rights restored, I, and all Saints everywhere, shall pursue our faith fully, as we have known it since the days of Joseph and Brigham, as we shall always know it, in these last days.

I, the undersigned, declare myself, and all those who share my convictions stated herein, the First and True Latter-day Saints, for that is what we are.

ELDER AARON WEBB
& Wives

Red Creek
Territory of Utah

THE CONVICTION OF JORDAN SCOTT

―――

"Officer Cunningham," I said, "I'm really sorry I'm late."

"You know the rules."

"I know, ten minutes' grace time, then that's it, appointment canceled. But I have a really good excuse."

"I'm listening."

"It's just that . . ." But where to start? And where to end? I stood in front of the metal detector, unable to come up with an explanation for any of this.

"Oh, what the heck. I don't know why I like you, but I do." She winked, and for a flash I could imagine her out of uniform, her gun and shield locked up, walking through her front door, receiving a hug from her husband and kids. I thanked her. I thanked her for everything.

"No mush, all right?" she said. "You know the drill: last cubicle in the row. Officer Kane'll bring her out."

It was just like before: the women, the babies, the glass screen. I waited on the stool, staring into the space that my mom would soon fill, looking at the yellow receiver, thinking about how lifeless it was and how in a few minutes it would crackle with her voice.

"Jordan," she said. "It feels like forever."

I told her everything that had happened, and it took a long time, and by the time I was done the wall clock said we had only a few minutes left.

"I'm not surprised to hear about Rita," she said.

"Why's that?"

She hesitated but she knew this wasn't the time to bite her tongue. "I'm not sure if you know that I replaced her. After I married your father, he stopped—how should I put this?—seeing her."

"Do you mean what I think you mean?"

Her cheeks flushed with shame. "He had his list," she said. "His list of wives. The wives he still—you know, visited. From the day I entered that house Rita treated me like I'd stolen something from her. She wanted to turn him against me, she was always trying to catch me doing something like ignoring my housework or forgetting my prayers or sneaking you more food than your share. When you were a baby she was really hard on me. You used to cry in church, and you know how the Prophet never liked that. She used to tell your father it was because of me—that I was holding you too tight or not changing you or whatever nonsense she could think of. You know your father, he never knew much about babies, so he didn't know what to believe. Over time I tried to be friends with her, I really tried. But all she'd do was lie to him about me."

"She was a total bitch."

Her lip crumpled. "I'm afraid you're right."

"Mom, I've seen the chart, but I can't really figure it out."

"It was his way of managing the wives, of keeping up."

"That, and Viagra."

"Don't be crude, Jordan. Not with me. I know everyone thinks we've lost our minds. The gals in here, they never use my name, the call me Nineteen. They make all sorts of cracks about orgies and whatnot. They have no idea who we are, they don't understand— they don't want to. I know the whole world thinks we're crazy or delusional or what have you. I'm sure a lot of people think I should be locked up. But I don't care. I don't care what anyone thinks about me. Except you. I don't know how I'll hold up if you start saying I'm crazy, too." The tip of her nose darkened and she turned to ask Officer Kane for a tissue.

"I didn't mean to make fun of you," I said.

She nodded. "I know." And then, sniffing, "Jordan?"

"Yeah."

"Do you think I'll get out of here?"

I thought about it for minute. "You might."

"If I do, it's all because of you."

"Maybe."

"No, it's because you believed me."

"There's more to it than that."

"No," she said. "That's the reason. It all boils down to that."

"Let's not get ahead of ourselves. There's still a lot we don't understand."

"I know, but we'll figure it out."

Was she right? To have so much faith? In me?

"Mom, let me ask you a question: Did Dad ever talk about his list?"

She took her time before answering, wiping up her face. "Only a little. I know there was a point for some of the wives when he decided he no longer wanted to be married to them, in that way, I mean, and he would tell them, just so it was clear, you know, expectations and all. From then on he always treated those wives a little different from the rest. We always knew when one wife was taken off the list—it was usually right before he married a new one—and when that happened we would look around and figure out who he was, well, not visiting as much."

"I had no idea it was so methodical."

"We never talked about it with the kids. It would break their hearts."

"Mom, what about you? Were you still on the list?"

She looked to the ceiling, the tears pooling in her eyes. "I never thought I'd have to talk to my own son about any of this."

"You don't have to. I understand."

"He no longer wanted to see me."

"It's OK," I said.

"I wish that were true. But now I'm worried about what's going to happen to me."

"I know, but I'm working on that."

"No, not in here, or in court, but after I'm gone. Oh, Jordan—

I'm so afraid of going to heaven without him. I'm afraid he won't be waiting for me there."

My mom, on the other side of the glass—she didn't have an ally in the world.

"That night," she said. "He told me that night. That's why I was down in the basement. He asked to see me. He asked me to come very late, so there wouldn't be any talk among the sister wives. But Rita saw me leave the basement. He was about to get married. He said the Prophet had granted him a new bride and he was going to marry her the next day. And so he told me that I could live the rest of my life in the house, but I was no longer his wife."

"I thought he had married someone that morning."

"This was someone else. Someone the Prophet wanted him to take."

"Who?"

"I don't know."

"And so he kicked you out of his bed."

She nodded slowly, as if she were just comprehending it now.

"Why didn't you tell Mr. Heber any of this?"

"I'm not a fool, I know how this looks. Everyone's going to think that was my reason for killing him. Except I didn't kill him. And no one believes me. Except you."

Then I saw it, everything, the numbers falling into place like lotto balls. "How many wives did he have?"

"Total? Between twenty and twenty-five, but I can't be sure. He never said. The Prophet told them never to say because when the battle came, our enemies would use the numbers against us. We each had our number, and we had a rough idea of where we fell on the list, but if you tried to add them up, it never made sense. There were gaps, and sometimes a wife would come and stay a year and then leave, and sometimes you'd get this feeling you were no longer the number you thought you were. It went like that, but the Prophet always said when we got to heaven we'd know."

She stopped. Her face cleared and her eyes dried out. She saw it, too. "That must be it."

It was all clear. Clear as the inch and a half slab of glass.

"You were no longer his nineteenth wife."

I called Tom. "He was about to marry some girl."

"I'm not following you."

"According to polygamy's wacky math, my mom wasn't his nineteenth wife anymore. Someone else was about to become number nineteen."

"What'd you say?"

"She didn't count anymore!" The connection was bad and getting worse. "If he wasn't screwing them, he didn't count them."

"He didn't what them?"

"The girl he was about to marry—that's who killed him!" I knew I had only a few more seconds before we lost the signal. "I'm almost there!"

"Where?"

"I feel like I'm five feet away from the answer."

The signal became good again and I could hear Tom breathing. "Maybe you should back off now. Let the cops take over."

"Not when I'm this close."

"At least go to Mr. Heber."

"He'll only slow things down."

"Jordan, I don't like this anymore. You're about to bump into a killer."

"Please don't worry about me."

"Too late."

"You know who knows the answer?"

"Who?" His voice was getting smaller.

"The Prophet."

"Jordan, I want you to come home."

"I'll call you as soon as I can."

"If something happens to you, I'm not sure I'll be able to forgive you."

"Oh, c'mon. Don't put that shit on me. It's not like we're—"

The call broke. A lost signal or did he hang up? I drove on to Mesadale, wondering if I'd ever find out.

At the turnoff a guard in a pickup motioned for me to stop. "What brings you out here?"

"I need to go to the post office."

"Why here?"

"I need to pay my electric bill," I lied. "It needs to be postmarked today."

The guy was an elder, silver hair buzzed down, red shiny lips. He fidgeted with his ammo vest, poking his finger in and out of an empty cartridge slot. "You tell Sister Karen hello."

I drove up the dirt road. Along the way I passed a couple of trucks parked in the dirt. Inside each a man was waiting, his left leg dangling out the open door. The trucks' gun racks were empty, which meant those guns were out somewhere being cradled. I expected one of the trucks to pull out in front of me, blocking the road, and then a team rushing from the brush. A little paranoid, I know, but something was happening even if I couldn't tell you what it was.

It was late afternoon, the sun burning the face of Mt. Jerusalem. Everywhere the red rocks were glowing and the mesas out in the direction of Arizona looked like they might combust. The Prophet used to talk a lot about the Apocalypse. "Any day now," he'd say. "Any day." I always imagined it would come at this time of day at this time of year, when the sun floods the desert and the thermometer keeps going up and you forget what it's like to be cold.

When I reached town there were Firsts everywhere. Men walking up the street, and some women, and a few couples, I mean real couples, one man, one wife, maybe with a kid. The women were wearing normal clothes. The girls, too. It looked like a busy afternoon in Anytown, USA, women shopping, kids playing, men bitching at the fence.

Sister Karen was at the counter, closing up her station.

"Why is everyone dressed like this? Why are you dressed like this?"

"I heard you need a stamp. I've got to close up in seven minutes"—she pointed to the wall clock—"so we don't have much time. What can I get you?"

"Actually, I don't really need—"

She tipped her chin to the security camera in the corner. "I've got some new stamps in. Here, you might like the superheroes and action figures." She showed me a sheet: Plastic Man contorting himself, Flash in a skimpy body suit, Superman ripping off his clothes. "If you want five, that would be . . . let me total that up real quick for you." On a scrap of paper she wrote *if you whisper the camera can't pick up your voice.*

"I need to see the Prophet."

"He isn't here."

"I know, but I need to see him."

"I have no idea where he is." And then in a regular voice: "Or do you want to see the American flags?" Sister Karen sorted through her stamp sheets. "Mind telling me why you need to see him?" she said under her breath. I began the whole story, but she interrupted. "You need to be out of here in less than four minutes, so make it short."

I told her my theory and she said, "You need to be very careful, Jordan. You don't know what you're dealing with here."

The door opened. "Sister Karen, you closing up?" It was the old fucker who'd been guarding the road.

"Right about now, Brother." She punched up my bill, her face straight. After I left the post office, she pulled a folding metal wall across the lobby, locking it into place. The brother stood on the slab of white concrete outside the post office, kicking the dirt from his heel, eyeing me and the road. Someone was driving into town; you could see the cloud rolling up our way.

"You expecting someone?" I said.

"This is not the day to mess around."

"Have a good one."

I sat in the back of the van for a while, thinking it all out. One of Johnny's t-shirts was wadded up on the futon. It smelled like feet. I kicked it into a garbage bag but then took it back out. I'd wash it at the laundromat and send it up to him. With a note. First I'd need to figure out what to say.

There was a knock on the side of the van. Then again. The van is such a tin can it sounded like a wooden spoon gonging a baking pan. I was sure it was the old brother, and I was sure it was a good idea to ignore him until I knew what I was going to say.

"Jordan?" But that wasn't the old guy's voice. "You in there?" A dog barked.

"Elektra?"

"Jordan?"

Elektra started scratching at the side of the van. Then Joey joined in, a gentle howl.

"Tom?"

"Jordan?"

"Elektra!"

"Tom!"

He stuck his head through the driver's window. "You all right?" The dogs shoved past him, leaping into the back, attacking with kisses from both sides. "We're here to help," said Tom. "And don't even try to say you don't need it."

"Who's taking care of the Malibu?"

"The assistant manager. It's no big deal."

But it was a big deal. I was about to solve a murder, and now here were Tom and the dogs. I had a crazy image of the three of them bound and gagged in a warehouse. I'd have to rescue them. Unlikely, I know, but I kept thinking about it and it was so clear in my mind it was as if it had already happened. "We need to be careful,"

I said.

"What we really need is for this whole thing to be over."

"Come on," I said. "Let's go."

Alton's patrol car was in front of Queenie's house, the sun glinting on the lightbar. "Is that good or bad?" said Tom.

"Good. I think."

We leashed up the dogs and headed to Queenie's front door. God, look at us: the gay couple out with their dogs. Except we were in the polygamy capital of America with a murderer on the loose, a Prophet on the run, and a bunch of wives freaking out. If it weren't so serious, it would be a joke, or a skit on *Saturday Night Live*. I know some gay people think polygamy and gay marriage are part of the same stay-out-of-my-bedroom political argument, and I'm generally a live-and-let-live kind of guy, but it's all different when there are kids, and sure, anyone should have the right to sleep with whoever, and marry whoever—this is America, after all—but you can't do whatever you want when you've got kids. You can't do whatever you want to kids. Have I said that before? I'm sorry. Political loudmouths are such a drag.

"My husband isn't here." Queenie was leaning into the door frame.

"His car's out front."

"He's down at the church. With the TV cameras, they all went down there."

"Mind if we wait?"

She looked at Tom, Joey, Elektra. "Sure, but not in the house. She's allergic to dogs," and she led us out to the garage.

"The new wife?"

"Who do you think?"

"How's it going with her?"

"Oh, just great. Nothing like listening to your husband screw another woman in the room next door."

"Queenie, what's wrong?"

"Everything."

"Is there something I can do?"

She laughed, and in laughing she softened up. "I'm sorry, Jordan. I didn't mean to be such a c-word. I'll be fine."

I asked if I could use the phone. She brought me the portable, but then she thought to ask, "Who're you calling?"

"Just someone."

I dialed, and on the fifth ring I worried maybe I'd forgotten the number, but then he answered. "Yeah, Alton?"

"No, it's me, Jordan Scott."

"What is this?"

"I need to see you."

"Jordan, what are you doing there?"

"It doesn't matter. I need to see you. Where can I meet you?"

"Jordan, it's too late."

"No, it's not too late."

"Please don't call me anymore."

"You were the one—"

Click.

"Was that the Prophet?" said Queenie.

"Yes."

"Shit, you guys should go. You're going to get me in a lot of trouble."

I told her to calm down, everything would be OK. "I know this is going to sound weird, but the Prophet and I, well, we're sort of working together."

"That didn't sound like working together."

"He's just freaking out because of the media and stuff."

She looked at me the way you look at someone you know has turned against you. There was a terrible silence in the garage, and leave it to Tom to fill it up. "So how many months are you?"

"It's still early, only two."

"Is that your little girl?" Tom pointed at the picture of Angela taped above the workbench. A little blond girl petting a cow. "So adorable," said Tom. "What about the next, boy or girl?"

"I'm hoping for a boy."

"A brother for Angela! How sweet." Tom had a starry look to him, like his daydreams were carrying him to a world where everyone was more or less good. He was too honest for this. Too kind. He deserved a tidy, reliable life. He wasn't equipped for the messier world of me. Look, there he was goo-gooing over baby pictures with Queenie and talking about boy names, and he was totally clueless she was lying. Last time I was here she was three months preggers.

"I've always wanted kids." Tom sighed, then looked at me. Why was he looking at me? It was so time to go.

In the van I said, "She's lying. She must be hiding something. I don't know what, but she was definitely lying."

"You're being paranoid."

"No, Tom, I'm not. I'm seeing things for what they are." I drove to the end of the block, turned the corner, and parked. "Alton was in there."

"How do you know?"

"I just do. He didn't want to see me. You stay here, I'm walking back."

"No way, I'm coming with you."

"You need to stay with the dogs."

"Speaking of which, it's their dinnertime."

"Fine, you feed them while I go back to the house. There's some kibble under the seat."

"Joey can't eat any old kibble. He needs his high-protein food. Let's go back to my car and I'll make their dinners and then we'll figure out what to do next."

"Tom, it doesn't work like that. I need to go in there now before he leaves."

"Goldens have sensitive stomachs."

"We don't have time for this."

"Look at Elektra, she's practically begging for her dinner."

"You've got to be shitting me." But let's face it, I was going to lose this argument. I drove down to the post office thinking, Tom shouldn't be here. I kept telling myself that. When we get to his car I'm going tell him to leave.

But before I could he got busy preparing the dogs' dinner. His trunk was like a pantry: tupperwares of organic dry food, water, bowls, squeaky toys, paw wipes, paper towels, and febreze. He set everything out on the hood and measured out the food down to the last kibble. I'm so not a smoker, but if I were, right about now I would've lit a cigarette and gone for a walk. I needed to step away from this. I strolled around to the other side of the post office. A thunderstorm rolled in the western sky, the clouds gray and green and blue. I leaned against the post office wall and shut my eyes.

That's when I heard something. Something like a box falling. And softly through the wall: "Oh, crud."

I stepped back to look at the post office. At the top of the wall, there was a long window running the length of the roofline. It was too high to see into, but the lights were on. I walked back to Tom. "Sister Karen's in there."

"In where?" Tom was cleaning up the dog bowls and putting everything away.

"We'll leave the dogs with her."

"I don't like that idea."

Too late. I was banging on the lobby's glass door. Eventually Karen rolled back the folding metal wall. "Can you take the dogs?"

"What?" she said through the glass door.

"I need someone to watch the dogs for twenty minutes, a half hour, max."

"Not today, it's a bad idea."

But I begged. And kept begging. Sensing an adventure, the dogs ran over to press their snouts to the glass. It took some more begging, but I knew she'd give in. She unlocked the door and led us into the back room. "I'm doing some organizing. They can stay with me. But please don't be long."

Tom's arms were full of supplies—bowls, water, a dog bed.

"Jesus, Tom, they're only going to be here a little while."

"Just in case." He arranged the bed in a corner and filled the water bowls. He moved with such precision and purpose, it was as if in the giant cosmic scheme of things he had been put on earth to tend to the needs of these two dogs.

That's when I saw them. And I kept looking at them in a way Sister Karen wouldn't notice I saw them. A shopping bag filled with little-girl clothes. And a duffel bag stuffed with pants and shirts.

Tom was giving Sister Karen a litany of instructions. "They shouldn't have to poop, but if Joey walks in a circle three times, that means he has to go. Here are some baggies." He had a whole list of doggy do's and don'ts.

The duffel was open and I kicked it open some more. My foot gently moved aside the white dress shirt on top. Beneath it was a dark blue shirt. The shoulder braiding confirmed it was a police uniform. I kicked the bag again, and now I could see half of a brass nameplate: Alt.

"You know what?" I said. "It's too much of an inconvenience."

"It's fine," said Sister Karen. "Just don't take all night."

"No, they're so fussy. I don't want to stick you with all their issues."

"Jordan," said Tom, "I just walked her through everything, they'll be fine."

Elektra chose this moment to decide she was tired. She yawned, walked over to the dog bed, and plopped down with an extended sigh. Joey followed suit, falling over on his side. His moist panting fogged up the linoleum tiles.

"Tom, please," I said. "It's too much to ask."

Tom turned to Sister Karen. "You tell us. Is this all right?"

"Look at them. They're going to be fine."

"Sister Karen, you really don't have to—" But she scooted us out the door.

In the car I said, "Why didn't you listen to me? Something

wasn't right."

"What? Sister Karen's on our side."

"I don't know if this has sides anymore." But Tom drove on, down the dark streets of Mesadale. He parked about a block from Queenie's.

"Maybe this isn't such a good idea," I said.

"No, it's a good idea. Until you figure this all out you're never going to get on with your life."

We walked up the road. It's hard to move silently on gravel, but we tried. Across from Queenie's house we stopped. The bedroom light was on, a gold outline around the drawn blinds. Everything else was dark. The storm clouds blotted out the moon and the yard was black, the patrol car a large dark shape. "What's the plan?" said Tom.

"I want to see if he's in there. Now be quiet. And follow me."

I crouched down, ran up the side of the yard to the house, pushing myself flat against the garage. Tom was right behind me. I mouthed, *Let's go round back.* We stayed close to the wall, bent at the waist. We continued along the wall until we were behind the house near a window. We crouched to our knees. I could hear Tom's heart in his chest. He whispered, "Are you OK?"

I brought my index finger to my lips. I wanted to listen. At first I couldn't hear anything. Then sounds of someone moving about, a door closing, a piece of furniture being dragged. I heard footsteps, then a second pair. Someone said, "Have everything?"

I waved to Tom, *Let's go.* We crouched back along the wall until we were beside the garage. "He's in there," I said.

"What do you want to do?"

"Ring the doorbell. Act casual. We don't want to startle them." We made our way along the front of the house until we were on the concrete porch. I rang the doorbell. No answer. I rang again. Eventually, "Yes?"

"Officer Alton?"

He opened the door. "Jordan. Hi. Queenie said you stopped by.

I didn't realize you were coming back."

"Do you have a second?"

Alton was blocking the door, his hand tight on the frame as if prepared to fight off an assault. "This really isn't a good time."

"That's the thing. This can't wait. I mean, you said to call if anything came up. And something's come up."

His lips twisted. "All right." He led us into the living room, turning on a floor lamp and pointing to the sofa. "So what's up?"

"You're about to leave town and I want to know why."

Tom looked at me like I was crazy. But Alton stayed cold. "Jordan, what's gotten into you?"

"Why are you sneaking off?"

He laughed once. He was sitting in a recliner with his legs open, relaxed but engaged, like he was watching a ball game on tv.

"I know what I know," I said.

"Look, I don't know what to tell you." He slapped his hands together. "I'm not going anywhere. And even if I were, what would that have to do with you?"

"I don't know, but I know it does."

"You're free to think whatever you want." He stood, moved to the door. Nothing threatening, more like a party host who has grown weary of his last guest.

"You told me to call if I needed you. Well, I need you. Actually, I need the Prophet. I need to see him. And something makes me think you're about to skip town with him."

Alton froze, then cocked his head. "Is that what you think?"

"Yes."

Tom stepped forward. "He's just trying to help his mom."

"I see," said Alton. "OK, why don't you sit down and tell me what's going on. You're right: I was going to see the Prophet tonight. I'll tell him anything you want."

So I told him my theory about my dad's latest wife, why I needed to find out who he was about to marry. When I finished I sat back on the couch. Alton looked bewildered. "You're quite the sleuth," he said. "That's some deduction work. Well, I'll tell you, I'll find out what you want to know. I'll go call him now."

Alton went into the garage. Tom shrugged. "That went all right."

A minute later Alton said, "Guys? Come on in here with me, OK?"

He stood in the door, his finger on the trigger of a semiautomatic. It was such a shocking sight—an off-duty police officer with a dumb-dude smile and a thick, muscled body one or two years away from fat standing in his socks aiming the muzzle of a gun. At me. It wasn't happening. That's all I said: "This isn't happening."

"What's going on?" said Tom.

"Don't say anything. Just come in here." We were too dumbfounded to get up from the couch. "I'm not joking. Get up. Now. . . . That's right. And don't try anything. Stay apart, just come on in here. Move slow and keep your hands up, that's right, just like that."

"Officer Alton," I said.

"Nope. Don't say a word."

Tom gave it a try. "Please, we really don't want—"

"Shut up. Right now. No more talking."

"Does Queenie know what you're doing?"

"I said shut up."

When we were in the garage, he pointed the muzzle at Tom. "You, Boyfriend. You see that?" He waved the gun at a loop of laundry line. "Take it down and tie him up."

"What?"

"You heard me. Tie him up."

"I don't know how."

"Start with his wrists."

"I can't."

Alton pushed the gun into my mouth and told me to kneel. "I think you can."

Tom took the rope and began measuring off a section.

"Now, Jordan," said Alton. "Put your arms together, wrists facing, and stick out your hands. . . . That's right, just like that. Now you, tie them up. Make it tight."

Tom looped the line around my wrists. "Jordan, I'm sorry," he said.

I tried to say it was OK but the gun barrel was heavy on my tongue.

"Guys, no talking." When the line was tight around my wrists, Alton said, "Now tie up his ankles."

"Why are you doing this?" said Tom.

"Just do what I say."

He stood up. "First I need to know what's going on." Alton pointed the gun at Tom.

"Tom, do what he says."

"Why should I?"

Alton pressed the gun to my chest. "Because you and I both don't want to see his heart splattered across your nice pair of khakis."

"You're bluffing."

"Are you really willing to risk finding that out?"

"Tom, please, do it."

Tom stood in place, his eyes burning. Then his jaw slackened and the light in his eyes went out. "All right."

"You, Jordan, lie down on your side so he can tie up your ankles." In five minutes I was looped together with forty feet of laundry line.

"You're next," said Alton. He yelled back into the house: "Queenie! I need you."

When she saw me she gasped. "Jordan, my God."

"Honey, tie him up." He pointed to a yellow nylon rope, then to Tom.

"Is he all right?"

"He's fine."

"Queenie," I said.

"Don't talk to him," said Alton.

She tried to ignore me, turning her head in the opposite direction, but our eyes met. She was scared, I could see that. Otherwise I had no idea what was going on. She got busy with Tom's wrists, then ankles. Soon we were both lying on our backs. "Now tie them together," said Alton. "At the ankle and wrist." We had to turn to face each other, then she tied up our hands. She was out of rope so she used a bungee cord to loop our ankles together. By the time she was done we were so close together I could feel his breath on my face. "Romantic," I said.

"Now gag them."

"Please, don't do this," Tom tried.

"Gag them." He handed her two rags, strips from an old flannel shirt. Tom resisted, shaking his head and sealing his lips. Alton laid his fingers around my throat. "I wouldn't do that if I were you."

Queenie gagged me next. There was no way she could do it without looking at me. Before she could get the rag in my mouth, I managed to say, "Why?"

"Honey, don't talk to him. Pretend it's someone else."

When she was finished Alton checked the knots. "Good job, everyone." He left the room.

The line pressed hard into my skin, and the gag made it difficult to breathe. But more than that was the fear. I suppose for everyone there's a moment when you realize you're about to die. For some people, the moment is extended over the course of a long illness. For others, it's just a few seconds before a flash. For my dad, it must've come once he saw the gun. Even people who die instantly, they must have a tiny, immeasurable moment of awareness. I like to think that. It seems only fair. And now here was mine. I didn't know how much time I had left, but I understood very clearly I would not survive the night. Tom had been very still until now. He saw me crying and his eyes filled too.

"I'm really very sorry about all this," said Queenie.

I looked at her. "Queenie!" called Officer Alton from the living room. "Let's go."

"I'm coming." She touched my cheek. "I never thought it would be like this." She kissed my forehead and her lips were warm. "You too," she said to Tom, stroking his ear. "You take care of him, all right? Give him what he deserves."

Tom yelled, the gag muffling his words.

"Don't yell," she said. "We can't leave if you're yelling."

"Queenie!"

"I'm coming." At the door she waited another moment, looking at us, her face flat with pity. "Good luck." She turned out the lights and shut the door.

I heard the front door close, then car doors slam, an engine turn. Tires on gravel. In my mind I could see the patrol car backing out of the drive, headlights sweeping the yard. I could see it as if I had seen it in a movie; everything about the scene was that clear. When Alton's cruiser was gone, the only sounds were Tom and me trying to breathe. It was too dark to see his expression, but his eyes were glowing. One of his fingers found one of mine. They clasped together, locked at the knuckle. I'm sorry, that's such a bunch of corn, but that's how it went—lying there on the concrete floor, bound and gagged, we reached out, our fingers found each other, and they linked. We were alone like that for a long time.

After some time we heard a car out front and a door slam. Then footsteps in the house. This is it, I kept thinking. This is it. Here we go.

The door to the living room opened and a head peered around. A pair of silver eyes. A fish-faced look of surprise. It was the Prophet. And he was shocked to see me like this. Really shocked, not fake shocked. This wasn't part of his plan. My face—well, I have no idea, but I bet I looked just as surprised. There we were. Two faces shaped by the same set of emotions at the same moment in time. We went on looking at each other for a while, saying nothing because there was nothing to say. That's how it goes, right? Eyes meeting up like that. Through a slab of glass. In the cineplex dark. At the Malibu Inn. Eyes saying good-bye in a garage. Who's to say what will come next? Who can say they know what it all means? You got to live with it. The not knowing. The wondering. The unanswered questions. The murk of life. You got to accept it— the why.

"Jordan," the Prophet said.

I said, They set up my mom. Except because of the gag my words were lost in my throat.

"What's this all about?"

I said, My mom. It's about my mom. Except I sounded like someone shouting into a towel.

I don't know how long we stared at each other like that. Tom's back was to the door. He was trying to maneuver himself to see who was there. He said something, but what?

The way the Prophet was peering around the door, I could see only his head and a hand. A dried spotted hand, knuckles yellow and white. And that sunken, tired face. An old man. Almost any old man.

The Prophet left, the door closing. The ghost of his face remained, hanging in the space where he'd been, an afterimage, or maybe even a dream. Then it too was gone and Tom and I were alone on the cold concrete floor.

June 12, 2006

President and Prophet Gordon Hinckley
The Church of Jesus Christ of Latter-day Saints
50 East North Temple
Salt Lake City, UT 84111

Dear President Hinckley,

I want to thank you for making the Church Archives available to me. My research into the complicated legacy of Ann Eliza Young and the end of LDS polygamy has been invaluably aided by the wealth of documents I was able to study thanks to your intervention. I hope you agree that your decision to open previously sealed records has been beneficial to our understanding of our history. I know some people think these matters should be left alone, but I have always found inspiration in the title of your book, *Truth Restored*.

 With your help, I have completed my archival research and will soon begin writing my thesis. I look forward to sending you a copy when I submit it for graduation next April. My conclusions may not be what you expect, but I can assure you they have been reached through careful study of the record.

 I also want you to know how helpful Deb Savidhoffer of the Archives has been. She is a friend to scholars, and to our beloved Church. I owe her much indeed.

Most Gratefully Yours,
KELLY DEE
Candidate for Master's Degree
Brigham Young University

I HAD NO IDEA

I know I need to explain what happened. It's pretty simple. You probably figured it out on your own. After two hours in the garage, Sister Karen found us. She knew something was wrong when we didn't come for the dogs. When she saw us like that—tied up on the concrete floor—she cried out in terror. That's how I know she didn't have anything to do with it. It's hard to fake fear in the voice.

Once she got over the shock, she started working to free us. First the gags. The old flannel pulled from my mouth. We told her what happened as she tried picking the knots loose. The knots wouldn't give. "In my pocket," I said, "I have a little knife."

She pulled out Johnny's knife and started cutting Tom free, then me. As she worked she told us what she knew. "You don't know what's going on, do you? I helped them escape tonight, Hiram and Queenie. The Prophet was coming down hard on them because Brother Hiram hadn't taken another wife."

"He just married someone."

"No, the Prophet was pressuring him to marry a girl, but he wouldn't, he loved Queenie too much. They knew they had to leave. It nearly killed them, but they had to go."

That didn't explain everything. "I guess it doesn't make much sense," Sister Karen said. "Unless . . ."

"Unless what?"

"I don't know."

On our way out we found the note on the living room sofa. I could've walked by it, but something told me to look over and there it was.

Jordan,

I never wanted to do anything like this to you but by the time
you find this we'll be on our way and everything will be better that
way. I'm sorry for doing this to you. And Tom. He seems like the
nicest guy in the world.

I love you,
Q

The second note arrived the next day at the Lincoln County
Sheriff's Office, postmarked Denver. It's all we needed.

Sheriff,

In regards to the death and murder of Brother Scott, husband
of Sisters Rita, BeckyLyn, and etc., I'm the one you want. He was
about to marry my wife. The Prophet didn't like me not having
more wives. As punishment he was taking Queenie away from me
and giving her to Brother Scott. She went to see him that night to
talk him out of it. I followed her and was real pissed. I didn't plan
on anything, but outside his door I heard him saying all sorts of
things you don't say to another man's wife, and I lost my head. I
picked up his Golden Boy and shot him. I don't know why he had
that suppressor on the gun but he did. It took as long to kill him
as it took me to write this sentence. He was gone. I didn't intend
any of this. We slipped out the well window. No one saw us come
and no one saw us go. I was always surprised they didn't notice the
open latch. Queenie had nothing to do with it. We never wanted
Sister BeckyLyn to take the heat. We figured they'd never know
who did it, so many had their reasons that they'd never arrest anyone over it. I was really upset when they arrested Sister BL. That's
not how we meant it. The only reason we tied up Jordan and his
friend was because they were stopping us. We were planning on
leaving tonight anyway and sending this note so the truth could be
known and Sister BL could go free. That's how it happened, I
swear by my love of God. How can you be sure? I was careful to
leave prints all over this note. They'll match those others you have

on the Golden Boy and all over the basement. I know you'll try to find Queenie and me but I'll tell you now, you never will. Feel free to start in Denver. Be my guest.

HIRAM ALTON
Formerly of the Firsts

XXI

———

EPILOGUES

THE 19TH WIFE:

—

Since the publication of *The 19th Wife* some thirty-three years ago, the Mormon Church has been forced to denounce its belief in plural marriage. Before his death in 1877, Brigham ordered his followers to fight until the Day of Judgment for the right to pursue their faith in full glory. This included the doctrine of plural marriage. He anticipated a future day when many pressures, from both outside and within, would persuade some Saints to abandon the doctrine for the sake of political and cultural expediency. He warned them never to succumb: "For the doctrine, as far as I know it, and as far as Joseph knew it, is and always will be the Word of God. Let no man tell you otherwise."

When Brigham passed on that hot August afternoon, felled by cholera morbus, his final word of life was a quiet call to his friend and Prophet. "Joseph," Brigham cried out. Then he was gone. He left behind a household of an unknowable number of wives and children—many of them estranged friends of mine—and an estate worth tens of millions of dollars. His unusual will categorized his wives into an inheritance pyramid, with Amelia, his favorite, placed proudly at the peak. Beneath her, the few favored wives. Beneath them, those he visited from time to time. And so on. The many wives he had abandoned in every sense but name received nothing more than lifetime room and board at the Lion House. That would have been me.

Brigham's legacy includes a vast colonization of the American West. In thirty years he erected an efficient, far-reaching civilization whose institutions stand as solidly as those in countries with five hundred years of history before them. He organized the immigration of more than seventy-five thousand men, women, and children to his desert kingdom, many of them penniless foreigners who had no hope in their original lands. Often Brigham waged peace with the American Indian, at a time when other national leaders preferred execution to accommodation, and thus set an example for our nation's future relations with our Native friends. Most important to him, I am sure, he provided spiritual comfort and moral direction to thousands of needy souls. These are few among his many achievements. They must be noted by all.

Yet upon quitting life on Earth, Brigham left another legacy, one of a darker, more ominous variety—a fervid population of Saints determined more than ever to defend polygamy.

Not surprisingly, Brigham's death heartened those fighting for the abolition of marital bondage, whether they lived inside Utah or out. The next decade brought about unprecedented changes in federal law, each a deeper nail in polygamy's coffin. By 1890, only thirteen years after Brigham's passing, President Wilford Woodruff, the fourth leader of the Latter-day Saints, recognized his Church was on the wrong end of a national moral battle. A savvy politician, he also understood Utah would never achieve statehood as long as the Mormons practiced polygamy. In his famous Manifesto of September 1890, he denounced polygamy forever, declaring it no longer the will of God. When I first read of this change, I was elated, believing the institution was at last dead. How wrong was I!

As they say, once a polygamist always a polygamist. A number of distraught and confused Saints denounced President Woodruff for abandoning the doctrine they held most dear. These dissenters included my brother Aaron, whose harem sweet Connie still ruled, and my half-sister, Diantha, whose husband had married in total six cheerful, youthful women, Diantha being the exception. After unsuccessfully petitioning the Church to reverse its position, Aaron and his followers broke from the Latter-day Saints, establishing themselves as the First Latter-day Saints, with their capital in the remote outpost of Red Creek, in the southern portion of Utah, just across the Arizona border. Here they remain today, practicing a faith they claim to be the true religion of Joseph Smith and Brigham Young. Polygamy stands at the center of everything they believe. The enmity between the Firsts and the leaders of the Mormon Church in Salt Lake will remind many of the animosity between the Reformation's Protestants and the Bishops denouncing them from the palace balconies of Rome. The full story of this new religious splintering has yet to be told. Many years must pass before we understand the outcome of this divide.

In recent years, it has come to light that many Latter-day Saints, including members of the leadership, have continued to marry plural wives in secret. In public they decried it, in private they swooped up wives numbers one, two, and three. Under pressure from Congress and elsewhere, in 1904 President Joseph F. Smith, the Mormon Church's sixth leader and nephew of the Prophet Joseph Smith, had to issue a Second Manifesto, reinforcing the Church's stance against polygamy. In this Manifesto, the Church warned its members that any man or woman caught in a plural marriage would face excommunication—the one fate all Saints feared. (I should know.) And yet, even today, stories of the man with a dozen wives upstairs continue to pour forth from Deseret. Although these abundant households are no longer sanctioned by the Church, they continue to exist. How can this be? Many leaders of the Mormon Church today are secret polygamists themselves, and thus they willfully look the other way.

Now, with the debate over polygamy revived, and commanding much of our nation's attention, I offer here a revised edition of my life, taking into account my full journey from daughter of polygamy to emancipator. I humbly offer these memories and political ideas to my Dear Readers everywhere, hoping they will sustain the women of Utah, now hidden from view, who continue to live in conjugal chains.

—Ann Eliza Young, 1908

From the Desk of
Lorenzo Dee, Eng.
Baden-Baden-by-the-Sea
Calif.
October 15, 1940

Professor Charles Green
Brigham Young University
Joseph Smith Building
Provo

Dear Professor Green,

Thank you for sending me a copy of your book. I took it down to my viewing bench at once to read. It was a still day, the sunshine on the flat ocean, but no sight of my friends. A good few hours passed before the sunset, and by nightfall, back in my study, with the steady crash of the ocean always in my ear, I finished your volume. First, let me offer my admiration and praise. You are a fine scholar—no, a courageous one—for it seems to me you have bravely unraveled the role of polygamy in your Church's history. I am only sorry to see, if I am to read your somewhat cryptic notes correctly, that the Church leadership denied you access to many important documents. It would be laughable if it weren't such a serious matter. There will be a time, I am sure, when they will open themselves up fully to an honest scholar. I am only sorry that this honest scholar has not been you. You are right, fifty years is a long time. But you are also wrong—fifty years is no time at all. Perhaps another fifty need to pass before the Church leaders, whoever they may be, can say to the world, Here are the facts, this is our history, we have nothing to hide.

I myself would be less than open if I failed to confess the disappointment, and sorrow, that overcame me after I closed your book. Since your first letter last year I have been carrying a bulky hope that you would take up the mystery of my mother's fate. It was difficult to discover that she plays no role in your narrative after the 1890 Manifesto. True, she gave up her crusade once she believed polygamy had been eradicated. But also true is she returned to the lecture stage in the first years of our century, once she saw that polygamy in fact lived on, whether secretly among the Mormons or defiantly among the Firsts. Granted, her role thereafter was of lesser importance. I am not criticizing your scholarship. No, I'm merely registering a son's regret about his mother. I must admit that since we began our correspondence my greatest fear has been that after your many efforts and investigations you would know no more about her fate than I already do, which is to say almost nothing. And so, upon closing your book, I realized this was the case. I am not faulting you, I am only acknowledging my grief. I am a son who has lost his mother, in every sense.

I have refrained from telling you any of this, for I did not want my pessimism nor my personal curiosities to color your investigation. Furthermore, I should have revealed something to you, Professor Green, in my first letter to you. Something about the relationship between my mother and myself. If I had done so, you would have been better equipped to spot my biases, which I humor myself into believing I do not nurse, but of course I do, for everyone does, and I am as guilty as the next man, perhaps more. I kept some important information from you and I was selfish to do so, probably just as selfish as those Church archivists, bent and gray with caution, were in denying you the right to read the dusty documents that could only illuminate the truth.

By the time I settled in California my mother and I had become estranged. It was over the subject of my wife, Rosemary. Her religion, to be precise. My mother, with her many blind spots, dismissed all Catholics as superstitious. I can understand the root of her suspicions, but what most angered me was her inability to pull beautiful Rosemary out of the lot. By that I mean my mother's inclination to cast judgment on an entire faith, an entire population, rather than come to know Rosemary for who she was. Rosemary, I must add, did not help the cause. Although she was a rebellious Catholic, she recognized at once my mother's hypocrisy and leapt at the chance to dismantle it. Rosemary, always mischievous, stood up to defend her faith as if she were Joan of Arc. After one unpleasant spat, I said to her—to Rosemary, that is—"You don't even believe half the things you said." She acknowledged I was correct, that she had a hundred bones to pick with the Pope. Even so, she was not going to let my mother's attacks fly without a response. You can see the position I was in. I am not the first to stand in the treacherous no-man's-land between mother and wife. There is no safe position. And so we decamped for California, as so many others have. This was in 1890, or was it 1891? I'd have to look it up to be sure. My, how the mind's cold fogs are beginning to roll in.

There was no formal estrangement between my mother and me, no final exchange or argument. This is often the case. We left and the communication dropped off to less than occasional. In 1908, when my mother published the revised, unsuccessful edition of *The 19th Wife*, I realized nearly ten years had passed since we had corresponded. I wrote her at her last address in Denver. The letter was forwarded to an address in El Paso, then returned. I meant to write her via her publisher, but time deceived me—I believed I had all of it in the world. When I finally contacted her, nearly a year later, I failed, for her publisher had gone out of business. It seems her editor, I don't know his name, it began with an E, had run off to South America with a street youth and the company's funds, what there were left of them. I was told the revised edition of *The 19th Wife* had failed to such an extent that it nearly bankrupted the little firm. The editor's thievery pushed the house over the brink. Quite simply, there were no files to search.

Again time played its trick on me. I pushed off the task of con-

tacting my mother for a few more years. Then, sometime just before the war, I started asking around; I made a trip east. I hired a
detective, a sincere man named Scotty Rivers; he was a gentle soul,
some terrible abuse had shaped him early in life, I am sure. After
two months Detective Rivers handed me an empty file and returned his fee. "The trail ends in 1908. She was leasing a cottage in
Arizona, the rent paid through the year. At the turn of 1909, the
landlord went for his rent but found the cottage cleared out. No
one could say when she left or where she went. After that I found
nothing, no insurance papers, no medical records, no police reports, nothing from an estate. One old woman, a neighbor, says she
remembers your mother talk of traveling east to promote the revised edition of her memoirs, but her mind is faulty, I discovered,
and her word can't be accepted as fact. Other than that I'm afraid I
don't have anything for you," the man said. "I won't take your
money."

I said to Rosemary, "How can someone vanish without a trace?"
But so she did. We never heard from my mother again.

I have to assume she's dead now, but where she rests I have no
idea. This outcome, no doubt, colors my perception of my mother.
To what degree, in what shade, I should say, I cannot say. If Rosemary were here, I would leave it to her to assess the effects of my
grief. I should have told you all this sooner. I did not want you to
think I am a man who thinks under the influence of sentiment. But
I suppose I do, for not a day passes without my wishing to speak to
my mother one last time. When I think of her now, I feel like that
little boy locked up in the Walker House, waiting for her return.

My mind tells me to end my letter here, yet my heart compels
me to continue hunting for the right letters on the typewriter. I
would like to share with you my speculative thoughts about my
mother's fate. You must put no more weight into them than you
would do so with the theories of a conspiracist.

First, I must lay out the three possible outcomes.

One, she died naturally somewhere, a once famous woman forgotten, penniless, laid to peace in a potter's field. With the failure of the second edition of *The 19th Wife*, and her career as a lecturer over, I cannot imagine how my mother sustained herself. No one wanted to hear her tale. Her Cassandra-like voice could not arouse the nation a second time. Rage is a candle, it will always burn out. And we must acknowledge that this was now the twentieth century, not the nineteenth. So much had already come to pass. And so a disease came upon my destitute mother, a quick and vicious illness, or a slow one, or a tumble down the stairs, or a reckless automobile ran her down on a sparkling afternoon—I cannot know the details. But something felled her and a quiet neighbor gave her a grave.

Two, an enemy murdered her, scattering her remains to the buzzards, or some other such thorough manner of disposal. This scenario, of course, leaves us with the very large question, Who? Your enemies, the antagonists of the Mormon Church, I mean, would say it was someone affiliated with the Saints. I cannot imagine it, for what cause? The old attacks on Brigham Young? Unlikely. More probable, it would seem to me—if this bleak scenario were true, which I have no evidence that it is—the break-away Saints, the Firsts they call themselves, I believe, those men and women splintered off in Red Creek and elsewhere, polygamous and paranoid, upon seeing my mother reemerge on the national stage with the second edition of *The 19th Wife* wrongly anticipated she would bring the law's wrath upon them to end their poly-amorous ways, just as she had done with the Mormons of Salt Lake. Any reader of mysteries will tell you the key to solving a crime is understanding the motive. So here is one, concocted by the imagination and a scarcity of facts.

Three, she is alive today, on the verge of her ninety-sixth birthday, rocking in a chair somewhere very far away. In this scenario she looks out upon a quiet landscape, the red desert, no doubt, pondering all that she has achieved. Her day will come soon, she knows, and she awaits it with a devotion that is tinted with anticipatory glee.

Change the details, and one of these three outcomes is more or less true. Which one, however, I cannot know with any kind of scientific certainty. Although I will never know the truth, it does not mean I have stopped pondering the puzzle of her last days. I am like the devoted but less than brilliant mathematician who knows he will never unlock a certain equation, yet still he keeps probing it diligently, trying again and again until his own final hour.

Since reasoning and logic have not helped me solve the mystery of my mother's disappearance, and I expect they never will, I will allow myself to tell you what my heart says, although I know I should not. Yet here I go. The first scenario and the last strike me as unlikely. The second, therefore, must be true. The Firsts of Red Creek silenced her. They had every reason. My uncle Aaron was their first Prophet. He never liked Ann Eliza, anyone will tell you that, their antagonism goes back to their youth. And so he removed her, or sent out his followers to remove her. I think of her fear, the terror of her final moment—the blade shining in the dark, the club falling through the air, the gun's muzzle taking aim of her, and the white flash when the trigger was pulled. I like to believe she understood what was happening to her. At the moment of her death, knowing the meaning of her fate was her only comfort. She saw the face of her enemy. In her last second on earth, she could hope her death would have significance. Then she was gone. Dead but not silenced, for *The 19th Wife* will always live on. Although I cannot prove this scenario, I know it—and isn't that the ultimate definition of faith? Knowing what we can't know. Seeing what isn't there.

And so there you have it, my friend—the end of Ann Eliza Young. All speculation and imagination, yet so true, so true.

Yours most fondly,

LORENZO DEE, SON

Women's Research Institute
Brigham Young University
Thesis for Master's Degree
Adviser, Professor Mary P. Sprague
April 13, 2007

WIFE #19:

A Desert Mystery

Introduction

My research into the life of Ann Eliza Young (1844–unknown) began more than two years ago. After studying her mother, Elizabeth Churchill Webb, and her father, Chauncey Webb, I turned to Ann Eliza herself and her complicated legacy in Church history. Fortunately for my scholarship many people, especially those closest to her, left written memories of her in the form of letters, diaries, depositions, testimonies, and news accounts.[1] In reading these, I have been able to construct what I hope is a complex view of the woman known as the notorious 19th Wife. My research has led me to form five conclusions about Ann Eliza and the role of polygamy in Church history.

One, her reports on the moral and spiritual debasement of the nineteenth-century plural wife are more accurate than generally

---

[1] Transcripts of the documents I have studied have been placed in the WRI's archives.

recognized. For many of us this is an uncomfortable truth, for it has been more convenient to dismiss her so-called exposé as an exaggerated depiction of how the plural wife lived. In truth, polygamy generally compromised the moral and spiritual development of its women and, equally important, its children. Ann Eliza Young's memoir, for the most part, tells it as it was. Certainly her depiction of Brigham Young is limited mostly to his role as polygamous husband and thus omits his many achievements as spiritual leader to thousands as well as those related to his colonization of the West. This partial portrait, by its very nature, is skewed. Yet her account of Brigham, in relation to her, her family, and her beloved sons, I regret to confirm is factually correct. As a husband and father, he failed many, including his so-called 19th wife.[2]

Two, by studying her father, Chauncey, and her half-brother Gilbert, I have come to realize that plural marriage could compromise the husband's soul as much as, if not more than, that of the plural wife. The false promise of sexual freedom, cloaked as it was in religious righteousness, led some men into an abundance of marriages they were not prepared to sustain financially, emotionally, or spiritually. This too is an awkward revelation, for it suggests our beloved leaders Joseph and Brigham, each of whom had at least half a hundred wives, were morally compromised by their conjugal indulgences. It brings me much pain to type this conclusion.

I often wonder how Brigham, who saved his people from mass extermination, who risked everything to deliver tens of thousands to the glory of Zion, could go on to nearly destroy his followers.

---

[2] A final note on numbers: My research shows Ann Eliza was most likely Brigham's 52nd of 55 wives. As far as I can tell, she was called the 19th because removed from the total tally were the wives who had died, who were barren, or whom Brigham no longer had sexual relations with. This discrepancy in marital accounting speaks volumes about Brigham's complicated relations with his spouses and polygamy's moral corrosion. If anyone still wonders why Ann Eliza was so ticked off, they need only consider this footnote.

Was it blind faith? A raging libido? I have an idea about it. I believe most men, even the greatest, can offer salvation only once in their lifetime; for if he succeeds (and most do not), he will overestimate his powers and thereafter will behave recklessly. Brigham achieved so much for us, assured us our survival and place on earth, yet he risked all in the name of polygamy. As Saints, we must consider this difficult truth. Its meaning resonates today.

Three, in bringing the issue of polygamy into the national debate, Ann Eliza Young indirectly saved the LDS Church from itself. She was not alone in this; many others played significant parts, yet her leadership in the campaign to end polygamy, and the impact of the first edition of *The 19th Wife*, cannot be denied. This is an awkward fact, for it means one of Brigham's fiercest enemies set the course for the Church's future—a future that we thrive in today. In this irony, however, I believe we can find many Christian truths.

Four, with the 1890 Manifesto, and the more forceful second Manifesto, issued in 1904, the LDS Church made its position on polygamy clear—any Saint participating in a plural marriage would face excommunication. Yet in abandoning polygamy, the Latter-day Saints were now burdened with an untenable theological problem. The doctrine Joseph and Brigham had preached as the Word of God was now being revised. If polygamy was no longer a divine doctrine, many in and out of the Church asked, what about the Doctrine & Covenants as a whole? And what about the Book of Mormon itself? Could it too be edited, revised, trimmed, amended, and otherwise altered by Church leaders in Salt Lake?

Furthermore, the revised Doctrine left many polygamists, including President Woodruff himself, who had five or six wives, in a legal and theological purgatory. If polygamy was no longer a religious doctrine, and no longer the path to salvation, what should a man with a dozen wives do? Abandon the last eleven? Live on as a historical curiosity? And how should a plural wife feel about herself now? To use Brigham's own uncharacteristically cruel words, was she now merely a social harlot? The Church was woefully inept in

guiding the Saints through these confusing days. This spiritual am-
biguity pushed many Saints, under the leadership of Aaron Webb,
to break away from the LDS Church, forming the so-called Firsts
in and around Red Creek, Utah, which later became known as
Mesadale.

Through my work at the Ann Eliza House I have come to know
many women and children whose lives have been defined by
polygamy today. I formally interviewed twenty-two of these,
recording their experiences.[3] These conversations were first done
for background purposes—to gain insight into the life of a child of
polygamy and the life of a plural wife. Yet the more women and
children I spoke to, the more pressing their stories became. At
some point, I saw the connection between Ann Eliza Young, nineteenth-century Mormon polygamy, and the polygamists of today.
Polygamists like the Firsts in Mesadale are not Mormons; we are
not of the same Church. This is not in dispute. Yet they are the unintended consequences of Joseph and Brigham's polygamous policies. To deny this is to deny the cold facts of history. To ignore their
stories is to abandon Christian principles. And so I could not look
away.

Five, to my profound disappointment, I was unable to determine
the fate of Ann Eliza Young. We know that after the publication of
The 19th Wife in 1875 she reconciled with her mother, who aposta-
tized after Brigham sought to destroy her daughter's reputation.
Elizabeth Churchill Webb died in 1884, presumably while living
with Ann Eliza. In 1890, after seeing the Church renounce
polygamy, Ann Eliza retired from the lecture circuit. She married a
wealthy Michigan industrialist, but the marriage soured after a few
years and they divorced. We know that by the late 1890s she was
living in Arizona, most probably on limited means. There is a large
gap in her biography until 1908, when she reemerged with the sec-

---

[3] Transcripts of these interviews are in the WRI's archives.

ond edition of *The 19th Wife* from a vanity press. It seems she spent most or all of her assets on the book's reissue, which failed to sell one thousand copies. Thereafter there are no reliable sources documenting her whereabouts. There are two reports of sightings: A son of James Dee, her first husband, claims to have seen her in Phoenix in 1915. One of Brigham's sons, John Willard Young, wrote that he passed her by near his apartment on Broadway in New York City the year before his death in 1923. Although intriguing, neither claim can be confirmed. Both strike me as unlikely.

Lorenzo Leonard Dee, Ann Eliza's second son (and my great-great-grand-uncle), believed that his mother was murdered by a member or members of the Firsts community. Certainly Aaron, or his followers, would have the most reason to silence polygamy's most effective opponent. Yet as tantalizing as this theory is, there is no evidence to support it, other than the distinct voice of a grieving son.

Then what happened to Ann Eliza Young? My searches through archives in Utah, California, New York, and Washington have turned up nothing regarding her last days. None of the local or national papers ever ran an obituary. As far as I know, there are no police reports, insurance records, estate papers, or any other clues concerning her fate. I have come to the conclusion, alas, that the mystery of her final outcome cannot be solved. Indeed, there are some mysteries that must exist without answer. In the end we must accept them for what they are: complex and many-sided, ornamented with clues and theories, yet ultimately unknowable—like life itself.

Thus, with these five conclusions formed, I submit what can only be described as an unorthodox thesis. After more than two years of research, I realized that a historical paper would not suffice. With this in mind, I have worked closely with a young man named Jordan Scott for several months. I interviewed him for nearly sixty hours about his life among the Firsts and, especially, his extraordinary relationship with his mother. At first, I tried to retell his story in an analytically detached way. Always, the results were cold and uninspired. Although his story offers much illumination on Ann Eliza and her legacy, my scholarly approach sucked the life out of his life. After many attempts I abandoned my voice for his. I edited the transcripts of our interviews into an early draft, then went back to him for more interviews. Together we edited the draft into a final narrative, *Wife #19:* A Desert Mystery.

Whether or not this will meet the thesis requirements is up to the Department. Yet I ask you to consider the questions *Wife #19 asks of the reader, and of itself. In my opinion these inquiries are serious and urgent and worthy of a scholar's attention. Although the words are Jordan's, it is shaped by my years of scholarship and thought, and a lifetime of open faith.*

WIFE #19:
EPILOGUE:
Focus on the Family

A week later Maureen and I went shopping. We were in a discount women's store, pushing a shopping cart down the aisle. Maureen had a firm sense of what we needed. "At least three pairs of shoes, one for dressier situations, one for every day, and one for walking and other activities. Any idea what color she likes?"

"Red," I said. "Mostly red."

"I'm afraid red can only go so far." Maureen inspected permanent press slacks, braided belts, t shirts with piped sleeves, nylon socks, and other basics. "Now let's go get her some bath things."

"I have some soap."

"A woman needs more than a bar of soap." She examined a jar of face cream. "I've gone ahead and made her an appointment at my beauty parlor. She'll need to figure out what to do with her hair."

An hour later we unpacked our purchases in Room 111. Maureen hummed about, snipping off tags and folding the shirts and slacks into a drawer she had lined with tissue. When she was done she clapped her hands. "All done. Now, if you need anything else . . ."

"I'm all set."

"I know, but if you ever need anything else, you let me know." She hugged me, her handbag clobbering me in the back.

"I couldn't've done this without you," I said.

"Of course you could've."

"No, actually, I couldn't."

"I'll just go say good-bye to Tom and the dogs." Then she was gone, a blur of blue.

The next morning at a quarter to eight, Tom and I waited at the security entrance of the jail. Officer Cunningham was manning the desk. "Big day," she said. "It'll only be another minute." We talked some about our dogs; she was taking her corgis to a show in Colorado next weekend and had their grooming on her mind.

At five to eight a photographer showed up, three cameras hanging around her neck. She gave her card to Officer Cunningham, who told her she could set up in the corner. The photographer opened a camera bag and changed her lenses, wiping them with a small tissue, readying everything so that when the moon-faced clock said it was exactly eight, she'd be all set to capture that picture everyone loves—a wrongly accused prisoner being freed.

I saw her face first through the chicken-wire glass in the door. Really, all I could see were her eyes. "There she is," said Tom. Officer Cunningham buzzed the door open, then an eternity—as if time stopped and whoever runs the universe went out for a smoke—and finally the door swung open.

"BeckyLyn, over here!"

My mom looked at the photographer. A flash, a click, another flash, more clicks.

"*St. George Register*," the photographer said. "Can you hold right there?" She wore the dusty pink prairie dress she'd been arrested in, the heavy stockings, the handmade shoes. Her steps were tentative, like she was learning to walk.

"Mom," I said, "this is Tom."

He couldn't help himself: he lunged to hug her. "I've heard so much about you!"

"BeckyLyn," the photographer called, "is that the son who saved you?" She took a picture with one camera, then the same picture with the next, and again the same shot with the third.

"Let's go," I said.

"How about a family reunion shot?"

"Time to go."

I led my mom out to the van. The photographer walked around us, crouching and stepping backward, click click click, saying *how*

do you feel? and *happy to be free?* and *this is great, just great.* When we
were in the van, the photographer stopped taking pictures. "Good
luck, BeckyLyn! Our readers love you!"

Tom was driving. He asked if she wanted the windows up or
down or if she needed water. "Or if you're hungry, we can stop now,
but Jordan and I thought we'd take you back to the Malibu first."

"I'm fine," she said. "Really." She was looking out the window at
the red sandstone cliffs, her face ghosted in the glass.

"Mom, how does it feel to be free?"

"I'm figuring that out right now."

"And *this*," said Tom, pushing the key card into the slot, "this is
your room. You've got a TV, cable, movie channels, a/c, the ice machine's down the hall. And *this*"—he pointed to an interior door—
"this door connects to our room."

Behind the door Elektra started barking, then Joey. Tom opened
the door and the second behind it. The dogs ran into Room 111,
snouts pointed right at my mom. Elektra jumped on her, pushing
her back onto the bed. After a lot of petting and licking, Elektra relented and my mom stood up and straightened out her dress. She
was laughing and saying, "Ah, what fun," and then her voice went
serious and she sat on the edge of the bed. "This is so nice of you,
but I'm not sure I'll be needing any of this."

"Mom. Tom and I, we want you to stay."

"As long as you like," said Tom. "I talked to the owner and we've
worked it all out."

"I appreciate it," she said. "I really do." And then, "But it's probably time for me to go."

"Go? Go where?"

"Back to Mesadale."

"I'm not taking you back there."

My phone rang. Roland. I don't know why I answered. "Honey,
I just read about you on the *Register*'s home page. You're like a lit-

tle Angela Lansbury out there. Now if only you could solve the mystery of my expanding waistline."

"Roland, I can't talk now."

"All right, but I want to hear all about it, especially that cute thing you picked up, Miss Utah. Leave it to you to solve a crime *and* find a hubby-hub."

"Not now, Roland."

"Anyway, when are you coming home?"

"Later."

"Oh no, don't tell me you're going all O Pioneer on me."

I hung up. "Mom, sorry, an old friend. Like I was saying, I didn't go through all this to drop you back in Mesadale."

The sunshine through the plate glass made her face look very round and very clean. It was a pure morning light, the kind that reveals everything for what it is. "God was right," she said. "He said you'd come, and he was right." She looked around. "This is such a nice place. And these clothes—I can't believe you bought them for me, they're so pretty. But I can't take them."

"Mom, you can."

"No, Jordan, I can't."

Right then, before she walked out the door, I felt like I had one last chance to save her. I opened the dresser, showing her the new slacks and blouses, the shoes lined up at the door, the face cream and beauty soap laid out on the vanity. I showed her the tv remote and promised to teach her how to use the internet in the lobby. "Mom, please, I want you to stay. Here. With me." I was trying to tell her we could pick up our lives in Rooms 111 and 112, get the second chance you almost never get. I was frantic to prove the Malibu Inn would make a nice home.

"And there's a pool! We didn't show you the pool! Right here, through the patio door." I opened the glass slider.

But I stopped. "Mom, please. I don't want you to go. You can stay here and do what you want. We won't get in your way."

"Jordan, I'm sorry."

"Mom, please."

"Jordan, I know you'll understand."

The thing was: I finally understood.

"What if I need to call you?"

"You won't."

"What if it's an emergency?"

"Then you'll know what to do."

"Will we ever see each other again?"

"I believe we will."

My mom and I drove over to Denny's for the breakfast special. We pushed around our eggs and searched for things to say. The truth was, we'd already said it, and twenty minutes later we were on the road to Mesadale in my van. My mom rolled down her window and the wind blew about the shrub of her hair. We passed the shot-up marker and the wasteland of scrub. I saw the stand of cotton-woods and pulled over to turn onto the road.

"I'll get out here," she said.

"I'm not going to leave you on the highway."

"I want to walk the rest of the way."

I turned off the engine and helped her down from the van. The sunlight was warm on my face and cast her skin in gold. The hot wind kicked up the sand and the dust and I could feel my throat drying out. "So I guess this is it," I said. "Mom, are you sure?"

She nodded. "I love you. I know you know that. That's why I can say good-bye."

We held each other for a while and at some point it was time to let go. She headed up the road, the dust collecting around her ankles, and the sun burned down, and it would burn hot and high on the desert until the last day.

I couldn't believe it. When I got back to Room 112, I found Johnny asleep on the bed. The dogs were curled up around him, and Tom was sitting on the other bed, reading. "Shhhh," he said. "They're sleeping."

"I can see that. What's he doing here?" Johnny's legs were scratched up, bug bites and a couple of bruises, but otherwise he looked all right.

"He ran away," he whispered. "I guess he missed you."

"What are we going to do with him?"

"Shhh, you'll wake him," he said. "We'll figure something out." And then, "Jordan."

"Tom."

"He can stay with us if he wants."

"Let's just see, all right? We have a lot going on."

"I know, but wouldn't it be nice if he stayed?"

"God, what a family we'd make."

"Sounds perfect," said Tom. "Now be quiet."

"He might not want to stay."

"He'll want to."

"I don't know."

"Jordan—"

"Tom—"

"Oh, for Christ's sake," said Johnny, sitting up. "Will you two birds shut the fuck up."

He cracked his smart-ass smile. Elektra moaned and reasserted her position on the bed. Joey swatted his tail. And Tom wound his arm around me. The sun was in the western sky and the room filled with its light. I tried to imagine my mom walking back into town—the dust in her hair, the hope in her eyes. The road, the post office, the mountain shadow. The excitement as someone recognized her, then someone else, then someone else again. Where would she go? Would she return to her old room? I grew tense and rolled back my shoulders. Would I wonder about her fate for the rest of my life? Burdened by its mystery? Then I saw four wives greet her, kiss her, take her inside the house. I saw three small children circling her skirt. I saw her old apron hanging on its peg. I saw her swing open the door to her room. I saw her move to the windowsill and stroke the leaf of her aloe plant. I saw my mother on her knees. I saw myself filling up her prayers.

It was enough. Knowing all that was enough.

"What are you thinking?" said Tom.

"Stuff."

"What kind of stuff?"

"You know what they say."

"What's that?"

"Endings are beginnings."

"Is that what they say?"

"In my book they do."

AUTHOR'S NOTE AND ACKNOWLEDGMENTS

———

This is a work of fiction. It is not meant to be read as a stand-in for a biography of Ann Eliza Young, Brigham Young, or any of the other historical figures who appear in it. Even so, it's human nature to wonder if a historical novel is based on real people and real events, and if so to what degree; and so I feel an obligation to the reader to begin to answer that question.

Ever since her apostasy from the Church of Jesus Christ of Latter-day Saints in 1873, Ann Eliza Young has been a figure of controversy among Mormons and non-Mormons alike. I don't expect to settle that controversy with this book. One reason the controversy has lingered is that she left us a substantial record of her experiences as a plural wife in her two memoirs and many public lectures. Her enemies and allies have used her words to denounce or support her, and thus anyone who writes about Ann Eliza Young must begin with her lectures and passionate memoirs, *Wife No. 19 (1876) and* Life in Mormon Bondage (1908). The books and lectures have their flaws. In them, Ann Eliza can come off as simultaneously hypercritical and hypersensitive. She is selective in her presentation of her story and Mormon history, carrying out an agenda with little subtlety or nuance. Too often her tone becomes strident and vengeful. Her portrait of Brigham Young lacks the complexity for which he was known. And she can get basic information wrong. Yet despite these limitations, her memoirs, as well as her public lectures upon which the memoirs are based, remain the best sources for the plot of her life and, just as important, for appreciating her point of view. If she had not spoken up there would be much about her life, and especially her marriage to

Brigham, that we could never know. It is one reason her story is so remarkable—she dared to reveal what thousands of other women bore in silence. Therefore I gratefully acknowledge her original efforts in autobiography—the lectures and memoirs. Without them, *The 19th Wife* would have been a far lesser, far more opaque book. My long process of thinking about Ann Eliza and her family, and the context of her life, began with the lectures and memoirs, and so it seemed only natural to begin my novel where she does, and then veer away.

The 19th Wife follows Ann Eliza's basic biographical arc as she describes it, although often I fill in where she skips in her accounts and I skip where she digresses. I continue past her conclusion and reinterpret where her point of view limits an understanding of her life and times. I also spend much time on members of her family, about whom she has little meaningful to say. It is with them—Chauncey, Elizabeth, Gilbert, and Lorenzo Leonard—that I take the most liberties because their biographies are less known and because of the novelist's need to weave the disparate into something unified. As for Brigham Young, my portrait of him is mostly consistent with that presented by a number of people who knew him, as well as the sermons, declarations, letters, and diaries he left. Often when he speaks in my narrative, especially at the pulpit, his words are inspired by a position we know, through the historical record, he took. I am sure his admirers will argue I linger too long on his egomaniacal tendencies as well as his appetites; and that by quoting him directly on the subject of blood atonement on pages ■■■. I am overemphasizing his calls for violence. Brigham's detractors, on the other hand, will probably say I let him off the hook. Thankfully the historical record is vast and accessible; the curious reader can visit the library or go online to form his or her own conclusions.

Which leads me to the documents (or "documents") that run throughout the novel—the newspaper articles, the letters, the Introduction by Harriet Beecher Stowe, the Wikipedia entry. Although I am the author of these, they are fictional representations of what it's like to spend time in the archives and online researching Ann Eliza Young, Brigham, and early LDS history. Many are inspired by an actual text or a kind of text. For example, my Howard Greenly interview with Joseph purposely evokes Horace Greeley's famous interview with Brigham in 1859; the devotional poem "In Our House" is my limp attempt at the sincere hymns the pioneers wrote to reflect their experiences; and the Wikipedia entry is (obviously) written in a style very much like a Wikipedia entry.

The mighty lens of history has enabled me to see Ann Eliza's life as she could not, and I have used this perspective to tell her story in a way that perhaps broadens it and connects it to our day. All of this is a long-winded answer to the original question, is *The 19th Wife* based on real people and real events? Yes. Have I invented much of it? Yes, for that is what novelists do.

Inevitably I relied on a variety of sources to write this book, each important to my task and worth acknowledging. Many times I turned to Irving Wallace's thorough biography, *The Twenty-Seventh Wife* (1961), itself indebted to Ann Eliza's original memoirs. I recommend it, along with *Wife No. 19*, for anyone who wants to know more about her life. In addition, the Irving Wallace Archive at the Honnold Library at the Claremont Colleges holds a fine collection on Ann Eliza Young; I'm grateful to Mr. Wallace for making his original research available to the public and to the archivists who maintain it today. Just as important were the archives of the Salt Lake *Daily Tribune*, one of Ann Eliza's most vocal allies. This paper published almost daily reports on her battle with Brigham, devoting hundreds of news columns to her story and dozens of editorials to support her cause, and reprinted most of the legal filings in their divorce case. Throughout the 1870s and '80s the *Tribune* featured a number of articles about the general conditions of polygamy in Utah and serialized sensational personal narratives, such as "Tied to the Stake; or Martyrs of Latter Days" by

Mrs. A. G. Paddock, many of which supported Ann Eliza's claims. This thorough repository—today housed on microfiche at the magnificent Salt Lake City Public Library—helped me with crucial details about Ann Eliza's life, as well as to better understand its historical context. On the other hand, the Deseret *News,* Ann Eliza's inevitable opponent, reported on her story from Brigham's perspective. While other local and national papers covered Ann Eliza's story in great (and often tabloid) detail, these two publications documented her life story and her apostasy from the Mormon Church as well as any periodical during her day.

Some people argue bibliographies have no place in fiction, but several books and documents have helped me with so many matters large and small that I want to give them the thanks they are due. I haven't included this list to show off the extent of my reading (or lack thereof) but to acknowledge a set of authors whose work I learned from: *Brigham Young: American Moses* by Leonard J. Arrington; *Twenty Years of Congress* by James G. Blaine; *No Man Knows My History* by Fawn M. Brodie; *Emma Lee* by Juanita Brooks; *The City of the Saints* by Sir Richard F. Burton; *The Pioneer Cookbook* by Kate Carter; *In Sacred Loneliness* by Todd Compton; "Forest Farm House and Forest Dale" by Edith Olsen Cowen; "Brigham Young, His Family and His Wives" compiled by the Daughters of the Utah Pioneers; "Unique Story—President Brigham Young" compiled by the Daughters of the Utah Pioneers; *Nauvoo Factbook* by George and Sylvia Givens; *By the Hand of Mormon* by Terry L. Givens; *The Mormon Question* by Sarah Barringer Gordon; *Solemn Covenant* by B. Carmon Hardy; "Eliza Jane Churchill Webb, Pioneer of 1848" by Olivette Webb Goe Henry; "Chauncey Griswold Webb, Pioneer of 1848" by Olivette Webb Goe Henry and Nina Beth E. Goe Cunningham; *Old Mormon Kirtland* by Richard Neitzel Holzapfel and T. Jeffrey Cottle; *Old Mormon Nauvoo* by Richard Neitzel Holzapfel and T. Jeffrey Cottle; III *Days to Zion* by Hal Knight and Dr. Stanley B. Kimball; *Under the Banner of Heaven* by Jon Krakauer; *The Story of the Mor-*

mons *from the Date of Their Origin to the Year 1901* by William Alexander Linn, especially Chapter IV, "The Hand-Cart Tragedy"; *Historic Dress in America* by Elizabeth McClellan; *Redburn* by Herman Melville, especially Chapter 38 for its vivid depiction of Liverpool's slums; *Eccentricities of Genius* by Major J.B. Pond; *The Book of Mormon,* translated by Joseph Smith, Jr.; *The Pearl of Great Price* by Joseph Smith, Jr.; *God Has Made Us a Kingdom* by Vickie Cleverley Speek; *Brigham Young at Home* by Clarissa Young Spencer and Mabel Harmer; *Mormon Country* by Wallace Stegner; *Expose of Polygamy in Utah* by Mrs. T.B.H. Stenhouse; *Tell It All* by Mrs. T.B.H. Stenhouse (it's worth noting that Stenhouse's books inspired Ann Eliza's memoirs in many ways); *Roughing It* by Mark Twain; *Mormon Polygamy* by Richard S. Van Wagoner; *Brigham Young* by M.R. Werner; *The Bold Women* by Helen Beal Woodward; *The Journal of Discourses, Volumes 3* and *4,* by Brigham Young; *Diary of Brigham Young, 1857, edited by Everett L. Cooley;* My Dear Sons: Letters of Brigham Young to His Sons, edited by Dean C. Jessee, and *The Complete Sermons of Brigham Young.*

I owe a great deal to the following institutions and their staffs for making their collections readily available through open stacks and policies of access. Each contains a variety of useful, idiosyncratic materials that I gladly co-opted for my use: the Salt Lake City Public Library; Brigham Young University's Harold B. Lee Library; the University of Utah's J. Willard Marriott Library; the Provo Public Library; the Washington County Library in St. George; the Daughters of the Utah Pioneers Museum; and the Nauvoo Research Center.

The Church of Jesus Christ of Latter-day Saints has devoted countless resources to creating and staffing dozens of historical museums, many of them free and open to the public. I visited these institutions several times, lingering to take notes and talk to the missionaries serving as docents and guides. Without the church's careful and abundant preservation of the past throughout Utah, as well as in Nauvoo, I could not have conjured up Ann Eliza's world.

I want to thank the Metropolitan Community Church of Las Vegas for warmly welcoming me into their sanctuary. Although the sermon on pages ███ is inspired by one I heard there on December 18, 2005, the scene itself is fictitious and does not depict this actual church or anyone in its loving congregation.

A number of people generously shared their stories with me. Without them I could not have written this novel as it is: Flora Jessop, Carmen Thompson, Steve Tripp, Mickey Unger, Beverly White, Kevin, Jimmy, Peter, and Susan. Thank you all.

Kari Main of the Pioneer Memorial Museum read the book in manuscript, correcting a number of errors. Her sharp, knowing eye fixed the book in many ways. She was an ideal reader and these few words are not enough thanks for her efforts.

The supremely talented Catherine Hamilton drew the illustration on page ███; it is based on an original 1876 etching by Stanley Fox.

Alexis Richland provided much needed editorial guidance on an early draft. Her thoughtful response helped solve some problems that had lingered in my mind for years. Mark Nelson read several drafts, each time raising important questions in need of resolution. I'm grateful for the many hours he devoted to this book, and for his unyielding friendship and support. Daryl Mattson, who has never tired of listening to me gab about almost anything, served as a sounding board for a number of ideas in this book, even when he wasn't aware of it. The name of the Internet café in St. George, A Woman Sconed, comes from him.

For ten years Elaine Koster has been a formidable agent, insightful editor, and loyal friend. Her unflagging encouragement helped bring this book from an early idea to the pages you now hold. I owe her much.

Lots of thanks are due to Marianne Velmanns and her colleagues at Transworld. They are the kind of publisher every writer hopes to have.

The thanks I want to offer to Random House are vast. So many people there have helped me over so many years that any list of names is bound to forget someone crucial. So I'll make a blanket but sincere expression of gratitude to everyone at 1745. I know how books are published, and I know that each of you played a part. I hope you'll forgive me for not printing the company roster. But I must thank my editor, Kate Medina. She is a brilliant reader, and her wise pencil made this book better in many, many ways. Frankie Jones and Jennifer Smith shouldered the burdens of turning a manuscript into a book; each did so with grace and generosity. Jynne Martin, publicity-goddess: it's an honor to be on your roster. And to my publisher, Gina Centrello, thank you for your support, which has shown itself in so many ways.

ABOUT THE AUTHOR

———

DAVID EBERSHOFF is the author of two novels, *The Danish Girl* and *Pasadena,* and a short-story collection, *The Rose City.* His fiction has won the Rosenthal Foundation Award from the American Academy of Arts and Letters and the Lambda Literary Award and has been translated into ten languages. He teaches in the graduate writing program at Columbia University and is an editor-at-large at Random House. He lives in New York City.

ABOUT THE TYPE

———

This book was set in Caslon, a typeface first designed in 1722 by William Caslon. Its widespread use by most English printers in the early eighteenth century soon supplanted the Dutch typefaces that had formerly prevailed. The roman is considered a "workhorse" typeface due to its pleasant, open appearance, while the italic is exceedingly decorative.

If you would like to share your thoughts on this book with us and your fellow booksellers, please do so here or send us an e-mail at RHTrademarketing@randomhouse.com

Title _____

_____

_____

_____

_____

Name: _____

Bookstore: _____

Address: _____

FOLD ALONG DOTTED LINE

RANDOM HOUSE

PLACE
STAMP
HERE

RANDOM HOUSE
1745 Broadway, MD 18-2
New York, NY 10019
Attn: K. Ruden

COLLEEN McCULLOUGH

Author of *THE THORN BIRDS* and *CAESAR'S WOMEN*

> "McCullough is terrific . . .
> Her characters quiver with life."
> —The New York Times Book Review

THE OCTOBER HORSE

A NOVEL OF CAESAR AND CLEOPATRA

ACCLAIM FOR COLLEEN McCULLOUGH'S
INTERNATIONALLY BESTSELLING NOVELS

The October Horse

"An intelligent page-turning epic that seamlessly mixes love, gore, and ambition."

—*Kirkus Reviews*

"McCullough is still going strong. . . . [A] panoply of richly imagined characters. . . . [A] heady novel . . . blessed with the same immediacy and breezy style that made the tumultuous first century B.C. come alive in previous volumes."

—*Publishers Weekly*

"McCullough boldly depicts the demise of the empire. . . . McCullough's vision of Julius Caesar [is that of] a man more charismatic, more intelligent, more visionary, and more dynamic than any other in history."

—*Library Journal*

"[A] swiftly moving story . . . packed full of political intrigue, romance, drama, and war, all pulled together by McCullough's seemingly effortless evocation of the excitement and turmoil present at the end of the republic. . . . [Her] legions of fans . . . won't be disappointed."

—*Booklist*

"The unbridled ambitions of the many great men and women who helped bring the Roman Republic to its knees are brilliantly brought to life."

—*The Daily Telegraph* (Sydney)

"Caesar and his rivals are splendidly brought to life."

—*Coventry Evening Telegraph* (U.K.)

"McCullough's knowledge of the era is encyclopedic. . . . McCullough's overall literary achievement shines brightly."

—*Calgary Herald*

Her breathtaking novel of the colonization of Australia . . .

Morgan's Run

"Compelling. . . . A stirring saga."

—*People*

"McCullough really shines."

—*The Washington Post*

"Fiction at its best."

—*Time*

"McCullough is terrific. . . . Her characters quiver with life."

—*The New York Times Book Review*

"[An] intricately researched, passionate epic. . . . Consistently entertaining."

—*Publishers Weekly*

"McCullough is a grand storyteller. . . . There are many perfectly stunning lyrical passages."

—*The Roanoke Times* (VA)

"Vivid. . . . [The narrative] detail sets McCullough's epic apart from the standard seafaring adventure."

—*The San Diego Union-Tribune*

"McCullough scores again."

—*St. Louis Post-Dispatch*

"A page-turner. . . . McCullough's account of the birth of a nation is utterly compelling."

—*Orlando Sentinel* (FL)

"McCullough is an obvious master of her craft. . . . The narrative triumphs."

—*Milwaukee Journal Sentinel*

"McCullough excels at creating richly textured characters who spring to life within a few sentences."

—*The Plain Dealer* (Cleveland)

"A rich, compelling epic."

—*Daily Mail* (UK)

Also by Colleen McCullough

On, Off

Angel Puss

The Touch

Morgan's Run

Roden Cutler, V.C. (*biography*)

The Song of Troy

Caesar: Let the Dice Fly

Caesar's Women

Fortune's Favorites

The Grass Crown

The First Man in Rome

The Ladies of Missalonghi

A Creed for the Third Millennium

An Indecent Obsession

The Thorn Birds

Tim

THE
OCTOBER
HORSE

Colleen McCullough

SIMON & SCHUSTER PAPERBACKS
New York London Toronto Sydney

SIMON & SCHUSTER PAPERBACKS
Rockefeller Center
1230 Avenue of the Americas
New York, NY 10020

This book is a work of fiction. Names, characters,
places, and incidents either are products of the
author's imagination or are used fictitiously. Any
resemblance to actual events or locales or persons,
living or dead, is entirely coincidental.

Copyright © 2002 by Colleen McCullough
All rights reserved, including the right to reproduce this book
or portions thereof in any form whatsoever. For information address
Simon & Schuster Subsidiary Rights Department,
1230 Avenue of the Americas, New York, NY 10020

This Simon & Schuster trade paperback edition November 2007

SIMON & SCHUSTER PAPERBACKS and colophon are registered trademarks
of Simon & Schuster, Inc.

For information regarding special discounts for bulk purchases,
please contact Simon & Schuster Special Sales at
1-800-456-6798 or business@simonandschuster.com

Manufactured in the United States of America

3   5   7   9   10   8   6   4   2

The Library of Congress has cataloged the hardcover edition as follows:
McCullough, Colleen, date.
The October horse : a novel about Caesar and Cleopatra / Colleen McCullough.
p.   cm.
1. Caesar, Julius—Fiction.   2. Cleopatra, Queen of Egypt, d. 30 B.C.—Fiction.
3. Rome—History—Republic, 265–30 B.C.—Fiction.   4. Egypt—History—332–30 B.C.—
Fiction.   5. Heads of state—Fiction.   6. Generals—Fiction.   7. Queens—Fiction.
I. Title.
PR9619.3.M32 O28 2002
823'.914—dc21   2002032753
ISBN   0-684-85331-0
ISBN-13: 978-1-4165-6665-6 (pbk)
ISBN-10:   1-4165-6665-1 (pbk)

For Ambassador Edward J. Perkins
Wm. J. Crowe Chair Professor of Political Science
the University of Oklahoma
for dedication to duty and all the unsung services
with love and admiration

GAIUS JULIUS CAESAR

The Ides of October marked the end of the campaigning season, and on that day a race was held on the grassy sward of the Campus Martius, just outside the Servian Walls of Republican Rome.

The year's best war horses were harnessed in pairs to chariots and driven at breakneck pace; the right-hand one of the winning pair became the October Horse, and was ritually killed with a spear by the *flamen Martialis*, the special priest of Mars, who was god of war. Then the October Horse's head and genitalia were amputated. The genitals were rushed to bleed on the sacred hearth in the Regia, Rome's oldest temple, after which they were given to the Vestal Virgins to burn to ashes in the sacred flame of Vesta; later these ashes were mixed into cakes offered on the anniversary of the founding of Rome by her first king, Romulus. The decorated head was tossed into the midst of two teams of humble citizens, one from the Subura district, one from the Sacra Via district, who fought strenuously for possession of it. If the Subura won, the head was nailed to the Turris Mamilia. If the Sacra Via won, the head was nailed to an outer wall of the Regia.

In this ritual so old that no one remembered how it had begun, the very best that Rome owned was sacrificed to the twin powers that ruled her: war and land. Out of them came her might, her prosperity, her everlasting glory. The death of the October Horse was at once a mourning of the past and a vision of the future.

I

Caesar in Egypt

From OCTOBER of 48 B.C.
until JUNE of 47 B.C.

CLEOPATRA

"I knew I was right—a very slight earthquake," Caesar said as he put the bundle of papers on his desk.

Calvinus and Brutus looked up from their own work, surprised.

"What has that to do with the price of fish?" Calvinus asked.

"The signs of my godhead, Gnaeus! The statue of Victory in that temple in Elis turning around, the clashing of swords and shields down in Antioch and Ptolemais, the drums booming from the temple of Aphrodite in Pergamum, remember? In my experience the gods don't interfere with the affairs of men, and it certainly didn't take a god on earth to beat Magnus at Pharsalus. So I made a few enquiries in Greece, northern Asia Province and Syria of the Orontes River. All the phenomena happened at the same moment on the same day—a slight earthquake. Look at our own priestly records in Italy, full of drums booming from the bowels of the earth and statues doing peculiar things. Earthquakes."

"You dim our light, Caesar," Calvinus said with a grin. "I was just beginning to believe that I'm working for a god." He looked at Brutus. "Aren't you disappointed too, Brutus?"

The large, heavy-lidded, mournful dark eyes didn't gleam with laughter; they stared at Calvinus thoughtfully. "Not disappointed or disillusioned, Gnaeus Calvinus, though I didn't think of a natural reason. I took the reports as flattery."

Caesar winced. "Flattery," he said, "is worse."

The three men were sitting in the comfortable but not luxurious room the *ethnarch* of Rhodes had given them as an office, as distinct from the quarters where they relaxed and slept. The window looked out across the busy harbor of this major trade route intersection linking the Aegean Sea with Cyprus, Cilicia and Syria; a pretty and interesting view, between the swarming ships, the deep blue of the sea and the high mountains of Lycia rearing across the straits, but no one took any notice.

Caesar broke the seal on another communication, read it at a glance, and grunted. "From Cyprus," he said before his companions could return to their work. "Young Claudius says that Pompeius Magnus has departed for Egypt."

"I would have sworn he'd join Cousin Hirrus at the court of the Parthian king. What's to be had in Egypt?" Calvinus asked.

"Water and provisions. At the snail's pace he's moving, the Etesian winds will be blowing before he leaves Alexandria. Magnus is going to join the rest of the fugitives in Africa Province, I imagine," Caesar said a little sadly.

"So it hasn't ended." Brutus sighed.

Caesar answered with a snap. "It can end at any time that Magnus and his 'Senate' come to me and tell me that I can stand for the consulship *in absentia*, my dear Brutus!"

"Oh, that's far too much like common sense for men of Cato's stamp," Calvinus said when Brutus failed to speak. "While Cato lives, you'll get no accommodations from Magnus or his Senate."

"I am aware of that."

Caesar had crossed the Hellespont into Asia Province three *nundinae* ago to work his way down its Aegean seaboard inspecting the devastation wreaked by the Republicans as they frantically gathered fleets and money. Temples had been looted of their most precious treasures, the strong rooms of banks, plutocrats and *publicani* tax farmers broken into and emptied; the governor of Syria rather than of Asia Province, Metellus Scipio had lingered there on his way from Syria to join Pompey in Thessaly, and had illegally imposed taxes on everything he could think of: windows, pillars, doors, slaves, a head count, grain, livestock, weapons, artillery, and the conveyance of lands. When they failed to yield enough, he instituted and collected provisional taxes for ten years to come, and when the locals protested, he executed them.

Though the reports reaching Rome dwelled more on evidence of Caesar's godhead than on such matters, in actual fact Caesar's progress was both a fact-finding mission and the initiation of financial relief for a province rendered incapable of prospering. So he talked to city and commercial leaders, fired the *publicani*, remitted taxes of all kinds for five years to come, issued orders that the treasures found in various tents at Pharsalus were to be returned to the temples whence they came, and promised that as soon as he had established good government in Rome, he would take more specific measures to help poor Asia Province.

Which, Gnaeus Domitius Calvinus thought, watching Caesar as he read on through the papers littering his desk here in Rhodes, is why Asia Province tends to regard him as a god. The last man who had understood economics and also had dealings with Asia had been Sulla, whose very fair system of taxation had been abolished fifteen years later by none other than Pompey the Great. Perhaps, Calvinus reflected, it takes one of the very old patricians to appreciate the duties

Rome owes her provinces. The rest of us don't have our feet so firmly anchored in the past, so we tend to live in the present rather than think about the future.

The Great Man was looking very tired. Oh, fit and trim as ever, but definitely the worse for wear. As he never touched wine or gourmandized from the table, he approached each day without the handicap of self-indulgence, and his ability to wake refreshed from a short nap was enviable; the trouble was that he had far too much to do and didn't trust most of his assistants enough to delegate them some of his responsibilities.

Brutus, thought Calvinus sourly (he disliked Brutus), is a case in point. He's the perfect accountant, yet all his energies are devoted to protecting his unsenatorial firm of usurers and tax farmers, Matinius et Scaptius. It should be called Brutus et Brutus! Everybody of importance in Asia Province owes Matinius et Scaptius millions, and so do King Deiotarus of Galatia and King Ariobarzanes of Cappadocia. So Brutus nags, and that exasperates Caesar, who loathes being nagged.

"Ten percent simple interest is just *not* an adequate return," he would say plaintively, "so how can you peg the interest rate at that when it's so deleterious to Roman businessmen?"

"Roman businessmen who lend at higher rates than that are despicable usurers," Caesar would reply. "Forty-eight percent compound interest, Brutus, is *criminal!* That's what your minions Matinius and Scaptius charged the Salaminians of Cyprus—then starved them to death when they couldn't keep up the payments! If our provinces are to go on contributing to Rome's welfare, they must be economically sound."

"It is not the fault of the moneylenders when the borrowers agree to contracts stipulating a higher than usual interest rate," Brutus would maintain with the peculiar stubbornness he reserved for financial matters. "A debt is a debt, and it must be repaid at the rate contracted for. Now you've made this illegal!"

"It should always have been illegal. You're famous for your epitomes, Brutus—who else can squeeze all of Thucydides into two pages? Haven't you ever tried to squeeze the Twelve Tables into one short page? If the *mos maiorum* is what provoked you into siding with your Uncle Cato, then you ought to remember that the Twelve Tables forbid levying *any* interest on a loan."

"That was six hundred years ago," Brutus would answer.

"If borrowers agree to exorbitant lending terms, then they're not suitable candidates for a loan, and you know it. What you're really complaining about, Brutus, is that I've forbidden Roman moneylenders to employ the governor's troops or lictors to collect their debts by force," Caesar would say, goaded into anger.

A conversation that was repeated at least once a day.

Of course Brutus was a particularly difficult problem for Caesar, who had taken him under his wing after Pharsalus out of affection for his mother, Servilia, and out of guilt at breaking Brutus's engagement to Julia in order to ensnare Pompey—it had broken Brutus's heart, as Caesar well knew. But, thought Calvinus, Caesar hadn't the slightest idea what kind of man Brutus is when he took pity on him after Pharsalus. He left a youth, he picked up the relationship twelve years later. Unaware that the pimply youth, now a pimply man of thirty-six, was a coward on a battlefield and a lion when it came to defending his staggering fortune. No one had dared to tell Caesar what everyone knew: that Brutus had dropped his sword unblooded at Pharsalus and hidden in the swamps before bolting to Larissa, where he was the first of Pompey's "Republican" faction to sue for a pardon. No, said Calvinus to himself, I don't like the craven Brutus, and I wish I could see the last of him. Calling himself a "Republican," indeed! It's just a high-sounding name whereby he and all the other so-called Republicans think to justify the civil war they pushed Rome into.

Brutus rose from his desk. "Caesar, I have an appointment."

"Then keep it," said the Great Man placidly.

"Does that mean the wormlike Matinius has followed us to Rhodes?" Calvinus asked the moment Brutus was gone.

"I fear so." The pale blue eyes, unsettling because of that black ring around the outside of each iris, crinkled at their corners. "Cheer up, Calvinus! We'll be rid of Brutus soon."

Calvinus smiled back. "What do you plan to do with him?"

"Ensconce him in the governor's palace at Tarsus, which is our next—and final—destination. I can't think of a more fitting punishment for Brutus than to make him go back to work for Sestius, who hasn't forgiven him for filching Cilicia's two legions and taking them to serve Pompeius Magnus."

Once Caesar issued the order to move, things happened in a hurry. The next day he set sail from Rhodes to Tarsus with two full legions and some 3,200 veteran soldiers amalgamated from the remains of his oldest legions, chiefly the Sixth. With him went 800 German cavalry troopers, their beloved Remi horses, and the handful of Ubii foot warriors who fought with them as spear snipers.

Ruined by the attentions of Metellus Scipio, Tarsus was limping along in the care of Quintus Marcius Philippus, younger son of Caesar's nephew-in-law and Cato's father-in-law, Lucius Marcius Philippus the fence-sitter and Epicure. Having commended young Philippus for his good sense, Caesar promptly put Publius Sestius back into the governor's curule chair and appointed Brutus his legate, young Philippus his proquaestor.

"The Thirty-seventh and the Thirty-eighth need a furlough," he said to Calvinus, "so put them in a good camp in the highlands above the Cilician Gates for six *nundinae*, then send them to me in Alexandria together with a war fleet. I'll wait there until they come, then I'm moving west to flush the Republicans out of Africa Province before they get too comfortable."

Calvinus, a tall, sandy-haired, grey-eyed man in his late forties, did not question these orders. Whatever Caesar wanted turned out to be the right thing to want; since joining Caesar a year ago he had seen enough to understand that this was the one man all wise men would adhere to if they wished to prosper. A conservative politician who should have chosen to serve Pompey the Great, Calvinus had elected Caesar after the blind enmity of men like Cato and Cicero had sickened him. So he had approached Mark Antony in Brundisium and asked to be ferried to Caesar. Very aware that Caesar would welcome the defection of a consular of Calvinus's standing, Antony had agreed instantly.

"Do you intend that I should remain in Tarsus until I hear from you?" he asked now.

"Your choice, Calvinus," Caesar answered. "I'd rather think of you as my 'roving consular,' if there is such a beast. As the dictator, I am empowered to grant imperium, so this afternoon I'll assemble thirty lictors to act as witnesses of a *lex curiata* granting you unlimited imperium in all lands from Greece eastward. That will enable you to outrank the governors in their provinces, and to levy troops anywhere."

"Have you a feeling, Caesar?" Calvinus asked, frowning.

"I don't get the things, if by that you mean some kind of preternatural gnawing inside my mind. I prefer to think of my—er—feelings as rooted in tiny events my thought processes have not consciously noted, but that are there nonetheless. All I say is that you should keep your eyes open for the sight of flying pigs and your ears tuned to the aether for the sound of singing pigs. If you see one or hear the other, something's wrong, and you'll have the authority to deal with it in my absence."

And on the following day, which was the second-last day of September, Gaius Julius Caesar sailed out of the river Cydnus into Our Sea with Corus blowing him south and east, ideal. His 3,200 veterans and 800 German horsemen were jammed into thirty-five transports; his warships he left being overhauled.

Two *nundinae* later, just as Calvinus the roving consular endowed with unlimited imperium was about to set out for Antioch to see what Syria was like after enduring Metellus Scipio as its governor, a courier arrived in Tarsus on a winded horse.

"King Pharnaces has come down from Cimmeria with a hundred thousand troops and is invading Pontus at Amisus," the man said when he was able. "Amisus is burning, and he's announced that he intends to win back all of his father's lands, from Armenia Parva to the Hellespont."

Calvinus, Sestius, Brutus and Quintus Philippus sat stunned.

"Mithridates the Great again," Sestius said hollowly.

"I doubt it," Calvinus said briskly, recovering from his shock. "Sestius, you and I march. We'll take Quintus Philippus with us and leave Marcus Brutus in Tarsus to govern." He turned to Brutus with such menace in his face that Brutus backed away. "As for you, Marcus Brutus, take heed of my words—there is to be no debt collecting in our absence, is that understood? You can have a propraetorian imperium to govern, but if you take so many as one lictor to enforce payments from Romans or provincials, I swear I'll string you up by whatever balls you have."

"And," snarled Sestius, who didn't like Brutus either, "it's due to you that Cilicia has no trained legions, so your chief job is recruiting and training soldiers—hear me?" He turned to Calvinus. "What of Caesar?" he asked.

"A difficulty. He asked for both the Thirty-seventh and the Thirty-eighth, but I daren't, Sestius. Nor I'm sure would he want me to strip Anatolia of all its seasoned troops. So I'll send him the Thirty-seventh after furlough and take the Thirty-eighth north with us. We can pick it up at the top of the Cilician Gates, then we march for Eusebeia Mazaca and King Ariobarzanes, who will just have to find troops, no matter how impoverished Cappadocia is. I'll send a messenger to King Deiotarus of Galatia and order him to gather whatever he can, then meet us on the Halys River below Eusebeia Mazaca. I'll also send messengers to Pergamum and Nicomedia. Quintus Philippus, find some scribes— *move!*"

Even having made his decision, Calvinus worried about Caesar. If Caesar had warned him in that oblique way that trouble was coming in Anatolia, then the same instincts had prompted him to want two full legions sent to him in Alexandria. Not receiving both might hamper his plans for going on to Africa Province as soon as maybe. So Calvinus wrote a letter to Pergamum addressed to a different son of Mithridates the Great than Pharnaces.

This was another Mithridates, who had allied himself with the Romans during Pompey's clean-up campaign in Anatolia after Rome's thirty years of war with the father. Pompey had rewarded him with the grant of a fertile tract of land around Pergamum, the capital of Asia Province. This Mithridates wasn't a king, but inside the boundaries of his little satrapy he was not answerable to Roman law. Therefore a client of Pompey's and bound to Pompey by the rigid laws of clientship, he had assisted Pompey in the war against Caesar, but after Pharsalus had sent a polite, apologetic missive to Caesar asking gracefully for forgiveness and the privilege of transferring his clientship to Caesar. The letter had amused Caesar, and charmed him too. He answered with equal grace, informing Mithridates of Pergamum that he was quite forgiven, and that he was henceforth enrolled in Caesar's clientele—but that he should hold himself ready to perform a favor for Caesar when it was asked of him.

Calvinus wrote:

Here's your chance to do Caesar that favor, Mithridates. No doubt by now you're as alarmed as the rest of us over your half brother's invasion of Pontus and the atrocities he has committed in Amisus. A disgrace, and an affront to all civilized men. War is a necessity, otherwise it would not exist, but it is the duty of a civilized commander to remove civilians from the path of the military machine and shelter them from physical harm. That civilians may starve or lose their homes is simply a consequence of war, but it is a far different thing to rape women and female children until they die of it, and torture and dismember civilian men for the fun of it. Pharnaces is a barbarian.

The invasion of Pharnaces has left me in a bind, my dear Mithridates, but it has just occurred to me that in you I have an extremely able deputy in formal alliance with the Senate and People of Rome. I know that our treaty forbids you to raise either army or militia, but in the present circumstances I must waive that clause. I am empowered to do so by virtue of a proconsular *imperium maius*, legally conferred by the Dictator.

You will not know that Caesar Dictator has sailed for Egypt with too few troops, having asked me to send him two more legions and a war fleet as soon as possible. Now I find that I can spare him only one legion and a war fleet.

Therefore this letter authorizes you to raise an army and send it to Caesar in Alexandria. Whereabouts you can find troops I do not know, as I will have picked the whole of Anatolia bare, but I have left Marcus Junius Brutus in Tarsus under orders to start recruiting and training, so you should be able to acquire at least one legion when your commander reaches Cilicia. I also suggest that you look in Syria, particularly in its southern extremities. Excellent men there, the best mercenaries in the world. Try the Jews.

When Mithridates of Pergamum received Calvinus's letter, he heaved a huge sigh of relief. Now was his opportunity to show the new ruler of the world that he was a loyal client!

"I'll lead the army myself," he said to his wife, Berenice.

"Is that wise? Why not our son Archelaus?" she asked.

"Archelaus can govern here. I've always fancied that perhaps I inherited a little of my father the Great's military skill, so I'd like to command in person. Besides," he added, "I've lived among the Romans and have absorbed some of their genius for organization. That my father the Great lacked it was his downfall."

 Oh, what bliss! was Caesar's initial reaction to his sudden removal from the affairs of Asia Province and Cilicia—and from the inevitable entourage of legates, officials, plutocrats and local *ethnarchs.* The only man of any rank he had brought with him on this voyage to Alexandria was one of his most prized *primipilus* centurions from the old days in Long-haired Gaul, one Publius Rufrius, whom he had elevated to praetorian legate for his services on the field of Pharsalus. And Rufrius, a silent man, would never have dreamed of invading the General's privacy.

Men who are doers can also be thinkers, but the thinking is done on the move, in the midst of events, and Caesar, who had a horror of inertia, utilized every moment of every day. When he traveled the hundreds, sometimes thousands, of miles from one of his provinces to another, he kept at least one secretary with him as he hurtled along in a gig harnessed to four mules, and dictated to the hapless man nonstop. The only times when work was put aside were those spent with a woman, or listening to music; he had a passion for music.

Yet now, on this four-day voyage from Tarsus to Alexandria, he had no secretaries in attendance or musicians to engage his mind; Caesar was very tired. Tired enough to realize that just this once he must *rest*—think about other things than whereabouts the next war and the next crisis would come.

That even in memory he tended to think in the third person had become a habit of late years, a sign of the immense detachment in his nature, combined with a terrible reluctance to relive the pain. To think in the first person was to conjure up the pain in all its fierceness, bitterness, indelibility. Therefore think of Caesar, not of I. Think of everything with a veil of impersonal narrative drawn over it. If *I* is not there, nor is the pain.

What should have been a pleasant exercise equipping Longhaired Gaul with the trappings of a Roman province had instead been dogged by the growing certainty that Caesar, who had done so much for Rome, was not going to be allowed to don his laurels in peace. What Pompey the Great had gotten away with all his life was not to be accorded to Caesar, thanks to a maleficent little group of senators who called themselves the *boni*—the "good men"—and had vowed to accord nothing to Caesar: to tear Caesar down and ruin him, strike all his laws from the tablets and send him into permanent exile. Led by Bibulus, with that yapping cur Cato working constantly behind the scenes to stiffen their resolve when it wavered, the *boni* had made Caesar's life a perpetual struggle for survival.

Of course he understood every reason why; what he couldn't manage to grasp was the mind-set of the *boni*, which seemed to him so utterly stupid that it beggared understanding. No use in telling himself, either, that if only he had relented a little in his compulsion to show up their ridiculous inadequacies, they might perhaps have been less determined to tear him down. Caesar had a temper, and Caesar did not suffer fools gladly.

Bibulus. He had been the start of it, at Lucullus's siege of Mitylene on the island of Lesbos, thirty-three years ago. Bibulus. So small and so soaked in malice that Caesar had lifted him bodily on to the top of a high closet, laughed at him and made him a figure of fun to their fellows.

Lucullus. Lucullus the commander at Mitylene. Who implied that Caesar had obtained a fleet of ships from the decrepit old King of Bithynia by prostituting himself—an accusation the *boni* had revived years later and used in the Forum Romanum as part of their political smear campaign. Other men ate feces and violated their daughters, but Caesar had sold his arse to King Nicomedes to obtain a fleet. Only time and some sensible advice from his mother had worn the accusation out from sheer lack of evidence. Lucullus, whose vices were disgusting. Lucullus, the intimate of Lucius Cornelius Sulla.

Sulla, who while Dictator had freed Caesar from that hideous priesthood Gaius Marius had inflicted on him at thirteen years of age—a priesthood that forbade him to don weapons of war or witness death. Sulla had freed him to spite the dead Marius, then sent him east, aged nineteen, mounted on a mule, to serve with Lucullus at Mitylene. Where Caesar had not endeared himself to Lucullus. When the battle came on, Lucullus had thrown Caesar to the arrows, except that Caesar walked out of it with the *corona civica*, the oak-leaf crown awarded for the most conspicuous bravery, so rarely won that its winner was entitled to wear the crown forever after on every public occasion, and have all and sundry rise to their feet to applaud him. How Bibulus had hated having to rise to his feet and applaud Caesar every time the Senate met! The oak-leaf crown had also entitled Caesar to enter the Senate, though he was only twenty years old; other men had to wait until they turned thirty. However, Caesar had already been a senator; the special priest of Jupiter Optimus Maximus was automatically a senator, and Caesar had been that until Sulla freed him. Which meant that Caesar had been a senator for thirty-eight of his fifty-two years of life.

Caesar's ambition had been to attain every political office at the correct age for a patrician and at the top of the poll—without bribing. Well, he couldn't have bribed; the *boni* would have pounced on him in an instant. He had achieved his ambition, as was obligatory for a Julian directly descended from the goddess Venus through her son, Aeneas. Not to mention a Julian directly descended from the god Mars through his son, Romulus, the founder of Rome. Mars: Ares, Venus: Aphrodite.

Though it was now six *nundinae* in the past, Caesar could still put himself back in Ephesus gazing at the statue of himself erected in the agora, and at its inscription: GAIUS JULIUS CAESAR, SON OF GAIUS, PONTIFEX MAXIMUS, IMPERATOR, CONSUL FOR THE SECOND TIME, DESCENDED FROM ARES AND APHRODITE, GOD MADE MANIFEST AND COMMON SAVIOR OF MANKIND. Naturally there had been statues of Pompey the Great in every agora between Olisippo and Damascus (all torn down as soon as he lost at Pharsalus), but none that could claim descent from any god, let alone Ares and Aphrodite. Oh, every statue of a Roman conqueror said things like GOD MADE MANIFEST AND COMMON SAVIOR OF MANKIND! To an eastern mentality, standard laudatory stuff. But what truly mattered to Caesar was *ancestry,* and ancestry was something that Pompey the Gaul from Picenum could never claim; his sole notable ancestor was Picus, the woodpecker totem. Yet there was Caesar's statue describing his ancestry for all of Ephesus to see. Yes, it mattered.

Caesar scarcely remembered his father, always absent on some duty or other for Gaius Marius, then dead when he bent to lace up his boot. Such an odd way to die, lacing up a boot. Thus had Caesar become *paterfamilias* at fifteen. It had been Mater, an Aurelia of the Cottae, who was both father and mother—strict, critical, stern, unsympathetic, but stuffed with sensible advice. For senatorial stock, the Julian family had been desperately poor, barely hanging on to enough money to satisfy the censors; Aurelia's dowry had been an insula apartment building in the Subura, one of Rome's most notorious stews, and there the family had lived until Caesar got himself elected Pontifex Maximus and could move into the Domus Publica, a minor palace owned by the State.

How Aurelia used to fret over his careless extravagance, his indifference to mountainous debt! And what dire straits insolvency had led him into! Then, when he conquered Long-haired Gaul, he had become even richer than Pompey the Great, if not as rich as Brutus. No Roman was as rich as Brutus, for in his Servilius Caepio guise he had fallen heir to the Gold of Tolosa. Which had made Brutus a very desirable match for Julia until Pompey the Great had fallen in love with her. Caesar had needed Pompey's political clout more than young Brutus's money, so . . .

Julia. All of my beloved women are dead, two of them trying to bear sons. Sweetest little Cinnilla, darling Julia, each just over the threshold of adult life. Neither ever caused me a single heartache save in their dying. Unfair, unfair! I close my eyes and there they are: Cinnilla, wife of my youth; Julia, my only daughter. The other Julia, Aunt Julia the wife of that awful old monster, Gaius Marius. Her perfume can still reduce me to tears when I smell it on some unknown woman. My childhood would have been loveless had it not been for her hugs and kisses. Mater, the perfect partisan adversary, was incapable of hugs and kisses for fear that overt love would corrupt me. She thought me too proud, too conscious of my intelligence, too prone to be royal.

But they are all gone, my beloved women. Now I am alone.

No wonder I begin to feel my age.

It was on the scales of the gods which one of them had had the harder time succeeding, Caesar or Sulla. Not much in it: a hair, a fibril. They had both been forced to preserve their *dignitas*—their personal share of public fame, of standing and worth—by marching on Rome. They had both been made Dictator, the sole office above democratic process or future prosecution. The difference between them lay in how they had behaved once appointed Dictator: Sulla had proscribed, filled the empty Treasury by killing wealthy senators and knight-businessmen and confiscating their estates; Caesar had preferred clemency, was forgiving his enemies and allowing the majority of them to keep their property.

The *boni* had forced Caesar to march on Rome. Consciously, deliberately—even gleefully!—they had thrust Rome into civil war rather than accord Caesar one iota of what they had given to Pompey the Great freely. Namely, the right to stand for the consulship without needing to present himself in person inside the city. The moment a man holding imperium crossed the sacred boundary into the city, he lost that imperium and was liable to prosecution in the courts. And the *boni* had rigged the courts to convict Caesar of treason the moment he laid down his governor's imperium in order to seek a second, perfectly legal, consulship. He had petitioned to be allowed to stand *in absentia*, a reasonable request, but the *boni* had blocked it and blocked all his overtures to reach an agreement. When all else had failed, he emulated Sulla and marched on Rome. Not to preserve his head; that had never been in danger. The sentence in a court stacked with *boni* minions would have been permanent exile, a far worse fate than death.

Treason? To pass laws that distributed Rome's public lands more equitably? *Treason?* To pass laws that prevented governors from looting their provinces? *Treason?* To push the boundaries of the Roman world back to a natural frontier along the Rhenus River and thus preserve Italy and Our Sea from the Germans? *These were treasonous?* In passing these laws, in doing these things, Caesar had betrayed his country?

To the *boni*, yes, he had. Why? How could that be? Because to the *boni* such laws and actions were an offense against the *mos maiorum*—the way custom and tradition said Rome worked. His laws and actions changed what Rome always had been. No matter that the changes were for the common good, for Rome's security, for the happiness and prosperity not only of all Romans, but of Rome's provincial subjects too: they were not laws and actions in keeping with the old ways, the ways that had been appropriate for a tiny city athwart the salt routes of central Italy six hundred years ago. Why was it that the *boni* couldn't see that the old ways were no longer of use to the sole great power west of the Euphrates River? Rome had inherited the entire western world, yet some of the men who governed her still lived in the time of the infant city-state.

To the *boni*, change was the enemy, and Caesar was the enemy's most brilliant servant ever. As Cato used to shout from the rostra in the Forum Romanum, Caesar was the human embodiment of pure evil. All because Caesar's mind was clear enough and acute enough to know that unless change of the right kind came, Rome would die, molder away to stinking tatters only fit for a leper.

So here on this ship stood Caesar Dictator, the ruler of the world. He, who had never wanted anything more than his due—to be legally elected consul for the second time ten years after his first consulship, as the *lex Genucia* prescribed. Then, after that second consulship, he had planned to become an elder statesman more sensible and efficacious than that vacillating, timorous mouse, Cicero. Accept a senatorial commission from time to time to lead an army in Rome's service as only Caesar could lead an army. But to end in ruling the world? That was a tragedy worthy of Aeschylus or Sophocles.

Most of Caesar's foreign service had been spent at the western end of Our Sea—the Spains, the Gauls. His service in the east had been limited to Asia Province and Cilicia, had never led him to Syria or Egypt or the awesome interior of Anatolia.

The closest he had come to Egypt was Cyprus, years before Cato had annexed it; it had been ruled then by Ptolemy the Cyprian, the younger brother of the then ruler of Egypt, Ptolemy Auletes. In Cyprus he had dallied in the arms of a daughter of Mithridates the Great, and bathed in the sea foam from which his ancestress Venus/ Aphrodite had been born. The elder sister of this Mithridatid lady had been Cleopatra Tryphaena, first wife of King Ptolemy Auletes of Egypt, and mother of the present Queen Cleopatra.

He had had dealings with Ptolemy Auletes when he had been senior consul eleven years ago, and thought now of Auletes with wry affection. Auletes had desperately needed to have Rome confirm his tenure of the Egyptian throne, and wanted "Friend and Ally of the Roman People" status as well. Caesar the senior consul had been pleased to legislate him both, in return for six thousand talents of gold. A thousand of those talents had gone to Pompey and a thousand more to Marcus Crassus, but the four thousand left had enabled Caesar to do what the Senate had refused him the funds to do—recruit and equip the necessary number of legions to conquer Gaul and contain the Germans.

Oh, Marcus Crassus! How he had lusted after Egypt! He had

to venture out to sea—the customs vessels that patrolled the seven mouths of river Nilus, he fancied. They had sighted none on their way south, but that was not to say that sharp eyes atop some lofty Delta tree hadn't spied this Roman fleet. Which would account for such readiness.

Hmmm. Quite a reception committee. Caesar had the bugler blow a call to arms, then followed that with a series of flags that told his ship's captains to stand and wait for further orders. He had his servant drape his *toga praetexta* about him, put his *corona civica* on his thinning pale gold hair, and donned his maroon senatorial shoes with the silver crescent buckles denoting a senior curule magistrate. Ready, he stood amidships at the break in the rail and watched the rapid approach of an undecked customs boat, a fierce fellow standing in its bows.

"What gives you the right to enter Alexandria, Roman?" the fellow shouted, keeping his vessel at a hailing distance.

"The right of any man who comes in peace to buy water and provisions!" Caesar called, mouth twitching.

"There's a spring seven miles west of the Eunostus Harbor—you can find water there! We have no provisions to sell, so be on your way, Roman!"

"I'm afraid I can't do that, my good man."

"Do you *want* a war? You're outnumbered already, and these are but a tenth of what we can launch!"

"I have had my fill of wars, but if you insist, then I'll fight another one," Caesar said. "You've put on a fine show, but there are at least fifty ways I could roll you up, even without any warships. I am Gaius Julius Caesar Dictator."

The aggressive fellow chewed his lip. "All right, you can go ashore yourself, whoever you are, but your ships stay right here in the harbor roads, understood?"

"I need a pinnace able to hold twenty-five men," Caesar called. "It had better be forthcoming at once, my man, or there will be big trouble."

A grin dawned; the aggressive fellow rapped an order at his oarsmen and the little ship skimmed away.

Publius Rufrius appeared at Caesar's shoulder, looking very anxious. "They seem to have plenty of marines," he said, "but the far-sighted among us haven't been able to detect any soldiers ashore, apart from some pretty fellows behind the palace area wall—the Royal Guard, I imagine. What do you intend to do, Caesar?"

"Go ashore with my lictors in the boat they provide."

"Let me lower our own boats and send some troops with you."

"Certainly not," Caesar said calmly. "Your duty is to keep our ships together and out of harm's way—and stop *ineptes* like Tiberius Nero from chopping off his foot with his own sword."

Shortly thereafter a large pinnace manned by sixteen oarsmen hove alongside. Caesar's eyes roamed across the outfits of his lictors, still led by the faithful Fabius, as they tumbled down to fill up the board seats. Yes, every brass boss on their broad black leather belts was bright and shiny, every crimson tunic was clean and minus creases, every pair of crimson leather *caligae* properly laced. They cradled their *fasces* more gently and reverently than a cat carried her kittens; the crisscrossed red leather thongs were exactly as they should be, and the single-headed axes, one to a bundle, glittered wickedly between the thirty red-dyed rods that made up each bundle. Satisfied, Caesar leaped as lightly as a boy into the craft and disposed himself neatly in the stern.

The pinnace headed for a jetty adjacent to the Akron theater but outside the wall of the Royal Enclosure. Here a crowd of what seemed ordinary citizens had collected, waving their fists and shouting threats of murder in Macedonian-accented Greek. When the boat tied up and the lictors climbed out the citizens backed away a little, obviously taken aback at such calmness, such alien but impressive splendor. Once his twenty-four lictors had lined up in a column of twelve pairs, Caesar made light work of getting out himself, then stood arranging the folds of his toga fussily. Brows raised, he stared haughtily at the crowd, still shouting murder.

"Who's in charge?" he asked it.

No one, it seemed.

"On, Fabius, on!"

His lictors walked into the middle of the crowd, with Caesar strolling in their wake. Just verbal aggression, he thought, smiling aloofly to right and left. Interesting. Hearsay is true, the Alexandrians don't like Romans. Where *is* Pompeius Magnus?

A striking gate stood in the Royal Enclosure wall, its pylon sides joined by a square-cut lintel; it was heavily gilded and bright with many colors, strange, flat, two-dimensional scenes and symbols. Here further progress was rendered impossible by a detachment of the Royal Guard. Rufrius was right, they were very pretty in their Greek hoplite armor of linen corselets oversewn with silver metal scales, gaudy purple tunics, high brown boots, silver nose-pieced helmets bearing purple horsehair plumes. They also looked, thought an intrigued Caesar, as if they knew how to conduct themselves in a scrap rather than a battle. Considering the history of the royal House of Ptolemy, probably true. There was always an Alexandrian mob out to change one Ptolemy for another Ptolemy, sex not an issue.

"Halt!" said the captain, a hand on his sword hilt.

Caesar approached through an aisle of lictors and came to an obedient halt. "I would like to see the King and Queen," he said.

"Well, you can't see the King and Queen, Roman, and that is that. Now get back on board your ship and sail away."

"Tell their royal majesties that I am Gaius Julius Caesar."

The captain made a rude noise. "Ha ha ha! If you're Caesar, then I'm Taweret, the hippopotamus goddess!" he sneered.

"You ought not to take the names of your gods in vain."

A blink. "I'm not a filthy Egyptian, I'm an Alexandrian! My god is Serapis. Now go on, be off with you!"

"I *am* Caesar."

"Caesar's in Asia Minor or Anatolia or whatever."

"Caesar is in Alexandria, and asking very politely to see the King and Queen."

"Um—I don't believe you."

"Um—you had better, Captain, or else the full wrath of Rome will fall upon Alexandria and you won't have a job. Nor will the King and Queen. Look at my lictors, you fool! If you can count, then count them, you fool! Twenty-four, isn't that right? And which Roman curule magistrate is preceded by twenty-four lictors? One only—the dictator. Now let me through and escort me to the royal audience chamber," Caesar said pleasantly.

Beneath his bluster the captain was afraid. What a situation to be in! No one knew better than he that there was no one in the palace who ought to be in the palace—no King, no Queen, no Lord High Chamberlain. Not a soul with the authority to see and deal with this up-himself Roman who did indeed have twenty-four lictors. Could he be Caesar? Surely not! Why would Caesar be in Alexandria, of all places? Yet here definitely stood a Roman with twenty-four lictors, clad in a ludicrous purple-bordered white blanket, with some leaves on his head and a plain cylinder of ivory resting on his bare right forearm between his cupped hand and the crook of his elbow. No sword, no armor, not a soldier in sight.

Macedonian ancestry and a wealthy father had bought the captain his position, but mental acuity was not a part of the package. Yet, yet— he licked his lips. "All right, Roman, to the audience room it is," he said with a sigh. "Only I don't know what you're going to do when you get there, because there's nobody home."

"Indeed?" asked Caesar, beginning to walk behind his lictors again, which forced the captain to send a man running on ahead to guide the party. "Where is everybody?"

"At Pelusium."

"I see."

Though it was summer, the day was perfect; low humidity, a cool breeze to fan the brow, a caressing balminess that carried a hint of perfume from gloriously flowering trees, nodding bell blooms of some strange plant below them. The paving was brown-streaked fawn marble and polished to a mirror finish—slippery as ice when it rains. Or does it rain in Alexandria? Perhaps it doesn't.

"A delightful climate," he remarked.

"The best in the world," said the captain, sure of it.

"Am I the first Roman you've seen here lately?"

"The first announcing he's higher than a governor, at any rate. The last Romans we had here were when Gnaeus Pompeius came last year to pinch warships and wheat off the Queen." He chuckled reminiscently. "Rude sort of young chap, wouldn't take no for an answer, though her majesty told him the country's in famine. Oh, she diddled him! Filled up sixty cargo ships with dates."

"Dates?"

"Dates. He sailed off thinking the holds were full of wheat."

"Dear me, poor young Gnaeus Pompeius. I imagine his father was not at all pleased, though Lentulus Crus might have been—Epicures love a new taste thrill."

The audience chamber stood in a building of its own, if size was anything to go by; perhaps an anteroom or two for the visiting ambassadors to rest in, but certainly not live in. It was the same place to which Gnaeus Pompey had been conducted: a huge bare hall with a polished marble floor in complicated patterns of different colors; walls either filled with those bright paintings of two-dimensional people and plants, or covered in gold leaf; a purple marble dais with two thrones upon it, one on the top tier in figured ebony and gilt, and a similar but smaller one on the next tier down; otherwise, not a stick of furniture to be seen.

Leaving Caesar and his lictors alone in the room, the captain hurried off, presumably to see who he could find to receive them.

Eyes meeting Fabius's, Caesar grinned. "What a situation!"

"We've been in worse situations than this, Caesar."

"Don't tempt Fortuna, Fabius. I wonder what it feels like to sit upon a throne?"

Caesar bounded up the steps of the dais and sat gingerly in the magnificent chair on top, its gold, jewel-encrusted detail quite extraordinary at close quarters. What looked like an eye, except that its outer margin was extended and swelled into an odd, triangular tear; a cobra head; a scarab beetle; leopard paws; human feet; a peculiar key; stick-like symbols.

"Is it comfortable, Caesar?"

"No chair having a back can be comfortable for a man in a toga, which is why we sit in curule chairs," Caesar answered. He relaxed and closed his eyes. "Camp on the floor," he said after a while; "it seems we're in for a long wait."

Two of the younger lictors sighed in relief, but Fabius shook his head, scandalized. "Can't do that, Caesar. It would look sloppy if someone came in and caught us."

As there was no water clock, it was difficult to measure time, but to the younger lictors it seemed like hours that they stood in a semicircle with their *fasces* grounded delicately between their feet, axed upper ends held between their hands. Caesar continued to sleep—one of his famous cat naps.

"Hey, get off the throne!" said a young female voice.

Caesar opened one eye, but didn't move.

"I said, get off the throne!"

"Who is it commands me?" Caesar asked.

"The royal Princess Arsinoë of the House of Ptolemy!"

That straightened Caesar, though he didn't get up, just looked with both eyes open at the speaker, now standing at the foot of the dais. Behind her stood a little boy and two men.

About fifteen years old, Caesar judged: a busty, strapping girl with masses of golden hair, blue eyes, and a face that ought to have been pretty—it was regular enough of feature—but was not. Thanks to its expression, Caesar decided—arrogant, angry, quaintly authoritarian. She was clad in Greek style, but her robe was genuine Tyrian purple, a color so dark it seemed black, yet with the slightest movement was shot with highlights of plum and crimson. In her hair she wore a gem-studded coronet, around her neck a fabulous jeweled collar, bracelets galore on her bare arms; her earlobes were unduly long, probably due to the weight of the pendants dangling from them.

The little boy looked to be about nine or ten and was very like Princess Arsinoë—same face, same coloring, same build. He too wore Tyrian purple, a tunic and Greek *chlamys* cloak.

Both the men were clearly attendants of some kind, but the one standing protectively beside the boy was a feeble creature, whereas the other, closer to Arsinoë, was a person to be reckoned with. Tall, of splendid physique, quite as fair as the royal children, he had intelligent, calculating eyes and a firm mouth.

"And where do we go from here?" Caesar asked calmly.

"Nowhere until you prostrate yourself before me! In the absence of the King, I am regnant in Alexandria, and I command you to come down from there and abase yourself!" said Arsinoë. She looked at the lictors balefully. "All of you, on the floor!"

"Neither Caesar nor his lictors obey the commands of petty princelings," Caesar said gently. "In the absence of the King, I am regnant in Alexandria by virtue of the terms of the wills of Ptolemy Alexander and your father Auletes." He leaned forward. "Now, Princess, let us get down to business—and don't look like a child in need of a spanking, or I might have one of my lictors pluck a rod from his bundle and administer it." His gaze went to Arsinoë's impassive attendant. "And you are?" he asked.

"Ganymedes, eunuch tutor and guardian of my Princess."

"Well, Ganymedes, you look like a man of good sense, so I'll address my comments to you."

"You will address me!" Arsinoë yelled, face mottling. "And get down off the throne! Abase yourself!"

"Hold your tongue!" Caesar snapped. "Ganymedes, I require suitable accommodation for myself and my senior staff inside the Royal Enclosure, and sufficient fresh bread, green vegetables, oil, wine, eggs and water for my troops, who will remain on board my ships until I've discovered what's going on here. It is a sad state of affairs when the Dictator of Rome arrives anywhere on the surface of this globe to unnecessary aggression and pointless inhospitality. Do you understand me?"

"Yes, great Caesar."

"Good!" Caesar rose to his feet and walked down the steps. "The first thing you can do for me, however, is remove these two obnoxious children."

"I cannot do that, Caesar, if you want me to remain here."

"Why?"

"Dolichos is a whole man. He may remove Prince Ptolemy Philadelphus, but the Princess Arsinoë may not be in the company of a whole man unchaperoned."

"Are there any more in your castrated state?" Caesar asked, mouth twitching; Alexandria was proving amusing.

"Of course."

"Then go with the children, deposit Princess Arsinoë with some other eunuch, and return to me immediately."

Princess Arsinoë, temporarily squashed by Caesar's tone when he told her to hold her tongue, was getting ready to liberate it, but Ganymedes took her firmly by the shoulder and led her out, the boy Philadelphus and his tutor hurrying ahead.

"What a situation!" said Caesar to Fabius yet again.

"My hand itched to remove that rod, Caesar."

"So did mine." The Great Man sighed. "Still, from what one hears, the Ptolemaic brood is rather singular. At least Ganymedes is rational—but then, he's not royal."

"I thought eunuchs were fat and effeminate."

"I believe that those who are castrated as small boys are, but if the testicles are not enucleated until after puberty has set in, that may not be the case."

Ganymedes returned quickly, a smile pasted to his face. "I am at your service, great Caesar."

"Ordinary Caesar will do nicely, thank you. Now why is the court at Pelusium?"

The eunuch looked surprised. "To fight the war," he said.

"What war?"

"The war between the King and Queen, Caesar. Earlier in the year, famine forced the price of food up, and Alexandria blamed the Queen—the King is but thirteen years old—and rebelled." Ganymedes looked grim. "There is no peace here, you see. The King is controlled by his tutor, Theodotus, and the Lord High Chamberlain, Potheinus. They're ambitious men, you understand. Queen Cleopatra is their enemy."

"I take it that she fled?"

"Yes, but south to Memphis and the Egyptian priests. The Queen is also Pharaoh."

"Isn't every Ptolemy on the throne also Pharaoh?"

"No, Caesar, far from it. The children's father, Auletes, was never Pharaoh. He refused to placate the Egyptian priests, who have great influence over the native Egyptians of Nilus. Whereas Queen Cleopatra spent some of her childhood in Memphis with the priests. When she came to the throne they anointed her Pharaoh. King and Queen are Alexandrian titles, they have no weight at all in Egypt of the Nilus, which is proper Egypt."

"So Queen Cleopatra, who is Pharaoh, fled to Memphis and the priests. Why not abroad from Alexandria, like her father when he was spilled from the throne?" Caesar asked, fascinated.

"When a Ptolemy flees abroad from Alexandria, he or she must depart penniless. There is no great treasure in Alexandria. The treasure vaults lie in Memphis, under the authority of the priests. So unless the Ptolemy is also Pharaoh—no money. Queen Cleopatra was given money in Memphis, and went to Syria to recruit an army. She has but recently returned with that army, and has gone to earth on the northern flank of Mount Casius outside Pelusium."

Caesar frowned. "A mountain outside Pelusium? I didn't think there were any until Sinai."

"A very big sandhill, Caesar."

"Ahah. Continue, please."

"General Achillas brought the King's army to the southern side of the mount, and is camped there. Not long ago, Potheinus and Theodotus accompanied the King and the war fleet to Pelusium. A battle was expected when I last heard," said Ganymedes.

"So Egypt—or rather, Alexandria—is in the midst of a civil war," said Caesar, beginning to pace. "Has there been no sign of Gnaeus Pompeius Magnus in the vicinity?"

"Not that I know of, Caesar. Certainly he is not in Alexandria. Is it true, then, that you defeated him in Thessaly?"

"Oh, yes. Decisively. He left Cyprus some days ago, I had believed bound for Egypt." No, Caesar thought, watching Ganymedes, this man is genuinely ignorant of the whereabouts of my old friend and adversary. Where *is* Pompeius, then? Did he perhaps utilize that spring seven miles west of the Eunostus Harbor and sail on to Cyrenaica without stopping? He stopped pacing. "Very well, it seems I stand *in loco parentis* for these ridiculous children and their squabble. Therefore you will send two couriers to Pelusium, one to see King Ptolemy, the other to see Queen Cleopatra. I require both sovereigns to present themselves here to me in their own palace. Is that clear?"

Ganymedes looked uncomfortable. "I foresee no difficulties with the King, Caesar, but it may not be possible for the Queen to come to Alexandria. One sight of her, and the mob will lynch her." He lifted his lip in contempt. "The favorite sport of the Alexandrian mob is tearing an unpopular ruler to pieces with their bare hands. In the agora, which is very spacious." He coughed. "I must add, Caesar, that for your own protection you would be wise to confine yourself and your senior staff to the Royal Enclosure. At the moment the mob is ruling."

"Do what you can, Ganymedes. Now, if you don't mind, I'd like to be conducted to my quarters. And you will make sure that my soldiers are properly victualed. Naturally I will pay for every drop and crumb. Even at inflated famine prices."

* * *

"So," said Caesar to Rufrius over a late dinner in his new quarters, "I am no closer to learning the fate of poor Magnus, but I fear for him. Ganymedes was in ignorance, though I don't trust the fellow. If another eunuch, Potheinus, can aspire to rule through a juvenile Ptolemy, why not Ganymedes with Arsinoë?"

"They've certainly treated us shabbily," Rufrius said as he looked about. "In palace terms, they've put us in a shack." He grinned. "I keep him away from you, Caesar, but Tiberius Nero is most put out at having to share with another military tribune—not to mention that he expected to dine with you."

"Why on earth would he want to dine with one of the least Epicurean noblemen in Rome? Oh, the gods preserve me from these insufferable aristocrats!"

Just as if, thought Rufrius, inwardly smiling, he were not himself insufferable or aristocratic. But the insufferable part of him isn't connected to his antique origins. What he can't say to me without insulting *my* birth *is* that he loathes having to employ an incompetent like Nero for no other reason than that he is a patrician Claudius. The obligations of nobility irk him.

For two more days the Roman fleet remained at anchor with the infantry still on board; pressured, the Interpreter had allowed the German cavalry to be ferried ashore with their horses and put into a good grazing camp outside the crumbling city walls on Lake Mareotis. The locals gave these extraordinary-looking barbarians a wide berth; they went almost naked, were tattooed, and wore their never-cut hair in a tortuous system of knots and rolls on top of their heads. Besides, they spoke not a word of Greek.

Ignoring Ganymedes's warning to remain within the Royal Enclosure, Caesar poked and pried everywhere during those two days, escorted only by his lictors, indifferent to danger. In Alexandria, he discovered, lay marvels worthy of his personal attention—the lighthouse, the Heptastadion, the water and drainage systems, the naval dispositions, the buildings, the people.

The city itself occupied a narrow spit of limestone between the sea and a vast freshwater lake; less than two miles separated the sea from this boundless source of sweet water, eminently drinkable even at this summer season. Asking questions revealed that Lake Mareotis was fed from canals that linked it to the big westernmost mouth of Nilus, the Canopic Nilus; because Nilus rose in high summer rather than in early spring, Mareotis avoided the usual concomitants of river-fed lakes—stagnation, mosquitoes. One canal, twenty miles long, was wide enough to provide two lanes for barges and customs ships, and was always jammed with traffic.

A different, single canal came off Lake Mareotis at the Moon Gate end of the city; it terminated at the western harbor, though its waters did not intermingle with the sea, so any current in it was diffusive, not propulsive. A series of big bronze sluice gates were inserted in its walls, raised and lowered by a system of pulleys from ox-driven capstans. The city's water supply was drawn out of the canal through gently sloping pipes, each district's inlet equipped with a sluice gate. Other sluice gates spanned the canal from side to side and could be closed off to permit the dredging of silt from its bottom.

One of the first things Caesar did was to climb the verdant cone called the Paneium, an artificial hill built of stones tamped down with earth and planted with lush gardens, shrubs, low palms. A paved spiral road wound up to its apex, and man-made streamlets with occasional waterfalls tumbled to a drain at its base. From the apex it was possible to see for miles, everything was so flat.

The city was laid out on a rectangular grid and had no back lanes or alleys. Every street was wide, but two were far wider than any roads

Caesar had ever seen—over a hundred feet from gutter to gutter. Canopic Avenue ran from the Sun Gate at the eastern end of the city to the Moon Gate at the western end; Royal Avenue ran from the gate in the Royal Enclosure wall south to the old walls. The world-famous museum library lay inside the Royal Enclosure, but the other major public buildings were situated at the intersection of the two avenues—the agora, the gymnasium, the courts of justice, the Paneium or Hill of Pan.

Rome's districts were logical, in that they were named after the hills upon which they sprawled, or the valleys between; in flat Alexandria the persnickety Macedonian founders had divided the place up into five arbitrary districts—Alpha, Beta, Gamma, Delta and Epsilon. The Royal Enclosure lay within Beta District; east of it was not Gamma, but Delta District, the home of hundreds of thousands of Jews who spilled south into Epsilon, which they shared with many thousands of Metics—foreigners with rights of residence rather than citizenship. Alpha was the commercial area of the two harbors, and Gamma, in the southwest, was also known as Rhakotis, the name of the village pre-dating Alexandria's genesis.

Most who lived inside the old walls were at best modestly well off. The wealthiest in the population, all pure Macedonians, lived in beautiful garden suburbs west of the Moon Gate outside the walls, scattered between a vast necropolis set in parklands. Wealthy foreigners like Roman merchants lived outside the walls east of the Sun Gate. Stratification, thought Caesar: no matter where I look, I see stratification.

Social stratification was extreme and absolutely rigid—no New Men for Alexandria!

In this place of three million souls, only three hundred thousand held the Alexandrian citizenship: these were the pure-blood descendants of the original Macedonian army settlers, and they guarded their privileges ruthlessly. The Interpreter, who was the highest official, had to be of pure Macedonian stock; so did the Recorder, the Chief Judge, the Accountant, the Night Commander. In fact, all the highest offices, commercial as well as public, belonged to the Macedonians. The layers beneath were stepped by blood too: hybrid Macedonian Greeks, then plain Greeks, then the Jews and Metics, with the hybrid Egyptian Greeks (who were a servant class) at the very bottom. One of the reasons for this, Caesar learned, lay in the food supply. Alexandria did not publicly subsidize food for its poor, as Rome had always done, and was doing more and more. No doubt this was why the Alexandrians were so aggressive, and why the mob had such power. *Panem et circenses* is an excellent policy. Keep the poor fed and entertained, and they do not rise. How blind these eastern rulers are!

Two social facts fascinated Caesar most of all. One was that native Egyptians were forbidden to live in Alexandria. The other was even more bizarre. A highborn Macedonian father would deliberately castrate his cleverest, most promising son in order to qualify the adolescent boy for employment in the palace, where he had a chance to rise to the highest job of all, Lord High Chamberlain. To have a relative in the palace was tantamount to having the ear of the King and Queen. Much though the Alexandrians despise Egyptians, thought Caesar, they have absorbed so many Egyptian customs that what exists here today is the most curious muddle of East and West anywhere in the world.

Not all his time was devoted to such musings. Ignoring the growls and menacing faces, Caesar inspected the city's military installations minutely, storing every fact in his phenomenal memory. One never knew when one might need these facts. Defense was maritime, not terrestrial. Clearly modern Alexandria feared no land invasions; invasion if it came would be from the sea, and undoubtedly Roman.

Tucked in the bottom eastern corner of the western, Eunostus, harbor, was the Cibotus—the Box—a heavily fortified inner harbor fenced off by walls as thick as those at Rhodes, its entrance barred by formidably massive chains. It was surrounded by ship sheds and bristled with artillery; room for fifty or sixty big war galleys in the sheds, Caesar judged. Not that the Cibotus sheds were the only ones; more lay around Eunostus itself.

All of which made Alexandria unique, a stunning blend of physical beauty and ingenious functional engineering. But it was not perfect. It had its fair share of slums and crime, the wide streets in the poorer Gamma-Rhakotis and Epsilon Districts were piled high with rotting refuse and animal corpses, and once away from the two avenues there was a dearth of public fountains and communal latrines. And absolutely no bathhouses.

There was also a local insanity. *Birds!* Ibises. Of two kinds, the white and the black, they were sacred. To kill one was unthinkable; if an ignorant foreigner did, he was dragged off to the agora to be torn into little pieces. Well aware of their sacrosanctity, the ibises exploited it shamelessly.

At the time Caesar arrived they were in residence, for they fled the summer rains in far off Aethiopia. This meant that they could fly superbly, but once in Alexandria, they didn't. Instead, they stood around in literal thousands upon thousands all over those wonderful roads, crowding the main intersections so densely that they looked like an extra layer of paving. Their copious, rather liquid droppings fouled every inch of any surface whereon people walked, and for all its civic pride, Alexandria seemed to employ no one to wash the mounting excreta away. Probably when the birds flew back to Aethiopia the city engaged in a massive cleanup, but in the meantime—! Traffic weaved and wobbled; carts had to hire an extra man to walk ahead and push the creatures aside. Within the Royal Enclosure a small army of slaves gathered up the ibises tenderly, put them into cages and then casually emptied the cages into the streets outside.

About the most one could say for them was that they gobbled up cockroaches, spiders, scorpions, beetles and snails, and picked through the scraps tossed out by fishmongers, butchers and pasty makers. Otherwise, thought Caesar, secretly grinning as his lictors cleared a path for him through the ibises, they are the biggest nuisances in all creation.

On the third day a lone "barge" arrived in the Great Harbor and was skillfully rowed to the Royal Harbor, a small enclosed area abutting on to Cape Lochias. Rufrius had sent word of its advent, so Caesar strolled to a vantage point from which he could see disembarkation perfectly, yet was not in close enough proximity to attract attention.

The barge was a floating pleasure palace of enormous size, all gold and purple; a huge, temple-like cabin stood abaft the mast, complete with a pillared portico.

A series of litters came down to the pier, each carried by six men matched for height and appearance; the King's litter was gilded, gem-encrusted, curtained with Tyrian purple and adorned with a plume of fluffy purple feathers on each corner of its faience-tiled roof. His majesty was carried on interlocked arms from the temple-cabin to the litter and inserted inside with exquisite care; a fair, pouting, pretty lad just on the cusp of puberty. After the King came a tall fellow with mouse-brown curls and a finely featured, handsome face; Potheinus the Lord High Chamberlain, Caesar decided, for he wore purple, a nice shade somewhere between Tyrian and the gaudy magenta of the Royal Guard, and a heavy gold necklace of peculiar design. Then came a slight, effeminate and elderly man in a purple slightly inferior to Potheinus's; his carmined lips and rouged cheeks sat garishly in a petulant face. Theodotus the tutor. Always good to see the opposition before they see you.

Caesar hurried back to his paltry accommodation and waited for the royal summons.

It came, but not for some time. Back to the audience chamber behind his lictors, to find the King seated not on the top throne but on the lower one. Interesting. His elder sister was absent, yet he did not feel qualified to occupy her chair. He wore the garb of Macedonian kings: Tyrian purple tunic, *chlamys* cloak, and a wide-brimmed Tyrian purple hat with the white ribbon of the diadem tied around its tall crown like a band.

The audience was extremely formal and very short. The King spoke as if by rote with his eyes fixed on Theodotus, after which Caesar found himself dismissed without an opportunity to state his business.

Potheinus followed him out.

"A word in private, great Caesar?"

"Caesar will do. My place or yours?"

"Mine, I think. I must apologize," Potheinus went on in a oily voice as he walked beside Caesar and behind the lictors, "for the standard of your accommodation. A silly insult. That idiot Ganymedes should have put you in the guest palace."

"Ganymedes, an idiot? I didn't think so," Caesar said.

"He has ideas above his station."

"Ah."

Potheinus possessed his own palace among that profusion of buildings, situated on Cape Lochias itself and having a fine view not of the Great Harbor but of the sea. Had the Lord High Chamberlain wished it, he might have walked out his back door and down to a little cove wherein he could paddle his pampered feet.

"Very nice," Caesar said, sitting in a backless chair.

"May I offer you the wine of Samos or Chios?"

"Neither, thank you."

"Spring water, then? Herbal tea?"

"No."

Potheinus seated himself opposite, his inscrutable grey eyes on Caesar. *He may not be a king, but he bears himself like one. The face is weathered yet still beautiful, and the eyes are unsettling. Dauntingly intelligent eyes, cooler even than mine. He rules his feelings absolutely, and he is politic. If necessary, he will sit here all day waiting for me to make the opening move. Which suits me. I don't mind moving first, it is my advantage.*

"What brings you to Alexandria, Caesar?"

"Gnaeus Pompeius Magnus. I'm looking for him."

Potheinus blinked, genuinely surprised. "Looking in person for a defeated enemy? Surely your legates could do that."

"Surely they could, but I like to do my opponents honor, and there is no honor in a legate, Potheinus. Pompeius Magnus and I have been friends and colleagues these twenty-three years, and at one time he was my son-in-law. That we ended in choosing opposite sides in a civil war can't alter what we are to each other."

Potheinus's face was losing color; he lifted his priceless goblet to his lips and drank as if his mouth had gone dry. "You may have been friends, but Pompeius Magnus is now your enemy."

"Enemies come from alien cultures, Lord High Chamberlain, not from among the ranks of one's own people. Adversary is a better word—a word allowing all the latitude things in common predicate. No, I don't pursue Pompeius Magnus as an avenger," Caesar said, not moving an inch, though somewhere inside him a cold lump was forming. "My policy," he went on levelly, "has been clemency, and my policy will continue to be clemency. I've come to find Pompeius Magnus myself so that I can extend my hand to him in true friendship. It would be a poor thing to enter a Senate containing none but sycophants."

"I do not understand," Potheinus said, skin quite bleached. No, no, I cannot tell this man what we did in Pelusium! We mistook the matter, we have done the unforgivable. The fate of Pompeius Magnus will have to remain our secret. Theodotus! I must find an excuse to leave here and head him off!

But it was not to be. Theodotus bustled in like a housewife, followed closely by two kilt-clad slaves bearing a big jar between them. They put it down and stood stiffly.

All Theodotus's attention was fixed on Caesar, whom he eyed in obvious appreciation. "The great Gaius Julius Caesar!" he fluted. "Oh, what an honor! I am Theodotus, tutor to his royal majesty, and I bring you a gift, great Caesar." He tittered. "In fact, I bring you *two* gifts!"

No answer from Caesar, who sat very straight, his right hand holding the ivory rod of his imperium just as it had all along, his left hand cuddling the folds of toga over his shoulder. The generous, slightly uptilted mouth, sensuous and humorous, had gone thin, and the eyes were two black-ringed pellets of ice.

Blithely unaware, Theodotus stepped forward and held out his hand; Caesar laid the rod in his lap and extended his to take the seal ring. A lion's head, and around the outside of the mane the letters CN POMP MAG. He didn't look at it, just closed his fingers on it until they clenched it, white-knuckled.

One of the servants lifted the jar's lid while the other put a hand inside, fiddled for a moment, then lifted out Pompey's head by its thatch of silver hair, gone dull from the natron, trickling steadily into the jar.

The face looked very peaceful, lids lowered over those vivid blue eyes that used to gaze around the Senate so innocently, so much the eyes of the spoiled child he was. The snub nose, the thin small mouth, the dented chin, the round Gallic face. It was all there, all perfectly preserved, though the slightly freckled skin had gone grey and leathery.

"Who did this?" Caesar asked of Potheinus.

"Why, we did, of course!" Theodotus cried, and looked impish, delighted with himself. "As I said to Potheinus, dead men do not bite. We have removed your enemy, great Caesar. In fact, we have removed two of your enemies! The day after this one came, the great Lentulus Crus arrived, so we killed him too. Though we didn't think you'd want to see *his* head."

Caesar rose without a word and strode to the door, opened it and snapped, "Fabius! Cornelius!"

The two lictors entered immediately; only the rigorous training of years disciplined their reaction as they beheld the face of Pompey the Great, running natron.

"A towel!" Caesar demanded of Theodotus, and took the head from the servant who held it. "*Get me a towel!* A purple one!"

But it was Potheinus who moved, clicked his fingers at a bewildered slave. "You heard. A purple towel. At once."

Finally realizing that the great Caesar was not pleased, Theodotus gaped at him in astonishment. "But, Caesar, we have eliminated your enemy!" he cried. "Dead men do not bite."

Caesar spoke softly. "Keep your tongue between your teeth, you mincing pansy! What do you know of Rome or Romans? What kind of men are you, to do this?" He looked down at the dripping head, his eyes tearless. "Oh, Magnus, would that our destinies were reversed!" He turned to Potheinus. "Where is his body?"

The damage was done; Potheinus decided to brazen it out. "I have no idea. It was left on the beach at Pelusium."

"Then find it, you castrated freak, or I'll tear Alexandria down around your empty scrotum! No wonder this place festers, when creatures like you run things! You don't deserve to live, either of you—nor does your puppet king! Tread softly, or count your days."

"I would remind you, Caesar, that you are our guest—and that you do not have sufficient troops with you to attack us."

"I am not your guest, I am your sovereign. Rome's Vestal Virgins still hold the will of the last legitimate king of Egypt, Ptolemy XI, and I hold the will of the late King Ptolemy XII," Caesar said. "Therefore I will assume the reins of government until I have adjudicated in this present situation, and whatever I decide will be adhered to. Move my belongings to the guest palace, and bring my infantry ashore today. I want them in a good camp inside the city walls. Do you think I can't level Alexandria to the ground with what men I have? Think again!"

The towel arrived, Tyrian purple. Fabius took it and spread it between his hands in a cradle. Caesar kissed Pompey's brow, then put the head in the towel and reverently wrapped it up. When Fabius went to take it, Caesar handed him the ivory rod of imperium instead.

"No, I will carry him." At the door he turned. "I want a small pyre constructed in the grounds outside the guest palace. I want frankincense and myrrh to fuel it. *And find the body!*"

He wept for hours, hugging the Tyrian purple bundle, and no one dared to disturb him. Finally Rufrius came bearing a lamp—it was very dark—to tell him that everything had been moved to the guest palace, so please would he come too? He had to help Caesar up as if he were an old man and guide his footsteps through the grounds, lit with oil lamps inside Alexandrian glass globes.

"Oh, Rufrius! That it should have come to this!"

"I know, Caesar. But there is a little good news. A man has arrived from Pelusium, Pompeius Magnus's freedman Philip. He has the ashes of the body, which he burned on the beach after the assassins rowed away. Because he carried Pompeius Magnus's purse, he was able to travel across the Delta very quickly."

So from Philip Caesar heard the full story of what had happened in Pelusium, and of the flight of Cornelia Metella and Sextus, Pompey's wife and younger son.

In the morning, with Caesar officiating, they burned Pompey the Great's head and added its ashes to the rest, enclosed them in a solid gold urn encrusted with red *carbunculi* and ocean pearls. Then Caesar put Philip and his poor dull slave aboard a merchantman heading west, bearing the ashes of Pompey the Great home to his widow. The ring, also entrusted to Philip, was to be sent on to the elder son, Gnaeus Pompey, wherever he might be.

All that done with, Caesar sent a servant to rent twenty-six horses and set out to inspect his dispositions. Which were, he soon discovered, disgraceful. Potheinus had located his 3,200 legionaries in Rhakotis on some disused land haunted by cats (also sacred animals) hunting myriad rats and mice, and, of course, already occupied by ibises. The local people, all poor hybrid Egyptian Greeks, were bitterly resentful both of the Roman camp in their midst and of the fact that famine-dogged Alexandria now had many extra mouths to feed. The Romans could afford to buy food, no matter what its price, but its price for the poor would spiral yet again because it had to stretch further.

"Well, we build a purely temporary wall and palisade around this camp, but we make it look as if we think it's permanent. The natives are nasty, very nasty. Why? Because they're hungry! On an income of *twelve thousand* gold talents a year, their wretched rulers don't subsidize their food. This whole place is a perfect example of why Rome threw out her kings!" Caesar snorted, huffed. "Post sentries every few feet, Rufrius, and tell the men to add roast ibis to their diet. I piss on Alexandria's sacred birds!"

Oh, he is in a temper! thought Rufrius wryly. How could those fools in the palace murder Pompeius Magnus and think to please Caesar? He's wild with grief inside, and it won't take much to push him into making a worse mess of Alexandria than he did of Uxellodunum or Cenabum. What's more, the men haven't been ashore a day yet, and they're already lusting to kill the locals. There's a mood building here, and a disaster brewing.

Since it wasn't his place to voice any of this, he simply rode around with the Great Man and listened to him fulminate. It is more than grief putting him out so dreadfully. Those fools in the palace stripped him of the chance to act mercifully, draw Magnus back into our Roman fold. Magnus would have accepted. Cato, no, never. But Magnus, yes, always.

An inspection of the cavalry camp only made Caesar crankier. The Ubii Germans weren't surrounded by the poor and there was plenty of good grazing, a clean lake to drink from, but there was no way that Caesar could use them in conjunction with his infantry, thanks to an impenetrably creepered swamp lying between them and the western end of the city, where the infantry lay. Potheinus, Ganymedes and the Interpreter had been cunning. But why, Rufrius asked himself in despair, do people *irritate* him? Every obstacle they throw in his path only makes him more determined—can they really delude themselves that they're cleverer than Caesar? All those years in Gaul have endowed him with a strategic legacy so formidable that he's equal to anything. But hold your tongue, Rufrius, ride around with him and watch him plan a campaign he may never need to conduct. But if he has to conduct it, he'll be ready.

Caesar dismissed his lictors and sent Rufrius back to the Rhakotis camp armed with certain orders, then guided his horse up one street and down another, slowly enough to let the ibises stalk out from under the animal's hooves, his eyes everywhere. At the intersection of Canopic and Royal Avenues he invaded the agora, a vast open space surrounded on all four sides by a wide arcade with a dark red back wall, and fronted by blue-painted Doric pillars. Next he went to the gymnasium, almost as large, similarly arcaded, but having hot baths, cold baths, an athletic track and exercise rings. In each he sat the horse oblivious to the glares of Alexandrians and ibises, then dismounted to examine the ceilings of the covered arcades and walkways. At the courts of justice he strolled inside, it seemed fascinated by the ceilings of its lofty rooms. From there he rode to the temple of Poseidon, thence to the Serapeum in Rhakotis, the latter a sanctuary to Serapis gifted with a huge temple amid gardens and other, smaller temples. Then it was off to the waterfront and its docks, its warehouses; the emporium, a gigantic trading center, received quite a lot of his attention, as did piers, jetties, quays curbed with big square wooden beams. Other temples and large public buildings along Canopic Avenue also interested him, particularly their ceilings, all held up by massive wooden beams. Finally he rode back down Royal Avenue to the German camp, there to issue instructions about fortifications.

"I'm sending you two thousand soldiers as additional labor to start dismantling the old city walls," he told his legate. "You'll use the stones to build two new walls, each commencing at the back of the first house on either side of Royal Avenue and fanning outward until you reach the lake. Four hundred feet wide at the Royal Avenue end, but five thousand feet wide at the lakefront. That will bring you hard against the swamp on the west, while your eastern wall will bisect the road to the ship canal between the lake and the Canopic Nilus. The western wall you'll make thirty feet high—the swamp will provide additional defense. The eastern wall you'll make twenty feet high, with a fifteen-foot-deep ditch outside mined with *stimuli,* and a water-filled moat beyond that. Leave a gap in the eastern wall to let traffic to the ship canal keep flowing, but have stones ready to close the gap the moment I so order you. Both walls are to have a watchtower every hundred feet, and I'll send you ballistas to put on top of the eastern wall."

Poker-faced, the legate listened, then went to find Arminius, the Ubian chieftain. Germans weren't much use building walls, but their job would be to forage and stockpile fodder for the horses. They could also find wood for the fire-hardened, pointed stakes called *stimuli*, and start weaving withies for the breastworks—wonderful wicker weavers, Germans!

Back down Royal Avenue rode Caesar to the Royal Enclosure and an inspection of its twenty-foot-high wall, which ran from the crags of the Akron theater in a line that returned to the sea on the far side of Cape Lochias. Not a watchtower anywhere, and no real grasp of the defensive nature of a wall; far more effort and care had gone into its decoration. No wonder the mob stormed the Royal Enclosure so often! This wouldn't keep an enterprising dwarf outside.

Time, time! It was going to take time, and he would have to fence and spar to fool people until his preparations were complete. First and foremost, there must be no indication apart from the activity at the cavalry camp that anything untoward was going on. Potheinus and his city minions like the Interpreter would assume that Caesar intended to huddle inside the cavalry fortress, abandon the city if attacked. Good. Let them think that.

When Rufrius returned from Rhakotis, he received more orders, after which Caesar summoned all his junior legates (including the hopeless Tiberius Claudius Nero) and led them through his plans. Of their discretion he had no doubts; this wasn't Rome against Rome, this was war with a foreign power not one of them liked.

On the following day he summoned King Ptolemy, Potheinus, Theodotus and Ganymedes to the guest palace, where he seated them in chairs on the floor while he occupied his ivory curule chair on a dais. Which didn't please the little king, though he allowed Theodotus to pacify him. *That one has started sexual initiation,* thought Caesar. *What chance does the boy have, with such advisers? If he lives, he'll be no better a ruler than his father was.*

"I've called you here to speak about a subject I mentioned the day before yesterday," Caesar said, a scroll in his lap. "Namely, the succession to the throne of Alexandria in Egypt, which I now understand is a somewhat different question from the throne of Egypt of the Nilus. Apparently the latter, King, is a position your absent sister enjoys, but you do not. To rule in Egypt of the Nilus, the sovereign must be Pharaoh. As is Queen Cleopatra. Why, King, is your co-ruler, sister *and* wife an exile commanding an army of mercenaries against her own subjects?"

Potheinus answered; Caesar had expected nothing else. The little king did as he was told, and had insufficient intelligence to think without being led through the facts first. "Because her subjects rose up against her and ejected her, Caesar."

"Why did they rise up against her?"

"Because of the famine," Potheinus said. "Nilus has failed to inundate for two years in a row. Last year saw the lowest reading of the Nilometer since the priests started taking records three thousand years ago. Nilus rose only eight Roman feet."

"Explain."

"There are three kinds of inundation, Caesar. The Cubits of Death, the Cubits of Plenty, and the Cubits of Surfeit. To overflow its banks and inundate the valley, Nilus must rise eighteen Roman feet. Anything below that is in the Cubits of Death—water and silt will not be deposited on the land, so no crops can be planted. In Egypt, it never rains. Succor comes from Nilus. Readings between eighteen and thirty-two Roman feet constitute the Cubits of Plenty. Nilus floods enough to spread water and silt on all the growing land, and the crops come in. Inundations above thirty-two feet drown the valley so deeply that the villages are washed away and the waters do not recede in time to plant the crops," Potheinus said as if by rote; evidently this was not the first time he had had to explain the inundation cycle to some ignorant foreigner.

"Nilometer?" Caesar asked.

"The device off which the inundation level is read. It is a well dug to one side of Nilus with the cubits marked on its wall. There are several, but the one of greatest importance is hundreds of miles to the south, at Elephantine on the First Cataract. There Nilus starts to rise one month before it does in Memphis, at the apex of the Delta. So we have warning what the year's inundation is going to be like. A messenger brings the news down the river."

"I see. However, Potheinus, the royal income is enormous. Don't you use it to buy in grain when the crops don't germinate?"

"Caesar must surely know," said Potheinus smoothly, "that there has been drought all around Your Sea, from Spain to Syria. We have bought, but the cost is staggering, and naturally the cost must be passed on to the consumers."

"Really? How sensible" was Caesar's equally smooth reply. He lifted the scroll on his lap. "I found this in Gnaeus Pompeius Magnus's tent after Pharsalus. It is the will of the twelfth Ptolemy, your father"— spoken to the lad, bored enough to doze—"and it is very clear. It directs that Alexandria and Egypt shall be jointly ruled by his eldest living daughter, Cleopatra, and his eldest son, Ptolemy Euergetes, as husband and wife."

Potheinus had jumped. Now he reached out an imperious hand. "Let me see it!" he demanded. "If it were a true and legal will, it would reside either here in Alexandria with the Recorder, or with the Vestal Virgins in Rome."

Theodotus had moved to stand behind the little king, fingers digging into his shoulder to keep him awake; Ganymedes sat, face impassive, listening. You, thought Caesar of Ganymedes, are the most able one. How it must irk you to suffer Potheinus as your superior! And, I suspect, you would far rather see *your* young Ptolemy, the Princess Arsinoë, sitting on the high throne. They all hate Cleopatra, but why?

"No, Lord High Chamberlain, you may not see it," he said coldly. "In it, Ptolemy XII known as Auletes says that his will was not lodged either in Alexandria or Rome due to—er—'embarrassments of the state.' Since our civil war was far in the future when this document was drawn up, Auletes must have meant events here in Alexandria." He straightened, face setting hard. "It is high time that Alexandria settled down, and that its rulers were more generous toward the lowly. I do not intend to depart this city until some consistent, humane conditions have been established for *all* its people, rather than its Macedonian citizens. I will not countenance festering sores of resistance to Rome in my wake, or permit any country to offer itself as a nucleus of further resistance to Rome. Accept the fact, gentlemen, that Caesar Dictator will remain in Alexandria to sort out its affairs—lance the boil, you might say. Therefore I sincerely hope that you have sent that courier to Queen Cleopatra, and that we see her here within a very few days."

And that, he thought, is as close as I go to conveying the message that Caesar Dictator will not go away to leave Alexandria as a base for Republicans to use. They must all be shepherded to Africa Province, where I can stamp on them collectively.

He rose to his feet. "You are dismissed."

They went, faces scowling.

"Did you send a courier to Cleopatra?" Ganymedes asked the Lord High Chamberlain as they emerged into the rose garden.

"I sent two," said Potheinus, smiling, "but on a very slow boat. I also sent a third—on a very fast punt—to General Achillas, of course. When the two slow couriers emerge from the Delta at the Pelusiac mouth, Achillas will have men waiting. I am very much afraid"—he sighed—"that Cleopatra will receive no message from Caesar. Eventually he will turn on her, deeming her too arrogant to submit to Roman arbitration."

"She has her spies in the palace," Ganymedes said, eyes on the dwindling forms of Theodotus and the little king, hurrying ahead. "She'll try to reach Caesar—it's in her interests."

"I am aware of that. But Captain Agathacles and his men are policing every inch of the wall and every wavelet on either side of Cape Lochias. She won't get through my net." Potheinus stopped to face the other eunuch, equally tall, equally handsome. "I take it, Ganymedes, that you would prefer Arsinoë as queen?"

"There are many who would prefer Arsinoë as queen," said Ganymedes, unruffled. "Arsinoë herself, for example. And her brother the King. Cleopatra is tainted with Egypt, she's poison."

"Then," said Potheinus, beginning to walk again, "I think it behooves both of us to work to that end. You can't have my job, but if your own chargeling occupies the throne, that won't really inconvenience you too much, will it?"

"No," said Ganymedes, smiling. "What is Caesar up to?"

"Up to?"

"He's up to something, I feel it in my bones. There's a lot of activity at the cavalry camp, and I confess I'm surprised that he hasn't begun to fortify his infantry camp in Rhakotis with anything like his reputed thoroughness."

"What annoys me is his high-handedness!" Potheinus snapped tartly. "By the time he's finished fortifying his cavalry camp, there won't be a stone left in the old city walls."

"Why," asked Ganymedes, "do I think all this is a blind?"

The next day Caesar sent for Potheinus, no one else.

"I've a matter to broach with you on behalf of an old friend," Caesar said, manner relaxed and expansive.

"Indeed?"

"Perhaps you remember Gaius Rabirius Postumus?"

Potheinus frowned. "Rabirius Postumus . . . Perhaps vaguely."

"He arrived in Alexandria after the late Auletes had been put back on his throne. His purpose was to collect some forty million sesterces Auletes owed a consortium of Roman bankers, chief of whom was Rabirius. However, it seems the Accountant and all his splendid Macedonian public servants had allowed the city finances to get into a shocking state. So Auletes told my friend Rabirius that he would have to earn his money by tidying up both the royal and the public *fiscus*. Which Rabirius did, working night and day in Macedonian garments he found as repulsive as he did irksome. At the end of a year, Alexandria's moneys were brilliantly organized. But when Rabirius asked for his forty million sesterces, Auletes and your predecessor stripped him as naked as a bird and threw him on a ship bound for Rome. Be thankful for your life, was their message. Rabirius arrived in Rome absolutely penniless. For a banker, Potheinus, a hideous fate."

Grey eyes were locked with pale blue; neither man lowered his gaze. But a pulse was beating very fast in Potheinus's neck.

"Luckily," Caesar went on blandly, "I was able to assist my friend Rabirius get back on his financial feet, and today he is, with my other friends the Balbi Major and Minor, and Gaius Oppius, a veritable plutocrat of the plutocrats. However, a debt is a debt, and one of the reasons I decided to visit Alexandria concerns that debt. Behold in me, Lord High Chamberlain, Rabirius Postumus's bailiff. Pay back the forty million sesterces at once. In international terms, they amount to one thousand six hundred talents of silver. Strictly speaking, I should demand interest on the sum at my fixed rate of ten percent, but I'm willing to forgo that. The principal will do nicely."

"I am not authorized to pay the late king's debts."

"No, but the present king is."

"The King is a minor."

"Which is why I'm applying to you, my dear fellow. Pay up."

"I shall need extensive documentation for proof."

"My secretary Faberius will be pleased to furnish it."

"Is that all, Caesar?" Potheinus asked, getting to his feet.

"For the moment." Caesar strolled out with his guest, the personification of courtesy. "Any sign of the Queen yet?"

"Not a shadow, Caesar."

Theodotus met Potheinus in the main palace, big with news. "Word from Achillas!" he said.

"I thank Serapis for that! He says?"

"That the couriers are dead, and that Cleopatra is still in her earth on Mount Casius. Achillas is sure she has no idea of Caesar's presence in Alexandria, though what she's going to make of Achillas's next action is anyone's guess. He's moving twenty thousand foot and ten thousand horse by ship from Pelusium even as I speak. The Etesian winds have begun to blow, so he should be here in two days." Theodotus chuckled gleefully. "Oh, what I would give to see Caesar's face when Achillas arrives! He says he'll use both harbors, but plans to make camp outside the Moon Gate." Not a very observant man, he looked at the grim-faced Potheinus in sudden bewilderment. "Aren't you pleased, Potheinus?"

"Yes, yes, that's not what's bothering me!" Potheinus snapped.

"I've just seen Caesar, who dunned the royal purse for the money Auletes refused to pay the Roman banker, Rabirius Postumus. The hide! The temerity! After all these years! And I can't ask the Interpreter to pay a private debt of the late king's!"

"Oh, dear!"

"Well," said Potheinus through his teeth, "I'll pay Caesar the money, but he'll rue the day he asked for it!"

"Trouble," said Rufrius to Caesar the next day, the eighth since they had arrived in Alexandria.

"Of what kind?"

"Did you collect Rabirius Postumus's debt?"

"Yes."

"Potheinus's agents are telling everybody that you've looted the royal treasury, melted down all the gold plate, and garnished the contents of the granaries for your troops."

Caesar burst out laughing. "Things are beginning to come to a boil, Rufrius! My messenger has returned from Queen Cleopatra's camp—no, I didn't use the much-vaunted Delta canals, I sent him at the gallop on horseback, a fresh mount every ten miles. No courier from Potheinus ever contacted her, of course. Killed, I imagine. The Queen has sent me a very amiable and informative letter, in which she tells me that Achillas and his army are packing up to return to Alexandria, where they intend to camp outside the city in the area of the Moon Gate."

Rufrius looked eager. "We begin?" he asked.

"Not until after I've moved into the main palace and taken charge of the King," said Caesar. "If Potheinus and Theodotus can use the poor lad as a tool, so can I. Let the cabal build its funeral pyre in ignorance two or three more days. But have my men absolutely ready to dash. When the time comes they have a great deal to do, and not much time to do it in." He stretched his arms luxuriously. "Ah, how good it is to have a foreign foe!"

On the tenth day of Caesar's stay in Alexandria, a small Nilus dhow slipped into the Great Harbor in the midst of Achillas's arriving fleet, and maneuvered its way between the clumsy transports unnoticed. It finally tied up at the jetty in the Royal Harbor, where a detachment of guards watched its advent closely to make sure no furtive swimmer left it. Only two men were in the dhow, both Egyptian priests—barefoot, shaven-headed, clad in white linen dresses that fitted tightly under the nipples and flared gently to a hemline at mid-calf. Both were *mete-en-sa*, ordinary priests not entitled to wear gold on their persons.

"Here, where do you think you're going?" asked the corporal of the guards.

The priest in the bow got out and stood with arms joined at the hands, palm to palm over his groin, a pose of subservience and humility. "We wish to see Caesar," he said in crooked Greek.

"Why?"

"We carry a gift to him from the U'eb."

"The who?"

"Sem of Ptah, Neb-notru, *wer-kherep-hemw*, Seker-cha'bau, Ptah-mose, Cha'em-uese," chanted the priest in a singsong voice.

"I am none the wiser, priest, and losing my patience."

"We carry a gift for Caesar from the U'eb, the high priest of Ptah in Memphis. That was his full name I spoke."

"What gift?"

"Here," said the priest, stepping back into the boat with the corporal on his heels.

A rush mat rolled into a flat cylinder lay in the bottom, a dowdy thing to a Macedonian Alexandrian, with its shabby colors and angular patterns. You could buy better in the meanest market of Rhakotis. Probably seething with vermin too.

"You're going to give Caesar *that*?"

"Yes, O royal personage."

The corporal unsheathed his sword and poked it at the mat, but gingerly.

"I wouldn't," said the priest softly.

"Why not?"

The priest caught the corporal's eyes and pinned them with his own, then did something with his head and neck that caused the man to back away, terrified. Suddenly he wasn't looking at an Egyptian priest, but at the head and hood of a cobra.

"Sssssssss!" hissed the priest, and stuck out a forked tongue.

The corporal leaped in one bound on to the jetty, face ashen. Swallowing, he found speech. "Doesn't Ptah like Caesar?"

"Ptah created Serapis, as he did all the gods, but he finds Jupiter Optimus Maximus an affront to Egypt," said the priest.

The corporal grinned; a lovely cash bonus from Lord Potheinus danced before his eyes. "Take your gift to Caesar," he said, "and may Ptah achieve his ends. Be careful!"

"We will, O royal personage."

The two priests bent, lifted the slightly floppy cylinder one at either end, and levered their burden neatly on to the jetty. "Where do we go?" asked the speaking priest.

"Just follow that path through the rose garden, first palace on your left past the small obelisk."

And off they trotted, the mat between them. A light thing.

Now, thought the corporal, all I have to do is wait until I hear that our unwelcome guest has died of snakebite. Then I'm going to be rewarded.

That podgy gourmet Gaius Trebatius Testa came waddling in, frowning; it went without saying that he would choose to serve with Caesar in this civil war, despite the fact that his official patron was Marcus Tullius Cicero. Quite why he had elected to sail to Alexandria he didn't know, save that he was always in search of new taste treats. But Alexandria didn't have any.

"Caesar," he said, "a rather peculiar object has arrived for you from Memphis, from the high priest of Ptah. *Not* a letter!"

"How intriguing," said Caesar, looking up from his papers. "Is the object in good condition? It hasn't been tampered with?"

"I doubt it ever was in good condition," Trebatius said with a moue of disapproval. "A dingy old mat. A *rug* it is not."

"Have it brought in exactly as it arrived."

"It will have to be your lictors, Caesar. The palace slaves took one look at its bearers and went paler than a German from the Cimbric Chersonnese."

"Just send it in, Trebatius."

Two junior lictors carried it between them, deposited it on the floor and gazed at Caesar in a rather minatory fashion.

"Thank you. You may go."

Manlius shifted uneasily. "Caesar, may we stay? This—er—thing arrived in the custody of two of the oddest fellows we've ever seen. The moment they got it inside the door, they bolted as if pursued by the Furies. Fabius and Cornelius wanted to open it, but Gaius Trebatius said no."

"Excellent! Now push off, Manlius. Out, out!"

Alone with the mat, the smiling Caesar toured it, then got down on his knees and peered into one end. "Can you breathe in there?" he asked.

Someone spoke from the interior, but unintelligibly. Then he discovered that either end of the mat was plugged with a thin strip of extra rush to make the thickness uniform from end to end. How ingenious! He pulled the padding out, unrolled Ptah's gift very gently.

No wonder she could hide in a mat. There was nothing to her. Where is all that big-boned Mithridatid blood? Caesar asked himself, going to a chair and sitting down to study her. Not five Roman feet tall, she would be lucky to weigh a talent and a half—eighty pounds if she wore lead shoes.

It was not his habit to waste his precious time speculating how unknown persons would look, even when said persons were of this one's status. Though he certainly hadn't expected a wispy little creature devoid of the slightest hint of majesty! Nor, he now discovered, amazed, did she care about her appearance, for she scrambled up like a monkey and never even looked around to see if there was a polished metal object she could use as a mirror. Oh, I like her! he thought. She reminds me of Mater—the same brisk, no-nonsense air to her. However, his mother had been called the most beautiful woman in Rome, whereas no one would ever call Cleopatra beautiful by any standard.

No breasts to speak of, nor any hips; just straight up and down, arms attached to stark shoulders like sticks, a long and skinny neck, and a head that reminded him of Cicero's—too big for its body.

Her face was downright ugly, for it bore a nose so large and hooked that it riveted all attention upon it. By comparison, the rest of her features were quite nice: a full but not too full mouth, good cheekbones, an oval face with a firm chin. Only the eyes were beautiful, very large and widely opened, dark lashes below dark brows, and having irises the same color as a lion's, golden yellow. Now where have I seen eyes that color? Among the offspring of Mithridates the Great, of course! Well, she is his granddaughter, but in no other way than the eyes is she a Mithridatid; they are big, tall people with Germanic noses and yellow hair. Her hair was pale brown and thin too, parted in rolled strips from forehead back to nape of neck like the rind on a melon, then screwed into a hard little knot. Lovely skin, a dark olive so transparent that the veins showed blue beneath it. She wore the white ribbon of the diadem tied behind her hairline; it was her only evidence of royalty, for her simple Greek dress was a drab fawn, and she wore no jewelry.

She was inspecting him just as closely, and in surprise.

"What do you see?" he asked solemnly.

"Great beauty, Caesar, though I expected you to be dark."

"There are fair Romans, medium Romans and dark Romans—also many Romans with red or sandy hair and lots of freckles."

"Hence your *cognomina*—Albinus, Flavus, Rufus, Niger."

Ah, the voice was wonderful! Low-pitched and so melodious that she seemed to sing rather than to speak. "You know Latin?" he asked, surprised in his turn.

"No, I've had no opportunity to learn it," Cleopatra said. "I speak eight languages, but they're all eastern—Greek, old Egyptian, demotic Egyptian, Hebrew, Aramaic, Arabic, Median and Persian." The feline eyes gleamed. "Perhaps you'll teach me Latin? I'm a very quick student."

"I doubt I'll have the time, child, but if you like, I'll send you a tutor from Rome. How old are you?"

"Twenty-one. I have sat on my throne for four years."

"A fifth of a lifetime. You're a veteran. Sit down, do."

"No, then I won't be able to see you properly. You're very tall," she said, prowling.

"Yes, right up there with the Gauls and the Germans. Like Sulla, I could pass for one if I had to. What happened to your height? Your brothers and sister are tall."

"Some of my shortness is inherited. My father's mother was a Nabataean princess, but she wasn't a full Arab. Her grandmother was the Parthian princess Rhodogune, another blood link to King Mithridates. They say the Parthians are short. However, my own mother blamed an illness I suffered as a babe. So I have always thought that Hippopotamus and Crocodile sucked my growth down their nostrils just as they do the river."

Caesar's mouth twitched. "Just as they do the river?"

"Yes, during the Cubits of Death. Nilus fails to rise when Taweret—Hippopotamus—and Sobek—Crocodile—suck the water down their nostrils. They do that when they're angry at Pharaoh," she said, absolutely seriously.

"Since you're Pharaoh, why are they angry at you? Nilus has been in the Cubits of Death for two years, I understand."

Her face became a study in indecision; she turned away, paced up and down, came back abruptly to standing directly in front of him, biting her lower lip. "The matter is extremely urgent," she said, "so I can see no point in striving to seduce you with woman's wiles. I had hoped you'd be an unattractive man—you're old, after all—and therefore amenable toward unbeautiful women like me. But I see that the tales are true, that you can have any woman you fancy despite your great age."

His head had gone to one side, and the aloof cold eyes were warm, though they didn't contain any lust. They simply drank her in, while his mind reveled in her. She had distinguished herself in adverse situations—the murder of the sons of Bibulus, the uprising in Alexandria, no doubt other crises as well. Yet she spoke as a virginal child. Of course she was a virgin. Clearly her brother/husband hadn't yet consummated their union, and she was a god on earth, she couldn't mate with mortal men. Hedged around with eunuchs, forbidden to be alone with an uncastrated man. Her situation is, as she said, extremely urgent, otherwise she would not be alone here with me, an uncastrated mortal man.

"Go on," he said.

"I have not fulfilled my duty as Pharaoh."

"Which is?"

"To be fruitful. To bear children. The first Inundation after I came to the throne was just inside the Cubits of Plenty because Nilus gave me the grace of time to prove my fruitfulness. Now, two Inundations later, I am still barren. Egypt is in famine and five days from now the priests of Isis at Philae will read the Elephantine Nilometer. The Inundation is due, the Etesian winds are blowing. But unless I am quickened, the summer rains will not fall in Aithiopai and Nilus will not inundate."

"Summer rains, not melting winter snows," Caesar said. "Do you know the sources of Nilus?" Keep her talking, let me have time to absorb what she's saying. My "great age" indeed!

"Librarians like Eratosthenes sent expeditions to discover Nilus's sources, but all they found were tributaries and Nilus himself. What they did find were the summer rains in Aithiopai. It is all written down, Caesar."

"Yes, I hope to have the leisure to read some of the books of the museum before I leave. Continue, Pharaoh."

"That's it," said Cleopatra, shrugging. "I need to mate with a god, and my brother doesn't want me. He wants Theodotus for his pleasure and Arsinoë for his wife."

"Why should he want her?"

"Her blood is purer than mine, she's his full sister. Their mother was a Ptolemy, mine was a Mithridatid."

"I fail to see an answer to your dilemma, at least not before this coming inundation. I feel for you, my poor girl, but what I can do for you, I don't know. I'm not a god."

Her face lit up. "But you are a God!" she cried.

He blinked. "There's a statue in Ephesus says it, but that's just—

er—flattery, as a friend of mine said. It's true that I am descended from two gods, but all I have are one or two drops of divine ichor, not a whole body full of it."

"You are the God out of the West."

"The god out of the west?"

"You are Osiris returned from the Realm of the Dead to quicken Isis-Hathor-Mut and sire a son, Horus."

"And you believe that?"

"I don't *believe* it, Caesar, it is a fact!"

"Then I have it right, you want to mate with me?"

"Yes, yes! Why else would I be here? Be my husband, give me a son! Then Nilus will inundate."

What a situation! But an amusing and interesting one. How far has Caesar gone, to arrive at a place where his seed can cause rains to fall, rivers to rise, whole countries to thrive?

"It would be churlish," he said gravely, "to refuse, but haven't you left your run a little late? With only five days until the Nilometer is read, I can't guarantee to quicken you. Even if I do, it will be five or six *nundinae* before you know."

"Amun-Ra will know, just as I, his daughter, will know. I am Nilus, Caesar! I am the living personification of the river. I am God on earth, and I have but one purpose—to ensure that my people prosper, that Egypt remains great. If Nilus stays in the Cubits of Death another year, the famine will be joined by plague and locusts. Egypt will be no more."

"I require a favor in return."

"Quicken me, and it is yours."

"Spoken like a banker! I want your complete co-operation in whatever I am called upon to do to Alexandria."

Her brow wrinkled, she looked suspicious. "Do *to* Alexandria? A strange way to phrase it, Caesar."

"Oh, a mind!" he said appreciatively. "I begin to hope for an intelligent son."

"They say you have no son at all."

Yes, I have a son, he thought. A beautiful little boy somewhere in Gaul whom Litaviccus stole from me when he murdered his mother. But I don't know what happened to him, and I never will know.

"True," he said coolly. "But having no son of one's body is of no importance to a Roman. We are at legal liberty to adopt a son, someone who shares our blood—a nephew or a cousin. During our lifetimes, or by testament after our deaths. Any son that you and I might have, Pharaoh, will not be a Roman because you are not a Roman. Therefore he cannot inherit either my name or my worldly goods." Caesar looked stern. "Don't hope for Roman sons—our laws don't work that way. I can go through a form of marriage with you if you wish, but the marriage won't be binding in Roman law. I already have a Roman wife."

"Who has no child at all, though you've been married long."

"I'm never home." He grinned, relaxed and looked at her with a brow raised. "I think it's time I moved to contain your older brother, my dear. By nightfall we'll be living in the big palace, and then we'll do something about quickening you." He got up and went to the door. "Faberius! Trebatius!" he called.

His secretary and his personal legate entered to stand with jaws dropped.

"This is Queen Cleopatra. Now that she's arrived, things begin to happen. Summon Rufrius at once, and start packing."

And off he went, his staff in his wake, leaving Cleopatra to stand alone in the room. She had fallen in love at once, for that was her nature; reconciled to espousing an old man even uglier than she was herself, to find instead someone who did indeed look the God he was filled her with joy, with feeling, with true love. Tach'a had cast the lotus petals upon the water in Hathor's bowl and told her that tonight or tomorrow night were the fertile ones in her cycle, that she would conceive if she looked on Caesar and found him worthy of love. Well, she had looked and found a dream, the God out of the West. As tall and splendid and beautiful as Osiris; even the lines graven upon his face were fitting, for they said that he had suffered much, just as Osiris had suffered.

Her lip quivered, she blinked at sudden tears. She loved, but Caesar did not, and she doubted that he ever would. Not for reasons grounded in lack of beauty or feminine charms; more that there was a gulf between them of age, experience, culture.

By nightfall they were in the big palace, a vast edifice that ramified down halls and up corridors, sprouted galleries and rooms, had courtyards and pools large enough to swim in.

All afternoon the city and the Royal Enclosure buzzed; five hundred of Caesar's legionaries had rounded up the Royal Guard and sent them to Achillas's mushrooming camp west of the Moon Gate with Caesar's compliments. That done, the five hundred men proceeded to fortify the Royal Enclosure wall with a fighting platform, proper breastworks and many watchtowers.

Other things were happening too. Rufrius evacuated the camp in

Rhakotis and evicted every tenant in the grand houses on either side of Royal Avenue, then stuffed the mansions with troops. While those affluent, suddenly homeless people ran about the city weeping and wailing, howling vengeance on Romans, hundreds of soldiers barged into the big temples, the gymnasium and the courts of justice, while a few left in Rhakotis went to the Serapeum. Under horrified Alexandrian eyes, they promptly tore out every beam from every ceiling and hustled them back to Royal Avenue. That done, they commenced work on the dockside structures—quays, jetties, the emporium—and carried off every useful piece of wood as well as all the beams.

By nightfall most of public Alexandria lay in ruins, anything useful or sizably wooden safely delivered to Royal Avenue.

"This is an outrage! *An Outrage!*" cried Potheinus when the unwelcome guest marched in accompanied by a century of soldiers, his staff, and a very smug-looking Queen Cleopatra.

"You!" shrilled Arsinoë. "What are you doing here? I am queen, Ptolemy has divorced you!"

Cleopatra walked up to her and kicked her viciously on the shins, then raked her nails down Arsinoë's face. "I am queen! Shut up or I'll have you killed!"

"Bitch! Sow! Crocodile! Jackal! Hippopotamus! Spider! Scorpion! Rat! Snake! Louse!" little Ptolemy Philadelphus was yelling. "Ape! Ape, ape, ape!"

"And you shut up too, you filthy little toad!" Cleopatra said fiercely, whacking him around the head until he blubbered.

Entranced by all this evidence of familial piety, Caesar stood and watched with arms folded. Twenty-one Pharaoh might be, but confronted by her littlest brother and her sister, she reverted to the nursery. Interesting that neither Philadelphus nor Arsinoë fought back physically: big sister cowed them. Then he grew tired of the unseemliness and deftly separated the three brawlers.

"You, madam, stay with your tutor," he ordered Arsinoë. "It is high time young princesses retired. You too, Philadelphus."

Potheinus was still ranting, but Ganymedes ushered Arsinoë away with an expressionless face. That one, Caesar thought, is far more dangerous than the Lord High Chamberlain. And Arsinoë is in love with him, eunuch or no.

"Where is King Ptolemy?" he asked. "And Theodotus?"

King Ptolemy and Theodotus were in the agora, as yet untouched by Caesar's soldiers. They had been dallying in the King's own quarters when a slave came running to tell them that Caesar was taking over the Royal Enclosure and that Queen Cleopatra was with him. Moments later Theodotus had himself and the boy dressed for an audience, Ptolemy in his purple hat complete with diadem; then the two entered the secret tunnel constructed by Ptolemy Auletes to permit escape whenever the mob materialized. It ran below ground and under the wall to emerge on the flank of the Akron theater, where it offered the opportunity to head for the docks or go deeper into the city. The little king and Theodotus elected to go into the city, to the agora.

This meeting place held a hundred thousand, and had been filling up since mid-afternoon, when Caesar's soldiers had started plundering beams. By instinct the Alexandrians went to it whenever tumult broke out, so when the pair from the palace appeared, the agora was already choked. Even so, Theodotus made the King wait in a corner; he needed time to coach the boy until he had a short speech off pat. After dark, by which time the mob spilled out on to the intersection and covered the arcade roofs, Theodotus led King Ptolemy to a statue of Callimachus the librarian and helped him climb up to its plinth.

"Alexandrians, we are under attack!" the King screamed, face ruddied by the flames of a thousand torches. "Rome has invaded, the whole of the Royal Enclosure is in Caesar's hands! But more than that!" He paused to make sure he was saying what Theodotus had drummed into him, then went on. "Yes, more than that! My sister Cleopatra the traitor has returned and is in league with the Romans! It is she who has brought Caesar here! All your food has gone to fill Roman bellies, and Caesar's prick is filling Cleopatra's cunt! They have emptied the treasury and murdered everyone in the palace! They have murdered everyone who lives on Royal Avenue! Some of your wheat is being tipped into the Great Harbor out of sheer spite, and Roman soldiers are tearing your public buildings apart! Alexandria is being wrecked, her temples profaned, her women and children raped!"

Dark in the night, the boy's eyes blazed a reflection of the crowd's mounting fury; a fury it had arrived with, a fury that the little king's words spurred to action. This was Alexandria, the one place in the world wherein a mob had become permanently conscious of the power a mob wielded, and wielded that power as a political instrument rather than in pure destructive rage. The mob had spilled many a Ptolemy; it could spill a mere Roman, tear him and his whore into pieces.

"I, your king, have been wrested from my throne by a Roman cur and a traitorous harlot named Cleopatra!"

The crowd moved, scooped King Ptolemy into its midst and put him upon a pair of broad shoulders, where he sat, his purple person on full display, urging his steed on with his ivory scepter.

It moved as far as the gate into the Royal Enclosure, where Caesar stood barring its passage, clad in his purple-bordered toga, his oak-leaf crown upon his head, the rod of his imperium on his right fore-arm, and twelve lictors to either side of him. With him was Queen Cleopatra, still in her drab fawn robe.

Unused to the sight of an adversary who faced it down, the crowd stopped moving.

"What are you doing here?" Caesar asked.

"We've come to drive you out and kill you!" Ptolemy cried.

"King Ptolemy, King Ptolemy, you can't do both," Caesar an-swered reasonably. "Either drive us out, or kill us. But I assure you that there's no need to do either." Having located the leaders in the front ranks, Caesar now directly addressed them. "If you've been told that my soldiers occupy your granaries, I ask that you visit the granaries and see for yourselves that there are none of my soldiers present, and that they are full to the brim. It is not my business to levy the price of grain or other foodstuffs within Alexandria—that is the business of your king, as your queen has been absent. So if you're paying too much, blame King Ptolemy, not Caesar. Caesar brought his own grain and supplies with him to Alexandria, he hasn't touched yours," he lied shamelessly. One hand went out to push Cleopatra forward, then it was extended to the little king. "Come down from your perch, Your Majesty, and stand here where a sovereign should stand—facing his subjects, not among them at their mercy. I hear that the citizens of Alexandria can tear a king to shreds, and it's you to blame for their plight, not Rome. Come to me, do!"

The eddies natural in such a host had separated the King from Theodotus, who couldn't make himself heard. Ptolemy sat on his steed's shoulders, his fair brows knitted in a frown, and a very real fear growing in his eyes. Bright he was not, but he was bright enough to understand that somehow Caesar was putting him in a wrong light; that Caesar's clear, carrying voice, its Greek now distinctly Macedon-ian, was turning the front ranks of the mob against him.

"Set me down!" the King commanded.

On his feet, he walked to Caesar and turned to face his irate sub-jects.

"That's the way," said Caesar genially. "Behold your king and queen!" he shouted. "I have the testament of the late king, father of these children, and I am here to execute his wishes—that Egypt and

Alexandria be ruled by his eldest living daughter, the seventh Cleopatra, and his eldest son, the thirteenth Ptolemy! His directive is unmistakable! Cleopatra and Ptolemy Euergetes are his legal heirs and must rule jointly as husband and wife!"

"Kill her!" Theodotus screamed: "Arsinoë is queen!"

Even this Caesar spun to his own advantage. "The Princess Arsinoë has a different duty!" he cried. "As the Dictator of Rome, I am empowered to return Cyprus to Egypt, and I hereby do so!" His tones oozed sympathy. "I know how hard it has been for Alexandria since Marcus Cato annexed Cyprus—you lost your good cedar timber, your copper mines, a great deal of cheap food. The Senate which decreed that annexation no longer exists. *My* Senate does not condone this injustice! Princess Arsinoë and Prince Ptolemy Philadelphus will be going to rule as satraps in Cyprus. Cleopatra and Ptolemy Euergetes will rule in Alexandria, Arsinoë and Ptolemy Philadelphus in Cyprus!"

The mob was won, but Caesar wasn't finished.

"I must add, people of Alexandria, that it is due to Queen Cleopatra that Cyprus is returned to you! Why do you think she has been absent? Because she traveled to me to negotiate the return of Cyprus! And she has succeeded." He walked foward a little, smiling. "How about a rousing cheer for your queen?"

What Caesar said was relayed swiftly through the crowd from front to back; like all good speakers, he kept his message short and simple when he addressed masses of people. So, satisfied, they cheered deafeningly.

"All very well, Caesar, but you can't deny that your troops are wrecking our temples and public buildings!" one of the mob's leaders called out.

"Yes, a very serious business," said Caesar, spreading his hands. "However, even Romans must protect themselves, and outside the Moon Gate sits a huge army under General Achillas, who has declared war on me. I am preparing myself to be attacked. If you want the demolition stopped, then I suggest you go to General Achillas and tell him to disband his army."

The mob reversed like soldiers drilling; the next moment it was gone, presumably to see Achillas.

Stranded, a shivering Theodotus looked at the boy king with tears in his eyes, then slunk to take his hand, kiss it.

"Very clever, Caesar," Potheinus sneered from the shadows.

Caesar nodded at his lictors and turned to walk back to the palace. "As I have told you before, Potheinus, I *am* clever. May I suggest that you cease your subversive activities among the people of your city and go back to running the Royal Enclosure and the royal purse? If I catch you spreading a false rumor about me and your queen, I'll have you executed the Roman way—flogging and beheading. If you spread *two* false rumors, it will be the death of a slave—crucifixion. *Three* false rumors, and it will be crucifixion without broken legs."

Inside the palace vestibule he dismissed his lictors, but put a hand out to rest on King Ptolemy's shoulder. "No more of these expeditions to the agora, young man. Now go to your rooms. I have had the secret tunnel blocked off at both ends, by the way." The eyes, very cold, looked over Ptolemy's tumbled curls to Theodotus. "Theodotus, you are banned from congress with the King. By morning I want you out of here. And be warned! If you try to reach the King, I'll give you the fate I described for Potheinus." A slight push, and King Ptolemy ran to weep in his quarters. Caesar's hand now went out to Cleopatra, took hers.

"It's bedtime, my dear. Good night, everybody."

She gave a faint smile and lowered her lashes; Trebatius stared at Faberius, staggered. Caesar and the Queen? But she wasn't his type at all!

Extremely experienced with women, Caesar found it no trouble to perform a very curious duty: a ritual mating of two gods for the sake of a country, and the girl god a virgin into the bargain. Not facts that provoked the heights of passion or stirred the heartstrings. An Oriental, she was delighted that he plucked all his body hair, though she deemed that evidence of his godhead when in reality it was simply his way of avoiding lice—Caesar was a cleanliness fanatic. In that respect she came up to his standard; plucked too, she smelled naturally sweet.

Oh, but there was scant pleasure in a naked, scrawny little mound that inexperience and nervousness rendered juiceless as well as uncomfortable! Her chest was almost as flat as a man's, and he was afraid that a hard hold would break her arms, if not her legs. In truth, the whole exercise was off-putting. No pedophile, Caesar had to exert all his massive will to push her undeveloped child's body out of his mind and get the business over and done with several times. If she was to conceive, then once was definitely not enough.

However, she learned quickly and ended in liking what he did very much, if the juices she produced later were anything to go by. A lubricious little creature.

"I love you" was the last thing she said before she fell into a deep slumber, lying curled against him with one stick across his chest, another stick over his legs. Caesar needs sleep too, he thought, and closed his eyes.

By the morning much of the work on Royal Avenue and the Royal Enclosure wall had been done. Mounted on his hired horse—he had not brought Toes with him, a mistake—Caesar set out to tour his dispositions and tell the legate of his cavalry camp to close the ship canal road, cut Alexandria off from the river Nilus.

What he was doing was actually a variation on his strategy at Alesia, where he had inserted himself and his 60,000 men inside a ring with both its inner and its outer walls heavily fortified to keep out the 80,000 Gauls camped on top of Alesia mount, and the 250,000 Gauls camped on the hills beyond him. This time he had a dumbbell, not a ring; Royal Avenue formed its shaft, the cavalry camp its swelling at one end, and the Royal Enclosure the swelling at its other end. The hundreds of beams plundered from all over the city were driven like horizontal piles from one mansion into the next to staple them together, and formed breastworks on top of the flat roofs, where Caesar mounted his smaller artillery; his big ballistas were needed on top of the twenty-foot wall on the eastern side of his cavalry camp. The Hill of Pan became his lookout, its bottom now a formidable rampart of blocks from the gymnasium, and huge stone walls cut off both sides of Canopic Avenue at its intersection with Royal Avenue. He could move his 3,200 veteran infantry from one end of Royal Avenue to the other at the double, and free of the ibis menace too; somehow those crafty birds sensed what was coming, and promptly flew the Roman coop. Good, thought Caesar, grinning. Let the Alexandrians try to fight without killing a sacred ibis! If they were Romans, they'd go to Jupiter Optimus Maximus and draft out a treaty whereby they could be temporarily exonerated of guilt upon payment of an appropriate sacrifice later. But I doubt that Serapis thinks like Roman Jupiter Optimus Maximus.

To the east of Caesar's dumbbell lay Delta and Epsilon Districts, all Jews and Metics; to the west lay the bulk of the city, Greek and Macedonian, by far the more dangerous direction. From the top of the Hill of Pan he could see Achillas—ye gods, he was slow!—trying to ready his troops, watch the activity in the Eunotus Harbor and the Cibotus as the warships came out of their sheds to splash into the water, replacing those that had come back from Pelusium and had to be put ashore for drying out. In a day or two—their admiral was as slow as Achillas—the galleys would row under the arches in the Heptastadion and sink all Caesar's thirty-five transports.

So he put two thousand of his men to demolishing all the houses behind those on Royal Avenue's west side, thus creating a four-hundred-foot-wide expanse of rubble larded with hazards like carefully covered pits with sharpened stakes at their bottoms, chains that rose from nowhere to loop around a neck, broken shards of Alexandrian glass. The other twelve hundred men formed up and invaded the commercial dockside of the Great Harbor, boarded every ship, loaded them with column drums from the courts of justice, the gymnasium and the agora, and proceeded to tip them into the water under the arches. In just two hours no ship, from pinnace to quinquereme, could sail through the Heptastadion from one harbor to the other. If the Alexandrians wanted to attack his fleet, they would have to do it the hard way—past the shoals and sandbars of the Eunostus, around the edge of Pharos Isle, and in through the Great Harbor passages. Hurry with my two legions, Calvinus! I need warships of my own!

Once the archways were blocked, Caesar's soldiers mounted the Heptastadion and ripped out the aqueduct that sent water to Pharos Isle, then stole the outermost row of artillery from the Cibotus. They met some hard resistance, but it was very clear that the Alexandrians lacked cool heads and a general; they flung themselves into the fray like Belgic Gauls in the old days before they learned the value of living to fight again another day. Not insuperable foes for these legionaries, all veterans of the nine-year war in Long-haired Gaul, and delighted to be pitted against foreigners as loathsome as the Alexandrians. Very good ballistas and catapults, those pinched from the Cibotus! Caesar would be pleased. The legionaries ferried the artillery back to the docks, then set fire to the ships moored at wharves and jetties. To rub it in, they lobbed flaming missiles from the captured ballistas among the warships in Eunostus and on top of the ship sheds. Oh, what a good day's work!

Caesar's work was different. He had sent messengers into Delta and Epsilon Districts and summoned three Jewish elders and three Metic leaders to a conference. He received them in the audience chamber, where he had put comfortable chairs, a nice meal laid out on side tables, and the Queen on her throne.

"Look regal," he instructed her. "None of this I-am-a-mouse rubbish—and take Arsinoë's jewels off her if you can't find any of your own. Try to look every inch a great queen, Cleopatra—this is a most important meeting."

When she entered, he found it hard not to gape. She was preceded by a party of Egyptian priests, clanking censers and chanting a low, monotonous dirge in a language he couldn't begin to identify. All of them were *mete-en-sa* save for their leader, who sported a gold pectoral studded with jewels and overlaid with a great number of amuleted gold necklaces; he carried a long, enameled gold staff which he rapped on the floor to produce a dull, booming sound.

"All pay homage to Cleopatra, Daughter of Amun-Ra, Isis Reincarnated, She of the Two Ladies Upper and Lower Egypt, She of the Sedge and Bee!" the high priest cried in good Greek.

She was dressed as Pharaoh, in finely pleated white-on-white striped linen covered by a short-sleeved, billowing coat of linen so fine it was transparent, and embroidered all over with designs in tiny, sparkling glass beads. On her head sat an extraordinary edifice that Caesar had already studied in the wall paintings, yet had not fully grasped until now, seeing it in three dimensions. A flaring outer crown of red enamel rose to a high shaft behind and at its front displayed a cobra's head and a vulture's head in gold, enamel and jewels. Inside it was a much taller, conical crown of white enamel with a flattish top and a curled band of gold springing out of it. Around her neck, a collar of gold, enamel and jewels ten inches wide; at her waist, an enameled gold girdle six inches wide; on her arms, magnificent gold and enamel bracelets in snake and leopard forms; on her fingers, dozens of flashing rings; perched on her chin and hooked behind her ears with gold wires, a false beard of gold and enamel; on her feet, jeweled gold sandals with very high, gilded cork soles.

Her face was painted into a mask with exquisite care, its mouth glossily crimson, its cheeks adorned with rouge, and its eyes replicas of the eye on her throne: rimmed with black *stibium* extending in thin lines toward her ears and ending in little triangles filled in with the coppery green that colored her upper lids all the way to her *stibium*-enhanced brows; below them a curled black line was drawn down onto each cheek. The effect of the paint was as sinister as it was stunning; one could almost imagine that the face beneath was not human.

Her two Macedonian attendants, Charmian and Iras, today were clad in Egyptian mode too. Because Pharaoh's sandals were so high, they assisted Cleopatra up the steps of the dais to her throne, where she sat, took the enameled gold crook and flail from them and crossed these symbols of her deity upon her breast.

No one, Caesar noticed, prostrated himself; a low bow seemed adequate.

"We are here to preside," she said in a strong voice. "We are

Pharaoh, you see our Godhead revealed. Gaius Julius Caesar, Son of Amun-Ra, Osiris Reincarnated, Pontifex Maximus, Imperator, Dictator of the Senate and People of Rome, proceed."

And that's it! he was thinking exultantly as she rolled the sonorous phrases out, that's it! Alexandria and things Macedonian don't even enter her ken. She's Egyptian to the core—once she dons this incredible regalia, she radiates power!

"I am overwhelmed at your majesty, Daughter of Ammon-Ra," he said, then indicated his delegates, rising from their bows. "May I introduce Simeon, Abraham and Joshua of the Jews, and Cibyrus, Phormion and Darius of the Metics?"

"Welcome, and be seated," said Pharaoh.

Whereupon Caesar quite forgot the occupant of the throne. Choosing to approach his subject tangentially, he indicated one laden side table. "I know that flesh has to be religiously prepared and that wine has to be properly Judaic," he said to Simeon, the chief elder of the Jews. "All has been done as your laws stipulate, so after we've spoken, don't hesitate to eat. Similarly," he said to Darius, *ethnarch* of the Metics, "the food and wine on the second table has been prepared for you."

"Your kindness is appreciated, Caesar," said Simeon, "but so much hospitality can't alter the fact that your fortified corridor has cut us off from the rest of the city—our ultimate source of food, our livelihoods, and the raw materials for our trades. We note that you've finished demolishing the houses at the rear of Royal Avenue's west side, so we must presume that you are about to demolish our houses on the east side."

"Don't worry, Simeon," Caesar said in Hebrew, "hear me out."

Cleopatra's eyes looked startled; Simeon jumped.

"You speak Hebrew?" he asked.

"A little. I grew up in a very polyglot quarter of Rome, the Subura, where my mother was the landlady of an insula. We always had a number of Jews among our tenants, and I had the run of the place when I was a child. So I picked up languages. Our resident elder was a goldsmith, Shimon. I know the nature of your god, your customs, your traditions, your foods, your songs, and the history of your people." He turned to Cibyrus. "I can even speak a little Pisidian," he said in that tongue. "Alas, Darius, I cannot speak Persian," he said in Greek, "so for the sake of convenience, let us have our talk in Greek."

Within a quarter of an hour he had explained the situation without apology; a war in Alexandria was inevitable.

"However," he said, "for my own protection I would prefer to fight the war on one side of my corridor only—the western side. Do nothing to oppose me and I'll guarantee that my soldiers don't invade you, that the war won't spread east of Royal Avenue, and that you'll continue to eat. As for the raw materials you need for your trades and the wages those of you who work on the west side will lose, I am not in a position to help. But there may be compensations for the hardships you're bound to suffer until I beat Achillas and subdue the Alexandrians. Don't hinder Caesar and Caesar will be in your debt. And Caesar pays his debts."

He rose from his ivory curule chair and approached the throne. "I imagine, great Pharaoh, that it is in your power to pay all who help you keep your throne?"

"It is."

"Then are you willing to compensate the Jews and Metics for the financial losses they will sustain?"

"I am, provided they do nothing to hinder you, Caesar."

Simeon stood, bowed deeply. "Great Queen," he said, "in return for our co-operation, there is one other thing we ask of you, as do the Metics."

"Ask, Simeon."

"Give us the Alexandrian citizenship."

A long pause ensued. Cleopatra sat hidden behind her exotic mask, her eyes veiled by coppery green lids, the crook and flail crossed on her breast rising and falling slightly as she breathed. Finally the shiny red lips parted. "I agree, Simeon, Darius. The Alexandrian citizenship for all Jews and Metics who have lived in the city for more than three years. Plus financial restitution for what this war will cost you, and a bonus for every Jewish or Metic man who actively fights for Caesar."

Simeon sagged in relief; the other five stared at one another incredulously. What had been withheld for generations was theirs!

"And I," said Caesar, "will add the Roman citizenship."

"The price is more than fair, we have a deal." Simeon beamed. "Furthermore, to prove our loyalty, we will hold the coast between Cape Lochias and the hippodrome. It isn't suitable for mass landings, but Achillas could get plenty of men ashore in small boats. Beyond the hippodrome," he explained for Caesar's benefit, "the swamps of the Delta begin, which is God's Will. God is our best ally."

"Then let's eat!" Caesar cried.

Cleopatra rose. "You don't need Pharaoh anymore," she said. "Charmian, Iras, your help."

* * *

"Oh, get me out of all this!" Pharaoh yelled, kicking off her shoes the moment she reached her rooms. Off came the incongruous false beard, the huge and weighty collar, a shower of rings and bracelets bouncing and rolling around the floor with fearful servants crawling after them, calling on one another to witness that nothing was purloined. She had to sit while Charmian and Iras battled to remove the mighty double crown; its enamel was layered over wood, not metal, but it was tailored to the shape of Cleopatra's skull so it could not fall off, and it was heavy.

Then she saw the beautiful Egyptian woman in her temple musician's garb, shrieked with joy and ran into her arms.

"Tach'a! Tach'a! My mother, my mother!"

While Charmian and Iras scolded and clucked because she was crushing her beaded coat, Cleopatra hugged and kissed Tach'a in a frenzy of love.

Her own mother had been very kind, very sweet, but always too preoccupied for love; something Cleopatra could forgive, herself a victim of that awful atmosphere in the palace at Alexandria. Mama's name had been Cleopatra Tryphaena, and she was a daughter of Mithridates the Great; he had given her as wife to Ptolemy Auletes, who was the illegitimate son of the tenth Ptolemy, Soter nicknamed Chickpea. She had borne two daughters, Berenice and Cleopatra, but no sons. Auletes had had a half sister, still a child when Mithridates forced him to marry Cleopatra Tryphaena, but that had been thirty-three years ago, and the half sister grew up. Until Mithridates died, Auletes was too afraid of his father-in-law to dispose of his wife; all he could do was wait.

When Berenice was twelve years old and little Cleopatra five, Pompey the Great ended the career of King Mithridates the Great, who fled to Cimmeria and was murdered by one of his sons, the same Pharnaces at present invading Anatolia. Freed at last, Auletes divorced Cleopatra Tryphaena and married his half sister. But the daughter of Mithridates was as pragmatic as she was shrewd; she managed to stay alive, continue to live in the palace with her own two daughters while her replacement gave Auletes yet another girl, Arsinoë, and finally two sons.

Berenice was old enough to join the adults, but Cleopatra was relegated to the nursery, a hideous place. Then, as the conduct of Auletes deteriorated, her mother sent little Cleopatra to the temple of Ptah in Memphis, where she entered a world that bore no resemblance to the palace at Alexandria. Cool limestone buildings in the ancient Egyptian style, warm arms to fold her close. For Cha'em, high priest of

Ptah, and his wife, Tach'a, took Cleopatra for their own. They taught her both kinds of Egyptian, Aramaic, Hebrew and Arabic, taught her to sing and play the big harp, taught her all that there was to know about Egypt of Nilus, the mighty pantheon of gods Creator Ptah had made.

More than sexual perversities and wine-soaked orgies rendered Auletes difficult to live with; he had scrambled on to the throne after his legitimate half brother, the eleventh Ptolemy, died without issue—but leaving a will that had bequeathed Egypt to Rome. Thus had Rome entered the picture, a fearsome presence. In Caesar's consulship Auletes had paid six thousand gold talents to secure Roman approval of his tenure of the throne, gold he had stolen from the Alexandrians. For Auletes was not Pharaoh, and had no access to the fabulous treasure vaults in Memphis. The trouble was that the Alexandrian income was in the purlieu of the Alexandrians, who insisted that their ruler pay them back. Times were hard, the price of food inflated, Roman pressures omnipresent and dangerous. Auletes's solution was to debase the Alexandrian coinage.

The people rose against him immediately, set the mob loose. His secret tunnel enabled Auletes to escape into exile by sailing away, but he left penniless. Which was of scant concern to the Alexandrians, who replaced him with his eldest daughter, Berenice, and her mother, Cleopatra Tryphaena. The situation in the palace was now reversed; it was Auletes's second wife and second family who had to take a back seat to the pair of Mithridatid queens.

And little Cleopatra was recalled from Memphis. A terrible blow! How she had wept for Tach'a, for Cha'em, for that idyllic life of love and scholarship beside the wide blue snake of Nilus! The palace in Alexandria was worse than ever; now eleven years old, Cleopatra was still in the nursery, which she shared with two biting, scratching, brawling little Ptolemies. Arsinoë was the worse, forever telling her that she was not "good enough"—too little Ptolemaic blood, and grandchild of a rascally old king who might have terrorized Anatolia for forty years, but still ended a broken man. Broken by Rome.

Cleopatra Tryphaena died a year after assuming the throne, so Berenice decided to marry. Something Rome didn't want. Crassus and Pompey were still plotting for annexation, aided and abetted by the governors of Cilicia and Syria. Wherever Berenice tried to find a husband, Rome was there before her to warn the fellow off. Finally she turned to her Mithridatid relatives, and among them found that elusive husband, one Archelaus. Caring nothing for Rome, he made the journey to Alexandria and married Queen Berenice. For a few short, sweet days they were happy; then Aulus Gabinius, the governor of Syria, invaded Egypt.

Ptolemy Auletes hadn't frittered away his time in exile, he had gone to the moneylenders (including Rabirius Postumus) and offered any governor of an eastern province ten thousand talents of silver to win back his kingdom. Gabinius agreed and marched for Pelusium with Auletes in his train. Another interesting man marched with Gabinius too: his commander of horse, a twenty-seven-year-old Roman noble named Marcus Antonius.

But Cleopatra had never set eyes on Mark Antony; the moment that Gabinius breached the Egyptian border, Berenice sent her little sister to Cha'em and Tach'a in Memphis. King Archelaus called up the Egyptian army intending to fight, but neither he nor Berenice was aware that Alexandria didn't approve of the Queen's marriage to yet another Mithridatid. The Alexandrian element in the army mutinied and killed Archelaus, which marked the end of Egyptian resistance. Gabinius entered Alexandria and put Ptolemy Auletes back on the throne; Auletes murdered his daughter Berenice before Gabinius had even quit the city.

Cleopatra had just turned fourteen, Arsinoë was eight, one little boy was six, and the other barely three. The scales had tipped; the second wife and the second family of Auletes were back on top again. Understanding that were Cleopatra to be sent home, she would be murdered, Cha'em and Tach'a kept her in Memphis until her father died from his vices. The Alexandrians hadn't wanted her on the throne, but the high priest of Ptah was the present holder of an office over three thousand years old, and he understood what to do. Namely, to anoint Cleopatra as Pharaoh before she left Memphis. If she returned to Alexandria as Pharaoh, no one would dare touch her, even a Potheinus or a Theodotus. Or an Arsinoë. For Pharaoh held the key to the treasure vaults, an unlimited supply of money, and Pharaoh was God in Egypt of Nilus, where Alexandria's food came from.

The chief source of the royal income was not Alexandria, but Egypt of the river. There, where sovereigns had existed for who knew how many thousands of years, everything belonged to Pharaoh. The land, the crops, the beasts and fowls of the field and farmyard, the honeybees, the taxes, duties and fares. Only the production of linen, in the province of the priests, did Pharaoh share; the priests received one-third of the income this finest linen in the world generated. Nowhere save in Egypt was linen woven so tenuously that it was sheer as faintly clouded glass, nowhere save in Egypt could it be pleated or dyed such magical colors, nowhere save in Egypt was it so brilliantly white. One other source of income was as unique as it was lucrative: Egypt produced paper from the papyrus plant that grew everywhere in the Delta, and Pharaoh owned the paper too.

Therefore Pharaoh's income amounted to over twelve thousand talents of gold a year, divided into two purses, the privy and the public. Six thousand talents in each. Out of the public purse Pharaoh paid his district governors, his bureaucrats, his police, his water police, his army, his navy, his factory workers, his farmers and peasants. Even when Nilus failed to inundate, that public income was sufficient to buy in grain from foreign lands. The privy purse belonged outright to Pharaoh and could not be touched for any but Pharaoh's personal needs and desires. In it were lumped the country's production of gold, gemstones, porphyry, ebony, ivory, spices and pearls. The fleets that sailed to the Horn of Africa for most of these belonged to—Pharaoh.

Little wonder then that Ptolemies like Auletes, denied the title of Pharaoh, lusted after it. For Alexandria was an entity entirely separate from Egypt; while the King and Queen took a goodly share of its profits in taxes, they did not own it or its assets, be they ships or glassworks or companies of merchants. Nor did they have title to the land on which it stood. Alexandria had been founded by Alexander the Great, who fancied himself a Greek, but was Macedonian through and through. The Interpreter, Recorder and Accountant collected all Alexandrian public income, and used much of it to feather their own nests, working through a system of privileges and perquisites that included the palace.

Veterans of Assyrian, Kushite and Persian dynasties before the arrival of Alexander the Great's marshal Ptolemy, the priests of Ptah in Memphis had come to an accommodation with Ptolemy and paid him Egypt's public purse on the condition that sufficient was spent on Egypt of Nilus to keep its people and temples thriving. If the Ptolemy were also Pharaoh, then he took the private income too. Except that it did not leave the treasury vaults in Memphis unless Pharaoh came in person to remove what he needed. Thus when Cleopatra had fled Alexandria, she didn't emulate her father by sailing out of the Great Harbor penniless; she went to Memphis and obtained the money to hire an army of mercenaries.

"Oh," said Cleopatra, freed from the last of her regalia, "it weighs me down so!"

"It may wear you down, Daughter of Amun-Ra, but it buoyed you up in Caesar's eyes," Cha'em said, tenderly smoothing her hair. "In Greek guise you're disappointing—Tyrian purple ill serves Pharaoh.

When all this is over and your throne is assured, you must robe yourself as Pharaoh even in Alexandria."

"Did I, the Alexandrians would tear me to pieces. You know how they loathe Egypt."

"The answer to Rome lies with Pharaoh, not with Alexandria," Cha'em said a little sharply. "Your first duty is to secure Egypt's autonomy once and for all, no matter how many Ptolemies left Egypt to Rome in their wills. Through Caesar you can do that, and Alexandria ought to be grateful. What is this city, except a parasite feeding off Egypt and Pharaoh?"

"Perhaps," Cleopatra said thoughtfully, "all that is about to change, Cha'em. I know you've just arrived by boat, but walk down Royal Avenue and see what Caesar's done to the city. He's wrecked it, and I suspect that what he's done so far is only the beginning. The Alexandrians are devastated, but in a very angry way. They'll fight Caesar until they can't fight anymore, yet I know they can't win. When the day comes that tames them, things will change forever. I've read the commentaries Caesar wrote of his war in Gaul—very detached, very unemotional. But since I've met him, I understand them far better. Caesar gives latitude and will continue to give latitude, but if he is constantly rebuffed, he changes. Mercy and understanding no longer exist, he will go to any lengths to kill all opposition. No one of his kind has ever warred with the Alexandrians." The strange eyes stared at Cha'em with some of Caesar's detachment. "When he is pushed to it, Caesar breaks spirits as well as backbones."

Tach'a shivered. "Poor Alexandria!"

Her husband said nothing, too intent upon his welling joy. Were Alexandria utterly crushed, it would be to the advantage of Egypt— power would return to Memphis. Those years Cleopatra had spent in the temple of Ptah were paying off; witnessing Alexandria humbled and ravaged would not cause her any anguish.

"No word yet from Elephantine?" Pharaoh asked.

"It is too early, Daughter of Amun-Ra, but we have come to be with you when the news arrives, as is our duty," Cha'em said. "You cannot come to Memphis at the moment, we know."

"True," Cleopatra said, and sighed. "Oh, how much I miss Ptah, Memphis and you!"

"But Caesar has married you," Tach'a said, clasping her dear girl's hands. "You are quickened, I can tell."

"Yes, I am quickened with a son, I know it."

The two priests of Ptah exchanged a glance, well satisfied.

*　*　*

Yes, I am quickened with a boy, but Caesar does not love me. I loved him the moment I set eyes upon him—so tall, so fair, so godlike. That I hadn't expected, that he would *look* Osiris. Old and young at once, father and husband. Filled with power, majesty. But I am a duty to him, something he can do with his earthly life that leads him in a new direction. In the past he has loved. When he isn't aware that I watch him, his pain shows. So they must be gone, the women he loved. I know his daughter died in childbirth. *I* will not die in childbirth, the rulers of Egypt never do. Though he fears for me, mistaking my exterior for inner frailty. What there is of me is tested metal. I will live to be very old, as is fitting for Amun-Ra's Daughter. Caesar's son out of my body will be an old man before he can rule with his wife rather than his mother. He too will live to be very old, but he will not be the only child. Next I must have Caesar's daughter, so that our son can marry his full sister. After that, more sons and more daughters, all married to each other, all fertile.

They will found a new dynasty, the House of Ptolemy Caesar. The son I am carrying will build temples up and down the river, we will both be Pharaoh. See to the choosing of the Buchis Bull, the Apis Bull, be at the Elephantine Nilometer every year to read the Inundation. Egypt is going to enjoy the Cubits of Plenty for generations upon generations; while ever the House of Ptolemy Caesar exists, Egypt will know no want. But more than that. The Land of the Two Ladies, of the Sedge and Bee, will regain all its past glories and all its past territories—Syria, Cilicia, Cos, Chios, Cyprus and Cyrenaica. In this child lies Egypt's destiny, in his brothers and sisters a wealth of talent and genius.

So when, five days later, Cha'em told Cleopatra that Nilus was going to rise twenty-eight feet into the Cubits of Plenty, she wasn't at all surprised. Twenty-eight feet was the perfect Inundation, just as hers was the perfect child. The son of two Gods, Osiris and Isis: Horus, Haroeris.

The war in Alexandria raged on into November, but was confined to the west side of Royal Avenue. The Jews and Metics proved doughty allies, marshaled soldiers of their own and turned all their small metal shops and foundries into armaments factories. A serious matter for the Alexandrians of Macedonian and Greek ancestry, for in other days they had welcomed the sequestration of nasty, smelly activities like metalworking to the east end, where all the skilled metalworkers lived anyway. Grinding his teeth in anguish, the Interpreter was forced to spend some of the city's funds on the importation of weapons of war from Syria, and do what he could to encourage anyone on the western side with any metal skills to start forging swords and daggers.

Achillas attacked across that no-man's-land time and time again, to no effect; Caesar's soldiers repulsed the sallies with the ease of veterans bolstered by their growing hatred of Alexandrians.

Arsinoë and Ganymedes escaped Caesar's palace net early in November and arrived in the western city, where the girl donned cuirass, helmet and greaves, waved a sword and produced a spate of stirring oratory. Thus capturing everyone's attention for long enough to let Ganymedes enter Achillas's camp, where the canny eunuch murdered Achillas at once. A survivor, the Interpreter promptly made Arsinoë queen and promoted Ganymedes to the general's tent. A wise decision; Ganymedes was made for the job.

The new general walked down to the bridge across Canopic Avenue, ordered the oxen to be harnessed to the capstans controlling the sluice gates, and shut off the water supply to Delta and Epsilon Districts. Though Beta District and the Royal Enclosure were spared, Royal Avenue was not. Then, using an ingenious combination of human treadmills and the good old Archimedes' screw, he pumped salt water from the Cibotus into the pipes, sat back and waited.

It took two days of steadily more brackish water for the Romans, Jews and Metics to realize what was happening; then they panicked. Caesar was obliged to deal with the frenzy in person, which he did by lifting the paving in the middle of Royal Avenue and digging a deep hole. As soon as it filled up with fresh water, the crisis was over; soon paving was being lifted in every Delta and Epsilon street and enough wells appeared to resemble the efforts of an army of moles. Capped by an admiration for Caesar that raised him to the status of a demigod.

"We're sitting on limestone," Caesar explained to Simeon and Cibyrus, "which always contains layers of fresh water because it's soft enough for underground streams to erode. After all, we're not very far from the world's biggest river."

While waiting to see what effect salt water would have on Caesar, Ganymedes concentrated on artillery fire, lobbing flaming missiles into Royal Avenue as fast as his men could load their ballistas and catapults. But Caesar had a secret weapon: men specially trained to fire small engines called scorpions. These shot short, pointed wooden bolts the artificers made by the dozens from templates guaranteed to produce uniform flights. The flat roofs of Royal Avenue made excellent platforms for scorpions; Caesar ranged them behind wooden beams right down the length of Royal Avenue's western mansions. The ballista operators were exposed targets; a good scorpion man could plug his target in chest or side every time he fired a bolt. Ganymedes was forced to shield his men behind iron screens, which spoiled their aim.

Just after the middle of November the long-awaited Roman fleet arrived, though no one in Alexandria knew it; the winds were blowing so hard that the ships were driven miles to the west of the city. A skiff stole into the Great Harbor and made for the Royal Harbor when its crew spotted the General's scarlet flag flying from the main palace pediment. It bore messages from the legate in charge of the fleet, and a letter from Gnaeus Domitius Calvinus. Though the messages said that the fleet was desperate for water, Caesar sat down first to read Calvinus's note.

> I am very sorry that it isn't possible to send you the Thirty-eighth Legion as well as the Thirty-seventh, but recent events in Pontus render that impossible. Pharnaces has landed at Amisus, and I am off with Sestius and the Thirty-eighth to see what I can do. The situation is very grim, Caesar. Though as yet I've only heard of the awful destruction, reports say that Pharnaces has upward of a hundred thousand men, all Skythians—formidable foes, if one can believe the memoranda of Pompeius Magnus.
>
> What I am able to do for you is to send you my entire fleet of warships, as it seems unlikely that they will be needed in the campaign against the King of Cimmeria, who has brought no navy with him. The best of my bunch are the ten Rhodian triremes—fast, maneuverable and bronze-beaked. They come under the command of a man you know well—Euphranor, the best admiral this side of Gnaeus Pompeius. The other ten warships are Pontic quinqueremes, very big and strong, though not speedy. I have also tricked out twenty transports as war vessels—rigged their bows with oaken beaks and added extra oar banks. I have no idea why I have a feeling that you're in need of a war fleet, but I do all the same. Of course, since you're now going to Africa Province, I daresay you'll run into Gnaeus Pompeius and his fleets soon enough. The latest news on that front is that the Republicans are definitely gathering there for another try. It is terrible to hear what the Egyptians did to Pompeius Magnus.
>
> The Thirty-seventh comes with plenty of good artillery, and I

thought you might be in need of provisions, as we hear that Egypt is in famine. I've loaded up forty merchantmen with wheat, chick-pea, oil, bacon, and some very nice dried beans, perfect for bean-and-dumpling soup. There are some barrels of salt pork for the soup.

I've also commissioned Mithridates of Pergamum to round up at least another legion of troops for you—thank you for the *imperium maius*, it enabled me to waive the stipulations of our treaty. Just when he'll turn up in Alexandria is in the lap of the gods, but he's a good fellow, so I'm sure he'll be hurrying. He'll be marching, not sailing, by the way. We are too short of transports. If he misses you, he can commandeer transports in Alexandria to follow you to Africa Province.

My next letter will be from Pontus. By the by, I left Marcus Brutus governing Cilicia—under *strict* orders to concentrate on troop recruitment and training rather than on debt collection.

"I think," said Caesar to Rufrius as he burned this missive, "that we'll pull a little wool over Ganymedes's eyes. Let's load every empty water barrel we can find aboard our transports, and take a little sea voyage to the west. We'll create as much fuss as we can—who knows? Ganymedes might gain the impression that his saltwater trick has worked, and Caesar is quitting the city with all his men except the cavalry, whom he has callously abandoned to their fate."

At first this was exactly what Ganymedes thought, but a detachment of his cavalry, scouting west of the city, stumbled upon a party of Caesar's legionaries wandering on the shore. They seemed nice, if naive, Romans; captured, they told the squadron leader that Caesar hadn't sailed away, he was just getting fresh water at the spring. Too eager to get back to Ganymedes and tell him this news, the horsemen galloped off, leaving their erstwhile prisoners to return to Caesar.

"What we forgot to tell them," said their junior centurion to Rufrius, "was that we're really here to meet a new fleet and a whole lot of warships. They don't know about that."

"We've got Ganymedes!" Caesar cried when Rufrius reported. "Our eunuch friend will have his navy in the roads off the Eunostus Harbor to waylay thirty-five humble transports returning loaded with fresh water. Sitting ducks for the Alexandrians ibises, eh? Where's Euphranor?"

Had the day been less advanced, the Alexandrian war might have ended there and then. Ganymedes had forty quinqueremes and quadriremes lying in ambush off the Eunostus Harbor when Caesar's transports hove in view, all rowing against the wind. Not too difficult a task with empty ships. Then, as the Alexandrians moved in for the kill, ten Rhodians, ten Pontics and twenty converted transports emerged from behind Caesar's fleet, rowing at ramming speed. With only two and a half hours of daylight left, the victory couldn't be complete, but the damage Ganymedes sustained was severe: one quadrireme and its marines captured, one sunk, two more disabled and their marines killed to a man. Caesar's warships were unhurt.

At dawn on the following day the troop transports and food ships belonging to the Thirty-seventh Legion sailed into the Great Harbor. Caesar wasn't out of boiling water yet, but he had successfully fought a defensive war against huge odds until these urgently needed reinforcements arrived. Now he also had 5,000 ex-Republican veteran soldiers, 1,000 noncombatants, and a war fleet commanded by Euphranor. As well as stacks of proper legionary food. How the men loathed Alexandrian rations! Especially oil made from sesame, pumpkin or croton seeds.

"I'll take Pharos Isle," Caesar announced.

Relatively easy; Ganymedes wasn't willing to expend any of his trained personnel to defend the island, though its inhabitants resisted the Romans bitterly. In the end, to no avail.

Rather than waste his resources on Pharos, Ganymedes concentrated on marshaling every ship he could put in the water; he was convinced that the answer to Alexandria's dilemma was a big victory at sea. Potheinus was sending information from the palace daily, though neither Caesar nor Ganymedes himself had told the Lord High Chamberlain that Achillas was dead; Ganymedes knew that did Potheinus know who was in command, his reports might dry up.

At the beginning of December, Ganymedes lost his informant in the palace.

"I can't permit any hint of my next move to reach Ganymedes, so Potheinus must die," said Caesar to Cleopatra. "Do you object to that?"

She blinked. "Not in the least."

"Well, I thought it polite to ask, my dear. He's *your* Lord High Chamberlain, after all. You might be running out of eunuchs."

"I have plenty of eunuchs, and will appoint Apollodorus."

Their time together was limited to an hour here and an hour there; Caesar never slept in the palace, or dined with her. All his energies were devoted to the war, an interminable business thanks to Caesar's lack of numbers. She hadn't told him yet about the baby growing in her womb. Time for that when he was less preoccupied. She wanted him to glow, not glower.

"Let me deal with Potheinus," she said now.

"As long as you don't torture him. A quick, clean death."

Her face darkened. "He deserves to suffer," she growled.

"According to your lights, definitely. But while I command, he gets a knife up under the ribs on the left side. I could flog and behead, but that's a ceremony I don't have time to conduct."

So Potheinus died with a knife up under his ribs on the left side, as ordered. What Cleopatra didn't bother to tell Caesar was that she showed Potheinus the knife a full two days before it was used. Potheinus did a lot of weeping, wailing and begging for his life in those two days.

The naval battle came on shortly into December. Caesar put his ships just seaward of the shoals outside the Eunostus Harbor without a center; the ten Rhodians on his right, the ten Pontics on his left, and a gap of two thousand feet between them in which to maneuver. His twenty converted transports lay well behind the gap. The strategy was his, the execution Euphranor's, and the preparations before the first galley left its moorings meticulously detailed. Each of his reserve vessels knew exactly which ship of the line it was to replace, each legate and tribune knew precisely what his duties were, every century of legionaries knew which corvus it would use to board an enemy ship, and Caesar himself visited every unit with cheery words and a crisp summary of what he intended to achieve. Long experience had shown him that trained and experienced ranker soldiers could often take matters into their own hands and wrest victory from defeat if they too had been told exactly what the General planned, so he always kept his rankers informed.

The corvus, a wooden gangway equipped with an iron hook under its far end, was a Roman invention dating back to the wars against Carthage, a naval power far more skilled than any Roman admiral of that time. But the new device turned a sea battle into a land one, and Rome had no peer on land. The moment the corvus plunked down on the deck of an enemy ship, the hook married it to the enemy ship and let Roman troops pour aboard.

Ganymedes arranged the twenty-two biggest and best of his warships in a straight line facing Caesar's gap, with twenty-two more behind them, and beyond this second line a great many undecked pinnaces and biremes. These last two kinds were not to fight; each held a small catapult to fire incendiary missiles.

The tricky part of the operation concerned the shoals and reefs; whichever side advanced first was the most at risk of being cut off and forced on to the rocks. While Ganymedes hung back, hesitating, Euphranor fearlessly rowed his vessels into the passage and skimmed past the hazards to engage. His leading ships were immediately surrounded, but the Rhodians were brilliant on the sea; no matter how he tried to manipulate his own clumsier galleys, Ganymedes couldn't manage to sink, or board, or even disable any of the Rhodians. When the Pontics followed the Rhodians in, disaster struck for Ganymedes, his fleet now in complete disorder and at Caesar's mercy—a quality Caesar wasn't famous for in battle.

By the time dusk broke the hostilities off, the Romans had captured a bireme and a quinquereme with all their marines and oarsmen, sunk three quinqueremes, and badly damaged a score of other Alexandrian ships, which limped back to the Cibotus and left Caesar in command of the Eunostus Harbor. The Romans incurred no losses whatsoever.

Now remained the Heptastadion mole and the Cibotus, heavily fortified and manned. At the Pharos end of the mole the Romans dug themselves in, but the Cibotus end was a different matter. Caesar's greatest handicap was the narrowness of the Heptastadion, which didn't permit more than twelve hundred men a foothold, and so few men were not enough to storm the Alexandrian defenses.

As usual when the going was hard, Caesar grabbed his shield and sword and mounted the ramparts to hearten his men, his scarlet *paludamentum* cloak marking him out for all to see. A huge racket in the rear gave his soldiers the impression that the Alexandrians had worked around behind them; they began to retreat, leaving Caesar stranded. His own pinnace sat in the water just below, so he leaped into it and directed it along the mole, shouting up to his men that there were no Alexandrians in their rear—keep going, boys! But more and more soldiers were jumping into the craft, threatening to capsize it. Suddenly deciding that today was not the day he was going to take the Cibotus end of the mole, Caesar dived off the pinnace into the water, his scarlet general's cloak clamped between his teeth. The *paludamentum* acted as a beacon while he swam; everyone followed it to safety.

So Ganymedes still held the Cibotus and the city end of the Heptastadion, but Caesar held the rest of the mole, Pharos Isle, all of the Great Harbor, and the Eunostus apart from the Cibotus.

The war entered a new phase and was waged on land. Ganymedes seemed to have concluded that Caesar had wreaked sufficient havoc on the city to make rebuilding a major task, so why not wreck more of it? The Alexandrians began to demolish another swath of houses beyond the no-man's-land behind the western mansions of Royal Avenue, and used the rubble to make a forty-foot-high wall with a top flat enough to hold big artillery. They then pounded Royal Avenue day and night, which didn't make much difference to Royal Avenue, whose luxurious, stoutly built houses held up under the pounding much like a *murus Gallicus* wall; the stone blocks from which they were built gave them rigid strength, while the wooden beams stapling them together gave them tensile strength. Very hard to knock down, and excellent shelter for Caesar's soldiers.

When this bombardment didn't succeed, a wooden siege tower ten stories high and mounted on wheels began to roll up and down Canopic Avenue contributing to the chaos, firing boulders and volleys of spears. Caesar put a counterattack on top of the Hill of Pan and shot enough flaming arrows and bundles of blazing straw into the tower to set it afire. A roaring inferno, hordes of screaming men toppling from it, it rolled away toward the haven of Rhakotis, and was seen no more.

The war had reached a stalemate.

After three months of constant urban battle that saw neither side in any position to impose terms of truce or surrender, Caesar moved back into the palace and left conduct of the siege to the competent Publius Rufrius.

"I detest fighting in cities!" he said savagely to Cleopatra, stripped to the padded scarlet tunic he wore under his cuirass. "This is exactly like Massilia, except that there I could leave the action to my legates and march off myself to wallop Afranius and Petreius in Nearer Spain. Here, I'm *stuck*, and every day that I'm stuck is one more day the so-called Republicans have to shore up resistance in Africa Province."

"Was that where you were going?" she asked.

"Yes. Though what I had really hoped was to find Pompeius Magnus alive and negotiate a peace that would have saved a great many precious Roman lives. But, thanks to your wretched, corrupt system of eunuchs and deviants in charge of children and cities—not to mention public moneys!—Magnus is dead and I am *stuck!*"

"Have a bath," she said soothingly. "You'll feel better."

"In Rome they say that Ptolemaic queens bathe in ass's milk. How did that myth originate?" he asked, sinking into the water.

"I have no idea," she said from behind him, working the knots out of his shoulders with surprisingly strong fingers. "Perhaps it goes back to Lucullus, who was here for a while before he went on to Cyrenaica. Ptolemy Chickpea gave him an emerald quizzing glass, I think. No, not a quizzing glass. An emerald etched with Lucullus's own profile—or was it Chickpea's profile?"

"I neither know nor care. Lucullus was a wronged man, though personally I loathed him," Caesar said, swinging her around.

Somehow she didn't look as wraithlike in the water; her little brown breasts broke its surface more plumply, nipples big and very dark, areolae more pronounced.

"You're with child," he said abruptly.

"Yes, three months. You quickened me that first night."

His eyes traveled to her flushed face, his mind racing to fit this astonishing news into his scheme of things. A child! And he had none, had expected to have none. How amazing. Caesar's child would sit on the Egyptian throne. Would be Pharaoh. Caesar had fathered a king or a queen. It mattered not an atom to him which sex the babe emerged with; a Roman valued daughters just as highly as sons, for daughters meant political alliances of huge importance to their sires.

"Are you pleased?" she asked anxiously.

"Are you well?" he countered, stroking her cheek with a wet hand, finding those beautiful lion's eyes easy to drown in.

"I thrive." She turned her head to kiss the hand.

"Then I am pleased." He gathered her close.

"Ptah has spoken, he will be a son."

"Why Ptah? Isn't Ammon-Ra your great god?"

"*Amun*-Ra," she corrected. "Ammon is Greek."

"What I like about you," he said suddenly, "is that you don't mind talking in the midst of touching, and you don't moan or carry on like a professional whore."

"You mean I'm an amateur one?" she asked, kissing his face.

"Don't be deliberately obtuse." He smiled, enjoying her kisses. "You're better pregnant, you look more like a woman than a little girl."

As January ended, the Alexandrians sent a deputation to Caesar at the palace. Ganymedes was not among its members; its spokesman was the Chief Judge, a worthy Ganymedes considered expendable if Caesar was in a mood to take prisoners. What none of them knew was that Caesar ailed, had succumbed to a gastric illness that grew worse with each passing day.

The audience was conducted in the throne room, which Caesar had not seen before. It paled every other chamber he had seen to insignificance. Priceless furniture stood around it, all Egyptian in style;

the walls were gem-encrusted gold; the floor was gold tiles; the ceiling beams were covered in gold. What the local craftsmen hadn't mastered was plastering, so there were no complicated cornices or ceilings honeycombed with detail—but with all that gold, who noticed? Most eye-catching of all was a series of solid gold statues larger than life and elevated on plinths: the pantheon of Egyptian gods, very bizarre entities. Most had human bodies, almost all had the heads of animals—crocodile, jackal, lioness, cat, hippopotamus, hawk, ibis, dog-faced baboon.

Apollodorus, Caesar noted, was dressed as an Egyptian rather than a Macedonian; he wore a long, pleated robe of linen dyed in red and yellow stripes, a gold collar bearing the vulture, and a cloth of gold *nemes* headdress, which was a stiffened, triangular cloth drawn tight across the forehead and tied behind the neck, with two wings that protruded from behind the ears. The court had ceased to be Macedonian.

Nor did Caesar conduct the interview. Cleopatra did, clad as Pharaoh: a great offense to the Chief Judge and his minions.

"We did not come to bargain with Egypt, but with Caesar!" he snapped, his head turned to look at a rather grey Caesar.

"I rule here, not Caesar, and Alexandria is a part of Egypt!" Cleopatra said in a loud, harsh, unmusical voice. "Lord High Chamberlain, remind this creature who I am and who he is!"

"You've abrogated your Macedonian inheritance!" the Chief Judge shouted, as Apollodorus forced him to kneel to the Queen. "Where is Serapis in this hideous menagerie of beasts? You're not the Queen of Alexandria, you're the Queen of Beasts!"

A description of Cleopatra which amused Caesar, seated below her on his ivory curule chair, placed where King Ptolemy's throne used to be. Oh, many shocks for a Macedonian bureaucrat! Pharaoh, not the Queen—and a Roman where the King should be.

"Tell me your business, Hermocrates, then you may leave the presence of so many beasts," Pharaoh said.

"I have come to ask for King Ptolemy."

"Why?"

"Clearly he isn't wanted here!" Hermocrates said tartly. "We are tired of Arsinoë and Ganymedes," he added, apparently unaware that he was feeding Caesar valuable information about morale among the Alexandrian high command. "This war drags on and on," the Chief Judge said with genuine weariness. "If we have custody of the King, it may be possible to negotiate a peace before the city ceases to exist. So many ships destroyed, trade in ruins—"

"You may negotiate a peace with me, Hermocrates."

"I refuse to, Queen of Beasts, traitor to Macedonia!"

"Macedonia," said Cleopatra, sounding equally tired, "is a place none of us has seen in generations. It's time you stopped calling yourselves Macedonians. You're Egyptians."

"Never!" said Hermocrates between his teeth. "Give us King Ptolemy, who remembers his ancestry."

"Bring his majesty at once, Apollodorus."

The little king entered in proper Macedonian dress, complete with hat and diadem; Hermocrates took one look at him and fell to his knees to kiss the boy's outstretched hand.

"Oh, your majesty, your majesty, we need you!" he cried.

After the shock of being parted from Theodotus had lessened, young Ptolemy had been thrown into the company of little brother Philadelphus, and had found outlets for his youthful energies which he had come to enjoy far more than the attentions of Theodotus. The death of Pompey the Great had pushed Theodotus into a premature seduction that had intrigued the lad in one way, yet repelled him in another. Though he had been with Theodotus—a crony of his father's—all his life, he saw the tutor through the eyes of childhood as unpalatably old, singularly undesirable. Some of the things Theodotus had done to him were pleasurable, but not all, and he could find no pleasure whatsoever in their author, whose flesh sagged, whose teeth were black and rotten, whose breath stank. Puberty was arriving, but Ptolemy wasn't highly sexed, and his fantasies still revolved around chariots, armies, war, himself as the general. So when Caesar had banished Theodotus, he turned to little Philadelphus as to a playmate in his war games, and had found a kind of life he was thoroughly enjoying. Lots of running around the palace and the grounds whooping, talks with the legionaries Caesar used to police those grounds, stories of mighty battles in Gaul of the Long-hairs, and a side to Caesar he had not suspected. Thus, though he saw Caesar rarely, he had transferred his hero worship to the ruler of the world, actually relished the spectacle of a master strategist making fools of his Alexandrian subjects.

So now he stared at the Chief Judge suspiciously. "Need me?" he asked. "What for, Hermocrates?"

"You are our king, majesty. We need you with us."

"With you? Where?"

"In our part of Alexandria."

"You mean I should leave my palace?"

"We have another palace ready for you, your majesty. After all, I see Caesar sitting in your place here. It's you we need, not the Princess Arsinoë."

The lad snorted with laughter. "Well, *that* doesn't surprise me!" he said, grinning. "Arsinoë's an arrogant bitch."

"Quite so," agreed Hermocrates. He turned not to Cleopatra, but to Caesar. "Caesar, may we have our King?"

Caesar wiped the sweat from his face. "Yes, Chief Judge."

Whereupon Ptolemy burst into noisy tears. "No, I don't want to go! I want to stay with you, Caesar! Please, please!"

"You're a king, Ptolemy, and you can be of service to your people. You must go with Hermocrates," said Caesar, voice faint.

"No, no! I want to stay with you, Caesar!"

"Apollodorus, remove them both," said Cleopatra, fed up.

Still howling and protesting, the King was hustled out.

"What was all that about?" Caesar asked, frowning.

When King Ptolemy reached his new quarters in an untouched, beautiful house in the grounds of the Serapeum, he still wept desolately; a grief exacerbated when Theodotus appeared, for Cleopatra had sent the boy's tutor back to him. To Theodotus's dismay, his overtures were rebuffed violently and viciously, but it was not Theodotus whom Ptolemy wanted to assault. He hungered to wreak vengeance on Caesar, his betrayer.

After sobbing himself to sleep, the boy woke in the morning hurt and hardened of heart. "Send Arsinoë and Ganymedes to me," he snapped at the Interpreter.

When Arsinoë saw him, she squealed in joy. "Oh, Ptolemy, you've come to marry me!" she cried.

The King turned his shoulder. "Send this deceitful bitch back to Caesar and my sister," he said curtly, then glared at Ganymedes, who looked careworn, exhausted. "Kill this *thing* at once! I shall take command of my army personally."

"No peace talks?" asked the Interpreter, stomach sinking.

"No peace talks. I want Caesar's head on a golden plate."

So the war went on more bitterly than ever, an increasing burden for Caesar, who suffered such terrible rigors and vomiting that he was incapable of command.

Early in February another fleet arrived; more warships, more food, and the Twenty-seventh Legion, a force composed of ex-Republican troops discharged in Greece, but bored with civilian life.

"Send out our fleet," Caesar said to Rufrius and Tiberius Claudius

Nero; he was wrapped in blankets, his whole body shaken with rigors. "Nero, as the senior Roman, you'll have the titular command, but I want it understood that the real commander is our Rhodian friend, Euphranor. Whatever he orders, you'll do."

"It is not fitting that a foreigner makes the decisions," Nero said stiffly, chin up.

"I don't care what's fitting!" Caesar managed to articulate, teeth chattering, face drawn and white. "All I care about are results, and you, Nero, couldn't general the fight for the October Horse's head! So hear me well. Let Euphranor do as he wants, and support him absolutely. Otherwise I'll banish you in disgrace."

"Let me go," Rufrius begged, foreseeing trouble.

"I can't spare you from Royal Avenue. Euphranor will win."

Euphranor did win, but the price of his victory was higher than Caesar was willing to pay. Leading the action as always, the Rhodian admiral destroyed his first Alexandrian ship and went after another. When several Alexandrian ships clustered around him, he flagged Nero for help. Nero ignored him; Euphranor and his ship went down with the loss of all hands. Both Roman fleets made it into the Royal Harbor safely, Nero sure that Caesar would never find out about his treachery. But some little bird on Nero's ship whistled a tune in Caesar's ear.

"Pack your things and go!" Caesar said. "I never want to see you again, you arrogant, conceited, irresponsible fool!"

Nero stood aghast. "But I won!" he cried.

"*You* lost. Euphranor won. Now get out of my sight."

Caesar had written one letter to Vatia Isauricus in Rome at the end of November, explaining that for the time being he was stuck in Alexandria, and outlining his plans for the coming year. For the moment he would have to continue as Dictator; the curule elections would just have to wait until he reached Rome, whenever that might be. In the meantime, Mark Antony would have to perform as Master of the Horse and Rome would have to limp along without higher magistrates in office than the tribunes of the plebs.

After that he wrote no more to Rome, trusting that his proverbial luck would keep the city from harm until he could get there in person and see to things. Antony had turned out well after a dubious period, he would hold the place together. Though why was it that only Caesar seemed able to gift places with political stability, functioning economies? Couldn't people stand off far enough away to see beyond their own careers, their own agendas? Egypt was a case in point. It cried out for firm tenure of the throne, a more caring and enlightened form of government, a mob stripped of power. So Caesar would have to remain there long enough to educate its sovereign to her responsibilities, ensure that it never became a refuge for renegade Romans, and teach the Alexandrians that spilling Ptolemies was no solution for problems rooted in the mighty cycles of good times and bad times.

The illness sapped him, for it refused to go away; a very serious malady that saw him lose weight by the pounds and pounds, he who carried not an ounce of superfluous flesh. Midway through February, and over his protests, Cleopatra imported the priest-physician Hapd'efan'e from Memphis to treat him.

"The lining of your stomach has become grossly inflamed," said this individual in awkward Greek, "and the only remedy is a gruel of barley starch mixed with a special concoction of herbs. You must live on it for a month at least, then we shall see."

"As long as it doesn't involve liver and eggs-in-milk, I'll eat anything," said Caesar fervently, remembering Lucius Tuccius's diet as he had recovered from the ague that had nearly put paid to his life while he had been hiding from Sulla.

Once he began this monotonous regimen, he improved dramatically, put on weight, regained his energy.

When he received a letter from Mithridates of Pergamum on the first day of March, he went limp with relief. His health now something that didn't cast a grey shadow at the back of his mind, he could bend it to what the letter said with his old vigor.

> Well, Caesar, I have come as far as Hierosolyma called Jerusalem, having picked up a thousand horse from Deiotarus in Galatia, and one legion of reasonable troops from Marcus Brutus in Tarsus. There was nothing to be had in northern Syria, but it seems that the Jewish king-without-a-kingdom, Hyrcanus, has a keen affection for Queen Cleopatra: he has donated three thousand crack Jewish soldiers and is sending me south in the company of his crony, Antipater, and Antipater's son Herod. In two *nundinae* we expect to reach Pelusium, where Antipater assures me that he will have the authority to collect Queen Cleopatra's army from Mount Casius—it consists of Jews and Idumaeans.
>
> You will know better than I whereabouts my army is likely to meet opposition. I gather from Herod, a very busy and subtle young man, that Achillas removed his army from Pelusium months ago to war against you in Alexandria. But Antipater,

Herod and I are all wary of entering the swamps and canals of the Delta without specific directives from you. So we will wait at Pelusium for instructions.

On the Pontic front, things are not good. Gnaeus Domitius Calvinus and the troops he managed to scrape up met Pharnaces near Nicopolis in Armenia Parva, and were defeated badly. Calvinus had no choice other than to retreat west toward Bithynia; had Pharnaces followed, Calvinus would have been annihilated. However, Pharnaces preferred to stay in Pontus and Armenia Parva, wreaking havoc. His atrocities are appalling. The last I heard before I marched myself, he was planning to invade Bithynia—but if so, then his preparations were slipshod and unorganized. He was ever the same, Pharnaces; I remember him when I was a youth.

By the time I reached Antioch, a new rumor caught me up: that the son Pharnaces left to govern in Cimmeria, Asander, waited until his daddy was thoroughly involved in Pontus, then declared himself king and his father an exile. So it may fall out that you and Calvinus will have an unexpected breathing space, if Pharnaces returns to Cimmeria first to put down this ungrateful child.

I await your reply with eagerness, and am your servant.

Rescue at last!

Caesar burned the letter, then had Trebatius write a new one purporting to be from Mithridates of Pergamum. Its contents were designed to tempt the Alexandrians into quitting the city for a quick campaign in the Delta. But first it had to reach Arsinoë in the palace in a way that led her to believe her agents had stolen it before Caesar opened it, that he didn't know reinforcements were at hand. The false letter was sealed with an impression of a coin issued by Mithridates of Pergamum and by devious ploys it duly reached Arsinoë, apparently unopened. Both letter and Arsinoë were gone from the palace within an hour. Two days later King Ptolemy, his army and the Macedonian element of Alexandria sailed away eastward toward the Delta. The city lay incapable of any fighting, its leading caste gone.

Caesar still wasn't entirely well, though he refused to admit it; watching him buckle himself into leather for the coming Delta campaign, Cleopatra fretted.

"Can't you let Rufrius deal with this?" she asked.

"Probably, but if I am to crush resistance totally and bring Alexandria permanently to its senses, I must be there in person," Caesar explained; the effort of dressing had him sweating.

"Then take Hapd'efan'e with you," she pleaded.

But the gear was on, he had managed unassisted, and his skin was regaining some color; the eyes he turned on Cleopatra were Caesar's eyes, in control of everything. "You concern yourself too much." He kissed her, his breath stale and sour.

Two cohorts of wounded troops were left to guard the Royal Enclosure; Caesar took the 3,200 men of the Sixth, the Thirty-seventh and the Twenty-seventh Legions, together with all the cavalry, and marched out of Alexandria on a route Cleopatra for one thought unduly circuitous. Instead of going to the Delta by way of the ship canal, he took the road south of Lake Mareotis, keeping it on his left; by the time he did turn toward the Canopic arm of Nilus, he was long out of sight.

A fast courier had galloped for Pelusium well ahead of King Ptolemy's army, his mission to inform Mithridates of Pergamum that he was to form one half of Caesar's pincers by moving down the east bank of the Pelusiac arm of Nilus, and that he was not to enter the Delta itself. They would nip Ptolemy between them near the apex, on solid ground.

So called because it had the shape of the Greek letter delta, the Delta of Nilus was larger than any other river mouth known: on Our Sea, a hundred and fifty miles from the Pelusiac to the Canopic arm; and from the coast of Our Sea to the bifurcation of Nilus proper just north of Memphis, over a hundred miles. The great river forked and forked and forked again into many branches, some larger than others, and fanned out to empty itself into Our Sea through seven interlinked mouths. Originally all the Delta waterways had been natural, but after the Greekly scientific Ptolemies came to rule Egypt, they connected Nilus's network of arms with thousands of canals, so that a piece of Delta land was nowhere farther than a mile from water. Why was it necessary to tend the Delta so carefully, when the thousand-mile course of Nilus from Elephantine to Memphis grew more than enough to feed Egypt and Alexandria? Because *byblos* grew in the Delta, the papyrus reed from which paper was made. The Ptolemies had a worldwide monopoly on paper, and all the profits of its sale went into Pharaoh's privy purse. Paper was the temple of human thought, and men had come to be unable to live without it.

This being the beginning of winter by the seasons, though the end of March by the Roman calendar, the summer flooding had receded, but Caesar had no desire to bog his army down in a labyrinth of waterways he didn't know nearly as well as Ptolemy's advisers and guides did.

Constant dialogues with Simeon, Abraham and Joshua during the months of war in Alexandria had dowered Caesar with a knowledge of the Egyptian Jews far superior to Cleopatra's; until his advent, she seemed never to have considered the Jews worth her notice. Whereas Caesar had huge respect for Jewish intelligence, learning and independence, and was already planning how best to turn the Jews into valuable allies for Cleopatra after he departed. Constricted by her upbringing and exclusivity she might be, but she had potential as a ruler once he had drummed the essentials into her; it had encouraged him when she had freely consented to give the Jews and Metics the Alexandrian citizenship. A start.

In the southeast of the Delta lay the Land of Onias, an autonomous enclave of Jews descended from the high priest Onias and his followers, who had been exiled from Judaea for refusing to prostrate themselves flat on the ground before the King of Syria; that, Onias had said, they did only to their god. King Ptolemy VI Philometor gave the Onians a large tract of land as their own in return for an annual tribute and soldiers for the Egyptian army. The news of Cleopatra's generosity had spread to the Land of Onias, which declared for her in this civil war and made it possible for Mithridates of Pergamum to occupy Pelusium without a struggle; Pelusium was full of Jews and had strong ties to the Land of Onias, which was vital to all Egyptian Jews because it held the Great Temple. This was a smaller replica of King Solomon's temple, even to a tower eighty feet tall and artificial gulches to simulate the Vales of Kedron and Gehenna.

The little king had barged his army down the Phatnitic arm of Nilus; it merged with the Pelusiac arm just above Leontopolis and the Land of Onias, which stretched between Leontopolis and Heliopolis. Here, near Heliopolis, King Ptolemy found Mithridates of Pergamum encased in a stout, Roman-style camp, and attacked it with reckless abandon. Hardly crediting his good luck, Mithridates promptly led his men out of the camp and waded into the fray so successfully that many Ptolemaians died and the rest scattered in panic. However, someone in Ptolemy's army owned common sense, for as soon as the post-battle frenzy evaporated, the Ptolemaians fell back to a naturally fortified position hedged in by a ridge, the Pelusiac Nilus, and a wide canal with very high, precipitous banks.

Caesar came up shortly after Ptolemy's defeat, more out of breath from the march than he cared to admit, even to Rufrius; he halted his men and studied Ptolemy's position intently. The chief obstacle for him was the canal, whereas for Mithridates, it was the ridge.

"We've found places where we can ford the canal," Arminius of the German Ubii told him, "and in other places we can swim it, the horses too."

The foot soldiers were directed to fell every tall tree in the neighborhood to build a causeway across the canal, which they did with enthusiasm, a hard day's march notwithstanding; after six months of war, Roman hatred of Alexandria and Alexandrians burned at white heat. To the last man they hoped that here would be the decisive battle, after which they could quit Egypt forever.

Ptolemy sent infantry and light-armed cavalry to block Caesar's advance, but the Roman infantry and the German cavalry poured across in such a rage that they fell on the Ptolemaians like worked-up Belgic Gauls. The Ptolemaians broke and fled, but were cut down; few escaped to seek shelter in the little king's fortress some seven miles away.

At first Caesar had thought to attack at once, but when he set eyes on Ptolemy's stronghold he changed his mind. Many old temple ruins in the vicinity had contributed a wealth of stone to buttress the site's natural advantages. Best put the men into camp for the night. They had marched over twenty miles before engaging at the canal crossing, they deserved a good meal and a sleep before the next clash. What he told nobody was that he himself felt faint, that Ptolemy's dispositions had pitched and heaved in his gaze like flotsam on a stormy sea.

In the morning he ate a small loaf of bread laced with honey as well as his barley gruel, and felt a great deal better.

The Ptolemaians—easier to call them that because they were by no means all Alexandrians—had fortified a nearby hamlet and joined it to their hill structure by stone bastions; Caesar threw the main brunt of his initial charge at the hamlet, intending to take it and carry on by natural impetus to take the fortress. But there was a space between the Pelusiac Nilus and the Ptolemaic lines that whoever commanded had made impossible to negotiate by directing a cross fire of arrows and spears into it; Mithridates of Pergamum, driving from the far side of the ridge, had problems of his own and could not help. Though the hamlet fell, Caesar couldn't extricate his troops from that lethal cross fire to storm the heights and finish the business.

Sitting his hired horse atop a mound, he noticed that the Ptolemaians had made too much of this minor victory, and had come down from the highest part of their citadel to help fire arrows at the beleaguered Romans. He summoned the hoary *primipilus* centurion of the Sixth Legion, Decimus Carfulenus.

"Grab five cohorts, Carfulenus, skirt the lower defenses and take the heights those idiots have vacated," he said crisply, secretly relieved that rest and food had restored his usual grasp of a military situation. Easy to see how to do it when he was feeling himself—oh, age! Is this the beginning of Caesar's end? Let it be quick, let it not be a slow dwindle into senescence!

Taking the heights provoked a generalized Ptolemaic panic. Within an hour of Carfulenus's occupation of the citadel, King Ptolemy's army was routed. Thousands were slain on the field, but some, harboring the little king in their midst, managed to reach the Pelusiac Nilus and their barges.

Of course it was necessary to receive Malachai, high priest of the Land of Onias, with due ceremony, introduce him to the beaming Mithridates of Pergamum, sit down with both of them and partake of sweet Jewish wine. When a shadow fell in the tent opening, Caesar excused himself and rose, suddenly very tired.

"News of little Ptolemy, Rufrius?"

"Yes, Caesar. He boarded one of the barges, but the chaos on the riverbank was so frenzied that his puntsmen couldn't push away before the barge became choked with men. Not far down the river, it capsized. The King was among those who drowned."

"Do you have his body?"

"Yes." Rufrius grinned, his seamed ex-centurion's homely face lighting up like a boy's. "We also have Princess Arsinoë. She was in the citadel and challenged Carfulenus to a duel, if you'd believe that! Waving her sword around and screaming like Mormolyce."

"What splendid news!" said Caesar genially.

"Orders, Caesar?"

"As soon as I can wriggle out of the formalities in there," Caesar said, nodding toward the tent, "I'm for Alexandria. I'll take the King's body and Princess Arsinoë with me. You and the good Mithridates can clean up, then follow me with the army."

"Execute her," said Pharaoh from the throne when Caesar presented her with a disheveled Arsinoë, still in her armor.

Apollodorus bowed. "At once, Daughter of Amun-Ra."

"Um—I am afraid not," said Caesar in apologetic tones.

The slight figure on the dais stiffened dangerously. "What do you mean, you're afraid not?" Cleopatra demanded.

"Arsinoë is my captive, Pharaoh, not yours. Therefore, as is Roman custom, she will be sent to Rome to walk in my triumph."

"While ever my sister lives, my life is imperiled! I say that she dies today!"

"*I* say she doesn't."

"You're a visitor to these shores, Caesar! You do not give commands to the throne of Egypt!"

"Rubbish!" said Caesar, annoyed. "I put you on the throne, and I command *whoever* sits on that expensive piece of furniture while ever I am a visitor to these shores! Attend to your own affairs, Pharaoh— bury your brother in the Sema, start rebuilding your city, take a trip to Memphis or Cyrene, nourish the child in your womb. For that matter, marry your remaining brother. You can't rule alone, it's neither Egyptian nor Alexandrian custom for a sovereign to rule alone!"

He walked out. She kicked off her towering sandals and ran after him, Pharaonic dignity forgotten, leaving a stunned audience to make what it would of that royal battle of wills. Arsinoë began to laugh wildly; Apollodorus looked at Charmian and Iras ruefully.

"Just as well I didn't summon the Interpreter, the Recorder, the Accountant, the Chief Judge and the Night Commander," the Lord High Chamberlain said. "However, I think we have to let Pharaoh and Caesar sort things out for themselves. And don't laugh, your highness. Your side lost the war—you will never be queen in Alexandria. Until Caesar puts you on a Roman ship, you're going to the darkest, most airless dungeon beneath the Sema—on bread and water. It is not Roman tradition to execute most of those who walk in a Roman triumph, so no doubt Caesar will free you after his, but be warned, your highness. If you ever return to Egypt, you will die. Your sister will see to that."

"How dare you!" Cleopatra shrilled. "How dare you *humiliate* Pharaoh in front of the court?"

"Then Pharaoh shouldn't be so high-handed, my dear," Caesar said, temper mended, patting his knee. "Before you announce any executions, ask me what I want first. Whether you like it or not, Rome has been a profound presence in Egypt for forty years. When I depart, Rome isn't going to depart too. For one thing, I intend to garrison Alexandria with Roman troops. If you want to continue to reign in Egypt and Alexandria, be politic and crafty, starting with me. That I am your lover and the father of your unborn child are of no significance to me the moment your interests conflict with Rome's."

"For Rome, infer Caesar," she said bitterly.

"Naturally. Come, sit down and cuddle me. It isn't good for a baby to endure tantrums. He doesn't mind it when we make love, but I'm sure he becomes extremely upset when we quarrel."

"You think he's a boy too," she said, unwilling yet to sit on his knee, but softening.

"Cha'em and Tach'a convinced me."

No sooner had he uttered those words than his whole body jerked. Caesar looked down at himself in amazement, then toppled out of the chair to lie with back arched, arms and legs rigidly extended.

Cleopatra screamed for help, tugging at the double crown as she ran to him, heedless of its fate when it flew off and crashed to the floor. By this, Caesar's face had gone a dark purple-blue and his limbs were in convulsion; still screaming, Cleopatra was knocked sprawling when she tried to restrain him.

As suddenly as it had come, it was over.

Thinking that the lovers were venting their spleen in physical violence, Charmian and Iras had not dared to enter until a certain note in their mistress's cries convinced them that something serious was happening. Then when the two girls added their shrieks to Cleopatra's, Apollodorus, Hapd'efan'e and three priests rushed in to find Caesar lying limply on the floor, breathing slowly and stertorously, his face the grey of extreme illness.

"What is it?" Cleopatra asked Hapd'efan'e, down on his knees beside Caesar sniffing at his breath, feeling for a heartbeat.

"Did he convulse, Pharaoh?"

"Yes, yes!"

"Very sweet wine!" the priest-physician barked. "Very sweet wine, and a supple reed that is well hollowed out. Quickly!"

While the other priests flew to obey, Charmian and Iras took hold of the howling, terrified Cleopatra, persuaded her to shed some of her pharaonic layers, the plethora of jewels. Apollodorus was roaring that heads were going to fall unless the hollow reed was found, and Caesar, comatose, knew nothing of the horror and terror in every breast—*what if the ruler of the world should die in Egypt?*

A priest came running from the mummification annex with the reed, normally used to perfuse the cranial cavity with natron. A snapped question reassured Hapd'efan'e that this reed had never been used. He took it, blew through it to see if it was patent, opened Caesar's mouth, slid the reed inside, stroked his throat, and gently pushed until a foot of it had vanished. Then he carefully trickled the very sweet wine into its lumen too slowly and thinly to cause an air block; not a lot of wine by volume, but the process seemed to last forever. Finally Hapd'efan'e sat back on his heels and waited. When his patient began to stir, the priest plucked the reed out and took Caesar into his arms.

"Here," he said when the eyes opened cloudily, "drink this."

Within a very few moments Caesar had recovered enough to stand unassisted, walk about and look at all these shocked people. Cleopatra, face smeared and wet with tears, sat staring at him as if he had risen from the dead, Charmian and Iras were bawling, Apollodorus was slumped in a chair with his head between his knees, several priests fluttered and twittered in the background, and all of this consternation apparently was due to him.

"What happened?" he asked, going to sit beside Cleopatra, and aware that he did feel rather peculiar.

"You had an epileptic fit," Hapd'efan'e said baldly, "but you do not have epilepsy, Caesar. The fact that sweet wine brought you around so quickly tells me that you have suffered a bodily change following that month of rigors. How long is it since you've eaten anything?"

"Many hours." His arm curled comfortingly around Cleopatra's shoulders, he gazed up at the thin, dark Egyptian and gave him a dazzling smile, then looked contrite. "The trouble is that when I'm busy I forget to eat."

"In future you must keep someone with you to remind you to eat," Hapd'efan'e said severely. "Regular meals will keep this infirmity at bay, but if you do forget to eat, drink sweet wine."

"No," said Caesar, grimacing. "Not wine."

"Then honey-and-water, or the juice of fruits—sweet syrup of some kind. Have your servant keep it on hand, even in the midst of battle. And pay attention to the warning signs—nausea, dizziness, faulty vision, faintness, headache, even tiredness. If you feel any of these, have a sweet drink immediately, Caesar."

"How did you get an unconscious man to drink, Hapd'efan'e?"

Hapd'efan'e held out the reed; Caesar took it and turned it between his fingers. "Through this," he said. "How did you know that you bypassed the airway to my lungs? The two passages are one in front of the other, and the oesophagus is normally closed to permit breathing."

"I didn't know for certain," Hapd'efan'e said simply. "I prayed to Sekhmet that your coma wasn't too deep, and stroked the outside of your throat to make you swallow when your gullet felt the pressure of the reed against it. It worked."

"You know all that, yet you don't know what's wrong with me?"

"Wrongnesses are mysterious, Caesar, beyond us in most cases. All medicine is based upon observation. Luckily I learned much about you when I treated your rigors"—he looked sly—"that, for instance, you regard having to eat as a waste of time."

Cleopatra was improving; her tears had turned to hiccoughs. "How do you know so much about the body?" she asked Caesar.

"I'm a soldier. Walk enough battlefields to rescue the wounded and count the dead, and you see everything. Like this excellent physician, I learn from observation."

Apollodorus lurched to his feet, wiped away the sweat. "I will see to dinner," he croaked. "Oh, thank every god everywhere in the world that you're all right, Caesar!"

That night, lying sleepless in Cleopatra's enormous goose-down bed, her warmth tucked against him in the mild chill of Alexandria's so-called winter, Caesar thought about the day, the month, the year.

From the moment he had set foot on Egyptian soil, everything had drastically altered. Magnus's head—that evil palace cabal—a kind of corruption and degeneracy that only the East could produce—an unwanted campaign fought up and down the streets of a beautiful city—the willingness of a people to destroy what had taken three centuries to build—his own participation in that destruction . . . And a business proposition from a queen determined to save her people in the only way she believed they could be saved, by conceiving the son of a god. Believing that he, Caesar, was that god. Bizarre. Alien.

Today Caesar had had a fright. Today Caesar, who is never ill, faced the inevitable consequences of his fifty-two years. Not merely his years, but how profligately he has used and abused them, pushed himself when other men would stop to rest. No, not Caesar! To rest has never been Caesar's way. Never will be either. But now Caesar, who is never ill, must admit to himself that he has been ill for months. That whatever ague or miasma racked his body with tremors and retches has left a malignancy behind. Some part of Caesar's machine has— what did the priest-physician say?—suffered a change. Caesar will have to remember to eat, otherwise he will fall in an epilepse, and they will say that Caesar is slipping at last, that Caesar is weakening, that Caesar is no longer unbeatable. So Caesar must keep his secret, must never let Senate and People know that *anything* is wrong with him. For who else is there to pull Rome out of her mire if Caesar fails?

Cleopatra sighed, murmured, gave one faint hiccough—so many tears, and all for Caesar! This pathetic little scrap loves me—loves *me*! To her, I have become husband, father, uncle, brother. All the twisted ramifications of a Ptolemy. I didn't understand. I thought I did. But I didn't. Fortuna has thrown the cares and woes of millions of people on her frail shoulders, offered her no choice in her destiny any more than I offered Julia a choice. She is an anointed sovereign in rites older and more sacred than any others, she is the richest woman in the world, she rules human lives absolutely. Yet she's a scrap, a babe. Impossible for a Roman to gauge what the first twenty-one years of her life have done to her—murder and incest as a matter of course. Cato and Cicero prate that Caesar hankers to be King of Rome, but neither of them has any concept of what true kingship is. True kingship is as far from me as this little scrap beside me, swollen with my child.

Oh, he thought suddenly, I must get up! I must drink some of that syrup Apollodorus so kindly brought—juice of melons and grapes grown in linen houses! How degenerate. My mind wanders, I am Caesar and I together, I cannot separate the two.

But instead of going to drink his juice of melons and grapes grown in linen houses, his head fell back upon the pillow and turned to look at Cleopatra. It wasn't very dark, for all that it was the middle of the night; the great panels in the outside wall were flexed sideways and light poured in from a full moon, turned her skin not to silver but to pale bronze. Lovely skin. He reached out to touch it, stroke it, feather the palm of his hand down across her six-months belly, not distended enough yet to be luminous, as he remembered Cinnilla's belly when she was close to term with Julia, with Gaius who was stillborn in the midst of her eclampsia. We burned Cinnilla and baby Gaius together, my mother, Aunt Julia, and I. Not Caesar. I.

She had budded delicious small breasts, round and firm as globes, and her nipples had darkened to the same plummy black as the skin of her Aethiopian fan bearers; perhaps she has some of that blood, for there's more in her than mere Mithridates and Ptolemy. Beautiful to feel, living tissue that has greater purpose than simply gratifying me. But I am part of it and her, she is carrying my child. Oh, we parent babes too young! Now is the time to relish them, adore their mothers. It takes many years and many heartaches to understand the miracle of life.

Her hair was loose and strayed in tendrils across the pillow, not dense and black like Servilia's, nor a river of fire he could wrap himself in like Rhiannon's. This was Cleopatra's hair, just as this was Cleopatra's body. And Cleopatra loves me differently from all the others. She returns me to my youth.

The leonine eyes were open, fixed on his face. Another time he would have closed his face immediately, excluded her from his mind with the automatic thoroughness of a reflex—never hand women the sword of knowledge, for they will use it to emasculate. But she is used to eunuchs, doesn't prize that kind of man. What she wants from me is a husband, a father, an uncle, a brother. I am her equal in power yet hold the additional power of maleness. I have conquered her. Now I must show her that it is no part of my intentions or compulsions to crush her into submission. None of my women has been a boot scraper.

"I love you," he said, gathering her into his arms, "as my wife, my daughter, my mother, my aunt."

She couldn't know that he was likening her to real women, not speaking in Ptolemaic comparatives, but she blazed inside with love, relief, utter joy.

Caesar had admitted her into his life.

Caesar had said he loved her.

The following day he put her atop a donkey and took her to see what six months of war had done to Alexandria. Whole tracts of it lay in ruins, no houses left standing, makeshift hills and walls sporting abandoned artillery, women and children scratching and grubbing for anything edible or useful, homeless and hopeless, clothing reduced to rags. Of the waterfront, almost nothing was left; the fires Caesar had set among the Alexandrian ships had spread to burn every warehouse, what his soldiers had left of the great emporium, the ship sheds, the docks, the quays.

"Oh, the book repository has gone!" she cried, wringing her hands, very distressed. "There is no catalogue, we'll never know what burned!"

If Caesar eyed her ironically, he said nothing to indicate his wonder at her priorities; she hadn't been moved by the heart-wrenching spectacle of all those starving women and children, now she was on the verge of tears over books. "But the library is in the museum," he said, "and the museum is perfectly safe."

"Yes, but the librarians are so slow that the books come in far faster than they can be catalogued, so for the last hundred years they've been piling up in a special warehouse. It's gone!"

"How many books are there in the museum?" he asked.

"Almost a million."

"Then there's very little to worry about," Caesar said. "Do cheer up, my dear! The sum total of all the books ever written is far less than a million, which means whatever was stored in the warehouse were duplicates or recent works. Many of the books in the museum itself must be duplicates too. Recent works are easy to get hold of, and if you need a catalogue, Mithridates of Pergamum has a library of a quarter-million books, most of fairly recent date. All you have to do is commission copies of works the museum doesn't have from Sosius or Atticus in Rome. They don't have the books in ownership, but they borrow from Varro, Lucius Piso, me, others who have extensive private libraries. Which reminds me that Rome has no public library, and I must remedy that."

Onward. The agora had suffered the least damage among the public buildings, some of its pillars dismantled to stop up the archways in the Heptastadion, but its walls were intact, as well as most of the arcade roofing. The gymnasium, however, was little more than a few foundations, and the courts of justice had entirely vanished. The beautiful Hill of Pan was denuded of vegetation, its streams and waterfalls dried up, their beds encrusted with salt, Roman artillery perched anywhere the ground was level. No temple had survived intact, but Caesar was pleased to see that none had lost its sculptures and paintings, even if they were stained and smirched.

The Serapeum in Rhakotis had suffered least, thanks to its distance from Royal Avenue. However, three massive beams were gone from the main temple, and the roof had caved in.

"Yet Serapis is perfect," Caesar said, scrambling over the mounds of masonry. For there he sat upon his jeweled golden throne, a Zeus-like figure, full-bearded and long-haired, with the three-headed dog Cerberus crouched at his feet, and his head weighed down by a gigantic crown in the form of a basket.

"It's very good," he said, studying Serapis. "Not up to Phidias or Praxiteles or Myron, but very good. Who did it?"

"Bryaxis," said Cleopatra, lips tight. She looked around at the wreckage, remembering the vast, beautifully proportioned building on its high podium of many steps, the Ionic columns all bravely painted and gilded, the metopes and pediment veritable masterpieces. Only Serapis himself had survived.

Is it that Caesar has seen so many sacked cities, so many charred ruins, so much havoc? This destruction seems to leave him quite composed, though he and his men have done most of it. My people confined themselves to ordinary houses, hovels and slums, things that are not important.

"Well," she said as he and his lictors escorted her back to the un-marred Royal Enclosure, "I shall scrape up every talent of gold and silver I can find to rebuild the temples, the gymnasium, the agora, the courts of justice, all the public buildings."

His hand holding the donkey's halter jerked; the animal stopped, its long-lashed eyes blinking. "That's very laudable," he said, voice hard, "but you don't start with the ornaments. The first thing you spend your money on is food for those left alive in this desolation. The second thing you spend your money on is clearance of the ruins. The third thing you spend your money on are new houses for the ordinary people, including the poor. Only when Alexandria's people are served can you spend money on the public buildings and temples."

Her mouth opened to rail at him, but before she could speak her outrage, she encountered his eyes. Oh, Creator Ptah! He *is* a God, mighty and terrible!

"I can tell you," he went on, "that most of the people killed in this war were Macedonians and Macedonian-Greeks. Perhaps a hundred thousand. So you still have almost three million people to care for—people whose dwellings and jobs have perished. I wish you could see that you have a golden opportunity to endear yourself to the *bulk* of your Alexandrian people. Rome hasn't suffered reduction to ruins since she became a power, nor are her common people neglected. You Ptolemies and your Macedonian masters have run a place far bigger than Rome to suit yourselves, there has been no spirit of philanthropy. That has to change, or the mob will return more angry than ever."

"You're saying," she said, pricked and confused, "that we at the top of the tower have not acquitted ourselves like a true government. You harp on our indifference to the lowly, the fact that it has never been our habit to fill their bellies at our expense, or extend the citizenship to all who live here. But Rome isn't perfect either. It's just that Rome has an empire, she can squeeze prosperity for her own lowly by exploiting her provinces. Egypt has no provinces. Those it did have, Rome took from it for her own needs. As for yourself, Caesar—your career has been a bloody one that ill equips you to sit in judgement on Egypt."

The hand tugged the halter; the donkey started walking. "In my day," he said in ordinary tones, "I have rendered half a million people homeless. Four hundred thousand women and children have died because of me. I have killed more than a million men on my fields of battle. I have amputated hands. I have sold a million more men, women and children into slavery. But all that I have done has been done in the knowledge that first I made treaties, tried conciliation, kept my end of the bargains. And when I have destroyed, what I have left behind will benefit future generations in far greater measure than the damage I did, the lives I ended or ruined."

His voice didn't increase in volume, but it became stronger. "Do you think, Cleopatra, that I don't see in my mind's eye the sum total of the devastation and upheaval I've caused? Do you think I don't grieve? Do you think that I look back on all of it—and look forward to more of it—without sorrow? Without pain? Without regret? Then you mistake me. The remembrance of cruelty is poor comfort in old age, but I have it on excellent authority that I will not live to be old. I say again, Pharaoh, rule your subjects with love, and never forget that it is only an accident of birth that makes you different from one of those women picking through the debris of this shattered city. You deem it Amun-Ra who put you in your skin. I *know* it was an accident of fate."

Her mouth was open; she put up her hand to shield it and looked straight between the donkey's ears, determined not to weep. So he believes that he will not live to be old, and is glad of it. But now I understand that I will never truly know him. What he is telling me is that everything he has ever done was a conscious decision, made in full knowledge of the consequences, including to himself. I will never have that kind of strength or perception or ruthlessness. I doubt anyone ever has.

A *nundinum* later Caesar called an informal conference in the big room he used as a study. Cleopatra and Apollodorus were there, together with Hapd'efan'e and Mithridates of Pergamum. There were Romans present: Publius Rufrius, Carfulenus of the Sixth, Lamius of the Fortieth, Fabricius of the Twenty-seventh, Macrinus of the Thirty-seventh, Caesar's lictor Fabius, his secretary Faberius, and his personal legate, Gaius Trebatius Testa.

"It is the beginning of April," he announced, looking very fit and well, every inch Caesar, "and reports from Gnaeus Domitius Calvinus in Asia Province have informed me that Pharnaces has gone back to Cimmeria to deal with his erring son, who has decided not to submit to *tata* without a fight. So matters in Anatolia lie dormant for at least the next three or four months. Besides, all the mountain passes to Pontus and Armenia Parva will be choked with snow until the middle of Sextilis—oh, how I hate the discrepancy between the calendar and the seasons! In that respect, Pharaoh, Egypt is right. You based your calendar on the sun, not on the moon, and I intend to have speech with your astronomers."

He drew a breath and returned to his subject. "There is no doubt in my mind that Pharnaces will return, however, so I will plan my future actions with that in mind. Calvinus is busy recruiting and training, and Deiotarus is extremely eager to atone for being in Pompeius Magnus's clientele. As for Ariobarzanes"—he grinned—"Cappadocia will always be Cappadocia. We'll get no joy from him, but nor will Pharnaces. I've told Calvinus to send for some of the Republican legions I returned to Italy with my own veterans, so when the time comes, we should be well prepared. It's to our advantage that Pharnaces is bound to lose some of his best soldiers fighting Asander in Cimmeria."

He leaned forward in his curule chair, eyes roaming the row of intent faces. "Those of us who have been marooned in Alexandria for the last six months have fought a particularly enervating campaign, and all troops are entitled to a winter rest camp. Therefore I intend to stay in Egypt for two more months, as long a winter camp as events allow. With Pharaoh's permission and co-operation, I am going to send my men to winter camp near Memphis, far enough away from Alexandria to permit of no memories. There are tourist attractions galore, and the issue of pay will give the men money to spend. Also, I am arranging to have Alexandria's surplus daughters shipped to the camp. So many potential husbands have died that the city will be burdened by too many women for years to come, and there is method in this provision. I do not intend these girls as whores, but as *wives*. The Twenty-seventh, the Thirty-seventh and the Fortieth are going to remain to garrison Alexandria for long enough to establish homes and families. I am afraid that the Sixth will not be able to form permanent liaisons."

Fabricius, Lamius and Macrinus looked at one another, not sure whether they welcomed this news. Decimus Carfulenus of the Sixth sat impassively.

"It is essential that Alexandria remains quiet," Caesar went on. "As time passes, more and more of Rome's legions will find themselves posted to garrison duty rather than active service. Which isn't to say that garrison duty consists of idleness. We all remember what happened to the Gabiniani whom Aulus Gabinius left behind to garrison Alexandria after Auletes was restored to his throne. They went native with a vengeance, and murdered the sons of Bibulus rather than return to active duty in Syria. The Queen dealt with that crisis, but it mustn't happen again. Those legions left in Egypt will conduct themselves as a professional army, keep up their soldier skills, and hold themselves ready to march at Rome's command. But men stranded in foreign places without a home life are discontented at first, then disaffected. What cannot happen is that they steal women from the people of Memphis. Therefore they will espouse the surplus Alexandrian women and—as Gaius Marius always said—spread Roman ways, Roman ideals and the Latin language through their children."

The cool eyes surveyed the three centurions concerned, each *primipilus* of his legion; Caesar never bothered with legates or military tribunes, who were noblemen and transient. Centurions were the backbone of the army, its only full-time officers.

"Fabricius, Macrinus, Lamius, those are your orders. Remain in Alexandria and guard it well."

No use complaining. It might have been a lot worse, like one of Caesar's thousand-mile marches in thirty days. "Yes, Caesar," said Fabricius, acting as spokesman.

"Publius Rufrius, you too will remain here. You'll have the high command as *legatus propraetore.*"

News that delighted Rufrius; he already had an Alexandrian wife, she was with child, and he hadn't wanted to leave her.

"Decimus Carfulenus, the Sixth will go with me when I march for Anatolia," Caesar said. "I'm sorry you won't have a permanent home, but you boys have been with me ever since I borrowed you from Pompeius Magnus all those years ago, and I prize you the more for being loyal to Pompeius after he took you back. I will plump your numbers out with other veterans as I go north. In the absence of the Tenth, the Sixth is my private command."

Carfulenus's beam revealed his two missing teeth, screwed up the scar he bore from one cheek to the other across a kind of a nose. His action in taking Ptolemy's citadel had saved a whole legion of troops pinned down by that cross fire, so he had received the *corona civica* when the army had been paraded for decorations, and, like Caesar, he was entitled to enter the Senate under Sulla's provisions for winners of major crowns. "The Sixth is deeply honored, Caesar. We are your men to the death."

"As for you lot," Caesar said affably to his chief lictor and his secretary, "you're permanent fixtures. Where I go, you go. However, Gaius Trebatius, I don't require any further duty from you that might handicap your noble status and your public career."

Trebatius sighed, remembering those awful walks in Portus Itius's extreme humidity because the General forbade his legates and tribunes to ride, remembering the taste of a Menapian roast goose, remembering those dreadful gallops in a pitching gig taking down notes while his pampered stomach heaved—oh, for Rome and litters, Baiae oysters, Arpinate cheeses, Falernian wine!

"Well, Caesar, as I imagine that sooner or later your path will take you to Rome, I shall defer my career decisions until that day comes," he said heroically.

Caesar's eyes twinkled. "Perhaps," he said gently, "you'll find the menu in Memphis more appealing. You've grown too thin."

He folded his hands in his lap and nodded briskly. "The Roman element is dismissed."

They filed out, the babble of their talk in full spate even as Fabius closed the door.

"You first, I think, good friend Mithridates," Caesar said, relaxing his pose. "You are the son and Cleopatra the granddaughter of Mithridates the Great, which makes you her uncle. If, say, you were to send for your wife and younger children, would you stay in Alexandria to supervise its rebuilding? Cleopatra tells me she will have to import an architect, and you're justly famous for what you've done down on the sea plain below Pergamum's acropolis." His face took on a wistful look. "I remember that sea plain very well. I used it to crucify five hundred pirates, much to the governor's displeasure when he found out. But these days it's a picture of walks, arcades, gardens, beautiful public buildings."

Mithridates frowned. A vigorous man of fifty, the child of a concubine rather than a wife, he took after his mighty father—heavyset, muscular, tall, yellow-haired and yellow-eyed. He followed Roman fashion in that he cropped his hair very short and was clean-shaven, but his garb tended more to the Oriental—he had a weakness for gold thread, plush embroidery and every shade of purple known to the dyers of *murex*. All foibles to be tolerated in such a loyal client, first of Pompey's, now of Caesar's.

"Frankly, Caesar, I would love to do it, but can you spare me? Surely with Pharnaces lurking, I am needed in my own lands."

Caesar shook his head emphatically. "Pharnaces won't get as far as Asia Province's borders, let alone Pergamum. I'll stop him in Pontus. From what Calvinus says, your son is an excellent regent in your absence, so take a long holiday from government, do! Your blood ties to Cleopatra will make you acceptable to the Alexandrians, and I note you've forged very strong links with the Jews. The skills of Alexandria repose with the Jews and Metics, and the latter will accept you because the Jews do."

"Then yes, Caesar."

"Good." Having gotten his way, the ruler of the world gave Mithridates of Pergamum the nod of dismissal. "Thank you."

"And I thank you," said Cleopatra when her uncle had gone. An uncle! How amazing! Why, I must have a thousand relatives through my mother! Pharnaces is my uncle too! And through Rhodogune and

Apama, I go back to Cambyses and Darius of Persia! Both once Pharaoh! In me, whole dynasties connect. What blood my son will have!

Caesar was speaking to her about Hapd'efan'e, whom he wanted to take with him as his personal physician. "I'd ask the poor fellow for myself," he said in Latin, which Cleopatra now spoke very well, "except that I've been in Egypt long enough to know that few people are genuinely free. Just the Macedonians. I daresay that Cha'em owns him, since he's a priest-physician of Ptah's consort, Sekhmet, and he seems to live in Ptah's precinct. But as you at least part-own Cha'em, he'll do as you say, no doubt. I need Hapd'efan'e, Cleopatra. Now that Lucius Tuccius is dead—he was Sulla's physician, then mine—I don't trust any physician practicing in Rome. If he has a wife and family, I'll happily carry them along as well."

Something she could do for him! "Hapd'efan'e, Caesar wants to take you with him when he goes," she said to the priest in the old tongue. "It would please Creator Ptah and Pharaoh if you consent to go. We in Egypt would have your thoughts as a channel to Caesar no matter where he might be. Answer him for yourself, and tell him about your situation. He's concerned for you."

The priest-physician sat with impassive face, his black, almond-shaped eyes fixed on Caesar unblinkingly. "God Caesar," he said in his clumsy Greek, "it is clearly Creator Ptah's wish that I serve you. I will do that willingly. I am *hem-netjer-sinw*, so I am sworn to celibacy." A gleam of humor showed in the eyes. "However, I would like to extend my treatment of you to include certain Egyptian methods that Greek physicians dismiss—amulets and charms possess great magic, so do spells."

"Absolutely!" Caesar cried, excited. "As Pontifex Maximus, I know all the Roman charms and spells—we can compare notes. I quite agree, they have great magic." His face became grave. "We have to clear one thing up, Hapd'efan'e. No 'god Caesar' and no falling to the floor to greet me! Elsewhere in the world I am not a god, and it would offend others if you called me one."

"As you wish, Caesar." In truth, this shaven-headed, still young man was delighted with the new turn in his life, for he had a natural curiosity about the world, and looked forward to seeing strange places in the company of a man he literally worshiped. Distance couldn't separate him from Creator Ptah and his wife, Sekhmet, their son Nefertem of the Lotus. He could wing his thoughts to Memphis from anywhere in the time it took a ray of sun to travel across the sacred pylon gates. So, while the talk between Caesar and Cleopatra proceeded in Greek too fast for him to follow, he mentally planned his equipment—a whole dozen carefully packed supple, hollowed reeds to start with, his forceps, trephines, knives, trocars, needles . . .

"What about the city officials?" Caesar was asking.

"The present lot have been banished," Apollodorus answered, "I put them on a ship for Macedonia. When I arrived with the new Royal Guard, I found the Recorder trying to burn all the bylaws and ordinances, and the Accountant trying to burn the ledgers. Luckily I was in time to prevent both. The city treasury is beneath the Serapeum, and the city offices are a part of the precinct. All survived the war."

"New men? How were the old chosen?"

"By sortition among the high Macedonians, most of whom have perished or fled."

"*Sortition?* You mean they cast lots for the positions?"

"Yes, Caesar, sortition. The lots are rigged, of course."

"Well, that's cheaper than holding elections, which is the Roman way. So what happens now?"

Cleopatra spoke. "We reorganize," she said firmly. "I intend to ban sortition and hold elections instead. If the million new citizens vote for a selection of candidates, it will reassure them that they do have a say."

"That surely depends on the selection of candidates. Do you intend to let all who declare themselves candidates stand?"

Her lids dropped, she looked cagey. "I haven't decided on the selection process yet," she hedged.

"Don't you think the Greeks will feel left out if the Jews and Metics become citizens? Why not enfranchise everybody, even your hybrid Egyptians? Call them your Head Count and limit their voting powers if you must, but allow them the simple citizenship."

But that, her face told him, was going way too far.

"Thank you, Apollodorus, Hapd'efan'e, you may go," he said, stifling a sigh.

"So we are alone," said Cleopatra, pulling him out of his chair and down beside her on a couch. "Am I doing well? I'm spending my money as you directed—the poor are being fed and the rubble cleared away. Every common builder has been contracted to erect ordinary houses. There is money enough to start the public building too because I've taken my own funds from the treasure vaults for that." The big yellow eyes glowed. "You are right, it is the way to be loved. Every day I set out with Apollodorus on my donkey to see the people, comfort them. Does this win your favor? Am I ruling in a more enlightened way?"

"Yes, but you have a long way to go. When you tell me that you've enfranchised *all* your people, you'll be there. You have a natural autocracy, but you're not observant enough. Take the Jews, for example. They're quarrelsome, but they have ability. Treat them with respect, always be good to them. In hard times they'll be your greatest support."

"Yes, yes," she said impatiently, tired of seriousness. "I have something else I want to talk about, my love."

His eyes crinkled at their corners. "Indeed?"

"Yes, indeed. I know what we're going to do with our two months, Caesar."

"If the winds were with me, I'd go to Rome."

"Well, they're not, so we're going to sail down Nilus to the First Cataract." She patted her belly. "Pharaoh must show the people that she is fruitful."

He frowned. "I agree that Pharaoh must, but I ought to stay here on Our Sea and try to keep abreast of events elsewhere."

"I refuse to listen!" she cried. "I don't care about events around Your Sea! You and I are setting out on Ptolemy Philopator's barge to see the real Egypt—Egypt of Nilus!"

"I dislike being pushed, Cleopatra."

"It's for your health, you stupid man! Hapd'efan'e says you need a proper rest, not a continuation of duty. And what greater rest can there be than a—a *cruise*? Please, I beg of you, grant me this! Caesar, a woman needs memories of an idyll with her beloved! We've had no idyll, and while ever you think of yourself as Caesar Dictator, we can't. Please! Please?"

 Ptolemy Philopator, the fourth of those who bore the first name of Ptolemy, hadn't been one of the more vigorous sovereigns of his house; he left Egypt only two tangible legacies: the two biggest ships ever built. One was seagoing and measured 426 feet in length and 60 feet in the beam. It had six banks of oars and forty men to each bank. The other was a river barge, shallower in the draft and having but two banks of oars, ten men to each oar, and measured 350 feet in length and 40 feet in the beam.

Philopator's river barge had been put away in a ship shed on the riverbank not far above Memphis, lovingly cared for during the hundred and sixty years since its construction—wetted and oiled, polished, constantly repaired, and used whenever Pharaoh sailed the river.

The Nilus Philopator, as Cleopatra called it, contained huge rooms, baths, an arcade of columns on the deck to join the stern and bow reception rooms, one for audiences, the other for banquets. Below deck and above the oar banks were Pharaoh's private quarters and accommodation for a multitude of servants. Cooking on board was limited to a screened-off area of braziers; the preparation of full meals was done ashore, for the great vessel cruised along at about the same speed as a marching legionary, and scores of servants followed it on the east bank; the west bank was the realm of the dead and of temples.

It was inlaid with gold, electrum, ivory, exquisite marquetry and the finest cabinet woods from all over the world, including citrus wood from the Atlas Mountains of the most wonderful grain Caesar had ever seen—no small opinion, when wealthy Romans had made the collection of citrus wood an art. Pedestals were made of chryselephantine—a mixture of gold and ivory—the statuary was Praxiteles, Myron, even Phidias, there were paintings by Zeuxis and Parrhasius, Pausias and Nicias, and tapestries of such richness that they vied with the paintings for reality of detail. The rugs which lay everywhere were Persian, the draperies of transparent linen dyed whatever colors were appropriate for the room.

Finally, old friend Crassus, thought Caesar, I believe your tales of the incredible wealth of Egypt. What a pity you can't be here to see this! A ship for a god on earth.

Progress down the river was by Tyrian purple sail, for the wind in Egypt always blew from the north; then, returning, oar power was assisted by the strong river current, flowing north to Our Sea. Not that he ever saw the oarsmen, had no idea what race they were, how they were treated; oarsmen everywhere were free men with professional status, but Egypt wasn't a place of free men. Every evening before sunset the Nilus Philopator tied up to the east bank at some royal wharf no other riverboat was allowed to contaminate.

He had thought to be bored, but he never was. River traffic was constant and colorful, hundreds of lateen-sailed dhows plying cargoes of food, goods brought overland from the Red Sea ports, great earthenware jars of pumpkin, saffron, sesame and linseed oils, boxes of dates, live animals, the floating shops of bumboats. All of it ruthlessly supervised by the swifter ships of the river police, who were everywhere.

It was easier to understand the phenomenon of the Cubits now he sailed Nilus, for the banks were seventeen feet high at their lowest, thirty-two feet high at their tallest; if the river didn't rise higher than the lowest banks, flooding wasn't possible, yet if it rose higher than

the tallest banks, the water poured over the valley in an uncontrollable spate, washed away villages, ruined the seed grain, took far too long to recede.

The colors were dramatic, sky and river a flawless blue, the distant cliffs that denoted the beginning of the desert plateau all shades from pale straw to deep crimson; the vegetation of the valley itself was every green imaginable. At this time of year, mid-winter by the seasons, the floodwaters of the Inundation had fully receded and the crops were sprouting like sheets of lush, rippling grass, hurtling on toward the earing and harvesting of spring. Caesar had imagined that no trees grew, but saw in surprise that there were whole groves of trees, sometimes small forests—the fruiting persea, a local sycamore, black-thorn, oak, figs—and that palms of all kinds grew besides the famous date.

At about the place where the southern half of Upper Egypt became the northern half of Upper Egypt, Nilus gave off an anabranch that ran north to Lake Moeris and formed the land of Ta-she, rich enough to grow two crops of wheat and barley a year; an early Ptolemy had dug a big canal from the lake back to Nilus, so that the water continued to flow. Everything throughout the thousand-mile length of Egyptian Nilus was irrigated; Cleopatra explained that even when Nilus failed to inundate, the people of the valley could manage to feed themselves by irrigating; it was Alexandria caused the famines—three million mouths to feed, more mouths than in the whole of Nilus's length.

The cliffs and the desert plateau were the Red Land; the valley, with its deep, dark, perpetually replenished soil, was the Black Land.

There were innumerable temples on both banks, all built on the same vast lines: a series of massive pylons connected by lintels above gateways; walls; courtyards; more pylons and gates farther in; always leading to the Holy of Holies, a small room where light was artificially guided in to appear magical, and there in it stood some beast-headed Egyptian god, or perhaps a statue of one of the great pharaohs, usually Rameses II, a famous builder. The temples were often faced with statues of a pharaoh, and the pylons were always joined by avenues of sphinxes, ram-headed, lion-headed, human-headed. All were covered in two-dimensional pictures of people, plants, animals, and painted in every color; the Egyptians loved color.

"Most of the Ptolemies have built, repaired or finished our temples," said Cleopatra as they wandered the wonderful maze of Abydos. "Even my father Auletes built extensively—he wanted so badly to be pharaoh! You see, when Cambyses of Persia invaded Egypt five hundred years ago, he considered the temples and the pyramid tombs sacrilegious, and mutilated them, sometimes quite destroyed them. So there's plenty of work for us Ptolemies, who were the first after the true Egyptians to *care*. I've laid the foundations of a new temple to Hathor, but I want our son to join me as its builder. He's going to be the greatest temple builder in Egypt's entire history."

"Why, when the Ptolemies are so Hellenized, have they built exactly as the old Egyptians did? You even use the hieroglyphs instead of writing in Greek."

"Probably because most of us have been Pharaoh, and certainly because the priests are so rooted in antiquity. They provide the architects, sculptors and painters, sometimes even in Alexandria. But wait until you see the temple of Isis at Philae! There we did slightly Hellenize—which is why, I think, it's generally held to be the most beautiful temple complex in all Egypt."

The river itself teemed with fish, including the oxyrhynchus, a thousand-pound monster which had a town named after it; the people ate fish, both fresh and smoked, as a meat staple. Bass, carp and perch abounded, and much to Caesar's amazement, dolphins streaked and gamboled, avoiding the predatory crocodiles with an almost contemptuous ease.

Many different animals were sacred, sometimes limited to a single town, sometimes universally revered. The sight of Suchis, a gigantic sacred crocodile, being force-fed honey cakes, roast meat and sweet wine had Caesar in fits of laughter. The thirty-foot-long creature was so tired of food that it would try to evade its priest feeders, to no avail; they would jack its jaws open and ram more food down while it groaned and sighed. He saw the Buchis Bull, the Apis Bull, their mothers, the temple complexes in which they lived out their pampered lives. The sacred bulls, their mothers, ibises and cats were mummified when they died, and laid to rest in vast underground tunnels and chambers. The cats and ibises were oddly sad to Caesar's foreign eyes—little amber parceled figures by the hundreds of thousands, dry as paper, stiff, immobile, while their spirits roamed the Realm of the Dead.

In fact, thought Caesar as the Nilus Philopator drew closer and closer to the most southern regions of Upper Egypt, it is no wonder that these people have made their gods part-human and part-animal, for Nilus is its own world, and animals are perfectly fused into the human cycle. Crocodile, hippopotamus and jackal are fearsome beasts—crocodile lurks waiting to snatch an imprudent fisherman or dog or child, hippopotamus lumbers ashore to destroy food plants with its mouth and huge trotters, jackal sneaks into houses and steals babies, cats. Therefore Sobek, Taweret and Anubis are malign gods. Whereas Bastet the cat eats rats and mice, Horus the hawk does the same, Thoth the ibis eats insect pests, Hathor the cow provides meat, milk and labor, Khnum the ram sires sheep for meat, milk and wool. To Egyptians, pent up in their narrow valley and sustained only by their river, gods must naturally be as much animal as human. Here, they understand that Man too is an animal. And Amun-Ra, the sun, shines every single day of the year; to us, the moon means rain or the women's cycle or changes of mood, whereas to them, the moon is just a part of Nut, the night sky that gave birth to the land. As for imagining their gods as we Romans do, forces that create pathways to link two different universes—no, they do not live in that kind of world. Here, it is sun, sky, river, human and animal. A cosmology containing no abstract concepts.

Fascinating to see the place where Nilus flowed out of its endless red canyon to become Egypt's river; in sere Nubia it watered nothing, flowing between vast rock walls, said Cleopatra.

"Nilus receives two branches in Aithiopai, where he is kind again," she explained. "These two branches collect the summer rains and are the Inundation, whereas Nilus himself flows down past Meroë and the exiled queens of the Sembritae, who once ruled in Egypt—they are so fat that they can't walk. Nilus himself is fed by rains that fall all year round somewhere far past Meroë, which is why he doesn't dry up in winter."

They inspected the first Nilometer at the isle of Elephantine on the little cataract, were taken upriver to the First Cataract itself, a place of roaring white waters and precipices. Then it was on south to the wells of Syene, where on the longest day of the year the sun at noon shone right down into the wells and saw his face reflected in the water far below.

"Yes, I've read my Eratosthenes," Caesar said. "Here at Syene the sun halts its northward course and starts to go south again. Eratosthenes called it the Tropic because it marked the turning point. A very remarkable man. As I remember, he blamed geometry and trigonometry on Egypt too—generations of little boys like me have wrestled their teachers and Euclid all because the Inundation obliterates the boundary stones of Egypt every single year, hence the Egyptian invention of surveying."

"Yes, but don't forget that it was the nosy Greeks who wrote it all down!" laughed Cleopatra, well schooled in mathematics.

* * *

The cruise was as much a discovery of Cleopatra as of Egypt. Nowhere in the world of Our Sea or the Parthians did a monarch receive the kind of absolute worship Pharaoh did as a matter of course rather than as a right or a reflex evoked by terror. The people flocked to the riverbank to throw flowers at the mighty barge sliding along, to prostrate themselves, rise and fall in one obeisance after another, to call her name. Pharaoh had blessed them with her divine presence, and the Inundation had been perfect.

Whenever she could, she would mount a dais on the deck to raise herself high enough and acknowledge her subjects very gravely, standing in profile so that they could see her pregnant belly. In every town she was sure to be there, the white crown of Upper Egypt on her head, the barge surrounded by rush canoes, little earthenware coracles and hide fishing boats, the deck sometimes awash in flowers. Though by now she was into her third trimester and not as comfortable or blooming as she had been during her second, her own needs did not matter. Pharaoh was all-important.

Despite the constant interruptions, they talked a great deal. This was a bigger pleasure for Caesar than for Cleopatra; his unwillingness to discuss just those aspects of his life she was on fire to learn about irked her, irked her, irked her. She wanted to know all the details of his relationship with Servilia (the whole world speculated about *that*!), his years-long marriage to a woman he had hardly cohabited with, the succession of broken-hearted women he had abandoned after he'd seduced them merely to cuckold their husbands, his political enemies. Oh, so many mysteries! Mysteries he refused to talk about, though he lectured her interminably on the art of ruling, from law to war, or would launch into fascinating stories about the Druids of Gaul, the lake temples at Tolosa and their cargo of gold a Servilius Caepio had stolen, the customs and traditions of half a hundred different peoples. As long as the subjects were not intimately personal, he was happy to talk. But the moment she started to fish in his emotional waters, he closed up.

Not unnaturally, Cleopatra left the precinct of Ptah until the end of their return journey north. Caesar had seen the pyramids from the barge, but now, mounted on a horse, he was conducted to the fields by Cha'em. Cleopatra, growing very heavy, declined to go.

"Cambyses of Persia tried to deface the outer polished stones, but became bored by chipping away and concentrated his destruction on temples," said Cha'em, "which is why so many of them are almost pristine."

"For the life of me, Cha'em, I cannot understand why a living man, even one who was a god, would devote so much time and toil to a structure of no use to him during life," Caesar said, genuinely puzzled.

"Well," Cha'em answered, smiling subtly, "you must remember that Khufu and the rest didn't do the actual *work*. Perhaps they came occasionally to see progress, but it never went further than that. And the builders were very skilled. There are about two million large stones in Khufu's *mer*, but most of the construction was done during the Inundation, when barges could bring the blocks to the bottom of the ramps up on to the plateau, and labor was not required in the fields. During planting and harvesting seasons, large-scale work virtually stopped. The polished outer casing is limestone, but once the top of each *mer* was sheathed in gold—plundered, alas, by the foreign dynasties. The tombs inside were broken into at the same period, so all the treasures are gone."

"Where then is the treasure of the living Pharaoh?"

"Would you like to see it?"

"Very much." Caesar hesitated, then spoke. "You must understand, Cha'em, that I am not here to loot Egypt. Whatever Egypt has will go to my son—or to my daughter, for that matter." He hunched his shoulders. "I can't be happy at the thought that in time to come my son might marry my daughter—incest is anathema to Romans. Though, oddly enough, I notice from overhearing what my soldiers say that Egypt's so-called beast gods upset them more than incest does."

"But you yourself understand our 'beast gods'—I see it in your eyes." Cha'em turned his donkey. "Now to the vaults."

Rameses II had built much of the half-square-mile of Ptah's precinct, approached through a long avenue of magnificent ram-headed sphinxes, and had flanked its west pylons with colossal statues of himself, meticulously painted.

No one, Caesar decided, even he, would ever have found the entrance to the treasure vaults without prior knowledge. Cha'em led him through a series of passageways to an interior room where painted, life-size statues of the Triad of Memphis stood in ghostly illumination. Ptah the Creator himself stood in the middle, shaven-headed, with a real skullcap of worked gold fitted tightly on his cranium. He was wrapped in mummy bandages from feet to neck save that his hands protruded to hold a staff on which were a terraced pillar, a large bronze ankh—a T-shaped object surmounted by a loop—and the crook of a scepter. To his right was his wife, Sekhmet, who had the body of a well-shaped woman but the head of a *nemes-maned* lion, with the disc of Ra and the cobra *uraeus* above the mane. On Ptah's left was their son, Nefertem, Guardian of the Two Ladies and Lord of the Lotus, a man wearing a tall blue lotus crown flanked on either side by a plume of white ostrich feathers.

Cha'em tugged at Ptah's staff and detached the ankh with the crook atop it, handed the very heavy object to Caesar, then turned and left the chamber to retrace the path from the outer pylons. On a nondescript section of corridor he stopped, knelt down and pushed with both palms on a cartouche just above the level of the floor; it sprang forward just enough for Cha'em to lever it free of the wall. Then he extended one hand and took the ankh from Caesar, inserted its blunt end into the space.

"We thought about this for a very long time," he said as he began to wind the ankh back and forth, using the crook on its end to apply considerable force. "Tomb robbers know all the tricks, so how to fool them? In the end we settled for a simple device and a subtle location. If you count all the corridors, they amount to many, many cubits. And this is just another corridor." He grunted with the effort, his words suddenly almost drowned by a groaning grinding. "The story of Rameses the Great unfolds along each wall, the cartouches of his many sons among the hieroglyphs and pictures. And the paving—why, it is like all the other paving."

Startled, Caesar looked to the source of the noise in time to see a granite flag in the center of the floor rise above the level of its neighbors.

"Help me," Cha'em said, abandoning the ankh, which remained protruding from the base of the wall.

Caesar knelt and lifted the flag clear of those around it, stared down into darkness. There was a pattern to the floor that enabled the pair of them to lift other, smaller flags around the middle one; they rested on two sides, the other two without any support, and when they were removed the hole in the floor was big enough for quite large objects to be passed through it.

"Help me," Cha'em said again, taking hold of a bronze rod with a flaring top in which the center flag had engaged.

It screwed free to permit of no impediment below, a rod some five feet in length. With an agile wriggle, Cha'em inserted himself into the hole, fiddled about and produced two torches. "Now," he said, emerging, "we go to the sacred fire and kindle them, for the vaults have no source of light whatsoever."

"Is there air enough for them to burn?" Caesar asked as they made their way to the fire in the Holy of Holies, a tiny room in which stood a seated statue of Rameses.

"As long as the flags are up, yes, provided we do not go too far. Were this designed to remove treasure, I would have other priests with me, and rig up a bellows to force air inside."

Torches burning sluggishly, they descended into the bowels of the earth beneath Ptah's sanctuary, down a flight of steps and into an antechamber which led into a maze of tunnels with small rooms opening off them—rooms filled with gold sows, chests of gems and pearls of every color and kind, rooms redolent with barks, spices, incenses, rooms of *laserpicium* and balsam, rooms stacked with elephant tusks, rooms of porphyry, alabaster, rock crystal, malachite, lapis lazuli, rooms of ebony wood, of citrus wood, of electrum, of gold coins. But no statues or paintings or what Caesar would have called works of art.

Caesar returned to the ordinary world with mind reeling; inside the vaults lay so much wealth that even the seventy treasure fortresses of Mithridates the Great paled into insignificance. It is true, what Marcus Crassus always said: that we of the western world have no idea of how much treasure Orientals accumulate, for we do not value it for its own sake. Of itself it is useless, which is why it lies here. Were it mine, I would melt the metals down and sell the jewels to fund a more prosperous economy. Whereas Marcus Crassus would have prowled, just looking at it, and crooned. No doubt it started as a nest egg, and hatched into a monster necessitating supreme guile to safeguard it.

Back in the corridor, they screwed the rod into its base five feet below and released the trip that had jacked the center slab upward; they then replaced the surrounding flags, and eased the center one into place, flush with the floor again. Caesar gazed up and down the paving, couldn't see the entrance no matter how hard he looked. An experimental stamp of his foot produced no hollow sound, for the flags were four inches thick.

"If one looks closely at the cartouche," he said as Cha'em replaced the ankh and scepter on Ptah's staff, "one would see that it has been tampered with."

"Not tomorrow," Cha'em said tranquilly. "It will be plastered, painted and aged to look exactly like the hundred others."

Once when a very young man, Caesar had been captured by pirates, who were secure enough in the anonymity of their Lycian cove to let him remain on deck as they sailed; but he had beaten them, counted the coves and returned to capture them after he was released on payment of a ransom. Just as with the treasure vaults. He had counted the cartouches between Ptah's sanctuary and the one that sprang free of the wall when pressed. It is one thing, he thought, following Cha'em into the daylight, not to know a secret, but quite another to be privy to the secret. To find the treasure vaults, robbers would have to tear the whole of the temple apart; but Caesar had had the opportunity to do a simple exercise in counting. Not that he had any intention of plundering what would one day belong to his son; only that a thinking man will always seize his chances.

5   At the end of May they were back in Alexandria to find the rubble entirely cleared away, and new houses going up everywhere. Mithridates of Pergamum had shifted himself to a comfortable palace with his wife, Berenice, and their daughter, Laodice, and Rufrius was busy building a garrison for the wintering troops to the east of the city near the hippodrome racetrack, thinking it prudent to quarter his legions adjacent to the Jews and Metics.

Caesar was full of advice and reminders.

"Don't be stingy, Cleopatra! Spend your money to feed your people, and *don't* pass on the cost to the poor! Why do you think Rome has so little trouble with its proletariat? Don't charge admission to the chariot racing, and think of a few spectacles you can put on in the agora free of charge. Bring companies of Greek actors to stage Aristophanes, Menander, the more cheerful playwrights—the common people don't like tragedies because they tend to live tragedies. They prefer to laugh and forget their troubles for an afternoon. Put in many more public fountains, and build some ordinary bathhouses. In Rome, a frolic in a bathhouse costs a quarter of a sestertius—people leave in a good mood as well as clean. Keep those wretched birds under control during summer! Hire a few men and women to wash the streets, and put in decent public latrines anywhere there's a running drain to carry the sewage away. Since Alexandria and Egypt are riddled with bureaucracies, institute citizen rolls that count heads as well as nobility, and establish a grain list that entitles the poor to one *medimnus* of wheat a month, plus a ration of barley so they can brew beer. The money you receive as income has to be distributed, not kept to molder—if you hoard it, you cause the economy to crash. Alexandria has been tamed, but it's up to you to keep it tamed."

And on, and on, and on. The laws she should pass, the bylaws and ordinances, the institution of a public auditing system. Reform Egypt's banks, owned and controlled by Pharaoh through a creaking bureaucracy that wouldn't do, just would *not* do!

"Spend more money on education, encourage pedagogues to set

up schools in public places and markets, subsidize their fees so more children can learn. You need bookkeepers, scribes—and when more books come in, put them straight into the museum! Public servants are a lazy lot, so police their activities more stringently—and don't offer them tenure for life."

Cleopatra listened dutifully, felt a little like a rag doll that nodded its head every time it was jiggled. Now into her eighth month, she dragged herself around, couldn't stay far from a chamber pot, had to endure Caesar's son beating and battering her from inside while Caesar beat and battered her mind. Willing to endure anything except the thought that very soon he would be leaving, that she would have to live without him.

Finally came their last night, the Nones of June. At dawn Caesar, the 3,200 men of the Sixth Legion and the German cavalry would march for Syria on the first leg of a thousand-mile journey.

She tried hard to make it a pleasant night, understanding that, though he did love her in his way, no woman could ever replace Rome in Caesar's heart, or mean quite as much to him as the Tenth or the Sixth. Well, they've been through more together. They are entwined among the very fibers of his being. But I too would die for him—I would, I would! He is the father I didn't have, the husband of my heart, the perfect man. Who else in this whole world can equal him? Not even Alexander the Great, who was an adventuring conqueror, uninterested in the mundanities of good government or the empty bellies of the poor. Babylon holds no lure for Caesar. Caesar would never replace Rome with Alexandria. Oh, I wish he would! With Caesar by my side, Egypt would rule the world, not Rome.

They could kiss and cuddle, but lovemaking was impossible. Though a man as controlled as Caesar isn't put out by that. I like the way he strokes me, so rhythmic and firm, yet the skin of his palm is smooth. After he goes, I will be able to imagine those hands, so beautiful. His son will be just like him.

"After Asia, will it be Rome?" she asked.

"Yes, but not for very long. I have to fight a campaign in Africa Province and finish the Republicans for good," he said, and sighed. "Oh, that Magnus had lived! Things might have turned out very differently."

She experienced one of her peculiar insights. "That's not so, Caesar. Had Magnus lived, had he reached an accommodation with you, nothing would have been different. There are too many others who will never bend the knee to you."

For a moment he said nothing, then laughed. "You're right, my love, absolutely right. It's Cato keeps them going."

"Sooner or later you'll be permanently in Rome."

"One of these days, perhaps. I have to fight the Parthians and get Crassus's Eagles back fairly soon, however."

"But I must see you again! I must! I had thought that as soon as your wars against the Republicans were over, you would settle to rule Rome. Then I could come to Rome to be with you."

He lifted himself on one elbow to look down at her. "Oh, Cleopatra, will you never learn? First of all, no sovereign can be away from their realm for months at a time, so you can't come to Rome. And secondly, it's your duty as a sovereign to rule."

"You're a sovereign, but you're away for ages at a time," she said mutinously.

"I am *not* a sovereign! Rome has consuls, praetors, an array of magistrates. A dictator is a temporary measure, no more. The moment I as the Dictator set Rome on her feet properly, I will step down. Just as Sulla did. It's not my constitutional prerogative to *rule* Rome. Were it, I wouldn't be away from Rome. Just as you can't absent yourself from Egypt."

"Oh, let's not quarrel on our last night!" she cried, her hand clasping his forearm urgently.

But to herself she was thinking, I am Pharaoh, I am God on earth. I can do whatever I want to do, nothing constrains me. I have Uncle Mithridates and four Roman legions. So when you have vanquished the Republicans and take up residence in Rome, Caesar, I will come to you.

Not rule Rome?

Of *course* you will!

II

THE MARCH OF CATO'S
TEN THOUSAND

From SEXTILIS (AUGUST) of 48 B.C.
until MAY of 47 B.C.

MARCUS PORCIUS CATO

Labienus brought the news of Pompey the Great's defeat at Pharsalus to Cato and Cicero; riding hard, he reached the Adriatic coast of Macedonia three days after the battle, his tenth horse on its last legs. Though he was alone and still in his dowdy, workmanlike war gear, the sentries at the camp gates did not need a second glance to recognize that dark, un-Roman countenance; Pompey's commander of cavalry was known—and feared— by every ranker soldier.

Assured that Cato was in the general's quarters, Labienus slid from his exhausted animal's back and strode off up the Via Principalis toward the scarlet flag stretched rigid in a stiff sea breeze, hoping against hope that Cato would be on his own. Now was not the moment to suffer Cicero's histrionics.

But that was not to be. The Great Advocate was within, his perfectly chosen, formally phrased Latin issuing out of the open door just as if it were a jury he addressed, rather than the dour, unimpressionable Cato. Who, Labienus saw in the instant that he crossed the threshold, was confronting Cicero with an expression that said his patience was being sorely tried.

Startled at this abrupt invasion, Cato and Cicero both jumped, mouths open to speak; Labienus's face silenced them.

"He trounced us in less than an hour," Labienus said curtly as he went straight to the wine table. Thirst made him drink the beaker's contents at a gulp, then he grimaced, shuddered. "Why is it, Cato, that you never have any decent wine?"

It was Cicero who did the squawking, the horrified trumpeting, the agitated flapping. "Oh, this is shocking, terrible!" he cried, tears beginning to course down his face. "What am I doing here? Why did I ever come on this hideous, ill-fated expedition? By rights I should have stayed in Italy, if not in Rome—there I might have been of some use—here, I am an impediment!" And more, and more. Nothing was known that could stem the spate of this wordsmith's verbosity.

Whereas Cato stood for many moments without a thing to say, conscious only of a numbness creeping through his jaws. The impossible had happened: Caesar was victorious. But how could that be? *How?* How could the wrong side have proven itself right?

Neither man's reaction surprised Labienus, who knew them too well and liked them too little; dismissing Cicero as a nothing, he focused his attention on Cato, the most obdurate of all Caesar's countless enemies. Clearly Cato had never dreamed that his own side—the Republicans, they called themselves—could be beaten by a man who had contravened every tenet of Rome's unwritten constitution, who had committed the sacrilege of marching on his own country. Now Cato was the bull struck by the sacrificial hammer, down on his knees without knowing how he had gotten there.

"He trounced us in less than an hour?" Cato finally said.

"Yes. Though he was heavily outnumbered, had no reserves and only a thousand horse, he trounced us. I've never known such an important battle to take so little time. Its name? Pharsalus."

And that, Labienus vowed to himself, is all you're going to hear about Pharsalus from me. I generaled for Caesar from the first to the last year of his exploits in Long-haired Gaul, and I was sure I could beat him. I had become convinced that without me, he couldn't have begun to conquer. But Pharsalus showed me that whatever he used to give me to do was given in the certainty that a skilled subordinate could not fail. He always reserved the strategy for himself, just turned Trebonius, Decimus Brutus, Fabius and the rest of us into tactical instruments of his strategic will.

Somewhere along the way between the Rubicon and Pharsalus I lost sight of that, so when I led my six thousand horse against Caesar's mere thousand Germans at Pharsalus, I deemed the battle already won. A battle *I* engineered because the great Pompeius Magnus was too worn down by the strife inside his own command tent to think of anything beyond self-pity. I wanted battle, his couch generals wanted battle, but Pompeius Magnus wanted Fabian warfare—starve the enemy, harry the enemy, but never fight the enemy. Well, he was right, we were wrong.

How many pitched battles has Caesar fought in? Very often, *literally* fought in, shield and sword among his front-line troops? Near enough to fifty. There is nothing he hasn't seen, nothing he hasn't done. What I do by inspiring fear—nay, terror!—in my soldiers, he does by making his soldiers love him better than they love their own lives.

A surge of bitterness drove him to crack his hand against the almost empty wine flagon, send it flying with a clang. "Did all the good wine go east to Thessaly?" he demanded. "Is there no drop worth drinking in this benighted place?"

Cato came to life. "I neither know nor care!" he barked. "If you want to swill nectar, Titus Labienus, go somewhere else! And," he added, with a sweep of his hand toward Cicero, who was still carrying on, "take him with you!"

Without waiting to see how they took this, Cato walked out his front door and made for the snakepath leading to the top of Petra hill.

Not months, but scant days. How many days, eighteen? Yes, it is only eighteen days since Pompeius Magnus led our massive army east to fresh ground in Thessaly. He didn't want me with him—does he think I don't know how my criticisms irk him? So he elected to take my dear Marcus Favonius with him in my stead, leave me behind here in Dyrrachium to care for the wounded.

Marcus Favonius, best of my friends—where is he? If he were alive, he would have returned to me with Titus Labienus.

Labienus! The butcher to end all butchers, a barbarian in Roman skin, a savage who took slavering pleasure in torturing fellow Romans simply because they had soldiered for Caesar rather than Pompeius. And Pompeius, who had the hubris to nickname himself "Magnus"—"Great"—never even made a token protest when Labienus tortured the seven hundred captured men of Caesar's Ninth Legion. Men whom Labienus knew well from Long-haired Gaul. That is the nucleus of it, that is why we lost the critical confrontation at Pharsalus. The right cause has been pursued by the wrong people.

Pompeius Magnus is Great no longer, and our beloved Republic has entered its death throes. In less than one hour.

The view from the heights of Petra hill was beautiful; a wine-dark sea beneath a softly misty sky and its watery sun, lush verdant hills that soared in the distance toward the high peaks of Candavia, the small terra-cotta city of Dyrrachium and its stout wooden bridge to the mainland. Peaceful. Serene. Even the miles upon miles upon miles of forbidding fortifications, bristling with towers and duplicating themselves beyond a scorched no-man's-land, were settling into the landscape as if they had always been there. Relics of a titanic siege struggle that had gone on for months until suddenly, in the space of a night, Caesar had vanished and Pompeius had deluded himself he was the victor.

Cato stood on Petra's pinnacle and looked south. There, a hundred miles away on Corcyra Island, was Gnaeus Pompeius, his huge naval base, his hundreds of ships, his thousands of sailors, oarsmen and marines. Odd, that Pompeius Magnus's elder son should have a talent for making war upon the sea.

The wind whipped at the stiff leather straps of his kilt and sleeves, tore his long and greying auburn hair to fluttering ribbons, plastered his beard against his chest. It was a year and a half since he had left Italy, and in all that time he had neither shaved nor cut his hair; Cato was in mourning for the crumbled *mos maiorum,* which was the way Roman things had always been and the way Roman things should always be, forever and ever. But the *mos maiorum* had been steadily eroded by a series of political demagogues and military marshals for almost a hundred years, culminating in Gaius Julius Caesar, the worst one of all.

How I hate Caesar! Hated him long before I was old enough to enter the Senate—his airs and graces, his beauty, his golden oratory, his brilliant legislation, his habit of cuckolding his political enemies, his unparalleled military skill, his utter contempt for the *mos maiorum*, his genius for destruction, his unassailably noble patrician birth. How we fought him in the Forum and the Senate, we who called outselves the *boni*, the good men! Catulus, Ahenobarbus, Metellus Scipio, Bibulus and I. Catulus is dead, Bibulus is dead— where are Ahenobarbus and that monumental idiot, Metellus Scipio? Am I the only one of the *boni* left?

When the perpetual rains of this coast suddenly began to fall, Cato returned to the general's house, to find it empty save for Statyllus and Athenodorus Cordylion. Two faces he could greet with genuine gladness.

Statyllus and Athenodorus Cordylion had been Cato's pair of tame philosophers for more years than any of them could remember; he boarded and paid them for their company. None but a fellow Stoic could have endured Cato's hospitality for more than a day or two, for this great-grandson of the immortal Cato the Censor prided himself on the simplicity of his tastes; the rest of his world just called him stingy. Which judgement did not upset Cato in the least. He was immune to criticism and the good opinion of others. However, Cato's was a household as much addicted to wine as to Stoicism. If the wine he and his tame philosophers drank was cheap and nasty, the supply of it was bottomless, and if Cato paid no more than five thousand sesterces for a slave, he could say with truth that he got as much work out of the man—he would have no women in his house—as he would have from one who cost fifty times that.

Because Romans, even those lowly enough to belong to the Head Count, liked to live as comfortably as possible, Cato's peculiar devotion to austerity had set him apart as an admired—even treasured— eccentric; this, combined with his quite appalling tenacity and incorruptible integrity, had elevated him to hero status. No matter how unpalatable a duty might be, Cato would perform it with heart and soul. His harsh and unmelodic voice, his brilliance at the filibuster and harangue, his blind determination to bring Caesar down, had all contributed to his legend. Nothing could intimidate him, and no one could reason with him.

Statyllus and Athenodorus Cordylion would not have dreamed of trying to reason with him; few loved him, but they did.

"Are we housing Titus Labienus?" Cato asked, going to the wine table and pouring himself a full beaker, unwatered.

"No," said Statyllus, smiling faintly. "He's usurped Lentulus Crus's old domicile, and scrounged an amphora of the best Falernian from the quartermaster to drown his sorrows."

"I wish him well of anywhere except here," Cato said, standing while his servant removed the leather gear from him, then sitting with a sigh. "I suppose the news of our defeat has spread?"

"Everywhere," Athenodorus Cordylion said, rheumy old eyes wet with tears. "Oh, Marcus Cato, how can we live in a world that Caesar will rule as a tyrant?"

"That world is not yet a foregone conclusion. It won't be over until I for one am dead and burned." Cato drank deeply, stretched out his long, well-muscled legs. "I imagine there are survivors of Pharsalus who feel the same—Titus Labienus, most definitely. If Caesar is still in the mood to issue pardons, I doubt he'll get one. *Issue pardons!* As if Caesar were our king. While all and sundry marvel at his clemency, sing his praises as a merciful man! Pah! Caesar is another Sulla—ancestors back to the very beginning, royal for seven centuries. More royal—Sulla never claimed to be descended from Venus and Mars. If he isn't stopped, Caesar will crown himself King of Rome. He's always had the blood. Now he has the power. What he doesn't have are Sulla's vices, and it was only Sulla's vices prevented him from tying the diadem around his head."

"Then we must offer to the gods that Pharsalus is not our last battle," Statyllus said, replenishing Cato's beaker from a new flagon. "Oh, if only we knew more about what happened! Who lives, who died, who was captured, who escaped—"

"This tastes suspiciously good," Cato interrupted, frowning.

"I thought—given this dreadful news, you understand—that just this once we wouldn't infringe our convictions if we followed Labienus's example," Athenodorus Cordylion said apologetically.

"To indulge oneself like a sybarite is not a right act, no matter how dreadful the news!" Cato snapped.

"I disagree," said a honeyed voice from the doorway.

"Oh. Marcus Cicero," Cato said flatly, face unwelcoming.

Still weeping, Cicero found a chair from which he could see Cato, mopped his eyes with a crisp, clean, large handkerchief—an indispensable tool for a courtroom genius—and accepted a cup from Statyllus.

I know, thought Cato with detachment, that his impassioned grief is genuine, yet it offends me almost to nausea. A man must conquer *all* his emotions before he is truly free.

"What did you manage to learn from Titus Labienus?" he rapped, so harshly that Cicero jumped. "Where are the others? Who died at Pharsalus?"

"Just Ahenobarbus," Cicero answered.

Ahenobarbus! Cousin, brother-in-law, indefatigable *boni* confrere. I shall never see that determined countenance again. How he railed about his baldness, convinced his shiny dome had set the electors against him whenever he ran for a priesthood . . .

Cicero was rattling on. "It seems Pompeius Magnus escaped, along with everybody else. According to Labienus, that happens in a rout. The conflicts which see men die on the field are those fought to a finish. Whereas our army caved in upon itself. Once Caesar shattered Labienus's cavalry charge by arming his spare cohorts of foot with siege spears, it was all over. Pompeius left the field. The other leaders followed, while the troops either dropped their weapons and cried quarter, or ran away."

"Your son?" Cato asked, feeling the obligation.

"I understand that he acquitted himself splendidly, but was not harmed," Cicero said, transparently glad.

"And your brother, Quintus, *his* son?"

Anger and exasperation distorted Cicero's very pleasant face. "Neither fought at Pharsalus—brother Quintus always said that he wouldn't fight for Caesar, but that he respected the man too much to fight against him either." A shrug. "That is the worst of civil war. It divides families."

"No news of Marcus Favonius?" Cato asked, keeping his tones suitably hard.

"None."

Cato grunted, seemed to dismiss the matter.

"What are we going to do?" Cicero asked rather pathetically.

"Strictly speaking, Marcus Cicero, that is your decision to make," Cato said. "You are the only consular here. I have been praetor, but not consul. Therefore you outrank me."

"Nonsense!" Cicero cried. "Pompeius left you in charge, not me! You're the one living in the general's house."

"My commission was specific and limited. The Law prescribes that executive decisions be taken by the most senior man."

"Well, I absolutely refuse to take them!"

The fine grey eyes studied Cicero's mutinous, fearful face—why will he always end a sheep, a mouse? Cato sighed. "Very well, I will make the executive decisions. But only on the condition that you vouch for my actions when I am called to account by the Senate and People of Rome."

"What Senate?" Cicero asked bitterly. "Caesar's puppets in Rome, or the several hundred at present flying in all directions from Pharsalus?"

"Rome's true Republican government, which will rally somewhere and keep on opposing Caesar the monarch."

"You'll never give up, will you?"

"Not while I still breathe."

"Nor will I, but not in your way, Cato. I'm not a soldier, I lack the sinew. I'm thinking of returning to Italy and starting to organize civilian resistance to Caesar."

Cato leaped to his feet, fists clenched. "Don't you dare!" he roared. "To return to Italy is to abase yourself to Caesar!"

"Pax, pax, I'm sorry I said it!" Cicero bleated. "But what are we going to *do*?"

"We pack up and take the wounded to Corcyra, of course. We have ships here, but if we delay, the Dyrrachians will burn them," Cato said. "Once we reach haven with Gnaeus Pompeius, we'll get news of the others and determine our final destination."

"Eight thousand sick men plus all our stores and supplies? We don't have nearly enough ships!" Cicero gasped.

"If," Cato said a little derisively, "Gaius Caesar could jam twenty thousand soldiers, five thousand noncombatants and slaves, all his mules, wagons, equipment and artillery into less than three hundred battered, leaky ships and cross ocean water between Britannia and Gaul, then there is no reason why I can't put a quarter of that number aboard a hundred good stout transports and sail close to shore in placid waters."

"Oh! Oh, yes, yes! You're quite right, Cato." Cicero rose to his feet, handed his beaker to Statyllus with trembling fingers. "I must start my own packing. When do you sail?"

"The day after tomorrow."

The Corcyra that Cato remembered from a previous visit had vanished, at least along its coasts. An exquisite island, the gem of the Adriatic, hilly and lush, a place of dreamy inlets and translucent, glowing seas.

A series of Pompeian admirals culminating in Gnaeus Pompey had remodeled Corcyra; every cove contained transport ships or war galleys, every small village had turned into a temporary town to service the demands of camps on their peripheries, the once pellucid sea was awash with human and animal excreta and stank worse than the mud flats of Egyptian Pelusium. To compound this lack of hygiene, Gnaeus Pompey had established his main base on the narrow straits facing the coast of the mainland. His reason: that this area yielded the best catches as Caesar tried to ferry troops and supplies from Brundisium to Macedonia. But the currents in the straits did not suck the filth away; rather, it accumulated.

Cato seemed not to notice the stench, whereas Cicero railed about it constantly, his handkerchief muffling his green face and affronted nostrils. In the end he removed himself to a decayed villa atop a hill where he could walk in a lovely orchard and pick fruits from the trees, almost forget the misery of homesickness. Cicero uprooted from Italy was at best a shadow of himself.

The sudden appearance of Cicero's younger brother, Quintus, and his son, Cicero's nephew Quintus Junior, only served to swell his woes. Unwilling to fight for either side, the pair had skulked from place to place all over Greece and Macedonia, then, upon Pompey the Great's defeat at Pharsalus, they had headed for Dyrrachium and Cicero. To find the camp deserted, and a general feeling in the neighborhood that the Republicans had sailed for Corcyra. Off they went to Corcyra.

"Now you know," Quintus snarled at his big brother, "why I wouldn't ally myself with that overrated fool, Pompeius Magnus. He's not fit to tie Caesar's bootlaces."

"What is the world coming to," Cicero riposted, "when the affairs of state are decided upon a battlefield? Nor, in the long run, can they be. Sooner or later Caesar has to return to Rome and pick up the reins of government—and I intend to be in Rome to make it impossible for him to govern."

Quintus Junior snorted. "*Gerrae*, Uncle Marcus! If you set foot on Italian soil, you'll be arrested."

"That, nephew, is where you're wrong," Cicero said with lofty scorn. "I happen to have a letter from Publius Dolabella *begging* me to return to Italy! He says that my presence will be welcome—that Caesar is anxious to have consulars of my standing in the Senate. He insists upon healthy opposition."

"How nice to have a foot in both camps!" Quintus Senior sneered.

"One of Caesar's chief minions your son-in-law! Though I hear that Dolabella isn't being a good husband to Tullia."

"All the more reason for me to go home."

"What about me, Marcus? Why should you, who openly opposed Caesar, be permitted to go home free and clear? My son and I—who have *not* opposed Caesar!—will have to find him and secure pardons because everyone thinks we fought at Pharsalus. And what are we going to do for money?"

Conscious that his face was reddening, Cicero tried to look indifferent. "That is surely your own business, Quintus."

"*Cacat!* You owe me millions, Marcus, *millions!* Not to mention the millions you owe Caesar! Cough some of it up right this moment, or I swear I'll slice you up the front from guts to gizzard!" Quintus yelled.

As he was not wearing his sword or dagger, an empty threat; but the exchange set the tenor of their reunion, which exacerbated Cicero's rudderlessness, worry for his daughter, Tullia, and indignation at the heartless conduct of his wife, Terentia, a termagant. Possessed of an independent fortune she had refused to share with the spendthrift Cicero, Terentia was up to every trick in the money book, from shifting the boundary stones of her land to declaring the most productive tracts sacred sites, thereby avoiding taxes. Activities Cicero had lived with for so long that he took them for granted. What he couldn't forgive her was the way she was treating poor Tullia, who had good cause to complain about her husband, Publius Cornelius Dolabella. But not as far as Terentia was concerned! If Cicero didn't know for a fact that Terentia had no feelings beyond satisfaction at making a profit, he would have said she was in love with Dolabella herself. Siding with him against her own flesh and blood! Tullia was ill, had been ever since she lost her child. My baby, my sweetheart!

Though, of course, Cicero didn't dare voice much of all that in his letters to Dolabella; he *needed* Dolabella!

Toward the middle of September (the very beginning of summer by the seasons that year), the Admiral of Corcyra called a small council in his headquarters.

Going on for thirty-two now, Gnaeus Pompey looked very much like his fabled father, though his hair was a darker shade of gold, his eyes were more grey than blue, and his nose was more Roman than Pompey the Great's despised snub. Command sat upon him easily; as he had his father's gift for organization, the task of manipulating a dozen separate fleets and many thousands of their servitors suited his talents. What he lacked were Pompey the Great's overweening conceit and inferiority complex; Gnaeus Pompey's mother, Mucia Tertia, was a high aristocrat with famous ancestors, so the dark thoughts of obscure Picentine origins which had so plagued poor Pompey the Great never crossed his son's mind.

Only eight men were present: Gnaeus Pompey, Cato, all three Cicerones, Titus Labienus, Lucius Afranius and Marcus Petreius.

Afranius and Petreius had generaled for Pompey the Great for many years, had even run both the Spains for him until Caesar had thrown them out last year. Grizzled they might be, but they were Military Men to the core, and old soldiers never die. Arriving in Dyrrachium just before the exodus to Corcyra, naturally they tagged along, delighted to see Labienus, a fellow Picentine.

They had brought more news—news which cheered Cato immensely, but cast Cicero down: resistance to Caesar was going to re-form in Roman Africa Province, still held by a Republican governor. Juba, King of neighboring Numidia, was openly on the Republican side, so all the survivors of Pharsalus were trying to head for Africa Province with as many troops as they could find.

"What of your father?" Cicero asked Gnaeus Pompey hollowly as he seated himself between his brother and his nephew. Oh, the horror of having to traipse off to Africa Province when all he yearned to do was go home!

"I've sent a letter to half a hundred different places around the eastern end of Our Sea," Gnaeus Pompey said quietly, "but so far I've heard nothing. I'll try again soon. There is a report that he was in Lesbos briefly to meet my stepmother and young Sextus, but if so, my letter there must have missed him. I have not heard from Cornelia Metella or Sextus either."

"What do you yourself intend to do, Gnaeus Pompeius?" asked Labienus, baring his big yellow teeth in the snarl as unconscious and habitual as a facial tic.

Ah, that's interesting, the silent Cato thought, eyes going from one face to the other. Pompeius's son dislikes this savage quite as much as I do.

"I shall remain here until the Etesian winds arrive with the Dog Star—at least another month," Gnaeus Pompey answered, "then I'll move all my fleets and personnel to Sicily, Melite, Gaudos, the Vulcaniae Isles. Anywhere I can gain a toehold and make it difficult for Caesar to feed Italy and Rome. If Italy and Rome starve for lack of grain, it will be that much harder for Caesar to inflict his will on them."

"Good!" Labienus exclaimed, and sat back contentedly. "I'm for Africa with Afranius and Petreius. Tomorrow."

Gnaeus Pompey raised his brows. "A ship I can donate you, Labienus, but why the hurry? Stay longer and take some of Cato's recovering wounded with you. I have sufficient transports."

"No," Labienus said, rising with a nod to Afranius and Petreius. "I'll go to Cythera and Crete first to see what I can pick up there by way of refugee troops—in your donated ship. If I find men to transport, I'll commandeer more ships and press crews if I have to, though the soldiers can row. Save your own resources for Sicily."

The next moment he was gone, Afranius and Petreius in his wake like two big, amiable, elderly hounds.

"So much for Labienus," said Cicero through his teeth. "I can't say I'll miss him."

Nor I, Cato wanted to say, but didn't. Instead he addressed Gnaeus Pompey. "So what of the eight thousand men I brought from Dyrrachium? A thousand at least are fit to sail for Africa at once, but the rest need more time to heal. None of them wants to give up the struggle, but I can't leave them here if you go."

"Well, it seems our new Great Man is more interested in Asia Minor than he is in the Adriatic." Lip lifted in contempt, Gnaeus Pompey snorted. "Kissing the ground at Ilium in honor of his ancestor Aeneas, if you please! Remitting Trojan taxes! Looking for the tomb of Hector!" Suddenly he grinned. "Not that leisure has lasted long. A courier came today and informed me that King Pharnaces has come down from Cimmeria to invade Pontus."

Quintus Cicero laughed. "Following in his dear old dad's footsteps, eh? Has Caesar moved to contain him?"

"No, Caesar's still heading south. It's that traitorous cur Calvinus has to contend with the son of Mithridates the Great. These oriental kings! Hydra-headed. Chop one off, and two more sprout from the stump. So I daresay Pharnaces means it's war as usual from one end of Anatolia to the other."

"Which gives Caesar plenty to do at the eastern end of Our Sea," Cato said with huge satisfaction. "We'll have sufficient time to grow strong again in Africa Province."

"You realize, Cato, that Labienus is trying to steal a march on you, and on my father, and on anyone else who might lay claim to the high command in Africa?" Gnaeus Pompey asked. "Why else is he so anxious to get there?" He pounded his fist against the palm of his other hand, anguished. "Oh, I wish I knew where my father is! I know him, Cato, I know how depressed he can get!"

"He'll turn up, have no fear," Cato said, leaning to clasp the Admiral's brawny arm with unusual demonstrativeness. "As for me, I have no desire to occupy the command tent." He jerked his head toward Cicero. "There sits my superior, Gnaeus Pompeius. Marcus Cicero is a consular, so when I leave for Africa, it will be under his authority."

Cicero emitted a squeak of outrage and leaped to his feet. "No, no, no, no! I've told you before, my answer is *no*! Go where you want and do what you want, Cato—appoint one of your philosopher toadies—or a baboon—or that painted whore who pesters you so—to the command tent, but don't appoint *me*! My mind is made up, I'm going home!"

Which brought Cato to tower at his full imposing height, looking down that even more imposing nose at Cicero as if he suddenly spied some noisome insect. "By virtue of your rank and your own windbag prating, Marcus Tullius Cicero, you are first and foremost the Republic's servant! What you *want* and what you *do* are two quite different horses! Not once in your lordly life have you genuinely done your duty! Especially when that duty requires you to pick up a sword! You're a Forum creature whose deeds don't begin to rival your words!"

"How dare you!" Cicero gasped, face mottling. "How dare you, Marcus Porcius Cato, you sanctimonious, self-righteous, pigheaded *monster*! It was you and no one else who brought us to this, it was you and no one else who—who *forced* Pompeius Magnus into civil war! When I came to him with Caesar's very reasonable and fair offer of terms, it was you who threw such a colossal tantrum that you literally terrified the life out of him! You screeched, screamed and howled until Magnus was a shivering heap of jelly—you had the man groveling and crawling to you more abjectly than Lucullus groveled and crawled to Caesar! No, Cato, I don't blame Caesar for this civil war, I blame you!"

Gnaeus Pompey was out of his chair too, white with rage. "What do you mean, Cicero, you ancestorless nobody from the back hills of Samnium? *My father* intimidated to jelly? *My father* groveling and crawling? Take that back, or I'll ram it between your rotting teeth with my fist!"

"No, I will not recant!" Cicero roared, beside himself. "I was there! I *saw* what happened! Your father, Gnaeus Pompeius, is a spoiled baby who toyed with Caesar and the idea of civil war to inflate his own opinion of himself, who never believed for one moment that Caesar would cross the Rubicon with one paltry legion! Who never believed that there are men with that kind of brazen courage! Who never believed in anything except his own—his own *myth*! A myth, son of Magnus, that started when your father blackmailed Sulla into giving him the co-command, and ended a month ago on a battlefield called Pharsalus! Much though it pains me to have to admit it, your father, son of Magnus, isn't Caesar's bootlace when it comes to war or politics!"

The stupefaction that had paralyzed Gnaeus Pompey almost audibly snapped; he launched himself at Cicero with a bellow, hands out to throttle him.

Neither of the Quintuses moved, too enthralled to care what Gnaeus Pompey did to the family tyrant. It was Cato who stepped in front of Pompey the Great's mortally insulted son and grasped both his wrists. The tussle between them was brief; Cato forced Gnaeus Pompey's arms down effortlessly and whipped them behind his back.

"That is enough!" he snapped, eyes blazing. "Gnaeus Pompeius, go back to caring for your fleets. Marcus Cicero, if you refuse to be the Republic's loyal servant, go back to Italy!"

"Yes, go!" Pompey the Great's son cried, and slumped into his chair to massage feeling back into his hands. Ye gods, who would ever have thought Cato so strong? "Pack your belongings, you and your kindred, and may I never see any of your faces again! A pinnace will be waiting at dawn tomorrow to take you to Patrae, from whence you can return to Italy, or take a trip to Hades to pat Cereberus's heads! Go! Get out of my sight!"

Head up, two scarlet spots in his cheeks, Cicero cuddled the massive folds of toga draped over his left shoulder and stalked out, his nephew by his side. Quintus Senior delayed a little to turn in the doorway.

"I shit on both your pricks," he said with grave dignity.

Which struck Gnaeus Pompey as exquisitely funny; he dropped his head into his hands and howled with mirth.

"I see nothing to laugh about," Cato said, inspecting the wine table. The last few moments had been thirsty work.

"You wouldn't, Cato," Gnaeus Pompey said when he was able. "By definition, a Stoic has no sense of humor."

"That is true," Cato agreed, sitting down again to nurse a goblet— no beakers or cups for Gnaeus Pompey—of excellent Samian wine. "However, Gnaeus Pompeius, we have not yet arrived at a conclusion about either me or the wounded."

"How many of your eight thousand do you really think will ever be fit to fight again?"

"At least seven thousand. Can you supply me with enough transports to get the thousand best of them across to Africa in four days' time?"

Gnaeus Pompey wrinkled his brow. "Wait until the Etesian winds come, Cato, they'll blow you straight to our Roman province. If you start before them, you'll be at the mercy of Auster—or Libotonus—or Zephyrus—or any other wind that Aeolus fancies letting out of his bag for a stretch and a canter."

"No, I must leave as soon as maybe, and ask that you send the rest of my men on before you shift traps yourself. Your work is vital, but it is different from mine. My task is to preserve the very brave soldiers your father placed in my care. For they are brave. If they were not, their wounds would be nonexistent."

"As you wish," said Gnaeus Pompey with a sigh. "There is a difficulty about those you want me to send on later—I'm going to need the transports back for my own use. If the Etesian winds are late, I can't guarantee that they'll reach Africa Province." He shrugged. "In fact, all of you could land anywhere."

"That is my worry," Cato said with all his usual sturdy resolution, but somewhat less of his usual shout.

Four days later fifty of the transports Cato had used to move his men, equipment and supplies from Dyrrachium were loaded and ready to go: 1,200 recovered soldiers formed into two cohorts, 250 noncombatant assistants, 250 pack mules, 450 wagon mules, 120 wagons, a month's supply of wheat, chickpea, bacon and oil, plus grindstones, ovens, utensils, spare clothing and arms—and, a gift from Gnaeus Pompey that traveled on Cato's own ship, a thousand talents of silver coins.

"Take it, I have plenty more," Gnaeus Pompey said cheerfully. "Compliments of Caesar! And," he went on, handing over a bundle of small rolls of paper, each tied and sealed, "these came from Dyrrachium for you. News of home."

Fingers trembling a little, Cato told the letters over, then tucked them inside the armhole of his light leather cuirass.

"Aren't you going to read them now?"

The grey eyes looked very stern, yet clouded, and the generous curve of Cato's mouth was drawn up as if with pain. "No," he said, at his loudest and most truculent, "I shall read them later, when I have the time."

Though it took all day to get the fifty transports out of an inadequate harbor, Gnaeus Pompey remained on the little wooden pier until the last ships went hull down over the horizon, until all that was left of them were hair-thin masts, black prickles against the opalescent skies of early evening.

Then he turned and trudged back to his headquarters; life would be more peaceful, certainly, but somehow when Cato was no longer a part of things, an emptiness entered. How Cato had awed him in his youth! How much his pedagogues and rhetors had harped on the different styles of the three greatest orators in the Senate: Caesar, Cicero and Cato. Names he had grown up with, men he could never forget; his father, the First Man in Rome, never a good orator, but a master at getting his own way. Now all of them were scattered while the same patterns went on aweaving, one life strand entwined with another until Atropos took pity and snipped this thread, that thread.

Lucius Scribonius Libo was waiting; Gnaeus Pompey stifled a sigh. A good man who had been Admiral after Bibulus died, then had yielded gracefully to Pompey the Great's son. As was fitting. The only reason this scion of the wrong branch of the Scribonius family had risen so high so quickly lay in the fact that Gnaeus Pompey had taken one look at his dimpled, ravishingly pretty daughter, divorced his boring Claudia, and married her. A match Pompey the Great had abhorred, deplored. But that was Father, himself obsessed with marrying only the most august aristocrats, and determined that his sons should do the same. Well, Sextus was still too young for marriage, and Gnaeus had tried for the sake of harmony until he'd set eyes on the seventeen-year-old Scribonia. Love, Pompey the Great's elder son reflected as he greeted his father-in-law, could destroy the best-laid plans.

They dined together, discussed the coming move to Sicily and environs, the potential resistance in Africa Province—and the possible whereabouts of Pompey the Great.

"Today's courier reported a rumor that he's taken Cornelia Metella and Sextus away from Lesbos, and is island-hopping down the Aegean," his elder son said.

"Then," said Scribonius Libo, preparing to depart, "I think it's time that you wrote again."

So when he had gone Gnaeus Pompey sat down resolutely at his desk, drew a blank double sheet of Fannian paper toward him, and picked up his reed pen, dipped it in the inkwell.

We are still alive and kicking, and we still own the seas. Please, I beg you, my beloved father, gather what ships you can and come either to me or to Africa.

But before Pompey the Great's brief reply could reach him, he learned of his father's death on the mud flats of Egyptian Pelusium at the hands of a torpid boy king and his palace cabal.

Of course. Of course. As cruel, as unethical as Orientals are, they killed him thinking to curry favor with Caesar. Not for one moment would it have occurred to them that Caesar hungered to spare him. Oh, Father! This way is *better*! This way, you are not beholden to Caesar for the gift of continued life.

When he was sure he could work without unmanning himself in front of his subordinates, Gnaeus Pompey sent 6,500 more of Cato's wounded to Africa, offering to the Lares Permarini, to Neptune and to Spes that they and Cato would find each other on that two-thousand-mile coast between the Nile Delta and Africa Province. Then he began the onerous task of removing himself, his fleets and men into bases around Sicily.

Its few natives unsure whether they were glad or sorry to see the Romans go, Corcyra slowly lost its scars and returned to its sweet oblivion. Slowly.

Cato had decided to use his soldiers and noncombatants as oarsmen; if he didn't push them too hard, splendid exercise for convalescents, he thought. Zephyrus was blowing fitfully from the west, so sails were useless, but the weather was tranquil and the sea flat calm, as always under that gentle breeze. Hate Caesar with implacable intensity he might, but he had pored over those crisp, impersonal commentaries Caesar himself had written about his war in Gaul of the Long-hairs, and not allowed his feelings to blind him to the many practical facts they contained. Most important, that the General had shared in the sufferings and the deprivations of his ranker soldiers—walked when they walked, lived on a few scraps of ghastly beef when they did, never held himself aloof from their company on the long marches and during the terrible times when they huddled behind their fortifications and could see no other fate than to be captured and burned alive in wicker cages. Politically and ideologically Cato had made great capital out of those same commentaries, but though his inwardly turned passions drove him to deride and dismiss Caesar's every action, a part of his mind absorbed the lessons.

As a child Cato had found it agony to learn; he didn't even have his half sister Servilia's ability to remember what he had been taught and told, let alone possess anything approaching Caesar's legendary memory. It was rote, rote, rote for Cato, while Servilia sneered contempt and his adored half brother Caepio sheltered him from her viciousness. That Cato had survived a hideous childhood as the youngest of that tempestuous, divided brood of orphans was purely due to Caepio. Caepio, of whom it had been said that he was not his father's child, but the love child of his mother, Livia Drusa, and Cato's father, whom she later married; that Caepio's height, red hair and hugely beaked nose were pure Porcius Cato; that therefore Caepio was Cato's full, not half, brother, despite the august patrician name of Servilius Caepio he bore, and the vast fortune he had inherited as a Servilius Caepio. A fortune founded on fifteen thousand talents of gold stolen from Rome: the fabulous Gold of Tolosa.

Sometimes when the wine didn't work and the daimons of the night refused to be banished, Cato would recall that evening when some minion of Uncle Drusus's enemies had thrust a small but wicked knife into Uncle Drusus's groin and twisted it until the damage within could not be repaired. A measure of how deadly the mixture of politics and love could become. The screams of agony that went on and on and on, the lake of blood on the priceless mosaic floor, the exquisite succor that the two-year-old Cato had felt enfolded within the five-year-old Caepio's embrace as all six children had witnessed Drusus's awful, lingering death. A night never to be forgotten.

After his tutor finally managed to teach him to read, Cato had found his code of living in the copious works of his great-grandfather Cato the Censor, a pitiless ethic of stifled emotions, unbending principles and frugality; Caepio had tolerated it in his baby brother, but never subscribed to it himself. Though Cato, who didn't perceive the feelings of others, had not properly understood Caepio's misgivings about a code of living which did not permit its practitioner the mercy of an occasional failure.

They could not be separated, even served their war training together. Cato never envisioned an existence without Caepio, his stout defender against Servilia as she heaped scorn on his auburn head because he was a descendant of Cato the Censor's disgraceful second marriage to the daughter of his own slave. Of course she was aware of Caepio's true parentage, but as he bore her own father's name, she focused all her malice on Cato.

Whose progeny he actually was had never worried Caepio, Cato thought as he leaned on the ship's rail to watch the myriad twinkling lights of his fleet throw dissolving gold ribbons across the black still waters. Servilia. A monstrous child, a monstrous woman. More polluted even than our mother was. Women are despicable. The moment some haughty beautiful fellow with impeccable ancestors and tomcat appeal strolls into view, they scramble to open their legs to him. Like my first wife, Attilia, who opened her legs to Caesar. Like Servilia, who opened her legs to Caesar, still does. Like the two Domitias, the wives of Bibulus, who opened their legs to Caesar. Like half of female Rome, who opened their legs to Caesar. *Caesar!* Always Caesar.

His mind strayed then to his nephew, Brutus. Servilia's only son. Undeniably the son of her husband at the time, Marcus Junius Brutus, whom Pompeius Magnus had had the gall to execute for treason. The fatherless Brutus had mooned for years over Caesar's daughter, Julia, even managed to become engaged to her. That had pleased Servilia! If her son was married to his daughter, she could keep Caesar in the family, didn't need to work so hard to hide her affair with Caesar from her second husband, Silanus. Silanus had died too, but of despair, not Pompeius Magnus's sword.

Servilia always said that I couldn't win Brutus to my side, but I did. I did! The first horror for him was the day that he found out his mother had been Caesar's mistress for five years; the second was the day Caesar broke his engagement to Julia and married the girl to Pompeius Magnus, almost old enough to be her grandfather—and Brutus's father's executioner. Pure political expediency, but it had bound Pompeius Magnus to Caesar until Julia died. And the bleeding Brutus—how *soft* he is!—turned from his mother to me. It is a right act to inflict punishment upon the immoral, and the worst punishment I could have found for Servilia was to take her precious son away.

Where is Brutus now? A lukewarm Republican at best, always torn between his Republican duty and his besetting sin, money. Neither a Croesus nor a Midas—too Roman, of course. Too steeped in interest rates, brokerage fees, sleeping partnerships and all the furtive commercial activities of a Roman senator, disbarred by tradition from naked moneymaking, but too avaricious to resist the temptation.

Brutus had inherited the Servilius Caepio fortune founded in the Gold of Tolosa. Cato ground his teeth, grasped the rail with both hands until his knuckles glistened white. For Caepio, beloved Caepio, had died. Died alone on his way to Asia Province, waiting in vain for me to hold his hand and help him cross the River. I arrived an hour too late. Oh, life, life! Mine has never been the same since I gazed on Caepio's dead face, and howled, and moaned, and yammered like one demented. I was demented. I am still—oh, still demented. *The pain!* Caepio was thirty to my twenty-seven; soon I will be forty-six. Yet Caepio's death seems like yesterday, my grief as fresh now as it was then.

Brutus inherited in accordance with the *mos maiorum;* he was Caepio's closest agnate male relative. Servilia's son, his nephew. I do not grudge Brutus one sestertius of that staggering fortune, and can console myself with the knowledge that Caepio's wealth could not have gone to a more careful custodian than he. I simply wish that Brutus was more a man, less a milksop. But with that mother, what else could I expect? Servilia has made him what she wanted—obedient, subservient, and desperately afraid of her. How odd, that Brutus actually got up the gumption to cut his leading strings and join Pompeius Magnus in Macedonia. That cur Labienus says he fought at Pharsalus. Amazing. Perhaps being isolated from his harpy of a mother has wrought great changes in him? Perhaps he'll even show his pimple-pocked face in Africa Province? Hah! I'll believe *that* when I see it!

Cato swallowed a yawn, and went to lie on his straw pallet between the miserably still forms of Statyllus and Athenodorus Cordylion—shockingly bad sailors, both of them.

Zephyrus continued to blow from the west, but veered around just sufficiently to the north to keep Cato's fifty transports heading in the general direction of Africa. However, he noted with sinking heart, far to the east of Africa Province. Instead of sighting first Italy's heel, then Italy's toe, and finally Sicily, they were pushed firmly against the west coast of the Greek Peloponnese all the way to Cape Taenarum, from whence they limped to Cythera, the beautiful island that Labienus had intended to visit in search of troops fleeing from Pharsalus. If he was still there, he didn't signal from the shore. Suppressing his anxiety, Cato sailed on toward Crete, and passed the stubby sere bluffs of Criumetopon on the eleventh day at sea.

Gnaeus Pompey had not been able to provide a pilot, but had sent Cato to spend a day with his six best men, all experienced mariners who knew the eastern end of Our Sea as well as had the Phoenicians of old. Thus it was Cato who identified the various landfalls, Cato who had an idea of where they were going.

Though they had sighted no other ships, Cato hadn't dared to stop and take on water anywhere in Greece, so on the twelfth day he anchored his fleet in unsheltered but placid conditions off Cretan Gaudos Isle, and there made sure that every barrel and amphora he owned was filled to the brim from a spring that gushed out of a cliff into the wavelets. Cretan Gaudos was the last lonely outpost before he committed them to the empty wastes of the Libyan Sea. Libya. They were going to Libya, where men were executed smeared with honey and lashed across an ant heap. Libya. A place of nomad Marmaridae—

marble people—and, if the Greek geographers were to be believed, perpetually shifting sands, rainless skies.

At Gaudos he had himself rowed in a tiny boat from one cluster of transports to the next, standing up to shout his little speech of cheer and explanation in that famously stentorian voice.

"Fellow voyagers, the coast of Africa is still far away, but here we must say farewell to the friendly breast of Mother Earth, for from now on we sail without sight of land amid the streams of tunnyfish and the whoofs of dolphins. Do not be afraid! I, Marcus Porcius Cato, have you in my hand, and I will hold you safely until we reach Africa. We will keep our ships together, we will row hard but sensibly, we will sing the songs of our beloved Italy, we will trust in ourselves and in our gods. We are Romans of the true Republic, and we will survive to make life hard for Caesar, so I swear it by Sol Indiges, Tellus and Liber Pater!"

A little speech greeted by frenzied cheers, smiling faces.

Then, though he was neither priest nor augur, Cato killed a bidentine ewe and offered it, as the Commander, to the Lares Permarini, the protectors of those who traveled on the sea. A fold of his purple-bordered toga over his head, he prayed:

"O ye who are called the Lares Permarini, or any other name ye prefer—ye who may be gods, goddesses or of no sex at all—we ask that ye intercede on our behalf with the mighty Father Neptune—whose offspring ye may or may not be—before we set out on our journey to Africa. We pray that ye will testify before all the gods that we are sincere as we ask ye to keep us safe, keep us free from the storms and travails of the deep, keep our ships together, and allow us to land in some civilized place. In accordance with our contractual agreements, which go back to the time of Romulus, we hereby offer ye the proper sacrifice, a fine young female sheep which has been cleansed and purified."

And on the thirteenth day the fleet weighed anchor to sail to only the Lares Permarini knew where.

Having attained his sea legs, Statyllus abandoned his bed and kept Cato company.

"Though I try valiantly, I can never understand the Roman mode of worship," he said, now enjoying the slight motion of a big, heavy ship riding a glossy sea.

"In what way, Statyllus?"

"The—*legality*, Marcus Cato. How can any people have legal contracts with their gods?"

"Romans do, always have done. Though I confess, not being a

priest, that I wasn't exactly sure when the contract with the Lares Per-marini was drawn up," Cato said very seriously. "However, I did remember that Lucius Ahenobarbus said the contracts with *numina* like the Lares and Penates were drawn up by Romulus. It's only the late arrivals like Magna Mater and"—he grimaced in disgust—"*Isis* whose legal agreements with the Senate and People of Rome are preserved. A priest would automatically know, it's a part of his job. But who would elect Marcus Porcius Cato to one of the pontifical colleges when he can't even get himself elected consul in a poor year of dismal candidates?"

"You are still young," Statyllus said softly, well aware of Cato's disappointment when he had failed to secure the consulship four years ago. "Once the true government of Rome is restored, you will be *senior* consul, returned by all the Centuries."

"That is as may be. First, let us get ourselves to Africa."

The days crept by as the fleet crept southeast, chiefly by oar power, though the huge single sail each ship bore aloft on a mast did swell occasionally, help a little. However, as a slack sail made rowing a harder business, sails were furled unless the day was one of frequent helpful puffs.

To keep himself fit and alert, Cato took a regular shift on an oar, plying it alone. Like merchant vessels, transports had but one bank of oars, fifteen to a side. All were fully decked, which meant the oarsmen sat within the hull, an ordeal more endurable because they were housed in an outrigger that projected them well over the water, made it easier and airier to row. Warships were entirely different, had several banks of oars plied by two to five men per oar, the bottom bank so close to the surface of the sea that the ports were sealed with leather valves. But war galleys were never meant to carry cargo or stay afloat between battles; they were jealously cared for and spent most of their twenty years of service sitting ashore in ship sheds. When Gnaeus Pompey quit Corcyra, he left its natives hundreds of ship sheds—*firewood!*

Because Cato believed that selfless hard work was one of the marks of a good man, he put his back to it, and inspired the other twenty-nine men who rowed with him to do the same. Word of the Commander's participation somehow spread from ship to ship, and men rowed more willingly, stroking to the beat of the *hortator's* drum. Counting every soul aboard those ships carrying soldiers rather than mules, wagons or equipment, there were men enough for two teams only, which meant a constant four hours on, four hours off, day and night.

The diet was monotonous; bread, the universal staple, had been off the menu except for that day spent at Cretan Gaudos. No ship could risk fire by stoking ovens. A steady fire was lit on a hearth of firebricks to heat a huge iron cauldron, and in that only one food could be cooked—thick pease porridge flavored with a small chunk of bacon or salt pork. Concerned about drinking water, Cato had issued an order that the porridge was to be eaten without additional salt, yet another blow for appetites.

However, the weather allowed all fifty ships to keep close together, and it seemed, Cato ascertained on his constant trips around them in his tiny boat, that his 1,500 men were as optimistic as he could have hoped for, given their healthy fear of an entity as secretive and mysterious as the sea. No Roman soldier was happy on the sea. Dolphins were greeted with joy, but there were sharks too, and schools of fish fled at the approach of all those whacking oars, which limited visual entertainment as well as guaranteed the absence of fish stew.

The mules drank more than Cato had estimated, the sun beat down every day, and the level of water in the barrels was dropping with appalling swiftness. Ten days out from Cretan Gaudos, he began to doubt that they would live to see land. As he took his tiny boat from ship to ship, he promised the men that the mules would go overboard long before the water barrels were empty. A promise his men did not welcome; they were soldiers, and mules to soldiers were quite as precious as gold. Each century had ten mules to carry what a man could not fit into his fifty-pound back load, and one four-mule wagon for the really heavy stuff.

Then Corus began to blow out of the northwest; whooping with delight, the men swarmed to break out the sails. In Italy, a wet wind, but not in the Libyan Sea. Their pace picked up, the oars were easier to pull, and hope blossomed.

At the middle of the fourteenth night since Cretan Gaudos, Cato woke and sat up in a hurry, the nostrils of his awesome beak flaring. The sea, he had long realized, had a smell all its own—sweetish, weedy, faintly fishy. But now a different perfume was smothering it. *Earth!* He could smell earth!

Sniffing ecstatically, he went to the rail and lifted his eyes to that magical indigo sky. It wasn't dark, had never really been dark. Though the orb of the moon had waned to invisibility, the vault was a richly glowing spangle of light from countless stars, spun in places like thin veils, all save the planets winking.

The Greeks say that the planets revolve around our globe much closer to it than the shimmering stars, which are an unimaginable distance away. We are blessed, for we are the home of the gods. We are the center of the whole universe, we hold court for all the celestial bodies. And, to worship us and the gods, they shine, lamps of the night reminding us that light is life.

My letters! My letters are still unread! Tomorrow we will land in Africa, and I will have to sustain the spirits of the men in a place of marble people and shifting sands. Like it or not, I must read my letters as soon as dawn pales the sky, before excitement spreads and I am caught up in it. Until then, I row.

From Servilia, a distillation of pure poison; mumbling his way through her conjoined words, Cato gave up on the seventh column, screwed her little scroll into a ball and tossed it overboard. So much for you, my detested half sister!

An oily missive from his father-in-law, Lucius Marcius Philippus, arch-fence-sitter and Epicure supreme. Rome was very quiet under the consul Vatia Isauricus and the urban praetor Gaius Trebonius. In fact, mourned Philippus in elegant prose, absolutely nothing was happening beyond wild reports that Pompeius had won a great victory at Dyrrachium and Caesar was on the run, a defeated man. It followed Servilia into the sea, danced away on the ripples created by the oar blades. So much for you too, Philippus, with your feet safely in both camps—nephew-in-law of Caesar, father-in-law of Cato, Caesar's greatest enemy. Your news is stale, it sticks in my gullet.

The real reason why he had never read his letters was the last one he read: the one from Marcia. His wife.

When Cornelia Metella defied tradition and set out to join Pompeius Magnus, I hungered desperately to follow her example. That I did not is Porcia's fault—why did you have to own a daughter as fiercely devoted to the *mos maiorum* as you are yourself? When she caught me packing, she flew at me like a harpy, then went around the corner to see my father and demanded that he forbid me to go. Well, you know my father. Anything for peace. So Porcia had her wretched way and I still sit here in Rome.

Marcus, *meum mel, mea vita,* I live alone in a vacuum of the spirit, wondering and worrying. Are you well? Do you ever think of me? Will I ever see you again?

It is not fair that I should have spent a longer time married to Quintus Hortensius than both my marriages to you put together. We have never spoken of that exile to which you sentenced me, though I understood immediately why you did it. You did it because you loved me *too* much, and deemed your love for me a betrayal of those Stoic principles you hold dearer than your life. Or your wife. So when sheer senescence prompted Hortensius to ask for me in marriage, you divorced me and gave me to him—with the connivance of my father, of course. I know that you took not one sestertius from the old man, but my father took ten million of them. His tastes are expensive.

I saw my exile with Hortensius as evidence of the depth of your love for me—four long, dreadful years! *Four years!* Yes, he was too old and enfeebled to force his attentions on me, but can you imagine how I felt as I sat for hours each day with Hortensius, cooing at his favorite pet fish, Paris? Missing you, longing for you, suffering your renunciation of me over and over again?

And then, after he died and you took me as your wife a second time, I had but a few short months with you before you left Rome and Italy on one of your remorseless acts of duty. Is that fair, Marcus? I am but twenty-six years old, I have been married to two men, one twice, yet I am barren. Like Porcia and Calpurnia, I have no child.

I know how much you detest reading my reproaches, so I will cease my complaining. If you were a different kind of man, I would not love you the way I do. There are three of us who mourn our missing men—Porcia, Calpurnia, and I. Porcia? I hear you ask. Porcia, missing dead Bibulus? No, not Bibulus. Porcia misses her cousin Brutus. She loves him, I believe, quite as much as you love me, for she has your nature—on fire with passions, all of them frozen by her absurd devotion to the teachings of Zeno. Who was Zeno, after all? A silly old Cypriot who denied himself all the glorious things that the gods gave us to enjoy, from laughter to good food. There speaks the Epicurean's child! As for Calpurnia, she misses Caesar. Eleven years his wife, yet only a few months actually with Caesar, who was philandering with your frightful sister until he left for Gaul. Since then—nothing. We widows and wives are poorly served.

Someone told me that you have neither shaved nor cut your hair since you left Italy, but I cannot imagine your wonderful, nobly Roman face as bewhiskered as a Jew's.

Tell me why, Marcus, we women are taught to read and write, yet are always doomed to sit at home, waiting? I must go, I cannot see for tears. Please, I beg of you, write to me! Give me hope.

The sun was up; Cato was a painfully slow reader. Marcia's scroll was crumpled up, then skimmed across the sparkling water. So much for wives.

His hands were shaking. Such a stupid, stupid letter! To love a woman with the consuming intensity of a funeral pyre is not a right act, cannot be a right act. Doesn't she understand that every one of her many letters says the same thing? Doesn't she realize that I will never write to her? What would I say? What is there to say?

No nose save his seemed to snuff that earthy tang in the air; everybody went about their business as if today were just another day. The morning wore on. Cato took a turn at the oars, then went back to stand at the rail straining his eyes. Nothing showed until the sun was directly overhead, when a thin, faint blue line appeared on the horizon. Just as Cato saw it, the sailor aloft at the masthead shrieked.

"Land! Land!"

His ship led the fleet, which swelled into a teardrop behind it. No time to step into his tiny boat himself, so he sent an eager *pilus prior* centurion, Lucius Gratidius, in his stead to instruct the captains not to get ahead of him, and to watch carefully for shoals, reefs, hidden rocks. The water had suddenly become very shallow and clear as the best Puteoli glass, with the same faintly blue sheen now that the sun was not glancing off it.

The land came up extremely fast because it was so flat, not a phenomenon Romans were used to, accustomed to sailing regions where high mountains reared in close proximity to the sea and thus made land visible many miles from shore. To Cato's relief, the westering sun revealed country more green than ocher; if grasses grew, then there was some hope of civilization. From Gnaeus Pompey's pilots he knew that there was only one settlement on the eight-hundred-mile coast between Alexandria and Cyrenaica: Paraetonium, whence Alexander the Great had set off south to the fabled oasis of Ammon, there to converse with the Egyptian Zeus.

Paraetonium, we must find Paraetonium! But is it west of here, or is it east?

Cato scraped in the bottom of a sack and managed to gather a small handful of chickpea—they had very little left—then threw the legumes into the water as he prayed:

"O all ye gods, by whichever name ye wish to be known, of whatever sex or no sex ye are, let me guess correctly!"

A brisk gust from Corus came on the echo of his plea; he went to the captain, stationed on a tiny poop between the rope-bound tillers of the massive rudder oars.

"Captain, we turn east before the wind."

Not four miles down the coast Cato's farsighted eyes took in the sight of two slight bluffs with the entrance to a bay between them, and one or two mud-brick houses. If this were Paraetonium, then the town had to be inside the harbor. The entrance was mined with rocks, but a clear passage lay almost in its middle; two sailors shoved at the tillers and Cato's ship turned, oars inboard for the maneuver, to sail into a beautiful haven.

He gasped, goggled. Three Roman ships already lay at anchor! Who, who? Too few for it to be Labienus, so who?

On the back reaches of the bay was a mud-brick, tiny town. Size didn't matter, though. Wherever people lived collectively, there was bound to be potable water and some provisions for sale. And he would soon find out which Romans owned the ships, all flying the SPQR pennant from their mastheads. Important Romans.

He went ashore in his tiny boat accompanied by the *pilus prior* centurion, Lucius Gratidius; the entire population of Paraetonium, some six hundred souls, was lined up along a beach, marveling at the sight of fifty big ships making port one at a time. That he might not be able to communicate with the Paraetonians did not occur to him; everyone everywhere spoke Greek, the *lingua mundi*.

The first words he heard, however, were Latin. Two people stepped forward, a handsome woman in her middle twenties and a stripling youth. Cato gaped, but before he could say anything the woman had fallen on his neck in floods of tears, and the youth was attempting to wring his hand off.

"My dear Cornelia Metella! And Sextus Pompeius! Does this mean that Pompeius Magnus is here?" he asked.

A question which caused Cornelia Metella to weep harder, and set Sextus Pompey to crying too. Their grief held a message: Pompey the Great was dead.

While he stood with Pompey the Great's fourth wife twined around his neck watering his purple-bordered toga and tried to extricate his hand from Sextus Pompey's grasp, a rather important-looking man in a tailored Greek tunic walked up to them, a small entourage in his wake.

"I am Marcus Porcius Cato."

"I am Philopoemon" was the answer, given with an expression that said Cato's name meant absolutely nothing to a Paraetonian.

Indeed this was the end of the world!

Over dinner in Philopoemon's modest house he learned the awful story of Pompey the Great in Pelusium, of the retired centurion Septimius who had lured Pompey into a boat and to his death, which Cornelia Metella and Sextus had witnessed from their ship. Worst news of all, Septimius had chopped off Pompey's head, put it in a jar, then left the body lying on the mud flats.

"Our freedman Philip and the boy who was his slave had gone in the dinghy with my father, but they survived by running away," Sextus said. "We could do nothing to help—Pelusium harbor was full of the Egyptian king's navy, and several warships were bearing down on us. Either we stayed to be captured and probably killed too, or we put to sea." He shrugged, his mouth quivering. "I knew which course my father would have wanted, so we fled."

Though her fountain of tears had dried up, Cornelia Metella contributed little to the conversation. How much she has changed, Cato thought, he who rarely noticed such things. She had been the haughtiest of patrician aristocrats, daughter of the august Metellus Scipio, first married to the elder son of Pompey's partner in two of his consulships, Marcus Licinius Crassus. Then Crassus and her husband had set out to invade the Kingdom of the Parthians, and perished at Carrhae. The widowed Cornelia Metella had become a political pawn, for Pompey was widowed too, the death of Caesar's Julia slipping rapidly into the past. So the *boni,* including Cato, had plotted to detach Pompey the Great from Caesar; the only way, they felt, to pull Pompey on to the *boni* side was to give him Cornelia Metella as his new wife. Extremely sensitive about his own obscure origins (Picentine, but with the awful stigma of Gaul added to that), Pompey always married women of the highest nobility. And who was higher than Cornelia Metella? A descendant of Scipio Africanus and Aemilius Paullus, no less. Perfect for *boni* purposes! The scheme had worked. His gratitude patent, Pompey had espoused her eagerly, and became, if not one of the *boni,* at least their close ally.

In Rome she had continued as she began, insufferably proud, cool if not downright cold, clearly regarding herself as her father's sacrificial animal. Marriage to a Pompeius from Picenum was a shocking comedown, even if this particular Pompeius was the First Man in Rome. He just didn't have the blood, so Cornelia Metella had gone secretly to the Vestal Virgins and obtained some of their medicine made from diseased rye, aborted a pregnancy.

But here in Paraetonium she was different, very different. Soft. Sweet. Gentle. When finally she did speak, it was to tell Cato of Pompey's plans after his defeat at Pharsalus.

"We were going to Serica," she said sadly. "Gnaeus had had his fill of Rome, of life anywhere around the margins of Our Sea. So we intended to enter Egypt, then journey to the Red Sea and take ship for Arabia Felix. From there we were going to India, and from India to Serica. My husband thought that the Sericans might be able to use the skills of a great Roman military man."

"I am sure they would have found a use for him," Cato said dubiously. Who knew what the Sericans might have made of a Roman? Certainly they would not have known him from a Gaul, a German or a Greek. Their land was so far away, so mysterious that the only information Herodotus had to offer about them was that they made a fabric from the spinnings of a grub, and that he called it *bombyx*. Its Latin name was *vestis serica*. On rare occasions a specimen had come through the Sarmatian trade routes of the King of the Parthians, but it was so precious that the only Roman known to have had a piece was Lucullus.

How far had Pompeius Magnus fallen, to contemplate such a course of action! Truly he was not a Roman of Rome.

"I wish I could go home!" Cornelia Metella sighed.

"Then go home!" Cato barked; this was the kind of evening he deemed wasted, when he had men to put into camp.

Shocked, she stared at him in dismay. "How can I go home when Caesar controls the world? He will proscribe—our names will be at the top of his proscription list, and our heads will bring some disgusting slave his freedom plus a small fortune for informing on us. Even if we live, we will be impoverished."

"*Gerrae!*" Cato said roundly. "My dear woman, Caesar is no Sulla in that respect. His policy is clemency—and very clever it is too. He intends to earn no hatred from businessmen or his fellow nobles, he intends that they kiss his feet in abject thanks for sparing their lives and letting them keep their property. I admit that Magnus's fortune will be confiscate, but Caesar won't touch your wealth. As soon as the winds permit it, I recommend that you go home." He turned sternly to Sextus Pompey. "As for you, young man, the choice is clear. Escort your stepmother as far as Brundisium or Tarentum, then join Caesar's enemies, who will gather in Africa Province."

Cornelia Metella swallowed. "There is no need for Sextus to escort me," she said. "I take your word for Caesar's clemency, Marcus Cato, and will sail alone."

Declining Philopoemon's offer of a bed, Cato drew the *ethnarch* of Paraetonium aside as he prepared to leave.

"Whatever you can spare us by way of water or food, we will pay for in silver coin," he said.

Philopoemon looked as much worried as delighted. "We can give you all the water you want, Marcus Cato, but we haven't much food to spare. There is famine in Egypt, so we haven't been able to buy in wheat. But we have sheep we can sell you, and cheese from our goats. While you're here, we can give your men green salads from several kinds of wild parsley, but it doesn't keep."

"Whatever you can spare will be appreciated."

On the morrow he left Lucius Gratidius and Sextus Pompey to deal with the men, himself preferring to have more conversation with Philopoemon. The more he could learn about Africa, the better.

Paraetonium existed to provide a port for the many pilgrims who journeyed to the oasis of Ammon to consult its oracle, as famous on this shore of Our Sea as Delphi was in Greece. Ammon lay two hundred miles to the south across a rainless desert of long sand dunes and outcrops of bare rocks; there the Marmaridae roamed from well to well with their camels and goats, their big leather tents.

When Cato asked of Alexander the Great, Philopoemon frowned. "No one knows," he said, "whether Alexander went to Ammon to ask a question of the oracle, or whether Ra, lord of the Egyptian gods, had summoned him to the oasis to deify him." He looked pensive. "All the Ptolemies since the first Soter have made the pilgrimage, whether on the throne of Egypt or satrap in Cyrenaica. We are tied to Egypt through its kings and queens, the oasis, but our blood is Phoenician, not Macedonian or Greek."

As Philopoemon chattered on, now about the herds of camels the town kept to hire out to pilgrims, Cato's thoughts strayed. No, we cannot stay here for very long, but if we sail while Corus is blowing, we will wind up in Alexandria. After hearing how the boy king dealt with Pompeius Magnus, I do not think Egypt is safe for Romans opposing Caesar.

"While Corus blows, impossible," he muttered.

Philopoemon looked puzzled. "Corus?"

"Argestes," Cato said, giving the wind its Greek name.

"Oh, Argestes! It will soon vanish, Marcus Cato. Aparctias is due any day."

Aparctias, Aquilo—the Etesian winds! Yes, of course! It is the middle of October by the calendar, the middle of Quinctilis by the seasons. The Dog Star is about to rise!

"Then," Cato said with a huge sigh of relief, "we will not need to abuse your hospitality much longer, Philopoemon."

Nor did they. The following day, the Ides of October, the Etesian winds arrived with the dawn. Cato busied himself in getting Cornelia

Metella aboard her three ships, then waved her off feeling unusually tender emotions; she had donated him Pompey the Great's nest egg, two hundred talents of silver coins. *Five million* sesterces!

The fleet set sail on the third day of the Etesians, the men happier than they had been since Pompey had enlisted them in his grand army of the civil war. Most were in their late twenties and had served Pompey in Spain for years—they were veterans, therefore enormously valuable troops. Like other rankers, they lived in ignorance of the hideous differences between Rome's political factions; ignorant too of Cato's reputation as a crazed fanatic. They thought him a splendid fellow—friendly, cheerful, compassionate. Not adjectives even Favonius would have attached to his dearest *amicus*, Marcus Porcius Cato. They had greeted Sextus Pompey with joy, and cast lots to see whose ship would carry him. For Cato had no intention of accommodating Pompey the Great's younger son on his own vessel; Lucius Gratidius and the two philosophers were as much company as he could stomach.

Cato stood on the poop as his ship led the fifty out of Paraetonium's bay with the wind on the leading edge of his sail and the first shift of oarsmen-soldiers pulling with a will. They had food enough for a twenty-day voyage; two of the local farmers had grown bumper crops of chickpea in good winter rains as well as enough wheat to feed Paraetonium. They had been happy to sell most of the chickpea to Cato. No bacon, alas! It took an Italian oak forest plump with acorns to breed good bacon porkers. Oh, pray that someone in Cyrenaica kept pigs! Salt pork was far better than no pork at all.

The five-hundred-mile voyage west to Cyrenaica took just eight days, the fleet far enough out to sea not to have to worry about reefs or shoals; Cyrenaica was a huge bump in the north African coast, thrusting it much closer to Crete and Greece than the interminably straight coast between it and the Nilus Delta.

Their first landfall was Chersonnesus, a cluster of seven houses festooned in fishing nets; Lucius Gratidius rowed ashore and learned that Darnis, immensely bigger, was only a few miles farther on. But "immense" to a village of fishermen turned out to be about the size of Paraetonium; there was water to be had, but no food other than catches of fish. Eastern Cyrenaica. About fifteen hundred miles to go.

Cyrenaica had been a fief of the Ptolemaic rulers of Egypt until its last satrap, Ptolemy Apion, had bequeathed it to Rome in his will. A reluctant heir, Rome had done nothing to annex it or so much as put a garrison there, let alone send it a governor. Living proof that lack of government simply allowed people to wax fat on no taxes and do what they always did with greater personal prosperity, Cyrenaica became a legendary backwater of the world, a kind of honeyed dreamland. As it was off the beaten track and had no gold, gems or enemies, it didn't attract unpleasant people. Then thirty years ago the great Lucullus had visited it, and things happened fast. Romanization began, the taxes were imposed, and a governor of praetorian status was appointed to administer it in conjunction with Crete. But as the governor preferred to live in Crete, Cyrenaica carried on much as it always had, a golden backwater, the only real difference those Roman taxes. Which turned out to be quite bearable, for the droughts which plagued other lands supplying grain to Italy were usually out of step with any droughts in Cyrenaica. A big grain producer, Cyrenaica suddenly had a market on the far side of Our Sea. The empty grain fleets came down from Ostia, Puteoli and Neapolis on the Etesian winds, and by the time the harvest was in and the ships loaded, Auster the south wind blew the fleets back to Italy.

When Cato arrived, it was thriving on the drought conditions that plagued every land from Greece to Sicily; the winter rains had been excellent, the wheat, almost ready for harvesting now, was coming in a hundredfold, and enterprising Roman grain merchants were beginning to arrive with their fleets.

A wretched nuisance for Cato, who found Darnis, small as it was, stuffed with ships already. Clutching his long hair, he was forced to sail on to Apollonia, the port serving Cyrene city, the capital of Cyrenaica. There he would find harbor!

He did, but only because Labienus, Afranius and Petreius had arrived before him with a hundred and fifty transports, and had evicted the grain fleets into the roads on the high seas. As Cato on the poop of his leading ship was an unmistakable figure, Lucius Afranius, in charge of the harbor, let him bring his fleet in.

"What a business!" Labienus snarled as he walked Cato at a fast clip to the house he had commandeered off Apollonia's chief citizen. "Here, have some *decent* wine," he said once they entered the room he had made his study.

The irony was lost on Cato. "Thank you, no."

Jaw dropped, Labienus stared. "Go on! You're the biggest soak in Rome, Cato!"

"Not since I left Corcyra," Cato answered with dignity. "I vowed to Liber Pater that I wouldn't touch a drop of wine until I brought my men safely to Africa Province."

"A few days here, and you'll be back guzzling." Labienus went to pour himself a generous measure, and downed it without pausing to breathe.

"Why?" Cato asked, sitting down.

"Because we're not welcome. The news of Magnus's defeat and death has flown around Our Sea as if a bird carried it, and all Cyrenaica can think about is Caesar. They're convinced he's hard on our heels, and they're terrified of offending him by seeming to aid his enemies. So Cyrene has locked its gates, and Apollonia is intent on doing whatever harm it can to us—a situation made worse after we sent the grain fleets packing."

When Afranius and Petreius entered with Sextus Pompey in tow, all that had to be explained again; Cato sat, wooden-faced, his mind churning. Oh, ye gods, I am back among the barbarians! My little holiday is over.

A part of him had looked forward to visiting Cyrene and its Ptolemaic palace, rumored to be fabulous. Having seen Ptolemy the Cyprian's palace in Paphos, he was keen to compare how the Ptolemies had lived in Cyrenaica against how they had lived in Cyprus. A great empire two hundred years ago, Egypt, which had even owned some of the Aegean islands as well as all Palestina and half of Syria. But the Aegean islands and the lands in Syria-Palestina had gone a century ago; all the Ptolemies had managed to hang on to were Cyprus and Cyrenaica. From which Rome had forced them out quite recently. Well do I remember, reflected Cato, who had been Rome's agent of annexation in Cyprus, that Cyprus had not welcomed Roman rule. From Orient to Occident is never easy.

Labienus had found 1,000 Gallic cavalry and 2,000 infantrymen lurking in Crete, rounded them up with his customary ruthlessness and appropriated every vessel Crete owned. With 1,000 horses, 2,000 mules and 4,000 men—he had noncombatants and slaves as well—crammed into two hundred ships, he sailed from Cretan Apollonia to Cyrenaican Apollonia (there were towns named after Apollo all over the world) in just three days, having had no other choice than to wait for the Etesian winds.

"Our situation goes from bad to worse," Cato told Statyllus and Athenodorus Cordylion as the three settled into a tiny house Statyllus had found abandoned; Cato refused to dispossess anyone, and cared not a rush for comfort.

"I understand," Statyllus said, fussing around the much older Athenodorus Cordylion, who was losing weight and developing a cough. "We should have realized that Cyrenaica would side with the winner."

"Very true," Cato said bitterly. He clutched at his beard, pulled it. "There are perhaps four *nundinae* of the Etesian winds left," he said, "so somehow I have to push Labienus into moving on. Once the south wind begins to blow, we will never reach Africa Province, and Labienus is more determined to sack Cyrene than he is to do anything constructive about continuing to wage war."

"You will prevail," said Statyllus comfortably.

That Cato did prevail was thanks to the goddess Fortuna, who seemed to be on his side. The following day word came from the port of Arsinoë, some hundred miles to the west; Gnaeus Pompey had kept his word and shipped another 6,500 of Cato's wounded to Africa. They had landed in Arsinoë and found the local inhabitants very glad to see them.

"Therefore we leave Apollonia and sail to Arsinoë," Cato said to Labienus in his harshest voice.

"A *nundinum* from now," said Labienus.

"Eight more days? Are you mad? Do what you like, you utter fool, but tomorrow I take my own fleet and leave for Arsinoë!"

The snarl became a roar, but Cato was no Cicero. He had cowed Pompey the Great, and he wasn't a bit afraid of barbarians like Titus Labienus. Who stood, fists clenched, teeth bared, his black eyes glaring into that cool grey steel. Then he sagged, shrugged.

"Very well, we leave for Arsinoë tomorrow," he said.

Where the goddess Fortuna deserted Cato, who found a letter from Gnaeus Pompey waiting for him.

> Things in Africa Province look very good, Marcus Cato. If I keep on going at the rate I am, I will have my fleets settled into good bases along the southern coast of Sicily, with one or two of the Vulcaniae Isles to deal with grain from Sardinia. In fact, things look so good that I have decided to leave my father-in-law Libo in charge, and take myself off to Africa Province with a great number of soldiers who have turned up in western Macedonia and asked me to let them fight on against Caesar.
>
> Therefore, Marcus Cato, though it pains me to do it, I must ask that you return *all* your ships to me at once. They are desperately needed, and I'm afraid that unwounded troops must take precedence over your own, wounded men. As soon as I can, I will send you another fleet large enough to get your fellows to Africa Province, though I warn you that you must sail far out to sea. The great bite in the African coast between Cyrenaica and

our province is not navigable—no charts, and waters choked with hazards.

I wish you well, and have made an offering that you and your wounded, having suffered so much, do reach us.

No ships. Nor, Cato knew, could they possibly return before Auster made it impossible for them to return.

"Be my fate as it may, Titus Labienus, I must insist that you send your ships to Gnaeus Pompeius as well," Cato brayed loudly.

"I will not!"

Cato turned to Afranius. "Lucius Afranius, as a consular you outrank us. Next comes Marcus Petreius, then me. Titus Labienus, though you have been a propraetor under Caesar, you were never an elected praetor. Therefore the decision does not rest with you. Lucius Afranius, what do you say?"

Afranius was Pompey the Great's man to the core; Labienus mattered only in that he was a fellow Picentine and a client of Pompey's. "If Magnus's son requires our ships, Marcus Cato, then he must have them."

"So here we sit in Arsinoë with nine thousand infantry and a thousand horse. Since you're so devoted to the *mos maiorum*, Cato, what do you suggest we do?" Labienus asked, very angry.

Well aware that Labienus knew that he was too loathed by the troops to appeal to them as a Caesar might have, Cato relaxed. The worst was over.

"I suggest," he said calmly, "that we walk."

No one had the wind to reply, though Sextus Pompey's eyes lit up, sparkled.

"Between reading Gnaeus Pompeius's letter and seeking this council," Cato said, "I made a few enquiries of the locals. If there is nothing else a Roman soldier can do, he can march. It seems the distance from Arsinoë to Hadrumetum, the first big town in Africa Province, is somewhat less than the fifteen hundred miles between Capua and Further Spain. About fourteen hundred miles. I estimate that resistance in Africa Province will not fully coalesce until May of next year. Here in Cyrenaica we have all heard that Caesar is in Alexandria and mired down in a war there, and that King Pharnaces of Cimmeria is running rampant in Asia Minor. Gnaeus Calvinus is marching to contain him, with two legions of Publius Sestius's and little else. I am sure you know Caesar in the field better than any of us, Labienus, so do you really think that, once he has tidied up Alexandria, he will go west when he leaves?"

"No," said Labienus. "He'll march to extricate Calvinus and give Pharnaces such a walloping that he'll flee back to Cimmeria with his tail between his legs."

"Good, we agree," Cato said, quite pleasantly. "Therefore, my fellow curule magistrates and senators, I will go to our troops and ask for a democratic decision as to whether we march the fourteen hundred miles to Hadrumetum."

"No need for that, Afranius can decide," Labienus said, and spat his mouthful of wine on to the floor.

"*No one* can make this decision except those we are going to ask to take this journey!" Cato yelled, at his most aggressive. "Do you really want ten thousand unwilling, resentful men, Titus Labienus? Do you? Well, I do not! Rome's soldiers are *citizens*! They have a vote in our elections, no matter how worthless that vote might be if they are poor. But many of them are not poor, as Caesar well knew when he sent them on furlough to Rome to vote for him or his preferred candidates. These men of ours are tried-and-true veterans who have accumulated wealth from sharing in booty—they matter politically as well as militarily! Besides, they lent every sestertius in their legion banks to help fund the Republic's war against Caesar, so they are our creditors too. Therefore I will go to them and ask."

Accompanied by Labienus, Afranius, Petreius and Sextus Pompey, Cato went to the huge camp on Arsinoë's fringe, had the troops assembled in the square to one side of the general stores, and explained the situation. "Think about it overnight, and have an answer for me at dawn tomorrow!" he shouted.

At dawn they had their answer ready, and a representative to deliver it: Lucius Gratidius.

"We will march, Marcus Cato, but on one condition."

"What condition?"

"That you are in the command tent, Marcus Cato. In a battle we will gladly take orders from our generals, our legates, our tribunes, but on a march through country no one knows, with no roads and no settlements, only one man can prevail—you," said Lucius Gratidius sturdily.

The five noblemen stared at Gratidius in astonishment, even Cato: an answer no one had expected.

"If the consular Lucius Afranius agrees that your request is in keeping with the *mos maiorum*, I will lead you," said Cato.

"I agree," Afranius said hollowly; Cato's comment about the fact that Pompey the Great was debtor to his own army had hit Afranius (and Petreius) hard; he had lent Pompey a fortune.

* * *

"At least," said Sextus to the housebound Cato the next day, "you administered such a kick to Labienus's arse that he got off it. Did he ever!"

"What are you talking about, Sextus?"

"He spent the night loading his cavalry and horses aboard a hundred of his ships, then sailed at dawn for Africa Province with the money, all the wheat Arsinoë would sell him, and his thumb to his nose." Sextus grinned. "Afranius and Petreius went as well."

A huge gladness invaded Cato, who actually forgot himself enough to grin back. "Oh, what a relief! Though I'm concerned for your brother, left a hundred ships short."

"I'm concerned for him too, Cato, but not concerned enough to want the *fellatores* marching with us—Labienus and his precious horses! You don't need a thousand horses on this expedition, they drink water by the amphora and they're fussy eaters." Sextus gave a sigh. "It's his taking all the money will hurt us most."

"No," Cato said serenely, "he didn't take all the money. I still have the two hundred talents your dear stepmother gave me. I just forgot to mention their existence to Labienus. Fear not, Sextus, we'll be able to buy what we need to survive."

"No wheat," Sextus said gloomily. "He cleaned Arsinoë out of the early harvest, and with the grain fleets hovering, we won't get any of the late harvest."

"Given the amount of water we'll have to carry, Sextus, we can't carry wheat as well. No, this expedition's food will be on the hoof, you might say. Sheep, goats and oxen."

"Oh, no!" Sextus cried. "*Meat?* Nothing but *meat?*"

"Nothing but meat and whatever edible greens we can find," Cato said firmly. "I daresay Afranius and Petreius decided to risk the sea because they suddenly wondered if, with Cato in the command tent, they'd be allowed to ride while others walked."

"I take it that no one is going to ride?"

"No one. Tempted at that news to hurry after Labienus?"

"Not I! Notice, by the way, that he took no Roman troops with him. The cavalry is Gallic, they're not citizens."

"Well," said Cato, rising to his feet, "having made my notes, it's time to start organizing the march. It is now the beginning of November, and I estimate that preparations will take two months. Which means we'll start out in early January."

"The beginning of autumn by the seasons. Still awfully hot."

"I am told that the coast is endurable, and we must stick to the coast or get hopelessly lost."

"Two months' preparation seems excessive."

"Logistics demand it. For one thing, I have to commission the weaving of ten thousand shady hats. Imagine what life would be like if Sulla had not made the shady hat famous! Its value in the sun of these latitudes is inestimable. Detest Sulla though all good men must, I have him to thank for that piece of common sense. The men must march as comfortably as possible, which means we take all our mules and those Labienus left behind. A mule can find forage wherever a plant can grow, and the local people have assured me that there will be forage along the coast. So the men will have pack animals for their gear. One thing about a march into uninhabited *terra incognita*, Sextus, is that mail shirts, shields and helmets need not be worn, and we need not build a camp every night. The few natives there are will not dare to attack a column of ten thousand men."

"I hope you're right," said Sextus Pompey devoutly, "because I can't imagine Caesar letting the men march unarmed."

"Caesar is a military man, I am not. My guide is instinct."

Yielding up ten talents of Cornelia Metella's gift enabled the men to eat bread during those two months of preparation, sop it in good olive oil; enquiries produced bacon, and Cato still had a great deal of chickpea. His own thousand men were superbly fit, thanks to almost a month of rowing, but between their wounds and inertia, the later arrivals were weaker. Cato sent for all his centurions and issued orders: every man intending to march had to submit himself to a rigorous program of drill and exercise, and if, when January arrived, he was not fit, he would be left in Arsinoë to fend for himself.

The *dioiketes* of Arsinoë, one Socrates, was a great help, a treasure house of good advice. Scholarly and fair-minded, his imagination had soared the moment Cato told him what he intended to do.

"Oh, Marcus Cato, a new *anabasis*!" he squawked.

"I am no Xenophon, Socrates, and my ten thousand men are good Roman citizen soldiers, not Greek mercenaries prepared to fight for the Persian enemy," Cato said, trying these days to moderate his voice and not offend people he needed. Thus he hoped that his tones were not indicative of the horror he felt at being likened to that other, very famous march of ten thousand men almost four hundred years ago. "Besides, my march will fade from the annals of history. I do not have Xenophon's compulsion to explain away treachery in writing because no treachery exists. Therefore I will write no commentary of *my* march of the ten thousand."

"Nonetheless, it is a very Spartan thing you do."

"It is a very sensible thing I do" was Cato's answer.

To Socrates he confided his greatest worry—that the men, raised on an Italian diet of starches, oils, greens and fruits, with the sole meat for a poor man a bit of bacon for flavoring, would not be able to tolerate a diet consisting of meat.

"But you must surely know of *laserpicium*," said Socrates.

"Yes, I know of it." What was visible of Cato's face between the hair and the beard screwed itself up in revulsion. "The kind of digestive men like my father-in-law pay a fortune for. It is said to help a man's stomach recover from a surfeit of"—he drew a breath, looked amazed—"*meat!* A surfeit of meat! Socrates, Socrates, I must have *laserpicium*, but how can I afford enough of it to dose ten thousand men every single day for months?"

Socrates laughed until the tears ran down his face. "Where you are going, Marcus Cato, is a wilderness of silphium, a scrubby little bush that your mules, goats and oxen will feast on. From silphium a people called the Psylli extract *laserpicium*. They live on the western edge of Cyrenaica, and have a tiny port town, Philaenorum. Were a surfeit of meat a dietary custom around Your Sea, the Psylli would be a great deal richer than they are. It is the canny merchants who visit Philaenorum who make the big profits, not the Psylli."

"Do any of them speak Greek?"

"Oh, yes. They have to, else they'd get nothing for their *laserpicium*."

The next day Cato was off to Philaenorum on a horse, with Sextus Pompey galloping to catch him up.

"Go back and be useful in the camp," Cato said sternly.

"You may order everyone around as much as you like, Cato," Sextus caroled, "but I am my father's son, and dying of curiosity. So when Socrates said that you were off to buy whole talents of *laserpicium* from people called Psylli, I decided that you needed better company than Statyllus and Athenodorus Cordylion."

"Athenodorus is ill," Cato said shortly. "Though I've had to forbid anyone to ride, I'm afraid I must relax that rule for Athenodorus. He can't walk, and Statyllus is his nursemaid."

Philaenorum turned out to be two hundred miles south, but the countryside was populated enough to procure a meal and a bed each night, and Cato found himself glad of Sextus's cheerful, irreverent company. However, he thought as they rode the last fifty miles, I see a hint of what we must contend with. Though there is grazing for stock, it is a barren wasteland.

"The one grace," said Nasamones, leader of the Psylli, "is the presence of groundwater. Which is why silphium grows so well. Grasses don't because their root systems can't burrow deeply enough to find a drink—silphium has a little taproot. Only when you cross the salt pans and marshes between Charax and Leptis Major will you need all the water you can carry. There is more salt desert between Sabrata and Thapsus, but that is a shorter distance and there is a Roman road for the last part of the way."

"So there are settlements?" Cato asked, brightening.

"Between here and Leptis Major, six hundred miles to the west, only Charax."

"How far is Charax?"

"Around two hundred miles, but there are wells and oases on the shore, and the people are my own Psylli."

"Do you think," Cato asked diffidently, "that I could hire fifty Psylli to accompany us all the way to Thapsus? Then, if we encounter people who have no Greek, we will be able to parley. I want no tribes afraid that we are invading their lands."

"The price of hire will be expensive," said Nasamones.

"Two silver talents?"

"For that much, Marcus Cato, you may have us all!"

"No, fifty of you will be enough. Just men, please."

"Impossible!" Nasamones shot back, smiling. "Extracting *laserpicium* from silphium is women's work, and that is what you must do—extract it as you march. The dose is a small spoonful per day per man, you'd never be able to carry half enough. Though I'll throw in ten Psylli men free of charge to keep the women in order and deal with snakebites and scorpion stings."

Sextus Pompey went ashen, gulped in terror. "*Snakes?*" He shuddered. "*Scorpions?*"

"In great numbers," Nasamones said, as if snakes and scorpions were just everyday nuisances. "We treat the bites by cutting into them deeply and sucking the poison out, but it is easier said than done, so I advise you to use my men, they are experts. If the bite is properly treated, few men die—only women, children, and the aged or infirm."

Right, thought Cato grimly, I will have to keep sufficient mules free of cargo to bear men who are bitten. But my thanks, gracious Fortuna, for the Psylli!

"And don't you dare," he said savagely to Sextus on the way back to Arsinoë, "say one word about snakes or scorpions to a single soul! If you do, I'll send you in chains to King Ptolemy."

The hats were woven, Arsinoë and the surrounding countryside denuded of its donkeys. For, Cato discovered from Socrates and Nasamones, mules would drink too much, eat too much. Asses, smaller and hardier, were the burden beasts of choice. Luckily no farmer or merchant minded trading his asses for mules; these were Roman army mules, bred from the finest stock. Cato acquired 4,000 asses in return for his 3,000 mules. For the wagons he took oxen, but it turned out that sheep were impossible to buy. In the end he was forced to settle for 2,000 cattle and 1,000 goats.

This is not a march, it is an emigration, he thought dourly; how Labienus, safe in Utica by now, must be laughing! But I will show him! If I die in the effort, I will get my Ten Thousand to Africa Province fit to fight! For ten thousand there were; Cato took his noncombatants with him as well. No Roman general asked his troops to march, build, fight *and* care for themselves. Each century held a hundred men, but only eighty of them were soldiers; the other twenty were noncombatant servants who ground the grain, baked the bread, handed out water on the march, cared for the century's beasts and wagon, did the laundry and cleaning. They were not slaves, but Roman citizens who were deemed unsuitable soldier material—mentally dull yokels who received a tiny share of the booty as well as the same wages and rations as the soldiers.

While the Cyrenaican women labored over the hats, Cyrenaican men were put to making water skins; earthenware amphorae, with their pointed bottoms and a shape designed for setting in a frame or a thick bed of sawdust, were too cumbersome to strap on panniers astride a donkey's back.

"No wine?" asked Sextus, dismayed.

"No, not a drop of wine," Cato answered. "The men will be drinking water, and so will we. Athenodorus will have to go without his little invalid fortification."

Two days into January the gigantic migration commenced its walk, cheered by the entire population of Arsinoë. Not a neat military column on the march, rather a wandering mass of animals and tunic-clad men with big straw hats on their heads moving among the animals to keep them more or less in one enormous group as Cato headed south for Philaenorum and the Psylli. Though the sun blazed down at lingering summer heat, the pace, Cato soon learned, would not enervate his men. Ten miles a day, set by the animals.

But though Marcus Porcius Cato had never generaled troops or been thought of by noble Rome, perpetually exasperated by his stubbornness and single-mindedness, as a person with any common sense whatsoever, Cato turned out to be the ideal commander of a migration. Eyes everywhere, he observed and adapted to mistakes no one, even Caesar, could have foreseen. At dawn on the second day his centurions were instructed to make sure every man's *caligae* were laced ruthlessly tight around his ankles; they were walking over unpaved land full of small potholes, often concealed, and if a man sprained an ankle or tore a ligament, he became a burden. By the end of the first *nundinum*, not yet halfway to Philaenorum, Cato had worked out a system whereby each century took charge of a certain number of asses, cattle and goats, designated its own property; if it ate too well or drank too much, it could not filch stock or water from another, more prudent century.

Each dusk the mass stopped, replenished its water from wells or springs, each man settling to sleep on his waterproof felt *sagum*, a circular cape with a hole in its middle through which, on a rainy or snowy march, he thrust his head. All the bread and chickpea Cato could carry went on this first segment of the march, for *laserpicium* would not be a part of the menu until Philaenorum. Ten miles a day. As well, then, that these first two hundred miles were through kinder country; they were the learning experience. After Philaenorum, things were going to get a lot worse.

When by some miracle they reached Philaenorum in eighteen rather than twenty days, Cato gave the men three days of rest in a slipshod camp just behind a long, sandy beach. So people swam, fished, paid a precious sestertius to some Psylli woman for sex.

All legionaries knew how to swim, it was a part of their boot-camp training—who knew when someone like Caesar would order them to swim a lake or a mighty river? Naked and carefree, the men frolicked, gorged on fish.

Let them, thought Cato, down swimming too.

"I say!" Sextus exclaimed, looking at the naked Cato, "I never realized how well you're built!"

"That," said the man with no sense of humor, "is because you are too young to remember the days when I wore no tunic under my toga to protest against the erosion of the *mos maiorum*."

* * *

Not required to herd animals or participate in century doings, the centurions had other duties. Cato called them together and issued instructions about *laserpicium* and the coming all-meat diet.

"You will eat no plant that the Psylli traveling with us say is inedible, and you will make sure that your men do the same," he yelled. "Each of you will be issued with a spoon and your century's supply of *laserpicium,* and every evening after the men have eaten their beef or goat, you will *personally* administer half of that spoon to each man. It will be your duty to accompany the Psylli women and two hundred noncombatants as they gather silphium and process it—I understand that the plant has to be crushed, boiled and cooled, after which the *laserpicium* is skimmed off the top. Which means we need firewood in country devoid of all trees. Therefore you will ensure that every dead plant and the dried crushed plants are collected and carried for burning. Any man who attempts to violate a Psylli woman will be stripped of his citizenship, flogged and beheaded. I mean what I say."

If the centurions thought he was finished, they were wrong. "One other point!" Cato roared. "Any man, no matter what his rank, who allows a goat to eat his hat, will have to go without a hat. That means sunstroke and death! As it happens, I have sufficient spare hats to replace those already eaten by goats, but I am about to run out. So let every man on this expedition take heed—no hat, no life!"

"That's telling them," said Sextus as he accompanied Cato to the house of Nasamones. "The only trouble, Cato, is that a goat determined to eat a hat is as difficult to elude as a whore with her sights on a rich old dodderer. How do you protect your hat?"

"When it is not on my head, I am lying flat with my hat under me. What does it matter if the crown is crushed? Each morning I plump it out again, and tie it firmly on my head with the ribbons those sensible women who made it, gave it."

"The word is out," Nasamones said, sorry that this wonderful circus treat was about to leave. "Until you reach Charax, my people will give you all the help they can." He coughed delicately. "Er—may I offer you a little hint, Marcus Cato? Though you will need the goats, you will never get to Africa Province alive if you continue to let the goats roam free. They will not only eat your hats, they will eat your very clothes. A goat will eat *anything*. So tie them together as you walk, and pen them at night."

"Pen them with what?" Cato cried, fed up with goats.

"I note that every legionary has a palisade stake in his pack. It is long enough to serve as a staff for help covering uneven ground, so each man can carry it. Then at night he can use it as part of a fence to pen up the goats."

"Nasamones," said Cato with a smile more joyous than any Sextus had ever seen, "truly I do not know what we would have done without you and the Psylli."

The beautiful mountains of Cyrenaica were gone; the Ten Thousand set off into a flat wilderness of silphium and little else, the ocher ground between those drab, greyish little bushes littered with rubble and fist-sized stones. The palisade stake staffs were proving invaluable.

Nasamones had been right; the wells and soaks were frequent. However, they were not multiple, so it was impossible to water ten thousand men and seven thousand beasts each night—that would have taken a river the size of the Tiber. So Cato had a century and its beasts refill their water skins at each well or soak they passed. This kept the spectacular horde moving, and at sundown everyone could settle for a meal of beef or goat boiled in seawater—the whole Ten Thousand collected dead bushes—and a sleep.

Apart from a brazen sky and silphium scrub, their constant companion was the sea, a huge expanse of polished aquamarine, fluffed with white where rocks lurked, breaking in gentle wavelets upon beach after beach after beach. At the pace the animals moved, men could take a quick dip to cool off and keep clean; if all they could cover were ten miles a day, it would be the end of April before they reached Hadrumetum. And, thought Cato with huge relief, by that time the squabbles as to who will be commander-in-chief of our armies will be over. I can simply slide my Ten Thousand into the legions—I myself will serve in some peaceful capacity.

No Roman ate beef, no Roman ate goat; cattle had but one use, the production of leather, tallow and blood-and-bone fertilizer, and goats were for milk and cheese.

One steer provided about five hundred pounds of edible parts, for the men ate all save the hide, the bones and the intestines. A pound of this per day per man—no one could force himself to eat more—saw the herd dwindle at the rate of twenty beasts a day for six days; the eight-day *nundinum* was made up with two days of goat, even worse.

At first Cato had hoped that the goats would yield milk from which cheese might be made, but the moment Philaenorum was left behind, the nanny goats nursing kids rejected them and dried up. No goat expert, he supposed this had something to do with too much silphium and no straw hats or other delicacies. The long-horned cattle ambled along without annoying the human complement, their hip bones protruding starkly from their nether regions like vestigial wings, shriveled empty udders swinging beneath the cows. No cattle expert either, he supposed that bulls were a nuisance, since all the male cattle were castrated. Be it a tomcat, a dog, a ram, a billy goat or a bull, a wholly male beast wore itself thin and stringy pursuing sex. Scatter the seed, reap a bumper crop of kittens, pups, lambs, kids or calves.

Some of this he voiced to Sextus Pompey, who was fascinated at aspects of the fanatical Marcus Porcius Cato that he fancied no other Roman had ever witnessed. Was this the man who had hectored his father into civil war? Who as a tribune of the plebs had vetoed any legislation likely to improve the way things worked? Who, when as young as Sextus was now, had intimidated the entire College of Tribunes of the Plebs into keeping that wretched column inside the Basilica Porcia? Why? Because Cato the Censor had put the column there; it was a part of the *mos maiorum* and could not be removed for any reason. Oh, all the stories he had heard about Cato the incorruptible urban quaestor—Cato the drinker—Cato the seller of his beloved wife! Yet here was that selfsame Cato musing about males and their hunger for sex, just as if he himself were not a male—and a very well-endowed male at that.

"Speaking for myself," Sextus said chattily, "I'm looking immensely forward to civilization. Civilization means *women*. I'm desperate for a woman already."

The grey eyes turned his way looked frosty. "If a man is a man, Sextus Pompeius, he should be able to control his baser instincts. *Four years* are nothing," Cato said through his teeth.

"Of course, of course!" Sextus said, beating a hasty retreat. Four years, eh? An interesting span to come up with! Marcia had spent four years as wife of Quintus Hortensius between two bouts of Cato. Did he love her, then? Did he suffer, then?

Charax was a village on an exquisite lagoon. Its inhabitants, a mixture of Psylli and an inland people called Garamantes, made a living diving for sponges and seed pearls; they consumed nothing but fish, sea urchins and a few vegetables grown in plots painstakingly watered by the women, who, upon seeing this appalling host descending, defended their produce shrilly, brandishing hoes and shrieking curses. Cato promptly issued an order forbidding the plundering of vegetables, then set to with the local chieftain to buy whatever greens he could. Nothing like enough, naturally, though the sight of his silver coins reconciled the women into harvesting everything larger than a sprout.

Romans knew well that humankind could not survive unless fruits and green vegetables were a part of the diet, but so far Cato hadn't noticed any prodromal signs of scurvy in the men, who had gotten into the habit of chewing a sprig of silphium as they walked, to have some saliva. Whatever else silphium contained besides *laserpicium* evidently had the same effect as greens. We are but four hundred miles along our way, he thought, but I know in my bones that we are going to make it.

One day off to swim and gorge on fish, then the Ten Thousand moved on into terrible country, flat as a planed board, a wearisome trek across salt pans and brackish marshes interspersed with a few stretches of silphium. Of wells or oases there were none for four hundred miles; forty days of pitiless sun, freezing nights, of scorpions and spiders. No one in Cyrenaica had mentioned spiders, which came as a horrific shock. Italy, Greece, the Gauls, the Spains, Macedonia, Thrace, Asia Minor—that part of the globe Romans marched around, across, up, down, and sideways—lacked big spiders. With the result that a highly decorated *primipilus* centurion, veteran of almost as many battles as Caesar, would faint dead away at the sight of a big spider. Well, the spiders of Phazania, as this region was called, were not big. They were enormous, as large in the body as a child's palm, with disgustingly hairy legs that folded under them malignly when they rested.

"Oh, Jupiter!" Sextus cried, shaking one of the things out of his *sagum* before he folded it one morning. "I tell you straight, Marcus Cato, that had I known such creatures existed, I would gladly have suffered Titus Labienus! I only half believed my father when he said that he turned back within three days of reaching the Caspian Sea because of spiders, but now I know what he meant!"

"At least," said Cato, who seemed unafraid, "their bite is merely painful because of the size of their nippers. They aren't poisonous like the scorpions."

Secretly he was as frightened and revolted as anyone, but pride would not let him betray what he felt; if the Commander screamed and ran, what would the Ten Thousand think? If only there were woody plants to make fires at night for warmth! Who would ever have dreamed that a place so scorching during the day could grow so cold after the sun set? Suddenly, dramatically. One moment frying, the next shivering until the teeth chattered. But what tiny supplies of driftwood they combed from the beaches had to be saved for the cooking fires, silphium and meat.

The Psylli men had earned their keep. No matter how the ground was scoured for scorpions, scorpions there were. Many men were stung, but after the Psylli had trained the century medics on how to slice into the flesh and suck vigorously, few men needed to ride donkeys. One Psylli woman, small and frail, was not so lucky. Her scorpion sting killed her, but not quickly, not kindly.

The more difficult the going became, the more cheerful Cato became. How he managed to cover as much territory as he did in a day escaped Sextus; it seemed that he visited every small group, paused for a chat and a laugh, told them how wonderful they were. And they would swell, grin, pretend that they were having a merry holiday. Then plod on. Ten miles a day.

The water skins shrank; not two days into that forty-day stretch had elapsed before Cato introduced water rationing, even to the animals. But if an occasional cow or steer keeled over, it was slaughtered on the spot to become that night's meal for some of the men. The asses, it seemed as indefatigable as Cato, just kept walking; that the water skin element in their cargoes was losing weight helped them. Yet thirst is terrible. The days and nights both reverberated to the anguished moos of cattle, the maas of goats, the sad squealing of donkeys. Ten miles a day.

Occasionally storm clouds in the distance would torment them, looming ever blacker, drawing closer; once or twice, the grey slanted curtain of falling rain. But never near the Ten Thousand.

For Cato, in between the spurts of energy that pushed him to make his rounds of the men, the journey had become a kind of glory. Somewhere inside his core the desolate wastes his Stoic ethic had made of his Soul reached out to embrace the desolate wastes his body traversed. As if he floated on a sea of pain, yet the pain was purifying, even beautiful.

At noon, when the sun turned the landscape to vast shimmering mists, he sometimes fancied that he saw his brother Caepio walking toward him, red hair glowing like a halo of flames, his unmistakable face a shining beacon of love. Once it was Marcia he saw, and once another, different dark woman; a stranger who he knew in his heart was his mother, though she had died two months after his birth, and he had never seen a portrait of her. Servilia transformed into goodness. Livia Drusa. Mama, Mama.

His last vision occurred on the fortieth day out from Charax, heralded at dawn by Lucius Gratidius to say that the water skins had shrunk to nothing. It was Caepio again, but this time the beloved figure came so close that his outstretched arms almost touched Cato's.

"Do not despair, little brother. There is water."

Someone shrieked. The vision popped out of existence in a sudden roar from ten thousand parched throats: *WATER!*

During the space of a short afternoon the countryside changed with all the drama and shock of a thunderclap. The water marked the boundary of this change, a small but running stream so recent that the plants along its perpendicular banks were still infantile. Only then did Cato realize that they had been under way for eighty days, that autumn was beginning to change into winter, that the rains were starting to fall. One of those taunting storms had dropped its liquid blessing inland at a place where the contours permitted it to run, gurgling and absolutely pure, all the way down to the sea. The cattle herd had shrunk to less than fifty beasts, the goat herd to about a hundred. Caepio had given his message just in time.

Humans and animals scattered along both banks of the rivulet for five miles to drink until sated, then, with stern warnings that no creature was to urinate or defecate anywhere near the stream, Cato allowed the Ten Thousand four days to fill the water skins, swim in the sea, fish, and sleep. He himself would have to find civilization and more food.

"The land of Phazania is behind us," he said to Sextus as they stretched out in the sand after a dip.

We have become brown as nuts, Sextus thought, gazing up and down the endless beach at the clusters of men. Even Cato, so fair, is deeply tanned. I daresay that means I look like a Syrian. "What land are we entering now?" he asked.

"Tripolitana," Cato said.

Why does he look so sad? Anyone would think that we have just walked out of the Elysian Fields, rather than out of Tartarus. Has he no idea that this water has come on the very last day before we started to die of thirst? That our food has run out too? Or did he conjure the water up out of his own will? Nothing about Cato surprises me anymore.

"Tripolitana," he echoed. "Land of the three cities. Yet I know of no cities between Berenice and Hadrumetum."

"The Greeks like things to sound familiar—look at all the towns named Berenice, Arsinoë, Apollonia, Heracleia. So I imagine that when they built three villages of a few houses here where the coast is more fertile, they called the land 'Three Cities.' Leptis Major, Oea and Sabrata, if Socrates and Nasamones are right. Odd, isn't it? The only Leptis I knew was Leptis Minor in our Africa Province."

Tripolitana wasn't a lush cornucopia of plenty like Campania or the Baetis River valley in Further Spain, but from that first stream onward the country began to look as if people might show their faces. Silphium still grew, but joined now by softer plants the Psylli pronounced edible. Occasional strange trees dotted the flatness, branches spread in planes like the layers in a slate ledge, sparsely leafed with yellow-green fernlike fronds; they reminded Cato of the two trees which used to be in Uncle Drusus's peristyle garden, trees said to have been brought back to Rome by Scipio Africanus. If so, then in spring or summer they must bear fabulous scarlet or yellow blossoms.

To Sextus Pompey, Cato appeared back to normal. "I think," he said, "that it's high time I hopped on an ass and trotted ahead to see which way the locals would like to see ten thousand men and a handful of goats go. Not, I am sure, through the middle of their wheat fields or peach orchards. I will try to buy some food. Fish is a pleasant change, but we need to replenish our stock of animals and—how I hope!—find grain for bread."

Astride an ass, Sextus thought, sitting ruthlessly on his laughter, Cato is ridiculous. His legs are so long that he looks as if he's paddling the thing, rather than riding it.

Ridiculous he may have appeared to Sextus, but when he came back four hours later the three men accompanying him were eyeing him in awed wonder. We have truly reached civilization, because they have heard of Marcus Porcius Cato.

"We have a route for when we move on," he announced to Sextus, scissoring off his donkey with more ease than a man stepped over a low fence. "Here are Aristodemus, Phazanes and Phocias, who will serve as our agents in Leptis Major. Twenty miles away, Sextus, and I have been able to buy a flock of hogget sheep. Meat, I know, but at least a different kind. You and I are moving into Leptis itself, so pack your stuff."

They passed through a village, Misurata, and so came to a town of twenty-thousand folk of Greek descent; Leptis Major or Magna. The harvest was all in, and it had been a good one. When Cato produced his silver coins, he bought enough wheat to put the men back on bread, and sufficient oil to moisten it.

"Only six hundred miles to Thapsus, another hundred up to Utica, and of those, but two hundred waterless ones between Sabrata and Lake Tritonis, the beginning of our Roman province." Cato broke open a loaf of fresh, crusty bread. "At least having crossed Phazania, Sextus, I know how much water we will need on our last stretch of desert. We'll be able to load some of the asses with grain, unearth the mills and ovens from the wagons, and make bread whenever there is firewood. Isn't this a wonderful place? This once, I'm going to fill up on *bread*."

The quintessential Stoic, thought Sextus, has feet of bread. But he's right. Tripolitana is a wonderful place.

Though the season for grapes and peaches had finished, the locals dried them, which meant raisins to munch by the handful, and leathery slices of peach to suck on. Celery, onions, cabbage and lettuce abounded in the wild, seeded from domestic gardens.

Women and children as well as men, the Tripolitanans wore tight trousers of densely woven wool and leather leggings over closed-toe boots as protection against snakes, scorpions and those massive spiders, known as *tetragnathi*. Almost all were engaged in agriculture—wheat, olives, fruit, wine—but kept sheep and cattle on common land deemed too poor for the plough. In Leptis there were businessmen and merchants, plus the inevitable contingent of Roman agents nosing to make a quick sestertius, but the feeling was of rustication, not of commerce.

Inland lay a low plateau that was the commencement of three thousand miles of desert stretching both east and west as well as farther to the south than anybody knew. The Garamantes roamed it on camels, herding their goats and sheep, living in tents to exclude not the rain—there was none—but the sand. A high wind blasted its grains with a force that could kill by suffocation.

A great deal more confident now that eight hundred miles lay behind them, the Ten Thousand left Leptis in high spirits.

The two-hundred-mile expanse of salt pans took only nineteen days to cross; though lack of firewood prevented the baking of bread, Cato had acquired as many sheep as cattle to vary the all-meat diet in a better way. No more goats! If I never see another goat again as long as I live, vowed Cato, I will count myself well satisfied. A sentiment his men echoed, especially Lucius Gratidius, upon whom had devolved the goats.

Lake Tritonis formed the unofficial boundary of the Roman African province—a disappointment, as its waters were bitter with natron, a substance akin to salt. Because an inferior sort of *murex* populated the sea just east of it, a factory for the manufacture of purple-dye sat on its shore alongside a stinking tower of empty shells and the rotting remains of the creatures that had lived inside them. The purple dye was extracted from a small tube in the *murex* body, which meant a lot of leftovers.

However, the lake marked the beginning of a properly surveyed and paved Roman road. Laughing and chattering, the Ten Thousand hustled past the festering factory as fast as they could, prancing all over the road. Where there was a road, was also Rome.

Outside Thapsus, Athenodorus Cordylion collapsed and died, so suddenly that Cato, elsewhere, didn't reach him in time to say good-bye. Weeping, Cato saw to the building of a driftwood pyre, offered libations to Zeus and a coin to Charon the ferryman, then took up his staff and set off again ahead of his men. So few left from the old days. Catulus, Bibulus, Ahenobarbus, and now dear Athenodorus Cordylion. How many more days do I have? If Caesar ends in ruling the world, I trust not many.

The march ended in a vast camp on the outskirts of Utica, always the capital of the Roman province. Another Carthage had been built adjacent to the site of the home of Hannibal, Hamilcar and Hasdrubal, but Scipio Aemilianus had razed that home so thoroughly that the new Carthage never rivaled Utica, possessed of an equally magnificent harbor.

A terrible wrench to part from the Ten Thousand, who mourned losing their beloved Commander; never organized into legions, the fifteen cohorts and extra noncombatants Cato had brought would be broken up and inserted into existing legions to plump them out. Still, that incredible march endowed every last participant in it with a luminousness akin to godhead in the eyes of their fellow Roman soldiers.

The only one Cato took with him and Sextus Pompey was Lucius Gratidius, who, if Cato had his way, would train civilians. On his last evening before he entered the governor's palace in Utica and re-entered a world he hadn't known for well over five months, Cato sat to write to Socrates, the *dioiketes* of Arsinoë.

I had the forethought, my dear Socrates, to find a few men whose natural double step measured exactly five feet, and I then deputed them to pace out our entire journey from Arsinoë to Utica. Averaging their tallies resulted in a figure of 1,403 miles. Given that we dallied for three days at Philaenorum, a day at Charax, and four days outside Leptis Major—a total of one *nundinum*—we actually walked for 116 days. If you remember, we left Arsinoë three days before the Nones of January. We have arrived in Utica on the Nones of May. I had thought until I sat to work all this out on my abacus that we traveled at the rate of ten miles per day, but it turns out we covered twelve miles per day. All save sixty-seven of my men survived the trip, though we also lost a Psylli woman to a scorpion bite.

This is just to tell you that we arrived and are safe, but also to tell you that were it not for you and Nasamones of the Psylli, our expedition would have foundered. We had naught but kindness and succor from those we encountered along the way, but the services you and Nasamones rendered us exceed all bounds. One day when our beloved Republic is restored, I hope to see you and Nasamones in Rome as my guests. I will do you public honor in the Senaculum.

The letter took a year to reach Socrates, a year during which much happened. Socrates read it through a wall of tears, then sat, the sheet of Fannian paper fallen to his lap, and shook his head.

"Oh, Marcus Cato, would that you were a Xenophon!" he cried. "Four months upon an uncharted course, and all you can regale me with are facts and figures. What a Roman you are! A Greek would have been making copious notes as foundation for his book; you merely kept a few men pacing and counting. The thanks are greatly appreciated and the letter will be treasured as a relic because you found the time to write it, but oh, what I would give for a narrative of the march of *your* Ten Thousand!"

3   Roman Africa Province wasn't unduly large, just extremely rich. After Gaius Marius had defeated King Jugurtha of Numidia sixty years earlier it had been augmented by some Numidian lands, but Rome preferred client-kings to governors, so King Hiempsal was allowed to retain most of his country. He had reigned for over forty years, and was succeeded by his eldest son, Juba. Africa Province itself owned one asset which made it necessary for Rome to govern it: the Bagradas River, a large stream of many and strong tributaries that permitted the cultivation of wheat on a grand scale. At the time that Cato and his Ten Thousand arrived there, its grain crop had become as important as Sicily's, and the owners of its huge grain farms were members of the Senate or the Eighteen, who were the most powerful knight-businessmen. The province also possessed another quality obligating Rome to govern it directly: it occupied a northward bulge in the African coast right below Sicily and the instep of the Italian foot, therefore it was a perfect jumping-off

point for an invasion of Sicily and Italy. In olden days, Carthage had done just that several times.

After Caesar crossed the Rubicon and gained largely peaceful control of Italy, the anti-Caesarean Senate fled their homeland in the train of Pompey the Great, appointed their commander-in-chief. Unwilling to devastate the Italian countryside in yet another civil war, Pompey had resolved to fight Caesar abroad, and chose Greece/Macedonia as his theater.

However, it was equally important to own the grain-producing provinces, particularly Sicily and Africa. Thus before it fled, the Republican Senate had dispatched Cato to hold Sicily, while Publius Attius Varus, governor of Africa Province, held that place in the name of the Republican Senate and People of Rome. Caesar sent his brilliant ex-tribune of the plebs, Gaius Scribonius Curio, to wrest both Sicily and Africa off the Republicans; he had to feed not only Rome, but also most of Italy, long incapable of feeding themselves. Sicily fell to Curio very quickly, for Cato was not a general of troops, simply a brave soldier. When he escaped to Africa, Curio and his army followed. But Attius Varus was not about to be cowed either by a couch general like Cato or a fledgling general like Curio. First he made Africa intolerable for Cato, who departed to Pompey in Macedonia, and then, aided by King Juba, Attius Varus led the overconfident Curio into an ambush. Curio and his army died.

So it fell out that Caesar controlled one wheat province, Sicily, while the Republicans controlled the other, Africa. Which gave Caesar ample grain in good years but insufficient in lean years—and there had been a succession of lean years due to a series of droughts from one end of Our Sea to the other. Complicated by the presence of Republican fleets in the Tuscan Sea, ready to pounce on Caesar's grain convoys; a situation bound to grow worse now that Republican resistance in the East was no more and Gnaeus Pompey had relocated his navy to the grain sea-lanes.

Having gathered in Africa Province after Pharsalus, the Republicans were well aware that Caesar had to come after them. While ever they could field an army, Caesar's mastery of the world remained debatable. Because he was Caesar, they expected him sooner rather than later; when Cato had started out from Cyrenaica, the general consensus had been June, as this date would give Caesar time to deal with King Pharnaces in Anatolia first. So when the Ten Thousand finished its march, Cato was amazed to find the Republican army at slothful ease, and no sign of Caesar.

* * *

Had the late Gaius Marius laid eyes on the governor's palace in Utica in this present year, he would have found it very little changed from the place he had occupied six decades ago. Its walls were plastered and painted dull red inside; apart from a largish audience chamber it was a warren of smallish rooms, though there were two nice suites in an annex for visiting grain plutocrats or front bench senators off on a sight-seeing trip to the East. Now it seethed with so many Republican Great Names that it threatened to burst at the seams, and its stuffy interior thrummed with the sounds of all these Republican Great Names at outs and at odds with each other.

A young and bashful tribune of the soldiers led Cato to the governor's office, where Publius Attius Varus sat at his walnut desk surrounded by paper-shuffling underlings.

"I hear you've survived a remarkable journey, Cato," Varus said, not getting up to shake hands because he detested Cato. A nod, and the minions rose to file out of the room.

"I could ill afford not to survive!" Cato shouted, back in shouting mode at mere sight of this churl. "We need soldiers."

"Yes, true."

A martial man of good—but not quite good enough—family, Varus counted himself a client of Pompey the Great's, but more than duty to his patron had pushed him on to the Republican side; he was a passionate Caesar-hater, and proud of it. Now he coughed, looked disdainful. "I'm very much afraid, Cato, that I can offer you no accommodation. Anyone who hasn't been at least a tribune of the plebs is dossing down in a corridor—ex-praetors like you rate a cupboard."

"I don't expect you to house me, Publius Varus. One of my men is searching for a small house at this very moment."

Recollections of Cato's standard of accommodation caused Varus to shudder; in Thessalonica, a three-roomed mud-brick hovel with three servants—one for himself, one for Statyllus, and one for Athenodorus Cordylion. "Good. Wine?" he asked.

"Not for me!" Cato barked. "I have taken a vow not to drink a drop until Caesar is dead."

"A noble sacrifice," said Varus.

The awkward visitor sat mum, his hair and beard a mess because he had not paused to bathe before reporting in. Oh, what did one say to such a man?

"I hear that all you've eaten for the past four months is meat, Cato."

"We managed to eat bread a part of the time."

"Indeed?"

"I have just said so."

"I also hear that there were scorpions and gigantic spiders."

"Yes."

"Did many die from their bites?"

"No."

"Are all of your men fully recovered from their wounds?"

"Yes."

"And—ah—did you get caught in any sandstorms?"

"No."

"It must have been a nightmare when you ran out of water."

"I did not run out of water."

"Were you attacked by savages?"

"No."

"Did you manage to transport the men's armaments?"

"Yes."

"You must have missed the cut and thrust of politics."

"There are no politics in civil wars."

"You missed noble company, then."

"No."

Attius Varus gave up. "Well, Cato, it's good to see you, and I trust you'll find suitable housing. Now that you're here and our troop tally is complete, I shall call a council for the second hour of daylight tomorrow. We have yet," he continued as he escorted Cato out, "to decide who is going to be commander-in-chief."

What Cato might have replied was not voiced, for Varus spotted Sextus Pompey leaning against the outer doorway deep in talk with the sentries, and squawked.

"Sextus Pompeius! Cato didn't say you were here too!"

"That doesn't surprise me, Varus. Nevertheless, I am here."

"*You* walked from Cyrenaica?"

"Under the aegis of Marcus Cato, a pleasant stroll."

"Come in, come in! May I offer you some wine?"

"You certainly may," said Sextus with a wink for Cato as he disappeared arm in arm with Varus.

Lucius Gratidius was lurking in the small square just outside the palace gates, chewing a straw and ogling the women busy doing their washing in the fountain. As he still wore nothing save a bedraggled tunic, no one on guard duty had realized that this skinny hulk was the *pilus prior* centurion of Pompey the Great's First Legion.

"Found you quite a comfortable place," he said, straightening as Cato walked out to stand blinking in the sun. "Nine rooms and a bath.

With a scrubwoman, a cook and two manservants thrown in, the price is five hundred sesterces a month."

To a Roman of Rome, a pittance, even were he as frugal as Cato. "An excellent bargain, Gratidius. Has Statyllus turned up yet?"

"No, but he will," Gratidius said cheerfully, directing Cato down a mean street. "He just wanted to make sure that Athenodorus Cordylion is going to rest easy. Lonely for a philosopher, I daresay, to have his ashes buried so far from any other philosopher's. You were right not to let Statyllus carry them to Utica. Not enough wood for a decent pyre, too many bone bits, too much marrow left."

"I hadn't quite looked at it that way," said Cato.

The apartment was the ground floor of a seven-story building right on the harbor front, its windows looking out over a forest of masts, tangles of silver-grey jetties and wharves, and that ethereally blue sea. Five hundred sesterces a month were indeed a bargain, Cato decided when he discovered that the two male slaves were obedient fellows pleased to fill him a warm bath. And, when Statyllus turned up in time for the late afternoon meal, he couldn't help but give a little smile. Statyllus's escort was none other than Sextus Pompey, who declined to share their bread, oil, cheese and salad, but ensconced himself in a chair and proceeded to give Cato the gleanings of his few hours with Varus.

"I thought you'd like to know that Marcus Favonius is safe," he started out. "He encountered Caesar at Amphipolis and asked for pardon. Caesar gave it to him gladly, it seems. Pharsalus must have done something to his mind, Cato, because he wept and told Caesar that all he wanted was to return to his estates in Italy and live a quiet, peaceful life."

Oh, Favonius, Favonius! Well, I could see this coming. While I lingered with the wounded in Dyrrachium, you had to endure those interminable quarrels between Pompeius's couch generals, ably assisted by that barbarian Labienus. Your letters told me all, but it doesn't surprise me that I've had no letter from you since Pharsalus. How you would dread informing me that you've abandoned the Republican cause. May you enjoy that quiet peace, dearest Marcus Favonius. I do not blame you. No, I cannot blame you.

"And," Sextus was rattling on, "my informant—who shall be nameless—told me that things are even worse in Utica than they were in Dyrrachium and Thessalonica. Even idiots like Lucius Caesar Junior and Marcus Octavius, who've never even been tribunes of the plebs, are saying that they deserve legatal status in our army. As for the really Big Names—ugh! Labienus, Metellus Scipio, Afranius and Governor Varus all think they should occupy the command tent."

"I had hoped that would be decided before I got here," Cato said, voice harsh, face expressionless.

"No, it's to be decided tomorrow."

"And what of your brother, Gnaeus?"

"Off applying a rod to *tata*-in-law Libo's arse somewhere on the south shore of Sicily. I predict," Sextus added with a grin, "that we won't see him until the command argument is settled."

"Sensible man" was Cato's comment. "And you, Sextus?"

"Oh, I'll stick to my stepmother's *tata* like a burr to a fleece. Metellus Scipio may not be bright or talented, but I do think my father would say I should serve with him."

"Yes, he would." The fine grey eyes lifted to look at Sextus sternly. "What of Caesar?" he asked.

A frown appeared. "That's the great mystery, Cato. As far as anyone knows, he's still in Egypt, though apparently not in Alexandria. There are all kinds of rumors, but the truth is that no one has heard a peep from Caesar since a letter written from Alexandria in November reached Rome a month later."

"I don't believe it," Cato said, mouth tight. "The man is a prolific correspondent, and now, above all other times in his life, he needs to be at the center of things. *Caesar*, silent? *Caesar*, not in touch? He must be dead. Oh, what a twist of fortune! To have Caesar die of some plague or peasant's spear in a backwater like Egypt! I feel—cheated."

"Definitely not dead, is what rumor says. In fact, rumor says that he's cruising down the river Nilus on a golden barge feet deep in flowers, with the Queen of Egypt by his side, enough harps to drown ten elephants trumpeting, dancing girls in skimpy veils, and baths full of ass's milk."

"Are you poking fun at me, Sextus Pompeius?"

"I, poke fun at *you*, Marcus Cato? Never!"

"Then it's a trick. But it makes sense of the inertia here in Utica. That autocratic piece of excrement, Varus, was not about to tell *me* anything, so I thank you for all this news. No, Caesar's silence has to be a trick." His lip curled. "What of the eminent consular and advocate, Marcus Tullius Cicero?"

"Stuck in Brundisium on the horns of his latest dilemma. He was welcomed back to Italy by Vatinius, but then Marcus Antonius returned with the bulk of Caesar's army, and ordered Cicero to leave. Cicero produced Dolabella's letter, and Antonius apologized. But you know the poor old mouse—too timid to venture any farther into Italy than Brundisium. His wife refuses to have a thing to do with him." Sextus giggled. "She's ugly enough to do duty as a fountain spout."

A glare from Cato sobered him. "And Rome?" Cato asked.

Sextus whistled. "Cato, it's a circus! The government is limping along on ten tribunes of the plebs because no one has managed to hold elections for the aediles, praetors or consuls. Dolabella got himself adopted into the Plebs and is now a tribune of the plebs. His debts are enormous, so he's trying to push a general cancellation of debts through the Plebeian Assembly. Every time he tries, that prime pair of Caesareans Pollio and Trebellius veto him, so he's copied Publius Clodius and organized street gangs to terrorize high and low alike," Sextus said, face animated. "As Caesar the Dictator is absent in Egypt, the head of state is his Master of the Horse, Antonius. Who is behaving shockingly—wine, women, avarice, malice and corruption."

"Pah!" Cato spat, eyes blazing. "Marcus Antonius is a rabid boar, a vulture—oh, this is wonderful news!" he cried, grinning savagely. "Caesar has finally overreached himself, to put a drunken brute like Antonius in control. Master of the Horse! Arse of the horse, more like!"

"You're underestimating Marcus Antonius," Sextus said, very seriously. "Cato, he's up to something. Caesar's veterans are camped around Capua, but they're restless and muttering about marching on Rome to get their 'rights'—whatever 'rights' might be. My stepmother—who sends you love, by the way—says it's Antonius working on the legions for his own ends."

"His own ends? Not Caesar's ends?"

"Cornelia Metella says Antonius has developed high ambitions, means to step into Caesar's shoes."

"How is she?"

"Well." Sextus's face puckered, was disciplined. "She built a beautiful marble tomb in the grounds of her Alban Hills villa after Caesar sent her my father's ashes. It seems he met our freedman Philip, who cremated the body on the beach at Pelusium. Caesar himself had the head cremated. The ashes came with a soft and graceful letter—Cornelia Metella's words—promising that she will be allowed to keep all her property and money. So she has it to show Antonius if and when he calls to tell her that everything is confiscate."

"I am at once astonished and deeply perturbed, Sextus," Cato said. "What *is* Caesar about? I need to know!"

Seventeen men gathered in the governor's audience chamber at the second hour of day on the morrow.

Oh, thought Cato, heart sinking, I am back in my old arena, but I have lost the taste for it. Perhaps it is a fault in my character that I abhor all high commands, but if it is a fault, then it has led me to a philosophy that sits inexorably upon my Soul. I know the precise parameters of what I must do. Men may sneer at so much self-denial, but self-indulgence is far worse, and what are high commands except a form of self-indulgence? Here we are, thirteen men in Roman togas, about to tear each other into shreds for the sake of an empty shell called a command tent. A metaphor, even! How many commanders actually inhabit a tent—or if they do, keep it austere and simple? Only Caesar. How I hate to admit that!

The four other men present were Numidians. One of them was clearly King Juba himself, for he was dressed from head to foot in Tyrian purple and wore the white ribbon of the diadem tied around his curled and flowing locks. Beard curled too, entwined with golden threads. Like two of the other three, he seemed about forty years of age; the fourth Numidian was a mere youth.

"Who are these—*persons?*" Cato demanded of Varus in his loudest and most obnoxious tones.

"Marcus Cato, lower your voice, please! This is King Juba of Numidia, Prince Masinissa and his son Arabion, and Prince Saburra," Varus said, embarrassed and indignant.

"Eject them, Governor! Immediately! This is a convocation of *Roman* men!"

Varus fought to keep his temper. "Numidia is our ally in the war against Caesar, Marcus Cato, and entitled to be present."

"Entitled to be present at a war council, perhaps, but not entitled to watch thirteen Roman noblemen make utter fools of themselves arguing about purely Roman matters!" Cato roared.

"The meeting hasn't started yet, Cato, but you're already out of order!" Varus articulated through his teeth.

"I repeat, this is a Roman convocation, Governor! Kindly send these foreigners outside!"

"I'm sorry, I can't do that."

"Then I remain here under protest, and will have nothing to say!" Cato bellowed.

While the four Numidians glowered at him, he retired to the back of the room behind Lucius Julius Caesar Junior, a pokered-up sprig of the Julian tree whose father was Caesar's cousin, right-hand man and staunchest supporter. Curious, thought Cato, eyes boring into Lucius Junior's back, that the son is a Republican.

"He doesn't get on with his *tata,*" Sextus whispered, sidling up to

Cato. "Outclassed, but without the sense to acknowledge that he will never be his *tata*'s bootlace."

"Shouldn't you be somewhere closer to the front?"

"At my tender age? Not likely!"

"I note a streak of levity in you, Sextus Pompeius, that ought to be eliminated," Cato said in his normal loud voice.

"I am aware of it, Marcus Cato, which is why I spend so much of my time with you," Sextus answered, equally loudly.

"Silence at the back! The meeting will come to order!"

"Order? *Order?* What do you mean, Varus? I can see at least one priest and one augur in this assembly! Since when has a legal convocation of Roman men met to discuss public business without first saying the prayers and taking the auspices?" Cato yelled. "Is this what our beloved Republic has descended to, that men like Quintus Caecilius Metellus Pius Scipio Nasica can stand here and not object to an illegal meeting? I cannot compel you to expel foreigners, Varus, but I *forbid* you to start proceedings without first honoring Jupiter Optimus Maximus and Quirinus!"

"If you would only wait, Cato, you'd see that I was about to call upon our good Metellus Scipio to say the prayers, and ask our good Faustus Sulla to take the auspices," Varus said, making a quick recovery that fooled no one except the Numidians.

Oh, has there ever been a meeting more doomed to fail than this one? Sextus Pompey asked of himself, thoroughly enjoying the spectacle of Cato making making mincemeat out of at least ten Romans and four Numidians. I am right, he has changed a great deal since I met him in Paraetonium, but today I catch a glimpse of what he must have been like in the House on one of those mad occasions when he went tooth and claw for everyone from Caesar to my father. You cannot shout him down and you cannot ignore him.

But, having made his protest and seen to it that the religious formalities were observed, Cato was true to his word and remained at the back in silence.

Competition for the command tent revolved around Labienus, Afranius, Metellus Scipio and none other than the governor, Varus. That so much dissension occurred was due to the fact that the nonconsular Labienus had the best battle record by far, whereas the consular and ex-governor of Syria, Metellus Scipio, had both the legal entitlement and the blood. That Afranius even entered the fray involved his commitment to Labienus, for he bolstered the claims of Caesar's ex-second-in-command as a fellow Military Man—and consular. Alas, like Labienus, he had no ancestors worth speaking of. The surprise candidate was Attius Varus, who took the line that he was the legal governor of his province, that the war was going to happen in his province, and that he outranked all others in his province.

To Cato, it was a manifestation of luck that the height of feelings made it impossible for some of the debaters to express themselves adequately in Greek, the latter a language that didn't permit insults to roll like thunder off the tongue the way Latin did. So the argument quickly lapsed into Latin. The Numidians lost the verbal track at once, which didn't please Juba, a subtle and crafty man who secretly detested all Romans, but had worked out that his chances of expanding his kingdom west into Mauretania were far better with this lot than they would have been with Caesar, no Juba-lover. Whenever Juba thought about that famous day in a Roman court when Caesar, disgusted at the lies, had lost his temper and pulled the royal beard, that selfsame beard smarted all over again.

Numidian resentments were fanned thanks to the fact that Varus had not imported any chairs; everyone was expected to stand, no matter how long the argument raged. An offended request for a chair to ease the royal feet was denied; apparently Romans in their congresses felt quite at home standing. Though I must co-operate with these Romans on the field, thought Juba, I also have to undermine Roman authority in their so-called African province. How enormously rich Numidia would be if I ruled the lands of the Bagradas River!

Four short spring hours of forty-five minutes each saw the argument still raging, a decision no closer, and acrimony growing with every drip of the water clock.

Finally, "There is no contest!" Varus cried, shaping up to Labienus truculently. "It was your tactics lost Pharsalus, so I spit on your contention that you're our best general! If you are, then what hope do we have of beating Caesar? It's time for new blood in the command tent— Attius Varus blood! I repeat, this is my province, legally bestowed on me by Rome's true Senate, and a governor in his province is the highest-ranking man."

"Arrant nonsense, Varus!" Metellus Scipio snapped. "I am the governor of Syria until I cross Rome's *pomerium* into the city, and that isn't likely to happen until after Caesar is defeated. What is more, the Senate gave me *imperium maius*! Your imperium is common old *propraetore*! You're small-fry, Varus."

"I may not have unlimited imperium, Scipio, but at least I can find better things to do with my time than wallow in little boys and pornography!"

Metellus Scipio howled and sprang at Varus while Labienus and Afranius folded their arms and watched the scuffle. A tall, well-built man once described as having a face like a haughty camel, Metellus Scipio gave a better account of himself than the younger Attius Varus had expected.

Cato shouldered Lucius Caesar Junior aside and strode to the center of the room to wrench the two men apart.

"I have had enough! *ENOUGH!* Scipio, go over there and stand absolutely still. Varus, come over here and stand absolutely still. Labienus, Afranius, unfold your arms and try to look who you are instead of a pair of barbered dancing girls trolling for arse outside the Basilica Aemilia."

He took a turn around the floor, hair and beard disheveled from clutching at them in despair. "Very well," he said, facing his audience. "It is clear to me that this could go on all day, all tomorrow, all next month and all next year, without a decision being reached. Therefore *I* am making the decision, right this moment. Quintus Caecilius Metellus Pius Scipio Nasica," he said, using Metellus Scipio's awesome full name, "you will occupy the command tent as supreme leader. I appoint you for two reasons, both valid under the *mos maiorum.* The first is that you are a consular with existing *imperium maius*, which—as you well know, Varus—overrides all other imperium. The second is that your name is Scipio. Be it superstition or fact, soldiers believe that Rome can't win a victory in Africa without a Scipio in the command tent. To tempt Fortuna now is stupid. However, Metellus Scipio, you are no better a general of troops than I am, so you will *not* interfere with Titus Labienus on the battlefield, is that fully understood? Your position is titular, and titular only. Labienus will be in military command, with Afranius as his second man."

"What about me?" Varus gasped, winded. "Whereabouts do I fit in your grand scheme, Cato?"

"Where you rightly belong, Publius Attius Varus. As governor of this province. Your duty is to ensure the peace, order and good government of its people, see that our army is properly supplied, and act as liaison between Rome and Numidia. It's obvious that you're thick with Juba and his minions, so make yourself useful in that area."

"You have no right!" Varus shouted, fists clenched. "Who are you, Cato? You're an ex-praetor who couldn't get himself elected consul, and very little else! In fact, did you not own a voice box made of brass, you'd be an utter nonentity!"

"I do not dispute that," said Cato, unoffended.

"*I* dispute your taking the decision even more than Varus!" Labienus snarled with teeth bared. "I'm fed up with doing the military dirty work minus a *paludamentum*!"

"Scarlet doesn't suit your complexion, Labienus," Sextus Pompey said, butting in cheekily. "Come, gentlemen, Cato is in the right of it. Someone had to take the decision, and, whether you admit it or not, Cato is the proper person because he doesn't want the command tent."

"If you don't want the command tent, Cato, what do you want?" Varus demanded.

"To be prefect of Utica," said Cato, voice quite moderate. "A job I can do well. However, Varus, you'll have to find me a suitable house. My rented apartment is too small."

Sextus whooped shrilly, laughed. "Good for you, Cato!"

"*Quin taces!*" snapped Lucius Manlius Torquatus, a Varus supporter. "Sew your mouth up, young Pompeius! Who are you, to applaud the actions of the great-grandson of a slave?"

"Don't answer him, Sextus," Cato growled.

"What is going on?" Juba demanded, in Greek. "Is it decided?"

"It is decided, King—except for you," Cato said in Greek. "Your function is to supply our army with additional troops, but until Caesar arrives and you can be of some personal use, I suggest that you return to your own domains."

For a moment Juba didn't answer, one ear cocked to hear what Varus whispered into it. "I approve of your dispositions, Marcus Cato, though not of the manner in which you made them," he said then, very regally. "However, I will not return to my kingdom. I have a palace in Carthage, and will live there."

"As far as I'm concerned, King, you can sit on your thumb and let your legs hang down, but I warn you—mind your own Numidian business, stay out of Roman affairs. Infringe that order, and I will send you packing," said Cato.

Thwarted and morose, his authority truncated, Publius Attius Varus concluded that the best way to deal with Cato was to give him whatever he asked for, and avoid being in the same room with him. So Cato was shifted to a fine residence on the main city square, adjacent to the waterfront, but not a part of it. The house's owner, an absentee grain plutocrat, had sided with Caesar and therefore was not in a position to object. It came complete with a staff and a steward aptly named Prognanthes, for he was too tall, had a gigantic lower jaw and an overhanging brow. Cato hired his own clerical help (at Varus's expense), but accepted the services of the house owner's agent, one Butas, when Varus sent him around.

That done, Cato called the Three Hundred together. This was Utica's group of most powerful businessmen, all Romans.

"Those of you with metal shops will cease to make cauldrons, pots, gates and ploughshares," he announced. "From now on, it's swords, daggers, the metal parts of javelins, helmets and some sort of mail shirt. All you can produce will be bought and paid for by me, as the Governor's deputy. Those in the building trade will commence work at once on silos and new warehouses—Utica is going to ensure the welfare of our army in every way. Stonemasons, I want our fortifications and walls strengthened to withstand a worse siege than Scipio Aemilianus inflicted upon old Carthage. Dock contractors will concentrate upon food and war supplies—to waste time on perfume, purple-dyes, fabrics, furniture and the like is hereby forbidden. Any ship with a cargo I deem superfluous to the war effort will be turned away. And, lastly, men between seventeen and thirty will be drafted to form a citizen militia, properly armed and trained. My centurion, Lucius Gratidius, will commence training in Utica's parade ground tomorrow at dawn." His eyes roamed the stunned faces. "Any questions?"

Since apparently they had none, he dismissed them.

"It was evident," he said to Sextus Pompey (who had resolved not to abandon Cato's company while ever Caesar was somewhere else) "that, like most people, they welcomed firm direction."

"A pity, then, that you keep maintaining you have no talent for generaling troops," Sextus said rather sadly. "My father always said that good generaling was mostly preparation for the battle, not the battle itself."

"Believe me, Sextus, I cannot general troops!" Cato barked. "It is a special gift from the gods, profligately dowered upon men like Gaius Marius and Caesar, who look at a situation and seem to understand in the tiniest moment where the enemy's weak points are, what the lie of the land will do, and whereabouts their own troops are likely to falter. Give me a good legate and a good centurion, and I will do what I am told to do. But think of what to do, I cannot."

"Your degree of self-knowledge is merciless," Sextus said. He leaned forward, hazel eyes sparkling eagerly. "But tell me, dear Cato, do I have the gift of command? My heart says that I do, but after listening to all those fools squabble about talents the biggest moron can see they do not own, am I wrong?"

"No, Sextus, you're not wrong. Go with your heart."

* * *

Within the space of two *nundinae* Utica fell into a new, more martial routine and seemed not to resent it, but on that second *nundinae* Lucius Gratidius appeared, looking worried.

"There's something going on, Marcus Cato," he said.

"What?"

"Morale isn't nearly as high as it should be—my young men are gloomy, keep telling me that all this effort will go for naught. Though I can discover no truth in it, they insist that Utica is secretly Caesarean in sympathies, and that these Caesareans are going to destroy everything." He looked grimmer. "Today I found out that our Numidian friend, King Juba, is so convinced of this nonsense that he's going to attack Utica and raze it to the ground to punish it. But I think it's Juba responsible for the rumors."

"Ahah!" Cato exclaimed, getting to his feet. "I agree with you entirely, Gratidius. It's Juba plotting, not nonexistent Caesareans. He's making trouble to force Metellus Scipio into giving him a co-command. He wants to lord it over Romans. Well, I'll soon scotch his ambitions! The cheek of him!"

Off went Cato in a temper and a hurry to the royal palace at Carthage where once Prince Gauda, a claimant to the Numidian throne, had moped and whined while Jugurtha warred against Gaius Marius. The premises were far grander than the governor's palace in Utica, Cato noted as he emerged from his two-mule gig, his purple-bordered *toga praetexta* folded immaculately. Preceded by six lictors in crimson tunics and bearing the axes in their *fasces* as the signal of his imperium, Cato marched up to the portico, gave the guards a curt nod, and swept inside as if he owned the place.

It works every single time, he thought: one look at lictors bearing the axes and the purple border on the toga behind them, and even the walls of Ilium would crumble.

Inside was spacious and deserted. Cato instructed his six lictors to remain in the vestibule, then marched onward into the depths of a house designed to envelop its denizens in a degree of luxury that he found nauseating. The invasion of Juba's privacy was not an issue; Juba had tampered with Rome's *mos maiorum*, he was a criminal.

The first person Cato encountered was the King, lying on a couch in a beautiful room with a splashing fountain and a vast window looking onto a courtyard, the sun streaming in delightfully. Walking across the mosaic floor in front of Juba in a demure parade were perhaps two dozen scantily clad women.

"This," barked Cato, "is a disgraceful sight!"

The King seemed to have a convulsion, stiffening and jerking as he levered himself off the couch to face the invader in shaking outrage, while the women shrieked and blundered, squalling, into any corner, there to huddle and hide their faces.

"Get out of here, you—you pervert!" Juba roared.

"No, you get out of here, you Numidian backstabber!" roared Cato at a volume that diminished the King's to a comparative whisper. "Get out, get out, get out! Quit Africa Province this very day, do you hear me? What do I care about your disgusting polygamy or your women, poor creatures devoid of any freedom? I am a monogamous Roman with a wife who manages her own business, can read and write, and is expected to conduct herself virtuously without the need for eunuchs and imprisonment! I spit on your women, and I spit on you!" Cato illustrated his point by spitting, not like a man getting rid of phlegm, but like a furious cat.

"Guards! Guards!" Juba yelled.

They piled into the room, the three Numidian princes hard on their heels. Masinissa, Saburra and young Arabion stood stunned at the sight of Cato with a dozen spears pressed against chest, back, sides. Spears Cato took absolutely no notice of, nor retreated an inch.

"Kill me, Juba, and you'll reap havoc! I am Marcus Porcius Cato, senator and *propraetore* commander of Utica! Do you think that you can intimidate me, when I have stood up to men like Caesar and Pompeius Magnus? Look well at this face, and know that it belongs to one who cannot be deflected from his course, who cannot be corrupted or suborned! How much are you paying Varus, that he stomachs the likes of you in his province? Well, Varus may do as his purse dictates, but don't even *think* of producing your moneybags to bribe me! Get out of Africa Province today, Juba, or I swear by Sol Indiges, Tellus and Liber Pater that I will go to our army, mobilize it in one hour, and give every last one of you the death of a slave—crucifixion!"

He pushed the spears aside contemptuously, turned on his heel and walked out.

By evening, King Juba and his entourage were on their way to Numidia. When appealed to, Governor Attius Varus had shivered and said that when Cato was in that sort of mood, the only thing to do was as one had been told.

The departure of Juba marked the end of Utica's attack of nerves; the city settled down to worship the ground Cato walked on, though had he known that, he would have assembled the entire populace and served it a diatribe on impiety.

For himself, he was happy. The civilian job suited him, he knew it was one he could do superbly well.

But where is Caesar? he asked himself as he strolled down to the harbor to watch the ceaseless comings and goings. When will he appear? Still no word of his whereabouts, and the crisis in Rome grows more dangerous every day. Which means that when he does pop into existence, he will have to deal with affairs in Rome as soon as he's evicted Pharnaces from Anatolia. His arrival is still months off; by the time he reaches Africa, we will be stale. Is *that* his trick? No one knows better than Caesar how divided our high command is. So it is up to me to keep all those stiff-necked fools from one another's throats for at least the next six months. While simultaneously damping down the savagery of barbarian Labienus, and depressing the intentions of our cunning King Juba. Not to mention a governor whose main ambition may well be to act as lord high chamberlain for a Numidian foreigner.

In the midst of these cheerless musings, he became aware that a young man was walking toward him with a hesitant smile on his face. Eyes narrowed (he was finding it hard to see at a distance since the march), he studied the familiar form until recognition burst on him like a bolt of lightning. *Marcus!* His only son.

"What are you doing here instead of skulking in Rome?" he asked, ignoring the outstretched arms.

The face, so like Cato's own, yet lacking its set planes of grim determination, twisted and crumpled.

"I thought, Father, that it was time I joined the Republican effort instead of skulking in Rome," young Cato said.

"A right act, Marcus, but I know you. What exactly provoked this tardy decision?"

"Marcus Antonius is threatening to confiscate our property."

"And my wife? You left her to Antonius's tender mercies?"

"It was Marcia insisted I come."

"Your sister?"

"Porcia is still living in Bibulus's house."

"My own sister?"

"Aunt Porcia's convinced that Antonius is about to confiscate Ahenobarbus's property, so she's bought a little house on the Aventine just in case. Ahenobarbus invested her dowry splendidly, she says—it's been accruing interest for thirty years. She sends her love. So do Marcia and Porcia."

How ironic, thought Cato, that the more able and intelligent of my two children should be the girl. My martial and fearless Porcia is soldiering on. What did Marcia say in that last letter I read? That Porcia is in love with Brutus. Well, I tried to match them for marriage, but Servilia wouldn't have it. *Her* dear precious emasculated son, marry his cousin, Cato's daughter? Hah! Servilia would kill him first.

"Marcia begs that you write to her," young Cato said.

His father's answer was oblique. "You'd best come home with me, boy, I have room for you. Do you still clerk well?"

"Yes, Father, I still clerk well." So much for the hope that once his father saw him again, he might be forgiven for his flaws. His failings. Impossible. Cato had no flaws, no failings. Cato never swerved from the path of the righteous. How terrible it is to be the son of a man without weaknesses.

III

PUTTING THINGS RIGHT
IN ASIA MINOR

From JUNE until SEPTEMBER of 47 B.C.

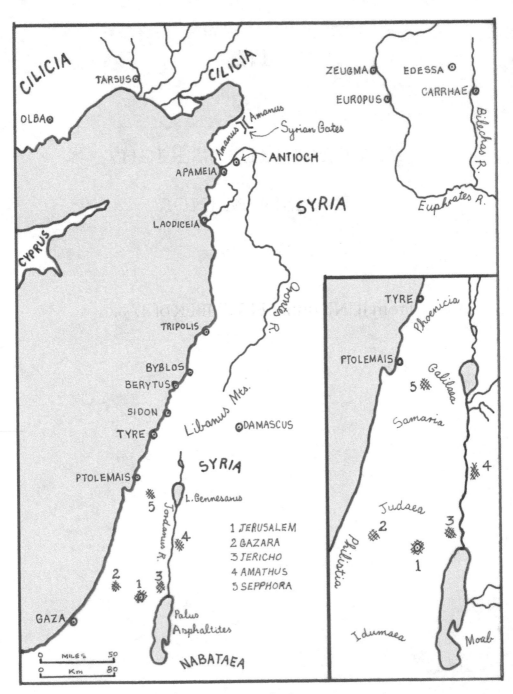

Roman Syria

Matters had not gone well for Judaea since the death of old Queen Alexandra in the same year Cleopatra had been born; the widow of the formidable Alexander Jannaeus, she managed to rule sitting in a disintegrating Syria. Among her own Jewish people, however, her efforts were not universally admired or appreciated, for her sympathies were entirely Pharisaic; whatever she did was unacceptable to the Sadducees, the schismatic Samaritans, the heretical up-country Galilaeans, and the non-Jewish population of the Decapolis. Judaea was in a state of religious flux.

Queen Alexandra had two sons, Hyrcanus and Aristobulus. After her husband's death she chose the elder, Hyrcanus, to succeed her, probably because he wouldn't give her any arguments. She made him high priest at once, but died before she could cement his power. No sooner was she buried than his younger brother seized both the high priesthood and the throne.

But the most naturally able man at the Jewish court was an Idumaean, Antipater; a great friend of Hyrcanus's, he had a long-standing feud with Aristobulus, so when Aristobulus usurped power, he rescued Hyrcanus and the pair of them fled. They took refuge with King Aretas in the Arab country of Nabataea, enormously rich because of its trade with the Malabar coast of India and the island of Taprobane. Antipater was married to King Aretas's niece, Cypros; it had been a love match that cost Antipater any chance of assuming the Jewish throne himself, for it meant that his four sons and one daughter were not Jewish.

The war between Hyrcanus/Antipater and Aristobulus raged on and on, complicated by the sudden appearance of Rome as a power in Syria; Pompey the Great arrived to make Syria a Roman province in the aftermath of the defeat of Mithridates the Great and his Armenian ally, Tigranes. The Jews rose and put Pompey's temper out dreadfully; he had to march on Jerusalem and take it instead of wintering comfortably in Damascus. Hyrcanus was appointed high priest, but Judaea itself was made a part of the new Roman Syrian province, stripped of all autonomy.

Aristobulus and his sons continued to make trouble, assisted by a series of ineffectual Roman governors of Syria. Finally there arrived Aulus Gabinius, a friend and supporter of Caesar's and no mean military man himself. He confirmed Hyrcanus as high priest and dowered him with five regions as an income—Jerusalem, Galilaean Sepphora, Gazara, Amathus and Jericho. An outraged Aristobulus contested him, Gabinius fought a short, sharp and effective war, and Aristobulus and one son found themselves on a ship for Rome a second time. Gabinius set out for Egypt to put Ptolemy Auletes back on his throne, fervently helped by Hyrcanus and his aide Antipater. Thanks to them, Gabinius had no difficulty forcing the Egyptian frontier north of Pelusium, whose Jewish population did not oppose him.

Marcus Licinius Crassus, boon companion of Caesar's and the next governor of Syria, inherited a peaceful province, even around Judaea. Alas for the Jews, Crassus was no respecter of local religions, customs and entitlements; he marched into the Great Temple and removed everything of value it contained, including two thousand talents of gold stored in the Holy of Holies. High priest Hyrcanus cursed him in the name of the Jewish god, and Crassus perished shortly thereafter at Carrhae. But the loot from the Great Temple was never returned.

Then came the unofficial governorship of a mere quaestor, Gaius Cassius Longinus, the only survivor of any importance from Carrhae. Despite his ineligibility, Cassius calmly assumed the reins of government in Syria, and started to tour the province to shore it up against certain Parthian invasion. In Tyre he met Antipater, who tried to explain the complications of religion and race in southern Syria, and why the Jews perpetually fought on two fronts—between religious factions, and against any foreign power which sought to impose discipline. When Cassius managed to round up two legions, he blooded them on an army of Galilaeans intent on destroying Hyrcanus. Shortly after that, the Parthians did invade, and the thirty-year-old quaestor Gaius Cassius was the only general between the Parthian army and its conquest of Syria. Cassius acquitted himself brilliantly, beat the Parthian hordes decisively, and drove Prince Pacorus of the Parthians out.

So when Caesar's *boni* enemy Marcus Calpurnius Bibulus finally deigned to arrive to govern Syria not long before the civil war broke out, Bibulus found a province at peace and all its books in order. How dare a mere quaestor do what Cassius had done? How dare a mere quaestor govern a province? In *boni* lights, a mere quaestor should have sat and twiddled his thumbs until the next governor arrived, no matter *what* happened to the province, including Jewish insurrections and Parthian invasions. Such was the mind-set of the *boni*. In consequence, Bibulus's manner was glacially cold toward Cassius, to whom he tendered no word of thanks. Rather, he ordered Cassius to quit Syria forthwith, but only after serving him a homily about taking things upon himself that were not a part of a quaestor's duties according to the *mos maiorum*.

* * *

Why then did Cassius choose the *boni* side in the civil war? Certainly not from love of his brother-in-law Brutus, though he adored Brutus's mother, Servilia. But she was neutral in the conflict, had close relatives on both sides. One reason lay in Cassius's instinctive antipathy toward Caesar: they were not unalike, in that both had taken military command upon themselves at an early age without the governor's approval—Caesar at Tralles in Asia Province, Cassius in Syria—and that both were physically brave, vigorous, no-nonsense men. To Cassius, Caesar had accreted too much glory to himself with that stunning nine-year war in Long-haired Gaul—how could Cassius, when *his* time came, find anything half as glamorous to do? Though that was nothing compared to the fact that Caesar had marched on Rome just as Cassius was entering on his tribunate of the plebs, scattered routine government to the winds, and ruined his chances of making a big splash in that most controversial and immortal of magistracies. Another reason compounded Cassius's detestation: Caesar was the natural father of Cassius's wife, Servilia's third daughter, Tertulla. Legally she was Silanus's daughter and came with a huge dowry from Silanus's fortune, but half of Rome—including Brutus—knew whose child Tertulla really was. Cicero had the temerity to make *jokes* about it!

After plundering a few temples to help fund the Republican war against Caesar, Cassius found himself sent to Syria to raise a fleet for Pompey. Sailing the high seas suited him a great deal more than being an insignificant member of Pompey's command chain; he found that his military talents extended to war on the sea, and ignominiously defeated a Caesarean fleet outside Sicilian Messana. Then off Vibo, in the Tuscan Sea, he intercepted the Caesarean admiral Sulpicius Rufus—and would have beaten him too, had it not been for Fortuna! A legion of Caesar's veterans were sitting on the shore watching the battle, and got fed up with Sulpicius's ineptitude. So they commandeered the local fishing fleet, rowed out to charge into the mass of dueling warships, and thrashed Cassius so soundly that he had to flee for his life aboard a strange ship—his own went down.

Licking his spiritual wounds, Cassius decided to retire east to revictual and raise a few more ships to replace those Caesar's veterans had demolished. But as he crossed the sea-lanes from Numidia his luck returned; he encountered a dozen merchantmen loaded with lions and leopards intended for sale in Rome. What a windfall! Worth a *huge* fortune! With the merchantmen in his custody, he called in to Greek Megara to take on water and food. Megara was a fanatically loyal Republican town, and promised to care for Cassius's lions and leopards until he could find somewhere more remote to conceal them; after Pompey was victorious, he would sell them to Pompey for his victory games. The caged felines ashore, Cassius sailed with a dozen empty merchantmen to donate to Gnaeus Pompey as transports.

At his next stop he learned of the defeat at Pharsalus. Stunned, he fled to Apollonia in Cyrenaica, where he found many refugees from Pharsalus—Cato, Labienus, Afranius, Petreius among them. None, however, was disposed to take any notice of a blooming young tribune of the plebs thrown out of office by civil war. So Cassius sailed off in high dudgeon, refusing to donate his ships to the Republican cause in Africa Province. They can shove Africa Province up their arses! I want no part of a campaign that involves Cato or Labienus! Or that toplofty turd Metellus Scipio!

Back he went to Megara to pick up his lions and leopards, only to find them gone. Quintus Fufius Calenus had come along to take the town for Caesar; the Megarans opened the cages and let the lions and leopards loose to eat Calenus's men. Instead, the lions and leopards ate the Megarans! Fufius Calenus rounded the beasts up, put them back into their cages and shipped them off to Rome for *Caesar's* victory games! Cassius was devastated.

He did learn one interesting fact in Megara, however: that Brutus had surrendered to Caesar after Pharsalus, had been freely pardoned, and was at present sitting in the governor's palace at Tarsus while Caesar himself had gone off in search of Pompey, and Calvinus and Sestius had marched to Armenia Parva to face Pharnaces.

Thus, with no better place to go, Gaius Cassius sailed for Tarsus. He would surrender his fleet to Brutus, his brother-in-law and co-eval—they were the same age within four months. If he couldn't stay in Tarsus, he could at least find out from Brutus what was real and what confabulation. Then perhaps he could more coolly decide what to do with the rest of his ruined life.

Brutus was so delighted to see him that Cassius found himself fervently hugged and kissed, ushered tenderly into the palace and given a comfortable suite of rooms.

"I insist that you remain here in Tarsus," said Brutus over a good dinner, "and wait for Caesar."

"He'll proscribe me," said Cassius, sunk in gloom.

"No, no, no! Cassius, you have my word that his policy *is* clemency! You're in similar case to me! You haven't gone to war against him after he's pardoned you, because he hasn't seen you to pardon you a first time! Truly, you'll find yourself forgiven! After which, Caesar will advance your career just as if none of this had ever happened."

"Except," muttered Cassius, "that I'll owe my future career to *his* generosity—*his* say-so—*his* condescension. What right has Caesar got to pardon me, when all's said and done? He's not a king, and I'm not his subject. We're both equal under the law."

Brutus decided to be frank. "Caesar has the right of the victor in a civil war. Come, Cassius, this isn't Rome's first civil war—we've had at least eight of them since Gaius Gracchus, and those on the winning side have never suffered. Those on the losing side certainly have. Until now. Now, in Caesar, we see a victor who is actually willing to let bygones be bygones. A first, Cassius, a first! What disgrace is there in accepting a pardon? If the word irks you, then call it by some other name—letting bygones be bygones, for example. He won't make you kneel to him or give you the impression that he considers you an insect! He was terribly kind to me, I didn't feel at all as if he deemed me in the wrong. What I felt was his genuine pleasure in being able to do such a little thing for me. That's how he looks at it, Cassius, honestly! As if siding with Pompeius were a little thing, and every man's right if he so saw his duty. Caesar has *beautiful* manners, and no—no—no need to aggrandize himself by making others look or feel insignificant."

"If you say so," said Cassius, head lowered.

"Well, though I was too much a constitutional man to dream of siding with Caesar," said Brutus, having no idea whatsoever of constitutionality, "the truth is that Pompeius Magnus was far more the barbarian. I saw what went on in Pompeius's camp, I saw him let Labienus behave—behave—oh, I can't even speak of it! If it had been Caesar in Italian Gaul when my late father was there with Lepidus, Caesar would never have murdered him out of hand, but Pompeius did. Whatever else you may or may not think about Caesar, he is a Roman to the core."

"Well, so am I!" Cassius snapped.

"And I am not?" asked Brutus.

"You're *sure*?"

"Absolutely, unshakably sure."

They passed then to news from home, but the truth was that neither of them had much of that to exchange; just gossip and hearsay. Cicero was reputed to have returned to Italy, Gnaeus Pompey to be making for Sicily, but no letters had come from Servilia, or Porcia, or Philippus, or anyone else in Rome.

Eventually Cassius calmed down sufficiently to allow Brutus to talk about matters in Tarsus.

"You can be of real help here, Cassius. I'm under orders to recruit and train more legions, but though I can recruit fairly capably, I'm hopeless at training. You've brought Caesar a fleet and transports, which he'll be grateful to have, but you can enhance your standing in his eyes by helping me train. After all, these troops are not for a civil war, they're for the war against Pharnaces. Calvinus has retreated to Pergamum, but Pharnaces is too busy laying waste to Pontus to be bothered following. So the more soldiers we can produce, the better. The enemy is foreign."

That had been January. By the time Mithridates of Pergamum passed through Tarsus late in February on his way to Caesar in Alexandria, Brutus and Cassius were able to donate him one full legion of reasonably well-trained troops. Neither of them had heard about Caesar's war in Alexandria, though word had come that Pompey had been foully murdered by King Ptolemy's palace cabal. Not from Caesar in Egypt, but in a letter from Servilia, who told them that Caesar had sent Pompey's ashes to Cornelia Metella. So conversant was Servilia with the deed that she even gave the names of the palace cabal—Potheinus, Theodotus and Achillas.

The two continued their work transforming civilian Cilicians into auxiliaries for Rome's use, waiting patiently in Tarsus for Caesar's return. Return he must, to deal with Pharnaces. Nothing was going to happen until the snows melted from the Anatolian passes, but when high spring arrived, so would Caesar.

Early in April came a ripple, a shiver.

"Marcus Brutus," said the captain of the palace guard, "we have detained a fellow at your door. Destitute, in rags. But he insists that he has important information for you from Egypt."

Brutus frowned, his melancholy eyes reflecting the doubts and indecisions which always plagued him. "Does he have a name?"

"He said, Theodotus."

The slight figure stiffened, sat up straight. "Theodotus?"

"That's what he said."

"Bring him in—and stay, Amphion."

Amphion brought a man in his sixties, indeed festooned in rags, but the rags were still faintly purple. His lined face was petulant, his expression fawning. Brutus found himself physically revolted by his un-Roman effeminacy, the simpering smile that showed blackened, rotting teeth.

"Theodotus?" Brutus asked.

"Yes, Marcus Brutus."

"The same Theodotus who was tutor to King Ptolemy of Egypt?"

"Yes, Marcus Brutus."

"What brings you here, and in such parlous condition?"

"The King is defeated and dead, Marcus Brutus." The lips drew back from those awful teeth in a hiss. "Caesar personally drowned him in the river after the battle."

"*Caesar* drowned him."

"Yes, personally."

"Why would Caesar do that if he had defeated the King?"

"To eliminate him from the Egyptian throne. He wants his whore, Cleopatra, to reign supreme."

"Why come to me with your news, Theodotus?"

The rheumy eyes widened in surprise. "Because you have no love for Caesar, Marcus Brutus—everyone knows that. I offer you an instrument to help destroy Caesar."

"Did you actually see Caesar drown the King?"

"With my own eyes."

"Then why are *you* still alive?"

"I escaped."

"A weak creature like you escaped Caesar?"

"I was hiding in the papyrus."

"But you saw Caesar personally drown the King."

"Yes, from my hiding place."

"Was the drowning a public event?"

"No, Marcus Brutus. They were alone."

"Do you swear that you are indeed Theodotus the tutor?"

"I swear it on my dead king's body."

Brutus closed his eyes, sighed, opened them, and turned his head to look at the captain of the guard. "Amphion, take this man to the public square outside the agora and crucify him. And don't break his legs."

Theodotus gasped, retched. "Marcus Brutus, I am a free man, not a slave! I came to you in good faith!"

"You are getting the death of a slave or pirate, Theodotus, because you deserve it. Fool! If you must lie, choose your lies more carefully— and choose the man to whom you tell them more carefully." Brutus turned his back. "Take him away and carry out the sentence immediately, Amphion."

* * *

"There's some pathetic old fellow hanging tied to a cross in the main square," said Cassius when he came in for dinner. "The guards on duty said you'd forbidden them to break his legs."

"Yes," said Brutus placidly, putting down a paper.

"That's a bit much, isn't it? They take days to die unless their legs are broken. I didn't know you had so much steel. Is an ancient slave a worthy target, Brutus?"

"He's not a slave," said Brutus, and told Cassius the story.

Cassius wasn't pleased. "Jupiter, what's the matter with you? You should have sent him to Rome in a hurry," he said, breathing hard. "The man was an eyewitness to murder!"

"*Gerrae,*" said Brutus, mending a reed pen. "You may detest Caesar all you like, Cassius, but many years of knowing Caesar endow me with sufficient detachment to dismiss Theodotus's tale as a tissue of lies. It isn't beyond Caesar to do murder, but in the case of Egypt's king, all he had to do was hand him over to his sister for execution. The Ptolemies love to murder each other, and this one had been at war with his sister. Caesar, to drown the boy in a river? It's not his style. What baffles me is why Theodotus thought that in mine, he'd find a pair of ears willing to listen. Or why he thought that any Roman would believe one of the three men responsible for Pompeius's hideous death. So too was the King responsible. I am not a vengeful man, Cassius, but I can tell you that it afforded me great satisfaction to crucify Theodotus one gasp at a time for days."

"Take him down, Brutus."

"No! Don't argue with me, Cassius, and don't bully me! *I* am governor in Cilicia, not you, and I say Theodotus dies."

But when Cassius wrote next to Servilia, he recounted the fate of Theodotus in Tarsus very differently. Caesar had drowned a fourteen-year-old boy in the river to please Queen Cleopatra. Cassius had no fear that Brutus would write his own version, for Brutus and his mother didn't get along, so Brutus never wrote to her at all. If he wrote to anyone, it would be Cicero. Two timorous mice, Brutus and Cicero.

2 There was only one road north from Pelusium. It followed the coast of Our Sea and ran through inhospitable, barren country until it entered Syria Palestina at the town of Gaza. After that the land grew a little kinder, and a series of hamlets began to appear fairly regularly. Too early in the year for grain, but Cleopatra had loaded them down with pack camels imported from

Arabia, odd creatures which groaned terribly but didn't need to drink every day like the Germans' horses.

Caesar wasted no time until he reached Ptolemais, a bigger town just beyond the northern headland of a wide bay. Here he stopped for two days to interview the Jewish contingent, whom he had summoned from Jerusalem by a letter that explained gracefully how pressed he was for time. Antipater, his wife, Cypros, and his two elder sons, Phasael and Herod, were waiting for him.

"No Hyrcanus?" Caesar asked, brows raised.

"The high priest cannot leave Jerusalem," Antipater said, "even for the Dictator of Rome. It is a religious prohibition that he feels sure the Pontifex Maximus of Rome can forgive."

The pale eyes twinkled. "Of course. How remiss of me!"

An interesting family, Caesar was thinking. Cleopatra had told him of them, explained that wherever Antipater went, there also went Cypros—a very devoted couple. Antipater and Phasael were handsome men, had the same clear dark skin as Cleopatra, but did not rejoice in her nose. Dark of eye, dark of hair, fairly tall. Phasael carried himself like a warrior prince, whereas his father had more the look of an energetic civil servant. Herod came from a different graft on the family tree; he was short, inclined to run to fat, and could have passed as a close cousin of Caesar's favorite banker, Lucius Cornelius Balbus Major from Spanish Gades. Phoenician stock—full mouth, hooked nose, wide yet heavy-lidded eyes. All three men were clean-shaven and had cropped hair, which Caesar took to mean that they were not Jewish in every way. Racially he knew they were Idumaeans who had fully espoused the Judaic faith, but he wondered how tenderly they were regarded by the Jews of Jerusalem. Cypros, a Nabataean Arab, was the one who looked most like Herod, though she had a peculiar charm her son quite lacked; her roundness was desirable, and her eyes liquid pools of sensuous delights. Though he speculated that perhaps Cypros went everywhere with Antipater to make sure that he remained hers and hers alone.

"You may tell Hyrcanus that Rome fully recognizes his high priesthood, and that he may call himself King of Judaea," Caesar announced.

"Judaea? Which Judaea is that? The kingdom of Alexander Jannaeus? Are we to have a port again at Joppa?" asked Antipater with more caginess than eagerness in his voice.

"I am afraid not," Caesar said gently. "Its boundaries are those laid down by Aulus Gabinius—Jerusalem, Amathus, Gazara, Jericho and Galilaean Sepphora."

"Five districts rather than continuous territory."

"True, but each district is rich, particularly Jericho."

"We need access to Your Sea."

"You have it, since Syria is governed as a Roman province. No one will prevent your using any number of ports." The eyes were growing colder. "Don't look a gift horse in the mouth, my dear Antipater. I will guarantee that no troops are billeted in any Judaean territory, and I exempt all Judaean territory from taxes. Considering the income from Jericho's balsam, it's a good bargain for Hyrcanus, even if he will have to pay port dues."

"Yes, of course," said Antipater, assuming a grateful look.

"You may also tell Hyrcanus that he is at liberty to rebuild the walls of Jerusalem, and fortify them."

"Caesar!" Antipater gasped. "That is very welcome news!"

"As for you, Antipater," Caesar went on, eyes warming a little, "I confer the Roman citizenship upon you and your descendants, remit you from all personal taxes, and appoint you Hyrcanus's chief minister in government. I understand that the duties of high priest are onerous, that he needs civil help."

"Too generous, too generous!" Antipater cried.

"Oh, there are conditions. You and Hyrcanus are to keep the peace in southern Syria, is that clear? I want no rebellions and no pretenders to the kingship. Whosoever of Aristobulus's line is left makes no difference to me. They've all been a bother to Rome and a constant source of local trouble. So let there be no need for any governor of Syria to march in Jerusalem's direction, is that understood?"

"It is, Caesar."

Neither son, Caesar noted, allowed any expression to show on his face. Whatever Phasael and Herod thought would not be forthcoming until the family was out of Roman earshot.

Tyre, Sidon, Byblos and the rest of the cities of Phoenicia did not fare nearly as well as Judaea; nor did Antioch when Caesar reached it. They had all sided enthusiastically with Pompey, had given him money and ships. Therefore, said Caesar, each would be fined the value of whatever it had given Pompey—as well as give Caesar the same as it had given Pompey. To make sure his orders were obeyed, he left his young cousin Sextus Julius Caesar in Antioch as the temporary governor of Syria. A post the highly flattered young man, grandson of Caesar's uncle, vowed to acquit himself in splendidly.

Cyprus, however, was not to be governed from Syria as part of it any longer. Caesar sent it a quaestor in the person of young Sextilius Rufus, but not exactly to govern.

"For the moment Cyprus won't be paying any Roman taxes or tributes, and its produce is to go to Egypt. Queen Cleopatra has sent a governor, Serapion. Your job, Rufus, is to make sure that Serapion behaves himself," said Caesar. "According to the lights of Rome, that is, not Egypt."

The removal of Cyprus from, as he saw it, Rome's empire, did not amuse Tiberius Claudius Nero, whom Caesar found skulking in Antioch still convinced that he had done no wrong in Alexandria.

"Does this mean," he asked Caesar incredulously, "that you have actually taken it upon yourself to give Cyprus back to the Crown of Egypt?"

"Had I, Nero, what business is that of yours?" Caesar asked very coldly. "Hold your tongue."

"You fool!" Sextilius Rufus said to Nero later. "He's giving nothing of Rome's away! All he's doing is allowing the Queen of Egypt to take timber and copper out of Cyprus to rebuild her city and fleets, and grain to ease the famine. If *she* believes Cyprus is Egyptian once more, then let her. Caesar knows better."

And so to Tarsus by the beginning of Quinctilis, having been a month on the march; disciplining Syria had taken time.

Thanks to the presence of Hapd'efan'e, Caesar himself was well. His weight had returned to normal and he suffered no prodromal dizziness or nausea. He had learned to drink whatever juice or syrup Hapd'efan'e tendered at regular intervals during the day, and suffered the flagon of the same that sat beside his bed.

Hapd'efan'e was thriving. He rode a donkey named Paser and carried his gear on three more named Pennut, H'eyna and Sut, their panniers loaded neatly with mysterious bundles and packets. Though Caesar had expected him to continue shaving his head and wearing his crisp white linen dresses, the priest-physician did not. Too noticeable, he said when asked. Cha'em had given him permission to dress like a Greek and wear his hair cropped like a Roman's. If they stopped in any kind of town for the night, he would be off to explore the herb stalls in the markets, or squat down to have an earnest conversation with some repulsive crone in a mouse-skull necklace and a girdle of dogs' tails.

Caesar had several freedmen servants to attend to his personal wants; he was most particular about the cleanliness of his garb, down to requiring fresh inner soles daily in his marching boots, and had a man to pluck his body hair, done now for so long that it had almost given up growing. Since they liked Hapd'efan'e and approved of his addition to the fold, they would rush around finding fruit for him, peel it or crush it or strain it at his bidding. What didn't occur to Caesar was that they loved Caesar greatly, and Hapd'efan'e now represented Caesar's well-being. So they taught the inscrutable priest Latin, improved his Greek out of sight, and even enjoyed those ridiculous donkeys.

At Antioch the camels were dispatched to Damascus, there to find buyers. Caesar was painfully aware that it was going to take a huge amount of money to set Rome on her feet again; every little helped, including the sale of prime camels to desert people.

A far richer source of income first manifested itself at Tyre, the world capital of the purple-dye industry, and hardest hit of all Syrian cities when it came to war reparations. There a party of horsemen caught up with the Romans and presented Caesar with a box from Hyrcanus, one from Antipater, and another from Cypros. Each contained a gold crown—not flimsy things of tissue-thin leaf, but extremely weighty objects no one could have worn without developing a bad headache. They were fashioned as olive wreaths, but the crowns that then began to arrive from the King of the Parthians were replicas of an eastern tiara, a towering edifice shaped like a truncated cone; even an elephant might have found it hard work to wear one, Caesar joked. After that, the crowns came thick and fast from every ruler of every minor satrapy along the Euphrates River. Sampsiceramus sent one in the form of a riband of braided gold studded with magnificent ocean pearls, the Pahlavi of Seleuceia-on-Tigris sent one of huge faceted and polished emeralds encased in gold. If this keeps on going, thought Caesar gleefully, I'll be able to pay for this war!

So when the Sixth, the Germans and Caesar arrived in Tarsus, they had twelve mules loaded with crowns.

Tarsus appeared to be prospering despite the absence of the governor Sestius and his quaestor Quintus Philippus. When Caesar saw the camp dispositions on the Cydnus plain he was astonished at Brutus's talent for military layout and facilities. A riddle answered when he entered the governor's palace and found himself face-to-face with Gaius Cassius Longinus.

"I know you won't require my intercession, Caesar, but I would like to intercede for Gaius Cassius just the same," Brutus said with that hangdog look only he could produce. "He's brought you a good fleet, and he's been a tremendous help in training the troops. He understands military matters much better than I do."

Oh, Brutus, with your philosophies and your pimples, your miseries and your moneylending! thought Caesar, inwardly sighing.

He couldn't remember ever meeting Gaius Cassius, whose older brother, Quintus, he knew well from the campaign against Afranius and Petreius in Nearer Spain; he had sent Quintus to govern in Further Spain afterward. This was not to say that he hadn't met Gaius. Simply that when last he had been in Rome with the time to look around, Gaius Cassius would have been a young man making tentative forays into the law courts to plead someone's case, therefore hardly worth noticing. Though he remembered how very pleased Servilia had been over his betrothal to Tertulla—ye gods, this man is the husband of my natural daughter! I hope he disciplines her—Julia used to say Servilia spoiled her too much.

Well, now Gaius Cassius was a man of thirty-six. Tall but not overly so, he was sturdily built and had a martial air to him, regular features that some women might call handsome, a humorous quirk to the corners of his mouth, a very determined chin, and the kind of hair that drove a barber mad—strong, springy, impossible to tame unless cut (as was Cassius's) close to the scalp. Light brown in color, as were his skin and eyes.

The eyes looked straight into Caesar's without flinching, a faint trace of scorn tinging the anger in them. Oho! thought Caesar. Cassius doesn't like being presented as a suppliant. If I give him the slightest excuse, he'll throw my pardon in my face, storm out and run his sword up under his rib cage. I see why Servilia is so fond of him. He's exactly what she wanted poor Brutus to be.

"I knew someone who's been around a few camps in his time engineered this one in Tarsus," Caesar said cheerfully, his smile open and his right hand out. "Gaius Cassius, of course! How can Rome thank you for keeping the Parthians out of Syria after poor Marcus Crassus died? I sincerely hope you've been made welcome, that you're comfortable?"

And so the moment passed without any mention of pardons on either side; Gaius Cassius had little choice save to take the hand held out so naturally, had little choice save to smile, to deprecate his doings in Syria a few years ago. This too handsome, too charming patrician had managed to pardon him with a handshake and a warmly personal greeting.

* * *

"I've sent ahead to Calvinus to meet us with whatever troops he can muster in Iconium in ten days," Caesar said over dinner. "Brutus and Cassius, you'll be marching with me. I'll need you as a personal legate, Brutus, but I'll be very glad to give you a legion of your own to command, Cassius. Calvinus is sending Quintus Philippus back to govern in Tarsus, so the moment he arrives, we head up the Cilician Gates to Iconium. Marcus Antonius has shipped two legions of ex-Republicans from Italy to Calvinus, who says he's ready to meet Pharnaces again." He smiled, his eyes looking at something far beyond the room. "Things will go differently this time. Caesar is here."

"His confidence is incredible!" snarled Cassius to Brutus later. "Does nothing ever dent it?"

Brutus blinked, remembering the day when Caesar had come to his mother's house dressed in the purple and crimson glory of the Pontifex Maximus's robes, then calmly announced that he was going to marry Julia to Pompeius Magnus. I fainted. Not so much at the shock of it—how much I loved her!—but at the prospect of facing Mama's rage. Caesar had done the unforgivable, rejected a Servilius Caepio in favor of Pompeius Magnus, the peasant from Picenum. Oh, she was angry! And of course she blamed me, not Caesar. I shiver at the memory of that day.

"No, nothing can dent Caesar's confidence," he said now to Cassius. "It is inborn."

"Then if nothing can, maybe the answer is to dent Caesar's chest with a knife," Cassius said between his teeth.

The pimples meant that Brutus couldn't shave, had to content himself with clipping his black beard as short as possible; as he heard this, he felt every one of those hairs stiffen. "Cassius! Don't even think of it!" he said in a terrified whisper.

"Why not? It's every free man's duty to kill a tyrant."

"He's not a tyrant! *Sulla* was a tyrant!"

"Then give me another name for him," Cassius sneered. His eyes roamed over Brutus's pinched face—the Furies take Servilia for making such a jelly out of her son! He shrugged. "Don't pass out, Brutus. Forget I ever said it."

"Promise me you won't! *Promise me!*"

For answer, Cassius went to his own quarters, there to pace up and down until his anger died.

By the time Caesar left Tarsus, he had collected a small group of penitent Republicans, all of whom received their pardons without the humiliation of hearing the word "pardon" spoken. In Antioch, young Quintus Cicero; in Tarsus, his father. They were the two who mattered most to Caesar. Neither was interested in joining the campaign against Pharnaces.

"I should get home to Italy," said Quintus Senior, sighing. "My foolish brother is still in Brundisium, not sure enough of his safety to venture farther, yet afraid to return to Greece." His brown eyes looked into Caesar's ruefully. "The trouble is, Caesar, that you were such a wonderful commander to campaign with. When the time came, I couldn't take up arms against you, no matter what Marcus said." He squared his shoulders. "We quarrelled dreadfully in Patrae before he sailed to Brundisium. Did you know that Cato tried to make him commander-in-chief of the Republican forces?"

Caesar laughed. "That's no surprise. Cato is an enigma to me. He has incredible strength of conviction, yet he's never formed any convictions for himself. And he refuses to take any responsibility for his own actions. It was he who forced Magnus into this war, but when Magnus reproached him with it, he had the gall to say that those who started the business should be the ones to finish it—he meant us military men! To Cato, politicians don't create wars. And that means he doesn't understand power."

"We're all what our upbringing makes of us, Caesar. How did you escape the taint?"

"I had a mother strong enough to resist me without crushing me. One in many millions, I suspect."

So the Quintus Cicerones waved them goodbye as they set out, a reasonable force of two Cilician legions, the Sixth, and the faithful Germans, who had been away from their misty forests for so long that they hardly ever thought of that old life.

The mountains of Anatolia were mostly over ten thousand feet in height, and impossible to negotiate save through infrequent passes. The Cilician Gates were one such corridor, a narrow, steep track through mighty pine forests, every cleft filled with roaring cascades from melting snow, and still very cold at night. Caesar's recipe for minor complaints like freezing temperatures and high altitudes was to push his army on at full marching pace, so that when evening camp was made, everyone was too exhausted to feel the cold, and too dizzy from the height to stay awake. He insisted on proper camps, unsure until he met Calvinus exactly whereabouts Pharnaces was; all Calvinus had told him in his one letter was that the King of Cimmeria had definitely returned.

Once through the pass the army descended to the high plateau which sat like a bowl in the center of Anatolia's vastness; hilly and grassy, at this time of year it was green and lush, ideal grazing for horses. Of which animals, Caesar noted, there were far too many. This was Lycaonia, not Galatia.

Iconium was a big town on a major trade route crossroads. It sat beneath the peaks of the Taurus on its south and looked north across the plateau in the direction of Galatia and western Pontus. One road led to Cappadocia and thence to the Euphrates; one to the Cilician Gates, thence to Tarsus, Syria, the eastern end of Our Sea; one to Asia Province and thence to the Aegean Sea at Smyrna; one to Ancyra in Galatia and thence to the Euxine Sea; and one to Bithynia, the Hellespont, and thence to Rome on the Via Egnatia. Traffic was caravan style, great strings of camels, horses and mules herded by heavily armed businessmen on the lookout for marauding bands of backwoods tribesmen. A caravan might be Roman, Asian Greek, Cilician, Arab, Armenian, Median, Persian or Syrian. Iconium saw expensive dyed wools, furniture, cabinet timber, wine, olive oil, paints and pigments and dyes, iron-bound Gallic wheels, iron sows, marble statues and Puteoli glass heading east; west came rugs, tapestries, tin for bronze, brass sows, dried apricots, lapis lazuli, malachite, camel-hair paintbrushes, furs, astrakhan and fine leathers.

What Iconium disliked were armies descending upon it, but such was its fate midway through Quinctilis: Caesar up from Tarsus with three legions and his German cavalry, Calvinus down from Pergamum with four good Roman legions. The abnormal number of horses was due to King Deiotarus, who had ridden from his own lands with two thousand Galatian horse troopers. It fell to Calvinus to provide the amalgamated army's food except for the Galatians, who brought their own.

Calvinus was full of news.

"When Pharnaces got home to Cimmeria, Asander proved clever enough to adopt Fabian tactics," he said, speaking to Caesar in private. "No matter where his father hounded him, Asander was one pace ahead. In the end Pharnaces decided that Asander would keep, loaded his troops back on board his transports, and sailed the Euxine to poor Amisus, which he sacked a second time. He's gone to earth in Zela, a part of Pontus I don't know, except that it's a fair way from the Euxine coast near Amaseia, where all the ancient Pontic kings are entombed in the cliffs. From what I hear, far kinder country than we encountered in Armenia Parva last December and January."

Head bent over a map inked and painted on Pergamum parchment, Caesar traced a route with one finger. "Zela, Zela, Zela . . . Yes, I have it." He frowned. "Oh, for some good Roman roads! They'll have to be the next governor of Pontus's first priority. I fear, Calvinus, that we'll have to loop around the eastern end of Lake Tatta and cross the Halys into more mountains. We'll need good guides, which I suppose means I'll have to forgive Deiotarus for pouring Galatian money and men into the Republican campaign."

Calvinus grinned. "Oh, he's here with Phrygian cap in hand, shitting himself in terror. Once Mithridates was defeated and Pompeius Magnus was all over Anatolia doling out land, Deiotarus expanded his kingdom in every direction, including at the expense of the old Ariobarzanes. After that Ariobarzanes died and the new one came to Cappadocia's throne—this one's a Philoromaios—there was hardly any decent territory left in Cappadocia."

"That may account for the money Cappadocia owes Brutus—oh, oops, did I say Brutus? I meant Matinius, of course."

"Fear not, Deiotarus is waist deep in debt to Matinius as well, Caesar. Magnus kept asking for money, money, money, and where was Deiotarus going to get it from?"

"Answer, a Roman usurer," said Caesar, and huffed in exasperation. "Why won't they ever learn? They gamble everything on the reward of additional lands, or the discovery of a ten-mile reef of pure gold."

"I hear that you're rather swimming in gold yourself—or at least, in gold crowns," said Calvinus.

"Indeed I am. So far I estimate that they'll melt down into about a hundred talents of gold, besides the value of the jewels in some of them. Emeralds, Calvinus! Emeralds the size of a baby's fist. I do wish they'd simply give me bullion. The workmanship in the crowns is exquisite, but who outside of the people who gave them to me are going to be interested in buying gold crowns? I have no choice other than to melt them down. Such a pity. Though I hope to sell the emeralds to Bogud, Bocchus and whoever inherits the throne of Numidia after Juba's defeated," said Caesar, ever practical. "The pearls aren't such a problem, I can sell them in Rome easily."

"I hope the ship doesn't sink," said Calvinus.

"Ship? What ship?"

"The one carrying the crowns to the Treasury."

Both fair brows flew up; Caesar's eyes twinkled. "My dear Calvinus, that foolish I am not. From all I hear of the situation in Rome, even if the ship didn't sink, the crowns would never see the inside of the Treasury. No, I'll keep them with me."

"Wise man" was Calvinus's response; they had spent some time discussing the reports about Rome that had come to Pergamum.

Deiotarus did indeed have a Phrygian cap—a fabric affair with a rounded point that flopped to one side. His, however, was made of Tyrian purple interwoven with gold thread, and he did hold it in his hand when Caesar received him. A twinge of mischief had prompted Caesar to make the audience a rather public one; not only Gnaeus Domitius Calvinus, but several legates, including Brutus and Cassius. Now let's see how you behave, Brutus! Here before Caesar stands one of your principal debtors.

Deiotarus was an old man now, but still vigorous. Like his people, he was a Gaul, a descendant of a Gallic migration eastward into Greece two hundred and fifty years earlier; deflected, most of the Gauls had gone home, but Deiotarus's people had continued east and finally occupied a part of central Anatolia where the country looked a dream to a horse people, rich in grass, and promising work for competent mounted warriors, of whom Anatolia had none. When Mithridates the Great had risen to power, he saw at once that the Galatians would have to go, invited all their chieftains to a feast, and massacred them. That had been in the time of Gaius Marius, sixty years ago. Deiotarus had escaped the massacre because he wasn't old enough to go to the feast with his father, but from the time he grew to manhood, Mithridates had a fierce enemy. He allied himself with Sulla, Lucullus and then Pompey, always against Mithridates and Tigranes, and finally saw his dreams come true when Pompey gave him huge territories and persuaded the Senate (with Caesar's connivance) to allow him to be called a king, his lands of Galatia a client-kingdom.

Not for one moment had it occurred to him that anyone could defeat Pompey the Great; no one had moved more strenuously to assist Pompey than Deiotarus. Now here he was in front of this stranger, Gaius Julius Caesar Dictator, his cap in his hand, his heart knocking frantically at his ribs. The man he saw was very tall for a Roman, and fair enough of hair and eye to be a Gaul, but the features were Roman of mouth, nose, shape of eyes, shape of face, those knife-edged high cheekbones. A more different man from Pompey the Great would be hard to imagine, yet Pompey had been Gallic fair too; maybe he had taken to Pompey from the time of first meeting because Pompey truly did look a Gaul, including his facial features.

If I had only seen this man first, I might have thought twice about giving Pompeius Magnus so much aid. Caesar is everything I have heard—royal enough to be a king, and those cold, piercing eyes look straight through a man to his marrow. O Dann! O Dagda! *Caesar has Sulla's eyes!*

"Caesar, I beg your merciful consideration," he began. "You must surely understand that I was in Pompeius Magnus's clientele—his loyalest and most obedient client at all times! If I assisted him, it was my cliental obligation to assist him—there was nothing personal in it! Indeed, finding money for his war chest has beggared me, I am in debt to"—his eyes went to Brutus, he hesitated—"certain firms of money-lenders. *Deeply* in debt!"

"Which firms?" Caesar asked.

Deiotarus blinked, shifted his trousered legs. "I am not at liberty to divulge their names," he said, swallowing.

Caesar's eyes slid sideways to where Brutus was sitting in a chair deliberately placed within the scope of Caesar's gaze. Ah! My Brutus is very concerned! So is brother-in-law Cassius. Does Cassius have shares in Matinius et Scaptius too? How amusing.

"Why not?" he asked coolly.

"It is a part of the contract, Caesar."

"I'd like to see that contract."

"I left it in Ancyra."

"Dear, dear. Would the name Matinius be in it? Scaptius?"

"I don't remember," Deiotarus whispered wretchedly.

"Oh, come, Caesar!" Cassius said sharply. "Leave the poor man alone! You're like a cat with a mouse. He's right, it's his business to whom he owes money. Just because you're the dictator doesn't mean you have the right to poke and pry into affairs that don't concern Rome's government! He's in debt, that's surely the only factor of relevance to Rome."

Had it been Tiberius Claudius Nero who said that, Caesar's answer would have been a barked order to get out, go back to Rome, go anywhere Caesar was not. But this was Gaius Cassius, who bore watching. Not afraid to speak his mind, and hot tempered.

Brutus cleared his throat. "Caesar, if I may, I would like to speak for King Deiotarus, whom I know from his visits to Rome. Don't forget that in him, Mithridates had an implacable enemy, that in him, Rome had a perpetual ally. Does it truly matter whose side King Deiotarus chose in this civil war? I too chose Pompeius Magnus, but I have been forgiven. Gaius Cassius chose Pompeius Magnus, but he has been forgiven. What is the difference? Surely Rome in the person of Caesar Dictator needs every ally possible in this coming struggle against Pharnaces? The King is here to offer his services, he's brought us two thousand horse troopers we desperately need."

"So you're advocating that I forgive King Deiotarus and let him go unpunished?" Caesar asked Brutus.

The big sad eyes were on fire: he sees his money vanishing.

"Yes," said Brutus.

A cat with a mouse. No, Cassius, not a cat with *a* mouse—a cat with three mice!

Caesar leaned forward in his curule chair and pinned Deiotarus on Sulla's eyes. "I do sympathize with your plight, King, and it's admirable for a client to assist his patron to the top of his bent. The only trouble is that Pompeius had all the clients, Caesar none. So Caesar had to fill his war chest from Rome's Treasury. Which must be paid back at ten percent simple interest—the only rate now legal from one end of the world to the other. Which ought to improve your lot considerably, King. It may be that I will allow you to keep most of your kingdom, but I hereby announce that I will not make any decisions until after Pharnaces is defeated. Caesar will be collecting every sestertius he can to pay the Treasury back, so Galatia's tribute will certainly increase, by somewhat less than the old rate of interest you were paying those anonymous usurers. Cherish that thought, King, until I call another council in Nicomedia after Pharnaces is defeated." He rose to his feet. "You are dismissed, King. And thank you for the cavalry."

A letter had come from Cleopatra, its advent contributing to the speed with which Caesar conducted his interview with Deiotarus. With the letter had come a camel train containing five thousand talents of gold.

> My darling, wonderful, omnipotent God on earth, my own Caesar, He of Nilus, He of the Inundation, Son of Amun-Ra, Reincarnation of Osiris, beloved of Pharaoh—I *miss* you!
>
> But all that is nothing, dearest Caesar, compared to the joyous news that on the fifth day of the last month of *peret* I gave birth to your son. Ignorance doesn't permit me to translate that perfectly into your calendar, but it was the twenty-third day of your June. He is under the sign of Khnum the Ram, and the horoscope you insisted I pay a Roman astrologer to draw for him says that he will be Pharaoh. A waste of money to learn that! The fellow was cagey, kept on muttering that there would be a crisis in his eighteenth year, but that the aspects didn't let him see clearly. Oh, dearest Caesar, he is beautiful! Horus personified. He was born before his due time, but perfectly formed. Just thin and wrinkled—he takes

after his *tata,* you perceive! His hair is gold, and Tach'a says his eyes will be blue.

I have *milk!* Isn't that wonderful? Pharaoh should always feed her babies herself, it is tradition. My little breasts ooze milk. His temper is very sweet, but he has a strong will, and I swear that the first time he opened his eyes to look at me, he smiled. He is very long, more than two Roman feet. His scrotum is large, so is his penis. Cha'em circumcised him according to Egyptian custom. My labor was easy. I felt the pains, squatted down on a thick pad of clean linen, and there he was!

His name is Ptolemy XV Caesar. Though we are calling him Caesarion.

Things go well in Egypt, even in Alexandria. Rufrius and the legions are well settled into their camp, and the women you gave them as wives seem to have accepted their lot. The rebuilding continues, and I have started the temple of Hathor at Dendera with the cartouches of Cleopatra VII and Ptolemy XV Caesar. We will do work at Philae too.

Oh, darlingest Caesar, I miss you so much! Were you here, you could do all the ruling with my good wishes—I *hate* having to be away from Caesarion to deal with litigious ship owners and crotchety landlords! My husband Philadelphus is growing more and more like our dead brother, whom I do not miss in the slightest. As soon as Caesarion is old enough, I will dispense with Philadelphus and elevate our son to the throne. I hope, by the way, that you are making sure that Arsinoë does not escape Roman custody. She's another would have me off my throne in a moment, could she.

Now here is the best news of all. With the garrison so settled, I spoke to Uncle Mithridates and secured his promise that when you are settled in Rome, he will rule in my absence while I visit you. Yes, I know you said Pharaoh shouldn't leave her country, but there is one reason compels her to—I must have more children with you, and sooner than your return to the East to war against the Parthians. Caesarion must have a sister to marry, and until he does, Nilus is in peril. For our next child might be another boy! They have to come often enough to ensure they are of both sexes. So, whether you like it or not, I am coming to see you in Rome the moment you have defeated the Republicans in Africa. A letter has come from Ammonius, my agent in Rome, to say that events there are going to tie you down in Rome for some time once you have established your rule beyond contest. I have authorized him to build me a palace, but I need you to make a grant of land. Ammonius says it's very difficult to set up a Roman citizen pretend-owner for prime land, so a grant from you would be quicker and easier. On the Capitol, near the temple of Jupiter Optimus Maximus. My choice. I asked Ammonius which location had the best views.

I am sending you five thousand gold talents with this letter in honor of our son. Please, please write to me! I miss you, I miss you, I miss you! Your hands especially. I pray for you every day to Amun-Ra, and to Montu, God of War. I love you, Caesar.

A son, apparently healthy. Caesar is absurdly pleased for an old man who ought to be welcoming the birth of grandchildren. But she has given the child a Greek name, Caesarion. Perhaps it's better. He isn't a Roman and he never can be a Roman. He will be the richest man in the world, and a powerful king. Oh, but the mother is immature! Such an artless letter, vain and vainglorious. Grant her land to build a palace on the Capitol, near the temple of Jupiter Best and Greatest— what a sacrilege, were it possible. She is determined to come to Rome, she will not be denied. Let it be upon her own head, then.

Caesar, you are too hard on her. No one can be more than the capacity of their mind and talents allow, and her blood is tainted, for all that at heart she is a nice little thing. Her crimes are natural to her background, her mistakes not due to arrogance as much as to ignorance. I fear she'll never have the gift of foresight, so I must offer that our son does.

But one thing Caesar has resolved: there will never be any sister for Caesarion to marry. Caesar will not quicken her again. *Coitus interruptus*, Cleopatra.

He sat down and wrote to her, half his attention on the sounds drifting into his room—sounds of legions pulling camp, of horses neighing, of men shouting and cursing, Carfulenus bellowing ghastly obscenities at a hapless soldier.

What good news, my dear Cleopatra. A son, just as was predicted. Would Amun-Ra dare disappoint his daughter on earth? Truly, I am very glad for you and Egypt.

The gold is welcome. Since emerging into the wide world again, I have come to a better understanding of how deeply Rome is in debt. Civil war brings no booty in its train, and war is profitable only if there is booty. Your contribution in the name of our son will not be wasted.

Since you insist upon coming to Rome, I will not stand in your way, only warn you that it will not be what you expect. I will arrange that you have land under the Janiculan Hill, adjoining my own pleasure gardens. Tell Ammonius to apply to the broker Gaius Matius.

I am not a man famous for his love letters. Just accept the love and know that I am indeed very pleased with you and our son. I will write to you again when I reach Bithynia. Take care of yourself and our boy.

And that was that. Caesar rolled the single sheet, plopped a blob of melted wax on its junction, and sealed it with his ring, a new one Cleopatra had given him not entirely from love. It was also a sly poke at his reluctance to discuss his past emotional history with her. The amethyst intaglio was of a sphinx in Greek form, having a human head and a lion's body, and instead of the usual abbreviated full name, it simply said CAESAR in mirrored block letters. He loved it. When he decided which of his nephews or close cousins would be his adopted heir, the ring would go to him along with the name. Ye gods, a sorry lot! *Lucius Pinarius?* Even Quintus Pedius, the best of his nephews, wasn't exactly inspiring. Among the cousins, there were the young fellow in Antioch, Sextus Julius Caesar—Decimus Junius Brutus—and the man most of Rome assumed would be his heir, Marcus Antonius. Who, who, who? For it could not be Ptolemy XV Caesar.

On his way out he gave the letter to Gaius Faberius. "Send this to Queen Cleopatra in Alexandria," he said curtly.

Faberius was dying to know if the baby had been born, but one look at Caesar's face decided him not to ask. The old boy was in the mood to fight, not wax lyrical about babies, even his own.

Lake Tatta was a huge, shallow body of bitterly salty water; perhaps, thought Caesar, studying the conglomerate shores, it was the remnant of some past inland sea, for ancient shells were embedded in the soft rock. Despite its desert nature, it was strikingly beautiful to behold; the scummy surface of the lake glowed with greens, acid yellows, reddish yellows, ribbons of one color coiling through another, and the sere landscape for many miles reflected some of that vivid spectrum.

Never having been in central Anatolia, Caesar found it both bizarre and splendid; the Halys River, the great red waterway that curled like an augur's *lituus* staff for hundreds of miles, lay in a narrow valley between high red cliffs that gave off extrusions and towers he thought reminiscent of a tall city. In other stretches of its course, the attentive Deiotarus told him, it flowed through a broad plain of fertile fields. The mountains began again, high and still smothered in snow, but the Galatian guides knew all the passes; the army weaved its way between them, a traditional Roman snake eight miles long, the cavalry dotting its flanks, the soldiers striding out singing their marching songs to keep the pace.

Oh, this is more like! A foreign foe, a true campaign in a strange new land whose beauty is haunting.

At which moment King Pharnaces sent his first gold crown to Caesar. This one resembled the Armenian rather than the Parthian tiara: mitered, not truncated, and encrusted with round, starred rubies all exactly the same small size.

"Oh, if only I knew someone who could buy it for what it's worth!" Caesar breathed to Calvinus. "It's heartbreaking to melt this down."

"Needs must," Calvinus said briskly. "Actually those little *carbunculi* will fetch an excellent price from any jeweler in the Porticus Margaritaria—I've never seen stars in them before. The gold hardly shows, there are so many. Like a cake rolled in nuts."

"Do you think our friend Pharnaces is becoming worried?"

"Oh, yes. The degree of his worry will show in how often he sends you a crown, Caesar." Calvinus grinned.

One every three days for the next *nundinum*, all the same in form and content; by that time Caesar was only five days' march from the Cimmerian camp.

The count at three crowns, Pharnaces sent an ambassador to Caesar with a fourth crown.

"A token of his regard from the King of Kings, great Caesar."

"King of Kings? Is that what Pharnaces has taken to calling himself?" Caesar asked, aping astonishment. "Tell your master that it's a title bodes ill for its holder. The last King of Kings was Tigranes, and look what Rome did to him in the person of Gnaeus Pompeius Magnus. Yet I defeated Pompeius Magnus, so what does that make me, Ambassador?"

"A mighty conqueror," said the ambassador, swallowing. Why didn't Romans look like mighty conquerors? No golden litter, no traveling harem of wives and concubines, no bodyguard of picked troops, no glittering garments. Caesar wore a plain steel cuirass with a red ribbon knotted around its lower chest, and looked, save for that ribbon, no different from a dozen others around him.

"Go back to your king, Ambassador, and tell him it's time he went home," said Caesar in businesslike tones. "But before he goes, I want sufficient gold bullion to pay for the damage he has done in Pontus and Armenia Parva. A thousand talents for Amisus, three thousand for the rest of those two countries. The gold will be used to repair his ravages, make no mistake. It is not for the Treasury of Rome."

He paused to turn his head and stare at Deiotarus. "However," he went on urbanely, "King Pharnaces was a client of Pompeius Magnus's, and did not honor his cliental obligations. Therefore I fine King Pharnaces two thousand gold talents for not honoring his cliental obligations, and that *will* go to the Treasury of Rome."

Deiotarus went purple, spluttered and choked, but said not a word. Did Caesar have no shame at all? Ready to punish Galatia for obeying its cliental obligations, equally ready to punish Cimmeria for *not* obeying its cliental obligations!

"If I do not hear from your king today, Ambassador, I will continue my advance across this beautiful valley."

"There isn't one-tenth that much gold in all of Cimmeria," said Calvinus, smothering his laughter at Deiotarus's outrage.

"You might be surprised, Gnaeus. Don't forget Cimmeria was an important part of the old king's realm, and he amassed whole mountains of gold. Not all of it was in those seventy fortresses Pompeius stripped bare in Armenia Parva."

"Did you hear him?" Deiotarus was squeaking to Brutus. *"Did you hear him?* A client-king can't do right, whichever course he elects! Oh, I don't believe his gall!"

"There, there," Brutus soothed. "It's his way of getting the money to pay for this war. He's right, he did have to burgle Rome's Treasury, which has to be paid back." The mournful eyes grew hard and minatory; Brutus stared at the King of Galatia like a father at a naughty son. "And you, Deiotarus, have to pay *me* back. I hope that's understood."

"And I hope you understand, Marcus Brutus, that when Caesar says ten percent simple interest, that's what he means!" Deiotarus said savagely. "That I'm willing to pay—if I keep my kingdom—but not one sestertius more. Do you want Matinius's books open to Caesar's auditors? And how do you think you can collect debts now that you can't commandeer legions for that purpose? The world has changed, Marcus Brutus, and the man who *dictates* how the new world will be run is not enamored of usurers, even among his own class. Ten percent simple interest—*if* I keep my kingdom. And keeping my kingdom may well depend upon how lyrically you and Gaius Cassius plead my cause at Nicomedia after we meet Pharnaces!"

* * *

Zela had taken Caesar's breath away. A high, rocky outcrop, it stood in the middle of a fifty-mile basin of springtime wheat as green as the emeralds in that crown, surrounded on all sides by soaring lilac mountains still covered in snow halfway down their sides, with the Scylax River, a broad, steely blue stream, winding from one side of the plain to the other.

The Cimmerian camp lay at the base of the outcrop, on top of which Pharnaces had put his command tents and harem; he had had a perfect view of the Roman snake as it had emerged from the northern pass, and sent his third crown. The ambassador returned after giving Caesar the fourth crown and delivered Caesar's message, but Pharnaces ignored it, convinced he was unbeatable. He watched Caesar put his legions and cavalry into a heavily fortified camp for the night, only a mile from his own lines.

At dawn Pharnaces attacked en masse; like his father and Tigranes before him, he couldn't believe that a smallish force, no matter how well organized, could withstand a hundred thousand warriors charging at it. He did better than Pompey at Pharsalus; his troops lasted four hours before they disintegrated. Just as in the early days in Belgic Gaul, the Skythians stayed to fight to the death, deeming it an unendurable disgrace to abandon a field of defeat alive.

"If Magnus's Anatolian foes were of this caliber," Caesar said to Calvinus, Pansa, Vinicianus and Cassius, "he doesn't deserve the epithet 'great.' It's no *great* task to beat them."

"I suppose the Gauls were infinitely *greater* adversaries," said Cassius between his teeth.

"Read my commentaries," Caesar said, smiling. "Bravery is not the issue. The Gauls owned two qualities today's adversaries don't have. First of all, they learned from their early mistakes. And secondly, they had an unquenchable patriotism that I had to work very hard to channel into avenues as useful to themselves as to Rome. But you did well, Cassius, led your legion like a true *vir militaris*. I'll have plenty of work for you in a few years, when I set out to deal with the Kingdom of the Parthians and bring our Eagles home. By then you'll have been consul, so you'll be one of my chief legates. I understand that you like waging war in dry places as well as on the sea."

This should have thrilled Cassius, but it angered him. He speaks as if it is all in his personal gift. What glory can there be in that for me, his minion?

The Great Man had wandered off to inspect the field, issue orders that mass graves be dug to bury the Skythians; there were too many to burn, even if Zela had owned any forests.

Pharnaces himself had fled, gathered his war chest and his treasures to gallop off northward, leaving the women of his harem dead. When Caesar was told, his only concern was for the women.

He donated the spoils to his legates, tribunes, centurions, legions and cavalry, declining to take the general's percentage; he had his crowns, they were enough. By the time the ceremony of dividing the spoils was over, the rankers found themselves ten thousand sesterces richer, and legates like Brutus and Cassius had amassed a hundred talents each. That was how much had lain around the Cimmerian camp, so who knew what Pharnaces had taken with him? Not that anybody received the money in his hand; it was an accounting exercise attended by elected representatives, for spoils were kept intact until they had been displayed in the general's triumph, after which the actual money was distributed.

Two days later the army marched for Pergamum, which greeted it with cheers and cascades of flowers. The threat of Pharnaces was no more, Asia Province could sleep peacefully. Though forty-two years had gone by, no one in Asia Province could forget the hundred thousand people Mithridates the Great had massacred when he invaded.

"I'll be sending Asia Province a very good governor as soon as I return to Rome," Caesar told Archelaus, the son of Mithridates of Pergamum, in a private interview. "He'll come knowing what has to be done to set the province on its feet. The days of the tax farming *publicani* are over for good. Each district will collect its own taxes and pay them directly to Rome after the five-year moratorium on taxes is over. However, none of that is why I asked to see you."

Caesar leaned forward, clasped his hands together on his desk. "I'll be writing to your father in Alexandria, yet Pergamum should know its fate now. I plan to shift the governor's seat to Ephesus—Pergamum is too far north, too out of things. So all of Pergamum will become the Kingdom of Pergamum, and be ruled as a client-state by your father. It won't be as large a realm as the one the last Attalus bequeathed to Rome in his will, but it will be larger than it currently is. I'm adding western Galatia, to give Pergamum sufficient land for growing and grazing. My feeling is that the provinces of Rome are becoming too bureaucratically necessary to Rome, perpetuating additional expenses from layers of middlemen and superfluous paperwork. Whenever I find a good, capable family of local citizens fit to rule a client-state, I shall create that client-state. You will pay taxes and tributes to Rome, but Rome won't have the bother of collection."

He cleared his throat. "There is a price. Namely, to hold Pergamum for Rome at all costs and against all foes. To remain not only Caesar's personal clients, but also the personal clients of Caesar's heir. To rule wisely and increase local prosperity for *all* your citizens, not merely the upper echelons."

"I've always known that my father is a wise man, Caesar," said the young man, amazed at this incredible gift, "but the wisest thing he ever did was to aid you. We are—oh, grateful is an inadequate word!"

"I'm not after gratitude," Caesar said crisply. "I'm after a more precious thing—loyalty."

From there it was north to Bithynia, the state along the southern shores of the Propontis, a vast lake forming a precursor to the mighty Euxine Sea, which filled it up through the straits of the Thracian Bosporus, upon which sat the ancient Greek city of Byzantium. The Propontis in its turn flowed south into the Aegean Sea through the straits of the Hellespont, thus linking the vast rivers of the Sarmatian and Skythian steppes with Our Sea.

Nicomedia lay upon a long, calm inlet of the Propontis that had the trick of forming a mirror for the world above it, from the cloud-puffed sky in its depths to the perfectly reversed images of trees, hills, people, animals—a place wherein the world seemed to go on as much below as above, like a miniature globe seen from its inside. To Caesar, it was one of the places he loved the most, for it was filled with heart-warming memories of an octogenarian king who wore a curled wig and elaborate face paint, kept an army of effeminate slaves to fulfill his every wish. No, they had never been lovers, the third King Nicomedes and Caesar! They had been something far better—dear friends. And big, booming old Queen Oradaltis, whose dog, Sulla, had bitten her on her behind the day a twenty-year-old Caesar had arrived. Their only child, Nysa, had been kidnaped by Mithridates the Great and held for years. Lucullus had freed her, aged fifty, and sent her back to her mother; the old king was dead then. When Rome made Bithynia a province, Caesar had diddled the governor, Juncus, by transferring Oradaltis's funds to a bank in Byzantium and moving her to a nice mansion in a fishing village on the Euxine coast. There Oradaltis and Nysa had lived out their days very happily, fishing with hand-lines from the pier and taking walks with their new dog, named Lucullus.

All dead now, of course. The palace he remembered so well had long been the governor's residence; its most priceless items had been removed by the first governor, Juncus, but the gilt and the purple marble were still in evidence. Juncus, Caesar reflected, had been the start of his determination to end gubernatorial peculations and looting.

Well, Verres first, but he had not been a governor. Verres was in a class all his own, as Cicero proved.

Men went out to govern provinces and make their fortunes at the expense of the provincials—sold the citizenship, sold tax exemptions, confiscated fortunes, regulated the grain prices, took every work of art they could put their hands on, took bribes from the *publicani* and loaned their lictors, even their troops, to Roman moneylenders collecting debts.

Juncus had done very well out of Bithynia, but some deity had taken offense at him or at his actions; he and his ill-gotten gains went to the bottom of Our Sea on the way home. Which does not put the statues and paintings back where they belong.

Oh, Caesar, you are old! That was another time, and the many memories playing around these walls have the shape and content of *lemures*, creatures of the underworld let loose two nights a year. Too much has happened far too fast. What Sulla did lives on, and Caesar is its latest victim. No man can be happy who has marched on his own country. Caesar's kindnesses are conscious, done for Caesar's benefit, and Caesar no longer sees the world as a place wherein magical things can occur. Because they can't. Men and women ruin it with their impulses, desires, thoughtlessness, lack of intelligence, cupidity. A Cato and a Bibulus can bring down good government. And a Caesar can get very tired of trying to put good government back together again. The Caesar who dueled wits with that naughty old king was a different man from this Caesar, who has become cold, cynical, utterly weary. This man has no passions. This man just wants to get through each day with his image unimpaired. This man grows dangerously close to being tired of the act of living. How can one man put Rome back together again? Especially a man who has turned fifty-three?

However, the days had to be gotten through, like it or not. One of Caesar's most promising protégés, Gaius Vibius Pansa, was appointed the governor of Bithynia; whereas, Caesar decided, for the moment Pontus should have its own governor rather than be ruled in tandem with Bithynia. He appointed another promising man, Marcus Coelius Vinicianus, governor of Pontus; it would be his task to repair the ravages of Pharnaces.

When the dispositions were finally completed, he shot the bolt on his study door and wrote letters: to Cleopatra and Mithridates of Pergamum in Alexandria, Publius Servilius Vatia Isauricus in Rome, Marcus Antonius his Master of the Horse, and, last but not least, to the oldest of his friends, Gaius Matius. They were the same age. Matius's father had rented the other ground-floor apartment of Aurelia's insula in the Subura, so the two boys had played together in the beautiful garden Matius's father had created at the bottom of the insula's light well. The son had inherited Matius Senior's genius for ornamental horticulture, and designed, in his nebulous spare time, Caesar's pleasure gardens across the Tiber. Matius had invented the art of topiary, and seized eagerly upon any chance to trim box and privet into birds, animals, wonderful shapes.

Caesar embarked upon this letter with his defenses down, for this recipient above all others had no axes to grind.

VENI, VIDI, VICI.

I came, I saw, I conquered. I am thinking of adopting that as my motto, it seems to happen so regularly, and the phrase itself is so succinct. At least this last episode of coming, seeing, and conquering has been against a foreigner.

Things in the East have been put right. What a mess! Thanks to rapacious governors and invading kings, Cilicia, Asia Province, Bithynia and Pontus are on their knees and groaning. I feel less sympathy for Syria. I've followed in the footsteps of that other dictator, Sulla—simply revived all his relief measures, which were remarkably perceptive. Since you're not in the tax farming business, my reforms in Asia Minor won't hurt you, but the fur will fly among the *publicani* and other Asian speculators when I reach Rome—I have clipped their wings back to stumps. Do I care? No, I do not. The trouble with Sulla was that he didn't know his political A B C. He resigned from his dictatorship without first making sure that his new constitution couldn't be overthrown. Believe me, Caesar won't make that mistake.

The last thing I want is a Senate stuffed with my own creatures, but I fear that is what must happen. You might think it sensible to have a compliant Senate, but it isn't, Matius, it isn't. While ever there is healthy political competition, the more feral among my adherents can be kept in order. But once governmental institutions are composed entirely of my own adherents, what is to stop a younger, more ambitious man than I from stepping over my carcass into the dictator's chair? Government must have opposition! What government does *not* need is the *boni,* who oppose for the sake of opposing, who don't understand what it is that they oppose. Therefore *boni* opposition was irrational, rather than soundly based in genuine, thoughtful analysis. Note that I switched to the past tense. The *boni* are no more, Africa Province will see to that. What I had hoped to see was the right kind of opposition: now I am afraid that all a civil war actually achieves is the murder of opposition. I am in a cleft stick.

From Tarsus onward I have had the dubious pleasure of the company of Marcus Junius Brutus and Gaius Cassius. Both now pardoned and working indefatigably for—themselves. No, not for Rome, and certainly not for Caesar. A potential healthy senatorial opposition, then? No, I fear not. Neither man cares more for his country than for his own personal agenda. Though being with that pair has had its entertaining side, and I have learned a lot about moneylending.

I have just concluded the rearrangement of Anatolia's client-kingdoms, chiefly Galatia and Cappadocia. Deiotarus needed a lesson, so I gave him one. Originally I had meant to pare Galatia back to a small area around Ancyra, but oh, oh, oh! Brutus suddenly roared like a lion and went to war to protect Deiotarus, who owes him millions upon millions. How *dare* I strip such a splendid fellow of three-quarters of his territories and turn a steady income into a permanent bad debt? Brutus just wouldn't have it. The eloquence, the rhetorical devices! Truly, Matius, had Cicero heard Brutus in full flight, he would have been tearing his hair out and gnashing his teeth in envy. With Cassius contributing his mite too, I add. They are more than mere brothers-in-law and old school chums.

In the end I let Deiotarus keep a great deal more than I had intended, but he lost western Galatia to the new client-kingdom of Pergamum, and Armenia Parva to Cappadocia. Brutus may not want much, but what he does want, he wants desperately. Namely, the preservation of his fortune.

Brutus's motives are as clear as Anatolian spring water, but Cassius is a far murkier individual. Arrogant, conceited and hugely ambitious. I shall never forgive him for that scurrilous report he sent back to Rome after Crassus died at Carrhae, extolling his own virtues and turning poor Crassus into nothing more than a money-grubber. I admit his weakness for money, but he was genuinely a great man.

What irked Cassius about my client-kingdom arrangements was that I did them by my dictate—without any debates in the House, without any laws on the tablets, without considering anybody's wishes save my own. In that respect it is terrific to be the Dictator—saves huge amounts of time in dealing with matters I know I've fixed in exactly the fairest and most proper way. But it doesn't please Cassius. Or put it this way: it would only please Cassius if *he* were the Dictator.

I am the father of a son. The Queen of Egypt presented me with a boy last June. Naturally he isn't a Roman, but his destiny is to rule Egypt, so I'm not complaining. As for the mother of my boy—meet her and decide for yourself. She insists upon coming to Rome after the Republicans—what a misnomer!—have gone down to final defeat. Her agent, one Ammonius, is going to come to you and ask that she be granted a tract of land next door to my Janiculan gardens, thereon to build a palace for her stay in Rome. When you deal with the conveyancing, put it in my name, though she can pay for it.

I have no intention of divorcing Calpurnia to marry her. That would be too churlish. Piso's daughter has been an exemplary wife. I may not have been in Rome for more than a few days since shortly after I married her, but I have my spies. Calpurnia is all that Caesar's wife must be—above suspicion. A nice girl.

I know I sound hard, a trifle facetious, somewhat cagey. But I have changed out of all recognition, Matius. It is not meet that a man should rise so far above his equals that he has no equal, and I fear that that is what has happened to me. The very men who might have given me a run for my money are all dead. Publius Clodius. Gaius Curio. Marcus Crassus. Pompeius Magnus. I feel like the lighthouse on Pharos—nothing stands half so tall. Which is not the way I would have it, did I have a choice.

When I crossed the Rubicon into Italy and marched on Rome, something broke in me. It isn't fair that they should have pushed me into that—did they genuinely think I would not march? I am Caesar, my *dignitas* is dearer to me than my very life. Caesar, to be convicted of a nonexistent treason and sent into an irreversible exile? Unthinkable. If I had it all to do again, I would do it all again. Yet something in me broke. I can never be what I wanted to be—consul for the second time in my year, Pontifex Maximus, elder statesman whose opinion is asked for first in the House after the consuls-elect and the consuls, Military Man without peer.

Now I am a god in Ephesus and a god in Egypt, I am Dictator of Rome and ruler of the world. But they are not my choice. You know me well enough to understand what I am saying. Few men do. They interpret my motives in the light of what their own motives would be were they in my place.

It came as a grievous shock to hear of Aulus Gabinius's death in Salona. A good man exiled for a wrong cause. Old Ptolemy

Auletes didn't have ten thousand talents to pay him, I doubt Gabinius ever got more than two thousand for the job. If Lentulus Spinther had gotten off his arse in Cilicia quickly enough to beat Gabinius to that particular contract, would *he* have been prosecuted? Of course not! He was *boni*, whereas Gabinius voted for Caesar. That is what has to stop, Matius—one law for one man, another law for another man.

On one subject my *inimicus* Gaius Cassius remains silent. When I told him that his brother Quintus had raped Further Spain, loaded his plunder on a ship and sailed for Rome before Gaius Trebonius arrived to govern, Cassius said not one word. Nor when I told him that the ship, very overloaded, capsized and sank in the Iberus estuary, and Quintus Cassius was drowned. I am not sure whether Gaius Cassius's silence is due to the fact that Quintus was my man, or that Quintus made the Cassii look bad.

I shall be in Rome around the end of September.

Caesar had written one letter from Zela straight after the battle, and sent it to Asander in Cimmeria. It repeated what the ambassador had been told: that Cimmeria owed Pontus four thousand gold talents, and the Treasury of Rome two thousand more. It also informed Asander that his father had fled to Sinope, apparently en route for home.

Just before Caesar left Nicomedia, he received an answer from Asander. It thanked him for his consideration, and was pleased to be able to tell Caesar Dictator that Pharnaces, having arrived in Cimmeria, had been put to death. Asander was now King of Cimmeria, and most desirous of being enrolled in Caesar's clientele. As evidence of good faith, the missive was accompanied by two thousand talents of gold; four thousand more had been sent to the new governor of Pontus, Vinicianus.

So when Caesar sailed down through the Hellespont, his ship held seven thousand talents of gold and a great number of crowns.

His first stop was the island of Samos, where he sought out one of the more moderate among his opponents, the great patrician consular Servius Sulpicius Rufus, who greeted him with pleasure and confessed that he was as unhappy as he was penitent.

"We wronged you, Caesar, and I am sorry for that. Sincerely, I never dreamed that matters would go so far," Sulpicius said.

"It wasn't your fault that they did. What I hope is that you'll return to Rome and resume your seat in the Senate. Not to suck up to me, but to consider my laws and measures in the light of their intrinsic worth."

Here on Samos, Caesar lost Brutus, whom Caesar had promised a priesthood; as Servius Sulpicius was a great authority on priestly law and procedure, Brutus wanted to stay and study with the expert. Caesar's only regret in leaving him behind was that he still had Gaius Cassius.

From Samos he sailed to Lesbos, where sat a far more obdurate opponent, the consular Marcus Claudius Marcellus. Who vehemently rebuffed all Caesar's overtures.

The next stop was Athens, which had been ardently Pompeian in its sympathies; it did not fare well at Caesar's hands. He imposed a huge fine, then spent most of his time in taking a trip to Corinth, on the isthmus dividing the Greek mainland from the Peloponnese. Gaius Mummius had sacked it generations before, and Corinth had never recovered. Caesar poked through its deserted buildings, climbed the great rearing citadel of the Akrocorinth; Cassius, ordered to accompany him, couldn't make out why the Great Man was so fascinated.

"The place is begging for a canal through the isthmus," the Great Man remarked, standing on the narrow spit of solid rock high above the water. "If there were a canal, ships wouldn't have to sail around Cape Taenarum at the mercy of its storms. They could go straight from Patrae to the Aegean. Hmmm."

"Impossible!" Cassius snorted. "You'd have to cut down two hundred and more feet."

"Nothing is impossible," Caesar said mildly. "As for the old city, it's begging for new settlers. Gaius Marius wanted to repopulate it with veterans from his legions."

"And failed," said Cassius shortly. He kicked at a stone, watched it bounce. "I'm planning to stay in Athens."

"I'm afraid not, Gaius Cassius. You'll go to Rome with me."

"Why?" Cassius demanded, stiffening.

"Because, my dear fellow, you're not an admirer of Caesar, and nor is Athens. I think it prudent to keep the pair of you well apart. No, don't flounce off, hear me out."

Feet already turned to walk away, Cassius paused, turned back warily. Think, Cassius, think! You may hate him, but he rules.

"I have a mind to advance you and Brutus, not because it is in my gift, but because both of you would have been praetors and consuls in or close to your year, therefore that should happen," Caesar said, holding Cassius's eyes. "Stop resenting me when you should be offering thanks to the gods that I am a merciful man. If I were Sulla, you'd be dead, Cassius. Convert your misdirected energies into the right channels and be of good use to Rome. I don't matter, you don't matter. *Rome* matters."

"Do you swear on your newborn son's head that you have no ambition to be the King of Rome?"

"I swear it," said Caesar. "King of Rome? I'd as soon be one of those mad hermits living in a cave above the Palus Asphaltites. Now look at the problem again, Cassius, and look at it dispassionately. A canal *is* possible."

IV

THE MASTER OF THE HORSE

From the end of SEPTEMBER to the end of
DECEMBER of 47 B.C.

MARCUS ANTONIUS

The Sixth Legion and the German cavalry had been sent from Pergamum to Ephesus to form the nucleus of Asia Province's army, so when Caesar set foot on Italian soil on Pompey the Great's birthday, he had only Decimus Carfulenus and a century of foot with him. As well as Aulus Hirtius, Gaius Cassius, his aide Gaius Trebatius, and a handful of other legates and tribunes all desirous of resuming their public careers. Carfulenus and his century were there to guard the gold, in need of an escort.

The winds had blown them around the heel to Tarentum, most vexatious! Had they landed as planned in Brundisium, Caesar could have seen Marcus Cicero with no inconvenience; as it was, he had to instruct the others to proceed up the Via Appia without him, and set out himself to backtrack to Brundisium in a fast gig.

As luck would have it, the four mules hadn't covered very many miles when they encountered a litter ambling toward them; Caesar whooped in delight. Cicero, it had to be Cicero! Who else would use a conveyance as slow as a litter in this kind of early summer heat wave? The gig drew up with a clatter, Caesar down from it before it stopped moving. He strode to the litter to find Cicero hunched over a portable writing table. For a moment Cicero gaped, then squawked and scrambled out.

"Caesar!"

"Come, walk with me a little."

The two old adversaries strolled off down the baking road in silence until they were out of earshot, then Caesar stopped to face Cicero, his eyes busy. Such terrible changes! Not so much to Cicero's exterior, though that was much thinner, more lined; to the spirit, showing nakedly in the fine, intelligent brown eyes, gone a little rheumy. Here is another who simply wanted to be an eminent consular, an elder statesman, censor perhaps, asked for his opinion early in the House debates. Like me, it's no longer possible. Too much water has flowed under the bridge.

"How has it been?" Caesar asked, throat tight.

"Ghastly," said Cicero without prevarication. "I've been stuck in Brundisium for a year, Terentia won't send me any money, Dolabella has dumped Tullia, and the poor girl had such a falling out with her mother that she fled to me. Her health is poor, and—why, I don't know!—she still loves Dolabella."

"Go to Rome, Marcus. In fact, I very much want you to take your seat in the Senate again. I need all the decent opposition I can get."

[223]

Cicero bridled. "Oh, I couldn't do *that!* I'd be seen as giving in to you."

A huge rush of blood; lips tightening, Caesar reined his temper in. "Well, let us not discuss it at the moment. Just pack your things and take Tullia to a more salubrious climate. Stay in one of your beautiful Campanian villas. Write a little. Think about things. Patch up matters with Terentia."

"Terentia? That's beyond patching up," Cicero said bitterly. "Would you believe that she's threatening to leave all her money to strangers? When she has a son and a daughter to provide for?"

"Dogs, cats or a temple?" Caesar asked gravely.

Cicero spluttered. "To leave her money to any of those, she would need a heart! I believe that her choice has fallen on persons dedicated to the—er—'wisdom of the East,' or some such. Tchah!"

"Oh, dear. Has she espoused Isis?"

"Terentia, put a whip to her own back? Not likely!"

They talked a little longer, keeping the subject to nothing in particular. Caesar gave Cicero what news of the two Quintuses he had, rather surprised that neither had yet turned up in Italy. Cicero told him that Atticus and his wife, Pilia, were very well, their daughter growing heartbreakingly fast. They moved then to affairs in Rome, but Cicero was reluctant to speak of troubles he clearly blamed on Caesar.

"What besides debt has bitten Dolabella?" Caesar asked.

"How would I know? Except that he's taken up with Aesopus's son, and the fellow is a shockingly bad influence."

"A tragic actor's son? Dolabella keeps low company."

"Aesopus," said Cicero with dignity, "happens to be a good friend of mine. Dolabella's company isn't *low,* it's just bad."

Caesar gave up, returned to his gig, and headed for Rome.

His cousin and dearest friend, Lucius Julius Caesar, met him at Philippus's villa near Misenum, not so very far from Rome. Seven years older than Caesar, Lucius looked a great deal like him in face and physique, though his eyes were a softer, kinder blue.

"You know, of course, that Dolabella has been agitating all year for a general cancellation of debts, and that an amazingly capable pair of tribunes of the plebs have opposed him adamantly?" Lucius asked as they settled to talk.

"Ever since I got out of Egypt. Asinius Pollio and Lucius Trebellius, two of my men."

"Two very good men! Though they take their lives in their hands every time, they keep vetoing Dolabella's bill in the Plebeian Assembly. Dolabella thought to cow them by reviving Publius Clodius's street gangs, added some ex-gladiators, and began to terrorize the Forum. It made no difference to Pollio and Trebellius, who are still vetoing."

"And your nephew and my cousin, Marcus Antonius, my Master of the Horse?" asked Caesar.

"Antonius is a wolfshead, Gaius. Indolent, gluttonous, bad-mannered, priapic, and a drunkard to boot."

"I am aware of his history, Lucius. But I had thought, given his good behavior during the war against Magnus, that he'd grown out of his bad habits."

"He will never grow out of his bad habits!" Lucius snapped. "Antonius's answer to the mushrooming violence in Rome was to quit the city and go elsewhere to—how did he put it?—'supervise affairs in Italy.' His idea of supervision consists in litters full of mistresses, wagons full of wine, a chariot harnessed to a quartet of lionesses, a retinue of dwarves, mummers, magicians and dancers, and an orchestra of Thracian Pan pipers and pitty-pat drummers—he fancies himself the new Dionysus!"

"The fool! I warned him," Caesar said softly.

"If you did, then he paid you no heed. Late in March word came from Capua that the legions camped there were restive, so Antonius set off with his circus to Capua, where, as far as I can gather, he's still conferring with the legions six months later. No sooner had he left Rome than Dolabella stepped up the violence. Then Pollio and Trebellius sent Publius Sulla and plain Valerius Messala to see you in person—you haven't seen them?"

"No. Continue, Lucius."

"Matters grew steadily worse. Two *nundinae* ago the Senate passed its Senatus Consultum Ultimum and ordered Antonius to deal with the situation in Rome. He took his time about responding, but when he did, what he did was unspeakable. Four days ago he marched the Tenth Legion from Capua straight into the Forum and ordered them to attack the rioters. Gaius, they drew their swords and waded into men armed only with cudgels! Eight hundred of them were killed. Dolabella called off his demonstrations immediately, but Antonius ignored him. Instead, he left the Forum reeking and sent some of the Tenth to round up a few men he called the ringleaders—on whose say-so, I have no idea. About fifty altogether, including twenty Roman citizens. He flogged and beheaded the non-citizens, and threw the citizens off the Tarpeian Rock. Then, having added those bodies to the total, Antonius marched the Tenth back to Capua."

Caesar's face was white, his fists clenched. "I've heard none of this," he said.

"I'm sure you haven't, though the news of it is all over the entire country. But who would tell Caesar Dictator, except me?"

"Where is Dolabella?"

"Still in Rome, but lying low."

"And Antonius?"

"Still in Capua. He says the legions are mutinous."

"And government, apart from Pollio and Trebellius?"

"Nonexistent. You've been away too long, Gaius, and you did too little in Rome before you left. *Eighteen months!* While Vatia Isauricus was consul things rubbed along fairly well, but this has not been a year to leave Rome without consuls or praetors, and so I tell you straight! Neither Vatia nor Lepidus has any authority, and Lepidus is a weakling into the bargain. From the moment that Antonius brought the legions back from Macedonia, the trouble started. He and Dolabella—what bosom friends they used to be!—seem determined to wreck Rome so effectively that even you won't be able to pick up the pieces—and if you can't pick up the pieces, Gaius, they'll fight it out to the finish to see which one of them will be the next dictator."

"Is that what they're after?" Caesar asked.

Lucius Caesar got to his feet and paced the room, his face grim. "Why," he demanded, spinning suddenly to confront Caesar, still sitting, "have you been away so long, cousin? It's unconscionable! Dallying in the arms of some Oriental temptress, boating down rivers, focusing your attention on the wrong end of Our Sea—Gaius, it is a year since Magnus died! *Where have you been?* Your place is in Rome!"

No one else could have said this to him, as Caesar well knew; no doubt Vatia, Lepidus, Philippus, Pollio, Trebellius and all those left in Rome had deliberately given the mission to the one man Caesar couldn't lash back at. His friend and ally of many years, Lucius Julius Caesar, consular, Chief Augur, loyalest legate of the Gallic War. So he listened courteously until Lucius Caesar ran down, then lifted his hands in a gesture of defense.

"Even I can't be in two places at one and the same moment," he said, keeping his voice level and detached. "Of course I knew how much work I had to do in Rome, and of course I realized that Rome must come first. But I was faced with two alternatives, Lucius, and I still believe that I chose the correct one. Either I left the eastern end of

Our Sea to become a hornet's nest of intrigue, Republican resistance, barbarian conquests and absolute anarchy, or I remained there and tidied the place because I just happened to be there when it all erupted. I decided to stay in the East, believing that Rome would survive until I could get home. My mistake is obvious now: I trusted Marcus Antonius too much. He can be so competent, Lucius, that's the most exasperating part of it! What did Julia Antonia do to those three boys, between her megrims and her vapors, her disastrous choice of husbands, and her inability to keep a properly Roman household? As you say, Marcus is a drunken, priapic wolfshead. Gaius is inept enough to qualify as a mental defective, and Lucius is so sly that he never lets his left hand know what his right is doing."

Blue eyes looked into blue; both pairs crinkled up. Family! The curse of every man.

"However, I am here now, Lucius. This won't happen again. Nor am I too late. If Antonius and Dolabella think to fight for the dictatorship over my corpse, they have another think coming. Caesar Dictator is not about to oblige them by dying."

"I do see your point about the East," Lucius said, a little mollified, "but don't let Antonius charm you, Gaius. You have a soft spot for him, but he's gone too far this time." He frowned. "There's something peculiar going on with the legions, and I know in my bones that my nephew is at the bottom of it. He won't allow anyone else in their vicinity."

"Have they reason to be discontented? Cicero hinted that they haven't been paid."

"I assume they have been, because I know Antonius took silver from the Treasury to mint into coin. Perhaps they're bored? They are your Gallic veterans. Pompeius Magnus's Spanish veterans are there too," Lucius Caesar said. "Inaction can't please them."

"They'll have work enough to do in Africa Province as soon as I've attended to Rome," Caesar said, and got to his feet. "We start for Rome this moment, Lucius. I want to enter the Forum at the crack of dawn."

"One other thing, Gaius," Lucius said as they left the room. "Antonius has moved into Pompeius Magnus's palace on the Carinae."

Caesar stopped in his tracks. "On whose authority?"

"His own, as Master of the Horse. He said his old house was too small for his needs."

"Did he now," said Caesar, moving again. "How old is he?"

"Thirty-six."

"Old enough to know better."

* * *

Every time Caesar comes back, Rome looks shabbier. Is it that Caesar visits so many other cities, cities planned and built by architecturally sophisticated Greeks who aren't afraid to rip things apart in the name of progress? Whereas we Romans revere antiquity and ancestors, cannot bear to demolish a public edifice simply because it's outgrown its function. For all her great size, she's not a glamorous lady, poor Roma. Her heart beats down in the bottom of a damp gulch that by rights should end in the swamps of the Palus Ceroliae, but doesn't because the rocky ridge of the Velia cuts clear across from Esquiline to Palatine, thereby turning the heart into a pond of its own. Did the Cloaca Maxima not flow directly beneath it, a pond it definitely would be. The paint is peeling everywhere, the temples on the Capitol are dingy, even Jupiter Optimus Maximus. As for Juno Moneta—how many centuries is it since anyone has refurbished her? The vapors from the mint in her basement are wreaking havoc. Nothing is well planned or laid out, it's an ancient jumble. Though Caesar is trying to improve it with his own privately funded projects! The truth is that Rome is exhausted from these decades of civil war. It cannot go on thus, it has to stop.

His eyes hadn't the leisure to seek out the public works he had begun seven years ago: the Forum Julium next door to the Forum Romanum, the Basilica Julia in the lower Forum Romanum where the two old basilicas Opimia and Sempronia used to be, the new Curia for the Senate, the Senate offices next door.

No, his eyes were too busy taking in the rotting bodies, the fallen statues, wrecked altars, desecrated nooks and crannies. The Ficus Ruminalis was scarred, two other sacred trees had their lower limbs splintered, and the Pool of Curtius was fouled by blood. Above, on the first rise of the Capitol, the doors to Sulla's Tabularium gaped wide, broken shards of stone littered around them.

"Did he make no attempt to clean up the mess?" Caesar asked.

"None," said Lucius.

"Nor has anyone else, apparently."

"The ordinary people have been too afraid to venture here, and the Senate didn't want the public slaves to take the bodies away until relatives had had a chance to reclaim them," Lucius said unhappily. "It's one more symptom of lack of government, Gaius. Who takes charge when there's no *praetor urbanus* or aediles?"

Caesar turned to his chief secretary, standing green-faced with a handkerchief plastered to his nose. "Faberius, go to the Port of Rome and offer a thousand sesterces to any man who's willing to cart putrefying bodies," he said curtly. "I want every corpse out of here by dusk, and they all go to the lime pits on the Campus Esquilinus. Though they were unjustifiably butchered, they were also rioters and malcontents. If their families haven't claimed them yet, too bad."

Desperately anxious to be elsewhere, Faberius hurried off.

"Coponius, find the superviser of the public slaves and tell him I want the entire Forum washed and scrubbed tomorrow," Caesar ordered another secretary; he blew through his nose, a sound of disgust. "This is the worst kind of sacrilege—it's senseless."

He walked between the temple of Concord and the little old Senaculum, and bent to examine the fragments lying around the Tabularium doors. "Barbarians!" he snarled. "Look at these, for pity's sake! Some of our oldest laws on stone, broken as fine as mosaic. Which is what we'll have to do—hire workers in that art to put the tablets back together again. I'll have Antonius's balls for this! Where is he?"

"Here comes one who might be able to answer that," Lucius said, watching the approach of a sturdy individual in a purple-bordered toga.

"Vatia!" Caesar cried, holding out his right hand.

Publius Servilius Vatia Isauricus came from a great plebeian family of noblemen, and was the son of Sulla's loyalest adherent; the father had prospered while ever Sulla's constitution remained in place, and was so wily that he managed to continue to prosper after it fell; he was still alive, retired to a country villa. That the son should choose to follow Caesar was something of a mystery to those who assessed Roman noblemen according to their family's political leanings—the Servilii Vatiae were extremely conservative, as indeed had Sulla been. This particular Vatia, however, had a gambling streak; he had fancied Caesar, the outside horse in the race for power, and was clever enough to know that Caesar was no demagogue, no political adventurer.

Grey eyes sparkling, lean face grinning, Vatia took Caesar's hand in both his own, wrung it fervently. "Thank the gods that you're back!"

"Come, walk with us. Where are Pollio and Trebellius?"

"On their way. We didn't expect you half so early."

"And Marcus Antonius?"

"He's in Capua, but sent word that he's coming to Rome."

They ended their tour at the massive bronze doors in the side of the very tall podium supporting the temple of Saturn, wherein lay the Treasury. After a very long, pounding assault, one leaf of the door finally opened a crack to reveal the frightened face of Marcus Cuspius, *tribunus aerarius*.

"Answering in person, Cuspius?" Caesar asked.

"Caesar!" The door was flung wide. "Come in, come in!"

"I can't see why you were so terrified, Cuspius," Caesar said as he walked up the dimly lit passageway leading to the offices. "The place is as empty as a bowel after an enema." He stuck his head into a small room, frowning. "Even the sixteen hundred pounds of *laserpicium* are gone. Who's been busy with the clyster?"

Cuspius did not pretend to be dense. "Marcus Antonius, Caesar. He has the authority as Master of the Horse, and he said he had to pay the legions."

"All I took to pay for a *war* were thirty million sesterces in minted coins and ten thousand silver talents in sows. That left twenty thousand talents of silver and fifteen thousand talents of gold," Caesar said evenly. "Sufficient to tide Rome over, I would have thought, were there two hundred legions to pay. More to the point, I had some rough calculations in my head that took into account what I estimated would be in the Treasury when I inspected it. I did not expect it to be empty."

"The gold is still here, Caesar," Marcus Cuspius said nervously. "I shifted it to the other side. A thousand talents of the silver were commissioned as coin during the consulship of Publius Servilius Vatia."

"Yes, I coined," Vatia said, "but only four million were put into circulation. The bulk came back here."

"I did try for some facts and figures, truly!"

"No one is blaming you, Cuspius. However, while the Dictator is in Italy, no one is to remove one sestertius unless he is present, is that clear?"

"Yes, Caesar, very clear!"

"You may expect a shipment of seven thousand talents of gold and a great many gold crowns the day after tomorrow. The gold is the property of the Treasury, and will be stamped thus. Hold the crowns against my Asian triumph. Good day to you."

Cuspius shut the door and sagged against it, gasping.

"What is Antonius up to?" Vatia asked the Caesars.

"I intend to find out," said Caesar Dictator.

Publius Cornelius Dolabella came from an old patrician family that had sunk into decay, a not uncommon story. Like another Cornelian, Sulla, Dolabella lived on his wits and little else. He had been a charter member of the old Clodius Club during the days when Clodius and his equally wild young cronies had set the more prudish elements of Rome by the ears with their scandalous goings-on. But almost seven years had elapsed since Milo had met Clodius on the Via Appia and murdered him, which had marked the disintegration of the club.

Some Clodius Clubbers went on to enjoy distinguished public careers: Gaius Scribonius Curio, for instance, had been Caesar's brilliant tribune of the plebs and was killed in battle just when his star was in ascendancy; Decimus Junius Brutus Albinus, always known as Decimus Brutus, had graduated from generaling Clodius's street gangs to generaling for Caesar with even greater genius, and was at present governing Long-haired Gaul; and, of course, Mark Antony had done so splendidly under Caesar that he was now the second-ranking man in Rome, the Dictator's Master of the Horse.

Whereas nothing grand had happened for Dolabella, who always seemed to be somewhere else when Caesar was handing the good jobs out, though he had declared for Caesar the moment the Rubicon was known to be a fact.

In many ways he and Mark Antony were very alike—big, burly, obnoxiously egotistical, loud-mouthed. Where they differed was in style; Dolabella was smoother. Both were chronically impoverished, both had married for money; Antony to the daughter of a rich provincial, and Dolabella to Fabia, the ex–Chief Vestal Virgin. The rich provincial died in an epidemic, Fabia proved too long a virgin to be a satisfactory wife, but the two men had emerged from their first essays into marriage considerably wealthier. Then Antony married Antonia, his own first cousin, daughter of the revolting Antonius Hybrida; she was as famous as her father for torturing slaves, but Antony soon beat it out of her. Whereas Dolabella had married the second time for love, to Cicero's quite bewitching daughter, Tullia—and what a letdown that had been!

While Antony worked as a senior legate for Caesar, commanding the embarkation in Brundisium and then in the field in Macedonia and Greece, Dolabella commanded a fleet in the Adriatic and was defeated so ignominiously that Caesar never bothered with him again. In fairness to Dolabella, his ships had been tubs and the Republican fleet composed of Liburnians, the best combat ships of all. But did Caesar take that into account? No. So while Mark Antony soared ever upward, Publius Dolabella moped aimlessly.

His situation became desperate. Fabia's fortune had long gone, and the dowry installments he had thus far received from Cicero never seemed to last one drip of the water clock. Living the same kind of life as Antony (if on a more modest scale), Dolabella's debts piled up and up. The moneylenders to whom the thirty-six-year-old rake owed millions began to dun him so persistently and unpleasantly that he hardly dared show his face in the better parts of Rome.

Then, at about the moment that Caesar vanished from the face of the earth in Egypt, Dolabella realized that the answer to his woes had been staring at him for years; he would take an example from Publius Clodius, founder of the Clodius Club, and seek election as a tribune of the plebs. Like Clodius, Dolabella was a patrician, and therefore not eligible to stand for this most eye- and ear-catching of public offices. But Clodius had gotten around disbarment by having himself adopted by a plebeian. Dolabella found a lady named Livia, and proceeded to have her adopt him. Now a bona fide plebeian, he could run for election.

Dolabella wasn't interested in using the office to cement political fame; he intended to legislate a general cancellation of debts. Given the current crisis, it wasn't as straw-plucking as it sounded. Groaning under the privations a civil war always brought in its train, Rome was filled with debt-ridden individuals and companies only too anxious to find a way out of their predicament that did not involve the payment of money. Dolabella ran on a platform of the general cancellation of debts, and came in at the top of the poll. He had been given a mandate.

What he hadn't taken into account were two other tribunes of the plebs, Gaius Asinius Pollio and Lucius Trebellius, who had the gall to veto him during the first *contio* he called to discuss his measure. *Contio* after *contio*, Pollio and Trebellius vetoed.

Dolabella reached into his grab bag of Clodian tricks and pulled out the street gang; the next thing the Forum Romanum was rocked by a wave of terror that ought to have driven Pollio and Trebellius into a self-imposed exile. It did not. They remained in the Forum, they remained on the rostra, they remained adamant. Veto, veto, veto. No general cancellation of debts.

March came, and the stalemate in the Plebeian Assembly continued. Until now Dolabella had kept his gangs under some degree of control, but clearly worse violence was needed. Knowing Mark Antony of old, Dolabella knew perfectly well that Antony was even more heavily in debt; it was very much in Antony's interests to see the general cancellation of debts pass into law.

"But the thing is, my dear Antonius, that I can't very well let my bully-boys loose in a *serious* way while the Dictator's Master of the Horse is in the neighborhood," Dolabella explained over a bucket or two of fortified wine.

Antony's curly auburn head went down; he burped hugely and

grinned. "Actually, Dolabella, the legions around Capua are restive, so I really ought to hie myself down there and do some investigating," he said. He pursed his lips to touch the tip of his nose, an easy trick for Antony. "It may well be that I'll find the situation so *serious* that I'll be stuck in Capua for—um—as long as it takes for you to pass your legislation."

And so it was arranged. Antony proceeded to Capua on his rightful business as Master of the Horse, while Dolabella unleashed havoc in the Forum Romanum. Trebellius and Pollio were physically mauled by the gangs, savagely manhandled, drubbed unmercifully; but, like other tribunes of the plebs before them, they refused to be intimidated. Every time Dolabella called a *contio* in the Plebeian Assembly, Pollio and Trebellius were there to veto, sporting black eyes and bandages, but also being cheered. The Forum frequenters loved courage, and the gangs were not made up of Forum frequenters.

Unfortunately for Dolabella, he couldn't possibly allow his bully-boys to kill—or even half kill—Pollio and Trebellius. They were Caesar's men, and Caesar would return. Nor would Caesar be in favor of a general cancellation of debts. Pollio in particular was dear to Caesar's heart; he had been there when the old boy crossed the Rubicon, and was busy writing a history of the last twenty years.

What Dolabella hadn't expected was a militant surge of strength on the part of the Senate, not populous enough these days to form a quorum. Knowing this, Dolabella had entirely dismissed the senior governing body from his calculations. And then what did Vatia Isauricus do? Called the Senate into session and forced it to pass the Senatus Consultum Ultimum! Tantamount to martial law. None other than Mark Antony was directed to end violence in the Forum. After waiting vainly for six months for the general cancellation of debts, Antony was fed up. Without bothering to warn Dolabella, he brought the Tenth into the Forum and set them loose on the gangs—and hapless Forum frequenters caught in the eye of the storm. Just who the men were Antony executed, Dolabella had no idea, and could only presume that Antony—typical!—simply grabbed the first fifty he saw in the alleyways of the Velabrum. Dolabella had always known that Antony was a butcher—and that he would never implicate one of his own class and inclinations.

Now here was Caesar back in Rome. Publius Cornelius Dolabella found himself summoned to the Domus Publica to see the Dictator.

It was Caesar's position as Pontifex Maximus that entitled him to live in the closest public building to a palace that Rome owned. Improved and enhanced first by Ahenobarbus Pontifex Maximus and then by Caesar Pontifex Maximus, it was a huge structure at the very center of the Forum, and had a peculiar dichotomy: on one side lived the six Vestal Virgins, on the other side the Pontifex Maximus. One of Rome's highest priest's duties was to supervise the Vestals, who didn't live an enclosed life, but whose intact hymens represented Rome's public well-being—indeed, Rome's luck. Inducted at six or seven years of age, a girl served for thirty years, then was free to go into the community at large, even marry if she so desired. As had Fabia, to Dolabella. Their religious duties were not onerous, but they also served as the custodians of Roman citizen wills, and at the time that Caesar returned to Rome, this meant that they had upward of three million documents on hand, all meticulously filed, numbered, regionalized. For even the poorest Roman citizens were prone to make a will, lodge it with the Vestals no matter whereabouts in the world they lived. Once the Vestals took your will, you knew it was sacrosanct, that no one would ever get their hands on it until came proof of death—and the person authorized to probate it.

Thus when Dolabella presented himself at the Domus Publica, he went not to the Vestal side, nor to the ornate main entrance with the new temple pediment Caesar had erected over it (the Domus Publica was an inaugurated temple), but to the private door of the Pontifex Maximus.

All the old folk from the days of Aurelia's insula in the Subura were dead, including Burgundus and his wife, Cardixa, but their sons and daughters-in-law still administered Caesar's many properties. The third of them, Gaius Julius Trogus, was in the steward's quarters at the Domus Publica, and admitted Dolabella with a slight bow. This brought his head down to the visitor's; a tall man, Dolabella wasn't used to being made to feel small, but Trogus dwarfed him.

Caesar was in his study, clad in the glory of his pontifical robes, a significant fact, Dolabella knew, but why escaped him. Both toga and tunic were striped in alternating bands of purple and crimson; in this room, brightly lit from a window and myriad lamps, the magnificent raiment echoed the color scheme of crimson and purple, its plastered cornices and ceiling touched with gilt.

"Sit down," Caesar said curtly, dropping the scroll he was reading to pin Dolabella on those awful eyes, cold, piercing, not quite human. "What have you to say for yourself, Publius Cornelius Dolabella?"

"That things got out of hand," Dolabella said frankly.

"You recruited gangs to terrorize the city."

"No, no!" Dolabella said earnestly, his blue eyes wide and innocent. "Truly, Caesar, the gangs were not my doing! I simply promulgated legislation for a general cancellation of debts, and the moment I did so, I discovered that most of Rome was so badly in debt people were desperate for it. My proposed bill gathered a following in much the same way as—as a snowball rolling down the Clivus Victoriae."

"Had you not proposed this irresponsible legislation, Publius Dolabella, it would never have snowed," said Caesar without humor. "Are your own debts so massive?"

"Yes."

"So your measure was intrinsically selfish."

"I suppose so. Yes."

"Did it not occur to you, Publius Dolabella, that the two members of your tribunician college who opposed the measure were not about to let you legislate?"

"Yes. Yes, of course."

"Then what was your tribunician duty?"

Dolabella blinked. "Tribunician duty?"

"I can see where your patrician birth must make it difficult for you to understand plebeian matters, Publius Dolabella, but you do have some small political experience. You must have known what your duty was once Gaius Pollio and Lucius Trebellius proved so obdurate in vetoing."

"Er—no."

The eyes never seemed to blink, they just kept boring into Dolabella's mind like two painful drills. "Persistence is a most admirable virtue, Publius Dolabella, but it goes only so far. When two of your own college members veto your every *contio* for three months, the message is plain. You withdraw your proposed legislation as unacceptable. Whereas you kept it going for *ten months*! There's not a scrap of use sitting there looking like a penitent child, either. Whether or not you were responsible for the organization of street gangs in the old Clodius manner or not, once they existed you were very happy to take full advantage of them—including standing by while they physically assaulted two men who are protected by the old plebeian tenets of inviolability and sacrosanctity. Marcus Antonius threw twenty of your fellow Roman citizens off the Tarpeian Rock, but not one of them was a hundredth as guilty as you are, Publius Dolabella. By rights I ought to order the same fate for you. So, for that matter, should Marcus Antonius, who had to know who was responsible. You and my Master of the Horse have been holding each other's pricks to piss for twenty years."

A silence fell; Dolabella sat with teeth clenched, feeling the sweat on his brow, praying the drops didn't roll into his eyes and force him to wipe them away.

"As Pontifex Maximus, Publius Cornelius Dolabella, it is my duty to inform you that your adoption into the Plebs was illegal. It did not have my consent, and it must under the relevant *lex Clodia*. You will therefore lay down your tribunate of the plebs immediately, and withdraw entirely from all public life until the Bankruptcy Court is back in session and you can apply to it to sort your affairs out. The Law does have mechanisms for situations like yours, and since the jury will be your peers, you should get off more lightly than you deserve. Now go." The head went down.

"That's all?" Dolabella asked incredulously.

A scroll was already between Caesar's hands. "That is all, Publius Dolabella. Do you think me stupid enough to apportion blame where it doesn't belong? You're not the prime mover in this, you're a simple cat's-paw."

Smarting yet relieved, the simple cat's-paw got up.

"One more thing," Caesar said, busy reading.

"Yes, Caesar?"

"You are forbidden all congress with Marcus Antonius. I have my sources of information, Dolabella, so I suggest that you don't try to infringe that prohibition. *Vale.*"

Two days later the Master of the Horse arrived in Rome. He came through the Capena Gate at the head of a squadron of German cavalry, riding the Antonian Public Horse, a big, showy beast as white as Pompey the Great's old Public Horse. Antony had gone one further than Pompey's scarlet leather tack; his mount wore leopard skin. As indeed did he, a short cloak slung around his neck on a golden chain, one side thrown back to reveal a scarlet lining the same as his tunic. His cuirass was gold, contoured to cuddle his magnificent pectoral muscles, and worked with a scene of Hercules (the Antonii traced their origins back to Hercules) slaying the Lion of Nemea; the scarlet leather straps of sleeves and kilt were emblazoned with gold medallions and bosses, and fringed with gold bullion. His gold Attic helmet with its dyed scarlet ostrich plumes (they had cost ten talents, for they were very rare in Rome) sat linked around the left posterior horn of his leopard skin saddle, for he wanted his head bare so that his gaping audience was in no doubt as to who was this powerful, godly figure. To add to his conceit, he had equipped his squadron of Germans with full scarlet tack for their uniformly black horses, and clad them in real silver with lion skins; the heads were draped over their helmets, the empty paws knotted across their chests.

Any woman in the crowd clustered to watch him ride through the Capena market square might have debated the question of his handsomeness: was he beautiful, or was he ugly? Opinions were usually evenly divided, for the body's height and musculature were beautiful, whereas the face was ugly. Antony's hair was very thick and curly, a good auburn in color, his face heavyset and roundish, his neck both short and so thick that it looked like an extension of his head. His eyes, the same auburn as his hair, were small, deep in their orbits and too close together. Nose and chin tried very hard to meet across his small, full-lipped mouth, one curving its beak downward, the other upward; women whom he had honored with his amorous attentions likened kissing him to being nipped by a turtle. What no one could deny was that he stood out in any crowd.

His fantasies were rich and fabulous; true of many men, but the difference between Antony and other men lay in the fact that Antony actually lived his fantasies in the real world. He saw himself as Hercules, as the new Dionysus, as Sampsiceramus the legendary eastern potentate, and he contrived to look and act like a combination of all three.

Though his riotously luxurious mode of living dominated his thoughts, he was neither stupid like his brother Gaius nor quite an oaf; inside Mark Antony was a shrewd streak of self-serving cunning which, when needed, had extricated him from many a precarious predicament, and he knew how to make his staggering masculinity work for him with other men, especially Caesar Dictator, who was his second cousin. Added to this, he possessed his family's ability to orate—oh, not in Cicero's or Caesar's class, but very definitely superior to most of the Senate. He did not lack courage or bravery, and he could think on a battlefield. What he lacked most was a sense of morality, of ethical behavior, of respect for life and human beings, yet he could be outrageously generous and tremendously good company. Antony was a bull at a gate, a creature of impulse and the flesh. What he wanted out of the noble life he had been born into was two-headed: on the one hand, he wanted to be the First Man in Rome; on the other hand, he wanted palaces, bonhomie, sex, food, wine, comedy and perpetual entertainments.

Since returning to Italy with Caesar's legions almost a year ago, he had been indulging himself in all these areas. As the Dictator's Master of the Horse, he was constitutionally the most powerful of all men in the Dictator's absence, and had been using that power in ways he knew very well Caesar would deplore. But he had also been living like an eastern potentate, and spending a great deal more money than he had. Nor had he cared about what a more prudent man would have understood right from the beginning—that the day would come when he would be called to account for his activities. To Antony, sufficient against the day. Except that now the day had arrived.

Politic, he decided, to leave his friends behind in Pompey's villa at Herculaneum. No point in upsetting Cousin Gaius more than necessary. Men like Lucius Gellius Poplicola, Quintus Pompeius Rufus the Younger and Lucius Varius Cotyla were known to Cousin Gaius, but not liked by Cousin Gaius.

His first stop in Rome was not the Domus Publica, or even Pompey's enormous mansion on the Carinae, now his abode; he went at once to Curio's house on the Palatine, parked his Germans in the garden attached to Hortensius's house, and strolled in asking to see the lady Fulvia.

She was the granddaughter of Gaius Sempronius Gracchus through her mother, Sempronia, who had married Marcus Fulvius Bambalio, an appropriate alliance considering that the Fulvii had been Gaius Gracchus's most ardent supporters, and had crashed too. Sempronia had taken her grandmother's huge fortune with her, despite the fact that women were forbidden to be major heirs under the *lex Voconia*. But Sempronia's grandmother was Cornelia the Mother of the Gracchi, powerful enough to procure a decree from the Senate waiving the *lex Voconia*. When Fulvius and Sempronia died, another senatorial waiver had allowed Fulvia to inherit from both her parents. She was the wealthiest woman in Rome. Not for Fulvia, the usual fate of heiresses! She chose her own husband, Publius Clodius the patrician rebel, founder of the Clodius Club. Why had she chosen Clodius? Because she was in love with her grandfather's demagogic image, and saw in Clodius great demagogic potential. Her faith was not misplaced. Nor was she a stay-at-home Roman wife. Even swollen in late pregnancy, she could be found in the Forum screaming encouragement at Clodius, kissing him obscenely, generally behaving like a harlot. In private life she was a full member of the Clodius Club, knew Dolabella, Poplicola, Antony—and Curio.

When Clodius was murdered she was heartbroken, but her old friend Atticus persuaded her to live for her children, and in time the terrible wound healed over a little. Three years into her widowhood she married Curio, another brilliant demagogue. By him she had a naughty little red-haired son, but their life together was cut tragically short when Curio died in battle.

At the time that Antony strolled through her door she was thirty-seven years old, the mother of five children—four by Clodius, one by Curio—and looked no more than twenty-five.

Not that Antony had much chance to assess her with his keen connoisseur's eye; she appeared in the atrium doorway, shrieked, and launched herself at him so enthusiastically that she bounced off his cuirass with a clang and fell on the floor laughing and crying together.

"Marcus, Marcus, Marcus! Oh, let me see you!" she said, his face between her hands, for he had followed her down. "You never seem to grow a single day older."

"Nor do you," he said appreciatively.

Yes, as desirable as ever. Seductively big breasts as firm as when she had been eighteeen, trim little waist—she was not one to conceal her sexual assets—no lines to mar that lovely clear-skinned face, with its black lashes and brows, its huge, dark-blue eyes. Her hair! Still that wonderful ice-brown. What a beauty! And all that money too.

"Marry me," he said. "I love you."

"And I love you, Antonius, but it's too soon." Her eyes filled with tears—not joy at Antony's advent, but grief at Curio's going. "Ask me again in a year."

"Three years between husbands as usual, eh?"

"Yes, it seems so. But don't make me a widow a third time, Marcus, I beg you! You constantly spoil for trouble, which is why I love you, but I want to grow old with someone I remember from my youth, and who is there left except you?" she asked.

He helped her up, but was too experienced to try to embrace her. "Decimus Brutus," he said, grinning. "Poplicola?"

"Oh, Poplicola! A parasite," she said scornfully. "If you marry me, you'll have to drop Poplicola, I won't receive him."

"No comment about Decimus?"

"Decimus is a great man, but he's—oh, I don't know, I see a light of ineradicable unhappiness around him. And he's too cold for me. Having Sempronia Tuditani for a mother ruined him, I think. She sucked cock better than anyone else in Rome, even the professionals." Fulvia was not a mincer of words. "I confess I was pleased when she finally dieted herself to death. So was Decimus, I imagine. He never even wrote from Gaul."

"I hear Poplicola's mother died too, speaking of *fellatrices*."

Fulvia pulled a face. "Last month. I had to hold her hand until it went stiff—ugh!"

They walked through to the peristyle garden, for it was a wonderful summer's day; she sat on the side of the fountain pool and played with the water, while Antony sat on a stone seat and watched her. By Hercules, she was a beauty! Next year . . .

"You're not popular with Caesar," she said abruptly.

Antony blew a derisive noise. "Who, old Cousin Gaius? I can handle him with one hand tied behind my back. I'm his pet."

"Don't be too sure, Marcus. Well do I remember how he used to manipulate my darling Clodius! While ever Caesar was in Rome, there wasn't one thing Clodius did that Caesar hadn't planted in his mind first, from Cato's trip to annex Cyprus to all those weird laws governing the religious colleges and religious law." She sighed. "It was only after Caesar went to Gaul that my Clodius began to run amok. Caesar could control him. And he will insist on controlling you too."

"He's family," Antony said, unperturbed. "I may get a tongue-lashing, but it won't be anything worse."

"You'd better offer to Hercules for that, Marcus."

From Fulvia's he went to Pompey's palace and his second wife, Antonia Hybrida. Oh, she wasn't too bad, though she had the Antonian face, poor thing. What looked good on a man definitely didn't on a woman. A strapping girl he had tired of very quickly, though not as quickly as he spent her considerable fortune. She had borne him a daughter, Antonia, now five years old, but the matching of first cousins had not been felicitous when it came to offspring. Little Antonia was mentally dull as well as dismally ugly and grossly fat. From somewhere he'd have to find a gigantic dowry, or else marry the girl off to some foreign plutocrat who'd give half his fortune for the chance to acquire an Antonian bride.

"You're in the boiling soup," said Antonia Hybrida when he found her in her sitting room.

"I'll emerge unscalded, Hibby."

"Not this time, Marcus. Caesar's livid."

"*Cacat!*" he said violently, scowling, fist up.

She flinched, shrank away. "No, please!" she cried. "I've done nothing—nothing!"

"Oh, stop whining, you're safe enough!" he snapped.

"Caesar sent a message," she said, recovering.

"What?"

"To report to him at the Domus Publica immediately. In a toga, not in armor."

"The Master of the Horse is armored all the time."

"I'm just relaying the message." Antonia Hybrida studied her husband, in a quandary; it might be months and months before she saw him again, even if he lived in this selfsame house. He had beaten her regularly when they were first married, but he had not broken her spirit, just broken her of her habit of torturing her slaves. "Marcus," she said, "I would like another child."

"You can like all you want, Hibby, but you're not getting another child. One mental defective is one too many."

"She was damaged in the birth process, not in the womb."

He walked to the big silver mirror Pompey the Great had once gazed into hoping to see the ghost of his dead Julia vanish into its depths, eyed himself with head to one side. Yes, impressive! *A toga!* No one knew better than Mark Antony that men of his physique didn't look impressive in a toga. Togas were for the Caesars of Rome's world—it took height and grace to wear one well. Not, mind you, he had to admit, that the old boy didn't wear armor with panache too. He simply looks what he is, royal. The family dictator. That's what we used to call him among ourselves when we were boys, Gaius, Lucius and I. Ran the lot of us, even Uncle Lucius. And now he's running Rome. As dictator.

"Don't expect me for dinner," he said, and clanked out.

"You look like Plautus's *miles gloriosus* in that ridiculous getup" was Caesar's opening remark. Seated behind his desk, he didn't rise, didn't attempt any kind of physical contact.

"The soldiers drink me up. They love to see their betters look their betters."

"Like you, their taste is in their arse, Antonius. I asked you to wear a toga. Armor's not appropriate inside the *pomerium*."

"As Master of the Horse, I can wear armor inside the city."

"As Master of the Horse, you do as the Dictator says."

"Well, do I sit down or keep standing?" Antony demanded.

"Sit."

"I'm sitting. What now?"

"An explanation of events in the Forum, I think."

"Which events?"

"Don't be obtuse, Antonius."

"I just want the jawing over and done with."

"So you know why I summoned you—to give you, as you so succinctly put it, a jawing."

"Isn't it?"

"Perhaps I object to your choice of words, Antonius. I was thinking along the lines of castration."

"That's not fair! What have I done, when it's all boiled down?" Antony asked angrily. "Your bum-boy Vatia passed the Ultimate Decree and instructed *me* to deal with the violence. Well, I did just that! As I see it, I did the job properly. There hasn't been a peep out of anyone since."

"You brought professional soldiers into the Forum Romanum, then you ordered them to use their swords to cut down men armed with wood. You slaughtered wholesale! Slaughtered Roman citizens in their own meeting place! Not even Sulla had the temerity to do that! Is it because you've been called upon to take your sword to fellow Romans on a battlefield that you turn the Forum Romanum into a battlefield? The Forum *Romanum*, Antonius! You slimed the stones where Romulus stood with citizen blood! The Forum of Romulus—of Curtius—of Horatius Cocles—of Fabius Maximus Verrucosus Cunctator—of Appius Claudius Caecus—of Scipio Africanus—of Scipio Aemilianus—of a thousand Romans more noble than you, more capable, more revered! You committed sacrilege!" Caesar said, biting off his words slowly and distinctly, his tones freezing, cutting.

Antony leaped to his feet, fists clenched. "Oh, I hate it when you're sarcastic! Don't come the orator with me, Caesar! Just say what you want to say, and have done with it! Then I can get back to my job, which is trying to keep your legions calm! Because they're not calm! They're very, very unhappy!" he shouted, a little red light of cunning at the back of his eyes. That should sidetrack the old boy—very sensitive about his legions.

It did not.

"*Sit down, you ignorant lump!* Shut your insubordinate mouth, or I'll cut your balls off here and now—and don't think that I can't! Fancy yourself a warrior, Antonius? Compared to me, you're a tyro! Riding a pretty horse in the stage armor of the vainglorious soldier! You don't stand and lay about in the front line, you never have! I could take your sword off you right now and chop you into cutlets!"

The temper was loose; Antony drew in a huge breath, shaken to the marrow. Oh, why had he forgotten Caesar's temper?

"How dare you be insolent to me? How dare you forget who exactly you are? You, Antonius, are *my* creature—I made you, and I can unmake you! If it were not for our blood ties, I'd have passed you over in favor of a dozen more efficient and intelligent men! Was it too much to ask that you comport yourself with a meed of discretion, of simple common sense? Obviously I asked too much! You're a butcher as well as a fool, and your conduct has made my task in Rome infinitely harder—I have inherited the mantle of your butchery! From the moment I crossed the Rubicon, my policy toward all Romans has been clemency, but what do you call this *massacre*? No, Caesar can't trust his Master of the Horse to behave like a civilized, educated, genuine Roman! What do you think Cato will make of this massacre when he hears of it? Or Cicero? You're an incubus suffocating my clemency, and I do not thank you for it!"

The Master of the Horse held up his hands in abject surrender. "Pax, pax, pax! I was in error! I'm sorry, I'm sorry!"

"Remorse is after the event, Antonius. There were at least half a hundred ways to deal with violence in the Forum without doing more than breaking one or two heads. Why didn't you arm the Tenth with shields and staves, as Gaius Marius did when he took on Saturninus's far vaster crowds? Hasn't it occurred to you that in ordering the Tenth to kill, you transferred a share of your guilt to their spirits? How am I to explain matters to them, let alone to the civilian populace?" The eyes were glacial, but they also bore revulsion. "I will never forget or forgive your action. What's more, it tells me that you enjoy wielding power in ways that might prove dangerous not only to the state, but to me."

"Am I fired?" Antony asked, beginning to ease his bottom out of the chair. "Are you done?"

"No, you are not fired, and no, I am not done. Put your arse back on the seat," Caesar said, still with that dislike. "What happened to the silver in the Treasury?"

"Oh, *that!*"

"Yes, that."

"I took it to pay the legions, but I haven't gotten around to coining it yet," Antony said, shrugging.

"Then is it at Juno Moneta's?"

"Um—no."

"Where is it?"

"At my house. I thought it was safer."

"*Your* house. You mean Pompeius Magnus's house?"

"Well, yes, I suppose so."

"What gave you to understand that you could move there?"

"I needed a bigger house, and Magnus's was vacant."

"I can see why you'd pick it—your taste is as vulgar as Magnus's was. But kindly move back to your own house, Antonius. As soon as I have the leisure, Magnus's house will be put up for auction to the highest bidder, as will the rest of his property," said Caesar. "The property of those who remain unpardoned after I deal with the resistance in Africa Province will be garnished by the state, though some can be dealt with sooner. But it will not be sold to benefit my own men, or my hirelings. I'll have no Chrysogonus in my service. If I find one, it won't take Cicero and a court case to bring about his—or her—downfall. Be very careful that you do not try to steal from Rome. Put the silver back in the Treasury, where it belongs. You may go." He let Antony get to the door, then spoke again. "By the way, how much back pay are my legions owed?"

Antony looked quite blank. "I don't know, Caesar."

"You don't know, but you took the silver. *All* the silver. As Master of the Horse, I suggest that you tell the legion paymasters to present their books directly to me here in Rome. My instructions to you when you took them back to Italy were to pay them once they were in camp. Have they not been paid at all since they returned?"

"I don't know," said Antony again, and escaped.

"Why didn't you fire him on the spot, Gaius?" Antony's uncle asked his cousin over dinner.

"I would have liked to, very much. However, Lucius, it isn't as simple as it looks, is it?"

Lucius Caesar's eyes stilled, then went pensive. "Explain."

"My mistake was in trusting Antonius in the first place, but to dismiss him out of hand would be an even bigger mistake," said Caesar, munching on a stick of celery. "Think about it. For close to twelve months Antonius has had the run of Italy and sole command of the veteran legions. With whom he's spent by far the major part of his time, especially since last March. I haven't seen the legions, and he's been mighty careful not to let any of my other representatives in Italy see them. There's evidence that they haven't been paid, so by now they're owed two years' money. Antonius pretended ignorance of the entire matter, yet eighteen thousand talents of silver were withdrawn from the Treasury and taken to Magnus's house. Apparently to go to Juno Moneta's for coining, though it hasn't."

"My heart's knocking at my ribs, Gaius. Go on, do."

"I don't have an abacus to hand, but my arithmetic isn't bad, even when I have to do the sums in my head. Fifteen legions times five thousand men times one thousand per capita per annum adds up to about seventy-five million sesterces. Which are three thousand talents of silver. Add another—say, three hundred talents to pay the noncombatants, and then double the figure to make it two years' pay, and you have six thousand, six hundred talents of silver. That is far short of the eighteen thousand Antonius removed," said Caesar.

"He's been living mighty high," said Lucius, sighing. "I know he's not paying rent for using Magnus's various residences, but that ghastly armor he's wearing would have cost a fortune to start with. Then there's the armor his sixty Germans wear. Plus the wine, the women, the entourage—my nephew, I think, is drowning in debt and decided he'd better empty the Treasury the moment he heard you were in Italy."

"He should have emptied it months ago," said Caesar.

"Do you think he's been working on the legions to disaffect them by not paying them and blaming you?" Lucius asked.

"Undoubtedly. Were he as organized as Decimus Brutus or as cognizantly ambitious as Gaius Cassius, we'd be deeper in the shit than we are. Our Antonius has high ideas, but no method."

"He's a plotter, not a planner."

"Indeed." A thick white goat's cheese looked appetizing; Caesar scooped some on to another stick of celery.

"When do you intend to pounce, Gaius?"

"I'll know because my legions will tell me," Caesar said. A spasm of pain crossed his face, he put the tidbit down quickly and pressed his hand against his chest.

"Gaius! Are you all right?"

How to tell a dear friend that the pain is not of the body? Not my legions! O Jupiter Optimus Maximus, not my legions! Two years ago it would not have occurred to me, but I learned from the mutiny of the Ninth. I trust none of them now, even the Tenth. *Caesar* trusts none of them now, even the Tenth.

"Just a touch of indigestion, Lucius."

"Then if you feel up to it, elucidate."

"I need the rest of this year to maneuver. Rome comes first, the legions second. I'll have six thousand talents minted for pay, but I'm not going to pay anybody yet. I want to see just what Antonius has been saying, and that won't happen until the legions tell me. If I went to Capua tomorrow, I could squash it in a day, but this is one boil that I think has to come to a head, and the best way to make it do that is to avoid seeing the legions in person." Caesar picked up the celery stick and began to eat again. "Antonius is swimming in very deep water, and his eyes are fixed on a bobbing lump of cork that spells salvation. He's not quite sure what form the salvation will take, but he's swimming very hard. Perhaps he's hoping I'll die—stranger things have happened. Or else he's hoping that I'll dash off to Africa Province ahead of my troops, and leave him a clear field to do whatever comes to his mind. He's a Fortuna man, he seizes his chance, he doesn't make his chance. I want him even farther from the shore before I strike, and

I want to know exactly what he's been doing and saying to my men. Having to give the silver back is a blow, he'll swim feverishly now. But I will be waiting behind the cork. Frankly, Lucius, I'm hoping that he'll continue to swim for two or three more months. I need time for Rome before I deal with the legions and Antonius."

"His actions are treasonable, Gaius."

Caesar reached a hand out to pat Lucius's arm. "Rest easy, there'll be no treason trials within the family. I'll cut our relative off from salvation, but I'll leave him his head." He chuckled. "*Both* his heads. After all, a great deal of his thinking is done with his prick."

When Sulla had returned from the East with his fabled beauty utterly destroyed, to march on Rome a second time, he was appointed (by his own arrangement, something he preferred not to mention) the Dictator of Rome.

For several *nundinae* he seemed to do nothing. But a few more observant people noticed a crabbed little old man muffled in a cloak walking all over the city, from Colline Gate to Capena Gate, from the Circus Flaminius to the Agger. It was Sulla, walking patiently up mean alleys and down main roads to see for himself what Rome needed—how he, the Dictator, was going to mend her, broken as she was by twenty years of foreign and civil wars.

Now Caesar was Dictator, a younger man whose beauty still sat fair upon him, and Caesar too walked from Colline Gate to Capena Gate, from the Circus Flaminius to the Agger, up mean alleys and down main roads, to see for himself what Rome needed—how he, the Dictator, was going to mend her, broken as she was by fifty-five years of foreign and civil wars.

Both Dictators had lived in the city's worst stews as children and young men, seen at first hand the poverty, the crime, the vice, the rough justice, the sunny acceptance of one's lot that seemed peculiar to the Roman temperament. But whereas Sulla had yearned for retirement to a world of the flesh, Caesar knew only that for as long as he lived, he must continue to work. His solace was work, for his life force was intellectual—he had no powerful urges of the flesh crying within him to be gratified, as had Sulla.

No need for Sulla's anonymity. Caesar walked openly and was happy to stop and listen to anyone, from the old crones who ran the public latrines to the latest generation of Decumii who ran the gangs selling protection to shops and small businesses. He talked to Greek freedmen, to mothers dragging children as well as produce, to Jews, to

Roman citizens of the Fourth and Fifth Classes, to Head Count labor-ers, to schoolteachers, to pasty vendors, bakers, butchers, herbalists and astrologers, landlords and tenants, makers of wax *imagines*, sculp-tors, painters, physicians, tradesmen. In Rome, a number of these peo-ple were women, who worked as potters, carpenters, physicians, all sorts; only upper-class women were not allowed to have jobs or a trade.

He himself was a landlord; he still owned Aurelia's insula apart-ment block, now in the charge of Burgundus's eldest son, Gaius Julius Arvernus, also his business manager. The half German, half Gallic Arvernus (born free) had been personally trained by Caesar's mother, who had the best head for figures and accounts of anyone he had ever known, even including Crassus and Brutus. So he talked to Arvernus a great deal.

This is what it is really all about, he would think exultantly as he left Arvernus's company—two absolutely barbarian ex-slaves in Bur-gundus and Cardixa had produced seven absolutely Roman sons! Oh, perhaps they had had a few extra advantages—owners who freed properly, popped them into rural tribes so their votes counted, edu-cated them and encouraged them to acquire status, but all that aside, they were Roman to the core.

And if that could work, as work it obviously did, why not the op-posite? Take Head Count Romans too poor to belong to one of the five Classes and ship them off into the world to settle in foreign places, bring Rome to the provinces, replace Greek with Latin as the *lingua mundi*. Old Gaius Marius had tried to do it, but it offended the *mos maiorum*, it destroyed Roman exclusivity. Well, that was sixty years ago, and everything had changed. Marius's mind had shattered, he degenerated into a butchering madman. Whereas Caesar's mind was growing ever sharper, and Caesar was the Dictator—there was no one to gainsay him, especially now that the *boni* were not a force in politics.

First and most important was to settle the question of debt. It had to take precedence over visits to see old friends as well as a meeting of the Senate, which he had not yet called. Four days after entering Rome he convoked the Popular Assembly, which was the *comitia* permitting the attendance of patricians as well as plebeians. The Well of the Comi-tia, a bowl in the lower Forum stepped down in tiers, used to be the place where the Assemblies met, but it was now in the process of being demolished to make way for Caesar's new Senate House, so Caesar called his meeting at the temple of Castor and Pollux.

Though his normal speaking voice was deep, Caesar pitched it high for public oratory; it traveled a great deal farther. Lucius Caesar, standing with Vatia Isauricus, Lepidus, Hirtius, Philippus, Lucius Piso, Vatinius, Fufius Calenus, Pollio and the rest of Caesar's adherents at the front of the big crowd, was amazed anew at his cousin's command of such masses of people. He'd always been able to do it, and the years hadn't spoiled his touch. If anything, he was even better. Autocracy suits him, thought Lucius. He knows his own power, yet he's not drunk on it, or overly enamored of it, or tempted to see how far he can go with it.

There would be no general cancellation of debts, he announced in tones that brooked no argument.

"How can Caesar possibly cancel debts?" he asked, hands out wryly. "In me, you see Rome's greatest debtor! Yes, I borrowed from the Treasury—a huge amount! It has to be paid back, *Quirites*, it has to be paid back at my new, uniform rate of interest on all loans—ten percent simple. And I won't have any objections to that either! Think! If the money *I* borrowed isn't paid back, where is the money for the grain dole to come from? The money to repair the Forum? The money to fund Rome's legions? The money to build roads, bridges, aqueducts? The money to pay the public slaves? The money to build more granaries? The money to fund the games? The money to add a new reservoir to the Esquiline?"

The crowd was quiet and attentive, not as disappointed or angry as it might have been with a different beginning.

"Cancel debt, and Caesar doesn't have to pay Rome back one sestertius! He can sit with his feet on his desk and sigh in content, he doesn't need to shed a tear because the Treasury is empty. He doesn't owe Rome any money, his debt is canceled along with all the other debts. Now we can't have that, can we? It's ridiculous! And so, *Quirites*, because Caesar is an honest man who believes that debts must be repaid, he must say no to a general cancellation."

Oh, very clever! thought Lucius Caesar, enjoying himself.

But, Caesar went on, there would be a measure of relief, there had to be. He understood how hard the times were. Roman landlords would have to accept a reduction of two thousand a year in rent, Italian landlords a reduction of six hundred. Later he would announce other measures of relief and negotiate a settlement of outstanding debts that would be of benefit to both sides of the debt equation. But they would have to be patient a little longer, because when relief came, it had to be absolutely fair and impartial, which took time to work out.

Next he announced a new fiscal policy, again not to come into effect immediately—oh, the paperwork! Namely, that the state would borrow money from private firms and individuals, and from other cities and districts throughout Italy and the whole Roman world. Client-kings would be asked if they would like to become Rome's creditors. Interest would be paid at the standard ten percent simple. The *res publicae*—the Things Public—said Caesar, could not be funded from the few taxes Rome levied: customs duties, a fee to free a slave, the income from provinces, the state's share of war booty, and that was it. No income tax, no head tax, no property tax, no banking tax— where *was* the money to come from? Caesar's answer was that the state would borrow, rather than institute new taxes. The poorest citizen could become Rome's creditor! What was the collateral? Why, Rome herself! The greatest nation on the face of the globe, rich and powerful, incapable of bankruptcy!

However, he warned, those frippery fellows and languid ladies who paraded around in Tyrian purple litters studded with ocean pearls had better count their days, because there was *one* tax he intended to bring in! No tax-free Tyrian purple, no tax-free extravagantly expensive banquets, no tax-free *laserpicium* to relieve the symptoms of over-indulgence!

In conclusion, he said quite chattily, it had not escaped his attention that there was a large amount of property belonging to persons who were now *nefas,* disbarred from Rome and citizenship due to crimes against the state. Their assets would be auctioned fairly and the proceeds put in the Treasury, which was filling up a trifle, thanks to the gift of five thousand talents of gold from Queen Cleopatra of Egypt and two thousand talents of gold from King Asander of Cimmeria.

"I will institute no proscriptions!" he cried. "No private citizens will profit from those unfortunates who abrogated their right to call themselves Roman citizens! I am not selling slave manumission for information, I am not handing out any rewards for information! I already know everything I need to know. Rome's knight-businessmen are the cause of her well-being, and it is to them that I look to help me heal these terrible scars." He lifted both hands above his head. "Long live the Senate and People of Rome! Long live Rome!"

A fine speech, couched simply and clearly, free of rhetorical devices. It did the trick; the thousands went away feeling as if Rome were under the care of someone who would genuinely help without shedding more blood. After all, Caesar had still been away when the massacre in the Forum happened—had he been here, it would not have happened. For, among the many other things he said, he apologized for the Forum slaughter and said that those responsible would be punished.

* * *

"He's as slippery as an eel," said Gaius Cassius to his mother-in-law, teeth showing.

"My dear Cassius, he has more intelligence in his ring finger than the rest of noble Rome put together," Servilia answered. "If you assimilate nothing more from Caesar's company than that, you'll benefit. How much cash can you lay your hands on?"

He blinked. "About two hundred talents."

"Have you touched Tertulla's dowry?"

"No, of course not! Her money's hers," he said indignantly.

"That never stopped many a husband."

"It stopped me!"

"Good. I'll tell her to have her money liquid."

"What exactly are you up to, Servilia?"

"Surely you've guessed. Caesar is about to auction some of the primest property in Italy—mansions in Rome, country and seaside villas, *latifundia* estates, probably a fish farm or two. I intend to buy, and I suggest you do the same," she said, a purr in her voice. "Though I do believe Caesar when he says he doesn't intend that he himself or his minions should profit, it will follow the pattern of Sulla's auctions nonetheless—there's only so much money available to buy. The plum properties will be sold first, and they'll fetch what they're worth. After a half dozen are gone, prices will fall until the run-of-the-mill pieces go for almost nothing. Then I'll buy."

Cassius leaped to his feet, face mottling. "Servilia, how can you? Do you think that I'd profit from the misfortunes of men I've messed with, fought alongside, shared common ideals with? Ye gods! I'd rather be dead than do that!"

"*Gerrae*," she said placidly. "Do sit down! Ethics are no doubt splendid abstractions, but it's sensible to face the fact that *someone* is going to benefit. If it comforts you, buy a piece of Cato's land and tell yourself that you're a better custodian than one of Caesar's—or Antonius's—leeches. Is it better that a Cotyla or a Fonteius or a Poplicola should own Cato's lovely estates in Lucania?"

"That's sophistry," he muttered, subsiding.

"It's plain good sense."

Her steward entered, bowing. "*Domina*, Caesar Dictator is asking to see you."

"Bring him in, Epaphroditus."

Cassius stood again. "That's it, I'm off." Before she could say a word, he slipped out of her sitting room toward the kitchen.

"My dear Caesar!" said Servilia, lifting her face for a kiss.

He obliged with a chaste salute and seated himself opposite her, his eyes derisive.

Older than he, she was pushing sixty now, and the years were finally beginning to show. Her beauty was night from her hair to her heart, he reflected, and that would never change. Now, however, two broad ribbons of pure white slashed through the masses of sooty hair and lent her a peculiar visual malignity that could be nothing new to her spirit. Crones and *veneficae* have such hair, but she has achieved the ultimate triumph of combining evil with good looks. Her waist had thickened and her once lovely breasts were bound up with ruthless severity, but she had not put on sufficient weight to destroy the clean lines of her jaw or plump out that faint sag of weakened muscles on the right side of her face. Her chin was pointed, her mouth small, full and enigmatic, her nose too short for Roman beauty, knobbed at its end. A fault everyone had forgiven because of the mouth and the eyes, which were wide yet heavy-lidded, dark as a moonless night, stern and strong and very intelligent. Her skin was white, her hands slender and graceful, with tapering fingers and manicured nails.

"How are you?" he enquired.

"I'll be happier when Brutus comes home."

"I imagine, knowing Brutus, that he's having a wonderful time in Samos with Servius Sulpicius. I promised him a priesthood, you see, so he's busy learning from an acknowledged authority."

"What a fool he is!" she snarled. "*You* are the acknowledged authority, Caesar. But of course he wouldn't learn from you."

"Why should he? I broke his heart when I took Julia away."

"My son," said Servilia deliberately, "is a pusillanimous coward. Not even a broom handle laced to his backbone could make him stand up straight." She nipped her bottom lip with her small white teeth and slewed her eyes sideways at her visitor. "I don't suppose his pimples have improved?"

"They haven't, no."

"Nor has he, your tone says."

"You underestimate him, my dear. There's a little cat in Brutus, a lot of ferret, and even a trace of fox."

She waved both hands in the air irritably. "Oh, let's not talk about him! How was Egypt?" she asked sweetly.

"Extremely interesting."

"And its queen?"

"For beauty, Servilia, she can't hold a candle to you—as a matter of fact, she's very thin, small, and ugly." His face took on a secretive smile, he veiled his eyes. "Yet she is fascinating. Her voice is pure music, her eyes belong to a lioness, her education is formidable, and her intellect above average for a woman. She speaks eight languages—well, nine now, because I taught her Latin. *Amo, amas, amat.*"

"What a paragon!"

"You may find out for yourself one of these days. She'll be in Rome when I finish with Africa Province. We have a son."

"Yes, I'd heard that you've finally produced one. Your heir?"

"Don't talk such rubbish, Servilia. His name is Ptolemy Caesar and he'll be Pharaoh of Egypt. A great destiny for a non-Roman, don't you think?"

"Indeed. So who will be your heir? Do you hope to get one from Calpurnia?"

"I doubt it at this stage."

"Her father's married again very recently."

"Has he? I haven't spoken much to Piso yet."

"Is Marcus Antonius your heir?" she persisted.

"As of this moment, no one is my heir. I have yet to make my will." The eyes gleamed. "How is Pontius Aquila?"

"Still my lover."

"How nice." He rose to his feet, kissed her hand. "Don't despair of Brutus. He may surprise you yet."

So that was one renewal of an old acquaintance off his list. Piso has married again? Interesting. Calpurnia said nothing about it to me. Still quiet and peaceful. I enjoy making love to her, but I'll make her no babies. How much longer have I left? Not enough time for fatherhood, if Cathbad is right.

Amid days filled with talks to plutocrats, bankers, Marcus Cuspius of the Treasury, the legion paymasters, major landlords and many others, amid nights filled with paperwork and the click-click-click of his ivory abacus, what time was there for social engagements? Now that Mark Antony had returned the silver, the Treasury was quite respectably full considering two years of war, but Caesar knew what he had yet to do, and one of those tasks was going to cost immense amounts of money: he would have to find the funds to pay good prices for thousands upon thousands of *iugera* of good land, land upon which to settle as many as thirty legions of veteran troops. The days of filching public lands from rebellious Italian towns and cities were virtually gone. His land would come expensive, for the legionaries were from Italy or from Italian Gaul and expected to retire on ten *iugera* of Italian land, not foreign land.

Gaius Marius, who first threw Rome's legions open to the propertyless Head Count, had dreamed of pensioning them off in the provinces, there to spread Roman customs and the Latin language. He had even begun that, on the big island of Cercina in the African bight adjacent to Africa Province. Caesar's father had been his principal agent in the business, spent most of his time at Cercina. But it all came to nothing in the aftermath of Marius's madness, the Senate's implacable opposition. So unless circumstances changed, Caesar's land would have to be in Italy and Italian Gaul—the most expensive real estate in the world.

At the end of October he did manage to have one dinner party in the Domus Publica *triclinium*, a beautiful dining room able to hold nine couches with ease. It opened on one side into the wide colonnade around the Domus Publica's main peristyle garden, and as the afternoon was mild and sunny, Caesar threw all the doors open. Inside, among the exquisite murals of the battle at Lake Regillus when Castor and Pollux themselves had fought for Rome, Pompey the Great had met Julia for the first time, and fallen in love. What a triumph that had been. How pleased his mother had been.

Gaius Matius and his wife, Priscilla, were there; Lucius Calpurnius Piso and his new wife, another Rutilia, were there; Publius Vatinius came with his adored wife, Caesar's ex-wife Pompeia Sulla; Lucius Caesar, a widower, came on his own—his son was with Metellus Scipio in Africa Province, a Republican in the Caesarean nest; Vatia Isauricus came with his wife, Junia, Servilia's eldest daughter; and Lucius Marcius Philippus arrived with a small army: his second wife, Atia, who was Caesar's niece; her daughter by Gaius Octavius, Octavia Minor; and her son, the young Gaius Octavius; his own daughter, Marcia, wife of Cato but great friend of Caesar's wife, Calpurnia; and his elder son, the stay-at-home Lucius. The notable absentees (who had been invited) were Mark Antony and Marcus Aemilius Lepidus.

The menu had been chosen with huge care, for Philippus was a famous Epicure, whereas Gaius Matius, for example, liked plain food. The first course consisted of shrimp, oysters and crabs from the fish farms of Baiae, some cooked in elegant sauces, some served natural, some lightly grilled; accompanied by salads of lettuce, cucumber and celery laced with various dressings of the best oils and aged vinegars; smoked freshwater eel; a perch doused with *garum* sauce; deviled eggs, fresh crusty bread, fine olive oil for dipping. The second course offered a variety of roast meats, from leg of pork with crisply crackled skin to many fowls and a suckling pig baked brown for hours in sheep's milk; delicate pork sausages coated with diluted thyme honey and gently broiled; a lamb stew redolent with marjoram and onion; a baby lamb roasted in a clay oven. The third course consisted of honey cakes, sweet pastries containing minced raisins soaked in spicy fortified wine, sweet omelets, fresh fruits including strawberries brought down from Alba Fucentia and peaches from Caesar's own Campanian orchards, both hard and soft cheeses, stewed prunes and bowls of nuts. The wines were vintage from the best Falernian grapes, red or white, and the water came from Juturna's spring.

To Caesar, a matter of indifference; he would have been far happier with bread-and-oil of any kind, some celery and a thick pease porridge boiled down with a chunk of bacon.

"I can't help it, I'm a soldier." He laughed, looking suddenly younger and more relaxed.

"Do you still drink vinegar in hot water in the mornings?" Piso asked.

"If there are no lemons, yes."

"What's that you're drinking now?" Piso persisted.

"Fruit juice. It's my new health regimen. I have an Egyptian priest-physician, and it's his idea. I've grown to enjoy it."

"You'd enjoy this Falernian far more," said Philippus, rolling the wine on his tongue.

"No, I've grown no fonder of wine."

The men's couches formed a large U, with the host's *lectus medius* at its blind end, and the tables, exactly the same height as the couches, sat flush against their fronts, thus enabling the diners to extend a hand and take whatever they fancied from the platters. There were bowls and spoons for anything too sloppy or sticky for the fingers, and the delicacies were presented already carved into bite-sized pieces; a diner desirous of rinsing his hands simply turned toward the back side of his couch and availed himself of a dish of water and a towel tendered by some attentive servant. Togas were abandoned as too clumsy to dine in, shoes were doffed and feet washed before the men reclined with the left elbow on a bolster for comfort.

On the opposite side of the U of tables the women's chairs were placed; in more modern establishments it was now considered chic for women to recline as well, but the old-fashioned ways still held in the Domus Publica, so the women sat. If anything about the dinner was novel, that lay in Caesar's letting his guests choose their own spots to recline or sit, with two exceptions: he directed his cousin Lucius to the *locus consularis* at the right-hand end of his own couch, and told his great-nephew, young Gaius Octavius, to insert himself between them. His favoring a mere lad was noted by all and a few brows were raised, but . . .

The impulse to distinguish young Gaius Octavius arose out of Caesar's surprise when he set eyes on the lad, who very correctly and unobtrusively located himself in his stepfather's shadow while Philippus, delighted to have been invited, made much of greeting all and sundry. Ah! thought Caesar. Now here's someone different! Of course he remembered Octavius well; they'd had some conversation two and a half years ago when he had stayed in Philippus's villa at Misenum.

How old would he be now? Sixteen, probably, though he still wore the purple-bordered toga of childhood, the *bulla* medallion of childhood on a thong around his neck. Yes, he was definitely sixteen, because Octavius Senior had made such a fuss about his birth during the year of Cicero's consulship, right in the midst of growing suspicion about Catilina's intention to overthrow the state. Late September, while the House waited for news of a revolt in Etruria and a defiant Catilina was still brazening it out in Rome. Good! His mother and stepfather had decided that he would celebrate his manhood on the feast of Juventas in December, when most Roman boys assumed the *toga virilis*, the plain white toga of a citizen. Some wealthy and pre-eminent parents allowed their sons a special manhood day on their actual birthdays, but this had not been accorded to young Gaius Octavius. Good! Unspoiled.

He was strikingly beautiful, enough so to be called epicene. His masses of softly waving, bright gold hair were worn a trifle long to hide his only real flaw, his ears; though not overly big, they stuck straight out like jug handles. A clever mother, not a vain son, for the boy didn't comport himself like one aware of his physical impact. Clear brown skin devoid of any blemishes, a firm mouth and chin, a longish nose with a sliding upward tilt to it, high cheekbones, an oval face, darkish brows and lashes, and a pair of remarkable eyes. Spaced well apart and very large, they were a light, luminous grey that had no hint of blue or yellow in it; a little unearthly, yet not in the Sulla or Caesar way, for they were neither cold nor unsettling. Rather, they warmed. Yet, thought Caesar, studying those orbs analytically, they give absolutely nothing away. *Careful* eyes. Who said that to me in Misenum? Or was it I found that particular word for myself?

Octavius wasn't going to be tall, but nor was he going to be unduly short. An average height, a slender physique, but well-muscled calves. Good! His parents have made him walk everywhere from infancy, to develop those calves. But his chest is on the small side, his rib cage restricted, which narrows the width of his shoulders. And the skin beneath those amazing eyes is blue with weariness. Now where have I seen that look before? I have, I know I have, but it was a very long time ago. Hapd'efan'e. I must ask Hapd'efan'e.

Oh, for that mop of hair! To be balding is no fate for a man whose cognomen, "Caesar," means a fine thick head of hair—he won't go bald, he has his father's thatch. We were very good friends, his father and I. We met at the siege of Mitylene and clubbed together with Philippus against that flea Bibulus. So it pleased me when Octavius married my niece—sound old Latin stock, immensely wealthy too. But Octavius died untimely, and Philippus took his place in Atia's life. Interesting, what's happened to Lucullus's junior military tribunes. Who would ever have thought that Philippus would turn out the way he has?

"Just what are you up to, Gaius?" Lucius whispered after Caesar put the lad between them.

A question his host ignored, too busy making sure that Atia was comfortable on the chair opposite him, and that Calpurnia was not going to make the mistake of seating herself and Marcia too close to Lucius Piso, whose enormously thick black brows were meeting across his nose in displeasure because he had to share this excellent dinner with Cato's wife, of all people! One or two deft juggles with chairs, and Marcia sat next to Atia with Calpurnia on her other side, while Piso's brows beetled at no more vulnerable targets than Matius's Priscilla, that beautiful idiot Pompeia Sulla, and his own Rutilia. This Rutilia, Caesar noted, was a sour-looking girl of no more than eighteen, possessed of her family's sandy hair and freckled skin. Buck teeth. A belly beginning to show a pregnancy. Piso might have a son at last.

"When do you plan to leave for Africa?" Vatinius asked.

"As soon as I can assemble enough ships."

"Am I a legate for this campaign?"

"No, Vatinius," Caesar said, turning up his nose at the fish and settling for a heel of bread, "you're staying in Rome as one of the consuls."

Conversation ceased; all eyes turned to Caesar, then to Publius Vatinius, who was sitting bolt upright, lost for words.

He was Caesar's client, a diminutive man with wasted lower legs and a large wen on his forehead that had once caused him to be rejected as an augur. His wit, cheerful disposition and high intelligence had made him much loved by those who came into contact with him in Forum, Senate or the courts, and despite his physical handicaps, Vatinius proved to be as able a soldier as he was a politician. Sent to relieve Gabinius in the siege at Salona in Illyricum, he and his legate Quintus Cornificius had not only taken the city, but then moved to crush the tribes of Illyricum before they could ally themselves with Burebistas and the tribes of the Danubius basin and become a bigger nuisance to Rome and Caesar than Pharnaces.

"It isn't much of a consulship, Vatinius," Caesar went on, "as it's just for the rump of this year. Under ordinary circumstances I wouldn't have bothered with consuls until the New Year, but there are reasons why I need two consuls in office immediately."

"Caesar, I would be happy to be consul for two *nundinae*, let alone two months," Vatinius managed to say. "Will you hold proper elections, or simply appoint me and—?"

"Quintus Fufius Calenus," said Caesar obligingly. "Oh, yes, I'll hold proper elections. Far be it from me to upset some of the senators I'm still hoping to win over."

"Will they be Sulla-style elections, or will you permit other men to run as well as Vatinius and Calenus?" Piso asked, scowling.

"I don't care if half of Rome wants to stand, Piso. I shall—ah—indicate my personal preferences, and leave the decision to the Centuries."

No one commented on that. In Rome's present condition, and after the marvelous speech about debt, the knight-businessmen of the Eighteen senior Centuries would be happy to elect a Tingitanian ape if Caesar nominated it.

"Why," Vatia Isauricus enquired, "is it so necessary to have consuls in office for the rump of this year when you're here in Rome yourself, Caesar?"

Caesar blandly changed the subject. "Gaius Matius, I have a favor to ask," he said.

"Anything, Gaius, you know that," said Matius, a quiet man with no political aspirations; his businesses had prospered thanks to his old friendship with Caesar, more than enough for him.

"I know that Queen Cleopatra's agent, Ammonius, approached you and secured a grant of land for her palace next to my gardens under the Janiculum. Would you give its gardens your personal touch? I'm *sure* the Queen will donate the palace to Rome later."

Matius knew perfectly well that she would; the property was in Caesar's name, as ordered. "I am delighted to help, Caesar."

"Is the Queen as beautiful as Fulvia?" Pompeia Sulla asked, well aware that she herself was more beautiful than Fulvia.

"No," Caesar said, his tone forbidding further discussion. He turned to Philippus. "Your younger son is a very capable man."

"I'm pleased that he has pleased, Caesar."

"I intend to have Cilicia governed as a part of Asia Province for the next year or two. If you don't mind his remaining in the East a while longer, Philippus, I'd like to leave him in Tarsus as deputy governor *propraetore*."

"Excellent!" Philippus beamed.

Caesar's eyes had gone to the elder son, now well into his thirties. Very handsome, reputedly quite as talented as Quintus, yet always stuck in Rome letting his opportunities go by without his father's excuse of Epicureanism. At that moment the reason broke on Caesar as a shock; Lucius's gaze was fixed hungrily on Atia, a look of hopeless love. But the look went unnoticed because the emotion clearly was not returned. Atia sat tranquilly, smiling at her husband from time to time in the way women do when they are perfectly satisfied with their marital lot. Hmmm. Undercurrents in the Philippus household. From Atia, Caesar transferred his attention to young Octavius, who thus far had not vouchsafed a single remark. Not from shyness, rather from a consciousness of his junior status. The lad was staring at his stepbrother with complete comprehension but rigid dislike and disapproval.

"Who's to govern Asia Province combined with Cilicia?" asked Piso, a question loaded with meaning.

He wants the job desperately, and in many ways he's a good man, but . . .

"Vatia, will you go?" Caesar asked.

Vatia Isauricus looked startled, then very exalted. "It would be an honor, Caesar."

"Good, then you have the job." He stared at the mortified Piso. "Piso, I have work for you too, but inside Rome. I'm still trying to get the debt relief legislation into order, but I won't have it anything like completed before I leave for Africa Province. As you're a brilliant legal draftsman, I'd like to collaborate with you on the subject and then leave it in your hands when I go." He paused, spoke very seriously. "One of the most inequitable aspects of Roman government concerns payment for services rendered. Why should a man be forced to make his fortune governing a province? That has led to shocking abuses, and I'll see an end to them. Why shouldn't a man be able to receive a governor's stipend for work he does at home, work of equal importance? What I propose is to pay you a proconsular governor's stipend for finishing the laws I draft roughly."

That shut him up!

"That shut him up," young Octavius said under his breath.

When the third course was removed from the tables and only the wine flagons and water pitchers remained, the women departed to Calpurnia's spacious quarters upstairs for a good gossip.

Now Caesar could focus on the most silent of his guests.

"Have you changed your mind about how you intend to pursue your public career, Octavius?" he asked.

"Keeping my counsel, you mean, Caesar?"

"Yes."

"No, I still think it suits my character."

"I remember you said that Cicero's tongue runs away with him too much. You're quite right. I encountered him on the Via Appia outside Tarentum the day I arrived back in Italy, and was rudely reminded of that fact."

Octavius answered obliquely. "It's said in the family, Uncle Gaius, that when you were about ten years old you acted as a kind of nurse-companion to Gaius Marius while he was recovering from a stroke. And that he talked, you listened. That you learned much about waging war from listening."

"I did indeed. However, Octavius, I still betrayed my talent for waging war, I am not sure how. Perhaps I listened *too* hard, and he sensed qualities in me I didn't know I had."

"He was jealous," Octavius said flatly.

"Very perceptive! Yes, he was jealous. His day was clearly over, mine hadn't begun. Old men struck down can be nasty."

"Yet though his day was clearly over, he returned to public life. His jealousy of Sulla was greater."

"Sulla was old enough to have demonstrated his ability. And Marius took care of my pretensions with remarkable cunning."

"By appointing you the *flamen Dialis* and marrying you to Cinna's tiny daughter. A lifelong priesthood that forbade you to touch a weapon of war or witness death."

"That is so." Caesar grinned at his great-nephew. "But I wriggled out of the priesthood—with Sulla's connivance. Sulla didn't like me at all, but though Marius was long dead by then, he still loathed Marius—oh, almost to mania. So he freed me to spite a dead man."

"You didn't try to wriggle out of the marriage. You refused to divorce Cinnilla when Sulla commanded it."

"She was a good wife, and good wives are rare."

"I shall remember that."

"Have you many friends, Octavius?"

"No. I'm tutored at home, I don't meet many other boys."

"You must meet them on the Campus Martius when you go there for the boys' military drills and exercises, surely."

The brown skin flushed crimson; Octavius bit his lip. "I hardly ever go to the Campus Martius."

"Does your stepfather forbid it?" Caesar asked, astonished.

"No, no! He's very good to me, very kind. I just—I just don't get to the Campus Martius often enough to make friends."

Another Brutus? Caesar was asking himself, dismayed. Does this fascinating boy avoid his military duties? During our conversation at Misenum he said he didn't have any military talent. Can that be it, a reluctance to betray his ineptitude? Yet he doesn't have the smell of a Brutus about him, I'd swear he isn't craven or uninterested.

"Are you a good student?" he asked, leaving sensitive subjects alone. There was time to investigate further.

"At mathematics, history and geography, very good, I think," Octavius said, regaining his composure. "It's Greek I can't seem to master. No matter how much Greek I read, write, or speak, I can never manage to *think* in it. So I have to think in Latin and then translate."

"That's interesting. Perhaps later, after six months living in Athens, you'll learn to think in Greek," Caesar said, hardly able to credit that anyone suffered this inability. He thought automatically in whichever language he was speaking.

"Yes, perhaps," Octavius said rather neutrally.

Caesar settled deeper into the couch, aware that Lucius was eavesdropping shamelessly. "Tell me, Octavius, how far do you want to rise?"

"To the consulship, returned by every Century."

"Dictator, even?"

"No, definitely, definitely not." This didn't sound critical.

"Why so emphatic?"

"Ever since they forced you to cross the Rubicon, Uncle Gaius, I've watched and listened. Though I don't know you well, I think that to be the dictator was the last thing you wanted."

"Rather any office than that," said Caesar grimly, "but rather that office than undeserved exile and ignominy."

"I shall offer regularly to Jupiter Optimus Maximus that I am never faced with that alternative."

"Would you dare it if you had to?"

"Oh, yes. In my heart I am a Caesar."

"A Gaius Julius Caesar?"

"No, merely a Julian of the Caesares."

"Who are your heroes?"

"You," Octavius said simply. "Just you." He slid off the back of the couch. "Please excuse me, Uncle Gaius, Cousin Lucius. My mother made me promise that I'd go home early."

The two men left on the *lectus medius* watched the slight figure leave the room without drawing attention to himself.

"Well, well, well," drawled Lucius.

"What do you think of him, Lucius?"

"He's a thousand years old."

"Give or take a century or two, yes. Do you like him?"

"It's plain you do, but do I? Yes—with reservations."

"Expatiate."

"He's not a Julian of the Caesares, much though he may think he is. Oh, there are echoes of the old Patriciate, but also echoes of a mind never shaped in the patrician mold. I can't catalogue his style, yet I know he has one. It may well be that Rome hasn't seen his style before."

"You're saying he's going to go far."

The vivid blue eyes twinkled. "A fool I am not, Gaius! If I were you, I'd take him as my personal *contubernalis* the moment he turns seventeen."

"So I thought when I met him at Misenum a few years ago."

"One thing I'd watch."

"What?"

"That he doesn't grow too fond of arses."

The paler blue eyes twinkled. "A fool I am not, Lucius!"

3   The storm brewing in the legionary camps around Capua tossed its first thunderbolt the day after Caesar's dinner party, at the very end of October. A letter came from Mark Antony.

Caesar, there's trouble. Big, big trouble. The really veteran veterans are wild with rage, and I can't reason with them—or rather, with their elected representatives. It's the Tenth and Twelfth are the worst. Surprised? Well, I was surprised, at any rate.

The pot boiled over when I issued orders that the Seventh, the Eighth, the Ninth, the Tenth, the Eleventh, the Twelfth, the Thirteenth and the Fourteenth were to pull stakes and march for Neapolis and Puteoli. I had all their elected representatives on my doorstep in Herculaneum (I'm living in Pompeius's villa there), telling me that no one was going anywhere until after they'd been formally notified about things like their date of discharge, their plots of land, their bounties and bonuses for this extra campaign— that's what they call it, an "extra campaign." Not usual duty. And they want to be paid.

They were set on seeing you, so they weren't too happy when I had to tell them that you're too busy in Rome to come to Campania. The next thing I knew, the Tenth and Twelfth went crazy, started looting and wrecking all the villages around Abella, where they're camped.

Caesar, I can't handle them anymore. I suggest you come yourself. Or, if you *really* can't come, send someone important to see them. Someone they know and trust.

Here it is, and it's too soon. Oh, Antonius, will you never learn patience? You've so much riding on this, yet you've just made a clumsy move, you've betrayed your insincerity. The only clever part, which is acting now rather than later, is simply due to your impatience. No, I can't leave Rome, as you well know! Though not for the reasons you think. I daren't leave Rome until I've held my elections, is the true reason. Have you divined why? I don't think so, despite your acting now. You're too unsubtle.

Use the tactics of delay, Caesar. Postpone the reckoning until after the elections, no matter whom you have to sacrifice.

He sent for one of his loyalest and most competent military men, Publius Cornelius Sulla. Sulla's nephew.

"Why not send Lepidus?" Publius Sulla asked.

"He hasn't enough clout with old warhorses like the Tenth and Twelfth," Caesar said curtly. "Better to send a man they know from Pharsalus. Explain that their land is on my agenda, Publius, but that the debt legislation has to come first."

"Do you want me to take the pay wagons, Caesar?"

"I think not. I have my reasons. The boil is coming to a head, balm like pay might cause it to subside untimely. Just do your best with the paltry ammunition I've given you," said Caesar.

Publius Sulla returned four days later, cut and bruised on face and arms. "They *stoned* me!" he snarled, stiff with fury. "Oh, Caesar, grind their faces into the dust!"

"The faces I want to grind into the dust are those belonging to whoever is working on them," Caesar said grimly. "The men are idle and more or less permanently drunk, I suspect—discipline hasn't been kept up either. That means they've been extended a lot of credit with the tavern keepers, and their centurions and tribunes are even drunker than the rankers. For all his continuous presence in Campania for months on end, Antonius has let this happen. Who else is going guarantor for so much wine on credit?"

Publius Sulla shot Caesar a look of sudden comprehension, but said not a word.

Next Caesar summoned Gaius Sallustius Crispus, a brilliant orator. "Choose two of your fellow senators, Sallustius, and try to make the *cunni* see sense. As soon as the elections are over, I'll see them in person. Just hold the fort for me."

The Centuriate Assembly finally met on the Campus Martius to vote for two consuls and eight praetors; no one was surprised when Quintus Fufius Calenus was elected senior consul and Publius Vatinius junior consul. Every candidate for praetor whom Caesar had personally recommended was also voted in.

It was *done!* Now he could deal with the legions—and with Marcus Antonius.

Shortly after dawn two days later Mark Antony rode into Rome, his German troopers escorting a litter strapped between a pair of mules. In it was a badly injured Sallust.

Antony was nervous and on edge. Now that his big moment had arrived, he was fretting about how exactly he should conduct himself during his interview with Caesar. That was the trouble in dealing with someone who'd kicked your arse when you were twelve years old and been metaphorically kicking it ever since. Gaining the advantage was difficult.

So he went about it aggressively, left Poplicola and Cotyla outside holding his Public Horse, barged into the Domus Publica and walked straight to Caesar's study.

"They're on their way to Rome," he announced as he strode in.

Caesar put down his beaker of vinegar and hot water. "Who?"

"The Tenth and the Twelfth."

"Don't sit down, Antonius. You're on report. Stand in front of my desk and report to your commander. Why are two of my oldest veteran legions on their way to Rome?"

His neckerchief wasn't covering a patch of skin where the gold chain holding his leopard cloak suddenly began to pinch; Antony reached up and tugged at the scarlet neckerchief, conscious of a slight patina of cold sweat. "They've mutinied, Caesar."

"What happened to Sallustius and his companions?"

"They tried, Caesar, but—"

The voice became glacial. "I've known times, Antonius, when you could summon words. This had better be one of them, for your own sake. Tell me what happened, if you please."

The "if you please" was worst. Concentrate, concentrate! "Gaius Sallustius called the Tenth and Twelfth to an assembly. They came in a very ugly mood. He started to say that everybody would be paid before embarkation for Africa and the land was under review, but Gaius Avienus intervened—"

"Gaius Avienus?" Caesar asked. "An unelected tribune of the soldiers from Picenum? That Avienus?"

"Yes, he's one of the Tenth's representatives."

"What did Avienus have to say?"

"He told Sallustius and the other two that the legions were fed up, that they weren't willing to fight another campaign. They wanted their discharges and their land right that moment. Sallustius shouted that you were willing to give them a bonus of four thousand if they'd just get on their ships—"

"That was a mistake," Caesar interrupted, frowning. "Go on."

Feeling more confident, Antony ploughed on. "Some of the worst hotheads shoved Avienus aside and started pelting stones. Well, rocks, actually. The next thing the air was full of them. I did manage to save Sallustius, but the other two are dead."

Caesar reared in his chair, shocked. "Two of my senators, dead? Their names?"

"I don't know," said Antony, sweating again. He searched wildly for something exculpatory, and blurted, "I mean, I haven't attended any meetings of the Senate since I've been back. I've been too busy as Master of the Horse."

"If you saved Sallustius, why isn't he here with you now?"

"Oh, he's flat out, Caesar. I carted him back to Rome in a litter. Terrible head injury, but he's not paralyzed or having seizures or anything. The army surgeons say he'll recover."

"Antonius, why did you let matters come to this? I feel I should ask you, give you the opportunity to explain."

The reddish-brown eyes widened. "It's not my fault, Caesar! The veterans came back to Italy so discontented that nothing I did or said pacified them. They're mortally offended that you gave all the work in

Anatolia to ex-Republican legions, and they don't approve of the fact that you're giving *them* land on retirement."

"Now you tell me. What do you think the Tenth and Twelfth intend to do when they reach Rome?"

Antony rushed to answer. "That's why I hustled myself back, Caesar! They're in the mood for murder. I think you should get out of the city for your own protection."

The lined, handsome face looked fashioned from flint. "You know perfectly well that I would never leave Rome in a situation like this, Antonius. Is it I they're in the mood to murder?"

"They will if they find you," Antony said.

"You're sure of that? You're not exaggerating?"

"No, I swear it!"

Caesar drained the beaker and rose to his feet. "Go home and change, Antonius. Into a toga. I'm summoning the Senate to meet in Jupiter Stator's on the Velia in one hour. Kindly be there." He went to the door and thrust his head around it. "Faberius!" he called, then glanced back at Antony. "Well, why are you standing there like a cretin? Jupiter Stator's in one hour."

Not too bad, thought Antony, emerging on to the Sacra Via, where his friends were still waiting.

"Well?" asked Lucius Gellius Poplicola eagerly.

"He's summoned the Senate to meet in an hour, though what good he thinks that will do, I have no idea."

"How did he take it?" asked Lucius Varius Cotyla.

"Since he always listens to bad news with the same expression as the Tarpeian Rock, I don't know how he took it," Antony said impatiently. "Come on, I have to get home to my old place and try to find a toga. He wants me at the meeting."

Their faces fell. Neither Poplicola nor Cotyla was a senator, though both were ostensibly eligible. That they were not lay in their social unacceptability; Poplicola had once tried to murder his father, the Censor, and Cotyla was the son of a man convicted and sent into exile by his own court. When Antony returned to Italy, they had tied their careers to his rising star, and looked forward to great advancement once Caesar was out of the way.

"Is he leaving Rome?" Cotyla asked.

"Him, leave? Never! Rest easy, Cotyla. The legions belong to me now, and in two days the old boy will be dead—they'll tear him apart with their bare hands. Which will throw Rome into *tumultus*, and I, as Master of the Horse, will assume the office of dictator." He stopped in his tracks, struck by amazement. "You know, I can't think why we didn't work out that this was what to do ages ago!"

"It wasn't easy to see a clear path until he came back to Italy," said Poplicola, and frowned. "One thing worries me . . ."

"What's that?" asked Cotyla apprehensively.

"He's got more lives than a cat."

Antony's mood was soaring; the more he thought about that interview with Caesar, the more convinced he became that he'd won his way through. "Even cats run out of lives sooner or later," he said complacently. "At fifty-three, he's past it."

"Oh, it will give me great satisfaction to proscribe that fat slug, Philippus!" Poplicola gloated.

Antony pretended to look scandalized. "Lucius, he's your half brother!"

"He cut our mother out of his life, he deserves to die."

Attendance in the temple of Jupiter Stator was thin; yet one more thing to do, plump out the Senate, thought Caesar. When he entered behind his twenty-four lictors, his eyes searched in vain for Cicero, who was in Rome and had been notified that there was an urgent meeting of the Senate. No, he couldn't attend Caesar's Senate! *That* would be seen as giving in.

The Dictator's ivory curule chair was positioned between the ivory curule chairs of the consuls on a makeshift dais. Since the people had burned the Curia Hostilia down with Clodius's body inside it, Rome's oligarchic senior governing institution was obliged to meet in temporary premises. The place had to be an inaugurated temple, and most were too small for comfort, though Jupiter Stator was adequate for the mere sixty men gathered there.

Mark Antony was present in a purple-bordered toga that looked the worse for wear—crumpled, marred by stains. Can Antonius not even control his own servants? Caesar asked himself, irritated.

As soon as Caesar entered, Antony came bustling up. "Where does the Master of the Horse sit?" he asked.

"You sound like Pompeius Magnus when he was consul for the first time," Caesar said acidly. "Have someone write you a book on the subject. You've been in the Senate for six years."

"Yes, but hardly ever in it physically except when I was a tribune of the plebs, and that was only for three *nundinae.*"

"Put your stool in the front row where I can see you and you can see me, Antonius."

"Why on earth did you bother electing consuls?"

"You're about to find out."

The prayers were said, the auspices taken. Caesar waited then until everyone had seated himself.

"Two days ago the consuls Quintus Fufius Calenus and Publius Vatinius entered office," Caesar said. "It is a great relief to see Rome in the care of her proper senior magistrates, the two consuls and eight praetors. The courts will be able to function, the *comitia* to meet in the prescribed manner." His tone changed, became even calmer and more matter-of-fact. "I've summoned this session to inform you, conscript fathers, that two mutinous legions, the Tenth and the Twelfth, are at this moment marching to Rome in—according to my Master of the Horse—a mood for murder."

No one stirred, no one murmured, though the shock was so palpable that the air seemed to vibrate.

"A mood for murder. *My* murder, apparently. In light of this, I wish to diminish my importance to Rome. Were the Dictator to be slain by his own troops, our country might well despair. Our beloved Rome might once again fill up with ex-gladiators and other ruffians. Business might slump drastically. Public works, so necessary for full employment and building contractors, might come to a halt, particularly those that I am personally paying for. Rome's games and festivals might not occur. Jupiter Optimus Maximus might show his displeasure by sending a thunderbolt to demolish his temple. Vulcan might visit Rome with an earthquake. Juno Sospita might vent her wrath on Rome's unborn babies. The Treasury might empty overnight. Father Tiber might flood and backwash the sewage onto the streets. For the murder of the Dictator is a cataclysmic event. Cat-a-clys-mic."

They were all sitting with their mouths open.

"However," he went on blandly, "the murder of a *privatus* is of little public moment. Therefore, conscript fathers of Rome's old and hallowed Senate, I hereby lay down my *imperium maius* and the dictatorship. Rome has two duly elected consuls who have been sworn in with the prescribed rituals, and no priest or augur found any flaws. Very gladly I hand Rome to them."

He turned to his lictors, standing against the closed doors, and bowed. "Fabius, Cornelius, all you others, I thank you most sincerely for your care of the Dictator's person, and assure you that if and when I am once more elected to public office, I will call upon your services." He walked between the senators and handed Fabius a clinking bag. "A small donative, Fabius, to be divided among yourselves in the customary proportions. Now go back to the College of Lictors."

Fabius nodded and opened the door, his face impassive. The twenty-four lictors filed out.

The silence was so profound that the sudden fluttering of a bird in the rafters made everyone jump.

"On my way here," Caesar said, "I procured a *lex curiata* confirming the fact that I have laid down my dictatorial powers."

Antony had listened in disbelief, not understanding exactly what Caesar was doing, let alone why he was doing it. For a while, in fact, he had fancied that Caesar was playing a joke.

"What do you mean, you've laid down your dictatorship?" he asked, voice cracking. "You can't do that with two mutinous legions on their way to Rome! You're *needed!*"

"No, Marcus Antonius, I am not needed. Rome has consuls and praetors in office. They are now responsible for Rome's welfare."

"That's rubbish! This is an emergency!"

Neither Calenus nor Vatinius had said a word; they exchanged a glance that mutually agreed on continued silence. Something more was going on than a simple abdication of power, and both men knew Caesar very well, as friend, fellow politician, and military commander. This had to do with Marcus Antonius: no one was deaf or blind, everyone knew Antonius had been a naughty boy with the legions. Therefore let Caesar play the act to its end. A decision men like Lucius Caesar, Philippus and Lucius Piso had also reached.

"Naturally," Caesar said, addressing the House, not Antony, "I don't expect the consuls to do my dirty work. I shall meet the two mutinous legions on the Campus Martius and discover why they are bent not only on my destruction, but on their own. But I will meet them as a *privatus*. As no more important than they." His voice rose. "Let all of it rest upon what happens there!"

"You can't resign!" Antony gasped.

"I have already resigned, *lex curiata* and all."

Whole body numb, having difficulty breathing, Antony lurched toward Caesar. "You've gone mad!" he managed to say. "Raving mad! In which case, the answer's obvious—in the absence of the Dictator's sanity, as his Master of the Horse, I declare myself the Dictator!"

"You can't declare yourself anything, Antonius," said Lucius Caesar from his stool. "The Dictator has resigned. The moment that happens, the office of Master of the Horse ceases to exist. You're a *privatus* too."

"No! No, no, no!" Antony roared, fists clenched. "As Master of the Horse, and in the absence of the Dictator's sanity, I am now the Dictator!"

"Sit down, Antonius," said Fufius Calenus. "You're out of order. You're not the Master of the Horse, you're a *privatus.*"

What had happened? Where had it all gone? Clutching the last vestige of his composure, Antony finally looked into Caesar's eyes, and saw contempt, derision, a certain enjoyment.

"Remove yourself, Antonius," Caesar whispered, took Antony's right arm and escorted him to the open doors, the babble of sixty voices behind them.

Once outside he dropped Antony's arm as if to touch it was an offense. "Did you think you fooled me, cousin?" he asked. "You don't have the intelligence. I know enough now to understand that you're utterly untrustworthy, that you cannot be relied on, that you are indeed what your uncle always calls you, a wolfshead. Our political and professional relationship is ended, and our blood kinship has become a mortification. An embarrassment. Get out of my sight, Antonius, and stay out of it! You're a mere *privatus*, and a *privatus* you'll remain."

Antony turned on his heel, laughing, trying to pretend he was in control again. "One day you'll need me, Cousin Gaius!"

"If I do, Antonius, I *will* use you. But always in the sure knowledge that you're not to be trusted an inch. So don't get too puffed up again. You're not a thinking man's anus."

A single lictor, dressed in a plain white toga and without the axe in his *fasces*, directed the Tenth and Twelfth around the city outside its walls to the Campus Martius; they had come up from the south, the Campus Martius lay north.

Caesar met them absolutely alone, mounted on his famous war horse with the toes, clad in his habitual plain steel armor and the scarlet *paludamentum* of the General. He wore the oak-leaf crown on his head to remind them that he was a decorated war hero, a front-line soldier of rare bravery. The very sight of him was enough to turn their knees to jelly.

They had sobered up on the long march from Campania, for the taverns along the Via Latina had bolted their doors, they had no money and Marcus Antonius's pledge wasn't good for a drink in this part of the country. Word that Caesar wasn't the dictator anymore and that Marcus Antonius had therefore lost his job came when they were still well short of Rome, a dampener. And somehow, as the miles passed by under their hobnailed *caligae*, their grievances seemed to dwindle, their memories of Caesar their friend and fellow soldier to blossom. So when they set eyes on him sitting Toes without a vestige of fear, all they could think was how they loved him. Always had, always would.

"What are you doing here, *Quirites*?" he asked coldly.

A huge gasp went up, spreading ever wider as his words were passed back. *Quirites*? Caesar was calling *them* ordinary civilian citizens? But they weren't ordinary civilians, they were his boys! He always called them his boys! They were his soldiers!

"You're not soldiers," he said scornfully, reproached by a hundred voices. "Even Pharnaces would hesitate to call you that! You're drunks and incompetents, pathetic fools! You've rioted! Looted! Burned! Wrecked! Stoned Publius Sulla, one of your commanders at Pharsalus! Stoned three senators, two of them to death! If my mouth wasn't dry as ashes, *Quirites*, I'd spit on you! Spit on the lot of you!"

They were beginning to moan, some of them to weep.

"No!" screamed a man from the ranks. "No, it's a mistake! A misunderstanding! Caesar, we thought you'd forgotten us!"

"Better to forget you than have to remember mutiny! Better you were all dead than present here as declared mutineers!"

The biting voice went on to inform them that Caesar had all of Rome to care for, that he had trusted them to wait for him because he had thought they knew him.

"But we love you!" someone cried. "You love us!"

"Love? Love? *Love?*" Caesar roared. "Caesar can't love mutineers! You're the professional soldiers of the Senate and People of Rome, their servants, their only defense against their enemies! And you've just proved that you're not professionals! You're rabble! Not fit to clean vomit off the streets! You've mutinied, and you know what that means! You've forfeited your share of the booty to be distributed after I celebrate my triumphs, you've forfeited your land upon discharge, you've forfeited any additional bonuses! You're Head Count *Quirites*!"

They wept, pleaded, beseeched, begged to be forgiven. No, not *Quirites*, not ordinary civilian citizens! Never *Quirites*! They belonged to Romulus and Mars, not to Quirinus!

The business took several hours, watched by half of Rome standing atop the Servian Walls and sitting on the roofs of the Capitol houses; the Senate, including the consuls, clustered a respectable distance from the *privatus* quelling a mutiny.

"Oh, he's a wonder!" sighed Vatinius to Calenus. "How did Antonius manage to delude himself that Caesar's soldiers would touch a hair of his head, scarce though they are?"

Calenus grinned. "I think Antonius was sure he'd replaced Caesar in their affections. You know what Antonius was like in Gaul, Pollio," he said to that individual. "Always prating that he'd inherit Caesar's legions when the old boy was past it. And for a year he's been buying them drinks and letting them loaf, which he equates with bliss. Forgetting that these men have willingly marched through six feet of snow for days on end just to please Caesar, not to mention never let him down on a field of battle, no matter how hard the fight."

Pollio shrugged. "Antonius thought his moment had arrived," he said, "but Caesar diddled him. I wondered why the old boy was so determined to hold rump of the year elections, and why he wouldn't visit Campania to calm the men down. It was Antonius he was after, and he knew how far he'd have to go to get him. I feel sorry for Caesar, it's a bitter affair whichever way you look at it. Though I hope he's learned the real lesson in this."

"What real lesson?" Vatinius asked.

"That even a Caesar can't leave veteran troops idle for so long. Oh, yes, Antonius stirred them, but so did others. There are always malcontents and natural troublemakers in any army. Idleness gives them fertile soil to till," said Pollio.

"I'll never forgive them!" Caesar said to Lucius Caesar, two red spots burning in his cheeks.

Lucius shivered. "But you did forgive them."

"I acted prudently, for the sake of Rome. But I swear to you, Lucius, that every man in the Tenth and Twelfth will pay for this mutiny. First the Ninth, now two more. The Tenth! I took them from Pomptinus at Genava—they were *always* my boys! For the moment I need them, but their own activities have shown me what I have to do—have a trusted agent or two in their ranks to take down the names of the ringleaders in this sort of thing. A rot has set in—certain among them have come to believe that the soldiers of Rome have power of their own."

"At least now it's over."

"Oh, no. There's more to come," Caesar said positively. "I may have drawn Antonius's fangs, but there are still some snakes lurking in the legion grass."

"On the subject of Antonius, I hear that he has the money to pay his debts," said Lucius, thought about that, then hastened to amend it. "At least some of his debts. He intends to bid for Pompeius's palace on the Carinae."

Brows pleating, Caesar looked alert. "Tell me more."

"To begin with, he looted Pompeius's premises wherever he

went. For instance, that solid gold grapevine Magnus was gifted with by Aristobulus of the Jews turned up the other day in the Porticus Margaritaria. It sold for a fortune in less time than it took Curtius to put it on display. And Antonius has another source of revenue—Fulvia."

"Ye gods!" Caesar cried, revolted. "After Clodius and Curio, what can she see in a gross specimen like Antonius?"

"A third demagogue. Fulvia falls in love with men who make trouble—and on that account, Antonius is very eligible. Take my word for it, Gaius, she'll marry Antonius."

"Has he divorced Antonia Hybrida?"

"No, but he will."

"Has Antonia Hybrida any money of her own?"

"Hybrida managed to conceal the existence of a lot of the grave gold he found on Cephallenia, and it's making his second exile most comfortable. Antonius spent her two-hundred-talent dowry, but I'm sure her father would be happy to settle another two hundred talents on her if you recall him from exile. I know he's execrable, and I well remember your suit against him, but it's a way of ensuring his daughter's future. She won't find a new husband. The child is such a sad case too."

"I'll recall Hybrida as soon as I return from Africa. What's one more, when I'm going to recall the Sullan exiles?"

"Is Verres coming home?" Lucius asked.

"Never!" Caesar said vehemently. "Never, never, never!"

The chastened legions were paid and shipped out of Neapolis and Puteoli gradually, destined for a primary camp around Lilybaeum in western Sicily, thence to Africa Province later.

No one, least of all the two consuls, asked any questions as to why—or how, legally—a *privatus* was calmly functioning as commander-in-chief of the forces intended to crush the Republicans in Africa Province. All would be made clear in time. As it was. At the end of November, Caesar held elections for next year's crop of magistrates, and graciously assented to pleas that he stand for the consulship. When asked if he had any preferences as to whom among his adherents he would like as fellow consul, he indicated that he would quite like his old friend and colleague, Marcus Aemilius Lepidus.

"I hope you understand your place, Lepidus," he said to that worthy after they had declared themselves consular candidates amid a cheering crowd at Vatinius's electoral booth.

"Oh, I think so," Lepidus said contentedly, not at all put out by

Caesar's bluntness. The promised consulship had been a while coming, but it was going to be his on New Year's Day, no doubt about that.

"Tell me, then."

"I am to hold Rome and Italy for you in your absence—keep both at peace—carry on with your program of legislation—make sure I don't insult the knights or depress business—continue to adlect senators according to your criteria—and watch Marcus Antonius like a hawk. Also watch Antonius's intimates, from Poplicola to the newest, Lucius Tillius Cimber," said Lepidus.

"What a splendid fellow you are, Lepidus!"

"Do you want to be dictator again, Caesar?"

"I would prefer not, but it may become necessary. If it does become necessary, would you be prepared to act as my Master of the Horse?" Caesar asked.

"Of course. Better me than some of the others. I never have had the knack of getting cozy with the troops."

 Brutus came home early in December, after Caesar had left for Campania to finish embarking his army. His mother looked him up and down sourly.

"You haven't improved" was her verbal conclusion.

"I think I have, actually," said Brutus, making no attempt to sit down. "The last two years have been highly educational."

"I hear you dropped your sword at Pharsalus and hid."

"If I had continued to hold it, I would have endangered my health. Does all of Rome know this story?"

"My, Brutus, you almost snapped at me! Whom do you mean by 'all of Rome'?"

"I mean, all of Rome."

"And Porcia in particular?"

"She's your niece, Mama. Why do you hate her so?"

"Because, like her father, she's the descendant of a slave."

"And a Tusculan peasant, you forgot to add."

"I hear you're to be a pontifex."

"Oh, Caesar came visiting, did he? Is the affair on again?"

"Don't be crass, Brutus!"

So Caesar hadn't renewed the affair, thought Brutus, escaping. From his mother's sitting room he went to his wife's. A daughter of Appius Claudius Pulcher, she had become his bride seven years ago, shortly after Julia's death, but had had little joy in the union. Brutus had managed to consummate the marriage, but with no pleasure, a worse factor than no love to poor Claudia. Nor had he entered her bed often enough to generate the children she yearned for. A good-natured young woman, and not ill looking, she had many friends and spent as much time as she could away from this unhappy house. When forced to be in it, she kept to her own apartment and her loom. Luckily she had no desire to administer the establishment, though technically it was her duty as the Master's wife to do so; Servilia was mistress, always.

Brutus pecked Claudia on the cheek, smiled at her absently and went to find his two tame philosophers, Strato of Epirus and Volumnius. Two welcoming faces at last! They had been with him in Cilicia, but he had sent them home when he joined Pompey; it might please Uncle Cato to drag his tame philosophers to a war, but Brutus wasn't made of such stern stuff, nor were Volumnius and Strato of Epirus. Brutus was an Academic, not a Stoic.

"The consul Calenus wants to see you," said Volumnius.

"Whatever for, I wonder?"

"Marcus Brutus, sit down!" said Calenus, looking glad to see him. "I was beginning to worry that you wouldn't return in time."

"In time for what, Quintus Calenus?"

"To take up your new duties, of course."

"New duties?"

"That's right. Caesar favors you highly—well, you know that— and said I was to be sure to tell you that he can think of no one as qualified as you to do this particular work."

"Work?" asked Brutus, a little blankly.

"Lots of it! Though you haven't been praetor yet, Caesar's given you a proconsular imperium and appointed you governor of Italian Gaul."

Brutus sat with jaw dropped. "Proconsular imperium? *Me?*" he squeaked, winded.

"Yes, you," said Calenus, who seemed undisturbed by this extraordinary business, didn't appear resentful or annoyed that such a plum post was going to an ex-Republican. "The province is at peace, so there won't be any military duties—in fact, at the moment there's no legion, even as a garrison."

The senior consul folded his hands on his desk and looked confiding. "You see, next year there's going to be a massive census in Italy and Italian Gaul, held on an entirely new basis. The census conducted two years ago no longer meets Caesar's—er—purposes, hence this new one." Calenus bent to lift a book bucket of scarlet leather, its flap sealed with purple wax, and handed it across the desk to Brutus, who looked at the seal curiously. A sphinx, with the word CAESAR around its margin.

When he went to take the bucket, he discovered that it was far heavier than most—it must be absolutely stuffed with very tightly wound scrolls. "What's inside?" he asked.

"Your orders, dictated by Caesar himself. He intended to give them to you in person, but of course you didn't show up in time." Calenus got up, came around his desk and shook Brutus's hand warmly. "Let me know the date you intend to set out, and I'll arrange for your *lex curiata* of imperium. It's a good job, Marcus Brutus, and I agree with Caesar—it's perfect for you."

Brutus left in a daze, his manservant carrying the book bucket as if it were made of gold. At first he stood in the narrow street outside Calenus's house and turned around several times, as if he wasn't sure whereabouts to go. Suddenly he squared his shoulders.

"Take the bucket home, Phylas, and lock it in my strong room at once," said Brutus to his manservant. He coughed, shuffled, looked embarrassed. "If the lady Servilia should see it, she may demand that you hand it over. I would prefer that she didn't see it, is that clear?"

Face expressionless, Phylas bowed. "Leave it to me, *domine*. It will go straight into your strong room undetected."

So the pair parted, Phylas to return to Brutus's house, and Brutus to walk the short distance to Bibulus's house.

Here he found chaos. Like many of the nicer premises on the Palatine, the back portions opened on to the lane-width street; entry put the newcomer in a small open room sheltering the porter, with the kitchens off to one side and the bathroom and latrine off to the other. Straight ahead was the big peristyle garden, surrounded on its three respectable aspects by a pillared walkway, off which opened the various suites of the inhabitants on right and left. At the far end lay the dining room, the master's study, and, beyond them, the huge atrium reception room, equipped with a loggia overlooking the Forum Romanum.

The garden was a muddle of crates and wrapped statues; a jumble of pots and pans tied together with twine littered the stones outside the kitchen, and the covered walkways were impeded by beds, couches, chairs, pedestals, different kinds of tables and cupboards. Linen lay in a heap, clothing in another.

Brutus stood in shock, understanding at once what was going on: though dead, Marcus Calpurnius Bibulus had been declared *nefas*, and his estates were confiscate. His surviving son, Lucius, was propertyless, and so too his widow. They were vacating the house, which must therefore be up for auction.

"*Ecastor, Ecastor, Ecastor!*" said a familiar voice, loud and harsh, deep enough to sound like a man's.

There she was, Porcia, clad in her usual awful brown tent of some coarse fabric, her mass of brilliant, waving red hair half falling down, tendrils escaping the pins.

"Put it all back!" Brutus cried, walking to her swiftly.

The next moment he was lifted off his feet, squashed in an embrace that drove the breath from his lungs, the smell of her in his nostrils—ink, paper, stale wool, leather of book buckets. Porcia, Porcia, Porcia!

How it happened he had no idea, for there was nothing novel about this greeting—she had been lifting him off his feet and squashing him for years. But his lips, pressed against her cheek, were suddenly seeking hers, and having found them, locked; a wave of fire and feeling crashed upon his spirit, he struggled to free his arms and slide them across her back. Then he kissed her with the first surge of passion he had ever known. She kissed him back, the taste of her tears mingled with the delicacy of her breath, untainted by wine or fancy foods. It seemed to go on for hours, and she didn't push him away or hold aloof. Her ecstasy was too great, her longing too old, her love too overwhelming.

"I love you!" he said when he could, his hands stroking her wonderful hair, his fingertips reveling in its crackling life.

"Oh, Brutus, I have always loved you! Always, always!"

They found two chairs abandoned on the colonnade, and sank into them handfast, gazing into each other's tear-filled eyes, smiling and smiling. Two children discovering enchantment.

"I have finally come home," he said, mouth trembling.

"It can't be real," she said, and leaned to kiss him again.

A dozen people had witnessed this passionate reunion, but they were all servants save for Bibulus's son, who winked at the steward and slipped away unnoticed.

"Put it all back," Brutus said again some time later.

"I can't. We've been served notice."

"I'll buy the place, so put it all back," he insisted.

Her lovely grey eyes grew stern; suddenly Cato looked out of them. "No, my father would not condone it."

"Yes, dearest, he would," Brutus said very seriously. "Come, Porcia, you know Cato! He would see it as a victory for the Republicans. He would deem it a right act. It is the duty of the family to look after the family. Cato, to render his daughter homeless? I condemn Caesar for this. Lucius Bibulus is too young to be a part of the Republican cause."

"His father was one of the great Republicans." She turned her face to present Brutus with her profile, the very image of Cato's; the huge, beaked nose was noble to his eyes, and the mouth distractingly beautiful. "Yes, I see the rightness," she said, then turned to look at him fearfully. "But others will be bidding too. What if someone else buys this house?"

He laughed. "Porcia! Who can outbid Marcus Junius Brutus? Besides, this is a nice house, but it doesn't compare with places like Pompeius Magnus's or Metellus Scipio's. The big money will be bid for the outstanding houses. I won't bid myself, I'll use an agent, so Rome won't gossip. And I shall bid for your father's estates in Lucania. Nothing else of his, just that. I'd like you to have something of his forever."

Tears dropped on her hands. "You speak as if he were dead already, Brutus."

"Many may get pardons, Porcia, but you and I know that Caesar will never reach an accommodation with any of the leaders who went to Africa Province. Still, Caesar won't live forever. He's older than Cato, who may be able to come home one day."

"Why did you beg a pardon from him?" she asked abruptly.

His face saddened, fell. "Because I am not Cato, my dearest girl. I wish I were! Oh, how I wish it! But if you truly love me, you must know what I am. As my mother says, a coward. I—I can't explain what happens to me when it comes to battle or defying people like Caesar. I just go to pieces."

"My father will say that it isn't a right act for me to love you because you gave in to Caesar."

"Yes, he will," Brutus agreed, smiling. "Does that mean we have no future together? I won't believe it."

She flung both arms around him fiercely. "I'm a woman, and women are weak, my father says. He won't approve, but I can't live without you, and I won't live without you!"

"Then you'll wait for me?" he asked.

"Wait?"

"Caesar has endowed me with a proconsular imperium. I am to go at once to govern Italian Gaul."

Her arms dropped, she moved away. "Caesar!" she hissed. "Everything goes back to Caesar, even your awful mother!"

His shoulders spasmed, hunched. "I have known that since I was a lad and first met him. When he came back from his quaestorship in Further Spain. He stood in the midst of all those women, looking like a god. So striking! So—*royal.* My mother was shot through the heart— he *slew* her! Her, with her pride! A patrician Servilia Caepionis. But she beggared her pride for him. After my stepfather Silanus died, she thought Caesar would marry her. He refused on the grounds that she was an unfaithful wife. 'With you, only with you!' she cried. It made no difference with whom she was unfaithful, he said. The fact remained that she was an unfaithful wife."

"How do you know that?" Porcia asked, fascinated.

"Because she came home roaring and screeching like Mormolyce. The whole house knew," said Brutus simply, and shivered. "But that is Caesar. It takes a Cato to resist him, and I am no Cato, my love." His eyes filled with tears, he took her hands. "Forgive me for my weakness, Porcia! A *proconsular* imperium, and I haven't even been a praetor yet! Italian Gaul! How can I say no to him? I don't have the strength."

"Yes, I understand," she said gruffly. "Go and govern your province, Brutus. I'll wait for you."

"Do you mind if I say nothing about us to my mother?"

She barked her strange laugh, but not in amusement. "No, dear Brutus, I don't mind. If she terrifies you, she terrifies me even more. Let's not wake the monster before we have to. Stay married to Claudia for the time being."

"Have you heard from Cato?" he asked.

"No, not a word. Nor has Marcia, who suffers terribly. She has to go home to her father now, of course. Philippus tried to intervene for Marcia's sake, but Caesar was adamant. Everything of my father's is confiscate, and she gave her dowry to him when he rebuilt the Basilica Porcia after Clodius's fire. Philippus isn't happy. She cries so, Brutus!"

"What of your dowry?"

"It went to rebuild the Basilica Porcia too."

"Then I'll lodge a sum with Bibulus's bankers for you."

"Cato would not approve."

"If Cato took your dowry, my love, he has forfeited his right to an opinion. Come," he said, drawing her to her feet, "I want to kiss you again, somewhere less public." At the door to her study he looked at her gravely. "We are first cousins, Porcia. Perhaps we shouldn't have children."

"Only *half* first cousins," she said reasonably. "Your mother and my father are only half sister and half brother."

* * *

A great deal of money came out of hiding when the property of the unpardoned Republicans came up for auction. Bidding through Scaptius, Brutus had no trouble in acquiring Bibulus's house, his big villa in Caieta, his Etrurian *latifundium* and his Campanian farms, vineyards; the best way to provide Porcia and young Lucius with an income, he had decided, was to buy all that Bibulus had. But he had no luck with Cato's Lucanian estates.

Caesar's agent, Gaius Julius Arvernus, bought every last piece of Cato's property. For more by far than it was worth; Brutus's Scaptius didn't dare keep on bidding once the sums became outrageous. Caesar's reasons were two: he wanted the satisfaction of seeing Cato's property fall to him, and he also wanted to use it to dower his three ex-centurions with enough to qualify for membership in the Senate. Decimus Carfulenus and two others had won the *corona civica,* and Caesar intended to honor Sulla's legislation that promoted all winners of major crowns of valor to the Senate.

"The odd thing is that I think my father would approve," said Porcia to Brutus when he came to bid her farewell.

"I'm very sure that Caesar wasn't aiming for Cato's approval," said Brutus.

"Then he misread my father, who esteems valor quite as much as Caesar."

"Given the hideous hatred between them, Porcia, neither man can read the other."

Pompey's mansion on the Carinae was knocked down to Mark Antony for thirty million sesterces, but when he casually told the auctioneers that he would defer payment until his finances were more flush, the head of the firm drew him aside.

"I am afraid, Marcus Antonius, that you must pay the entire amount immediately. Orders from Caesar."

"But it would clean me out!" said Antony indignantly.

"Pay now, or forfeit the property and incur a fine."

Antony paid, cursing.

Whereas Servilia, new owner of Lentulus Crus's *latifundium* and several lucrative vineyards in Falernian Campania, fared much better at Caesar's hands.

"Our instructions are to give you a third off the price," the chief auctioneer said when she presented herself at the booth to make arrangements for payment. She hadn't bothered to use an agent, it was more fun by far to bid in person, especially as she was a women and not supposed to be so publicly forward.

"Instructions from whom?" she asked.

"Caesar, *domina*. He said you would understand."

Most of Rome understood, including Cicero, who almost fell off his chair laughing. "Oh, well done, Caesar!" he cried to Atticus (another successful bidder), visiting to give him all the news. "A third off! A *third!* You have to admit that the man's witty!" The joke, of course, lay in the fact that Servilia's third girl, Tertulla, was Caesar's child.

The witticism hadn't amused Servilia in the least, but her umbrage was not sufficient to spurn the discount. Ten million was ten million, after all.

Gaius Cassius, who bid for nothing, was not amused either. "How dared he draw attention to my wife!" he snarled. "Everyone I meet puns on Tertulla's name!"

More than his wife's relationship to Caesar was annoying Cassius; while Brutus, the same age and at exactly the same level on the *cursus honorum*, was going to govern Italian Gaul as proconsul, he, Gaius Cassius, had been palmed off with an ordinary propraetorian legateship in Asia Province. Though Vatia the governor was his own brother-in-law, he wasn't one of Cassius's favorite people.

V

The Sting in Winning

From JANUARY until QUINCTILIS (JULY) of 46 B.C.

FULVIA

PORCIA

CALPURNIA

Publius Sittius was a Roman knight from Campanian Nuceria, of considerable wealth and education; among his friends he had numbered Sulla and Cicero. Several unfortunate investments during the years after Pompey the Great and Marcus Crassus had been consuls for the first time had caused him to join Catilina's conspiracy to overthrow Rome's legitimate government; what had attracted him was Catilina's promise that he would bring in a general cancellation of debts. Though Sittius didn't think so at the time, it turned out to be for the best that his financial embarrassments grew too pressing to linger in Italy waiting for Catilina's bid at power. He was forced to flee to Further Spain at the beginning of the Cicero/Hybrida consulship, and when that didn't prove far enough away from Rome, he then migrated to Tingis, the capital of western Mauretania.

This most distressing series of events brought out qualities in Publius Sittius that he never knew he owned; the businessman with a tendency to speculate transformed himself into a sweet-talking, immensely capable freebooter who undertook to reorganize King Bocchus's army, and even to provide the ruler of western Mauretania with a nice little navy. Though Bocchus's kingdom was farther from Numidia than his brother, Bogud's, kingdom of eastern Mauretania, Bocchus was terrified of the expansionist ideas churning around in King Juba of Numidia's head. Juba was determined to be another Masinissa, and since the Roman African province lay on Numidia's eastern borders, the only direction to expand was west.

Once he had Bocchus's forces up to strength, Sittius did the same for Bogud's forces. His rewards were gratifying; money, his own palace in Tingis, a whole harem of delectable women, and no business worries. Definitely the life of a talented freebooter was preferable to flirting with conspiracies in Italy!

When King Juba of Numidia declared for the Republicans after Caesar crossed the Rubicon, it was inevitable that Bocchus and Bogud of Mauretania would declare for Caesar. Publius Sittius stepped up Mauretanian military preparedness and sat back to see what would happen. A great relief when Caesar won at Pharsalus, then a huge shock when the Republican survivors of Pharsalus decided to make Africa Province their next focus of resistance. Too close to home!

So Sittius hired a few spies in Utica and Hadrumetum to keep himself informed on Republican doings, and waited for Caesar to invade, as Caesar must.

* * *

But Caesar's invasion began unhappily in several ways. He and his first fleet were forced to land at Leptis Minor because every seaport to the north of it was too strongly fortified by the Republicans to think of trying to get ashore. As there were no port facilities at Leptis Minor, the ships had to be brought in very close to a long beach and the troops ordered to jump into shallow water, wade ashore. Caesar went first, of course. But his fabled luck deserted him; he jumped, tripped and fell full length in the knee-deep water. A terrible omen! Every single pair of watching eyes widened, a thousand throats gasped, rumbled.

Up he came with the agility of a cat, both hands clenched into fists above his head, sand trickling from them down his arms.

"Africa, I have you in my hold!" he shouted, turning the omen into a propitious one.

Nor had he neglected the old legend that Rome couldn't win in Africa without a Scipio present. The Republicans had Metellus Scipio in the command tent, but Caesar's purely titular second-in-command was Scipio Salvitto, a disreputable scion of the family Cornelius Scipio whom he had plucked out of a Roman brothel. A complete nonsense, Caesar knew; Gaius Marius had conquered in Africa without a Scipio in sight, though Sulla *was* a Cornelian.

None of which had much significance compared to the fact that his legions were continuing to mutiny. The Ninth and Tenth were joined by the Fourteenth in a mutiny first quelled in Sicily, but which flared up again the moment they were landed in Africa. He paraded them, flogged a few and concentrated upon the five men, including the un-elected tribune of the soldiers Gaius Avienus, who had done most of the damage. The five were put aboard a ship with all their belongings and sent back to Italy, disgraced, discharged and stripped of every en-titlement from land to booty.

"If I were a Marcus Crassus, I would decimate you!" he cried to the assembled men. "You deserve no mercy! But I *cannot* execute men who have fought for me bravely!"

Naturally the news that Caesar's legions were disaffected reached the Republicans; Labienus began to whoop in delight.

"What a situation!" Caesar said to Calvinus, with him as usual. "Of my eight legions, three consist of raw, unblooded recruits, and of my five veteran legions, three are untrustworthy."

"They'll fight for you with all their customary verve," Calvinus said comfortably. "You have a genius for handling them that fools like Marcus Crassus never had. Yes, I know you loved him, but a general who decimates is a fool."

"I was too weak," Caesar said.

"A comfort to know you have weaknesses, Gaius. A comfort to them as well. They don't think the worse of you for clemency." He patted Caesar's arm. "There won't be any more mutinies. Go and drill your raw recruits."

Advice that Caesar followed, to discover that his luck was back. Exercising his three legions of raw recruits, he stumbled by chance upon Titus Labienus and a larger force, and evaded defeat by typical Caesarean boldness. Labienus ceased to whoop.

Reports of all this had percolated to Publius Sittius; he and his two kings began to fear that Caesar, very outnumbered, would be overpowered.

What, wondered Sittius, could Mauretania do to help? Nothing in Africa Province because the Mauretanian army was similar to the Numidian one: it consisted of lightly armed cavalry who fought as lancers rather than at close quarters. Nowhere near enough ships were available to transport troopers and horses a thousand miles by sea. Therefore, Publius Sittius decided, the best thing to do was to invade Numidia from the west and lure King Juba back to defend his own kingdom. That would leave the Republicans very short of cavalry and deny them one of their sources of supplies.

The moment he heard that the impudent Sittius had invaded, Juba panicked and withdrew westward in a hurry.

"I do not know how long we can keep Juba out of the way," said Sittius in a letter to Caesar, "but my kings and I hope that his absence will at least give you a breathing space."

A breathing space that Caesar utilized to good effect. He sent Gaius Sallustius Crispus and one legion to the big island of Cercina in the bight, where the Republicans had amassed huge stores of grain. Though it was after harvest time, the African province's grain was denied him, for the Bagradas River's wheat *latifundia* lay west of the Republican lines; Caesar's territory around Leptis Minor was the poorest land in the province, and south to Thapsus it was even poorer.

"What the Republicans have forgotten," Caesar said to Sallust, recovered from his stoning at Abella, "is that Gaius Marius settled Cercina with his veterans. My father was the one who did it for him, so the Cercinans know the name of Caesar very well. You have this job, Sallustius, because you can draw the birds down from the trees with words. What you have to do is remind the children and grandchildren of Gaius Marius's veterans that Caesar is Marius's nephew, that their loyalties must lie with Caesar. Talk well, and you won't have to fight. I want the Cercinans to hand over Metellus Scipio's hoard of grain willingly. If we have it, we'll eat for however long we're in Africa."

While Sallust sailed off with his legion on the short voyage to Cercina, Caesar fortified his position and started to send letters of commiseration to the wheat plutocrats of the Bagradas and the Catada, whom Metellus Scipio was needlessly antagonizing. Having taken sufficient grain to feed his troops without bothering to pay for it, Metellus Scipio, for reasons best known to himself, pursued a scorched-earth policy, burned the fields wherein the coming year's crops were sprouting.

"It rather sounds," said Caesar to his nephew Quintus Pedius, "as if Metellus Scipio thinks the Republicans are going to lose."

"Whoever wins must lose," said Quintus Pedius, a farmer to his very core. "We'd better hope this business finishes itself in time to plant a second time. The bulk of the winter rains are still to come, and burned stubble ploughed in is beneficial."

"Let's hope Sallustius succeeds" was Caesar's answer.

Two *nundinae* after his departure, Sallust and his legion were back, Sallust wreathed in smiles. Apprised of the situation, the Cercinans unanimously declared for Caesar, undertook to keep the major part of the grain there, defend it against Republican grain transports when they came, and send it to Caesar as he needed it.

"Excellent!" said Caesar. "Now all we have to do is force a general engagement and get this wretched affair over with."

Easier said than done. With Juba absent, neither Metellus Scipio in the command tent nor Labienus in the field wanted a general engagement with someone as slippery as Caesar, even if his veterans were disaffected.

Caesar wrote to Publius Sittius and told him to withdraw.

More time actually dragged on than the calendar indicated, for the College of Pontifices at Caesar's direction had declared an intercalation following the month of February: twenty-three extra days. This little month, called Mercedonius, had to be taken into account when both sides said that March seemed as if it would never end. The Republican legions, camped around Hadrumetum, and the Caesarean legions, camped around Leptis Minor, had to suffer two full months of relative inertia while Juba in western Numidia tried to lay his hands on the wily Publius Sittius, who finally received Caesar's letter and withdrew toward the end of March. Juba hurried back to Africa Province.

* * *

Even so, Caesar had to force an engagement, the Republicans were so wary of him. They skirmished, then withdrew, skirmished, then withdrew. Very well, they would have it thus! Caesar must attack Thapsus from its landward side. Not very far south of Leptis Minor, the city was already under massive blockade from the sea, but Labienus had fortified it heavily, and it still held out.

Shadowed by Metellus Scipio and Labienus in joint command of the entire Republican army, including Juba and his squadron of war elephants, Caesar marched his legions out of Leptis Minor in the direction of Thapsus at the beginning of April.

A typical feature of that brackish, inhospitable coastline gave Caesar his long-awaited chance: a flat, sandy spit about a mile and a half wide and several miles long. On one side of it lay the sea, on the other a huge salt lagoon. Inwardly exulting, Caesar led his army on to the spit, and kept marching in very tight formation until every man he had was penned into the spit.

What he gambled on was that Labienus wouldn't divine why he marched in a modified *agmen quadratum* instead of the usual eight-man-wide snake; *agmen quadratum* was a march in wide columns of troops, which reduced the length of the forces while it increased their breadth. Knowing Labienus, he would simply assume that Caesar expected to be attacked by the shadowing Republican army, and wanted to hustle his men off the spit as quickly as he could. In reality, it was Caesar who intended to attack.

The moment Caesar marched into the spit, Labienus saw what he had to do, and raced to do it. While the bulk of his infantry under Afranius and Juba closed Caesar off from retreat out of the spit, Labienus and Metellus Scipio led the cavalry and the fast-moving veteran legions around the landward side of the lagoon and positioned themselves at the far end of the spit to meet Caesar's advance head-on.

Caesar's bugles sounded: his army promptly split into two halves, with Gnaeus Domitius Calvinus leading the half which reversed its direction and charged at Afranius and Juba behind, while Caesar and Quintus Pedius led the half still moving forward in a charge at Labienus and Metellus Scipio. All Caesar's crack legions were at the head and rear of his army, with the raw recruits in the middle. The moment the two halves went in opposite directions, the recruits were behind the crack troops.

Thapsus, as the battle came to be called, was a rout. All smarting from Caesar's disapproval allied to his clemency, his veterans, particularly the Tenth, fought perhaps better than in all their long careers. By the end of the day, ten thousand Republican dead littered the field, and organized resistance in Africa was over. The most disappointing thing about Thapsus to Caesar was the dearth of prominent captives. Metellus Scipio, Labienus, Afranius, Petreius, Sextus Pompey, the governor Attius Varus, Faustus Sulla and Lucius Manlius Torquatus all fled, as did King Juba.

"I very much fear it will go on somewhere else," Calvinus said to Caesar afterward. "In Spain, perhaps."

"If it does, then I'll go to Spain," Caesar said grimly. "The Republican cause *has* to die, Calvinus, otherwise the Rome I want to make will revert back to the *boni* conception of the *mos maiorum.*"

"Then the one you have to eliminate is Cato."

"Not eliminate, if by that you mean kill. I don't want *any* of them dead, but most particularly Cato. The rest may see the error of their ways, Cato never will. Why? Because that part of his mind is missing. Yet he must stay alive, and he must enter my Senate. I need Cato as an exhibit."

"He won't consent to that."

"He won't know that he is," Caesar said positively. "I'm going to write a protocol governing conduct in the Senate and the *comitia*—no filibustering, for example. Time limits for speeches. And no allegations about fellow members without definite proof."

"We march for Utica, then?"

"We march for Utica."

 A courier from Metellus Scipio brought the news of the defeat at Thapsus to Utica, but the man was not more than a few hours ahead of refugees from the battlefield, none of them having higher rank than a junior military tribune.

"Lucius Torquatus, Sextus Pompeius and I are joining Gnaeus Pompeius's fleet in Hadrumetum," said Metellus Scipio's brief note. "As yet we have no idea of our next destination, but it will not be Utica unless you request that, Marcus Cato. If you can rally enough men to resist Caesar, then we will fight with you."

"But Caesar's troops were disaffected," Cato said hollowly to his son. "I was *sure* we'd beat him!"

Young Cato didn't answer: what was there to say?

After writing to Metellus Scipio to tell him not to bother with Utica, Cato sat drawn up into himself for the rest of that awful day, then at dawn of the next he took Lucius Gratidius and set out to see the Thapsus refugees, who had clustered together in an old camp on Utica's outskirts.

"There are enough of us to give Caesar one more fight," he said to their senior, a minor legate named Marcus Eppius. "I have five thousand good, trained young men in the city who are willing to join those of you here. And I can rearm you."

Eppius shook his head. "No, Marcus Cato, we've had enough." He shivered, lifted his hand in the sign to ward off the Evil Eye. "Caesar is invincible, we know that now. We captured one of the Tenth's centurions, Titius, whom Quintus Metellus Scipio examined himself. Titius admitted that the Ninth, the Tenth and the Fourteenth had mutinied twice since leaving Italy. Even so, when Caesar sent them into battle, they fought like heroes for him."

"What happened to this centurion Titius?"

"He was executed."

And that, thought Cato, is really why I ought never have put Metellus Scipio in the command tent. Or Labienus. Caesar would have pardoned a brave captive centurion. As should all men.

"Well, I suggest that all of you make your way to Utica's harbor and board the transports waiting there," Cato said cheerily. "They belong to Gnaeus Pompeius, who I gather is thinking of going west to the Baleares and Spain. I'm sure he won't insist that you accompany him, so if you prefer to return to Italy, tell him."

He and Lucius Gratidius returned to Utica.

Yesterday's panic had settled, though the city wasn't going about its wartime business as it had during the months of Cato's prefecture. The three hundred most prominent citizens were already waiting in the marketplace for Cato to tell them what he wanted them to do. They genuinely loved him, as did almost all Uticans, for he had been scrupulously fair, willing to listen to their grievances, unfailingly optimistic.

"No," he said, quite gently for Cato, "I can no longer make decisions for you. You must decide for yourselves whether to resist Caesar or sue for pardon. If you want to know what I think you should do, I think you should sue for pardon. The alternative would be to withstand siege, and your fate would be no different from the fates of Carthage, Numantia, Avaricum, Alesia. Caesar is an even greater master of siege than Scipio Aemilianus. The result would be the destruction of this beautiful, immensely rich city, and the deaths of many of its citizens. Caesar will levy a huge fine, but you'll have the ongoing prosperity to pay it. Sue for pardon."

"If we freed our slaves and put them to military service as well, Marcus Cato, we might survive a siege," said one citizen.

"That would be neither moral nor legal," Cato said sternly. "No government should have the authority to order any man to free his slaves if he doesn't want to."

"What if the freeing were voluntary?" another asked.

"Then I would condone it. However, I urge you not to resist. Talk about it among yourselves, then summon me back."

He and Gratidius walked across to sit on the stone coping of a fountain, where young Cato joined them.

"Will they fight, Father?"

"I hope not."

"I hope they do," said Gratidius, a little tearfully. "If they don't, I'm out of a job. I hate the thought of submitting tamely to Caesar!"

Cato did not reply, his eyes on the debating Three Hundred.

The decision was swift: Utica would sue for pardon.

"Believe me," said Cato, "it is the best way. Though I above all men have no cause to love Caesar, he is a merciful man who has been clement since the beginning of this sad business. None of you will suffer physical harm, or lose your property."

Some of the Three Hundred had decided to flee; Cato promised them that he would organize transport for them from among the ships belonging to the Republican cause.

"And that's that," he said with a sigh when he, young Cato and Gratidius were ensconced in the dining room. Statyllus came in, looking apprehensive.

"Pour me some wine," said Cato to Prognanthes, his steward.

The others stilled, turned wondering eyes on the master of the house, who took the clay beaker.

"My task is done, why shouldn't I?" he asked, sipped, and retched. "How extraordinary!" he exclaimed. "I've lost my taste for wine."

"Marcus Cato, I have news," Statyllus said.

The food came in on the echo of his words: fresh bread, oil, a roast fowl, salads and cheeses, some late grapes.

"You've been away all morning, Statyllus," Cato said, biting into a leg of roast fowl. "How good this tastes! What news are you so afraid of?"

"Juba's horsemen are looting the countryside."

"We could expect nothing else. Now eat, Statyllus."

Next day came word that Caesar was approaching rapidly, and that Juba had gone in the direction of Numidia. Cato watched from his window as a deputation from the Three Hundred rode out to treat with the conqueror, then turned his eyes to the harbor, a frenzy of activity as refugees and soldiers boarded ships.

"This evening," he said, "we'll have a nice dinner party. Just the three of us, I think. Gratidius is a good man, but he doesn't appreciate philosophy."

He said it with such pleasure that young Cato and Statyllus stared at each other in puzzlement; was he indeed so glad that his task was over? And what did he intend to do now that it was over? Surrender to Caesar? No, that was inconceivable. Yet he had issued no orders to pack their few clothes and books, made no attempt to secure passage room on a ship.

The prefect's fine house on the main square contained a proper bathroom; in midafternoon Cato ordered the bath filled, and went to enjoy a leisurely soak. By the time he emerged the dining room was set for the party, and the two other diners were reclining, young Cato on the couch to the right, Statyllus on the couch to the left, with the middle one for Cato. When he walked in, young Cato and Statyllus stared at him openmouthed. The long hair and beard were gone, and Cato wore his senatorial tunic with the broad purple band of the *latus clavus* down its right shoulder.

He looked magnificent, years younger, though all trace of red was gone from his hair, combed now in its customary style. The many months of abstention from wine had returned his grey eyes to their old luminousness, and the lines of dissipation were gone.

"Oh, I'm so hungry!" he said, taking the *lectus medius*. "Prognanthes, food!"

It wasn't possible to be gloomy; Cato's mood was too infectious. When Prognanthes produced a superior vintage of a smooth red wine, he tasted it gingerly, pronounced it good, and sipped occasionally from his goblet.

When only the wine, two fine cheeses and some grapes remained on the tables, and all the servants save Prognanthes had gone, Cato settled into his couch with his elbow comfortably disposed on a bolster, and gave a huge sigh of satisfaction.

"I shall miss Athenodorus Cordylion," he said, "but you'll have to take his place, Marcus. What did Zeno think was real?"

Oh, I am back at school! thought young Cato, and answered automatically. "Material things. Things that are solid."

"Is my couch solid?"

"Yes, of course."

"Is God solid?"

"Yes, of course."

"And did Zeno think the Soul was solid?"

"Yes, of course."

"Which came first of all solid things?"

"Fire."

"And after fire?"

"Air, then water, then earth."

"What must happen to air, water and earth?"

"They must return to fire at the end of the cycle."

"Is the Soul fire?"

"Zeno thought so, but Panaetius didn't agree."

"Where else can we look for the Soul than Zeno and Panaetius?"

Young Cato floundered, looked for help to Statyllus, who was gazing at Cato in growing consternation.

"We can look at Socrates through Plato," Statyllus said, his voice trembling. "Though he found great fault with Zeno, Socrates was the perfect Stoic. He cared nothing for his material welfare, nor for heat and cold, nor for passions of the flesh."

"Do we look for the Soul in the *Phaedrus* or the *Phaedo?*"

Statyllus spoke, drawing a gasping breath. "The *Phaedo*. In it, Plato discusses what Socrates said to his friends just before he drank the cup of hemlock."

Cato laughed, flung his hands out. "All good men are free, all bad men are slaves—let's look at the Paradoxes!"

The subject of the Soul seemed forgotten as the three embarked upon one of Cato's favorite subjects. Statyllus was deputed to adopt the Epicurean point of view, young Cato the Peripatetic, while Cato, true to himself, remained a Stoic. The arguments flew back and forth amid laughter, a quick give-and-take of premises so well known that each answer was automatic.

A growl of distant thunder came; Statyllus got up and went to look out the south window at the mountains.

"A terrible storm is coming," he said; then, more softly, "A terrible storm." He reclined again to take up the cudgels about freedom and slavery on behalf of the Epicureans.

The wine was working insidiously on Cato, who hadn't noticed its creeping effects. Suddenly, violently, he pitched his goblet out the south window. "No, no, no!" he roared. "A free man who consents to slavery of *any* kind is a bad man, and that's that! I don't care what form the slavery takes—lascivious pleasure—food—wine—punctuality— making money—the man who enslaves himself to it is a bad man! Wicked! *Evil!* His Soul will leave his body so fouled, so encrusted with filth that she sinks down, down, down to Tartarus, and there she stays forever! Only the good man's Soul can soar into the aether, into the realms of God! Not *the* gods, but *God!* And the good man never succumbs to any kind of slavery! Any kind! Any kind!"

Statyllus had scrambled up during this impassioned speech, gone to huddle next to young Cato. "If you get a chance," he whispered, "go to his sleeping room and steal his sword."

Young Cato jumped, turned terrified eyes on Statyllus. "Is that what all this is about?"

"Of course it is! He's going to kill himself."

Cato ran down, sat shuddering and glaring at his audience. Without warning he lurched to his feet and reeled to his study, where the two sitting on the couch could hear him rummaging among his pigeonholes of books, throwing scrolls around.

"*Phaedo, Phaedo, Phaedo!*" he was calling, giggling too.

Eyes rolling in his head, young Cato gaped at Statyllus, who gave him a push.

"Go, Marcus! Steal his sword now!"

Young Cato dashed to his father's roomy sleeping quarters and snatched the sword, hanging by its baldric from a hook on the wall. Back to the dining room, where he saw Prognanthes standing with the wine flagon in his hand. "Here, take this and hide it!" he said, giving the steward Cato's sword. "Hurry! Hurry!"

Prognanthes left just in time; Cato reappeared with a scroll in his hand. He threw it down on the *lectus medius* and turned in the direction of the atrium. "It's coming on dusk, I have to give the password to the gate sentries," he said curtly, and vanished, shouting for a waterproof *sagum*; it was going to rain.

The storm was drifting closer; flashes of lightning began to bathe the dining room in glowing blue-white flickers, for no one had yet lit the lamps. Prognanthes came in with a taper.

"Is the sword hidden?" young Cato asked him.

"Yes, *domine*. The master won't find it, rest assured."

"Oh, Statyllus, he *can't!* We mustn't let him!"

"We won't let him. Hide your sword too."

Some time later Cato returned, threw his wet cape into a corner, and picked up the *Phaedo* from the couch. Then he went to Statyllus, embraced him and kissed him on both cheeks.

After that it was young Cato's turn. How utterly alien, the feeling of his father's arms around him, those dry lips on his face, his mouth. Inside his mind were only memories of the day he had howled into Porcia's rough dress when his father had called them to his study to inform them that he had divorced their mother for adultery with Caesar, and that they would never, never see her again. Even for a moment. Even to say goodbye. Little Cato had wept desolately for his mama, and his father had told him not to unman himself. That to unman himself for such a paltry reason was not a right act. So many memories of a hard father, one who inflicted his own pitiless ethic upon all those around him. And yet—and yet—how *proud* he was to be the great Cato's son! So now he unmanned himself and wept.

"Please, Father, don't!"

"What?" Cato asked, eyes widening in surprise. "Not retire to read my *Phaedo?*"

"It doesn't matter." Young Cato mourned. "It doesn't matter."

The Soul, the Soul, whom the Greeks thought female. How right it seemed, listening to the storm outside, that the natural world should echo the tempest within his—heart? mind? body? We do not even know that, so how can we know anything about the Soul, her purity or lack of purity? Her immortality? I need to have her proved to me, proved beyond a shadow of a doubt!

Several multiple lamps burning, he sat down in a chair and opened the scroll between his hands, reading the Greek slowly; it was always easier for Cato to separate the words in a Greek text than a Latin one, why he didn't know. Reading the words of Socrates as he asked Simmias one of his famous questions: Socrates taught by asking questions.

> "Do we believe in death?"
> "Yes," said Simmias.
> "Death is the separation of Soul and body. To be dead is the end result of this separation."

Yes, yes, yes, it must be so! What I am is more than mere body, what I am contains the white fire of my Soul, and when my body is dead, my Soul is free. Socrates, Socrates, reassure me! Give me the strength and purpose to do what I must do!

> "To enjoy pure knowledge, we must shed our bodies. . . .
> The Soul is made in the image of God, and is immortal, and has intelligence, and is uniform, and cannot change. She is immutable. Whereas the body is made in the image of humankind. It is mortal. It has no intelligence, it has many shapes, and it disintegrates. Can you deny this?"
> "No."

"So if what I say is true, then the body must decay, but the Soul cannot."

Yes, yes, Socrates is right, she is immortal! She will *not* dissolve when my body dies!

Enormously relieved, Cato put the book in his lap and looked at the wall, his eyes seeking his sword. At first he thought what he saw was the aftereffect of the wine, then his mortal eyes, so filled with false visions, acknowledged the truth: his sword had gone. He transferred the book to his side table and rose to strike a copper gong with a muted hammer. The sound thrummed away into the darkness, torn by lightning, enhanced by thunder.

A servant came.

"Where is Prognanthes?" Cato asked.

"The storm, *domine*, the storm. His children are crying."

"My sword is gone. Fetch me my sword at once."

The servant bowed and vanished. Some time later, Cato struck the gong again. "My sword is gone. Fetch it at once."

This time the man looked afraid, nodded and hurried off.

Cato picked up the *Phaedo* and continued to read it to its end, but the words didn't impinge. He struck the gong a third time.

"Yes, *domine*?"

"Send every servant to the atrium, including Prognanthes."

He met them there and looked angrily at his steward. "Where is my sword, Prognanthes?"

"*Domine*, we have searched and searched, but it cannot be found."

Cato moved so fast that no one actually saw him stride across the room to punch Prognanthes, just heard the *crack!* of Cato's fist against the steward's massive jaw. He fell unconscious, but no servant went to help him, just stood shivering, staring at Cato.

Young Cato and Statyllus erupted into the room.

"Father, please, please!" Young Cato wept, throwing his arms about his father.

Who shook him off as if he stank. "Am I a madman, Marcus, that you deny me my protection against Caesar? Do you deem me incompetent, that you dare to take my sword? I don't need it to take my own life, if that's what's worrying you—taking my own life is simple. All I have to do is hold my breath or dash my head against a wall. My sword is my right! *Bring me my sword!*"

The son fled, sobbing wildly, while four of the servants took hold of the inanimate Prognanthes and carried him away. Only two of the lowliest slaves remained.

"Bring me my sword," he said to them.

The noise of its coming preceded it, for the rain had died to a gentle murmur; the storm was passing out to sea. A toddling child brought it in, both hands around its ivory eagle hilt, the tip of the blade making a scraping sound as the little fellow dragged it doggedly behind him across the floor. Cato bent and picked it up, tested its point and edges; still razor sharp.

"I am my own man again," he said, and returned to his room.

Now he could reread the *Phaedo* and make sense of it. Help me, Socrates! Show me that my fear is needless!

"Those who love knowledge are aware that their Souls are no more than attached to their bodies as with glue or pins. Whereas those who do not love knowledge are unaware that each pleasure, each pain is a kind of nail fastening the Soul to the body like a rivet, so that she emulates the body, and believes that all her truths arise from the body . . . Is there an opposite to life?"

"Yes."

"What is it?"

"Death."

"And what do we call the thing that owns no death?"

"Immortal."

"Does the Soul own death?"

"No."

"Then the Soul is immortal?"

"Yes."

"The Soul cannot perish when the body dies, for the Soul does not admit of death as a part of herself."

There it is, manifest, the truth of all truths.

Cato rolled and tied the *Phaedo*, kissed it, then lay down upon his bed and fell into a deep, dreamless sleep while the storm muttered and grumbled into a profound calm.

In the middle of the night his right hand woke him, stabbing, throbbing; he gazed at it in dismay, then struck the gong.

"Send for the physician Cleanthes," he told the servant, "and summon Butas here to see me."

His agent came with suspicious celerity; Cato eyed him with irony, realizing that at least a third of Utica knew that its prefect had demanded his sword. "Butas, go down to the harbor and make sure that those trying to board vessels are all right."

Butas went; outside he paused to whisper to Statyllus. "He can't be thinking of suicide, he's too concerned with the present. You imagine things."

So the household cheered up, and Statyllus, who had been on the point of fetching Lucius Gratidius, changed his mind. Cato wouldn't thank him for sending a centurion to plead with him!

When the physician Cleanthes arrived, Cato held out his right hand. "I've broken it," he said. "Splint it so I can use it."

While Cleanthes worked at an impossible task, Butas returned to inform Cato that the weather had played havoc with the ships, and that many refugees were in a state of confusion.

"Oh, poor things!" said Cato. "Come back at dawn and let me know more, Butas."

Cleanthes coughed delicately. "I have done the best I can, *domine,* but may I remain in your house a while longer? I am told that the steward Prognanthes is still unconscious."

"Oh, him! His jaw is like his name—a rocky shelf. He broke my hand, a wretched nuisance. Yes, go and tend him if you must."

He was awake when Butas reported at dawn that the situation on the waterfront had settled down. As the agent left, Cato lay down on his bed.

"Close the door, Butas," he said.

The moment the door shut, he took the sword from where he had propped it against the end of his narrow bed and attempted to maneuver it into the traditional position, drive it upward under his rib cage into his chest just to the left of the sternum. But the broken hand refused to obey, even when he tore the splint off it. In the end he simply plunged the blade into his belly as high as he could, and sawed from side to side to enlarge the rent in his abdomen wall. As he groaned and hacked, determined to succeed, to liberate his pure and unsullied Soul, his traitorous body suddenly snatched control from his will, jerked massively; Cato fell off the bed and sent an abacus flying into the gong with a clatter and a huge, sonorous boom.

The household came running from all directions, Cato's son in the lead, to find Cato on the floor in a spreading lake of blood, entrails strewn around him in steaming heaps. The grey eyes were wide open, unseeing.

Young Cato was howling hysterically, but Statyllus, too far into shock to weep, saw Cato's eyes blink.

"He's alive! He's still alive! Cleanthes, he's alive!"

The physician was already kneeling beside Cato; he glared up at Statyllus. "Help me, you idiot!" he barked.

Together they gathered up Cato's bowels and put them back inside his abdomen, Cleanthes cursing and pushing, shaking the mass until it settled and he could draw the edges of the wound together comfortably. Then he took his curved needle and some clean linen thread and sewed the awful gash tightly, each stitch separate but in close proximity; dozens of them.

"He's so strong he might live," he said, standing back to review his handiwork. "It all depends how much blood he's lost. We must thank Asklepios that he's unconscious."

Cato came up out of a peaceful place into a terrible agony. A hideous wail of pain erupted, neither shriek nor groan; his eyes opened to see many people crowded around him, his son's face repulsive with tears and snot, Statyllus emitting whimpers, the physician Cleanthes turning with wet hands from a bowl of water, and clusters of slaves, a crying babe, keening women.

"You will live, Marcus Cato!" Cleanthes cried triumphantly. "We have saved you!"

The cloud cleared from Cato's eyes. They traveled downward to the bloody linen towel across his middle. His left hand moved, twitched, pulled the towel away to see the Tyrian purple, distended expanse of his belly gashed from side to side in a ragged tear, now neatly sewn up with crimson embroidery.

"My Soul!" he screamed, shuddered, and screwed up every part of himself that had always fought, fought, fought, no matter what the odds; both hands went to the stitches, ripped and tore with frenzied strength until the wound was gaping open, then he began to pull the shiny, pearly intestines out, fling them away.

No one moved to stop him. Paralyzed, his son and his friend and his physician watched him destroy himself piece by piece, his mouth gaping silently. Suddenly he spasmed hugely. The grey eyes, still open, took on the look of death, irises fled before the expanding black pupils; finally came a faint gold sheen, death's ultimate patina. Cato's Soul was gone.

The city of Utica burned him the next day on a huge pyre of frankincense, myrrh, nard, cinnamon and Jericho balsam, his body wrapped in Tyrian purple and cloth-of-gold.

He would have hated it, Marcus Porcius Cato, the enemy of all ostentation.

He had done as much as he could, given the shortness of the time at his disposal to prepare for death; there were letters for his poor devastated son, for Statyllus, and for Caesar, gifts of money for Lucius Gratidius and Prognanthes the steward, still inanimate. But he left no word for Marcia, his wife.

When Caesar rode into the main square mounted on Toes, his scarlet *paludamentum* carefully draped across the handsome chestnut horse's haunches, the ashes had been collected from the pyre, but the pyre itself still sat, a blackened, aromatic heap, in the midst of a silently watching populace.

"What is this?" Caesar asked, skin crawling.

"The pyre of Marcus Porcius Cato Uticensis!" shrilled the voice of Statyllus.

The eyes were so cold they looked eerie, inhuman; without any change of expression Caesar slid from the horse to the paving stones, his cloak falling behind him gracefully. To Utica, he looked every inch the conqueror.

"His house?" he asked Statyllus.

Statyllus turned and led the way.

"Is his son here?" Caesar asked, Calvinus entering behind him.

"Yes, Caesar, but very upset by his father's death."

"Suicide, of course. Tell me about it."

"What is there to tell?" Statyllus asked, shrugging. "You know Marcus Cato, Caesar. He would not submit to any tyrant, even a clement one." A fumble inside the sleeve of his black tunic produced a slender scroll. "He left this for you."

Caesar took it, examined the seal, a cap of liberty with the words M PORC CATO around it. Not a reference to his own fight against what he saw as tyranny, but a reference to his great-grandmother, the daughter of a slave.

> I refuse to owe my life to a tyrant, a man who flouts the Law by pardoning other men, just as if the Law gave him the right to be their master. The Law does not.

Dying to read it, Calvinus despaired that he would ever get the chance. Then the strong, tapering fingers crushed the note, threw it away. Caesar looked down at his fingers as if at a stranger's, drew a breath that was neither sigh nor growl.

"I grudge you your death, Cato, just as you grudged me your life," he said harshly.

Young Cato shuffled out, supported by two servants.

"Could you not persuade your father to wait, at least to see me, talk to me?"

"You know Cato a great deal better than I do, Caesar," the young man said. "He died as he lived—very hard."

"What do you plan to do now that your father's dead? You know that all his property is confiscate."

"Ask you for a pardon and make a living somehow. I am not my father."

"You're pardoned, just as he would have been."

"May I ask a favor, Caesar?"

"Yes, of course."

"Statyllus. May he travel to Italy with me? My father left him the money to go to Marcus Brutus, who will take him in."

"Marcus Brutus is in Italian Gaul. Statyllus may join him."

And that was the end of it. Caesar swung on his heel and walked out, Calvinus behind him—after he'd retrieved the note. A valuable archive.

Outside, Caesar threw off the mood as if it had never been. "Well, I could expect nothing else from Cato," he said to Calvinus. "Always the worst of my enemies, always out to foil me."

"An absolute fanatic, Caesar. From the day of his birth, I suspect. He never understood the difference between life and philosophy."

Caesar laughed. "The difference? No, my dear Calvinus, not the difference. Cato never understood *life*. Philosophy was his way of dealing with something he didn't have the ability to grasp. Philosophy was his manual of behavior. That he chose to be a Stoic reflected his nature—purification through self-denial."

"Poor Marcia! A cruel blow."

"The cruel blow was in loving Cato, who refused to be loved."

 Among the Republican high command, only Titus Labienus, the two Pompeys and governor Attius Varus reached Spain.

Publius Sittius was back in action for Kings Bocchus and Bogud of the Mauretanias; the moment he received word of Caesar's victory at Thapsus, he sent out his trusty fleet to sweep the seas and himself invaded Numidia by land.

Metellus Scipio and Lucius Manlius Torquatus sailed aboard a group of ships that elected to hug the African coast; Gnaeus and Sextus Pompey, in Gnaeus's original fleet, decided to strike across open water and revictual in the Balearic Isles. Labienus sailed with them, not trusting Metellus Scipio's judgement, and loathing the man besides.

Publius Sittius's fleet encountered the Africa-hugging ships and attacked with such enthusiasm that capture was inevitable. Like Cato, Metellus Scipio and Torquatus chose suicide over a pardon from Caesar.

In hopeless disarray, the Numidian army of light armed horse was no match for the invading Sittius, who swept them up before him and advanced inexorably through Juba's kingdom.

Marcus Petreius and King Juba had gone to Juba's capital of Cirta, only to find its gates locked and the populace too afraid of Caesar's vengeance to let them inside. The two men sought shelter in a villa Juba kept not far from Cirta, and there agreed to fight a duel to the death as the most honorable way left. The outcome was a foregone conclusion: Juba was much younger and stronger than Petreius, who had grown old and grizzled in Pompey the Great's service. Petreius died in the duel, but when Juba tried to inflict the death stroke upon himself, he found that his arms were too short. A slave held his sword, and Juba ran on it.

The most distressing tragedy of all was Lucius Caesar's son, who was captured and released on his own cognizance to stay in a villa on the outskirts of Utica until Caesar had time to deal with him. It was staffed by some of Caesar's own servants, and in its grounds were a few cages of wild animals found among Metellus Scipio's abandoned baggage; Caesar took them to use in the games he planned to celebrate in his dead Julia's honor, for a vindictive Senate had denied her funeral games. Cato and Ahenobarbus.

Perhaps the aura of suspicion surrounding this only member of the Julii Caesares who had sided with the Republicans had eaten into his core, or perhaps some innate mental instability had always been there; whatever the reason, Lucius Caesar Junior was soon joined by a group of Republican legionaries, took over the villa, and tortured Caesar's servants to death. Having no more human victims, Lucius Caesar Junior then tortured the animals to death. When the legionaries decamped, Lucius Caesar Junior did not. A horrified tribune sent to check on him found him wandering the villa covered in blood, mumbling and raving alternately. Like Ajax after the fall of Troy, he seemed to think the beasts were his enemies.

Caesar decided that he would have to stand trial, deeming it absolutely necessary that his cousin's only son be dealt with publicly, and trusting that the military court would see for itself that Lucius

Caesar Junior was hopelessly demented. Pending trial, he was left locked inside the villa under guard.

Oh, shades of Publius Vettius! When some soldiers came to put Lucius Caesar Junior into chains and bring him to Utica for the court-martial, they discovered him dead—but not by his own hand. Who had sneaked in and murdered him remained a mystery, but not even the most insignificant member of Caesar's staff thought Caesar implicated. Many were the rumors about Caesar Dictator, yet that particular calumny was never put forward. After conducting the funeral as Pontifex Maximus, Caesar sent Lucius's son's ashes home to him with as much explanation as he thought Lucius could bear.

Utica was pardoned too, but Caesar reminded the Three Hundred that during his first consulship thirteen years ago he had passed a *lex Julia* which had greatly benefited the city.

"The fine is levied at two hundred million sesterces, to be paid in six-monthly installments over a period of three years. Not to me, citizens of Utica. Directly to the Treasury of Rome."

A huge fine! Eight thousand talents of silver. Since Utica could not deny that it had aided the Republicans and had lauded, adored and gladly harbored Cato, Caesar's most obdurate enemy, the Three Hundred accepted its fate meekly. What could they do about it, especially when the money had to be paid directly to the Roman Treasury? This was one tyrant not out to enrich himself.

Republican owners of wheat *latifundia* in the Bagradas and Catada valleys suffered too; Caesar auctioned their properties at once, thus ensuring that those who continued to farm wheat on a large scale in Africa Province were very definitely his clients. An action he regarded as vital for Rome's welfare—who knew what the future might hold?

From Africa Province he proceeded to Numidia, where he put up all Juba's personal property for auction before dismantling the kingdom of Numidia completely. The eastern portion, which was the most fertile, was incorporated into the African province as Africa Nova; Publius Sittius received a fine strip of territory on Africa Nova's western boundary as his personal fief—provided that he held it for the Rome of Caesar and Caesar's heir. Bogud and Bocchus received the western end of Numidia, but Caesar left it up to the two kings to sort out the boundaries between themselves.

On the last day of May he quit Africa for Sardinia, leaving Gaius Sallustius Crispus behind to govern the Roman provinces.

That hundred-and-fifty-mile voyage took twenty-seven days; the seas were mountainous, his ship leaked, had to put into every tiny isle on the way, was blown far to the east, then blown far to the west. Exasperating, not because Caesar was prone to seasickness—he was not—but because the ship moved too much for him to read, write, or even think lucidly.

Harbor made at last, he raised Republican Sardinia's tithe to one-eighth, and levied a special fine of ten million sesterces on the town of Sulcis for actively abetting the Republicans.

Two days into Quinctilis and he was ready to sail for Ostia or Puteoli, whichever port the winds and weather made feasible; then the equinoctial gales began to roar as if what had plagued his ship on the way to Sardinia had been but a gentle zephyr. Caesar looked at Carales harbor and condescended to heed his captain's plea not to sail. The gales blew for three *nundinae* without let, but at least sitting on dry land he could read and write, catch up on the mountain of correspondence.

Time for thought didn't come until finally he set sail for Ostia; the wind was blowing from the southwest, so Ostia at the mouth of the Tiber it would be.

The war will go on, unless Gaius Trebonius in Further Spain can capture Labienus and the two Pompeii before they have time to organize fresh resistance. A better man than Trebonius does not exist, but the pity of it is that when he arrived in his province he found it in no mood to co-operate after the predatory governorship of Quintus Cassius. That is the trouble, Caesar. You cannot do everything yourself, and for every Gaius Trebonius, there is a Quintus Cassius. For every Calvinus, there is an Antonius.

Spain is on the lap of the gods, there's no point in wasting time fretting about Spain at the moment. Think rather, that so far the war has gone all Caesar's way, and that Africa confirms Pharsalus in the world's eyes. So many dead! So much talent and ability wasted on battlefields.

And what about the *Phaedo*, eh? It took time to get the story out of Statyllus, but a hint that perhaps Caesar would renege on his promise to let Statyllus go to Brutus soon had the whole of that unspeakable suicide laid bare for Caesar's inspection. Oh, immensely cheering to learn that the tempered, indestructible steel of Cato's *persona* was so totally fractured underneath. When the time came to die, he feared to die. Had first to convince himself that he would live forever by reading the *Phaedo*. How fascinating. It is some of the most beautiful, poetic

Greek ever written, but the man who wrote it was speaking at second hand, and neither he nor Socrates, the supreme philosopher, was valid in logic, in reason, in common sense. *Phaedo, Phaedrus* and the rest are full of sophistry, sometimes downright dishonest, and commit the same old philosophical crime: they arrive at conclusions that suit them and please them, rather than at the truth. As for Stoicism, what philosophy is narrower, what other code of spiritual conduct can breed the ultimate fanatic so successfully?

What it boils down to is that Cato couldn't do the deed without first knowing that he would enjoy a life thereafter. And sought confirmation in the *Phaedo*. This comforts Caesar, who craves no life hereafter. What can death be, except an eternal sleep? The only immortality a man can ever have is to live on in the memories and stories of the *gens humana* for time immemorial. A fate sure to happen for Caesar, but a fate that Caesar will exert every effort to make sure does not happen for Cato. Without Cato, there would have been no civil war. It is for that I cannot ever forgive him. It is for that *Caesar* cannot forgive him.

Ah, but Caesar's life grows lonelier, even with the death of Cato. Bibulus, Ahenobarbus, Lentulus Crus, Lentulus Spinther, Afranius, Petreius, Pompeius Magnus, Curio. Rome has become a city of widows, and Caesar has no real competition. How can Caesar excel without opposition to drive him? Though not, though *never*, opposition from his legions.

Caesar's legions. Ninth, Tenth, Twelfth, Fourteenth, their standards loaded down with honors, their share of booty sufficient to give the rankers Third Class status in the Centuries, their centurions Second Class status. Yet they mutinied. Why? Because they were idle, poorly supervised and prey to the mischief men like Avienus cannot resist making. Because some men within them have given them the notion that they can dictate terms of service to their generals. Their mutiny is not forgiven—but, more important, it is not forgotten. No man from a mutinous legion will ever get land in Italy, or a full share of the booty after Caesar triumphs.

After Caesar triumphs. Caesar has waited fourteen years to triumph, cheated out of his Spanish one when he came back from Further Spain as praetor. The Senate forced him to cross the *pomerium* into the city to declare his candidacy for the consulship, so he lost his imperium and his triumph. But this year he will triumph, so splendidly that Sulla's and Pompeius Magnus's triumphs will seem mean, small. This year. Yes, this year. There will be time, for this year Caesar will put the calendar to rights at last, tie the seasons to the months in a proper 365-day year, with an extra day every four years to keep both in perfect step. If Caesar does no more for Rome than that, his name will live on long after he himself is dead.

That is all that immortality can ever be. Oh, Cato, with your longing for an immortal soul, your fear of dying! What is there to be afraid of, in dying?

The ship heeled, quivered; the wind was changing, getting up, swinging around to the southeast. He could almost smell Egypt of Nilus on its breath—the sweet, slightly fetid stench of inundation-soaked black soil, the alien blossoms in alien gardens, the fragrance of Cleopatra's skin.

Cleopatra. Caesar does miss her, though he thought he would not. What will the little fellow look like? She says in her letters, like Caesar, but Caesar will see him more dispassionately. A son for Caesar, but not a Roman son. Who will be Caesar's Roman son, the son he adopts in his will? Wherever Caesar's life is going, it is time and more than time that he made his will. Yet how can a man poise the balance between an untried, unknown sixteen-year-old and a man of thirty-seven?

Pray there is time to poise the balance.

The Senate has voted Caesar the dictatorship for ten years, with the powers of a censor for three years and the right to let his preferences be known when the candidates apply for election as magistrates. A good letter to receive before leaving Africa.

A voice whispers: where are you going, Gaius Julius Caesar? And why does it seem to matter so little? Is it that you have done all that you wanted to do, though not in the way and with the constitutional sanction you yearned for? No sense in ruing what has been done and cannot be undone. No, it cannot be undone, even for a million gold crowns studded with rubies or emeralds or ocean pearls the size of pebbles.

But without rivals, victory is hollow. Without rivals, how can Caesar shine?

The sting in winning is to be left the only one alive on the field.

VI

TRYING TIMES, THANKLESS TASKS

From SEXTILIS (AUGUST) until the end of
DECEMBER of 46 B.C.

MARCUS TULLIUS CICERO

The Domus Publica had changed for the better on its exterior. Its ground floor was built of tufa blocks and had the old, rectangular windows, then Ahenobarbus Pontifex Maximus had added an *opus incertum* upper story faced with bricks and having arched windows. Caesar Pontifex Maximus added a temple pediment over the main entrance and gave the entire outside of the ugly building a more uniform look by facing it in polished marble. Inside it maintained its venerable beauty, for Caesar, Pontifex Maximus now for seventeen years, permitted no neglect.

Time, he thought, having finally returned from Sardinia, to start giving receptions, to suggest to Calpurnia that she host the Bona Dea celebrations in November; if Caesar Dictator was to be stranded in Rome for many months, he may as well create a splash.

His own quarters were on the ground floor; a bedroom and study, and, where his mother used to live, two offices for his chief secretary, Gaius Faberius. Who greeted him with slightly overdone pleasure, and wouldn't meet his eyes.

"Are you so offended that I didn't take you to Africa? I'd thought to give you a rest from travel, Faberius," Caesar said.

Faberius jumped, shook his head. "No, Caesar, of course I wasn't offended! I was able to get a great deal of work done in your absence, and see something of my family."

"How are they?"

"Very happy to move to the Aventine. The Clivus Orbius has gone sadly downhill."

"Orbian hill—downhill. Good pun," said Caesar, and left it at that. But with a mental note to find out what was worrying this oldest among his secretaries.

When he entered his wife's quarters upstairs he wished he had not, for Calpurnia had guests: Cato's widow, Marcia, and Cato's daughter, Porcia. Why did women choose peculiar friends? Still, it was too late to retreat now. Best to brazen it out. Calpurnia, he noticed, was growing into her beauty. At eighteen she had been a pleasant-looking girl, shy and quiet, and he knew perfectly well that her conduct during the years of his absence had been irreproachable. Now in her late twenties, she had a better figure, a great deal more composure, and was arranging her hair in a new, highly flattering style. His advent didn't fluster her in the least, despite the vexation that being caught with these two women must have caused her.

"Caesar," she said, rising and coming to kiss him lightly.

"Is that the same cat I gave you?" he asked, pointing to a rotund ball of reddish fur on a couch.

"Yes, that's Felix. He's getting old, but his health is good."

Caesar had advanced to take Marcia's hand and smile at Porcia in a friendly way.

"Ladies, a sad meeting. I would have given much to ensure a happier one."

"I know," said Marcia, blinking away tears. "Was he—was he well before—?"

"Very well, and much loved by all of Utica. So much so that the people of that city have given him a new cognomen—Uticensis. He was very brave," said Caesar, making no attempt to sit.

"Naturally he was brave! He was Cato!" said Porcia in that same loud, harsh voice her father had owned.

How like him she was! A pity that she was the girl, young Marcus the boy. Though she would never have begged a pardon—would be fleeing to Spain, or dead.

"Are you living with Philippus?" he asked Marcia.

"For the time being," she said, and sighed. "He wants me to marry again, but I don't wish to."

"If you don't wish to, you shouldn't. I'll speak to him."

"Oh yes, by all means do that!" Porcia snarled. "You're the King of Rome, whatever you say must be obeyed!"

"No, I am not the King of Rome, nor do I want to be," Caesar said quietly. "It was meant kindly, Porcia. How are you faring?"

"Since Marcus Brutus bought all Bibulus's property, I live in Bibulus's house with Bibulus's youngest son."

"I'm very glad that Brutus was so generous." Taking in the sight of several more cats, Caesar used them as an excuse to bolt. "You're lucky, Calpurnia. These creatures make my eyes water and my skin itch. *Ave*, ladies."

And he escaped.

Faberius had put his important correspondence on his desk; frowning, he noted one scroll whose tag bore a date in May. Vatia Isauricus's seal. Before he opened it, he knew it held bad news.

Syria is without a governor, Caesar. Your young cousin Sextus Julius Caesar is dead.

Did you by any chance meet a Quintus Caecilius Bassus when you passed through Antioch last year? In case you did not, I had better explain who he is. A Roman knight of the Eighteen, who took up residence in Tyre and went into the purple-dye business after serving with Pompeius Magnus during his eastern campaigns. He speaks fluent Median and Persian, and it is now being bandied about that he has friends at the court of the King of the Parthians. Certainly he is enormously rich, and not all his income is from Tyrian purple.

When you imposed those heavy penalties on Antioch and the cities of the Phoenician coast for so strongly supporting the Republicans, Bassus was gravely affected. He went to Antioch and looked up some old friends among the military tribunes of the Syrian legion, all men who had served with Pompeius Magnus. The next thing, governor Sextus Caesar was informed that you were dead in Africa Province and the Syrian legion was restive. He called the legion to an assembly intending to calm its men down, but they murdered him and hailed Bassus as their new commander.

Bassus then proclaimed himself the new governor of Syria, so all your clients and adherents in northern Syria fled at once to Cilicia. As I happened to be in Tarsus visiting Quintus Philippus, I was able to act swiftly, sent a letter to Marcus Lepidus in Rome, and asked him to send Syria a governor as quickly as possible. According to his reply, he has dispatched Quintus Cornificius, who should answer well. Cornificius and Vatinius fought a brilliant campaign in Illyricum last year.

However, Bassus has entrenched himself formidably. He marched to Antioch, which shut its gates and refused to let him in. So our friend the purple merchant marched down the road to Apameia: in return for many trade favors, it declared for Bassus, who entered it and has set himself up there, calling Apameia the capital of Syria.

He has worked a great deal of mischief, Caesar, and he is definitely in league with the Parthians. He's made an alliance with the new king of the Skenite Arabs, one Alchaudonius—who, incidentally, was one of the Arabs with Abgarus when he led Marcus Crassus into the Parthian trap at Carrhae. Alchaudonius and Bassus are very busy recruiting troops for a new Syrian army. I imagine that the Parthians are going to invade, and that Bassus's Syrian army will join them to move against Rome in Cilicia and Asia Province.

This means that both Quintus Philippus and I are also recruiting, and have sent warning to the client-kings.

Southern Syria is quiet. Your friend Antipater is making sure the Jews stay out of Bassus's plans, and has sent to Queen Cleopatra in Egypt for men, armaments and food supplies against the day when the Parthians invade. The rebuilding and fortification of Jerusalem's walls may turn out to be more vital than even you envisioned.

There have been Parthian raids up and down the Euphrates, though the territory of the Skenite Arabs has not suffered. You may have thought that the eastern end of Our Sea was pacified, but I doubt that Rome will ever be able to say that about any part of her world. There's always someone lusting to take things off her.

Poor young Sextus Caesar, the grandson of his uncle, Sextus. That branch of the family—the elder branch—had had none of Caesar's fabled luck. The patrician Julii Caesares used three first names—Sextus, Gaius and Lucius. If a Julius Caesar had three sons, the first was Sextus, the second Gaius, and the third Lucius. His own father was the second son, not the first, and only the marriage of his father's elder sister to the fabulously wealthy New Man Gaius Marius had given his father the money to stay in the Senate and ascend the *cursus honorum,* the ladder to the senior magistracies. His father's younger sister had married Sulla, so Caesar could rightly say that both Marius and Sulla were his uncles. Very handy through the years!

His father's elder brother, Sextus, had died first, of a lung inflammation during a bitter winter campaign of the Italian civil war. *Lungs!* Suddenly Caesar remembered where he had previously seen the stigmata he had noticed in young Gaius Octavius. Uncle Sextus! He'd had the same look about him: the same narrow rib cage, small chest. There had not been a moment to ask Hapd'efan'e, and now he could offer the priest-physician more information. Uncle Sextus had suffered from the wheezes, used to go to the Fields of Fire behind Puteoli once a year to inhale the sulphur fumes that belched out of the earth amid splutters of lava and licks of flame. He remembered his father saying that the wheezes cropped up from time to time in a Julius Caesar, that it was a family trait. A family trait young Gaius Octavius had inherited? Was *that* why the lad didn't attend the youths' drills and exercises on the Campus Martius regularly?

Caesar summoned Hapd' efan'e.

"Has Trogus given you a nice room, Hapd'efan'e?" he asked.

"Yes, Caesar. A beautiful guest suite that overlooks the big peristyle. I have the space to store my medicaments and my instruments, and Trogus has found me a lad for my apprentice. I like this house and I like the Forum Romanum—they are *old*."

"Tell me about the wheezes."

"Ah!" said the priest-physician, dark eyes widening. "You mean a wheezing noise when a patient breathes?"

"Yes."

"But on expiration, not on inspiration."

Caesar wheezed experimentally. "Breathing out, definitely."

"Yes, I know of it. When the air is still and reasonably dry and the season is neither blossoms nor harvest, the patient is quite well unless some painful emotion troubles him. But when the air is full of pollen or little bits of straw or dust, or is too humid, the patient is distressed when he breathes. If he is not removed from the irritation, he goes into a fully fledged attack of wheezing, coughs until he retches, goes blue in the face as he struggles for every breath. Sometimes he dies."

"My Uncle Sextus had it, and did die, but apparently of a lung inflammation due to exposure to extreme cold. Our family physician called it dyspnoea, as I remember," said Caesar.

"No, it is not dyspnoea. That is a constant struggle for breath, rather than episodic," said Hapd'efan'e firmly.

"Can this episodic non-dyspnoea run in families?"

"Oh, yes. The Greek name for it is asthma."

"How best to treat it, Hapd'efan'e?"

"Certainly not the way the Greeks do, Caesar! They advocate bloodletting, laxatives, hot fomentations, a potion of hydromel mixed with hyssop, and lozenges made from galbanum and turpentine resin. The last two may help a little, I admit. But in our medical lore, it is said that asthmatics are suffused with sensitive feelings, that they take things to heart when others do not. We treat an attack with inhalation of sulphur fumes, but work more on avoiding attacks. We advise the patient to stay away from dust, tiny particles of grass or straw, animal hair or fur, pollen, heavy sea vapors," said Hapd'efan'e.

"Is it present for life?"

"In some cases, Caesar, yes, but not always. Children who suffer from it sometimes grow out of it. A harmonious home life and general tranquillity are helpful."

"My thanks, Hapd'efan'e."

One of his worries about young Gaius Octavius had just been elucidated, though finding a solution would be hugely difficult. The boy shouldn't be let near horses or mules—yes, that had been true of Uncle Sextus as well! Military training was going to be almost impossible, yet it was absolutely obligatory for a man with aspirations to be consul. All very well for Brutus! His family was so powerful, so ancestor-rich, and his fortune so vast that no colleague or peer would ever be indelicate enough to refer to Brutus's lack of martial spirit. Whereas Octavius lacked imposing ancestors on his father's side, and bore his father's name. The patrician Julian blood was distaff blood, not manifest in his name. Poor fellow! His road to the consulship would prove hard, perhaps insuperable. *If* he lived to get that far.

Caesar got up to pace, bitterly disappointed. There didn't seem to be enough of a chance that Gaius Octavius would survive to warrant making the lad Caesar's heir. Back to Marcus Antonius—what a hideous prospect!

Lucius Marcius Philippus had extended an invitation to dinner at his spacious house on the Palatine to "celebrate your return to Rome" said the gracefully written note.

Cursing the waste of time but aware that family obligations insisted they attend, Caesar and Calpurnia arrived at the ninth hour of daylight to find themselves the only guests. Equipped with a dining room able to hold six couches, Philippus usually filled all six, but not today. Some warning alarm sounded; Caesar doffed his toga, made sure his thin layer of hair covered his scalp—he grew it long forward from the crown—and let the servant offer him a bowl of water to wash his feet. Naturally he was put in the *locus consularis,* the place of honor on Philippus's own couch, with young Gaius Octavius at its far end from Caesar; Philippus took the middle position. His elder son wasn't present—was that the reason for his sense that something was wrong? Caesar wondered. Was he here to be informed that Philippus was divorcing his wife for adultery with his son? No, no, of course not! That wasn't the kind of news passed on at a dinner party with the wife sitting there. Marcia wasn't present either; just Atia and her daughter, Octavia, joined Calpurnia on the three chairs opposite the only occupied couch.

Calpurnia looked delicious in an artfully draped lapis blue gown that echoed the color of her eyes; she was wearing the new sleeves, cut open from the shoulder and pinched together at intervals down the outer arm with little jeweled buttons. Atia had chosen a lavender blue that suited her fair beauty, and the young girl was exquisitely garbed in pale pink. How like her brother she was! The same masses of waving golden hair, his oval face, high cheekbones and nose with the sliding upward tilt. Her eyes alone were different, a clear aquamarine.

When Caesar smiled at Octavia she smiled back to reveal perfect teeth and a dimple in her right cheek; their eyes met, and Caesar drew an involuntary breath of astonishment. Aunt Julia! Aunt Julia's gentle, peaceful soul looked out at him, warmed him to the marrow. She is Aunt Julia all over again. I shall give her a bottle of Aunt Julia's perfume and rejoice. This girl will inspire love in all who meet her, she is a pearl beyond price. From her face he turned to gaze at her brother, to see an unqualified affection. He adores her, this elder sister.

The meal was quite up to Philippus's standards, and included his favorite party fare—a smooth, yellowish mass of cream churned with eggs and honey inside an outer barrel filled with a mixture of snow and salt. It was brought at the gallop from the Mons Fiscellus, Italy's highest mountain. The two young people spooned up the icy, melting poultice ecstatically, as did Calpurnia and Philippus. Caesar refused it. So did Atia.

"Between the eggs and the cream, Uncle Gaius, I simply dare not," she laughed, but nervously. "Here, have some strawberries."

"For Philippus, out of season means nothing," said Caesar, growing ever more intrigued at the apprehension in the air. He lay back against his bolster and eyed Philippus mockingly, one fair brow raised. "There has to be a reason for this occasion, Lucius. Enlighten me."

"As my note said, a celebration of your return to Rome. Ah—however, there is an additional reason to celebrate, I admit," said Philippus as smoothly as his iced cream.

Caesar braced himself. "Since my great-nephew has been a man for nearly eight months, it can't concern him. Therefore it must concern my great-niece. Is she betrothed?"

"She is," said Philippus.

"Where's the prospective bridegroom?"

"On his Etrurian estates."

"May I ask his name?"

"Gaius Claudius Marcellus Minor," said Philippus airily.

"Minor."

"Well, it couldn't be Major! He's still abroad, unpardoned."

"I wasn't aware that *Minor* had been pardoned."

"Since he did nothing wrong and remained in Italy, why does he need a pardon?" Philippus asked, beginning to sound truculent.

"Because he was senior consul when I crossed the Rubicon, and made no attempt to persuade Pompeius Magnus and the *boni* to reach an accommodation with me."

"Come, Caesar, you know he was ill! Lentulus Crus did all the work, though as junior consul he didn't hold the *fasces* for January. Once sworn in, Marcellus Minor was obliged to take to his bed, and there he remained for many moons. Since none of the physicians could find a reason for his sickness, I've always been of the opinion that it was Minor's way of avoiding the displeasure of his far more militant brother and first cousin."

"A coward, you're implying."

"No, *not* a coward! Oh, sometimes you're too much the lawyer, Caesar! Marcellus Minor is simply a prudent man with the foresight to see that you can't be beaten. It's no disgrace for any man to deal craftily with his more unperceptive relatives," said Philippus, grimacing. "Relatives can be a terrible nuisance—look at me, handicapped with a mother like Palla and a half brother who tried to murder his own father! Not to mention *my* father, who tergiversated perpetually. They're the reasons why I adopted Epicureanism and have remained resolutely neutral all my political life. And look at you, with Marcus Antonius!"

Philippus scowled and clenched his fists, then disciplined himself to relax. "After Pharsalus, Marcellus Minor made a good recovery, and he's been attending the Senate ever since you left for Africa. Not even Antonius objected to his presence, and Lepidus welcomed him."

Caesar kept his face expressionless, but his eyes didn't thaw. "Does this match please you, Octavia?" he asked, looking at her, and remembering that Aunt Julia had gone to Gaius Marius in a spirit of self-sacrifice, though apparently she had loved him. Caesar preferred to remember the pain Marius caused her.

Octavia shivered. "Yes, it pleases me, Uncle Gaius."

"Did you ask for this match?"

"It is not my place to ask," she said, the pink fading from her cheeks and lips.

"Have you met him, this forty-five-year-old?"

"Yes, Uncle Gaius."

"And you can look forward to married life with him?"

"Yes, Uncle Gaius."

"Is there anyone you would prefer to marry?"

"No, Uncle Gaius," she whispered.

"Are you telling me the truth?"

The big, terrified eyes lifted to his; her skin was ashen now. "Yes, Uncle Gaius."

"Then," said Caesar, putting down his strawberries, "I offer you my felicitations, Octavia. However, as Pontifex Maximus, I forbid marriage *confarreatio*. An ordinary marriage, and you will retain the full control of your dowry."

As pale as her daughter, Atia rose to her feet with rare clumsiness. "Calpurnia, come and see Octavia's wedding chest."

The three women left very quickly, heads down.

Voice conversational, Caesar addressed Philippus. "This is a very strange alliance, my friend. You have betrothed Caesar's great-niece to one of Caesar's enemies. What gives you the right to do that?"

"I have every right," Philippus said, dark eyes burning. "I am the *paterfamilias*. You are not. When Marcellus Minor came to me with his offer, I considered it by far the best I've had."

"Your status as *paterfamilias* is debatable. Legally I would have said she's in her brother's hand, now he's of age. Did you consult her brother?"

"Yes," said Philippus between his teeth, "I did."

"And what was your answer, Octavius?"

The official man slid off the couch and transferred himself to the chair opposite Caesar, a place from which he could look at his great-uncle directly. "I considered the offer carefully, Uncle Gaius, and advised my stepfather to accept it."

"Give me your reasons, Octavius."

The lad's breathing had become audible, a moist rattle on every expiration, but he was clearly not about to back down, even though the emotional strain, according to Hapd'efan'e, was of an order to produce wheezing.

"First of all, Marcellus Minor had come into possession of the estates of his brother, Marcus, and his first cousin, Gaius Major. He bought them at auction. When you listed the estates confiscate, Uncle, you did not list Minor's, so my stepfather and I assumed Minor was an eligible suitor. Thus his wealth was my first reason. Secondly, the Claudii Marcelli are a great family of plebeian nobles with consuls going back many generations, and strong ties to the patrician Cornelii of the Lentulus branch. Octavia's children by Marcellus Minor will have great social and political clout. Thirdly, I do not consider that the conduct of either this man or his brother, Marcus the consul, has been dishonest or unethical, though I admit that Marcus was a terrible enemy to you. But he and Minor adhered to the Republican cause because they deemed it right, and you of all men, Uncle Gaius, have never castigated men for that. Had the suitor been Gaius Marcellus Major, my decision would have been different, for he lied to the Senate and lied to Pompeius Magnus. Offenses you and I—and all decent men—find abhorrent. Fourthly, I watched Octavia very closely when they met, and talked to her afterward. Though you may not like him, Uncle, Octavia liked him very well. He is not ill looking, he is well-read, cultured, good-natured and besottedly in love with my sister. Fifthly, his future position in Rome depends heavily upon your favor. Marriage to Octavia strengthens that position. Which leads me to my sixth point, that he will be an excellent husband. I doubt Octavia will ever be able to reproach him for infidelity or treatment I for one would find repellent."

Octavius squared his narrow shoulders. "Such are my reasons for thinking him a suitable husband for my sister."

Caesar burst out laughing. "Good for you, young man! Not even Caesar could have been more dispassionate. I see that when I call the Senate to a meeting, I'll have to make much of Gaius Claudius Marcellus Minor, crafty enough to pretend illness, shrewd enough to buy his brother's and his first cousin's property, and enterprising enough to cement his position with Caesar Dictator by a politic marriage." He straightened on the couch. "Tell me, Octavius, if the situation were to change and an even more desirable marriage offer for your sister were to surface, would you break off the engagement?"

"Of course, Caesar. I love my sister very much, but we take pains to make our women understand that they must always help us enhance our careers and our families by marrying where they are instructed to marry. Octavia has wanted for nothing, from the most expensive clothes to an education worthy of Cicero. She is aware that the price of her comfort and privilege is obedience."

The wheezing was dying away; Octavius had come through his ordeal relatively unscathed.

"What's the gossip?" Caesar asked Philippus, who had sagged in relief.

"I hear that Cicero is at his villa in Tusculum writing a new masterpiece," Philippus said uneasily. This had not been a restful dinner, and he could already feel a need for *laserpicium*.

"I detect a note of ominousness. The subject?"

"A eulogy on Cato."

"Oh, I see. From that, I deduce that he still refuses to take his place in the Senate?"

"Yes, though Atticus is trying to make him see sense."

"No one can!" said Caesar savagely. "What else?"

"Poor little Varro is beside himself. While Master of the Horse Antonius used his authority to strip Varro of some of his nicer estates, which he put in his own name. The income is handy now that he isn't Master of the Horse. The moneylenders are dunning him for repayment of the loan he took out to buy that monument to bad taste, Pompeius's palace on the Carinae."

"Thank you for that snippet of information. I will attend to it," Caesar said grimly.

"And one other thing, Caesar, which I think you should know about, though I'm afraid it will come as a blow."

"Deal the blow, Philippus."

"Your secretary, Gaius Faberius."

"I knew something was wrong. What's he done?"

"He's been selling the Roman citizenship to foreigners."

Oh, Faberius, Faberius! After all these years! It seems no one save Caesar himself can wait one or two months more for his share of the booty. My triumphs are imminent, and Faberius's share would have earned him knight's status. Now he gets nothing.

"Is his graft on a grand scale?"

"Grand enough to buy a mansion on the Aventine."

"He mentioned a house."

"I wouldn't exactly call Afranius's old place a mere house."

"Nor would I." Caesar swung himself backward on the couch and waited for the servant to slip on his shoes, buckle them. "Octavius, walk me home," he commanded. "Calpurnia can stay to talk to the women a little longer—I'll send a litter for her. Thank you, Philippus, for the welcome home party—and for the gossip. Most illuminating."

The awkward guest gone, Philippus donned backless slippers and shuffled to his wife's sitting room, where he found Calpurnia and Octavia examining piles of new clothing while Atia watched.

"Did he settle down?" Atia whispered, coming to the door.

"Once Octavius spoke his piece, his mood became sanguine. Your son is a remarkable fellow, my dear."

"Oh, the relief! Octavia really does want this marriage."

"I think Caesar will make Octavius his heir."

Her face went to stark terror. "*Ecastor*, no!"

As Philippus's commodious house lay on the Circus Maximus side of the Palatine and looked more west than north, Caesar and his companion, both togate, walked down to the upper Forum, then turned at the shopping center corner to descend the slope of the Clivus Sacer to the Domus Publica. Caesar stopped.

"Tell Trogus to send a litter for Calpurnia, would you?" he asked Octavius. "I want to inspect my new additions."

Octavius was back in a moment; they resumed their walk down into the gathering shadows. The sun was low, bronzing the arched stories of the Tabularium and subtly changing the colors of the temples encrusting the Capitol above it. Though Jupiter Optimus Maximus

Campus Martius

VIA LATA FLAMINIA
VIA SALARIA VETUS

SAEPTA

VILLA PUBLICA

Servian Walls

CIRCUS FLAMINIUS

Campus Martius

ARX
5

Subura

Tiber Island

CAPITOL

4

6

7
8

ARGILETUM

FAUCES SUBURAE

VIA AURELIA

FORUM

VICUS IUGARIUS

9

FORUM ROMANUM

CLIVUS ORBIUS

PONS
AEMILIA

HOLITORIUM

10

Carinae

14

VELABRUM

VICUS TUSCUS

11

12

Transtiberim

FORUM BOARIUM

Germalus

Palus Ceroliae
Swamps

Palatine

13

VIA SACRA

Luperal

Steps
of Cacus

PORT OF ROME

15

Lane to the
Ox Heads

Aventine

Palatine

CIRCUS MAXIMUS

VIA TRIUMPHALIS

1 POMPEY'S THEATER
2 HUNDRED-PILLARED PERISTYLE
3 POMPEY'S SENATORIAL CURIA
4 T. JUPITER OPTIMUS MAXIMUS
5 T. JUNO MONETA
6 FORUM JULIUM
7 CURIA HOSTILIA & SENATE OFFICES
8 T. SATURN & TREASURY
9 BASILICA JULIA
10 T. CASTOR & POLLUX
11 DOMUS PUBLICA
12 PORTICUS MARGARITARIA
13 T. JUPITER STATOR
14 T. TELLUS
15 T. CERES

Servian Walls

← CAPENA GATE

dominated the higher hump and Juno Moneta the Arx, which was the lower hump, almost every inch of space was occupied by a temple to some god or aspect of a god, the oldest among them small and drab, the newest glowing with rich colors and glittering with gilding. Only the slight depression between the two humps, the Asylum, contained any free ground, planted with pencil pines and poplars, several ferny trees from Africa.

The Basilica Julia was completely finished; Caesar stood to regard its size and beauty with great satisfaction. Of two high stories, his new courthouse had a façade of colored marbles, Corinthian columns separated by arches in which stood statues of his ancestors from Aeneas through Romulus to that Quintus Marcius Rex who had built the aqueduct, and Gaius Marius, and Sulla, and Catulus Caesar. His mother was there, his first wife, Cinnilla, both Aunts Julia, and Julia, his daughter. That was the best part about being ruler of the world; he could erect statues of whomever he liked, including women.

"It's so wonderful that I come to look at it often," said Octavius. "No more postponing the courts because of rain or snow."

Caesar passed to the new Curia Hostilia, home of the Senate. The Well of the Comitia had gone to make room for it; he had built a new, much taller and larger rostra that faced up the full length of the Forum, adorned with statues and the columns that held the captured ships' beaks from which the rostra had gotten its name. There had been mutters that he was disturbing the *mos maiorum* with so much change, but he ignored them. Time that Rome looked better than places like Alexandria and Athens. Cato's new Basilica Porcia remained at the foot of the Hill of the Bankers because, though it was small, it was very recent and sufficiently attractive to warrant preserving.

Beyond the Basilica Porcia and the Curia Hostilia was the Forum Julium, a huge undertaking that had meant resuming the business premises facing on to the Hill of the Bankers and excavating the slope to flatness. Not only that, but the Servian Walls had intruded upon its back, so he had paid to relocate these massive fortifications in a jog that went around his new forum. It was a rectangular open space paved in marble and surrounded on all four sides with a colonnade of splendid Corinthian pillars of purple marble, their acanthus leaf capitals gilded. A magnificent fountain decorated with statues of nymphs played in the middle of the space, while its only building, a temple to Venus Genetrix, stood at the back atop a high podium of steps. The same purple marble, the same Corinthian pillars, and atop the peak of the temple's pediment, a golden *biga*—a statue of Victory driving two winged horses. The sun was almost gone; only the *biga* now reflected its rays.

Caesar produced a key and let them into the *cella*, just one big room with a glorious honeycombed ceiling ornamented by roses. The paintings hung on its walls made Octavius catch his breath.

"The 'Medea' is by Timomachus of Byzantium," Caesar said. "I paid eighty talents for it, but it's worth much more."

It certainly is! thought the awed Octavius. Startlingly lifelike, the work showed Medea dropping the bloody chunks of the brothers she had murdered into the sea to slow her father down and enable her and Jason to escape.

"The Aphrodite arising from the sea foam and the Alexander the Great are by the peerless Apelles—a genius." Caesar grinned. "However, I think I'll keep the price I paid to myself. Eighty talents wouldn't cover one of Apelles's seashells."

"But they're here in Rome," Octavius said fervently. "That alone makes a matchless painting worth the price. If Rome has them, then Athens or Pergamum don't."

The statue of Venus Genetrix—Venus the Ancestress—stood in the center of the back wall of the *cella*, painted so well that the goddess seemed about to step down off her golden pedestal. Like the statue of Venus Victrix atop Pompey's theater, she bore Julia's face.

"Arcesilaus did it," Caesar said abruptly, turning away.

"I hardly remember her."

"A pity. Julia was"—his voice shook—"a pearl beyond price. Any price at all."

"Who did the statues of you?" Octavius asked.

A Caesar in armor stood to one side of Venus, a togate Caesar on the other.

"Some fellow Balbus found. My bankers have commissioned an equestrian statue of me to go in the forum itself, on one side of the fountain. I commissioned a statue of Toes to go on the other side. He's as famous as Alexander's Bucephalus."

"What goes there?" Octavius asked, pointing to an empty plinth of some black wood inlaid with stones and enamel in most peculiar designs.

"A statue of Cleopatra with her son by me. She wanted to donate it, and as she says it will be solid gold, I didn't like to put it outside, where someone enterprising might start shaving bits off it," Caesar said with a laugh.

"When will she arrive in Rome?"

"I don't know. As with all voyages, even the last, it depends on the gods."

"One day," said Octavius, "I too will build a forum."
"The Forum Octavium. A splendid ambition."

Octavius left Caesar at his door and commenced the uphill battle to Philippus's house, never more conscious of his chronic shortness of breath than when toiling uphill. Dusk was drawing in, a chill descending; day's trappings going, night's coming, thought Octavius as the whirr of small bird wings was replaced by the ponderous flap of owls. A vast, billowing cloud reared above the Viminal, shot with a last gasp of pink.

I notice a change in him. He seems tired, though not with a physical weariness. More as if he understands that he will not be thanked for his efforts. That the petty creatures who creep about his feet will resent his brilliance, his ability to do what they have no hope of doing. "As with all voyages, even the last"—why did he phrase it so?

Just beyond the ancient, lichen-whiskered columns of the Porta Mugonia the hill sloped more acutely; Octavius paused to rest with his back pressed to the stone of one, thinking that the other looked like a brooding *lemur* escaped from the underworld, between its tubby body and its mushroom-cap hat. He straightened, struggled on a little farther, stopped opposite the lane that led to the Ox Heads, certainly the worst address on the Palatine. I was born in a house on that lane; my father's father, a notorious miser, was still alive and my father hadn't come into his inheritance. Then before we could move, he was dead, and Mama chose Philippus. A lightweight to whom the pleasures of the flesh are paramount.

Caesar *despises* the pleasures of the flesh. Not as a philosophy, like Cato, simply as unimportant. To him, the world is stuffed with things that need setting to rights, things that only he can see how to fix. Because he questions endlessly, he picks and chews, gnaws and dissects, pulls whatever it is into its component parts, then puts them together again in a better, more practical way.

How is it that he, the most august nobleman of them all, is not impaired by his birth, can see beyond it into illimitable distances? Caesar is classless. He is the only man I know or have read about who comprehends both the entire gigantic picture and every smallest detail in it. I want desperately to be another Caesar, but I do not have his mind. I am not a universal genius. I can't write plays and poems, give brilliant extemporaneous speeches, engineer a bridge or a siege platform, draft great laws effortlessly, play musical instruments, general flawless battles, write crisp commentaries, take up shield and sword to fight in the front line, travel like the wind, dictate to four secretaries at once, and all those other legendary things he does out of the vastness of his mind.

My health is precarious and may grow worse, I stare that in the face every day. But I can plan, I have an instinct for the right alternative, I can think quickly, and I am learning to make the most of what few talents I have. If we share anything in common, Caesar and I, it is an absolute refusal to give up or give in. And perhaps, in the long run, that is the key.

Somehow, some way, I am going to be as great as Caesar.

He started the plod up the Clivus Palatinus, a slight figure that gradually merged into the gloom until it became a part of it. The Palatine cats, hunting for mouse or mate, slunk from shadow to shadow, and an old dog, half of one ear missing, lifted its leg to piss on the Porta Mugonia, too deaf to hear the bats.

Gaius Faberius, who had been with Caesar for twenty years, was dismissed in disgrace; Caesar convened a meeting of the Popular Assembly to witness the destruction of the tablets upon which the names of Faberius's false citizens were inscribed.

"Due note has been taken of these names, and none will ever receive our citizenship!" he told the crowd. "Gaius Faberius has refunded the moneys paid to him by the false citizens, and said moneys will be donated to the temple of Quirinus, the god of all true Roman citizens. Furthermore, Gaius Faberius's share of my booty will be put back into the general pool for division."

Caesar took a stroll across his new, taller rostra, went down its steps and escorted the tiny figure of Marcus Terentius Varro on to its top. "Marcus Antonius, come here!" he called. Knowing what was coming, the scowling Antony ascended, stood to face Varro as Caesar informed the listening assembly that Varro had been a good friend to Pompey the Great, but never involved in the Republican conspiracy. The Sabine nobleman, a great scholar, received the deeds of his properties back, plus a fine of one million sesterces Caesar levied against Antony for causing Varro such distress. Then Antony had publicly to apologize.

"It's not important," Fulvia crooned when Antony stalked into her house immediately after the meeting. "Marry me, and you'll have the use of my fortune, darling Antonius. You're divorced now, there's no impediment. Marry me!"

"I hate to be obligated to a woman!" Antony snapped.

"*Gerrae!*" she gurgled. "Look at your two wives."

"They were forced on me, you're not. But Caesar's finally set the dates for his triumphs, so I'll be getting my share of the Gallic booty in less than a month. Therefore I'll marry you."

His face twisted into hate. "Gaul first, then Egypt for King Ptolemy and Princess Arsinoë, then Asia Minor for King Pharnaces, and finally Africa for King Juba. Just as if Caesar's never heard of the word Republicans! What a farce! I could kill him! I mean, he appoints me his Master of the Horse, which cuts me out of any of the booty for Egypt, Asia Minor or Africa—I had to sit in Italy instead of serving with him! And have I had any thanks? No! He just shits on me!"

An agitated nursemaid hurried in. "*Domina, domina*, little Curio has fallen over and hit his head!"

Fulvia gasped, threw her hands in the air and was off at a run. "Oh, that child! He'll be the death of me!" she wailed.

Three men had witnessed this rather unromantic interlude: Poplicola, Cotyla and Lucius Tillius Cimber.

Cimber had entered the Senate as a quaestor the year before Caesar crossed the Rubicon, and supported his cause in the House. Unlike Antony, he could look forward to a share of the Asian and African booty, but they were nothing compared to what Antony would collect for Gaul. His vices were expensive, his association with Poplicola and Cotyla of some years' duration, and his acquaintance with Antony had burgeoned since Antony's return to Italy after Pharsalus. What he hadn't realized until this illuminating scene was the depth of Antony's hatred for his cousin Caesar; he truly did look as if he could do murder.

"Didn't you say, Antonius, that you're bound to be Caesar's heir?" Poplicola asked casually.

"I've been saying it for years, what's that to the point?"

"I think Poplicola is trying to find a way to introduce the matter into our conversation," Cotyla said smoothly. "You're Caesar's heir, correct?"

"I have to be," Antony said simply. "Who else is there?"

"Then if it irks you to depend on Fulvia for money because you love her, you do have another source, not so? Compared to Caesar, Fulvia's a pauper," Cotyla said.

Arrested, eyes gleaming redly, Antony looked at him. "Are you implying what I infer, Cotyla?"

Cimber moved quietly out of Antony's line of sight, drawing no attention to his presence.

"We're both implying it," Poplicola said. "All you have to do to get out of debt permanently is kill Caesar."

"*Quirites*, that's a brilliant idea!" Antony's fists came up, clenched in exultation. "It would be so easy too."

"Which one of us should do it?" Cimber asked, inserting himself back into the action.

"I'll do it myself. I know his habits," Antony said. "He works until the eighth hour of night, then goes to bed for four hours and sleeps like the dead. I can go in over the top of his private peristyle wall, kill him and be out again before anybody knows I'm there. The tenth hour of night. And later, if there are any enquiries, the four of us will have been sitting drinking in old Murcius's tavern on the Via Nova."

"When will you do it?" asked Cimber.

"Oh, tonight," Antony said cheerfully. "While I'm still in the mood."

"He's a close kinsman," said Poplicola.

Antony burst into laughter. "What a thing for you to say, Lucius! You tried to murder your own father."

All four men laughed uproariously; when Fulvia returned, she found Antony in an excellent humor.

Well after midnight Antony, Poplicola, Cotyla and Cimber staggered into old Murcius's tavern very much the worse for wear, and usurped the table right at the back with the excuse that it was handy to the window in case anyone wanted to vomit. When the Forum watchman's bell announced the tenth hour of night, Antony slipped out of the window while Cotyla, Cimber and Poplicola clustered around their table and continued their rowdy banter as if Antony were still a part of it.

They expected him to be away some small while, as the Via Nova was perched atop a thirty-foot cliff; Antony would have to run a short distance to the Ringmakers' Steps, which would bring him to the back of the Porticus Margaritaria and the Domus Publica.

He returned quite quickly, looking furious. "I don't believe it!" he gasped, out of breath. "When I got to the peristyle wall, there were servants sitting on top of it with torches!"

"Is this a new thing, for Caesar to mount a watch?" Cimber asked curiously.

"I don't know, do I?" snarled Antony. "This is the first time I've ever tried to sneak into the place during the night."

Two days later Caesar summoned the Senate to the very first meeting of that body since his return; the venue was Pompey's Curia on the Campus Martius behind his hundred-pillared courtyard and the vast bulk of his theater. Though it meant a fairly long walk, those summoned breathed a sigh of relief. Pompey's Curia had been specifically built for meetings of the Senate, and could accommodate everyone in comfort and proper gradation. As it lay outside the *pomerium*, in the days when the Curia Hostilia of the Forum had existed, it was mostly used for discussing foreign war, a subject considered inappropriate for *pomerium*-confined meetings.

Caesar was already ensconced on the podium in his curule chair, a folding table in front of him loaded with documents he had to find time to read, wax tablets and a steel stylus used to gouge writing in the wax. He took no notice as men dribbled in, had their slaves set up their stools on the correct tier: the top one for *pedarii*, senators allowed to vote but not speak; the middle one for holders of junior magistracies, namely ex-aediles and ex-tribunes of the plebs; and the front, lowest tier for ex-praetors and consulars.

Only when Fabius, his chief lictor, tapped him on the shoulder did Caesar lift his head and gaze about. Not too bad on the back benches, he thought. So far he had appointed two hundred new men, including the three centurions who had won the *corona civica*. Most were scions of the families who made up the Eighteen senior Centuries, but some were from prominent Italian families, and a few, like Gaius Helvius Cinna, from Italian Gaul. The "unsuitable" appointments had not met with approval from those of Rome's old noble families who regarded the Senate as a body purely for them. The word had gone around that Caesar was filling the Senate with trousered Gauls and ranker legionaries, along with rumors that he intended to make himself King of Rome. Every day since he had come back from Africa someone asked Caesar when he was going to "restore the Republic"—a question he ignored. Cicero was being very vocal about the deteriorating exclusivity of the Senate, an attitude heightened by the fact that he himself was not a Roman of the Romans, but a New Man from the country. The more of his like filled the Senate, the less his own triumph in attaining it against all the odds. He was, besides, a colossal snob.

A few men Caesar had yearned to see there were sitting on the front benches: the two Manius Aemilius Lepiduses, father and son; Lucius Volcatius Tullus the elder; Calvinus; Lucius Piso; Philippus; two members of the Appius Claudius Pulcher *gens*. And some men not so yearned for: Marcus Antonius and Octavia's betrothed, Gaius Claudius Marcellus Minor. But no Cicero. Caesar's lips thinned. No doubt too busy eulogizing Cato to attend.

The podium was quite crowded. Himself and Lepidus, the two consuls, and six of the praetors, including his staunch ally Aulus Hirtius and Volcatius Tullus's son. That boor Gaius Antonius had his behind on the tribunician bench, along with the other, equally uninspiring, holders of the tribunate of the plebs.

Enough, thought Caesar, counting more than a quorum. He rose to pull a fold of toga over his head and say the prayers, waited for Lucius Caesar to take the auspices, then got down to business.

"Some sad news first, conscript fathers," he said in his usual deep voice; the acoustics in Pompey's Curia were good. "I have had word that the last of the Licinii Crassi, Marcus the younger son of the great consular, has died. He will be missed."

He swept on without looking as if his next item of news was going to cause a sensation, and so caught the senators unaware. "I have to draw a second unpleasantness to your attention. Namely, that Marcus Antonius has made an attempt on my life. He was seen trying to enter the Domus Publica at an hour when I am known to be asleep, and the interior deserted. His garb was not formal—a tunic and a knife. Nor was his mode of entry formal—the wall of my private peristyle."

Antony sat, rigid with shock—how did Caesar *know*? No one had seen him, no one!

"I mention this with no intention of pursuing the matter. I simply draw your attention to it, and take leave to inform all of you that I am not as unprotected as I may seem. Therefore those of you who do not approve of my dictatorship—or of my methods!—had best think twice before deciding that you will rid Rome of this tyrant Caesar. I tell you frankly that my life has been long enough, whether in years or renown. However, I am not yet so tired of it that I will do nothing to avert its being terminated by a deed of murder. Remove me, and I can assure you that Rome will suffer far greater ills than Caesar Dictator. Rome's present situation is much the same as it was when Lucius Cornelius Sulla took up the dictatorship—she needs one strong hand, and in me she has that hand. Once I have set my laws in place and made sure that Rome will survive to grow ever greater, I will lay down my dictatorship. However, I will not do that until my work is entirely finished, and that may take many years. So be warned, and cease these pleas that I 'return the Republic' to its former glory.

"*What glory?*" he thundered, making his appalled audience jump. "I repeat, *what glory?* There was no glory! Just a fractious, obstinate, conceited little group of men jealously defending their privileges. The privilege of going to govern a province and rape it. The privilege of granting business colleagues the opportunity to go to a province and rape it. The privilege of having one law for some, and another law for others. The privilege of putting incompetents in office simply because they bear a great name. The privilege of voting to quash laws that are desperately needed. The privilege of preserving the *mos maiorum* in a form suitable for a small city-state, but not for a worldwide empire."

They were sitting bolt upright, their faces slack. For some, it had been a long time since this Caesar had last bellowed his radical ideas to the House; for others, this was the first time.

"If you believe that all Rome's wealth and privilege should remain in the Eighteen from which you come, senators, then I will cut you down to size. I intend to restructure our society to distribute wealth more equally. I will make laws encouraging the growth of the Third and Fourth Classes, and enhance the lot of the Head Count by encouraging them to emigrate to places where they can rise into higher classes. Further to this, I am introducing a means test on the distribution of free grain so that men who can afford to buy grain will no longer be able to obtain it free. At present there are three hundred thousand recipients of the free grain dole. I will cut that figure in half overnight. I will also make it impossible for a man to free slaves in order to benefit from the grain dole. How am I going to do this? By holding a new kind of census in November. My census agents will go from door to door throughout Rome, Italy, and all the provinces. They will assemble mountains of facts about housing, rents, hygiene, income, population, literacy and numeracy, crime, fire, and the number of children, aged and slaves in every family. My agents will also ask members of the Head Count if they would like to emigrate abroad to the colonies I will found. Since Rome now has a huge surplus of troop transport ships, I will use them."

Piso spoke. "Be he rich or poor, Caesar, every Roman citizen is entitled to the free grain dole. I warn you that I will oppose any attempt to impose a means test!" he said loudly.

"Oppose all you like, Lucius Piso, the law will come into effect anyway. *I will not be gainsaid!* Nor do I advise you to oppose—it will harm your career. The measure is fair and just. Why should Rome pay out her precious moneys to men like you, well able to buy grain?" asked Caesar, voice hard.

There were mutterings, dark looks; the old, high-handed, arrogant Caesar was back with a vengeance. However, the faces on the back benches, though alarmed, were not angry. They owed their position to Caesar, and they would vote for his laws.

"There will be innumerable agrarian laws," Caesar continued, "but there's no need for fury, so don't get furious. Any land I buy in Italy and Italian Gaul for retiring legionaries will be paid for up-front and at full value, but most of the agrarian legislation will involve foreign land in the Spains, the Gauls, Greece, Epirus, Illyricum, Macedonia, Bithynia, Pontus, Africa Nova, the domain of Publius Sittius, and the Mauretanias. At the same time as some of our Head Count and some of our legionaries go to settle in these colonies, I will also grant the full citizenship to deserving provincials, physicians, schoolteachers, artisans and tradesmen. If resident in Rome, they will be enrolled in the four urban tribes, but if resident in Italy, in the rural tribe common to the district wherein they live."

"Do you intend to do anything about the courts, Caesar?" asked the praetor Volcatius Tullus in an attempt to calm the House.

"Oh, yes. The *tribunus aerarius* will disappear from the jury list," the Dictator announced, willing to be sidetracked. "The Senate will be increased to one thousand members, which will, with the knights of the Eighteen, provide more than enough jurors for the courts. The number of praetors will go to fourteen per year to enable swifter hearings in the busier courts. By the time that my legislation is done, there will hardly be any need for the Extortion Court, because governors and businessmen in the provinces will be too hamstrung to extort. Elections will be better regulated, so the Bribery Court will also stultify. Whereas ordinary crimes like murder, theft, violence, embezzlement and bankruptcy need more courts and more time. I also intend to increase the penalty for murder, but not in a way that disturbs the *mos maiorum*. Execution for crime and imprisonment for crime, two concepts alien to Roman thought and culture, will not be introduced. Rather, I will increase the time of exile and make it absolutely impossible for a man sentenced to exile to take his money with him."

"Aiming for Plato's ideal republic, Caesar?" Piso sneered; he was taking the greatest offense.

"Not at all," Caesar said genially. "I'm aiming for a just and practical Roman republic. Take violence, for example. Those desirous of organizing street gangs will find it much harder, for I am going to abolish all clubs and sodalities save those that are harmless of intent— Jewish synagogues, trade and professional guilds—and the burial clubs, of course. Crossroads colleges and other places where troublemakers can meet on a regular basis will disappear. When men have to buy their own wine, they drink less."

"I hear," said Philippus, who was a huge landowner, "a tiny rumor that you have plans to break up *latifundia*."

"Thank you for reminding me, Lucius Philippus," said Caesar, smiling broadly. "No, *latifundia* will not be broken up unless the state has bought them for soldier land. However, in future no owner of a *latifundium* will be allowed to run it entirely on slaves. One-third of his employees must be free men of the region. This will help the jobless rural poor as well as local merchants."

"That's ridiculous!" yelled Philippus, dark face flushed. "You're going to introduce legislation to tamper with *everything!* A man will soon have to apply for permission to fart! You, Caesar, are deliberately setting out to strip Rome of any kind of First Class! Where do you get these insane ideas from? Help the rural poor indeed! A man has rights, and one of them is the right to run his businesses and enterprises exactly how he wants! Why should I have to pay *wages* to one-third of my *latifundia* workers when I can buy cheap slaves and not pay them at all?"

"Every man should pay his slaves a wage, Philippus. Can't you see," Caesar asked, "that you have to buy your slaves? Then you have to build *ergastula* to house them, buy food to feed them, and use up twice as many workers to supervise these unwilling men? If you were any good at arithmetic or you had agents who could add up two and two, you'd soon realize that employing the free is cheaper. You don't have the initial outlay, and you don't need to house or feed free men. They go home each night and eat out of their own gardens because they have wives and children to grow for them."

"*Gerrae!*" Philippus growled, subsiding.

"What, no sumptuary laws?" Piso asked.

"Sheaves of them," Caesar answered readily. "Luxuries will be severely taxed, and while I will not forbid the erection of expensive tombs, the man who builds one will have to pay Rome's Treasury the same amount of money he pays his tomb builder."

He looked down at Lepidus, who hadn't said a word, and raised a brow. "Junior consul, just one more thing and you can dismiss the meeting. There will be *no* debate."

He turned back to the House and proceeded to tell it that he intended to bring the calendar into line with the seasons for perpetuity, so this year would be 455 days long: Mercedonius was over, but a 67-day period called Intercalaris would also be added following the last day of December. New Year's Day, when eventually it came, would be exactly where it was supposed to be, one-third of the way through winter.

"There isn't a name for you, Caesar," Piso declared as he left, his whole body trembling. "You're a—a—a *freak!*"

Miming injured innocence to those who stared at him, Antony waited to get Caesar to himself. "What do you mean, Caesar, to come out with that assassination rot? Then you barged on about returning the Republic to its days of glory without even giving me a chance to defend myself!" He pushed his face aggressively close to Caesar's. "First you humiliate me in public, now you've accused me of attempted murder in the Senate! It isn't true—ask any of the three men I was with all that night at Murcius's tavern!"

Caesar's eyes wandered to Lucius Tillius Cimber, descending from the top left-hand tier with his stool slave following him. What an interesting man. Full of useful information.

"Do go away, Antonius," he said wearily. "As I've already indicated, I have no intention of pursuing the matter. However, I felt that your playing the fool with murder was an excellent excuse to inform the House that I'm not so easily gotten rid of. In the financial soup worse than ever, eh?"

"I'm marrying Fulvia and shortly I'll have my share of the Gallic booty," Antony countered. "Why do I need to murder you?"

"One question, Antonius—how do you know which night the attempt was made if you didn't make it? I neglected to mention the date. Of course you tried! In a temper, following the Varro apology. Now go away."

"I despair for Antonius," said Lucius Caesar, approaching.

Almost to the doorway, his lictors passed outside, Caesar turned to look back down the ostentatious hall with its splendid marbles and not-quite-right color scheme—typical of its author! And there at the rear of the platform accommodating the curule magistrates stood the statue of Pompey the Great in his white marble toga with the purple marble border, his face, hands, right arm and calves painted to the perfect tones of his skin, even including the faint freckles. The bright gold hair was superbly done, the vivid blue eyes seeming to sparkle with life.

"A very good likeness," Lucius said, following his cousin's gaze. "I hope you don't mean to emulate Magnus and put a statue of yourself behind the curule magistrates in your new Curia?"

"It's not a bad idea, Lucius, when you think about it. If I were away for ten years, every time the Senate met in its Curia it would be reminded of the fact that I'll be back."

They moved outside, passed through the colonnade and emerged on the road back to town.

"One thing I meant to ask you, Lucius. How did young Gaius Octavius go when he served as city prefect?"

"Didn't you ask him in person, Gaius?"

"He didn't mention it, and I confess it slipped my mind."

"You need have no fears, he did very well. *Praefectus urbi* notwithstanding, he occupied the urban praetor's booth with a lovely mixture of humility and quiet confidence. He handled the inevitable one or two contentious situations like a veteran—very cool, asked all the right questions, delivered the proper verdict. Yes, he did very well."

"Did you know that he suffers the wheezing sickness?"

Lucius stopped. "*Edepol!* No, I didn't."

"It represents a dilemma, doesn't it?"

"Oh, yes."

"Yet I think it has to be him, Lucius."

"There's time enough." Lucius put an arm around Caesar's shoulders, squeezed them comfortingly. "Don't forget Caesar's luck, Gaius. Whatever you decide carries Caesar's luck with it."

2   Cleopatra arrived in Rome at the end of the first *nundinum* in September. She was conveyed from Ostia in a curtained litter, an enormous procession of attendants before her and behind her, including a detachment of the Royal Guard in their quaint hoplite gear, but mounted on snow-white horses with purple tack. Her son, a little unwell, traveled in another litter with his nursemaids, and a third one held King Ptolemy XIV, her thirteen-year-old husband. All three litters had cloth-of-gold curtains, the jewels in the gilded woodwork flashing in the bright sun of a beautiful early summer's day, ostrich-feather plumes caked in gold dust nodding at all four corners of the faience-tiled roofs. Each was borne by eight powerfully built men with plummy black skin, clad in cloth-of-gold kilts and wide gold collars, big feet bare. Apollodorus rode in a canopied sedan chair at the head of the column, a tall gold staff in his right hand, his *nemes* headdress cloth-of-gold, his fingers covered with rings, the chain of his office around his neck. The several hundred attendants wore costly robes, even the humblest among them; the Queen of Egypt was determined to make an impression.

They had started out at dawn with a good percentage of Ostia escorting them, and as Ostia drew farther away, others took their place; anyone who had occasion to be on the Via Ostiensis that morning thought it more fun to join the royal parade than go about normal business. Cornelius the lictor, deputed to act as guide, picked them up a mile from the Servian Walls and viewed his charge with an awe bordering on profound—oh, what a tale he'd have to tell when he got back to the College of Lictors! It was noon by this time, and Apollodorus stared at the looming ramparts in relief. But then Cornelius led them around the outskirts of the Aventine to the wharves of the Port of Rome, there to halt. The Lord High Chamberlain began to frown; why were they not entering the city, why was her majesty in this decrepit, seedy neighborhood?

"We boat across the river here," Cornelius explained.

"Boat? But the city is to our right!"

"Oh, we're not entering the city," Cornelius said in affable inno-

cence. "The Queen's palace is across the Tiber at the foot of the Janicu-lan Hill, which makes this the easiest place to cross—wharves on both sides."

"Why isn't the Queen's palace inside the city?"

"Tch, tch, that would *never* do," said Cornelius. "The city is forbid-den to any anointed sovereign because to enter it means crossing the sacred *pomerium* and laying down all imperial power."

"*Pomerium?*" asked Apollodorus.

"The invisible boundary of the city. Within it, no one has im-perium except the dictator."

By this time half the Port of Rome had gathered to gawk, as had grooms, stablehands, slaughtermen and shepherds from the Campus Lanatarius. Cornelius was wishing that he had brought other lictors to keep the crowds at bay—what a circus! And so Rome's lowly regarded it, a wonderful, unexpected circus on an ordinary working day. Luck-ily for the Egyptians a succession of barges drew into the wharf; the lit-ters and sedan chair were quickly conveyed on board the first of them, and the horde of attendants pushed on to the others with the Royal Guard bringing up the rear, dismounted and soothing their fractious horses.

Apollodorus's frown gathered mightily when they were off-loaded into the mean alleys of Transtiberim, where he was forced to order the Royal Guards into tight formation around the litters to pre-vent the dirty, ragged inhabitants from gouging jewels out of the litter posts with their knives—even the women seemed to carry knives. Nor was he amused when, after yet another long plod, he found that the Queen's palace had no walls to keep the Transtiberini out!

"They'll give up and go home," said the unconcerned Cornelius, leading the way through an arch into a courtyard. Apollodorus's an-swer was to swing the Royal Guard across this entrance and tell it to stay there until the Transtiberini went home. What kind of place was this, that there were no walls to exclude the dross of humanity from the residences of their betters? And what kind of place was this, that her majesty's only deputed escort was one lictor minus his *fasces?* Where was Caesar?

The Queen's belongings had preceded her by sufficient time to en-sure that when she emerged from her litter and walked into the vast atrium, her eyes could rest on a properly outfitted interior, from paint-ings and tapestries on the walls to rugs, chairs, tables, couches, stat-ues, her huge collection of pedestals containing busts of all the Ptolemies and their wives—an air of inhabited comfort.

She was not in a good mood. Naturally she had peeked between the curtains at this alien landscape of rearing hills, seen the massive Servian Walls, the terra-cotta roofs dotting the hills inside them, the tall thin pines, the leafy trees, the pines shaped like parasols. A shock for her as well as Apollodorus when they bypassed the city and entered a dockland dominated by a tall mount of broken pots and festering rubbish. Where was the guard of honor Caesar should have sent? Why had she been ferried across that—that *creek* to a worse slum, then hustled to nowhere? For that matter, why hadn't Caesar answered any of the barrage of notes she had sent him since arriving in Ostia, save for the first? And that terse communication simply told her to move into her palace as soon as she wished!

Cornelius bowed. He knew her from Alexandria, though he was inured enough to eastern rulers to understand that she would not recognize him. Nor did she; her majesty was in a huff. "I am to give you Caesar's compliments, your majesty," he said. "As soon as he finds the time, he'll visit you."

"As soon as he finds the time, he'll visit me," she echoed to Cornelius's receding back. "He'll *visit!* Well, when he does, he'll wish he hadn't!"

"Calm down and behave yourself, Cleopatra," said Charmian firmly; brought up from infancy with their queen, she and Iras stood in no fear of her, divined her every mood.

"It's very nice," Iras contributed, gazing about. "I love the huge pool in the middle of the room, and how cunning to put dolphins and tritons in it." She looked up at the sky with less approval. "You'd think they'd put a roof over it, wouldn't you?"

Cleopatra sat on her temper. "Caesarion?" she asked.

"He's been taken straight to the nursery, but don't worry, he's improving."

For a moment the Queen stood uncertainly, chewing her lip; then she shrugged. "We are in a strange land of high mountains and peculiar trees, so I suppose we must expect the customs to be equally strange and peculiar. Since apparently Caesar isn't going to come at a run to welcome me, there's no point in keeping my regalia on. Where are the nursery and my private rooms?"

Changed into a plain Greek gown and reassured that Caesarion was indeed improving, she toured the palace with Charmian and Iras. On the small side, but adequate, was their verdict. Caesar had given her one of his own freedmen, Gaius Julius Gnipho, as her Roman steward, who would be in charge of things like purchasing food and household items.

"Why are there no gauze curtains to shield the windows, and none around the beds?" Cleopatra asked.

Gnipho looked bewildered. "I'm sorry, I don't understand."

"Are there no mosquitoes here? No night moths or bugs?"

"We have them aplenty, your majesty."

"Then they must be kept outside. Charmian, did we bring any linen gauze with us?"

"Yes, more than enough."

"Then see it's put up. Around Caesarion's cot at once."

Religion had not been neglected; Cleopatra had carried a select pantheon with her, of painted wood rather than solid gold, dressed in their proper raiment—Amun-Ra, Ptah, Sekhmet, Horus, Nefertem, Osiris, Isis, Anubis, Bastet, Taweret, Sobek and Hathor. To care for them and her own needs she had brought a high priest, Pu'em-re, and six *mete-en-sa* to assist him.

The agent, Ammonius, had been to Ostia to see his queen on several occasions, and had made sure that the builders provided one room with plastered walls; this would be the temple, once the *mete-en-sa* had painted the walls with the prayers, the spells and the cartouches of Cleopatra, Caesarion and Philadelphus.

Her mood dropping inexorably toward depression, Cleopatra fell to abase herself before Amun-Ra. The formal prayer, in old Egyptian, she spoke aloud, but after it was finished she remained on her knees, hands and brow pressed to the cold marble floor, and prayed silently.

God of the Sun, bringer of light and of life, preserve us in this daunting place to which we have taken your worship. We are far from home and the waters of Nilus, and we have come only to keep faith with thee, with all our gods great and small, of the sky and the river. We have journeyed into the West, into the Realm of the Dead, to be quickened again, for Osiris Reincarnated cannot come to us in Egypt. Nilus inundates perfectly, but if we are to maintain the Inundation, it is time that we bear another child. Help us, we pray, endure our exile among these unbelievers, keep our Godhead intact, our sinews taut, our heart strong, our womb fruitful. Let our Son, Ptolemy Caesar Horus, know his divine Father, and grant us a sister for him so that he may marry and keep our blood pure. Nilus must inundate. Pharaoh must conceive again, many times.

When Cleopatra had set out from Alexandria with her fleet of ten warships and sixty transports, her excitement had infected everyone who traveled with her. For Egypt in her absence she had no fears; Publius Rufrius guarded it with four legions, and Uncle Mithridates of Pergamum occupied the Royal Enclosure.

But by the time they put into Paraetonium for water, her excitement had evaporated—who could have imagined the boredom of looking at nothing but sea? At Paraetonium the fleet's speed increased, for Apeliotes the East Wind began to blow and pushed them west to Utica, very quiet and subdued after Caesar's war. Then Auster, the South Wind, came along to blow them straight up the west coast of Italy. When the fleet made harbor in Ostia, it had been at sea from Alexandria for only twenty-five days.

There in Ostia the Queen had waited aboard her flagship until all her goods had been brought ashore and word came that her palace was ready for occupation. Bombarding Caesar with letters, standing at the rail every day hoping to see Caesar being borne out to see her. His terse note had said only that he was in the midst of drafting a *lex agraria*, whatever that might be, and could not spare the time to see her. Oh, why were his communications always so unemotional, so *unloving*? He spoke as if she were some ordinary suppliant ruler, a nuisance for whom he would find time when he could. But she wasn't ordinary, or a suppliant! She was Pharaoh, his wife, the mother of his son, Daughter of Amun-Ra!

Caesarion had chosen to come down with a fever while they were moored in that ghastly, muddy harbor. Did Caesar care? No, Caesar didn't care. Hadn't even replied to *that* letter.

Now here she was, as close to Rome as she was going to get, if Cornelius the lictor was right, and still no Caesar.

At dusk she consented to eat what Charmian and Iras brought her—but not until it had been tasted. A member of the House of Ptolemy did not simply give a little of the food and drink to a slave; a member of the House of Ptolemy gave the food and drink to the child of a slave known to love his children dearly. An excellent precaution. After all, her sister Arsinoë was here in Rome, though, not being an anointed sovereign, no doubt she lived within its walls. Housed by a noblewoman named Caecilia, Ammonius had reported. Living on the fat of the land.

The air was different, and she didn't like it. After dark it held a chill she had never experienced, though it was supposed to be early summer. This cold stone mausoleum contributed to the miasma that curled off the so-called river, which she could see from the high loggia. So damp. So foreign. And no Caesar.

Not until the middle hour of the night by the water clock did she go to bed, where she tossed and turned until finally she fell asleep after cock crow. A whole day on land, and no Caesar. Would he ever come?

What woke her was an instinct; no sound, no ray of light, no change in the atmosphere had the power Cha'em had inculcated in her as a child in Memphis. When you are not alone, you will wake, he had said, and breathed into her. Since then, the silent presence of another person in the room would wake her. As it did now, and in the way Cha'em had taught her. Open your eyes a tiny slit, and do not move. Watch until you identify the intruder, only then react in the appropriate way.

Caesar, sitting in a chair to one side of the bed at its foot, looking not at her but into that distance he could summon at will. The room was light but not bright, every part of him was manifest. Her heart knocked at her ribs, her love for him poured out in a huge spate of feeling, and with it a terrible grief. He is not the same. Immeasurably older, so very tired. His bones are such that his beauty will persist beyond death, but something is gone. His eyes have always been pale, but now they are washed out, making that black ring around the irises starker still. All her own resentments and irritations seemed suddenly too petty to bear; she curved her lips into a smile, pretended to wake and see him, lifted her arms in welcome. It is not I who needs succor.

His eyes came back from wherever they had been and saw her; he smiled that wonderful smile, twisted out of the enveloping toga as he rose in a way she could never fathom. Then his arms were around her, clutching her like a drowning man a spar. They kissed, first an exploration of the softness of lips, then deeply. No, Calpurnia, he is not like this with you. If he were, he would not need me, and he needs me desperately. I sense it all through me, and I answer it all through me.

"You're rounder, little scrag," he said, mouth in the side of her neck, smooth hands on her breasts.

"You're thinner, old man," she said, arching her back.

Her thoughts turned inward to her womb as she opened herself to him, held him strongly but tenderly. "I love you," she said.

"And I you," he said, meaning it.

There was divine magic in mating with an anointed sovereign, he had never felt that so intensely before, but Caesar was still Caesar; his mind never entirely let go, so though he made ardent love to her for a long time, he deprived her of his climax. No sister for Caesarion, never a sister for Caesarion. To give her a girl was a crime against all that Jupiter Optimus Maximus was, that Rome was, that he was.

She wasn't aware of his omission, too satisfied herself, too swept out of conscious thought, too devastated at being with him again after almost seventeen months.

"You're sopping with juice, time for a bath," he said to reinforce her delusion; Caesar's luck that she produces so much moisture herself. Better that she doesn't know.

"You must eat, Caesar," she said after the bath, "but first, a visit to the nursery?"

Caesarion was fully recovered, had woken his usual cheerful, noisy self. He flew with arms outstretched to his mother, who picked him up and showed him proudly to his father.

I suppose, thought Caesar, that once I looked much like this. Even I can see that he's inarguably mine, though I recognize it mostly in the way he echoes my mother, my sisters. His regard is the same steady assessment Aurelia gave her world, his expression isn't mine. A beautiful child, sturdy and well nourished, but not fleshy. Yes, that's genuine Caesar. He won't run to fat the way the Ptolemies do. All he has of his mother are the eyes, though not in color. Less sunk in their orbits than mine, and a darker blue than mine.

He smiled, said in Latin, "Say *ave* to your *tata*, Caesarion."

The eyes widened in delight, the child turned his head from this stranger to his mother's face. "That's my *tata*?" he asked in quaintly accented Latin.

"Yes, your *tata*'s here at last."

The next moment two little arms were reaching for him; Caesar took him, hugged him, kissed him, stroked the fine, thick gold hair, while Caesarion cuddled in as if he had always known this strange man. When she went to take him from Caesar, he refused to go back to his mother. In his world he has missed a man, thought Caesar, and he needs a man.

Dinner forgotten, he sat with his son on his lap and found out that Caesarion's Greek was far better than his Latin, that he did not indulge in baby talk, and uttered his sentences properly parsed and analyzed. Fifteen months old, yet already an old man.

"What do you want to be when you grow up?" Caesar asked.

"A great general like you, *tata*."

"Not Pharaoh?"

"Oh, pooh, Pharaoh! I have to be Pharaoh, and I'll be that *before* I grow up," said the child apparently not enamored of his regnant destiny. "What I want to be is a general."

"Whom would you war against?"

"Rome's and Egypt's enemies."

"All his toys are war toys," Cleopatra said with a sigh. "He threw away his dolls at eleven months and demanded a sword."

"He was talking then?"

"Oh yes, whole sentences."

Then the nursemaids bore down and took him off to feed him; expecting tears and protests, Caesar saw in some amazement that his son accepted the inevitable quite happily.

"He doesn't have my pride or temper," he said as they walked through to the dining room, having promised Caesarion that *tata* would be back. "Sweeter natured."

"He's God on earth," she said simply. "Now tell me," she said, settling into Caesar's side on the same couch, "what is making you so tired."

"Just people," he said vaguely. "Rome doesn't appreciate the rule of a dictator, so I'm continually opposed."

"But you always said you wanted opposition. Here, drink your fruit juice."

"There are two kinds of opposition," he said. "I wanted an atmosphere of intelligent debate in the Senate and *comitia,* not endless demands to 'bring back the Republic'—as if the Republic were some vanished entity akin to Plato's Utopia. Utopia!" He made a disgusted sound. "The word means 'Nowhere'! When I ask what's wrong with my laws, they complain that they're too long and complicated to read, so they won't read them. When I ask for good suggestions, they complain that I've left them nothing to suggest. When I ask for co-operation, they complain that I force them to co-operate whether they want to or not. They admit that many of my changes are highly beneficial, then turn around and complain that I change things, that change is wrong. So the opposition I get is as devoid of reason as Cato's used to be."

"Then come and talk to me," she said quickly. "Bring me your laws and I'll read them. Tell me your plans and I'll offer you constructive criticism. Try out your ideas on me and I'll give you a considered opinion. If another mind is what you need, my dearest love, mine is the mind of a dictator in a diadem. Let me help you, please."

He reached out to take her hand, held it to his lips and kissed it, the shadow of a smile filling his eyes with some of the old vigor and sparkle. "I will, Cleopatra, I will." The smile grew, his gaze became more sensuous. "You've budded into a very special beauty, my love. Not a Praxiteles Aphrodite, no, but motherhood and maturity have turned you into a deliciously desirable woman. I missed your lion's eyes."

* * *

Said Cicero to Marcus Junius Brutus in a letter written two *nundinae* later:

> You will miss the Great Man's triumphs, my dear Brutus, sitting up there amid the Insubres. Lucky you. The first one, for Gaul, is to be held tomorrow, but I refuse to attend. Therefore I see no reason to delay this missive, bursting as it is with news amorous and marital.
>
> The Queen of Egypt has arrived. Caesar has set her up in high style in a palace beneath the Janiculan Hill far enough upstream to look across Father Tiber at the Capitol and the Palatine rather than at the stews of the Port of Rome. None of us was privileged to see her own private triumphal parade as she came up the Via Ostiensis, but gossip says it was awash in gold, from the litters to the costumes.
>
> With her she brought Caesar's presumed son, a toddling babe, and her thirteen-year-old husband, King Ptolemy the something-or-other, a surly, adipose lad with nothing to say for himself and a very healthy fear of his big sister/wife. Incest! The game the whole family can play. I said that about Publius Clodius and his sisters once, I remember.
>
> There are slaves, eunuchs, nursemaids, tutors, advisers, clerks, scribes, accountants, physicians, herbalists, crones, priests, a high priest, minor nobles, a royal guard two hundred strong, a philosopher or four, including the great Philostratus and the even greater Sosigenes, musicians, dancers, mummers, magicians, cooks, dishwashers, laundresses, dressmakers, and various skivvies. Naturally she carries all her favorite pieces of furniture, her linens, her clothing, her jewels, her money chests, the instruments and apparatuses of her *peculiar* religious worship, fabrics for new robes, fans and feathers, mattresses, pillows, bolsters, carpets and curtains and screens, her cosmetics, and her own supply of spices, essences, balms, resins, incenses and perfumes. Not to forget her books, her mirrors, her astronomical tools and her own private Chaldaean soothsayer.
>
> Her retinue is said to number well over a thousand, so of course they don't fit into the palace. Caesar has built them a village on the periphery of Transtiberim, and the Transtiberini are *livid*. It is war to the death between the natives and the interlopers, so much so that Caesar has issued an edict promising that all Transtiberini who raise a knife to slice the nostrils or ears of a de-

tested foreigner will be transported to one of his new colonies whether they like it or not.

I have met the woman—incredibly haughty and arrogant. She threw a reception for us Roman peasants with Caesar's official blessing, had some sumptuous barges pick us up near the Pons Aemilius and then, upon disembarking, we were ferried in litters and sedan chairs *spewing* cushions and fur rugs. She held court—an exact description—in the huge atrium, and invited us to make free of the loggia as well. She's a pathetic dab of a thing, comes up to my navel, and I am not a tall man. A beak of a nose, but the most extraordinary eyes. The Great Man, who is infatuated, calls them lion's eyes. It shamed me to witness his conduct with her—he's like a boy with his first prostitute.

Manius Lepidus and I prowled around a little and found the temple. My dear Brutus, we were aghast! No less than twelve statues of these *things*—the bodies of men or women, but the heads of beasts—hawk, jackal, crocodile, lion, cow, et cetera. The worst was female, had a grossly swollen belly and great pendulous breasts, all crowned with a hippopotamus's head—absolutely revolting! Then the high priest came in—he spoke excellent Greek—and offered to tell us who was who—better to say, which was which—in that bizarre and off-putting pantheon. He was shaven-headed, wore a pleated white linen dress, and a collar of gold and gems around his neck that must be worth as much as my whole house.

The Queen was dolled up in cloth-of-gold from head to foot—*her* jewels could buy you Rome. Then Caesar came out of some inner sanctum carrying his child. Not at all shy! Smiled at us as if we were new subjects, greeted us in Latin. I must say that he looks very like Caesar. Oh yes, it was a *royal* occasion, and I begin to suspect that the Queen is working on Caesar with a view to making him the King of Rome. Dear Brutus, our beloved Republic grows ever farther away, and this landslide of new legislation will end in stripping the First Class of all its old entitlements.

On a different note, Marcus Antonius has married Fulvia—now there's a woman I really loathe! I daresay you have heard that Caesar said *in the House* that Antonius had tried to murder him. Much as I deplore Caesar and all he stands for, I am glad that Antonius didn't succeed. If Antonius were the dictator, things would be much worse.

More interesting still is the marriage between Caesar's great-niece Octavia and Gaius Claudius Marcellus Minor. Yes, you read aright! He's done very well for himself, while his brother and first cousin sit in exile, their property gone—Marcellus Minor's way, I add. There has been one extremely fascinating consequence of this alliance that almost made me wish I could bend my principles and attend the Senate. It happened during a meeting of the Senate Caesar convoked to discuss his first group of agrarian laws. As the senators dispersed afterward, Marcellus Minor asked Caesar to pardon his brother, Marcus, who is still on Lesbos. When Caesar said no several times, would you believe that Marcellus Minor *fell to his knees and begged?* With that repellent man Lucius Piso adding his voice, though he didn't fall to his knees. They say that Caesar looked utterly taken aback, quite horrified. Retreated until he collided with Pompeius Magnus's statue, roaring at Marcellus Minor to get up and stop making a fool of himself. The upshot was that Marcus Marcellus is now pardoned. Marcellus Minor is going around saying that he intends to return all brother Marcus's estates to him. He won't be able to do the same for cousin Gaius Marcellus, as I hear he has expired of some creeping disease. Brother Marcus will come home after visiting Athens, we are told by Marcellus Minor.

Of course I am not enamored of any of the Claudian Marcelli, as you know. Whatever caused them to renounce their patrician status and join the Plebs is too far in the past to be known, but the fact that they did that does say something about them, doesn't it?

I will write again when I have more news.

After Caesar explained Rome's aversion to kings and queens and the religious significance in crossing the *pomerium*, the Queen of Egypt's natural indignation at not being able to go inside the city faded. Every place had its taboos, and Rome's were all tied to the notion of the Republic, to an abhorrence of absolute rule that verged on the fanatical—and could—and did—breed fanatics like Marcus Porcius Cato Uticensis, whose appalling suicide was still the talk of Rome.

To Cleopatra, absolute rule was a fact of life, but if she couldn't enter the city, then she couldn't enter the city. When she wept at the thought that she wouldn't see Caesar triumph, he told her that a knight friend of his banker Oppius's, one Sextus Perquitienus, had offered to let her share his loggia with him. As his house was built on the back cliff of the Capitol overlooking the Campus Martius, Cleopatra would be able to see the start of the parade, and follow it until it turned the corner of the Capitol back cliff to enter the city through the Porta Triumphalis, a special gate opened solely for triumphs.

The veteran legionaries from the Gallic campaign were to march in this first triumph, which actually meant a mere five thousand men; only a few in each of the legions numbered during Gallic War times were still under the Eagles, as Rome still did not maintain a long-serving regular army. Though the eldest of the Gallic War veterans was but thirty-one years old if he had enlisted at seventeen, the natural attrition of war weariness, wounds and retirement had taken a huge toll.

But when the order of march was issued, the Tenth found to its dismay that it would not be in the lead. The Sixth had been given that honor. Having mutinied three times, the Tenth had fallen from Caesar's favor, and would go last.

The original eleven legions numbered between the Fifth Alauda and the Fifteenth contributed these five thousand veterans, kitted in new tunics, with new horsehair plumes in their helmets, and carrying staves wreathed in laurels—actual weapons were not allowed. The standard-bearers wore silver armor, and the Aquilifers, who carried each legion's silver Eagle, wore lion skins over their silver armor. No compensation to the unhappy Tenth, which decided to take a peculiar revenge.

This was one triumph that the consuls of the year could participate in, as the triumphator, whose imperium had to outweigh all others, was Dictator. Therefore Lepidus sat with the other curule magistrates upon the podium of Castor's in the Forum. The rest of the Senate led the parade; most of them were Caesar's new appointees, so the senators at around five hundred made an imposing body of marchers—too few in purple-bordered togas, alas.

Behind the Senate came the *tubilustra*, a hundred-strong band of men blowing the gold horse-headed trumpets an earlier Ahenobarbus had brought back from his campaign in Gaul against the Arverni. Then came the carts carrying the spoils, interspersed with large flat-topped drays that served as floats to display incidents from the campaign played by actors in the correct costumes and surrounded by the right props. The staff of Caesar's bankers, who had had the gigantic task of organizing this staggering spectacle, had been driven almost to the point of madness trying to find sufficient actors who looked like Caesar, for he featured prominently in most of the float enactments, and everyone in Rome knew him.

All the famous scenes were there: a model of the siege terrace at Avaricum; an oaken Veneti ship with leather sails and chain shrouds; Caesar at Alesia going to the rescue of the camp where the Gauls had broken in; a map of the double circumvallation at Alesia; Vercingetorix sitting cross-legged on the ground as he submitted to Caesar; a model of the mesa top and its fortress at Alesia; floats crowded with out-landish long-haired Gauls, said long hair stiffened into grotesque styles with limey clay, their tartans bright and bold, their longswords (of silvered wood) held aloft; a whole squadron of Remi cavalry in their brilliant outfits; the famous siege of Quintus Cicero and the Seventh against the full might of the Nervii; a depiction of a Britannic stronghold; a Britannic war chariot complete with driver, spearman and pair of little horses; and twenty more pageants. Every cart or float was drawn by a team of oxen garlanded with flowers, trapped in scarlet, bright green, bright blue, yellow.

Intermingled with all these fabulous displays, groups of whores danced in flame-colored togas, accompanied by capering dwarves wearing the patchwork coats of many colors called *centunculi*, musicians of every kind, men blowing gouts of fire from their mouths, magicians and freaks. No gold crowns or wreaths were exhibited, as the Gauls had tendered none to Caesar, but the carts of spoils glittered with gold treasures. Caesar had found the accumulated hoard of the Germanic Cimbri and Teutones at Atuatuca, and had also plundered centuries of precious votives held by the Druids at Carnutum.

Next came the sacrificial victims, two pure white oxen to be offered to Jupiter Optimus Maximus when the triumphator reached the foot of the steps to his temple on the Capitol. A destination some three miles away, for the procession wended a path through the Velabrum and the Forum Boarium, then into the Circus Maximus, went once right around it, up it again and out its Capena end to the Via Triumphalis, and finally down the full length of the Forum Romanum to the foot of the Capitoline mount, where it stopped.

Here those prisoners of war doomed to die were taken to be strangled in the Tullianum; here the floats and lay participants disbanded; here the gold was put back into the Treasury; and here the legions turned into the Vicus Iugarius to march back to the Campus Martius through the Velabrum, there to feast and wait until their money was distributed by the legion paymasters. It was only the Senate, the priests, the sacrificial animals and the triumphator who continued up the Clivus Capitolinus to Jupiter Optimus Maximus, escorted now by special musicians who blew the *tibicen*, a flute made from the shinbone of a slain enemy.

The two white oxen were smothered in garlands and ropes of flowers and had gilded horns and hooves; they were shepherded, already drugged, by the *popa*, the *cultarius*, and their acolytes, who would expertly perform the killing.

After them came the College of Pontifices and the College of Augurs in their particolored togas of scarlet and purple stripes, each augur bearing his *lituus*, a curliqued staff that distinguished him from the pontifices. The other, minor sacerdotal colleges in their specific robes followed, the *flamen Martialis* looking very strange in his heavy circular cape, wooden clogs, and ivory *apex* helmet. At Caesar's triumphs there would be no *flamen Quirinalis*, as Lucius Caesar marched as Chief Augur instead of his other role; and also no *flamen Dialis*, for that special priest of Jupiter was actually Caesar, long since released from his duties.

The next section of the parade was always very popular with the crowd, as it consisted of the prisoners. Each was clad in his or her very best regalia, gold and jewels, looking the picture of health and prosperity; it was no part of the Roman triumph to display prisoners ill-treated or beaten down. For this reason, they were kept hostage in some rich man's house while they waited for their captor to triumph. Rome of the Republic did not imprison.

King Vercingetorix came first; only he, Cotus and Lucterius were to die. Vercassivellaunus, Eporedorix and Biturgo—and all the other, more minor prisoners of war—would be sent back to their peoples unharmed. Once, many years earlier, Vercingetorix had wondered at the prophecy which said he would wait six years between his capture and his death; now he knew. Thanks to civil war and other things, it had taken Caesar six years to achieve his triumph over Long-haired Gaul.

The Senate had decreed a very special privilege for Caesar: he was to be preceded by seventy-two rather than the Dictator's usual twenty-four lictors. Special dancers and singers were to weave their way between the lictors, hymning Caesar Triumphator.

So by the time that Caesar's turn to move actually came, the procession had already been under way for two long summer hours. He rode in the triumphal chariot, a four-wheeled, extremely ancient vehicle more akin to the ceremonial car of the King of Armenia than to the two-wheeled war chariot; his was drawn by four matched grey horses with white manes and tails, Caesar's choice. Caesar wore triumphal regalia. This consisted of a tunic embroidered all over in palm leaves and a purple toga lavishly embroidered in gold. On his head he wore the laurel crown, in his right hand he carried a laurel branch, and in his left the special twisted ivory scepter of the triumphator, surmounted by a gold eagle. His driver wore a purple tunic, and at the back of the roomy car stood a man in a purple tunic who held a gilded oak-leaf crown over Caesar's head, and occasionally intoned the warning given to all triumphators:

"Respice post te, hominem te memento!"*

Though Pompey the Great had been too vain to subscribe to the old custom, Caesar did. He painted his face and hands with bright red *minim*, an echo of the terra-cotta face and hands possessed by the statue of Jupiter Optimus Maximus in his temple. The triumph was as close to emulating a god as any Roman ever came.

Right behind the triumphal car walked Caesar's war horse, the famous Toes with the toes (actually the current one of several such over the years—Caesar bred them from the original Toes, a gift from Sulla), the General's scarlet *paludamentum* draped across him. To Caesar it would have been unthinkable to triumph without giving Toes, the symbol of his fabled luck, his own little triumph.

After Toes came the throng of men who considered that Caesar's Gallic campaign had liberated them from enslavement; they all wore the cap of liberty on their heads, a conical affair that denoted the freed man.

Next, those of his Gallic War legates in Rome at this time, all in dress armor and mounted on their Public Horses.

And, in last place, the army, five thousand men from eleven legions who shouted *"Io triumphe!"* as they marched. The bawdy songs would come later, when there were more ears to hear them and chuckle.

When Caesar stepped into the triumphal car its left front wheel came off, pitching him forward on to the front wall, sending the triumphal intonator toppling, and setting the horses to nervous whinnying and rearing.

A collective gasp went up from all those who saw it happen.

"What is it? Why are people so shocked?" Cleopatra asked of Sextus Perquitienus, who had gone chalk white.

"A frightful omen!" he whispered, holding up his hand in the sign to ward off the Evil Eye.

Cleopatra followed suit.

The delay was minimal; as if by magic, a new wheel appeared and was fitted swiftly. Caesar stood to one side, his lips moving. Though Cleopatra could not know it, he was reciting a spell.

Lucius Caesar, Chief Augur, had come running.

"No, no," Caesar said to him, smiling now. "I will expiate the omen by climbing the steps of Jupiter Optimus Maximus on my knees, Lucius."

"*Edepol*, Gaius, you can't! There are fifty of them!"

---

* "Look behind thee, remember that thou art a mortal man!"

"I can, and I will." He pointed to a flagon strapped to the car wall on its inside. "I have a magic potion to drink."

Off went the triumphal chariot, and soon the army was marching to bring up the parade's rear, two miles behind the Senate.

In the Forum Boarium the triumphator had to stop and salute the statue of Hercules, always naked save on a triumphal day, when he too was clad in triumphal regalia.

A hundred and fifty thousand people were jammed into the long bleachers of the Circus Maximus; the roars and cheers which went up when Caesar entered could be heard by Cleopatra's servants in her palace. But by the time that the car had made its way up one side of the *spina*, around its Capena end, down the other side, then up again toward the Capena exit, the army was all inside, and the crowd was worn out by cheering. So when the Tenth began to sing its new marching song, everyone quietened to listen.

> *"Make way for him, seller of whores*
> *Take note of his fine head of hair*
> *His other head bangs cunty doors*
> *He fucks 'em all, in bed or chair*
> *In Bithynia he sold his arse*
> *His admiral was short some fleets*
> *So Caesar shit a fleet of class*
> *Between the kingly linen sheets*
> *He's never lost a single battle*
> *Though his tally's about fifty*
> *He rounds 'em up like mooing cattle*
> *Our King of Rome neat and nifty!"*

Caesar called to Fabius and Cornelius, tailing the seventy-two lictors ahead of him.

"Go tell the Tenth that if they don't stop singing that song, I'll strip them of their share of the booty and discharge them minus their land!" he snapped.

The message was conveyed and the ditty promptly ceased, but many were the debates in the College of Lictors as to which of the verses gave Caesar the most offense; the conclusion Fabius and Cornelius reached was that the reference to selling his arse had gotten under Caesar's skin, but a few of the other lictors were in favor of the "King of Rome" phrase. Certainly it wasn't the bawdiness of the Tenth's song; that was standard practice.

* * *

By the time the long business had ended, night was falling. Division of the spoils would have to wait until the morrow. The Field of Mars turned into a camp, for all the retired veterans were there too, having watched the triumph from the crowds. A man's share had to be collected in person unless, as happened in the case of Caesar's triumph, many of the veterans lived in Italian Gaul. Groups of them had clubbed together and armed one representative with an authorizing document, which would contribute to the difficulties the legion paymasters inevitably suffered.

The rankers each received 20,000 sesterces (more than the pay for twenty years of service); junior centurions received upward of 40,000 sesterces, and the top centurions 120,000 sesterces. Huge bonuses, more than any army's in history, even the army of Pompey the Great after he conquered the East and doubled the entire contents of the Treasury. Despite this bounty, the soldiers of all ranks went away angry. Why? Because Caesar had set aside a small percentage and given it to the free poor of Rome, who each received 400 sesterces, 36 pounds of oil, and 15 *modii* of wheat. What had the free poor done to deserve a share? Though the free poor were ecstatic, the army was anything but.

The general military consensus was that Caesar was up to something, but what? After all, there was nothing to stop a free poor man from enlisting in the legions, so why was Caesar gifting men who hadn't?

The triumphs for Egypt, Asia Minor and Africa followed in quick succession, none as spectacular as Gaul, but nonetheless above the standard of nine out of ten triumphs. The Asia triumph contained a float of Caesar at Zela surrounded by all his crowns: above the scene was a large, beautifully lettered placard that read VENI, VIDI, VICI. Africa was last, and the least approved of by Rome's elite, for Caesar let his anger destroy his common sense and used the floats to deride the Republican high command. There was Metallus Scipio indulging in pornography, Labienus mutilating Roman troops, and Cato guzzling wine.

The triumphs were not the end of the extra entertainments that year. Caesar also gave magnificent funeral games for his daughter, Julia, who had been very much loved by the ordinary Roman people; she had grown up in the Subura, surrounded by the ordinary people, and never held herself above them. Which was why they had burned her in the Forum Romanum, and why her ashes lay in a magnificent tomb on the Campus Martius—unheard of.

There were plays in Pompey's stone theater and in temporary wooden ones erected wherever there was space enough; the comedies of Plautus, Ennius and Terence were popular, but everyone liked the simple Atellan mime best. This was a farce stuffed with ludicrous stock characters and played minus masks. However, all tastes had to be catered for, so one small venue was reserved for highbrow drama by Sophocles, Aeschylus and Euripides.

Caesar also instituted a competition for new plays, and offered a generous prize for the best effort.

"You really ought to write plays as well as histories, my dear Sallustius," he said to Sallust, whom he liked very much. As well for Sallust that he did; Sallust had been recalled from his governorship of Africa Province after he plundered the place unashamedly. The matter had been hushed up when Caesar personally paid out millions in compensation to aggrieved grain and business plutocrats; yet here was Caesar, still liking Sallust.

"No, I'm not a playwright," said Sallust, shaking his head in revulsion at the mere thought. "I'm too busy writing a very accurate history of Catilina's conspiracy."

Caesar blinked. "Ye gods, Sallustius! Then I hope that you're lauding Cicero to the skies."

"Anything but," said the unrepentant looter of his province cheerfully. "I blame the whole affair on Cicero. He manufactured a crisis to distinguish his consulship above banality."

"Rome might become as hot as Utica when you publish."

"Publish? Oh no, I daren't publish, Caesar." He giggled. "At least, not until after Cicero's dead. I hope I don't have to wait twenty years!"

"No wonder Milo horsewhipped you for philandering with his darling Fausta," said Caesar, laughing. "You're incorrigible."

Plays were not the entirety of Julia's funeral games. Caesar tented in the whole of the Forum Romanum and his own Forum Julium and gave gladiatorial games, wild-beast shows, combats between condemned prisoners of war, and exhibitions of the latest martial craze, fencing with long, whippy swords useless in a battle.

After which he gave a public banquet for all of Rome on no less than 22,000 tables. Among the delicacies were 6,000 fresh water eels he had to borrow from his friend Lucilius Hirrus, who refused to sell them; his price was replacement. The wines flowed like water, the tables groaned with food, and there was enough left over to enable the poor to heft home sacks of goodies to augment their menu for some time to come.

* * *

Cicero was still writing to Brutus in Italian Gaul.

I know I've already told you about Caesar's *disgraceful* lampooning of the Republican heroes in Africa, but I am still fulminating about it. How can the man have such excellent taste when it comes to things like games and shows, yet make a mockery out of worthy Roman opponents?

However, that is not why I write. I have divorced that termagant Terentia at last—thirty years of misery! So I am now an eligible sixty-year-old bachelor, a very strange and freeing sensation. So far I have been offered two widows, one the sister of Pompeius Magnus, the other his daughter. You do know that Publius Sulla died very suddenly? It upset the Great Man, who always liked him—why escapes me. Anyone whose father was adopted by a man like Sextus Perquitienus Senior and was brought up in *that* household cannot help but be a cur. So his Pompeia is a widow. However, I prefer the other Pompeia—for one thing, she's thirty years younger. For another, she seems to be a fairly sanguine widow, isn't mourning Faustus Sulla overmuch. That's probably because the Great Man permitted her to keep all her property, which is vast. I shall not marry a poor woman, my dear Brutus, but nor, after Terentia, will I marry a woman who is in complete control of her own fortune. So perhaps neither Pompeia Magna is a good choice. We Romans allow women too much autonomy.

There has been another divorce in the ranks of the Tullii Cicerones. My darling Tullia has finally severed her union to that rabid boar Dolabella. I requested that her dowry payments be returned, as I am entitled to when the wife is the injured party. To my surprise, Dolabella said yes! I think he's trying to get back into favor with Caesar, hence the promised repayment. Caesar is a stickler for women being treated properly, witness his concern for Antonia Hybrida. Then what happens? Tullia informs me that she is with child by Dolabella! Oh, what is the matter with women? Not only that, but Tullia is so terribly downcast, doesn't seem to be interested in the coming baby, and has the temerity to blame *me* for the divorce! Says I nagged her into it. I give up.

No doubt Gaius Cassius has written to tell you that he is coming home from Asia Province. I rather gather that he and Vatia Isauricus have nothing in common save their wives, your sisters. Well, Vatia hewed to Caesar and cannot be pried loose. From what Cassius tells me in his letter, Vatia is a very strict governor, has regulated the taxes and tithes of Asia Province (not due to be enforced for several more years) to make it impossible for a *publicanus* or any other sort of Roman businessman to make one sestertius of profit from the Amanus to the Propontis. I ask you, Brutus, what does Rome have provinces for, if not to let Romans make a sestertius or two out of them? Truly, I think Caesar believes Rome should pay her provinces, not the other way around!

Gaius Trebonius has arrived in Rome—driven out of Further Spain by Labienus and the two Pompeii, it seems. He was struggling after Quintus Cassius's deplorable conduct when he was governor—a regular Gaius Verres, they say. The three Republicans landed to hysterical joy, and have been raising legions with marked success. Having moored his many ships in Balearic waters, Gnaeus Pompeius is now living in Corduba as the new Roman governor. Labienus is the commander of military matters.

I wonder what Caesar plans to do?

"I think Caesar will be going to Spain as soon as his present legislation is done with," said Calpurnia to Marcia and Porcia.

Porcia's eyes lit into a blaze, her face suffused with hope. "This time it will be different!" she cried, smacking her right fist into her left palm jubilantly. "Every day that passes sees Caesar's legions more disaffected, and since the time of Quintus Sertorius, the Spanish have produced legionaries every bit as good as those Italy produces. You wait and see, Spain will be the end of Caesar. I *pray* for it!"

"Come, Porcia," Marcia said, her eyes meeting Calpurnia's ruefully, "remember our company."

"Oh, really!" Porcia snapped, her hand going out to clench Calpurnia's. "Why should poor Calpurnia care? Caesar spends all his time across the Tiber with That Woman!"

Very true, thought Calpurnia. The only nights he occupies his Domus Publica bed are those before a meeting of the Senate at dawn. Otherwise, he's there with *her*. I'm jealous and I hate feeling jealous. I hate her too, but I still love Caesar.

"I believe," she said with composure, "that the Queen is extremely knowledgeable about government, and that very little of his time with her is devoted to love. From what he says, they talk of his laws. And political matters."

"You mean he has the gall to mention her name to his wife?" Porcia demanded incredulously.

"Yes, often. That's why I don't worry very much about her. Caesar doesn't act one scrap differently toward me than he ever has. I am his wife. At best, she's his mistress. Though," said Calpurnia wistfully, "I would love to see the little boy."

"My father says he's a beautiful child," Marcia offered, then frowned. "The interesting thing is that Atia's boy, Octavius, detests the Queen and refuses to believe that the child is Caesar's. Though my father says the child undoubtedly is Caesar's, he's very like him. Octavius calls her the Queen of Beasts because of her gods, which apparently have the heads of beasts."

"Octavius is jealous of her," said Porcia.

Calpurnia's eyes widened. "Jealous? But why?"

"I don't know, but my Lucius knows him from the drills on the Campus Martius, and says he makes no secret of it."

"I didn't know Octavius and Lucius Bibulus were friends," said Marcia.

"They're the same age, seventeen, and Lucius is one of the few who doesn't sneer at Octavius when he goes to the drills."

"Why should anyone sneer?" asked Calpurnia, puzzled.

"Because he wheezes. My father," Porcia went on, transfigured at the mere mention of Cato, "would say that Octavius ought not to be punished for an infliction of the gods. My Lucius agrees."

"Poor lad. I didn't know," said Calpurnia.

"Living in that house, I do," Marcia said grimly. "There are times when Atia despairs for his life."

"I still don't understand why he should be jealous of Queen Cleopatra," Calpurnia said.

"Because she's stolen Caesar," Marcia contributed. "Caesar was spending considerable time with Octavius until the Queen came to Rome. Now, he's forgotten Octavius exists."

"My father," Porcia brayed, "condemns jealousy. He says that it destroys inner peace."

"I don't think we're terribly jealous, yet none of us enjoys inner peace," said Marcia.

Calpurnia picked up a kitten wandering around the floor and kissed its sleek, domed little skull. "I have a feeling," she said, cheek against its fat tummy, "that Queen Cleopatra is not at peace either."

A shrewd guess; having learned that Caesar was going to Spain to deal with the Republican rebellion there, Cleopatra was filled with a rather royal dismay.

"But I can't live in Rome without you!" she said. "I refuse to let you leave me here alone!"

"I'd say, go home, except that autumnal and winter seas are perilous between here and Alexandria," Caesar said, keeping his temper. "Stick it out, my love. The campaign won't be long."

"I heard that the Republicans have thirteen legions."

"I imagine at least that many."

"And you've discharged all but two of your veteran legions."

"The Fifth Alauda and the Tenth. But Rabirius Postumus, who has consented to act as my *praefectus fabrum* again, is recruiting in Italian Gaul, and a lot of the discharged veterans there are bored enough to re-enlist. I'll have eight legions, sufficient to beat Labienus," Caesar said, and leaned to kiss her with lingering enjoyment. She's still miffed. Change the subject. "Have you looked at the census data?" he asked.

"I have, and they're brilliant," she said warmly, diverted. "When I return to Egypt, I shall institute a similar kind of census. What fascinates me is how you managed to school thousands of men to take it door-to-door."

"Oh, men love to ask nosy questions. The training lies more in teaching them how to deal with people who resent nosy questions."

"Your genius staggers me, Caesar. You do everything so efficiently, yet so swiftly. The rest of us toil in your wake."

"Keep paying me compliments, and my head won't fit through your door," he said lightly, then scowled. "At least yours smack of sincerity! Do you know what those idiots put on that wretched gold *quadriga* they erected in Jupiter Optimus Maximus's porticus?"

She did know. While she approved of it and agreed with it, she knew Caesar well enough by now to understand why it had so angered him. The Senate and the Eighteen had commissioned a gold sculpture of Caesar in a four-horse chariot atop a globe of the world, another of the honors they heaped upon him against his will.

"I am on the horns of a dilemma about these honors," he had said to her some time ago. "When I refuse them, I'm apostrophized as churlish and ungrateful, yet when I accept them, I'm apostrophized as regal and arrogant. I told them I refused to condone this awful construction, but they've gone ahead with it anyway."

He hadn't seen the "awful construction" until this morning, when it was unveiled. The sculptor, Arcesilaus, had done well; his four horses were superb. Pleasantly surprised, Caesar had toured around it with equanimity until he noticed the plaque affixed to the front wall of the chariot. It said, in Greek, exactly what the statue of him in the Ephesus agora said—GOD MADE MANIFEST and all the rest.

"Take that abomination off!" he snapped.

No one moved to obey.

One of the senators was wearing a dagger on his belt; Caesar snatched it and used it to dig into the chased gold surface until the plaque came off. "Never, never say such things about me!" he said, and walked out, so furious that the plaque, thrown away, was crushed and crumpled into a ball of metal.

So now Cleopatra said pacifically, "Yes, I know about it. And I am sorry it offended you."

"I do not want to be the King of Rome, and I do not want to be a god!" he snarled.

"You are a God," she said simply.

"No, I am not! I am a mortal man, and I will suffer the fate of all mortal men, Cleopatra! I—*will*—*die!* Hear that? Die! Gods don't die. If I were to be made a god after my death, that would be different—I'd be sleeping the eternal sleep, and not know I was a god. But while I am mortal, I cannot be a god. And why," he demanded, "do I *need* to be King of Rome? As Dictator, I can do whatever has to be done."

"He's like a bull being tormented by a crowd of little boys safely on the other side of the stall railings," said Servilia to Gaius Cassius with great satisfaction. "Oh, I am enjoying it! So is Pontius Aquila."

"How is your devoted lover?" Cassius asked sweetly.

"Working for me against Caesar, but very subtly. Of course Caesar doesn't *like* him, but fair-mindedness is one of Caesar's weaknesses, so if a man shows promise, he's advanced, even if he is a pardoned Republican—and Servilia's lover," she purred.

"You're such a bitch."

"And I always was a bitch. I had to be, to survive Uncle Drusus's household. You know Drusus confined me to the nursery and forbade me to leave the premises until I married Brutus's *tata*, don't you?" she asked.

"No, I didn't. Why would a Livius Drusus do that?"

"Because I spied for my father, who was Drusus's enemy."

"At what age?"

"Nine, ten, eleven."

"But why were you living with your mother's brother instead of your own father?" Cassius asked.

"My mother committed adultery with Cato's father," she said, her face twisting hideously even at so old a memory, "and my father chose to deem all his own children by her as someone else's."

"That would do it," said Cassius clinically. "Yet you spied for him?"

"He was a patrician Servilius Caepio," she said, as if that explained it all.

Knowing her, Cassius supposed it did.

"What happened with Vatia in Africa Province?" she asked.

"He wouldn't let me collect my or Brutus's debts."

"Oh, I see."

"How is Brutus?"

Her black brows rose, she looked indifferent. "How would I know? He doesn't write to me any more than he writes to you. He and Cicero dribble words to each other. Well, why not? Both of them are old women."

Cassius grinned. "I saw Cicero in Tusculum on my way, stayed with him overnight. He's very busy writing a paean to Cato, if you like that idea. No, I thought you wouldn't. However, the war looming in the Spains had him twittering and fluttering, which surprised me, given his detestation for Caesar. I asked him why, and he said that if the Pompeius boys beat Caesar, he thought they would be far worse masters for Rome than Caesar is."

"And what did you reply to that, Cassius dear?"

"That, like him, I'd settle for the easygoing old master I know. The Pompeii hail from Picenum, and I've never known a Picentine who wasn't cruel to the marrow. Scratch a Picentine, and you reveal a barbarian."

"That's why Picentines make such wonderful tribunes of the plebs. They love to strike when the back is turned, and they're never happier than when they can make mischief. Pah!" Servilia spat. "At least Caesar is a Roman of the Romans."

"So much so that he has the blood to be King of Rome."

"Just like Sulla," she agreed. "However—and also like Sulla!—he doesn't want to be the King of Rome."

"If you can say that so positively, then why are you and certain others trying very hard to make it seem as if Caesar itches to tie on the diadem?"

"It passes the time," Servilia said. "Besides, I must have a tiny bit of Picentine in me. I adore making mischief."

"Have you met her majesty?" Cassius asked, feeling his own Romanness expand. Oh, it was good to be home! Tertulla might be half Caesar's, but the other half was pure Servilia, and both halves made for a fascinatingly seductive wife.

"My dear, her majesty and I are *bosom* friends," Servilia cooed. "What fools Roman women can be! Would you believe that most of my female peers have decided to label the Queen of Egypt *infra dignitatem*? Silly of them, isn't it?"

"Why don't you find her beneath your dignity?"

"It's more interesting to stand on good terms with her. As soon as Caesar leaves for Spain, I shall bring her into fashion."

Cassius frowned. "I'm sure your motives aren't admirable, Mama-in-law, but whatever they are, they elude me. You know so little about her. She might be a wilier snake than you."

Servilia lifted her arms above her head and stretched. "Oh, but there you're quite wrong, Cassius. I know a great deal about Cleopatra. You see, her younger sister spent almost two years here in Rome—Caesar exhibited her as his captive in his Egyptian triumph. She was put to live with old Caecilia, and as Caecilia is a good friend of mine, I came to know Princess Arsinoë well. We chatted for hours about Cleopatra."

"That triumph's almost three months into the past. Where's Princess Arsinoë now?" Cassius peered about theatrically. "I'm surprised she isn't living here with you."

"She would be, had I had half a chance. Unfortunately Caesar put her on a ship bound for Ephesus the day after his triumph. I hear she's to serve Artemis in the temple there. The moment she escapes, she can be killed for a nice reward. Apparently he gave Cleopatra his word that he'd clip Arsinoë's wings. Such a pity! I was *so* looking forward to reuniting the two sisters."

He shivered. "There are times, Servilia, when I am profoundly glad that you like me."

In answer, she changed the subject. "Do you really prefer Caesar as your master, Cassius?"

His face darkened. "I would prefer to have no master. To acknowledge a master is an offense against Quirinus," he snarled.

VII

The Cracks Appear

From INTERCALARIS of 46 B.C.
until SEPTEMBER of 45 B.C.

DECIMUS JUNIUS BRUTUS

GAIUS TREBONIUS

Caesar's nephew Quintus Pedius and Quintus Fabius Maximus had marched four "new" legions from Placentia in western Italian Gaul during November, and arrived in Further Spain a month later. By the seasons it was late summer, very hot; to their delight, they found the province not entirely at the beck and call of the three Republican generals, so were able to make a good camp on the upper Baetis River and buy the harvest of the region. Caesar's orders were to wait for him and use the time laying in supplies, even though he didn't expect a long campaign. Better to be safe than sorry was always Caesar's motto when it came to logistics.

Then at the beginning of the sixty-seven days of Intercalaris which followed the end of December, this comfortable situation changed; Labienus appeared with two legions of well-trained Roman men and four legions of raw local troops, and proceeded to besiege the camp. In a pitched battle Caesar's legates Pedius and Fabius Maximus would have fared well, but in a siege situation Labienus could use his superior strength to best advantage, and did. Safe was definitely preferable to sorry; besieged or no, Caesar's troops could still eat. Unsure of the water from the stream that ran through the camp, the four penned-up legions dug wells for groundwater and settled down to wait for Caesar and rescue.

With the Tenth, the Fifth Alauda and two fresh legions largely made up of bored veterans, Caesar set out from Placentia at the same moment as his two legates in Further Spain came under siege. The distance to Corduba on the Via Domitia was one thousand miles, and it was a typically Caesarean march: it took twenty-seven days at an average of thirty-seven miles a day, assisted by the fact that it was no longer necessary to build a camp each night. Gaul of the Via Domitia was so pacified that even Caesar could see no need for a camp with walls, ditches and palisades. That changed when they came down through the pass from Laminium in Nearer Spain to Oretum in Further Spain, but by then there were only a hundred and fifty miles to go.

The moment Caesar appeared, Labienus vanished.

Sextus Pompey was holding the heavily fortified capital of Corduba while older brother Gnaeus took the bulk of the army and went to besiege the town of Ulia, defiantly anti-Republican. But the moment Labienus sent word that Caesar was already marching to take Corduba before Sextus could bring up reinforcements, Gnaeus Pompey packed up his siege to return to Corduba. Just in time!

"We have thirteen legions, Caesar eight," said Gnaeus Pompey to Labienus, Attius Varus and Sextus Pompey. "I say we face him now and beat him for once and for all!"

"Yes!" cried Sextus.

"Yes," said Attius Varus, though less eagerly.

"Absolutely not," said Labienus.

"Why?" asked Gnaeus Pompey. "Let's finish it, *please!*"

"At the moment Caesar can eat, but winter's on the way, and according to the locals, it's going to be a hard one," Labienus said, tones reasonable. "Leave Caesar to face that winter. Harry him, prevent his foraging, make him use up his supplies."

"We outnumber him by five legions," Gnaeus said, unconvinced. "Four of our thirteen are veteran Roman troops, another five are almost as good, which leaves four only of recruits, and they're not all that bad—I've heard you say so yourself, Labienus."

"What you don't know and I do, Gnaeus Pompeius, is that Caesar also has *eight thousand* Gallic cavalry. They were some days behind him through the pass, but they're here now. The year's been dry, the grazing isn't wonderful, and if the upper Baetis gets snow this winter, Caesar will lose them. You know Gallic cavalry—" He stopped, grunted, looked wry. "No, of course you don't. Well, I do. I worked with them for eight years. Why do you think that Caesar came to prefer Germans? When their precious horses start to suffer, Gallic cavalry ride home. Therefore we leave Caesar alone until spring. Once the horses begin starving, it's goodbye to Caesar's cavalry."

The news broke on the two Pompeys as a bitter disappointment, but they were their father's sons; Pompey the Great had never fought unless his forces heavily outnumbered the enemy's. Eight thousand horse meant Caesar outnumbered them.

Gnaeus Pompey sighed, banged a frustrated fist on the table. "All right, Labienus, I see your point. We spend the winter denying Caesar any chance to work down out of the Baetis foothills to find snowless grazing."

"Labienus is learning," Caesar remarked to his legates, now augmented by Dolabella, Calvinus, Messala Rufus, Pollio, and his admiral, Gaius Didius. Inevitably, he also had Tiberius Claudius Nero, whose only value was his name; Caesar needed all the old patricians he could find to dignify his cause. "It's going to be hard finding sufficient fodder for the horses. They're such a wretched nuisance on any campaign, but with Labienus in the field, we're going to need them.

His Spanish cavalry are excellent, and he has several thousand at least. He can also get more."

"What do you intend to do, Caesar?" Quintus Pedius asked.

"Sit tight here in the upper Baetis for the moment. Once winter really cracks down, I have a few ideas. First, we have to convince Labienus that his tactics are working." Caesar looked at Quintus Fabius Maximus. "Quintus, I want your junior legates to fill in their idle moments by finding trustworthy men among my centurions, and use them to monitor feelings in my legions. I've sensed no mutinous rumbles, but the days when I believed in my troops are over. Most of the men Ventidius enlisted in Placentia are veterans, and he sifted them thoroughly for malcontents, I know. Be that as it may, everyone keep his ear to the ground."

An uncomfortable silence fell. How terrible to realize that Caesar, the soldier's general, thought that way these days! Yet he was right to think that way. Mutiny was insidious. Once the men who manipulated the ranks learned that it was possible, it became a way to control the general. Things military had been in a state of flux since Gaius Marius admitted the propertyless Head Count to the legions, and mutiny was just a new symptom of that state of flux. Caesar would find a solution.

At the beginning of January, calendar and seasons now in perfect step, Caesar implemented one of his ideas when he moved to besiege the town of Ategua, a day's march south of Corduba on the river Salsum. Right into the lion's jaws. Ategua contained a huge amount of food, but more important, it held Labienus's winter fodder for his horses.

The weather was bitter, Caesar's march as secret as unexpected; by the time that Gnaeus Pompey found out and moved his troops from Corduba to prevent Ategua's capture, Caesar had circumvallated the town in the style of Alesia: a double ring of fortifications, the inner one surrounding the town, the outer one keeping Gnaeus Pompey's relief force at bay. Caesar's eight legions sat within the ring, while his eight thousand Gallic cavalry harassed Gnaeus Pompey continuously. Titus Labienus, who had been absent on a mission, arrived and looked dourly at Caesar's circumvallation.

"You can't assist Ategua or break into the ring, Gnaeus," Labienus said. "All you're doing is losing men to Caesar's cavalry. Withdraw to Corduba. Ategua's a lost cause."

When the town fell despite heroic resistance, it was a blow to the

Republicans in more ways than one. Not only did Caesar feed his horses, but Labienus now had to move closer to the coast to graze his, and the Spanish locals began to lose faith. Desertions in the Spanish levies increased dramatically.

For Caesar, what ought to have been a great satisfaction was blighted by a letter and a book bucket from Servilia.

>I thought you'd get as big a kick out of the enclosed, Caesar, as I did. After all, you're the only other person I know whose loathing of Cato rears as high as Mount Ararat. This *gem* has been authored by that utter peasant, Cicero, and published, naturally, by Atticus. When I chanced to meet the hypocritical plutocrat who manages to stay on good terms with you *and* your enemies, I served him a tongue-lashing he won't forget in a hurry.
>
>"You're a parasite as well as a hypocrite, Atticus!" I said. "The quintessential middleman who makes all the profits without owning any personal talents. Well, I'm delighted that Caesar's put one of his biggest colonies for the Roman Head Count on your *latifundium* in Epirus—that will teach you to start a business on public land! I hope you rot while you're still alive, and I hope Caesar's poor *wreck* your *latifundium!*"
>
>I couldn't have found a better way to alarm him than that. Apparently he and Cicero thought they'd deflected your colony to somewhere farther from Atticus's cattle and tanneries than Buthrotum. Now they find out that it's still Buthrotum. Caesar, don't you dare let Atticus talk you out of that site for your colony! Atticus doesn't own the land, he doesn't pay rent on the land, and he deserves everything he gets from you and the Head Count! Publishing this revolting paean of praise for the worst man who ever sat in the Senate! I am *livid!* When you read Cicero's "Cato," you'll be livid too. Of course my idiot son thinks it's just wonderful—it seems he'd written a little pamphlet extolling Uncle Cato, but tore it up after he read Cicero's panegyric.
>
>Brutus says he's coming back to Rome as soon as Vibius Pansa arrives to govern Italian Gaul in his place. Honestly, Caesar, where do you find these nobodies? Still, Pansa's rich enough to have married Fufiius Calenus's daughter, so I daresay Pansa will go far. There are a number of your old legates from Gaul in Rome at the moment, from praetor Decimus Brutus to ex-governor Gaius Trebonius.
>
>I know that Cleopatra writes to you about four times a day, but

I thought you might like a more dispassionate tone from someone else. She's managing to survive, but she's so utterly miserable without you. How dared you tell her it would be a short campaign? Rome won't see you for a year, is my estimate. And why on earth did you put her in that marble mausoleum? The poor creature is permanently frozen! This winter is cold and early—ice on the Tiber, snow in Rome already. I gather that the Alexandrian winter is about like late spring in Rome. The little boy fares better, thinks that playing in the snow is the best fun ever invented.

Now to gossip. Fulvia is with child by Antonius, looks her usual glowing self. Imagine it! Issue, probably male, for the third of her bully-boy rowdies! Clodius, Curio, and now Antonius.

Cicero—oh, I cannot get away from that man!—married his seventeen-year-old ward, Publilia, the other day. What do you think about that? Disgusting.

Read the "Cato." Cicero badly wanted to dedicate it to Brutus, by the by, but Brutus declined this signal honor. Why? Because he knew that if he accepted, I'd murder him.

He read the "Cato" with at least as much rage and indignation as Servilia, his fury white-hot by the time he finished it. Cato, said Cicero, was the noblest Roman who ever lived, the loyalest and most unswerving servant of the extinct Republic, the enemy of all tyrants like Caesar, the constant protector of the *mos maiorum,* the hero even in his death, the perfect husband and father, the brilliant orator, the frugal master of his bodily appetites, the true Stoic to the end, and more, and more, and more. Perhaps had Cicero gone no further, Caesar might have stomached the "Cato." But Cicero had gone much further. The entire emphasis of the work was on the contrast between the superlative virtues of Marcus Porcius Cato and the unspeakable villainies of Caesar Dictator.

Trembling with anger, Caesar sat stiffly in his chair and bit his lips until they bled. So that is what you think, Cicero, is it? Well, Cicero, your day is done. Caesar will never ask anything of you ever again. Nor will you ever sit in Caesar's Senate, even if you beg on your knees. As for you, Atticus, the publisher of this unjust piece of malice, Caesar will do as Servilia suggests. The immigrant poor will *flock* into Buthrotum!

Caesar had whiled away the time on his march to Further Spain by writing a poem. It was titled *"Iter"*—"The Journey"—and, on rereading it, he had found it far better than he had originally thought. The best thing he'd written in years. Good enough to warrant publication.

Of course he had intended to send it to Atticus, whose small army of copy scribes did beautiful work. But now *"Iter"* would go to the Brothers Sosius for publication. Nor would Atticus receive any dictatorial favors in future. It wasn't necessary to be King of Rome to exact reprisals. Dictator of Rome was quite sufficient.

Rage not cooled but rather gone to icy determination, Caesar began to write a refutation of Cicero's "Cato" that would take every point Cicero made and turn it on its head. Couched in prose that would have Cicero squirming at his own inadequate talents. The "Cato" could not be ignored. Those who read it would deem Caesar worse than any Greek tyrant, yet it was a warped, one-sided piece of rubbish. It *must* be answered!

Usually it was Caesar who looked for a pitched battle to end a war quickly, but in Spain it was the Republicans; Caesar was too involved in his "Anti-Cato" to think about battles.

Sextus Pompey had hugely relished Cicero's "Cato," though he was very disappointed that it had nothing to say about Cato's march, which to Sextus Pompey represented the last time he had been truly happy. Africa Province had been detestable, and Spain was worse. He couldn't like Titus Labienus, and found Attius Varus a venal nonentity. Only poor Gnaeus was worth fighting for, yet Gnaeus seemed to have lost his old zest for the Republican struggle.

"I'm no good on land, Sextus, and that's the truth," Gnaeus said gloomily as they walked to a meeting with Labienus and Attius Varus. It was the first day of March; Corduba was thawing, the Spanish sun had some warmth again. "I'm an admiral."

"I find I'm more comfortable on the sea too," Sextus said. "What's going to happen?"

"Oh, we'll try to force a battle with Caesar as soon as we possibly can." Gnaeus stopped, grasped his young brother's wrist strongly. "Sextus, make me a promise?"

"Anything, you know that."

"If I should fall on the field, or meet some other sticky end, will you marry Scribonia?"

Skin tight and prickling, Sextus broke free of the grip and reversed it. "Ny-Ny!" he cried, a small child again. "That's absolutely ridiculous! Nothing is going to happen to you!"

"I have a premonition."

"You and every other man going into battle!"

"I agree that it may be a fancy, but what if it isn't? I don't want my darling Scribonia to fall captive to Caesar, she has no money and no relatives on Caesar's side." Gnaeus's blue eyes held a desperate and convinced sincerity that Sextus had seen before, in his father's eyes when he had spoken of fleeing to far-off Serica. "Somehow, Sextus, I don't have any premonition about you. Whether we win or lose the fight with Caesar, you'll live and escape. Please, I beg of you, take Scribonia with you! Have our father's grandchildren by her, for I haven't managed to. Say you will! *Promise!*"

Not wanting Gnaeus to see his tears, Sextus embraced him, a convulsion of love and sorrow. "I promise, Ny-Ny."

"Good. Now let's see what Labienus has to say."

The war council agreed that the army should leave the vicinity of Corduba and move south to lure Caesar farther away from his bases and his supplies. To Gnaeus Pompey, the profoundest shock came from Labienus, who refused to take field command.

"I don't have Caesar's luck," he said simply. "It's taken me two battles to see it, but I do now. Every time the strategy has been left up to me, we go down. So now it's your turn, Gnaeus Pompeius. I'll command the cavalry and do whatever you order."

Pompey the Great's elder son stared at the greying Labienus in horror; if this battered, aging eagle of a man could say that, what was going to happen? Well, he knew what was going to happen. Labienus might blame it on Caesar's luck, but Gnaeus Pompey thought it was more Caesar's ability.

An assumption confirmed five days into March, when the battle came on near a town called Soricaria. Gnaeus Pompey discovered that he didn't have his father's skills or instincts when it came to war on land. He and his infantry went down badly, but the engagement wasn't decisive despite the Republican losses. Gnaeus Pompey drew off to lick his wounds, his confidence further eroded when a slave reported to him that his Spanish tribunes and soldiers were sneaking away. Not sure if it was the right thing to do, he had the would-be deserters detained overnight; in the morning, shrugging his shoulders, he let them go. If men weren't willing to fight, why keep them?

"There are too few of us dedicated to the cause," he said to Sextus, eyes shining with tears. "There's no one on the face of the globe has the genius to beat Caesar, and I'm tired." His hand went out, gave Sextus a small paper. "This arrived from Caesar at dawn. I haven't shown it to Labienus or Attius Varus yet, but I must."

To Gnaeus Pompeius, Titus Labienus, the legates and men of the Republican army: Caesar's clemency is no more. Let this communication serve notice of that fact upon you. There will be no more pardons, even for men who have never been pardoned. The Spanish levies will be considered equally culpable and will suffer accordingly, as will all the towns that have assisted the Republican cause. Any men of an age to fight who are found in any towns will be executed without trial.

"Caesar's *terribly* angry!" said Sextus in a whisper. "Oh, Gnaeus, I feel as if we've kicked a hornet's nest like a toy ball! Why is he so angry? Why?"

"I have no idea," said Gnaeus, and went to show the note to Labienus and Attius Varus.

Labienus knew. Brow glistening with sweat, he looked at the two Pompeys out of stony black eyes. "He's reached the end of his tether. The last time he did that was at Uxellodunum, where he amputated the hands of four thousand Gauls and sent them to beg from one end of Gaul to the other."

"Ye gods, why?" asked Sextus, appalled.

"To show Gaul that if it continued to resist, there would be no more mercy. Eight years, he thought, was enough mercy. You're of an age to remember Caesar's temper, Gnaeus. When he reaches the end of his tether, he breaks it. Nothing can break him."

"What should I do?" asked Gnaeus.

"Read it out to the army just before we fight." Labienus squared his shoulders. "Tomorrow we look for the right place to give battle. We fight to the death, and I for one will make it the hardest battle of Caesar's unparalleled career."

They found their ground near the town of Munda, on the road from Astigi to the coast at Calpe, the Pillar of Hercules on the Spanish side of the straits. A low mountain pass, Munda offered the Republicans excellent downhill terrain; for Caesar, who ran up the battle flag joyously when he arrived, an uphill fight. It was Caesar's plan to hold his position with infantry until his huge cavalry force, massed on his left wing, could roll up the Republican right and come around behind the whole Republican army. Not easy with uphill terrain and an enemy served formal notice that there would be no quarter during battle, no clemency after battle.

The two sides met shortly after dawn, and what fell out was a grim, interminably long, bloody engagement of the most basic kind. There were no opportunities for brilliant or innovative tactics at Munda, perhaps the most straightforward battle Caesar had ever fought. It was also the one he came closest to losing, for the Republicans refused to yield ground and wouldn't permit Caesar to deploy his cavalry. Munda was a slugging match, toe-to-toe, with Caesar, fighting uphill with four fewer legions of foot, severely disadvantaged. Gnaeus Pompey's troops had taken Caesar's message to heart and fought doggedly, desperately.

Eight hours later and Munda was still not decided. Sitting Toes atop a good observation mound, Caesar saw his front line begin to waver and break; he was down off Toes in an instant, took his shield, drew his sword and pushed his way through the ranks to the front line, where the Tenth wasn't holding.

"Come on, you mutinous *cunni*, they're mere children!" he shrieked, laying about him. "If you can't do better than this, then it's the last day of life for you and me both, because I'll die alongside you!" The Tenth responded, closed ranks, and struggled on with Caesar in their midst.

Thus, with sunset imminent and no decision in sight, it was Quintus Pedius on the observation mound. Caesar-trained, he saw the cavalry's chance and ordered it to charge Gnaeus Pompey's right, a young tribune named Salvidienus Rufus in the lead. The Gauls, strengthened by a thousand Germans, followed Salvidienus, crashed into Labienus's horse, rolled the flank up, and fell on Gnaeus Pompey's rear.

As darkness fell, the bodies of 30,000 Republicans and their Spanish allies littered the field. Of Caesar's Tenth Legion, hardly a man survived. They had finally expiated mutiny. Titus Labienus and Publius Attius Varus fell in battle, quite deliberately, whereas the two Pompeys got away.

Gnaeus fled to Hispalis and tried to find shelter there, but Caesennius Lento, a minor legate of Caesar's, pursued him, killed him, cut off his head and nailed it up in the marketplace. Gaius Didius, mopping up, found it and sent it to Caesar, who he knew would not be pleased at this barbarity; Caesennius Lento was going to experience a rapid fall from Caesar's favor for this deed.

Almost blinded by fatigue, Sextus scrambled on to a riderless horse and instinctively headed for Corduba, where Gnaeus had left Scribonia. Obliged to slink from place to place because the Spanish were heartily ruing their choice of the Republicans, Sextus had ridden over a hundred circuitous miles before he saw Corduba in the distance; it was the second night after Munda.

The noise of a party trotting down the road sent him into a grove of trees, from which he peered into the moonlit expanse as the men passed him by. There, high on a spear, he saw the head of his brother, glaucous eyes rolled upward at the sky, mouth drawn into a grimace of pain. Ny-Ny, Ny-Ny!

Gnaeus's premonition had been a true one. My father, now my brother. Both headless. Is decapitation to be my fate too? If so, then I swear by Sol Indiges, Tellus and Liber Pater that I will outlive Caesar and be a merciless enemy to his successors. For the Republic will never return, I know it in my bones. My father was right to think of fleeing to Serica, but it is too late for that. I am going to remain in the world of Our Sea—but on it. Gnaeus still has his fleets in the Baleares. Picus, our own Picentine deity, preserve his fleets for me!

Outside the gates of Corduba he found Gnaeus Pompeius Philip, the same freedman retainer who had burned his father's body on the beach at Pelusium, and left Cornelia Metella's service to be with the two sons in Spain. Armed with a lamp, walking up and down, too elderly to attract any notice.

"Philip!" Sextus whispered.

The freedman fell upon his shoulder and wept. "*Domine*, they have killed your brother!"

"Yes, I know. I saw him. Philip, I promised Gnaeus that I would take care of Scribonia. Have they detained her yet?"

"No, *domine*. I have hidden her."

"Can you smuggle her out to me? With a little food? I'll try to find a second horse."

"There is a conduit through the walls, *domine*. I will bring her within an hour." Philip turned and vanished.

Sextus used the time to prowl in search of horses; like most cities, Corduba was not equipped with much stabling within its walls, and he knew exactly where Corduban mounts were kept. When Philip returned with Scribonia and her maidservant, Sextus was ready.

The poor, pretty little girl was rocked by grief and clung to him in a frenzy.

"No, Scribonia, there's no time for that! Nor can I take your maid. It's you and I alone. Now dry your eyes. I've found you a gentle old horse, all you have to do is sit astride it and hang on. Come, be brave for Gnaeus's sake."

Philip had brought him the kind of clothing a Spanish man would wear, and had made Scribonia wear something unremarkable. The two of them tried to put her on the horse, but she refused—oh, no, it was too immodest to sit astride anything! *Women!* So Sextus had to find her a donkey, which took time. Eventually he was able to kiss

Philip goodbye, take the halter of Scribonia's donkey, and ride off into the last of the darkness. Just as well Gnaeus's wife was pretty; her mind was about the size of a pea.

They hid by day and rode by night on local tracks, passed to the coast well above New Carthage, and headed into Nearer Spain, Pompey the Great's old fief. Philip had given Sextus a bag of money, so when the food ran out they bought more from lonely farmhouses as they worked their way the hundreds of miles north, skirting around Caesar's occupation forces. Once they crossed the Iberus River, Sextus sighed with relief; he knew exactly where he was going. To the Laccetani, among whom his father had kept his horses for years. He and Scribonia would be safe there until Caesar and his minions left the Spains. Then he would go to Maior, the big Balearic isle. Take command of Gnaeus's fleets, and marry Scribonia.

"I think we may safely conclude that Munda was the end of all Republican resistance," Caesar said to Calvinus as they rode for Corduba. "Labienus dead at last. Still, it was a good battle. I would never ask for a better. I fought on the field among my men, and they're the ones I remember." He stretched, winced in pain. "However, I confess that at fifty-four, I feel it." His voice grew colder. "Munda also solved my problem with the Tenth. What very few are left will be in no mood to dispute whereabouts I choose to settle them."

"Where will you settle them?" Calvinus asked.

"Around Narbo."

"Word of Munda will reach Rome by the end of March," Calvinus said with some pleasure. "When you return, you'll find Rome has accepted the inevitable. The Senate will probably vote you in as dictator for life."

"They can vote me whatever they like," Caesar said, sounding indifferent. "This time next year, I'll be on my way to Syria."

"*Syria?*"

"With Bassus occupying Apameia, Cornificius occupying Antioch, and Antistius Vetus on his way to govern and see what he can do to sort the mess out, the answer is obvious. The Parthians are bound to invade within two years. Therefore I must invade the Kingdom of the Parthians first. I have a desire to emulate Alexander the Great, conquer from Armenia to Bactria and Sogdiana, Gedrosia and Carmania to Mesopotamia, and throw India in for good measure," said Caesar calmly. "The Parthians have learned to covet territory west of the Euphrates, therefore we must learn to covet territory east of the Euphrates."

"Ye gods, you're talking a minimum of five years away!" gasped Calvinus. "Can you afford to leave Rome to her own devices for so long, Caesar? Look what happened when you disappeared in Egypt, and that was for a matter of months, not years. Caesar, you can't expect Rome to thrive while you gad off conquering!"

"I am not," said Caesar through his teeth, "gadding off! I am surprised, Calvinus, that you haven't yet grasped the fact that civil wars cost money—money Rome doesn't have! Money that I must find in the Kingdom of the Parthians!"

They entered Corduba without a fight; the city opened its gates and begged for mercy, some of Caesar's famous clemency. It did not receive any. Caesar rounded up every man of military age within it and executed them on the spot, then ordered the city to pay a fine as big as the one levied on Utica.

A severe lung inflammation had struck Gaius Octavius the day before he was due to leave for Spain to serve as Caesar's personal *contubernalis*, so it was not until midway through February that he was well enough to quit Rome, and then under strong protest from his mother. The calendar was in perfect step with the seasons for the first time in a hundred years, so setting forth in February meant snowy mountain passes and bitter winds.

"You won't get there alive!" Atia cried despairingly.

"Yes, Mama, I will. What harm can I come to in a good mule carriage with hot bricks and plenty of rugs?"

Thus, over her protests, the young man set off, discovering as he progressed that a journey at this time of year (provided he kept warm) did not provoke the asthma, as he had learned to call his malady. Caesar had sent Hapd'efan'e to see him, and he had been given a mine of sensible advice to follow. With snow on the roads, there was no dust or pollen in the air, the mule hair didn't fly, and the cold was crisp rather than damp. He found to his pleasure that when the carriage became stuck in snow halfway through the Mons Genava Pass on the Via Domitia, he was able to take a shovel and help clear a way for it, and that he felt better for the exercise. The only respiratory distress he suffered came as he negotiated the causeway through the marshes at the mouth of the Rhodanus River, but that lasted a mere hundred miles. At the top of the pass through the coastal Pyrenees he paused to look at Pompey the Great's trophies, growing battered and tattered by the weather, then descended into Nearer Spain of the Laccetani to find an early spring. Even so, he experienced no asthma attack; the spring was fairly wet and windless.

At Castulo he learned that there had been a decisive battle at Munda and that Caesar was in Corduba, so to Corduba he went.

He arrived on the twenty-third day of March to find the city a reeking mess of blood and the smoke from dozens of multiple funeral pyres, but luckily the governor's palace sat in a citadel above the aftermath of what he assumed had been mass executions. Surprised at his own sinew, he found that he could view what he saw with equanimity; at least in that respect he didn't seem to be less than other men, a fact that pleased him very much. Very conscious that his looks branded him a pretty weakling, he had been terrified that the sight and smell of slaughter would unman him.

Inside the palace foyer sat a young man in military dress, apparently doing duty as a kind of reception or filtration unit; the sentries outside, observing the richness of Octavius's small entourage and private carriage, had let him through unchallenged, but this youth was obviously not prepared to be so obliging.

"Yes?" he barked, looking up from beneath bushy brows.

Octavius stared at him wordlessly. Here was a soldier in the making! Exactly what Octavius himself yearned to be, yet never would be. As he rose to his feet he revealed that his height was up there with Caesar's, that his shoulders were like twin hills and his neck as thick and corded as a bull's. But all that was as nothing compared to his face, strikingly handsome yet absolutely manly; a thatch of fairish hair, bushy dark brows, stern and deeply set hazel eyes, a fine nose, a strong firm mouth and chin. His bare arms were muscular, his hands the kind of big, well-shaped members that suggested he was capable of doing forceful or sensitive work with them.

"Yes?" he asked again, more mildly, a trace of amusement in his eyes. An Alexander type, he was thinking of the stranger ("beauty" was not a word in his vocabulary for describing males), but very delicate and precious looking.

"I beg your pardon," the visitor said courteously, yet with a faint trace of kingliness. "I am to report to Gaius Julius Caesar. I am his *contubernalis*."

"What great aristocrat sent you?" the reception committee asked. "You'll have a hard time of it once he sets eyes on you."

Octavius smiled, which removed the touch of royalty from his expression. "Oh, he already knows what I look like. He asked for me himself."

"Oh, *family!* Which one are you?"

"My name is Gaius Octavius."

"Doesn't mean a thing to me."

"What's your name?" Octavius asked, very drawn to him.

"Marcus Vipsanius Agrippa. Quintus Pedius's *contubernalis*."

"Vipsanius?" Octavius asked, brows knitted. "What a peculiar *nomen*. Whereabouts do you come from?"

"Samnite Apulia, but the name's Messapian. I'm usually just called by my *cognomen*, Agrippa."

" 'Born feet first.' You don't look as if you limp."

"My feet are perfect. What's your *cognomen?*"

"I have none. I'm simply Octavius."

"Up the stairs, down the corridor to the left, third door."

"Will you watch my stuff until I can collect it?"

The "stuff" was coming in; Agrippa eyed the new *contubernalis* ironically. He had enough "stuff" to be a senior legate. Which member of the family was he? Some sort of remote cousin-by-marriage, no doubt. Seemed nice enough—not conceited, yet in an odd way he had a high opinion of himself. A potential military man he was certainly not! If he reminded Agrippa of anyone, it was of the fellow in the story about Gaius Marius—a cousin-by-marriage of Marius's who had been killed by a ranker soldier for making homosexual advances. Instead of executing the soldier, Marius had decorated him! Not that this young fellow quite suggested *that*.

Gaius Octavius . . . Latium, for sure. There were plenty of Octavii in the Senate, even among the consuls. Agrippa shrugged and went back to checking his list of the executed.

"Come," said Caesar's voice when Octavius knocked.

The face Caesar turned to the door was flinty, but softened when its eyes took in who stood there. The pen went down, he rose. "My dear nephew, you lasted the distance. I'm very glad."

"I'm glad too, Caesar. I'm just sorry I missed the battle."

"Don't be. It wasn't one of my tactical finest, and I lost too many men. Therefore I hope it isn't my last battle. You seem well, but I'll have Hapd'efan'e see you to make sure. Much snow in the passes?"

"Mons Genava, yes, but the Pyreneae Pass was fairly good." Octavius sat down. "You were looking particularly grim when I came in, Uncle."

"Have you read Cicero's 'Cato'?"

"That piece of spiteful twaddle? Yes, it enlivened my sickbed in Rome. I hope you're answering it?"

"That was what I was doing when you knocked." Caesar sighed. "People like Calvinus and Messala Rufus don't think I should deign to answer. They believe anything I write will be called petty."

"They're probably right, but it still has to be answered. To ignore it is to admit there's truth in it. The people who will call it petty won't want to believe your side anyway. Cicero has charged you with permanently killing the democratic process—a Roman's right to run his own life without interference of any kind—*and* Cato's death. Later on, when I have the money, I'll deal with it by buying up every copy of the 'Cato' in existence and burning the lot," said Octavius.

"What an interesting ploy! I could do that myself."

"No, people would guess who was behind it. Let me do it at some time in the future, after the sensation has died down. How are you approaching your refutation?"

"With a few well-aimed barbs at Cicero to begin with. From them, I pass to assassinating Cato's character better than Gaius Cassius did Marcus Crassus's. From the stinginess to the wine to the tame philosophers to the disgraceful way he treated his wives, it will all be there," said Caesar, a purr in his voice. "I am sure that Servilia will be happy to furnish me with the less well-known incidents that have dotted Cato's life."

Which was the commencement of a cadetship for Gaius Octavius that was far removed from the usual. Hoping that he would have an opportunity to further his acquaintance with the fascinating Marcus Vipsanius Agrippa, Octavius discovered the day after he arrived that Caesar had other ideas than permitting this *contubernalis* to associate with his fellows.

Once Fortuna landed Caesar in a place, he refused to quit it until it was properly organized. In the case of Further Spain, long a Roman province, the work Caesar undertook was mostly the establishment of Roman colonies. Save for the Fifth Alauda and the Tenth, all the legions he had brought with him to Spain were to be settled in the Further province on generous allotments of very good land taken from Spanish owners who had sided with the Republicans. A colony for Rome's urban poor was to be founded at Urso, rejoicing in the name *Colonia Genetiva Julia Urbanorum*, but the rest were for veteran soldiers. One was near Hispalis, one near Fidentia, two near Ucubi, and three near New Carthage. Four more were to be the west in the lands of the Lusitani. Every colony was to have the full Roman citizenship, and freedmen were to be allowed to sit on the governing council, the latter provision very rare.

It became Octavius's job to accompany Caesar in his galloping gig as he went from one site to the next, supervising the division of land, making sure that those who would carry on with the work knew how to do it, issuing the charters outlining colonial laws, bylaws and ordinances, and personally choosing the first lot of citizens who would sit on each governing council. Octavius understood that he was on trial: not only was his competence under review, so too was his health.

"I hope," he said to Caesar as they returned from Hispalis, "that I'm of some help to you, Uncle."

"Remarkably so," said Caesar, sounding a little surprised. "You have a mind for minutiae, Octavius, and a genuine pleasure in what many men would deem the more boring aspects of this work. If you were lethargic, I'd call you an ideal bureaucrat, but you aren't a scrap slothful. In ten years' time, you'll be able to run Rome for me while I do the things I'm better suited for than running Rome. I don't mind drafting the laws to make her a more functional and functioning place, but I fear I'm not really very suited for staying in one place for years at a time, even if the place is Rome. She rules my heart, but not my feet."

By this time they stood on very comfortable terms, and had quite forgotten that more than thirty years lay between them. So Octavius's luminous grey eyes lit with laughter, and he said, "I know, Caesar. Your feet have to march. Can't you postpone the Parthian expedition until I'm a little further along the way to being of real use to you? Rome wouldn't lie down under a mere youth, but I doubt that those you'll have to depute to govern in your absence will lie down either."

"Marcus Antonius," said Caesar.

"Quite so. Or Dolabella. Calvinus perhaps, but he's not an ambitious enough man to want the job. And Hirtius, Pansa, Pollio and the rest don't have good enough ancestors to keep Antonius or Dolabella in their place. Must you cross the Euphrates so soon?"

"There are only two places with the wealth to drag Rome out of her present precarious financial position, nephew—Egypt and the Kingdom of the Parthians. For obvious reasons I can't touch Egypt, therefore it has to be the Kingdom of the Parthians."

Octavius put his head back against the seat and turned his face toward the flying countryside, unwilling to let Caesar see it in case it betrayed his inner thoughts. "In that respect, I understand why it has to be the Kingdom of the Parthians. After all, Egypt's wealth can't possibly compete."

A statement which caused Caesar to laugh until he wiped away tears of mirth. "If you'd seen what I've seen, Octavius, you couldn't say that."

"What have you seen?" Octavius asked, looking like a boy.

"The treasure vaults," said Caesar, still chuckling.

And that would do for the moment. Hasten slowly.

"What a weird job you've got," said Marcus Agrippa to Octavius later that day. "More a secretary's than a cadet's, isn't it?"

"To each his own," said Octavius, not resenting the comment. "My talents aren't military, but I think I do have some gifts for government, and working with Caesar so closely is an education in that respect. He talks to me about everything he does, and I—why, I listen very hard."

"You never told me he's your real uncle."

"Strictly speaking, he isn't. He's my great-uncle."

"Quintus Pedius says you're his favorite of favorites."

"Then Quintus Pedius is indiscreet!"

"I daresay he's your first cousin or something. He mutters to himself sometimes," Agrippa said, trying to patch up his own indiscretion. "Are you here for a while?"

"Yes, for two nights."

"Then come and mess with us tomorrow. We don't have any money, so the food's not much good, but you're welcome."

"Us" turned out to be Agrippa and a military tribune named Quintus Salvidienus Rufus, a red-haired Picentine in his middle to late twenties.

Salvidienus eyed Octavius curiously. "Everybody talks about you," he said, making room for the guest by shoving various bits of military impedimenta off a bench on to the floor.

"Talks about me? Why?" asked Octavius, perching on the bench, an item of furniture he had had little acquaintance with before.

"You're Caesar's favorite, for one thing. For another, our boss Pedius says you're delicate—can't ride a horse or do proper military duty," Salvidienus explained.

A noncombatant brought in the food, which consisted of a tough boiled fowl, a mush of chickpea and bacon, some reasonable bread and oil, and a big dish of superb Spanish olives.

"You don't eat much," Salvidienus observed, wolfing food.

"I'm *delicate*," said Octavius, a little waspishly.

Agrippa grinned, slopped wine into Octavius's beaker. When the guest sipped it, then abandoned it, his grin grew wider. "No taste for our wine?" he asked.

"I have no taste for wine at all. Nor does Caesar."

"You're awfully like him in a funny way," Agrippa said.

Octavius's face lit up. "Am I? Am I really?"

"Yes. There's something of him in your face, which is more than I can say for Quintus Pedius. And you're slightly regal."

"I've had a different upbringing," Octavius explained. "Old Pedius's father was a Campanian knight, so he grew up down there. Whereas I've been brought up in Rome. My father died some years ago. My stepfather is Lucius Marcius Philippus."

A very well-known name; the other two looked impressed.

"An Epicure," said Salvidienus, more knowledgeable than young Agrippa. "Consular too. No wonder you have enough gear for a senior legate."

Octavius looked embarrassed. "Oh, that's my mother," he said. "She's always convinced I'm going to die, especially when I'm away from her. I don't honestly need it or use it. Philippus may be an Epicure of the Epicures, but I'm not." He gazed about at the untidy, impoverished room. "I envy you," he said simply, then sighed. "It's no fun being delicate."

"Did you have an enjoyable time?" Caesar asked when his *contubernalis* returned, aware that he gave the lad little chance to mingle with his fellows.

"Yes, I did, but it made me realize how privileged I am."

"In what way, Octavius?"

"Oh, plenty of money in my purse, everything I need, your favor," said Octavius frankly. "Agrippa and Salvidienus have neither money nor favor, yet they're two very good men, I think."

"If they are, then they'll rise under Caesar, rest assured. Ought I to take them on the Parthian campaign?"

"Definitely. But on your own staff, Caesar. With me, since I won't be old enough to run Rome in your absence."

"You really want to come? The dust will be frightful."

"I still have much to learn from you, so I'd like to try."

"Salvidienus I know. He led the cavalry charge at Munda, and won nine gold *phalerae*. A typical Picentine, I suspect—very brave, a superior military mind, capable of plotting. Whereas Agrippa I can't place. Tell him to be present when we leave in the morning, Octavius," said Caesar, curious to see what kind of confrere Octavius would choose as a friend.

Meeting Agrippa was a revelation. Privately Caesar thought him one of the most impressive young men he had ever seen. Had he been homelier, there was a great deal of Quintus Sertorius in him, but the good looks put him in a category all his own. If he had gone to a big

Roman school for the sons of knights, he would inevitably have been the head prefect. The sort you could trust always to give of his best—infinitely reliable, utterly devoid of fear, athletic, and extremely intelligent. A stalwart. A pity his education hadn't been better. Also his blood, very mediocre. Both would retard any hope of a public career in Rome. One reason why Caesar was determined to change Rome's social structure sufficiently to permit the rise of men as eminently capable as the seventeen-year-old Agrippa promised to be. For he wasn't a prodigy like Cicero, nor did he have the ruthlessness of a Gaius Marius, two New Men who had gotten there. What he would need was a patron, and that Caesar himself would be. His great-nephew had an eye for choosing good men, a comfort.

While Agrippa stood stiffly to attention and answered Caesar's pleasant but probing questions, Octavius, observed Caesar out of the corner of his eye, stood and stared at Agrippa adoringly. Not the same kind of adoring looks he gave Caesar by any means. Hmmm.

Sometimes a secretary traveled with them in their gig, but this morning Caesar elected that he and Octavius should be alone. Time for that talk, postponed because Caesar wasn't looking at all forward to it.

"You like Marcus Agrippa very much," Caesar commenced.

"Better than anyone I've ever met," said Octavius instantly.

When you have to lance a boil, cut deep and cruelly. "You're a very pretty fellow, Octavius."

The startled Octavius didn't take that as a compliment. "I hope to grow out of it, Caesar," he said in a small voice.

"I see no evidence that you ever will, because you can't exercise long enough and hard enough to develop Agrippa's kind of physique—or mine, for that matter. You're always going to be much as you look now—a very pretty fellow, and rather willowy."

Octavius's face was growing red. "Do you mean what I think you mean, Caesar? That I appear effeminate?"

"Yes," Caesar said flatly.

"So that's why men like Lucius Caesar and Gnaeus Calvinus eye me the way they do."

"Quite so. Do you cherish any tender feelings toward your own sex, Octavius?"

The red was fading, the skin now too pale. "Not that I have noticed, Caesar. I admit that I might look at Marcus Agrippa like a ninny, but I—I—I admire him so."

"If you cherish no tender feelings, then I suggest that the ninny looks cease. Make sure you never do develop tender feelings. Nothing can retard a man's public career more effectively than that particular failing, take it from one who knows," said Caesar.

"The accusation about King Nicomedes of Bithynia?"

"Precisely. An unjustified accusation, but unfortunately I hadn't endeared myself to my commanding officer, Lucullus, or to my colleague Marcus Bibulus. They took great delight in using it as a political slur, and it was *still* haunting me at my triumph."

"The Tenth's song."

"Yes," said Caesar, lips thin. "They have paid."

"How did you counter the accusation?" Octavius asked, curious.

"My mother—a remarkable woman!—advised me to cuckold my political rivals, the more publicly, the better. And never to befriend any among my colleagues with that rumor around them. Never, she said, give anyone the tiniest particle of evidence that the accusation was more than spite," said Caesar, looking straight ahead. "And don't, she said, spend time in Athens."

"I remember her very well." Octavius grinned. "She terrified the life out of me."

"And out of me too, from time to time!" Caesar reached to take Octavius's hands, clasp them strongly. "I am passing her advice on to you, though in a different vein, as we are very, very different sorts of men. You don't have the kind of appeal to women that I did when I was young. I made them yearn to tame me, to capture my heart, while making it all too plain to everyone that I could not be tamed and had no heart. That you can't do, you don't have the arrogance or self-assurance. Deservedly or not, you do exude a slight air of effeminacy. I blame it on your illness, which has worried your mother into cosseting you. It has also prevented your attending the boys' drills regularly enough to permit your peers to know you well. In every generation there are individuals like your cousin Marcus Antonius, who deem all men effeminate if they can't lift anvils and sire a bastard every *nundinum*. Thus Antonius actually got away with kissing his boon companion Gaius Curio in public—no one could ever credit that Antonius and Curio were genuine lovers."

"And were they?" Octavius asked, fascinated.

"No. They just liked to scandalize the stuffy. Whereas if you did that, the response would be very different, and Antonius would be your first accuser."

Caesar drew a breath. "Since I doubt you have the stamina or the physical presence to make a reputation as a great philanderer, I recommend a different ploy. You should marry young, and build a reputation as a faithful husband. Some may deem you a dull dog, but it works, Octavius. The worst that will be said of you is that you are un-adventurous and under the cat's foot. Therefore choose a wife with whom you can enjoy domestic peace, yet a woman who gives onlook-ers the impression that she rules the roost." He laughed. "That's a tall order and one you may not be able to fill, but keep it in mind. You're far from stupid, and I've noticed that you usually manage to get your own way. Are you following me? Do you understand what I'm saying?"

"Oh, yes," said Octavius. "Oh, yes."

Caesar released his hands. "So no looking at Marcus Agrippa with naked adoration. I realize why you do, but others won't be so percep-tive. Cultivate his friendship, by all means, but always remain a little aloof. I say cultivate his friendship because he is exactly your own age, and one day you'll need adherents like him. He shows great promise, and if he owes his advancement to you, he'll give you his complete loyalty because that's the kind of man he is. I say remain at a slight dis-tance from him because he should never gain the impression that he is an intimate of yours on equal terms with you. Make him *fides Achates* to your Aeneas. After all, you have the blood of Venus and Mars in your veins, whereas Agrippa is a Messapian Oscan of no ancestry. All men should be able to aspire to be great and do great things, and I would build a Rome that allowed them to fulfill their destinies. But some of us have the additional gift of birth, which endows us with an additional burden—we must prove ourselves worthy of our ances-tors, rather than found an ancestry."

The countryside was rolling by; shortly they would cross the Baetis River on their long journey to the Tagus River. Octavius stared out the window, not seeing a thing. Then he licked his lips, swallowed, and turned to look directly into Caesar's eyes, which were kind, sym-pathetic, caring.

"I understand everything you've said, Caesar, and I thank you more than you can ever know. It is absolutely sensible advice, and I will follow it to the letter."

"Then, young man, you will survive." Caesar's eyes twinkled. "I've noticed, by the way, that though we've flown around all of Fur-ther Spain throughout this spring, you haven't suffered one attack of asthma."

"Hapd'efan'e explained it," said Octavius, who felt lighter, more confident, shriven. "When I'm with you, Caesar, I feel *safe*. Your ap-proval and protection wrap around me like a blanket, and I experience no anxieties."

"Even when I speak on distasteful subjects?"

"The more I know you, Caesar, the more I regard you as my father. My own died before I needed him to talk about men's cares and difficulties, and Lucius Philippus—Lucius Philippus—"

"Lucius Philippus gave up the duties of fatherhood at around the time that you were born," said Caesar, absurdly delighted at the result of a conversation he had dreaded. "I too lacked a father, but I was better served with my particular mother. Atia is *all* a mother. Mine was as much a father. So if I can be of help in paternal matters, I'm pleased to be of help."

It isn't fair, Octavius was thinking, that I should get to know Caesar so late. If I had known him like this when I was a child, perhaps I wouldn't suffer the asthma at all. My love for him is boundless, I would do anything for him. Soon we will be done in the Spains, and he'll go back to Rome. Back to that awful woman across the Tiber, with her ugly face and her beast-gods. Because of her and the little boy, he won't touch Egypt's wealth. How clever women are. She has enslaved the ruler of the world and ensured the survival of her kingdom. She will keep its wealth for her son, who is not a Roman.

"Tell me about the treasure vaults, Caesar," he said aloud, and turned big grey eyes, filled with innocence, to his idol.

Relieved to have a new subject, Caesar obliged. It was a subject he couldn't air to any Roman save this one, a mere lad who thought of him as a father.

To Cicero, that first properly calated year went from one sorrow and misery to another.

Tullia gave birth to a sickly, too-premature child early in January; baby Publius Cornelius received the *cognomen* of his grandmother's branch of the Cornelii—Lentulus. It was Cicero who suggested it; as Dolabella had skipped off to Further Spain to join Caesar, he wasn't present to insist that his son bear his own *cognomen*. A way of getting back at Dolabella, who had gone without paying Tullia's dowry back.

She ailed, wasn't interested in her baby, refused to eat or exercise; midway through February she quietly died, it seemed to all who knew her of unrequited love for Dolabella. For Cicero, a terrible grief made worse by the indifference of her mother and the rather pettish behavior of his new wife, Publilia, who could not begin to understand why Cicero wept, mourned, ignored her. Publilia was, besides, quite disillusioned with this marriage to such a famous man, as she was quick to tell her mother and her underage brother whenever they came to visit. Visits that the wildly grief-stricken Cicero came to dread so much that he found reasons to be elsewhere the moment his in-laws arrived.

The letters of condolence came flooding in, one from Brutus in Italian Gaul written just before he left to return to Rome; Cicero had opened it eagerly, sure that this man, so close to him in philosophy and political leanings, would find exactly the right words to heal his battered *animus*. Instead, he found a cold, passionless, stereotyped expression of sympathy that in effect informed him that his grief was too florid, too excessive, too intemperate. A blow rendered more telling when Caesar's letter came and held all the exquisite comfort Cicero had wanted from Brutus. Oh, why had the wrong man written the right letter?

The wrong man, the wrong man, the wrong man! A viewpoint reinforced when he received a curt communication from Lepidus, who, as senior patrician in the Senate, was its leader, the Princeps Senatus. It demanded to know why Cicero wasn't attending meetings of the House, and reminded him that under Caesar's new laws, a man *had* to attend on pain of forfeiting his seat. Since the founding of the Republic, the oligarchs of the Senate had enjoyed the title of senator without ever needing to sit in the House or serve on a jury unless they wanted to. Now it was different. Senators had to serve on juries when they were told, and had to be physically present in the House. If illness were Cicero's reason for absenting himself, then he would have to obtain three affidavits from three senators to that effect.

Illness was the only valid excuse for absence if a senator was in Italy. Further, a senator now had to petition the House to leave Italy! Everywhere a man looked, there were rules and regulations that insulted his entitlements as a member of Rome's most august governing body—oh, it was *intolerable!* Half dazed by grief, half fuming with anger, Cicero was forced to seek out three fellow senators and ask them to swear to Lepidus that Marcus Tullius Cicero was incapable of assuming his seat in the House due to severe illness of long-standing duration.

To add insult to injury, having decided that Tullia must have a glorious monument set in public gardens, Cicero discovered that the ten-talent tomb designed by Clautius the architect would cost him twenty talents; Caesar's sumptuary laws stipulated that whatever a tomb cost must also be paid to the Treasury. That one, the lawyer found a way to avoid: all he had to do was call Tullia's tomb a shrine, and it became tax-free. Therefore Tullia would have a shrine, not a tomb. Sometimes those thirty years of marriage to Terentia paid off—she knew how to avoid any tax even a Caesar could dream up.

Of course there were palliatives for his misery, particularly the very favorable reception his "Cato" had received. A letter from Aulus Hirtius, governing Narbonese Gaul for Caesar, told Cicero that Caesar was planning to write an "Anti-Cato"—oh, do, Caesar, please do! It will damage your *dignitas* immeasurably.

News from Further Spain trickled in; so slow was it that Hirtius, writing from Narbo on the eighteenth day of April, did not know that Gnaeus Pompey had been found and his head severed. But Munda was known, and it was a fact that all of Rome had to accept. Republican resistance was permanently over, there was nothing to stop Caesar enacting his disgraceful laws aimed at the First Class. Even Atticus, so long fair-minded about Caesar, was worried. Though he was still working to make sure that the Head Count poor were not going to be shipped to Buthrotum, he could get no absolute assurances that they would go elsewhere. Caesar's staff refused to commit themselves.

"We'll have to wait until Caesar comes home," said Cicero. "One thing is certain—shipping the Head Count overseas isn't done in an hour, no one will sail before Caesar comes home." He paused. "You'll have to know, Titus, so better now. I'm going to divorce Publilia. I can't stand her or her family a moment longer."

Titus Pomponius Atticus eyed his friend with wry sympathy. A great aristocrat of the *gens Caecilia*, he could have had an illustrious public career, risen to the consulship, but the love of his heart was commerce, and a senator could not indulge in business unconnected to land ownership. A discreet lover of young boys, he had earned the nickname "Atticus" because of his devotion to Athens, a place which found no fault with this kind of love; he had made it his second home, and limited his activities to his time there. Four years older than Cicero, he had married late, to a cousin, Caecilia Pilia, and had produced his heir, his much-loved daughter, Caecilia Attica. His ties to Cicero went deeper than friendship, for his sister, Pomponia, was married to Quintus Cicero. That union, a stormy one, teetered perpetually on the brink of divorce. All in all, he reflected, the two Cicerones had not had happy marriages; they had been obliged to marry for money, to heiresses. What neither brother had counted on was the tendency of Roman heiresses to control their own money, which the law did not stipulate they had to share with their husbands. The pity of it was that both women loved their Cicerones; they just didn't know how to show it, and were, besides, frugal women who deplored the Ciceronian tendency to spend money.

"I think it's wise to divorce Publilia," Atticus said gently.

"Publilia was so unkind to Tullia when she was sick."

Atticus sighed. "Well, Marcus, it's very difficult to be more than ten years younger than your stepdaughter. Not to mention how hard it is to live with a legend older than your grandfather."

Baby Publius Cornelius Lentulus died at the beginning of June, just six months into his tenuous life. Born on the cusp between seven and eight months *in utero,* he had sufficient of Dolabella's strength to try to live, but his wet nurses found his scrawny, red little person repulsive, couldn't love him the way his mother might have, had she not loved his father to the exclusion of all else. So he gave up the fight as quietly as Tullia had, passing from a nightmare to a dream. Cicero mingled his ashes with his mother's and resolved to inter them in the shrine together—if he could only find the right piece of land for this monument.

In an odd way the child's death sealed the chapter of Tullia in Cicero's mind; he began to recover, a process accelerated when he finally got his hands on a copy of Caesar's "Anti-Cato." It had not yet been published, but he knew the Sosius Brothers were about to do so. Cicero found it malicious, spiteful, plain nasty. Where *had* Caesar obtained some of his information? It contained juicy tales of Cato's unrequited love for Metellus Scipio's wife, Aemilia Lepida, snippets of the abysmally bad poetry he had written following her rejection of him, excerpts from his (never filed) lawsuit against Aemilia Lepida for breach of promise, a highly evocative recounting of Cato's telling his two young children that they would never be allowed to see their mother again. Even Cato's most intimate secrets were revealed! As Caesar was the man with whom Cato's first wife had committed adultery, it was the height of impropriety for him to divulge the sordid details of Cato's lovemaking techniques! The man was *dead!*

Oh, but the prose! Why, Cicero asked himself miserably, am I incapable of prose half that good? And Caesar's poem, *"Iter,"* was being hailed as a masterpiece by everyone from Varro to Lucius Piso, a great literary connoisseur. It isn't fair that one man should be so gifted, so I am glad that his hatred for Cato has gotten the better of him.

Then Cicero found himself having to side with Caesar, not a comfortable position. One, however, that justice demanded.

Marcus Claudius Marcellus, whom Caesar had pardoned after his brother, Gaius Marcellus Minor, went down on his knees and begged, had left Lesbos and gone to Athens, where he was murdered in the Pi-raeus. Certain persons who were well known to detest Caesar began to bruit it abroad that Caesar had paid to have Marcus Marcellus mur-dered. A calumny that Cicero could not condone, for all his own detes-tation of Caesar. Hating having to do it, he announced publicly to all and sundry that Caesar could not have had anything to do with the murder. Caesar was a murderer of character, witness his "Anti-Cato," but never one who murdered in mean back alleys. Cicero's stand went a long way toward scotching the rumor.

By now the tale of Gnaeus Pompey's severed head was all over Rome, complete with its sequel. The decapitator, Caesennius Lento, had been an up-and-coming man on Caesar's staff, but when Caesar had received the head from the disgusted Gaius Didius, Caesennius Lento was immediately stripped of his share of the booty and sent back to Rome with Caesar's caustic dressing down still ringing in his ears. There would be no advancement up the *cursus honorum* for such a gross barbarian; in fact, Caesennius Lento would find himself ex-pelled from the Senate when Caesar had time for the censor's duties he had inherited along with many other honors.

So there you had Caesar, thought Cicero: on the one hand, scrupu-lously civilized; on the other, a deliberate traducer of virtue. But a man who would pay to murder? Never. Thus Cicero displayed some un-derstanding of Caesar; just not enough. What Cicero could never be brought to see was that it was his own impulsive and thoughtless gy-rations that antagonized Caesar most. Had he refrained from traduc-ing Caesar in his "Cato," Caesar would not have traduced Cato in his "Anti-Cato." Cause and effect.

Where *did* the money go? Though Mark Antony's share of the Gallic booty had amounted to a thousand sil-ver talents, when he set out to pay his creditors he discov-ered that he owed more than twice that much. His debts amounted to seventy million sesterces, and Fulvia didn't have the cash reserves to pay them, having already outlaid thirty million before they married. The trouble was that Caesar's confiscated property auctions had re-duced the price of prime land for the time being, and to sell prime land was the only way she could raise cash until more income flowed in. This third husband was an expensive one.

Fulvia's massive fortune had originally been set up by her great-grandmother, Cornelia the Mother of the Gracchi, a Roman woman of the old kind. Her granddaughter, who was Fulvia's mother, had seen no reason to change the arrangements. Thus Fulvia's many properties and businesses were buried in sleeping partnerships or nominally held by someone else. So selling capital assets wasn't easy, took a lot of time, and was opposed by her banker, Gaius Oppius, who knew perfectly well where the cash was going.

"The trouble is that I didn't get to Gaul soon enough," said Antony gloomily to Decimus Brutus and Gaius Trebonius.

The three of them were sitting in Murcius's tavern atop the Via Nova, having encountered each other on the Vestal Steps.

"That's right, you didn't arrive until after Vercingetorix rose," said Trebonius, who had been with Caesar for five years, and had received ten thousand talents. "Even then," he added with a grin, "you were late, as I remember."

"Oh, the pair of you should talk!" Antony growled. "You were Caesar's marshals, I was a mere quaestor. I'm always just a bit too young to come into the real money."

"Age has nothing to do with it," Decimus Brutus drawled, one fair brow flying upward.

Antony frowned. "What does that mean?" he asked.

"I mean that our age no longer gives us a *fighting* chance at being elected consul. My election as a praetor this year was as big a farce as Trebonius's was three years ago. We have to wait on the Dictator's dictate to see when we'll be *allowed* to be consuls. Not the electors' choice, Caesar's choice. I've been promised the consulship in two years' time, but look at Trebonius—he should have been consul last year, but he isn't consul yet. People like Vatia Isauricus and Lepidus have more clout and have to be placated first," said Decimus Brutus, the drawl lessening as his temper built.

"I didn't know you felt so strongly," Antony said slowly.

"All real men do, Antonius. I'll grant Caesar anything you like when it comes to competence, brilliance, a gigantic appetite for work—yes, yes, the man's a total genius! But *you* must know how it feels to be overshadowed when your birth says you ought not to be. You're half Antonius and half Julius, I'm half Junius Brutus and half Sempronius Tuditanus—we both have the blood, we should both have a *fighting* chance to get to the top. Out there in our chalk-whitened togas smarming to the voters, promising them the world, lying and smiling. Instead, we wait on Caesar Rex, the King of Rome. What we receive is by his grace and favor, not by our own endeavors. I hate it! *I hate it!*"

"So I see," Antony said dryly.

Trebonius sat and listened, wondering if Antonius and Decimus Brutus had any idea what they were actually saying. As far as he, Trebonius, was concerned, it didn't matter a rush what a man's ancestors entitled him a *fighting* chance to do, because he didn't have any ancestors. He was wholly Caesar's creature, could never have gotten a tenth so high without Caesar there to push him. It had been Caesar who bought his services as a tribune of the plebs and bribed him into that office; it had been Caesar who spotted his military potential; it had been Caesar who trusted him with independent maneuvers during the Gallic War; it had been Caesar who gave him his praetorship; it had been Caesar who awarded him the governorship of Further Spain. I, Gaius Trebonius, am Caesar's man, bought and paid for a thousand times over. My riches I owe to him, my pre-eminence I owe to him. Had Caesar not noticed me, I would be an absolute nobody. Which makes my resentment of Caesar all the greater, for every time I put my foot forward on a venture, I am aware that the moment that foot takes a wrong step, it is in Caesar's power to strike me down to nothing. High aristocrats like this pair can be forgiven an occasional slip, but nobodies like me have no redress. I failed Caesar in Further Spain, he thinks I didn't try hard enough to eject Labienus and the two Pompeii. So when he and I met in Rome, I had to throw myself on his mercy, beg him for forgiveness. As if I were one of his women. He chose to be gracious, to chide me for begging, to say forgiveness wasn't an issue, but I know, I could tell. He will have no further use for me, I'll never be a full consul, just a suffect.

"Did you really try to murder Caesar, Antonius?" he asked now.

Antony blinked, turned his head Trebonius's way. "Um—yes, as a matter of fact," he said, and shrugged.

"What inspired you?" Trebonius asked, intrigued.

Antony grinned. "Money, what else? I was with Poplicola, Cotyla and Cimber. One of them—I don't remember which—reminded me that I'm Caesar's heir, so it seemed like a good idea to come into Caesar's money then and there. Didn't come to anything—the old boy had guards posted everywhere around the Domus Publica, so I couldn't get in." He snarled. "What I want to know is who gave me away, because someone did. Caesar said in the House that I was seen, but I know I wasn't. My guess is Poplicola."

"Caesar's your close kinsman, Antonius," said Decimus Brutus.

"I know *that!* At the time I didn't care, but Fulvia wormed the story out of me after Caesar mentioned it in the House, and made me promise that I'd never lift a hand against him again." He grimaced. "She made me swear on my ancestor Hercules."

"Caesar's my kinsman too," Decimus Brutus mused, "but I've not sworn any oaths."

Gaius Trebonius had a naturally mournful countenance, rather ordinary to look at, and a pair of sad grey eyes. They lifted to Antony's face. "The thing is," he said, "would you do a Poplicola and tattle to Caesar if you heard of a plot to murder him?"

A silence fell. Arrested, Antony stared at Trebonius; so too did Decimus Brutus.

"I don't tattle, Trebonius, even about murder plots."

"I didn't think you would. Just making sure," said Trebonius.

Decimus slapped his hand loudly on the table. "This isn't getting us anywhere, so I suggest we change the subject," he said.

"To what?" asked Trebonius.

"We're none of us enjoying Caesar's esteem at the moment, for one reason or another. He made me praetor this year, but not for anything decent, so why didn't he ask me to go to Further Spain with him? I'd have commanded better than logs like Quintus Pedius! But I can't please Caesar. Instead of patting my back for putting down the Bellovaci uprising, he said I was too hard on them." His face, so blond that it was curiously featureless, twisted. "Whether we like it or not, we utterly depend on the Great Man's favor, and I have ground to make up. I want that consulship, even if it is by his grace and favor. You, Trebonius, deserve a consulship. And you, Antonius, have a lot of crawling and smarming to do if you're ever going to get ahead."

"Where is this going?" Antony demanded impatiently.

"To the fact that we daren't remain in Rome like three cringing bitches," Decimus said, returning to his habitual drawl. "We have to go to meet him on his way home—the sooner, the better. Once he reaches Rome, he'll be buried under such a landslide of sycophancy that we'll never get his ear. We're all men he's worked with for years, men he knows can general troops. It's common knowledge that he intends to invade the Kingdom of the Parthians—well, we have to get to him quickly enough to secure senior legateships in that campaign. After Asia, Africa and Spain, he has dozens of men he knows can general troops, from Calvinus to Fabius Maximus. To some extent we're has-beens, *amici*—Gaul is years in the past. So we have to reach him and remind him that we're better than Calvinus or Fabius Maximus."

The other two were listening avidly.

"I did very well out of Gaul," Decimus Brutus continued, "but Parthian plunder would make me as rich as Pompeius Magnus used to be. Like you, Antonius, I have very expensive tastes. And since it's the height of bad manners to murder a kinsman, we'll have to find another source of money than Caesar's will. I don't know what you plan to do, but tomorrow I'm leaving to meet Caesar."

"I'll come with you," Antony said instantly.

"And I," said Trebonius, leaning back contentedly.

The subject had been broached, and the reaction of Caesar's two kinsmen not unsatisfactory by any means. Just when Trebonius had decided that Caesar must die he wasn't sure, for it had stolen up out of some layer of his mind where things went on beneath the level of thought, and it had nothing to do with noble intentions. It was founded in pure, unadulterated hatred: the hatred of the man with nothing for the man with everything.

When Brutus had finally returned from Italian Gaul he seemed, to his mother at any rate, in a very strange mood. That he had much enjoyed the work Caesar had given him was patent, yet he was more than usually absentminded, didn't notice when Servilia picked and carped, wasn't pierced by her barbs.

Most fascinating of all the changes in him was his skin. It had cleared up so dramatically that he was able to shave closely, and only the pockmarks remained to testify to that noisome affliction that had plagued him for almost twenty-five years. He and Gaius Cassius would be forty next year, ought to be candidates for the praetorship this year. A gift that now lay in Caesar's purlieu.

Caesar! Caesar, who was inarguably the ruler of the world, as Servilia's lover, Lucius Pontius Aquila, said to her at least once every time they met. A tribune of the plebs at the moment, Aquila chafed unbearably at his impotence; with a dictator in office, he could veto nothing the Dictator promulgated as a law, and burned to find something he could do to indicate his loathing of all that Caesar was and stood for.

As for Gaius Cassius, he grumbled around Rome with nothing much to do and little hope of that praetorship, frittered away his time with men like Cicero and Philippus. Much to Rome's surprise, Cassius had suddenly abrogated Stoicism and espoused Epicureanism, for no reason Servilia could see beyond the fact that it devastated Brutus so much that Brutus was avoiding him. Not easy, when both of them visited Cicero interminably!

So Servilia devoted most of her own time to congress with Queen Cleopatra, desperately lonely in her marble mausoleum. Of course the Queen knew very well that Servilia had been Caesar's mistress for years, but had made it plain that this did not affect their friendship. Rather, she seemed to regard it as a bond. An attitude of mind Servilia understood.

"Do you think he'll ever come home?" she asked Servilia as May drew toward its end.

"I agree with Cicero—he has to," Servilia stated firmly. "If he's planning on going off to fight the Parthians, he has a great deal to do in Rome first."

"Oh, Cicero!" said Cleopatra with a moue of distaste. "I don't know when I've met a bigger poseur than Cicero."

"He doesn't like you either," said Servilia.

"Mama," cried Caesarion, galloping in astride a hobbyhorse, "Philomena says I can't go outside!"

"If Philomena says you can't go outside, my son, then you can't go outside," said Cleopatra.

"I can't believe how like Caesar he is," said Servilia with a hard lump in her throat. Oh, why wasn't it I to give him a son? Mine would have been Roman, and patrician through and through.

The little boy galloped off with his usual sunny acceptance of Mama's authority.

"To look at, yes," said Cleopatra, smiling tenderly, "but can you imagine Caesar so obedient, even at that age?"

"Actually, no. Why can't he go outside? It's a perfect day for playing in the sun, and sunlight's good for him."

Cleopatra's face clouded. "Yet another reason why I wish his father would return. The Transtiberini have been eluding my guards, and they prowl the grounds bent on mischief. They carry knives, and use them to slice up the nostrils or cut off ears. Some of our children Caesarion's age have suffered, as well as my women servants."

"My dear Cleopatra, what do you have guards for? Send the boy out under guard, don't coop him up inside!"

"He'd insist on playing with the guards."

"Why not?" asked Servilia, astonished.

"He can only play with his equals."

Servilia pursed her lips. "My ancestry, Cleopatra, is very much better than yours, but even I can see no sense in that. He will soon learn to distinguish his equals, but in the meantime he will have sun, air and exercise."

"I have a different solution," said Cleopatra, looking stubborn.

"I can't wait to hear it."

"I'm going to have a high wall built all around my estate."

"That won't keep the Transtiberini out."

"Yes, it will. I'll have every cubit of it patrolled."

Eyes rolling, Servilia gave up. Some months of Cleopatra's company had shown her how different Roman women were from eastern ones. The Queen of Egypt might rule millions, but she didn't have a particle of common sense. First meeting had demonstrated one very soothing fact: that whatever he felt for her, Caesar was not fathoms deep in love with Cleopatra. Probably, knowing him, he was intrigued at the thought of fathering a king he was acknowledged the father of; Caesar had bedded several queens, but they were all the wives of someone else. Whereas this queen was his, and his alone. Oh, she had her attractions. Though she had no common sense, she understood laws and government. But the longer Servilia knew her, the less she worried about Queen Cleopatra.

Brutus was visiting a far different woman from Cleopatra; his first port of call upon returning to Rome had been Porcia, who had welcomed him ecstatically, but not offered her lips or one of those bear hugs that lifted Brutus clean off his feet. The reason was not lack of love, or second thoughts: the reason had a name. Statyllus.

Though he had originally been going to Brutus in Placentia, Statyllus ended in getting no farther than Rome, where he presented himself at Bibulus's house and beseeched young Lucius Bibulus to take him in. As Lucius never thought to ask his stepmama what she thought, Porcia found herself back in an odd facsimile of Cato's house during her childhood, taking a back seat to an eternally tippling philosopher, and watching Statyllus insidiously persuading Lucius to tipple as well. Oh, it wasn't fair! Why hadn't she pushed harder to send young Lucius off to Gnaeus Pompeius in Spain? He was old enough to be a *contubernalis* now, but he had been so disconsolate at Cato's death that she had not felt it right to push. Once Statyllus arrived, she rued that.

Thus, her eyes drinking Brutus in but very aware of Statyllus in the background, Porcia held aloof.

"Dear Brutus, your skin has cleared up," she said, dying to reach out and stroke his smooth, clean-shaven jaw.

"I think it's you," he said, a smile lighting his eyes.

"Your mother must be pleased."

He snorted. "*Her?* She's too busy huddling heads with that revolting foreigner across the Tiber."

"Cleopatra? You do mean Cleopatra?"

"I certainly do. Servilia practically lives there."

"I would have thought she'd be the last one Servilia wanted to stand on good terms with," Porcia said, flabbergasted.

"I also, but apparently we're wrong. Oh, I have no doubt that she has something nasty up her sleeve, but I have no idea what. She simply says that Cleopatra entertains her."

Thus that first meeting got no further than a meeting of eyes, a shy exchange of glances; nor did any of the other meetings that followed progress beyond visual caresses. Sometimes it was just Statyllus standing watch, at other times Statyllus and Lucius.

In June, Brutus drew Porcia out of earshot and spoke with painful directness. "Porcia, will you marry me?" he asked.

She turned into a pillar of flame, alight from head to foot. "Yes, yes, yes!" she cried.

Brutus went home to send Claudia packing on the spot, so eager to divorce her that it never occurred to him to cite proper grounds, like childlessness. He just summoned her, handed her the bill of divorcement, and had her conveyed in a litter to her older brother, who roared loudly enough to be heard on the far side of the city, then came around to see the unfeeling husband.

"You can't do this!" Appius Claudius shouted, striding up and down the atrium, too angry to wait until Brutus could shoo him into a more private environment.

Curious to see who was making such a fuss, Servilia appeared immediately; Brutus found himself facing an irate brother-in-law and an even more irate mother.

"You can't do this!" Servilia echoed.

Perhaps it was his suddenly respectable face endowed Brutus with courage, or perhaps it was his love for Porcia; he himself wasn't sure. Whatever the basis, he confronted both of them with chin up and eyes hard.

"I have already done it," he said, "and that is the end of it. I do not like my wife. I have never liked my wife."

"Then give her dowry back!" Appius Claudius Pulcher yelled.

Brutus raised his brows. "What dowry?" he asked. "Your late father never provided one. Now go away!" He turned on his heel, marched to his study, and bolted himself in.

"Nine years of marriage!" he could hear Appius Claudius saying to Servilia. "Nine years of marriage! I'll have him in court!"

An hour later Servilia started pounding on the study door in a way that told the listening Brutus that she was prepared to go on pounding forever if necessary. Best get it over and done with—well, some of it, anyway. News of his plans for Porcia could wait. He opened the door with a resolute gesture and stood back.

"You fool!" Servilia snapped, black eyes flashing. "What did you do that for? You can't divorce a woman as well liked and nice as Claudia for no reason!"

"I don't care if all Rome likes her, I don't like her."

"You won't earn any friends for this."

"I don't expect to, or want to."

"This will set Rome by the ears! Brutus, she's a Claudian of the highest rank! And dowryless! At least settle something on her so she has some financial independence," Servilia said, her mood calming a little. Her eyes narrowed suddenly. "Just what are you up to?"

"I'm putting my house in order," said Brutus.

"Settle some money on her."

"Not a sestertius."

Servilia ground her teeth, a sound which in the old days had reduced him to a shivering wreck. Now he endured it without any change in expression.

"Two hundred talents," said Servilia.

"Not one sestertius, Mama."

"You odious skinflint! Do you *want* all Rome to condemn you?"

"Go away," said the worm, turned at last.

Which meant that it was Servilia who sent Claudia two hundred talents in an attempt to silence the clacking tongues. Lentulus Spinther the younger had just divorced his wife in scandalous circumstances too, but the sensation that had caused paled to insignificance beside the hitherto inoffensive Brutus's coldhearted rejection of his poor, blameless, sweet little wife. And though he was universally condemned for it, Brutus went about unconcerned.

Very much aware that she had lost her ascendancy over her son, Servilia retired to the shadows to watch and wait. He *was* up to something, and time would reveal exactly what. His skin had quite healed; so, it seemed, had the spirit within him. But if he was under the illusion that his mother had no tricks left, he would soon learn otherwise.

Oh, what was the matter with her life? One disappointment after another for as long as she could remember.

Servilia might have been pardoned for presuming that when her son left Rome the next day for his villa in Tusculum, he did so to avoid her, but such was not the case. There was no room in his mind for his mother. Traveling the fifteen miles in a comfortable hired *carpentum*,

Brutus had more agreeable things to think about: his new wife, Porcia, sat beside him.

With none but Lucius Caesar's freedmen for witnesses, they had been married by the Chief Augur and *flamen Quirinalis* at his house; judging by his calm reception of their request that he marry them, Lucius Caesar might conduct unexpected weddings every day. He bound their hands together with his red leather strap, told them that they were now husband and wife, and wished them well at his front door. Though there was no one in Rome with whom he wished to share this fascinating piece of news, no sooner was the happy couple gone than he was at his desk writing to Cousin Gaius, en route from Spain to Rome.

Because it was so close to Rome, Tusculum was not possessed of those massive villas Rome's mighty or wealthy owned in places like Misenum, Baiae and Herculaneum; Tusculan villas tended to be smallish and old, fairly close to the neighbors. On one boundary Brutus's villa had Livius Drusus Nero's place, on another Cato's place (now the property of a decorated ex-centurion senator), the Via Tusculana on its third side, and Cicero's villa on the fourth. This last was a nuisance, as Cicero was always popping around when he knew Brutus was in occupation, but when Brutus and Porcia arrived late in the afternoon, Brutus knew that Cicero's schedule would not bring him knocking on their door that evening, even were he aware that Brutus was in residence.

The servants had prepared a meal which neither of the diners had the appetite to eat; as soon as it was proper to abandon the wedding feast, Brutus took Porcia on a tour of the house, then, quite terrified, led his new wife to her marriage bed. He knew from those talks with Porcia after she had married Bibulus that her opinion of connubial intimacy was not high, and he knew that his own sexual prowess was minimal.

The flesh had never plagued Brutus during adolescence and young manhood the way it seemed to plague most men; what natural urges he had experienced had been channeled into intellectual pursuits. A great deal of this had been Cato's fault, for Cato believed that a man should go to his wife quite as virginal as she; that was the old Roman way, as well as a part of Cato's interpretation of Stoicism. But some of it had been due to Servilia, whose contempt for his lack of masculinity had stripped him of confidence in all the avenues of his life. And then there had been Julia, whom he had loved so ardently for so long. Nine years younger than he, Julia was never the recipient of anything more than a chaste kiss; then, when she was seventeen and

Brutus's wait almost over, Caesar had married her to Pompey the Great. A terrible business, made worse because Servilia had taken huge pleasure in telling him that Julia was ardently in love with her old man, that she had found Brutus boring and ugly.

Despite marriage to Bibulus, Porcia was hardly better prepared for this wedding night than Brutus, for Bibulus had been married twice before, to two Domitias of the Ahenobarbi, both of whom that arch-predator, Caesar, had seduced. Eighteen years old, she had been given to Bibulus by her father arbitrarily, and found herself the bride of an embittered man in his late forties, a man who already had two sons by his first Domitia, and then Lucius by his second Domitia. Enormously flattered though Bibulus was by Cato's gift of his only daughter, she didn't exactly suit his tastes. For one thing, she was six feet tall to his five feet four; for another, Porcia was not every man's idea of a beautiful woman.

Bibulus had done his duty in a rather indifferent way, made no attempt to please her, and then sat back to revel in the fact that his third wife was Cato's daughter: that this was one wife Caesar could never plunder. Only the gods knew what might have happened had Bibulus returned to Rome after governing Syria; his two elder sons were murdered in Alexandria, which left him Lucius. Had he returned, he may well have decided to sire children by Porcia. But he didn't, of course. Caesar had crossed the Rubicon while Bibulus lingered in Ephesus, and Rome never saw him again. Porcia became a widow without ever being a well-used wife.

So they sat side by side on the edge of the bed, wordless and afraid. Very much in love with each other, but having no idea how intimacy would affect that love. The light outside was still high and bright, for this was midsummer; finally Brutus turned his head and took in that wealth of brilliant red hair, experienced a desire she would surely not find repugnant.

"May I let down your hair?" he asked.

Her grey eyes, Cato's except for the fright, widened. "If you like," she said. "Just don't lose the pins because I think I forgot to pack any."

Not to lose the pins was a facet of Brutus's careful nature anyway; he plucked them out one by one and put them in a heap on the bedside table, going about his task with burgeoning delight. It really did feel alive, such masses of it, and never once cut; his fingers ran through it, then shook it out into a cascade of fire that puddled on the bed.

"Oh, it's so beautiful!" he whispered.

No one had ever called anything about her beautiful; Porcia shivered with pleasure. Then his hands were plucking at her awful homespun dress, pulled its sash off, unbuttoned the placket up its back and tugged it down over her shoulders, tried to work her arms out of its sleeves. She helped him until she realized her breasts were bared, and clutched its folds across her chest.

"Please let me look," he begged. "Please!"

This was so new—why would anyone want to look? Still, when his hands covered hers and gently persuaded them downward, she let him, gritted her teeth and stared straight ahead.

Brutus gazed enraptured. Who would ever have guessed that her ghastly tentlike dresses contained these exquisite, small and firm breasts with such deliciously pink little nipples?

"Oh, they're beautiful!" he breathed, and kissed one.

Her skin leaped, a warmth kindled and spread through her.

"Stand up, let me see all of you," he commanded in a voice he hadn't known he possessed—strong, rich, throaty.

Amazed at it, amazed at herself, she obeyed; the dress fell around her feet, leaving her clad only in her coarse linen undergarment. He disposed of that too, but so reverently that she felt no urge to hide that part of herself that Bibulus had never bothered to inspect. Well, both his Domitias had been red-haired.

"You're fire *everywhere!*" said Brutus, awed.

Then he reached out his arms and gathered her to him, she still standing, he with his face on her belly, and he began to move it back and forth against her skin, pressing kisses on her, his hands moving over her back, stroking her flanks. She fell forward on to the bed as he struggled with his tunic; now it was her turn to help. Gasping at the shock of it, they felt the wonder of true contact, couldn't get enough, wrapped their arms about each other and kissed hungrily, passionately. He slipped inside her smoothly, filling Porcia with joy, with strange feeling she had never known, sensations that worked up and up and up until she cried out even as he cried out.

"I love you," he said, still erect.

"And I have always loved you, always!"

"Again?"

"Yes, yes! Forever again!"

With no Brutus to pick at, Servilia went to visit Cleopatra after her son departed for Tusculum. She found Lucius Caesar there, a real pleasure; he was one of the most cultivated men in Rome. The three of them settled to a lively discussion of the "Cato" and the "Anti-Cato," all on Caesar's side, of course, though Servilia and Lucius Caesar were dubious of the wisdom of the "Anti-Cato."

"Especially," said Servilia, "because of its literary merit. That has guaranteed it a wide audience."

"Lucius Piso says he doesn't care what it says, the prose is superb, Caesar at his best," said Cleopatra.

"Yes, but that's Piso, who'd read a book about a beetle if the prose were superb," Lucius Caesar objected. He raised a brow at Servilia. "Was it you who supplied Caesar with the anecdotes no one knew about?" he asked.

"Naturally," purred Servilia, "though I don't have Caesar's gift for picking the eyes out of, for instance, Cato's poetry. I just sent him the lot. There were drawers full of it, you know."

"It tempts the gods to speak ill of the dead," Lucius remarked.

The two women stared at him in astonishment.

"I fail to see that," Cleopatra said. "If people are horrible while they're alive, why should the Gods oblige one to be mealymouthed about them just because they've had the consideration to die? I can assure you that when my father died, I offered thanks to the Gods. I certainly didn't change my opinion of him—or of my elder brother. And after Arsinoë dies, I won't be saying any nice things about her."

"I agree," said Servilia. "Hypocrisy is detestable."

Lucius Caesar retreated, hands up in surrender. "Ladies, ladies! I'm merely echoing most of Rome!"

"Including my stupid son," Servilia snarled. "He actually had the temerity to write an 'Anti-Anti-Cato,' or whatever one calls a refutation of a refutation."

"I can understand that," said Lucius. "He's very tied to Cato, after all."

"Not anymore," said Servilia grimly. "Cato's dead."

"You don't think Brutus's marriage to Porcia constitutes a continuing tie to Cato?" Lucius asked in all innocence.

How could a large, airy, light-filled room suddenly darken as if the sun outside was totally eclipsed? For the room did darken, its atmosphere fizzing with sparks of invisible lightning that emanated from Servilia, who had gone absolutely rigid.

Cleopatra and Lucius Caesar sat gaping for a moment, then Cleopatra moved to her friend's side.

"Servilia! Servilia! What is it?" she asked, picking up a hand to chafe it.

The hand was snatched away. "Marriage to Porcia?"

"Surely you know," Lucius floundered.

The air was now suffused with blackness. "I do *not* know! How do you know?"

"I married them this morning."

Servilia got up jerkily and walked out, screaming for her litter, her servants.

"I was sure she knew!" said Lucius to Cleopatra.

Cleopatra drew a breath. "I am not famous for my pity, Lucius, but I pity Brutus and Porcia."

By the time that Servilia arrived home it was too late to set out for Tusculum. One look at her face had the servants shaking in fear; that cloud of darkness surrounded her impenetrably.

"Bring me an axe, Epaphroditus," she said to the steward, whom she never addressed by his unabbreviated name unless there was huge trouble. Alone among the staff, Epaphroditus was a veteran of the crucifixion of the nursery maid who had dropped baby Brutus; he raced to find that axe.

Servilia stalked to Brutus's study and proceeded to destroy it, hacking at the desk, couches and chairs, sending the wine and water flagons flying with one blow, smashing the Alexandrian glass goblets to fragments. She tore every scroll out of the pigeonholes, emptied the book buckets, piled them in a heap on the floor. Then she marched to a multiple lamp, shook the oil out of it on to the pile, and set fire to it. Epaphroditus smelled the smoke and hunted the petrified servants to fetch buckets of sand from the kitchen, buckets of water from the peristyle fountain and the atrium *impluvium*, praying that the mistress would quit the room before the fire caught hold too strongly to be put out. The moment she erupted from the study he went to work, more afraid of fire than of the Klytemnestra dragging her axe.

Only when Brutus's sleeping cubicle and all his favorite statues were demolished did Servilia pause, still so consumed by rage that she just wished there was more of his to destroy. Ah! The bronze bust of a boy by Strongylion! His pride and delight! In the atrium! Off she went, seized the piece—it was so heavy that only her fury enabled her to lift it—and lugged it to her own sitting room, where she sat it on a table and stared at it. How did one ruin solid bronze without a furnace?

"Ditus!" she roared.

Epaphroditus was there in an instant. "Yes, *domina?*"

"See this?"

"Yes, *domina.*"

"Take it down to the river and drop it in at once."

"But it's *Strongylion!*" he bleated.

"I don't care if it's Phidias or Praxiteles! Do as I say!" The black eyes, cold as obsidian, wormed into him. "Do as I say, Epaphroditus. Hermione!" she roared.

Her personal maid appeared instantly out of nowhere.

"Accompany Epaphroditus to the river and make sure he throws this—this *thing* into it. Otherwise, it's crucifixion."

It took the two old retainers to pick the bust up and totter away carrying it between them.

"What has happened?" Hermione whispered. "I haven't seen her like this since Caesar told her he wouldn't marry her!"

"I don't know what's happened, but I do know she'll crucify us unless we obey her," said Epaphroditus, giving the bust to a young, strong slave. "Down to the Tiber, Phormion. Quickly!"

A hired carriage was at the door as dawn broke; Servilia entered it without a change of clothes or a servant.

"Gallop the whole way," she told the *carpentarius* curtly.

"*Domina*, I can't do that! You'd be jolted to death!"

"Listen, you moron," she said between her teeth, "when I say gallop, I mean gallop. I don't care how often you have to change mules— when I say gallop, I mean gallop!"

Having risen disgracefully late, Brutus and Porcia were at break-fast when Servilia walked through the door.

"You *cunnus!* You slimy, slithering snake!" Servilia hissed. With-out breaking stride, she marched straight up to Porcia, drew back her arm, and punched her new daughter-in-law over the temple with her clenched fist. Stunned, Porcia fell to the floor, where Servilia began systematically to kick her from head to feet, paying particular atten-tion to groin and breasts.

It took Brutus and two male slaves to pull her away.

"How could you do this, you ingrate?" Servilia screamed at her son, struggling, lashing out with her feet, trying to bite.

Apparently not much injured, Porcia got up unaided, leaped at Servilia, grabbed her hair, held her by it with one hand and used the other to strike her repeatedly across the face.

"Don't you use gutter language to me, you stuck-up patrician monster!" Porcia shouted. "And don't you dare touch me! Or Brutus! I am Cato's daughter, and every bit your equal! Touch me again, and I'll make you wish you'd never been born! Go suck up to your foreign queen and leave us alone!"

By the end of this speech three other servants had managed to haul Porcia out of striking distance; bruised and disheveled, the two women glared at each other with teeth bared.

"*Cunnus!*" Servilia snarled.

Brutus put himself between them.

"Mama, Porcia, I am the master here, and I will be obeyed! It is not in your province to choose my wife, Mama, and as you can see, I have chosen one for myself. You will be civil to her, and you will welcome her to my house, or I will evict you. I mean what I say! It is a man's duty to house his mother, but I will not go on housing you if you won't be civil to my wife. Porcia, I apologize for my mother's conduct, and can only beg that you forgive her." He stepped aside. "Is all that understood? If it is, then these men will release you."

Servilia shrugged her captors off, put her hands up to her hair. "Grown a backbone, have we, Brutus?" she asked mockingly.

"As you see, yes," he said stiffly.

"How did you trap him, you harpy?" she asked Porcia.

"You're the harpy, Servilia. Brutus and I," said Porcia, moving to him, "were made for each other."

Handfast, they looked at Servilia defiantly.

"Think you have the situation under control, do you, Brutus? Well, you haven't," said Servilia. "If you think for one moment that I'll be civil to the descendant of a Celtiberian slave and a dirty old Tusculan peasant, you've got another think coming! Evict me, and I'll smear you with so much mud your career will be over—Brutus the coward who avoided the boys' drills and dropped his sword at Pharsalus! Brutus the moneylender who starves old men to death! Brutus who divorced his blameless wife of nine years and refused to compensate her! I still have Caesar's ear, and I still have influence in the Senate! As for you, you great hulking lump, you're not fit to clean my son's shoes!"

"And you're not fit to lick Cato's excrement, you malicious adulterer!" yelled Porcia.

"*Ave, ave, ave!*" caroled a voice from the open doorway; in walked Cicero blithely, glistening eyes going from one to another of the players in this delicious drama.

Brutus handled it very well, smiled broadly, brushed past his wife and his mother to shake Cicero warmly by the hand. "My dear Cicero, what a pleasure," he said. "Actually, I'm glad to see you, because I find I need your advice on one or two points. I've started an epitome of Fannius's rather odd history of Rome, and Strato of Epirus says it's a futile exercise . . ." His voice ceased when he shut his study door.

"You won't live to be old, Porcia!" Servilia howled.

"I'm not afraid of you!" Porcia answered at a shout. "You're all bluff!"

"I don't bluff! I survived the Livius Drusus household without anyone to shield me or hold my hand, but your father couldn't say the same. *He* clung to our brother Caepio. My mother was a whore, Porcia, with your grandfather, so don't come the moralist with me! At least my adultery was with a man who has the blood to be the King of Rome, but no one could say that of a turd named Cato. You'd better not plan a family, my dear. Any brats Brutus might sire on you won't live long enough to be weaned."

"Threats, idle threats! You're hollow as a reed, Servilia!"

"Actually it isn't Fannius I want to talk about," Brutus said while the women's voices ripped through the wood of the door.

"I didn't think it was," Cicero said, ears cocked. "Oh, by the way, congratulations on your marriage."

"News gets around rapidly."

"News like that gets around faster than lightning, Brutus. I heard it from Dolabella this morning."

"Dolabella? Isn't he with Caesar?"

"He was with Caesar, but having obtained what he wanted, he came back to pacify his creditors."

"What did he want?" Brutus asked.

"The consulship and a good province. Caesar promised that he would be consul next year, and then go to Syria," said Cicero, and sighed. "Try though I may, I can't ever manage to dislike Dolabella, even now that he refuses to pay back Tullia's dowry. He says her death nullifies any agreement. I fear he's right."

"No Roman should have the power to promise a consulship," Brutus said, face puckering.

"I couldn't agree more. What did you want to discuss?"

"A subject I've touched on before. That I think it behooves me to go to meet Caesar on his way home."

"Oh, Brutus, I wish you wouldn't!" Cicero cried. "There's a cloud of dust a mile high from all those hurrying out of Rome to meet the Great Man. Don't demean yourself by joining the herd."

"I think I must. Cassius too. But what ought I to say to him, Cicero? How can I discover what he intends?"

Cicero looked blank. "There's no use asking me, my dear Brutus. Nor will I be a part of the herd. I'm staying here."

"What I plan," said Brutus, "is to talk about you as well as about myself—make it plain to Caesar that I've discussed things with you, and that you think as I do."

"No, no, no!" Cicero yelled, appalled. "Absolutely not! My name won't do your cause any good, especially after the 'Cato.' If it angered him enough to write that imprudent reply, then I am definitely *persona non grata* with Caesar Rex." He brightened. "I've begun to call him 'Rex.' Well, he acts like a king, doesn't he? Gaius Julius Caesar Rex has a marvelous ring to it."

"I am sorry you feel that way, Cicero, but it can't alter my decision to meet Caesar in Placentia," said Brutus.

"Well, you must do as you see fit." Cicero rose. "Time I strolled back to my own place. Such a parade of visitors these days. I don't think there's anyone doesn't pop in to see me." He bustled to the door, relieved to hear silence on its far side. "Did I tell you that I had a very strange letter a little while ago? From some fellow who claims to be Gaius Marius's grandson. Begging assistance from me, if you please. I wrote back and said that I thought, with Caesar for a relative, he didn't need my poor help." He was still talking at the front door. "My dear son is in Athens—yes, you know that, of course—and wants to buy a carriage. I ask you, a carriage! What were we provided with feet for, my dear Brutus, if not to get from place to place, especially at that age?" He giggled. "I wrote back and told him to ask his mother for the money. Fat chance!"

No sooner had Cicero disappeared than Servilia appeared.

"I'm going back to Rome," she said shortly.

"An excellent idea, Mama. I hope that by the time I bring Porcia to her new home, you will be more reconciled." He handed her into the *carpentum*. "I am quite serious, you know. If you offend me, I will evict you."

"I have every intention of offending, but you won't evict me. Try to, and you'll find how much control I still have over your fortune. The only man who has ever bested me is Caesar, and you, my son, are not Caesar's little finger."

Stomach roiling, he went to find Porcia, profoundly glad that the two least welcome of the day's potential visitors were already in the past. Mama and my fortune? But how? Through whom? My banker, Flavius Hemicillus? No. My director Matinius? No. It's my director Scaptius. He was always her creature.

His wife was sitting in the garden, contemplating the peaches ripening on a tree. When she heard him she turned, face alight with pleasure, and held out her hands. Oh, Porcia, I do love you so much! My pillar of fire.

* * *

"What do you think about it?" Servilia demanded of Cassius.

"I can certainly understand why you object, Servilia, but in many ways Brutus and Porcia suit each other," said Cassius. "Yes, I know you hate to admit there are similarities, but that doesn't mean to say they don't exist. They're a rather humorless pair, very earnest, boringly narrow. That's the real reason why I've given up Stoicism. I just couldn't stand the narrowness."

Servilia eyed her favorite male relative with complete love. He was so martial, so manly, so crisp and decisive. How glad she was to have him in the family! Vatia Isauricus, married to Junia Major, and Lepidus, married to Junia Minor, were a pair of stiff, punctilious aristocrats who never seemed to be able to reconcile their adherence to Caesar with their mother-in-law's adultery with Caesar. Whereas Cassius, more immediately affected thanks to Tertulla's paternity, didn't let it interfere with his liking.

"Tertulla says you're off to see Caesar," she said.

"Yes, I am. With Brutus, I hope, if Porcia doesn't change his mind." Cassius grinned. "I can't credit that she'll approve of Brutus's smarming to Caesar."

"Oh, he'll just go without telling her," said Servilia. "But why exactly is it necessary?"

"Munda," he said simply. "I was so relieved when Caesar won. I've always detested the uncrowned King of Rome, but at least he forced a final decision. The Republican cause is now too dead to be resurrected. As a pardoned man who has never put a foot wrong since Caesar implied that pardon—he was far too clever to speak the actual words—I intend to have my share of the perquisites, much though it sticks in my throat to be civil to him. I want to be praetor next year, so does Brutus, but by the time the Great Man reaches Rome, all the jobs will be gone." He eyed Servilia ironically; they had no secrets. "As—er—Caesar's unofficial son-in-law, I think I deserve a good job. In fact, I think that I deserve Syria more than Dolabella does. Don't you agree?"

"Absolutely," she said. "Go with my blessing."

While Caesar and Octavius, talking incessantly, made their way up the coast of Nearer Spain to cross the Pyrenees, the seaport of Narbo was experiencing more excitement than it had since Lucius Caesar had used it as his base while Cousin Gaius fought the Long-haired Gauls. An attractive city at the mouth of the Atax River, it was famous for its seafood, particularly the world's most succulent fish, a very flat creature that lived on the estuary sea floor and had to be dug out of hiding: hence its name, dug-mullet.

However, Narbo didn't really think that the sixty-odd Roman senators who descended upon it at the end of June were visiting in order to dine on dug-mullets. Narbo knew that Caesar was coming, and that these important men were there to see him. That they had chosen Narbo lay in the fact that there was no other place of sufficient size to accommodate so many in a proper degree of comfort. Senators like Decimus Brutus, Gaius Trebonius, Marcus Antonius and Lucius Minucius Basilus were well known from the days of Caesar's Gallic War; arriving first, the four promptly moved into Lucius Caesar's mansion, which he had kept in the hope that one day he would have a chance to return to a place he loved dearly. The rest distributed themselves around the better inns or begged shelter with some prosperous Roman merchant; Narbo had a good many, as it served as the port for a lush hinterland that stretched as far as Tolosa, a fine inland city downstream from the headwaters of the Garumna River.

Recently Narbo's status had risen even higher; Caesar had created a new province, Narbonese Gaul, which extended from west of the Rhodanus River to the Pyrenees, and from Our Sea to Oceanus Atlanticus where the Duranius and the Garumna met at the Gallic *oppidum* of Burdigala. It thus incorporated the lands of the Volcae Tectosages and the Aquitani. As the capital, Narbo had a fine new governor's palace where Caesar and his staff would stay after they arrived. Its first incumbent, already in residence, was Caesar's brave and scholarly legate, Aulus Hirtius.

Mark Antony slept in Lucius Caesar's house only the one night before Hirtius invited him to the governor's palace. Which left Gaius Trebonius, Decimus Brutus and Basilus in Lucius Caesar's house, a state of affairs that suited Trebonius, relieved him. He had decided that it was time to start feeling out certain men on the subject of an untimely death for Caesar.

He started with Decimus Junius Brutus Albinus, sustained by that little chat in Murcius's tavern.

"The only way we're ever going to have that fighting chance in the elections you talked of, Decimus, is if Caesar no longer rules Rome," he said as they walked the busy quayside.

"I am aware of that, Trebonius."

"If you are, then how do you think we can end Caesar's rule?"

"There's only one way. Kill him."

"Once upon a time," Trebonius said in his mournful voice, staring at a ship anchoring in the roads, "Caesar prosecuted Antonius's uncle Hybrida for atrocities he committed in Greece. It created a bit of an uproar because of Caesar's connection to the Antonii, but the Great Man—not so great in those days—said it didn't infringe the unwritten tenets of families because the connection was through marriage only."

"I remember the case. Hybrida invoked tribunician protection and halted proceedings, but Caesar had rendered him so odious that he had to go into exile anyway," Decimus said. "*My* connection to the Julii is by blood, but it's quite remote—through a Popillia who was the mother of Catulus Caesar's father."

"Is that remote enough to consider joining a group of men dedicated to killing Caesar?"

"Oh, yes," said Decimus Brutus without hesitation. He walked on, wrinkling his nose at the smell of fish, seaweed and ships. "However, Trebonius, why do you need a group of men?"

"Because I have no intention of sacrificing my own life and career in the cause," Trebonius said frankly. "I want enough very important men involved to make it seem a patriotic act, one that the Senate won't have the courage to punish."

"So you're not thinking of doing it here in Narbo?"

"All I intend to do in Narbo is sound people out—but only after a lot of listening and observation. I'm asking you here and now because that makes two of us to listen and observe."

"Ask Basilus, and there will be three of us."

"I had thought of him. Do you think he'll be in it?"

"In a flash," said Decimus. His lip curled, but not from the smells. "He's another Hybrida, he tortures his slaves. I heard that his activities have come to Caesar's ears, and that he'll have no further advancement. Caesar paid him out instead."

Trebonius frowned. "A history like that won't add any distinction to our group."

"Very few know. To senatorial sheep, he's important."

Which was true enough. Lucius Minucius Basilus was a Picentine landowner who claimed that his family could trace its origins back to the days of Cincinnatus, though he could offer no proof beyond a flat statement. Having discovered that a flat statement was all that most of his fellow First Class required as proof, he had gone far. A Caesar-appointed praetor this year, he had looked forward to the consulship until word leaked back to him that his secret vice had been reported to Caesar. With a tortured slave to testify. When he had received Caesar's curt letter informing him that his public career was over, Basilus turned from a Caesar worshiper to a Caesar hater. After four years as one of Caesar's legates in Gaul, a rude shock to find himself excluded from the inner circle. He had come to Narbo to plead his case, but with little hope.

When Trebonius and Decimus Brutus sounded him out, he agreed to join what Decimus had nicknamed the Kill Caesar Club with alacrity, even jubilation.

Three. Now who else?

Lucius Staius Murcus had come to Narbo confidently, for he knew he stood high in Caesar's favor; his talents lay on the sea, and he had admiraled fleets for Caesar with flair. However, he had sided with Caesar for the most basic of reasons: he knew that Caesar would win, and he wanted to be on the winning side. The trouble was that he disliked Caesar intensely, and sensed that the emotion was reciprocated. Therefore standing high in Caesar's favor was a state of being that could change, especially now that there were no more battles to be fought. He had been praetor, he wanted to be consul, yet was edgily aware that, with only two consuls each year, and many men high in Caesar's favor, his own chances were slender.

Basilus suggested him, but they agreed not to approach Staius Murcus in Narbo. Narbo was for noting names, not approaching.

Certain others in Narbo went on the list of potential Kill Caesar Club members, but all mere *pedarii* senators, backbenchers with little clout. Decimus Turullius, the brothers Caecilius Metellus and Caecilius Buciolanus, the brothers Publius and Gaius Servilius Casca were noted down. So was a very angry Caesennius Lento, the beheader of Gnaeus Pompey.

On the third day of Quinctilis, Caesar's party descended on Narbo at last, accompanied by the remnants of the Tenth Legion and the somewhat plumper Fifth Alauda.

Caesar, noted Mark Antony, was looking in the pink of health.

"My dear Antonius," said Caesar cordially, kissing his cheek, "what a pleasure to see you. And Aulus Hirtius, of course."

Antony didn't notice what Caesar went on to say, his eyes on the slender figure emerging from Caesar's gig. Young Gaius Octavius? Yes, it was! But there had been *big* changes. He'd never really taken any notice of his second cousin, dismissed him as a future bum-boy who'd be one of the family disgraces, but the lad, though as precious and pretty as ever, now exuded a quiet confidence that said he was doing very well as Caesar's cadet.

Caesar turned to Octavius with a smile and drew him forward. "As you see, I have just about the entire family with me. All we needed to be complete was Marcus Antonius." Caesar slipped an arm about Octavius's shoulders and gave him a slight hug. "Go inside, Gaius, and see where they've put me."

Octavius smiled at Antony unself-consciously and did as he was told. Quintus Pedius was approaching; Antony had to act fast, and did. "I'm here to apologize, Caesar. And beg forgiveness."

"I accept the one and grant the other, Antonius."

The next thing they were all there, from Quintus Pedius to young Lucius Pinarius, Caesar's other great-nephew, a *contubernalis* with his cousin, Pedius. Plus Quintus Fabius Maximus, Calvinus, Messala Rufus, and Pollio.

"I'd better move out," said Antony to Hirtius, counting the entourage. "I can stay at Uncle Lucius's place."

"There's no need," said Caesar genially. "We'll put Agrippa, Pinarius and Octavius together in a cupboard somewhere."

"Agrippa?" asked Antony.

"There," said Caesar, pointing. "Did you ever see a more promising military man in all your life, Antonius?"

"Quintus Sertorius with a face," Antony said instantly.

"Exactly what I thought. He's a *contubernalis* with Pedius, but I'm transferring him to my own staff when I leave for the East. And one of Pedius's military tribunes, Salvidienus Rufus. He led the cavalry charge at Munda, and did brilliantly."

"Nice to know that Rome's still producing good men."

"Not Rome, Antonius. *Italy!* Think more broadly, do!"

"I've counted sixty-two senators come to bow and scrape," said Antony as they went indoors together. "Most of them are your own appointees, *pedarii* lobby fodder, but Trebonius and Decimus Brutus are here, so are Basilus and Staius Murcus." He stopped to look at Caesar quizzically. "You seem mighty fond of that young *saltatrix tonsa*, Octavius," he said abruptly.

"Don't let appearances fool you, Antonius. Octavius is far from a barbered dancing girl. He has more political acumen in his little finger than you have in your entire hulking body. He's been my constant companion since shortly after Munda, and I don't remember when I've enjoyed a young fellow so much. He's sickly and he'll never be a military man, but the head on his shoulders is old and wise. A pity his name's Octavius, really."

A stab of alarm pierced Antony; he stiffened. "Thinking of making his name Julius Caesar by adoption, are you?" he asked.

"Alas, no. I told you, he's sickly. Too sickly to make old bones," Caesar said lightly.

Octavius appeared. "Up the stairs, the suite right at the end of the corridor, Caesar," he said. "You won't need me now, so if you don't mind, I'll see where Agrippa and Pinarius are stowing their gear. Is it all right if I stay with them?"

"I had planned it thus. Enjoy Narbo, and don't get into any trouble. You're on leave."

The large, beautiful grey eyes rested on Caesar's face with patent adoration, then the lad nodded and vanished.

"He thinks the sun shines out of your arse," said Antony.

"It's very pleasant to know that *someone* does, Antonius. Particularly a member of my own family."

"Go on! Pedius doesn't fart unless you tell him to."

"What of your farts, cousin?"

"Treat me well, Caesar, and I'll treat you well."

"I've accepted your apology, but you're on probation, and it would be wise to remember that. Are you out of debt?"

"No," said Antony gruffly, "but I was able to pay the usurers enough to shut them up. Once Fulvia's flush again, they'll get more, and I'm counting on a share of the Parthian booty to finish the business."

They had reached Caesar's suite, where Hapd'efan'e was paring some fruit. Antony eyed the Egyptian physician with revulsion.

"I have other plans for you," Caesar said, swallowing a peach.

Antony stopped dead and glared at Caesar furiously. "Oh, no, not again!" he snapped. "Don't expect me to sit on Rome for you for five years, because I won't! I want a decent campaign with some decent booty!"

"You will have it, Antonius, but not with me," Caesar said, keeping his voice level. "Next year you will be consul, and after that you'll go to Macedonia with six good legions. Vatinius will remain in Illyricum, and the two of you will fight a joint campaign north into the lands of the Danubius and Dacia. I have no desire to see Rome's frontiers threatened by King Burebistas while I'm absent. You and Vatinius will conquer from the Savus and Dravus all the way to the Euxine Sea. And your share of the booty will be the general's, not a legate's."

"But it won't be Parthian booty," Antony growled.

"If the puny campaigns of the previous governors of Macedonia are anything to go by, Antonius," said Caesar, keeping his temper, "I predict you'll emerge from the campaign as rich as Croesus. The Danubian tribes are gold-rich peoples."

"I'll still have to share with Vatinius," said Antony.

"You'd have to share the Parthian spoils with two dozen men of equal rank. And have you forgotten that as the general, you take all the proceeds from the sale of slaves? Do you know how much I made out of the sale of Gallic slaves? Thirty *thousand* talents!" Caesar eyed him mockingly. "You, Antonius, are a glaring example of a Roman boy who never did his homework and never mastered arithmetic. You're also a born glutton."

Caesar remained in Narbo for two *nundinae*, setting up the new province of Narbonese Gaul and allocating generous, fertile portions of land to the few survivors of the Tenth Legion; the Fifth Alauda was to march east with him to the Rhodanus valley, where he intended to settle its men on equally good land. They were a priceless gift for Gaul, these matchless legionaries, who would marry Gallic women and commingle the blood of two superlative warrior peoples.

"He's always been royal," said Gaius Trebonius to Decimus Brutus as they watched Caesar move among the fawning senators, "but it grows in leaps and bounds. Caesar Rex! If we convince all the Romans who matter that he intends to crown himself King of Rome, we'll get away free, Decimus. Rome has never punished regicides."

"We need someone closer to him to convince the Romans who matter that he will crown himself King of Rome," Decimus said thoughtfully. "Someone like Antonius, who I hear is to be one of next year's consuls. I know Antonius won't do the deed, but I always have a feeling that he'll not condemn the deed either. Perhaps he'd go as far as making the deed look respectable?"

"Perhaps," said Trebonius, smiling. "Shall I ask him?"

As Antony was making a huge effort to stay sober and be of some use to Caesar, it wasn't easy to get him on his own, but on their last evening in Narbo, Trebonius managed by inviting Antony to look at a particularly beautiful horse.

"The beast's up to your weight, Antonius, and well worth what the owner's asking. I know you're in to the bloodsuckers for millions, but the consul needs a better Public Horse than your old fellow, which must be due for retirement. The Treasury pays for a Public Horse, don't forget."

Antony took the bait, and was delighted when he saw the animal, tall and strong without being lumbering, and a striking mixture of light and dark grey dapples. The deal concluded, he and Trebonius walked back to the town.

"I'm going to do some talking," said Trebonius, "but I don't want you to answer me. All I ask is that you listen. Nor do you need to tell me that I'm putting my life in your hands by broaching this particular subject. However, whether you agree with me or not, I refuse to believe that you'll tattle to Caesar. Of course you know what the subject is. Killing Caesar. There are now a number of us who are convinced that the deed *must* be done if Rome is ever to be free again. But we can't hurry, because we have to appear to the First Class as the champions of liberty—as truly patriotic men doing Rome a great service."

He paused while two senators passed. "The oath you swore to Fulvia can't be broken, so I'm not asking you to belong to the Kill Caesar Club. Decimus thought of the name, which could be a joke as easily as a conspiracy—walls have ears? What I'm going to do is to ask you to help in ways that don't affect your oath. Namely, by making it seem as if Caesar is about to don the diadem. There are people already saying that, but it's generally held to be spite invented by Caesar's avowed enemies, so it hasn't impressed people like Flavius Hemicillus and Atticus, any of the other real plutocrats. As Decimus says, someone close to Caesar has to make the King of Rome option look a foregone conclusion."

Two more senators passed by; Trebonius was overheard talking eagerly about Antony's new Public Horse.

"Now, the rumor is out that next year you will be consul," Trebonius resumed, "and that when Caesar leaves Rome for the war against the Parthians, you're to stay in Rome to govern until the end of the year, then start a campaign into Dacia with Vatinius—don't ask me how I know, just believe I do. I imagine you're not as pleased as maybe Caesar thinks you are, and I understand why. Booty will be hard to come by. There's no German treasure like the one in Atuatuca, nor is there a Druid center of worship full of gold votives. You'll have to force the barbarians to reveal the sites of their burial mounds, and you're not a Labienus, are you? As for the sale of slaves, who's going to buy them? The biggest market is the Kingdom of the Parthians, and they're not going to be buying any slaves while Caesar's breathing down their necks. But if Caesar is dead, all that changes, doesn't it?"

Antony stopped, bent to tie his boot; his fingers, Trebonius noted, were trembling. Yes, the message was being absorbed.

"Anyway, as consul-elect for the rump of this year and consul in fact next year, you're in a perfect position to perform little acts that will make it appear as if Caesar intends to be Caesar Rex. There's talk of putting a statue of Caesar in Quirinus's, but what if the Senate voted to give Caesar a palace on the Quirinal alongside Quirinus's, and put a temple pediment on it? What if there was to be a cult to Caesar's clemency, only it looked more like a god cult? If *you* were the *flamen*, people would have to take it seriously, wouldn't they?"

Trebonius paused to draw breath, then went on. "I have a great many ideas along those lines, and I'm sure you're capable of thinking of plenty for yourself. What we have to do is make it seem as if Caesar will never step down, never abrogate his power, and is aiming at being a god on earth. The first step to that is to be a king, so the two can be worked together. You see, none of the members of the Kill Caesar Club wants to be tried for *perduellio* treason, or even to be castigated for the deed. We aim to be *heroes*. But that requires the generation of a mood in the First Class, which is the only Class that matters. Anyone lower than that thinks Caesar is a god and a king already, and they love it and love him. He gives them work, opportunities, prosperity—do they care who rules them, or how? No, they don't. Even the Second Class. What we have to do is turn the First Class implacably against Caesar Rex."

They were approaching Lucius Caesar's mansion. "Don't say a word, Antonius. Your actions are all the answer we need."

Trebonius nodded and smiled as if they had just enjoyed a meaningless conversation, and slipped inside. Mark Antony walked on to the governor's palace. He too was smiling.

When the huge cavalcade departed from Narbo the next day at dawn, Caesar invited Antony to share his gig. Not at all put out, Gaius Octavius joined Decimus Brutus in another gig.

"We're remote relatives, young Octavius," Decimus Brutus said, settling himself into his seat with a sigh of weariness. The time in Narbo had been a strain, and the strain was going to continue until he could be sure that Antony had not tattled.

"Indeed we are," said Octavius sunnily.

The exchange constituted the prelude to a journey of innocuous talk that ended three days later in Arelate, where Caesar stayed a *nundinum* to get the Fifth Alauda organized. When the gigs commenced the haul up the Via Domitia to the Mons Genava Pass, Octavius was back in Caesar's gig, and Mark Antony traveled with Decimus Brutus. No, he hadn't tattled. The relief!

"Out of favor already?" Decimus asked. "Truly, Antonius, you need a muzzle."

Antony grinned. "No, I'm standing well with the Great Man. The trouble is that I'm too big for him to have a secretary there too. The pretty little pansy bum-boy doesn't take up much room. He's something, isn't he?"

"Oh, yes," said Decimus instantly, "but not in the way you mean it. Gaius Octavius is *very* dangerous."

"You're joking! The strain of waiting to see if I'd tattle has warped your thinking, Decimus."

"Far from it, Antonius. Do you remember the tale of Sulla's remark to Aurelia when she begged for Caesar's life? He wasn't much older then than Octavius is now. 'Very well, have it your own way! I will spare him! But be warned! In this young man I see many Mariuses.' Well, in this boy I see many Mariuses."

"You're definitely touched in the head," said Antony with a rude noise, and changed the subject. "Our next stop's Cularo."

"What happens there?"

"A gathering of the Vocontii. The Great Man is bestowing the traditional Vocontii lands on them for their absolute own in honor of old Gnaeus Pompeius Trogus."

"That's one thing I have to grant Caesar," said Decimus Brutus. "He never forgets a good turn. Trogus was a wonderful help to us through all the years in Gaul, and the Vocontii have earned Friend and Ally status. After Trogus joined the staff, they stopped those awful raids on us. Never joined Vercingetorix either."

"I'm going ahead when we reach Taurasia," Antony announced.

"Why's that?"

"Fulvia's due and I'd like to be there."

Decimus Brutus burst out laughing. "Antonius! You're under the cat's foot at last! How many children have you got already?"

"Only the one in wedlock, and she's a dolt. All Fadia's died with her in that epidemic, don't forget. Not that they were any loss, with a Fadia for a mother. Fulvia's different. This sprog will be able to say he's the great-grandson of Gaius Gracchus."

"What if it's a girl?"

"Fulvia says she's carrying a boy, and she'd know."

"Two boys and two girls by Clodius, a boy by Curio—you're right, she'd know."

The Via Domitia came down to the vast river plain of the Padus at Placentia, which was the capital of Italian Gaul and the seat of the governor, Gaius Vibius Pansa, one of Caesar's loyalest clients. He had succeeded Brutus, so when Brutus and Cassius arrived in Placentia, he hailed them delightedly.

"My dear Brutus, you did a brilliant job," he said warmly. "To succeed you has left me with practically nothing to do beyond follow your *edicta*. Here to see Caesar?"

"Yes, as a matter of fact, which means you'll be crowded out with boarders," Brutus said, a little astonished at so much praise. "Gaius Cassius and I will stay at Tigellius's inn."

"Nothing of the kind! No, no, I won't hear of it! I've had a message from Caesar that says his party will consist of himself, Quintus Pedius, Calvinus, and three *contubernales*. Decimus Brutus and Gaius Trebonius are traveling straight on to Rome, so are the others who've managed to keep up with Caesar," said Pansa.

"Then thank you, Pansa," Cassius said briskly. "I hope," he said to Brutus when they took possession of a suite of four rooms, "that we don't have a long wait. Pansa is *tedious*."

"Um," said Brutus absently; his mind was on Porcia, whom he was missing badly. Not to mention that he was suffering from guilt because he hadn't dared tell her whereabouts he was going.

The wait was minimal; Caesar turned up the next day in time for dinner. His reaction to their presence was perhaps a little too imperious for Cassius's taste, but his gladness was genuine.

Seven of them reclined to take the meal: Caesar, Calvinus, Quintus Pedius, Pansa, Brutus, Cassius and Gaius Octavius. In accordance with tradition, Pansa's wife, Fufia Calena, had not accompanied him to his province, so there were no women present to slow the conversation down with small talk.

"Where's Quintus Fabius Maximus?" Pansa asked Caesar.

"Gone ahead with Antonius. He did very well in Spain, so he will be triumphing. As will Quintus Pedius."

Cassius's lips tightened, but he said nothing. The idea of holding triumphs for victories over purely Roman foes had not occurred to him—surely Caesar wasn't going to call it a Spanish revolt! Not enough of the Further province had risen for that, and the Nearer one hadn't participated at all.

"You'll be triumphing yourself?" Pansa asked.

"Naturally," said Caesar with a slightly malicious smile.

He's not even going to bother trying to disguise the fact that the enemy was Roman, thought Cassius. He's going to revel in this pathetic victory! I wonder did he pickle Gnaeus Pompey's head so he can display it in his parade?

A silence fell while everybody concentrated upon the food; Cassius was not the only one rendered uncomfortable by the fact that the enemy had been Roman.

"Been writing anything lately, Brutus?" Caesar asked.

Brutus's sad brown eyes lifted to Caesar's face, startled out of his reverie about Porcia. "Why, yes," he said. "No less than three dissertations, as a matter of fact."

"Three."

"Yes, I like to keep several projects going at once. As luck would have it," he went on before his mind could stop him, "the manuscripts were at Tusculum, so didn't perish in the fire."

"Fire?"

Brutus went scarlet, bit his lip. "Er—yes. There was a fire in my study in Rome. All my books and papers were burned."

"*Edepol!* Is your house in ashes?"

"No, the house is intact. Our steward acted very promptly."

"Epaphroditus. Yes, a gem, as I remember. You say that *all* your books and papers perished? I mean, a man's books and papers are scattered around the four walls of his study, not to mention the tables and desk," said Caesar, munching on nuts.

"True," said Brutus, his misery visibly increasing.

The intelligence behind the pale eyes had clearly grasped at a mystery—may even, Cassius decided, have divined what really happened. But Brutus was unworthy prey for this big cat, so the subject was dropped with a lordly command:

"Do tell us about the manuscripts at Tusculum."

"Well, one dissertation is on virtue, one is on submissive endurance, and one on duty," said Brutus, recovering.

"What do you have to say about virtue, Brutus?"

"Oh, that virtue alone is sufficient to ensure a happy life. If a man be truly virtuous, then poverty, sickness or exile cannot destroy his happiness, Caesar."

"Do tell! You amaze me, considering the wealth of your experience. A Stoic's argument that should please Porcia. My most sincere congratulations on your marriage," said Caesar gravely.

"Oh, thank you. Thank you."

"Submissive endurance—is *it* a virtue?" Caesar asked, then answered his own question. "Absolutely not!"

Calvinus laughed. "A Caesarean answer."

"A *man's* answer," said a voice from the end of the far couch. "Endurance is a genuine virtue, but submissiveness is a quality admirable only in women," Octavius declared.

Cassius's eyes went from Brutus's discomfiture to the lad, their brown depths surprised. It was on the tip of his tongue to say that he didn't consider anyone as womanish as this presumptuous sprig an authority on men's answers, but again he suppressed his impulse. What stopped him was Caesar's face. Ye gods, our ruler is *proud* of this pansy ninny! What's more, respects his opinion!

The last course was carried out; only the wine and water remained. What a curious dinner, how fraught with hidden tensions. Cassius found it difficult to decide exactly where the source of these stresses was located. At first, inevitably, he had blamed Caesar, but the longer the meal went on, the more he thought that young Gaius Octavius was the guilty party. He stood on incredibly good terms with his great-uncle, so much was evident. What he said—when he said anything—was listened to as if he were a legate, not a lowly cadet. Nor was it Caesar alone; Calvinus and Pedius hung upon Octavius's lips too. Yet Cassius couldn't call the youth impudent, rude, forward, even conceited. Most of the time he lay among the shadows, left the conversation to his elders. Except for those sudden, uncannily prescient, occasionally barbative, remarks. Uttered quietly but firmly. You, Gaius Octavius, said Cassius to himself, are a deep one.

"Now to business," said Caesar, so unexpectedly that Cassius was jerked out of his ruminations about Gaius Octavius.

"Business?" Pansa asked, startled.

"Yes, but not provincial business, Pansa, so relax. Marcus Brutus—Gaius Cassius—I have praetorships going begging next year," Caesar said. "Brutus, I'm offering you *praetor urbanus.* Cassius, I'm offering you *praetor peregrinus.* Will you accept?"

"Yes, please!" cried Brutus, lighting up.

"Yes, I accept," said Cassius, less joyfully.

"I believe that urban praetor best suits your talents, Brutus, whereas foreign praetor suits Cassius better. With your love of meticulous work, you'll issue the right kind of *edicta* and stick to them," said Caesar to Brutus. He turned then to Cassius. "As for you, Cassius, you've had a great deal of experience with non-citizens, you travel hard and fast, and you think on your feet. Therefore, foreign praetor."

Ah! thought Cassius, lying back limply. It has been worth the trip. So Dolabella thinks to have Syria, does he?

Brutus was in a state of exaltation. Urban praetor! The top job! Oh, Porcia will understand, I know she will!

They look, thought Octavius, like cats in a lake of cream.

 When Caesar left Placentia, he traveled alone; even Gaius Octavius was told that he would have to make his own way back to Rome. Thus the little clutch of gigs which galloped off down the Via Aemilia Scauri to the coast and the Via Aurelia of Etruria contained Caesar's secretaries, servants, and Hapd'efan'e.

Well into Sextilis already, which meant less than seven months before he departed for Syria and a *decent* war. That meant two lots of work: what still had to be done for Rome and Italy, as well as the myriad preparations that went into planning a five-year campaign involving fifteen legions of infantry and ten thousand German, Gallic and Galatian cavalry. Gaius Rabirius Postumus was acting as *praefectus fabrum*, and the trusty old muleteer, Publius Ventidius, was busy recruiting and training. This campaign would see no raw troops; luckily a year of retirement was about as much peace and quiet as any old legionary could stomach, so the re-enlistment ratio was very high. With Ventidius supervising, the re-enlisting veterans would be carefully culled and juggled so that the very best of them went into making six crack legions, while the rest were apportioned to make the other nine legions uniformly experienced. Artillery. A hundred pieces per legion, not counting the small stuff. Artificers and skilled noncombatants of all kinds . . .

The time on the road passed swiftly, spent in dictating to shuffled arrays of secretaries, now about military matters, now about Rome, now about Italy, now about public works crying out to be done, from that canal through the Isthmus of Corinth to a new harbor at Ostia. Drain the Pomptine marshes, build more aqueducts into Rome, divert the Tiber so that the Campus Martius and the Campus Vaticanus were both on Rome's side of the river. Italy owned no Via Julia Caesaris, so one must be constructed between Rome and Firmum Picenum to open up the least accessible parts of the Apennines . . .

Get those wretched land commissioners off their arses so that those of his veterans being settled in Italy weren't kept around waiting years for their land. He had legislated to protect them from the depredations of greedy wives, confidence tricksters and gobbling landowners by forbidding them to sell their portions for twenty years. Something Brutus had said to him in Placentia had annoyed him, for Brutus knew so little of human nature ("submissive endurance" indeed!) that he actually believed Caesar had instituted the twenty-year prohibition to stop the soldiers selling their land to buy wine and whores. That's how Brutus thought the lower classes behaved. Brutus, who knew nothing of poverty, sickness or exile, yet could dismiss them as incapable of destroying happiness! The entire Palatine ought to grow up amid poverty, as Caesar had. Not desperately poor himself, as Sulla had been, but witness to the suffering poverty brought in its train, the lives it blighted . . .

Fascinating, that a year governing Italian Gaul had cured Brutus's pimples. Authority had freed him from his own miseries—and freed him from Servilia at last. So much so that upon his return he had divorced his Claudia and married Cato's daughter. Caesar knew as surely as if he had been present how that fire in Brutus's study had started . . .

It was time that Italian Gaul was made a part of Italy, ceased to be governed as a province. Every inhabitant was now a full citizen, so why was there an artificial barrier in existence? Why did Rome send it a governor, instead of governing it directly? Sicilians ought to be granted the full citizenship, though that would be bitterly opposed, even by his own creatures. Too many of Greek descent—but wasn't that equally true of Italy south of Rome? Smaller and darker . . .

It wasn't right that Alexandria had a library of close to a million copies, while Rome had no public library at all. Varro! The perfect job for Marcus Terentius Varro, to collect multiple copies of all the books extant and put them under one roof . . .

The problem he didn't share with his secretaries through the medium of dictation was the fate of Rome in his absence. It had plagued him from the moment the situation in Syria had informed him that, if the world of Our Sea was to remain Occidental, the Kingdom of the Parthians would have to be eliminated. The fact that he knew he was the only man capable of invading and crushing the Parthian empire was not evidence of overweening conceit, but simple knowledge of himself—of his will, abilities, genius. The truth was not conceit.

If Caesar did not conquer the Parthians, they would remain a threat that one day would invade the western world. Few political men were gifted with foresight, but Caesar had it in huge measure; the coming centuries unfolded within his mind, and he cared more about them than he did about the centuries already written down in the history books. The Parthians were warlike, a disparate collection of remotely related peoples united by a king and a central government. Rather like Rome, really, save that Rome had no king. But should one man with one idea unite the peoples of that vast empire into a whole that thought the same way, then all other civilizations would be overrun. Only Caesar could prevent that happening, for no one else owned the vision to see what was coming.

The trouble was that Rome wasn't an indissoluble whole, so Rome in his absence was a ghastly problem. He had decided that the only way to prevent the disintegration of what he had thus far achieved was to give the heart of his universe a system of checks and balances aimed at preventing another man from doing what he had done. Sulla had tried by establishing a new constitution, but it had toppled within fifteen years because it wasn't new, it was an attempt to revert to the past.

Caesar's solution was more complex. The *res publica* was in much better condition now than it had been when he had taken up his first dictatorship. The laws were settling into place, and they were *good* laws, even if some of the First Class didn't think so. Business had re-covered so well that no one agitated for a general cancellation of debts anymore; his solution of Rome's financial woes had benefited both debtors and creditors, was hailed by both sides as brilliant. The courts were functioning properly for the first time in decades, juries were no difficulty, privilege was harder to defend, the Assemblies were finally coming to understand their role in Rome's government, and the Sen-ate was less liable to be dominated by a tiny group like the *boni*.

The real heart of the problem didn't lie in any group; if Caesar had failed anywhere, it was in the fact that he had done what he did virtu-ally single-handedly. As an autocrat. And there were other men who believed that they could do the same. In keeping the dictatorship for so long, Caesar had created a changed climate, and he knew it very well. Nor had he found a solution, save to continue as Dictator for the rest of his life, and hope that after he died, Rome would have learned enough to move onward rather than backward. But onward to what? That, he didn't know. All he could do was demonstrate the excellence of his changes, and trust that those who followed him would see their excellence clearly enough to preserve them.

Which didn't solve the problem of his five-year absence. At first he had thought that the best way was to take Marcus Antonius with him. Antonius was an instinctive abuser of power. But he had made trouble with the legions, had wanted control of the army in order to make himself the First Man in Rome, if not Dictator. Therefore to take Anto-nius with him was to run the risk of massive troop mutinies the mo-ment the going got hard. His expedition might turn out to be Lucullus and Clodius in eastern Anatolia all over again. No, Antonius would have to be left behind, which meant giving him the consulship, fol-lowed by a proconsular command that saw him the general of his own army far enough away from Italy to keep his thoughts away from Italy.

Only how to control Antonius the consul? First, by keeping his dictatorship, thus leaving whatever forces remaining in Italy under the control of a Master of the Horse. Who would never again be Marcus Antonius. Lepidus would do nicely, save that Lepidus would insist on going to govern a province. Calvinus would have to replace him as Master of the Horse. Secondly, make sure that Antonius was the *junior* consul. Caesar himself would be the senior consul until he left for the East; after that, the senior consul would have to be a man who didn't like Antonius—a man who would take great pleasure in keeping Antonius in his place until he went to his proconsular command in Macedonia. There was really only one candidate for this job: Publius Cornelius Dolabella.

Nor would there be any experienced legions in Italy or Italian Gaul. Caesar would garrison the provinces with the professional legions he didn't take with him, confine military presence within the semi-circle of the Alps to recruitment and training. Sextus Pompeius was abroad in Spain and Carrinas was contending with him, but Sextus wouldn't submit tamely. Alone as he was, he didn't present a major threat, but nonetheless it was necessary to put strong governors in the Spains and the Gauls. Men he could trust, men who didn't like Marcus Antonius.

The time flew so fast that he arrived at his villa outside Lanuvium before he had concluded his deliberations. For one more task still had to be done, a task he didn't dare postpone any longer: the making of his will. Which was why he had elected to bypass Rome, only twenty miles away. He needed isolation to wrestle with the matter.

The Caesars had always owned estates in Latium, but this villa he had bought from Fulvia after she began selling property to pay Antony's debts. She had inherited it from Publius Clodius, an architectural marvel left uncompleted because his murder had occurred as he returned from visiting its construction site. Fulvia had hated it ever after, refused to do any further work on it. But Caesar, its new owner, had finished it. It lay in the Alban Hills some way out of Lanuvium and well off the Via Appia, and was suspended over a cliff on hundred-foot-high piers. From its loggia the view was breathtaking, for it looked out over rugged country to the Latin plain and the dreamy reaches of the Tuscan Sea, saw wonderful sunsets every time Aetna or the Vulcaniae Isles erupted and poured smoke into the air, a frequent occurrence. Varro, an expert on natural phenomena, insisted that some huge cataclysm was brewing in Italy's chain of volcanoes, for the Fields of Fire behind Puteoli and Neapolis were becoming more violent.

Who, who, who? Who would be Caesar's heir?

* * *

Oddly, he had abandoned all ideas of Antonius the moment he saw that familiar figure waiting in the courtyard of the governor's palace in Narbo. Though his remorseless physical excesses had never had the power to destroy Antonius's body, with its barrel chest, huge shoulders and arms, its flat belly, bulging thighs and calves, when Caesar laid eyes on him illuminated by a westering sun, he saw terrible signs of inner decay, of moral erosion and impoverished emotions. Too much high living, yes, but also too much worry over debts, too much brute ambition allied to too little common sense.

Quintus Pedius, excellent man though he was, would always remain a Campanian knight, and that blood was throwing true; his sons were in his mode, neither looked nor behaved like Julians, for all that their mother was a patrician Valeria Messala. Nor was young Lucius Pinarius promising. The Pinarii, once powerful patricians, had foundered long ago. His sister Julia Major had married Pinarius's grandfather, a wastrel who died soon after; fed up with women choosing poor husbands, Caesar had married her to Quintus Pedius's father, to whom she had objected at first, then discovered how nice it was to be a rich old man's darling. His younger sister, Julia Minor, hadn't been allowed to pick her own husband. Caesar the youthful *paterfamilias* had found her a very wealthy Latin knight from Aricia, Marcus Atius Balbus, by whom she had had a son and a daughter, that Atia who first married Gaius Octavius from Velitrae in the Latin heartlands, then the eminent Philippus. Atia's brother had died without issue.

The choice finally came down to Decimus Junius Brutus Albinus or Gaius Octavius.

Decimus Brutus was in his prime, and had never put a foot wrong. Generaled brilliantly in Long-haired Gaul on land and on sea, and had been a distinguished praetor in the murder court. The one thing Caesar condemned in him was his ruthlessness after the Bellovaci rose while he was governing Long-haired Gaul, but he had accepted Decimus's explanation that the Bellovaci alone had conserved their strength until after Caesar was long gone, thinking that whoever governed would not have Caesar's strength of purpose.

Decimus would have to be given the consulship soon. Yet another he had no intention of taking east with him, for very different reasons than Antonius. He needed Decimus Brutus, whom he trusted implicitly, to keep an eye on Rome and Italy. After he had been consul he would go to govern Italian Gaul, the most strategic of all the provinces when it came to keeping an eye on Rome and Italy.

Gaius Octavius would turn eighteen in latish September, and he loved the lad dearly. But he was too young and too sick. A long talk with Hapd'efan'e hadn't allayed his fears about Octavius's asthma, though he had hoped it would, given that there had been almost no asthma during those months in Spain, on the way home. That, said Hapd'efan'e, was because Octavius felt so secure in Caesar's vicinity. While ever Caesar was a part of Octavius's world, he would thrive, including on this expedition to the East.

But Caesar's heir would come into his inheritance after Caesar's death. Caesar's heir would be stripped of Caesar's presence. And death, thought Caesar, cannot be too far away, if Cathbad the Chief Druid was right. He had promised Caesar that Caesar would not live to be a crabbed old man, that he would die in his prime. Caesar has turned fifty-five and has perhaps ten years left of his prime . . .

He closed his eyes and conjured up their faces.

Decimus Brutus, so blond that he looked bland. Yet on close examination the eyes were steely and intelligent, the mouth firm and strong, the facial planes those of a man to be reckoned with. What told against him was his mother's *fellatrix* blood. Yes, the Sempronii Tuditani were dissolute, and he had heard tales about Decimus Brutus.

The Alexandrine face of Gaius Octavius. Faintly womanish, rather too graceful, the over-long hair not a help save to hide those jug-handle ears. Yet on close examination the eyes showed a formidable and subtle person, the mouth and chin were strong, firm. What told against him was the asthma.

Caesar, Caesar, make up your mind!

What was it that Lucius had said? Something to the effect that Caesar's luck went with Caesar's name, that Caesar's luck was all Caesar needed to trust in.

"Let the dice fly high!" he said in Greek, for the second time in his life. The first had been just before he crossed the Rubicon.

He drew a sheet of paper forward, dipped his reed pen in the inkwell, and commenced to write.

VIII

FALL OF A TITAN

From OCTOBER of 45 B.C. until the end of
MARCH of 44 B.C.

MARCUS JUNIUS BRUTUS

Ensconced in the Domus Publica and with preparations for his triumph over Further Spain going nicely, Caesar took a trip out of the city to see Cleopatra, who greeted him with frantic joy.

"My poor girl, I haven't treated you very well," he said to her ruefully after a night of love that hadn't seen the slightest chance of a sister or brother for Caesarion.

Her eyes filled with dismay. "Did I complain so much in my letters?" she asked anxiously. "I tried not to worry you."

"You never have worried me," he said, kissing her hand. "I have other sources of information than your own letters, you know. You have a great champion."

"Servilia," she said instantly.

"Servilia," he agreed.

"It doesn't anger you that I've made a friend of her?"

"Why should it?" His face lit with his beautiful smile. "In fact, it was very clever of you to befriend her."

"She befriended me, I think."

"Whatever. The lady is a dangerous enemy, even for a queen. As it is, she genuinely likes you, and she'd certainly far rather that I intrigued with foreign queens than Roman rivals."

"Like Queen Eunoë of Mauretania?" she asked demurely.

He burst out laughing. "I do love gossip! How on earth was I supposed to bed her? I didn't even get as far as Gades while I was in Spain, let alone cross the straits to see Bogud."

"I worked that out for myself, actually." She frowned, put a hand on his arm. "Caesar, I'm trying to work something else out for myself too."

"What?"

"You're a very secretive man, and it shows in all sorts of ways. I never know when you finish yourself—*patratio?*" She looked hunted, but determined. "I produced Caesarion, so I know you must, but it would be nice if I knew when."

"That, my dear," he drawled, "would give you too much power."

"Oh, you and your mistrust!" she cried.

The exchange might have proceeded to a quarrel, but Caesarion saved the day by trotting in with his arms held wide. *"Tata!"*

Caesar scooped him up, tossed him into the air amid shrill whoops of bliss, kissed him, cuddled him.

"He's grown like a weed, Mama."

"Hasn't he? I can't see a thing of myself in him, for which I thank Isis."

"I love the way you look, Pharaoh, and I love you, even if I am secretive," he said, eyes quizzing her.

Sighing, she abandoned that contentious subject. "When do you plan to set out on your Parthian campaign?"

"*Tata*, may I go with you as your *contubernalis*?"

"Not this time, my son. It's your job to protect Mama." He rubbed the child's back, looking at Cleopatra. "I plan to leave three days after the Ides of March next year. It's time you were thinking of going home to Alexandria anyway."

"It will be easier to see you from Alexandria," she said.

"Indeed."

"Then I shall stay here until after you go. It's time we celebrated your being in Rome for six months, Caesar. I've settled in a little, and made a few friends above and beyond dear Servilia. I have such plans!" she went on artlessly. "I want Philostratus to give lectures, and I've succeeded in hiring the services of your favorite singer, Marcus Tigellius Hermogenes. Do say we can entertain!"

"Happily." Still holding Caesarion, he strode across the room to the colonnade outside, and gazed at the topiary garden Gaius Matius had created. "I'm glad you didn't put up that wall, my love. It would have broken Matius's heart."

"It's odd," she said, looking puzzled. "The Transtiberini were such a nuisance for the longest time, then, just as I was about to put up the wall, they disappeared. I was so afraid for our son! Did Servilia tell you, for I swear I didn't?"

"Yes, she told me. There's no need to fret anymore. The Transtiberini are gone." He smiled, but not pleasantly. "I've wished them on Atticus in Buthrotum. They can carve the noses and ears of his cattle for a change."

As Cleopatra liked Atticus, she stared at Caesar in consternation. "Oh, is that fair?" she asked.

"Extremely," he said. "He and Cicero have already been to see me about my colony for the Head Count—I ordered the Transtiberini shipped months ago, and of course they've now arrived."

"What did you say to Atticus?"

"That my migrants *thought* they were remaining at Buthrotum, but are being moved on," said Caesar, ruffling Caesarion's hair.

"And what's the truth?"

"They stay at Buthrotum. Next month I'm sending another two thousand to join them. Atticus won't be a happy man."

"Did publishing Cicero's 'Cato' offend you so much?"

"So much and more," Caesar said grimly.

THE OCTOBER HORSE

* * *

The Spanish triumph was held on the fifth day of October; the First Class loathed it, the rest of Rome loved it. Caesar made no attempt whatsoever to play down the fact that the defeated enemy was Roman, though he committed no solecisms like displaying Gnaeus Pompey's head. When he passed his new rostra in the lower Forum Romanum, all the magistrates seated upon it rose to their feet to honor the triumphator—except for Lucius Pontius Aquila, who had finally found a way to distinguish his tribunate of the plebs. Aquila's gesture of contempt angered Caesar greatly; so did the feast laid out in the temple of Jupiter Optimus Maximus afterward. Stingy and unworthy, was his verdict. He gave another feast at his own expense on the next religiously proper day, but Pontius Aquila was told not to attend. Caesar was making it plain that Servilia's lover would receive no further public advancement.

Gaius Trebonius promptly strolled around to Aquila's house and added another member to the Kill Caesar Club—but made him take an oath not to say a word about it to Servilia.

"I'm not a fool, Trebonius," said Aquila, one auburn brow flying up. "She's a marvel in bed, but do you think I don't know that she's still in love with Caesar?"

Some other men had also joined: Decimus Turullius, whom Caesar disliked intensely; the brothers Caecilius Metellus and Caecilius Buciolanus; the brothers Publius and Gaius Servilius Casca of a plebeian sept of the *gens Servilia*; Caesennius Lento, the murderer of Gnaeus Pompey; and, most interestingly, Lucius Tillius Cimber, a praetor in this year along with several other praetors—Lucius Minucius Basilus, Decimus Brutus, and Lucius Staius Murcus—all members of the club.

In October another man was accepted into the Kill Caesar Club: Quintus Ligarius, whom Caesar loathed so much that he had forbidden Ligarius to return to Rome from Africa, though he had cried pardon. Pressure from many influential friends caused Caesar to relent and recall him, but Ligarius, successfully defended in court on charges of treason by Cicero, knew that he was another doomed not to advance in public life.

Yes, the collection of would-be assassins was growing, but it still lacked men of real clout, names that the entire First Class knew well enough to respect wholeheartedly. Trebonius had little choice other than to bide his time. Nor had Mark Antony made it appear as if Caesar were aiming for kingship and godhead; he was too delighted at the birth of his son by Fulvia, Marcus Antonius Junior, whom the besotted pair addressed as Antyllus.

* * *

On the day after his triumph Caesar stepped down as consul—but not as Dictator—and had Quintus Fabius Maximus and Gaius Trebonius appointed the suffect consuls for the rump of the year, less than three months. Calling them "suffect" dispensed with the need for an election; a senatorial decree was enough.

He announced his governors for the following year: Trebonius was to replace Vatia Isauricus in Asia Province; Decimus Brutus was to go to Italian Gaul; another Kill Caesar Club member, Staius Murcus, was to succeed Antistius Vetus in Syria; and yet another, Tillius Cimber, was to govern Bithynia combined with Pontus. The strong array of governors in the western provinces went from Pollio in Further Spain through Lepidus in Nearer Spain and Narbonese Gaul to Lucius Munatius Plancus in Gaul of the Long-hairs and Gaul of the Rhodanus, and ended with Decimus Brutus in Italian Gaul.

"However," said Caesar to the House, "I cannot step down as Dictator yet, which means I must replace my present Master of the Horse, Marcus Aemilius Lepidus, governing next year. His successor will be Gnaeus Domitius Calvinus."

Antony, listening smugly and expecting to hear his own name— he was behaving himself perfectly, after all!—felt the rebuff like a plunge into icy water. Calvinus! A far harder man to bully and baffle than Lepidus, and a man who made no effort to conceal his dislike of Marcus Antonius. Damn Caesar! Was nothing to come easily?

It appeared not. Caesar then proceeded to announce next year's consuls. Himself as senior consul until he departed for the East, and Marcus Antonius as junior consul for the entire year. The senior consul after Caesar left would be Publius Cornelius Dolabella.

"Oh, no, you don't!" roared Antony, on his feet. "Be junior to *Dolabella?* I'd rather be dead!"

"Let us see what the elections bring, Antonius," said Caesar, quite unruffled. "If the voters wish to return you ahead of Dolabella in the polls, well and good. Otherwise, lump it."

Dolabella, a handsome man quite as tall and almost as heavily built as Antony, leaned back on his stool, folded his hands behind his head and grinned complacently. He knew as well as Antony did that his own activities in Rome were a great deal harder to prove than those of a man who had killed eight hundred Roman civilians in the Forum Romanum with armed troops.

"Your deeds will come back to haunt you, Antonius," he said, and began to whistle.

"It won't happen!" said Antony through his teeth.

Cassius listened keenly, on anybody's side rather than that brute Antonius—at least Caesar had *some* sense! Dolabella was venal and could behave like a fool, but he'd grown up somewhat during the past year, and he wasn't about to be cowed by Antonius, so much was sure. Perhaps Rome would survive. Cassius was, besides, still glowing; he had been notified that he was to be inducted into the College of Augurs, a significant honor.

Brutus listened with growing hope; as he reported to the absent Cicero later, Caesar's dispositions made him think that eventually Caesar intended to restore the full Republic.

"Sometimes, Brutus," Cicero snapped, "you talk utter rubbish! Just because Caesar has made you urban praetor, you suddenly think the man is a wonder. Well, he's not. He's an ulcer!"

It was after this meeting of the Senate that the honors given to Caesar suddenly began to multiply. Many of them had been mooted, even legalized by senatorial *consulta,* yet nothing had been done to implement them. Now all that changed; the statue of Caesar currently being made to go into the temple of Quirinus was to bear a plaque that said TO THE UNCONQUERABLE GOD—a reference, said Antony during a meeting of the Senate that Caesar didn't attend, to Quirinus, not to Caesar. At the same meeting funding was granted for an ivory statue of Caesar riding in a golden car to appear at all state parades; yet another statue of him was to be put alongside the ones of the Kings of Rome and the Founder of the Republic, Lucius Junius Brutus. Caesar's palace on the Quirinal, with its temple pediment, also received a vote of money.

With the Parthian invasion looming, Caesar in fact didn't have the time to attend many meetings of the Senate, and at the beginning of December he was obliged to spend some time in Campania dealing with the allocation of veterans' land. Antony and Trebonius seized their chance immediately, though they were astute enough to have other, lesser men propose their decrees. In future, the month of Quinctilis would be called the month of Julius. A thirty-sixth tribe of Roman citizens was to be created and called the Tribus Julia. A third college of *luperci* was to come into being as the Luperci Julii, and Mark Antony, already a *lupercus,* was to be its prefect. A temple was to be built to Caesar's Clemency, and Mark Antony was to be *flamen* of the new cult of Caesar's Clemency. Caesar was to sit on a curule chair made of gold and wear a golden wreath adorned with gems at the games. His ivory statue was to be carried in the parade of the gods and have an identical pulvinar base. All these decrees were to be inscribed in gold letters on pure silver tablets, to show how Caesar had filled the Treasury to over-flowing.

"I object!" Cassius cried when Trebonius, now consul with the *fasces*, moved for a division of the House on the proposals. "I say again, I object! Caesar is *not* a god, but you're behaving as if he were! Did he vanish down to Campania so that he wouldn't be present to look bashful and be obliged for form's sake to protest? It certainly looks that way to me! Strike these motions, consul! They are sacrilegious!"

"If you object, Gaius Cassius, then stand to the left of the curule dais" was Trebonius's response.

Fuming, Cassius went to the left, traditionally the direction that was more likely to lose in a division: ill-omened. That day it was. Only a handful of men, including Cassius, Brutus, Lucius Caesar, Lucius Piso, Calvinus and Philippus, stood to the left. But almost the entire House, Antony in its lead, went right.

"I don't think the price of my praetorship is worth it, if I am to bear these godlike honors," said Cassius to Brutus, Porcia and Tertulla over dinner.

"Nor do I!" Porcia declared in ringing tones.

"Give Caesar time, Cassius, please!" Brutus begged. "I don't believe that any of these honors were proposed at his instigation, I really don't. I think he's going to be appalled."

"They shame him," said Tertulla, who hovered perpetually between pleasure at knowing she was Caesar's daughter and pure pain that he never acknowledged her, however informally.

"Of course they were passed at Caesar's instigation!" cried Porcia, flicking Brutus an exasperated glance.

"No, my love, you're wrong," Brutus insisted. "They were proposed by men trying to curry favor with him, and passed by a House that probably does think he wants them. But there are two significant things. One, that Marcus Antonius is up to his eyes in whatever is going on, and the other, that the proposers waited until Caesar definitely couldn't be present."

But it was to be some time before Caesar became aware of the new honors, for the simplest of reasons: the amount of work he had to do was so great that he pushed the minutes of senatorial meetings held in his absence to one side, unread. As it was, he irritated Cleopatra by reading all through her dazzling receptions, eating hardly anything because he was too busy.

"You try to do too much!" she snapped. "Hapd'efan'e tells me you're neglecting to drink your syrup now that it isn't made of fruit juice. Caesar, even if you do dislike it, you *must* drink it! Do you want to fall over in a fit in public?"

"I'll be all right," he said absently, eyes on a paper.

She snatched it away and held a glass of liquid under his nose. "Drink!" she snarled.

The ruler of the world meekly obeyed, but then insisted on going back to his paperwork, lifting his head only when Marcus Tigellius Hermogenes began a series of arias he had composed to the words of Sappho, accompanying himself on a lyre.

"Music is the one thing that can divert his attention from work," Cleopatra whispered to Lucius Caesar.

Lucius squeezed her hand. "At least something does."

The honors went on. Mark Antony's youngest brother, Lucius, became a tribune of the plebs on the tenth day of December, and distinguished himself by proposing to the Plebeian Assembly that Caesar be given the right to recommend half the candidates for every election except that for the consuls—and the right to appoint all the magistrates, including the consuls, while he was away in the East. It went into law at first *contio*, which was unconstitutional, but sanctioned by the consul Trebonius.

"For Caesar, nothing is unconstitutional," said Trebonius, a statement that only men like Cicero, informed of it later, found a little peculiar coming from so stout a Caesarean.

Midway through December, Caesar named the consuls for the year after next—Aulus Hirtius and Gaius Vibius Pansa—and the year after that—Decimus Junius Brutus and Lucius Munatius Plancus. None a man who would support Antony.

Then the Senate appointed Caesar Dictator for the fourth time, though his third term had not yet elapsed.

The tribune of the plebs Lucius Cassius apparently had little knowledge of the law; he put a plebiscite before the Plebeian Assembly that allowed Caesar to appoint new patricians. Quite illegal, as the Patriciate had absolutely nothing to do with the Plebs. Caesar appointed one new patrician, and one only: his great-nephew, Gaius Octavius, busy getting ready to accompany him abroad as his *contubernalis*. Patrician he might now be, but his military rank had not been elevated, as Philippus rather snappishly informed him. Octavius accepted the reprimand with equanimity, more concerned with dissuading his mother from loading him down with comforts and luxuries he now knew branded him a lightweight.

* * *

On the first day of January the new consuls and praetors entered office, and all went well. The night watches for omens were unremarkable, the sacrificial white bulls went to the knife properly drugged, and the feast held in the temple of Jupiter Optimus Maximus atop the Capitol was a good one. Now junior consul, Mark Antony strutted around importantly and managed to ignore Dolabella, smirking in the background because he would be Antony's senior after Caesar left for the East.

One of the duties of the senior consul on New Year's Day was to set the date of the Latin Festival, the feast of Jupiter Latiaris held upon the Alban Mount. Usually it was held in March, just before the start of the campaigning season, but Caesar, who wanted to preside himself, announced that this year it would take place on the Nones of January.

The Julii were the hereditary priests of Alba Longa, a town older by far than the founding of Rome; when the senior consul happened to be a Julian, as this year, he could wear the regalia of the King of Alba Longa to celebrate the Latin Festival. Of course there had been no King of Alba Longa since infant Rome had leveled the town to the ground, for it had never been rebuilt. But it had been founded by Iulus, the son of Aeneas, and the Julii, his direct descendants, had been its kings, who also were its high priests.

When Caesar obtained the clothing of the King of Alba Longa and opened the redolent cedar chest to inspect the robes, he found them in perfect condition. They had last been worn fifteen years ago, when he had been consul for the first time. A very tall man, he had been obliged then to have a new pair of the high, bright scarlet boots made. Now they looked a little warped. Best try them on, he thought, and did so. Walking about in them, he noticed that the pain he had been experiencing in his lower legs for some time magically vanished, and went to see Hapd'efan'e.

"Why didn't I think of that?" the priest-physician asked, sounding chagrined.

"Think of what?"

"Caesar, you have varicose veins, and Roman boots are too short to give the distended blood vessels proper support. These boots lace up tightly to just below the knee. That's why the pain in your legs has eased. You must wear high boots."

"*Edepol!*" Caesar exclaimed, and laughed. "I'll send for my bootmaker at once, but, since my family are the priests of Alba Longa, there's no reason why I can't wear these until I have a few pairs made in ordinary brown. Well done, Hapd'efan'e!"

Off went Caesar to seat himself on the rostra, where he was dealing with complaints relating to the *fiscus*.

Here junior consul Mark Antony, ex–junior consul Trebonius, ex-praetor Lucius Tillius Cimber, ex-praetor Decimus Brutus, and twenty carefully chosen *pedarii* senators came in solemn procession to see him. Six of the junior men each carried a glittering silver tablet about the size of a sheet of paper. Irritated at the interruption, Caesar glanced up with mouth open to banish them, but Antony got in first, going down reverently on one knee.

"Caesar," he hollered, "as your Senate decreed, we present you with six new honors, each inscribed in gold on silver!"

Ooohs and aaahs from the gathering crowd.

Decimus Turullius, new quaestor, came forward and presented his tablet on one knee—the month of Julius.

Caecilius Metellus presented the new tribe, Julia.

Caecilius Buciolanus presented the Luperci Julii.

Marcus Rubrius Ruga presented Caesar's Clemency.

Cassius Parmensis presented the gold curule chair and wreath.

Petronius presented the ivory statue in the parade of gods.

Through all of it, witnessed by the rapidly growing crowd, Caesar sat as if graven from stone, so confounded that he could neither speak nor move, his lips still parted. Finally, when all six tablets had been presented and the group stood around him expectantly, each face beaming with pride at its owner's cleverness, Caesar shut his mouth. Try though he did, he could not manage to rise to his feet, felt the weakness and dizziness of his affliction.

"I cannot accept these," he said, "they're honors that ought not to be paid to a man. Take them away, melt them down and put the metal back where it belongs—in the Treasury."

The delegation's members drew themselves up in outrage.

"You insult us!" Turullius cried.

Ignoring him, Caesar turned to Antony, who looked quite as put out as the rest. "Marcus Antonius, you should know better. As consul with the *fasces*, I am convoking the Senate to meet in the Curia Hostilia in one hour." He beckoned to his syrup slave, took the beaker and drained it. A close thing.

The new Curia Hostilia owned a far less pretentious interior than Pompey's Curia on the Campus Martius, but it was, a peeking Cicero had admitted with a twinge of regret that he wouldn't be sitting there, in exquisite taste. Just simple white marble tiers and curule dais, plastered walls painted white with a few decorative curliques, and a black-and-white tesselated marble floor; the roof, just like the old one, was naked cedar rafters with the bellies of the terra-cotta tiles showing through. Save for age, it was a twin of the old Curia Hostilia, thus no one objected to its having the same name.

Summoned at such short notice, the House was by no means full, but when Caesar entered behind his twenty-four lictors, he counted a comfortable quorum. As it was a court day, all the praetors were there; most of the tribunes of the plebs; a few quaestors besides that worm Turullius; two hundred backbenchers; Dolabella, Calvinus, Lepidus, Lucius Caesar, Torquatus, Piso. It was obvious that word of his rejection of the silver tablets had gotten around, for the buzz when he entered increased rather than diminished. I am getting old indeed, he thought; I am not even in a temper over this, I am just very tired. They're wearing me down.

Caesar distinguished the new pontifex, Brutus, by having him take the prayers, and the new augur, Cassius, by having him take the auspices. Then he moved to the front of the curule dais and stood in his *corona civica* while the House applauded. He waited until his three crowned ex-centurion senators were applauded in turn, then began to speak.

"Honored junior consul, consulars, praetors, aediles, tribunes of the plebs and conscript fathers of the Senate, I have summoned you to inform you that these honors you insist upon showering on me must cease forthwith. It is fitting that the Dictator of Rome should receive *some* honors, but only those honors appropriate for a man. *A man!* An ordinary member of the *gens humana*, neither a king nor a god. Today some of you presented me with honors that infringe our *mos maiorum*, and in a public manner I found extremely distasteful. Our laws are inscribed on bronze, not on silver, and bronze all laws must be. These were silver inscribed in gold, two precious metals with more useful purpose than as law tablets. I ordered them destroyed and the metal returned to the Treasury."

He paused, his eyes meeting Lucius Caesar's. Lucius tilted his head infinitesimally toward Antony, behind Caesar on the dais. His own head nodded: yes, I understand your message.

"Conscript fathers, I give you notice that these ridiculous, sycophantic gestures must stop. I have not asked for them, I do not crave them, and I will not accept them. That is my dictate, and will be obeyed. I will have no decrees passed in this House that may be interpreted as an attempt to crown me King of Rome! That is a title we abrogated when the Republic came into being, and it is a title I abhor. *I have no need to be the King of Rome!* I am Rome's legally appointed Dictator, which is all I need to be."

There was a stir as Quintus Ligarius got to his feet. "If you have no wish to be the King of Rome," he shouted, pointing at Caesar's right leg, "why are you wearing the high scarlet boots of a king?"

Caesar's mouth went thin, two red spots flaring in his cheeks. Admit to this lot that he had varicose veins? Never! "As priest of Jupiter Latiaris, it is my right to wear the priestly boots, and I'll have no false assumptions made on that sort of premise, Ligarius! Are you finished? If so, sit down."

Ligarius subsided, scowling.

"That's all I have to say to you on the subject of honors," he said. "However, to further make my point, to demonstrate to all of you conclusively that I am no more than a Roman man and have no wish to be more than my rank entitles me to be, I hereby dismiss my twenty-four lictors. Kings must have bodyguards, and a curule magistrate's lictors represent the republican equivalent of a bodyguard. Therefore I will go about my official business without them while ever I am within one mile of Rome." He turned to Fabius, sitting with his fellows on the side steps to the right of the curule dais. "Take your men back to the College of Lictors, Fabius. I will notify you when I need you."

Horrified, Fabius put out a hand in protest, let it drop. Caesar's lictors rose and left the chamber in a profound silence.

"To dismiss one's lictors is legal," Caesar said. "It is not the *fasces* or their bearers who empower a curule magistrate. His power resides in the *lex curiata*. As this is a busy day, go about your affairs. Just remember what I have said. Under no possible circumstances will I entertain the thought of ruling Rome as her king. Rex is a word, nothing more. Caesar does not need to be Rex. To be Caesar is enough."

Not all the tribunes of the plebs were bent on sucking up to Caesar. One, Gaius Servilius Casca, was already a member of the Kill Caesar Club, and two others had come under review by the club's founders: Lucius Caesetius Flavus and Gaius Epidius Marullus. However, Trebonius and Decimus Brutus had decided not to invite Flavus and Marullus to join the club, much though they both hated Caesar. They were notorious blabbers, and neither had an ounce of genuine clout with the First Class.

On the day after Caesar let the Senate know how he felt about becoming the King of Rome, Flavus and Marullus just happened to be in the vicinity of the new rostra, which, as Caesar had built it at his own expense, held a bust of the Great Man on a high, hermed pedestal. Though the day was dull and cold, the Forum frequenters were out and about, wandering to see if there was an interesting court case going on inside the Basilica Julia—such a comfort to be under shelter if one was!—eating snacks from the stalls and booths tucked in out-of-the-way corners, hoping that some new orator would decide to mount a vacant set of steps or tribunal and declaim—in other words, an ordinary early January day.

Suddenly Flavus and Marullus started shouting and yelling, making such a fuss that they quickly drew a large crowd.

"Look! Look!" Marullus was screaming, pointing.

"A disgrace! A crime!" Flavus was screaming, pointing.

Both jabbing fingers were leveled at the bust of Caesar, a good one painted to lifelike verisimilitude; around its pale brow and thinning blond hair someone had tied a broad white ribbon, knotted it on the nape of the neck and strayed the two ends over the bust's vestigial shoulders.

"He wants to be the King of Rome!" Marullus shrieked.

"A diadem! A diadem!" Flavus shrieked.

After a great deal more of the same, the two tribunes of the plebs tore the ribbon off the bust and trampled it showily beneath their feet, then ostentatiously ripped it into several pieces.

One day later, the Nones, the Latin Festival was held on the Alban Mount with Caesar officiating, clad in the ancient regalia of the Alban priest-kings, as was his Julian right.

It was a relatively brief affair, over and done with in short enough time for the celebrants to ride out of Rome at dawn and return to Rome by sunset. Riding Toes, Caesar led the procession of magistrates back to the city, where, for the second time, the new young patrician Gaius Octavius had acted as *praefectus urbi* in the absence of the consuls and praetors. For the ordinary people it was a popular occasion; those who lived adjacent to the Alban Mount went there and afterward attended a public feast, while those in Rome contented themselves with lining the Via Appia to watch the magistrates return.

"*Ave, Rex!*" someone called from the roadside crowd as Caesar rode by. "*Ave, Rex! Ave, Rex!*"

Caesar threw back his head and laughed. "No, you have the *cognomen* wrong! I'm Caesar, not Rex!"

Marullus and Flavus spurred their horses down the line from where the tribunes of the plebs rode to where Caesar was; mounts rearing and plunging spectacularly, they started to yell, pointing into the throng.

"Lictors, remove the man who called Caesar a king!" Marullus shouted several times.

When Antony's lictors started to move, Caesar held up his hand to halt them. "Stay where you are," he ordered curtly. "Marullus, Flavus, go back to your places."

"He called you a king! If you don't do something about it, Caesar, then you *want* to be king!" Marullus screamed.

By now the entire parade had come to a stop, horses milling, lictors and magistrates watching fascinated.

"Remove the man and prosecute him!" Flavus was shouting.

"Caesar *wants* to be king!" Marullus was shouting.

"Antonius, have your lictors put Flavus and Marullus where they belong!" Caesar snapped, red kindling in his cheeks.

Antony sat his horse, looking contemplative.

"Do it, Antonius, or tomorrow you'll be a *privatus!*"

"Hear that? Hear that? Caesar *is* a king, he orders the consul around like a servant!" Marullus yelled as Antony's lictors took hold of his horse's bridle and led him back down the line.

"Rex! Rex! Rex! Caesar Rex!" Flavus was howling.

"Call the Senate into session tomorrow at dawn" was Caesar's parting remark to Antony as he reached the Domus Publica.

This time his temper was up.

The prayers and auspices were over in a trice, the applause for the crown winners cut ruthlessly short.

"Lucius Caesetius Flavus, Gaius Epidius Marullus, come out!" he rapped. "Front and center of the floor, *now!*"

The two tribunes of the plebs lifted their buttocks off the tribunician bench in front of the curule dais and marched to face Caesar, chins up, eyes hard.

"I am fed up with being put in the wrong! Do you hear me? Do you understand me?" Caesar thundered. "I am fed up! I will have no more of it! Flavus, Marullus, you disgrace your office!"

"Rex! Rex! Rex! Rex!" they began to bark.

"*Tacete, ineptes!*" Caesar roared.

How he did it, no one ever knew when they thought about it afterward; simply that when Caesar got a certain look on his face and roared in a certain tone, the whole world quailed. He wasn't a king. He was nemesis. All of a sudden every senator started remembering what a dictator could do without needing to be a king. Like flog. Decapitate.

"What has the tribunate of the plebs descended to, when a pair like you think you can behave worse than two scruffy schoolboys?"

Caesar demanded. "If someone ties a white ribbon on my image, then take it off, by all means! That would win my approbation! But to make such a business out of it that a thousand people collect to hear you scream and shout—that is unacceptable conduct for any Roman magistrate, even the most unabashed demagogue who ever called himself a tribune of the plebs! And if some fellow in a crowd makes a smart remark, then let him! A soft answer and a joke turn him off, he's rendered ridiculous! What the pair of you did on the Via Appia was unconscionable—you transformed some *scurra* in the crowd into a circus! What did you want to prosecute him for? High treason? Minor treason? Impiety? Murder? Theft? Embezzlement? Bribery? Extortion? Violence? Inciting violence? Bankruptcy? Witchcraft? Sacrilege? To the best of my knowledge, they are the sum total of crimes under Roman law! It is *not* a crime for a man to come out with a provocative remark! It is *not* a crime for a man to slander other men! It is *not* a crime for a man to calumniate other men! If it were, then Marcus Cicero would be in permanent exile for calling Lucius Piso a sucking whirlpool of greed, among many other things! Along with every other member of this House for calling some other member of this House anything from an eater of feces to a violator of his own children! How dare you blow trivial incidents up into major crimes? How dare you traduce me by making much out of nothing? I'll have an end to it! Hear me? *Do you hear me?* If one single member of this body ever again implies—let alone says outright!—that I want to be King of Rome, let him beware! Rex is a word! It has connotations, but no reality in our Roman sphere! Rex? Rex? If I did want to be your absolute ruler in perpetuity, why should I bother to call myself Rex? Why not plain Caesar? Caesar is a word too! It could as easily mean king as rex does! So beware! As Dictator, I can strip any one of you of your citizenship and your property! I can flog and behead you! I do not need to be Rex! And believe me, conscript fathers, you tempt me! *You tempt me!* That is all. You are dismissed. Go!"

The silence was more thunderous than the sound of that huge voice booming off the rafters, echoing around the walls.

Gaius Helvius Cinna rose from the tribunician bench and went to a place from which he could see both Caesar and the miscreants, who stood shivering in their senatorial shoes.

"Conscript fathers, as president of the College of Tribunes of the Plebs," he said, "I move that Lucius Caesetius Flavus and Gaius Epidius Marullus cease forthwith to be tribunes of the plebs. I further move that they be expelled from the Senate."

The House broke into tumult, fists waving. "Expel! Expel!"

"You can't do this!" cried Lucius Caesetius Flavus Senior, rising to his feet. "My son doesn't deserve this!"

"If you had any sense, Caesetius, you'd disinherit your son for sheer stupidity!" Caesar snapped. "Now go, all of you! Go! Go! I don't want to see your faces again until you can start to behave like responsible Roman men!"

Helvius Cinna promptly marched outside, convened the Plebeian Assembly and enacted the dismissal of Flavus and Marullus from the College of Tribunes of the Plebs and the Senate. He then conducted a brisk election: Lucius Decidius Saxa and Publius Hostilius Saserna became tribunes of the plebs.

"I hope you realize, Cinna," said Caesar gently to Helvius Cinna when the meeting was over, "that today is *feriae*. You'll have to do it all again tomorrow, when the *comitia* can meet. Still, I appreciate the gesture. Come and have a goblet of wine at my house, and tell me about the new poetry."

The "King of Rome" campaign suddenly died as if it had never been. Those who had not heard Caesar explain that there was no reason why "Rex" and "Caesar" couldn't mean the same were apprised of his remark, and swallowed convulsively. As Cicero said to Atticus (they were still getting nowhere with the Buthrotum immigrants), the trouble was that people tended to forget what kind of man Caesar actually was until he lost his temper.

Perhaps as a result of that memorable meeting, on the Kalends of February the House met under Mark Antony's auspices, and voted Gaius Julius Caesar the Dictator Perpetuus. Dictator for life. No one, from Brutus and Cassius to Decimus Brutus and Trebonius, had the courage to stand to the left of the curule dais when the division was called. The decree passed unanimously.

Twenty-one men now belonged to the Kill Caesar Club: Gaius Trebonius, Decimus Brutus, Staius Murcus, Tillius Cimber, Minucius Basilus, Decimus Turullius, Quintus Ligarius, Antistius Labeo, the brothers Servilius Casca, the brothers Caecilius, Popillius Liguriensis, Petronius, Pontius Aquila, Rubrius Ruga, Otacilius Naso, Caesennius Lento, Cassius Parmensis, Spurius Maelius, and Servius Sulpicius Galba. Apart from his loathing of Caesar, Spurius Maelius had given a peculiar, if logical, reason for joining the club. Four hundred years earlier, his ancestor, also named Spurius Maelius, had tried to make himself King of Rome; to kill Caesar was a way to remove the lingering odium from his family, which hadn't prospered since. The acquisition of Galba had delighted the club's founders, for he was patrician, an ex-praetor, and had enormous clout. During the early period of Caesar's Gallic War, Galba had conducted a campaign in the high Alps and bungled it so badly that Caesar quickly dispensed with his services; Galba was, besides, one of Caesar's cuckolds.

Six of the members could claim some sort of distinction, but unfortunately the rest were, as Trebonius said despondently to Decimus Brutus, a pathetic bunch of would-bes and has-beens.

"About the best one can say is that they've all been mighty close-lipped about it—I haven't heard a whisper that the Kill Caesar Club exists."

"Nor I," said Decimus Brutus. "If we could only get two more members with Galba's clout, I'd call the club big enough. Once it gets over twenty-three, the business would turn into a free-for-all worse than the fight for the October Horse's head."

"The business bears some similarity to the October Horse," Trebonius said reflectively. "When you think about it, that's what we aim to do, isn't it? Kill the best war horse Rome owns."

"I concede your point. Caesar's in a class all by himself, no one can hope to eclipse him. If hope existed, there would be no need to kill him. Though Antonius has grand delusions—pah! We should kill Antonius as well, Trebonius."

"I don't agree," Trebonius said. "If we want to live and prosper, we have to make it *scream* patriotism! Kill even one of Caesar's minions, and we stand as rebels and outlaws."

"Dolabella will be there, and he's a man you can deal with," Decimus Brutus said. "Antonius is a wolfshead."

Decimus Brutus's steward knocked on the study door.

"*Domine*, Gaius Cassius is asking to see you."

The two exchanged an uneasy glance.

"Send him in, Bocchus."

Cassius entered rather hesitantly, which seemed odd; he was ordinarily anything but hesitant.

"I'm not intruding?" he asked, sniffing something in the air.

"No, no," said Decimus Brutus, drawing up a third chair. "A little wine? Some refreshments?"

Cassius sat with a thump, linked his hands and twisted them. "Thank you, I need nothing."

A silence fell that was curiously difficult to break; when finally it did, it was Cassius who spoke.

"What do you think of our dictator for life?" he asked.

"That we've made a rod for our own backs," said Trebonius.

"That we'll never be free again," said Decimus Brutus.

"My sentiments exactly. And those of Marcus Brutus, though he doesn't believe there's a thing we can do about it."

"Whereas you believe there is, Cassius?" Trebonius asked.

"If I had my way, I'd kill him!" said Cassius. He lifted his amberish brown eyes to Trebonius's face and saw things in its dismal planes that made him catch his breath. "Yes, I'd kill this millstone around our necks."

"Kill him how?" Decimus Brutus asked, as if puzzled.

"I don't—I don't—I don't know," stammered Cassius. "It's a new thought, you understand. Until we all voted to make him the dictator for life, I suppose I had reconciled myself to a number of years of him, but he's *indestructible!* He'll still be attending meetings of the House when he's ninety—his health is fantastic and that mind will never let go." As he spoke, Cassius's voice grew stronger; the two pairs of light eyes staring intently at him were echoing everything his roiling thoughts had been turning over. He understood that he was among friends, and visibly relaxed. "Am I the only one?" he asked.

"By no means," said Trebonius. "In fact, join the club."

"Club?"

"The Kill Caesar Club. We called it that because, if its existence became known, we could explain it away as a joke name for a group of men who don't like Caesar, and have clubbed together to kill him politically," Trebonius said. "So far it contains twenty-one members. Are you interested in joining?"

Cassius made up his mind with the same speed he had at that meeting along the Bilechas River when he had decided to abandon Marcus Crassus to his fate and gallop for Syria. "Count me in," he said, and sat back. "Now I'd appreciate some wine."

Nothing loath, the two founders proceeded to acquaint Cassius with the club, its duration, its aims, why they had resolved to kill the October Horse. Cassius listened eagerly until he was told the names of the members.

"A paltry lot," he said flatly.

"You're right," said Decimus, "but they lend us one important thing—bulk. It could be a political alliance—there were never many *boni*, for example. At least they're all senators, and there are too many to indicate a feel-in-the-dark conspiracy. Conspiracy is the one word we don't want attached to our club."

Trebonius took over. "Your participation is a bonus we had despaired of earning, Cassius, because you have real clout. But even a Cassius and a patrician Sulpicius Galba may not be enough to imbue the deed with the—the *heroism* it must have. I mean, we're tyrannicides, not murderers! That's how we must look when the deed is done, when it's over. We have to be able to march down to the rostra and declare to the whole of Rome that we've lifted the curse of tyranny from our beloved homeland, that we have no apologies to make and expect no retaliations. Men who free their homeland from a tyrant should be lauded. Rome's rid herself of tyrants before, and the men who did it have passed down as Rome's greatest men ever. Brutus, who banished the last king and executed his own sons when they tried to bring the monarchy back! Servilius Ahala, who killed Spurius Maelius when he tried to make himself King of Rome—"

"Brutus!" Cassius cried, interrupting. "*Brutus!* Now that Cato is dead, we have to have Brutus in the club! The direct descendant of the first Brutus, and, through his mother, the heir of Servilius Ahala as well! If we can persuade Brutus to join us, we're free and clear—no one would dream of prosecuting us."

Decimus Brutus stiffened, eyes flashing cold fire. "I am a direct descendant of the first Brutus too—do you think we haven't already thought of that?" he demanded.

"Yes, but you're not connected to Servilius Ahala," Trebonius said. "Marcus Brutus outranks you, Decimus, and there's no use getting angry about it. He's the richest man in Rome, so his clout is colossal, he's a Brutus and a patrician Servilius—Cassius, we have to have him! Then we'll have two Brutuses, we can't fail!"

"All right, I see that," Decimus said, anger dying. "Yet can we get him, Cassius? I admit I don't know him very well, but what I do know of him suggests he wouldn't be a party to tyrannicide. He's so docile, so tame, so *anemic*."

"You're correct, he's those and more," Cassius said gloomily. "His mother rules him—" He stopped, brightening. "Until, that is, he married Porcia. Oh, the fights! There's no doubt that Brutus has more gumption since he married Porcia. And the Dictator Perpetuus decree horrified him. I'll work on him, persuade him that it's his moral and ethical duty as a Junius Brutus and a Servilius Ahala to rid Rome of her present tyrant."

"Do we dare approach him?" Decimus Brutus asked warily. "He might run straight to Caesar."

Cassius looked astonished. "Brutus? No, never! Even if he decides not to join us, I'd stake my life on his silence."

"You will be," said Decimus Brutus. "You will be."

* * *

When the Dictator Perpetuus convened the Centuries on the Campus Martius to "elect" Publius Cornelius Dolabella the senior consul in Caesar's absence, the voting went swiftly and smoothly; there was no reason why it should not, since there was only one candidate, but the vote of each Century still had to be counted, at least right through the First Class and as far into the Second Class as necessary to obtain a majority; the Centuries were very heavily weighted in favor of the First Class, so in an "election" like today's, no one from the Third, Fourth or Fifth Classes even bothered to turn up.

Both Caesar and Mark Antony attended, Caesar as supervising magistrate, Antony in his function as augur. It took the junior consul an inordinately long time to complete his auspication; the first sheep was rejected as unclean, the second had too few teeth. Only when he came to the third did he decide it met his purposes, which were to inspect the victim's liver according to a strict protocol both written down and on display as a three-dimensional bronze model. There was no mystical element in Rome's auguries, hence no need to find mystical men to act as augurs.

Impatient as always, Caesar ordered the voting to proceed while Antony fussed and probed.

"What's the matter?" he asked, coming to Antony's side.

"The liver. It looks terrible."

Caesar looked, turned it over with a stylus, counted the lobes and verified their shapes. "It's perfect, Antonius. As Pontifex Maximus and a fellow augur, I declare the omens auspicious."

Shrugging, Antony walked away as the augural acolytes began to clean up, and stood staring into the distance. A smile playing about his lips, Caesar went back to supervising.

"Don't sulk, Antonius," he said. "It was a good try."

About half the votes of the necessary ninety-seven Centuries had been registered when Antony suddenly jumped and squawked, then strode to the *saepta* side of the supervising tower, where he could see the long lines of white-clad figures filing to the baskets.

"A fireball! The omens are inauspicious!" he bellowed in his stentorian voice. "As official augur on this occasion, I order the Centuries to go home!"

It was brilliantly done. Caught unprepared, Caesar hadn't time to start enquiring who else had seen this evanescent meteor before the Centuries, full of men who would rather be elsewhere, began to leave in a hurry.

Dolabella came running from his constant soliciting of the Centuries lined up to vote, his face purple with rage. "*Cunnus!*" he spat at the grinning Antony.

"You go too far, Antonius," Caesar said, mouth thin.

"I saw a fireball," Antony maintained stubbornly. "On my left, low on the horizon."

"I presume that this is your way of informing me that there is no point in holding another election? That it too will fail?"

"Caesar, I'm simply telling you what I saw."

"You're an incontinent fool, Antonius. There are other ways," Caesar said, turned on his heel and walked down the tower steps.

"Fight, you prick!" Dolabella yelled, shaping up.

"Lictors, restrain him," Antony barked, following Caesar.

Cicero scuttled up importantly, eyes sparkling. "That was so stupid, Marcus Antonius," he announced. "You acted illegally. You should have watched the skies as consul, not as augur. Augurs must be formally commissioned to watch the skies, consuls not."

"Thank you, Cicero, for telling Antonius the correct way to screw up future elections!" Caesar snapped. "I would remind you that Publius Clodius made it illegal for consuls to watch the skies without commission too. Before you pontificate, look up the laws passed while you were in exile."

Cicero sniffed and marched off, mortified.

"I doubt," said Caesar to Antony, "that you'll have the gall to block Dolabella's appointment as suffect consul."

"No, I won't do that," Antony said agreeably. "As a suffect consul, he can't outrank me."

"Antonius, Antonius, your law is as bad as your arithmetic! Of course he can, if the consul he replaces is the senior consul. Why do you think I went to the trouble of having a suffect consul appointed for a few hours when Fabius Maximus, the *senior* consul, died on the last day of last December? Law is not only what is written on the tablets, it is also valid on uncontested precedents. And I set the precedent a little over a month ago. Neither you nor anybody else objected. You may think you caught me out today, but, as you now know, I am always one step ahead of you." Caesar smiled sweetly and went to join Lucius Caesar, glaring fiercely at Antony.

"What can we do with my nephew?" Lucius asked in despair.

"In my absence? Sit on him, Lucius. He's actually well contained, if you think about it. Dolabella's dislike for him won't diminish after today, will it? Calvinus as Master of the Horse, the Treasury completely in the hands of Balbus Major and Oppius—yes, Antonius is well contained."

* * *

Quite aware that he was effectively muzzled, Antony stalked home in a towering rage. It wasn't fair, it wasn't right! The cunning old fox was master of every trick in the political and legal manuals, plus a few tricks he'd invented. Soon every last senator would be compelled to swear a mortal oath to uphold all of Caesar's laws and dictates in his absence. It would be administered under the open sky of the temple of Semo Sancus Dius Fidius, and as Pontifex Maximus the old boy had gotten around things like holding a stone in the hand to negate the oath—Caesar had been around too long to be fooled by *anything.*

Trebonius. I need to talk to Gaius Trebonius. Not Decimus Brutus, but Trebonius. Somewhere very private.

He made contact after the Senate met to appoint Dolabella the suffect consul after Caesar stepped down. Suffect, but senior.

"My horse has arrived from Spain. Want to take a walk out to the Campus Lanatarius and see him?" Antony asked jovially.

"Certainly," said Trebonius.

"When?"

"There's no time like the present, Antonius."

"Where's Decimus Brutus?"

"Keeping Gaius Cassius company."

"That's an odd friendship."

"Not these days."

They walked on in silence until they passed through the Capena Gate, heading for the area which contained Rome's stables, as well as the stockyards and slaughterhouses.

The day was cold, a bitter wind blowing; inside the Servian Walls they hadn't felt it as much, but once beyond the city, their teeth began to chatter.

"Here's a nice little tavern," said Antony. "Clemency can wait, I need wine and a warm fire."

"Clemency?"

"My new Public Horse. After all, I am the *flamen* of the new cult of Caesar's Clemency, Trebonius."

"Oh, he was angry when we gave him the silver tablets!"

"Don't remind me. The first time I ever met him, he kicked my arse so hard I couldn't sit down for a *nundinum.*"

The few occupants of the tavern looked at the newcomers and gaped; never in all the place's history had two men in purple-bordered togas walked through the door! The landlord rushed to escort them to his best table, evicting three merchants who were too awed to protest, then hunted for his best amphora of wine, put bowls of pickled onions and plump olives down for them to munch.

"We'll be safe here, this lot's as Latin as Quirinus," said Trebonius in Greek. He sipped experimentally at his beaker of wine, looked surprised, and waved his approval at the beaming landlord. "What's on your mind, Antonius?"

"Your little plot. Time's running out. How's it going?"

"Well in one way, not so well in another. There are enough of us at twenty-two, but we lack a figurehead, which is a worry. There's no point in doing this particular deed if we can't survive it in an odor of sanctity. We're tyrannicides, not murderers," said Trebonius, uttering his favorite sentence. "However, Gaius Cassius has joined us, and he's going to try to persuade Marcus Brutus to be the figurehead."

"*Edepol!*" Antony exclaimed. "He'd be all of that."

"I'm not sanguine about Cassius's chances of success."

"How about," said Antony, pulling layers off an onion, "some additional guarantees in case you don't get your figurehead?"

"Guarantees?" Trebonius asked, looking alert.

"Don't forget I'll be consul—and don't think for a moment that Dolabella's going to be a problem, because I won't let him. If You-know-who is dead, he'll lie down, roll over, and present me with his belly," said Antony. "What I'm proposing is to smooth things over for you with the Senate and People. My brother Gaius is a praetor and my brother Lucius is a tribune of the plebs. I'm happy to guarantee that none of the participants will be brought to trial, that none will be deprived of his magistracy, province, estates or entitlements. Don't forget that I'm Caesar's heir. *I'll* control the legions, who love me a great deal more than they do Lepidus or Calvinus or Dolabella. No one will dare to go against me in the Senate or the Assemblies."

The ugly, attractive face turned feral. "I'm not nearly as big a fool as Caesar deems me, Trebonius. If he's killed, why not kill me—and Uncle Lucius—and Calvinus—and Pedius? My life is in jeopardy too. So I'll make a bargain with you—with you, and you alone! It's your scheme, and you're the one who'll hold the rest together. What I'm saying to you is between you and me, it's not for dissemination to the others. You make sure that I'm not a target and I'll make sure that no one suffers for the deed."

Moist grey eyes reflective, Trebonius sat and thought. He was being made an offer too good to spurn. Antonius was an administrative sloth, not a maniac for work like Caesar. He'd be content to let Rome slide back into her old ways as long as he could strut around calling himself the First Man in Rome—and as long as he had Caesar's staggering fortune to spend.

"It's a deal," said Gaius Trebonius. "Our secret, Antonius. What the rest don't know won't hurt them."

"That goes for Decimus too? I remember him from Clodius Club days, and he's maybe not as stable as most people think."

"I won't tell Decimus, you have my oath on it."

Early in February, Caesar got his *casus belli*. News came from Syria that Antistius Vetus, sent to replace Cornificius, had blockaded Bassus inside Apameia thinking it would be a short, swift siege. But Bassus had fortified his Syrian "capital" very efficiently, so the siege became protracted. Worse than that, Bassus had sent to King Orodes of the Parthians for help, and help had arrived; a Parthian army under Prince Pacorus had just invaded Syria. The whole of the northern end of the province was being overrun, and Antistius Vetus was penned up in Antioch.

Since no one could now possibly argue that Syria ought not to be defended or the Parthians contested, Caesar rifled the Treasury for a great deal more than he had originally intended, and sent the war chest to Brundisium to await his arrival; for safety, it was stored in the vaults of his banker Gaius Oppius. He issued orders that all the legions were to assemble in Macedonia as fast as the transports could ferry them there from Brundisium; his cavalry were shipped from Ancona, the closest port to Ravenna, where they were camped. Legates and staff were told to get to Macedonia yesterday, and he informed the House that he would step down as consul on the Ides of March.

A startled Gaius Octavius suddenly found himself served a curt notice from Publius Ventidius to go to Brundisium, where he was to embark at the end of February with Agrippa and Salvidienus Rufus. The order was a welcome one, for his mother was weeping and wailing that she would never see her beloved only son again, and Philippus was, thanks to her dramatics, unusually testy. Deliberately abandoning two-thirds of what she had put together for him, he hired three gigs and two carts with a view to setting off down the Via Latina immediately. Freedom! Adventure! *Caesar!*

Who managed to see him for a very brief farewell the evening before he departed.

"I expect you to continue your studies, Octavius, because I don't think your destiny is a military one," said the Great Man, who seemed tired, unusually harassed.

"I will, Caesar, I will. I'm taking Marcus Epidius and Arius of Alexandria to polish my rhetoric and knowledge of the law, and Apollodorus of Pergamum to keep me struggling with my Greek." He pulled a face. "It is improving a little, but no matter how hard I try, I still can't think in it."

"Apollodorus is an old man," said Caesar, frowning.

"Yes, but he assures me that he's fit enough to travel."

"Then take him. And start educating Marcus Agrippa. That's one young man I'm anxious to see capable of a public career as well as a military one. Has Philippus arranged for you to stay with someone in Brundisium? The inns will be overflowing."

"Yes, with his friend Aulus Plautius."

Caesar laughed, looked suddenly boyish. "How convenient! You can keep an eye on the war chest, young Octavius."

"The war chest?"

"It takes many millions of sesterces to keep an army eating, marching and fighting," Caesar said gravely. "A prudent general takes his funds with him when he goes—if he has to send back to Rome for more money, the Senate can prove very difficult. So my war chest of many millions of sesterces is sitting in Oppius's vaults right next door to Aulus Plautius's house."

"I'll keep an eye on the war chest, Caesar, I promise."

A quick handshake, a light kiss on the cheek, and Caesar was gone. Octavius stood staring at the empty doorway with an ache in his heart he couldn't define.

One more little King of Rome ploy, thought Mark Antony on the day before the festival of the Lupercalia. This year three teams would participate, with Antony leading the Luperci Julii.

The Lupercalia was one of the oldest and most beloved feast days Rome owned, its archaic rituals fraught with sexual overtones that the prudish segment of the Roman upper classes preferred not to see.

In the cliff on the corner of the Palatine Mount that faced the end of the Circus Maximus and the Forum Boarium was a small cave and spring called the Lupercal. Here, adjacent to the shrine of the Genius Loci and under an aged oak tree (though in her time it had been a fig tree), the she-wolf had suckled the abandoned twins Romulus and Remus. Romulus had gone on to found the original city on the Palatine, and executed his brother for some peculiar treason described as "jumping over the walls." One of Romulus's oval thatched huts was still preserved on the Palatine, just as the people of Rome still reverenced the Lupercal cave and prayed to Rome's spirit, the Genius Loci.

It had all happened over six hundred years ago, but it continued to live, never more so than on the feast of Lupercalia.

The men of the three colleges of *luperci* met at the cave, and there outside it, all stark naked, killed sufficient billy goats and one male dog. The three prefects of Luperci Julii, Fabii and Quinctilii supervised their teams as they cut the victims' throats, then stood while the bloody knives were wiped across their foreheads, roaring with obligatory crazy laughter. Neither of the other two prefects laughed as loudly or as crazily as Mark Antony, blinking the blood out of his eyes until the members of his team cleaned the blood away with hanks of wool dipped in milk. The goats and dog were skinned and the gory hides hacked into strips which all the *luperci* then wrapped around their loins, making sure that a section of this gruesome drape was long enough to use as a flail.

Few of the many thousands who came to Lupercalia were able to see this part of the ceremony, between the piers of houses above and the roofs of temples and shrines below; the Palatine had become too built up. Once the *luperci* were dressed, they offered little salt cakes called *mola salsa* to the faceless deities who safeguarded the People of Rome. The cakes were made by the Vestal Virgins from the first ears of the last Latin harvest, and constituted the real sacrifice; the goats and dog were killed to provide *luperci* apparel, albeit ritually. After which the three dozen fit, athletic men lay on the ground and ate a "feast" washed down by watered wine—a sparse meal, actually, for as soon as it concluded the *luperci* commenced a run over two miles long.

With Antony in their lead, they came down the Steps of Cacus from the Lupercal to plough into the huge throng below, laughing as they grasped the long pieces of their drapes and whipped them about. A path was cleared for them; they began their run up the Circus Maximus side of the Palatine, around the corner into the wide avenue of the Via Triumphalis, down to the swamps of the Palus Ceroliae, then up the hill to the Velia at the top of the Forum Romanum, down the Forum to the rostra on the Sacra Via, then ended by backtracking a short distance to Rome's first temple, the tiny old Regia. Every foot of the way, the run was made more difficult because the path through the crowd was barely wide enough to give one man passage at a time, and hordes of people dashed across it constantly, presenting themselves to be flailed.

There was solemn purpose in the flail; whoever it struck was assured of procreating, so those who despaired of having children— men as well as women—implored to be let through the crush so that one of the *luperci* would lash them with his bloody whip. To Antony it was a simple fact of life; Fulvia's mother, Sempronia the daughter of Gaius Gracchus, had reached thirty-nine years of age without conceiving. Not knowing what else was left to do, she went to the Lupercalia and was struck. Nine months later she gave birth to Fulvia, her only child. So Antony swished and lashed his flail generously despite the additional labor it involved, roaring with laughter, pausing to drink water some kind soul in the press offered, thoroughly enjoying himself.

He provided the crowd with more than this, however; as soon as he came into sight people screamed and swooned deliriously, for alone among the *luperci* he had made no attempt to cover his genitalia with the piece of hide; the most formidable penis and the largest scrotum in Rome were there for all to see, a treat in itself. Everybody loved it! Oh, oh, oh, strike me! *Strike me!*

Nearing the finish of the run, the *luperci* streamed down the hill to the lower Forum with Antony still in the lead; ahead, sitting on his curule chair atop the rostra, was Caesar Dictator, for once not immersed in paperwork. He too was laughing, making jokes and exchanging pleasantries with the people thronging the whole area. When he saw Antony he made some remark—directed at Antony's exposed genitals, it was obvious—that had men and women falling on the ground in mirth. Witty *mentula*, Caesar, no one could deny it. Well, Caesar, take this flail!

As he reached the bottom of the rostra Antony stretched out his left hand, took something from a hand in the crowd; suddenly he leaped up the steps and was behind Caesar, was tying a white ribbon around Caesar's head, already crowned with oak leaves. Caesar acted like lightning. The ribbon came off without marring the oak leaves, and on his feet, the diadem in his right hand, held on high, he cried out in a huge voice:

"Jupiter Optimus Maximus is the only king in Rome!"

The crowd began to cheer deafeningly, but he held up both his hands to hush them.

"*Quiris*," he said to a young, togate man below him, "take this to the temple of Jupiter Optimus Maximus and lay it at the base of the Great God's statue as a gift from Caesar."

The people cheered again as the young man, clearly overcome at the honor, ascended the rostra to accept the diadem. Caesar smiled at him, said a few words to him that no one could hear, then, dazed and uplifted, the *Quiris* descended and began the walk up the Clivus Capitolinus to the temple.

"You haven't finished your run yet, Antonius," Caesar said to

Antony, standing with chest heaving and a slight erection that had women whimpering. "Do you want to be the last man at the Regia? After you've had a bath and covered yourself, you have another job to do. Convene the Senate for dawn tomorrow in the Curia Hostilia."

The Senate met, shivering in dread, to find Caesar looking his usual self.

"Let it be inscribed on bronze," he said levelly, "that on the day of the Lupercalia in the year of the consulship of Gaius Julius Caesar and Marcus Antonius, the consul Marcus Antonius did offer Caesar a diadem, and that Caesar did refuse it publicly, to great applause from the people."

"Well played, Caesar!" said Antony heartily as the House went off about other business. "Now the whole of Rome has seen you refuse to wear a diadem. Admit that I've performed a great service for you."

"Kindly leave your philanthropy at that, Antonius. Otherwise *one* of your heads might part company from your body. My problem is, which head holds your thinking apparatus?"

Twenty-two was not a very large number, but getting twenty-two men together under one roof for a meeting of the Kill Caesar Club was depressingly difficult. None of the members—they did not think of themselves as conspirators—had a big enough dining room to accommodate so many diners, and it was too wintry for chats in a peristyle or public garden. Guilt and apprehension contributed to their reluctance to be seen together, even before a meeting of the Senate.

Had Gaius Trebonius not been a distinguished tribune of the plebs in his day and maintained an interest above and beyond the normal in the history of the Plebs, the club may well have foundered for the lack of a safe place to meet. Luckily Trebonius was archiving the records of the Plebs, which were stored under the temple of Ceres on the Aventine Mount. Here, in what was held to be Rome's most beautiful temple, the club could meet unnoticed after dark, provided that said meetings were not held frequently enough to make a nosy female curious as to where her spouse or son or son-in-law was going.

Like most temples, behind its exquisite façade of columns on all four sides, Ceres was a windowless building with close-fitting double bronze doors; once they were shut, no lights showed to indicate that anyone was inside. The *cella* was huge, dominated by a twenty-foot-high statue of the goddess, arms full of sheaves of emmer wheat, clad in a gloriously painted robe patterned in summer's beauties from roses to pansies and violets. Her golden hair was crowned by a wreath of flowers, cornucopias overflowing with fruits clustered at her feet. However, the most striking feature of the temple was a gigantic mural depicting a priapic Pluto carrying Proserpina off to rape and exile in Hades, while a tearful, disheveled Ceres wandered a sere, blasted winter landscape searching vainly for her beloved daughter.

All the members came on the night that fell two days after Caesar's dictate that his rejection of the diadem be recorded on a bronze tablet. They were edgy and irritable, some to the point of mild panic; telling over their faces, Trebonius wondered how he was ever going to keep them together.

Cassius charged into speech. "In less than a month, Caesar will be gone," he said, "and so far I've not seen a particle of evidence that any one of you is really serious about this business. It's all very well to talk! What we need is action!"

"Are *you* getting anywhere with Marcus Brutus?" Staius Murcus asked waspishly. "There's more at stake than action, Cassius! I'm supposed to have left for Syria already, and our master is looking at me sideways because I'm still in Rome. My friend Cimber can say the same."

Cassius's touchiness was a direct consequence of his failure with Brutus; between his extraordinary passion for Porcia and the war that Porcia and Servilia were pursuing relentlessly, Brutus had time for so little else that even his cherished but illicit commercial activities were suffering.

"Give me another *nundinum*," Cassius said curtly. "If that doesn't do it, count him out. But that's not what's worrying me. Killing Caesar isn't going far enough. We have to kill Antonius and Dolabella as well. Also Calvinus."

"Do that," Trebonius said calmly, "and we'll be declared *nefas* and sent into permanent exile without a sestertius—if we keep our heads. Civil war isn't possible because there are no legions in Italian Gaul for Decimus to use, and every legion camped between Capua and Brundisium is on the move to Macedonia. This isn't a conspiracy to overthrow Rome's government, it's a club to rid Rome of a tyrant. As long as we confine ourselves to Caesar, we can claim that we acted rightly, within the law and in keeping with the *mos maiorum*. Kill the consuls and we're *nefas*, make no mistake."

Marcus Rubrius Ruga was a nonentity of a family that had produced a governor of Macedonia unlucky enough to have to cope with a young Cato; of morals, ethics and principles he had none. "Why," he asked now, "are we going through all this? Why don't we simply waylay Caesar in secret, kill him, and never tell?"

The silence hung like a pall until Trebonius spoke. "We are honorable men, Marcus Rubrius, that's why. Where's the honor in a simple murder? To do it and not admit to it? No! Never!"

The growls of agreement that erupted from every throat had Rubrius Ruga shrinking into a dark corner.

"I think Cassius has a point," said Decimus Brutus with a glance of contempt for Rubrius Ruga. "Antonius and Dolabella will come after us—they're too attached to Caesar not to."

"Oh, come, Decimus, how can you say that of Antonius? He pecks at Caesar remorselessly," Trebonius objected.

"For his own ends, Gaius, not our ends. Don't forget that he swore an oath to Fulvia on his ancestor Hercules that he'd never touch Caesar," Decimus countered. "Which makes him doubly dangerous. If we kill Caesar and leave Antonius alive, he'll start to wonder when his turn will come."

"Decimus is right," Cassius said strongly.

Trebonius sighed. "Go home, all of you. We'll meet here again in one *nundinum*—hoping, Cassius, that you bring Marcus Brutus with you. Concentrate on that, not on a bloodbath that would see no one left to sit on the curule dais, and Rome plunged into utter chaos."

Since he held the key, Trebonius waited until the others had departed, some in groups, some singly, then went around snuffing the lamps, the last one in his hand. It's doomed, he thought. It's doomed. They sit there listening, hopping and leaping at the slightest noise, they offer not one word of encouragement, they have no opinions worth listening to—sheep. Baa, baa, baa. Even men like Cimber, Aquila, Galba, Basilus. Sheep. How can twenty-two sheep kill a lion like Caesar?

The next morning Cassius went around the corner to Brutus's house and marched him into his study, where he bolted the door and stood glaring at the stupefied Brutus.

"Sit down, brother-in-law," he said.

Brutus sat. "What is it, Gaius? You look so strange."

"As well I might, given Rome's condition! Brutus, when is it going to occur to you that Caesar is already the King of Rome?"

The round shoulders slumped; Brutus looked down at his hands and sighed. "It has occurred to me, of course it has occurred to me. He was right when he said that 'rex' is just a word."

"So what are you going to do about it?"

"Do about it?"

"Yes, do about it! Brutus, for the sake of your illustrious ancestors, wake up!" Cassius cried. "There's a reason why Rome at this very moment owns a man descended from the first Brutus and Servilius Ahala both! Why are you so blind to your duty?"

The dark eyes grew round. "Duty?"

"Duty, duty, *duty!* It's your duty to kill Caesar."

Jaw dropped, face a mask of terror, Brutus gaped. "My duty to kill Caesar? *Caesar?*"

"Can you do nothing other than make what I say into questions? If Caesar doesn't die, Rome is never going to be a republic again—he's already its king, he's already established a monarchy! If he's let continue to live, he'll choose an heir within his lifetime, and the dictatorship will pass to his heir. So there are some of us determined to kill Caesar Rex. Including me."

"Cassius, no!"

"Cassius, yes! The other Brutus, Decimus. Gaius Trebonius. Cimber. Staius Murcus. Galba. Pontius Aquila. Twenty-two of us, Brutus! We need you to make it twenty-three."

"Jupiter, Jupiter! I can't, Cassius! I can't!"

"Of course you can!" a voice boomed. Porcia strode in from the colonnade door, face and eyes alight. "Cassius, it is the only thing to do! And Brutus *will* make it twenty-three."

The two men stared at her, Brutus confounded, Cassius in a stew of apprehension. Why hadn't he remembered the colonnade?

"Porcia, swear on your father's body that you won't say one word about this to anyone!" Cassius cried.

"I swear it gladly! I'm not stupid, Cassius, I know how dangerous it is. Oh, but it's a right act! Kill the king and bring back Cato's beloved Republic! And who better to do the deed than my Brutus?" She began to stride up and down, shivering with joy. "Yes, a right act! Oh, to think I can help to avenge my father, bring back his Republic!"

Brutus found words. "Porcia, you know that Cato wouldn't approve—would *never* approve! Murder? Cato, condone murder? It is not a right act! Through all the years that Cato opposed Caesar, never once did he contemplate murder! It would—it would denigrate him, destroy the memory of him as liberty's champion!"

"You're wrong, wrong, wrong!" she shouted fiercely, coming to loom over him like a warrior, eyes blazing. "Are you craven, Brutus? Of course my father would approve! When Cato was alive, Caesar was a threat to the Republic, not its executioner! But now Caesar is its executioner! Cato would think as I think, as Cassius and all good men must think!"

Brutus clapped his hands over his ears and fled the room.

"Don't worry, I'll push him to it," Porcia said to Cassius. "By the time I finish with him, he'll do his duty." Her lips thinned, she stood frowning. "I know exactly how to do it, I really do. Brutus is a thinker. He'll have to be hunted into doing, he can't be given a moment to think. What I have to do is make him more afraid *not* to do it than do it. Hah!" she trumpeted, and walked out, leaving Cassius standing fascinated.

"She's Cato's image," he breathed.

"What on earth is going on?" Servilia demanded the next day. "Look at it! Disgraceful!"

The bust of the first Brutus, archaically bearded, wooden of expression, was covered with a graffito: BRUTUS, WHY HAVE YOU FORGOTTEN ME? I BANISHED ROME'S LAST KING!

Pen in hand, Brutus emerged from his study prepared for the hundredth time to make peace between his wife and his mother, to find no sign of the one and the other indignant for an unrelated reason. Oh, Jupiter!

"Paint! *Paint!*" said Servilia wrathfully. "It will take a bucket of turpentine to remove it, and the proper paint will come off too! Who did this? And what does it mean, 'why have you forgotten me?' Ditus! Ditus!" she called, marching away.

But that was only the beginning. When Brutus went to the urban praetor's tribunal in the Forum accompanied by a host of clients, he found it daubed with graffiti too: BRUTUS, WHY DO YOU SLEEP? BRUTUS, WHY ARE YOU FAILING ROME? BRUTUS, WHAT SHOULD YOUR FIRST EDICT BE? BRUTUS, WHERE IS YOUR HONOR? BRUTUS, WAKE UP!

The statue of the first Brutus that stood next to the statues of the kings of Rome bore the words BRUTUS, WHY HAVE YOU FORGOTTEN ME? I BANISHED ROME'S LAST KING! And the statue of Servilius Ahala, close by, said BRUTUS, DON'T YOU REMEMBER ME? I KILLED MAELIUS WHEN HE TRIED TO BE KING!

The stall in the general marketplace which sold turpentine ran out of it; Brutus had to send servants all over Rome to buy up turpentine, its price suddenly soaring.

He was terrified, mostly because he was sure that Caesar, who noticed everything, would notice those graffiti and query their purpose, which to Brutus's appalled eyes was glaringly apparent: he was being urged to kill the Dictator Perpetuus.

And at dawn on the following day when Epaphroditus let in his clients, not only was the original graffito back on the faded, ruined bust of the first Brutus, but his own bust now said STRIKE HIM DOWN, BRUTUS! all over it, and the bust of Servilius Ahala said I KILLED MAELIUS! AM I THE ONLY PATRIOT IN THIS HOUSE? Neatly printed across a tesselated panel on the atrium wall was CALL YOURSELF BRUTUS? UNTIL YOU STRIKE, YOU DO NOT DESERVE THAT ILLUSTRIOUS, IMMORTAL NAME!

Servilia was screeching and stamping around, Porcia was in fits of wild laughter, the clients were huddled bewildered in the atrium, and poor Brutus felt as if some dreadful *lemur* had escaped from the underworld to haunt him into madness.

Not to mention Porcia's perpetual nagging. Instead of the sweet bliss of her body against his in their bed, he lay next to a yapping, harping termagant who never let up.

"No, I refuse!" he shouted over and over and over. "I will not do murder!"

Finally she literally dragged him into her sitting room, dumped him in a chair, and produced a small knife. Thinking she meant to use it on him, Brutus shrank away, but she yanked up her dress and plunged the blade into her white, fleshy thigh.

"See? See? You may be afraid to strike, Brutus, but I am not!" she howled, the wound gushing blood.

"All right, all right, all right!" he gasped, ashen. "All right, Porcia, you win! I'll do it. I'll strike."

Porcia fainted.

And so it came to pass that the Kill Caesar Club gained its precious figurehead, Marcus Junius Brutus Servilius Caepio. He was too intimidated to go on refusing, and too horribly aware that the longer Porcia's campaign of nagging and graffiti went on, the more Rome talked.

"I am not blind and I am not deaf, Brutus," Servilia said to him after the surgeon had ministered to Porcia. "Nor am I stupid. All this is an attempt to murder Caesar, isn't it? Whoever is plotting the deed needs your name to do it. Having said that, I insist upon every detail. Talk, Brutus, or you're dead."

"I know of no plot, Mama," Brutus managed to say, even looked into her eyes as he said it. "Someone is trying to destroy my reputation, discredit me with Caesar. Someone very malign and quite mad. I suspect it's Matinius."

"Matinius?" she asked blankly. "Your own business director?"

"He's been peculating. I fired him several days ago, but I neglected to tell Epaphroditus that he wasn't to be admitted to the house." He smiled sheepishly. "It's been a little hectic."

"I see. Go on."

"Now that Epaphroditus knows, Mama, I think you'll find that the graffiti will cease," Brutus went on, growing more and more confident. It was true that Matinius had peculated and been fired, that was the lucky part. "What's more, I shall see Caesar this morning and explain. I've hired ex-gladiators to watch my tribunal and the public statues night and day, so that should be the end of Matinius's campaign to get me in trouble with Caesar."

"It makes sense," Servilia said slowly.

"Nothing else does, Mama." He tittered nervously. "I mean, do *you* honestly think I'm capable of murdering Caesar?"

Her head went back, she laughed. "Honestly? A mouse like you? A rabbit? A worm? A spineless nonentity under the thumb of an atrocious monster of a wife? I can credit *she'd* murder him, but you? It's far easier to believe in flying pigs."

"Quite so, Mama."

"Well, don't stand there looking like a moron! Go and see Caesar before he has you charged with plotting his murder."

Brutus did as he was told—well, didn't he always? In the end, it was the best alternative.

"So that's what happened, Caesar," he said to the Dictator Perpetuus in his study at the Domus Publica. "I apologize for the worry it must have caused you."

"It intrigued me, Brutus, but it didn't worry me. Why should the thought of death worry any man? There's little I haven't done or achieved, though I trust I'll live long enough to conquer the Kingdom of the Parthians." The pale eyes were permanently washed out these days, the pressure of work almost too much even for a Caesar. "If it isn't conquered, our western world will rue it sooner or later. I do confess I won't be sorry to leave Rome." A smile lit the eyes. "Not the right thing for a man who aspires to be king to say, is it? Oh, Brutus, what man in his right mind would want to king it over a contentious, fractious, prickly lot of Romans? Not I!"

Brutus blinked at sudden tears, lowered his lashes. "A good question, Caesar. I wouldn't want to king it either. The trouble is that the graffiti have started rumors that there's a plot afoot to kill you. Start using your lictors again, please."

"I don't think so," Caesar said cheerfully, ushering his visitor out. "If I did, people would say I was afraid, and I can't have that. The worst part of it is that Calpurnia has heard the rumors, and frets. So does Cleopatra." He laughed. "Women! Let them, and they'd have a man shrinking like a violet."

"How very true," said Brutus, and walked back to his house to face his wife.

"Is it right, what Servilia said?" Porcia demanded ferociously.

"I don't know until you tell me what she said."

"That you've been to see Caesar."

"After the rash of graffiti in so many public places, Porcia, I could do little else," Brutus said stiffly. "There's no need to fly into a rage—Fortuna is smiling on your cause. I am able to blame Matinius. If that satisfied Mama, which it did, it couldn't help but satisfy our ruler." He took Porcia's hands in his own, squeezed them. "My dear girl, you must learn discretion! If you don't, we cannot succeed in this enterprise. Hysterical scenes and self-mutilation have to stop, hear me? If you genuinely love me, then protect me, don't incriminate me. Having seen Caesar, I now have to see Cassius, who must be as worried as I am. Not to mention the others involved. What was a secret is now being talked about everywhere, thanks to you."

"I had to get you to do it," she said.

"Granted, but you did. Your mood is too unstable. Have you forgotten that my mother lives here? She was Caesar's mistress for years, and she still loves him desperately." His face twisted. "Please believe me, my dearest one, when I say that I have no love for Caesar. All my pain is because of him. Were I a Cassius, to kill him would be easier than lifting a feather. But what you will not understand is that I am not a Cassius. To speak of murder and to do murder are two very different things. In all my life I have never killed a creature bigger than a spider. But to kill Caesar?" He shuddered. "That is like deliberately stepping into the Fields of Fire. A right act in one way, I can see that, but in another—oh, Porcia, I cannot convince myself that killing him will benefit Rome or bring back the Republic. My instincts say that to kill him will only make matters worse. Because to kill him is to tamper with the will of the gods. All murder does that."

She heard part of it, but only what her unruly heart would let her hear. Her light died, she drooped. "Dear Brutus, I see the justice in your criticisms of me. I am too unstable, my moods do get out of control. I will behave, I promise. But to kill *him* is the rightest act in Rome's history!"

February over, Caesar convened the Senate on the Kalends of March, intending it to be the last meeting before he stepped down as consul on the Ides. Shipment of the legions across the Adriatic continued at a furious pace; on the Macedonian side of that sea they were camped between Dyrrachium and Apollonia, with Caesar's personal staff located in Apollonia. Dyrrachium was the northern and Apollonia the southern terminus of the Via Egnatia, the Roman road east to Thrace and the Hellespont. An eight-hundred-mile march that the legions were expected to complete in a month.

At the meeting on the Kalends Caesar outlined the intended campaign of Publius Vatinius and Marcus Antonius against King Burebistas of the Dacians, necessary because, said Caesar, he was going to plant colonies of Roman Head Count all around the margins of the Euxine Sea. As soon as the year was over, he went on, Publius Dolabella would go to Syria as governor and keep Caesar supplied during his campaigns. The House, quite sparsely attended, was polite enough to listen to this old news.

"When the Senate convenes on the Ides, it will do so outside the *pomerium*, as the subject will be my war. In the Curia Pompeia, rather than in Bellona. Bellona is too small. At that meeting I will also allocate provinces to this year's praetors."

That night the Kill Caesar Club gathered at the temple of Ceres. When Cassius walked in with Marcus Brutus, the rest of the members stared in disbelief, including Gaius Trebonius.

"Knock me over with a pine needle!" Publius Casca exclaimed. Like everybody else, he was extremely apprehensive, for the rumors of a conspiracy to kill Caesar were increasing. "Did you give us away to Caesar when you saw him, Brutus?"

"Well, did you?" his brother, Gaius Casca, demanded.

"We discussed the peculations of a colleague of mine," Brutus said coolly as he moved with Cassius to a bench beneath Pluto. He had gone beyond fear, was reconciled to what was going to happen, though setting eyes on some of these faces was no joy. Lucius Minucius Basilus! Did any noble purpose need such dross to fuel it? An upstart who claimed descent from Cincinnatus's Minucius and tortured his slaves! And Petronius, an insect whose father had been a dealer in mine and quarry slaves! Caesennius Lento, already a murderer of the great! And Aquila, his mother's lover, who was younger than her son! Oh, what a *wonderful* little group!

"Order, order!" Trebonius said sharply; he too was feeling the strain. "Marcus Brutus, welcome." He walked to the center of the floor beneath the plinth of Ceres and looked at the twenty-two faces, ruddied by the lamplight, grotesquely shadowed, ominous and unfamiliar. "Tonight we have to make some decisions. There are but fourteen days left until the Ides of March. Though Caesar says he'll remain three further days in Rome after that, we can't count on it. If word should come from Brundisium that he's needed, he'll go at once. Whereas until the Ides, he has to be in Rome."

He took a turn about the *cella*, an ordinary man of the most undistinguished kind, slight in build, average in height, drab of coloring and mien. Yet, as all the men present knew, remarkably able. If his brief consulship had been humdrum, it was only because Caesar had left him nothing of note to do. He was governor-designate of Asia Province, not a military command, admittedly, but a difficult job thanks to the province's financial distress. His greatest asset was his peculiarly Roman intelligence—a mixture of pragmatism, an instinct for the right moment to act, a nose sensitive to brewing trouble, and superlative logistical skills. Therefore they settled down to listen to him feeling less queasy, less unsure.

"For Marcus Brutus's benefit, I had better outline what has already been decided, namely, the location of the deed. The fact that Caesar has no lictors is of immeasurable importance, but he is still surrounded by hundreds of clients whenever he goes about the city. That narrowed our opportunity to one location—the long lane between Cleopatra's palace and the Via Aurelia, because he takes no one with him when he goes to visit her except two or three secretaries. Now that the Transtiberini have been thinned out by his migrant pursuits, the area is deserted. So that is where we will ambush him. The date has not yet been decided."

"Ambush?" asked Brutus, sounding amazed. "Surely you're not going to *ambush* Caesar? How will people know who did it?"

"Ambush is the only way," said Trebonius blankly. "To prove we did it, we take his head and we go to the Forum, where we soften everybody up with a couple of magnificent speeches, call the Senate into session and demand that it commend us for ridding Rome of a tyrant. If we have to, we kidnap Cicero into attending—he'll back us up, nothing surer."

"That is absolutely appalling!" Brutus cried. "Disgusting! Sickening! *Caesar's head?* And why isn't Cicero a part of this?"

"Because Cicero's chickenhearted and incapable of keeping his mouth shut!" Decimus Brutus snapped, hackles up. "We'll use him afterward, not before or during. How do you envision killing Caesar, Brutus? In public?"

"Yes, in public," Brutus said without hesitation.

A collective gasp went up.

"We'd be lynched on the spot," said Galba, swallowing.

"This is tyrannicide, not murder," said Brutus in the tone that told Cassius that Brutus's mind was irrevocably made up. "It *must* be a public deed, out in the open. Anything furtive brands us as assassins. I was led to believe that we're acting in the spirit of the first Brutus and Ahala, who were liberators, and hailed as such. Our motives are pure, our intentions noble. We're ridding Rome of a tyrant king, and that calls for the courage of our convictions. Don't you see?" he asked, hands out in appeal. "We *cannot* be applauded for this deed if it has been done secretly, by stealth!"

"Oh, I do see," Basilus sneered. "We meet Caesar on the, say, Sacra Via, in the midst of a thousand of his clients, we part the sea of people, stroll up to him casually and say, '*Ave*, Caesar, we are honorable men who are about to kill you. Now just stand there, drop the toga off your left shoulder, and present your heart for our daggers.' What utter rot! Whereabouts do you live, Brutus? Among the clouds of Olympus? Plato's ideal republic?"

"No, but I don't busy myself with hot irons and pincers for my own amusement either, Basilus!" Brutus snarled, astonished at his own fierce anger. Pushed into this by Porcia he might have been, but he was not about to pander to the likes of a Minucius Basilus for a thousand Catos! Irrevocably committed, he found now that he *cared*.

Listening to an obdurate Brutus had an unexpected effect on Cassius; from self-preservation he went to a sudden enormous desire to offer his very life on the altar of Brutus's making. Brutus was right! What better way to kill Caesar than out in the open? They would all die for it on the spot, but Rome would put their statues among the gods forever. There were worse fates.

"*Tacete*, the lot of you!" he yelled, entering the fray. "He is right, you fools! We do the deed in public! It's my experience that things clandestine are more likely to go wrong—straight ahead is the way to go, not down some crooked lane. Naturally we don't just walk up to Caesar and announce our intentions, Basilus, but a knife can kill as surely in public as anywhere else. What's more, it gives us the chance to kill all three of them in one swoop. Caesar has a habit of standing with his junior consul on one side and his suffect consul on the other." He hit the palm of one hand with the other's fist—*smack!* "We get rid of Antonius and Dolabella as well as Caesar."

"No!" Brutus shouted. "No, no! We're tyrannicides, not mass murderers! I won't hear of killing Antonius and Dolabella! If they happen to be flanking him, let them. We kill the king—*only* the king! Crying out even as we do it that we are freeing Rome of a tyrant! Then we drop our daggers and we go to the rostra, where we speak to everyone proudly, unashamedly, jubilantly! Our best orators will have to make mountains move and gorgons weep, but we have orators in our ranks able to do that. We will call ourselves Rome's liberators, and stand there wearing caps of liberty to reinforce our action."

Oh, why did I ever think that Marcus Brutus would prove an asset? Trebonius asked himself, listening to this nonsense with a leaden heart. His eyes met Decimus Brutus's, who rolled his upward in despair. No matter if Brutus was howled down, the plan was in tatters, its integrity undermined. To do the deed in secret and confess to it at a prearranged moment, with Antonius already apprised, was one thing. What Brutus suggested was sheer suicide. Antonius would *have* to retaliate by killing them! Mind racing, Trebonius tried to pluck something out of the debris that would retrieve the plan.

"Wait! Wait! I have it!" he hollered, so loudly that the developing argument ceased. Every face turned to him. "It can be done publicly, yet safely," he said. "On the Ides of March, in the Curia Pompeia—is that public enough for you, Brutus?"

"A curia of the Senate is exactly the right kind of public place," Brutus gasped, eyes distended, sweat rolling off his brow. "I didn't mean to imply that it should necessarily be done in the midst of a huge Forum crowd, only that there must be witnesses of the highest repute present—men able to swear on sacred oath to our sincerity, our honorable intentions. A meeting of the House would fulfill all my criteria, Trebonius."

"Then that solves *where* we do it and *when* we do it," Trebonius said thankfully. "Caesar always goes straight inside, he never pauses to chat. Usually he spends the time between his entry and the House's seating itself in his eternal paperwork. But he never infringes the House rules by bringing any secretaries in, and he has no lictors. Once he enters the curia, he's totally unprotected. I agree with you entirely, Brutus, that we kill Caesar and Caesar alone. That means we have to keep the other curule magistrates outside until the deed is done, because they all have lictors. Lictors don't think, they act. Let any men raise a hand against Caesar in the presence of anyone's lictors, and they'll leap to his defense. We won't succeed. So it is vital that we keep the other curule magistrates outside."

The faces were beginning to lighten; Trebonius was devising a new plan that had the merit of immediacy. Not one of the club members had been looking forward to doing the deed and confessing to it later, at the propitious moment, by producing a grisly trophy like Caesar's head. Some among them had already begun to wonder if all twenty-three would have the dedication and the courage to own up.

"We have to strike fast," Trebonius went on. "There are sure to be backbenchers inside, but we'll be clustered around Caesar, and most won't realize what's going on until it's too late. And we will be right where we can make the most of our situation with oratory, caps of liberty, whatever. Everyone's first reaction will be shock, and shock paralyzes. By the time that Antonius gets his breath back, Decimus—I think we all agree that he's our best orator—will be in full spate. If he's nothing else, Antonius is a practical man. What's done will be done as far as he's concerned, Caesar's cousin or not. The House will take its attitude from him, not from Dolabella. Everyone knows there's bad blood between Caesar and Antonius. Truly, fellow members of our club, I am *sure* that Antonius will be prepared to listen, that he won't exact reprisals."

Oh, Trebonius, Trebonius! What do you know that the rest of us don't? Decimus asked himself at the conclusion of this breathless but effective speech. You've struck a deal with our Antonius, haven't you? How clever of you! And how clever of Antonius! He gets what he wants without lifting a finger against Cousin Gaius.

"I still say kill Antonius too," Cassius said stubbornly.

Decimus answered. "No, I don't think so. Trebonius is right. If we're unapologetic about our deed of liberation—an excellent word, Brutus, I think we should call ourselves the Liberators!—then Antonius has many reasons to accommodate us. For one thing, he'll lead the invasion of the Parthians."

"Isn't that to take Caesar's place?" Cassius grumbled.

"It's a war, and Antonius likes making war. But take Caesar's place? He'll never do that, he's too lazy. The only strife will be between him and Dolabella over who's the senior consul," said Staius Murcus. "But I do suggest that one of us runs off to get Cicero, who won't be there while Caesar's in the House, but will be only too happy to be there to look on his dead body."

"There's a more important problem," Decimus said, "namely, keeping Antonius, Dolabella and the other curule magistrates outside the curia itself while we do the deed. One of us will have to stay in Pompeius's garden. He has to be the one on best terms with Antonius, the one Antonius will be glad to linger with, talk to. If Antonius doesn't move to go inside, nor will any of the others, including Dolabella." He drew a long breath. "I nominate Gaius Trebonius to stay in the garden."

When Trebonius jumped, Decimus walked up to him, took his hand and clasped it strongly. "Those of us from the Gallic War know that you're not afraid to use a dagger, so no one will call you craven, my dear Gaius. I think it has to be you who stays outside, even if that means you won't have the opportunity to strike a blow for liberty."

Trebonius returned the grip. "I'm willing, on condition that every one of you votes me in, and that you, Decimus, strike an extra blow for me. Twenty-three men, twenty-three blows. That way, no one will ever know whose dagger actually killed Caesar."

"I'll do that gladly," said Decimus, eyes shining.

The vote was taken: Gaius Trebonius was unanimously elected the man who stayed outside to detain Marcus Antonius.

"Is there any need to meet again before the Ides?" Caecilius Buciolanus asked.

"None," said Trebonius, smiling broadly. "What I do insist upon is that all of us congregate in the garden an hour after dawn. It doesn't matter if we huddle together and talk too earnestly to invite company, because as soon as the deed is done, everyone will know what we were talking about. We'll run through it then in greater detail. Caesar won't be on time. It's the Ides, don't forget, which means that Caesar will have to fill in for our nonexistent *flamen Dialis* and lead his sheep down the Sacra Via, then climb the steps to sacrifice it on the Arx. He'll also have unavoidable business, given that he leaves Rome so soon afterward—or would, if he were still alive."

They laughed dutifully, save for Brutus and Cassius.

"I predict that we'll have some hours to discuss the deed before Caesar turns up," Trebonius continued. "Decimus, it would be a good idea if you presented yourself at the Domus Publica at dawn, then go with him to Jupiter's ceremony and wherever else he chooses. As soon as he starts for the Campus Martius, send us a warning. Be open about it—tell him he's so late that it might be prudent to notify the senators that he's actually on his way."

"In his high red boots." Quintus Ligarius giggled.

At the doors of Ceres they all shook hands solemnly, looked into each other's eyes, then melted into the darkness.

"Gaius, I wish that you'd recall your lictors," Lucius Caesar said to his cousin, encountering him leaving the Treasury. "And don't you *dare* ignore me to dictate a letter! This mania for work is becoming ridiculous."

"I would love to be able to take an hour off, Lucius, but it is quite impossible," Caesar said, banishing the secretary to walk in his rear. "There are a hundred and fifty-three separate pieces of agrarian legislation, thanks to our lack of public land and the cantankerousness of every *latifundium* owner my commission's buying from—there are almost as many colonies on foreign land as that, all of which have to be individually legislated—in my function as censor, I have innumerable state contracts to let—every day thirty or forty petitions come in from citizens of this town or that, all with serious grievances—and that is but the surface of my work mountain. My senators and magistrates are either too lazy, too haughty or too disinterested in the machinery of government to act as deputies, and so far I haven't had the time to create the bureaucratic departments which will have to come in before I can step down as dictator."

"I'm here and willing to help, but you don't ask me," Lucius said a little stiffly.

Caesar smiled, squeezed his arm. "You're a venerable, not so young consular, and your services to me in Gaul alone must excuse you from the plod of paperwork. No, it's high time that the back-benchers were given something more to do than merely sit mum during infrequent meetings of the House and spend the rest of their days touting for juicy criminal lawsuits that benefit them but not Rome."

Lucius looked mollified, consented to walk with Caesar as they passed between the Well of Juturna and the little round *aedes* of Vesta, heading a huge crowd of Caesar's clients, who were a part of a great man's burden. One that Lucius Caesar was glad to see now that his cousin refused to be escorted by lictors.

Though stalls and booths had largely been banished from the Forum Romanum save for the impermanent barrows vending snacks to Forum frequenters, there were no laws on the tablets to prevent people from usurping a tiny spot of Forum ground, thereon to pursue an activity usually to do with the occult. Romans were a superstitious lot, loved astrologers, fortune-tellers and eastern magi, a number of whom dotted the margins of the area. Cross any of a dozen palms with a silver coin and you could find out what the morrow held, or why your business venture had failed, or what kind of future your new-born son could hope for.

Old Spurinna enjoyed an unparalleled reputation among these soothsayers. His place was adjacent to the public entrance to the Vestal Virgin side of the Domus Publica, the door through which any Roman citizen desirous of depositing his or her will with the Vestals might enter and lodge it. An excellent site for one in the soothsaying business, for men and women with death on their minds and wills in their hands were always tempted to pause, give old Spurinna a denarius, and learn how much longer they had to live. His appearance inspired confidence in his mystical gift, for he was skinny, dirty, unkempt, seamed of face.

As the two Caesars passed by him without noticing him—he had been a fixture there for decades—Spurinna got to his feet.

"Caesar!" he cried.

Both Caesars stopped, both looked at him.

"Which Caesar?" Lucius asked, grinning.

"There is only one Caesar, Chief Augur! His name will come to mean the man who rules Rome," Spurinna shrilled, dark irises ringed with the white halo that heralded the approach of death. " 'Caesar' means 'king'!"

"Oh, no, not again." Caesar sighed. "Who's paying you to say that, Spurinna? Marcus Antonius?"

"It isn't what I want to say, Caesar, and no one paid me."

"Then what do you want to say?"

"Beware the Ides of March!"

Caesar fumbled in the purse attached to his belt, flipped a gold coin that Spurinna caught deftly. "What's going to happen on the Ides of March, old man?"

"Your life will be imperiled!"

"I thank you for the warning," Caesar said, and walked on.

"He's usually uncannily right," Lucius said with a shiver. "Caesar, *please* recall your lictors!"

"And let all of Rome know that I pay attention to rumors and ancient visionaries? Admit I am afraid? Never," said Caesar.

Caught in the web of his own making, Cicero had no choice but to sit in the spectators' bleachers while legislation, policy making and senatorial decrees went on without him. All he had to do was walk into the curia, have his slave unfold his stool, and put his bottom on it among the most senior consulars of the front benches. But pride, stubbornness and his detestation of Caesar Rex forbade it. Worse still, he was feeling the full force of Caesar's enmity since the publication of his "Cato," and Atticus too was unpopular with Caesar. No matter how they tried, or through whom, the migrant poor of Rome's seediest areas kept on flooding into the colony outside Buthrotum.

It was Dolabella who first told him that there was a rumor going about that Caesar was to be assassinated.

"Who? When?" he asked eagerly.

"That's just it, no one really knows. It's a typical rumor—'they say' and 'I heard that' and 'there's a feeling in the air'—no substance that I've managed to find. I know you can't stand him, but I'm Caesar's man through and through," Dolabella declared, "so I'm looking hard and listening harder. If anything happened to him, I'd be all to pieces. Antonius would run rampant."

"No whisper of names, even *a* name?" Cicero asked.

"None."

"I'll pop around to see Brutus," Cicero said, and shooed his ex-son-in-law out.

"Have you heard any stories that someone is plotting to assassinate Caesar?" Cicero demanded as soon as a goblet of wine-and-water was put into his hand.

"Oh, that business!" Brutus said, sounding slightly angry.

"So there is something to it?" Cicero asked eagerly.

"No, there's absolutely nothing to it, that's what irritates me. As far as I know, it started because that madman Matinius daubed graffiti all over Rome instructing *me* to kill Caesar."

"Oh, the graffiti! I didn't see them myself, but I heard. Is *that* all? How disappointing."

"Yes, isn't it?" asked Brutus.

"Dictator Perpetuus. You'd think there were some men in Rome with enough gumption to rid us of this Caesar."

The dark eyes, sterner than of yore, held Cicero's with some irony in their depths. "Why don't *you* rid us of this Caesar?"

"*I?*" Cicero gasped, clutching dramatically at his chest. "My dear Brutus, it's not my style. My assassinations are done with a pen and a voice. To each his own."

"Staying out of the Senate has silenced your pen and voice, Cicero, that's the trouble. There's no one left in that body to aim a verbal dagger at Caesar. You were our only hope."

"Enter the House with *that man* in a dictator's chair? I'd rather die!" Cicero declared in ringing tones.

A small, uncomfortable silence fell, broken by Brutus.

"Are you in Rome until the Ides?" he asked.

"Definitely." Cicero coughed delicately. "Is Porcia well?"

"Not very, no."

"Then I trust your mother is?"

"Oh, she's indestructible, but she isn't here at the moment. Tertulla is with child, and Mama thought some country air might benefit her, so they've gone to Tusculum," said Brutus.

Cicero departed, convinced he was being palmed off, though why or because of what escaped him.

In the Forum he encountered Mark Antony deep in conversation with Gaius Trebonius. For a moment he thought they were going to ignore him, then Trebonius started, smiled.

"Cicero, how good to see you! In Rome for a while, I hope?"

Antony being Antony simply grunted something, gave Trebonius a casual flip of his hand, and walked off toward the Carinae.

"I detest that man!" Cicero exclaimed.

"Oh, he's more bark than bite," Trebonius said comfortably. "His whole trouble is his size. It must be very hard to think of oneself as an ordinary man when one is so—well endowed."

A notorious prude, Cicero flushed. "Disgraceful!" he cried. "Absolutely disgraceful!"

"The Lupercalia, you mean?"

"Of course the Lupercalia! *Exposing* himself!"

Trebonius shrugged. "That's Antonius."

"And offering Caesar a diadem?"

"I think that was a put up job between the pair of them. It enabled Caesar to engrave his public repudiation of the diadem on a bronze tablet which, I am reliably informed, will be attached to his new rostra. In Latin *and* in Greek."

Cicero spotted Atticus emerging from the Argiletum, farewelled Trebonius and hurried off.

It's done, thought Trebonius, glad to be rid of a nosy gossip like Cicero. Antonius knows when and where.

On the thirteenth day of March, Caesar finally managed to find the time to visit Cleopatra, who welcomed him with open arms, kisses, feverish endearments. As tired as he was, that wretched traitor in his groin insisted upon immediate gratification, so they retired to Cleopatra's bed and made love until well into the afternoon. Then Caesarion had to have his play with *tata*, who enjoyed the little fellow more each time he saw him. His Gallic son by Rhiannon, vanished without a trace, had also looked very like his father, but Caesar remembered him as a rather limited child who had not been able to name the fifty men inside his toy Trojan horse. Caesar had commissioned another for this boy, discovering in delight that he could identify every one of them after a single lesson. It boded well for his future, it meant he wasn't stupid.

"Only one thing worries me," said Cleopatra over a late meal.

"What's that, my love?"

"I am still not with child."

"Well, I haven't been able to get across the Tiber nearly as often as I had hoped," he said calmly, "and it seems I am not a man who impregnates his women the moment he doffs his toga."

"I fell with Caesarion immediately."

"Accidents do happen."

"It must be because I don't have Tach'a with me. She could read the petal bowl, she knew the days to make love."

"Offer to Juno Sospita. Her temple is outside the sacred boundary," he said easily.

"I have offered to Isis and Hathor, but I suspect they don't like being so far from Nilus."

"Never mind, they'll be home again soon."

She rolled over on the couch, her big golden eyes raised to his face. Yes, he was terribly tired, and sometimes forgetful of his sweet drink. There had been one public episode when he fell and twitched, but luckily Hapd'efan'e had been there and got the syrup down before he needed to intubate. Caesar, recovered, had blamed it on muscle cramps, which seemed to satisfy his audience. The one good thing about it was that it had given him a fright, so he had been more mindful since, Hapd'efan'e more alert.

"You've grown so beautiful in my eyes," he said, rubbing one palm on her belly. Poor little girl, deprived of her issue because a Roman man, Pontifex Maximus, could not condone incest. Purring and stretching, she lowered her long black lashes, reached out a hand to touch him.

"Me, with my great beaky nose and my scrawny body?" she asked. "Even at sixty, Servilia is more beautiful."

"Servilia is an evil woman, make no mistake about that. Once I did think her beautiful, but what kept me in her toils was never beauty. She's intelligent, interesting, and devious."

"I've found her a very good friend."

"For her own purposes, believe me."

Cleopatra shrugged. "What do her purposes matter? I'm not a Roman woman she can ruin, and you're right, she's intelligent and interesting. She saved me from dying of boredom while you were in Spain. Through her, I actually met a few more Roman women. That Clodia!" She giggled. "A female rake, very good company. And she brought me Hortensia, surely the most intelligent woman here."

"I wouldn't know. After Caepio died—and that's over twenty years ago—she donned widow's weeds and refused every suitor who dangled after her. I'm surprised she mixes with Clodia."

"Perhaps," said Cleopatra demurely, "Hortensia prefers to have lovers. Perhaps she and Clodia sit together and choose them from among the naked young swimmers in the Trigarium."

"One thing about that family of Claudians, they never have cared about their reputations. Do they still visit, Clodia and Hortensia?"

"Often. In fact, I see more of them than I do of you."

"A reproach?"

"No, I understand, but that doesn't make your absences any easier to bear. Though since you've been back, I see more Roman men. Lucius Piso and Philippus, for instance."

"And Cicero?"

"Cicero and I don't get along," said Cleopatra, pulling a face. "What I want to know is, when will you bring some of the more famous Roman men to visit me? Like Marcus Antonius. I'm dying to meet him, but he ignores my invitations."

"With Fulvia for wife, he wouldn't dare accept them." Caesar grinned. "She's very possessive."

"Well, don't tell her he's coming." After a small pause she said, wistfully, "Won't I see you again until the Ides are gone? I'd hoped for tomorrow too."

"I can sleep in your bed tonight, my love, but at dawn I must get back to the city. Too much work."

"Then tomorrow night?" she pressed.

"I can't. Lepidus is having a men's dinner I daren't miss. I'll have to work through it, but at least I'll have a chance to shake a few hands I mightn't otherwise. It would be churlish to tell Brutus and Cassius about their provinces for the first time in the full glare of the Senate."

"Two more famous men I've never met."

"Pharaoh, you're twenty-five years old now, therefore quite old enough to realize why a great many of Rome's most prominent men and women are reluctant to make your acquaintance," Caesar said levelly. "They call you the Queen of Beasts, and blame you for my reputed desire to become the King of Rome. You're deemed a corrupting influence."

"How idiotic!" she cried, sitting up indignantly. "There's no one in the world could influence your thinking."

Marcus Aemilius Lepidus had done very well for himself since Caesar had been declared Dictator. The youngest of the three sons of that Lepidus who, with Brutus's father, had rebelled against Sulla, he had been born with a caul over his face; this was considered a mark of lifelong good fortune. Certainly he had been lucky to be too young to become embroiled in his father's revolt; the oldest boy had died in it, and the second boy, Paullus, had spent many years in exile. The family was patrician and immensely august, but after Lepidus Senior died of a broken heart, there didn't seem to be any chance that it would retrieve its position among the greatest of the Famous Families of Rome. Then Caesar had bribed the recalled Paullus into a consulship he had hoped to see enable him to be elected consul himself without crossing the *pomerium* to declare his candidacy. Unfortunately Paullus was a slug, not worth the enormous sum Caesar had paid him; Curio, bought more cheaply, had proven of better value.

But none of Caesar's ploys to avoid unmerited prosecution had worked; crossing the Rubicon into rebellion, always his last resort, became the only alternative. And Marcus Lepidus, the youngest of those three sons, had immediately seen his opportunity, allied himself with Caesar, and never looked back. In personality he was easygoing and unobservant, was prone to seek the least taxing way to do things, and was generally regarded as a political lightweight. To Caesar, however, he had two great virtues: he was Caesar's man through and through, and a high enough aristocrat to give Caesar's faction some much needed respectability.

His first wife had been a Cornelia Dolabellae who had owned no dowry, but died shortly thereafter in childbirth. His next bride came with five hundred talents; she was the middle daughter of Servilia and her second husband, Silanus. Junilla had married him some years before Caesar crossed the Rubicon, years during which her money kept Lepidus afloat. When civil war came, his mother-in-law, Servilia, was quite happy to have him and Vatia Isauricus in Caesar's camp, since Brutus and Tertulla were in Pompey's camp. No matter to Servilia which side won the war—she couldn't lose.

Lepidus was the son-in-law she liked the least, principally because his birth was so lofty that he never bothered to flatter her. But Lepidus, a tall, handsome man whose blood links to the Julii Caesares showed in his face, cared nothing for Servilia's good opinion. Nor did Junilla, who happened to love Lepidus very much. They had two sons and a daughter, all still children.

Enriched through allegiance to Caesar, Lepidus had bought an imposingly large residence on the Germalus of the Palatine, overlooking the Forum, and owned a dining room large enough to hold six couches. His cooks were quite as good as Cleopatra's, his wine cellar commended by those privileged to sample its contents.

Well aware that Caesar was likely to quit Rome the moment the meeting of the Senate on the Ides was over, Lepidus had gotten in early and secured Caesar for his dinner party on the evening before the Ides. He also invited Antony, Dolabella, Brutus, Cassius, Decimus Brutus, Trebonius, Lucius Piso, Lucius Caesar, Calvinus and Philippus; he had badly wanted Cicero, who declined "due to my grievous state of health."

Much to his surprise, Caesar arrived first.

"My dear Caesar, I thought you'd be the last to come and the first to go," Lepidus said, greeting him in the awesome atrium.

"There's method in my madness, Master of the Horse," Caesar said, one hand indicating the retinue behind him, which included his Egyptian physician. "I'm afraid I'm going to be unpardonably rude by working all the way through dinner, so I came early enough to ask that you allocate me your meanest couch all to myself. Put whomsoever you like in the *locus consularis,* just give me an end couch where I can read, write and dictate without driving the rest of your guests to distraction."

Lepidus took this with good humor unruffled. "Whatever you want shall be yours, Caesar," he said, leading the awkward guest of honor into the dining room. "I'll bring a fifth couch, then take your pick."

"How many are we?"

"Twelve, including you and me."

"*Edepol!* That will leave you with two men only on one of your couches," Caesar said.

"Not to worry, Caesar. I'll put Antonius on my couch in the *locus consularis* and no one between us," Lepidus said with a grin. "He's such a hulk that three on his couch is a tight squeeze."

"Actually, I'm going to even you up," Caesar said as servants carried a fifth couch in and put it beyond the lone couch to the left of the host's *lectus medius,* which formed the crosspiece of the U. "I'll take it, it will suit me nicely. Plenty of room to spread my papers out, and, if you would, a chair behind it for my secretary. I'll use one man at a time, the rest can wait outside."

"I'll see to it that they have comfortable chairs and plenty to eat," Lepidus said, hurrying away to call his steward.

Thus it was that when the others began to arrive, they found Caesar already ensconced on the least enviable couch, a secretary on a chair behind him and the rest of his couch littered with piles of papers and scrolls.

"Poor Lepidus!" said Lucius Caesar, eyes dancing. "You'd do best to put Calvinus, Philippus and me on the couch opposite this impolite reprobate. None of us is timid enough to leave him alone, and who knows? He might actually talk a little."

When the first course was carried in, Mark Antony and Lepidus reclined alone on the *lectus medius;* Dolabella, Lucius Piso and Trebonius reclined to the immediate right, with Philippus, Lucius Caesar and Calvinus beyond them; on the immediate left lay Brutus, Cassius and Decimus Brutus, with Caesar beyond them.

Naturally Caesar's industriousness came as no surprise to any of the diners, so the meal and the conversation proceeded merrily, aided by an excellent Falernian white to accompany the fishier, more nibbly first course, a superb Chian red to accompany the meaty, more substantial main course, and a sweetish, slightly effervescent white wine from Alba Fucentia to accompany the desserts and cheeses which formed the third, final course.

Philippus was ecstatic over a new dessert Lepidus's cooks had devised, a gelatinous mixture of cream, honey, pulped early strawberries, egg yolks, and egg whites beaten stiffly, the whole turned out of a chilled mold shaped like a peacock and decorated with piped whipped cow's cream dyed in pinks, greens, blues, lilacs and yellows from leaf and petal juices.

"Tasting this," he mumbled, "I admit that my Mons Fiscellus ambrosia is too sickly-sweet. This is *perfect!* Absolute ambrosia! Caesar, do have some!"

Caesar glanced up, grinned, took a spoonful and looked quite astonished. "You're right, Philippus, it is ambrosia. Clause ten: it shall not be lawful to sell, barter, gift or otherwise dispose of a free grain chit, on penalty of fifty *nundinae* throwing lime into the paupers' pits of the necropolis." He ate another spoonful. "Very good! My physician would approve. Clause eleven: upon the death of a holder of a free grain chit, it shall be returned to the plebeian aedile's booth together with proof of death . . ."

"I thought," said Decimus Brutus, "that the free grain dole legislation was already in place, Caesar."

"Yes, it is, but upon rereading it, I found it too ambiguous. The best laws, Decimus, contain no loopholes."

"I like the punishment," said Dolabella. "Shoveling lime on stinking mass graves will deter anybody from almost anything."

"Well, I had to think of *a* deterrent, which is very difficult when people have no money to pay fines and no property to impound. Holders of free grain chits are very poor," said Caesar.

"Now that your head is up from your papers, answer me one question," said Dolabella. "I note you want a hundred pieces of artillery per legion for the Parthian campaign. I know you're an ardent exponent of artillery, Caesar, but isn't that excessive?"

"Cataphracts," said Caesar.

"Cataphracts," asked Dolabella, frowning.

"Parthian cavalry," said Cassius, who had seen them in their thousands at the Bilechas River. "Clad in chainmail from head to foot. They ride giant horses clad in chainmail too."

"Yes, I remembered in your report to the Senate, Cassius, that you said they couldn't charge at a full gallop, and it occurred to me that they would suffer terribly from heavy bombardment in the early stages of a battle," said Caesar, looking pensive. "It may also be possible to bombard the trains of camels bringing spare arrows up to the Parthian archer cavalry. If my ideas are wrong, I'll put however much of the artillery into storage, but somehow I don't think I'm wrong."

"Nor do I," said Cassius, looking impressed.

Antony, who detested all-men dinners populated by the stuffier among his peers, listened to this with his eyes roving thoughtfully over the three men on the *lectus imus* to his left—Brutus, Cassius and Decimus Brutus—and then onward to Caesar. Tomorrow, my dear cousin, tomorrow! Tomorrow you will be dead at the hands of these three men and that unappreciated genius facing them, Trebonius. He's stuck to it, and it's going to happen. Did you ever see a more miserable face than Brutus's? Why is he in it, if he's so terrified? I bet he never plunges *his* dagger in!

"Returning to lime pits, necropolises and death," Antony said suddenly and loudly, "what's the best way to die?"

Brutus jumped, went white, put his spoon down quickly.

"In battle," said Cassius instantly.

"In one's sleep," said Lepidus, thinking of his father, forced to divorce the wife he worshiped, pining away for her so slowly.

"Of sheer old age," said Dolabella, chuckling.

"With the taste of something like this coating one's tongue," said Philippus, licking his spoon.

"With one's children around one," said Lucius Caesar, whose only son had been such a disappointment. There was no fate worse than outliving one's children.

"Feeling vindicated," said Trebonius, casting Antony a look of loathing. Was this boor about to betray them?

"In the act of reading a new poem better than Catullus's," said Lucius Piso. "I think Helvius Cinna might do it one day."

Caesar looked up, brows raised. "The way doesn't matter," he said, "as long as it's sudden."

Calvinus, who had been shifting and grunting for some time, gave a moan and clutched at his chest. "I fear," he said, face grey, "that *my* death is arriving. The pain! The pain!"

Instead of abandoning his work to tell Brutus and Cassius of their provinces next year, Caesar had to summon Hapd'efan'e from the atrium; the matter was forgotten as the guests clustered to view Calvinus with concern, Caesar in their forefront.

"It is a spasm of the heart," said Hapd'efan'e, "but I do not think he will die. He must be taken home and treated."

Caesar supervising, Calvinus was put into a litter.

"An ill-omened subject!" Caesar snapped at Antony.

More ill-omened than you realize, said Antony silently.

Brutus and Cassius walked most of the way home together, not speaking until they came to Cassius's door.

"We're all meeting tomorrow morning half an hour after dawn at the foot of the Steps of Cacus," Cassius said. "That leaves plenty of time to get out to the Campus Martius. I'll see you there and then."

"No," said Brutus, "don't wait for me. I'd prefer to go on my own. My lictors will be company enough."

Cassius frowned, peered at the pale face. "I hope you're not thinking of backing out?" he asked sharply.

"Of course not." Brutus drew a breath. "It's just that poor Porcia has worked herself into such a state—she knows—"

Came the sound of Cassius grinding his teeth. "That woman is a menace!" He banged on his door. "Just don't renege, hear me?"

Brutus trudged around the corner to his own house, knocked on its door and was admitted by the porter, praying as he tiptoed through the corridors toward the master's sleeping cubicle that Porcia would be asleep.

She was not. The moment the wan light of his lamp showed in the doorway she leaped out of their bed, threw herself at him and clasped him convulsively.

"What is it, what is it?" she whispered loudly enough for the whole house to hear. "You're so early! Is it discovered?"

"Hush, hush!" He closed the door. "No, it is not discovered. Calvinus took seriously ill, so the party broke up." He shed his toga and tunic, left them lying on the floor, sat on the edge of the bed to unbuckle his shoes. "Porcia, go to sleep."

"I can't sleep," she said, sitting beside him with a thump.

"Then take some syrup of poppies."

"It constipates me."

"Well, you're rapidly sending me the other way. Please, oh, please, just get into your own side of the bed and *pretend* you're asleep! I need peace."

Sighing and grumbling, she did as she was told; Brutus felt his bowels move, got up, put on his tunic, some slippers.

"What is it, what is it?"

"Nothing except a bellyache," he said, took the lamp and went to the latrine. There he remained until he was sure that he had nothing left to evacuate, then, shivering in the icy night, he stood on the colonnade until the coldness drove him back in the direction of his cubicle and Porcia. On the way he passed Strato of Epirus's door: closed, no light beneath it. Volumnius's door: closed, no light beneath it. Statyllus's door: slightly open, a light showing. The moment he scratched, Statyllus was there, drawing him inside.

It hadn't struck him as odd after he married Porcia that she should ask if Statyllus could come to live with them, and she had not told him that her reason was to separate Lucius Bibulus from Statyllus and the tippling. It was a delight to Brutus to have Cato's philosopher friend in his house. Never more so than now.

"May I lie on your couch?" Brutus asked, teeth chattering.

"Of course you may," said Statyllus.

"I can't face Porcia."

"Dear, dear."

"She's hysterical."

"Dear, dear. Lie down, I'll get some blankets."

None of the three philosophers knew of the plot to kill Caesar, though all of them knew something was wrong. Their conclusion was that Porcia was going mad. Well, who could blame Cato's daughter, so highly strung and sensitive, with Servilia verbally cutting and slashing at her as soon as Brutus went out? Statyllus, however, had watched Porcia grow up, the other two had not. When he realized that she loved Brutus, he had tried to prevent its bearing fruit. Some of his opposition was due to jealousy, but most of it was due to his fear that she would wear Brutus down with her fits and starts. What he hadn't taken into account was Servilia's enmity, though he should have— how much she had hated Cato! And now here was poor Brutus, too intimidated to face his wife. So Statyllus clucked and crooned, settled Brutus on his couch, then sat with a lamp to guard him.

Brutus drifted into a light sleep, moaned and tossed, woke suddenly when the dream of stabbing Caesar reached its bloody, awful climax. Still sitting in the chair, Statyllus had nodded off, but snapped to attention the moment Brutus swung his feet on to the floor.

"Rest again," the little philosopher said.

"No, the Senate is meeting and I can hear cocks crowing, so it can't be more than an hour from dawn," Brutus said, stood up. "Thank you, Statyllus, I needed a refuge." He sighed, took his lamp. "Now I'd better see how Porcia is." At the door he paused, gave a peculiar laugh. "Thank all the gods that my mother won't be back from Tusculum until this afternoon."

Porcia too had found solace in sleep; she was lying on her back, her arms above her head, the signs of copious tears on her face. His bath was ready; Brutus went to it, lay in the warm water and soaked for a little while, his imperturbable manservant standing by to drape him in a soft linen towel as he emerged. Then, feeling better, he dressed in a clean tunic, put on his curule shoes, and went to his study to read Plato.

"Brutus, Brutus!" Porcia yelled, erupting into the room with her hair in tangled skeins around her, eyes starting from her head, a robe falling off her shoulders. "Brutus, it is today!"

"My dear, you're not well," he said, not getting up. "Go back to bed and let me send for Atilius Stilo."

"I don't need a physician! There's nothing wrong with me!" Unaware that her every gesture and expression contradicted this statement, she skittled around the perimeter, rummaged in the sadly empty pigeonholes, grabbed a pen from a beaker of them sitting on the desk, began to stab the air with it. "Take that, you monster! And that, you murderer of the Republic!"

"Ditus!" Brutus shouted. "Ditus!"

The steward came immediately.

"Ditus, find the lady Porcia's women and send them to her. She's unwell, so send for Atilis Stilo too."

"I am not unwell! Take that! Die, Caesar! Die!"

Epaphroditus cast her a frightened look and fled, returned suspiciously quickly with four womenservants.

"Come, *domina*," said Sylvia, who had been with Porcia since childhood. "Lie down until Atilius comes."

Porcia went, but against her will, struggling so strongly that two male slaves had to help.

"Lock her in her rooms, Ditus," Brutus said, "but make sure that her scissors and paper knife are removed. I fear for her sanity, I really do."

"It is very sad," said Epaphroditus, more worried on Brutus's behalf; he looked frightful. "Let me get you something to eat."

"Has dawn broken yet?"

"Yes, *domine*, but only just. The sun hasn't risen."

"Then I'll have some bread and honey, and a drink of that herb tea the cook makes. I have a sore belly," said Brutus.

Atilius Stilo, one of Rome's fashionable medics, was at the door when Brutus departed, draped in his purple-bordered toga, his post-assassination speech clutched in his right hand.

"Whatever else you do, Stilo, give the lady Porcia a potion to calm her down," said Brutus, and stepped into the lane, where his six lictors were waiting, *fasces* shouldered.

The sun's rays were just touching the gilded statues atop Magna Mater's temple as he hurried down the Steps of Cacus into the Forum Boarium and turned toward the Porta Flumentana, the gate in the Servian Walls which led into the Forum Holitorium, already bustling with vegetable and fruit vendors putting their wares on display for early shoppers. This was the shortest route to Pompey the Great's vast theater complex upon the Campus Martius if one lived upon the Palatine—no more than a quarter-hour walk.

Mind a teeming jumble of thoughts, Brutus was conscious with every step he took of that dagger residing upon his belt, for it was long enough to thrust its sheathed tip into the top of his thigh, and in all his life he had never worn a dagger under his toga. He knew it was going to happen, yet it seemed to have no reality save for that dagger. Dodging between the carts loaded with cabbages and kale, parsnips and turnips, celery and onions, whatever could be grown in the market gardens of the outer Campus Martius and the Campus Vaticanus at this turning season of the year, Brutus was surprised to find the ground muddy and pooled with water—had it rained during the night? How stolid lictors were! Just walked.

"Terrible storm!" said a gardener, standing in the back of his cart pitching bunches of radishes to a woman.

"I thought the world would end," she answered, deftly catching.

A storm? Had there been a storm? He hadn't heard it, not a mutter of thunder nor a reflection of lightning. Was the storm in his heart so cataclysmic that it had blotted out a real storm?

Once past the Circus Flaminius, Pompey the Great's gigantic marble theater dominated the greensward of the Field of Mars, the semi-circle of the theater itself towering farthest west. Behind it going east was a magnificent rectangular peristyle garden hemmed in on all four sides by a colonnade that contained exactly one hundred fluted pillars with Corinthian capitals, lavishly gilded, painted in shades of blue; the walls behind were painted scarlet between a series of murals. One short end of the garden abutted on to the straight stage wall of the theater; the other was equipped with shallow steps that led upward into the Curia Pompeia, Pompey's consecrated senatorial meeting house.

Brutus entered the hundred-pillared colonnade through its south doors and paused, blinking in the sudden shade, to see where the Liberators were gathered. Hanging on to that word was all that had steeled him to come—they were not murderers, they were liberators. *The* Liberators. There! Out in the garden itself, in a sunny spot sheltered from the wind, close by the ornate fountain that played winter and summer through heated water pipes. Cassius waved, left the group to meet him.

"How's Porcia?" he asked.

"Not well at all. I sent for Atilius Stilo."

"Good. Come and listen to Gaius Trebonius. He's been waiting for you to arrive."

Caesar had heard the storm, the first of the equinoctial season, with its high winds and tormented weather, gone out into the main peristyle to watch the fantastic lacework of lightning in the clouds, the huge cracks of thunder as the storm drifted directly over Rome. When the rain began to come down in sheets he retreated to his sleeping cubicle, lay down and had those four precious hours of deep, dreamless sleep. Two hours before dawn, the storm gone, he was awake again and the early shift of secretaries and scribes was reporting for duty. At dawn Trogus brought him freshly baked, crusty bread, some olive oil and his habitual hot drink—lemon juice at this time of year, far nicer than vinegar, especially now that Hapd'efan'e insisted it be sweetened by honey.

He felt well, refreshed, all of him profoundly glad that his time in Rome was finally drawing to an end.

Calpurnia came in as he was finishing his breakfast, eyes heavy and ringed with the blackness of fatigue; he got up at once and went to greet her with a kiss, then put one hand beneath her chin and looked into her face, his own concerned.

"My dear, what is it? Did the storm frighten you?"

"No, Caesar, my dream did that," she said, and clasped his arm anxiously.

"A nasty dream?"

She shuddered. "A terrible dream! I saw some men surround you and stab you to death."

"*Edepol!*" he exclaimed, feeling rather helpless. How did one calm worried wives? "Just a dream, Calpurnia."

"But it was so real!" she cried. "In the Senate, though not in the Curia Hostilia. Pompeius's curia, because it happened near his statue. Please, Caesar, don't go to the meeting today!"

He disengaged her hands, held them and chafed them. "I have to go, my dear. Today I step down as consul, it's the end of my official business in Rome."

"Don't! Please don't! It was so *real!*"

"Then I thank you for the warning, and will endeavor not to be stabbed in Pompeius's curia," he said, gently but firmly.

Trogus came in with his *toga trabea;* already clad in his crimson-and-purple-striped tunic, the high red boots upon his feet, Caesar stood while Trogus draped the massive garment about his body, arranged the folds over his left shoulder so that they would not tumble down his left arm as he moved it.

How magnificent he looks, thought Calpurnia; purple and red become him more than white. "What are you doing as the Pontifex Maximus?" she asked. "Can't you use that as an excuse?"

"No, I can't," he said, sounding a little exasperated. "It's the Ides, a brief sacrifice."

And off he went to join the procession waiting outside on the Sacra Via; a quick check of the sheep, and he was away down the hill toward the lower Forum and the Arx of the Capitol.

Within an hour he was back to change, discovering with a sigh that the reception room was thronged with clients, some of whom would have to be seen before he could set out on his rounds. He found Decimus Brutus in his study, chatting to Calpurnia.

"I hope," Caesar said, coming in wearing his purple-bordered toga, "that you've managed to convince my wife that I stand in no danger from assassins today?"

"I've been trying, though I'm not sure I've succeeded," Decimus said, his rump and palms propped on the edge of Caesar's malachite desk, his ankles casually crossed.

"I have to see some fifty clients, none for very long, and none privately, if you want to stay. What brings you here so bright and early?"

"I thought you might be visiting Calvinus on your way to the meeting, and I'd like to see him," Decimus said easily. "If I showed up there on my own, I'd likely be refused, whereas if I show up with you, I can't be refused."

"Clever." Caesar chuckled. He looked at Calpurnia, brows up. "Thank you, my dear, I have work to do."

"Decimus, take care of him!" she begged from the door.

Decimus smiled broadly—such a comforting smile! "Don't worry, Calpurnia, I promise I'll take care of him."

Two hours later the pair of them left the Domus Publica to walk up the Vestal Steps on to the Palatine, a host of clients in their wake. As they turned the corner of the house to head for Vesta's *aedes,* they passed old Spurinna, squatting in his usual spot beside the Door of Wills.

"Caesar! Beware the Ides of March!" he called.

"The Ides of March are here, Spurinna, and as you see, I am perfectly fit and well." Caesar laughed.

"The Ides of March are here, yes, but they haven't gone."

"Silly old fool," Decimus muttered.

"He's many things, Decimus, but not that," Caesar said.

At the foot of the Vestal Steps the crowd pressed in on them; a hand thrust a note at Caesar. Decimus intercepted it, took the note and put it inside the sinus of his toga. "Let's get a move on," he said. "I'll give it to you to read later."

At Gnaeus Domitius Calvinus's door they were admitted, taken straight to where Calvinus lay on a couch in his study.

"Your Egyptian physician is a marvel, Caesar," Calvinus said as they entered. "Decimus, what a pleasure!"

"You look much better than you did last night," Caesar said.

"I feel much better."

"We're not staying, but I needed to see you for myself, old friend. Lucius and Piso say they're skipping the meeting today to come and keep you company, but if they tire you, throw them out. What was the trouble?"

"A heart spasm. Hapd'efan'e gave me an extract of digitalis and I settled down almost at once. He said my heart was—well, the word he used was 'fluttering'—very evocative! Apparently I have some fluid accumulated around the organ."

"As long as you recover enough to be Master of the Horse. Lepidus leaves for Narbonese Gaul today, so there's yet another won't be in the House. Nor Philippus, who overindulged yesterday—him and his ambrosias! So I fear the front benches will be sparsely populated for my last appearance," said Caesar. Rather surprisingly, he leaned to kiss Calvinus on the cheek. "Look after yourself."

Then he was gone, Decimus Brutus in his wake.

Calvinus lay frowning; his eyelids drooped, he dozed.

As they passed the Circus Flaminius, picking their way between the puddles, Decimus spoke.

"Caesar, may I send word ahead that we're coming?"

"Of course."

One of Decimus's servants sped off.

When they entered the colonnade they found some four hundred senators dotted around the garden, some reading, some dictating to scribes, some stretched out asleep on the grass, some clustered in chattering, laughing groups.

Mark Antony strode to meet them and shook Caesar's hand. "*Ave,* Caesar. We had about given up on you until Decimus's messenger came running in."

Caesar dropped Antony's hand with a cold look that said it was nobody's business how late the Dictator was, and bounded up the steps to the Curia Pompeia, two servants in his wake, one with his ivory curule chair and a folding table, the other with wax tablets and a sack full of scrolls. They set up his chair and table at the front of the curule dais, received a nod of dismissal and left. Satisfied the furniture was correctly placed, Caesar emptied the sack of its contents a few at a time, setting the scrolls neatly one on top of the other along the back of the table, then seated himself with the wax tablets stacked to his left and a steel stylus beside them in case he wished to take notes.

"He's working already," said Decimus, joining the twenty-two others at the foot of the steps. "About forty *pedarii* are inside, none near the curule end. Trebonius, time to act."

Trebonius moved immediately to join Antony, who had decided that the best way to keep Dolabella outside was to stay with him and make an effort to be civil. Their lictors, twelve each, were standing some distance away, the *fasces* (which belonged to the senior, Dolabella, as this was March) grounded. Though the meeting was outside the *pomerium*, it was within one mile of the city, so the lictors were togate and had no axes in their bundles of rods.

A refinement had occurred to Trebonius during the night, and he put it into effect as soon as Brutus came in with his six lictors. Namely, that out of respect for Caesar, lictorless for some *nundinae* by now, all the praetors and the two curule aediles should dismiss their lictors forthwith, attend the meeting without them. None objected as Cassius went the rounds of the other curule magistrates; glad of this unexpected holiday, the praetorian and aedilician lictors hurried back to their college, which was located behind the inn on the Clivus Orbius, and therefore handy for a thirsty lictor.

"Stay outside with me a while," Trebonius said cheerfully to Antony, "there's something I need to discuss with you."

Dolabella had spied a crony playing dice with two others, nodded to his lictors that they still had time to waste, and went to join the dice game; he was feeling lucky today.

While Antony and Trebonius talked earnestly at the foot of the steps, Decimus led the Liberators inside. Had any of the senators left in the garden thought to look at them, he might have wondered at the gravity of their faces, the slightly furtive manner they had unconsciously adopted; but no one looked.

Lagging behind, Brutus felt a tug at his toga and turned to see one of his house servants standing red-faced and panting.

"Yes, what is it?" he asked, unbearably happy that something delayed his embarkation upon tyrannicide.

"*Domine*, the lady Porcia!" The man gasped.

"What about her?"

"She's dead!"

The world didn't rock, heave, or spin; Brutus stared at the slave in disbelief. "Nonsense," he said.

"*Domine*, she's dead, I swear she's dead!"

"Tell me what happened," Brutus said calmly.

"Well, she was in a terrible state—running around like one demented, screaming that Caesar was dead."

"Hadn't Atilius Stilo seen her?"

"Yes, *domine*, but he became angry and left when she refused to drink the potion he mixed for her."

"And?"

"She fell over, stone dead. Epaphroditus couldn't find one single sign of life—nothing! She's dead! Dead! Come home, please come home, *domine!*"

"Tell Epaphroditus that I will come when I can," Brutus said, putting a foot on the bottom step. "She isn't dead, I promise you. I know her. It's a fainting spell." And mounted the next step, leaving the slave to gape at his back.

The chamber, large enough to hold six hundred when crammed, looked very empty despite the few backbencher senators already seated, scholarly men who seized any opportunity to read. None had put his stool at the curule dais end, for the light from a series of clerestory grilles streamed in best near the outer doors, but the readers were fairly evenly distributed between the two sides of the House, right top tier and left top tier. Very good, thought Decimus, shepherding his flock ahead of him, glancing back to see Brutus still outside—lost his courage, had he?

Caesar sat with his head bent over an unfurled scroll, lost to the world. Suddenly he moved, but not to look at the group walking down the center of the floor. His left hand plucked the top tablet off his stack, flipped it open, while his right picked up the stylus, began to inscribe the wax quickly and deftly.

Within ten feet of the dais the group came to a confused halt; it didn't seem proper that Caesar failed to notice his assassins. Decimus's eyes went to Pompey's statue, very tall on its four-foot plinth, nestled into its alcove at the back of the platform, which was expansive, as it had to hold between sixteen and twenty men seated on curule chairs. Fingers suddenly clumsy, Decimus felt for his dagger, withdrew it, held it hidden by his side. He could sense the others doing the same, saw Brutus scuttle up the chamber out of the corner of his eye—he'd found the courage after all.

Lucius Tillius Cimber walked up the lictors' step seats at the side of the dais, his dagger on naked display.

"Wait, you impatient cretin, wait!" Caesar barked irritably, his head still down, steel stylus still gouging at the wax.

Lips tightening in outrage, Cimber cast his fellow Liberators a fierce glare—see what a boor our Dictator is?—and strode forward to yank the toga away from the left side of Caesar's neck. But Gaius Servilius Casca, pushing up on Cimber's left, got in first, driving down from behind at Caesar's throat. The blow glanced off the collarbone, inflicted a superficial wound at the top of the chest. Caesar was on his feet so quickly that the movement was a blur, striking out instinctively with his steel stylus. It plunged into Gaius Casca's arm as the rest of the Liberators, emboldened, pressed forward with daggers raised.

Though he fought strenuously, Caesar neither cried out nor spoke. The table went flying, scrolls raining everywhere, the ivory chair followed, and spattering drops of blood. Now some of the senators on the top tiers were looking, exclaiming in horror, but none moved to come to Caesar's aid. Retreating backward, he encountered Pompey's plinth just as Cassius pushed to the fore, sank his blade into Caesar's face, screwed it around, enucleating an eye and rendering that beauty nonexistent. A furore descended as the Liberators crowded in, daggers rising and falling, blood spurting now. Suddenly Caesar ceased to struggle, accepting the inevitable; that unique mind directed its flagging energies to dying with dignity unimpaired. His left hand came up to pull a fold of toga over his face and hide it, his right clenched the toga so that when he fell his legs would be decently covered. No one among this carrion should see what Caesar thought as he died, nor be able to jeer at the memory of Caesar's legs bared.

Caecilius Buciolanus stabbed him in the back, Caesennius Lento in the shoulder. Bleeding terribly, Caesar still stood as the flurry of blows continued. Second-last and cool warrior that he was, Decimus Brutus put everything he had into the first of his two stabs, deep into the left side of Caesar's chest. As the dagger went home to his heart, Caesar collapsed in a heap, Decimus following him down to deal his second blow, for Trebonius. And Brutus, the last to strike, blinded by sweat, palsied by fear, knelt to jab his knife at the genitals his mother had so adored, its tip piercing the many folds of toga because, entirely by accident, Brutus had aimed directly downward. He heard the metal grind and crunch on bone, retched, and scrambled to his feet as a searing pain crossed the back of his hand; someone had cut him.

The deed was done. All twenty-two men had wounded Caesar somewhere, Decimus Brutus twice. Face and legs covered, Caesar lay beneath Pompey's statue, the creamish-white toga sliced to ribbons around his chest and back, soaking up the brilliantly red blood spreading over the white marble of the platform until it seemed there couldn't possibly be more blood to come, there was so much of it pouring everywhere. Everywhere. Some skipped to avoid it, but Decimus didn't notice it until it flowed around his shoes and percolated inside; he whimpered, sure it burned him.

Sobbing for breath, the Liberators stared at one another, eyes wild, Brutus absorbed in trying to staunch his bleeding hand. As if by instantaneous yet unvoiced consent, they turned and ran for the doors, Decimus as panicked as the rest. The *pedarii* who had witnessed the deed were already outside, screaming that he was dead, Caesar was dead! The panic became universal as the Liberators emerged into the garden, togas bloody, knives still in their sticky fists.

Men fled in all directions save into the Curia Pompeia; senators, lictors and slaves took to their heels, howling that Caesar was dead, Caesar was dead, Caesar was dead!

All their grand plans for speeches and thundering oratory forgotten, the Liberators fled too. Who among them could ever have believed that the reality would be so different from the dream, that staring at Caesar dead was such a terrible end to ideas, to philosophies, to aspirations? Only after the deed was done did any of them, even Decimus Brutus, truly understand its meaning. The titan had fallen, the world was so changed that no Republic could ever spring fully armed from its brow. The death of Caesar was a liberation, but what it had liberated was chaos.

By sheer instinct the Liberators ran for asylum to the temple of Jupiter Optimus Maximus, legs driving like mill shafts across the grass of the Campus Martius, up the back steps of the Capitol on to Romulus's original Asylum, then up the final slope and all those steps to the temple. There, inside, groaning for breath, knees given way, the twenty-two men fell to the floor. Above them reared fifty feet of the Great God in gold and ivory splendor, his bright red terra-cotta face smiling that asinine, shut-mouthed, ear-to-ear smile.

*   *   *

As soon as the first *pedarius* bolted out of the Curia Pompeia shrieking that Caesar was assassinated, Mark Antony let out a yelp and began to run as well—out of the peristyle in the direction of the city! Staggered by Antony's utterly unexpected reaction, Trebonius ran in his wake, shouting at him to stop, return and convene the Senate. But it was too late. Dolabella and his lictors were fleeing, all the senators, stool slaves—and the Liberators. All Trebonius could do was attempt to catch Antony.

Inside was absolute silence. Unable to look down at what lay at its feet, the statue of Pompey gazed up the chamber at the open doors, its pupils already pinpoints against the blinding glare because the artist had wanted overwhelming blueness. Caesar huddled partly on his right side, his face veiled by a fold of toga, the flow of blood finally come to a halt forming a tiny cascade over one side of the dais. Sometimes a small bird flew in, fluttered vainly around the honeycombed roses of the ceiling until the light drew it out again into freedom. The hours dripped on, but no man or woman ventured inside. Caesar and Pompey did not move.

It was well into the afternoon when Calvinus's steward came into his master's study, where the invalid, very much better, was talking to Lucius Caesar and Lucius Piso. On the steward's heels came the Egyptian physician, Hapd'efan'e.

"Not another examination!" Calvinus exclaimed, feeling so much like himself that he could resent medical interruptions.

"No, *domine*. I asked Hapd'efan'e to be here just in case."

"Just in case of what, Hector?"

"The whole city is buzzing with a horrible rumor." Hector hesitated, then blurted it out. "Everyone is saying that Caesar has been murdered."

"Jupiter!" Piso cried as Calvinus leaped off the couch.

"Where? How? Speak, man, speak!" Lucius Caesar snapped.

"Lie down, lord Calvinus, please lie down," Hapd'efan'e was beseeching Calvinus while Hector answered Lucius Caesar.

"No one seems to know, *domine*. Just that Caesar's dead."

"Back on the couch, Calvinus, and no arguments. Piso and I will investigate," said Lucius Caesar, halfway out the door.

"Keep me informed!" Calvinus yelled.

"It can't be, it can't be," Lucius Caesar was muttering as he went down the Vestal Steps five at a time, Piso keeping up.

They burst into the Pontifex Maximus's reception room, the first room inside, to find Quinctilia and Cornelia Merula pacing about;

Calpurnia sat limply on a bench with Junia supporting her. When the men entered, all the women ran to them.

"Where is he?" Lucius Caesar demanded.

"No one knows, Chief Augur," said Quinctilia, a fat, jolly woman who was Chief Vestal. "It's just that the whole Forum is saying that he's been murdered."

"Did he come home from the meeting at the Curia Pompeia?"

"No, he didn't."

"Has anyone of authority been here?"

"No, no one."

"Piso, hold the fortress," Lucius Caesar commanded. "I'm off to the Curia Pompeia to see if anyone's still there."

"Take some lictors with you!" Piso shouted.

"No, Trogus and some of his sons will do."

Lucius moved at the double through the Velabrum—run, trot, walk, run, trot, walk—with Gaius Julius Trogus and three of his sons. People were clustered in groups everywhere, some wringing their hands, some weeping, but no one he barked a question at knew anything more than that Caesar was dead, Caesar had been murdered. Past the Circus Flaminius, out to the theater, into the hundred-pillared colonnade; clutching at a stitch in his side, Lucius paused to get his breath back. No one, but there were many signs that a large number of men had left in a hurry.

"Stay here," he said curtly to Trogus, walked up the steps and into the Curia Pompeia.

He smelled it before he saw it: unmistakable to a soldier, the smell of old, congealing blood. The ivory chair was in small pieces around the purple-and-white marble floor, a folding table had come to rest against the bottom tier on the right side—they had attacked from the left, then—there were scrolls scattered for many feet around, and a body lay on the bare curule dais, absolutely still. When he bent over it he could see that Caesar had been dead for some hours, but he peeled the fold of toga gently away from the head, gasped, choked. The left side of the face was a ruin of blood and flesh, white bone glistening, the eye a runny mess. Oh, Caesar!

"Trogus!" he screamed.

Trogus came running, started to wail like a child.

"There's no time for that, man! Send two of your sons to the Forum Holitorium and commandeer a hand cart. Go on, man, do it! Cry afterward."

He heard two of the young men run off; when Trogus and his remaining lad came into the chamber, Lucius waved them away.

"Wait outside," he said, and slumped on to the edge of the curule dais where he could see his beloved cousin, so still, in such a welter of blood. To have produced so much of it, the wound that killed him must have been among the last.

"Oh, Gaius, that it should have come to this! What will we do? How can the world go on without you? It would be easier to lose our gods." The tears began to pour down his face; he wept for the years, the memories, the joy, the pride, the sheer *waste* of this luminous, peerless Roman. Caesar reduced all others to insignificance. Which was why they had killed him, of course.

But when Trogus came to say that the barrow had arrived, Lucius Caesar arose dry-eyed.

"Bring it in," he said.

It came, an unpainted old wooden cart perched on two wheels, its flat tray very narrow but long enough to take a body, two handles at one end to push it. Lucius absently plucked a few scraps of leaf out of it, brushed some particles of soil away with his hands, made sure that the wrecked face was covered.

"Pick him up gently, lads, lie him on it."

He hadn't begun to stiffen yet; now that he was lying on his back, one arm and hand refused to stay by his side, insisted upon flopping off the barrow. Lucius shrugged himself out of his purple-bordered toga and spread it over Caesar, tucked it in all around. Let the arm and hand dangle free; they would tell the world what kind of burden the old hand cart carried.

"Let's take him home."

Trebonius ran after Antony frantically, shouting at him to calm down, help deal with the situation, call the House into session. But Antony, who could move like the wind despite his size, tore through the Forum with his lictors and kept on going.

Angry and frustrated, Trebonius gave up trying to catch him. Striving to collect himself, he instructed his stool slave to return to the Curia Pompeia and find out what was going on there, then come to report to him at Cicero's house; that done, he ascended the Palatine and asked to see Cicero.

Who wasn't in, but was expected back at any moment. Trebonius sat down in the atrium, accepted wine and water from the steward, and prepared to wait. His stool slave came first, to inform him that the Curia Pompeia was deserted, and that the Liberators had fled en masse to seek asylum in Jupiter Optimus Maximus's.

Stupefied, Trebonius put his head in his hands and tried to work out what had gone wrong. Why had they sought asylum when they ought to be on the rostra proclaiming their deed?

"My dear Trebonius, what is it?" boomed Cicero's golden voice some time later, alarmed at nothing more than the sight of Gaius Trebonius with his head in his hands; he had been playing marriage counselor with Quintus's wife, Pomponia, and had heard no rumors.

"In private," said Trebonius, rising.

"Well?" asked Cicero, shutting the door quickly.

"A group of senators killed Caesar in the Curia Pompeia four hours ago," Trebonius said calmly. "I wasn't one of them, but I was their commanding officer."

The aging, shrunken face lit up like the Alexandrian Pharos; Cicero whooped, clapped his hands together in wild applause, then wrung Trebonius's hand ecstatically. "Trebonius! Oh, what wonderful, wonderful news! Where are they? On the rostra? Still in the Curia Pompeia talking?"

Trebonius wrenched his hand away. "Hah! I should hope!" he snarled savagely. "No, they're not at the Curia Pompeia! No, they're not on the rostra! First that dolt Antonius panicked and ran for the Carinae, I imagine, as he certainly didn't stop in the Forum! He was supposed to spearhead the campaign to extol Caesar's elimination, not scuttle home as if the Furies chased him!"

"*Antonius* was a part of it?" Cicero breathed incredulously.

Remembering to whom he was speaking, Trebonius tried to mend this fence at least. "No, no, of course not! But I knew he wasn't very fond of Caesar, so I thought I could talk him into seeing the sense in smoothing the killing over once it was a fact, that's all. When he wouldn't stop running, I came to find you, which was what I planned to do anyway. Thinking that you'd lend us your support."

"Gladly, gladly!"

"It's too late!" Trebonius cried despairingly. "Do you know what they did? They panicked! *Panicked!* Men like Decimus Brutus and Tillius Cimber panicked! My trusty band of tyrannicides came charging out of the Curia Pompeia and fled to Jupiter Optimus Maximus's, where they're cowering like whipped dogs! Leaving four hundred *pedarii* to fly in all directions screaming that Caesar was dead, murdered, then presumably rush home to lock themselves in. The ordinary folk are down in the Forum milling about, and there's no one in authority to tell them anything."

"Decimus Brutus? No, he'd never panic!" Cicero whispered.

"I tell you, he panicked! They all did! Cassius—Galba—Staius Murcus—Basilus—Quintus Ligarius—there are twenty-two men up there on the Capitol praying to Jupiter's statue and shitting themselves in fear! It all went for nothing, Cicero," Trebonius said grimly. "I thought that bringing them up to the mark would be the hard part—I never even took into account what might happen afterward! Panic! The scheme's in ruins, no one can retrieve our position now. They did the deed, yes, but they didn't hold their ground. Fools, fools!" Trebonius groaned.

Cicero squared his shoulders and patted Trebonius's. "It may not be too late," he said briskly. "I'm off to the Capitol at once, but I suggest you round up some of Decimus Brutus's troupe of gladiators—they're in Rome for some ancestor's funeral games—or at least that's what he told me the other day. With this in the wind, perhaps he brought them in as bodyguards for after." He extended a hand to Trebonius. "Come, my dear fellow, cheer up! You go and find them some protection, and I'll get them down to the rostra." He whooped again, chuckled with glee. "Caesar is dead! Oh, what a gift for liberty! They must be extolled, they must be praised to the skies!"

It was late afternoon when Cicero walked into the temple of Jupiter Optimus Maximus, his beloved freedman Tiro in his wake.

"Congratulations!" he roared. "Fellow senators, what a feat! What a victory for the Republic!"

That huge voice had them jumping, squawking, scrambling into the corners of the *cella*. Eyes adjusting to the gloom, Cicero told them over in astonishment. *Marcus Brutus?* Ye gods! How had they managed to talk him into this? But how terrified they were! Killing Caesar had utterly unmanned them, even Cassius, even Decimus Brutus, even that wolfshead Minucius Basilus.

So he settled to talk them out of their panic, only to find that nothing he said could persuade them to emerge from the temple, declaim upon the rostra. Finally he sent Tiro to buy wine, and when it came he dished it out in the rude clay beakers the vendor had supplied, watched them drink it so thirstily that it was gone in a trice.

When Trebonius walked in he was still trying to jolly them. "The gladiators are outside," Trebonius said briefly, then snorted in disgust. "As I feared, Antonius ran home and has bolted himself in. So has Dolabella and every member of the Senate who knows." He turned on the Liberators in exasperated anger. "Why did you panic?" he demanded. "Why aren't you down there on the rostra? People are gathering like flies on a carcass, but there's no one to tell them what's happened."

"He looked so *awful!*" Brutus moaned, rocking back and forth. "How could anyone so alive be dead? Awful, awful!"

"Come," said Cicero suddenly, pulled Brutus to his feet and crossed to where Cassius sat, head between his knees. Cassius too was hauled up. "The three of us are going down to the rostra, and I'll hear no arguments. Someone has to speak to the people, and, since we lack Antonius or Dolabella, yours are the two best-known faces. Move! Come on, move!"

One hand in Cassius's, the other in Brutus's, Cicero dragged the pair out of the temple and propelled them down the Clivus Capitolinus, thrust them up on to the rostra. A crowd gathered, not a huge one; its mood was docile, bewildered, aimless. As he looked at it, Brutus regained sufficient composure to understand that Cicero was right, that something had to be said. His cap of liberty on his dark curls, his toga long gone, he stepped to the front of the rostra.

"Fellow Romans," he said in a small voice, "it is true that Caesar is dead. That he should continue to live had become intolerable to all men who love freedom. So some of us, including me, decided to free Rome from Caesar's dictatorial tyranny." He held his dagger aloft in his bloody hand, its makeshift bandage emphasizing the redness. A moan went up, but the crowd, growing rapidly as word spread that someone was speaking from the rostra, made no move, evinced no rage.

"Caesar couldn't be let strip land off men who have held it for centuries just to settle his veterans in Italy," Brutus said in the same small voice. "We, the Liberators, who killed Caesar Dictator, the King of Rome, understand that Rome's soldiers must have land to retire on, and we love Rome's soldiers just as much as Caesar did, but we love Rome's landowners too, and what were we to do, I ask you? Caesar leaned too much one way, so Caesar had to go. Rome is more than merely veterans, though we, who have liberated Rome from Caesar, love Rome's veterans—"

He wandered and meandered, all about veteran soldiers and their land, which meant very little to this urban crowd, and told them virtually nothing about why or how Caesar had died. No one who tried to decipher what Brutus was saying was sure who these Liberators were, or who had freed whom from what. Cicero stood listening with a leaden heart. He couldn't speak until Brutus finished anyway, but the longer Brutus dribbled on, the less he wanted to speak at all. Phrases like "committing verbal suicide" danced through his mind; the trouble was that this wasn't his arena, he needed the resonance of a good hall to bounce his voice around—and he needed to look at intelligent faces, not masses.

Run down, Brutus stopped very suddenly. The crowd remained still and silent.

A scream shattered that silence, ripping from the direction of the Velabrum, then was followed by another, closer, from the shadows the Basilica Julia's bulk cast on the Vicus Iugarius. Another scream, another. On the rostra, Brutus saw what was coming through a widening gap in the throng—a vegetable cart pushed by two very tall, strong young men who looked like Gauls. On it lay something covered in a purple-bordered toga, and off one side of the barrow hung a limply flopping hand and lower arm, white as chalk. Behind the two Gauls pushing this burden walked two more, and in their wake, Lucius Julius Caesar in a tunic.

Brutus began to shriek, terrible sounds of horror and pain. Then, before Cicero could restrain him, he was running, Cassius too, off the rostra, back up the hill of the Capitol to the temple. Not knowing what else to do, Cicero followed them.

"He's in the Forum! He's dead, he's dead, he's dead, he's dead! I've seen him!" Brutus howled as he reached the *cella*, fell on the floor and began to weep like one demented. Not in much better case, Cassius crawled to his corner and sobbed. The next thing all of them were crying, moaning.

"I give up," said Cicero to Trebonius, who looked exhausted. "I'm going to get them some food and decent wine. You stay here, Trebonius. Sooner or later they have to come to their senses, but not before morning, I think. I'll send blankets too—it's cold in here." At the doorway he tilted his head, stared at Trebonius dolefully. "Hear that? Mourning, not jubilation. It seems that those in the Forum would rather have Caesar than liberty."

They took Caesar to the Pontifex Maximus's bathroom first; Hapd'efan'e, who had returned from Calvinus's, hung on to his physician's composure and peeled the tattered toga off, the tunic beneath it; no togate man wore a loincloth. While Trogus took off the high red boots of the Alban kings, Hapd'efan'e began to wash away the blood, Lucius Caesar watching. He was a beautifully made man, Caesar, even at fifty-five, his skin always white where the sun hadn't weathered it, but utterly white now, for all his blood had poured away.

"Twenty-three wounds," said Hapd'efan'e, "but if he had had immediate attention, none would have killed him except that one, there." He pointed to the most professionally administered blow, not very large, but right over the heart. "He died the moment it fell, I don't have to open his chest to know that the blade went right inside the heart. Two of his assailants had something very personal to say—there"— pointing to the face—"and there." He pointed to the genitals. "They knew him much better than the others. His beauty and his virility offended them."

"Can you mend him well enough to display his body?" Lucius asked, wondering which two had hated Caesar so personally, for as yet he had no idea who the assassins were.

"I am trained in mummification, lord Lucius. I know that is not necessary for a people who cremate, but even his face will be whole again when I have finished," said Hapd'efan'e. He hesitated, his very dark, slightly sloed eyes staring at Lucius painfully. "Pharaoh—does she know?" he asked.

"Oh, Jupiter! Probably not," said Lucius, and sighed. "Yes, Hapd'efan'e, I'll go and see her now. Caesar would want that."

"His poor women," said Hapd'efan'e, and went on working.

So Lucius Caesar, wrapped in one of his cousin's togas, set out with two of Trogus's mourning sons to see Cleopatra. He didn't bother boating across the river, he took the Pons Aemilia and the Via Aurelia, not sorry for the solitude of the long walk. Gaius, Gaius, Gaius . . . You were tired, so tired. I've seen it descending upon you like a dense fog a little at a time, ever since they forced you to cross the Rubicon. That was never what you wanted. All you wanted was your due. The men who denied you that were small, petty, mean-spirited, devoid of a particle of common sense. Their emotions drove them, not their intellects. That's why they could never understand you. A man with your kind of detachment is an indictment of irrational stupidity. Oh, but I will miss you!

Somehow Cleopatra knew; she met him clad in black.

"Caesar is dead," she said very steadily, her chin up, those remarkable eyes tearless.

"Did you hear the rumor, even out here?"

"No. Pu'em-re saw it when he spilled the sands and sifted them. He did that after we found Amun-Ra turned on his pedestal to the west, and Osiris broken into pieces on the ground."

"An earth tremor on this side of the river. There was none in the city that I know of," Lucius said.

"Gods move the earth when they die, Lucius. I mourn him in my body, but not in my soul, for he is not dead. He has gone into the west, from whence he came. Caesar will be a God, even in Rome. Pu'em-re saw it in the sands, saw his temple in the Forum. Divus Julius. He was murdered, wasn't he?" she asked.

"Yes, by little men who couldn't bear to be eclipsed."

"Because they thought he wanted to be a king. But they did not know him, did they? A terrible deed, Lucius. Because they murdered him, the whole world will take a different course onward. It is one thing to murder a man, quite another to murder a God on earth. They will pay for their crime, but all the peoples of the world will pay far more. They tampered with the Will of Amun-Ra, who is Jupiter Optimus Maximus and Zeus. They played the God game."

"How will you tell his son?"

"Honestly. He is Pharaoh. Once we return to Egypt, I will put my brother down like the jackal he is, and raise Caesarion to the throne beside me. One day he will inherit Caesar's world."

"But he can't be Caesar's heir," Lucius said gently.

The yellow eyes widened, looked scornful. "Oh, Caesar's heir must be a Roman, I know that. But it is Caesarion who is Caesar's blood son, who will inherit all that Caesar was."

"I can't stay," Lucius said, "but I urge you to leave for Egypt as soon as possible. The men who killed Caesar might thirst for other blood."

"Oh, I intend to go. What is left here for me?" Her eyes shimmered, but no tears fell. "I didn't have a chance to say goodbye."

"None of us did. If there's anything you need, come to me."

She let him out into the cold night, and sent torchbearers with him armed with spare ones; her torches were dipped in the fine asphalt from the Palus Asphaltites in Judaea, but no torch lasted very long. Just as no life lasted very long. Only the Gods lived forever, and even they could be forgotten.

How calm she is! thought Lucius. Perhaps sovereigns are different from other men and women. Caesar was, and he had been a natural sovereign. It is not the diadem, it is the spirit.

On the Pons Aemilius he met Caesar's oldest friend, the knight Gaius Matius, whose family had occupied the other ground-floor apartment in Aurelia's Suburan insula.

They fell on each other's shoulders and wept.

"Do you know yet who did it, Matius?" Lucius asked, wiping his eyes and putting an arm around Matius's shoulders as they walked.

"I've heard some names, which is why Piso asked me to go to meet you. Marcus Brutus, Gaius Cassius—and two of his own Gallic marshals, Decimus Brutus and Gaius Trebonius. Pah!" Matius spat. "They owed him everything, and this is how they thank him."

"Jealousy is the worst vice of all, Matius."

"The idea was Trebonius's," Matius went on, "though he didn't strike a blow. His job was to keep Antonius out of the House while the rest did the deed. No lictors inside. It was very clever, but it fell down afterward. They panicked and went to earth in Jupiter Optimus Maximus's."

Lucius felt a coldness growing in the pit of his belly. "Was Antonius a part of the plot?"

"Some say yes, some say no, but Lucius Piso doesn't think so, nor does Philippus. There's no real reason to suppose it, Lucius, if Trebonius was obliged to stay outside and detain him." A sob, several more, then Matius broke into a fresh spate of tears. "Oh, Lucius, what will we do? If Caesar, with all his genius, couldn't find a way out, then who is there left to try? We're lost!"

Servilia had had an irritating day, between Tertulla, who continued to be poorly, and the local Tusculan midwife, who had advised against the jolting journey back to an unhealthy, grimy city—the lady Tertulla was *sure* to have a miscarriage! So Servilia traveled alone, and arrived in Rome after dark.

Sweeping past the porter, she never noticed that his lips were parted to give her a message; up the women's side of the colonnade she marched her stumpy legs, her ears offended by the sounds of jubilation emanating from the three suites on the opposite side where those useless, parasitic philosophers lived—on the wine again, no doubt. Were it left to her, they'd be roosting on top of the rubbish dump near the Agger lime pits. Or, better still, hanging from three crosses in the peristyle rose beds.

Her maidservant running to keep up, she entered her own suite of rooms and dumped her voluminous wrap on the floor; conscious that her bladder was full to bursting, she debated whether to return to the latrine to empty it, then shrugged and went onward to the corridor between the dining room and Brutus's study, looking for him. The lamps were all lit; Epaphroditus came to meet her, wringing his hands.

"Don't tell me!" she barked, not in a good mood. "What's the wretched girl done now?"

"This morning we thought her dead, *domina,* and sent to the master at the Curia Pompeia, but he was right. He said it was a fainting fit, and it was."

"So he's been sitting by her bedside all day when he should have been in the House?"

"That's just it, *domina!* He sent a message back with the servant that it was only a fainting fit—he didn't come home!" Epaphroditus burst into noisy tears. "Oh, oh, oh, and now he can't come home!" he wailed.

"What do you mean, *can't* come home?"

"He means," cried Porcia, running in, "that Caesar is dead, and that my Brutus—*my* Brutus!—killed him!"

Shock paralyzed Servilia; she stood feeling warm urine gush down her legs, numb to the marrow, breath suspended, mouth agape, eyes goggling.

"Caesar's dead, my father is avenged! Your lover's dead because your son killed him! And I made Brutus do it—*I* made him!"

The power to move returned. Servilia leaped at Porcia and punched her with fist closed. Down Porcia went in a sprawl while Servilia got both hands in that mass of hair and dragged her to the pool of urine, scrubbed her face in it until she came to, choking. "*Meretrix mascula! Femina mentula!* Filthy, crazy, lowborn *verpa!*"

Porcia heaved herself to her feet and went for Servilia with teeth and nails; the two women swayed, locked in furious, silent combat as Epaphroditus shrieked for assistance. It took six men to separate them.

"Shut her in her room!" Servilia panted, very pleased because she had gotten by far the best of the tussle. It was Porcia all bleeding and scratched, Porcia all bitten and torn. "Go on, do it!" she roared. "Do it, or I'll have the lot of you crucified!"

The three tame philosophers had tumbled out of their doors to gape, but none ventured close, and none protested as the howling, screaming Porcia was dragged to her room and locked in.

"What are you looking at?" the lady of the house demanded of the three philosophers. "Anxious to hang on crosses, are you, you wine-soaked leeches?"

They bolted back into their suites, but Epaphroditus stood his ground; when Servilia was like this, best to see it out.

"Is what she said true, Ditus?"

"I fear so, *domina*. Master Brutus and the others have sought sanctuary in the temple of Jupiter Optimus Maximus."

"The others?"

"A number, it seems. Gaius Cassius is an assassin too."

She tottered, grabbed at the steward. "Help me to my room, and have someone clean this mess up. Keep me informed, Ditus."

"Yes, *domina*. The lady Porcia?"

"Stays right where she is. No food, no drink. Let her rot!"

The maidservant banished, Servilia slammed her door, dropped on to a couch, rocked with grief. Caesar, dead? No, it couldn't be! But it was. Cato, Cato, Cato, may you roll boulders for all eternity in Tartarus for this! It's your doing, no one else's. It's you brought that piss-puss up, it's you put the idea in Brutus's head to marry her, it's you and the *mentula* who fathered you have ruined my life! Caesar, Caesar! How much I have loved you. I will always love you, I cannot scour it out of my mind.

She leaned back, lashes fanning down over her pallid cheeks, dreaming first of how she was going to kill Porcia—oh, what a day that would be! Then, eyes opening dull and black and fierce, she started to work on a far more important problem—how to retrieve Brutus from this insane catastrophe, how to make sure that the family Servilius Caepio and the family Junius Brutus would emerge from it with fortunes and reputations intact. Caesar dead, but family ruin wouldn't bring him back.

"It's been dark for two hours," Antony said to Fulvia. "I should be safe by now."

"Safe for what?" Fulvia asked, purplish-blue eyes gone murky in the dimness. "Marcus, what are you going to do?"

"Go to the Domus Publica."

"Why?"

"To see for myself that he's really dead."

"Of course he's dead! If he weren't, someone would have come to tell you. Stay here, please! Don't leave me alone!"

"You'll be all right."

And he was gone, a winter cloak thrown around his shoulders.

An exclusive district of large houses, the Carinae was a fork of the Esquiline Mount that traveled toward the Forum, divided from the festering stews behind it by several temple sanctuaries and a grove of oaks. Therefore Antony hadn't far to walk. Lamps flickered down the Sacra Via toward the Forum; there were many people out and about, all going to Rome's heart to wait for news of Caesar. Face covered, he slipped in among them and shuffled along. Some kept moving to the lower Forum, but the area around the Domus Publica was thronged; he was obliged to push through the crowd and hammer on the Pontifex Maximus's door in a more public way than he had hoped. But no one moved to restrain him. Most of the people wept desolately, and all were ordinary Romans. No senators waited outside Caesar's residence.

Seeing the face, Trogus opened the door just enough to let Antony squeeze inside, then closed it quickly. Lucius Piso stood behind him, swarthy face bleak.

"Is he here?" Antony asked, tossing the cloak at Trogus.

"Yes, in the temple. Come," said Piso.

"Calpurnia?"

"My daughter's in bed. That odd Egyptian fellow mixed her a sleeping draft."

The temple lay between the two sides of the Domus Publica, a huge room without an idol, for it belonged to Rome's *numina*, the shadowy gods without faces or human forms that preceded Greek ideas by centuries and still formed the true nucleus of Roman worship; they were the forces that governed functions, actions, entities like larders, granaries, wells, crossroads. It was lit to brilliance with chandeliers, its great double bronze doors open at either end, one set on to the colonnade around the main peristyle, the other on to the mysterious vestibule of the Kings, with its two *amygdalae* and its three downward sloping mosaic pathways to yet another set of doors. Along either side of the chamber stood the *imagines* of the Chief Vestals since the time of the first Aemilia, lifelike wax masks encased in miniature temples, each perched on a costly pedestal.

Caesar sat upright on a black bier in the exact middle, and looked as if he slept. Only Hapd'efan'e knew that the upper left side of his face was carefully tinted wax smeared on a bed of gauze; the eyes were closed, so too the mouth. More shocked and afraid than he had thought to be, Antony inched up to the bier and looked into the dreaming countenance. His toga and tunic were the crimson and purple of the Pontifex Maximus, his head adorned with the oak-leaf crown. The only ring he had ever worn was his seal, but it was gone; the long, tapering fingers were folded on each other in his lap, nails trimmed and polished.

Suddenly the sight was too much; Antony turned away, left the *cella* to go to Caesar's study, Piso following.

"Is there any money here?" Antony asked abruptly.

Piso looked blank. "How would I know?" he asked.

"Calpurnia will. Wake her."

"I beg your pardon?"

"Wake Calpurnia! She'll know where he keeps his money." As he spoke Antony opened a desk drawer, began to rummage inside it.

"Antonius, stop that!"

"I'm Caesar's heir, it will all be mine anyway. What's the difference between taking a bit now or later? I'm being dunned, I have to find enough to satisfy the moneylenders tomorrow."

Piso angry was a terrifying sight; his unfortunate face had a naturally villainous cast, and when he bared his rotten, broken teeth in a snarl, they looked like fangs. Angry now, he wrested Antony's hand out of the drawer, slammed it shut. "I said, stop that! Nor am I waking my poor daughter!"

"I'm Caesar's heir, I tell you!"

"And I am Caesar's executor! You do nothing, you take nothing until I've seen Caesar's will!" Piso declared.

"All right, that can be arranged."

Antony strode to the temple, where Quinctilia, the Chief Vestal, had taken up residence on a chair to keep vigil over Caesar.

"You!" Antony barked, yanking her roughly off the chair. "Fetch me Caesar's will!"

"But—"

"I said, fetch me Caesar's will—*now!*"

"Don't you dare molest Rome's luck!" Piso growled.

"It will take a few moments," Quinctilia babbled, frightened.

"Then don't waste them here! Find it and bring it to Caesar's study! *Move,* you fat, stupid sow!"

"Antonius!" Piso roared.

"He's dead, what does he care?" Antony asked, flapping a hand at Caesar's body. "Where's his seal ring?"

"In my possession," Piso whispered, too angry to yell.

"Give it to me! I'm his heir!"

"Not until I see that for myself."

"He must have scrip, deeds, all sorts of things," said Antony, ransacking the study pigeonholes.

"Yes, he does, but not here, you impious, avaricious fool! Everything is kept with his bankers—he's no Brutus, to have his own strong room!" Piso usurped the desk before Antony could. "I pray," he said coldly, "that you die very slowly and horribly."

Quinctilia appeared with a scroll in her hand, bound with wax and heavily sealed. When Antony went to grab it, she skipped past him with surprising agility and handed it to Piso, who took it and held it to a lamp, examined the seal.

"Thank you, Quinctilia," Piso said. "Please ask Cornelia and Junia to come and act as witnesses. This ingrate insists that I open Caesar's testament now."

The three Vestals, clad in white from head to foot, hair crowned with seven circlets of wool beneath their veils, clustered at one side of the desk while Piso broke the seal and unfurled the short, small document.

A good reader, and assisted by the dot that Caesar always put over the top letter of a new word, Piso scanned it quickly, his arm deliberately obscuring it from Antony's gaze. Without any warning, he threw his head back and roared with laughter.

"What? *What?*"

"You're not Caesar's heir, Antonius! In fact, you don't get a mention!" Piso managed to say, fumbling for his handkerchief to wipe away his tears, half grief, half mirth. "Well done, Caesar! Oh, well done!"

"I don't believe you! Here, give it to me!"

"There are three Vestal witnesses, Antonius," Piso warned as he handed it over. "Don't attempt to destroy it."

Fingers trembling, Antony read only enough to see a ghastly name, didn't get to the adoption clause. "*Gaius Octavius?* That simpering, mincing little pansy? It's a joke! Either that, or Caesar was mad when he wrote it. I'll contest!"

"By all means try," Piso said, snatching the will back. He smiled at the three Vestals, as delighted as he at this wonderful retribution. "It's watertight, Antonius, and you know it. Seven-eighths to Gaius Octavius, one-eighth to be divided between—um, Quintus Pedius, Lucius Pinarius, Decimus Brutus—that won't hold up, he's one of the assassins—and my daughter, Calpurnia."

Piso leaned back and closed his eyes as Antony stormed out. *He has to be worth at least fifty thousand talents,* he thought to himself, still smiling. *One-eighth of that is six thousand, two hundred and fifty talents . . . Ignoring Decimus Brutus, who can't inherit as the result of a crime, that gives my Calpurnia something over two thousand talents. Well, well, well! He's tied it up for her as a decent husband should, too. I can't touch it—without her consent, at any rate.*

He opened his eyes to find he was alone; the Vestals had gone back to their vigil, no doubt. Popping the will into the sinus of his toga, he rose to his feet. Two thousand talents! That made Calpurnia a major heiress. As soon as her official mourning period of ten months was over, he could marry her to someone powerful enough to be a big help for his infant son. Wouldn't Rutilia be thrilled?

Interesting, however, that Caesar had made no provision for a child of Calpurnia's body. *That means he knows there won't be one— or that if there is, it doesn't belong to him. Too busy across the river* with Cleopatra. Gaius Octavius was going to be the richest man in Rome.

Having heard the news of Caesar's assassination as he passed through Veii, not far north of Rome, Lepidus arrived at Antony's house at dawn. Grey with shock and fatigue, he accepted a goblet of wine and stared at Antony.

"You look worse than I feel," Lepidus said.

"I feel worse than I look."

"Odd, I didn't think Caesar's death would hit you so hard, Antonius. Think of all that money you're inheriting."

Whereupon Antony began to laugh insanely, walking back and forth, slapping his thighs, stomping his huge feet on the floor. "*I am not Caesar's heir!*" he hollered.

Jaw dropped, Lepidus gaped. "You're joking!"

"I am not joking!"

"But who else is there to leave it to?"

"Think of the least likely candidate."

Lepidus gulped. "Gaius Octavius?" he whispered.

"Gaius Cunnus Octavius," said Antony. "It all goes to a girl in a man's toga."

"Jupiter!"

Antony collapsed on to a chair. "I was so sure," he said.

"But Gaius Octavius? It makes no sense, Antonius! What is he, about eighteen or nineteen?"

"Eighteen. Sitting across the Adriatic in Apollonia. I wonder did Caesar tell him? They were mighty thick in Spain. I didn't read that far, but no doubt he's been adopted."

"More important," said Lepidus, leaning forward, "what's going to happen now? Shouldn't you be talking to Dolabella? He's the senior consul."

"We'll see about that," Antony said grimly. "Did you bring any troops with you?"

"Yes, two thousand. They're on the Campus Martius."

"Then the first thing is to garrison the Forum."

"I agree," Lepidus was saying when Dolabella walked in.

"Pax, pax!" Dolabella cried, holding up his hands, palms out. "I've come to say that I think you should be senior consul now Caesar's dead, Antonius. This shock changes everything. If we don't present a united front, the gods know what might brew up."

"That's the first piece of good news I've heard!"

"Go on, you're Caesar's heir!"

"*Quin taces!*" Antony snarled, swelling.

"He's not Caesar's heir," Lepidus explained. "Gaius Octavius is. You know, his great-nephew? The pretty pansy?"

"Jup-i-ter!" said Dolabella. "What are you going to do?"

"Stall the bloodsuckers for the moment, and get some money out of the Senate. Now that Caesar's dead, his dictate about who can pull money out of the Treasury will have to go—you do agree, I hope, Dolabella?"

"Definitely," Dolabella said cheerfully. "I owe money too."

"And what about me?" Lepidus asked ominously.

"Pontifex Maximus, for a start," Antony said.

"Oh, that will please Junilla! I can sell my house."

"What are we going to do about the assassins? Do we know yet how many of them there are?" Dolabella asked.

"Twenty-three, if you include Trebonius," Antony said.

"*Trebonius?* But he—"

"Stayed outside to keep me out, and therefore you out. No lictors inside. They carved the old boy into mincemeat. Why don't you know any of this? Lepidus has come from Veii, and he knows."

"Because I've been shut in my house!"

"So have I, but *I* know!"

"Oh, stop arguing!" said Lepidus. "Knowing Cicero, he's been to see you already, am I right?"

"You're right. Now there's a happy man! He wants an amnesty for all of them, of course," Antony said.

"No, a thousand times no!" Dolabella shouted. "I'm not going to let them get away with murdering Caesar!"

"Calm down, Publius," said Lepidus. "Think, man, think! If we don't handle this in the most peaceful way possible, there's certain to be another civil war, and that's the last thing anybody wants. We have to get Caesar's funeral over and done with, which means convoking the Senate—he'll have to have a state ceremony. Have you seen the crowds in the Forum? They're not angry, but the numbers are growing in leaps and bounds." He got up. "I'd best get out to the Campus Martius and deploy my men. When for the Senate meeting? Where?"

"Tomorrow at dawn—next door in Tellus. We'll be safe," said Antony.

"Pontifex Maximus!" Lepidus said gleefully. "Wasn't it odd?" he asked at the door. "When we were talking about the way to die at my dinner. 'As long as it's sudden,' he said. I'm rather glad he got his wish. Can you imagine Caesar dying by inches?"

"He'd fall on his sword first," Dolabella said gruffly, and winked away tears. "Oh, I shall miss him!"

"Cicero told me that the assassins—they call themselves the Liberators, can you believe it?—are wrecks," said Antony. "That's why we ought to go easy on them. The more we try to persecute them, the angrier men like Decimus Brutus might get—he can general troops. Softly, softly, Dolabella."

"For the time being" was as far as Dolabella was prepared to go. "When I have half a chance, Antonius, they'll pay!"

Cicero was pleased with everything except the sad performance of the Liberators in oratory. Twice that day he had persuaded Brutus to speak, the first time from the rostra, the second from the steps of the temple—dismal, doleful, ineffectual, silly! When he didn't ramble in circles about privately owned land being given to the veterans, but how much he loved the veterans, he was maintaining that the Liberators had not forsworn their oaths to safeguard Caesar, because the oaths were invalid. Oh, Brutus, Brutus! Cicero's tongue itched to take over, but his instinct for self-preservation was stronger, and kept him silent. He was also, truth to tell, miffed that they hadn't taken him into their confidence beforehand—if he had known, this shocking mess would not exist, and most of the First Class would not be locked inside their Palatine houses fearing revolution and murder.

What he did do was spend a lot of time talking to Antony, Dolabella and Lepidus, pushing them gently into admitting that, after all, the assassination of Caesar Dictator wasn't the worst crime ever committed.

When the Senate met in the temple of Tellus on the Carinae at dawn of the second day after Caesar's death, the Liberators were not in attendance; they were still living in the temple of Jupiter Optimus Maximus, still refusing to come out. Most other senators were there, but not Lucius Caesar, not Calvinus, and not Philippus. Tiberius Claudius Nero opened proceedings by asking that special honors be granted to the Liberators for freeing Rome from a tyrant, which provoked howls of outrage from the *pedarii*.

"Sit down, Nero, no one asked you for your opinion on anything," Antony said, and swept on into a very reasonable, dulcetly phrased speech that acquainted the conscript fathers with the way the Roman wind was going to blow from the curule dais: the deed was done, the deed could not be undone, and yes, it was misguided, but no, there could be no doubt that the men who slew Caesar were as honorable as they were patriotic. By far the most important aspect, Antony kept hammering, was that government should continue with himself, the *senior* consul Marcus Antonius, in command. If some stared at Dolabella in astonishment, Dolabella simply nodded agreement.

"That is what I want, and that is what I must insist upon," Antony said in no-nonsense tones. "However, it is essential that the House should confirm Caesar's laws and dictates, including those he intended to pass, but didn't."

Many grasped the tenor of that: that whenever he needed to do something, Antony would pretend that Caesar was going to bring it into law later, hadn't gotten around to it before he died. Oh, how Cicero yearned to dispute that! But he couldn't, he had to devote his speech to a plea for the Liberators, who were well intentioned and honorable, must be excused their zeal in killing Caesar. Amnesty was essential! His only reference to Caesar's unpromulgated laws and dictates came at the end, when he protested that he didn't think it was wise to consider things Caesar had not yet mooted.

The meeting broke up with the resolution that government should continue under the aegis of Marcus Antonius, Publius Cornelius Dolabella and the praetors; and a *senatus consultum* that the Liberators, all patriotic men, should go unpunished.

From the temple of Tellus the senior magistrates, together with Aulus Hirtius, Cicero and some thirty others, walked to the temple of Jupiter Optimus Maximus. There Antony informed the dirty, unshaven Liberators that the Senate had decreed a general amnesty, that they were perfectly safe from retribution. Oh, the *relief!* Then the whole party ascended the rostra and publicly shook hands with each other under the sullen eyes of the enormous crowd, watching silently. Not for, but not against. Passive.

"To cement our pact," said Antony as they left the rostra, "I suggest that each of us ask one Liberator to dinner today. Cassius, will you be my guest?"

Lepidus asked Brutus, Aulus Hirtius asked Decimus Brutus, Cicero asked Trebonius, and so on, until every Liberator had an invitation to dinner that afternoon.

"I can't believe it!" whooped Cassius to Brutus as they toiled up the Vestal Steps. "Home free!"

"Yes," said Brutus absently; he had just that moment remembered that Porcia might be dead. This was the first moment since he had left the slave to walk into the Curia Pompeia that he had even thought of her name. But of course she was alive. Were she dead, Cicero would have been the first to tell him.

Servilia met him just beyond the porter's lodge, standing as

Klytemnestra must have done just after killing Agamemnon. All she lacked was the axe. Klytemnestra! That is who my mother is.

"I've locked your wife up," she greeted him.

"Mama, you can't do that! This is my house," he bleated.

"This is my house, Brutus, and it will be until the day I die. That monstrous incubus is no concern of mine, including at law. She drove you to murder Caesar."

"I freed Rome from a tyrant," he said, wishing with every fiber of his being that he could—just this once!—gain the better of her. Wish on, Brutus, that will never happen. "The Senate has decreed an amnesty for the Liberators, so I am still the urban praetor. I still have my wealth and estates."

She started to laugh. "Don't tell me you believe that?"

"It is a fact, Mama."

"The murder of Caesar is a fact, my son. Senatorial decrees are not worth the paper they're written upon."

Decimus Brutus's mind was in a turmoil so chaotic that he wondered about his sanity. He had panicked! Surely that fact alone said his thought processes were quite unhinged. Panic! He, Decimus Junius Brutus, to panic? He, the veteran of many battles, of many life-threatening situations, had looked down at Caesar's body and panicked. He, Decimus Junius Brutus, had run away.

Now he was going to dine with another veteran of the Gallic War: the clerkly warrior Aulus Hirtius, as good with a pen as with a sword, inarguably Caesar's loyalest adherent. Next year Hirtius would be consul with Vibius Pansa if Caesar's dictate held up. But Hirtius is a peasant, a nobody. I am a Junius Brutus, a Sempronius Tuditanus. Loyalty is something I owe first and foremost to myself. And to Rome, of course. That goes without saying. I slew Caesar because he was ruining the Rome of my ancestors. Knitting up a Rome none of us wanted. Decimus, stop deluding yourself! You *are* going mad! You killed Caesar because he outshone you so brilliantly that you realized the only way that men would ever remember your name was if you killed him. *That* is the truth. You'll be in the history books, thanks to Caesar.

It was hard to meet Hirtius's eyes, a nondescript shade of grey-blue-green, peaceful yet stern; the sternness was uppermost, but Hirtius extended his hand cordially and drew Decimus into his very nice house—bought, like Decimus's own, out of the spoils from Long-haired Gaul. They dined alone, a great relief for Decimus, who had dreaded the presence of others.

Finally, the last course and the servants gone, the wine and water remaining, Hirtius turned himself on his end of the couch so that he could see Decimus more comfortably.

"This is a shocking mess you've gotten yourself into," he said as he poured unwatered wine.

"Why say that, Aulus? The Liberators have been granted a general amnesty, things will go on as they always have."

"I'm afraid not. Things have been started that can't go on as they were, because they didn't exist. They're entirely new."

Startled, Decimus spilled a little of his wine. "I don't understand what you're saying."

"Come with me, I'll show you." Hirtius swung his legs off the couch, slid his feet into backless slippers.

Bewildered, Decimus followed suit, walked with Hirtius through the atrium and out on to the loggia, which had a fine view of the lower Forum. The sun was still well up, the sea of people manifest. As far as the eye could travel, masses and masses of people. Just standing there, hardly moving, hardly talking.

"So?" Decimus asked.

"There are plenty of women there, but look at the men. Look at them properly! What do you see?"

"Men," said Decimus, bewilderment growing.

"Decimus, is it really so long ago? Look at them! Half of the men in that crowd are old soldiers—Caesar's old soldiers. Old in terms of soldiering, but not old in years. Twenty-five, thirty, thirty-five, no more. Old, yet still young. The word is spreading up and down Italy that Caesar is dead, murdered, and they've come to Rome for his funeral. Thousands of them. The House hasn't even discussed a date for the funeral yet, but look at how many of them there are already. By the time that Caesar is burned, Lepidus's men will be hopelessly out-numbered." Shivering, Hirtius turned. "It's cold. We can go inside again."

Back on the couch, Decimus downed half a goblet of wine, then stared at Hirtius very levelly. "Do you want my blood, Aulus?"

"I grieve deeply for Caesar," Hirtius answered. "He was my friend as well as my benefactor. But the world can't run backward. If we who are left don't stick together, there'll be another civil war—and that, Rome can't afford. But," Hirtius went on with a sigh, "we're edu-cated, wealthy, privileged, and to some extent detached. It's the veter-ans you have to worry about, Decimus, not men like me or Pansa, much though we loved Caesar. I don't want your blood, but the veter-ans will. And if the veterans want it, then those in power will have to oblige them. The moment the veterans start baying for your blood, so will Marcus Antonius."

Decimus broke into a cold sweat. "You're exaggerating."

"No, I am not. You served with Caesar. You know how his soldiers felt about him. It was a love affair, pure and simple. Even the mutinies. Once the funeral's over, they'll turn ugly. So will Antonius. Or if not Antonius, someone else with power. Dolabella. That slippery eel, Lepidus. Or someone we haven't taken into account as a power because he's waiting in the wings."

More wine, and he felt better. "I'll stick it out in Rome," Decimus muttered, almost to himself.

"I doubt you'll be let stick it out in Rome. The Senate will renege on its amnesty because the people and the veterans will insist it does. The ordinary people loved him too—he was a part of them. And once he rose high, he never forgot them, always had a cheerful word for them, stopped to listen to their woes. What does the abstract concept of political liberty mean to a man or woman of the Subura, Decimus, tell me that? Their votes don't even count in an election of Centuries, People, or Plebs. Caesar *belonged* to them. None of us ever have or ever will."

"If I leave Rome, then I admit that I did wrong."

"That's true."

"Antonius is strong. He's been remarkably decent to us."

"Decimus, don't trust Marcus Antonius!"

"I have very good reason to trust him," Decimus said, knowing what Hirtius could not know: that Marcus Antonius had contrived at the murder of Caesar.

"I believe that he wants to protect you, yes. But the people and the veterans won't let him. Besides, Antonius wants Caesar's power, and any man who aspires to that courts the same fate as Caesar. This assassination has set a precedent. Antonius will begin to fear that he'll be the next man cut down." Hirtius cleared his throat. "I don't know what he'll do, but whatever it is, take it from me, it won't benefit the Liberators."

"You're hinting," Decimus said slowly, "that the Liberators should find honorable, legitimate excuses to leave the city. For me, that's easy. I can go to my province at once."

"You can go. But you won't keep Italian Gaul long."

"Nonsense! The House moved that Caesar's laws and dictates be upheld, and Caesar himself gave me Italian Gaul to govern."

"Believe me, Decimus, you'll keep your province only as long as it suits Antonius and Dolabella."

* * *

The moment he got home Decimus Brutus sat and wrote in haste to Brutus and Cassius, told them what Hirtius had told him, and, back in that blind panic again, announced that he intended to quit Rome and Italy for his province.

As he wrote, the letter grew more and more garbled, talked wildly of a mass migration of the Liberators to Cyprus or the most remote regions of Spanish Cantabria. What could they do except flee? he asked. They had no general like Pompeius Magnus to lead them, not one of them had any clout with the legions or foreign rulers. Sooner or later they were going to be declared public enemies, which would cost them their citizenship and their heads, or at best they would be tried and sent into permanent exile without the funds to live. In the midst of which he was begging them to work very hard on Antonius, assure him that no Liberator had any designs on the state or intention of killing the consuls.

He ended by asking that the three of them meet around the fifth hour of night at a place of their choosing.

So they met at Cassius's house, speaking in whispers with the shutters closed in case some servant grew curious. Brutus and Cassius were stunned by the extent of Decimus's mania, and therefore were not convinced that he knew what he was talking about. Perhaps, Cassius suggested, Hirtius was, for reasons of his own, trying to frighten them into bolting? For the moment they left Rome, they were admitting they had committed a crime. So no, Brutus and Cassius wouldn't leave Rome, and no, they refused to start gathering their liquid assets together either.

"Have it your own way," Decimus said, rising. "Go or stay, I don't care anymore. I'm off to my province as soon as I can make arrangements. If I'm well entrenched in Italian Gaul, then Antonius and Dolabella might decide to leave me alone. Though I think I'll safeguard myself by doing a little secret recruiting of troops among the veterans up there. Just in case."

"Oh, this is terrible!" Brutus cried to Cassius after the obsessed Decimus had gone. "My mother has ill-wished me, Porcia hasn't said two sensible words—Cassius, we've lost our luck!"

"Decimus is wrong," Cassius said confidently. "I'm the one who had dinner with Antonius, so I can assure you that he's totally wrong. It struck me that Antonius was thrilled to see the end of Caesar." His teeth flashed in a grin. "Except, that is, for the contents of Caesar's will."

"Are you going to the Senate meeting tomorrow?" Brutus asked.

"Very definitely. We all should—in fact, we must. And don't worry, Decimus will be there too, I'm sure."

Lucius Piso had called the meeting to discuss Caesar's funeral. Entering the dilapidated interior of Tellus's hesitantly, the Liberators met with no overt hostility, though not one of the backbenchers would go near them in case he should inadvertently touch them. Caesar's obsequies were fixed for two days hence, the twentieth day of March.

"So be it," said Piso, and looked at Lepidus. "Marcus Lepidus, is the city secure?" he asked.

"The city is secure, Lucius Piso."

"Then isn't it time you read Caesar's will publicly, Piso?" Dolabella asked. "I gather it contains a public bequest."

"Let us go to the rostra now," said Piso.

With one accord the House rose and walked to the rostra amid that sea of people. Shrinking, haunted, shuddering, Decimus noted how right Aulus Hirtius was: many of those present were veteran soldiers, more today than yesterday. There were also professional Forum frequenters present, men who knew every prominent face in the First Class. When Brutus and Cassius mounted the rostra with Antony and Dolabella, the Forum frequenters whispered among their less knowledgeable neighbors. A growl began in one throat after another, ominously swelling; Dolabella, Antony and Lepidus made a great show of friendliness toward Brutus, Cassius and Decimus Brutus until the growling eventually died away.

Lucius Calpurnius Piso read Caesar's will out in full. Not only did it name Gaius Octavius as his heir, it also formally adopted him as Caesar's son, to be known henceforward as Gaius Julius Caesar. Murmurs of amazement rose from the crowd; no one knew who this Gaius Octavius was, the Forum frequenters able to give his origins, but unable to describe his appearance. When Decimus Brutus was mentioned as a minor heir, another growl went up, but Piso nimbly hopped to the bequest of most interest—three hundred sesterces to every Roman citizen man, and public use of Caesar's gardens across the Tiber. The news was greeted with an alarming silence. No one cheered, no one threw objects into the air, no one applauded. After Piso concluded by announcing the date of the funeral, the Senate left the vicinity of the rostra very quickly, each member escorted by six of Lepidus's soldiers.

It was as if the whole world waited for Caesar's funeral, as if no man or woman in Rome was prepared to make a judgement until

Caesar's last rites were over. Even when Antony told the Senate the next day in Jupiter Stator's that he was permanently expunging the office of dictator from the constitution, only Dolabella reacted with enthusiasm. Apathy, everywhere apathy! And the crowds grew thicker, denser. After dark the whole of the Forum and the streets leading to it were ablaze with lights from lamps and campfires; worried residents in the surrounding insulae didn't sleep for fear of fire.

A relief then, when the day of Caesar's funeral dawned.

A special shrine had been erected on an open piece of ground slightly down-Forum from the side of the Domus Publica and the little round *aedes* of Vesta; it was an exact but smaller replica of the temple of Venus Genetrix in Caesar's Forum, made from wood painted to look like marble. Atop it was a platform accessed by steps to one side, its supports made to look like pillars too.

After long consultation with the Senate, the two in charge of the funeral arrangements, Lucius Caesar and Lucius Piso, had decided that the rostra was just too dangerous a site for the public display of the body and the eulogy. This site at mid-Forum was safer. From it, the funeral procession could turn straight into the Vicus Tuscus and the Velabrum without invading the nucleus of the crowd. Once the cortege reached the Circus Flaminius, it would enter and proceed down its length; as this circus held fifty thousand spectators in its bleachers, Rome's citizens would have a good opportunity to mourn Rome's most beloved son. And from there it would be on to the Campus Martius, where the body would be burned, several hundred litters of aromatics bought at state expense to fuel the pyre.

The procession commenced at the fringes of the Palus Ceroliae swamps, where there was room for every participant to gather. Caesar's bier would join it as it passed the Domus Publica. All Lepidus's two thousand soldiers kept the crowds off the Sacra Via itself, and defended a space around the viewing and eulogy site large enough to accommodate the huge pageant.

Fifty gilded black chariots drawn by pairs of black horses carried the actors wearing the wax masks of Caesar's ancestors—from Venus and Aeneas and Mars through Iulus and Romulus to his uncles by marriage, Gaius Marius and Lucius Cornelius Sulla—down from the Velia to stand in a triple semi-circle in front of the platformed shrine. One hundred of the many hundreds of litters piled with frankincense, myrrh, nard and other costly, burnable aromatics were stacked as a fence between the back row of chariots and the crowd, with shoulder-to-shoulder soldiers as an additional barrier. Interspersed with the chariots and litters as the procession came down from the Velia were black-robed professional mourners beating their breasts, tearing their hair, emitting eldritch wails and keening dirges.

The crowd was gigantic, the greatest number of people since the famous gathering of Saturninus. When Caesar appeared on his bier from out of the doors to the vestibule of the Kings, a moan went up, a sigh, a tremble as of a million leaves. Lucius Caesar, Lucius Piso, Antony, Dolabella, Calvinus and Lepidus carried him, each clad in a black tunic and toga. Behind it the masses closed in. The soldiers standing with their backs pressed against the fence of litters started to look at each other uneasily, feeling the litters begin to wobble and creak as the crowd behind them pushed inexorably. Their worry communicated itself to the chariot horses, which grew restive, and that in turn had the actors shivering.

Caesar sat upright upon the black cushions of the bier in the glory of his pontifical robes, head crowned with the *corona civica*, face serene, eyes closed. He rode on high like a mighty king, for all six of his pallbearers were imposingly tall, and looked the great noblemen they were.

The pallbearers climbed the steps smoothly; Caesar hardly moved as they compensated for the slope. The bier was set down upon the platform so that Caesar was on full display.

Mark Antony went to the front of the edifice and looked out across that ocean, a corner of his appalled mind noting the many Jews with their corkscrew curls and beards, the foreigners of all descriptions— and the veterans, who had chosen to wear a sprig of laurel on their black togas. What was always a white crowd, for Romans at public affairs were togate, had become a black crowd. Fitting, thought Antony, intending to give the greatest speech of his career to the greatest audience any speaker since Saturninus had ever owned.

But it was never given. All Antony managed to say were the opening words inviting Rome to mourn for Caesar. Screams of terrible grief erupted from countless thousands of throats, and the crowd moved as if seized by a single convulsion. Those in the forefront of the crush laid hands upon the hundred litters of aromatics as the chariot horses began to plunge and rear, the actors to scramble for their lives. Suddenly the air was full of chunks of flying wood, bark, resin, raining down on the platform, thrown inside the shrine, around it in growing heaps. The pallbearers, including Antony, fled down the platform steps and ran for the Domus Publica.

Someone threw a torch, and the whole area burst into a pillar of flames. Like his daughter before him, Caesar burned at the wish of the people, not by decree of the Senate.

And after so many days of silence, the crowd shouted for the blood of the Liberators.

"Kill them! Kill them! Kill them!" on and on and on.

Yet there was no riot. Thundering for Liberator blood, the masses stood watching the platform, bier and shrine dissolve into a wall of solid fire, not moving again until the blaze died away and the whole of Rome was filled with the dizzying, beautiful smell of burning aromatics.

Only then did anger erupt into violence. Ignoring Lepidus's soldiers, the masses raced in all directions looking for victims. Liberators! Where were the Liberators? Death to the Liberators! Many poured up on to the Palatine, where doors were bolted in anonymous rows down dozens of narrow alleys and no one knew behind which one lived a Liberator. A Forum frequenter, crazed with grief, spotted Gaius Helvius Cinna, poet senator, running like one possessed, and mistook him for the other Cinna, Lucius Cornelius Cinna, who had once been Caesar's brother-in-law and was rumored to be a Liberator. Innocent of any wrongdoing, Helvius Cinna was literally torn into small pieces.

With night falling, and balked of any other positive prey, the weeping, anguished mobs dispersed.

The Forum Romanum lay deserted under a pall of sweet smoke.

On the morrow the undertakers searched for Caesar's ashes, put what tiny fragments of charred bones they could find into a gem-studded golden urn.

And on the following day, dawn revealed that the blackened flags where shrine and platform had been were covered with little bunches of early spring flowers, and little woollen dolls, and little woollen balls. Soon the little bunches of flowers, the little woollen dolls and the little woollen balls lay a foot thick. Those who left the flowers were women; those who left the dolls were Roman citizen men; and those who left the balls were slaves. The offerings had specific religious significance, and showed how far love for Caesar percolated through every stratum of the city. Of all five Classes, only the First had not universally loved him. And the Head Count, too lowly to have a Class at all, had loved him most. Slaves had no heads to count, hence the balls, but there were just as many little woollen balls as little woollen dolls.

Who can tell why some men are loved, and others not? To a very angry Mark Antony, it was a mystery he had no hope of solving, though, had he asked Aulus Hirtius, Hirtius would have said that all who set eyes on him remembered Caesar, that he radiated some powerfully attractive force impossible to define, that, perhaps, he was simply the personification of the legendary hero.

An angry Antony ordered the removal of the flowers, dolls and balls, but it turned out to be an exercise in futility. For every lot hauled away, twice as many appeared. Baffled, Antony had to give up, to close his eyes to the hundreds upon hundreds of people who were always there around the place where Caesar had burned to pray to him, to offer to him.

Three days after the funeral, the dawn light revealed a magnificent marble altar on the spot where Caesar had burned, and the flowers, the dolls and the balls spread right down the Forum to the rostra.

Eight days after the funeral, a twenty-foot-high column of pure white Proconnesian marble reared alongside the altar. All done in the night marches. Lepidus's soldiers hadn't seen a thing, they protested; they loved Caesar too. Caesar, who was being worshiped as a god by almost all of Rome.

Lucius Caesar didn't stay in Rome to witness most of this. He came down with pain in every limb, climbed laboriously into a litter and set off for his villa near Neapolis. On the way, he visited Cleopatra.

The palace had become a sparsely furnished desert of bleak polished stone and wooden crates; the barges were already moving things downstream to Ostia.

"Are you so ill, Lucius?" she enquired anxiously.

"I am ill in the spirit, Cleopatra. I just couldn't bear to be in a city that allows two blatant murderers in purple-bordered togas to go about their praetorian business."

"Brutus and Cassius. Though I believe that they haven't yet had the courage to go about their praetorian business."

"They daren't until the veterans have left Rome. You heard that poor Helvius Cinna was killed? Piso is desolate."

"Instead of the other Cinna, yes. Was the other Cinna truly one of the assassins?"

"That ingrate? No. He merely thanked Caesar for recalling him from exile by stripping off his praetorian insignia in public because *Caesar* gave them to him. It gave him a day in the sun."

"It's the end of everything, isn't it?" she asked.

"Either an end, or a beginning."

"And Caesar adopted Gaius Octavius." She shivered. "That was brilliant of him, Lucius. Gaius Octavius is very dangerous."

Lucius laughed. "An eighteen-year-old boy? I think not."

"At eight. At eighty."

She looks, Lucius thought, blighted yet entire. Well, she was reared in a cruel nest. She will survive.

"Where's Caesarion?" he asked.

"Gone with his nursemaids and Hapd'efan'e. It's not politic to put two Ptolemies aboard the same ship, or even in the same fleet of ships. We go in two segments. I shall wait another two *nundinae*. Charmian and Iras have remained, and Servilia visits. Oh, Lucius, how she suffers! She blames Porcia for Brutus's share in it, probably with justice. But it's Caesar's death eats at her. She loved him more than anyone."

"More than you loved him?"

"Past tense? No, always present tense. Her love is different from mine. I have a country to care for, and Caesar's blood son."

"Will you marry again?"

"I will have to, Lucius. I am Pharaoh, I must have issue to nurture Nilus and my people."

So Lucius Julius Caesar went on his way to Neapolis, feeling the grief of Caesar's going more now than in the beginning. Matius is right. If Caesar, with all his genius, could not find a way out, who is there left to try? An eighteen-year-old? Never. The wolves of Rome's First Class will tear Gaius Octavius into tinier bits than the Head Count did Helvius Cinna. We of the First Class are our own worst enemies.

IX

Caesar's Heir

From APRIL until DECEMBER of 44 B.C.

GAIUS OCTAVIUS

Legates, military tribunes and prefects of all ranks, even *contubernales*, since they came from families with clout or had distinguished themselves in some way, were not subject to the restrictions and disciplines placed on ranker soldiers and their centurions; it was, for instance, their right to leave military service at any time.

Thus, having arrived in Apollonia at the beginning of March, Gaius Octavius, Marcus Agrippa and Quintus Salvidienus were not obliged to live in the enormous leather-tented camps that stretched from Apollonia all the way north to Dyrrachium. The fifteen legions Caesar had assembled for his campaign went about their camping business indifferent to the presence of the upper-class men who would later assume a sometimes purely nominal command of their battle activities. Save for battle, the twain rarely met.

For Octavius and Agrippa, accommodation was not an issue; they went to the house in Apollonia set aside for Caesar and moved into a small, undesirable room. The penurious Salvidienus, eight years their senior and unsure of his duties or even his rank until Caesar defined them, reported to the quartermaster-general, Publius Ventidius, who assigned him to a room in a house rented for junior military tribunes not yet old enough to stand for election as tribunes of the soldiers. The problem was that the room already had a tenant, another junior military tribune named Gaius Maecenas, who went to Ventidius and explained that he didn't want to share his room or his life with another fellow, especially a Picentine.

The fifty-year-old Ventidius was another Picentine, and had a personal history more ignominious by far than Salvidienus's. As a little boy he had walked as a captive in a triumphal parade Pompey the Great's father had celebrated for victories over the Italians in the Italian War. Childhood afterward had been a parentless ordeal, and only marriage to a wealthy widow from Rosea Rura country had given him a chance to rise. As the Rosea Rura bred the best mules in the world, he went into the business of breeding and selling army mules to generals like Pompey the Great. Thus his contemptuous nickname, Mulio, "the muleteer." Lacking education and the proper background, he had hungered in vain for a military command, knowing in his bones that he could general troops. By the time Caesar crossed the Rubicon he was well known to Caesar; he attached himself to Caesar's cause and waited for his chance. Unfortunately Caesar preferred to give him quartermaster's duties than command of a legion, but, being Ventidius, he applied himself to this organizational job with dour efficiency.

Be it regulating the lives of junior military tribunes or doling out food, equipment and arms to the legions, Publius Ventidius did it well, still hoping in his heart for that opportunity to general. It was getting closer. Caesar had promised him a praetorship next year, and praetors commanded armies, didn't serve as quartermasters.

Understandably, when the wealthy, privileged Gaius Maecenas came complaining about a squalid Picentine moving into his room, Ventidius was not impressed.

"The answer's easy, Maecenas," he said. "Do what others in the same situation do—rent yourself a house at your own expense."

"Do you think I wouldn't, if there were any to rent?" gasped Maecenas. "My servants are living in a hovel as it is!"

"Hard luck" was Ventidius's unsympathetic reply.

Maecenas's reaction to this lack of official co-operation was typical of a wealthy, privileged young man: he couldn't keep Salvidienus out, but nor was he prepared to move over for him.

"So I'm living in about a fifth of a room that's plenty big enough for two ordinary tribunes," Salvidienus said to Octavius and Agrippa in disgust.

"I'm surprised you haven't just pushed him into his half and told him to lump it," said Agrippa.

"If I do that, he'll go straight to the legatal tribunal board and accuse me of making trouble, and I can't afford to earn a reputation as a troublemaker. You haven't seen this Maecenas—he's a fop with connections to all the higher-ups," said Salvidienus.

"Maecenas," Octavius said thoughtfully. "An extraordinary name. Sounds as if he goes back to the Etruscans. I'm curious to meet this Gaius Maecenas."

"What a terribly good idea," said Agrippa. "Let's go."

"No," said Octavius, "I'd rather fish on my own. The pair of you can spend your day on a picnic or a nice long walk."

So when Gaius Octavius strolled alone into the room in one of the junior military tribunes' buildings, Gaius Maecenas glanced up from his writing with a puzzled frown.

Four-fifths of the space was crammed with Maecenas's gear: a proper bed with a feather mattress, portable pigeonholes full of scrolls and papers, a walnut desk inlaid with some very good marquetry, a matching chair, a couch and low table for dining, a console table that held wine, water and snacks, a camp bed for his body servant, and a dozen large wood-and-steel trunks.

The owner of all this clutter was anything but a martial type. Maecenas was short, plump, quite homely of face, clad in a tunic of expensive patterned wool, with felt slippers upon his feet. His dark hair was exquisitely barbered, his eyes were dark, his moist red lips in a permanent pout.

"Greetings," said Octavius, perching on a trunk.

Clearly one look had informed Gaius Maecenas that he confronted a social equal, for he got up with a welcoming smile. "Greetings. I'm Gaius Maecenas."

"And I'm Gaius Octavius."

"Of the consular Octavii?"

"The same family, yes, though a different branch. My father died a praetor when I was four years old."

"Some wine?" Maecenas asked.

"Thank you, but no. I don't drink wine."

"Sorry I can't offer you a chair, Octavius, but I had to move my guest's chair out to make room for some oaf from Picenum."

"Quintus Salvidienus, you mean?"

"That's him. Faugh!" said Maecenas with a moue of distaste. "No money, only one servant. I'll get no contributions toward decent dinners there."

"Caesar favors him highly," Octavius said idly.

"A Picentine nobody? Nonsense!"

"Appearances can be very deceiving. Salvidienus led the cavalry charge at Munda and won nine gold *phalerae*. He'll be attached to Caesar's personal staff when we set out." How very nice it was to be in a position of superior knowledge when it came to command affairs! thought Octavius, crossing his legs and linking his hands around one knee. "Have you had any military experience?" he asked sweetly.

Maecenas flushed. "I was Marcus Bibulus's *contubernalis* in Syria," he said.

"Oh, a Republican!"

"No. Bibulus was simply a friend of my father's. We elected," Maecenas said stiffly, "to stay out of the civil war, so I returned from Syria to my home in Arretium. However, now that Rome's more settled, I intend to enter public life. My father thought it—er—politic— that I gain additional military experience in a foreign war. So here I am," he concluded airily, "in the army."

"But very much on the wrong foot," said Octavius.

"Wrong foot?"

"Caesar is no Bibulus. In his army, rank has few privileges. Senior legates like his nephew Quintus Pedius don't travel in the luxury I see here. I'll bet you have a stable of horses too, but since Caesar walks, so does everybody else, even his senior legates. One horse for battle is mandatory, but more will earn you censure. As will a whole large wagon full of personal possessions."

The liquid eyes gazing at this most unusual youth were growing more and more confused, the redness beneath the skin was deepening. "But I am a Maecenas from Arretium! My ancestry *obliges* me to emphasize my status!"

"Not in Caesar's army. Look at his ancestry."

"Just who do you think you are, to criticize me?"

"A friend," said Octavius, "who would dearly like to see you shift from the wrong foot to the appropriate one. If Ventidius has decided that you and Salvidienus are to share, then you'll continue to share for many moons. The only reason why Salvidienus hasn't beaten the daylights out of you is because he doesn't want to earn a reputation as a troublemaker before the campaign begins. Think about it, Maecenas," said that persuasive voice. "Once we've seen action a couple of times, Salvidienus will stand even higher in Caesar's estimation than he does now. Once that happens, he *will* beat the daylights out of you. Perhaps under your soft exterior, you are a military lion, but I doubt it."

"What do you know? You're only a boy!"

"True, but I don't live in ignorance of what kind of general—or man—Caesar is. I was with him in Spain, you see."

"A *contubernalis!*"

"Precisely. One who knows his place, what's more. However, I'd like to see peace in our little corner of Caesar's campaign, which means you and Salvidienus will have to learn to get along. Salvidienus matters to us. You're a pampered snob," Octavius said genially, "but for some reason, I've taken a fancy to you." He waved his hand at the hundreds of scrolls. "What I see is a man of letters, not of the sword. If you take my advice, you'll apply to Caesar when he arrives for a position as one of his personal assistants on the secretarial front. Gaius Trebatius isn't with him, so there's scope for you to advance that public career as a man of letters with Caesar's help."

"Who *are* you?" Maecenas asked hollowly.

"A friend," Octavius said with a smile, and got up. "Think about what I've said, it's good advice. Don't let your wealth and education prejudice you against men like Salvidienus. Rome needs all kinds of men, and it's to Rome's advantage if different kinds of men tolerate one another's quirks and dispositions. Send all of this except your literature back to Arretium, give Salvidienus half of your quarters, and don't live like a sybarite in Caesar's army. He's not *quite* as strict as Gaius Marius, but he's strict."

A nod, and he was gone.

When Maecenas got his breath back, he stared at his furniture through a veil of tears. Several fell when his eyes reached his big, comfortable bed, but Gaius Maecenas was no fool. The lovely lad had exuded a strange authority. No arrogance, no hauteur, no coldness. Nor the slightest hint of an invitation, though Octavius had revealed a degree of perception about behavior that must surely have informed him that Gaius Maecenas, lover of women, was also a lover of men. He hadn't referred to this by word or look, but he definitely understood that the principal reason Maecenas had tried to eject Salvidienus lay in a need for privacy above and beyond mere literary pursuits. Well, on this campaign it would have to be women, none but women.

So when Salvidienus returned several hours later, he found the room stripped of its trappings, and Gaius Maecenas seated at a plain folding table, his ample behind on a folding stool.

Out came a manicured hand. "I apologize, my dear Quintus Salvidienus," said Maecenas. "If we're to live together for many moons, then we'd best learn to get along. I'm soft, but I'm not a fool. If I annoy you, tell me. I'll do the same."

"I accept your apology," said Salvidienus, who understood a few things about behavior too. "Octavius visited, did he?"

"Who is he?" Maecenas asked.

"Caesar's nephew. Have you been issued orders?"

"Oh, no," said Maecenas. "That's not his style."

The fact that Caesar didn't arrive in Apollonia toward the end of March was generally blamed on the equinoctial gales, now blowing fitfully. Stuck in Brundisium, was the consensus.

On the Kalends of April, Ventidius sent for Gaius Octavius.

"This just came for you by special courier," he said, his tone disapproving; in Ventidius's catalogue of priorities, mere cadets didn't receive specially couriered letters.

Octavius took the scroll, which bore Philippus's seal, with a stab of alarm that had nothing to do with his mother or his sister. White-faced, he sank without permission into a chair to one side of Ventidius's desk and gazed at the trusty muleteer, a helpless agony in his eyes that silenced Ventidius's tongue.

"I'm sorry, my knees have gone," he said, and wet his lips. "May I open this now, Publius Ventidius?"

"Go ahead. It's probably nothing," Ventidius said gruffly.

"No, it's bad news about Caesar." Octavius broke the seal, unfurled the single sheet, and read it laboriously. Finished, he didn't look up, just thrust the paper across the desk. "Caesar is dead, assassinated."

He knew before he opened it! thought Ventidius, snatching the letter. Having mumbled his way through it in disbelief, he stared at its recipient in numbed horror. "But why to you, news like this? And how did you know? Are you prescient?"

"Never before, Publius Ventidius. I don't know how I knew."

"Oh, Jupiter! What will happen to us now? And why hasn't this news been conveyed to me or Rabirius Postumus?" Tears gathered in the muleteer's eyes; he put his face upon his arms and wept bitterly.

Octavius got to his feet, his breath suddenly whistling. "I must return to Italy. My stepfather says he'll be waiting for me in Brundisium. I'm sorry that the news came to me first, but perhaps the official notification was delayed by events."

"Caesar dead!" came Ventidius's muffled voice. "Caesar dead! The world has ended."

Octavius left the office and the building, went down to the quays to hire a pinnace, laboring over the short walk as he hadn't labored for months. Come, Octavius, you can't suffer an attack of the asthma now! Caesar is dead, and the world is ending. I must know it all as soon as possible, I can't lie here in Apollonia gasping for every breath.

"I'm for Brundisium today," he told Agrippa, Salvidienus and Maecenas an hour later. "Caesar has been assassinated. Whoever wants to come with me is welcome, I've hired a big enough pinnace. There won't be any expedition to Syria."

"I'll come with you," Agrippa said instantly, and left the common room to pack his single trunk, call his single servant.

"Maecenas and I can't just leave," said Salvidienus. "We'll have work to do if the army is to be stood down. Perhaps we'll meet again in Rome."

Salvidienus and Maecenas stared at Octavius as if at a total stranger; he had walked in looking blue around the mouth and wheezing, but absolutely calm.

"I haven't time to deal with Epidius and my other tutors," he said now, producing a fat purse. "Here, Maecenas, give this to Epidius and tell him to get everybody and everything to Rome."

"There's a gale coming," Maecenas said anxiously.

"Gales never stopped Caesar. Why should they stop me?"

"You're not well," Maecenas said courageously, "that's why."

"Whether I'm on the Adriatic or in Apollonia, I won't be well, but sickness wouldn't stop Caesar, and it isn't going to stop me."

He went off to supervise the packing of his trunk, leaving Salvidi-enus and Maecenas to look at each other.

"He's too calm," said Maecenas.

"Maybe," Salvidienus said pensively, "there's more of his uncle in him than meets the eye."

"Oh, I've known *that* since the moment I met him. But he does a balancing act on a nervous tightrope that nothing in the history books says Caesar did. The history books! How terrible, Quintus, to think he's now relegated to the history books."

"You're not well," said Agrippa as they walked down to the quays in the teeth of a rising wind.

"That subject is forbidden. I have you, and you're enough."

"Who would *dare* to murder Caesar?"

"The heirs of Bibulus, Cato and the *boni*, I imagine. They won't go unpunished." His voice dropped until it became inaudible to Agrippa. "By Sol Indiges, Tellus and Liber Pater, I swear that I will exact retri-bution!"

The open boat put out into a heaving sea, and Agrippa found him-self Octavius's nursemaid, for Scylax the body servant Octavius chose to go with him succumbed to seasickness even faster than his master did. As far as Agrippa was concerned, Scylax could die, but that couldn't be Octavius's fate. Between his shivering bouts of retching and an attack of the asthma that had him greyish-purple in the face, it did look to the worried Agrippa as if his friend might die, but they had no alternative save to go westward for Italy; wind and sea insisted upon pushing them in that direction. Not that Octavius was a trouble-some or demanding patient. He simply lay in the bottom of the boat on a board to keep him clear of the foul water slopping there; the most Agrippa could do for him was to keep his chin up and his head to one side so that he couldn't aspirate the almost clear fluid he vomited.

Agrippa now discovered convictions in himself that he hadn't known he possessed: that this sickly fellow scant months younger than he wasn't going to die, or disappear into obscurity now that his all-powerful uncle was no longer there to push him upward. At some point in the distant future, Octavius was going to matter to Rome, when he had grown to maturity and could emulate the earlier mem-bers of his family by entering the Senate. He will need military men like Salvidienus and me, he will need a paper man like Maecenas, and we must be there for him, despite whatever happens during the years that must elapse between now and when Gaius Octavius comes into his own. Maecenas is too exalted to be a client, but as soon as Octavius improves, I am going to ask him if I may become his first client, and advise Salvidienus to be his second client.

When Octavius fought to sit upright, Agrippa took him into his arms and held him where his feeble gestures indicated that he could breathe easiest, a *sagum* sheltering him from the rain and spume. At least, thought Agrippa, it's not going to be a long passage. We'll be in Italy before we know it, and once we're on dry land he's bound to lose the seasickness, if not the asthma. Whoever heard of something called asthma?

But landfall when it came was a bitter disappointment; the storm had blown them to Barium, sixty miles north of Brundisium.

In charge of Octavius's purse—as well, for he had no money of his own—Agrippa paid the pinnace owner and carried his friend ashore, leaving Scylax to totter in his wake supported by his own man, Phormion, who to Agrippa represented the difference between utter penury and some pretensions to gentility.

"We must hire two gigs and get to Brundisium at once," said Octavius, who looked much better just for leaving the sea.

"Tomorrow," said Agrippa firmly.

"It's barely dawn. Today, Agrippa, and no arguments."

The asthma improved only a little on the journey, over the sealed Via Minucia but behind two molting mules, but Octavius refused to stop for longer than it took to change teams; they reached the house of Aulus Plautius on nightfall.

"Philippus couldn't come, he has to stay closer to Rome," Plautius said, showing Agrippa where to put Octavius, "but he's sent a letter at the gallop, and there's one from Atia too."

Breathing easier with each passing moment, Octavius lay propped on pillows on a comfortable couch and extended his hand to the anxious Agrippa.

"You see?" he asked, his smile as beautiful as Caesar's. "I knew I'd be safe with Marcus Agrippa. Thank you."

"When did you last eat?" asked Plautius.

"In Apollonia," said the famished Agrippa.

"Where are my letters?" Octavius demanded, more interested in reading than eating.

"Hand them over for the sake of peace," Agrippa said, used to him. "He can read and eat at the same time."

Philippus's letter was longer than the brief note sent to Apollonia, and included a full list of the Liberators as well as the news that Caesar had named Gaius Octavius as his heir, and had also adopted him in his will.

I cannot understand Antonius's toleration of these loathsome men, let alone what seems to be implied approval of their act. They have been granted a general amnesty, and though Brutus and Cassius have not yet appeared on their tribunals to resume their praetorian duties, it is being said that they will do this very shortly. Indeed, I imagine that they would already be back at work, had it not been for the advent of a fellow who appeared three days ago at the spot where Caesar's body was summarily burned. He calls himself Gaius Amatius, and insists that he is Gaius Marius's grandson. Certainly he has considerable oratorical skill, which argues against a purely peasant origin.

First he informed the crowds—they continue to gather every day in the Forum—that the Liberators are utter villains, and must be killed. His anger is directed at Brutus, Cassius and Decimus Brutus more than at the others, though my own opinion is that Gaius Trebonius is the biggest villain. He didn't participate in the actual murder, but he masterminded the plot. On that first day Amatius inspired the crowd to anger: it began, as happened at the funeral, to howl for Liberator blood. His second appearance was even more effective, and the crowd grew really ugly.

But yesterday's appearance, Amatius's third, was worse. He accused Marcus Antonius of complicity in the deed! Said that Antonius's accommodation of the Liberators (oddly enough, Antonius did use the word "accommodation") was deliberate. Antonius was publicly patting the Liberators on the back, rewarding them. They walk around as free as birds, yet they murdered Caesar—Antonius was thick as thieves with Brutus and Cassius, hadn't the people seen that for themselves? All this, and more. So the crowd grew riotous.

I am leaving for my villa at Neapolis, where I will meet you, but I have just heard that some of the Liberators have decided since the appearance of this Gaius Amatius to leave Italy. Cimber has gone to his province in a huge hurry, so have Staius Murcus, Trebonius and Decimus Brutus.

The Senate met to discuss the provinces, and Brutus and Cassius attended, expecting to hear where they would be sent to govern next year. Instead, Antonius discussed only his province, Macedonia, and Dolabella's province, Syria. No talk of pursuing

Caesar's war against the Parthians, however. Antonius has laid claim to the six crack legions encamped in western Macedonia, insists they are now his. For war against Burebistas and the Dacians? He didn't say so. I think he is simply ensuring his own survival if things come to yet another civil war. No decisions were taken about the other nine legions, which have not been recalled to Italy.

The Senate, aided and abetted by Cicero—who was back in the House the moment Caesar died, praising the Liberators to the skies—is busy starting to unravel Caesar's laws, which is a tragedy. There's no *thought* behind it. They remind me of a child getting its hands on mama's sewing halfway through shaping a sleeve.

One other subject I must mention before closing—your inheritance. Octavius, I *beg* you not to take it up! Come to an agreement with the one-eighth heirs whereby the estate is more equitably split up, and decline to be adopted. To take up your inheritance is to court death. Between Antonius, the Liberators and Dolabella, you won't live out the year. They will crush you, an eighteen-year-old. Antonius is beside himself with rage at being cut out of the will, especially by a mere lad. I do not say he did conspire with Caesar's assassins, for there is no proof of it, but I do say that he has few scruples and no ethics. So when I see you, I will expect to hear you say that you have decided to decline Caesar's bequest. Live to be an old man, Octavius.

Octavius put the letter down, chewing hungrily on a chicken leg. Thank all the gods, the asthma was lifting at last. He felt curiously invigorated, able to deal with anything.

"I am Caesar's heir," he said to Plautius and Agrippa.

Working his way through the very generous meal as if it were his last, Agrippa paused, the eyes beneath that jutting, thick-browed forehead gleaming. Plautius, who evidently knew this already, looked grim.

"Caesar's heir," said Agrippa. "What exactly does that mean?"

"It means," Plautius answered, "that Gaius Octavius inherits all Caesar's money and estates, that he will be rich beyond any imagination. But Marcus Antonius expected to inherit, and isn't pleased."

"Caesar also adopted me. I am no longer Gaius Octavius, I am Gaius Julius Caesar Filius." As he announced this, Octavius seemed to swell, his grey eyes as brilliant as his smile. "What Plautius didn't say was that, as Caesar's son, I inherit his enormous clout—and his clientele. I will have at least a quarter of Italy as my clients—my legal followers, pledged to do my bidding—and almost everyone in Italian Gaul, because Caesar absorbed all Pompeius Magnus's clients there as well as having multitudes of his own."

"Which is why your stepfather doesn't want you to take up this terrible inheritance!" Plautius cried.

"But you will," Agrippa said, grinning.

"Of course I will. Caesar *trusted* me, Agrippa! In giving me his name, Caesar said that he thinks I have the strength and the spirit to continue his struggle to put Rome on her feet. He knew that I don't have the ability to inherit his military mantle, but that didn't matter as much to him as Rome does."

"It's a death sentence." Plautius groaned.

"The name Caesar will never die, I will make sure of that."

"Don't, Octavius!" Plautius implored. "Please don't!"

"Caesar trusted me," Octavius repeated. "How can I betray that trust? If he were my age and this was given to him to do, would he abrogate it? No! And nor will I."

Caesar's heir broke the seal on his mother's letter, glanced at it, tossed it into the brazier. "Silly," he said, and sighed. "But then, she always is."

"I take she's begging you not to take up your inheritance either?" asked Agrippa, back into the food.

"She wants a living son, she says. Pah! I do *not* intend to die, Agrippa, no matter how much Antonius might want me to. Though why he should, I have no idea. No matter how the estate's divided, he's not an heir. Maybe," Octavius went on, "we wrong Antonius. Perhaps his chief desire isn't Caesar's money, but Caesar's clout and clientele."

"If you don't intend to die, then eat," said Agrippa. "Go on, Caesar, eat! You're not a tough, stringy old bird like your namesake, and you've nothing in your stomach at all. *Eat!*"

"You can't call him Caesar!" Plautius bleated. "Even if he is adopted, his name becomes Caesar Octavianus, not plain Caesar."

"I'm going to call him Caesar," said Agrippa.

"And I will never, never forget that the first person to call me Caesar was Marcus Agrippa," the debatably named heir said, gaze soft. "Will you cleave to me through thick and thin?"

Agrippa took the outstretched hand. "I will, Caesar."

"Then you will rise with me. So I pledge it. You will be famous and powerful, have your pick of Rome's daughters."

"You're both too young to know what you're doing!" Plautius moaned, wringing his hands.

"We're not, you know," said Agrippa. "I think Caesar knew what he was doing too. He chose his heir wisely."

Because Agrippa was right, Octavian* ate, his mind putting aside this extraordinary fate in favor of a more immediate and pressing concern: his asthma. Again, Caesar had come to his rescue in providing Hapd'efan'e, who had explained his malady to him in simple yet unoptimistic terms. Something no physician had done before. If he was in truth to survive, then he must follow Hapd'efan'e's advice in all ways, from avoiding foods like honey and strawberries to disciplining his emotions into positive channels. Dust, pollen, chaff and animal hair would always be hazards, there was nothing he could do about those beyond try to avoid them, and that wouldn't always be possible. Nor would he ever be a good sailor, between the heavy air and the seasickness. What he had to banish was fear, not easy for one whose mother had inculcated it in him so firmly. Caesar's heir should know no fear, just as Caesar had known no fear. How can I assume Caesar's name and massive *dignitas* if I stand there in public whistling like a bellows and blue in the face? I *will* conquer this handicap, because I must. Exercise, Hapd'efan'e had said. Good food. And a placid frame of mind. How can the owner of Caesar's name have a placid frame of mind?

Very tired, he slept dreamlessly from just after that late dinner until two hours before dawn, not sorry that Plautius's spacious house permitted him and Agrippa to have separate rooms. When he woke, he felt well and breathed easily. A drumming sound brought him to the window, where he found Brundisium in the grasp of driving rain; a glance up at the faint outline of the clouds ascertained that they were ragged, scudding before a high wind. There would be nobody on the streets today, for this weather had set in. Nobody on the streets today . . .

An idle thought, it wandered aimlessly through his mind and bumped into a fact he hadn't remembered until the two collided. From what Plautius had said, all of Brundisium knew that he was Caesar's heir, just like the rest of Italy. The news of Caesar's death had spread

---

* To avoid confusion, it is not possible to start calling Gaius Octavius "Caesar" in narrative. By tradition he is known in these early years to history and historians as "Octavianus," often rendered in English as "Octavian." I shall use the simpler Octavian. The "ianus" suffix in Latin denotes that this name, put last, was the family to which the adopted man originally belonged. Thus, strictly speaking, Gaius Octavius became Gaius Julius Caesar Octavianus. Octavian's own habit in the early days of adding "Filius" to Caesar's name simply indicates "son of."

like wildfire, so the news of Caesar's heir, this eighteen-year-old nephew (he would forget the "great"), had gone after it with equal speed. That meant that whenever he showed his face, people would defer to him, especially if he announced himself as Gaius Julius Caesar. Well, he *was* Gaius Julius Caesar! He would never again call himself anything else, save perhaps to tack "Filius" on to it. As for the Octavianus—a useful way to tell friend from enemy. Those who called him Octavianus would be those who refused to acknowledge his special status.

He remained at the window watching the thick rods of rain angle down before the wind, his face, even his eyes, composed into a tranquil mask that gave nothing of his thoughts away. Inside that bulbous cranium—the same huge skull Caesar and Cicero both owned—his thoughts were very busy, but not tumultuous. Marcus Antonius was desperate for money, and there would be none from Caesar. The contents of the Treasury were probably fairly safe, but right next door in the vaults of Gaius Oppius, chief banker to Brundisium and one of Caesar's loyalest adherents, lay a vast sum of money. Caesar's war chest. Possibly in the neighborhood of thirty thousand talents of silver, from what Caesar had said—take it all with you, don't rely on sending back to the Senate for more because you mightn't get it. Thirty thousand talents amounted to seven hundred and fifty million sesterces.

How many talents can one of those massive wagons I saw in Spain carry if it's drawn by ten oxen? These will be Caesar's wagons here too—the very best from axle grease to stout, iron-bound Gallic wheels. Could one wagon carry three, four, five hundred talents? Now that's the kind of thing Caesar would know at once, but I do not. How fast does a groaning wagon travel?

First I have to get the war chest out of the vaults. How? Unabashed. Just walk in and ask for it. After all, I *am* Gaius Julius Caesar! I have to do this. Yes, I *must* do this! But even supposing I managed to spirit it away, where to hide it? That's easy—on my own estates beyond Sulmo, estates my grandfather had as spoils from the Italian War. Useful only for the timber they bear, logged and sent to Ancona for export. So cover the silver with a layer of wooden planks. I have to do this! I *must!*

Holding a lamp, he went to Agrippa's room and woke him. A true warrior, Agrippa slept like the dead, yet was fully alert at a soft word.

"Get up, I need you."

Agrippa slipped a tunic over his head, ran a comb through his hair, bent to lace on boots, grimacing at the sound of rain.

"How many talents can a heavy army wagon carry, and how many oxen are needed to pull it?" asked Octavian.

"One of Caesar's wagons, at least a hundred with ten oxen, but a lot depends on how the load is distributed—the smaller and more uniform the components, the heavier the cargo can be. Roads and terrain are factors too. If I knew what you were after, Caesar, I could tell you more."

"Are there any wagons and teams in Brundisium?"

"Bound to be. The heavy baggage is still in transit."

"Of course!" Octavian slapped his thigh in vexation at his own density. "Caesar would have conveyed the war chest from Rome in person, it's still here because he'll take it on in person, so the wagons and oxen are here too. Find them for me, Agrippa."

"Am I allowed to ask what and why?"

"I'm appropriating the war chest before Antonius can get his hands on it. It's Rome's money, but Antonius would use it to pay his debts and run up more. When you find the teams and wagons, bring them into Brundisium in a single line, then dismiss their drivers. We'll hire others after they're loaded. Park the leading one outside Oppius's bank next door. I'll organize the labor," said Octavian briskly. "Pretend you're Caesar's quaestor."

Agrippa departed wrapped in his waterproof circular cape, and Octavian went to break his fast with Aulus Plautius.

"Marcus Agrippa has gone out," he said, looking very ill.

"In this weather?" Plautius asked, then sniffed. "Looking for a whorehouse, no doubt. I hope you have more sense!"

"As if asthma were not enough, Aulus Plautius, I feel a sick headache coming on, so it's bed for me in absolute silence. I'm sorry I won't be able to keep you company on such an awful day."

"Oh, I shall curl up on my study couch and read a book, which is why I've sent my wife and children to my estates—peace and quiet to read. I intend to best Lucius Piso—oh, you've eaten nothing!" cried Plautius, clucking. "Off you go, Octavius."

Off the young man went, into the rain. The living rooms opened on to the back lane to avoid the noise of wagons rumbling up and down the main street; if Plautius became immersed in his book, he'd hear nothing. Fortuna is my partner in this enterprise, thought Octavian; the weather is perfect for this, and the Lady of Good Luck loves me, she will see me through. Brundisium is used to strings of wagons and moving armies.

* * *

Two cohorts of troops were camped in a field on the outskirts of the city, all veterans not yet incorporated into legions, having enlisted too late or come too far to reach Capua before the legions left. Whatever military tribune was in charge of them had abandoned them to their own devices, which in weather like this consisted of dice, knucklebones, board games and talk; wine was off legionary menus since the Tenth and Twelfth had mutinied. These men, who had belonged to the old Thirteenth, had no sympathy with mutiny and had only enlisted again because they loved Caesar and fancied a good long campaign against the Parthians. Having heard of his awful death, they grieved, and wondered what was going to happen to them now.

No expert on legionary dispositions, the rather small, hooded and caped visitor had to enquire of the sentries whereabouts the *primipilus* centurion lived, then trudged down the rows of wooden huts to knock on the door of a somewhat larger structure. The noise of voices inside ceased; the door opened. Octavian found himself looking up at a tall, burly fellow who wore a red, padded tunic. Eleven other men sat around a table, all in the same gear, which meant that the visitor surveyed the entire centurion complement of two cohorts.

"Shocking weather," said the door opener. "Marcus Coponius at your service."

Engaged in doffing his *sagum*, Octavian didn't reply until he was done, then stood in his trim leather cuirass and kilt, mop of golden hair damp but not wringing wet. There was something about him that brought the eleven other centurions to their feet, quite why they didn't know.

"I'm Caesar's heir, so my name is Gaius Julius Caesar," said Octavian, big grey eyes welcoming their hard-bitten faces, a smile on his lips that was hauntingly familiar. A collective gasp went up, the men stiffened to attention.

"Jupiter! You look just like him!" Coponius breathed.

"A smaller edition," Octavian said ruefully, "but I hope I still have some growing to do."

"Oh, it's terrible, terrible!" said one at the table, tears gathering. "What will we do without him?"

"Our duty to Rome," said Octavian, matter-of-fact. "That's why I'm here, to ask you to do a duty for Rome."

"Anything, young Caesar, anything," said Coponius.

"I have to get the war chest out of Brundisium as soon as I possibly can. There won't be any campaign to Syria, I'm sure you realize that, but so far the consuls haven't indicated what's going to happen to the legions over the waves in Macedonia—or men like you, still waiting to be shipped. My job is to collect the war chest on behalf of Rome. My adjutant, Marcus Agrippa, is rounding up the wagons and oxen that carry the war chest, but I need loading labor, and I don't trust civilians. Will your men put the money on board the wagons for me?"

"Oh, gladly, young Caesar, gladly! There's nothing worse than wet weather without no work to do."

"That's very kind of you," said Octavian with the smile so reminiscent of Caesar's. "I'm the closest thing Brundisium has to a commanding officer at the moment, but I wouldn't like you to think that I have imperium, because I don't. Therefore I ask humbly, I don't command that you help me."

"If Caesar made you his heir, young Caesar, and gave you his name, there's no need to command," said Marcus Coponius.

With a thousand men at his beck and call, many more than one of the sixty wagons were loaded simultaneously. Caesar had devised a knacky way to carry his money—it was money, not unminted sows. Each talent, in the form of 6,250 denarii, was stored in a canvas bag equipped with two handles, so that two soldiers could easily carry a one-talent bag between them. Swiftly loading while the rain poured down unabated and all Brundisium remained indoors, even on this usually busy street, the wagons moved onward steadily to a timber yard where sawn planks were carefully placed over the bags to look as if sawn planks were all the wagons carried.

"It's sensible," said Octavian glibly to Coponius, "to disguise the cargo, because I don't have the imperium to order a military escort. My adjutant is hiring drivers, but we won't let them know what we're really hauling, so they won't get here until after you're gone." He pointed to a hand cart that held a number of smaller linen bags. "This is for you and your men, Coponius, as a token of my thanks. If you spend any of it on wine, be discreet. If Caesar can help you in any way in the future, don't hesitate to ask."

So the thousand soldiers pushed the hand cart back to their camp, there to discover that Caesar's heir had gifted them with two hundred and fifty denarii for each ranker, one thousand for each centurion, and two thousand for Marcus Coponius. The unit for accounting was the sestertius, but the denarius was far more convenient to mint, at four sesterces to the denarius.

"Did you believe all that, Coponius?" asked one of the very gratified centurions.

Coponius eyed him in scorn. "What d'you take me for, an Apulian hayseed? I don't have no idea what young Caesar's up to, but he's his *tata*'s son, that's for sure. A thousand miles ahead of the opposition. And whatever he's up to ain't none of our business. We're Caesar's veterans. As far as I'm concerned, for one, anything young Caesar does is all right." He put his right index finger to the side of his nose and winked. "Mum's the word, boys. If someone comes asking, we don't know nothing, because we was never out in the rain."

Eleven heads nodded complete agreement.

So the sixty wagons rolled out in the pouring rain on the deserted Via Minucia almost to Barium, then set off cross-country on hard, stony ground toward Larinum, with Marcus Agrippa in civilian dress shepherding this precious load of timber planks. The drivers, who walked alongside their leading beasts rather than sat holding reins, were being paid very well, but not so excessively that they were curious; they were simply glad for the work at this slack season. Brundisium was the busiest harbor in all Italy, cargo and armies came and went incessantly.

Octavian left Brundisium a full *nundinum* later and took the Via Minucia to Barium. There he left it to join the wagons, still plodding north in the direction of Larinum at surprising speed considering that they hadn't used a road since before Barium. When he found them, he learned that Agrippa had been pushing them along while ever there was a moon to see by, as well as all day.

"It's flat ground without hazards. It won't be so easy once we get into the mountains," Agrippa said.

"Then follow the coast, don't turn inland until you see an unsealed road ten miles south of the road to Sulmo. You'll be safe enough on that road, but don't use any others. I'm going ahead to my lands to make sure there are no chattering locals and a good but accessible hiding place."

Luckily chattering locals were few and far between, for the estate was forest in a land of forests. Having discovered that Quintus Nonius, his father's manager, still occupied the staff quarters of the comfortable villa where Atia used to bring her ailing son for a summer in mountain air, Octavian decided that the wagons would be safe in a clearing several miles beyond the villa. Logging, said Nonius, was going on in a different area, and people didn't prowl; there were too many bears and wolves.

Even here, Octavian was astonished to learn, people already knew that Caesar was dead and that Gaius Octavius was Caesar's heir. A fact that delighted Nonius, who had loved the quiet, sick little boy and

Italy's Roads

his anxious mother. However, few if any of the locals knew who owned these timber estates, still referred to as "Papius's place" after their original Italian owner.

"The wagons belong to Caesar, but people who aren't entitled to them will be looking for them everywhere, so no one must know that they're here on Papius's place," he explained to Nonius. "From time to time I may send Marcus Agrippa—you'll meet him when the wagons arrive—to pick up one or two of them. Dispose of the oxen as you think best, but always have twenty beasts on hand. Luckily you use oxen to tow logs to Ancona, so the presence of oxen won't seem unusual. It's important, Nonius—so important that my life may depend upon your and your family's silence."

"Don't you worry, little Gaius," said the old retainer. "I'll look after everything."

Convinced that Nonius would, Octavian backtracked to the junction of the Via Minucia and the Via Appia at Beneventum, picked up the Via Appia there and resumed his journey to Neapolis, where he arrived toward the end of April to find Philippus and his mother in a fever of worry.

"Where have you been?" Atia cried, hugging him to her and watering his tunic with tears.

"Laid low with asthma in some mean inn on the Via Minucia," Octavian explained, removing himself from his mother's clutches, feeling an irritation he was at some pains to hide. "No, no, leave me be, I'm well now. Philippus, tell me what's happened, I've had no news since your letter to Brundisium."

Philippus led the way to his study. A man of high coloring and considerable good looks, he seemed to his stepson's eyes to have aged a great deal in two months. Caesar's death had hit him hard, not least because, like Lucius Piso, Servius Sulpicius and several others among the thin ranks of the consulars, Philippus was trying to steer a middle course that would ensure his own survival no matter what happened.

"Gaius Marius's so-called grandson, Amatius?" Octavian asked.

"Dead," said Philippus, grimacing. "On his fourth day in the Forum, Antonius and a century of Lepidus's troops arrived to listen. Amatius pointed at him and screamed that there stood the real murderer of Caesar, whereupon the troops took Amatius into custody and marched him off to the Tullianum." Philippus shrugged. "Amatius never emerged, so the crowd eventually went home. Antonius went straight to a meeting of the Senate in Castor's, where Dolabella asked him what had happened to Amatius. 'I executed him,' said Antonius. Dolabella protested that the man was a Roman citizen and ought to have been tried, but Antonius said Amatius wasn't a Roman, he was an escaped Greek slave named Hierophilus. And that was the end of it."

"Which rather indicates what kind of government Rome has," Octavian said thoughtfully. "Clearly it isn't wise to accuse dear Marcus Antonius of anything."

"So I think," Philippus agreed, face grim. "Cassius tried to bring up the subject of the praetors' provinces again, and was told to shut up. He and Brutus tried to occupy their tribunals several times, but desisted. Even after Amatius was executed, the crowd didn't welcome them, though their amnesty holds up. Oh, and Marcus Lepidus is the new Pontifex Maximus."

"They held an election?" Octavian asked, surprised.

"No. He was adlected by the other pontifices."

"That's illegal."

"There's no definition of legal anymore, Octavius."

"My name isn't Octavius, it's Caesar."

"That is still undecided." Philippus got up, went to his desk and withdrew a small object from its drawer. "Here, this has to go to you—for the time being only, I hope."

Octavian took it and turned it over between trembling hands, awed. A singularly beautiful seal ring consisting of a flawless, royally purple amethyst set in pink gold. It bore a delicately carved intaglio sphinx and the word CAESAR in mirrored capitals above the sphinx's human head. He slipped it on to his ring finger, to find that it fitted perfectly. The bigger Caesar's fingers had been slender, his own were shorter, thicker, more spatulate. A curious feeling, as if its weight and the essence of Caesar it had drawn into itself were suffusing into his own body.

"An omen! It might have been made for me."

"It was made for Caesar—by Cleopatra, I believe."

"And I am Caesar."

"Defer that decision, Octavius!" Philippus snapped. "A tribune of the plebs—the assassin Gaius Casca—and the plebeian aedile Critonius took Caesar's Forum statues from their plinths and pedestals and sent them to the Velabrum to be broken up. The crowd caught them at it, went to the sculptor's yard and rescued them, even the two that had already been attacked with mallets. Then the crowd set fire to the place, and the fire spread into the Vicus Tuscus. A shocking conflagration! Half the Velabrum burned. Did the crowd care? No. The intact statues were put back, the two broken ones given to another sculptor to repair. Then the crowd started to roar, demanding that the consuls produce Amatius. Of course that wasn't possible. A terrible riot erupted—the worst I ever remember. Several hundred citizens and fifty of Lepidus's soldiers were killed before the mob was dispersed. A hundred of the rioters were taken prisoner, divided into citizens and non-citizens, then the citizens were thrown from the Tarpeian Rock, and the non-citizens were flogged and beheaded."

"So to demand justice for Caesar is treason," Octavian said, drawing in a breath. "Our Antonius is showing his true colors."

"Oh, Octavius, he's just a brute! I don't think it occurs to him that some might interpret his actions as anti-Caesar. Look at what he did in the Forum when Dolabella was deploying his street gangs. Antonius's answer to public violence is slaughter because it's his nature to slaughter."

"I think he's aiming to take Caesar's place."

"I disagree. He abolished the office of dictator."

"If 'rex' is a simple word, so too is 'dictator.' So I take it that no one dares to laud Caesar, even the crowd?"

Philippus laughed harshly. "Antonius and Dolabella should hope! No, nothing deters the common people. Dolabella had the altar and column removed from the place where Caesar burned when he discovered that people were openly calling Caesar 'Divus Julius.' Can you *imagine* that, Octavius? They started worshiping Caesar as a god before the very stones where he burned were cold!"

"Divus Julius," Octavian said, smiling.

"A passing phase," said Philippus, misliking that smile.

"Perhaps, but why can't you see its significance, Philippus? The people have started worshiping Caesar as a god. *The people!* No one in government started it—in fact, everyone in government is doing his best to stamp it out. The people loved Caesar so much that they cannot bear to think of him gone, so they have resurrected him as a god— someone they can pray to, look to for consolation. Don't you see? They're telling Antonius, Dolabella and the Liberators—pah, how I hate that name!—and everyone else at the top of the Roman tree that they refuse to be parted from Caesar."

"Don't let it go to your head, Octavius."

"My name is Caesar."

"I will never call you that!"

"One day you will have no choice. Tell me what else goes on."

"For what it's worth, Antonius has betrothed his daughter by Antonia Hybrida to Lepidus's eldest boy. As both children are years off marriageable age, I suspect it will last only as long as their fathers are holding each other's pricks to piss. Lepidus went to govern Nearer Spain and Narbonese Gaul over two *nundinae* ago. Sextus Pompeius is now fielding six legions, so the consuls decided that Lepidus had better contain his Spanish province while he could. Pollio is still holding Further Spain in good order, so we hear. If we can believe what we hear."

"And that wonderful pair, Brutus and Cassius?"

"Have quit Rome. Brutus has given the urban praetor's duties to Gaius Antonius while he—er—recovers from severe emotional stress. Whereas Cassius can at least pretend to continue his foreign praetor's duties as he wafts around Italy. Brutus took both Porcia and Servilia with him—I hear that the battles between the two women are Homeric—teeth, feet, nails. Cassius gave out that he needs to be nearer to his pregnant Tertulla in Antium, but no sooner did he leave Rome than Tertulla arrived back in Rome, so who knows what the true story is in that marriage?"

Octavian cast his stepfather an unsettlingly shrewd glance. "There's trouble brewing all over the place and the consuls aren't handling it skillfully, are they?"

A sigh from Philippus. "No, they're not, boy. Though they're getting along better together than any of us believed possible."

"And the legions, with regard to Antonius?"

"Are being brought back from Macedonia gradually, I hear, apart from the six finest, which he's keeping there for when he goes to govern. The veterans still waiting for their land in Campania are growing restless because the moment Caesar died—"

"—was murdered—" Octavian interrupted.

"—died, the land commissioners stopped allocating the parcels to the veterans and packed up their booths. Antonius has been obliged to go to Campania and get the land commissioners back to work. He's still there. Dolabella is in charge of Rome."

"And Caesar's altar? Caesar's column?"

"I told you, gone. Just where is your mind going, Octavius?"

"My name is Caesar."

"Having heard all this, you still believe you'll survive if you take up your inheritance?"

"Oh, yes. I have Caesar's luck," said Octavian with a very secretive smile. Enigmatic. If one's seal ring bore a sphinx, to be an enigma was mandatory.

Octavian went to his old room to find that he had been promoted to a suite. Even if Philippus did intend to talk him out of taking up his inheritance, that arch-fence-sitter was clever enough to understand that one didn't put Caesar's heir in accommodations fit for the master's stepson.

His thoughts were disciplined, even if they were fantastic. The rest of what Philippus had had to say was interesting, germane to how he conducted himself in the future, but paled before the story of Divus Julius. A new god apotheosized by the people of Rome for the people of Rome. In the face of obdurate opposition from the consuls Antonius and Dolabella, even at the cost of many lives, the people of Rome were insisting that they be allowed to worship Divus Julius. To Octavian, a beacon luring him on. To be Gaius Julius Caesar Filius was wonderful. But to be Gaius Julius Caesar Divi Filius—the son of a *god*—was miraculous.

But that is for the future. First, I must become known far and wide as Caesar's son. Coponius the centurion said I was his image. I am not, I know that. But Coponius looked at me through the eyes of pure sentiment; the tough, aging man he had served under—and probably never seen at really close quarters—was golden-haired and light of eye, was handsome and imperious. What I have to do is convince people, including Rome's soldiers, that when he was my age, Caesar looked just like me. I can't cut my hair that short because my ears are definitely not Caesar's, but the shape of my head is. I can learn to smile like him, walk like him, wave my hand exactly as he used to, radiate approachability and careless consciousness of my exalted birth. The ichor of Mars and Venus flows in my veins too.

But Caesar was very tall, and in my heart I know that I have scant growing left to do. Perhaps another inch or two, but that will still fall far short of his height. So I will wear boots with soles four inches thick, and to make the device look less obvious, they will always be proper boots, closed at the toe. At a distance, which is how the soldiers will see me, I will tower like Caesar—still not nearly as tall, but close enough to six feet. I will make sure that the men around me are all short. And if my own Class laughs, let them. I will eat the foods that Hapd'efan'e said elongate the bones—meat, cheese, eggs—and I will exercise by stretching. The high boots will be difficult to walk in, but they will give me an athletic gait because walking in them will require great skill. I will pad the shoulders of my tunics and cuirasses. It's Caesar's luck that Caesar was not a hulk like Antonius; all I have to be is an actor.

Antonius will try to block my inheriting. The *lex curiata* of adoption won't come quickly or easily, but a law doesn't really matter as long as I behave like Caesar's heir. Behave like Caesar himself. And the money will be difficult to lay my hands on too because Antonius will block probate. I have plenty of my own, but I may need far more. How fortunate that I appropriated the war chest! I wonder when that oaf Antonius will remember that it exists, and send for it? Old Plautius lives in blissful ignorance, and while Oppius's manager will say that Caesar's heir collected it, I shall deny that. Protest that someone very clever impersonated me. After all, the appropriation happened the day after I arrived from Macedonia—how could I have done it so swiftly? Impossible! I mean, an eighteen-year-old think of something so audacious, so—breathtaking? Ha ha ha, what a laugh! I am an asthmatic, and I had a sick headache too.

Yes, I will feel my way and keep my counsel. Agrippa I can trust with my very life; Salvidienus and Maecenas, less so, but they'll prove good helpmates as I tread this precarious path in my high-soled boots. First and foremost, emphasize the likeness to Caesar. Concentrate on that ahead of anything else. And wait for Fortuna to toss me my next opportunity. She will.

Philippus moved to his villa at Cumae, where the seemingly endless stream of visitors began, all anxious to see Caesar's heir.

Lucius Cornelius Balbus Major came first, arrived convinced that the young man would not prove up to the task Caesar had given him, and departed in a very different frame of mind. The lad was as subtle as a Phoenician banker, and did have an uncanny look of Caesar despite the manifest discrepancies in features and stature. His fair brows were mobile in Caesar's exact fashion, his mouth had the same humorous curve, his facial expressions echoed Caesar's, so did the way his hands moved. His voice, which Balbus remembered as light, had deepened. The only concrete information Balbus prised out of him was that he definitely intended to be Caesar's heir.

"I was fascinated," Balbus said to his nephew and business partner, Balbus Minor. "He has his own style, yes, but he has all Caesar's steel, never doubt it. I am going to back him."

Next came Gaius Vibius Pansa and Aulus Hirtius, destined to be consuls next year if Antonius and Dolabella didn't decide that Caesar's appointments should be overturned. Knowing this, both were worried men. Both had met Octavian: Hirtius in Narbo, Pansa in Placentia. Neither had thought much about him, but now their eyes rested on him in puzzled wonder. Had he reminded them of Caesar then? He definitely did now. The trouble was that the living Caesar cast all others in the shade, and the *contubernalis* had been self-effacing. Hirtius ended in liking Octavian greatly; Pansa, remembering that dinner in Placentia, reserved judgement, convinced that

Antonius would cut the boy's ambitions to ribbons. Yet neither man thought Octavian afraid, and neither man thought that his lack of fear was due to ignorance of what lay in store. He had Caesar's unswerving determination to see things through to the end, and seemed to contemplate his probable fate with a quite unyouthful equanimity.

Cicero's villa, where Pansa and Hirtius were staying, was right next door. Octavian did not make the mistake of waiting for Cicero to call on him. He called on Cicero.

Who eyed him rather blankly, though the smile—oh, *so* like Caesar's!—tugged at his heart. Caesar had possessed an irresistible smile, therefore resisting it had been a hard business. Whereas when it came from such an inoffensive, likeable boy as Gaius Octavius, he could respond to it without reserve.

"You are well, Marcus Cicero?" Octavian asked anxiously.

"I've been better, Gaius Octavius, but I've also been worse." Cicero sighed, unable to discipline that treacherous tongue into silence. When one was born to talk, one would talk to a post, and Caesar's heir was no post. "You've caught me in the midst of personal upheavals as well as upheavals of the state. My brother, Quintus, has just divorced Pomponia, his wife of many years."

"Oh, dear! Isn't she Titus Atticus's sister?"

"She is," Cicero said sourly.

"Acrimonious, was it?" Octavian asked sympathetically.

"Dreadfully so. He can't pay her dowry back."

"I must offer my condolences for the death of Tullia."

The brown eyes moistened, blinked. "Thank you, they are most welcome." A breath quivered. "It seems half a lifetime ago."

"Much has happened."

"Indeed, indeed." Cicero shot Octavian a wary look. "I must offer you condolences for Caesar's death."

"Thank you."

"I never could like him, you know."

"That's understandable," said Octavian gently.

"I couldn't grieve at his death, it was too welcome."

"You had no reason to feel otherwise."

So when Octavian took himself off after a properly short visit, Cicero decided that he was charming, quite charming. Not at all what he had expected. Those beautiful grey eyes held no coldness or arrogance; they caressed. Yes, a very sweet, decently humble young fellow.

So when Octavian paid several more visits to Cicero, he was received warmly, allowed to sit and listen to the Great Advocate talk for some time on each occasion.

"I do believe," Cicero said to his newly arrived houseguest, Lentulus Spinther Junior, "that the lad is really devoted to me." He preened. "Once we're all back in Rome, I shall take Octavius under my wing. I—ah—hinted that I would, and he was enraptured. So different from Caesar! The only similarity I find is the smile, though I've heard others call him Caesar's living image. Well, not everyone is gifted with my degree of perception, Spinther."

"Everyone is saying that he means to take up his inheritance," said Spinther.

"Oh, he will, no doubt about that. But it doesn't worry me in the least—why should it?" Cicero asked, nibbling a candied fig. "Who inherits Caesar's vast fortune and estates doesn't matter a"—he brandished his snack—" fig. Who matters is the man who inherits Caesar's far vaster army of clients. Do you honestly think that *they* will cleave to an eighteen-year-old as raw as freshly killed meat, as green as grass, as naive as an Apulian goatherd? Oh, I don't say that young Octavius doesn't have potential, but even *I* took some years to mature, and *I* was an acknowledged child prodigy."

The acknowledged child prodigy was invited, together with Balbus Major, Hirtius and Pansa, to dinner at Philippus's villa.

"I'm hoping that the four of you will support Atia and me in persuading Gaius Octavius to refuse his inheritance," Philippus said as the meal began.

Though he itched to correct his stepfather, Octavian said nothing about wanting to be called Caesar; instead, he reclined in the most junior spot on the *lectus imus* and forced himself to eat fish, meat, eggs and cheese without saying anything at all unless asked. Of course he was asked; he *was* Caesar's heir.

"You definitely shouldn't," said Balbus. "Too risky."

"I agree," said Pansa.

"And I," said Hirtius.

"Listen to these august men, little Gaius," Atia pleaded from the only chair. "Please listen!"

"Nonsense, Atia." Cicero chuckled. "We may say what we like, but Gaius Octavius isn't going to change his mind. It's made up to accept your inheritance, correct?"

"Correct," said Octavian placidly.

Atia got up and left, on the verge of tears.

"Antonius expects to inherit Caesar's enormous clientele," Balbus said in his lisping Latin. "That would have been automatic had he been named Caesar's heir, but young Octavius here has—er—complicated the picture. Antonius must be offering to Fortuna in gratitude that Caesar didn't name Decimus Brutus."

"Quite so," said Pansa. "By the time that you're old enough to challenge Antonius, my dear Octavius, he'll be past his prime."

"Actually I'm rather surprised that Antonius hasn't come to congratulate his young cousin," Cicero said, diving into the mound of oysters that had been living in Baiae's warm waters that dawn.

"He's too busy sorting out the veterans' land," Hirtius said. "That's why brother Gaius in Rome is enacting new agrarian laws. You know our Antonius—too impatient to wait for anything, so he's decided to legislate reluctant sellers into giving up their land for the veterans. With little or no financial recompense."

"That wasn't Caesar's way," said Pansa, scowling.

"Oh, Caesar!" Cicero waved a dismissive hand. "The world has changed, Pansa, and Caesar is no longer in it, thank all the gods. One gathers that most of the silver in the Treasury went into Caesar's war chest, and of course Antonius can't touch the gold. There's not the money for Caesar's system of compensation, hence Antonius's more draconian measures."

"Why doesn't Antonius repossess the war chest, then?" asked Octavian.

Balbus sniggered. "He's probably forgotten it."

"Then someone ought to remind him," said Octavian.

"The tributes are due from the provinces," Hirtius remarked. "I know Caesar was planning to use them to continue buying land. Don't forget he levied huge fines on Republican cities. The next installments ought to be in Brundisium by now."

"Antonius really ought to visit Brundisium," said Octavian.

"Don't worry your head about where Antonius is going to find money," Cicero chided. "Fill it with rhetoric instead, Octavius. That's the way to the consulship!"

Octavian flashed him a smile, resumed eating.

"At least we six here can console ourselves with the fact that none of us owns land between Teanum and the Volturnus River," said Hirtius, who was amazingly knowledgeable about everything. "I gather that's where Antonius is garnishing his land. *Latifundia* only, not vineyards." He then proceeded to drop sensational news into the conversation. "Land, however, is the least of Antonius's concerns. On the Kalends of June he intends to ask the House to let him swap Macedonia for two of the Gauls—Italian Gaul and Further Gaul excluding Lepidus's Narbonese province, as Lepidus is to continue governing next year. It seems Pollio in Further Spain will also continue next year, whereas Plancus and Decimus Brutus are to be required to step down." Discovering every eye fixed on him in horror, Hirtius made things even worse. "He is also going to ask the House to let him keep those six crack legions in Macedonia, but ship them to Italy in June."

"This means Antonius doesn't trust Brutus and Cassius," said Philippus slowly. "I admit they've issued *edicta* saying they did Rome and Italy a great service in killing Caesar, and begging the Italian communities to support them, but if I were Antonius, I'd be more afraid of Decimus Brutus in Italian Gaul."

"Antonius," said Pansa, "is afraid of everybody."

"Oh, ye gods!" cried Cicero, face paling. "This is idiocy! I can't speak so certainly for Decimus Brutus, but I *know* that Brutus and Cassius don't even dream of raising rebellion against the present Senate and People of Rome! I mean, I myself am back in the Senate, which shows everybody that *I* support this present government! Brutus and Cassius are patriots to the core! They would never, never, never incite an uprising in Italy!"

"I agree," said Octavian unexpectedly.

"Then what's going to happen to the campaign with Vatinius against Burebistas and his Dacians?" asked Philippus.

"Oh, that died with Caesar," said Balbus cynically.

"Then by rights Dolabella ought to have the best legions for Syria—in fact, they're needed there now," said Pansa.

"Antonius is determined to have the six best right here on Italian soil," said Hirtius.

"To achieve *what?*" Cicero demanded, grey and sweating.

"To protect himself against anyone who tries to tear him off his pedestal," said Hirtius. "You're probably right, Philippus—the trouble when it comes will be from Decimus Brutus in Italian Gaul. All he has to do is find some legions."

"Oh, will we never be rid of civil war?" cried Cicero.

"We were rid of it until Caesar was murdered," Octavian said dryly. "That's inarguable. But now that Caesar's dead, the leadership is in flux."

Cicero frowned; the boy had clearly said "murdered."

"At least," Octavian continued, "the foreign queen and her son are gone, I hear."

"And good riddance!" Cicero snapped savagely. "It was she who filled Caesar's head with ideas of kingship! She probably drugged him too—he was always drinking some medicine that shifty Egyptian physician concocted."

"What she couldn't have done," said Octavian, "was inspire the common people to worship Caesar as a god. They thought of that for themselves."

The other men stirred uneasily.

"Dolabella put paid to that," Hirtius said, "when he took the altar and column away." He laughed. "Then hedged his bets! He didn't destroy them, he popped them into storage. True!"

"Is there anything you don't know, Aulus Hirtius?" Octavian asked, laughing too.

"I'm a writer, Octavianus, and writers have a natural tendency to listen to everything from gossip to prognostication. And consuls musing on the state of affairs." Then he dropped another piece of shocking news. "I also hear that Antonius is legislating the full citizenship for all of Sicily."

"Then he's taken a massive bribe!" Cicero snarled. "Oh, I begin to dislike this—this *monster* more and more!"

"I can't vouch for a Sicilian bribe," Hirtius said, grinning, "but I do know that King Deiotarus has offered the consuls a bribe to return Galatia to its pre-Caesar size. As yet they haven't said yes or no."

"To give Sicily the full citizenship endows a man with a whole country of clients," Octavian said thoughtfully. "As I am a mere youth, I have no idea what Antonius plans, but I do see that he's giving himself a lovely present—the votes of our closest grain province."

Octavian's servant Scylax entered, bowed to the diners, then moved deferentially to his master's side. "Caesar," he said, "your mother is asking for you urgently."

"*Caesar?*" asked Balbus, sitting up quickly as Octavian left.

"Oh, all his servants call him Caesar," Philippus growled. "Atia and I have talked ourselves hoarse, but he insists upon it. Haven't you noticed? He listens, he nods, he smiles sweetly, and then he does precisely what he meant to do anyway."

"I am just profoundly grateful," Cicero said, suppressing his unease at hearing this about Octavius, "that the lad has you to guide him, Philippus. I confess that when I first heard that Octavius had returned to Italy so quickly after Caesar's death, I thought immediately what a convenient rallying point he'd make for a man intent upon overthrowing the state. However, now that I've actually met him, I don't fear that at all. He's delightfully humble, yes, but not fool enough to allow himself to be used as somebody else's cat's-paw."

"I'm more afraid," said Philippus gloomily, "that it's Gaius Octavius will use others as *his* cat's-paws."

After Decimus Brutus, Gaius Trebonius, Tillius Cimber and Staius Murcus left for their provinces, Rome's attention became focused on the two senior praetors, Brutus and Cassius. A few shrinking ventures into the Forum to test the atmosphere with a view to presiding at their tribunals had convinced the pair that to absent themselves was more sensible. The Senate had granted each of them a fifty-man bodyguard of lictors minus *fasces*, which served only to increase their visibility.

"Leave Rome until feelings die down," Servilia advised. "If your faces aren't seen, people will forget them." She gave a snort of laughter. "Two years from now, you could run for consul without anyone's remembering that you murdered Caesar."

"It was not murder, it was a right act!" Porcia shouted.

"Shut up, you," Servilia said placidly; she could afford to be generous, she was well and truly winning the war. Porcia had handed it to her on a platter by growing steadily madder.

"To leave Rome is to admit guilt," said Cassius. "I say we have to stick it out."

Brutus was torn. The public half of him agreed with Cassius, whereas the private half dwelled wistfully upon an existence without his mother, whose mood hadn't improved after she gave Pontius Aquila his marching orders. "I'll think about it," he said.

His way of thinking about it was to seek an interview with Mark Antony, who looked as if he was capable of containing all opposition. The result, Brutus decided, of the fact that the Senate, full of Caesar's creatures, had turned to Antony as to its guiding star. Comforting then to know that Antony really had accommodated the Liberators in every way. He was on their side.

"What do you think, Antonius?" Brutus asked, big brown eyes as sad as ever. "It's no part of our intention to contest you—or proper, ethical Republican government. Personally, I found your abolition of the dictatorship enormously reassuring. If you feel that good government would be assisted by our absence, then I'll talk Cassius into going."

"Cassius has to go anyway," Antony said, frowning. "He's a third of his way into the foreign praetorship and he hasn't yet heard a case anywhere except in Rome."

"Yes, I understand that," said Brutus, "but for me, it's a different matter. As urban praetor, I can't leave Rome for more than ten days at a time."

"Oh, we can find a way around that," Antony said comfortably. "My brother Gaius has been acting as urban praetor ever since the Ides of March—not hard, as you'd issued your *edicta*—which, by the way, he says are excellent. He can go on doing the job."

"For how long?" Brutus asked, feeling as if he were being swept along on an irresistible tide.

"Between you and me?"

"Yes."

"At least four more months."

"But," Brutus protested, aghast, "that would mean I wouldn't be in Rome to hold the *ludi Apollinares* in Quinctilis!"

"Not Quinctilis," Antony said gently. "Julius."

"You mean Julius is to stay in place?"

Antony's little white teeth gleamed. "Certainly."

"Would Gaius Antonius be willing to celebrate Apollo's games in my name? Naturally I will be funding them."

"Of course, of course!"

"Stage the plays I specify? I have definite ideas."

"Of course, my dear fellow."

Brutus made up his mind. "Then will you ask the Senate to excuse me from my duties for an indefinite period of time?"

"First thing tomorrow," said Antony. "It's really better this way," he added as he accompanied Brutus to the door. "Let the people grieve for Caesar without reminders."

"I was wondering how long Brutus would last," Antony said to Dolabella later that same day. "The number of Liberators still inside Rome is steadily declining."

"With the exception of Decimus Brutus and Gaius Trebonius, they're paltry men," Dolabella said contemptuously.

"I'll grant you Decimus and Trebonius, but Trebonius isn't a problem now he's scuttled off to Asia Province. The one who does worry me is Decimus. He's a cut above the others for ability as well as birth, and we shouldn't forget that under Caesar's dictates he's consul with Plancus the year after next." Antony's frown gathered. "He could prove very dangerous. As one of Caesar's heirs, he has the power to collect at least some of Caesar's clients. While he's up there in Italian Gaul, he's among vast quantities of them."

"*Cacat!* So he is!" cried Dolabella.

"Caesar secured the full citizenship for those who live on the far side of the Padus, and now that Pompeius Magnus is out of the client equation, Caesar's inherited those who live on this side of the Padus as well. Would you care to bet that Decimus isn't going among them wooing them into *his* clientele?"

"No," said Dolabella very seriously, "I wouldn't care to bet one sestertius on it. Jupiter! Here was I thinking of Italian Gaul as a province without any legions, when all the time it's stuffed with Caesar's veterans! The best of them, at that—those who have already been allocated land, and those who have family holdings. Italian Gaul was Caesar's best recruiting ground."

"Exactly. What's more, I've heard that those among them who enlisted under Caesar's Eagles for the Parthian war are starting to go home already. My crack legions are holding, but the other nine are definitely losing cohorts from Italian Gaul. And they're not coming home through Brundisium. They're marching through Illyricum, a few at a time."

"Are you saying Decimus is recruiting already?"

"I honestly don't know. All I'm prepared to say is that it behooves me to keep a close eye on Italian Gaul."

Brutus left Rome on the ninth day of April, but not alone. Porcia and Servilia insisted upon coming too. After an extremely trying night spent in the main hostelry at Bovillae—just fourteen miles down the Via Appia from the Servian Walls of Rome—Brutus had had enough.

"I refuse to travel with you one moment longer," he said to Servilia. "Tomorrow you have two choices. Either you will enter the carriage I've hired to take you to Tertulla in Antium, or tell the driver to take you back to Rome. Porcia is going with me, but you are not."

Servilia gave a twisted smile. "I shall go to Antium and wait until you admit that you can't make the right decisions without me," she said. "Without me, Brutus, you're an utter idiot. Look at what's happened to you since you listened to Cato's daughter ahead of your mother."

Thus Servilia went to Tertulla at Antium, while Brutus and Porcia moved on a little way from Bovillae to his villa outside the small Latin town of Lanuvium, where, had they wished to look up the mountainside, they might have gazed at Caesar's daring villa on its massive piers.

"I think Caesar's choosing an eighteen-year-old as his heir was very clever," said Brutus to Porcia as they dined alone.

"*Clever?* I think it was remarkably foolish," said Porcia. "Antonius will make mincemeat out of Gaius Octavius."

"That's just the point. Antonius doesn't need to," Brutus said patiently. "Loathe the man I might, but the only mistake Caesar ever

made was in dismissing his lictors. Don't you see, Porcia? Caesar settled on someone so young and inexperienced that no one, no matter
how deluded by imagined persecutions, will consider him a rival. On
the other hand, the youth possesses all Caesar's money and estates.
Perhaps for as many as twenty years, Gaius Octavius will seem no
danger to anyone. He'll have time to grow and mature. Instead of se-
lecting the biggest tree in the whole forest, Caesar planted a seed for
the future. His money and estates will water that seed, give it nourishment, permit it to grow quietly and provoke no one to chop it down. In
effect, his message to Rome and to his heir is that in time there will be
another Caesar." He shivered. "The lad must have many traits in common with Caesar, many qualities that Caesar saw and admired. So
twenty years from now, another Caesar will emerge from the forest's
shadows. Yes, very clever."

"They say Gaius Octavius is an effeminate weakling," Porcia said,
kissing her husband's wrinkled brow.

"I doubt that very much, my dear. I know my Caesar better than I
know my Homer."

"Are you going to lie down tamely under this banishment?" she
demanded, returning to her favorite topic.

"No," Brutus said calmly. "I've sent Cassius a message that I intend to draft a statement on both our behalves, addressed to all of
Italy's towns and communities. It will say that we acted in their best
interests, and beg for their support. I don't want Antonius to think that
we're without support just because we gave in and left Rome."

"Good!" said Porcia, pleased.

Not every town and rural district in Italy had loved Caesar; in
some areas Republican sentiments had caused the loss of much public
land, in others no Roman was loved or trusted. So the two Liberators
found their statement well received in certain places, were even offered young men as troops if they wished to take up arms against
Rome and all Rome stood for.

A state of affairs that perturbed Antony, particularly after he left
Rome himself to deal with veteran land in Campania; the Samnite
parts of that lush region were seething with talk of a new Italian War
under the aegis of Brutus and Cassius. So Antony sent Brutus a stiff
letter informing him that he and Cassius were, consciously or unconsciously, stirring up revolt and courting a trial for treason. Brutus and
Cassius answered him with another public statement that implored
the discontented parts of Italy not to offer them any troops, to leave
things as they lay.

Setting Samnite hatred for Rome aside, there were still nests of ardent Republicans who looked to the pair as to saviors, which was unfortunate for Brutus and Cassius, genuinely not interested in stirring up revolt. In one such nest sat Pompey the Great's friend, *praefectus fabrum* and banker, Gaius Flavius Hemicillus, who approached Atticus and asked that canny plutocrat to put himself at the head of a consortium of financial magicians willing to lend the Liberators money for purposes Hemicillus left unspecified. Atticus courteously refused.

"What I am willing to do privately for Servilia and Brutus is one thing," he told Hemicillus, "but public odium is quite another."

Then Atticus informed the consuls of Hemicillus's overtures.

"That settles it," said Antony to Dolabella and Aulus Hirtius. "I'm not governing Macedonia next year, I'm going to remain right here in Italy—with my six legions."

Hirtius raised his brows. "Italian Gaul as your province?" he asked.

"Definitely. On the Kalends of June I'll ask the House for Italian Gaul and Further Gaul apart from the Narbonese province. Six crack legions camped around Capua will deter Brutus and Cassius—*and* make Decimus Brutus think twice. What's more, I've written to Pollio, Lepidus and Plancus and asked them if they'll place their legions at my disposal if Decimus tries to raise rebellion in Italian Gaul. None of them will back Decimus, that's certain."

Hirtius smiled, but didn't voice his thought: they'll wait and see, then back the stronger man. "What about Vatinius in Illyricum?" he asked aloud.

"Vatinius will back me," Antony said confidently.

"And Hortensius caretaking in Macedonia? He has long-standing ties to the Liberators," said Dolabella.

"What can Hortensius do? He's a bigger lightweight than our friend and Pontifex Maximus, Lepidus." Antony huffed contentedly. "There'll be no uprisings. I mean, can you see Brutus and Cassius marching on Rome? Or Decimus, for that matter? There's not a man alive with the guts to march on Rome—except me, that is, and I don't need to, do I?"

To Cicero, the world had gotten ever crazier since Caesar's death. He couldn't work out why, except that he blamed the failure of the Liberators to seize government on their not taking him into their confidence. He, Marcus Tullius Cicero, with all his wisdom, his experience, his knowledge of the law, had not been asked for advice by one single man.

That included his brother. Quintus, free of Pomponia but unable to pay back her dowry, had filched a solution from Cicero and married a nubile young heiress, Aquilia. That way he could pay off his first wife and still have something to live on. Which had outraged his son to the point of huge temper tantrums. Quintus Junior ran to Uncle Marcus for support, but was silly enough to declare to Cicero that he still loved Caesar, would always love Caesar, and would kill any of the assassins foolish enough to appear in his vicinity. So Cicero had had a temper tantrum of his own and sent Quintus Junior packing. Having nowhere else to go, the young man attached himself to Mark Antony, an even worse insult.

All Cicero could do after that was write letter after letter, to Atticus (in Rome), Cassius (on the road), and Brutus (still in Lanuvium), asking why people couldn't see that Antonius was a bigger tyrant than Caesar? His laws were hideous travesties.

"Whatever you do, Brutus," he said in one letter, "you *must* return to Rome to take your seat in the House on the Kalends of June. If you're not there, it will be the end of your public career, and worse disasters will follow."

One rumored disaster had him ecstatic, however; apparently Cleopatra, her brother Ptolemy and Caesarion had been shipwrecked on the way home and had all drowned.

"And have you heard," he asked the visiting Balbus in his Pompeian villa—Cicero was an incessant villa-hopper—"what Servilia is doing?" He uttered a theatrical gasp, mimed horror.

"No, what?" asked Balbus, lips twitching.

"She's actually staying *alone* with Pontius Aquila in his villa down the road! Sleeping in the same bed, they say!"

"Dear, dear. I heard that she'd broken with him after she found out he was a Liberator," said Balbus mildly.

"She did, but then Brutus threw her out, so this is her way of embarrassing him and Porcia. A woman in her sixties, and he's younger than Brutus!"

"More distressing by far is the declining prospect of peace in Italy," Balbus said. "I despair of it, Cicero."

"Not you too! Truly, neither Brutus nor Cassius intends to start another civil war."

"Antonius doesn't agree with you."

Cicero's shoulders slumped, he sighed, looked suddenly eighty years old. "Yes, things are drifting warward," he admitted sadly. "Decimus Brutus is the main threat, of course. Oh, why didn't any of them seek counsel from me?"

"Who?"

"The Liberators! They did the deed with the *courage* of men, but about as much *policy* as four-year-olds. Like nursery children stabbing their rag doll to death."

"The only one who might help is Hirtius."

Cicero brightened. "Then let's both see Hirtius."

Octavian entered Rome on the Nones of May, accompanied only by his servants; his mother and his stepfather had declined to take any part in this insane venture. At the fourth hour of day he passed through the Capena Gate and commenced the walk to the Forum Romanum, clad in a spotless white toga with the narrow purple band of a knight on the exposed right shoulder of his tunic. Thanks to many hours of practicing how to walk in his high-soled boots, he made sufficient impression on the people he encountered to cause them to turn and watch his progress admiringly, for he was tall, dignified, and possessed of a straight-backed posture that forbade mincing or undulating; to do either would see him flat on his face. Head up, waving masses of golden hair gleaming, a slight smile on his lips, he proceeded along the Sacra Via with that easy mien of friendliness Caesar had made his own.

"That's Caesar's heir!" one of his servants would whisper to a group of onlookers.

"Caesar's heir has arrived in Rome!" another would murmur.

The day was fine and the sky cloudless, but the humidity was suffocatingly high; so much water vapor saturated the air that the vault was leached of its blueness. Around the sun but some distance from it was a brilliant halo that had people pointing and wondering audibly what this omen meant. Rings around the full moon everybody had seen at some time, but a ring around the sun? Never! An extraordinary omen.

It was easy to find the spot where Caesar had burned, for it was still covered with flowers, dolls, balls. Octavian turned off the Clivus Sacer and went to its margin. There, while the crowd continued to gather, he pulled a fold of toga over his head and prayed silently.

Beneath the nearby temple of Castor and Pollux lay offices used by the College of Tribunes of the Plebs. Lucius Antonius, who was a tribune of the plebs, came out of Castor's basement door just in time to see Octavian tug the toga off his mop of hair.

The youngest of the three Antonii was generally deemed the most intelligent of them, but he owned handicaps that militated against his ever standing as high in public favor as his eldest brother: he had a tendency to run to fat, he was quite bald, and he had a sense of the ridiculous that had gotten him into trouble with Marcus on more than one occasion.

He stopped to watch the praying sprig, suppressing an urge to hoot with laughter. What a sight! So this was the famous Caesar's heir! None of the Antonii mixed in Uncle Lucius's circle and he never remembered setting eyes on Gaius Octavius, but this was he, all right. Couldn't be anyone else. For one thing, he knew that his brother Gaius, acting urban praetor, had received a letter from Gaius Octavius asking for permission to speak publicly from the rostra when he arrived in Rome on the Nones of May.

Yes, this was Caesar's heir. What a figure of fun! Those boots! Who did he think he was fooling? And didn't he have a barber? His hair was longer than Brutus's. A proper little dandy—look at the way he was primping the toga back into place. Is this the best you could do, Caesar? You preferred this perfect pansy to *my brother?* Then you were touched in the head when you made your will, Cousin Gaius.

"*Ave,*" he said, strolling up to Octavian with his hand out.

"Is it Lucius Antonius?" Octavian asked with Caesar's smile—unsettling, that—and enduring the bone-crushing handshake with no change of expression.

"Lucius Antonius it is, Octavius," Lucius said cheerfully. "We're cousins. Has Uncle Lucius seen you yet?"

"Yes, I visited him in Neapolis some *nundinae* ago. He's not well, but he was glad to see me." Octavian paused, then asked, "Is your brother Gaius on his tribunal?"

"Not today. He awarded himself a holiday."

"Oh, too bad," said the young man, still smiling for the crowd, oohing and aahing. "I wrote to ask him if I might speak to the people from the rostra, but he didn't answer."

"S'all right, I can give you permission," Lucius said, his brown eyes sparkling. Something in him was loving this poseur's gall, a typically Antonian reaction. Yet looking into those big, long-lashed eyes revealed nothing whatsoever; Caesar's heir kept his thoughts to himself.

"Can you keep up with me in those brothel pounders?" Lucius asked, pointing to the boots.

"Of course," said Octavian, striding out beside him. "My right leg is shorter than my left, hence the built up footware."

Lucius guffawed. "As long as your *third* leg measures up is the important thing!"

"I really have no idea whether it measures up," Octavian said coolly. "I'm a virgin."

Lucius blinked, faltered. "That's a stupid secret to blurt out," he said.

"I didn't blurt it out, and why should it be a secret?"

"Hinting that you want to throw your leg over, eh? I'll be happy to take you to the right place."

"No, thank you. I'm very fastidious and discriminating, is what I was implying."

"Then you're no Caesar. He'd hump anything."

"True, I am no Caesar in that respect."

"Do you *want* people to laugh at you, coming out with things like that, Octavius?"

"No, but I don't care if they do. Sooner or later they'll be laughing on the other side of their faces. Or crying."

"Oh, that's neat, very neat!" Lucius exclaimed, laughing at himself. "You've turned the table on me."

"Only time will prove that, Lucius Antonius."

"Hop up the steps, young cripple, and stand midway between the two columns of beaks."

Octavian obeyed, turned to stand confronting his first Forum audience: a considerable one. What a pity, he was thinking, that the way the rostra is oriented prevents a speaker from standing with the sun behind him. I'd dearly love to be standing with that halo around my head.

"I am Gaius Julius Caesar Filius!" he announced to the throng in a surprisingly loud and carrying voice. "Yes, that is my name! I am Caesar's heir, formally adopted by him in his will." He put his hand up and pointed to the sun, almost overhead. "Caesar has sent an omen for me, his son!"

But then, without pausing to endow the omen with a ponderous significance, he went smoothly to discuss the terms of Caesar's bequest to the people of Rome. This he dwelled upon at length, and promised that as soon as the will was probated, he would distribute Caesar's largesse in Caesar's name, for he *was* Caesar.

The crowd lapped him up, Lucius Antonius noted uneasily; no one down on the flags of the Forum cared about the high-soled right boot (the left was quite hidden by a toga cut so that it fell just short of the ground), and no one laughed at him. They were too busy marveling at his beauty, his manly bearing, his magnificent head of hair, his startling likeness to Caesar from smile to gestures to facial expressions. Word must have spread very quickly, for a great many of

Caesar's old, faithful people had appeared—Jews, foreigners, Head Count.

Not only his appearance helped Gaius Octavius; he spoke very well indeed, indicating that in time to come he would be one of Rome's great orators. When he was done, he was cheered for a long time; then he walked down the steps and into the crowd fearlessly, his right hand out, that smile never varying. Women touched his toga, almost swooned. If he really is a virgin—I am beginning to think he was just taking the piss out of me—he can alter that state with any female in this crowd, thought Lucius Antonius. The cunning little *mentula* pulled the wool over my eyes beautifully.

"Off to Philippus's now?" Lucius Antonius asked Octavian as he began to move toward the Vestal Steps up on to the Palatine.

"No, to my own house."

"Your father's?"

The fair brows rose, a perfect imitation of Caesar. "My father lived in the Domus Publica, and had no other house. I've bought a house."

"Not a palace?"

"My needs are simple, Lucius Antonius. The only art I fancy, I would dower on Rome's public temples, the only food I fancy is plain, I do not drink wine, and I have no vices. *Vale*," Octavian said, and began to climb the Vestal Steps lithely. His chest was tightening, the ordeal was over and he had done well. Now the asthma would make him pay.

Lucius Antonius made no move to follow him, just stood frowning.

"The cunning little fox, he pulled the wool over my eyes beautifully," Lucius said to Fulvia a little later.

She was with child again, and missing Antony acutely, which made her short-tempered. "You shouldn't have let him speak," she said, her face somber enough to reveal a few unflattering lines. "Sometimes you're an idiot, Lucius. If you've reported his words accurately, then what he said when he pointed to the ring around the sun implied that Caesar is a god and he the son of a god."

"D' you really think so? I just thought it was crafty," said Lucius, still chuckling. "You weren't there, Fulvia, I was. He's a born actor, that's all."

"So was Sulla. And why inform you he's a virgin? Youths don't do that, they'd rather die than admit that."

"I suspect he was really informing me that he's not a homosexual. I mean, he's so pretty any man would get ideas, but he denied having *any* vices. His needs are simple, he says. Though he's a good orator. Impressed me, actually."

"He sounds dangerous to me, Lucius."

"Dangerous? Fulvia, he's *eighteen!*"

"Eighteen going on eighty, more like. He's after Caesar's clients and adherents, not after noble colleagues." She got up. "I shall write to Marcus. I think he ought to know."

When Fulvia's letter about Caesar's heir was followed two *nundinae* later by one from the plebeian aedile Critonius telling Antony that Caesar's heir had tried to display Caesar's golden curule chair and gem-studded gold wreath at the games in honor of Ceres, Mark Antony decided it was time to return to Rome. The little mongrel hadn't gotten his way—Critonius, in charge of the *ludi Ceriales*, had forbidden any such displays. So young Octavius had then demanded that the parade show the diadem Caesar had refused! Another no from Critonius saw him defeated, but not penitent. Nor cowed. What's more, said Critonius, he insisted on being addressed as "Caesar"! Was going all over Rome talking to the ordinary people and calling himself "Caesar"! Wouldn't be addressed as "Octavius," and even declined "Octavianus"!

Accompanied by a bodyguard of veterans several hundred strong, Antony clattered into Rome upon a blown horse twenty-one days into May. His rump was sore and his temper the worse for a grueling ride, not to mention that he had had to interrupt vitally important work—if he didn't keep the veterans on his side, what might the Liberators do?

One other item dumped a colossal amount of fuel on his rage. He had sent to Brundisium for the tributes from the provinces and Caesar's war chest. The tributes had duly arrived in Teanum, his base of operations—a great relief, as he could go on buying land and paying something off his debts. Antony wasn't fussy about using Rome's moneys for his private purposes. As consul, he simply sent Marcus Cuspius of the Treasury a statement saying he owed that establishment twenty million sesterces. But the war chest didn't come to Teanum because it wasn't in Brundisium. It had been commandeered by Caesar's heir in Caesar's name, the bewildered bank manager informed Antony's legate, the ex-centurion Cafo. Aware that he couldn't go back to Campania armed with no more than this, Cafo made extensive enquiries all over Brundisium and its suburbs, even the surrounding countryside. What he learned amounted to nothing. The day the money disappeared had been one of torrential rain, no one had been out and about, two cohorts of veterans in a camp said no one in his right mind would have been out in that kind of weather, and no one had seen a train of sixty wagons anywhere. Aulus Plautius when applied to looked utterly blank and was prepared to swear on his family's heads that Gaius Octavius had had nothing to do with any thefts from the bank next door. He had only arrived from Macedonia the day before, and was terribly ill in the bargain—blue in the face. So Cafo rode back to Teanum after deputing several of his men to start asking after a train of wagons north to Barium or west to Tarentum or south to Hydruntum, while others enquired if any laden ships had put out to sea as soon as the gale eased.

By the time Antony rode for Rome, all these investigations had yielded nothing. No train of wagons had been seen anywhere, no ships had put out. The war chest had disappeared off the face of the earth, or so it seemed.

Since it was too late in the day to summon Gaius Octavius, Antony soaked his sore rump in a mineral bath, then had a lusty all-over bath with Fulvia, saw the sleeping Antyllus, ate a huge meal washed down by plenty of wine, then went to bed and slept.

Dolabella, he was informed at dawn, had gone out of town for a few days, but Aulus Hirtius arrived as he was breaking his fast and didn't look in a good mood either.

"What do you mean, Antonius, bringing fully armed soldiers into Rome?" he demanded. "There are no civil disturbances, and you don't have Master of the Horse privileges. The city is alive with rumors that you intend to arrest the Liberators still here—I've had seven of them visit me already! They're writing to Brutus and Cassius—you're *provoking* war!"

"I don't feel safe without a bodyguard," Antony snarled.

"Safe from whom?" Hirtius asked blankly.

"That snake in the grass Gaius Octavius!"

Hirtius flopped on to a chair. "*Gaius Octavius?*" Unable to stifle it, he laughed. "Oh, come, Antonius, really!"

"The little *cunnus* stole Caesar's war chest in Brundisium."

"*Gerrae!*" said Hirtius, laughing harder.

A servant appeared. "Gaius Octavius is here, *domine.*"

"Let's ask him, then," said the scowling Antony, temper not improved at Hirtius's patent disbelief. The trouble was that he didn't dare antagonize Hirtius, the loyalest and most influential of Caesar's adherents in Rome. Carried huge weight in the Senate, and would be consul next year too.

The high-soled boots came as a surprise to Hirtius and Antony both, and didn't contribute to metaphors like snakes in the grass. This demure, togate youth with his odd pretensions, a danger? Worthy of an escort of several hundred armed troops? Hirtius threw Antony a speaking, mirthful glance, leaned back in his chair and prepared to observe the clash of the titans.

Antony didn't bother to rise or extend his hand. "Octavius."

"Caesar," Octavian corrected gently.

"You are not Caesar!" Antony bellowed.

"I am Caesar."

"I forbid you to use that name!"

"It is mine by legal adoption, Marcus Antonius."

"Not until the *lex curiata* of adoption has been passed, and I doubt it ever will be. I'm senior consul, and I'm in no hurry to convene the Curiate Assembly to ratify it. In fact, *Gaius Octavius*, if I have anything to do about it, you'll never see a *lex curiata* passed!"

"Go easy, Antonius," said Hirtius softly.

"No, I will not! You stinking little pansy, who do you think you are, to defy me?" Antony roared.

Octavian stood expressionless, eyes wide and completely opaque, nothing in his pose betraying fear or even tension. His hands, left cuddling folds of toga, right by his side, were curved in a relaxed manner, and his skin was free of sweat.

"I am Caesar," he said, "and, as Caesar, I wish to have that part of Caesar's fortune intended to go to the People of Rome as their inheritance."

"The will hasn't been probated, you can't have it. Pay the people out of Caesar's war chest, Octavius." Antony sneered.

"I beg your pardon?" Octavian asked, allowing himself to look astonished.

"You stole it from Oppius's vaults in Brundisium."

Hirtius sat up, eyes gleaming.

"I beg your pardon?" Octavian repeated.

"You stole Caesar's war chest!"

"I can assure you that I didn't."

"Oppius's manager will testify that you did."

"He can't, because I didn't."

"You deny that you presented yourself to Oppius's manager, announced that you were Caesar's heir, and requested the thirty thousand talents of Caesar's war chest?"

Octavian began to smile delightedly. *"Edepol!* Oh, what a clever thief!" He chuckled. "I'll bet he didn't produce any proof, because even I didn't have any in Brundisium. Perhaps Oppius's manager stole it himself. Dear, dear, what an embarrassment for the state! I do hope you find it, Marcus Antonius."

"I can put your slaves to torture, Octavius."

"I had only one with me in Brundisium, which will make your task easier—*if* you charge me. When did this heinous crime take place?" Octavian asked coolly.

"On a day of terrible rain."

"Oh, that exonerates me! My slave was still prostrate from seasickness, and I from asthma and a sick headache. I do wish," said Octavian, "that you would accord me my due and call me Caesar."

"I will *never* call you Caesar!"

"I must serve you notice, Marcus Antonius, since you are the senior consul, that I intend to celebrate Caesar's victory games after the *ludi Apollinares*, but still during Julius. That is why you see me this morning."

"I forbid it," Antony said harshly.

"Here, you can't do that!" Hirtius said indignantly. "I'm one of Caesar's friends prepared to contribute funds, and I would hope you'll be contributing yourself, Antonius! The boy's right, he's Caesar's heir and has to celebrate them."

"Oh, get out of my sight, Octavius!" Antony snapped.

"My name is Caesar," said Octavian as he departed.

"You were intolerably rude," said Hirtius. "What possessed you to rant and rave at him? You never even asked him to sit down."

"The only thing I'd ask him to sit down on is a spike!"

"Nor can you deny him his *lex curiata*."

"He can have his *lex curiata* when he produces the war chest."

That set Hirtius to laughing again. "*Gerrae, gerrae, gerrae!* If someone did indeed steal the war chest, then it had to be an undertaking that must have been *nundinae* in the planning and execution, Antonius, as you well know. You heard Octavianus, he'd only just arrived from Macedonia, and he was ill."

"Octavianus?" asked Antony, still scowling.

"Yes, Octavianus. Whether you like it or not, his name is Gaius Julius Caesar Octavianus. I shall call him Octavianus. No, I won't go so far as to call him Caesar, but Octavianus gives him his due as Caesar's heir," said Hirtius. "He's remarkably cool and clever, isn't he?"

When Hirtius walked out into the peristyle of the palace on the Carinae, he found Antony's veteran escort gathered in it, apparently waiting on the senior consul's orders. And there in the middle of them was Octavianus, smiling Caesar's smile, moving his hands like Caesar, it seemed capable too of Caesar's wit, for they were all laughing at whatever he was saying in that deep voice that sounded more like Caesar's every time Hirtius heard him.

Before Hirtius reached the group, Octavianus was gone with a Caesarean wave.

"Oh, he's lovely!" sighed one old stager, wiping his eyes.

"Did you see him, Aulus Hirtius?" another asked, eyes equally misty. "Caesar's image, young Caesar!"

What game is he playing? wondered Hirtius, heart sinking. Not one of these men will be in the ranks by the time Octavianus comes into his own, as he certainly will. It must be their sons he wants. Is he capable of that much planning?

The loss of Caesar's war chest had a profound effect upon Antony's plans, plans he wasn't prepared to outline in full to men like Aulus Hirtius. Land for the veterans wasn't an insuperable problem; it could always be legislated away from private ownership and put into the *ager publicus*. Even the most powerful knights of the Eighteen, who would be the victims of all such laws (along with many senators), were lying low and not doing too much complaining since the death of Caesar. Nor were his own debts what worried Antony most.

Since Caesar had crossed the Rubicon, another factor had crept into being, escalating to the point where every soldier in every legion expected to be paid hefty bonuses for fighting. Ventidius was recruiting two new legions in Campania, and every enlisting man wanted a cash gift of a thousand sesterces simply to join up. Not only was it going to cost the state the inevitable sums for equipment, it was going to cost ten million sesterces in cash, payable immediately. The six crack legions still in Macedonia had held together, but their representatives were now in Teanum dropping hints. With the loss of the Parthian spoils, was it going to be worth soldiering? Would the Dacian spoils be equal to the Parthian? How could Antony tell them that there were not going to be any Dacian spoils either, because they were coming back to Italy to shore up the consul's power? Before he gave them that news, he had to find them ten thousand sesterces each in cash bonuses payable on landing in Brundisium. Leaving out the extra money their centurions would cost, that was three hundred million sesterces.

But he didn't have the money, and he couldn't get the money. The provincial tributes had to cover a great many ordinary governmental expenses apart from the cost of legions. With Caesar dead, no man alive could hold legionary loyalty without cash bonuses; if his exertions in Campania had told him nothing else, they had told him that.

"What about the emergency hoard in the temple of Ops?" asked Fulvia, to whom he confided everything.

"There isn't one," Antony said gloomily. "It's been raided by everybody from Cinna and Carbo to Sulla."

"Clodius said it was paid back. If he hadn't managed to pass his law to annex Cyprus to pay for the free grain dole, he planned to garnish the money from Ops. After all, she's Rome's plenty, the fruits of the earth, so he considered Ops a properly legal source for free grain. As it was, his law passed, so he never needed to raid Ops."

Antony swooped on her and kissed her thoroughly. "What would I do without you, my own personification of Ops?"

Opsiconsiva's temple on the Capitol was only moderately old; though she was *numen* and therefore faceless, disembodied, belonging to the days when Rome first emerged, her original temple had been burned to the ground, and this one erected by a Caecilius Metellus a hundred and fifty years ago. It wasn't large, but the Caecilii Metelli had kept it painted and clean. The single *cella* contained no image, nor was it the site of sacrifices to Ops, for she had an altar in the Regia of more importance to the state religion. Like all Roman temples, Ops of the Capitol stood atop a tall podium because these basements were sacrosanct, protected by the deity above, therefore were often used to store precious objects and items, including money or bullion.

Moving after dark and accompanied only by his henchmen, Mark Antony forced the door to Ops's basement and let his lamp play across the great stacks of tarnished silver sows, breath suspended. Ops had been paid back with interest! He had his money.

Which he proceeded to remove in broad daylight, not all at once and not very far. Just across the Capitol, through the Asylum, and into Juno Moneta's basement, where the mint was located. There, day and night, the silver sows were converted into silver denarii. He could pay his legions for a long time to come, and even pay off his debts. Ops had held twenty-eight thousand silver talents—seven hundred million sesterces.

Things moved into place for the Kalends of June, when he would ask the Senate to exchange his provinces. And after that, he would have brother Lucius use the Plebeian Assembly to strip Italian Gaul off Decimus Brutus at once.

A letter from Brutus and Cassius had him snarling.

It would please us greatly to be present in the Senate on the Kalends of June, Marcus Antonius, but we must seek assurances from you that we will be safe. It grieves us that, though we are the two senior praetors, neither you nor any other magistrate keeps us informed about what is happening in Rome. We appreciate your concern for our welfare, and thank you once again for your many accommodations since the Ides of March. However, it has come to our attention that the city is full of Caesar's old soldiers, and that they intend to re-erect the altar and column to Caesar which the consul Dolabella so rightly dismantled.

Our question is: will we be safe if we come to Rome? Please, we humbly beg, give us assurances that our amnesties remain in place, and that we will be welcome in Rome.

Feeling very much better now that his financial worries were a thing of the past, Antony replied to this almost obsequious plea with scant consideration for Liberator sentiments.

I cannot give you assurances of safety, Marcus Brutus, Gaius Cassius. It's true that the city is full of Caesar's old soldiers, who are holidaying here while they wait for their land or debate whether to re-enlist in the legions I am recruiting in Campania. As to their intentions regarding what I call Caesar-worship, you may have assurances from me that Caesar-worship will not be encouraged.

Come to Rome for the meeting on the Kalends of June, or do not come. The choice is entirely yours.

There! That would tell them what their place was in the Antonian scheme of things! And also tell them that, should they decide to take advantage of Samnite discontent, there would be legions in the neighborhood to put rebellion down. Yes, by Ops, excellent!

His mood plummeted on the Kalends of June when he entered the Curia Hostilia to find attendance so thin that he had no quorum. Had Brutus, Cassius and Cicero been there, he would have scraped in, but they were not.

"All right," he said to Dolabella through his teeth, "I'll go straight to the Plebeian Assembly. Lucius!" he called to his brother, leaving arm in arm with Gaius Antonius. "Convoke the Plebeian Assembly for two days hence!"

The Plebeian Assembly, also thinly attended, had no quorum regulations. If one member of each tribe turned up, the meeting could proceed, and two hundred–odd had turned up, spread across the thirty-five tribes. The pace was fast and Antony's mood furious, so none of the Plebs was prepared to argue with Lucius Antonius, and none of his fellow tribunes of the plebs were prepared to interpose a veto. In short order the Plebs awarded Italian Gaul and Further Gaul minus the Narbonese province to Marcus Antonius for a period of five years with unlimited imperium, then went on to award Syria to Dolabella for five years with unlimited imperium. This *lex Antonia de permutatione provinciarum* went into immediate effect, which meant that Decimus Brutus was stripped of his province.

The Plebeian Assembly's work wasn't done; the first fruits of Antony's deal with the legions became evident when Lucius Antonius brought in yet another law, this one providing a third type of juror to staff the courts: high ranking ex-centurions, who were not required to have a knight's income to qualify for jury duty. Antony's youngest brother followed this up with another land bill, this one to distribute *ager publicus* to the veterans through the medium of a seven-member commission comprising Mark Antony, Lucius himself, Dolabella, and four minions who included the Liberator Caesennius Lento, busy smarming to Antony.

If Hirtius had heard rumors that King Deiotarus of Galatia was bribing Antony, he saw those rumors confirmed when Armenia Parva was taken off Cappadocia and added to Galatia.

The two consuls had found their feet and proclaimed their style of government: corruption and self-service. A brisk trade in tax exemptions and privileges dated from the Kalends of June, and all those permanently banned from the citizenship by Caesar after he discovered that Faberius was selling the citizenship now could buy it after all. While the mint kept on coining silver sows from Ops.

"What," asked Antony of Dolabella, "is power for, if not to use to one's own best advantage?"

The Senate met again five days into June, this time with a quorum present. To the astonishment of Lucius Piso, Philippus and the few on the front benches, Publius Servilius Vatia Isauricus Senior sat there among them. Sulla's greatest friend and political ally, Vatia Senior had been retired from public life for so long that most had quite forgotten his existence; his Roman house was occupied by his son, Caesar's friend at present returning from governing Asia Province, while Vatia Senior contemplated the beauties of Nature, Art and Literature in his villa at Cumae.

Once the prayers were said and the auspices taken, Vatia Senior rose to his feet, the sign that he wished to speak. As the most senior and august among the consulars, it was his entitlement to do so.

"Later," said Antony curtly, to a chorus of gasps.

Dolabella turned his head to glare ferociously at Antony. "I hold the *fasces* in June, Marcus Antonius, therefore this is *my* meeting! Publius Vatia Senior, it is an honor to welcome you back to the House. Please speak."

"Thank you, Publius Dolabella," Vatia Senior said, voice a little thready, but quite audible. "When do you mean to discuss provinces for the praetors?"

"Not today," Antony answered before Dolabella could.

"Perhaps we should discuss them, Marcus Antonius," Dolabella said stiffly, determined not to be overridden.

"I *said*, not today! It is postponed," snarled Antony.

"Then I ask that you give special consideration to two of the praetors," said Vatia Senior. "Marcus Junius Brutus and Gaius Cassius Longinus. Though I cannot condone their taking the law into their own hands to kill Caesar Dictator, I am concerned for their welfare. While ever they remain in Italy, their lives are threatened. Therefore I move that Marcus Brutus and Gaius Cassius be voted provinces at once, no matter how long the other praetors must wait. I further move that Marcus Brutus be awarded the province of Macedonia, since Marcus Antonius has relinquished it, and that Gaius Cassius be awarded the province of Cilicia, together with Cyprus, Crete and Cyrenaica."

Vatia Senior stopped, but didn't sit; an imperfect silence fell, disturbed by ominous mutters from the top tiers, where Caesar's appointees had no love for Caesar's assassins.

Gaius, the praetor Antonius, rose to his feet, looking angry. "Honored consuls, da-de-da the rest," he shouted impudently, "I agree with the consular Vatia Senior, in that it is high time we saw the backs of Brutus and Cassius! While ever they remain in Italy, they represent a threat to government. Since this House voted them an amnesty, they can't be tried for treason, but I refuse to see them given provinces while innocent men like me are told we must wait! I say, give them quaestor's duties! Give them commissions to buy in grain for Rome and Italy. Brutus can go to Asia Minor, Cassius to Sicily. Quaestor's duties are all that they deserve!"

A debate followed that showed Vatia Senior how unpopular his cause was; if he needed further proof, he received it when the House voted to give Brutus and Cassius grain commissions in Asia Minor and Sicily. Then, to rub it in, Antony and his minions poked fun at him, mocked his age and his old-fashioned ideas. So as soon as the meeting was over, he went back to his villa in Campania.

Once home, he asked his servants to fill his bath. Then Publius Servilius Vatia Isauricus Senior stretched out in the water with a sigh of bliss, opened the veins of both wrists with a lancet, and drifted into the warm, infinitely welcome arms of death.

"Oh, how can I bear such a homecoming?" Vatia Junior asked Aulus Hirtius. "Caesar murdered, my father suicided—" He broke down again, wept bitterly.

"—and Rome in the clutches of Marcus Antonius," Hirtius said grimly. "I wish I could see a way out, Vatia, but I can't. No one can stand against Antonius, he's capable of anything from blatant illegality to summary execution without trial. And he has the legions on his side."

"He's *buying* the legions," said Junia, very glad to see her husband home. "I could kill my brother Brutus for setting all of this in motion, but Porcia pulls his strings."

Vatia wiped his eyes, blew his nose. "Will Antonius and his tame Senate let you be consul next year, Hirtius?" he asked.

"He says so. I'm careful not to thrust my face under his nose too often—it's wiser to stay invisible. Pansa thinks the same. That's why we don't attend many meetings."

"So there's no one with the clout to oppose him?"

"Absolutely no one. Antonius is running wild."

 And thus it did seem to Rome's and Italy's leading men of business and politics during that dreadful spring and summer after the Ides of March.

Brutus and Cassius wandered from place to place around the Campanian coast, Porcia fastened to Brutus as by a rivet. On the one occasion when they found themselves in the same villa as Servilia and Tertulla, the five of them bickered constantly. News had come of the grain commissions, which mortally offended them—how dare Antony palm them off with duties befitting mere quaestors?

Cicero, calling on them, found Servilia convinced that she still possessed enough power in the Senate to have the decision reversed, Cassius in the mood for war, Brutus utterly despondent, Porcia carping and nagging as usual, and Tertulla in the depths of despair because she had lost her baby.

He went away shattered. It's a shipwreck. They don't know what to do, they can't see a way out, they exist from day to day waiting for some axe or other to fall. The whole of Italy is foundering because malign children are running it and we less malign children have no defenses against their kind of chaos. We have become the tools of professional soldiers and the ruthless brute of a man who controls them. Was this what the Liberators envisioned when they conspired to eliminate Caesar? No, of course not. They could see no further than eliminating Caesar—they genuinely thought that once he was gone, everything would go back to normal. Never understanding that they themselves would have to take the tiller of the ship of state. And in not taking it, they have let it run on the rocks. A shipwreck. Rome is done for.

The two sets of games in the new month of Julius, first those of Apollo, then those dedicated to Caesar's victories, diverted and amused the people, who poured into Rome from as far afield as Bruttium, the toe, and Italian Gaul, the rump atop the leg. It was high summer, very dry and hot—time for a month of holiday. Rome's population almost doubled.

Brutus, the absentee celebrant of the *ludi Apollinares*, had staked his all on a performance of the *Tereus*, a play by the Latin author Accius. Though the common people preferred the chariot races that opened and closed the seven days of the games, and in between thronged to the big theaters staging Atellan mimes and the musically rich farces of Plautus and Terence, Brutus was convinced that the *Tereus* would serve as a meter to tell him what the common people thought about the assassination of Caesar. The play was replete with tyrannicide and the reasons behind it—a tragedy of epic proportions. Therefore it didn't appeal in the least to the common people, who didn't go to see it—a fact that Brutus's ignorance of the common people rendered him incapable of grasping. The audience was an elite one, stuffed with literati like Varro and Lucius Piso, and the play was received with almost hysterical approval. After this news was relayed to Brutus, he went around for days convinced that he was vindicated, that the common people condoned Caesar's assassination, that soon a full reinstatement would come for the Liberators. Whereas the truth was that the production of the *Tereus* was a brilliant one, the acting superb, and the play itself so rarely staged that it came as a welcome change to dramatically jaded elite palates.

Octavian, the celebrant of the *ludi Victoriae Caesaris*, had implanted no gauges to monitor popular response to his games, but was gifted with one by Fortuna herself. His games ran for eleven days, and were somewhat different in structure from the other games Rome saw fairly regularly throughout the warmer months. The first seven days were devoted to pageants and scenes, with the opening day's pageant, a re-enactment of Alesia, situated in the Circus Maximus—a cast of thousands, mock battles galore, an exciting and novel display organized and directed by Maecenas, who demonstrated a rare talent for this sort of activity.

To the principal funder of the games went the honor of giving the signal that they should begin, and Octavian, standing in the box, seemed to the enormous crowd to be a reincarnation of Caesar; much to Antony's annoyance, Octavian was cheered for a full quarter of an hour. Though this was immensely satisfying, Octavian well knew that it was not an indication that Rome belonged to him; it was an indication that Rome had belonged to Caesar. *That* was what upset Antony.

Then, about an hour before sunset on the opening day, just as Vercingetorix sat cross-legged at Caesar's feet, a huge comet appeared in the northern skies above the Capitol. At first no one noticed it, then a few fingers pointed at the *stella critina*, and suddenly the whole two hundred thousand jammed into the Circus were on their feet, screaming wildly.

"Caesar! The star is Caesar! Caesar is a god!"

The next day's pageants and scenes, like the five more after them, were relegated to smaller venues around the city, but every day the comet rose about an hour before sunset, and shone through most of the night with eerie brilliance. Its head was as big as the moon, its tail swept behind it in two shimmering trails right across the northern heavens. And during the wild-beast hunts, the horse races, the chariot races and the other magnificent spectacles held in the Circus Maximus for the last four days of the games, the long-haired star personifying Caesar continued to shine. The very moment the games were over, it disappeared.

Octavian had acted quickly. By the second day of the games, Caesar's statues throughout the city bore gilded stars on their foreheads.

Thanks to Caesar's star, Octavian had won more than he lost, for Antony himself had forbidden the display of Caesar's golden chair and wreath in the parade, and Caesar's ivory statue was not carried in the procession of the gods. On the second day of the games, Antony had delivered a stirring speech to the audience in Pompey's theater, vigorously defending the Liberators and playing down Caesar's importance. But with that uncanny comet shining, all Antony's countermeasures went for nothing.

To those who offered him comments or asked him questions, Octavian replied that the star *must* indicate Caesar's godhead; otherwise, why did it appear on the first day of his victory games and vanish the moment those games were over? Unanswerable in any other way. Inarguable. Even Antony could not contradict such unimpeachable evidence, while Dolabella chewed his nails down to the quick and thanked his primal instincts for not destroying Caesar's altar and column. Though he didn't re-erect them.

Inside himself, Octavian looked at Caesar's star differently. Naturally it endowed Caesar's heir with some of Caesar's godly mystery; if Caesar were a god, then he was the son of a god. He saw that reflected in many eyes as he deliberately walked around Rome's less salubrious neighborhoods. This child of Palatine exclusivity had been quick to understand that to remain exclusive was no way to inspire love in the ordinary people. Nor would it have occurred to him that to stage a play full of droning terror and high-flown dialogue would tell him anything about the people who lived in Rome's less salubrious neighborhoods. No, he walked and talked, told those he met that he wished to learn about his father, Caesar—please tell me *your* story! And many of the people he met were Caesar's veterans, in Rome for the two sets of games. They really liked him, deemed him humble, grateful, very ready to listen to anything they had to say. More important, Octavian discovered that Antony's public rudeness to him over the course of the games had been noticed, was strongly condemned.

A core of invulnerable security was forming in him, for Octavian knew perfectly well what Caesar's star really meant. It was a message to him from Caesar that his destiny was to rule the world. His desire to rule the world had always seemed to be there, but so tenuous, so manifestly impossible that he had called it a daydream, a fantasy. But from the moment the long-haired star had appeared, he knew otherwise. The sense of destiny had suddenly become certainty. Caesar meant him to rule the world. Caesar had passed to him the task to heal Rome, enhance her empire, endow her with unimaginable power. Under his care, under his aegis. I am the man. I *will* rule the world. I have time to be patient, time to learn, time to rectify the mistakes I must surely make, time to grind opposition down, time to deal with everyone from the Liberators to Marcus Antonius. Caesar made me heir not just to money and estates, but to his clients and adherents, his power, his destiny, his godhead. And by Sol Indiges, by Tellus, and by Liber Pater, I will not disappoint him. I will be a worthy son. I will be Caesar.

* * *

At the end of the eighth day of the games, which was the first back in the Circus Maximus, a delegation of centurions cornered Antony as he left the Circus after doing everything he could to make it clear to the crowd that he despised Caesar's heir.

"It's got to stop, Marcus Antonius," said the spokesman, who happened to be Marcus Coponius, chief centurion of those two cohorts present in Brundisium when Octavian had needed help to remove the war chest. The two cohorts were now destined to join the Fourth.

"What's got to stop?" Antony snarled.

"The way you treat dear young Caesar, sir. It ain't right."

"Are you asking for a court-martial, centurion?"

"No, sir, definitely not. All I'm saying is that there's a great big hairy star in the sky called Caesar, who's gone to live with the gods. He's shining on his son, young Caesar—a sort of a thank you for putting on these terrific games, we see it. It ain't me complaining, Marcus Antonius, sir. It's all of us. I got fifty men here with me, all centurions or ex-centurions from the old boy's legions. Some have re-enlisted, like me. Some have land Caesar gave them. I got land Caesar gave me last time I was discharged. And we notice how you treat the dear young chap. Like he was dirt. But he ain't dirt. He's young Caesar. And we say it's got to stop. You've got to treat young Caesar right."

Uncomfortably aware that he was in a toga, not in armor, and therefore less impressive in legionary eyes, Antony stood with a storm of feelings crossing his ugly-handsome face—feelings the delegation pretended not to see. His frustration had gotten the better of him, his impatience had led him into conduct that he hadn't realized would be so offensive to men he needed desperately. The trouble was that he had viewed himself as Caesar's natural heir, and had believed that Caesar's veterans would agree that he was. A mistake. At heart they were children. Brave and strong, great soldiers. But children nonetheless. Who wanted their adored Marcus Antonius to smarm and cuddle up to a pretty pansy in high-soled boots because said pretty pansy was Caesar's adopted son. They didn't see what he saw. They saw someone that sentiment had convinced them was how Caesar must have looked at eighteen.

I never knew Caesar at eighteen, but maybe he did look like a pretty pansy. Maybe he *was* a pretty pansy, if there's any truth in the story about King Nicomedes. But I refuse to believe that Gaius Octavius is an embyronic Caesar! No one could change that much. Octavius doesn't have Caesar's arrogance, style, or genius. No, he gets his way by deceit, honey-sweet words, sympathy and smiles. He says himself that he can't general troops. He's a lightweight. But these idiots want me to be nice to him because of a wretched comet.

"What's your definition of treating Gaius Octavius right?" he asked, managing to look more interested than angry.

"Well, for a start, we think you ought to proclaim in public that you're friends," said Coponius.

"Then all who are interested should show up on the Capitol at the foot of the steps to Jupiter Optimus Maximus at the second hour on the day after the games finish," said Antony with as much good grace as he could muster. "Come, Fulvia," he said to his wife, standing fearfully behind him.

"You'd better watch your step with that little worm," she said as she toiled up the Steps of Cacus, the babe in her womb growing large enough to be a handicap. "He's dangerous."

Antony put his hand in the flat of her back and began to push her upward, a help. That was one of the nicest things about him; another husband would have ordered a servant to assist her, but he saw no loss of dignity in doing it himself.

"My mistake was in thinking I didn't need my bodyguard for the games. Lictors are useless." This was said loudly, but the next statement was muttered. "I thought the legions would be on my side in this. They belong to me."

"They belonged to Caesar first," puffed Fulvia.

So on the day after Caesar's victory games ended, over a thousand veterans clustered on the Capitol anywhere that they could see the steps of Jupiter Optimus Maximus. Defiantly in armor, Mark Antony arrived first, early because he wanted to pass among the assembled men, chat to them, joke with them. When Octavian arrived he was togate—and in ordinary shoes. Smiling Caesar's smile, he walked swiftly through the ranks to stand in front of Antony.

Oh, cunning! thought Antony, sitting ruthlessly on his impulse to smash that pretty face to pulp. Today he wants everybody to see how *small* he is, how harmless and inoffensive. He wants me to look a bully, a churl.

"Gaius Julius Caesar Octavianus," Antony began, hating with every part of him to speak that odious name, "it's been drawn to my attention by these good fellows that I—er—haven't always given you a proper measure of respect. For which I sincerely apologize. It was done unintentionally—I've got too much on my mind. Will you forgive me?"

"Gladly, Marcus Antonius!" Octavian cried, smile broader than ever, and thrust out his hand.

Antony shook it as if it were made of glass, red eyes roving over the faces of Coponius and the original fifty to see how this nauseating performance was going down. All right, but not enough, their faces said. So, holding in his gorge, Antony put his hands on Octavian's shoulders and drew him into an embrace, kissed him smackingly on both cheeks. That did it. Sighs of content arose, then the whole crowd applauded.

"I'm only doing this to please them." Antony whispered into Octavian's right ear.

"Ditto," whispered Octavian.

The pair of them left the Capitol by walking through the men, Antony's arm about Octavian's shoulders, so far beneath his own that the worm looked an innocent, gorgeous child.

"Lovely!" said Coponius, weeping unashamedly.

The big grey eyes met his, a ghost of a different smile in their limpid depths.

Sextilis came in with a new, equally unpleasant shock for Antony. Brutus and Cassius issued a praetorian edict to all the towns and communities of Italy which differed greatly in content from the two they had issued in April. Couched in prose that had Cicero drooling, it announced that, while they wished to absent themselves from Rome to govern provinces, they were not about to be palmed off with quaestorian duties like buying in grain. To buy in grain, they said, was a gross insult to two men who had already governed provinces, and governed them well. Cassius at a mere thirty years of age had not only governed Syria, but had also defeated and driven out a large Parthian army. And Brutus had been Caesar's personal choice to govern Italian Gaul with a proconsular imperium, though he hadn't yet been praetor. Further, the edict went on, it had come to their ears that Marcus Antonius was accusing them of preaching sedition to the Macedonian legions returning to Italy. This was a false accusation that they insisted Antonius retract forthwith. They had *always* acted in the interests of peace and liberty, never at any time had they tried to incite civil war.

Antony's response was a devastating letter to them.

Who do you think you are, putting up your notices in every town from Bruttium and Calabria to Umbria and Etruria? I have issued a consular edict that will go up in the place where yours will be torn down, from Bruttium and Calabria to Umbria and Etruria. It will tell the people of Italy that the pair of you are acting in your own private interests, that your edict does not have praetorian authority. It will go on to warn its readers that should more unofficial notices go up under your names, such notices will be seriously regarded as potentially treasonous, and that their authors may well find themselves designated public enemies.

That's what I will say in public. In this letter I will go further. You *are* behaving treasonously, and you have no right to demand anything from the Senate and People of Rome. Instead of whining and bleating about your grain commissions, you ought to be fawning at the Senate's feet saying a series of abject thank-yous for being given any kind of official duties. After all, you deliberately murdered the man who was legally the head of the Roman state— did you really expect to be dowered with gold curule chairs and gem-studded gold wreaths for committing treason? Grow up, you stupid, pampered adolescents!

And how dare you accuse me publicly of saying that you've tried to tamper with my Macedonian legions? Why on earth should I start those sorts of rumors, tell me that? Shut up and pull your heads in, or you'll be in even bigger trouble than you already are.

On the fourth day of Sextilis, Antony had a reply from Brutus and Cassius, addressed to him privately. He had expected profuse apologies, but he didn't get them. Instead, Brutus and Cassius stubbornly maintained that they were legal praetors, could legally issue any edicts they wanted to issue, and could not be accused of anything other than consistently working for peace, harmony and liberty. Antony's threats, they said, held no terrors for them. Hadn't their own conduct proved that their liberty was more precious to them than any friendship with Marcus Antonius?

They ended with a Parthian shot: "We would remind you that it is not the length of Caesar's life that is the issue, but rather, the briefness of his reign."

What had happened to his luck? wondered Antony, feeling more and more that events were conspiring against him. Octavian had publicly forced him into a corner which had informed him that his control of the legions wasn't as complete as he had thought; and two praetors were busy telling him that it lay in their power to end his career in the same way they had ended Caesar's. Or so he took that defiant letter, chewing his lips and fuming. The briefness of a reign, eh? Well, he could deal with Decimus in Italian Gaul, but he couldn't deal with a war on two fronts, one with Decimus in the far north and another with

Brutus and Cassius south in Samnite Italy, always ready to have another go at Rome.

Octavian could have told him why he had lost his luck, but of course it never occurred to Antony to enquire of his most gnatlike enemy. He had lost it on that first occasion when he had been rude to Octavian. The god Caesar hadn't liked it.

Time then, Antony decided, to concede enough to Brutus and Cassius to be rid of them so that he could concentrate on Decimus Brutus. So he convened the Senate the day after he received their letter and had the Senate award them a province each. Brutus was to govern Crete, and Cassius to govern Cyrenaica. Neither place possessed a single legion. They wanted provinces? Well, now they had provinces. Goodbye, Brutus and Cassius.

 Cicero despaired, grew gloomier with every day that passed. This, despite the fact that he and Atticus had finally managed to evict the urban poor from Caesar's colony at Buthrotum. They had applied to Dolabella, who was very happy, after a long talk with Cicero, to take a huge bribe from Atticus that ensured the survival of the leather, tallow and fertilizer empire in Epirus. Atticus had needed some good news, for his wife had come down with the summer paralysis, and was gravely ill. Little Attica mourned because no one would let her see her mother, who had to stay in Rome while Atticus sent his daughter and her servants to isolation in his villa at Pompeii.

Money had again become a terrible problem for Cicero, due in large measure to young Marcus, still on his Grand Tour and perpetually writing home for additional funds. Neither of the Quintuses was speaking to him, his brief marriage to Publilia hadn't yielded as much revenue as he had thought thanks to her wretched brother and mother, and Cleopatra's agent in Rome, the Egyptian Ammonius, was refusing to pay the Queen's promissory note. And after he had gone to so much trouble to have all his speeches and dissertations copied on the best paper, complete with marginal illustrations and exquisite script! It had cost him a fortune that her promissory note clearly said she was willing to refund him. Ammonius's grounds for refusing to pay up: that Caesar's death had caused her to decamp before the collected Ciceroniana was delivered! Then here it is, send it to her! was Cicero's reply. Ammonius just raised his brows and retorted that he was sure the Queen, home again safely in Egypt (the rumored shipwreck hadn't happened), had better things to do than read thousands of pages of Latin prating. So here he was with the finest edition of his entire works ever made, and no one willing to buy it!

What he wanted to do, he had decided, was to leave Italy, go to Greece, confront young Marcus and then wallow in Athenian culture. His beloved freedman Tiro was working indefatigably toward this end, but where was the money to come from? Terentia, sourer than ever, was busy piling up the sesterces, but when applied to, had answered that at last count he had owned ten fabulous villas from Etruria to Campania, all stuffed with the most enviable art works, so if he was strapped for cash, sell a few villas and statues, don't write asking *her* to pay for his ridiculous follies!

His encounters with Brutus went round and round without ever seeming to go anywhere; Brutus too was thinking of going to Greece. What he absolutely refused to do was to accept a grain-buying commission! Then the silly fellow sailed off with Porcia to the little island of Nesis, not far from the Campanian coast. Whereas Cassius had elected to take up his grain commissionership in Sicily, and was busy assembling a fleet; harvest was nearing.

Then Dolabella, delighted at the promptness with which Atticus had paid his bribe, agreed to give Cicero permission to leave Italy—how disgraceful, to think that a consular of his standing had to apply for permission to go abroad! Such was Caesar's dictate, which the consuls had not rescinded. Swallowing his ire, Cicero sold a villa in Etruria he never visited; now he had the money to go as well as the permission.

What thrust him into actually going was the change in name of the month Quinctilis to the month Julius. When receiving letters dated Julius became utterly intolerable, Cicero hired a ship and sailed from Puteoli, where Cassius's grain fleet was assembling. But nothing was intended to proceed smoothly! Cicero's ship got as far as Vibo, off the coast of Bruttium, and couldn't make further headway because of high, contrary winds. Taking this as a message that he was not destined to leave Italy at this time, Cicero disembarked at the fishing village of Leucoptera, a hideously stinking, awful place. It was always the same; somehow the moment leaving Italy arrived, he couldn't bear to go. His roots were just too deeply implanted in Italian soil.

Tired and in need of real hospitality, Cicero turned in at the gates of Cato's old estates in Lucania, expecting to find no one there. The lands had gone to one of Caesar's three ex-centurion crown-winning senators, who hadn't wanted estates so far from his home ground of Umbria, and sold them to an unknown buyer. It was the seventeenth day of Sextilis when Cicero's litter entered the gates; this awful summer was wearing down at last. Once inside, he saw that the lamps dotting the gardens were lit—someone was home! Company! A good meal!

And there at the door to welcome him was Marcus Brutus. His eyes suddenly brimming with tears, Cicero fell on Brutus's neck and hugged him fervently. Brutus had been reading, for he still had a scroll in his hand, and was very taken aback at the effusion of Cicero's greeting until Cicero explained his odyssey and its pain. Porcia was with her husband, but didn't join them for supper, a relief as far as Cicero was concerned. A very little Porcia went a very long way.

"You won't know that the Senate has granted Cassius and me provinces," said Brutus. "I have Crete, Cassius has Cyrenaica. The news came just as Cassius was about to sail, so he decided not to be a grain commissioner, and handed his fleet over to a prefect. He's in Neapolis with Servilia and Tertulla."

"Are you pleased?" Cicero asked, warm and content.

"Not very, no, but at least we do have provinces." Brutus gave a sigh. "Cassius and I haven't been getting along together lately. He derided my interpretation of the reception of the *Tereus*, could talk about nothing except young Octavianus, who tried Antonius's temper dreadfully over those victory games in Caesar's honor. And of course the *stella critina* appeared over the Capitol, so all Rome's teeming hordes are calling Caesar a god, with Octavianus egging them on."

"The last time I saw young Octavianus I was startled at the change in him," Cicero contributed, burrowing comfortably into his couch. How wonderful to enjoy a cozy meal with one of the few civilized men in Rome! "Very sprightly—very witty—very sure of himself. Philippus wasn't at all happy, confided to me that the young fool is becoming hubristic."

"Cassius deems him dangerous" was Brutus's comment. "He tried to display Caesar's gold chair and wreath at his games, and when Antonius said no, he stood up to the *senior consul* as if he were Antonius's equal! Quite unafraid, extremely outspoken."

"Octavianus won't last because he can't last." Cicero cleared his throat delicately. "What of the Liberators?"

"Despite our being granted provinces, I think the prospects are grim," Brutus said. "Vatia Isauricus is back from Asia and fit to be tied, between Caesar's death and his father's suicide—Octavianus is insisting that the Liberators must be punished—and Dolabella is everybody's enemy, as well as his own worst enemy."

"Then I shall go on to Rome at dawn," said Cicero.

True to his word, he was ready to depart at first light, not really pleased that Porcia was there to farewell him too. He knew perfectly well that she despised him, considered him a braggart, a poseur, a man of straw. Well, he considered her a mannish freak who, like every other woman, had formed no opinions that hadn't belonged to a man first—in her case, her father.

Cato's villa was not pretentious, but it did have some truly magnificent murals. As they stood in the atrium, the increasing light fell upon a wall filled by a tremendous painting of Hector saying farewell to Andromache before going out to fight Achilles. The artist had caught Hector in the act of giving his son, Astyanax, back to his mother, but instead of looking at the child, she was gazing piteously at Hector.

"Wonderful!" Cicero cried, drinking in the painting avidly.

"Is it?" asked Brutus, staring at it as if he had never seen it until that moment.

Cicero began to quote:

> *"Restless spirit, do not distress yourself*
> *with thoughts of me! No man sends me*
> *into the underworld untimely;*
> *yet no man can escape his fate either,*
> *be he coward or hero.*
> *Go home and look after your sort of work,*
> *loom and spindle. Supervise your servants*
> *so they spin and weave too. War*
> *is men's work, and the men of Troy*
> *must cleave to it, especially me."*

Brutus laughed. "Oh, come, Cicero, you don't expect me to say that to Cato's daughter, do you? Porcia is the equal of any man in courage and high intent."

Her face lighting up, Porcia turned to Brutus and pulled his hand against her cheek, which embarrassed him in front of Cicero; yet he made no move to take his hand away.

Eyes blazing rather madly, Porcia said:

"I have no father and mother now. . . . So you, my Brutus, are father and mother both to me, as well as my most beloved husband."

Brutus detached his hand and left her side, gave Cicero a tight grimace that seemed the closest he could get to a smile. "You see how erudite she is? She's not content to paraphrase—she picks the eyes out of eyeless Homer. No mean feat."

Laughter booming, Cicero blew a kiss to Andromache in the painting. "If she can pick the eyes out of blind old Homer, my dear Brutus, then you and she are well matched. Goodbye, my two epitomators, and may we meet again in better times."

Neither waited at the door to watch him enter his litter.

Toward the end of Sextilis, Brutus took ship from Tarentum to Patrae in Greece; he left Porcia behind with Servilia.

Mark Antony sent a message to Cicero, arrived in Rome, that he was to present himself in the Senate for the obligatory first-day-of-the-month meeting. When Cicero didn't turn up, an irate Antony left for Tibur to attend to some urgent business.

With Antony safely out of town, Cicero went to the Senate the next day; the House had prorogued its meeting to finish its early September agenda. And in its chamber the vacillating, vainglorious consular Marcus Tullius Cicero finally found the courage to embark upon what was to be his life's work: a series of speeches against Marcus Antonius.

No one expected this first speech; everyone was staggered, and many were frightened out of their wits. The softest and most subtle of the series, the first was the most telling, in part because it came out of the blue.

He started kindly enough. Antony's actions after the Ides of March had been moderate and conciliatory, said Cicero; he hadn't abused possession of Caesar's papers, had restored no exiles, had abolished the dictatorship forever, and suppressed disorder among the common people. But from May onward, Antony began to change, and by the Kalends of June a very different man stood revealed. Nothing was done through the Senate anymore, everything was done through the People in their tribes, and sometimes even the will of the People was ignored. The consuls-elect, Hirtius and Pansa, did not dare to enter the Senate, the Liberators were virtually exiled from Rome, and the veteran soldiers were actively encouraged to seek fresh bonuses and fresh privileges. Cicero protested at the honors being paid to Caesar's memory and thanked Lucius Piso for his speech on the Kalends of Sextilis, deploring the fact that Piso had found no support for his motion to make Italian Gaul a part of Italy proper. He condoned the ratification of Caesar's acts, but condemned the ratification of mere promises or casual memoranda. He went on to enumerate those of Caesar's laws that Antony had transgressed, and made much of the fact that Antony tended to transgress Caesar's *good* laws, uphold the bad ones. In his peroration he exhorted both Antony and

Dolabella to seek genuine glory rather than dominate their fellow citizens through a reign of terror.

Vatia Isauricus followed Cicero and spoke to the same effect—just not nearly as well. The old master was back, and the old master had no peer. Significantly, the House dared to applaud.

With the result that Antony returned to Rome from Tibur to find a new mood in the Senate and all kinds of rumors circulating in the Forum, where the frequenters were abuzz with discussions about Cicero's brilliant, timely, most welcome, very brave speech.

Antony reacted with a towering temper tantrum and demanded that Cicero be present in the House to hear his answer on the nineteenth day of September; but Antony's rage contained palpable fear, had an element of bluster no one had seen or heard before. For Antony knew that if two consulars as prestigious as Cicero and Vatia Isauricus dared to speak out openly against him in the House, then his ascendancy was waning. A conclusion reinforced midway through the month when he put a new statue of Caesar, star on its brow, in the Forum bearing an inscription which denied that Caesar was a god of any kind. The tribune of the plebs Tiberius Cannutius spoke against the inscription to a crowd; suddenly, Antony realized, even the mice were growing fangs.

If he blamed the change in attitude on anyone in particular, it was on Octavian, not on Cicero. That sweet, demure, fetching boy was working against him on all fronts. Starting on the day when he had been forced by the centurions to apologize publicly to Octavian, Antony had come to understand that he was not dealing with a pretty pansy—he was dealing with a cobra.

So when the House met on the nineteenth day of September, he thundered a tirade against Cicero, Vatia, Tiberius Cannutius and everyone else who was suddenly presuming to criticize him openly. He didn't mention Octavian—that would have been to make a fool of himself—but he did get on to the subject of the Liberators. For the first time, he condemned them for striking down a great Roman, for acting unconstitutionally, for doing outright murder. This change of face didn't go unremarked; the balance was beginning to tip against the Liberators when even Marcus Antonius found it necessary to speak against them.

For which Antony blamed Octavian and no one else. Caesar's heir was saying unequivocally to all prepared to listen that while ever the Liberators continued to go unpunished, Caesar's shade was unappeased. Didn't the *stella critina* say with the force of a clap of thunder that Caesar was a god? A *Roman* god! Of massive power and moment to Rome, yet unappeased! Nor did Octavian limit his categorical statements to the common people. He said them to the upper classes too. What were Antony and Dolabella going to do about the Liberators? Was overt treason to be condoned, even extolled? The months since the Ides of March, said Octavian to all and sundry, had seen nothing but a permissive passivity; the Liberators walked around free men, yet had killed a Roman god. A god who received no official sacrifices, and was unappeased.

Toward the end of the first *nundinum* in October, Antony's mushrooming sense of persecution caused him to purge his bodyguard of veteran soldiers. He arrested some of them on the charge of attempting to assassinate him, and went so far as to allege that Octavian had paid them to assassinate him. A highly indignant Octavian got up on the rostra in front of a suspiciously large audience and denied the allegation passionately. In a very good speech. Everybody listening believed him completely. Antony got the message, had to content himself with dismissing the men he had accused; he didn't dare execute them. Did he, he would do himself irreparable harm in the eyes of soldiers and civilians alike. The day after Octavian's address, fresh deputations from the legions and the veterans came to see him and inform him that they wouldn't stand for Antony's harming one single hair of Octavian's darling golden head. Somehow, though it was a mystery to Antony quite how, Caesar's heir had become a talisman of the army's good luck; he had fused himself into legionary worship alongside the Eagles.

"I don't *believe* it!" he cried to Fulvia, pacing up and down like a caged beast. "He's a—a child! How does he do it, for I swear he has no Ulysses whispering in his ear how to do it!"

"Philippus?" she suggested.

Antony blew a derisive noise. "Not he! He's too careful of his skin, and it runs in that family for generations. There's no one, Fulvia, no one! The artfulness, the guile—they're him! I don't even understand how Caesar saw what he is!"

"You're boxing yourself into a corner, my love," Fulvia said with conviction. "If you stay in Rome, you'll end in massacring everyone from Cicero to Octavianus, and that would be your downfall. The best thing you can do is go and fight Decimus Brutus in Italian Gaul. A victory or two against the prime mover among the Liberators, and you'll retrieve your position. It's vital that you retain control of the army, so put your energies into that. Face the fact that you're not by nature a politician. It's Octavianus who is the politician. Draw his fangs by absenting yourself from Rome and the Senate."

*   *   *

Six days before the Ides of October, Mark Antony and a swollen Fulvia left Rome together to go to Brundisium, where four of the six crack Macedonian legions were due to land.

Antony had at least a partial *casus belli,* for Decimus Brutus was ignoring the directives both of the Senate and the Plebeian Assembly by maintaining that he was the legal governor of Italian Gaul, and by continuing to recruit soldiers. Before he left Rome to go to Brundisium, Antony sent a curt order to Decimus Brutus to quit his province, as Antony was coming to replace him as the new governor. If Decimus refused to obey, then Antony had a complete *casus belli.* And Antony was sure Decimus had no intention of obeying; did he, his public career was over and the prospect of trial for treason inevitable.

Not to be outmaneuvered, Octavian left Rome the day after Antony and Fulvia, bound for the legionary camps in Campania. A number of legions shipped from Macedonia were bivouacked there, as well as some thousands of veterans and young men now of age who had enlisted when Ventidius began to recruit.

With him Octavian took Maecenas, Salvidienus and the Apennine-hopping Marcus Agrippa, recently returned with two wagons full of wooden planks. The banker Gaius Rabirius Postumus also tagged along, together with the most prominent citizen in Latin Velitrae, one Marcus Mindius Marcellus, an Octavian relative of huge wealth.

They started in Casilinum and Calatia, two small towns on the Via Latina in northern Campania. Those in the area who had enlisted, be they veteran or youngster, received two thousand sesterces on the spot, and were promised twenty thousand more later if they swore to hew to Caesar's heir. Within the space of four days, Octavian had five thousand soldiers willing to march anywhere with him. What a wonderful thing a war chest was!

"I don't believe," he said to Agrippa, "that it's necessary to recruit a whole army. I don't have the experience or the talent to go to war against Marcus Antonius. What I'm doing is making it look to the rest of the legions as if I am in need of *one* legion to protect myself *from* Antonius. And that's what Maecenas and his agents are going to be doing—spreading the word that Caesar's heir doesn't want to fight, he simply wants to live."

In Brundisium, Antony wasn't faring nearly as well. When he offered the men of the four newly disembarked crack legions four hundred sesterces each as a bonus, they laughed at him and said that they could get more from young Caesar. To Antony, this came as a colossal shock; he had no idea that those two cohorts of troops under the centurion Marcus Coponius still encamped on Brundisium's outskirts were fraternizing with the new arrivals—and talking big money from Caesar's heir.

"The little prick!" he said savagely to Fulvia. "I turn my back, and he's buying my soldiers! Paying them hard cash, would you believe? Where did he get the money? I can tell you that—he did steal Caesar's war chest!"

"Not necessarily," Fulvia answered reasonably. "Your courier says he has Rabirius Postumus with him, which means he must have access to Caesar's money, even if the will hasn't been probated."

"Well, I know how to deal with mutiny," Antony snarled, "and it won't be as gently as Caesar dealt with it!"

"Marcus, don't do anything rash!" she entreated.

Antony ignored her. He paraded the Legio Martia, cut every tenth man out of its ranks, and executed every fifth one of them for insubordination. By no means a decimation, but twenty-five legionaries died, so randomly that all were innocent of troublemaking. The Legio Martia and the other three crack legions fell quiet, but Marcus Antonius was now loathed.

When another of the crack legions arrived from Macedonia, Antony sent the Legio Martia and two others up the Adriatic coast of the peninsula toward Italian Gaul. The remaining two, one of which was the Legio Alauda, Caesar's old Fifth Legion, he marched up the Via Appia in the direction of Campania, hoping to catch Octavian in the act of suborning the consul's troops.

But the two legions were humming with stories about young Caesar and his audacity—also his stunning generosity. And they were more knowledgeable about young Caesar's activities than Mark Antony was, for they knew that he wasn't suborning the consul's legions, he had contented himself with one legion of new troops in order to protect himself. Since Antony's action with the Legio Martia, these two legions sympathized with young Caesar. So fresh trouble erupted not far up the Via Appia. Again, Antony's way of dealing with it was to execute the hapless victims of a blind count, not the ringleaders. However, the dark looks which followed him as he rode at the head of his troops decided him that it was not wise to enter Campania. Instead, he turned and marched up the Adriatic coast.

* * *

It was, thought Cicero, a nightmare. So much happened during October and November that his head spun. Octavian was incredible! At his age, and without any kind of experience, he was dreaming of going to war against Marcus Antonius! Rome rumbled with rumors of approaching war, of Antonius heading for Rome with two legions, of Octavian and his unorganized troops, only a legion in number, milling around in northern Campania without a definite objective. Did Octavian actually think to oppose Antonius in Campania, or was he intending to march on Rome? Privately Cicero hoped that the boy would march on Rome: it was the smart thing to do. How did Cicero know so much? Because Octavian wrote to him constantly.

"Oh, Brutus, where are you?" Cicero mourned. "What a golden opportunity you're missing!"

Word had come to Rome of disquieting events in Syria too, via a slave of the rebel Caecilius Bassus, still penned up in Apameia. The slave had traveled with Brutus's director, Scaptius, and told Servilia, who went to see Dolabella. There were now six legions in Syria, she told Rome's at-home consul, all concentrated around Apameia. First of all, she told Dolabella, they were disaffected, as were the four legions garrisoning Egyptian Alexandria. And, a second, more amazing fact, all these legions expected *Cassius* to arrive as the new governor! If Bassus's slave were to be believed, said Servilia, all ten legions desperately wanted to see Cassius the governor of Syria.

Dolabella panicked. Within the space of a day, he had packed up and set off for Syria, leaving Rome in charge of the urban praetor, Gaius Antonius, and without so much as bothering to write a note to Antony or tell the Senate that he was leaving. As far as Dolabella was concerned, Cassius must have been making secret overtures to the Syrian and Alexandrian legions, so it was vital that he reach his province ahead of Cassius. Servilia maintained that he was quite mistaken, that Cassius had voiced no desire to usurp governance of Syria illegally, but Dolabella refused to heed her. He sent his legate Aulus Allienus by separate ship to Alexandria with orders to bring him those four legions to Syria, and himself took ship from Ancona to western Macedonia; it was no time of year to sail the seas, so he would march overland.

Cicero knew as well as Servilia that Cassius was not en route for Syria, but as October turned into November, he was far more worried about events in Campania. Octavian's letters indicated that he was definitely thinking of marching on Rome, as they kept begging Cicero to remain in Rome. He needed Cicero in the Senate, he wanted to act constitutionally through the Senate to depose Antony—*please* make sure that the moment he arrived outside the Servian Walls, the Senate convened so that he could address it and state his case against Antony!

"I don't trust his age and I don't honestly know what kind of disposition he possesses," Cicero said to Servilia, so frantic with worry that he could think of no better confidant than a woman. "Brutus couldn't have chosen a less opportune moment to go to Greece—he should be here to defend himself and the rest of the Liberators. In fact, were he here, it's possible that he and I together could swing the Senate and People right away from Antonius and Octavianus both, and restore the Republic."

Servilia eyed him a trifle cynically; her mood wasn't the best because that sow Porcia was back in residence, and madder than ever. "My dear man," she said wearily, "Brutus doesn't belong to himself or to Rome. He belongs to Cato, though Cato's been dead now for over two years. Reconcile yourself to the fact that Antonius has gone too far, and Rome has had enough of him. He hasn't Caesar's intelligence or charisma, he's a bull charging blindly. As for Octavianus—he's a nothing. Rat cunning, I give you, but not Caesar's bootlace. I liken him to the young Pompeius Magnus, head full of dreams."

"The young Pompeius Magnus," Cicero said dryly, "bluffed Sulla into the co-command and went on to become Rome's undisputed First Man. Caesar was a late bloomer, when you think about it. Never did anything remarkable until he went to Long-haired Gaul."

"Caesar," Servilia snapped tartly, "was a constitutional man! Everything *in suo anno*, everything according to the Law. When he did act unconstitutionally, it was only because not to do so would have seen the end of him, and that patriotic he wasn't."

"Well, well, let's not argue about a dead man, Servilia. His heir is very much alive, and a mystery to me. I suspect he is to everyone, even Philippus."

"The mystery boy is busy in Campania organizing his soldiers into cohorts, so I'm told," said Servilia.

"With other children as his helpers—I ask you, whoever heard of Gaius Maecenas or Marcus Agrippa?" Cicero chuckled. "In many ways, all three remind me of absolute yokels. Octavianus firmly believes that the Senate will meet at his command if he marches on Rome, though I keep telling him in my letters that it cannot meet without either consul in Rome to head it."

"I confess I'm dying to meet Caesar's heir."

"Apropos of nothing, have you heard—well, you must have, as the wife of the new Pontifex Maximus is your daughter!—that poor

Calpurnia has bought a little house on the outer Quirinal and is living there with none other than Cato's widow?"

"Naturally," said Servilia, whose hair was now a fascinating mixture of jet-black and snow-white stripes; she smoothed it with one beautiful hand. "Caesar left her well provided for, and Piso can't persuade her to remarry, so he's washed his hands of her—or rather, his wife has. As for Marcia, she's another of the faithful widow, Cornelia-the-Mother-of-the-Gracchi breed."

"And you've inherited Porcia."

"Not for very long," Servilia said cryptically.

When Octavian learned that Antony had changed his mind about driving for Rome through Campania and turned to follow his first three legions up the Adriatic coast to Italian Gaul and Decimus Brutus, he decided to march on Rome. Though everyone from his stepfather, Philippus, to his epistolary adviser, Cicero, deemed him a feckless youth without any comprehension of reality, Octavian was well aware how perilous was this alternative. It was not undertaken with any illusions, nor was he sure what its outcome would be. But long hours of thought had convinced him that the one fatal mistake was to do nothing. If he remained in Campania while Mark Antony drove north on the wrong side of the Apennines, both the legions and Rome would conclude that Caesar's heir was a talker rather than a doer. His model was always Caesar, and Caesar dared everything. The last thing Octavian wanted was a battle, for he knew he didn't have the manpower or the skill to defeat a seasoned campaigner like Mark Antony. However, if he moved on Rome, he was telling Antony that he was still very much a player in the game, that he was a force to be reckoned with.

No army lying in wait to oppose him, he marched up the Via Latina, took the *diverticulum* that led around the outside of the Servian Walls to the Campus Martius, set up a camp there, put his five thousand men into it, then led two cohorts into Rome and peacefully occupied the Forum Romanum.

There he was greeted by the tribune of the plebs Tiberius Cannutius, who welcomed this new patrician on behalf of the Plebs and invited him to mount the rostra, speak to the very thin crowd.

"No Senate?" he asked Cannutius.

Cannutius sneered. "Fled, Caesar, every last one of them, including all the consulars and senior magistrates."

"So I cannot appeal for a legal deposition of Antonius."

"They're too afraid of him to do it."

After a word to Maecenas to send out his agents and try to drum up a decent audience, Octavian went to his house and changed into his toga and high-soled boots, then returned to the Forum to find about a thousand hardened Forum frequenters assembled. He climbed on to the rostra and proceeded to give a speech that came as a gratifying surprise to the audience; it was lyrical, precise, structured, delivered with every rhetorical gesture and device perfect—and a treat to listen to. He began by praising Caesar, whose exploits he lauded for what they were—done for the greater glory of Rome, ever and always for the greater glory of Rome.

"For what is Rome's greatest man, if he is not the glory of Rome herself? Until the day he was murdered he remained Rome's most faithful servant—the bringer of riches, the enhancer of empire, the living personification of Rome!"

After the hysterical cheers died down, he went on to discuss the Liberators and demanded justice for Caesar, struck down by a paltry group of little men obsessed with their perquisites of office and their First Class privileges, not with the greater glory of Rome. Proving himself as good an actor and impersonator as Cicero, he went through them one by one, starting with Brutus and miming his cowardly behavior at Pharsalus; talked of the ingratitude of Decimus Brutus and Gaius Trebonius, who owed all that they were to Caesar; imitated Minucius Basilus in the throes of torturing a slave; told how he himself had seen the amputated head of Gnaeus Pompeius after Caesennius Lento had done that deed. Not one of the twenty-three assassins escaped his merciless derision, his razor wit.

After which he asked the crowd why Marcus Antonius, who was Caesar's close cousin, had been so compassionate, so tolerant of the Liberators? Hadn't he, Caesar Filius, seen Marcus Antonius huddled with Gaius Trebonius and Decimus Brutus in Narbo, where the plot was hatched? Wasn't it true that Marcus Antonius again had huddled with Gaius Trebonius outside the Curia Pompeia while the rest went inside and used their daggers on Caesar? Hadn't Antonius murdered hundreds of unarmed Roman citizens in the Forum? Hadn't Antonius accused him, Caesar Filius, of attempted murder without a shred of proof? Hadn't Antonius thrown Roman citizens from the Tarpeian Rock without trial? Hadn't Antonius abused his office by selling everything from the Roman citizenship to tax exemptions?

"But I have bored you for long enough," he concluded. "All I have left to say is that *I am Caesar!* That I intend to win for myself the public standing and legal offices that my beloved father won! My beloved father, who is now a god! If you do not believe me, look now to the spot where Caesar was burned and see that Publius Dolabella admitted

Caesar's godhead by re-erecting his altar and column! Caesar's star in the heavens said everything! Caesar is Divus Julius, and I am his son! I am Divi Filius, and I will live up to everything that the name Caesar embodies!"

Drawing a long breath, he turned amid the cheering and walked from the rostra to Caesar's altar and column, there to pull a fold of toga over his head and stand praying to his father.

It was a memorable performance, one that the troops he had brought into the city never forgot, and were assiduous in spreading to every soldier they came into contact with in later times.

That was the tenth day of November. Two days later, word came that Mark Antony was fast approaching Rome on the Via Valeria with the Legio Alauda, which he put into camp at Tibur, not far away. Hearing that all Antony had was one legion, Octavian's men started hoping for battle.

That was not to be. Octavian went to the Campus Martius, explained that he refused to fight fellow Romans, pulled stakes and marched his troops north on the Via Cassia. At Arretium, the home of Gaius Maecenas, who belonged to its ruling family, he went to earth among friends and waited to see what Mark Antony would do.

Antony's first move was to summon the Senate, intending to have Octavian declared *hostis*—a formal public enemy who was stripped of citizenship, was not entitled to trial, and could be killed on sight. But the meeting never took place; he received horrific news that forced him to leave the city immediately. The Legio Martia had declared for Octavian, had turned off the Adriatic road and was heading for Rome on the Via Valeria, thinking that Octavian was still in Rome.

Having acted so precipitately that he had brought no soldiers with him, when Antony met the Legio Martia at Alba Fucentia he was in no condition to punish them as he had in Brundisium. No mean orator, he was obliged instead to try to make the legionaries see reason, talk them out of this mutiny. To no avail. The men apostrophized him as cruel and stingy, said flatly that they would fight for Octavian and no one else. When Antony offered them two thousand sesterces each, they refused to take the money. So he contented himself with informing them that they weren't worth a legionary's pinch of salt and returned to Rome thwarted, while the Legio Martia hied itself off to join Octavian at Arretium. The one thing Antony had learned from the Legio Martia was that none of the soldiers on Octavian's side or on his side would fight each other if he tried to bring on a battle. The little snake who was now openly calling himself Divi Filius could sit in Arretium inviolate.

Once back in Rome, Antony proceeded to do something unconstitutional yet again: he summoned the Senate to a night meeting in the temple of Jupiter Optimus Maximus on the Capitol. The Senate was forbidden to conduct a meeting after sundown, but it went ahead anyway. Antony forbade the three tribunes of the plebs Tiberius Cannutius, Lucius Cassius and Decimus Carfulenus to attend, and moved once more to have Octavian declared *hostis*. But before he could call for a division, more horrific news arrived. The Fourth Legion had declared for Octavian too, and with it went his quaestor, Lucius Egnatuleius. For a second time he was unable to outlaw Caesar's heir, and to rub that in, Tiberius Cannutius sent him a message that, in the event of a bill of attainder against Octavian, he would have great pleasure in vetoing it when it came before the Plebs for ratification.

So, while the Fourth Legion marched for Octavian in Arretium, Antony's meeting of the Senate ended in discussing petty subjects. Antony praised Lepidus lavishly for reaching an agreement with Sextus Pompeius in Nearer Spain, then took the province of Crete off Brutus and the province of Cyrenaica off Cassius. His own ex-province of Macedonia (now minus most of its fifteen legions) he gave to his praetor brother, Gaius Antonius.

Worst of all, Antony didn't have Fulvia to advise him. She had gone into labor while he spoke in the House, and for the first time in a laudably large number of births, she suffered badly. Antony's second son by her was eventually born, leaving Fulvia seriously ill. He decided to call the boy Iullus, which was a direct slap at Octavian, as it emphasized the Julian blood in the Antonii. Iullus (or Iulus) was Aeneas's son, the founder of Alba Longa, the Roman people—and the Julians.

All his self-serving cronies had gone into hiding, abandoning Antony to the counsel of his brothers, no help or consolation. Events had become so complex and unnerving that he just couldn't handle them, especially now that that dog Dolabella had deserted his post to rush off to Syria. In the end Antony decided that the only possible thing to do was to march for Italian Gaul to eject Decimus Brutus, who had replied to his order to quit the province with a curt refusal. That was what Fulvia had always suggested, and she had a habit of being right. Octavian would just have to wait until he had defeated Decimus; it had occurred to him that the moment Decimus was crushed, he would inherit Decimus's legions, who would feel no loyalty to Caesar's heir. Then he'd act!

He hadn't had the wisdom or the patience to behave as he ought when Octavian had come on the scene—welcome him and get to know him. Instead he had rebuffed the boy, who had turned nineteen on the twenty-third day of September. So now he found himself with an adversary whose quality was as unproven as it was unguessable. The best he could do before he left for Italian Gaul was to issue a series of edicts denouncing Octavian's army as a private one, therefore treasonous, and calling it Spartacist rather than Catilinarian, thus deriding Octavian's thoroughly Roman men as a rabble of slaves. The edicts also contained juicy canards about Octavian's homosexuality, his stepfather's gross gluttony, his mother's unchastity, his sister's reputation as a whore, and his blood father's puerile ineffectuality. Rome read them and laughed in disbelief, but Antony was not present to witness how they were received. He was on his way north.

Once Antony was gone, Cicero embarked on his second attack against Antony. It could not be called a speech, because he never delivered it; he published it instead. But it answered all the charges against Octavian, and went on to feed its avid readers with a mountain of dirt about the senior consul. His intimates were gladiatorial stars like Mustela and Tiro, freedmen like Formio and Gnatho, actress-whores like Cytheris, actors like Hippias, mimes like Sergius, and gamblers like Licinius Denticulus. He made very serious allegations that Antony had been a part of the conspiracy to assassinate Caesar, hence his reluctance afterward to prosecute them. He accused Antony of stealing Caesar's war chest as well as the seven hundred million from the temple of Ops, and stated that it had all gone to pay his debts. After that, he detailed the wills of men who had left Antony everything, and paid Antony back for calling Octavian a homosexual by describing in lavish detail his years-long affair with Gaius Curio, later one of his wife's husbands. The carousing was dwelled upon lovingly, from the litterloads of mistresses to the lion-drawn chariot to the vomiting upon the rostra and in other public places. Rome had a field day reading it.

With Antony absent—he was investing the town of Mutina, in which Decimus Brutus had barricaded himself—and Octavian still in Arretium, Rome now belonged at last to Cicero, who continued to deliver his diatribes against Antony with increasing baldness and savagery. A tinge of admiration for Octavian began to creep into them: if Octavian hadn't marched on Rome, Antony would have massacred every consular left and set himself up as an absolute ruler, so Rome owed Octavian a great debt. As with all Cicero's rhetoric, written or spoken, the facts were inaccurate if that served his purposes, and the truth elastic.

The influence of the Catonians and the Liberators had quite disappeared from the Senate, which was now splitting into two new factions—Antony's and Octavian's. This, despite the fact that one was senior consul, and the other not even a junior senator. To be neutral was becoming extremely difficult, as Lucius Piso and Philippus were finding out. Naturally a major part of Rome's attention was focused on Italian Gaul, where a hard winter was descending; military action was therefore going to be slow and indecisive until spring.

Toward the end of December, his three legions comfortably camped in the neighborhood of Arretium, Octavian returned to Rome, where his family greeted him with uneasy gladness. Philippus, who steadfastly refused to commit himself to Octavian in public, was not so behindhand in private, and spent hours and hours with his wayward stepson, telling him that he must be cautious, that he mustn't ever commit himself to a civil war against Antony, that he mustn't keep insisting that he be called Caesar, or—horrors!—Divi Filius. Octavia's husband, Marcellus Minor, had come to the conclusion that young Octavian was a major political force who was not about to wait for maturity to claim high office, and started cultivating him assiduously. Caesar's two nephews, Quintus Pedius and Lucius Pinarius, indicated that they were firmly on Octavian's side. There were also three more men on the fringes of the family, for Octavian's father had been married before he married Atia, and had a daughter, also named Octavia. This older Octavia had espoused one Sextus Appuleius, and had two adolescent sons, Sextus Junior and Marcus. The Appuleii too began to nose around the nineteen-year-old who had assumed family leadership.

Lucius Cornelius Balbus Major and Gaius Rabirius Postumus had been the first of Caesar's bankers to take up Octavian's cause, but by the end of the year the rest were in his camp too: Balbus Minor, Gaius Oppius (who was convinced Octavian had stolen the war chest), and Caesar's oldest friend, the plutocrat Gaius Matius. As well as his blood father's relative, Marcus Mindius Marcellus. Even that cagey individual Titus Atticus was taking Octavian very seriously, warned his colleagues to be nice to Caesar's heir.

"The first thing I have to do," said Octavian to Agrippa, Maecenas and Salvidienus, "is get myself adlected to the Senate. Until I am, I have to operate as a complete *privatus*."

"Is it possible?" asked Agrippa dubiously. He was enjoying himself immensely, for upon him and Salvidienus devolved the army duties, and he was discovering in himself a competence quite the equal of the older Salvidienus. The troops of the Fourth and the Legio Martia had taken a strong fancy to him.

"Oh, very possible," said Maecenas. "We'll work through Tiberius Cannutius, even though his term as a tribune of the plebs is finished. We'll also buy a couple of the new ones. Additionally, Caesar, you have to go to work on the new consuls the moment they step into office on New Year's Day. Hirtius and Pansa belong to Caesar, not to Antonius. Once Antonius ceases to be consul, they'll get up more courage. The Senate has reinforced their appointment—and stripped Macedonia off Gaius Antonius. All promising for you, Caesar."

"Then," said Octavian, smiling Caesar's smile, "we'll just have to wait and see what the New Year brings. I have Caesar's luck, so I'm not about to go down. The only direction I'm going is up, up, up."

When Brutus reached Athens at the end of Sextilis, he finally found the adulation he had expected for assassinating Caesar. The Greeks had a very soft spot for a tyrannicide, and so they regarded Brutus. Much to his embarrassment, he discovered that statues of himself and Cassius were already under construction, and would go up on imposing plinths in the agora right next to the statues of the great Greek tyrannicides, Aristogeiton and Harmodius.

With him he had taken his three tame philosophers, Strato of Epirus, Statyllus and the Latin Academic, Publius Volumnius, who wrote a little and sponged a lot. The four of them entered into Athenian intellectual life with enthusiasm and delight, spent their time going from this talk to that, and sitting at the feet of the current philosophical idols, Theomnestus and Cratippus.

Which puzzled Athens very much. Here was the tyrannicide behaving like any other Roman with intellectual pretensions, skipping from theaters to libraries to lectures. For Athens had assumed that Brutus was there to raise the East and throw Rome out. Instead—nothing!

A month later Cassius too reached Athens, and the pair moved into a commodious house; of Brutus's vast fortune, hardly any was left in Rome or Italy. It came east with him, and Scaptius was every bit as good a manager as Matinius. In fact, Scaptius intended to be better than Matinius. Thus there was no shortage of money, and the three tame philosophers lived terrifically well. For Statyllus, used to Cato, a welcome change.

"The first thing you have to do is come and see our statues in the agora," Brutus said eagerly, almost pushing Cassius out the front door. "Oh, I am awed! Such wonderful work, Cassius! I look like a god. No, no, I'm not suffering from Caesar's complaint, but I can tell you that a good Greek statue of oneself is far superior to anything the Velabrum workshops can produce."

When Cassius set eyes on them, he fell on the ground laughing, had eventually to move to a place from which he couldn't see them before he could regain his equanimity. Both statues were full length, and absolutely nude. The spindling, round-shouldered, unathletic Brutus looked like a Praxiteles boxer, bulging with muscles, and suitably endowed with an imposing penis, plump long scrotum. No wonder he thought it marvelous! As for himself—well, maybe he was as well endowed as his effigy—and as splendid in body—but to see himself there for all homophilic Athens to drool over was just terribly, terribly funny. Brutus flew into a huff and marched them home without saying another word.

One day in Brutus's company told Cassius that his brother-in-law was idyllically happy living the life of a wealthy Roman in this cultural capital of the world, whereas Cassius itched to do something, get on with something significant. Servilia's news that Syria expected *him* as its governor had given him his idea; he would go to govern Syria.

"If you have the sense you're born with," he told Brutus, "you'll go to Macedonia and govern it *before* Antonius finishes pulling all its legions out. Grab the legions still there, and you'll be inviolable. Write to Quintus Hortensius in Thessalonica and ask him what's happening."

But before Brutus could, Hortensius wrote to him and told him that as far as he, Quintus Hortensius, was concerned, Marcus Brutus was welcome to come and govern Macedonia. Antonius and Dolabella weren't true consuls, they were wolfsheads. With a prod from Cassius, Brutus wrote back to Hortensius and said yes, he would come to Thessalonica, bringing a couple of young men who could act as legates—Cicero's son, Marcus, and Bibulus's young son, Lucius. Plus others.

Within a *nundinum* Cassius had taken ship to island-hop the Aegean to Asia Province, leaving the hesitant Brutus hovering between what he saw as his duty, to go to Macedonia, and his true inclination, to stay in Athens. So he didn't hurry north, as he should have, especially after he heard that Dolabella was rushing through the province on his way to Syria.

And, of course, he had to write letters from Athens before he started out; the proximity of Servilia and Porcia worried him. So he wrote to Servilia and warned her that from this time on he would be difficult to contact, but that whenever he could, he would send Scaptius to see her. Writing to Porcia was far harder; all he could do was beg her to try to get along with her mother-in-law, and tell her that he loved her, missed her. His pillar of fire.

Thus it was the end of November before Brutus arrived in Thessalonica, the capital of Macedonia; Hortensius greeted him ecstatically, and promised that the province would stand by him. But Brutus quibbled. Was it right to take Hortensius's place before the New Year? Hortensius was due to step down then, but if he acted prematurely, the Senate might decide to send an army to deal with a usurping quasi-governor. Four of Antony's crack legions were gone, but the other two, said Hortensius, seemed likely to remain in Dyrrachium for some time to come. Even so, Brutus procrastinated, and a fifth crack legion left.

The one fascinating piece of news from Rome was Octavian's march on the city, which puzzled Brutus greatly. Who was this extremely young man? How did he think he could get away with defying a boar like Marcus Antonius? Were all the Caesars cut from the same cloth? In the end he decided that Octavian was a nonentity, that he would be eliminated by the New Year.

Very much out of things, Publius Vatinius the governor of Illyricum sat in Salona with his two legions and waited for news from Mark Antony that the drive into the lands of the Danubius River was to take place. Finally late in November he received a letter from Antony that ordered him to take his men and march south to assist Gaius Antonius in taking charge of western Macedonia. Unaware of the degree of Antony's unpopularity, Vatinius did as he was told, alarmed by Antony's insistence that Brutus was aiming to snatch Macedonia, and that Cassius was on his way to Syria to snatch it from Dolabella.

So Vatinius marched south to occupy Dyrrachium at the very end of December, his progress an ordeal of snow and ice; winter was early and unusually severe. He found all but two legions gone, one crack and one not so crack, but at least Dyrrachium was a comfortable base. He settled down to wait for Gaius Antonius, as far as he knew the legitimate governor of Macedonia.

* * *

Brutus still waited for news from Rome, which Scaptius brought midway through December. Octavian had gone to earth in Arretium, and a bizarre situation was developing. Two of Antony's legions had mutinied in favor of Octavian, yet nobody's troops would fight, not Octavian's against Antony, or Antony's against Octavian. Caesar's heir, said Scaptius, was now called plain Caesar by almost everyone, and he had a distinct look of Caesar about him. Two attempts by Antony to have Octavian declared *hostis* had failed, so Antony had gone off to Italian Gaul to invest Mutina, where Decimus Brutus was holed up. How extraordinary!

More to the point for him, he learned that the Senate had stripped him of Crete, and Cassius of Cyrenaica. They were not yet declared public enemies, but Macedonia had been given to Gaius Antonius to govern, and Vatinius was ordered to help him.

According to Servilia and Vatia Isauricus, Antony's intentions were grandiose. Armed with a five-year *imperium maius*, he would crush Decimus Brutus, then sit north of the Italian border with Rome's very best legions for five years, having guaranteed himself a continuous frontier westward through Plancus and Lepidus to Pollio, plus eastward through Vatinius to Gaius Antonius. He had ambitions to rule Rome, yes, but understood that the presence of Octavian meant that he couldn't for perhaps another five years.

Finally Brutus acted. He left Hortensius in Thessalonica and marched west on the Via Egnatia with Hortensius's one legion and a few cohorts of Pompey the Great's veterans who had settled in the country around the capital. Young Marcus Cicero and Lucius Bibulus went with him; so did the tame philosophers.

But the weather was appalling, Brutus's progress painfully slow. He battled on at a snail's pace, and was still in the Candavian highlands at the end of the year Caesar died.

Cassius got to Smyrna in Asia Province early in November, to find Gaius Trebonius in residence and well ensconced as governor. With him was another of the assassins, Cassius Parmensis, who was serving as Trebonius's legate.

"I make no secret of it," Cassius said to them. "I intend to beat Dolabella to Syria and take the province off him."

"Good for you," said Trebonius, beaming approval. "Have you any money?"

"Not a sestertius," Cassius confessed.

"Then I can give you some to start off your war chest," said Trebonius. "What's more, I can give you a small fleet of galleys, and I'll donate you the services of two handy legates, Sextilius Rufus and Patiscus. Both good admirals."

"I'm a good admiral too," said Cassius Parmensis. "If you can use me, I'll go with you as well."

"Can you really spare *three* good men?" Cassius asked Trebonius.

"Oh, yes. Asia Province is nothing if not peaceful. They'll be glad of some activity."

"I have less palatable information, Trebonius. Dolabella is going to Syria by land, so you're bound to see him."

Trebonius shrugged. "Let him come. He has no authority in my province."

"Since I'm going on as soon as possible, I'd be grateful if you could round up those war galleys," said Cassius.

They appeared at the end of November. Cassius sailed with his three admirals, determined that he was going to acquire more ships en route. With him went a cousin, one of the many Lucius Cassiuses, and a centurion named Fabius. No tame philosophers for Gaius Cassius!

In Rhodes he had no luck whatsoever. True to form, the city of Rhodus refused him ships or money, explaining that they wanted no part of internecine Roman strife.

"One day," he said pleasantly to the *ethnarch* and the harbormaster of Rhodus, "I'll make you pay for this. Gaius Cassius is a bad enemy, and Gaius Cassius doesn't forget an insult."

In Tarsus he met the same response, and made the same reply. After which he sailed on to northern Syria, though he was too clever to leave his fleet moored where it might encounter a fleet belonging to Dolabella when he arrived.

Caecilius Bassus occupied Apameia, but the assassin Lucius Staius Murcus occupied Antioch and had those six restless, disaffected legions. When Cassius appeared, Murcus handed over the reins gladly and paraded his troops to show them that they now had the governor they wanted, Gaius Cassius.

"I feel as if I've come home," he said in a letter to Servilia, always his favorite correspondent. "Syria is where my heart is."

All of which was a subtle beginning to civil war, if indeed civil war was to emerge from this confused hodgepodge of provinces and would-be governors. Everything depended upon how those in Rome handled the situation; at this stage of affairs, neither Brutus nor Cassius nor even Decimus Brutus really presented major threats to the Senate and People of Rome. Two good consuls and a strong Senate could quash all these pretensions to imperium, and no one had actually challenged the central government on its own turf.

But did Gaius Vibius Pansa and Aulus Hirtius have the clout to control the Senate—or Marcus Antonius—or his martial allies to east and west—or Brutus—or Cassius—or Caesar's heir?

When the old year died, that awful year of the Ides of March, no one knew what might happen.

X

ARMIES ALL OVER THE PLACE

From JANUARY until SEXTILIS (AUGUST) of 43 B.C.

Who Marched Where

1   Exactly twenty years after his own memorable consulship, during which (as he would tell anyone prepared to listen) he had saved his country, Marcus Tullius Cicero found himself at the center of events again. Fear for his own safety had muzzled him many times over the course of those twenty years, and the one time he had desperately tried to save the Republic—when he had almost talked Pompey the Great out of civil war—he had failed, thanks to Cato. But now, with Marcus Antonius gone north, Cicero could look around Rome and see no one with the steel or the sinew to prevent his carrying all before him. At long last a golden tongue would prove more telling than military might and brute force!

Though he had hated Caesar and worked constantly to undermine him, a part of him had always known that Caesar was the phoenix—capable of rising from his own ashes. Ironically vindicated after he was physically burned, when that star had risen to tell all of Rome's world that Caesar would never, never go away. But Antony was better to work against because Antony provided so much ammunition: coarse, intemperate, cruel, impulsive, thoughtless. And, swept away on the power of his own rhetoric, Cicero set out to destroy Antony in the sure knowledge that this was one target without the ability to rise again.

His head was stuffed with visions of the Republic restored to its old form, in the charge of men who revered its institutions, stood forth as champions of the *mos maiorum*. All he had to do was convince the Senate and People that the Liberators were the true heroes, that Marcus Brutus, Decimus Brutus and Gaius Cassius—the three Antony had singled out as Rome's worst enemies—were in the right of it. That it was Antony in the wrong. And if, in this simplistic equation, Cicero neglected to incorporate Octavian, then he had good reason: Octavian was a nineteen-year-old youth, a minor piece to be used on the game board as a lure, carrying within him the seeds of his own destruction.

When Gaius Vibius Pansa and Aulus Hirtius were inaugurated the new consuls on New Year's Day, Mark Antony's status shifted. He was no longer consul, but consular, and whatever powers he had accrued could be chipped away. Like others before him, he hadn't bothered to obtain his governorship and imperium from the body constitutionally able to endow them, the Senate; he had gone to the Plebs in its tribal assembly. Therefore one could argue that the *whole* People had not consented because all patricians were excluded from the Plebeian Assembly. Unlike the other *comitia* and the Senate, the Plebs was not constrained by religious precursors; the prayers were not said, the auspices were not taken. A tenuous argument after men like Pompey the Great, Marcus Crassus and Caesar had obtained provinces and imperium from the Plebs, but one that Cicero used nonetheless.

Between the second day of September and New Year's Day he had spoken against Mark Antony four times, to telling effect. The Senate, full of Antony's creatures, was beginning to waver, for Antony's own conduct made the position of his creatures difficult. Though not accompanied by tangible evidence, the allegation that Antony had conspired with the Liberators to kill Caesar held enough logic to damage him, and his rudeness to Caesar's heir put his creatures in a cleft stick, as they were mostly Caesar's appointees. Antony had come to power as Caesar's heir, even if he wasn't mentioned in Caesar's will; a mature man, he was the natural inheritor of the staggering army of Caesar's clients, and had walked off with enough of them to cement his position. But now Caesar's real heir was wooing them to *his* service—from the bottom up. Octavian couldn't say yet that the majority of senators rued their connection to Antony, but Cicero was intent upon helping him there—for the time being. Once the senators were detached from Antony, he, Cicero, would gradually swing them not to Octavian but to the Liberators. Which meant making it look as if Octavian himself preferred the Liberators to Mark Antony, so unacceptable was Mark Antony. In this, Cicero was immeasurably helped by the fact that Octavian wasn't a senator, therefore found it hard to deny the attitude Cicero was bestowing upon him for Cicero's ends.

The Great Advocate had embarked upon this tack at a meeting of the Senate held toward the end of December; a groundswell had developed against Antony that he couldn't fight because he wasn't in Rome. Which put both Octavian and Antony in the same bind, at the mercy of a master senatorial tactician.

Cicero had a powerful ally in Vatia Isauricus, who blamed Antony for his father's suicide, and implicitly believed that Antony was one of the assassination conspirators. Vatia's clout was enormous, including on the back benches, for he had been, with Gnaeus Domitius Calvinus, Caesar's staunchest aristocratic supporter.

Now, commencing on the second day of January, Cicero set out to discredit Antony so completely that the Senate would endorse Decimus Brutus as the true governor of Italian Gaul, vote to fire Antony and declare him *hostis*, a public enemy. After both Cicero and Vatia spoke, the senators were definitely wavering. All each really wanted was to hang on to what little power he had, and to stick to a lost cause would imperil that.

Were they ripe? Were they ready? Was this the moment to call for a division on the motion that Marcus Antonius be declared *hostis*, an official enemy of the Senate and People of Rome? The debate seemed to be over, and looking at the faces of the hundreds of *pedarii* on the top tiers, it was easy to see where the vote was going to go: against Antony.

What Cicero and Vatia Isauricus overlooked was the right of the consuls to ask others to speak before a division. The senior consul was Gaius Vibius Pansa, who therefore held the *fasces* for the month of January, and was chairing the meeting. He was married to the daughter of Quintus Fufius Calenus, Antony's man to the death, and loyalty dictated that he should do what he could to protect his father-in-law's friend Marcus Antonius.

"I call," came Pansa's voice from the chair, "upon Quintus Fufius Calenus for his opinion!" There. He had done what he could; it was up to Calenus now.

"I suggest," said Calenus craftily, "that before the House sees a division upon Marcus Cicero's motion, an embassage be sent to Marcus Antonius. Its members should be empowered to command Antonius to lift his siege at Mutina and submit to the authority of the Senate and People of Rome."

"Hear, hear!" cried Lucius Piso, a neutral.

The *pedarii* stirred, started to smile: a way out!

"It is madness to send ambassadors to see a man whom this House declared an outlaw twelve days ago!" roared Cicero.

"That's stretching it, Marcus Cicero," said Calenus. "The House *discussed* outlawry, but it wasn't formally implemented. If it were, what's today's motion all about?"

"Semantic quibbling!" Cicero snapped. "Did the House on that day—or did it not?—commend the generals and soldiers opposing Marcus Antonius? The men of Decimus Brutus, in other words? Decimus Brutus himself, in other words? Yes, it did!"

From there he launched into his usual diatribe against Mark Antony: he passed invalid laws, blocked the Forum with armed troops, forged decrees, squandered the public moneys, sold kingdoms, citizenships and tax exemptions, besmirched the courts, introduced bands of brigands into the temple of Concord, massacred centurions and troops at and near Brundisium, and threatened to kill anyone who stood up to him.

"To send an embassage to see such a man is only to delay the inevitable war and weaken the indignation rampant in Rome! I move that a state of *tumultus* be declared! That the courts and other governmental business be suspended! That civilians don military garb! That a levy to raise soldiers be instituted throughout the whole of Italy!

That the welfare of the state be entrusted to the consuls by an Ultimate Decree!"

Cicero paused to wait out the hubbub this ringing peroration brought in its wake, shivering in exultation and oblivious to the fact that his oratory was thrusting Rome into yet another civil war. Oh, this was *life!* This was his own consulship all over again, when he had said much the same about Catilina!

"I also move," he said when he could be heard, "that a vote of thanks be tendered to Decimus Brutus for his forbearance, and a second vote of thanks be tendered to Marcus Lepidus for making peace with Sextus Pompeius. In fact," he added, "I think a gilded statue of Marcus Lepidus should be erected on the rostra, for the last thing we need is a *double* civil war."

As no one knew whether he was serious or not, Pansa ignored the gilded statue of Marcus Lepidus and very shrewdly set Cicero's motions aside.

"Is there any other business the House should consider?"

Vatia rose immediately and commenced a long speech in praise of Octavian that had to be adjourned when the sun set. The House would sit again on the morrow, said Pansa, and for however many days it took to settle all business.

Vatia resumed his panegyric of Octavian on the morrow. "I admit," he said, "that Gaius Julius Caesar Octavianus is extremely young, but there can be no getting away from certain facts—first, that he is Caesar's heir—secondly, that he has displayed maturity far beyond his years—thirdly, that he has the loyalty of a great many of Caesar's veteran troops. I move that he be adlected into the Senate immediately, and that he be allowed to stand for the consulship ten years ahead of the customary age. As he is a patrician, the customary age is thirty-nine. That means he will qualify as a candidate ten years from now, when he turns twenty-nine. Why do I recommend these extraordinary measures? Because, conscript fathers, we are going to need the services of all Caesar's veteran soldiers not attached to Marcus Antonius. Caesar Octavianus has two legions of veteran troops and a third legion of mixed troops. Therefore I further ask that Caesar Octavianus, in possession of an army, be given a propraetor's imperium and assigned one-third of the command against Marcus Antonius."

That set the cat among the pigeons! But it showed a great many of the backbenchers that they could no longer support Mark Antony in as whole a way as they hoped; the most they could do was refuse to declare him *hostis.* So the debate raged until the fourth day of January, on which date several resolutions were passed. Octavian was adlected into the Senate and given a one-third command of Rome's armies; he was also voted the money he had promised his troops as bonuses. The governance of all Rome's provinces were to remain as at Caesar's dictate, which meant that Decimus Brutus was officially Italian Gaul's governor, and his army the official one.

Matters on that fourth day were enlivened by the appearance of two women in the portico outside the Curia Hostilia doors: Fulvia and Julia Antonia. Antony's wife and mother were dressed in black from head to foot, as were Antony's two little sons, the toddler Antyllus holding his grandmother's hand, the new babe Iullus in his mother's arms. The four of them wept and howled without let, but when Cicero demanded that the doors be shut, Pansa wouldn't allow it; he could see that Antony's women and children were having an effect on the backbenchers, and he didn't want Antony declared *hostis*, he wanted that embassage sent.

The ambassadors chosen were Lucius Piso, Lucius Philippus and Servius Sulpicius Rufus, three *eminently* eminent consulars. But Cicero fought the embassage tooth and nail, insisted that it go to a division. Whereupon the tribune of the plebs Salvius vetoed a division, which meant that the House had to approve the embassage. Mark Antony was still a Roman citizen, albeit one acting in defiance of the Senate and People of Rome.

Fed up with sitting on their stools, the senators disposed of the embassage swiftly. Piso, Philippus and Servius Sulpicius were instructed to see Antony at Mutina and inform him that the Senate wished him to withdraw from Italian Gaul, not to advance within two hundred miles of Rome with his army, and to submit to the authority of the Senate and People. Having delivered this message to Antony, the embassage was then to seek an audience with Decimus Brutus and assure him that he was the legitimate governor and had the Senate's sanction.

"Looking back on it," said Lucius Piso gloomily to Lucius Caesar, present in the House again, "I don't honestly know how any of this has happened. Antonius acted stupidly and arrogantly, yes, but tell me one thing he's done that someone else hasn't?"

"Blame Cicero," said Lucius Caesar. "Men's emotions get the better of their good sense, and no one can stir the emotions like Cicero. Though I doubt that anyone reading what he says can have any idea what it's like actually to hear him. He's a phenomenon."

"You would have abstained, of course."

"How could I not? Here I am, Piso, between a wolfshead of a nephew and a cousin for whom I can find no comparison in the entire animal kingdom. Octavianus is a completely new creation."

* * *

Knowing what was coming, Octavian marched north from Arretium to the Via Flaminia, and had reached Spoletium when the Senate's commission caught up with him. The nineteen-year-old senator's propraetorian imperium was right there for all his three legions to see: six lictors clad in crimson tunics, bearing the axes in their *fasces*. The two leading lictors were Fabius and Cornelius, and all had served Caesar since his days as a praetor.

"Not bad, eh?" he asked Agrippa, Salvidienus and Maecenas, sounding complacent.

Agrippa grinned proudly, Salvidienus began to plan military action, and Maecenas asked a question.

"How did you manage it, Caesar?"

"With Vatia Isauricus, you mean?"

"Well, yes, I suppose that's what I mean."

"I asked to marry Vatia's eldest daughter as soon as she's of age," said Octavian blandly. "Luckily that won't happen for several years, and a lot can happen in several years."

"You mean you don't want to marry Servilia Vatia?"

"I don't want to marry anyone, Maecenas, until I'm smitten, though it mightn't work out that way."

"Will it come to a battle with Antonius?" Salvidienus asked.

"I sincerely hope not!" Octavian said, smiling. "And most definitely not while I'm the senior magistrate in the neighborhood. I'm perfectly happy to defer to a consul. Hirtius, I imagine."

Aulus Hirtius had commenced his junior consulship a sick man, had struggled through the inauguration ceremony and then retired to his bed to recover from a lung inflammation.

So when the Senate notified him that he was to lead three more legions in Octavian's wake, catch the new young senator up and assume the co-command of their combined forces, Hirtius was in no fit condition to take the field. Which didn't stop this loyal and selfless man; he wrapped himself up in shawls and furs, chose a litter as his conveyance, and commenced the long journey north on the Via Flaminia into the teeth of a bitter winter. Like Octavian, he didn't want a battle against Antony, was determined to pursue any other course that presented itself.

He and Octavian joined forces on the Via Aemilia inside the province of Italian Gaul, southeast of the big city of Bononia, and went into camp between Claterna and Forum Cornelii, much to the delight of these two towns, assured of fat army profits.

"And here we stay until the weather improves," said Hirtius to Octavian through chattering teeth.

Octavian eyed him in concern. It was no part of his plans to let the consul die; the last thing he wanted was too high a profile. So he agreed to this ultimatum eagerly, and proceeded to supervise Hirtius's nursing, armed with the knowledge of lung ailments which he had soaked up from Hapd'efan'e.

Mobilization in Italy proper was going ahead at full speed; hardly anyone in Rome had realized the enmity Antony had generated among large elements of the Italian communities, which had suffered more at his hands than Rome herself had. Firmum Picenum promised money, the Marrucini of northern Adriatic Samnium threatened to strip Marrucine objectors of their property, and hundreds of rich Italian knights subsidized the equipping of troops. The groundswell was greater outside Rome than inside.

A delighted Cicero took the opportunity to speak out against Antony again at the end of January, when the House met to discuss trivia. By this time, the betrothal of Octavian and Vatia's eldest daughter was generally known, and heads nodded while lips smirked. The fine old custom of making political alliances through marriage still flourished, a cheering thought when so much had changed.

Word had traveled ahead of the returning embassage that it had gotten nowhere with Antony, though just what Antony had told it wasn't known. Which didn't deter Cicero from delivering his seventh oration against Antony. This time he attacked Fufius Calenus and other Antonian partisans savagely for manufacturing reasons why Antony couldn't possibly agree to the Senate's terms.

"He must be declared *hostis!*" roared Cicero.

Lucius Caesar objected. "That's not a word we should bandy about lightly," he said. "To declare a man *hostis* is to deprive him of his citizenship and offer him up as sword fodder to the first patriotic man who sees him. I agree that Marcus Antonius was a bad consul, that he did many things that disadvantaged and disgraced Rome, but *hostis?* Surely *inimicus* is punishment enough."

"Naturally you'd think so! You're Antonius's uncle," Cicero retorted. "I won't permit the ingrate to retain his citizenship!"

The argument raged on into the next day, Cicero refusing to back down. *Hostis* it must be.

At which moment two of the three ambassadors returned; Servius Sulpicius Rufus had succumbed to the freezing weather, and died.

"Marcus Antonius refuses to meet the Senate's conditions," said

Lucius Piso, looking pinched and worn, "and has issued some of his own. He says he will give up Italian Gaul to Decimus Brutus—*if* he can retain Further Gaul until after Marcus Brutus and Gaius Cassius have been consuls four years hence."

Cicero sat stunned. Marcus Antonius was stealing his thunder! He was proclaiming to the Senate that he was switching sides, that he acknowledged the entitlements of the Liberators, that they must have everything Caesar had given them before they killed him! But that was his, Cicero's, ploy! To oppose Antonius was to oppose the Liberators.

Cicero's interpretation was not the only one. The Senate chose to see Antony's ploy as a repeat of Caesar's before he took the fatal step and crossed the Rubicon. Therefore it opposed Antony and ignored his references to Brutus and Cassius. For the choice was the same as with Caesar: to accede to Antony's demands was to admit that the Senate couldn't control its magistrates. So the House declared a state of *tumultus,* which meant civil war, and authorized the consuls Pansa and Hirtius to meet Antony on a field of battle by passing the Ultimate Decree. It refused, however, to declare Antony *hostis.* He was *inimicus.* A victory for Lucius Caesar, albeit a Pyrrhic one. All Antony's laws as consul were invalidated, which meant that his praetor brother, Gaius, was no longer governor of Macedonia, that his seizure of the silver in Ops was illegal, that his land allocations for the veterans fell by the wayside—the repercussions went on and on.

Just before the Ides of February a letter came from Marcus Brutus to inform the Senate that Quintus Hortensius had confirmed him as governor of Macedonia, and that Gaius Antonius was now shut up in Apollonia as Brutus's prisoner. All the legions in Macedonia, said Brutus, had hailed him as governor and their commander.

Dreadful news! Horrific! Or—was it? By this, the Senate was in total disarray, didn't know what to do. Cicero advocated that the House officially confirm Marcus Brutus the governor of Macedonia, and asked the Antonians why they were so against the two Brutuses, Decimus and Marcus?

"Because they're murderers!" Fufius Calenus shouted.

"They're patriots," said Cicero. "Patriots."

On the Ides of February the Senate made Brutus the governor of Macedonia, gave him a proconsular imperium, then added Crete, Greece and Illyricum to his provinces. Cicero was ecstatic. Now he had only two things left to do. The first, to see Antony a beaten man on a battlefield in Italian Gaul. The second, to see Syria taken off Dolabella and given to Cassius to govern.

The first anniversary of Caesar's assassination brought a new horror, for it was on the Ides of March that Rome learned of the atrocities committed by Publius Cornelius Dolabella. En route to Syria, Dolabella had plundered the cities of Asia Province. When he reached Smyrna, where the governor Trebonius was residing, he entered the city by stealth at night, took Trebonius prisoner, and demanded to know where the province's moneys were stored. Trebonius refused to tell him, even after Dolabella resorted to torture. Not the worst pain Dolabella could inflict had the power to loosen Trebonius's tongue; Dolabella lost his temper, killed Trebonius, cut off his head and nailed it to the plinth of Caesar's statue in the agora. Thus Trebonius became the first assassin to die.

The news devastated the Antonians. How could they defend him when his colleague had behaved like a barbarian? When Pansa called the House into immediate session, Fufius Calenus and his cronies had no choice other than to vote with the rest that Dolabella be stripped of his imperium and declared *hostis*. All his property was confiscated, but it amounted to nothing; Dolabella had never managed to clear himself of debt.

Then a fresh wrangle broke out, thanks to the fact that Syria was now a vacant governorship. Lucius Caesar proposed that Vatia Isauricus be given a special commission to take an army east and deal with Dolabella. This peeved the senior consul Pansa greatly.

"Aulus Hirtius and I have already been given the East for our provinces next year," he told the House. "Hirtius is to govern Asia Province and Cilicia, I am to govern Syria. This year our armies are committed to fighting Marcus Antonius in Italian Gaul, we can't fight Dolabella in Syria as well. Therefore I recommend that this year be devoted to the war in Italian Gaul, and next year to war in Syria against Dolabella."

The Antonians saw this proposal as their best bet. Antony still had to be beaten, and they were convinced he couldn't be beaten. Pansa's proposition would keep the legions already in Italy there for the rest of the year, by which time Antony would have thrashed Hirtius, Pansa and Octavian, and the legions would all belong to him. Then *he* could go to Syria.

Cicero had a different answer. Give Syria to Gaius Cassius to govern! Now, right this moment! As no one knew whereabouts Cassius was, this proposal came as a shock. Did Cicero know something the rest of the Senate didn't know?

"Don't give this job to a slug like Vatia Isauricus, and don't pop it in the cellar to store for Pansa next year either!" said Cicero, forgetting protocol and manners. "Syria has to be attended to *now*, not later, and by a young, vigorous man in his prime. A young, vigorous man who already knows Syria well, and has even dealt with the Parthians. Gaius Cassius Longinus! The best and only man for this governorship! What's more, give him the power to make military requisitions in Bithynia, Pontus, Asia Province and Cilicia. Give him unlimited imperium for five years. Our consuls Pansa and Hirtius have their work cut out for them in Italian Gaul!"

Of course from there it was on to Antony. "Do not forget that this Marcus Antonius is a traitor!" Cicero cried. "When he handed Caesar a diadem on the day of the Lupercalia, he showed the whole world that *he* was Caesar's real murderer!"

A look at the faces of his audience showed him that he hadn't hammered Cassius home enough. "I judge Dolabella as Antonius's equal in barbarity! Give Syria to Gaius Cassius immediately!"

But that Pansa was not about to allow. He forced a motion through the House which gave him and Hirtius command of the war against Dolabella as soon as the war in Italian Gaul was over. He was now absolutely committed to the war in Italian Gaul and had to get it over and done with quickly so he at least could leave for Syria during this year, not next. So Pansa handed the care of Rome over to the praetors and took more legions to Italian Gaul.

The day after Pansa left, the governor of Further Gaul, Lucius Munatius Plancus, and of Nearer Spain and Narbonese Gaul, Marcus Aemilius Lepidus, sent letters to the Senate that said they would deeply appreciate it if the Senate would come to an accommodation with Marcus Antonius, a Roman as loyal as they were. The message was implicit: the Senate ought not to forget that there were two big armies sitting on the far side of the Alps, and that these two armies were under the command of governors who favored Marcus Antonius.

Blackmail! said Cicero to himself, and took it upon himself to sit down and write to Plancus and Lepidus, though he had no authority to do so. With eleven speeches delivered against Mark Antony, he had entered a state of exaltation that forbade his climbing down in any way, so what he said to Plancus and Lepidus was injudiciously arrogant—stay out of things you're too far away to know about, mind your own provincial business, and don't stick your noses into Rome's affairs! Not a high aristocrat, Plancus took Cicero's rebuke with his sangfroid intact, whereas Lepidus reacted as if punctured by an ox goad—how dare that New Man nobody Cicero upbraid an Aemilius Lepidus!

After March came in, the weather in Italian Gaul improved a little; Hirtius and Octavian pulled up stakes and moved closer to Mutina, forcing Antony, who had control of Bononia, to abandon that city and concentrate all his legions around Mutina.

When news came that Pansa was on his way from Rome with three legions of recruits, Hirtius and Octavian elected to wait for him before offering Antony battle. But Antony also knew that Pansa was approaching, and struck at Pansa before he could join forces with his two co-commanders. The engagement took place at Forum Gallorum, some seven miles from Mutina, and the decision went to Antony. Pansa himself was badly wounded, but managed to get a message to Hirtius and Octavian that he was under attack. The official dispatches to Rome later said that Hirtius had ordered Octavian to remain behind and defend their camp while he went to Pansa's aid, but the truth was that Octavian had come down with asthma.

What kind of general Antony was he demonstrated very clearly at Forum Gallorum. Having trounced Pansa, he made no attempt to form up his ranks and march to shelter; instead he let his men run wild, ransack Pansa's baggage train, scatter in all directions. Coming up without warning, Hirtius caught him in no condition to fight, and Antony went down so badly that he lost the better part of his army, extricated himself only with great difficulty. So the overall honors of the day went to Aulus Hirtius, Caesar's beloved clerkly marshal.

Some days later, the twenty-first one of April, Hirtius and Octavian tricked Antony into a second battle and defeated him so decisively that he had no choice other than to evacuate his siege camps around Mutina, flee westward on the Via Aemilia. It had been Hirtius in command, Hirtius's battle plan Octavian followed, but even so, he divided his share of the legions into two and put Salvidienus in charge of one half, Agrippa of the other. He had not lost sight of the fact that he was no general, but he also had no intention of putting legates in command of his legions who had the necessary birth and seniority to claim his half of the victory for themselves.

Though they had won—and the assassin Lucius Pontius Aquila, fighting for Antony, was killed—Fortuna was not completely on Octavian's side. Supervising the battle atop a horse on a mound, Aulus Hirtius was felled by a spear and died on the spot. The next day Pansa died of his wounds, which left Caesar Octavianus the only commander the Senate and People of Rome retained.

Except for Decimus Brutus, liberated from the siege of Mutina, and very upset that he hadn't had a chance to fight Antony himself.

"The only legion Antonius managed to save unharmed is the Fifth Alauda," Octavian said to Decimus Brutus when they met inside Mutina, "but he has some stray cohorts from the remainder of his forces, and he's moving westward very swiftly indeed."

For Octavian, this was an unpleasant encounter; as the Senate's lawful commander, he was obliged to be friendly and cooperative in his relations with this murderer. So he was stiff, reserved, cold. "Do you intend to follow Antonius?" he asked.

"Only after I see what develops," Decimus answered, liking Octavian no better than Octavian liked him. "You've come a long way since you were Caesar's personal *contubernalis,* haven't you? Caesar's heir, a senator, a *propraetore* imperium—my, my!"

"Why did you kill him?" Octavian asked.

"Caesar?"

"Who else's death would interest me?"

Decimus shut his pale eyes, put his pale head back, and spoke with dreamy detachment. "I killed him because all that I or any other Roman nobleman had was by his grace and favor—at his dictate. He took upon himself the authority of a king, if not the title, and deemed himself the only man capable of governing Rome."

"He was right, Decimus."

"He was wrong."

"Rome," said Octavian, "is a world empire. That means a new form of government. The annual election of a group of magistrates won't work anymore, nor even five-year imperiums to govern in the provinces, which was Pompeius Magnus's answer. Caesar's too, in the beginning. But Caesar saw what had to be done long before he was murdered."

"Aiming to be the next Caesar?" Decimus asked maliciously.

"I *am* the next Caesar."

"In name, that's all. You won't be rid of Antonius easily."

"I am aware of that. But I will be rid of him, later if not sooner," said Octavian.

"There will always be an Antonius."

"I disagree. Unlike Caesar, I will show those who oppose me no clemency, Decimus. That includes you and the other assassins."

"You're a cocksure child in need of a spanking, Octavianus."

"I am not. I am Caesar. And the son of a god."

"Oh yes, the *stella critina*. Well, Caesar is far less of a danger now he's a god than when he was a living man."

"True. However, as a god he's there to be made capital out of. And I will make capital out of him—as a god."

Decimus burst out laughing. "I hope I live long enough to see Antonius administer that spanking!"

"You won't," said Octavian.

Though Decimus Brutus tendered the invitation with apparent sincerity, Octavian declined to move into his house in Mutina; he remained in his camp to hold the funerals of Pansa and Hirtius, return their ashes to Rome.

Two days later Decimus came to see him, very perturbed.

"I've heard that Publius Ventidius is on the march to join Antonius with three legions he's recruited in Picenum," he said.

"That's interesting," Octavian observed casually. "What do you think I ought to do about it?"

"Stop Ventidius, of course," Decimus said blankly.

"That's not up to me, it's up to you. You're the one with proconsular imperium, you're the Senate's designated governor."

"Have you forgotten, Octavianus, that my imperium doesn't permit me to enter Italy proper? Whoever stops Ventidius *must* enter Italy proper, because he's traveling through Etruria and marching for the Tuscan coast. Besides," said Decimus frankly, "my legions are all raw recruits who can't stand up to Ventidius's Picentines—his are all Pompeius Magnus's old veterans Magnus settled on his own lands in Picenum. Your own men are veterans and the recruits Hirtius and Pansa brought are either veterans or blooded here. So it has to be you who goes after Ventidius."

Octavian's mind raced. He knows I can't general, he wants me to get that spanking. Well, I think Salvidienus could do it, but that's not my problem. I daren't budge from here. If I do, the Senate will see me as another young Pompeius Magnus, indeed cocksure and overweeningly ambitious. Unless I tread carefully, I will be removed, and not merely from my command. From life itself. How do I do it? How do I say no to Decimus?

"I refuse to move my army against Publius Ventidius," he said coolly.

"*Why?*" gasped Decimus, staggered.

"Because the advice has been tendered to me by one of my father's assassins."

"You've got to be joking! We're on the same side in this!"

"I am never on the same side as my father's assassins."

"But Ventidius *has* to be stopped in Etruria! If he meets up with Antonius, we have it to do all over again!"

"If that be the case, then so be it," said Octavian.

He watched Decimus stalk off in high dudgeon, sighing with relief; now he had a perfect excuse not to move. An assassin had told him what to do, and his troops would back him in his refusing to take Decimus's advice.

He didn't trust the Senate as far as he could throw it. Men in that body were hungering for a pretext to declare Caesar's heir *hostis*, and if Caesar's heir entered Italy proper with his army, that was a pretext. When I enter Italy proper with an army, said Octavian to himself, it will be to march on Rome a second time.

A *nundinum* later he received confirmation that his instincts had been correct. Word came from the Senate hailing Mutina as a wonderful feat of arms. But the triumph it awarded for the victory went to Decimus Brutus, *who had taken no part in the fighting!* It also instructed Decimus to take the high command in the war against Antony, and gave him all the legions, including those belonging to Octavian, whose reward was an ignominious minor triumph, the ovation. The *fasces* of the dead consuls, said the Senate, had been returned to the temple of Venus Libitina until new consuls could be elected—but it mentioned no date for an election, and Octavian's impression was that no election would ever be held. To further rebuff Octavian, the Senate had reneged on paying the bonuses to his troops. It was forming a committee to dicker with the legion representatives face-to-face, bypassing their commanders, and neither Octavian nor Decimus was to be on this committee.

"Well, well, well!" said Caesar's heir to Agrippa. "We know where we stand, don't we?"

"What do you intend to do, Caesar?"

"*Nihil.* Nothing. Sit pat. Wait. Mind you," he added, "I don't see why you and a few others can't quietly inform the legion representatives that the Senate has arbitrarily reserved the right to decide for itself how much cash my soldiers will get. And emphasize that senatorial committees are notoriously miserly."

Hirtius's legions were camped on their own, whereas Pansa's three legions were camped with Octavian's three. Decimus took command of Hirtius's legions at the end of April, and demanded that Octavian hand over his own and Pansa's forces. Octavian politely but firmly refused, stoutly maintaining that the Senate had given him his commission, and that its letter was not specific enough to convince him that Decimus really was empowered to take command and legions off him.

Very angry, Decimus issued a direct order to the six legions, whose representatives told him flatly that they belonged to young Caesar and would prefer to stay with young Caesar. Young Caesar paid decent bonuses. Besides, why should they soldier for a man who had murdered the old boy? They'd stick with a Caesar, wanted no part of assassins.

Thus Decimus was obliged to move westward after Antony with some of his own troops from Mutina and Hirtius's three legions of Italian recruits, well blooded at Mutina and therefore the best men he had. But oh, for the six legions with Octavian!

Octavian retired to Bononia, and there sat down to hope that Decimus ruined himself. A general Octavian might not be, but a student of politics and power struggles he was. His own options were few and inauspicious if Decimus didn't ruin himself; Octavian knew that if Antony merged with Ventidius and then succeeded in drawing Plancus and Lepidus on to his side, all Decimus had to do was reach an accommodation with Antony. That done, the whole pack of them would then turn on him, Octavian, and rend him. His one hope was that Decimus would be too proud and too shortsighted to see that refusing to join Antony spelled his ruin.

The moment he received Cicero's presumptuous letter telling him to mind his own provincial business, Marcus Aemilius Lepidus marshaled his legions and moved all of them to the vicinity of the western bank of the Rhodanus River, the border of his Narbonese province. Whatever was going on in Rome and in Italian Gaul, he intended to be positioned so that he could demonstrate to upstarts like Cicero that provincial governors were quite as large a part of *tumultus* as anyone else. It was Cicero's Senate had declared Marcus Antonius *inimicus*, not Lepidus's Senate.

Lucius Munatius Plancus in Further Gaul of the Long-hairs was not quite sure whose Senate he supported, but a state of *tumultus* in Italy was serious enough for him to marshal all his ten legions and start marching down the Rhodanus. When he reached Arausio he halted in a hurry; his scouts reported that Lepidus and his army of six legions were camped a mere forty miles away.

Lepidus sent Plancus a friendly message that said, in effect, "Come on over and visit!"

Though he knew that Antony had been defeated at Mutina, the wary Plancus didn't know about Ventidius and the three Picentine legions marching to Antony's aid, or about Octavian's refusal to co-operate with Decimus Brutus; thus Plancus decided to ignore Lepidus's friendly overtures. He reversed his direction of march and moved north a little to see what happened next.

In the meantime, Antony had hustled himself to Dertona and there took the Via Aemilia Scauri to the Tuscan Sea coast at Genua, where he met Ventidius and the three Picentine legions. The pair then laid a false scent for the pursuing Decimus Brutus, deluding him into believing that they were on the Via Domitia to Further Gaul rather than down on the coast. The ruse worked. Decimus passed Placentia and took the Via Domitia across the high Alps, far to the north of Antony and Ventidius.

Who followed the coast road and sat down at Forum Julii, one of Caesar's new veteran colonies. Where Lepidus, moving east from the Rhodanus River, arrived on the opposite bank of the local stream and sat his army down casually. In close contact, the troops of both armies fraternized—with some help from two of Antony's legates. A new version of the Tenth was with Lepidus, and the Tenth had developed a tradition of liking Antony ever since the days when he had stirred mutiny in Campania. So it was easy for Antony at Forum Julii; Lepidus accepted the inevitable and joined forces with him and Ventidius.

By this time May was wearing down into its second half and even in Forum Julii there were rumors that Gaius Cassius was busy taking over Syria. Interesting, but not of great moment. The movements of Plancus and his huge army up the Rhodanus were more important by far than Cassius in Syria.

Plancus had been edging his legions closer to Antony, but when his scouts reported that Lepidus was also at Forum Julii, Plancus panicked and retreated to Cularo, well north of the Via Domitia, and sent a message to Decimus Brutus, still on the Via Domitia. When Decimus received this letter, he struck off toward Plancus, reaching Cularo early in June.

There the two decided to amalgamate their armies and cleave to the Senate of the moment, Cicero's. After all, Decimus had its full mandate, and Plancus was a legal governor. When he then heard that Lepidus had also been declared *inimicus* by Cicero's Senate, Plancus congratulated himself that he had chosen rightly.

The problem was that Decimus had changed terribly, lost all his old panache, that marvelous military ability he had displayed so consistently during Caesar's war against the Long-hairs. He wouldn't hear of their moving from around Cularo, fretted about the unblooded state of the majority of their troops, insisted that they do nothing to provoke a confrontation with Antony. Their fourteen legions were just not enough—not nearly enough!

So everybody played a waiting game, unsure of success if it came to a pitched battle. This was not a clear cut ideological contest between two sides whose soldiers believed ardently in what they were fighting for, and there were no lions anywhere.

At the beginning of Sextilis the scales tipped Antony's way; Pollio and his two legions arrived from Further Spain to join him and Lepidus. Why not? asked a grinning Pollio. Nothing exciting was going on in his province now that Cicero's Senate had given command of Our Sea to Sextus Pompey—what a stupid thing to do!

"Truly," said Pollio, shaking his head in despair, "they go from bad to worse. Anyone with a particle of sense can see that Sextus Pompeius is simply gathering strength to hold Rome to ransom over the grain supply. Still, it has made life extremely boring for an historian like me. There'll be more to write about if I'm with you, Antonius." He gazed around in delight. "You do pick good camps! The fish and the swimming are superb, the Maritime Alps a magnificent backdrop— much nicer than Corduba!"

If life was offering Pollio a wonderful time, it was not doing nearly as well by Plancus. For one thing, he couldn't get away from Decimus Brutus's eternal complaints. For another, when the listless Decimus wouldn't, it fell to him to write to the Senate trying to explain why he and Decimus hadn't moved against Antony and his fellow *inimicus*, Lepidus. He had to make Octavian his chief butt, blame Octavian for not stopping Ventidius, and condemn him for refusing to give up his troops.

The moment Pollio arrived, the two *inimici* sent Plancus an invitation to join them; abandoning Decimus Brutus to his fate, Plancus accepted with relief. He marched for Forum Julii and its gala atmosphere, failing to notice as he came down the eastern slopes of the Rhodanus valley that everything was unnaturally dry, that the crops of this fertile region weren't forming ears.

The terrible panic and depression he had experienced after Caesar's death had returned to haunt Decimus Brutus; after Plancus deserted, he threw his hands in the air and abdicated his military duty and his imperium. Leaving his bewildered legions where they were in Cularo, he and a small group of friends set off overland to join Marcus Brutus in Macedonia. Not an unfeasible endeavor for Decimus, who was fluent in many Gallic tongues, and envisioned no problems en route. It was high summer, all the alpine passes were open, and the farther east they traveled, the lower and easier the mountains became.

He did well until he entered the lands of the Brenni, who inhabited the heights beyond that pass into Italian Gaul bearing their name. There the party was taken prisoner by the Brenni and brought before their chieftain, Camilus. Thinking that all Gauls must loathe Caesar, their conqueror, and thinking to impress Camilus, one of Decimus's friends told the chieftain that this was Decimus Brutus, who had killed the great Caesar. The trouble was that among the Gauls Caesar was passing into folklore alongside Vercingetorix, was loved as a supreme martial hero.

Camilus knew what was going on, and sent word to Antony at Forum Julii that he held Decimus Junius Brutus captive—what did the great Marcus Antonius want done with him?

"Kill him" was Antony's curt message, accompanied by a fat purse of gold coins.

The Brenni killed Decimus Brutus and sent his head to Antony as proof that they had earned their money.

On the last day of June the Senate declared Marcus Aemilius Lepidus *inimicus* for joining Antony, and confiscated his property. The fact that he was Pontifex Maximus created some confusion, as Rome's highest priest could not be stripped of his high priesthood, nor could the Senate deny him the big emolument he received from the Treasury every year. *Hostis* would have done it, *inimicus* didn't. Though Brutus, writing from Macedonia, deplored his sister Junilla's descent to pauperdom, the truth was that she continued to live very comfortably in the Domus Publica, and had the use of any villa she fancied between Antium and Surrentum. No one appropriated Junilla's jewelry, wardrobe or servants, nor would Vatia Isauricus, married to her elder sister, have condoned any financial measures on the part of the state that affected her well-being. All Brutus was doing was playing politics in the proper fashion; some of the donkeys would believe him, and weep.

The Liberators left in Rome were dwindling. Deriving an obscene pleasure from torturing a slave, Lucius Minucius Basilus found himself tortured and killed when his slaves rose up against him en masse. His death was not felt to be a loss, especially by those Liberators remaining, from the brothers Caecilius to the brothers Casca. They still attended the Senate, but privately wondered for how long: Caesar Octavianus lurked, in the person of his agents. Rome seemed filled with them, and all they did was ask people why the Liberators were still unpunished.

Indeed, Antony, Lepidus, Ventidius, Plancus, Pollio and their twenty-three legions worried those in Rome far less than Octavian did. Forum Julii seemed an eternity away compared to Bononia, right on the junction of the Via Aemilia and the Via Annia—two routes to Rome. Even Brutus in Macedonia considered Octavian a far greater threat to peace than he did Mark Antony.

The object of all this apprehension sat placidly in Bononia and did nothing, said nothing. With the result that he became shrouded in mystery; no one could say with any conviction that he knew what Caesar Octavianus was after. Rumor said he wanted the consulship— still vacant—but when applied to, his step-father, Philippus, and his brother-in-law, Marcellus Minor, just looked inscrutable.

By now people knew that Dolabella was dead and Cassius was governing in Syria, but, like Forum Julii, Syria was an eternity away compared to Octavian in Bononia.

Then, much to Cicero's horror (though secretly he toyed with the idea), another rumor started: that Octavian wanted to be the junior consul to Cicero's senior consul. The young man sitting at the feet of the wise, venerable older man, there to learn his craft. Romantic. Delicious. But even though exhausted by the great series of speeches against Mark Antony, Cicero retained sufficient good sense to feel that the picture this conjured up was utterly false. Octavian couldn't be trusted an inch.

Toward the end of Julius, four hundred centurions and hoary veterans arrived in Rome and sought an audience with the full Senate, bearing a mandate from their army and proposals from Gaius Julius Caesar Filius. For themselves, the promised bonuses. For Caesar Filius, the consulship. The Senate said a resounding no to both.

On the last day of the month renamed in his adopted father's honor, Octavian crossed the Rubicon into Italy with eight legions, then forged ahead with two legions of handpicked troops. The Senate flew into a panic and sent envoys to beg that Octavian halt his march. He would be allowed to stand for the consulship without needing to present himself inside the city, so there was no real reason to continue!

In the meantime, two legions of veterans from Africa Province arrived in Ostia. The Senate snatched at them eagerly and put them in the fortress on the Janiculum, from which they could look down on Caesar's pleasure gardens and Cleopatra's vacant palace. The knights of the First Class and the upper end of the Second Class donned armor, and a militia of young knights was raised to man the Servian Walls.

All of it was no more than a clutching at straws; those in nominal control had no idea what to do, and those with a status lower than the Second Class went serenely about their business. When the mighty fell out, the mighty did the bleeding. The only time the common people suffered was when they rioted, and not even the lowliest were in a mood to riot. The grain dole was being issued, commerce went on so jobs were safe, next month would see the *ludi Romani*, and nobody in his or her right mind ventured into the Forum Romanum, which was where the mighty usually bled.

The mighty went right on clutching at straws. When a rumor arose that two of Octavian's original legions, the Martia and the Fourth, were about to desert him and help the city, a huge sigh of relief went up—only to turn into a wail of despair when the rumor was found to be baseless.

On the seventeenth day of Sextilis, Caesar's heir entered Rome unopposed. The troops stationed in the Janiculan fortress reversed swords and *pila* and went over to the invader amid cheers and flowers. The only blood that was spilled belonged to the urban praetor, Marcus Caecilius Cornutus, who fell on his sword when Octavian walked into the Forum. The common people hailed him with hysterical joy, but of the Senate there was no sign. Very properly, Octavian withdrew to his men on the Campus Martius, there to receive anyone who asked to see him.

The next day the Senate capitulated, humbly asked if Caesar Octavianus would be a candidate for the consular elections, to be held immediately. As the second candidate, the senators timidly suggested Caesar's nephew, Quintus Pedius. Octavian graciously acceded, and was elected senior consul, with Quintus Pedius as his junior.

Nineteen days into Sextilis and still more than a month off his twentieth birthday, Octavian offered up his sacrificial white bull on the Capitol and was inaugurated. Twelve vultures circled overhead, an omen so portentous and awesome that it had not been seen since the time of Romulus. Though his mother and sister were barred from this all male gathering, Octavian was perfectly happy to count the faces present, from his doubting stepfather to the appalled senators. What the bewildered Quintus Pedius thought, his young cousin didn't know—or care about.

This Caesar had arrived on the world stage, and was not going to leave it untimely.

XI

THE SYNDICATE

From SEXTILIS (AUGUST) until
DECEMBER of 43 B.C.

MARCUS AEMILIUS LEPIDUS

LUCIUS JULIUS CAESAR

1. To Marcus Vipsanius Agrippa had fallen the role of most faithful follower, a role he continued to welcome as much as he relished it. Not for Agrippa the pangs of envy or ambition to be first; his feelings for Octavian remained unalloyed love, total admiration, tender protectiveness. Others might condemn Octavian, or loathe him, or deride him, but Agrippa alone understood exactly who and what Octavian was, thought no worse of him for the extremes in his character. If Caesar's intellect had lifted him into the aether, Octavian's very different mentality, Agrippa decided, enabled him to descend into the underworld. No human failing escaped his notice, no weakness was ignored, no chance remark went unweighed. His instincts were reptilian, in that he preserved his immobility while others made the mistake of moving. When he did move, it was so fast that it was a blur, or else so slow that it seemed an illusion.

Agrippa interpreted his job as making sure that Octavian survived to achieve the great destiny he perceived as his right, as the natural outcome of who and what he was. And for Agrippa, the highest reward was to be Octavian's best friend, the one in whom he confided. He did nothing to deflect his idol's attention from men like Salvidienus and Maecenas, others like Gaius Statilius Taurus rising to the rank of intimate friend; there was no need, for Octavian's own instincts kept them at one remove from his innermost thoughts and desires. Those he reserved for Agrippa's ear, and Agrippa's alone.

"The first thing I must do," Octavian said to Agrippa, "is have you, Maecenas, Salvidienus, Lucius Cornificius and Taurus put into the Senate. There's no time for quaestorian elections, so adlection it will have to be. Philippus can move it. Then we set up a special court to try the assassins. You will indict Cassius, Lucius Cornificius will indict Marcus Brutus. One of my friends for each assassin. Naturally I expect every juror to return a verdict of CONDEMNO. If any juror should vote ABSOLVO, I want to know his name. For future reference, you understand. It always pays to know the men who have the courage of their convictions." He laughed. "Or their exonerations."

"You'll legislate the court personally?" Agrippa asked.

"Oh, no, that wouldn't be wise. Quintus Pedius can do it."

"It sounds," said Agrippa, brows meeting, "as if you mean this to happen quickly, but it's high time that I returned to a certain place for another load of wooden planks."

"No more wood for the moment, Agrippa. The Senate agreed to pay each of my original legionaries twenty thousand in bonuses, therefore the money will come out of the Treasury."

"I thought the Treasury was empty, Caesar."

"Not quite, but it isn't healthy. Nor do I intend to strip it. By tradition, the gold is never touched. However, the reports of the plebeian aediles are alarming," said Octavian, revealing that he wasn't wasting any time wading into the work; this was one consul who intended to be hands-on. "Last year's harvest was a poor one, but this year's is disastrous. Not only in our grain provinces, but all the way from the western ocean to the eastern ocean. Nilus isn't inundating, the Euphrates and the Tigris are low, and there have been no spring rains anywhere. A colossal drought. That's why my asthma is rather bad."

"It's better than it used to be," soothed Agrippa. "Perhaps you're growing out of it."

"I hope so. I detest having to appear in the House looking blue around the gills and wheezing, but appear I must. Though I do think the terrible attacks are less frequent."

"I'll offer to Salus."

"I do, every day."

"The harvest?" Agrippa prompted, heeding the message: he too must offer to Salus every day.

"It seems there literally won't be one. What grain there is will fetch huge prices, so Quintus Pedius is going to have to bring some emergency measures into law forbidding the sale of grain to private vendors ahead of the state. That's why I can't strip the Treasury. It's no part of my strategy to impoverish business, but grain will have to be a special case. Despite my father's colonies for the urban poor, there are still a hundred and fifty thousand free grain chits issued, and that must continue. Cicero and Marcus Brutus wouldn't agree with me, but I value the esteem of the Head Count. It gives Rome most of her soldiers."

"Why not pay the legion bonuses in wood, Caesar?"

"Because there's a principle involved," Octavian said in tones that brooked no argument. "Either I run the Senate, or the Senate runs me. Were it a body of wise men, I'd be grateful for its counsel, but it's nothing but factions and frictions."

"Do you plan to abolish it?" Agrippa asked, fascinated.

Octavian looked genuinely shocked. "No, never! What I have to do is re-educate it, Agrippa, though *that* won't be done in a single day—or a single consulship. The Senate's proper function is to recommend decent laws and leave executive government to the elected magistrates."

"What about the wagons of wood, then?"

"They stay where they are. Things are going to get worse long before they get better, and I want a reserve of money against far more daunting situations than a drought and Marcus Antonius. This time tomorrow I become Caesar Filius in law, the *lex curiata* will be passed. That means I'll have Caesar's fortune—minus his gift to the people, which I'll pay immediately. But I don't mean to squander anything I have from my father, be it wood or investments. For the moment I have Rome to myself, but do you think I don't realize that must end? The contents of the Treasury are going to have to pay for everything while wastrels like Antonius exist." He stretched contentedly, smiling Caesar's smile for Agrippa's eyes alone. "I wish," he remarked, "that I had the Domus Publica as an office. My house is too small."

Agrippa grinned. "Buy a bigger one, Caesar. Or hold a proper election and get yourself voted in as Pontifex Maximus."

"No, Lepidus can stay Pontifex Maximus. I have my eye on a bigger house, but not the Domus Publica. Unlike my father, I have no desire to make a huge splash in Rome's pond. He reveled in magnificence because it suited his nature. He *enjoyed* notoriety. I do not," said Octavian.

"But," Agrippa objected, still haunted by the specter of legionary bonuses, "you have over three hundred million to pay the legions. That's twelve thousand talents of silver. I don't see how you can do it, Caesar, without using wood."

"I don't intend to pay all of it," Octavian said nonchalantly. "Just half of it. I'll owe them the rest."

"They'll change sides!"

"Not after I talk to them and explain that payment over time guarantees a future income. Especially if there's ten percent interest payable on it. Do not fret so, Agrippa, I know what I'm doing. I'll talk them into it—*and* keep their loyalty."

He will too, thought Agrippa, awed. What a plutocrat he'd make! Atticus would have to look to his laurels.

Two days later Philippus held a family dinner in honor of the new consuls, shrinking at the prospect of having to inform them that his younger son, Quintus, was making overtures to Gaius Cassius in Syria. Oh, for a life devoted to the pleasures of the table, of books, of a beautiful, cultured wife! Instead, he had been inflicted with a juvenile power grabber who apparently had no brakes. That, he remembered vaguely, was what Caesar's mother, Aurelia, had always said about *her* Caesar: he had no brakes. Nor did this second edition. Such a charming, inoffensive, quiet, sick little boy he had been! Now it was he, Philippus, who was sick. That long ambassadorial journey to Italian Gaul during the depths of winter had not only killed Servius Sulpicius; it was threatening to kill him and Lucius Piso too. Piso's ailment was pulmonary, his was rotting toes. The frostbite he had suffered had turned to something so unpleasant that the physicians shook their heads and the surgeons recommended amputation, which Philippus had rejected with horror. So the Philippus who greeted his guests wore slippers over socks stuffed with sweet-smelling herbs to disguise the stench of his blackened toes.

The men outnumbered the women because three of the men were bachelors—his elder son, Lucius, who stubbornly refused every bride Philippus suggested—Octavian—and Marcus Agrippa, whom Octavian had insisted upon bringing. When Philippus set eyes on this unknown Agrippa, his breath caught. So handsome, yet so much a man! Nearly as tall as Caesar had been, shoulders like Antonius, a soldierly bearing that endowed him with massive presence. Oh, Octavianus! cried Philippus within his mind, this young man will take it all off you! But by the time the dinner concluded, he had changed his mind. Agrippa belonged whole and entire to Octavianus. Not that he could level a charge of unchastity or indecency; they never touched, even when they walked together, and cast each other no caressing or languishing looks. Whatever this natural leader of men saw in Octavianus, it completely negated his own ambitions. My stepson is building a faction among men in his age group, and more shrewdly than Caesar, who always stood apart, held himself aloof from intimate friendships with men. Well, that old canard about King Nicomedes had done it, of course, but if Caesar had had an Agrippa, no one could have murdered him. My stepson is far different. He doesn't care about canards, they bounce off him like stones off a hippopotamus.

For Octavian the dinner was a delight because his sister had come. Of all the people in his life, including his mother, Octavia lay closest by far to his heart. How she had bloomed! Her fair beauty shone Atia's down, though her nose wasn't as lovely, nor her cheekbones as high. It was all in her eyes, the most wonderful eyes any woman had ever owned, wide apart, widely opened, the color of an aquamarine, as revealing as his were shut away. Her nature was entirely love and compassion, and it looked out of her eyes. She only had to appear in the Porticus Margaritaria to shop, and everyone who saw her loved her at a single glance. My father had his daughter, Julia, as a conduit to the common people; I have Octavia. I will treasure her and shelter her for all my days as my good spirit.

The three women were in a merry mood, Atia because her darling son was proving such a prodigy—why had she never suspected it? After nearly twenty years of worrying herself to the point of illness over someone she had thought too frail to hang on to life, she was beginning to discover that her little Gaius was a huge force to be reckoned with. For all his wheezing, it came as a shock to realize that he would probably outlive everyone, even that magnificent Marcus Agrippa.

Octavia was in a merry mood because her brother was there; his affection for her was fully returned. She was three years older than he, and wonderfully healthy herself; he had always been a superior kind of doll, toddling around in her wake beaming at her, plying her with questions, seeking haven with her when their mother fussed and clucked too unbearably. Octavia had always seen what Rome and her family were only now beginning to see: the strength, the determination, the brilliance, the ineradicable sense of specialness. She supposed that all of these were his Julian inheritance, but understood too that he possessed a hardheaded, frugal, down-to-earth side from their blood father's impeccably Latin stock. How composed he is! *My brother will rule the world.*

Valeria Messala was in a merry mood because suddenly her life had opened up. The sister of Messala Rufus the augur, she had been wife to Quintus Pedius for thirty years, given him two sons and a daughter; one son was grown, the younger of *contubernalis* age, and the girl sixteen. Her chief beauty was her mass of red hair, though her swampy green eyes attracted attention too. She and Quintus Pedius had married as part of Caesar's network of political connections. A patrician, she was of much better family than the Pedii of Campania, though not of the Julii, and she had found that she and Quintus suited each other very well. If anything had bothered Valeria Messala, it was her husband's absolute loyalty to Caesar, who hadn't advanced him as rapidly as she felt proper. Now that he was junior consul, her every wish was answered. Her sons came from consular stock on both sides, and her daughter, Pedia Messalina, would make a truly splendid marriage.

Oblivious to the masculine conversation, the women chattered about babies. Octavia had borne a girl, Claudia Marcella, last year, and was pregnant again. This time, she hoped, with a son.

Her husband, Gaius Claudius Marcellus Minor, found himself in a curious position for one whose family had so obdurately and persistently opposed Caesar. He had retrieved his expectations—and preserved his large fortune—by marrying Octavia, whom he loved passionately because one couldn't not. But who would ever have dreamed that his wife's little brother would be senior consul at nineteen? And whereabouts was it all going to go? Somehow, he thought, to dizzying heights. Octavianus radiated success, though not in the flamboyant style of his great-uncle.

"Do you think," Marcellus Minor asked Octavian and Pedius, "that it's the right time to prosecute the Liberators?" He caught the red look in Octavian's eyes at his use of this detested name, and amended it hastily. "The assassins, I mean, of course. Most of Rome uses 'Liberator' as an ironical device, not sincerely. But to go on with what I was saying, Caesar Octavianus, you have Marcus Antonius and the western governors to deal with, so is this the right time for trials, which are so drawn out?"

"And from what I hear," said Philippus, coming to Marcellus Minor's rescue, "Vatinius isn't going to contest Marcus Brutus in Illyricum, he's coming home. That strengthens Brutus's position. Then there's Cassius in Syria, another threat to peace. Why try the assassins and exacerbate the situation? If Brutus and Cassius are tried and found guilty, they're outlaws and can't come home. *That* might tempt them into war, and Rome doesn't need yet another war. Antonius and the western governors are war enough."

Quintus Pedius listened, but had no intention of answering. A most unhappy man, he was permanently embroiled in the affairs of the Julii, and hated it. His nature he had inherited from his country squire father, but his fate he had inherited from his mother, Caesar's eldest sister. All he wanted was a quiet life on his vast estates in Campania, not the consulship. Then his eyes fell on his wife, so animated, and he sighed. Patricians will always be patricians, he reflected wryly. Valeria loves being the consul's wife, talks of nothing but hosting the Bona Dea.

"The assassins *must* be prosecuted," Octavian was saying. "The scandal lies in the fact that they weren't prosecuted the day after they did the deed. Had they, the present situation could never have arisen. It's Cicero and the Senate responsible for legalizing Brutus's position, which rather flows on to Cassius's, but it's Antonius and *his* Senate that didn't prosecute."

"Which is my point," Marcellus Minor said. "If they weren't prosecuted immediately afterward—indeed, were given a general amnesty—will people understand?"

"I don't care if people don't, Marcellus. Senate and People have to learn that a group of noblemen can't excuse the murder of a fellow nobleman in a legal office on patriotic grounds. Murder is murder. If the assassins had reason to believe that my father intended to make himself King of Rome, then they should have prosecuted him in a court of law," said Octavian.

"How could they possibly have done that?" Marcellus asked. "Caesar was Dictator Perpetuus, above the law, inviolable."

"All they had to do was strip him of his dictatorship—it was voted to him, after all. But they didn't even try to strip him of it. The assassins voted in favor of Dictator Perpetuus."

"They were afraid of him," said Pedius. He had been too.

"Nonsense! Afraid of what? When did my father ever take a Roman life except in battle? His policy was clemency—a mistake, but a reality nonetheless. Pedius, he had *pardoned* most of his assassins, some of them twice over!"

"Still and all, they were afraid of him," said Marcellus.

The young, smooth, beautiful face hardened, took on the mien of a cold, mature purveyor of terror. "They have more reason to be afraid of *me!* I won't rest until the last assassin is dead, his reputation in ruins, his property confiscated, his women and children paupers."

A queer silence fell upon the men. Philippus broke it.

"There are fewer and fewer to prosecute," he said. "Gaius Trebonius, Aquila, Decimus Brutus, Basilus—"

"But why," Marcellus interrupted, "is Sextus Pompeius to be prosecuted? He wasn't an assassin, and he's now officially Rome's proconsul of the seas."

"His proconsular status is about to end, as you well know. I have a dozen witnesses to testify that his ships raided the African grain fleet two *nundinae* ago. That makes him a traitor. Besides, he's Pompeius Magnus's son," Octavian said flatly. "I will be rid of *all* Caesar's enemies."

His auditors knew that the Caesar he meant was himself.

The trials of the Liberators came on within the first month of the consulship of Gaius Julius Caesar Octavianus and Quintus Pedius; even though there were twenty-three separate hearings (the dead were tried too), the whole process was over within one *nundinum.* The jurors unanimously condemned each Liberator, who was declared *nefas.* All his property was confiscated by the state. Those Liberators like the tribune of the plebs Gaius Servilius Casca who were still in Rome fled, but pursuit was slow. Suddenly Servilia and Tertulla were homeless, though not for long. Their private fortunes had always been invested with Atticus, who bought Servilia a new house on the Palatine and took a great deal of undeserved credit for supporting the two women.

When the subsidiary prosecution convicted Sextus Pompey of treason, one of the thirty-three jurors returned a tile marked A for AB-SOLVO; the rest obediently said C for CONDEMNO.

"Why did you do that?" Agrippa asked the man, a knight.

"Because Sextus Pompeius is not a traitor" was the answer.

Octavian filed away the name, rather pleased at the size of the man's fortune. He would keep.

The bequests were distributed to the people, and Caesar's parks and gardens thrown open; Romans from all walks of life loved to stroll and picnic in verdant but tamed places. Octavian was pleased to hire Cleopatra's palace out to ambitious members of the First Class desirous of giving large feasts for their clients. Their names went into his "Items of Interest" file too.

He secured the election of two intimates as tribunes of the plebs: Marcus Agrippa and Lucius Cornificius, for with Casca's flight, the College held two vacancies. Publius Titius, already a tribune of the plebs and anxious to stand high with Octavian, saved Octavian's life when the foreign praetor, Quintus Gallus, tried to murder him. Gallus was stripped of his office, the galvanized Senate condemned him to death without a trial, and the ordinary people were allowed to loot his house. Tiny shock waves were radiating through the First Class, who now began to ask themselves if Octavianus was any better than Antonius?

True to his word, the new senior consul took enough money from the Treasury to pay his original three legions ten thousand sesterces each. Their representatives had readily agreed to his proposal that the other half should wait and accrue interest as a guarantee of future income. Though, with centurion extras, this amounted to less than four thousand talents, he took six thousand—as much as he dared with grain prices spiraling—and split the remainder up among his three later legions. He also recruited sixty humble rankers in each legion to work as his private agents, one man per century; their job was to spread word of Caesar's generosity and constancy, and also report any troublemakers. They were told to speak about the army as a long-term career sure to leave a soldier a relatively wealthy man at the end of fifteen or twenty years' service. Largesse was good, but secure, well-paid, all-expenses-founded, steady employment was better, was Octavian's message. Be loyal to Rome and Caesar and Rome and Caesar will always look after you, even if there are no wars to be fought. Garrison duty permitted family life on post. The army was an *attractive* career! Thus, even at this very early stage, Octavian began to prepare the legionaries for the idea of a permanent, standing army.

* * *

On the twenty-third day of September, which was his twentieth birthday, Octavian took eleven legions and marched north to contend with Mark Antony and the western governors.

With him he took the tribune of the plebs Lucius Cornificius, an extraordinary action—to care for the interests of his troops, all plebeians, he explained. Behind him in Rome he left Pedius to govern, with his two other tribunes of the plebs, Agrippa and Titius, to push Pedius's laws through the Plebeian Assembly. His more invisible helper, Gaius Maecenas, remained in Rome on less obvious business, chiefly concerned with recruiting innovative men of the lower classes.

Agrippa hadn't liked abandoning Octavian. "You'll get into trouble if I'm not with you," he said.

"I'll manage, Agrippa. I need you in Rome to gain experience in unwarlike matters, and learn about lawmaking. Believe me, I stand in no danger on this campaign."

"But you're taking a tribune of the plebs," Agrippa objected.

"One less known to be my loyalest follower," said Octavian.

The march was fairly leisurely and ended at Bononia, where Octavian made camp and sent to Mutina for the six legions of raw recruits Decimus Brutus had deemed so hopeless that he left them behind when he chased Antony westward. Salvidienus was charged with drilling and training all recruits remorselessly while the army waited for Mark Antony to find it.

Octavian had no intention of fighting Antony when he came, and had formulated a plan he thought had a fair chance of success, depending upon how persuasively he could talk. What he knew was that it was up to him to unite all the factions of Caesar's old civil war alliance; if he didn't, Rome would go to Brutus and Cassius, now controlling every province east of the Adriatic. A state of affairs that had to be terminated, but impossible to terminate unless all Caesar's adherents were united.

Early in October, Mark Antony took seventeen of his legions out of camp in Forum Julii, leaving six behind with Lucius Varius Cotyla to garrison the West. After their halcyon summer the men were fit, well rested, and spoiling for some action. All three governors marched with him: Plancus, Lepidus and Pollio. But of master plans there were none. Antony was well aware of Brutus and Cassius in the East and understood that they would have to be put down, but his thinking lumped Octavian in with the two Liberators as yet another unacceptable, obnoxious player in the power game. He was not enamored of losing valuable troops in battle against Octavian, but saw no alternative. Once Octavian was knocked out of the game, he would pick up Octavian's troops, but their loyalty would always be suspect, he knew. If the Martia and the Fourth could leave Marcus Antonius for a baby who reminded them of Caesar, what would they think of that selfsame Marcus Antonius when their baby Caesar lay dead at Marcus Antonius's hands?

So he took the Via Domitia and crossed into Italian Gaul at Ocelum in a sour mood, not improved by his bedtime reading, the series of speeches Cicero had delivered against him. Though he despised Octavian, he *hated* Cicero. Were it not for Cicero, his position would be secure, his public enemy status would not exist, and Octavian wouldn't be a problem. It had been Cicero who encouraged Caesar's heir, Cicero who turned the Senate against him until even Fufius Calenus didn't dare speak up for him. Confiscation of his property hadn't been an issue, for though his debts were paid off, he had no money worth speaking of. Much as they might hunger to, the senators didn't dare touch Fulvia or his palace on the Carinae—she was the granddaughter of Gaius Sempronius Gracchus, and under the protection of Atticus.

Fulvia. He missed her, and he missed his children by her. Full of news and well written, her letters had kept him informed of every event in Rome, and he had cause to be grateful to Atticus. Her hatred of Cicero was even greater than his own, if that were humanly possible.

When Antony reached Mutina, twenty miles from Octavian's camp on the outskirts of Bononia, he was met by the third tribune of the plebs, Lucius Cornificius. A holder of that office was the best of all envoys; even a Mark Antony had sufficient sense to understand that his cause would not be improved by the manhandling of a tribune of the plebs. They were sacrosanct and inviolate when acting for the Plebs, as Cornificius insisted he was, despite the fact that his boss belonged to the Patriciate.

"The consul Caesar," said Cornificius, twenty-one years old, "wishes to confer with Marcus Antonius and Marcus Lepidus."

"Confer, or surrender?" Antony sneered.

"Confer, definitely confer. I bear an olive branch, not a reversed standard."

Plancus and Lepidus were very much against the idea of any meeting with Octavian, whereas Pollio thought it excellent. So, after thinking things over, did Antony.

"Tell Octavianus that I'll consider his proposal," Antony said.

Lucius Cornificius did a lot of galloping back and forth over the next several days, but eventually it was agreed that Antony, Lepidus and Octavian would meet to confer on an island in the middle of the swift, strong Lavinus River near Bononia. It was Cornificius named the site on his last mission.

"All right, that will do," said Antony after considering it from all sides, "provided that Octavianus moves his camp to the Bononian side of the river, while I move my camp to the Mutinan bank. If there's any treachery, we can fight it out on the spot."

"Let Pollio and me come with you and Lepidus," Plancus said, unhappy because he knew that whatever was discussed would affect his whole future. "It ought to be more public, Antonius."

Bright eyes twinkling, Gaius Asinius Pollio gazed at Plancus in amusement. Poor Plancus! A *beautiful* writer, an erudite man, but incapable of seeing what he, Pollio, saw plainly. What do men like Plancus and Pollio matter? What, really, does silly Lepidus matter? It's between Antonius and Octavianus. A man of forty versus a man of twenty. The known versus the unknown. Lepidus is merely their sop to throw to good dog Cerberus, their way to enter Hades undevoured. How terrific it is to be an eyewitness of great events when one is an historian! First the Rubicon, now the Lavinus. Two rivers, and Pollio was there.

The island was small and grassy, shaded by several lofty poplars; there had been some willows too, but a party of sappers hauled them out so that the observers on each bank could have an unimpeded view of proceedings. The meeting place for the three negotiators—marked by three curule chairs beneath a poplar—was far enough away from the bevy of servants and secretaries who occupied the island's far end, there to distribute refreshments or wait to be summoned to take something down in writing.

Antony and Lepidus were rowed across from their bank, both clad in armor, whereas Octavian chose his purple-bordered toga and maroon senatorial shoes with consular crescent buckles rather than his special boots. The audience was vast, for both armies lined the banks of the Lavinus and watched raptly while the three figures sat, stood, paced, gesticulated, looked at each other or stared pensively at the swirling waters.

The greetings were typical: Octavian was suitably deferential, Lepidus amiable, Antony curt.

"Let's get down to business," Antony said, and sat.

"What do you think our business is, Marcus Antonius?" asked Octavian, waiting until Lepidus sat before taking his own chair.

"To help you crawl out of the hole you've dug for yourself," said Antony. "You know if it comes to battle you'll lose."

"We each have seventeen legions, and mine contain quite as many veterans, I believe," Octavian said coolly, fair brows up. "However, you have the advantage of a more experienced command."

"In other words, you want to crawl out of that hole."

"No, I'm not thinking of myself. At my age, Antonius, I can afford to suffer an occasional humiliation without its coloring the rest of my career. No, I'm thinking of *them*." Octavian indicated the watching soldiers. "I asked for this conference to see if we can work out a way to avoid shedding one drop of their blood. Your men or mine, Antonius, makes no difference. They're all Roman citizens, and all entitled to live, to sire sons and daughters for Rome and Italy, which my father believed were the same entity. Why should they have to shed their blood simply in order to decide whether you or I is the leader of the pack?"

A question so unanswerable that Antony shifted uncomfortably, spoke uncomfortably. "Because your Rome isn't my Rome," he said.

"Rome is Rome. Neither of us owns her. Both of us are her servants, we can't be her master. Everything you do, everything I do, should go to her greater glory, enhance her power. That is equally true of Brutus and Cassius. If you, and I, and Marcus Lepidus, vie for anything, it should be for the distinction of contributing the most to Rome's greater glory. We ourselves are mortal, whether we die here on a field of battle, or later, at peace with each other. Rome is eternal. Rome owns us."

A grin showed. "I'll say this for you, Octavianus, you can talk. A pity you can't general troops."

"If talk is my specialty, then I chose my field of action very well," said Octavian, smiling Caesar's smile. "Truly, Antonius, I do not want bloodshed. What I want is to see all of us who followed Caesar united again under one banner. The assassins did us no favor in murdering our undisputed leader. Since his death, we've split asunder. I blame no small part of it on Cicero, who is every Caesarean's enemy, just as he was Caesar's enemy. To me, if we spill blood here, we will have betrayed Caesar. *And* betrayed Rome. Rome's real enemies are not here in Italian Gaul. They're in the East. The assassin Marcus Brutus holds all of Macedonia, Illyricum, Greece, Crete, and through minions Bithynia, Pontus and Asia Province. The assassin Gaius Cassius holds Cilicia, Cyprus, Cyrenaica, Syria, perhaps even Egypt by now."

"I agree with you about Brutus and Cassius," said Antony, who was visibly relaxing. "Continue, Octavianus."

"What I am asking for, Marcus Antonius, Marcus Lepidus, is an alliance. A reunification of all Caesar's loyal adherents. If we can sort out our differences and achieve that, then we can deal with the real enemies, Brutus and Cassius, from a position of power equal to theirs. Otherwise, Brutus and Cassius will win, and Rome will pass away. For Brutus and Cassius will hand the provinces back to the *publicani* and squeeze the *socii* so tightly that they will prefer barbarian or Parthian rule to Roman rule."

Lepidus listened while Octavian expatiated upon his theme and Antony interpolated an occasional comment. Somehow it all sounded so reasonable and logical when Octavian explained it, though quite why that was, Lepidus didn't know, since nothing the young man said was novel or extraordinary.

"It isn't that I'm afraid to fight, rather that I plain don't want to fight," Octavian reiterated. "We should conserve every bit of our combined strength for the real adversaries."

"Hit them so hard that they don't have a chance to do what happened after Pharsalus," said Antony, getting into stride. "What exhausted Rome was the prolongation of the struggle against the Republicans. Pharnaces, then Africa, then Spain."

And so it started, though it took the rest of that day to reach wholehearted agreement that all the factions of Caesar's adherents should reunite, for there were more men to please than the three who conferred. Both Antony and Octavian knew full well that if Antony had grown tired of being dominated by Caesar, then he had already passed the mark whereat he might agree to share leadership with a twenty-year-old newcomer whose only assets were his relationship to Caesar and the power stemming out of it. The best that might be accomplished was a temporary cessation in the contest for ultimate supremacy. What Octavian could do, and did on the island in the Lavinus River, was to give Antony the impression that Caesar's heir would yield supremacy until Antony's age negated it. If he thinks that, said Octavian to himself, it will sustain both of us until Brutus and Cassius are crushed. After that, we shall see. One thing at a time.

"Of course my legions won't consent to a settlement that looks as if you've won," said Antony when discussions resumed on the second day.

"Nor mine a settlement that looks as if I've lost," Octavian riposted, looking rueful.

"And my legions, and Plancus's, and Pollio's," said Lepidus, "will want *us* to have a share of the leadership."

"Plancus and Pollio will have to be content with consulships in the near future," said Antony harshly. "The stage is populated enough by the three sitting here." He had spent most of the night thinking, and he was far from stupid; his chief intellectual disabilities lay in his impulsiveness, his hedonism and his lack of interest in the art of politics. "How about," he asked, "if we split the leadership of Rome more or less equally between the three of us?"

"That sounds interesting," said Octavian. "Do go on."

"Um—well . . . None of us should be consul, yet all of us should be something better than consul. You know, like three to share the dictatorship."

"You abolished the dictatorship," Octavian said gently.

"True, and I don't mean to imply that I regret that!" Antony snapped, bristling. "What I'm trying to say is that Rome can't be run by a succession of mere consuls until the Liberators are finished, yet a genuine dictator is too offensive to everyone who believes in democracy. If three of us share the control by having partial dictatorial powers, then we exert a measure of control over each other as well as running Rome the way she needs to be run for the time being."

"A syndicate," said Octavian. "Three men. *Triumviri rei publicae constituendae.* Three men forming a syndicate to set the affairs of the Republic in order. Yes, it has a good ring to it. It will soothe the Senate and appeal to the People enormously. All of Rome knows that we embarked on military action. Imagine how splendid it will look when the three of us return to Rome the best of friends, our legions safe and unharmed. We'll show everybody that Roman men *can* sort out their differences without resorting to the sword—that we care more about the Senate and the People than we do about ourselves."

They sat back in their chairs and stared at each other with huge content. Yes, it was splendid! A new era.

"It also," said Antony, "shows the People that we are their true government. There won't be any grumbling about civil war for the sake of civil war when we go east to fight Brutus and Cassius. That was a good idea to try and condemn the Liberators for treason, Octavianus. We can say that we're not fighting other Romans, we're fighting men who abrogated their citizenship."

"We do more than that, Antonius. We keep agents circulating throughout Italy to reinforce indignation about the murder of their beloved Caesar. And when prosperity declines, we can blame Brutus and Cassius, who have appropriated Rome's revenues."

"Prosperity declines?" asked Lepidus in dismay.

"It is already declining," Octavian said flatly. "You're a governor, Lepidus. You must surely have noticed that the crops in your provinces haven't come in this year."

"I haven't been in my provinces since early summer," Lepidus excused himself.

"I've noticed that it's suddenly very expensive to feed my legions," said Antony. "Drought?"

"Everywhere, including the East. So Brutus and Cassius must be suffering too."

"What you're really saying is that we're going to run out of money," snarled Antony, glaring at Octavian. "Well, you pinched Caesar's war chest, so you can fund our campaign in the East!"

"I did not steal the war chest, Antonius. I spent my entire patrimony on bonuses for my legions when I arrived in Italy, and I've had to take money from the Treasury to part-pay the bonuses I still owe my men. I'm in debt to them, and will be for a long time. I've no idea who took the war chest, but don't blame me."

"Then it has to be Oppius."

"You can't be sure. Some Samnite might as easily have done it. The solution doesn't lie in the past, Antonius. It's vital that we keep Rome and Italy fed and entertained, two very pricey undertakings, and we also have to keep a great number of legions in the field. How many do you think we'll need?"

"Forty. Twenty to go with us, twenty more for garrison duty in the West, in Africa, and for dropping in our wake as we march. Plus ten or fifteen thousand cavalry."

"Including noncombatants and horse, that's over a quarter of a million men." The big grey eyes looked glassy. "Think of the quantities of grain, chickpea, lentil, bacon, oil—a million and a quarter *modii* of wheat a month at fifteen sesterces the *modius* is seven hundred and fifty talents a month for wheat alone. The other staples will double it, perhaps more in this drought."

"What a fantastic *praefectus fabrum* you'd make, Octavianus!" said Antony, eyes dancing.

"Joke if you must, but what I'm saying, Antonius, is that we can't do it. Not and feed Rome, feed Italy as well."

"Oh, I know a way," Antony said too casually.

"I'm all ears," said Octavian.

"That you are, Octavianus!"

"Are you done with the jokes?"

"Yes, because the solution's no joke. We proscribe."

The last word fell into a silence broken only by the faint rushing of the river, the rattle of golden poplar leaves waiting for the winter winds to blow them down, the far-off murmur of thousands of troops, the whinnying of horses.

"We proscribe," Octavian echoed.

Lepidus looked ready to faint—pale, shaking. "Antonius, we daren't!" he cried.

The reddish-brown eyes stared him down fiercely. "Oh, come, Lepidus, don't be a bigger fool than your mother and father made you! How else can we fund a state and an army through a drought? How else could we fund them even if there wasn't a drought?"

Octavian sat looking thoughtful. "My father," he said, "was famous for his clemency, but it was his clemency killed him. Most of the assassins were pardoned men. Had he killed them, we would have no need to worry about Brutus and Cassius, Rome would have all the eastern revenues, and we'd be free to sail into the Euxine to buy grain from Cimmeria if we could get it nowhere else. I agree with you, Marcus Antonius. We proscribe, exactly as Sulla did. A one-talent reward for information from a free man or a freedman, a half-talent reward plus his freedom for a slave. But we don't make the mistake of documenting our rewards. Why give some aspiring tribune of the plebs of the future the chance to force us to punish our informants? Sulla's proscriptions netted the Treasury sixteen thousand talents. That's our target."

"You're a perpetual surprise, my dear Octavianus. I thought I'd have a long job talking you into it," said Antony.

"I'm first and foremost a sensible man." Octavian smiled. "Proscription is the only answer. It also enables us to rid ourselves of enemies, real or potential. All those with Republican sentiments or sympathy for the assassins."

"I *can't* agree!" wailed Lepidus. "My brother Paullus is a die-hard Republican!"

"Then we proscribe your brother Paullus," said Antony. "I have a few relatives of mine who'll have to be proscribed, some in conjunction with cousin Octavianus here. Uncle Lucius Caesar, for example. He's a very rich man, and he's been no help to me."

"Or to me," said Octavian, nodding. He frowned. "However, I suggest that we don't render ourselves odious by executing our relatives, Antonius. Neither Paullus nor Lucius is a threat to our lives. We'll just confiscate their property and money. I think we'll both have to sacrifice some third cousins."

"Done!" Antony made a purring noise. "But Oppius dies. I *know* he pinched Caesar's war chest."

"We don't touch any of the bankers or top plutocrats," said Octavian, tones uncompromising.

"*What?* But that's where the big money is!" Antony objected.

"Precisely, Antonius. Think about it, please. Proscription is a short-term measure to fill the Treasury, it can't go on forever. The last thing we want is a Rome deprived of her money geniuses. We're going to need them forever. If you believe that a Greek freedman like Sulla's Chrysogonus is a replacement for an Oppius or an Atticus, you're touched in the head. Look at that freedman of Pompeius Magnus's, Demetrius—rolling in wealth, but not Atticus's bootlace when it comes to turning money over. So we proscribe Demetrius, but we don't proscribe Atticus. Or Sextus Perquitienus, or the Balbi, or Oppius, or Rabirius Postumus. I grant you that Atticus and Perquitienus play both ends against the middle, but the bankers I've mentioned have been Caesareans ever since Caesar became a force in politics. No matter how tempting the size of their fortunes, we do not touch our own. Especially if they have the ability to keep money turning over. We can afford to proscribe Flavius Hemicillus, and perhaps Fabius—both are Brutus's banking minions. But those Rome will need in the future must be sacrosanct."

"He's right, Antonius," said Lepidus feebly.

Antony had listened; now he thought, lips moving in and out, auburn brows meeting. Finally, "I see what you mean." His head hunched into his shoulders, he gave a mock shudder. "Besides, if I touched Atticus, Fulvia would kill me. He's been very good to her since the decree outlawing me. But Cicero goes—and I mean head from neck, understood?"

"Completely," Octavian said. "We concentrate on the rich, but only *some* of the fabulously rich. If enough men are proscribed, the amount of cash will add up quickly. Of course when it comes to property, we won't garner anything like the actual worth of the property we auction. Caesar's auctions have proven that as much as Sulla's did. But we'll be able to pick up some good estates for ourselves and our friends dirt cheap. Lepidus has to be compensated for the loss of his villas and estates, so he ought not to have to pay a sestertius for anything until his losses have been remedied."

The appalled Lepidus began to look less appalled; this was an aspect of proscription that hadn't occurred to him.

"Land for our veterans," said Antony, who loathed agrarian activity. "I suggest we confiscate the public lands of towns and *municipia* we can classify as inimical to Caesar or that made overtures of friendliness to Brutus and Cassius when they were issuing their edicts. Venusia, dear old Capua yet again, Beneventum, a few other Samnite nests. Cremona hasn't pulled its weight in Italian Gaul, and I know how to prevent Bruttium from offering aid to Sextus Pompeius. We'll put some soldier colonies around Vibo and Rhegium."

"Excellent!" Octavian exclaimed. "I recommend too that we don't discharge all the legions after the war against Brutus and Cassius is over. We should retain a certain number of them as a standing army, have the men sign up for, say, fifteen years. This business of having to recruit every time we need troops may be the Roman way and a part of the *mos maiorum*, but it's a costly nuisance. Every time a man is discharged, he gets a piece of land. Some men have been in and out so many times over the last twenty years that they've accumulated a dozen plots of land which they rent out to tenant farmers or graziers. A standing army can garrison the provinces, be there to be called into service when and where it's needed without the perpetual expenses of recruiting and equipping fresh legions, or finding land on discharge."

But that dissertation was a little much for Mark Antony, who shrugged, bored; his attention span was not the equal of the painstaking, minutiae-fixated Octavian's. "Yes, yes, but time is getting on, and I want to finish this business today, not next month." He assumed a crafty expression. "Of course we'll have to have some evidence of each other's good faith. Lepidus and I have affianced two of our children. You're single, Octavianus. How about a marriage bond with me?"

"I'm engaged to Servilia Vatia," Octavian said woodenly.

"Oh, Vatia won't care if you break it off! My Fulvia's eldest girl, Claudia, is eighteen. How about her? Terrific set of ancestors for your children! Julian, Gracchan, Claudian, Fulvian. You can't do better than a girl of Fulvia's and Publius Clodius's, now can you?"

"No, I can't," said Octavian without hesitation. "Consider me betrothed to Claudia, provided Vatia consents."

"Not betrothed, *married*," Antony said firmly. "Lepidus can conduct the ceremony as soon as we return to Rome."

"If you wish."

"You'll have to step down from the consulship," said Antony, riding high.

"Yes, I rather imagined I'd have to do that. Whom do you suggest as suffect consuls for the rump of the year?"

"Gaius Carrinas for senior, Publius Ventidius for junior."

"Your men."

Ignoring this, Antony swept on. "Lepidus for a second term next year, with Plancus as his junior."

"Yes, we'll definitely have to have one of the Triumvirs as senior consul next year. And the year after?"

"Vatia as senior, my brother Lucius as junior."

"I am sorry about Gaius Antonius."

Eyes filling with tears, Antony swallowed convulsively. "I will make Brutus pay for killing my brother!" he said savagely.

Privately Octavian thought that Brutus had done efficiency and success a great service in ridding Rome of Gaius Antonius, bungler supreme, but he looked grieved and sympathetic, then changed the subject. "Have you thought how best to legislate our triumviral syndicate?" he asked.

"Through the Plebs, it's become custom. *Supra*consular powers— *imperium maius*, even inside Rome—for five years. Together with the right to nominate the consuls. Inside Italy we should all three have equal powers and govern equally, but outside Italy I think we should divide the provinces up. I'll take Italian Gaul and Further Gaul. Lepidus can have Narbonese Gaul and both the Spains, because I'm going to use Pollio as my legate in my provinces, let him do the actual governing."

"Which leaves me," said Octavian, looking particularly sweet and humble, "the Africas, Sicily, Sardinia and Corsica. The—er—grain supply. Not a happy group of provinces, from what I hear. The governor of Africa Vetus is having a little private war with the governor of Africa Nova, and Sextus Pompeius has been using all those ships the Senate gave him to raid our grain fleets since well before Pedius's court condemned him."

"Not pleased with your lot, Octavianus?" Antony asked.

"Put it this way, Antonius. I won't complain about my lot provided that I have full and equal co-command with you when we go east to deal with Brutus and Cassius."

"No, I won't agree to that."

"You don't have any choice in the matter, Antonius. My own legions will insist on it, and you can't go east without them."

Antony leaped out of his chair and strode to the water's edge, Lepidus following in alarm.

"Come, Antonius," Lepidus whispered to him, "you can't have it all your own way. He's made big concessions. And he's right about his legions, they won't follow you."

A long pause ensued, Antony scowling at the river, Lepidus with one hand on Antony's arm. Then Antony swung about, returned.

"All right, you can have full co-command, Octavianus."

"Good. Then we have a pact," Octavian said cordially, and held out his hand. "Let's shake on it to show the men that we've reached accord and there'll be no battle."

The three walked to the very middle of the island, there to shake hands with each other. Cheers erupted from the throat of every watcher; the Triumvirate was a reality.

Only one other difference of opinion arose, on the next day: namely, the order in which the Triumvirs would enter Rome.

"Together," said Lepidus.

"No, on three succeeding days," Antony contradicted. "I go first, Octavianus goes second, you go third, Lepidus."

"I go first," Octavian said firmly.

"No, I do," said Antony.

"I go first, Marcus Antonius, because I am the senior consul and no laws have as yet been passed that give you or Marcus Lepidus any rights whatsoever. You're still public enemies. Even if you weren't, the moment you cross the *pomerium* into Rome, you give up your imperium and become mere *privati*. It is inarguable. I must go first, to preside over the removal of your outlaw status."

Very put out he might be, but Mark Antony had no choice other than to agree. Octavian must enter Rome first.

2 Most of Italian Gaul was a flat alluvial plain watered by the Padus River and its many tributaries; when rain didn't fall, the local farmers could irrigate extensively, so the region had crops, full granaries. The most exasperating thing about the country, so close to Italy proper, was that it couldn't feed Italy proper. The Apennine mountain chain crossed the top of the leg from east to west and fused with the Maritime Alps in Liguria, thus forming a barrier too formidable for the transport of freight by land. Nor could Italian Gaul's grains and pulses be sent by sea; the winds were always contrary shipping from north to south. For this reason, the Triumvirs decided to leave their legions in Italian Gaul, and set out for Rome accompanied only by a few hand picked troops.

"However," said Octavian to Pollio (they were sharing a gig), "since feeding Rome and Italy has fallen to me, I shall start sending wagon trains of wheat from the west of the province through Dertona to travel down the Tuscan coast. The gradients are not impossible on that route, it just hasn't been done."

Pollio eyed him with fascination, having realized since they started out from Bononia that the young man never stopped thinking. His mind, Pollio decided, was precise, factual, preoccupied with logistics ahead of logic—what interested him was how to get ordinary things done. If you gave him a million chickpeas to count, thought Pollio, he would stick at it until he did it—and not make a mistake in his count. No wonder Antonius despises him! While Antonius dreams of military glory and of being the First Man in Rome, Octavianus dreams of how to feed people. While Antonius spends money profligately, Octavianus looks for the cheapest way to do things. Octavianus isn't a plotter, he's a planner. I do hope I live long enough to see what he ultimately becomes.

So Pollio led Octavian on to speak on many subjects, including the fate of Rome.

"What's your greatest ambition, Octavianus?" he asked.

"To see the whole Roman world at peace."

"And what would you do to achieve that?"

"Anything," said Octavian simply. "Anything at all."

"It's a laudable objective, but hardly likely to happen."

The grey eyes turned to look into Pollio's amber orbs, their expression genuinely surprised. "Why?"

"Oh, perhaps because war is ingrained in Romans. War and conquest add to Rome's revenues, most men think."

"Her revenues," said Octavian, "are already great enough for her needs. War drains the Treasury dry."

"That's not Roman thinking! War plumps the Treasury out—look at Caesar and Pompeius Magnus, not to mention Paullus, the Scipios, Mummius," said Pollio, enjoying himself.

"Those days are over, Pollio. The great treasures have all been absorbed into Rome already except for one."

"The Parthian treasures?"

"No!" Octavian said scornfully. "That's a war only Caesar could have contemplated. The distances are enormous and the army would have to live on forage for years, surrounded on all sides by enemy and formidable terrains. I mean the Egyptian treasure."

"And would you approve of Rome's taking that?"

"I will take it. In time," said Octavian, sounding smug. "It's a feasible objective, for two reasons."

"And they are?"

"The first, that it isn't necessary for a Roman army to get far from Our Sea. The second, that, apart from the treasure, Egypt produces grain that our growing population will need."

"Many say the treasure doesn't exist."

"Oh, it exists," said Octavian. "Caesar saw it. He told me all about it when I was with him in Spain. I know where it is and how to get it. Rome will need it *because* war drains her dry."

"Civil war, you mean."

"Well, think about it, Pollio. During the last sixty or so years, we've fought more civil wars than properly foreign ones. Romans against Romans. Conflicts over ideas of what constitutes the Roman Republic. Ideas of what constitutes liberty."

"Wouldn't you be Greek and go to war for an idea?"

"No, I would not."

"What about going to war to ensure peace?"

"Not if it means warring against fellow Romans. The war we fight against Brutus and Cassius must be the last civil war."

"Sextus Pompeius might not agree with you. There's no doubt he flirts with Brutus and Cassius, but he won't commit himself to them entirely. He'll end in waging his own war."

"Sextus Pompeius is a pirate, Pollio."

"So you don't think he'll gather the remnants of Liberator forces after Brutus and Cassius are defeated?"

"He's chosen his ground, and it's water. That means he can never mount a full campaign," said Octavian.

"There's another prospect of civil war," said Pollio slyly. "What if the Triumvirs should fall out?"

"Like Archimedes, I will shift the globe to avoid that. I assure you, Pollio, that I will *never* go to war against Antonius."

And why, asked Pollio of himself, do I believe that? For I do.

Octavian entered Rome toward the end of November, on foot and togate, escorted by singers and dancers hymning peace between the Triumvirs, and surrounded by hordes of cheering, delighted people, at whom he smiled Caesar's smile, waved Caesar's wave, his feet in those high-soled boots. He went straight to the rostra and there announced the formation of the *triumviri rei publicae constituendae* in a short, moving speech that gave the crowds no doubt of his pivotal role in reconciling all parties in the pact. He was Caesar Peacemaker, not Caesar Warmaker.

Then he went to the Senate, waiting in the Curia Hostilia to hear this news in more comfort and privacy. Publius Titius was instructed to convene the Plebeian Assembly immediately and revoke the legislation outlawing Antony and Lepidus. Though Quintus Pedius thus learned publicly that his consulship was about to end, Octavian saved the news of the proscriptions to tell him afterward.

"Titius will enact the laws setting up the Triumvirate in the Plebs," he said to Pedius in Pedius's study, "but he'll also pass other, equally necessary measures."

"What other, equally necessary measures?" Pedius asked warily, misliking the expression on his cousin's face, which was set.

"Rome is bankrupt, therefore we proscribe."

Flinching, Pedius put up his hands to ward off some invisible menace. "I refuse to condone proscription," he said, voice thin. "As consul, I will speak against it."

"As consul, you will speak in favor. Oppose it, Quintus, and yours will be the first name on the list Titius will post upon the rostra and the Regia. Come, my dear fellow, be sensible," said Octavian softly. "Do you want a Valeria Messala widowed and homeless, her children prohibited from inheriting, from taking their rightful places in public life? *Caesar's* great-nephews? Quintus Junior will soon be standing for election as a tribune of the soldiers. And if you are proscribed, we'll have to proscribe Messala Rufus too." Octavian got up. "Think well before you say anything, cousin, I do implore you."

Quintus Pedius thought well. That night, after his household was asleep, he fell on his sword.

Summoned at dawn, Octavian had firm words to say to Valeria Messala, weeping and distraught. And to her augur brother. "I will give out that Quintus Pedius died in his sleep, worn out by his consular duties. Please understand that I have cogent reasons for wanting his death so described. If you value your lives, the lives of your children, and your property, obey my wishes. You'll know why soon enough."

Antony entered the city in more state than Octavian, aware that his thunder was stolen. He wore his ornate armor and his leopard-skin cloak and tack on his new Public Horse, Clemency, was escorted by his guard of German cavalry, and was extremely pleased at his reception. Octavian had been right; the Roman people wanted no military conflict between factions. So when Lepidus entered the next day, he too was greeted joyously.

Toward the end of November, Octavian resigned his consulship and was succeeded by two grizzled victims of the Italian War, Gaius Carrinas and Publius Ventidius. The moment the suffect consuls were installed, Publius Titius went to the Plebs. First he legislated the Triumvirate into official existence with the consent of every tribe, then enacted public-enemy laws that echoed Sulla's in almost every detail, from the rewards for information to the publicly posted list of the proscribed. One hundred and thirty names were on the first list, headed at Antony's request by Marcus Tullius Cicero. Most of the other men on it were already dead or fled; Brutus and Cassius were also named. The reason for proscription was "Liberator sympathies."

The First and Second Classes were caught unawares and flew into a panic fueled by the arrest and execution of the tribune of the plebs Salvius as soon as the comitial meeting was over. The heads of the victims were not displayed, simply dumped with the bodies in the lime pits of the Campus Esquilinus necropolis. Octavian had persuaded Antony that a climate of terror was more endurable if visible reminders were not in evidence. The sole exception would be Cicero, if he was found still in Italy.

Lepidus had proscribed his brother Paullus, Antony his uncle Lucius Caesar and Octavian cousins, though none was executed. A proviso not made for Pollio's father-in-law or Plancus's praetor brother, both killed. Three other proscribed praetors died, as did the tribune of the plebs Publius Appuleius, not as lucky as Gaius Casca, fled with his brother to the East. Vatinius's old legate, the unflagging Quintus Cornificius, went on the list and was executed.

Atticus and the bankers had been privately informed that they were not to be proscribed, which did much to keep money from going into hiding, always a danger in trying times. The Treasury cells, empty of all but the precious gold and ten thousand talents of silver, began slowly to fill with the cash reserves and liquid investments of Lucius Caesar, several Appuleii, Paullus Aemilius Lepidus, the two assassin brothers Caecilius, the venerable consular Marcus Terentius Varro, the very wealthy Gaius Lucilius Hirrus, and hundreds more.

Not everyone died. Quintus Fufius Calenus took in old Varro and defied the proscription authorities (the proscriptions were, as in Sulla's time, bureaucratically run) to kill him until he could get to Antony and secure his life. Lucilius Hirrus fled the country with his slaves and clients by fighting his way to the sea, and the town of Cales bolted its gates and refused to give up Publius Sittius's brother. Cato's beloved Marcus Favonius was proscribed, but managed to escape from Italy, as did others. Provided that the money was left behind, the Triumvirs didn't care deeply about the fate of the persons to whom it had belonged.

Except, that is, for Cicero, whom Antony was determined to bring to a nasty end. Charged with this mission, the tribune of the soldiers Gaius Popillius Laenas (a very famous name) left Rome with a party of soldiers and a centurion, Herennius, to check Cicero's villas. The loyal Caesareans Quintus Cicero and his son had gone on the second proscription list, informed on by a slave who swore that their sentiments had changed, that they now were bent on fleeing the country to join the Liberators. So Laenas had three targets, though the great Marcus Cicero was by far the most important, must be attended to first.

The outcome of Octavian's second march on Rome had stunned Cicero, who had gone to the new senior consul and begged that he be excused from attending future meetings of the Senate.

"I am tired and ill, Octavianus," he had explained, "and I would very much like to be able to go to my estates whenever I wish. Is that possible?"

"Of course!" Octavian had said warmly. "If I can excuse my stepfather from meetings, I can certainly excuse you and Lucius Piso. Philippus and Piso are still suffering the aftermath of that terrible winter journey, you know."

"I opposed the sending of that embassage."

"Indeed you did. A pity the Senate ignored you."

Looking at this beautiful young man, whose exterior had not changed one iota since landing in Brundisium all those months ago, Cicero suddenly realized that Octavian had dedicated himself to the pursuit of power at all costs. How had he ever deluded himself that he could influence this pitiless pillar of ice? Caesar had owned feelings, including a shocking temper, but Octavian mimed feelings. His likeness to Caesar was an acted-out sham.

From that moment Cicero had abandoned all hope, even of persuading Brutus to come home. In his last letters Brutus had turned so critical and acerbic that Cicero felt no urge to write to him, apprise him what he thought of the consulship of Caesar Octavianus and Quintus Pedius.

From his interview with the new senior consul, Cicero had gone at once to see Atticus. "I won't visit you again," he had said, "nor am I going to write to you. Truly, Titus, it is better this way, for both our sakes. Look after Pilia, little Attica and yourself. Do *nothing* to antagonize Octavianus! When he made himself consul, the Republic died for good. Neither Brutus nor Cassius—nor even Marcus Antonius—will prevail. Our old, clement master has had the last laugh. He knew exactly what he was doing when he made Octavianus his heir. Octavianus will complete his work, believe me."

Atticus had gazed at him through a mist of tears. How old he was looking! Fallen away to skin and bone, those wonderful dark eyes as hunted as a deer's surrounded by baying wolves. Of the vast presence that had so dominated and awed Rome's law courts for forty years, nothing was left. When his dearest, most exasperating and impulsive friend had embarked upon that series of invectives aimed at Marcus Antonius, Atticus had hoped to see Cicero healed, back to normal after so many bitter disappointments, griefs, and that constant loneliness devoid of daughter and wife, of brotherly affection. But the advent of Octavianus had killed his revival; it is now Octavianus, thought Atticus, whom Cicero fears the most.

"I shall miss our correspondence," Atticus had said, not knowing what else to say. "Not one of your letters to me isn't treasured and preserved."

"Good. Publish them when you dare, please."

"I will, Marcus, I will."

After that, Cicero had retired completely from public life, nor wrote a single letter. When he learned of the triumviral pact in Bononia, he quit Rome, leaving the faithful Tiro behind to send him reports of everything that happened.

First he went to Tusculum, but the old farmhouse was too full of memories of Tullia and Terentia and his pleasure-loving, martial son. Thank all the gods that young Marcus was now with Brutus! And pray to all the gods that Brutus would win!

When Tiro sent an urgent note to tell him that proscription had come in and his was the first name on the list, he packed up and took the byways and lanes to his villa at Formiae, still using his litter, a painfully slow mode of transport, but the only one Cicero could bear. His intention was to take a ship from the nearest port, Caieta, to flee to Brutus or perhaps to Sextus Pompey in Sicily—he wasn't sure, couldn't make up his mind.

It seemed Fortuna favored him, for there was a ship for hire in Caieta harbor, and its master agreed to take him despite his proscribed status; the proscription notices had gone up in every town throughout Italy.

"You're a special case, Marcus Cicero," the master said. "I can't condone the persecution of one of Rome's greatest men."

But it was the beginning of December, and winter weather had arrived with gales, a little sleet; the ship put out to sea and was forced back inshore several times, though its master refused to give up, insisted they could make it at least to Sardinia.

A terrible depression invaded Cicero, a weariness so draining that he understood its message: there was to be no leaving Italy for Marcus Tullius Cicero, whose very heartstrings were tied to it.

"Put in to Caieta and set me ashore," he said.

A servant was sent running to his villa, about a mile away upon the heights of Formiae, and returned three hours after dawn on the seventh day of December with Cicero's litter and bearers. Wet and shivering, Cicero climbed into its cushioned, welcoming shelter and lay back to wait for whatever was to come.

I am going to die, but at least I will die in the country I have worked so hard and so often to save. I succeeded with that cur Catilina, but then Caesar ruined my victory with his speech—I did *not* act unconstitutionally by executing Rome's enemies without a trial! Even Cato said as much. But Caesar's speech stuck like a burr, and some men looked at me with contempt ever after. Even so, life since has been a shadow, a phantasm, except for my speeches against Marcus Antonius. I am tired of living. I no longer want to endure life's cruelties, its travesties.

Gaius Popillius Laenas and his men caught the litter on its slow ascent of the hill, dismounted and encircled it. The centurion Herennius drew his sword, two feet of razor-sharp, double-edged efficiency. Cicero poked his head out of the litter to look.

"No, no!" he called to his servants. "Don't try to fight! Submit quietly and save your lives, please."

Herennius approached him and raised the sword to the boiling, sullen sky. Gazing at it, Cicero noted that its shade of grey was duller, darker than the vault, and did not glitter. He put his palms upon the litter's margin and pushed his shoulders out of it, then extended his neck as much as he could manage.

"Strike well," he said.

The sword descended and took Cicero's head from his body in one neat blow; the stump gouted blood, the body tensed and did a short, recumbent dance as the head hit the muddy path and rolled a little distance, then stopped. The servants were keening and weeping, but Popillius Laenas's party ignored them. Herennius bent to pick up the head by its back hair, grown long so Cicero could comb it forward over his bald spot. A soldier produced a box, the head was dropped into it.

Concentrating upon this, Laenas didn't notice two of his men haul the rapidly exsanguinating body out of the litter until he heard the scrape of swords coming out of scabbards.

"Here, what do you think you're doing?" he asked.

"Was he right- or left-handed?" a soldier demanded.

Laenas looked blank. "I don't know," he said.

"Then we'll cut off both his hands. One of them wrote awful things about Marcus Antonius."

Laenas considered this, then nodded. "Go ahead. Put them in the box, then let's get moving."

The men rode back to Rome without stopping, their horses foamed and blown by the time they reached Antony's palace on the Carinae, where a startled steward let them into the peristyle. Carrying the box, Laenas strode into the atrium to find Antony and Fulvia waiting, wrapped in night robes, blinking the last of sleep from their eyes.

"You wanted this, I believe," said Popillius Laenas, giving Antony the box.

Antony withdrew the head and held it up, laughing. "Got you at last, you vindictive old *cunnus!*" he shouted.

Far from being revolted, Fulvia snatched at the head. "Give it to me, give it to me, give it to me!" she shrilled while Antony kept holding it just out of her reach, laughing and teasing.

"My men brought you something else," said Laenas. "Look in the box, Marcus Antonius."

So Fulvia succeeded in grabbing the head; Antony was busy removing and inspecting the two hands.

"We didn't know if he was right- or left-handed, so we brought you both of them to be sure. As my men said, they wrote awful things about you."

"You've earned an extra talent." Antony grinned. He glanced at Fulvia, who had put the head down on a console table and was busy scrabbling among its untidy contents—scrolls, papers, ink, pens, wax tablets. "What are you doing?" he asked her.

"Ah!" she exclaimed, holding up a steel stylus.

Cicero's eyes were closed, his mouth wide open. Antony's wife thrust her long-nailed fingers between the lips and fished about, then squeaked with triumph and yanked. Out came Cicero's tongue, held by her nails. She took the thick strap of flesh in a harder hold and skewered it with the stylus, which lay athwart the mouth and kept the tongue protruding.

"That's what I think of his gift of the gab," she said, eyeing her work with huge satisfaction.

"Fix up a wooden frame and nail it to the rostra," Antony ordered Laenas. "The head in the middle, a hand to either side."

So when Rome awoke at dawn, it saw Cicero's head and hands nailed to the rostra on a wooden frame.

The Forum frequenters were devastated. Since his twelfth birthday Cicero had walked the flags of the Forum Romanum without rhetorical peer. The trials! The speeches! The sheer wonder of his words!

"But," said one frequenter, mopping his tears, "dear Marcus Cicero is still champion of the Forum."

The two Quintus Cicerones perished shortly thereafter, though their heads were not displayed. What the divorced Pomponia felt, at least for her son, an appalled Rome soon learned. She kidnaped the slave who had informed on them and killed him by making him carve slices off his own body, broil them, and eat them.

The barbarity of Antony's revenge on Cicero did not sit well with Octavian, but, since there was nothing he could do about it, he made no reference to it in public or in private; he simply avoided Antony's company whenever possible. When he had first set eyes on Claudia, he had thought that perhaps he could learn to love her, for she was very pretty, very dark (he liked dark women), and suitably virginal. But after he saw Cicero's skewered tongue and listened to Fulvia's describing the pleasure she had taken in doing this particular indignity to Cicero's flesh, Octavian decided that Claudia was not going to bear any children of his.

"Therefore," he said to Maecenas, "she will be my wife in name only. Find six big, strapping German women slaves and make sure that Claudia is never left alone. I want her a virgin against the day when I can return her to Antonius and her vulgar harpy of a mother."

"You're sure?" asked Maecenas, knitting his brows.

"Believe me, Gaius, I would as soon touch a decayed black dog as any daughter of Fulvia's!"

Because Philippus chose to die on the same day, the wedding itself was a very quiet affair; Atia and Octavia couldn't come, and the moment the ceremony was over, Octavian joined his mother and sister, leaving his wife alone with her German guards. The bereavement gave him an excellent excuse for not consummating the marriage.

But as time went on it became obvious to Claudia that consummation was unlikely to occur at all. She found her husband's attitude—and her guards—inexplicable; on meeting him, she had thought him handsome, alluringly aloof. Now she lived as a virtual prisoner, untouched and apparently undesired.

"What do you expect me to do about it?" Fulvia asked when appealed to for help.

"Mama, take me home!"

"I can't do that. You're a peace offering between Antonius and your husband."

"But he doesn't *want* me! He doesn't even *talk* to me!"

"That sometimes happens with arranged marriages." Fulvia got up, chucked her daughter under the chin bracingly. "He'll come to his senses in time, girl. Wait him out."

"Ask Marcus Antonius to intercede for me!" Claudia pleaded.

"I'll do no such thing. He's far too busy to be bothered with trivialities." And off went Fulvia, absorbed in her latest family; Clodius had been a long time ago.

With no one left to whom she could appeal, Claudia had no choice other than to suffer her existence, which did improve after Octavian bought Quintus Hortensius's enormous old mansion at the proscription auctions. Its size allowed her a suite of rooms to herself, which removed her entirely from Octavian's vicinity; youth being resilient, she made friends of her German women, and set out to have as happy a life as a married virgin could.

Octavian was not sleeping alone. He had taken a mistress.

Never plagued by strong sexual impulses, the youngest of the Triumvirs had contented himself with masturbation until after his marriage, when the perceptive and subtle Maecenas took a hand. It was high time, he decided, that Octavian had a woman. So he cruised the premises of Mercurius Stichus, famous for his sex slaves, and found Octavian's ideal woman. A girl of twenty who had a small boy child, she hailed from Cilicia, had been the toy of a pirate chieftain in Pamphylia, and bore the name of Sappho, just like the poet. Ravishingly pretty, dark of hair and eye, round and cuddly, she had, said Mercurius Stichus, a sweet nature. Maecenas brought her home and popped her into Octavian's bed on his first night in Hortensius's old mansion. The ploy worked; there was no disgrace in a slave, no possibility of her gaining ascendancy over a master like Octavian. He liked her docile submission, he appreciated her situation, he let her have time with her child, he esteemed the new maturity taking sexual liberties gave him.

In fact, were it not for Sappho, Octavian's life during the early days of the Triumvirate would have been extremely unpleasant. Controlling Antony was always difficult, sometimes—as in the affair of Cicero's death—impossible. The proscription auctions weren't fetching nearly enough, and it fell to Octavian to cull the informants' lists to see who had sufficient ready money to warrant posting as a Liberator sympathizer. Additional taxes had to be found, hints dropped to the inviolate plutocrats and bankers that they had better start giving large donations toward buying grain, the price of which kept spiraling. Not very many days into December, all the Classes from First to Fifth discovered that they had to pay the state a year's income in cash forthwith.

But even that wasn't enough. At the end of December the tribune of the plebs Lucius Clodius, a creature of Antony's, brought in a *lex Clodia* that compelled all women who were *sui iuris*—in control of their own money—to pay a year's income forthwith.

This annoyed Hortensia very much. The widow of Cato's half brother Caepio and the mother of Caepio's only daughter (married to the son of Ahenobarbus), Hortensia had inherited far more of her father's famous rhetorical skills than had her brother, now proscribed because he had offered Macedonia to Brutus. With Cicero's widow, Terentia, and a group of women who included Marcia, Pomponia, Fabia the ex–Chief Vestal, and Calpurnia, Hortensia marched into the Forum and mounted the rostra, the others in her wake. And there they stood, wearing chain mail shirts, helmets on their heads, shields at rest on the ground, swords in their hands. Such an extraordinary sight that every Forum frequenter collected; so too, though at first it wasn't remarked upon, did a great many women from all walks of life, including a good number of professional whores in flame-colored togas, gaudy wigs and paint.

"I am a Roman citizen!" Hortensia roared in a voice that was audible in the Porticus Margaritaria. "I am also a woman! A woman of the First Class! And what exactly does that mean? Why, that I go to my marriage bed a virgin, and then become the chattel of my husband! Who can execute me for unchastity, though I cannot reproach him for having sex with other women—or men! And when I am widowed, I am not supposed to marry again. Instead, I must depend upon the charity of my family to house me, for under the *lex Voconia* I cannot inherit any fortunes, and if my husband wants to plunder my dowry, it is very hard to prevent him!"

Boom! came the sound of the flat of her sword against the boss of her shield; the audience jumped.

"That is the lot of a woman of the First Class! But how would it differ were I a woman of a lower Class, or if I had no Class at all? I would still be a Roman citizen! I would still be a virgin when I went to my marriage bed, and I would still be the chattel of my husband! I would still have to depend upon the charity of my family when I was widowed. But at least I would have the opportunity to espouse more than a man! I could espouse a profession, a trade, a craft. I could earn a living for myself as a painter or a carpenter, a physician or a herbalist. I could sell the produce of my garden or my hen house. If I wished, I could sell my body by working as a whore. I could save a little of what I earned and put it away for my old age!"

Boom! This time all the swords on the rostra thumped the shield bosses; the female segment of the audience stood rapt, the male segment scandalized.

"Therefore, as a Roman citizen and a woman, I feel entitled to register the outrage of every Roman citizen woman who earns an income of any kind and has the power to control her income! I stand here on behalf of my own First Class, whose income is derived from dowry or meager inheritance, and on behalf of all those women of lower Class or no Class whose income is derived from eggs!—vegetables!—plumbing!—painting!—construction!—whoredom!—et cetera, et cetera! For all of us are to lose a year's income to fund the insanities of Roman men! Insanities I say, and insanities I mean!"

Boom! Boom! Boom! This time the swords on shields were joined by the cymbals of whores, the feet of women in the crowd, and went on longer. The Forum frequenters looked angrier and angrier, were growling and shaking their fists.

Up went Hortensia's sword, waved around her head. "Do the citizen women of Rome vote?" she yelled. "Do we elect magistrates? Do we vote for or against laws? Did we have a chance to vote against this disgraceful *lex Clodia* that says we must pay a year's income to the Treasury? No, we did *not* have a chance to vote against this insanity! An insanity sponsored by a trio of smug, privileged, moronic men named Marcus Antonius, Caesar Octavianus and Marcus Lepidus! If Rome wants to tax us, then Rome must give us the franchise as well as citizenship! If Rome wants to tax us, then Rome will have to let us vote for magistrates, vote for or against laws!"

Up went the sword again, this time joined by all the other swords, and accompanied by shrill cheers from the listening women, howls of rage from the listening Forum frequenters.

"And just how are the idiots who run Rome going to collect this iniquitous tax?" Hortensia demanded. "The men of the five Classes are enrolled by the censors, their incomes written down! But we Roman citizen women aren't entered on any rolls, are we? So how are the idiots who run Rome going to decide what our incomes are? Is some brute of a Treasury agent going to stride up to some poor little old woman in the marketplace selling her embroideries or her lamp wicks or her eggs, and ask her what she earns in a year? Or, even worse, arbitrarily decide what she earns on the evidence of his own bigoted misogynism? Are we to be badgered and bullied, browbeaten and bludgeoned? Are we? *Are we?*"

"No!" screamed several thousand female throats. "No, no!" The male throats were suddenly silent; it had suddenly dawned on the Forum frequenters that they were shockingly outnumbered.

"I should think not! All of us standing on the rostra are widows— Caesar's widow, Cato's widow, Cicero's widow among us! Did Caesar tax women? Did Cato tax women? Did Cicero tax women? No, they did not! Cicero and Cato and Caesar understood that women have no public voice! The only power at law we have is the right to own our little bit of money free and clear, and now this *lex Clodia* is going to strip us even of that! Well, we refuse to pay this tax! Not one sestertius! Unless we are accorded different rights—the right to vote, the right to sit in the Senate, the right to stand for election as magistrates!"

Her voice was drowned in a huge cheer.

"And what of the Triumvir Marcus Antonius's wife, Fulvia?" thundered Hortensia, eyes noting the entire College of Lictors appear at the back of the crowd and start to push their way toward the rostra. "Fulvia is the richest woman in Rome, and *sui iuris!* But is she to pay this tax? No! No, she is not! Why? Because she's given Rome seven children! By, I add, three of the most reprehensible villains ever to mount a rostra or a woman! While we, who obeyed the *mos maiorum* and remained widowed, are to pay!"

She strode to the edge of the rostra and thrust her face at the lictors, nearing the front. "Don't you dare try to arrest us!" she roared. "Go back to your masters and tell them from Quintus Hortensius's daughter that the *sui iuris* women of Rome from highest to lowest will not pay this tax! *Will not pay it!* Go on, shoo! Shoo, shoo!"

The women in the crowd took it up: "Shoo! Shoo!"

"I'll have the sow proscribed! I'll proscribe *all* the sows!" snarled Antony, livid.

"You will not!" snapped Lepidus. "You'll do nothing!"

"And say nothing," Octavian growled.

The next day a red-faced Lucius Clodius went back to the Plebeian Assembly to repeal his law and bring in a new one that compelled every *sui iuris* woman in Rome, including Fulvia, to pay the Treasury one-thirtieth of her income. But it was never enforced.

XII

EAST OF THE ADRIATIC

From JANUARY until DECEMBER of 43 B.C.

GAIUS CASSIUS LONGINUS

After an arduous winter passage across the Candavian mountains, Brutus and his little force arrived outside Dyrrachium on the third day of January. Ordered down from Salona by Mark Antony, the governor of Illyricum, Publius Vatinius, had occupied Petra camp with one legion. Nothing daunted, Brutus moved his troops into one of the many fortresses dotting the circumvallations built five years ago when Caesar and Pompey the Great had waged siege war there. But Brutus's action proved hardly necessary. Not four days later Vatinius's soldiers opened the gates of Petra camp and went over to Brutus. Their commander Vatinius, they said, had already gone back to Illyricum.

Suddenly Brutus owned a force of three legions and two hundred cavalrymen! No one was more surprised than he, no one less sure how to general an army. However, he did understand that fifteen thousand men required the services of a *praefectus fabrum* to ensure that they were kept fed and equipped, so he wrote to his old friend, the banker Gaius Flavius Hemicillus, who had done this duty for Pompey the Great—would he do the same for Marcus Brutus? That out of the way, the new warlord decided to move south to Apollonia, where sat the official governor of Macedonia, Gaius Antonius.

And money just fell into his lap! First came the quaestor of Asia Province, young Lentulus Spinther, carrying its tributes to the Treasury; no lover of Mark Antony, Spinther promptly turned the cash over to Brutus and returned to his boss, Gaius Trebonius, to tell him that the Liberators were not going to lie down tamely after all. No sooner had Spinther departed than the quaestor of Syria, Gaius Antistius Vetus, arrived en route to Rome with Syria's tributes. He too turned the cash over to Brutus, then elected to stay—who knew what was going on in Syria? Nicer by far in Macedonia.

In mid January the city of Apollonia surrendered without a fight, its legions announcing that they much preferred Brutus to the loathesome Gaius Antonius. Though men like young Cicero and Antistius Vetus urged Brutus to execute this least talented and unluckiest of the three Antonian brothers, Brutus refused. Instead, he allowed the captive Gaius Antonius the run of his camp, and treated him with great courtesy.

Brutus's cup ran over when Crete, originally senatorially assigned to him, and Cyrenaica, originally assigned to Cassius, both notified him that they were content to function in the interests of the Liberators, if in return they might be sent proper governors. Brutus delightedly obliged.

Now he had six legions, six hundred horse, and no less than three provinces—Macedonia, Crete and Cyrenaica. Almost before he could assimilate this bounty, Greece, Epirus and coastal Thrace declared for him. Amazing!

Oozing content, Brutus wrote to the Senate in Rome and let it know these facts, with the result that on the Ides of February the Senate officially confirmed him as governor of all these territories, then added Vatinius's province of Illyricum to his tally. He was now governor of almost half the Roman East!

At which moment came news from Asia Province. Dolabella, he learned, had tortured and beheaded Gaius Trebonius in Smyrna, an horrific deed. Oh, but what had happened to the gallant Lentulus Spinther? Shortly thereafter he received a letter from Spinther telling him that Dolabella had pounced in Ephesus and tried to find out where Trebonius had hidden the province's money. But Spinther had played dense and stupid so well that the frustrated Dolabella simply ordered him to get out before moving on into Cappadocia.

Brutus was now in a fever of apprehension over Cassius, from whom he had heard nothing. He wrote to various places warning Cassius that Dolabella was bearing down on Syria, but had no idea whether or not they reached their target.

Through all of this, Cicero was writing to beg Brutus to return to Italy, a tempting alternative now that he was in official favor. In the end, however, Brutus decided that the best thing he could do was to retain control of the Roman land route east across Macedonia and Thrace—the Via Egnatia. Then if Cassius needed him, he could march to his assistance.

By now he had a trusty little band of noble followers who included Ahenobarbus's son, Cicero's son, Lucius Bibulus, the son of the great Lucullus by Servilia's younger sister, and yet another defecting quaestor, Marcus Appuleius. Though most were in their twenties, some barely that old, Brutus made them all legates, distributed them through his legions, and counted himself very fortunate.

The worst of not being in Italy was the uncertainty of the news from Rome. A dozen people were writing to Brutus regularly, but what each had to say conflicted with what everyone else said. Their perspectives were different, sometimes contradictory; often they tendered mere rumors as incontrovertible fact. After the deaths of Pansa and Hirtius on the battlefield in Italian Gaul, he was told that Cicero would be the new senior consul with the nineteen-year-old Octavianus as his junior. This was followed by an assurance that Cicero already *was* consul! Time proved that none of it was true, but how was he to know fact from fiction at this removed distance? Porcia badgered him with tales of her woes at Servilia's hands, Servilia sent him an infrequent, curt missive informing him that his wife was a madwoman, Cicero protested that he wasn't consul nor would be consul, but that too many honors were being heaped upon young Octavianus. So when the Senate itself ordered Brutus back to Rome, Brutus ignored the directive. Who was telling the truth? What *was* the truth?

Unappreciative of Brutus's courtesy, Gaius Antonius was giving trouble, had taken to donning his purple-bordered toga and haranguing Brutus's soldiers about his unjust captivity, his governor's status. When Brutus forbade Gaius Antonius to wear his purple-bordered toga, he switched to a plain white one and went right on haranguing. Which forced Brutus to confine him to his quarters and set a guard on him. So far he hadn't impressed the troops, but Brutus was too insecure a commander to let him be.

When big brother Mark Antony sent crack troops to Macedonia to extricate Gaius, they went over to Brutus instead; his tally was now seven legions and a thousand horse!

Bolstered by his military strength, Brutus decided that it was time he headed east to rescue Cassius from Dolabella. Behind him in Apollonia he left the original Macedonian legion as a garrison; Antony's brother he left in the custody of Gaius Clodius, one of the very many Clodiuses of that wayward patrician clan, Claudia.

Having started his march from Apollonia on the Ides of May, he reached the Hellespont toward the end of June, an indication that he wasn't a swift mover. The Hellespont crossed, he made for Nicomedia, the capital of Bithynia, where he ensconced himself in the governor's palace. His fellow Liberator, the governor Lucius Tillius Cimber, had picked up his traps and moved east to Pontus, and Cimber's Liberator quaestor, Decimus Turullius, had mysteriously disappeared; no one, thought Brutus wryly, wants to become involved in a civil war.

Then came a letter from Servilia.

> I have some bad news for you, even if it is good news for me. Porcia is dead. As I told you in earlier correspondence, she had not been well since your departure. I gather that others have told you this also.
>
> First she began to neglect her appearance, then to refuse to eat. When I promised her that I would have her tied down and fed by force if necessary, she relented and ate enough to keep living,

though every bone ended in showing. Next came bouts of talking to herself. She wandered around the house jabbering and gibbering—about what, no one could tell. Nonsense, pure nonsense.

Though I was having her closely watched, I confess that she was too cunning for me. I mean, how could one ever guess why she asked for a brazier? It was three days after the Ides of June, and the weather was on the cool side. I simply assumed that starvation caused her to feel cold. Certainly she was shivering, and her teeth were chattering.

Her servant Sylvia found her dead about an hour after the fire tripod was delivered to her sitting room. She had eaten red-hot coals, still had one in her hand. Apparently the kind of food she craved, wouldn't you say?

I have her ashes, but am not sure what you want to do with them—mix them with Cato's now they're finally home from Utica, or save them to mix with your own? Or just build a tomb for her alone? You can pay for it if that is your wish.

Brutus dropped the letter as if it too burned, eyes wide but vision turned inward. Watching inside his mind as Servilia tied his wife to a chair, jacked her mouth wide open, and forced the coals down her throat.

Oh, yes, Mama, it was you. You conceived the idea out of your threat to force-feed my poor tormented girl. Its horrific cruelty would have appealed to you—you are the cruelest person I know. Do you think me a fool, Mama? No one, no matter how mad, can commit suicide that way. Bodily reflexes alone would prevent it. You tied her down and fed them to her. *The agony!* Oh, Porcia, my pillar of flame! My dearly beloved, core of my being. Cato's daughter, so full of courage, so alive, so passionate.

He didn't weep. He didn't even destroy the letter. Instead he walked out on to the balcony overlooking that mirrored sound of water and stared sightlessly at the forested hill on its far side. I curse you, Mama. May you be visited daily by the Furies. May you never again know a moment's peace. A comfort for me to know that Aquila your lover died at Mutina, but you never cared for him. Leaving aside Caesar, the ruling passion of your entire life has been your hatred of Cato, your own brother. But your killing Porcia is a signal to me. That you do not expect ever to see me again. That you deem my cause hopeless and my chances of success nonexistent. For if I ever did see you again, I would tie you down and feed you hot coals.

* * *

When King Deiotarus sent Brutus a legion of infantry and said that he would do whatever lay in his power to aid the Liberators, Brutus wrote (vainly, as it turned out) to all the cities of Asia Province and demanded that they give him troops, ships—and money. From Bithynia he asked two hundred warships and fifty transports, but there was no one to implement his request, nor would the local *socii* co-operate; Cimber's quaestor, Turullius, he now discovered, had taken everything the province could offer and gone to serve Cassius.

News from Rome continued to be alarming: Mark Antony was a second-class public enemy, so was Lepidus. Then Gaius Clodius, the legate Brutus had left in charge of Apollonia, wrote to tell Brutus that he had heard for absolute certain that Mark Antony was in the act of mounting a full-scale invasion of western Macedonia to rescue his brother. Clodius's response had been to lock himself and the Legio Macedonica inside Apollonia—and to kill Gaius Antonius. His logic was impeccably Clodian: once Antony learned that his brother was dead, he'd cancel his invasion.

Oh, Gaius Clodius, why did you do that? Marcus Antonius is *inimicus*, he's in no position to mount any rescue invasions!

Terrified nonetheless of what Antony might do when he found out that his brother was dead, Brutus put some of his legions into camp along the river Granicus in Bithynia, and ordered the rest to march back into the west as far as Thessalonica while he himself raced ahead to see exactly what was happening on the Adriatic coast of Macedonia.

Nothing. When he reached Apollonia late in Julius, he found the Legio Macedonica enthusiastically investigating reported landings of Antonian troops here, there, and everywhere.

"But every last report is spurious," said Gaius Clodius.

"Clodius, you should not have executed Gaius Antonius!"

"Of course I should," said Gaius Clodius, unrepentant. "In my view, the world is well rid of the *cunnus*. Besides, as I said to you in my letter, I was sure that if Marcus knew his brother was dead, he wouldn't bother trying to rescue a corpse. And I was right."

Brutus threw his hands in the air—who could reason with a Clodius? They were all mad. So he backtracked east again to Thessalonica, where he found his legions and Gaius Flavius Hemicillus already at work.

Cassius was finally in contact, informing the astonished Brutus that Syria was uncontestably his. Dolabella was dead, and he was planning to invade Egypt and punish its queen for not helping him. That would take two months, said Cassius, after which he would start mounting an expedition to invade the Kingdom of the Parthians.

Those seven Roman Eagles taken from Crassus at Carrhae had to be wrested from their pedestals in Ecbatana.

"Cassius's work is cut out for him for some time to come," said Hemicillus, one of those people noble Rome could produce by the dozens: meticulous, efficient, logical, canny. "While he is so engaged, it would benefit your troops greatly if you were to blood them in a small campaign."

"A small campaign?" Brutus asked warily.

"Yes, against the Thracian Bessi."

It turned out that Hemicillus had befriended a Thracian prince named Rhascupolis, whose tribe was subject to King Sadala of the Bessi, the major people of inland Thrace.

"I want," said Rhascupolis, introduced to Brutus, "independent status for my tribe and the title Friend and Ally of the Roman People. In return for that, I will help you conduct a successful war against the Bessi."

"But they're fearsome warriors," Brutus objected.

"Indeed they are, Marcus Brutus. However, they have their weaknesses, and I know every one of them. Use me as your mentor, and I promise you victory over the Bessi within a single month, as well as plenty of spoils," said Rhascupolis.

Like other coastal Thracians, Rhascupolis did not look like a barbarian; he wore proper clothes, was not tattooed, spoke Attic Greek, and conducted himself like any other civilized man.

"Are you the chieftain of your tribe, Rhascupolis?" Brutus asked, sensing that something was being withheld.

"I am, but I have an older brother, Rhascus, who thinks he should be chieftain," Rhascupolis confessed.

"And where is this Rhascus?"

"Gone, Marcus Brutus. He is not a danger."

Nor was he. Brutus led his legions into the heart of Thrace, a huge area of country between the Danubius and Strymon Rivers and the Aegean Sea, more lowland than highland, and, as he soon learned, capable of producing wheat even in the midst of this drought, which seemed to exist almost everywhere. Feeding his troops had become an expensive exercise, but with the Bessi grain in his enormous cavalcade of ox wagons, Brutus could look forward to winter in better spirits.

The campaign had lasted throughout the month of Sextilis, and at the end of it Marcus Junius Brutus, Caesar's unmartial paper shuffler, had blooded his army with minimal losses. That army had hailed him imperator on the field, which entitled him to celebrate a triumph; King Sadala had made his submission, and would walk in his parade. Rhascupolis became undisputed ruler of Thrace, was assured that he would receive Friend and Ally status as soon as the Senate answered Brutus's communication. It did not occur either to Rhascupolis or to Brutus to wonder what had become of Rhascus, the older brother ejected from the chieftainship. Nor, for the moment, did Rhascus, safe in hiding, intend to tell them that his mind was applied to the problem of how to become King Rhascus of Thrace.

Brutus crossed the Hellespont for the second time that year around the middle of September, and picked up the legions he had left camped along the Granicus River.

Then he heard that Octavian and Quintus Pedius were the new consuls, and wrote frantically to Cassius, urging him to abandon any campaigns against Egypt or the Parthians. What he had to do was march north and join their forces, said Brutus, for with the monstrous Octavian in control of Rome, everything had changed. A destructive child had been given the world's biggest and most complex toy to play with.

In Nicomedia, Brutus learned that the Liberator governor, Lucius Tillius Cimber, had marched from Pontus to join Cassius, but had left Brutus a fleet of sixty warships.

So Brutus set out for Pergamum, where he demanded tribute, though he made no attempt to tamper with Caesar's dispositions anent Mithridates of Pergamum, who was allowed to keep his little fiefdom provided that he made a hefty donation to Brutus's hungry war chest. Caught, Mithridates gave the hefty donation.

Brutus finally arrived in Smyrna in November, there to sit himself down and wait for Cassius. All the ready money in Asia Province had long gone; there remained only temple wealth in the form of gold or silver statuary, objects of arts, plate. Stifling his qualms, Brutus confiscated everything from everywhere, melted his loot down and minted coins. If Caesar, he thought, could put his profile on coins minted during his lifetime, so too could Marcus Brutus. Thus Brutus's coins displayed his profile, with various laudations of the Ides of March on their reverse sides: a cap of liberty, a dagger, the words EID MAR.

More and more men had joined his cause. Marcus Valerius Messala Corvinus—a son of Messala Niger—arrived in Smyrna with Lucius Gellius Poplicola, once Antony's intimate. The Casca brothers appeared; so did Tiberius Claudius Nero, Caesar's least favorite incompetent, accompanied by a close Claudian relative, Marcus Livius Drusus Nero. Importantly, Sextus Pompey, who controlled the seas west of Greece, had indicated that he would not hinder the Liberators.

The only staff problem Brutus had was Labienus's son, Quintus, who bade fair to outdo his father when it came to barbaric savagery. What, asked Brutus of himself, am I to do with Quintus Labienus before his conduct ruins me? It was Hemicillus gave an answer:

"Send him to the court of the King of the Parthians as your ambassador," said the banker. "He'll feel right at home there."

So Brutus did, a decision that was to have far-reaching consequences in the fairly distant future.

Of more concern was the news that the consuls in Rome had tried all the Liberators, who were now *nefas*, stripped of their citizenships and property; the Casca brothers had brought it. There could be no going back now, no hope of reaching an accommodation with Octavian's Senate.

 By the middle of January, Cassius owned six legions and the province of Syria save only for Apameia, wherein the rebel Caecilius Bassus was still holed up. Then Bassus threw open the gates of Apameia and offered Cassius his two good legions, which swelled Cassius's army to eight. The moment each district in the province learned that the legendary Gaius Cassius was back, local faction fighting ceased.

Antipater came hurrying from Judaea to assure Cassius that the Jews were on his side, and was sent back to Jerusalem under orders to raise money and make sure that no hostile elements among the Jews made trouble. They had always favored Caesar, a Jew lover; Cassius was no Jew lover, but intended to make full use of this awkward, fractious people.

When news reached Antipater that Aulus Allienus, sent to obtain Alexandria's four legions for Dolabella, was on the march north with these troops, he immediately couriered word to Cassius in Antioch. Cassius came south, met Antipater, and together they had no trouble persuading Allienus to surrender his four legions. Cassius's army now held twelve experienced legions and four thousand horsemen, the best force in the Roman world. Did he have ships, his happiness would have been unalloyed, but he had no ships at all. Or so he thought.

Unbeknownst to him, young Lentulus Spinther had met up with the admirals Patiscus, Sextilius Rufus and the Liberator Cassius Parmensis, and gone to war against the fleets of Dolabella, in full sail for Syria. Dolabella himself had marched overland through Cappadocia: when he crossed the Amanus and entered Syria, he had no idea that Spinther, Patiscus and the others were busy defeating his fleets, then commandeering most of the vessels for Cassius's use.

The horrified Dolabella found every hand in Syria turned against him; even Antioch shut its gates and announced that it belonged to Gaius Cassius, Syria's true governor. Grinding his teeth, Dolabella flounced off to make an offer to the elders of the port city of Laodiceia: if Laodiceia gave Dolabella aid and sanctuary, he would make it Syria's capital once he had taught Cassius a much-needed lesson. The elders accepted with alacrity. While he went to work fortifying Laodiceia, Dolabella sent agents to suborn Cassius's troops—to no avail. Every soldier hewed stoutly to his hero, Gaius Cassius. Who was this Dolabella? A brawling drunkard who had tortured a Roman governor, beheaded him.

April saw Cassius still in ignorance of the maritime success Spinther and the others were enjoying. Sure that Dolabella would soon be possessed of hundreds of ships, Cassius sent envoys to Queen Cleopatra to demand a huge fleet of warships and transports from Egypt, to be delivered to Cassius yesterday. Cleopatra's reply was in the negative: Egypt was in the throes of famine and pestilence, she said, therefore in no position to help. Her regent on Cyprus did send ships, as did Tyre and Aradus in Phoenicia—but not enough to content Cassius, who resolved to invade Egypt and show its Caesarean queen that a Liberator was not to be taken lightly.

Sure that his fleets would arrive soon, and sure too that Mark Antony was even then sending him additional troops, Dolabella barricaded himself inside Laodiceia. He had no idea that Antony was now *inimicus* rather than the proconsul of Italian Gaul.

Laodiceia stood on the swollen end of a bulbous promontory connected to the Syrian mainland by an isthmus only four hundred yards wide. Which made the city extremely difficult to besiege. Dolabella's legions were camped outside its walls, a section of which was torn down and re-erected across the isthmus. And by mid-May a few ships began to turn up, their masters assuring Dolabella that the great bulk of them weren't far behind.

But nobody really knew what anybody else was doing, which contributed as much to the fortunes of the war in Syria as any brilliant feats of command. Spinther had gone to the Pamphylian city of Perge to pick up the dead Trebonius's cache of money for Cassius, while his colleagues Patiscus, Sextilius Rufus and Cassius Parmensis chased Dolabella's fleets off the high seas. A state of affairs neither Dolabella nor Cassius knew about as Cassius brought a segment of his army up to Laodiceia; he went to work to build an awesome rampart across the isthmus just outside Dolabella's wall, which it overlooked. That done, he put artillery atop it and bombarded Dolabella's camp remorselessly.

At which moment Cassius finally discovered that he owned all the fleets. Cassius Parmensis arrived with a flotilla of quinqueremes, broke the chain on Laodiceia's harbor, entered, and sent every ship of Dolabella's moored inside to the bottom. Blockade was now complete. No supplies could reach Laodiceia.

Starvation set in, as did disease, but the city held out until the beginning of Julius, when the day commander of Dolabella's wall opened the doors and gates in it to admit Cassius's troops. By the time they reached Laodiceia itself, Publius Cornelius Dolabella was dead by his own hand.

Syria now belonged to Cassius from the Egyptian border to the Euphrates River, beyond which the Parthians skulked, unsure what was going on, and unwilling to invade with Cassius around.

Amazed at his good fortune—but positive that it was well deserved—Cassius wrote to Rome and to Brutus, his mood soaring until he felt himself invincible. He was better than Caesar.

Now, however, he had to find the money to keep his enterprise going, not an easy matter in a province denuded first by Pompey the Great's Metellus Scipio, then by Caesar in retaliation. He adopted Caesar's technique, demanding the same sum from a city or district as it had paid to Pompey, knowing very well that he was not going to get anything like the amounts stipulated. However, when he settled for less, he appeared a merciful, temperate man.

Having been so loyal to Caesar, the Jews were hit hardest. Cassius demanded seven hundred talents of gold, which the people of Judaea just didn't have. Crassus had stolen their gold from the Great Temple, and no Roman since had given them the chance to accumulate more. Antipater did what he could, dividing the task of obtaining the bullion between his sons Phasael and Herod, and one Malichus, a secret supporter of a faction determined to rid Judaea of King Hyrcanus and his Idumaean sycophant Antipater.

Of the three collectors, Herod did best. He took one hundred talents of gold to Cassius in Damascus, presenting himself to the governor in a humble, charming fashion. Cassius remembered him well from his earlier days in Syria; then a youth, Herod had nonetheless made an impression, and Cassius was fascinated now to see how the ugly young man had turned out. He found he liked the wily Idumaean, doomed never to qualify as king because his mother was a gentile. A pity, thought Cassius. Herod was an ardent advocate of Rome's presence in the East, and would have made loyal allies out of the Jews did he rule them. For at least Rome was akin to Judaea; the alternative, rule by the King of the Parthians, was more hideous by far.

The other two gold raisers did poorly. Antipater was able to scrape together enough to make Phasael's contribution look respectable, but Malichus failed miserably because Malichus wasn't about to give the Romans anything. Determined to show that he meant business, Cassius summoned Malichus to Damascus and condemned him to death. Antipater came hurrying with a further hundred talents and begged Cassius not to carry out the sentence; the mollified Cassius spared Malichus, whom Antipater bore back to Jerusalem, unaware that Malichus had wanted to be a martyr.

Some communities, like Gompha, Laodiceia, Emmaus and Thamna were sacked and razed to the ground, their peoples sent to the slave markets of Sidon and Antioch.

All of which meant that Cassius now had the leisure to think about invading Egypt. This was not merely to punish its queen; it was also due to the fact that Egypt was said to be the richest country on the face of the globe, except perhaps for the Kingdom of the Parthians. In Egypt, thought Cassius, he would find the funds to rule Rome. Brutus? Brutus could be the head of his bureaucracy. Cassius no longer believed in the Republican cause, he deemed it deader than Caesar. He, Gaius Cassius Longinus, would be the King of Rome.

Then he got Brutus's letter.

Terrible news from Rome, Cassius. I am sending this at the gallop in the hope that it reaches you before you set out to invade Egypt. That is now quite impossible.

Octavianus and Quintus Pedius are consuls. Octavianus marched on Rome and the city gave in without a murmur. It seems likely that there will be civil war between them and Antonius, who has allied himself with the governors of the western provinces. Antonius and Lepidus are both outlawed, and the Liberators tried and condemned *nefas* in Octavianus's court. All our property is forfeit, though Atticus writes assuring me that he is looking after Servilia, Tertulla and Junilla. Vatia Isauricus and Junia will have nothing to do with them. Decimus Brutus is defeated in Italian Gaul and has fled, no one knows where.

This is our best opportunity to win Rome. If Antonius and Octavianus should patch up their differences (though I admit that does not seem likely), then we will spend the rest of our lives outlawed. Therefore I say that if you haven't yet started for Egypt, don't. We have to stick together and make a move to take Italy and Rome. We might have been able to conciliate Antonius one day, but Octavianus? Never. Caesar's heir is obdurate, all the Liberators must die disenfranchised and poverty-stricken.

Leave what legions you deem necessary to garrison Syria in your absence and march to join me as soon as you can. I conquered the Bessi and have a great quantity of grain and other foodstuffs, so our combined army will eat. Some parts of Bithynia and Pontus have also produced crops, which will belong to us, not to Octavianus to keep Rome pacified. I hear that Italy and the West are as dry as all Greece, Africa and Macedonia. We must act now, Cassius, while we can feed our men—and while we still have money in our war chests.

Porcia is dead. My mother says suicide. I am desolate.

Cassius wrote back immediately. Yes, he would march for Asia Province, probably inland through Cappadocia and Galatia. Was it Brutus's intention to go to war against Octavianus and then hope to make a deal with Antonius?

An answer came swiftly: yes, that was what Brutus hoped to do. March at once, we will meet in Smyrna in December. Send as many ships as possible.

Cassius picked his two best legions and sat them down, one in Antioch, one in Damascus, then appointed his loyalest follower, an ex-centurion named Fabius, as temporary governor. Leaving noblemen to govern, in Cassius's experience, only meant trouble. A sentiment Caesar would have echoed heartily.

Just before he left the vicinity of Antioch to head north, he learned from Herod that the ingrate Malichus had poisoned his benefactor Antipater in Jerusalem, and rejoiced in his deed.

"I have him prisoner," wrote Herod. "What shall I do?"

"Have your revenge" was Cassius's answer.

Herod did. He took the fanatically Judaic Malichus to Tyre, home of the purple-dye industry and home of the hated god Baal. Therefore a religiously anathematic place to a Jew. Two of Cassius's soldiers led the naked and barefoot Malichus out into the middle of a stinking mass of putrefying shellfish carcasses, and there very slowly killed him while Herod watched. The body was left to rot among the *murex*.

Learning of Herod's revenge on Malichus, Cassius laughed softly. Oh, Herod, you are a very interesting man!

At the pass through the Amanus range called the Syrian Gates, Tillius Cimber, the Liberator governor of Bithynia and Pontus, joined Cassius with a legion of Pontic troops. That brought the army up to eleven legions, plus three thousand cavalry—as many horses as the practical Cassius thought the countryside would bear this side of grassy Galatia.

Cimber and Cassius agreed that their progress would have to be leisurely enough to squeeze as much money as possible out of every land they traversed.

In Tarsus they fined the city the fantastic sum of fifteen hundred gold talents, and insisted that it be paid before they left. The terrified city councillors melted down every precious object in the temples, then sold the free Tarsian poor into slavery; even that didn't begin to approach the sum, so they went on selling Tarsians into slavery, ascending the social ladder. When they managed to gather five hundred gold talents, Cassius and Cimber pronounced themselves satisfied and departed up through the Cilician Gates to Cappadocia.

They had sent their cavalry on ahead to demand money from Ariobarzanes, who said flatly that he had none, and pointed to the holes in his doors and window shutters where once golden nails had resided. The old king was killed on the spot and his palace plus the temples of Eusebeia Mazaca plundered to little effect. Deiotarus of Galatia donated infantry and cavalry as his share, then stood aside and watched his temples and palace pillaged. You can tell, he thought wearily, that Brutus and Cassius are in the moneylending business. Nothing is sacred except money.

At the beginning of December, Cassius, Cimber and the army entered Asia Province through the wild and beautiful mountains of Phrygia, then followed the course of the Hermus River down to the Aegean Sea. Reunion with Brutus was only a short ride down a good Roman road. If everyone they encountered looked poor and downtrodden, if every temple and public building looked shabby and neglected, they chose not to notice. Mithridates the Great had made a far worse chaos of Asia Province than any Roman.

3   When Cleopatra had arrived in Alexandria that June three months after the death of Caesar, she had found Caesarion safe and well in the custody of Mithridates of Pergamum, wept on her uncle's bosom, thanked him lovingly for his care of her realm, and sent him home to Pergamum laden down with a

thousand talents of gold. Gold that Mithridates was to find very handy when Brutus demanded tribute; he paid the specified amount and said nothing about the large surplus of bullion still in his secret coffers.

Now three years of age, Cleopatra's son was tall, golden-haired, blue of eye and growing more like Caesar every day. He could read and write, discuss affairs of state a little, and was fascinated by the work his birth had made his lot. A happy chance. Time then to say goodbye to Ptolemy XIV Philadelphus, Cleopatra's half brother and husband. The fourteen-year-old boy was handed over to Apollodorus, who had him strangled and gave out to the citizens of Alexandria that their king had died of a familial trouble. True enough. Caesarion was elevated to the throne as Ptolemy XV Caesar Philopator Philomator— Ptolemy Caesar, father-loving and mother-loving. He was anointed Pharaoh by Cha'em, high priest of Ptah, and became Lord of the Two Ladies, He of the Sedge and Bee; he was also given his own physician, Hapd'efan'e.

But Caesarion could not marry Cleopatra. Father-daughter or mother-son incest was religiously unacceptable. Oh, for the daughter Caesar had never given her! A mystery and clearly the will of the Gods, but why? Why, why? She, the personification of Nilus, had not quickened, even during those last months when she and Caesar were together in Rome for many nights of love. When her menses began to flow as her ship had put out from Ostia, she had fallen to the deck and howled, screeched, torn her hair, lacerated her breasts. She had been late, been *sure* she was with child! Now there would never be a full sister—or brother—for Caesarion.

In about the time that it would have taken for news that Egypt had a new king to travel from Alexandria to Cilicia and back again, Cleopatra received a letter from her sister Arsinoë. Despite Caesar's plans that she would spend the rest of her days in service to Artemis of Ephesus, Arsinoë had escaped as soon as she learned of Caesar's assassination. She had gone to earth in the temple kingdom of Olba, where, it was said, the descendants of Ajax's archer brother, Teucer, still ruled. It was described in some of the Alexandrian texts, which Cleopatra had consulted the moment she learned Arsinoë's whereabouts, hoping to find a clue as to how she could eliminate her sister. Hauntingly beautiful, said the texts, with its gorges, white and racing rivers, jagged peaks of many colors; its people lived in roomy houses cut inside the cliffs, warm in winter, cool in summer, and made exquisite lace that procured an income for Olba. What she read discouraged

Cleopatra. Arsinoë was safe enough there to think herself inviolate, untouchable.

Her letter asked that she be allowed to return to Egypt and take up her rightful place as a princess of the House of Ptolemy. Not, swore Arsinoë on the paper, to attempt to usurp the throne! There was no need for that. Let her come home, she begged, to marry her nephew, Caesarion. That would mean children of the true blood for Egypt's throne within little more than a decade.

Cleopatra wrote one word back: NO!

She then issued an edict to all her subjects that forbade the Princess Arsinoë to enter Egypt. If she did, she was to be put to death at once and her head sent to the Pharaohs. This edict found favor with her subjects of Nilus, but not with her Macedonian and Greek subjects in Alexandria, whom Caesar had tamed beyond any thought of insurrection, but who still thought it a good idea for Caesarion to have a suitably Ptolemaic bride. After all, he couldn't marry someone without a drop of the same blood in her veins!

On the Ides of Julius, the priests read the first Nilometer, at Elephantine on the Nubian border. The news was sent down the length of the mighty river to Memphis in a sealed packet that Cleopatra opened with a leaden heart. She knew what it would say: that Nilus was not going to inundate, that this year of Caesar's death would see the river in the Cubits of Death. Her foreboding was confirmed. Nilus measured twelve feet, well and truly down in the Cubits of Death.

Caesar was dead, and Nilus had failed. Osiris was returned to the West and the Realm of the Dead, carved up in twenty-three chunks, and Isis searched for the pieces in vain. Though she saw the wonderful comet not long after on the far northern horizon, she did not know that it had coincided with Caesar's funeral games in Rome, nor was she to learn that for two more months, by which time its spiritual significance had faded.

Well, business must go on, and a ruler's business was to rule, but Cleopatra had no heart for it as the year wore down. Her sole joy was Caesarion, who shared her life more and more. She needed a new husband and more children desperately, but whom could she marry? Someone of either Ptolemaic or Julian blood. For a while she toyed with the idea of her cousin Asander in Cimmeria, but abandoned him with little regret; none of her people, Egyptian or Alexandrian, would take kindly to a grandson of Mithridates the Great as the husband of a granddaughter of Mithridates the Great. Too Pontic, too Aryan. The line of the Ptolemies was finished. Therefore her husband would have to be of Julian blood—quite impossible! They were Romans, laws unto themselves.

All she could do was send agents to winkle Arsinoë out of Olba, which finally happened after a gift of gold. Shipped first to Cyprus, she was then shipped back to the precinct of Artemis in Ephesus, where Cleopatra had her watched closely. Killing her was out of the question, but while ever Arsinoë lived, there were Alexandrians who saw her as preferable to Cleopatra. Arsinoë could marry the King, Cleopatra could not. Some might have asked why Cleopatra was so opposed to the idea of a marriage between Arsinoë and her son: the answer was simple. Once Arsinoë was the wife of Pharaoh, it would be so easy for her to eliminate her older sister. A potion, a knife in the dark, a royal cobra, even a coup. The moment that Caesarion had a wife acceptable to Alexandria and Egypt, his mother was expendable.

No one in the Royal Enclosure expected that the famine when it came would be so terrible, for the usual recourse was to buy in grain from elsewhere than Egypt. This year, however, every land around Our Sea had seen its crops fail, so there was no grain to buy in to feed that massive parasite, Alexandria. A desperate Cleopatra sent ships into the Euxine Sea and managed to buy some wheat from Asander of Cimmeria, but an unknown person—Arsinoë?—then whispered to him that his cousin Cleopatra didn't think him good enough to share her throne. The Cimmerian supply dried up. Where else, where else? Ships sent to Cyrenaica, usually capable of producing grain when other places couldn't, returned empty to say that Brutus had taken the Cyrenaican grain to feed his gigantic army, and that his partner in crime, Cassius, had afterward taken by force what the Cyrenaicans had kept to feed themselves.

In March, when the harvest ought to have been filling the granaries to overflowing, the field rats and field mice of the Nilus valley had no gleanings to pick through, no precious little hoards of wheat and barley and pulses to tide them over. So they quit the fields and moved into the villages of Upper Egypt between Nubia and the beginning of the anabranch that enclosed the land of Ta-she. Every dwelling was mud brick with an earthen floor, be it the meanest hovel or the mansion of the *nomarch*. Into all these premises came the field rodents and their cargo of fleas, which hopped off their bony, anemic hosts and hopped into bedding, mats, clothes, there to feast upon human blood.

The rural workers of Upper Egypt sickened first, came down with chills and high fevers, splitting headaches, aching bones, tenderly painful bellies. Some died within three days spitting copious, putrid phlegm. Others did not spit, but rather developed hard, fist-sized lumps in groins and armpits, hot and empurpled. Most who had this form of the disease died at the lump stage, but some survived long enough for the lumps to burst and produce cupfuls of foul pus. They were the lucky ones, who mostly got better. But no one, even the temple physician-priests of Sekhmet, had any idea how the frightful epidemic was transmitted.

The people of Nubia and Upper Egypt died in thousands upon thousands, and the plague began to move slowly down the river.

The tiny harvest that had been gathered stayed inside piles of jars on the river's wharves; the local people were too sick and too few to load it on to barges and send it to Alexandria and the Delta. When word of the plague reached Alexandria and the Delta, no one volunteered to venture down the river and do the loading either.

Cleopatra faced a hideous dilemma. There were three million people in and around Alexandria, and another million in the Delta. Disease had closed the river to both these hungry hordes, and all the gold in the treasure vaults could not buy grain from abroad. Word went to the Arabs of southern Syria that there would be huge rewards for those men willing to go down Nilus and load grain, but the rumors of a terrible plague kept the Arabs away too. The desert was their shield against whatever was going on in Egypt; travel between southern Syria and Egypt dwindled and then ceased, even by sea. Cleopatra could feed her urban millions for many months to come on what the granaries still contained from last year's harvest, but if the next Nilus inundation were also in the Cubits of Death, Alexandria would starve, even if the more rural Delta people survived.

One of the few consolations was the appearance of Dolabella's legate Aulus Allienus, to remove those four legions from garrison duty in Alexandria. Expecting to meet opposition, Allienus was baffled when he found the Queen eager to oblige him—yes, yes, take them! Take them *tomorrow!* Without them, there would be thirty thousand fewer mouths to feed.

She had to make some decisions. Caesar had nagged her to think ahead, but she wasn't by nature that kind of person. Nor did anyone, least of all a cosseted monarch, know the mechanics of plague. Cha'em had told her that the priests would contain the disease, that it would not spread north of Ptolemais, where all river and road traffic had been stopped. Except of course that traffic among field rodents proceeded, albeit at a slower rate. Understandably, Cha'em was too busy marshaling his priest army to go to Alexandria and see Pharaoh, who didn't travel south to see him either. She had no one to advise her, and absolutely no idea what she ought to do.

Plunged into gloom anyway by Caesar's passing, Cleopatra couldn't summon the necessary detachment for decision making. Assuming from the usual pattern that next year's Inundation would also be in the Cubits of Death, she issued an edict that inside the city only those with the Alexandrian citizenship would be allowed to buy grain. The Delta people would be allowed to buy grain only if they were engaged in agricultural pursuits or the production of paper, a royal monopoly that had to be continued.

There were a million Jews and Metics in Alexandria. Caesar had gifted them with the Roman citizenship, and Cleopatra had matched his generosity by granting them the Alexandrian citizenship. But, after Caesar sailed away, the million Greeks of the city had insisted that if the Jews and Metics had the citizenship, they ought to have it too. In the end the only residents of the city who didn't have the citizenship, once confined to just three hundred thousand Macedonians, were the hybrid Egyptians. If the citizenship were to exist as it did at the moment, then the granaries would have to provide something over two million *medimni* of wheat or barley every month. Could that be cut to something over one million *medimni* every month, the prospect was brighter.

So Cleopatra reneged on her promise and stripped the Jews and Metics of the Alexandrian citizenship while allowing the Greeks to keep it. Her wisdom as a ruler was running backward: she had never taken Caesar's advice and issued free grain to the poor, and now she removed the franchise from a third of the city's populace in order, as she saw it, to save the lives of those most entitled to dwell in Alexandria by right of bloodline. No one in the Royal Enclosure said a word against the edict; autocracy bred its own disadvantages, one of which was that autocrats preferred to associate with people who agreed with them, didn't like people who disagreed with them unless they were on a level with Caesar—and who in Alexandria was, to Cleopatra?

The edict fell upon the Jews and Metics like a thunderbolt. Their sovereign, in whose service they had toiled, for whom they had given up much, including precious lives, was going to let them starve. Even if they sold everything they owned, they would still not be allowed to buy grain, the staple of existence. It was reserved for the Macedonian and Greek Alexandrians. And what else was there for an urban populace to eat in time of famine? Meat? There were no animals in drought. Fruit? Vegetables? The markets had none in drought, and despite the presence of Lake Mareotis, nothing grew in that sandy soil. Alexandria, the artificial graft on the Egyptian tree, just could not feed itself. Those in the Delta would eat something, those in Alexandria would not.

People began to leave, especially out of Delta and Epsilon Districts, but even that was not easy. The moment rumors of plague ran around the ports of Our Sea, Alexandria and Pelusium ceased to see foreign ships dock, and Alexandrian merchantmen voyaging abroad found that they were not allowed to dock in foreign ports. In its little corner of the world, Egypt was quarantined by no edict save the ages-old fear and horror of plague.

The riots began when the Alexandrians of Macedonian and Greek extraction barricaded the granaries and mounted huge numbers of guards wherever food was stockpiled. Delta and Epsilon Districts boiled, and the Royal Enclosure became a fortress.

To compound her woes, Cleopatra also had Syria to worry about. When Cassius sent asking for warships and transports, she had to decline because she still hoped to find a source of grain somewhere in the world, would need every ship to bring it back including war galleys—how else was she going to ensure that her transports would be allowed to dock and load?

As summer began, she learned that Cassius intended to invade. On the heels of that, word came from the first Nilometer that, as she had expected, the Inundation was down in the Cubits of Death again. There would be no harvest, even if sufficient people along Nilus were alive to plant the seed, which was debatable. Cha'em sent her figures that said sixty percent of the population of Upper Egypt was dead. He also told her that he thought the plague had crossed the frontier the priests had erected athwart the valley at Ptolemais, though now he hoped to arrest it below Memphis. What to do, what to do?

Around the end of September things suddenly improved a little. Limp with relief, Cleopatra learned that Cassius and his army had gone north to Anatolia; there would be no invasion. Unaware of Brutus's letter, she assumed that Cassius had heard how bad the plague was, and had decided not to risk exposure to it. At almost the same moment, an envoy from the King of the Parthians arrived and offered to sell Egypt a large amount of barley.

So distraught was she that at first she could only babble to the envoys about the difficulties she would have importing it; with Syria, Pelusium and Alexandria closed, the barley would have to be barged down the Euphrates to the Persian Sea, brought around Arabia and into the Red Sea, then all the way up to the very top of the gulf that separated Sinai from Egypt. With plague all along Nilus, she babbled to the expressionless envoys, it could not be unloaded at Myos Hormos or the usual Red Sea ports because it couldn't go overland to the river. Babble, babble, babble.

"Divine Pharaoh," the leader of the Parthian delegation said when she let him get a word in, "that isn't necessary. The acting governor of Syria is a man called Fabius, who can be bought. *Buy him!* Then we can send the barley overland to Nilus Delta."

A large amount of gold changed hands, but gold Cleopatra had in enormous quantities; Fabius graciously accepted his share of it, and the barley came overland to the Delta.

Alexandria would eat a little longer.

News from Rome was scanty, thanks to the general ban on Pelusium and Alexandria, but not long after the Parthian envoys departed (to tell their royal master that the Queen of Egypt was an incompetent fool), Cleopatra received a letter from Ammonius, her agent in Rome.

Gasping, she discovered that Rome hovered on the brink of at least two separate civil wars: one between Octavianus and Marcus Antonius, one between the Liberators and whoever was in control of Rome when their armies reached Italy. No one knew what was going to happen, said Ammonius, except that Caesar's heir was senior consul, and everybody else was outlawed.

Gaius Octavius! No, Caesar Octavianus. A twenty-year-old? Senior consul of Rome? It beggared description! She remembered him well—a very pretty boy with a faint hint of Caesar about him. Grey eyed, very calm and quiet, yet she had sensed a latent power in him. Caesar's great-nephew, and therefore a cousin of Caesarion's.

A cousin of Caesarion's!

Mind whirling, Cleopatra walked to her desk, sat down, drew paper forward and picked up a reed pen.

> I congratulate you, Caesar, on your election as Rome's senior consul. How wonderful to think that Caesar's blood lives on in such a peerless individual as yourself. I remember you well, when you came with your parents to my receptions. Your mother and stepfather are well, I trust? How proud they must be!
>
> What news can I give you that might assist you? We are in famine in Egypt, but so, it seems, is the whole world. However, I have just received the happy news that I can buy barley from the King of the Parthians. There is also a frightful plague in Upper

Egypt, but Isis has spared Lower Egypt of the Delta and Alexandria, from which city I write this on a beautiful day of sun and balmy air. I pray that the autumnal air of Rome is equally salubrious.

You will, of course, have heard that Gaius Cassius has left Syria in the direction of Anatolia, probably, we think, to conjoin with his fellow criminal, Marcus Brutus. Whatever we can do to help you bring the assassins to justice, we will.

It may be that, after your consulship has ended, you might choose Syria as your province. To have such a charming neighbor would please me very much. Egypt is close, and well worth a visit. No doubt Caesar told you of his travels on Nilus, of the sights and wonders to be seen only in Egypt. Do, dear Caesar, think about visiting Egypt in the near future! All that it has is yours for the asking. Delights beyond your wildest imagination. I repeat, *all that Egypt has is yours for the asking.*

The letter was sent off the same day on a fast trireme, no expense spared, direct for Rome. With the letter went a tiny box in which reposed one enormous, perfect, pink ocean pearl.

Dear Isis, prayed Pharaoh, brow upon the floor, bent as low as the meanest of her subjects, dear Isis, send this new Caesar to me! Give Egypt life and hope again! Let Pharaoh bear sons and daughters of Caesar's blood! Safeguard my throne! Safeguard my dynasty! Send this new Caesar to me, and pour into me all the arts and wiles of the countless Goddesses who have served you, and Amun-Ra, and all the Gods of Egypt, as Pharaoh.

She could expect a reply within two months, but first came a letter from Cha'em to tell her that the plague had reached Memphis and was killing thousands. For some inexplicable reason, the priests in the temple precinct of Ptah were being spared; only those priest-physicians whom Sekhmet governed were sickening, and that because they had gone into the city to minister. The strong contagious element had prompted them not to return to Ptah's temple, but to stay where they were. A great sorrow to Cha'em. But be warned, he said. The disease would now spread into the Delta and into Alexandria. The Royal Enclosure must be sealed off from the city.

"Perhaps," said Hapd'efan'e thoughtfully when Cleopatra showed him Cha'em's letter, "it has to do with stone. The temple precinct is stone, its grounds are flagged. Whatever it is that carries the plague might not like such a barren environment. If so, then this stone palace will be a protection. And, if so, then the garden soil will be dangerous. I must consult the gardeners and have them plant the flower beds with wormwood."

Octavian's reply reached Alexandria before the plague did, at the end of November.

> Thank you for your good wishes, Queen of Egypt. It may please you to know that the number of living assassins is dwindling. I will not rest until the last one is dead.
>
> In the New Year I expect my task will be to deal with Brutus and Cassius.
>
> My stepfather, Philippus, is dying by inches. We do not expect him to live out the month. His toes have rotted and the poison is in his bloodstream. Lucius Piso is also dying, of an inflammation of the lungs.
>
> I write this from Bononia in Italian Gaul, where the autumnal air is freezing and full of sleet. I am here to meet Marcus Antonius. As I do not like traveling, I will never visit Egypt as a tourist. Your offer is most kind, but I must refuse it.
>
> The pearl is beautiful. I have set it in gold and will put it around the neck of Venus Genetrix in her temple in Caesar's forum.

Meet Marcus Antonius? *Meet?* What precisely does he mean by that? And what an answer. Consider yourself slapped on the face, Cleopatra. Octavianus is an icy man, not interested in Egyptian affairs, even of the heart.

So it can't be Caesar's heir. He has rejected me. I adore Lucius Caesar, but he would never make love where Caesar made love. Who else is there with Julian blood? Quintus Pedius. His two sons. Lucius Pinarius. The three Antonian brothers, Marcus, Gaius and Lucius. A total of seven men. It will have to be whichever of them comes first to my end of Their Sea, for I cannot travel to Rome. Seven men. Surely they can't all be as cold a fish as Octavianus. I will pray to Isis to send me a Julian, and sisters and brothers for Caesarion.

The plague reached Alexandria in December, and cut the city's population by seventy percent—Macedonians, Greeks, Jews, Metics, hybrid Egyptians perished in roughly equal numbers. Those who survived would eat well; Cleopatra had drawn the hatred of a million people upon her head for nothing.

"God," said Simeon the Jew, "does not discriminate."

XIII

Funding an Army

From JANUARY until SEXTILIS (AUGUST) of 42 B.C.

Greece, Thrace, Macedonia and Asia Province

1 "You can't possibly think of invading Italy without a great deal more money," said Hemicillus to Brutus and Cassius.

"*More* money?" gasped Brutus. "But there's no more to be had!"

"Why?" asked Cassius, frowning. "Between what I squeezed out of Syria and what Cimber and I collected on the way here, I must have two thousand gold talents." He turned on Brutus with a snarl. "Have you managed to collect none, Brutus?"

"Far from it," Brutus said stiffly, resenting the tone. "Mine is all in coin, about two-thirds silver, a third gold, and amounts to—?" He looked at Hemicillus enquiringly.

"Two hundred million sesterces."

"All up, then, we have four hundred million sesterces," said Cassius. "That's enough to mount an expedition to conquer Hades."

"You forget," Hemicillus said patiently, "that there will be no spoils, always the difficulty in civil war. Caesar took to giving his troops cash donatives in lieu of a share of spoils, but what he gave out was nothing compared to what soldiers demand now. Octavianus promised his legions twenty thousand per man, a hundred thousand for centurions of highest rank down to forty thousand for a junior centurion. Word travels. The men *expect* big money."

Brutus got up and walked to the window, looked out across the port, filled with hundreds of warships and transports.

His appearance had surprised Cassius, used to the mournful dark mouse; this Brutus was brisker, more—martial. His success against the Bessi had endowed him with much needed confidence, and Porcia's death had hardened him. The recipient of most of Servilia's letters, Cassius too had been appalled by her callous acceptance of Porcia's horrible suicide, but, unlike Brutus, he believed it had been a suicide. The Servilia he loved was not the woman Brutus had known and feared since memory began. Nor had Brutus voiced his conviction of murder to Servilia's favorite male relative, who would have rejected it adamantly.

"What has happened to Rome?" Brutus asked the multitude of ships. "Where is patriotism? Loyalty?"

"Still there," Cassius said harshly. "Jupiter, you're a fool, Brutus! What do ranker soldiers know about warring factions among their leaders? Whose definition of patriotism is a ranker soldier going to believe? Yours, or the Triumvirs'? All men know is that when they draw their swords, it will be against fellow Romans."

"Yes, of course," said Brutus, turning with a sigh. He sat down and stared at Hemicillus. "Then what do we do, Gaius?"

"Find more money," Hemicillus said simply.

"Where?"

"To start with, in Rhodes," said Cassius. "I've been talking to Lentulus Spinther, who tried several times to prise ships and money out of the Rhodians without getting either. So did I. According to Rhodes, their treaties with Rome don't include providing a specific side in a civil war with any aid whatsoever."

"And," said Hemicillus, "another part of Asia Minor that has never really been tapped—Lycia. Too difficult for the governors of Asia Province to get at to be bothered trying."

"Rhodes and Lycia," said Brutus. "I presume we're going to have to go to war to persuade them to help our enterprise?"

"In the case of Rhodes, definitely," said Cassius. "It may be that a simple request to—say, Xanthus, Patara and Myra—will suffice, if they know the alternative is invasion."

"How much should we ask from Lycia?" Brutus asked Hemicillus.

"Two hundred million sesterces."

"Rhodes," Cassius said grimly, "can give us twice that and still have some left over."

"Do you think that one thousand million will see us through to Italy?" Brutus asked.

"I'll do my sums later, when I know exactly what our strength will be," said Hemicillus.

Wintering in Smyrna was comfortable, even in this dry year. Of snow there was none, of wind little, and the broad valley of the Hermus enabled the Liberators to scatter their massive army over sixty miles of separate camps, each of which soon acquired its satellite community providing wine, whores and entertainment for the soldiers. Small farmers brought vegetables, ducks, geese, chickens and eggs to sell to eager buyers, sticky confections of oily pastry and syrup, an edible snail of the region, even plump frogs from the marshes. Though the big merchants in the urban settlements did not profit much from an army that had its own staples with it, these commercially unversed yet enterprising peasants, taxed to poverty, began to see a trace of prosperity return.

For Brutus and Cassius, living in the governor's residence alongside Smyrna port, the chief advantage of this winter location was the swiftness of news from Rome. So they had learned, aghast, of the formation of the Triumvirate, and understood that Octavian deemed the

Liberators a far greater threat to *his* Rome than he did Marcus Antonius. The Triumviral intention was clear: Brutus and Cassius would have to be eliminated. War preparations were going on all over Italy and Italian Gaul, and none of the forty-plus legions the Triumvirs could call upon had been discharged from service. Rumor said that Lepidus, now senior consul with Plancus as his junior, was to remain in Rome to govern, while Antony and Octavian were to deal with the Liberators; the most quoted commencement date for their campaign was May.

More horrifying even than all this was the news that Caesar had officially been declared a god, and that the cult of Divus Julius, as he was to be known, would be propagated all over Italy and Italian Gaul, with temples, priests, festivals. Octavian now openly called himself "Divi Filius," and Mark Antony had not voiced an objection. One of the Triumvirs was the son of a god, their cause *must* be the right one! So much had Antony's attitude changed since his own disastrous consulship that he now joined with Octavian in forcing the Senate to swear an oath to uphold all of Divus Julius's laws and dictates. And an imposing temple to Divus Julius was being built in the Forum Romanum on the site where his body had been burned. The People of Rome had won their battle to be allowed to worship Caesar.

"Even if we beat Antonius and win Rome, we're going to have to suffer Divus Julius forever," Brutus said miserably.

"The place has gone downhill," Cassius answered, scowling. "Can you imagine some lout raping a *Vestal Virgin?*"

That news had come too, that Rome's most revered women, used to walking freely about the city unaccompanied, now had to take a lictor as a bodyguard; Cornelia Merula, strolling alone to visit Fabia on the Quirinal, had been attacked and molested, though rape was Cassius's word, not mentioned in Servilia's letter. In all the history of Rome, the Vestals, clad in their unmistakable white robes and veils, had been free to come and go without fear.

"It represents a milestone," Brutus said sadly. "The old values and taboos are no longer respected. I'm not even sure I want to enter Rome ever again."

"If Antonius and Octavianus have anything to do with it, you won't, Brutus. All I know is that they'll have to fight hard to prevent *my* entering Rome," said Cassius.

With nineteen legions, five thousand cavalry and seven hundred ships at his disposal, Cassius sat down to work out how to extract six hundred million sesterces out of Rhodes and the cities of Lycia. Brutus was present, but had learned over the preceding few *nundinae* to be suitably deferential when Cassius had command on his mind; to Cassius, Brutus had simply had a stroke of luck in Thrace rather than generaled an authentic campaign.

"I'll take Rhodes," he announced, "which means a maritime war, at least to begin with. You'll invade Lycia, a land business, though you'll have to bring your troops in by sea. I doubt that there's much use for horse in either case, so I suggest that we send all but a thousand of our cavalry to Galatia for the spring and summer." He grinned. "Let Deiotarus bear their cost."

"He's been very generous and helpful" from Brutus, timidly.

"Then he can be even more generous and helpful" from Cassius.

"Why can't I march overland from Caria?" Brutus asked.

"I suppose you could, but why would you want to?"

"Because Roman foot hate sea voyages."

"All right, please yourself, but you can't muddle along at a snail's pace, and you'll have some nasty mountains to cross."

"I understand that," Brutus said patiently.

"Ten legions and five hundred horse for scouting."

"No baggage train if there are nasty mountains. The army will have to use pack mules, which means it can't afford to be on the march for longer than six *nundinae*. I'll have to hope that Xanthus has sufficient food to feed me when I get there. I do think Xanthus ought to be my first target, don't you?"

Cassius blinked, rather startled. Who would have thought to hear so much military common sense from Brutus? "Yes, Xanthus first," he agreed. "However, there's nothing to stop you sending more food by sea and picking it up when you reach Xanthus."

"Good idea," said Brutus, smiling. "And you?"

"As I said, sea battles, though I'll need four legions—who will board transports and endure the deep whether they like it or not," said Cassius.

Brutus set out with his ten legions and five hundred cavalry in March, following a good Roman road south through the valley of the Maeander River to Ceramus, where he negotiated the coast for as long as he could. The route offered him plenty of forage, for the granaries still contained wheat from last year's lean harvest, and he didn't care if his confiscations left the local people hungry, though he was sensible enough to heed their pleas that he must leave them enough seed to plant this year's crops. Unfortunately the spring rains hadn't come, a bad omen; the fields would have to be watered by hand from the rivers. How, asked the farmers piteously, were they to do that if they were too weak from hunger?

"Eat eggs and poultry," said Brutus.

"Then don't let your men steal our chickens!"

Deeming this reasonable, Brutus tightened up on illicit plundering of farmyard animals by his troops, who were beginning to discover that their commander was tougher than he looked.

The Solyma Mountains of Lycia were formidable, towering eight thousand feet straight up from the water's edge; it was thanks to them that no governor of Asia Province had ever bothered to regulate Lycia, determine a tribute or send legates to enforce his edicts. Long a haven for pirates, it was a place where the settlements were confined to a series of narrow river valleys, and all communication between settlements went on by sea. The land of Sarpedon and Glaucus of *Iliad* fame commenced at the town of Telmessus, where the good Roman road stopped. From Telmessus onward, there was not so much as a goat track.

Brutus simply made his own road as he marched, cycling the duty of going ahead to hack and dig with picks and shovels through his legions, whose men groaned and whined at the labor, but put their backs to it when their centurions administered the knobbed ends of their vine rods.

The dryness meant beautiful weather, no danger of landslides and no mud to slow the pack mules down, but camps were a thing of the past; each night the men curled up where they were along the ten-foot-wide rubble of the road, indifferent to the spangled nets of stars in the sky, the soaring, lacy cataracts of boiling little rivers, the pine-smothered peaks scarred by mighty hollows where whole flanks had fallen away, the pearly mists that coiled around the blackish-green trees at dawn. On the other hand, they had all noticed the big, shiny chunks of jet-black rock their picks turned over, but only because they had thought this some rare gemstone; the moment they were informed that it was just unworkable glass, they cursed it along with everything else on that grueling road-making exercise through the Solyma.

Only Brutus and his three philosophers had the temperament— and the leisure—to appreciate the beauties that unfolded by day, continued in mysterious form after dark, when creatures screamed from the forest, bats flitted, night birds hung silhouetted against the moon-silvered vault. Apart from appreciating the scenery, they each had their preferred activities: for Statyllus and Strato of Epirus, mathematics; for the Roman Volumnius, a diary; whereas Brutus wrote letters to dead Porcia and dead Cato.

It was a mere twenty miles from Telmessus to the valley of the Xanthus River, but those twenty miles occupied more than half of the thirty-day, hundred-and-fifty-mile march. Both Lycia's biggest cities, Xanthus and Patara, stood on this river's banks—Patara at its mouth, Xanthus fifteen miles upstream.

Brutus's army spilled off its homemade road into the valley closer to Patara than Xanthus, Brutus's first target. Unluckily for him, a stray shepherd had warned the cities, whose people used the hours to good advantage; they razed the countryside, evacuated the suburbs and shut the gates. All the granaries were inside, there were springs of fresh water, and the walls of Xanthus in particular were massive enough bastions to keep the Romans out.

Brutus's two chief legates were Aulus Allienus, a skilled soldier from a family of Picentine nobodies, and Marcus Livius Drusus Nero, a Claudian aristocrat adopted into the Livian clan; his sister, Livia, was betrothed to Tiberius Claudius Nero, though not yet old enough to marry this insufferable dolt whom Caesar had loathed and Cicero had wanted as his son-in-law. Using both Allienus and Drusus Nero as his advisers, Brutus put his military machine into siege mode. The scorched earth had annoyed him, as it removed vegetables from his legionary menu; he wouldn't bother starving the Xanthians out, he'd try to take the city quickly.

Considered by his peers to be extraordinarily erudite, Brutus actually was well versed in only a very few subjects—philosophy, rhetoric, certain literature. Geography bored him, as did non-Roman history save for titans like Thucydides, so he never read earth-people like Herodotus. Thus he knew nothing about Xanthus, apart from a tradition that said it had been founded by the Homeric King Sarpedon, who was worshiped as the city's principal god and had the most imposing temple. But Xanthus had another tradition too, unknown to Brutus. Twice before it had been besieged, first by a general of Cyrus the Great of Persia's named Harpagus the Mede, then by Alexander the Great. When it fell, as fall it did, the entire population of Xanthus had committed suicide. Among the frenzied activities the Xanthians had pursued during that period of grace the shepherd's warning gave them was the gathering of a huge amount of firewood; as the Roman siege swung into operation, the people inside the city heaped the wood into pyres in every open space.

The towers and the earthworks went up in the proper Roman manner, and the various pieces of artillery were wheeled into position; ballistas and catapults rained missiles of all kinds except blazing bundles—the city had to fall intact. Then the three rams arrived, the last items hauled along the new road. They were made of seasoned oak swung on thick yet supple ropes attached to a portable framework that was rapidly assembled, each fronted by a great bronze ram's head, beautifully fashioned from curled horns to sneering lips to menacing, half-closed eyes.

There were only three gates in the walls, ram-proof because they were mighty openwork portcullises of oak plated with very heavy iron; when pounded, they bounced like springs. Undeterred, Brutus put the rams to work on the walls themselves, which had not the tensile strength to resist, and slowly began to crumble. Too slowly, for they were very thick.

When Allienus and Drusus Nero judged that the Xanthians felt threatened enough to become desperate, Brutus withdrew his forces as if tired of trying, apparently off to see what he could do to Patara. Armed with torches, a thousand beleaguered men streamed out of Xanthus intent upon burning the artillery and siege towers. The lurking Brutus pounced and the Xanthians fled, only to find themselves shut out of the city because the prudent gate guards had lowered the portcullises. All thousand raiders perished.

Next day at noon the Xanthians tried again, this time making sure their gates remained open. Beating a hasty retreat as soon as the torches were thrown, they discovered that the portcullis machinery was far too slow; the Romans, in hot pursuit, poured inside until the gate operators chopped through the hoist ropes and the portcullises crashed down. Those beneath died instantly, but two thousand Roman legionaries had managed to get inside. They didn't panic. Instead, they formed up into tortoises and migrated to the main square, there to take refuge in the temple of Sarpedon, which they barred and defended.

The sight of those falling portcullises had a profound effect on the besiegers. Legionary camaraderie was very powerful; the thought of two thousand of their fellows trapped inside Xanthus moved Brutus's army to anguished madness. A level-headed, cool madness.

"They will have banded together and sought shelter," said Allienus to an assemblage of senior centurions, "so we'll assume that for the time being they're safe enough. What we have to do is work out how to get inside and rescue them."

"Not the portcullises," said *primipilus* Malleus. "The rams are useless, and we've nothing to cut through that iron plate."

"Still, we can make it look as if we *think* we can break them down," Allienus said. "Lanius, start." He raised his brows. "Any other ideas?"

"Ladders and grapples everywhere. They can't man every inch of the walls with pots of hot oil, and they don't have enough siege spears, the fools. We'll probe for weak spots," said Sudis.

"Get it done. What else?"

"Try to find some locals left outside the walls and—um—ask them *nicely* if there are any other ways to get in," said the *pilus prior* Callum.

"Now you're talking!" said Allienus with a grin.

Shortly afterward Callum's party came back with two men from a nearby hamlet. It didn't prove necessary to be *nice* to them; they were furiously angry because the Xanthians had burned their market gardens and orchards.

"See there?" asked one, pointing.

A main reason why Xanthus's bastions were so impregnable lay in the fact that the back third of the city had been built flush against the crags of a cliff.

"I see, but I don't see," said Allienus.

"The cliff isn't half as bad as it looks. We can show you a dozen snake paths that will put you among the outcrops on the cliff face. That isn't getting inside, I know, but it's a start for you clever chaps. You won't find any patrols, though you'll find defenses." The orchardist spat. "Cocksucking shits that they are, they burned our apples in flower, and all our cabbages and lettuces. All we got left are onions and parsnips."

"Rest assured, friend, that when we've taken the place, your village will get first pick of whatever's in there," said Callum. "Edible, I mean." He shaded his brow beneath the helmet with its immense sideways ruff of scarlet horsehair and tapped his thigh with his vine staff. "Right, all the limber ones for this. Macro, Pontius, Cafo, your legions are young, but I don't want any ninnies that get dizzy on heights. Go on, move!"

By noon the cliff swarmed with soldiers, high enough to look down over the walls and see what awaited them inside: a dense palisade of spikes many feet wide. Some of the men produced iron pegs and hammered them into the rock, then tied long ropes to them that dangled over a concave section of precipice; a man would grasp the end of the rope, his fellows would start pushing him as a father pushed a child on a swing, until momentum had him soaring over the deadly palisade to drop beyond it on to paving.

All afternoon soldiers penetrated the back defenses in dribs and drabs, forming into a tight square. When enough men had made it, the men split into two squares and fought their way to the two gates most convenient for the army waiting outside, and went to work on the portcullises with saws, axes, wedges and hammers; the inside faces had not been reinforced with iron plates. Hacking and hewing in a frenzy, they got through the oak in a superbly organized assault on the top and both sides of the portcullis until the iron outside was bared. Then they took long crowbars and twisted the plates until the whole portcullis tumbled to lie on the ground. The army cheered deafeningly, and charged.

But the Xanthians had a tradition to uphold, and did. The streets were full of pyres, so were the light wells of every insula and the peristyles of all the houses. The men killed their women and children, threw them on to the wood, set fire to it and climbed on top to finish themselves with the same bloody knives.

All of Xanthus went up in flames, not one square foot of it was spared. The soldiers marooned in Sarpedon's temple managed to carry out what valuables they could, and other groups did the same, but Brutus ended in obtaining less from Xanthus than the siege had cost him in time, food, lives. Determined that his Lycian campaign wasn't going to begin in utter ignominy, he waited until the fires died out and had his men comb every inch of the charred wreckage for melted gold and silver.

He did better at Patara, which defied the Romans when the artillery and siege equipment first appeared, but it had no suicidal tradition like Xanthus, and eventually surrendered without the pain of undergoing protracted siege. The city turned out to be very rich, and yielded fifty thousand men, women and children for sale into slavery.

The appetite of the world for slaves was insatiable, for, as the saying went, you either owned slaves, or were slaves. No people anywhere disapproved of slavery, which varied from place to place and people to people. A Roman domestic slave was paid a wage and was usually freed within ten or fifteen years, whereas a Roman mine or quarry slave was worked to death within one year. Slavery too had its social gradations: if you were an ambitious Greek with a skill, you sold yourself into slavery to a Roman master knowing you would prosper, and end a Roman citizen; if you were a hulking German or some other barbarian defeated and captured in battle, you went to the mines or quarries and died. But by far the largest market for slaves was the Kingdom of the Parthians, an empire larger than the world of Our Sea plus the Gauls. King Orodes was eager to take as many slaves as Brutus could send him, for the Lycians were educated, Hellenized, skilled in many crafts, and a handsome people whose women and girl children would be popular. His majesty paid in hard cash through his own dealers, who followed Brutus's army in their own fleet of ships like vultures the depredations of a barbarian horde on the move.

Between Patara and Myra, the next port of call, lay fully fifty miles of the same gorgeous but awful terrain the army had covered to get this far. Building another road was no answer; Brutus now understood why Cassius had advocated sailing, and commandeered every ship in Patara harbor as well as the transports he had sent around from Miletus with food. Thus he sailed to Myra, at the mouth of the well-named Cataractus River.

Sailing proved a bonus in another way than convenience. The Lycian coast was as famous for pirates as the coasts of Pamphylia and Cilicia Tracheia, for in the groins of the mighty mountains lay coves fed by streamlets, ideal for pirate lairs. Whenever he saw a pirate lair, Brutus sent a force ashore and collected a huge amount of booty. So much booty, in fact, that he decided not to bother with Myra, turned his fleet around and sailed west again.

With three hundred million sesterces in his war chest from the Lycian campaign, most of it garnished from pirates, Brutus brought his army back to the Hermus valley in June. This time he and his legates took up residence in the lovely city of Sardis, forty miles inland and more ascetically pleasing than Smyrna.

The coast of Asia Province was not only rugged; it also thrust a series of peninsulas out into the Aegean Sea, which made voyages tedious for merchantmen sailing close inshore, always having to traipse around another rocky protrusion. The last such peninsula on the way to Rhodes was the Cnidan Cheronnese, with the port of Cnidus on its very tip; the entire very long, thin finger of land was simply referred to by the city's name, Cnidus.

For Cassius, Cnidus was handy. He took four legions from the Hermus valley and put them into camp there, while he marshaled his fleets at Myndus on the next peninsula up, just west of the fabulous city of Halicarnassus. He was using a vast number of big, slow galleys from quinquereme down to trireme, nothing any smaller, which he knew the Rhodians, masters of maritime warfare, would deem easy game. His admirals were the same trusty fellows who had made mincemeat out of Dolabella's men: Patiscus, the two Liberators Cassius Parmensis and Decimus Turullius, and Sextilius Rufus. The command of his land army was split between Gaius Fannius Caepio and Lentulus Spinther.

Of course the Rhodians heard about all this activity and sent an innocent-looking pinnace to spy on Cassius; when its crew reported back about the mammoth craft Cassius was employing, the Rhodian admirals had a good laugh. They preferred taut, trim triremes and biremes, usually undecked, with two banks of oars in outriggers and very businesslike bronze beaks for ramming. Rhodians never used marines or soldiers to board the enemy, they simply raced around clumsy warships in deft circles and either forced these leviathans to collide with each other, or got up a good straight run and rammed them so hard they were holed; they were also experts at coming alongside a ship and shearing off its oars.

"If Cassius is stupid enough to attack with his elephants of ships," said the wartime chief magistrate, Alexander, to the wartime chief admiral Mnaseas, "he'll go the way of Poliorketes and King Mithridates the so-called Great, ha ha ha. *Ignominious* defeat! I agree with the Carthaginians of old—no Roman ever born can fight on the sea when the enemy's a seafaring people."

"Yes, but in the end the Romans crushed the Carthaginians," said Archelaus the Rhetor, who had been brought to the city of Rhodus from his idyllic rural retreat because he had once taught Cassius rhetoric when Cassius had been a youth in the Forum.

"Oh, yes!" sneered Mnaseas. "But only after a hundred and fifty years and three wars! And then they did it on land."

"Not entirely," Archelaus persisted stubbornly. "Once they invented the corvus gangplank and could board troops in number, Carthage's fleets didn't do very well."

The two wartime leaders glared at the old pedant and began to wish that they had left him to his bucolic maunderings.

"Send Gaius Cassius an embassage," Archelaus pleaded.

So the Rhodians sent an embassage to see Cassius at Myndus, more to shut Archelaus up than because they thought it would achieve anything. Cassius received the deputation arrogantly and loftily told its members that he was going to wallop them.

"So when you get home," he said, "tell your council to start thinking about negotiating a peace settlement."

Back they went to tell Alexander and Mnaseas that Cassius had sounded so confident! Perhaps it might be best to negotiate? Alexander and Mnaseas hooted in derision.

"Rhodes *cannot* be beaten at sea," said Mnaseas. He lifted his lip in contempt and looked thoughtful. "To illustrate the point, I note that Cassius has his ships out exercising every day, so why don't we show him what Rhodes can do? Catch him sitting on the latrine, dreaming that Roman drill can beat Rhodian skill."

"You're a poet," said Archelaus, who really was a nuisance.

"Why don't you hop off to Myndus and see Cassius yourself?" Alexander suggested.

"All right, I will," said Archelaus.

Who took a pinnace to Myndus and saw his old pupil, pulling all his rhetorical brilliance out of his magical speaking hat to no avail. Cassius heard him out unmoved.

"Go back and tell those fools that their days are numbered" was as much satisfaction as Archelaus could get.

"Cassius says your days are numbered," he told the wartime commanders, and was sent back to his rustic villa in disgrace.

Cassius knew exactly what he was doing, little though Rhodes thought that. His drills and exercises went on remorselessly; he supervised them himself, and punished severely when his ships did not perform up to expectations. A great deal of his time was filled in shuttling back and forth between Myndus and Cnidus, which he could do while supervising, for the land army had to be fit for action too, and he believed in the personal touch.

Early in April the Rhodians picked out their thirty-five best vessels and sent them out on a surprise raid, their quarry Cassius's busily exercising fleet of unwieldy quinqueremes. At first it looked as if the Rhodians would win easily, but Cassius, standing in his pinnace flagging messages to his captains, was not at all flustered. Nor did his captains panic, start to run into each other or present a tempting beam to the enemy. Then the Rhodians realized that the Roman ships were herding them into a smaller and smaller area of water, until finally they could not turn, ram, or perform any of the brilliant maneuvers for which they were so famous. Darkness enabled the Rhodians to break out of the net and dash for home, but behind them they left two ships sunk and three captured.

Rhodes sat ideally poised at the eastern bottom corner of the Aegean Sea; eighty miles long, the lozenge-shaped, hilly, fertile island was large enough to feed itself, as well as to form a barrier to ongoing sea traffic heading for Cilicia, Syria, Cyprus and all points east. The Rhodians had exploited this natural bounty by going to sea, and relied upon their naval superiority to protect their island.

Cassius's land army sailed on the Kalends of May in a hundred transports, with Cassius himself leading eighty war galleys that also carried marines. He was ready on all fronts.

When it saw this huge armada bearing down, out came the entire Rhodian fleet, only to succumb to the same tactics Cassius had used off Myndus; while the sea battle raged, the transports slipped past unharmed, allowing Fannius Caepio and Lentulus Spinther to land their four legions safely on the coast to the west of Rhodus city. Not only were there twenty thousand well-equipped, mail-shirted soldiers forming up into rank and column, but cranes were winching and gangways were rolling staggering amounts of artillery and siege machines ashore! Oh, oh, oh! The horrified Rhodians had no land army of their own, and no idea how to withstand a siege.

Alexander and the Rhodian council sent a frantic message to Cassius that they would capitulate, but even as this was being done, the ordinary people inside Rhodus were busy opening all the gates and doors in the walls to admit the Roman army.

The only casualty was a soldier who fell and broke his arm.

Thus the city of Rhodus was not sacked, and the island of Rhodes sustained little damage.

Cassius set up a tribunal in the agora. Wearing a wreath of victory laurels on his cropped light brown hair, he mounted it clad in his purple-bordered toga. With him were twelve lictors in crimson tunics bearing the axed *fasces*, and two hoary veteran *primipilus* centurions in decorations and shirts of gold scales, one bearing a ceremonial spear. At a gesture from Cassius, the centurion rammed the spear into the tribunal deck, a signal that Rhodes was the prisoner of the Roman war machine.

He had the other centurion, owner of a famously stentorian voice, read out a list of fifty names, including those of Mnaseas and Alexander, had them brought to the foot of his tribunal and executed on the spot. The centurion then read out twenty-five more names; they were exiled, their property confiscated along with the property of the fifty dead men. After which Cassius's impromptu herald bawled out in bad Greek that every piece of jewelry, every coin, every gold or silver or bronze or copper or tin sow, every temple treasure and every item of valuable furniture or fabric were to be brought to the agora.

Those who obeyed willingly and honestly would not be molested, but those who tried to flee or conceal their possessions would be executed. Rewards for information were offered to free men, freedmen, and slaves.

It was a perfect act of terrorism that achieved Cassius's ends immediately. The agora became so piled with loot that the soldiers couldn't carry it away fast enough. Very graciously he allowed Rhodes to keep its most revered work of art, the Chariot of the Sun, but he allowed it to keep nothing else. A legate entered every dwelling in the city to make sure no precious thing remained, while Cassius himself led three of the legions into the countryside and stripped it barer than carrion birds a carcass. Archelaus the Rhetor lost nothing for the most logical of reasons: he had nothing.

Rhodes yielded an incredible eight thousand gold talents, which Cassius translated as six hundred million sesterces.

On his return to Myndus, Cassius issued an edict to all of Asia Province that each city and district was to pay him ten years' tributes or taxes in advance—and that included every community previously enjoying an exempt status. The money was to be presented to him in Sardis.

Though he didn't leave at once for Sardis. Word had come through the regent of Cyprus, the very frightened Serapion, that Queen Cleopatra had assembled a large fleet of warships and merchant vessels for the Triumvirs, even including some of the precious barley she had bought from the Parthians. Neither famine nor pestilence had prevented her making this decision, said Serapion, one of those who wanted Arsinoë on the throne.

Cassius detached Lucius Staius Murcus the Liberator and sixty big galleys from his fleets and ordered him to lie in wait for the Egyptian ships off Cape Taenarum at the foot of the Greek Peloponnese. An efficient man, Staius Murcus did as he was told swiftly, but he waited in vain. Finally a message reached him that Cleopatra's fleet had encountered a violent storm off the coast of Catabathmos, turned and limped back to Alexandria.

However, said Staius Murcus in a note to Cassius, he didn't think he could be of much use in the eastern end of Our Sea, so he was going to take himself and his sixty galleys off to the Adriatic around Brundisium. There, he thought, he could make plenty of mischief for the Triumvirs, attempting to get their armies across to western Macedonia.

Sardis had been the capital of the ancient kingdom of Lydia, and so immensely rich that its king of five hundred years ago, Croesus, was still the standard by which wealth was measured. Lydia fell to the Persians, then passed into the hands of the Attalids of Pergamum, and so, by the testament of the last King Attalus, into Rome's fold in the days when much of the territory Rome owned had been bequeathed to her in wills.

It rather tickled Brutus to choose King Croesus's city as headquarters for the vast Liberator enterprise, the place from which his and Cassius's armies would embark upon their long march westward. To Cassius when he arrived, an irksome nuisance.

"Why aren't we on the sea?" he demanded the moment he had shed his leather traveling cuirass and kilts.

"I'm fed up with looking at ships and smelling fish!" Brutus snapped, caught off guard.

"Therefore I have to make a hundred-mile round trip every time I want to visit my fleets, just to soothe your nose!"

"If you don't like it, go live with your wretched fleets!"

Not a good beginning to the vast Liberator enterprise.

Gaius Flavius Hemicillus, however, was in an excellent mood. "We will have enough funds," he announced after several days in the company of a large staff and many abacuses.

"Lentulus Spinther is to send more from Lycia," said Brutus. "He writes that Myra yielded many riches before he burned it. I don't know why he burned it. Pity, really. A pretty place."

Yet another reason why Brutus was grating on Cassius. What did it matter if Myra was *pretty?*

"Spinther sounds a great deal more effective than you were," Cassius said truculently. "The Lycians didn't offer to pay over ten years' tribute to *you.*"

"How could I ask for something the Lycians had never paid? It didn't occur to me," Brutus bleated.

"Then it should have. It did to Spinther."

"Spinther," Brutus said haughtily, "is an unfeeling clod."

Oh, what's the matter with the man? asked Cassius silently. He has no more idea how to run a war than a Vestal. And if he moans about Cicero's death one more time, I'll throttle him! He hadn't one good thing to say about Cicero for months before his death, now the passing of Cicero is a tragedy outranking the best Sophocles can do.

Brutus wafts along in a world all his own, while I have to do all the real work.

But it wasn't only Brutus who nettled Cassius; Cassius was nettling Brutus quite as much, chiefly because he harped and he harped about Egypt.

"I should have gone south to invade Egypt when I intended to," he would say, scowling. "Instead, you palmed me off with Rhodes—a mere eight thousand gold talents, when Egypt would have yielded a thousand thousand gold talents! But no, don't invade Egypt! Go north and join me, you wrote, as if Antonius was going to be on Asia's doorstep within a *nundinum*. And I *believed* you!"

"I didn't say that, I said now was our chance to invade Rome! And we have money enough from Rhodes and Lycia anyway," Brutus would answer stiffly.

And so it went, neither man in charity with the other. Part of it was worry, part of it the manifest differences in their natures: Brutus cautious, thrifty and unrealistic; Cassius daring, splashy and pragmatic. Brothers-in-law they might be, but in the past they had spent mere days living together in the same house, and that not often. Besides the fact that Servilia and Tertulla had always been there to damp the combustible mixture down.

Though he had no idea he wasn't helping the situation, poor Hemicillus didn't help, always appearing to voice the latest rumor about how much the troops expected as cash donatives, fuss and fret because he'd have to recalculate their expenses.

Then, toward the end of Julius, Marcus Favonius appeared in Sardis asking to join the Liberator effort. After escaping from the proscriptions he had gone to Athens, where he had lingered for months wondering what to do; when his money ran out, he realized that the only thing he could do was go back to war on behalf of Cato's Republic. His beloved Cato was dead four years, he had no family worth speaking of, and both Cato's son and Cato's son-in-law were under arms.

Brutus had been delighted to see him, Cassius far less so, but his presence did compel the two Liberators to put a better face on their constant differences. Until, that is, Favonius walked into the midst of a terrible quarrel.

"Some of your junior legates are behaving shockingly toward the Sardians," Brutus was saying angrily. "There's no excuse for it, Cassius, no excuse at all! Who do they think they are, to push Sardians rudely off their own pathways? Who do they think they are, to walk into taverns, guzzle expensive wine, then refuse to pay for it? You should be punishing them!"

"I have no intention of punishing them," Cassius said, teeth bared in a snarl. "The Sardians need teaching a lesson, they're arrogant and unappreciative."

"When my legates and officers behave that way, I punish them, and you should punish yours," Brutus insisted.

"Shove," said Cassius, "your punishment up your arse!"

Brutus gasped. "You—you *typical* Cassian! There's not a Cassius alive who isn't an oaf, but you're the biggest oaf of all!"

Standing unnoticed in the doorway, Favonius decided that it was time to break the quarrel up, but even as he moved, Cassius swung a fist at Brutus. Brutus ducked.

"Don't, please don't! Please, please, please!" Favonius squawked, arms and hands flapping wildly as Cassius pursued the cringing Brutus with murder written on his face. Desperate to head Cassius off, Favonius threw himself between the two men in an unconsciously wonderful imitation of a panicked fowl.

Or at least that was how the mercurial Cassius saw Favonius as his rage cleared; he burst into howls of laughter while the terrified Brutus dodged behind a desk.

"The whole house can hear you!" Favonius cried. "How can you command an army when you can't even command your own feelings?"

"You're absolutely right, Favonius," said Cassius, wiping the tears of mirth from his eyes.

"You're insufferable!" the unmollified Brutus said to Cassius.

"Insufferable or not, Brutus, you have to suffer me, just as I have to suffer you. Personally I think you're a gutless cocksucker—you'll always provide the orifice! At least I'm the one shoves it in, which makes me a *man*."

In answer, Brutus stalked from the room.

Favonius gazed at Cassius helplessly.

"Cheer up, Favonius, he'll get over his snit," Cassius said, clapping him lustily on the back.

"He had better, Cassius, or your enterprise will come to an abrupt end. All Sardis is talking about your rows."

"Luckily, old friend, all Sardis will soon have other things to talk about. Thank all the gods, we're ready to march."

The great Liberator enterprise got under way two days into Sextilis, the army marching overland to the Hellespont while the fleets made sail for the island of Samothrace. Word had come from Lentulus Spinther that he would meet them on the Hellespont at Abydos, and word had come from Rhascupolis of the Thracians that he had found an ideal site for a mammoth camp on the Gulf of Melas, only a day's march beyond the straits.

No Caesars when it came to rapid movement, Brutus and Cassius pushed their land forces north and west at a pace that saw them take a month to reach the Gulf of Melas, a mere two hundred miles from Sardis. The actual ferrying of troops across the Hellespont, however, took a full *nundinum* of that. Thence they took the sea-level pass that fractured the precipitous terrain of the Thracian Chersonnese, and so came down to the fabulously rich, dreamy expanse of the Melas River valley, where they pitched a more permanent camp. Cassius's admirals left their flagships to join the conference the two commanders held in the little town of Melan Aphrodisias.

And here Hemicillus did his final totting up, for here, the Liberators had resolved, they would pay their land and sea forces those cash bonuses.

Though none of their legions was at full strength, averaging 4,500 men per legion, Brutus and Cassius had 90,000 Roman foot soldiers distributed over 19 legions; they also had 10,000 foreign foot soldiers under Roman Eagles. In cavalry they were extremely well off, having 8,000 Roman-run Gallic and German horse, 5,000 Galatian horse from King Deiotarus, 5,000 Cappadocian horse from the new King Ariarathes, and 4,000 horse archers from the small kingdoms and satrapies along the Euphrates. A total of 100,000 foot and 24,000 horse. On the sea, they had 500 warships and 600 transports moored around Samothrace, plus Murcus's fleet of 60 and Gnaeus Ahenobarbus's fleet of 80 hovering in the Adriatic around Brundisium. Murcus and Ahenobarbus themselves had come to the conference on behalf of their men.

In Caesar's time, it had cost 20 million sesterces to equip one full strength legion with everything: clothing, personal arms and armor, artillery, mules, wagons, oxen teams, tack, tools and implements for the artificers, and supplies of wood, iron, firebricks, molds, cement and other items a legion might need for the manufacture of gear on the march or under siege. It cost a further 12 million to keep a legion in the field for twelve continuous months in good, cheap grain years, what with food, clothing replacements, repairs, general wear and tear and army pay. Cavalry was less expensive because most horse troopers were the gift of foreign kings or chieftains, who paid to outfit them and keep them in the field. In Caesar's case, that had not held true after he dispensed with the Aedui and grew to rely on German cavalry; that, he had to fund himself.

Brutus and Cassius had had to bear the cost of creating and equipping fully half their legions, and also bore the cost of those 8,000 Roman-run horse troopers plus the 4,000 horse archers. Thus what money they had before the campaigns against Rhodes and Lycia had gone on equipping. It was the latter two sources of income that would pay at Melas; with what Lentulus Spinther had squeezed out of Lycia in Brutus's wake, and what the cities and regions of the East had managed to scrape together, the Liberators had 1,500 million sesterces in their war chest.

But there were more men to pay than the legionaries and the horse troopers: they also had to pay the army noncombatants; and the men of the fleets, who included oarsmen, sailors, marines, masters, specialist sailors, artificers and noncombatants. About 50,000 men altogether on the sea, and 20,000 land noncombatants.

It was true that Sextus Pompey didn't charge a fee for his help in the West, where he now virtually controlled the grain sea lanes from the grain provinces to Italy. But he did charge for the grain he sold the Liberators at ten sesterces the *modius* (he was charging the Triumvirs fifteen per *modius*). It took five *modii* to feed a soldier for a month. Between selling Rome back the wheat he stole from her grain fleets and what he sold the Liberators, Sextus Pompey was becoming fabulously rich.

"I have worked out," said Hemicillus to the assembled war council in Melan Aphrodisias, "that we can afford to pay the Roman rankers six thousand each, going up to fifty thousand for a *primipilus* centurion—say—averaging out over the tortuous gradations of centurion rank—twenty thousand per centurion, and there are sixty per legion. Six hundred million for the rankers, a hundred and fourteen million for the centurions, seventy-two million for the horse, and two hundred and fifty million for the fleets. That comes to something over one thousand million, which leaves us with something under four hundred million in the war chest for provisions and ongoing expenses."

"How did you arrive at six hundred million for the rankers?" asked Brutus, frowning as he did the sums in his head.

"Noncombatants have to be paid a thousand each, and there are ten thousand non-citizen foot soldiers to pay as well. I mean, troops need water on the march, their needs have to be catered for—you don't want to run the risk of noncombatants neglecting their duties, do you, Marcus Brutus? They're free Roman citizens too, don't forget. The Roman legions don't use any slaves," Hemicillus said, a trifle offended. "I've done my computations well, and I do assure you that, having taken many more things into account than I have enumerated here, my figures *are* correct."

"Don't quibble, Brutus," said Cassius wearily. "The prize is Rome, after all."

"The Treasury will be empty," Brutus said despondently.

"But once we have the provinces up and running again, it will soon fill" from Hemicillus. He cast a furtive eye around to make sure that no representative from Sextus Pompey sat there, and coughed delicately. "You do realize, I hope, that once you have put Antonius and Octavianus down, you will have to scour the seas of Sextus Pompeius, who may call himself a patriot, but acts like a common pirate. Charging patriots for grain, indeed!"

"When we beat Antonius and Octavianus, we'll have the contents of their war chest," said Cassius comfortably.

"What war chest?" from Brutus, determined to be miserable. "We'll have to go through the belongings of every legionary to find their money, because it will be where our money will be—in the belongings of every legionary."

"Well, actually, I was going to talk about that," said the indefatigable Hemicillus, with another little cough. "I recommend that, having paid your army and navy, you then ask to borrow the money back at Caesar's ten percent simple interest. That way, I can invest it with certain companies and earn something on it. If you just pay it over, it will sit there in legionary belongings earning nothing, which would be a tragedy."

"Who can afford to hire the money in this dreadful economic climate?" Brutus asked gloomily.

"Deiotarus, for one. Ariarathes, for another. Hyrcanus in Judaea. Dozens of little satrapies in the East. A few Roman firms I know that are looking for liquid assets. And if we ask fifteen percent, who's to know except us?" Hemicillus giggled. "After all, we won't have any trouble collecting on the debts, will we? Not with our army and navy our creditors. I also hear that King Orodes of the Parthians is having cash flow troubles. He sold a good deal of barley last year to Egypt, though his own lands are in famine too. I think his credit is good enough to consider him a loan prospect."

Brutus had cheered up tremendously as he listened to this. "Hemicillus, that's wonderful! Then we'll talk to the army and navy representatives and see what they say." He sighed. "I would never have believed how expensive it is to make war! No wonder generals like spoils."

That done, Cassius settled to make his dispositions. "The main base for the fleets will be Thasos," he said briskly. "It's about as close to Chalcidice as ships in any number can go."

"My scouts," said Aulus Allienus smoothly, knowing that Cassius respected him, even if Brutus thought him a Picentine upstart, "tell me that Antonius is marching east along the Via Egnatia with a few legions, but that he's in no fit state to give battle until he's reinforced."

"And that," said Gnaeus Ahenobarbus smugly, "isn't likely to happen in a hurry. Murcus and I have the rest of his army stuck in Brundisium under blockade."

Odd, thought Cassius, that the son had followed the father; Lucius Ahenobarbus had liked the sea and fleets too.

"Keep up the good work," he said, winking. "As for those of our fleets around Thasos, I predict that we'll soon find Triumvir fleets trying to interrupt our supply lines and grab the food for themselves. The drought last year was bad enough, but this year there's no grain to be had in Macedonia or Greece. Which is why I hope not to have to give battle. If we adopt Fabian tactics, we'll starve Antonius and his minions out."

XIV

Philippi: Everything by Halves

From JUNE until DECEMBER of 42 B.C.

GAIUS JULIUS CAESAR OCTAVIANUS

MARCUS VIPSANIUS AGRIPPA

Mark Antony and Octavian had forty-three legions at their command, twenty-eight of them in Italy. The fifteen legions elsewhere were distributed between the provinces the Triumvirs controlled, save for Africa, which was so cut off and absorbed in its local war that, for the moment, it had to wait.

"Three legions in Further Spain and two in Nearer Spain," Antony said to his war council on the Kalends of June. "Two in Narbonese Gaul, three in Further Gaul, three in Italian Gaul, and two in Illyricum. That puts a good curtain between our provinces and the Germani and the Dacians—will deter Sextus Pompeius from raiding the Spains—and, should the opportunity arise, Lepidus, will give you troops for Africa." He grunted. "Food, of course, is the main strain on our purse strings, between the legions and the three million people of Italy, but you should be able to manage in our absence, Lepidus. Once we get hold of Brutus and Cassius, we'll be in better financial condition."

Octavian sat and listened as Antony went on to fill out his plans in greater detail, well content with the first six months of this three-man dictatorship. The proscriptions had put almost twenty thousand silver talents in the Treasury, and Rome was very quiet, too busy licking her wounds to offer trouble, even among the least co-operative elements in the Senate. Thanks to the sale of those distinctive maroon leather shoes to men desirous of senatorial rank, that body had grown back to Caesar's thousand members. If some of them hailed from the provinces, why not?

"What of the situation in Sicily?" Lepidus asked.

Antony grinned sourly and squiggled his brows expressively at Octavian. "Sicily is your province, Octavianus. What do you suggest in our absence?"

"Common sense, Marcus Antonius," Octavian answered levelly. He never bothered to ask Antony to call him Caesar; he knew what the response would be. Antony would keep.

"Common sense?" asked Fufius Calenus, blinking.

"Certainly. For the moment we should permit Sextus Pompeius to regard Sicily as his private fief, and buy grain from him as if he were a legitimate grain vendor. Sooner or later the huge profits he's making will return to Rome's coffers, namely when we have the leisure to deal with him the way an elephant deals with a mouse—*splat!* In the meantime, I suggest that we encourage him to invest some of his ill-gotten gains inside Italy. Even inside Rome. If that leads him to assume that one day he'll be able to return and enjoy his father's old status, well and good."

Antony's eyes blazed. "I hate paying *him!*" he snapped.

"So do I, Antonius, so do I. However, since the state does not own Sicily's grain, we have to pay someone for it. All the state has ever done is tithe, though we can't do that now. In this time of poor harvests, he's asking fifteen sesterces the *modius*, which I agree is extortionate." That sweet and charming smile showed; Octavian looked demure. "Brutus and Cassius pay ten sesterces the *modius*—a discount, but not free grain by any means. Sextus Pompeius, like a few other people I know, will keep."

"The boy's right," said Lepidus.

Another grate on Octavian's hide. "The boy" indeed! You too will keep, you haughty nonentity. One day you'll *all* call me by my rightful name. If, that is, I let you live.

Lucius Decidius Saxa and Gaius Norbanus Flaccus had already taken eight of the twenty-eight legions across the Adriatic to Apollonia, under orders to march east on the Via Egnatia until they found an impregnable bolt-hole in which they could sit and wait for the bulk of the army to catch them up. It was good strategy on Mark Antony's part. When Brutus and Cassius marched west on the same road, they had to be halted well east of the Adriatic, and a formidably entrenched force eight legions strong would bring them to an abrupt stop, no matter how enormous their own army was.

Word from Asia Province was patchy and unreliable; some sources insisted that the Liberators were many months off their invasion, others that they would commence any day now. Both Brutus and Cassius were at Sardis, their spring campaigns a stunning success—what was there to delay them? Time was money when one waged a war.

"We have twenty more legions to ship to Macedonia," Antony went on, "and that will have to be in two segments—we lack the transports to do it all at once. I don't plan on using all the twenty-eight in my attack force. Western Macedonia and Greece proper have to be garrisoned so we get whatever food there is."

"Precious little," grumbled Publius Ventidius.

"I'll take my seven remaining legions directly to Brundisium on the Via Appia," Antony said, ignoring Ventidius. "Octavianus, you'll take your thirteen down the Via Popillia on the west side of Italy in conjunction with all the warships we can muster. I don't want Sextus Pompeius in the vicinity of Brundisium while we're shuttling troops, so that means it's your job to keep him in the Tuscan Sea. I don't think he's terribly interested in events east of Sicily, but I also don't want him tempted. He'd find it easier to re-establish himself in a Liberator Rome than a Triumviral one."

"Who for admiral?" asked Octavian.

"Your command, you pick one."

"Salvidienus, then."

"Good choice," said Antony, approving, and smirked at the old hands like Calenus, Ventidius, Carrinas, Vatinius, Pollio.

He went home to Fulvia well pleased with the way things were going. "I haven't heard a peep out of Pretty Boy," he said, his head cushioned on her breasts as they shared a dining couch; no one else to dinner, a pleasant change.

"He's too quiet," she said, popping a shrimp in his mouth.

"I used to think so, but I've changed my mind, *meum mel*. He can give me twenty years, and he's settled for that. Oh, he's sly and devious, I grant you, but he's not in Caesar's league when it comes to staking his all on a single gamble. Octavianus is a Pompeius Magnus—he likes to have the odds on his side."

"He's patient," she said thoughtfully.

"But definitely not in a position to challenge me."

"I wonder if he ever thought he was?" she asked, and made a slurping noise. "Oh, these oysters are delicious! Try them."

"When he marched on Rome and made himself senior consul, you mean?" Antony laughed, sucked in an oyster. "You're right—perfect! Oh yes, he thought he had me beaten, our Pretty Boy."

"I'm not so sure," Fulvia said slowly. "Octavianus moves in strange ways."

"I'm definitely not in a position to challenge Antonius," Octavian was saying to Agrippa at much the same moment in time.

They too were dining, but sitting on hard chairs at either side of a small table holding a plate of crusty bread, some oil in dipping bowls, and a pile of plain broiled sausages.

"When do you plan to challenge him?" Agrippa asked, chin shining with sausage fat. He had spent most of his day playing medicine ball with Statilius Taurus, and was starving. The plain fare suited his palate, though it never ceased to surprise him that a high aristocrat like Caesar also liked plain fare.

"I won't say boo until after I return to Rome on an equal footing with him as far as the army and the people are concerned. My main obstacle is Antonius's greed. He'll try to steal all the victory laurels when we beat Brutus and Cassius. Oh, we will beat them, I've no doubt of that! But when the two sides meet, my troops have to contribute as much to our victory as Antonius's troops—and I have to lead them," Octavian said, wheezing.

Agrippa stifled a sigh; this awful weather was taking its toll, what with the grit and chaff on every puff of wind. Caesar wasn't well, wouldn't be well until after some good rains had laid the dust and prompted some green growth. Still, he knew better than to remark on the wheezing. All he could do was be there for Caesar.

"I heard today that Gnaeus Domitius Calvinus has come out of his retirement," Agrippa said, pulling the crunchy brown ends off a sausage and saving them to eat last; he had been brought up in a frugal household, treasured treats.

Octavian sat up straighter. "Has he, now? To ally himself with whom, Agrippa?"

"Antonius."

"A pity."

"I think so."

Octavian shrugged, wrinkled his nose. "Well, they're old campaigning comrades."

"Calvinus is to command the embarkation at Brundisium. All the transports are back from Macedonia safe and sound, though it can't be long before some enemy fleet tries to blockade us."

Gnaeus Domitius Ahenobarbus arrived to blockade Brundisium harbor as Antony left Capua with his seven legions, and had been joined by Staius Murcus before Antony reached his destination. With close to a hundred and fifty galleys cruising offshore and the Triumviral fleet accompanying Octavian and his troops down Italy's west coast, Antony had no choice other than to sit and wait for a chance to break out. What he needed was a good stiff sou'wester, as this wind would give him a chance to outdistance pursuit provided Murcus and Ahenobarbus were where blockading ships usually were, off to the south. But no sou'wester blew.

Aware that Caesar's heir should emulate his divine father in speed of movement, Octavian hustled his thirteen legions and reached the lower section of the Via Popillia in Bruttium by the middle of June, with Salvidienus's fleet shadowing him a mile out to sea. Some of Sextus Pompey's handy triremes appeared, but Salvidienus did surprisingly well in the series of skirmishes that followed between Vibo and Rhegium. For those on land, the march was wearisome; it was three times as long as the Via Appia route to Brundisium, hugging the littoral of the Italian foot all the way to Tarentum.

Then, with Sicily clearly visible across the Straits of Messana, came a curt note from Antony: Ahenobarbus and Murcus had him penned up, he couldn't get one single legionary or mule across the Adriatic.

Therefore Octavian would have to forget trying to contain Sextus Pompey, send the fleet to Brundisium in a tearing hurry.

The only problem in obeying that order was Sextus Pompey, whose major fleet chose to block the southern outlet of the straits not long after Octavian had flagged Salvidienus to break out the oars and sails and make haste for Brundisium. Caught in the midst of one chaos by another bearing down on him, the unlucky Salvidienus was too slow bringing his ships into battle formation, and found the fastest of Sextus Pompey's galleys in among his own before he could do more than order up the next rank of vessels. So the early phases of the conflict went all Sextus Pompey's way, but not as decisively as he had hoped; the young Picentine military man was no sloth on the sea either.

"I could do better," muttered Agrippa under his breath.

"Eh?" asked Octavian, beside himself with anxiety.

"Maybe it's sitting on shore watching, Caesar, but I can see how Salvidienus should be doing things, and isn't. For one thing, he has that squadron of Liburnians in the rear, when they ought to be in the front rank—they're faster and nippier than anything Sextus Pompeius has," said Agrippa.

"Then next time, the fleet is yours. Oh, what wretched bad luck! Quintus Salvidienus, extricate yourself! We need your fleet in Brundisium, not on the sea bottom!" Octavian cried, arms rigidly by his sides, fists clenched.

He's *willing* Salvidienus out of it! thought Agrippa.

Suddenly a wind came up out of the northwest that pushed Salvidienus's heavier ships through Sextus Pompey's hordes and allowed his lighter ships to follow in their wake; the Triumviral fleet bore away to the south with two holed triremes making for port in Rhegium, and only minor damage to a few other galleys.

"Statilius," Octavian barked at Gaius Statilius Taurus, "take a pinnace and catch Salvidienus. Tell him he has to get to Brundisium as quickly as possible, then return to me. The army will follow as best it can. Helenus—where's Helenus?" This last query was to his favorite freedman, Gaius Julius Helenus.

"Here, Caesar."

"Take this letter down:

"This is all rather silly, Sextus Pompeius. I am Gaius Julius Caesar Divi Filius, in command of that army your sea captains must surely have reported to you as heading down the Via Popillia in company of a fleet. I gladly concede you the honors of the maritime engagement, but was wondering if there is any possibility that we could meet for a parley? Just the two of us? Preferably neither at sea nor in a place I would have to reach by sea. I am sending you four hostages with this note, in the hope that you will agree to meet me in one *nundinum* at Caulonia."

Gaius Cornelius Gallus, the Brothers Cocceius and Gaius Sosius were chosen to go as hostages; Cornelius Gallus, not a patrician Cornelian but of a family from Ligurian Gaul, was so well known to be one of Octavian's intimates that even an exile like Sextus Pompey would appreciate his value to Octavian. The note, Gallus and the others boarded a second pinnace; the little craft raced off across the deceptively placid waters wherein lurked the awful monsters Scylla and Charybdis.

The army now had to reach Caulonia, on the sole of the Italian foot, in just eight days—only eighty miles, but who knew what the road would be like? This was not a legionary route, and the chain of the Apennines plunged into the Sicilian Sea through high, rugged countryside. The ox wagons and artillery had gone with the rest to be shipped from Ancona, so only men and mules made the march.

Which turned out to be an easy one. The road was in good condition save for an occasional small landslide, and the army reached Caulonia in three days. Octavian sent it onward under the command of another nicknamed Gallus, Lucius Caninius Gallus. His first choice had been Agrippa, but that worthy refused to leave him attended by, as he put it,

"Servants and fools. Who knows whether this son of Pompeius Magnus is honorable? I'm staying with you. So are Taurus and a cohort of the Legio Martia."

Sextus Pompey arrived off Caulonia so suspiciously soon after dawn on the eighth day that the reception committee assumed he had moored somewhere in the neighborhood overnight. His lone ship, a sleek bireme, was faster than anything sitting in what passed for a harbor, and he came ashore in a small boat accompanied by a crew of oarsmen who dragged the boat up on the shingle, then went off in search of a good breakfast.

Octavian advanced to meet him with a smile and his right hand extended.

"I see what the gossip means," said Sextus, shaking it.

"Gossip?" asked Octavian, escorting his guest to the *duumvir*'s house, Agrippa in their wake.

"It says you're very young and very pretty."

"The years will take care of both."

"True."

"You're quite like your father's statues, but darker."

"Did you never see him, Caesar?"

Acknowledgment! Octavian, prone to like Sextus anyway, liked him even more. "In the distance, when I was a child, but he didn't mix with Philippus and the Epicures."

"No, he didn't."

They entered the house, were received by an awed *duumvir*, and taken to his reception room.

"We're not very different in age, Caesar," said Sextus, seating himself. "I'm twenty-five. You are—?"

"Twenty-one in September."

Helenus waited on their needs, but a vigilant Marcus Agrippa stood just inside the door, sword in scabbard and face set.

"Does Agrippa have to be here?" Sextus asked, breaking fresh bread eagerly.

"No, but he thinks he does," Octavian said tranquilly. "He's no gossip. Whatever we say will go no further."

"Ah, there's nothing like new bread after four days at sea!" said Sextus, crunching and tearing with gusto. "Don't like the sea, eh?"

"I hate it," Octavian said frankly, shuddering.

"Well, some men do hate it, I know. I'm the opposite, never happier than when the water's busy."

"A little mulled wine?"

"Yes, but just a little," Sextus said warily.

"I made sure the poker was white-hot, so it won't addle your wits, Sextus Pompeius. Myself, I like a warm drink first thing in the morning, and mulled wine is far preferable to my father's vinegar in hot water."

And so the conversation went while they ate, pleasant and unprovocative. Then Sextus Pompey clasped his hands between his knees and looked up at Octavian from under his brows.

"Just why did you ask to parley, Caesar?"

"Well, I'm here, you see, and it might be years before I get another opportunity to talk to you," said Octavian, face unclouded. "I'm marching on this route with my army and our fleet in order to keep you in the Tuscan Sea. Not unnaturally, we want to ship our forces across the Adriatic in time to stop the Liberators short of Macedonia proper, and Marcus Antonius is of the opinion that you'd rather a Liberator than a Triumviral Rome. Thus he doesn't want you sniffing up Brundisium's arse as well as the Liberator fleets."

"You make it sound," said Sextus, grinning, "as if you yourself are not so sure that I'm a Liberator supporter."

"I keep my options open, Sextus Pompeius, and it's occurred to me that you probably do the same. Therefore I don't automatically suppose you a Liberator supporter. My feeling is that you're a Sextus Pompeius supporter. So I thought that two such open-minded young men as you and I should parley on our own, without any of those elderly, terrifically experienced warriors of the battlefield and the Forum present to remind us of our tender years and our naïveté." Octavian smiled broadly. "Our provinces are, you might say, much the same. I am *supposed* to be in charge of the grain supply, whereas, in actual fact, you are."

"Well put! Go on, I'm agog."

"The Liberator faction is huge and august," said Octavian, holding Sextus's eyes. "So huge and august that even a Sextus Pompeius is liable to be buried beneath a plethora of Junii, Cassii, patrician Claudii and Cornelii, Calpurnii, Aemilii, Domitii—need I go on?"

"No," said Sextus Pompey between his teeth.

"Admittedly you have a large and competent fleet to offer the Liberators, but little else apart from grain—which, my agents say, is not a commodity in short supply for the Liberators, who stripped inland Thrace and all Anatolia—and have a nice deal in place with King Asander of Cimmeria. Therefore it seems to me that your best course is *not* to ally yourself with the Liberators. Indeed, to hope that Rome does not end up a Liberator Rome. They don't need you as badly as I do."

"You, Caesar. What about Marcus Antonius and Marcus Lepidus?"

"They're elderly, terrifically experienced warriors of the battlefield and the Forum. As long as Rome and Italy are fed, and we can buy grain for our forces, they don't really care what I do. Or with whom I dicker, Sextus Pompeius. May I ask you a question?"

"Go ahead."

"What do *you* want?"

"Sicily," said Sextus. "I want Sicily. Without a fight."

The golden head nodded sagely. "A practical ambition for a maritime man positioned on the grain route. An *achievable* one."

"I'm halfway there," said Sextus. "I own the coasts and I've forced Pompeius Bithynicus to—er—hail me as his co-governor."

"Of course he's a Pompeius," Octavian said smoothly.

The olive skin flushed. "Not one of *my* family!" he snapped.

"No. He's the son of Junius Juncus's quaestor when Juncus was governor of Asia Province and my father brought Bithynia into the Roman fold. They made a deal. Juncus took the loot, Pompeius took the name. The first Pompeius Bithynicus wasn't much either."

"Am I correct in thinking that, were I to assume command of the Sicilian militia and spill Pompeius Bithynicus Filius, you would confirm me as governor of Sicily, Caesar?"

"Oh, absolutely," said Octavian blandly. "Provided, that is, that you agree to sell Sicily's grain to Rome of the Triumvirs for ten sesterces the *modius*. After all, you'll completely eliminate the middlemen if you own the *latifundia* and the transports. I do trust that's what you aim for?"

"Oh, yes. I'll own the harvest and the grain fleet."

"Well then . . . You'll have so few overheads, Sextus Pompeius, that you'll make more selling to the Treasury for ten sesterces the *modius* than you currently do selling to all and sundry for fifteen sesterces the *modius*."

"That's true."

"Another, very important question—is there going to be a harvest in Sicily this year?" Octavian asked.

"Yes. Not an enormous harvest, but a harvest nonetheless."

"Which leaves us with the vexed question of Africa. Should Sextius in the New province manage to overcome Cornificius in the Old province and African grain flows to Italy again, naturally you will intercept it. Would you agree to sell it to me for the same ten sesterces the *modius*?"

"Provided that I'm left alone in Sicily, and that the veteran colonies around Vibo and Rhegium in Bruttium are abolished, yes," said Sextus Pompey. "Vibo and Rhegium need their public lands."

Out went Octavian's hand. "Done!"

Sextus Pompey took it. "Done!"

"I'll write to Marcus Lepidus at once and have the veteran colonies relocated on the Bradanus around Metapontum and the Aciris around Heracleia," said Octavian, very pleased. "We tend rather to forget these lands in Rome—the instep's so remote. But the locals are of Greek descent, and lack political power."

The two young men parted on the best of terms, each aware that this amicable verbal treaty had a tenuous time span; when events permitted, the Triumvirs (or the Liberators) would have to strip Sicily from Sextus Pompey and drive him off the seas. But for the moment, it would do. Rome and Italy would eat for the old grain price, and sufficient grain would come to keep them eating. A better bargain than Octavian had envisioned in a time of such terrible drought. For the fate of Aulus Pompeius Bithynicus he cared not a fig; the man's father had offended Divus Julius. As for Africa, Octavian had been busy there too, written off to Publius Sittius and his family in their Numidian fief and begged, for Divus Julius's sake, that Sittius aid Sextius, in return for which, Sittius's brother would come off the proscription list and see his property fully restored. Cales could open its gates.

Having released the four hostages, Sextus Pompey sailed.

"What do you think of him?" Octavian asked Agrippa.

"That he's a worthy son of a great man. His downfall as well as his advantage. He won't share power, even if he considered any of the Triumvirs or the assassins his equal on the sea."

"A pity I couldn't make a loyal adherent out of him."

"You'll not do that," Agrippa said emphatically.

"Ahenobarbus has disappeared, where to or for how long I can't find out," said Calvinus to Octavian when he arrived in Brundisium. "That leaves Murcus's sixty ships on blockade. They're very good, and so is Murcus, but Salvidienus is in the offing, just out of sight. We have reason to believe that Murcus doesn't know. So I think, Octavianus—and Antonius agrees—that we should load every transport we have to the gunwales and make a run for it."

"Whatever you wish," said Octavian. Now, he realized, was not the moment to trumpet his successful negotiations with Sextus; he took himself off to write again to Lepidus in Rome to make sure that slug got the message.

The port of Brundisium had a wonderful harbor containing many branches and almost limitless wharfage, so the groaning, whining soldiers were put aboard the four hundred available transports in the space of two days. Somehow the cursing centurions managed to stuff eighteen of the twenty legions into them; men and mules were packed so tightly that the less seaworthy vessels lay too low in the water to survive a minor gale.

In the absence of Ahenobarbus, Staius Murcus's technique was to hide behind the island at the harbor's narrow mouth and pounce on any ships venturing out. It gave him the advantage of the wind at this time of year, for the only wind that would have benefited the Triumvirs was a westerly, and it was not the season of the Zephyr, it was the season of the Etesians.

The transports sailed in their literal hundreds on the Kalends of Sextilis, swarming out of the harbor just as far apart as their oars permitted. At the same moment as the mass exodus began, Salvidienus brought his fleet in from the northeast ahead of a good wind and swung it in a semi-circle around the island to pen Murcus up. He could get out, yes, but not without a naval battle, and he wasn't at Brundisium to engage in naval battles—he was there to sink transports. Oh, why had Ahenobarbus rushed off on the hunt for a rumored second Egyptian expedition?

Impotent, Murcus had to watch while four hundred transports streamed out of Brundisium all day and far into the night, their way lit by bonfires atop tall rafted towers Antony had originally built as offensive weapons—a vain business, but they came in handy now. Western Macedonia was eighty miles away; half the ships were destined for Apollonia, half for Dyrrachium, where, with any luck, the cavalry, heavy equipment, artillery and the baggage train, all sent from Ancona earlier in the year, would be waiting.

If Italy was dry, Greece and Macedonia were far worse, even on this notoriously wet Epirote shore. The rains that had so dogged other generals from Paullus to Caesar hadn't fallen, wouldn't fall, and the hooves of Antony's cavalry horses plus the oxen and spare mules had trodden whatever grass there was into superfine chaff that the Etesians picked up and blew in the direction of Italy.

Their transport hadn't shaken free of the harbor before the shrinking Octavian began to wheeze loudly enough to be heard as one more component of the noises aboard a rickety ship on a perilous voyage. The hovering Agrippa decided that seasickness was not contributing to Octavian's malady; the water was board-flat and the vessel so overloaded that it sat like a cork, hardly rolling even after it heeled to bear northeast under oar power. No, all he suffered was the asthma.

Neither young man had wanted to seem unduly exclusive when their ship was stuffed with ranker soldiers, so their accommodation was limited to a tiny section of deck just behind the mast, out of the way of the tillers and the captain, but surrounded by men. Here Agrippa had insisted that Octavian place a peculiar-looking bed that had one end sloping upward at a sharp angle. It bore quite a few blankets to cushion the hard wood, but no mattress. Under the frightened eyes of legionaries he didn't know (Legio Martia had been one of the two units left behind in Brundisium), Agrippa propped Octavian in a sitting position on the bed to help him catch his breath. An hour later, sailing free on the Adriatic, held now within Agrippa's arms, he labored fiercely and stubbornly to draw enough air into his lungs, his hands clenched around Agrippa's so strongly that it was to be two days before all the feeling came back. The spasms of coughing racked him until he retched, which seemed to give him a slight temporary relief, but his face was both livid and grey, his eyes turned inward.

"What is it, Marcus Agrippa?" asked a junior centurion.

They know my name, so they know who he is. "An illness from

Mars of the Legions," said Agrippa, thinking quickly. "He's the son of the god Julius, and it's a part of his inheritance to take all your illnesses upon himself."

"Is *that* why we're not seasick?" asked a ranker, awed.

"Of course," lied Agrippa.

"How about we promise offerings to Mars and Divus Julius for him?" someone else asked.

"It will help," said Agrippa gravely. He looked about. "So would some kind of shield against the wind, I believe."

"But there's no wind," the junior centurion objected.

"The air's laden with dirt," said Agrippa, improvising again. "Here, take these two blankets"—he wrenched them from under himself and the oblivious Octavian—"and hold them up around us. It will stop the dirt getting in. You know what Divus Julius always used to say—dirt is a soldier's enemy."

It can't do any harm, Agrippa thought. The important thing is that these fellows don't think any the worse of their commander for being ill—they have to believe in him, not dismiss him as a weakling. If Hapd'efan'e is right about dirty air, then he's not going to get much better as this campaign goes on. So I'm going to harp about his being Divus Julius's son—that he's set himself up as the universal victim in order to bring the army victory, for Divus Julius is not only a god to the People of Rome, he's a god to Rome's armies.

Toward the end of the voyage and after a long night afloat in a vast nothingness, it seemed, Octavian began to recover. He came out of his self-induced trance and gazed at the ring of faces, then, smiling, held out his right hand to the junior centurion.

"We're almost there," he wheezed. "We're safe."

The soldier took his hand, pressed it gently. "You brought us through, Caesar. How brave you are, to be ill for us."

Startled, the grey eyes flew to Agrippa's. Seeing a stern warning in their greenish depths, he smiled again. "I do whatever is necessary," he said, "to nurture my legions. Are the other ships safe?"

"All around us, Caesar," said the junior centurion.

Three days later, every legion safely landed because, rumor had it, Caesar Divi Filius had offered himself up in their place, the two Triumvirs realized that communication with Brundisium had been cut.

"Probably permanently," said Antony, visiting Octavian in his house on top of Petra camp's hill. "I imagine that Ahenobarbus's fleet has returned, so nothing is going to get out, even a small boat. That means news from Italy will have to come through Ancona." He tossed

Octavian a sealed letter. "This came for you that way, along with letters from Calvinus and Lepidus. I hear you've cut a deal with Sextus Pompeius that guarantees the grain supply—very clever!" He huffed irritably. "The worst of it is that some fool of a legate in Brundisium held the Legio Martia and ten cohorts of stiffening troops until last, so we don't have them."

"A pity," said Octavian, clutching his letter. He was lying on a couch propped up with cushions, and looked very sick. The wheezing was still present, but the height of his house in Petra camp had meant some relief from the chaffy dust. Even so, he had lost enough weight to look thinner, and his eyes were sunk into two black hollows of exhaustion. "I needed the Legio Martia."

"Since it mutinied in your favor, I'm not surprised."

"That's water under the bridge, Antonius. We are both on the same side," said Octavian. "I take it that we forget what's still in Brundisium, and head east on the Via Egnatia?"

"Definitely. Norbanus and Saxa are not far to the east of Philippi, occupying two passes through the coastal mountains. It seems Brutus and Cassius are definitely on the march from Sardis to the Hellespont, but it will be some time before they encounter Norbanus and Saxa. We'll be there first. Or at least, I will." The reddish-brown eyes studied Octavian shrewdly. "If you take my advice, you'll stay here, O good luck talisman of the legions. You're too sick to travel."

"I'll accompany my army," said Octavian in mulish tones.

Antony flicked his thigh with his fingers, frowning. "We have eighteen legions here and in Apollonia. The five least experienced will have to stay to garrison western Macedonia—three in Apollonia, two here. That gives you something to command, Octavianus, if you stay."

"You're implying that they have to be from *my* legions."

"If yours are the least experienced, yes!" snapped Antony.

"So of the thirteen going on, eight will belong to you and five to me. As well then that Norbanus's four legions up ahead are mine," said Octavian. "You're in the majority."

Antony barked a short laugh. "This is the oddest war since wars began! Two halves against two halves—I hear that Brutus and Cassius don't work any better in tandem than you and I."

"Equal co-commands tend to be like that, Antonius. Some halves are bigger than others, is all. When do you plan to move?"

"I'll take my eight in one *nundinum's* time. You'll follow me six days later."

"How are our supplies of food? Our grain?"

"Adequate, but not for a long war, and we won't get any from

Greece or Macedonia, there's no harvest whatsoever. The locals are going to starve this winter."

"Then," said Octavian thoughtfully, "it behooves Brutus and Cassius to wage Fabian war, doesn't it? Avoid a decisive battle at all costs and wait for us to starve."

"Absolutely right. Therefore we force a battle, win it, and eat Liberator food." A brusque nod, and Antony was gone.

Octavian turned his letter over to study the seal, which was Marcellus Minor's. How peculiar. Why would his brother-in-law need to write? Came a stab of anxiety: Octavia must surely be due to have her second child. No, not my Octavia!

But the letter was from Octavia.

> You will be happy to know, dearest brother, that I have given birth to a beautiful, healthy baby boy. I suffered hardly at all, and am well.
>
> Oh, little Gaius, my husband says that it is my duty to write before someone who loves you less gets in first. I know it should be Mama to write, but she will not. She feels her disgrace too much, though it is more a misfortune than a disgrace, and I love her just the same.
>
> We both know that our stepbrother Lucius has been in love with Mama ever since she married Philippus. Something she either chose to ignore or else genuinely didn't see. Certainly she has nothing to reproach herself with through the years of her marriage to Philippus. But after he died, she was terribly alone, and Lucius was always there. You were so busy, or else not in Rome, and I had little Marcella, and was expecting again, so I confess I was not attentive enough. Therefore what has happened I must blame on my neglect. I am to blame. Yes, I am to blame.
>
> Mama is pregnant to Lucius, and they have married.

Octavian dropped the letter, conscious of a creeping, awful numbness in his jaws, of his lips drawing back from his teeth in a rictus of disgust. Of shame, rage, anguish. Caesar's niece, little better than a whore. *Caesar's niece!* The mother of Caesar Divi Filius.

Read the rest, Caesar. Finish it, and finish with her.

> At forty-five, she didn't notice, dearest brother, so when she did notice, it was far too late to avoid scandal. Naturally Lucius was eager to marry her. They had planned to marry anyway when

her period of mourning for Philippus was over. The wedding took place yesterday, very quietly. Dear Lucius Caesar has been very good to them, but though his *dignitas* is undiminished among his friends, he has no weight with the women who "run Rome," if you know what I mean. The gossip has been malicious and bitter, the more so, my husband says, because of your exalted position.

Mama and Lucius have gone to live in the villa at Misenum, and will not be returning to Rome. I write this in the hope that you will understand, as I do, that these things *happen,* and do not indicate depravity. How can I not love Mama, when she has always been everything a mother ought to be? And everything a Roman matron ought to be.

Would you write to her, little Gaius, and tell her that you love her, that you understand?

When Agrippa came in some time later he found Octavian lying on his couch, propped against the pillows, his face wet with tears, his asthma worse.

"Caesar! What is it?"

"A letter from Octavia. My mother is dead."

Brutus and Cassius moved westward from the Gulf of Melas in September, not expecting to meet the Triumviral armies until they reached Macedonia proper, somewhere between Thessalonica and Pella. Cassius was adamant that the enemy would not advance east of Thessalonica in this terrible year, for to do so would stretch their supply lines intolerably, given that the Liberator fleets owned the seas.

Then, just after the two Liberators crossed the Hebrus River at Aenus, King Rhascupolis appeared with some of his nobles, riding a beautiful horse and clad in Tyrian purple.

"I came to warn you," he said, "that there is a Roman army about eight legions strong divided between two passes through the hills east of Philippi." He swallowed, looked miserable. "My brother Rhascus is with them, and advising them."

"What's the nearest port?" Cassius asked, not perturbed about what couldn't be remedied.

"Neapolis. It's connected to the Via Egnatia by a road that meets it between the two passes."

"Is Neapolis far from Thasos Island?"

"No, Gaius Cassius."

"I see Antonius's strategy," Cassius said after a moment's thought. "He intends to keep us out of Macedonia, so he's sent eight legions to do that. Not by giving battle, by preventing our going forward. I don't believe Antonius wants a battle, it's not in his best interests, and eight legions aren't enough, he knows that. Who's in command of this advance force?"

"A Decidius Saxa and a Gaius Norbanus. They're very well situated and they'll be hard to dislodge," said Rhascupolis.

The Liberator fleets were ordered to occupy the port of Neapolis as well as Thasos Island, thus ensuring the rapid transfer of supplies to the Liberator army when it arrived.

"As arrive we must," said Cassius in council with his legates, admirals and a silent Brutus, down in the dumps again for some inexplicable reason. "Murcus and Ahenobarbus have the Adriatic closed and Brundisium under blockade, so it will be Patiscus, Parmensis and Turullius in charge of maritime operations around Neapolis. Is there any danger of a Triumviral fleet coming up?"

"Absolutely none," Turullius said emphatically. "Their only fleet—a very big one, but not big enough—enabled them to break most of their army out of Brundisium, but then Ahenobarbus returned, which forced their fleet to retire to Tarentum. Their army will get nothing but grief in the Aegean, rest assured."

"Which confirms my hypothesis that Antonius won't bring the bulk of his army east of Thessalonica," said Cassius.

"Why are you so sure that the Triumvirs don't want a battle?" Brutus asked Cassius in private later.

"For the same reason we don't want one," Cassius said, voice carefully patient. "It's not in their best interests."

"I fail to see why, Cassius."

"Then take my word for it. Go to bed, Brutus. Tomorrow we march west."

Many square miles of salt marsh and a range of tall, jagged hills compelled the Via Egnatia to dive ten miles inland on the plain of the Ganga River, above which stood the old town of Philippi on its rocky mesa. In the massif of nearby Mount Pangaeus, Philip, father of Alexander the Great, had funded his wars to unite Greece and Macedonia; Pangaeus had been extremely rich in gold, long since mined out. That Philippi itself still survived was due to a fertile, if flood prone, hinterland, though its population had dwindled to fewer than a thousand souls when the Liberators and the Triumvirs met there two and a half years after Caesar's death.

Saxa had put himself and four legions in the Corpilan Pass, the more easterly of the two, while Norbanus occupied the Sapaean Pass with his four legions.

Riding out with Cassius, Rhascupolis and the legates to see just how Saxa had dug himself in, Brutus noticed that Saxa had no view of the sea, whereas Norbanus in the more westerly Sapaean Pass had two watchtowers well able to spot any maritime activity.

"Why," said Brutus timidly to Cassius, "don't we lure Saxa out of the Corpilan Pass by loading one of our legions aboard transports and making them cluster along the landward rails so that it looks as if half our army is sailing to Neapolis to march up the road and out-flank him?"

Thunderstruck at this unexpected evidence of military acumen, Cassius blinked. "Well, if either of them is in Caesar's class as a commander it won't work, because sitting between them isn't prising either of them out, but if they're not in Caesar's class, it just might panic them. We'll try it. Congratulations, Brutus."

When a huge fleet stuffed with soldiers hove in sight of Norbanus's watchtowers and cruised toward Neapolis, Norbanus sent a frantic message to Saxa imploring him to withdraw in a hurry. Saxa did as he was told.

The Liberators marched through the Corpilan Pass, which meant they had direct contact with Neapolis, but there ground to a halt. United in the Sapaean Pass, Saxa and Norbanus had fortified their position so formidably that they could not be dislodged.

"In Caesar's class they're not, but they know we can't land our forces west of them before Amphipolis. We're still stuck," said Cassius.

"Can't we just bypass them and land at Amphipolis?" asked Brutus, rather emboldened by his last bright idea.

"What, and put ourselves in the middle of a pincer? Antonius would move east of Thessalonica in a mighty hurry if he knew he had eight legions to fall on our rear," Cassius said, his tones long-suffering.

"Oh."

"Um, if I may speak, Gaius Cassius, there's a goat track along the heights above the Sapaean Pass," said Rhascupolis.

A remark that no one paid any attention to for three days, both commanders having forgotten their school history lessons on Thermopylae, where the stand of Leonidas and his Spartans had finally been thwarted by a goat track called Anopaea. Then Brutus remembered it because Cato the Censor had done the same thing in the same gorge, outflanked the defenders.

"It is a literal goat track," Rhascupolis explained, "so to accommodate troops it will have to be widened. That can be done, but only if the excavators are very quiet and carry water with them. Believe me, there is no water until the goat track ends at a stream."

"How long would the work take?" asked Cassius, failing to take account of the fact that Thracian noblemen were not experts on manual labor.

"Three days," said Rhascupolis, making a wild guess. "I'll go with the road makers myself to prove that I'm not lying."

Cassius gave the job to young Lucius Bibulus, who set off with a party of seasoned sappers, each of whom took three days' water with him. The work was extremely dangerous, for it had to be done right above Saxa and Norbanus in the bottom of the ravine—nor, once he commenced, did Lucius Bibulus think of turning back. This was his chance to shine! At the end of three days the water ran out, but no stream manifested itself. Parched and frightened, the men needed to be coaxed and wheedled into carrying on when the fourth day dawned, but young Lucius Bibulus was too like his dead father to coax and wheedle. Instead, he ordered his work force to continue on pain of a flogging, whereupon they mutinied and began to stone the hapless Rhascupolis. Only a faint sound of trickling water brought them to their senses; the sappers raced to drink, then finished the road and returned to the Liberator camp.

"Why didn't you just send back for more water?" Cassius asked, stunned by Lucius Bibulus's stupidity.

"You said there was a stream" came the answer.

"Remind me in future to put you somewhere that's suited to your mentality!" snarled Cassius. "Oh, the gods preserve me from noble blockheads!"

Since neither Brutus nor Cassius wanted a battle, their army marched over the new high road making as much noise as possible, with the result that Saxa and Norbanus pulled out in good order and retired to Amphipolis, a large timber seaport fifty miles west of Philippi. There, well ensconced—but cursing Prince Rhascus, who hadn't told them of the goat track—they sent word to Mark Antony, rapidly approaching.

Thus by the end of September, Brutus and Cassius owned both passes, and could advance on to the Ganga River plain to make a spacious camp. No fear of floods this year.

"It's a good position here at Philippi," said Cassius. "We hold the Aegean and the Adriatic—Sicily and the waters around it belong to our friend and ally Sextus Pompeius—there's widespread drought—and the Triumvirs won't find food anywhere. We'll settle here for a while, wait for Antonius to realize he's beaten and retreat back to Italy, then we'll invade. By then his troops will be so hungry—and all of Italy so fed up with Triumviral rule—that we'll have a bloodless victory."

They proceeded to make a properly fortified camp, but in two separate halves. Cassius took the hill to the south side of the Via Egnatia for his camp, his exposed flank protected by miles of salt marsh, beyond which lay the sea. Brutus occupied the twin hill on the north side of the Via Egnatia, his exposed flank protected by cliffs and impassable defiles. They shared a main gate on the Via Egnatia itself, but once through that common entrance, two separate camps with separate fortifications existed; free access between them was impossible anywhere, which meant that troops couldn't be shuttled between north and south of the road.

The distance between the summit of Cassius's hill and the summit of Brutus's hill was almost exactly one mile, so between these two rises they built a heavily fortified wall on the west side. This wall didn't travel in a straight line; it bent backward in the middle where it crossed the road at the main gate, giving it the shape of a great curved bow. Within that wall, each camp had its own inner lines of fortification, which then traveled down either side of the Via Egnatia to the commencement of the Sapaean Pass.

"Our army is just too big to put into one camp," Cassius explained to his and Brutus's legates in council. "Two separate camps mean that if the enemy should penetrate one, it can't get inside the other. That gives us time to rally. The side road to Neapolis makes it easy for us to bring up supplies, and Patiscus is in charge of making sure we get those supplies. Yes, when all is said and done, in the highly unlikely event that we should be attacked, our dispositions will answer very well."

No one present contradicted. What was preying on every mind at the council was the news that Mark Antony had reached Amphipolis with eight more legions and thousands of cavalry. Not only that, but Octavian was at Thessalonica and not stopping either, despite reports that he was so ill his conveyance was a litter.

Cassius gave the best of everything to Brutus. The best of the cavalry, the best legions of old Caesarean veterans, the best artillery. He didn't know how else to shore up this hesitant, timid, unmartial partner in the great enterprise. For Brutus was those things, no matter how many occasional tactical inspirations he might have. Sardis had shown Cassius that Brutus cared more for abstractions than he did for the practical necessities war brought in its train. It wasn't *quite* cowardice on Brutus's part, it was more that war and battles appalled him, that he couldn't flog up interest in military matters. When he should have been poring over maps and visiting his men to jolly them along, he was huddled with his three tame philosophers debating something or other, or else writing one of those chilling letters to a dead wife. Yet if he were taxed with his moods and chronic depression, he denied suffering them! Or else he started up about Cicero's murder, and how he *had* to bring the Triumvirs to justice, no matter how unsuited for the task he was. He had a kind of blind faith in rightness as he saw rightness, nor could he credit that evil men like Antonius and Octavianus stood a chance of winning. His stand was for the restoration of the old Republic and the liberties of free Roman noblemen, causes that couldn't possibly lose. Himself very different, Cassius shrugged his shoulders and simply did what he could to protect Brutus from his weaknesses. Let Brutus have the best of everything, and offer to Vediovis, god of doubts and disappointments, that they would be enough.

Brutus never even noticed what Cassius had done.

Antony arrived on the Ganga River plain on the last day of September and pitched camp a scant mile from the western, bow-shaped wall of the Liberators.

He was acutely aware how bad his position was. He had no burnable fuel and the nights were freezingly cold, the baggage train's better food was lagging behind by some days, and the wells he dug in search of more potable water turned out to be as foul and brackish as the river. The Liberators, he deduced, must have access to good springs in that rocky chain of hills behind them, so he sent parties to explore Mount Pangaeus, where he managed to find fresh water—then had to transport it to his camp until his engineers, using troops as laborers, built a makeshift aqueduct.

However, he proceeded to do what any competent Roman general would: protect and fortify his position with walls, breastworks, towers and ditches, then manned them with artillery. Unlike Brutus and Cassius, he built one camp for his and Octavian's foot soldiers, and tacked a smaller camp on either side of it for that fraction of his cavalry whose horses would drink the brackish water. Then he put his two worst legions in the seaward small camp, where his own quarters were located, and left sufficient room in the other small camp for two of Octavian's legions when they arrived. They would act as reserves.

After studying the lie of the land, he decided that any battle hereabouts was going to be an infantry one, so secretly, at dead of night, he sent all but three thousand willing drinkers among his cavalry back to Amphipolis. In locating Octavian's personal headquarters as a mirror image of his own in the other small camp, it did not occur to him that Octavian's illness was affected by the proximity of horses; it simply filled him with fury that the legions thought no worse of the little coward for his girly complaint—indeed, they seemed to think that he was interceding with Mars on their behalf!

Still in a litter, Octavian drew up with his five legions early in October, and the baggage train a day later. When he saw where Antony had put him, he rolled his eyes despairingly at Agrippa, but had too much sense to protest to Antony.

"He wouldn't understand anyway, his own health is too rude. We'll pitch my tent on the outer palisades at the very back, where I might get a sea wind across those marshes and—I hope, I hope!—blow the dust from trampling hooves away from me."

"It will help," Agrippa agreed, amazed that Caesar had gotten this far. The will inside him, he thought, is truly more than mortal. He refuses to quit, let alone die—if only because, should he do either, Antonius would be the chief beneficiary.

"If the wind changes or the dust increases, Caesar," Agrippa added, "you can slip through that little gate there and make your way into the marshes themselves for relief."

Both sides had nineteen legions at Philippi and could marshal about a hundred thousand foot, but the Liberators had over twenty thousand horse, while Antony had reduced his thirteen thousand to a mere three.

"Things have changed since Caesar's time in Gaul," he said to Octavian over a shared dinner. "He thought himself superbly well off if he had two thousand horse to pitch against half of Gaul and a few levies of Sugambri to boot. I don't think he ever fielded more than one horseman to the enemy's three or four."

"I know you're milling your troopers around as if you still had thousands upon thousands of them, Antonius, but you don't," said Octavian, forcing down a piece of bread. "Yet our opponents have a vast cavalry camp up the valley, so Agrippa tells me. Why is that? Something to do with Caesar?"

"I can't find forage," said Antony, wiping his chin, "so I'm betting that what cavalry I have will be enough. Just like Caesar. It's going to be a foot-slogger battle."

"Do you think they'll fight?"

"They don't want to, that I know. But eventually they'll have to, because we're not going away until they do."

Antony's abrupt arrival had shattered Brutus and Cassius, positive that he would skulk at Amphipolis until he realized that he was doing himself no good in Thrace. Yet here he was, it seemed spoiling for a battle.

"He won't get one," said Cassius, frowning at the salt marshes.

The very next day he started work on his exposed salt marsh flank, bent on extending his fortifications right out into their middle, thus rendering it impossible for the Triumvirs to get around behind his lines. At the same time the gate across the Via Egnatia began to put forth ditches, extra walls and palisades; previously Cassius had thought that the Ganga River, flowing right in front of their two hills, would provide sufficient protection, but every day its level visibly dropped in this cold, rainless autumn of a cold, rainless year. Men could not only cross it, they could now fight in it. Therefore, more defenses, more fortifications.

"Why are they so busy?" Brutus asked Cassius as they stood atop Cassius's hill, his hand pointing to the Triumviral camp.

"Because they're preparing for a major engagement."

"Oh!" gasped Brutus, and gulped.

"They won't get one," said Cassius, tones reassuring.

"Is that why you've extended your defenses into the swamp?"

"Yes, Brutus."

"I wonder what they're thinking about all this in Philippi town when they look down on us?"

Cassius blinked. "Does what Philippi town thinks matter?"

"I suppose not," said Brutus, sighing. "I just wondered."

October dragged on, saw nothing beyond a few minor skirmishes between foraging parties. Every day the Triumvirs stood waiting for battle, every day the Liberators ignored them.

To Cassius it seemed that this daily brandishing of arms was all the Triumvirs were doing, but he was wrong. Antony had decided to outflank Cassius in the marshes, and had put more than a third of the whole army to laboring in them. The noncombatants and baggage train attendants were clad in armor and made to imitate soldiers at the brandishing of arms ritual, while the soldiers toiled. To them, the work was a signal that battle was in the offing, and any soldier worth his salt looked forward to battle. Their mood and their attitude were sanguine, for they knew that they were well generaled and that most men lived through a fight. Not only did they have the great Marcus Antonius, they also had Caesar Divi Filius, who was their sacrificial victim as well as their darling.

Antony began to cut a negotiable channel through the marshes alongside Cassius's extended flank, his plan to come around behind and block the road to Neapolis as well as attack Cassius's underbelly. Every day for ten days he pretended to call his men to assemble for battle, while more than a third of them sweated in the marshes, hidden from Cassius by swamp grass and reeds. They labored to build a firm roadway, even driving piles to throw stout bridges across bottomless fens—and all in utter silence. As they progressed they equipped the road with salients ready to receive fortifications that would turn them into redoubts complete to towers and breastworks.

But Cassius saw none of it, heard none of it.

On the twenty-third day of October, Cassius turned forty-two; Brutus was four and a half months younger than he. By rights he ought to have been consul this year; instead, he was at Philippi out-waiting a determined enemy. Just how determined, he learned at dawn on this birth anniversary; Antony abandoned secrecy and sent a column of shock troops to occupy all the salients, use the materials put there to turn them into redoubts.

Aghast, Cassius raced to cut Antony off by trying to extend his fortifications all the way to the sea; he used his entire army, and drove them ruthlessly. Nothing else entered his mind, even the possibility that this was the start of something far bigger than one army trying to outflank the other. Had he only stopped to think, he might have realized what was really in the wind, but he didn't. So he threw battle preparedness away among his own troops, and completely forgot all about Brutus and his troops, to whom he sent no word, let alone orders. Not having heard a word from Cassius, Brutus assumed as the racket built that he was to sit pat and do nothing.

At noon Antony attacked on two fronts, using most of the combined army; only Octavian's two most inexperienced legions were held in reserve inside his small camp. Antony lined his men up facing east at Cassius's camp, then swung half of his line south to charge Cassius's men as they worked desperately in the swamps, while the other half charged at the main gate across the road, but on Cassius's side of it. Those at the main gate front had ladders and grapples, and fell to with great enthusiasm, delighted that the battle had finally come on.

The truth was that even as Antony attacked, Cassius was still convinced that Antony didn't want a battle. Though he and Antony were much the same age, they had not mixed in the same circles as children, or youths, or men. Antony the bully-boy demagogue riddled with vices, Cassius the martial scion of an equally old noble plebeian family doing everything the correct way: when they met at Philippi, neither man knew how the other's mind worked. So Cassius failed to take Antony's recklessness into account, he assumed that his opponent would act as he would himself. Now, with battle thrust upon him, it was too late to organize his resistance or send word to Brutus.

Antony's troops ran at Cassius's marsh wall under a hail of missiles and routed Cassius's front line, men drawn up outside the wall on dry ground. As soon as the front line fell, the Triumviral soldiers stormed Cassius's outer defenses and cut off those still toiling in the marshes. Good legionaries that they were, they had their arms and armor with them; they scrambled for battle and rushed up to join the fight, but Antony dealt with them by wheeling a few cohorts and driving them, leaderless, back into the swamps. There his shock troops manning the redoubts took over and rounded most of them up like sheep. Some managed to evade capture, sneaked around behind Cassius's hill, and sought shelter in Brutus's camp.

With the marsh attack an assured success, Antony turned his attention to the assault on Cassius's camp alongside the main gate, where his men had part of the wall down, were up and over to tackle Cassius's inner line of fortifications.

Thousands of soldiers stood along the Via Egnatia wall of Brutus's camp in full war gear, ears straining for the sound of a bugle or the bellowing of a legate. In vain. No one gave them the order to go to Cassius's rescue. So at two in the afternoon, the watchers tooks matters into their own hands. Without orders, they unsheathed their swords, dropped from Brutus's ramparts and charged Antony's men as they tore down Cassius's inner defenses. They did well until Antony brought up some of his reserves and threw them into a line between his own men and Brutus's men, at a disadvantage because they were attacking uphill.

These men of Brutus's were the hoary old veteran Caesareans; the moment they saw their cause was hopeless, they gave up that fight and embarked upon another. There stood Octavian's small camp, so they turned and charged it, literally romped into it. It held those two reserve legions, the bulk of the baggage train and a few cavalrymen. No match for the attackers. Brutus's hoary old Caesarean veterans took the camp, killed those defenders who stood up to them, and proceeded into the main camp, where there were no defenders at all. Having thoroughly looted the Triumviral camps, at six o'clock they turned and went home in the darkness to Brutus's hill.

At the start of the conflict a huge pall of dust had arisen, so dry was the ground outside the marshlands; never was a battle so befogged as First Philippi. For which fact Octavian could give thanks, for it spared him the ignominy of being captured; feeling the asthma worsening, with Helenus's assistance he had gotten himself through the small gate and made his way to the marshes, where he could face the sea and *breathe*.

But for Cassius the opaque cloud meant total loss of contact with what was going on now that the swamp battle had gone all Antony's way. Even atop the hill inside his camp, he could see nothing. Brutus's camp, such a short distance away, was blotted from sight, utterly invisible. What he did know was that the enemy was penetrating his defenses along the Via Egnatia, and that his camp was inevitably doomed. Was Brutus under the same ferocious assault? Was Brutus's camp doomed too? He had to presume so, but he couldn't see.

"I'm going to try to find a vantage spot," he said to Cimber and Quinctilius Varus, with him. "Get yourselves away, I think we're defeated. I think—but I don't *know!* Titinius, will you come with me? We might be able to see from Philippi itself."

So at half after four in the afternoon, Cassius and Lucius Titinius mounted a pair of horses and rode out the back gate, around the rear of Brutus's hill, and came to the road that led up to Philippi's mesa. An hour later, with dusk closing in, they reached the heights above the dust cloud and looked down. To see that the light below had died and the pall lay like a higher level, flat, featureless plain.

"Brutus must be done for as well," said Cassius to Titinius, his voice dull. "We've come so far, and all for nothing."

"We still don't really know," Titinius comforted.

Then a group of horsemen emerged from the brown fog, coming up the hill toward them at a gallop.

"Triumviral cavalry," said Cassius, peering.

"They could as easily be ours—let me intercept them and find out," said Titinius.

"No, they look like Germans to me. Don't go, please!"

"Cassius, we have German troopers too! I'm going."

Kicking his horse in the ribs, Titinius turned and rode down to meet the newcomers. Cassius, watching, saw them surround his friend, take hold of him—the noise of cries drifted up to him.

"He's taken," he said to Pindarus, his freedman who bore his shield, and dismounted, struggling to unbuckle his cuirass. "As a free man, Pindarus, you owe me nothing except my death." His dagger came free of its sheath, the same knife he had twisted so cruelly in Caesar's face—odd, all he could think of at this moment was how much he had hated Caesar at that moment. He held the dagger out to Pindarus. "Strike well," he said, baring his left side for the blow.

Pindarus struck well. Cassius pitched forward to lie in the road; his freedman stared down, weeping, then scrambled on to his horse and spurred it away toward the town above.

But the German cavalry troopers belonged to the Liberators, and had come to tell Cassius that Brutus's men had stormed the Triumviral camp, won a victory. First Philippi was a draw. With Titinius in their midst, they came up the slope to find Cassius alone and dead, his horse nosing at his face. Tumbling from the saddle, Titinius ran to him, held him close and wept.

"Cassius, Cassius, it was *good* news! Why didn't you wait?"

There seemed no point in continuing to live if Cassius was dead. Titinius pulled his sword and fell on it.

Brutus had spent the whole of that frightful afternoon on top of his hill, trying vainly to see the field. He had no idea what was happening, had no idea that several of his legions had taken matters into their own hands and won a victory, had no idea what Cassius expected him to do. Nothing, was what he presumed, and "Nothing, I presume" was what he told his legates, friends, all those who came badgering him to do *something*, do *anything!*

It was the disheveled and breathless Cimber who told him of his victory, the spoils his legions had dragged across the Ganga River whooping in jubilation.

"But—but Cassius didn't—didn't order that!" said Brutus with a stammer, eyes dismayed.

"They did it anyway, and good for them! Good for us too, you doleful stickler!" Cimber snapped, patience tried.

"Where's Cassius? The others?"

"Cassius and Titinius rode for Philippi town to see if they could discern what's happening in this fog. Quinctilius Varus thought all was lost, and fell on his sword. About the rest, I don't know. Oh, was there ever such a mess?"

Darkness fell, and slowly, very slowly, the dust cloud began to settle. No one on either side would be able to assess the results of this day until the morrow, so those Liberators who had survived it gathered to eat in Brutus's wooden house, bathed and changed into warm tunics.

"Who died today?" Brutus asked before the meal was served.

"Young Lucullus," said Quintus Ligarius, assassin.

"Lentulus Spinther, fighting in the marshes," said Pacuvius Antistius Labeo, assassin.

"And Quinctilius Varus," Cimber, assassin, added.

Brutus wept, especially for the unflappable and innovative Spinther, son of a more torpid, less worthy man.

Came the sound of a commotion; young Cato burst into the room, eyes wild. "Marcus Brutus!" he cried. "Here! Out here!"

His tone brought the dozen men present to their feet, then to the door. On the ground just outside, the bodies of Gaius Cassius Longinus and Lucius Titinius lay on a rough litter. A thin scream erupted from Brutus, who fell to his knees and began to rock, his hands covering his face.

"How?" asked Cimber, taking command.

"Some German cavalry brought them in," young Marcus Cato said, standing stiffly, pose martial; his father would not have known him. "It seems Cassius thought they were Antonius's troopers come to take him prisoner—he and Titinius were on the road at Philippi. Titinius went to intercept them and found out that they were ours, but Cassius killed himself while Titinius was away. He was dead when they reached him. Titinius fell on his sword."

"And where," roared Mark Antony, standing amid the ruins of his camp, "were you while all this was going on?"

Leaning on Helenus—he dared not look at the silent Agrippa, whose hand was on his sword—Octavian stared into the small, angry eyes without flinching. "In the marshes trying to breathe."

"While those *cunni* stole our war chest!"

"I'm quite sure," Octavian wheezed, lowering his long fair lashes, "that you'll get it back, Marcus Antonius."

"You're right, I will, you useless, pathetic ninny! You mama's boy, you waste of a good command! Here was I thinking I'd won, and all the time some renegades from Brutus's camp were plundering my camp! *My camp!* And several thousand men dead into the bargain! What's the point in killing eight thousand of Cassius's men when I lose men *inside my own camp?* You couldn't organize a bun fight!"

"I never claimed I could organize a bun fight," Octavian said calmly. "You made the dispositions for today, I didn't. You hardly bothered to tell me you were attacking, and you certainly didn't invite me to your council."

"Why don't you give up and go home, Octavianus?"

"Because I am co-commander of this war, Antonius, no matter how you feel about that fact. I've contributed the same number of men—they were *my* infantry died today, not yours!—and more of the money than you have, for all your bellowing and your blustering. In future, I suggest that you include me in your war councils and make better provision for safeguarding our camp."

Fists clenched, Antony hawked and spat on the ground at Octavian's feet, then stormed away.

"Let me kill him, please," Agrippa pleaded. "I could take him, Caesar, I know I could! He's getting old, and he drinks too much. Let me kill him! It can be fair, I'll fight a duel!"

"No, not today," said Octavian, turning to walk back to his battered tent. Noncombatants were digging pits by torchlight, as there were many horses to bury. A dead horse meant a cavalryman who couldn't fight, as Brutus's soldiers well knew. "You were in the thick of things, Agrippa— Taurus told me. What you need is sleep, not a duel with a vulgar gladiator like Antonius. Taurus told me that you won nine gold *phalerae* for being the first over Cassius's wall. It should have been a *corona vallaris*, but Taurus says Antonius quibbled because there were two walls, and you weren't first over both of them. Oh, that makes me so proud! When we fight Brutus, you'll be commanding the Fourth Legion."

Though he swelled with happiness for the praise, Agrippa was more worried about Caesar than concerned with himself. After that undeserved dressing-down from a boar like Antonius, he thought, Caesar should be black in the face and dying. Instead, the roaring out seemed to act like a magical medicine, improved his condition. How controlled he is. Never turned a hair. He has his own sort of bravery. Nor will Antonius get anywhere if he tries to undermine Caesar's reputation among the legions by mocking him for cowardice today. They know Caesar is ill, and they will think that his illness today helped them win a great victory. For it is a great victory. The troops we lost were our worst. The troops the Liberators lost were Cassius's best. No, the legions won't believe Caesar a coward. It's inside Rome among Antonius's cronies and the senatorial couch generals that men will believe Antonius's lying stories. There, he'll forget to mention illness.

Brutus's camp was full to overflowing; perhaps twenty-five thousand of Cassius's soldiers had made it to haven inside. Some of them were wounded, most were merely exhausted from laboring in the marshes and then trying to fight. Brutus had extra rations broken out of Stores, made the noncombatant bakers work as hard as the soldiers had in the swamps, laid on fresh bread and lentil soup laced with plenty of bacon. It was so cold, and firewood was hard to come by because trees felled from the hills behind were too green to burn yet. Hot soup and bread-and-oil would put some warmth into them.

When he thought of how the troops were going to react to the death of Cassius, Brutus panicked. He bundled all the noble bodies into a cart and secretly sent them to Neapolis in the charge of young Cato, whom he instructed to cremate them there and send the ashes home before returning. How terrible, how unreal to see Cassius's face leached of life! It had been more alive than any other face he had ever set eyes on. They had been friends since school days, they became brothers-in-law, their lives inextricably intertwined even before killing Caesar had fused them together for better or worse. Now he was alone. Cassius's ashes would go home to Tertulla, who had so wanted children, but never managed to carry them. It seemed a fate common to Julian women; in that, she had taken after Caesar. Too late for children now. Too late for her, too late for Marcus Brutus as well. Porcia is dead, Mama alive. Porcia is dead, Mama alive. Porcia is dead, Mama alive.

Then after Cassius's body had gone, a peculiar strength flowed into Brutus; the enterprise had entirely passed to him, he was the one Liberator left who mattered to the history books. So he wrapped a cloak around his thin, stooped frame and set out to do what he could to comfort Cassius's men. They felt their defeat bitterly, he discovered as he went from one group to another to talk to them, calm them down, soothe them. No, no, it wasn't your fault, you didn't lack valor or determination, Antonius the unprincipled sneaked up on you, didn't behave like a man of honor. Of course they wanted to know how Cassius was, why it wasn't he visiting them. Convinced that news of his death would utterly demoralize them, Brutus lied: Cassius was wounded, it would be some days before he was back on his feet. Which seemed to work.

As dawn neared, he summoned all his own legates, tribunes and senior centurions to a conference in the assembly place.

"Marcus Cicero," he said to Cicero's son, "it is your job to confer with my centurions and attach Cassius's soldiers to my legions, even if they go to over-strength. But find out if any of his legions survived intact enough to retain their identities."

Young Cicero nodded eagerly; the most painful aspect of being the great Cicero's son was that he ought by rights to have been Quintus

Cicero's son, and young Quintus the great Cicero's. For Marcus Junior was warlike and unintellectual, whereas Quintus Junior had been clever, bookish and idealistic. The task Brutus had just given him suited his talents.

But having comforted Cassius's men, the peculiar strength drained out of Brutus to be replaced by the old despondency.

"It will be some days before we can offer battle," said Cimber.

"Offer battle?" Brutus asked blankly. "Oh no, Lucius Cimber, we won't be offering battle."

"But we must!" cried Lucius Bibulus the noble blockhead.

The tribunes and centurions were exchanging glances, looking sour; everyone, it was clear, wanted a battle.

"We sit here where we are," said Brutus, drawing himself up with as much dignity as he could muster. "We do not—I repeat, *we do not!*—offer battle."

Dawn saw Antony lined up for battle, however. Disgusted, Cimber summoned the Liberator army to do the same. There was actually an attempt at an engagement, broken off when Antony withdrew; his men were tired, his camps in dire need of much attention. All he had intended to do was to show Brutus that he meant business, he was not going to go away.

The day after that, Brutus called a general assembly of all his infantry and addressed them in a short speech that left them feeling winded, wronged. For, said Brutus, he had no intention of giving battle at any time in the future. It wasn't necessary, and his first priority was to protect their precious lives. Marcus Antonius had bitten off more than he could chew because all he had to chew was air; there were no crops or animals in Greece, Macedonia and western Thrace, so he was going to starve. The Liberator fleets controlled the seas, Antonius and Octavianus could bring supplies from nowhere!

"So relax and be comfortable, we have plenty to eat until next year's harvest, if necessary," he concluded. "However, long before then, Marcus Antonius and Caesar Octavianus will be dead from lack of food."

"That," said Cimber between his teeth, "went down very badly, Brutus! They want a fight! They don't want to sit comfortably and eat while the enemy starves—*they want a fight!* They're soldiers, not Forum frequenters!"

Brutus's answer was to open his war chest and give each and every soldier a cash donative of five thousand sesterces as thanks for their bravery and loyalty. But the army took it as a bribe, and lost whatever respect they might have felt for Marcus Brutus. He tried to sweeten the gift by promising them a lucrative, short campaign in Greece and Macedonia after the Triumvirs had scattered to eat straw, insects, seeds—think of sacking Spartan Lacedaemon, Macedonian Thessalonica! The two richest cities left untouched.

"The army doesn't want to sack cities, it wants to fight!" said Quintus Ligarius, furious. "It wants to fight here!"

But no matter who said what to him, Brutus refused to fight.

By the beginning of November, the Triumviral army was in severe trouble. Antony sent foraging parties as far afield as Thessaly and the valley of the river Axius far above Thessalonica, but they came back with nothing. Only a sally into the lands of the Bessi along the river Strymon produced grain and pulses, for Rhascus, smarting because he hadn't remembered the goat track in the Sapaean Pass, offered to show them where to go. The presence of Rhascus hadn't improved relations between Antony and Octavian: the Thracian prince refused to deal with Antony, insisted on talking to *Caesar*. Who handled him with a deference Antony could not have summoned up. Octavian's legions returned with enough edibles to last another month, but no longer.

"It's time," said Antony shortly thereafter, "that you and I conferred, Octavianus."

"Sit down, then," said Octavian. "Confer about what?"

"Strategy. You're not a commander's bootlace, boy, but you're definitely a crafty politician, and maybe a crafty politician is who we need. Have you any ideas?"

"A few," said Octavian, maintaining an expressionless face. "To begin with, I think we should promise our troops a twenty-thousand bonus."

"You're joking!" Antony gasped, sitting upright in a hurry. "Even with our losses, that would amount to eighty thousand silver talents, and there isn't that much money this side of Egypt."

"That's absolutely true. Nevertheless, I think we should go ahead and make that promise. Sufficient unto the day, my dear Antonius. Our men aren't fools, they know that we don't have the money. However, if we can take Brutus with his camp in one piece and the road to Neapolis closed, we'll find many thousands of silver talents. Our troops are clever enough to realize that too. An extra incentive to force a battle."

"I see your point. All right, I agree. Anything else?"

"My agents inform me that there's a great deal of doubt in Brutus's mind."

"Your agents?"

"One does what one's physical and mental equipment make it possible to do, Antonius. As you constantly reiterate, neither my physical nor my mental equipment makes me a general's bootlace. However, there's a strong streak of Ulysses in me, so, like that interestingly devious man, I have spies in our own Ilium. One or two quite high up the command chain. They feed me information."

Jaw dropped, Antony stared. "Jupiter, you're deep!"

"Yes, I am," Octavian agreed blandly. "My agents say that it preys on Brutus's mind that so many of his troops once belonged to Caesar. He's not sure of their loyalty. Cassius's troops also worry him—he thinks they have no faith in him."

"And how much of Brutus's state of mind is due to the whispers of your agents?" Antony asked shrewdly.

Caesar's smile dawned. "A little, for sure. He's vulnerable, our Brutus. A philosopher and a plutocrat all in one. Neither half believes in war—the philosopher because it's repulsive and destructive, the plutocrat because it ruins business."

"What's that to the point you're obviously trying to make?"

"That Brutus is vulnerable. He can be pressured into giving battle, I think." Octavian leaned back with a sigh. "As to how we provoke his men into insisting upon battle, I leave to you."

Antony got up, looked down at the golden head with a frown. "One more question."

"Yes?" asked Octavian, looking up with lambent eyes.

"Do you have agents in our army?"

Another of Caesar's smiles. "What do you think?"

"I think," Antony snarled, peeling back the tent flap, "that you're warped, Octavianus! You're too crooked to lie straight in bed, and that's something no one could ever say about Caesar. He was straight as an arrow, always. I despise you."

As November wore on, Brutus's dilemma grew. No matter which way he turned, every face was set against him, for every man wanted one thing, and one thing only—a battle. To compound his woes, Antony marched his army out every day and lined it up, whereupon those in its front ranks began to howl like hungry curs, yammer like rutting curs, whine like kicked curs. Then they shrieked insults at the Liberator soldiers—they were cowards, spineless weaklings, afraid of a fight. The din penetrated every inch of Brutus's camp, and all who heard what the Triumviral troops were screaming gritted their teeth, hated it—and hated Brutus for not consenting to battle.

Ten days into November, and Brutus began to waver; not only his fellow assassins, his other legates and his tribunes were at him constantly, but the centurions and rankers had joined the perpetual chorus. Not knowing what else to do, Brutus shut his door and sat inside his house, his head in his hands. The Asian cavalry was leaving in droves, not even bothering to conceal the fact; since before First Philippi, grazing had been a problem and water was available only in the hills, to which every horse had to be led once a day for a drink. Like Antony, Cassius had known that the combat would not involve much cavalry, so he had begun to send them home. Now, after First Philippi, the trickle had become a spate. If battle did come, Brutus wouldn't be able to field more than five thousand horse, and didn't understand that even this number was too large. He thought it far too small.

When he did venture out of his house, only because he thought he must occasionally, those whispers and shouts all seemed aimed at pointing out that so many of his troops used to belong to dead Caesar, and that every day they could see the yellow thatch of Caesar's heir as he walked up and down the front line smiling and joking with his troops. So back Brutus would go to hide, sit with his head in his hands.

Finally, the day after the Ides, Lucius Tillius Cimber barged unannounced into the room, marched across to the startled Brutus and yanked him to his feet.

"Whether you want to or not, Brutus, you're going to fight!" Cimber yelled, beside himself with rage.

"No, it would be the end of everything! Let them starve," Brutus whimpered.

"Issue battle orders for tomorrow, Brutus, or I'll relieve you of the command and issue them myself. And don't think that I've just taken it upon myself to say this—I have the backing of all the Liberators, the other legates, the tribunes, the centurions, and the soldiers," said Cimber. "Make up your mind, Brutus—do you want to retain the command, or are you going to give it to me?"

"So be it," said Brutus dully. "Give the battle orders. But remember when it's over and we're beaten that I didn't want this."

At dawn the Liberator army came out of Brutus's camp and lined up on their side of the river. An anxious and fretful Brutus had badgered his tribunes and centurions to make sure that the men were never too far from free ingress to the camp, that all had a safe avenue of retreat—both tribunes and centurions looked amazed, proceeded to ignore him. What was he doing, trying to tell the men that the battle was lost before it began?

But Brutus managed to get that message to the ranks anyway. While Antony and Octavian strode down their lines shaking hands with the soldiers, smiling, joking, wishing them the protection of Mars Invictus and Divus Julius, Brutus mounted a horse and rode down his lines telling his soldiers that it was their own fault if they lost today. It was they had insisted upon this battle, he himself wanted no part of it, he had been forced into it against his better judgement. Face mournful, eyes teary and sad, shoulders sagging. By the time he ended his ride, most of his troops were wondering why they had ever enlisted under this defeatist misery.

A sentiment they had plenty of time to voice among themselves when no bugle call sounded battle. From dawn they stood in rank and file, leaning on their shields and *pila*, glad that it was a cloudy, late autumn day. Noncombatants brought food around at noon and both sides ate at their posts, went back to leaning on their shields and *pila*. What a farce! Plautus couldn't have written a more ludicrous one.

"Give battle, Brutus, or take off the general's cape," said Cimber at two in the afternoon.

"Another hour, Cimber, just one more hour. Then it will have come on too late to be decisive, because the light will soon be gone. Two-hour battles can't kill too many, or be decisive," said Brutus, convinced he had dreamed up another of those inspirations that had even awed Cassius.

Cimber stared, confounded. "What about Pharsalus? You were *there*, Brutus! Less than one hour was long enough."

"Yes, but very few died. I'll sound the bugles in another hour, not a moment before," said Brutus stubbornly.

So at three the bugles sounded. The Triumviral army gave a cheer and charged; the Liberator army gave a cheer and charged. An infantry battle once again; the cavalry on the fringes of the field did little save cruise around each other.

The two massive collections of foot came together fiercely, with huge strength and vigor. There were no preliminary sallies with *pila* or arrows, the men lusted too passionately to have at each other, smash bodies and thighs with upthrust short swords. From the start it was hand-to-hand fighting, for both sides had waited too long to clash. The slaughter was immense; neither side gave an inch. When men in the front ranks fell, those behind moved up to take their places perched atop the dead and badly wounded, shields around, hoarse from screaming war cries, sword blades flickering thrust, stab, thrust, stab.

Octavian's five best legions formed Antony's right wing, with Agrippa and his Fourth Legion closest to the Via Egnatia. Since it had been Octavian's troops lost the camps, these five legions had a score to settle with Brutus's veterans, opposite them on Brutus's left wing. After almost an hour of a struggle that neither yielded nor gained any ground, Octavian's five legions began to pile on so much weight that they literally pushed Brutus's left wing back by sheer brute force.

"Oh!" cried the watching Octavian to Helenus, enraptured. "They look as if they're turning some massive machine around! Push, Agrippa, push! Turn them!"

Very slowly Brutus's old Caesareans began to yield ground, the pressure on them increasing until it was so remorseless they were compelled to break ranks. Even so, there was no panic, no flight from the field. Simply that as the rear ranks realized that the front ranks were giving way, they too began to retreat.

An hour after the two armies met, the strain became too much to bear. Suddenly the speed of the retreat on Brutus's left turned into a stampede, with Octavian's legions so close behind that they were still in sword contact. Ignoring the rain of stones and darts from the ramparts above them, Agrippa's Fourth stormed the main gate and its fortifications across the Via Egnatia, and closed Brutus's camp to his fleeing soldiers. Scattering, they ran for the salt marshes or the gulches behind his hill.

Second Philippi lasted very little longer than Pharsalus, but saw a very high death rate; fully half of the Liberator army perished, or was never heard from again by anyone in the world of Our Sea. Later, it would be said that some survived to go into the service of the King of the Parthians, but not to the fate of the ten thousand from Carrhae who now garrisoned the frontier of Sogdiana against the steppe hordes of the Massagetae. For the son of Labienus, Quintus Labienus, was a trusted minion of King Orodes, and Quintus Labienus invited them to help him coach the Parthian army in Roman fighting techniques.

Brutus and his own party had watched from the summit of his hill, able to see today because the dust stayed confined within the heaving, densely packed bodies. When it was obvious that the battle was lost, the tribunes of his four senior legions came to him and asked him what they should do.

"Save your lives," said Brutus. "Try to get through to the fleets at Neapolis, or else try to get to Thasos."

"We should escort you, Marcus Brutus."

"No, I prefer to go alone. Leave now, please."

Statyllus, Strato of Epirus and Publius Volumnius were with him; so were his three most cherished freedmen—his secretaries Lucilius and Cleitus and his shield bearer, Dardanus—plus a few others. Perhaps twenty in all, including the slaves.

"It is over," he said, watching Agrippa's Fourth assaulting his walls. "We had better hurry. Are we packed, Lucilius?"

"Yes, Marcus Brutus. May I beg a favor?"

"Ask."

"Give me your armor and scarlet cape. We're the same size and coloring, I can pass for you. If I ride up to their lines and say I am Marcus Junius Brutus, it will delay pursuit," said Lucilius.

Brutus thought for a moment, then nodded. "All right, but on one condition: that you surrender to Marcus Antonius. On no account let them take you to Octavianus. Antonius is an untutored oaf, but he has a sense of honor. He won't harm you when he finds out he's been deceived. Whereas I think that Octavianus would have you killed on the spot."

They exchanged garb; Lucilius mounted Brutus's Public Horse and rode off down the hill toward the front gate, while Brutus and his party rode off down the hill toward the back gate. The light was fading, the camp walls were still being torn down by Agrippa's men. So no one saw them leave, enter the nearest defile and negotiate it and others until they emerged on the Via Egnatia well to the east of the Neapolis road, which Antony had captured a few days after First Philippi.

With darkness closing in, Brutus chose to leave the road inside the Corpilan Pass, ascend the heavily forested slopes below the gorge escarpment.

"Antonius will surely have cavalry out looking for escapees," Brutus said in explanation. "If we settle on this ledge for the night, we can see our best course in the morning."

"If we put someone on lookout, we can have a fire," Volumnius said, shivering. "It's too cloudy to see without torches, so we need only douse the fire when our lookout sees approaching torches."

"The sky is clearing," said Statyllus, sounding desolate.

They gathered around a briskly blazing fire of dead wood to find that they were too thirsty to eat; no one had remembered to carry water.

"The Harpessus has to be nearby," said Rhascupolis, getting up. "I'll take two spare horses and bring water back, if I can empty the grain out of these jars and store it in sacks."

Brutus hardly heard, so abstracted that the activity went on around him as if seen through a thick mist and heard through ears stuffed with wadding.

This is the end of my road, the end of my time on this awful, tormented globe. I was never cut out to be a warrior, it isn't in my blood. I do not even know how the military mind works. If I did, I might have understood Cassius better. He was so dedicated and *aggressive*. That's why Mama always preferred him to me. For she is the most aggressive person I have ever known. Prouder than the towers of Ilium, stronger than Hercules, harder than *adamas*. She's doomed to outlive all of us—Cato, Caesar, Silanus, Porcia, Cassius, and me. She will outlive all save perhaps that serpent Octavianus. It was he who forced Antonius to persecute the Liberators. Had it not been for Octavianus, we would all be living in Rome, and be consuls in our proper year. This year!

Octavianus owns the guile of a man four times his age. Caesar's heir! The roll of Fortuna's dice we none of us took into consideration. Caesar, who started it all when he seduced Mama—shamed me—tore my Julia away to marry her to an old man. Caesar the self-server. Shuddering, he thought of a line from the *Medea* of Euripides, cried it aloud:

" 'Almighty Zeus, remember who is the cause of so much pain!' "

"What was that?" asked Volumnius, trying to store everything up until he could next make an entry in his diary.

Brutus didn't answer, so Volumnius had to wrestle with the quotation until Strato of Epirus enlightened him. But Volumnius assumed Brutus referred to Antonius, didn't even think of Caesar.

Rhascupolis came back with the water; everyone save Brutus drank greedily, parched. After that they ate.

Somewhat later a noise in the distance made them stamp out the fire; they sat rigid while Volumnius and Dardanus went off to investigate. A false alarm, said the pair on their return.

Suddenly Statyllus leaped to his feet, clapping his hands around himself to generate a little warmth. "I can't stand it!" he cried. "I'm going back to Philippi to see what's happening. If I find the hill inside the camp deserted, I'll light the big beacon fire. From this height, you should see it well—after all, it was designed to warn the guards in both passes if the Triumvirs outflanked Neapolis. What is it, five miles? You should see it in about an hour if I hurry. Then you'll know whether Antonius's men are doing more sleeping than hunting."

Off he went, while those left behind huddled together to ward off the cold. Only Brutus remained aloof, sunk in thought.

This is the end of my road, and it was all for nothing. I was so sure that if Caesar died, the Republic would return. But it didn't. All his death accomplished was the unleashing of worse enemies. My heart's strings are the binding of the Republic, it is fitting that I die.

"Who," he asked suddenly, "died today?"

"Hemicillus," Rhascupolis said into the darkness. "Young Marcus Porcius Cato, fighting very gallantly. Pacuvius Labeo, by his own hand, I believe."

"Livius Drusus Nero," said Volumnius.

Brutus burst into tears, wept into the silence while the rest stayed very still, wishing they were elsewhere.

How long he wept, Brutus didn't know, only that when the tears dried, he felt as if he had emerged from a dream into a far wilder, more beautiful and fascinating dream. On his feet now, he walked to the middle of the clearing and lifted his head to the sky, where the clouds had dissipated and the stars shone in their myriads. Only Homer had the words to describe what his eyes and his dazzled mind took in, awestruck.

" 'There are nights,' " he said, " 'when the upper air is windless and the stars in heaven stand out in their full splendor around the bright moon; when every mountain top and headland and ravine starts into sight, as the infinite depths of the sky are torn open to the very firmament.' "*

It marked a transition, all of them knew it, stiffening and pricking as their round eyes, long adjusted to the inky gloom, followed the shadow of Brutus walking back to them. He went to the bundles of belongings, picked up his sword and pulled it from its scabbard. He extended it to Volumnius.

"Do the deed, old friend," he said.

Sobbing, Volumnius shook his head and backed away.

Brutus held out the sword to each of them in turn, and each of them refused to take it. Last was Strato of Epirus.

"Will you?" asked Brutus.

It was over in an instant. Strato of Epirus took the weapon in a blur of movement, seemed to prolong the gesture in a sudden lunge that saw the blade go in up to its eagle hilt under Brutus's rib cage on the left side. A perfect thrust. Brutus was dead before his knees hit the leafy ground.

"I'm for home," said Rhascupolis. "Who's with me?"

No one, it seemed. The Thracian shrugged, found his horse, mounted it and disappeared.

When the wound had done bleeding—a very little only—there

---

* Homer's *Iliad*, Book VIII, 558. Prose translation by Dr. E. V. Rieu, Penguin Classics.

was a leap of flame in the west; Statyllus had kindled the camp bea-con. So they waited as the constellations wheeled overhead and Bru-tus lay very peacefully on the pungent carpet, his eyes closed, the coin in his mouth—a gold denarius with his own profile on its obverse side.

Finally Dardanus the shield bearer stirred. "Statyllus is not com-ing back," he said. "Let us take Marcus Brutus to Marcus Antonius. He would wish it so."

They loaded the limp body across Brutus's own horse and, as dawn broke faintly in the east, commenced the plod back to the battle-field of Philippi.

A prowling cavalry squadron conducted them to Mark Antony's tent, where the victor of Philippi was already up and about, his robust health more than equal to the feast of last night.

"Put him there," said Antony, pointing to a couch.

Two German troopers carried the very small bundle to the couch and laid it down gently, straightened its limbs until once more it as-sumed the form of a man.

"My *paludamentum*, Marsyas," said Antony to his body servant.

The scarlet cape of the general was brought; Antony shook it out and let it flutter to cover all but Brutus's face, stark and white, the scars of those decades of acne pitting its skin, the lank black curls crowning his scalp like silky feathers.

"Have you money to go home?" he asked Volumnius.

"Yes, Gaius Antonius, but we would like to take Statyllus and Lu-cilius too."

"Statyllus is dead. Some guards caught him in Brutus's camp and thought he was there to loot. I've seen his corpse. As for the false Bru-tus—I've a mind to keep Lucilius in my own service. Loyalty is hard to find." Antony turned to his body servant. "Marsyas, arrange passes for any of Brutus's people who wish to go to Neapolis."

Which left him alone with Brutus, mute company. Brutus and Cas-sius dead. Aquila, Trebonius, Decimus Brutus, Cimber, Basilus, Ligar-ius, Labeo, the Casca brothers, a few more of the assassins. That it should have come to this, when it all might have blown over and Rome gone on in its same old slipshod, imperfect way! But no, that hadn't satisfied Octavianus the arch-manipulator, the nightmare Cae-sar had conjured up out of nowhere to exact a full and bloody revenge.

As if the thought were father to the reality, Antony looked up to see Octavian standing in the light-filled triangle of the tent flap, with his impassive, stunningly handsome coeval Agrippa right behind him. Wrapped in a grey cloak, that hair glittering in the lamp flames like the tumbled surface of a pile of gold coins.

"I heard the news," Octavian said, coming to stand beside the couch and gaze down at Brutus; a finger came out, touched the waxen cheek as if to assess its substance, then withdrew to be wiped fastidiously on the grey cloak. "He's a wisp."

"Death shrinks us all, Octavianus."

"Not Caesar. Death has enhanced *him*."

"Unfortunately that's true."

"Whose *paludamentum* is that? His?"

"No, it's mine."

The slight frame went rigid, the big grey eyes narrowed and blazed cold fire. "You do the cur too much honor, Antonius."

"He's a Roman nobleman, the commander of a Roman army. I'll do him even greater honor at his funeral later today."

"*Funeral*? He deserves no funeral!"

"My word rules here, Octavianus. He'll be burned with full military honors."

"Your word does not rule! He's Caesar's assassin!" Octavian hissed. "Feed him to the dogs, as Neoptolemus did Priam!"

"I don't care if you howl, whine, screech, whimper or mew," Antony said, little teeth bared, "Brutus will be burned with full military honors, and I expect your legions to be present!"

The smooth, beautiful young face turned to stone, suddenly so much the face of Caesar in a temper that Antony took an involuntary step backward, appalled.

"My legions can do as they please. And if you insist upon your honorable funeral, then conduct it. But not the head. The head is mine. Give it to me! *To me!*"

Antony looked on Caesar at the height of his power, saw a will incapable of bending. Thrown completely off balance, he found himself unable to tower, to roar, to bully. "You're mad," he said.

"Brutus murdered my father. Brutus led my father's assassins. Brutus is my prize, not yours. I will ship his head to Rome, where I will impale it on a spear and fix it at the base of Divus Julius's statue in the Forum," said Octavian. "Give me the head."

"Do you want Cassius's head too? You're too late, it's not here. I can offer you a few others who died yesterday."

"Just the head of Brutus," Octavian said, voice steel.

The advantage lost, he didn't honestly know how, Antony was reduced to pleading, then to begging, then to exhortations in his best oratory, then to tears. He ran the gamut of the softer emotions, for if there was one thing this joint expedition had shown him, it was that Octavianus the weakling, the sickly ninny, was impossible to cow, dominate, overwhelm. And with that shadow Agrippa always just behind him, unkillable too. Besides, the legions wouldn't condone it.

"If you want it, then you take it!" he said in the end.

"Thank you. Agrippa?"

It was done in the time it took lightning to strike. Agrippa drew his sword, stepped forward, swung it and chopped through the neck clear to the cushions beneath, which parted and spat a shower of goose down. Then Octavian's coeval caught the black curls in his fingers and let the head hang by his side. His face never changed.

"It will rot before it reaches Athens, let alone Rome," said Antony, nauseated and disgusted.

"I commandeered a jar of pickling brine from the butchers," Octavian said coolly, walking to the tent flap. "It doesn't matter if the brain melts to a runny mess, as long as the face is recognizable. Rome must know that Caesar's son has avenged his chief murderer."

Agrippa and the head disappeared, Octavian lingered. "I know who's dead, but who has been taken prisoner?" he asked.

"Just two. Quintus Hortensius and Marcus Favonius. The rest chose to fall on their swords—it's not hard to see why," Antony said, flicking one hand at Brutus's headless body.

"What do you intend to do with the captives?"

"Hortensius gave the governorship of Macedonia to Brutus, so he dies on my brother Gaius's tomb. Favonius can go home—he's completely harmless."

"I insist that Favonius be executed immediately!"

"In the name of all our gods, Octavianus, *why*? What has he ever done to you?" Antony cried, clutching at his hair.

"He was Cato's best friend. That's reason enough, Antonius. He dies today."

"No, he goes home."

"Execution, Antonius. You need me, my friend. You can't do without me. And I insist."

"Any more orders?"

"Who got away?"

"Messala Corvinus. Gaius Clodius, who murdered my brother. Cicero's son. And all the fleet admirals, of course."

"So there are still a few assassins to bring to justice."

"You won't rest until they're all dead, eh?"

"Correct." The flap parted; Octavian was gone.

"Marsyas!" Antony bellowed.

"Yes, *domine*?"

Antony plucked at the scarlet cape to twitch a fold over the grisly neck, oozing fluid. "Find the senior tribune on duty and tell him to have a funeral pyre prepared. We burn Marcus Brutus today with full military honors—and don't let anyone know that Marcus Brutus no longer has his head. Find a pumpkin or something that will do, and send ten of my Germans to me now. They can put him on his bier inside this tent, put the pumpkin where the head ought to be, and pin the cape down firmly. Understood?"

"Yes, *domine*," said the ashen Marsyas.

While the Germans and the shivering body servant dealt with the corpse of Marcus Brutus, Antony sat turned away, nor said a word. Only after Brutus was gone did he stir, blink away sudden, inexplicable tears.

The army would eat until it got home, there was so much food in the two Liberator camps, and more by far in Neapolis; the admirals had sailed the moment they heard the result of Second Philippi, leaving everything behind. A house full of silver one-talent sows, stuffed granaries, smokehouses of bacon, barrels of pickled pork, a warehouse of chickpea and lentil. The haul would amount to at least a hundred thousand talents in coin and sows, so the promised bonuses could be paid. Twenty-five thousand of the Liberator troops had volunteered to join *Octavianus's* legions. No one wanted to join Antonius's, though it was Antonius had won the two battles.

Calm down, Marcus Antonius! Don't let that cold-blooded cobra Octavianus sink his fangs into you. He's right, and he knows it. I need him, I can't do without him. I've an army to get back to Italy, where the three Triumvirs have it all to do again. A new pact, an extended commission to set Rome in order. And it will give me great pleasure to dump all the dirty work on Octavianus. Let *him* find land for a hundred thousand veterans and feed three million Roman citizens with Sextus Pompeius owning Sicily and the seas. A year ago I would have said he couldn't do it. Now, I'm not so sure. Agents, for pity's sake! He's hatched a small army of snakelets to whisper, and spy, and promulgate his causes, from the worship of Caesar to securing his own position. But I can't live in the same city with him. I'm going to find a more congenial place to live, more congenial things to do than wrestle with an empty Treasury, hordes of veterans, and the grain supply.

"Is the head snugged down for its passage home?" Octavian asked Agrippa when he entered his tent.

"Perfectly, Caesar."

"Tell Cornelius Gallus to take it to Amphipolis and hire a seaworthy ship. I don't want it traveling with the legions."

"Yes, Caesar," said Agrippa, turning to leave.

"Agrippa?"

"Yes, Caesar?"

"You did superbly at the head of the Fourth." He smiled, his breathing light and easy, his pose relaxed. "Brave Diomedes to my Ulysses. So may it always be."

"So will it always be, Caesar."

And today I too won a victory. I faced Antonius down, I beat him. Within a year he'll have no choice but to call me Caesar to the whole Roman world. I will take the West and give Antonius the East wherein to ruin himself. Lepidus can have Africa and the Domus Publica, he's no threat to either of us. Yes, I have a stout little band of adherents—Agrippa, Statilius Taurus, Maecenas, Salvidienus, Lucius Cornificius, Titius, Cornelius Gallus, the Coccei, Sosius . . . The nucleus of an expanding new nobility. That was my father's great mistake. He wanted to preserve the old nobility, wanted his faction adorned by all the great old names. He couldn't establish his autocracy within an ostensibly democratic framework. But I won't make that mistake. My health and my tastes don't run to splendor, I can never rival his magnificence as he stalked through the Forum in the garb of the Pontifex Maximus with his valorous crown upon his head and that inimitable aura of invincibility around him. Women looked on him, and swooned. Men looked on him, and their inadequacies gnawed at them, their impotence drove them to hate him.

Whereas I will be their *paterfamilias*—their kind, steady, warm and smiling daddy. I will let them think they rule themselves, and monitor their every word and action. Turn the brick of Rome into marble. Fill Rome's temples with great works of art, re-pave her streets, deck her squares, plant trees and build public baths, give the Head Count full bellies and all the entertainment they could wish for. Wage war only when necessary, but garrison the peripheries of our world. Take the gold of Egypt to revitalize Rome's economy. I am so young, I have the time to do it all.

But first, find a way to eliminate Marcus Antonius without murdering him, or going to war against him. It can be done: the answer lies in the mists of time, just waiting to manifest itself.

3 When no ship's captain in Amphipolis could be prevailed upon to take a fat fee and put out into winter seas bound for Rome, Cornelius Gallus brought the big, swilling jar back to the camp at Philippi to find the army still mopping up.

"Then," said Octavian, sighing, "take it all the way across to Dyrrachium and find a ship there. Go now, Gallus. I don't want it traveling with the army. Soldiers are superstitious."

Cornelius Gallus and his squadron of German cavalry arrived in Dyrrachium at the end of that momentous year; there he found his ship, its master willing to make the voyage across the Adriatic to Ancona. Brundisium was no longer under blockade, but there were many fleets roaming, their Liberator admirals rudderless as they debated what to do. Mostly, join Sextus Pompey.

It was no part of Gallus's orders to accompany the jar; he handed it over to the captain and rode back to Octavian. But someone in his party whispered what the cargo was before he left, for it had generated much interest. A whole ship, hired at great expense, just to ferry a big ceramic jar to Italy? It hadn't made any sense until the whisper surfaced. The head of Marcus Junius Brutus, murderer of Divus Julius! Oh, the Lares Permarini protect us from this evil cargo!

In the middle of the sea the merchantman encountered a storm worse than any the crew had ever experienced. The head! *It was the head!* When the stout hull sprang a bad leak, the crew was sure that the head was determined to kill them too. So the oarsmen and sailors wrested the jar from the captain's custody and threw it overboard. The moment it vanished, the storm blew into nothing.

And the jar containing the head of Marcus Junius Brutus sank like the heavy stone it was, down, down, down, to lie forever on the muddy bottom of the Adriatic Sea somewhere between Dyrrachium and Ancona.

FINIS

Author's Afterword

Marking as it does the passing of the last great Republican mover and shaker, Gaius Julius Caesar, *The October Horse* brings my series of novels about Republican Rome to an end.

Octavius/Octavian/Augustus more properly belongs to the Imperium than to the Republic, so, having dealt with his childhood and his emergence on to the stage of world affairs, I think it is appropriate to call a halt to what has been an enormously enjoyable creative exercise: breathing life into history without distorting it more than the limitations of my scholarship make inevitable.

Provided that history is adhered to and the writer can resist the temptation to visit his or her own modern attitudes, ethics, morals and ideals upon the period and its characters, the novel is an excellent way to explore a different time. It permits the writer to climb inside the characters' heads and wander the maze of their thoughts and emotions: a luxury not permitted to professional historians, but one that can render understandable events that are otherwise inexplicable, mysterious or incongruous. During the course of these six books, I have taken the external events of some very famous lives and attempted to create rounded, believable human beings endowed with all the complexities common sense dictates they must have possessed.

What attracted me to the period was threefold: first of all, that it hadn't been done to death by other writers; secondly, its relevance to modern western civilization in that so much of our own systems of justice, government and commerce stem out of the Roman Republic; and, last but by no means least, that rarely have so many extraordinarily gifted men walked history's stage in close enough temporal proximity to one another to have known one another as living men. Marius, Sulla and Pompey the Great were all known to Caesar, and all, in one way or another, shaped the course of his life, as did other famous historical figures like Cato Uticensis and Cicero. But by the end of *The October Horse* they are all gone, including Caesar. What remains is their legacy to the ongoing Roman experience: Caesar's great-nephew, Gaius Octavius, who was to become Caesar Imperator, and then Augustus. If I don't stop now, I never will!

Now to some specifics.

The specter of William Shakespeare must always overshadow our preconceptions of Brutus, Cassius, Mark Antony, and Caesar's assassination. With apologies to the Bard, I have decided to follow the ancient sources that state that Caesar said nothing before he died, and that Mark Antony didn't have a chance to make a great funeral oration before the crowd surged.

The etymology of the word "assassin" is younger than this period, but I have chosen to use it in my text because of its specificity to modern readers. Occasionally a more modern word is more satisfactory than any word a Latin speaker may have had at his or her command, but I have endeavored to keep this sort of thing to a minimum. Some words are untranslatable, and appear in the text in Latin, such as *pomerium, mos maiorum* and *contio*.

The reader may be intrigued by some of the less well-known events of these generally best known years: Cato's overland march to Africa Province, and the fate of Brutus's head, for example. Others, like the battle of Philippi, are so confused that making head or tail of them is difficult. The two most widely read ancient sources, Plutarch and Suetonius, must be supplemented by dozens and dozens of others, including Appian, Cassius Dio and Cicero's letters, speeches and essays. A bibliography is available if any interested party cares to write to me at P.O. Box 333, Norfolk Island, via Australia.

One liberty I have taken with history concerns the reputed cowardice of Octavian during the campaign that culminated in the battle of Philippi. The more I delved into his early life, the less credible cowardice seemed. So many other aspects of his career at this stage indicate that he did not lack courage; he had quite astonishing sticking power, and tackled undertakings like two marches on Rome as a teenager with all the aplomb of a Sulla or a Caesar. I am in good company, incidentally, when I have the lad steal Caesar's war chest; Sir Ronald Syme thought he did too.

Getting back to the so-called cowardice, it struck me that there might be a physical reason for his behavior. What intrigued me was the statement that Octavian "hid in the marshes" during First Philippi, a battle we know produced so much dust that Cassius couldn't even see Brutus's camp from his own. In that conduct, I believe, lies the answer to the riddle. What if Octavian suffered from asthma? Asthma is a disorder that can imperil life, may diminish (or increase) with age, and is affected by foreign matter in the air, from dust to pollen to water vapor, and by emotional stress. It fits very well with what we know of the young Caesar Augustus. Maybe, after he had cemented his power, enjoyed a more stable private life, and had the gold of Egypt to put the Empire back on its feet, he suffered fewer or even no asthmatic attacks. Though he traveled, he was not an inveterate traveler like Caesar, nor does he seem to have experienced Caesar's rude health. Did Octavian have asthma, it makes everything that happened to him during that campaign in Macedonia logical, including his fleeing to the sea breezes and cleaner air of the salt marshes while dry ground was fogged by a suffocating pall of chaffy dust. My recourse to asthma is not an excuse aimed at making Octavian look good, it is simply an attempt to explain his conduct in a reasonable, possible way.

On the subject of Caesar's "epilepsy," I have professional experience to assist me. In a day and age when anticonvulsant medication was not available, Caesar's mental acuity, including at the end of his life, militates against a long-term epileptic condition of generalized nature, though the only seizure described in the ancient sources seems to have been a generalized one. Many altered physiological states can cause a rare seizure in persons who do not have regular seizures, for epilepsy is a symptom rather than a disease. Trauma, space-occupying lesions of the brain, cerebral inflammation, severe electrolyte imbalances and acute hypoglycemia, among other things, can cause seizures. Since the ancient sources harp a little on Caesar's indifference to food, I elected to attribute his seizure to an attack of hypoglycemia (low blood sugar) following a systemic illness that may have involved the pancreas.

So much has been written about the significance of Caesar's wearing the high red boots of the Alban Kings in the last two months of his life that a spirit of mischief led me to gift him with varicose veins. The Roman boot was a low affair that would not afford support for varicosities, whereas a high, tightly laced boot would. I am as likely to be right as wrong!

Health and disease are, not unnaturally, often misinterpreted by historians, whose academic inclinations lie far from medicine. It just seems to me that, particularly in times when knowledge of and treatment of ailments was less adept than it is now, many famous historical characters must surely have suffered common maladies like diabetes, asthma, varicose veins, heart failure, and Napoleon's notorious hemorrhoids. Cancer was common, pneumonia often fatal, and poliomyelitis stalked Rome's seven hills every summer. The description of the plague in Egypt sounds suspiciously like a close cousin to the Black Death, or else was it.

There are aspects of Cleopatra's relationship with Caesar and her subsequent relationship with Mark Antony that are overlooked, though they should not be.

One must always be skeptical about Cleopatra, whom the mature Octavian/Augustus found it politic to malign; he didn't dare have a civil war with Antony, so in her he found his foreign foe. The first master of propaganda, Octavian is responsible for her reputation as sexually promiscuous, up to and including denying that Caesarion was her son by Caesar. The truth is that her royal situation would have insisted that she be a virgin, but more than that: a Ptolemy, she would never have lowered herself to mate with a mere mortal. Circumstances like inundations in the Cubits of Death and an unavailable Ptolemaic husband made Caesar an eligible husband; he was generally regarded as a god throughout the eastern end of the Mediterranean when he landed in Alexandria.

But having introduced a new strain of godly blood into her line, Cleopatra was then faced with the problem of reinforcing that new, Julian blood. Her first choice to achieve this would have been a full sister for Caesarion to marry, but when that did not happen, she had to find another source of Julian blood. Mark Antony's mother was a Julia, so he qualified. There can be no doubt that, had he lived, Caesarion would have married his half sister by Antony, Cleopatra Selene. The only other answer to Cleopatra's dilemma than a Julian bride for Caesarion was marriage to her own half sister, Arsinoë: an alternative she could not condone, as it would have led to her own murder.

There were thus excellent dynastic reasons why Cleopatra espoused Mark Antony and had children by him. To do so ensured the House of Ptolemy Caesar. But, of course, Octavian destroyed all Cleopatra's hopes by killing Caesarion before his little half sister was old enough for marriage. This child, Cleopatra Selene, was reared by Octavia and was eventually married to King Juba II of Numidia. Her twin brother, Ptolemy Helios, and their small brother, Ptolemy Philadelphus, were also raised by Octavia.

Now to the drawings.

Rarely has a people pre-dating the candid camera left such an immensely rich legacy of "warts and all" portraiture as the Romans. Identification of the busts depends largely upon coin profiles, as the busts were almost never labeled with a name. These unflattering likenesses were painted in the manner of a waxworks figure, which means that we do not see them today as they were in antiquity. It is for this reason that I have tried to bring the busts to life by drawing them. As I am no artist, I beg to be excused their faults. Most have lost their necks, so I fall down badly on necks. The hair I have kept stylized because to do so emphasizes the genius of the Roman barber, who seems to have catered for the individual mutiny of his master's hair amazingly well.

First, the authenticated busts.

Good busts of Caesar all possess certain similarities: the frown lines, the creases at the outer corners of the eyes, the ears, the extraordinary cheekbones, and the slightly uptilted lips.

The Cassius is drawn from the Montreal bust, and confirms the impression one must get from Cicero's famous "shipwreck" letter, that Cassius did not look lean and hungry!

There are many busts of Caesar Augustus, and of all ages save old age. Though they do have vague echoes of Alexander the Great, inspection always reveals the prominent ears and unclassical nose.

Cato we know is Cato thanks to a labeled bust found in North Africa, where he was adored.

The young Cleopatra is from the marble head in Berlin, but none of her extant likenesses do the enormous beaked nose of her coin portraits justice. It was truly immense.

Lepidus, Cicero and Agrippa are authentic.

The Brutus is the bust in the Prado at Madrid; note the fascinating muscle wasting in the right cheek.

Marcus Antonius is an elusive character; perhaps no other famous Roman has as many so-called likenesses as he, all very different from one another—and from the coin profile, which depicts a huge nose and chin striving to meet across a thick-lipped mouth. I have chosen to draw from the bust that most resembles the coin profile.

Now come a group of three drawings that are not authentic, but bear similarities to some well-authenticated people. The Lucius Caesar is said to be a bust of the great Caesar, but is not: the frown lines are absent, so are the creases in the outer corners of the eyes; the shape of the skull and face are wrong, and there is a general asymmetry that Caesar's face does not have. Whether this is Lucius Caesar, I don't know, but the subject certainly looks like a Julian.

The Calpurnia reminded me of an authenticated bust of her father, Lucius Calpurnius Piso. I can say the same for Porcia.

The rest of the drawings are from busts of the proper date, but anonymous. They are there because it's fun to put a name to a face, and I maintain that my casting is better than Hollywood's.

GLOSSARY

ABSOLVO   The term employed by a court jury when delivering a verdict of acquittal.

adamas   Diamond, known to be the hardest of all substances.

Acadamic   An adherent of Platonic philosophy.

aedes   The house of a god not called a temple because it had not been used for augury at the time of its consecration.

aedile   A Roman magistrate. There were four: two were plebeian aediles, two were curule aediles.

The plebeian aediles were set up in 493 B.C. to assist the tribunes of the plebs (q.v.), particularly to guard the right of the Plebs to its headquarters in the temple of Ceres. They were elected by the Plebeian Assembly, served for one year, and were not entitled to sit in the curule chair or have lictors.

Two curule aediles were created in 367 B.C. to give the patricians a share in this office. They were elected by the Popular Assembly, served for one year, and had the right to sit in the curule chair. They were preceded by two lictors.

All four became responsible for the care of Rome's streets, squares, water supply, drains and sewers, traffic, public buildings, building standards and regulations for private construction, public monuments and facilities, markets, weights and measures (standard sets of these were housed in the basement of the temple of Castor and Pollux), some games and the public grain supply.

They had the power to fine citizens and non-citizens alike for infringements of any regulations, and used the money to help fund their games.

Aeneas   The son of King Anchises of Trojan Dardania and the goddess Venus/Aphrodite, he fled the burning city of Troy (Ilium) with his aged father on his shoulders and the Palladium tucked under one arm. After many adventures en route, he arrived in Latium and founded the race which produced the Romans. His son Iulus by his Latin wife, Lavinia, became the first King of Alba Longa; the Julians traced their descent from Venus through him.

aether   That part of the upper atmosphere permeated by godly forces, or the air immediately surrounding a god. It also meant the blue sky of daylight.

ager publicus   Land vested in Roman public ownership. It became politically contentious after the Gracchi (q.v.) and Marius (q.v.) began to seize it to divide up among the poor or poor soldiers as a kind of pension. This was bitterly opposed by the Senate.

agora   An open space in a Greek city, usually surrounded by colonnades, used as a meeting place.

agrarian   Pertaining to land; in this book, farmland.

Alexander the Great   King of Macedonia, the third of that name. He was born in 356 B.C. and succeeded his father, Philip II, when twenty years old; haunted by the specter of the Persians, he vowed to deal them a blow so hard that they would never again be able to invade Europe. In 334 B.C. he led an army across the Hellespont. His odyssey between this date and his death in Babylon at thirty-two took him, always victorious, as far as the Indus River in modern Pakistan. When he tried to go farther east, his army mutinied, so he was forced to turn back. His tutor as a boy was Aristotle. Dying without a true successor, his empire did not survive him as a single entity, but he seeded Hellenic kings in the persons of his marshals, who divided most of Asia Minor, Egypt, Syria, Media and Persia among them.

amicus, amici   Friend, friends.

Amisus   Modern Samsun, on the Black Sea in Turkey.

amo, amas, amat   "I love, thee loves, he/she/it loves."

amygdalae   Almond-shaped objects or spaces.

Anatolia   Roughly, modern Asian Turkey.

animus   Quoting the Oxford Latin Dictionary: "The mind as opposed to the body, the mind or soul as constituting with the body the whole person." To a Roman, it probably did not mean an immortal soul; it was simply the force that animated, endowed life.

Apollonia   The southern terminus of the Via Egnatia on the west (Adriatic) coast of Macedonia. It lay near the mouth of the modern Vijosë River in Albania.

Apulia   That region of southeastern Italy where the Apennines flatten somewhat and the boot's "spur" is located. Its people were considered by the Romans to be backward bumpkins.

aquilifer The best soldier in a legion, he carried the silver Eagle and was expected to keep it safe from enemy capture. As a mark of his distinction, he wore a wolf or lion skin.

Arabia Felix Happy, or Lucky, Arabia. That part of the Arabian peninsula at the south end of the Red Sea.

Arelate Modern Arles, in France.

Armenia Parva Little Armenia. It lay west of Armenia proper around the headwaters and upper course of the Euphrates River, and was high, extremely mountainous and inhospitable.

Arretium Modern Arezzo, situated on the Arno River in Italy.

Assembly In Latin, *comitium, comitia*. Any gathering of Roman citizen men convoked to deal with governmental, legislative, electoral or judicial matters. There were three major Assemblies, of the Centuries, the People and the Plebs.

The **Centuriate Assembly** consisted of the People in their Classes, which were defined by a means test and were economic in nature. It met to elect the consuls, the praetors and (every five years) the censors. It also met to hear trials of *perduellio* treason (q.v.).

The other two major Assemblies were tribal in nature, rather than economic.

The **Assembly of the People** or **Popular Assembly** allowed the full participation of patricians, and it met in the thirty-five tribes among which all Roman citizens were distributed. It was convoked by a consul or a praetor, could formulate laws, and elected the curule aediles, quaestors and tribunes of the soldiers. It could also conduct trials. Like the Centuriate Assembly, it was religiously constrained; prayers had to be said and the auspices taken before the meeting could begin.

The **Plebeian Assembly** did not allow the participation of patricians, and was convoked only by a tribune of the plebs. No prayers were said or auspices taken. It had the power to enact laws and conduct trials, and elected the tribunes of the plebs and the plebeian aediles.

No Roman Assembly used an individual citizen's vote directly. In the Centuriate Assembly his vote was credited to his Century of his Class, the single vote of his Century going the way of the majority of its members. In the Popular and Plebeian Assemblies, his vote was credited to his tribe, the single vote of the tribe going the way of the majority of its members. The only time a man's vote counted directly was in a court jury.

Atropos There were three goddesses of Fate. Clotho spun the thread, Lachesis wove it in a pattern, and Atropos cut the thread with her shears, thus regulating the origin, course, and end of life.

augur, auspices The augur was a priest whose duties concerned div-ination rather than prognostication, and was elected (for life). He in-spected the proper object or signs to ascertain whether or not the projected undertaking had the approval of the gods, be it a meeting, a war, a proposed new law, or any other public business. A protocol governing interpretation existed, so an augur "went by the book" rather than claimed to have psychic powers.

auxiliaries Troops serving in a Roman army but not owning the Roman citizenship. Cavalrymen were usually auxiliaries.

Baetis River The modern Guadalquivir, in Spain. According to the geographer Strabo, the Baetis valley was the most fertile and produc-tive land in the world.

ballista In Republican times, a piece of artillery designed to hurl stones and boulders. The missile was put in a spoon-shaped arm that was put under extreme tension by a tightly wound rope spring; when the spring was released, the arm shot into the air and came to rest against a thick pad, propelling the missile a considerable distance. It was accurate when expertly used.

barbarian Derived from a Greek word having strong onomatopoeic overtones; the Greeks had fancied, upon hearing the tribal peoples of the north speak, that they barked like dogs—"bar-bar." The word was not applied to any Mediterranean or Middle Eastern people. It re-ferred to the peoples of the steppes and forests, who were deemed un-civilized, lacking in any desirable or admirable culture.

Barium Modern Bari, on the Adriatic coast of Italy.

basilica A large building devoted to public activities such as courts of law or to commercial activities. The basilica was clerestory-lit and was erected at the expense of some civic-minded Roman nobleman, usually of consular status. His basilica bore his name.

beak In Latin, *rostrum*. The beak, of oak or bronze, projected forward of a warship's bows just below the waterline, and was used to hole or damage an enemy vessel during an activity called "ramming."

Belgae The fearsome confraternity of tribes inhabiting northwestern and Rhineland Gaul. Of mixed Germano-Celtic blood, they comprised tribes like the Nervii, who fought on foot, and the Treveri, who fought from horseback.

biga A chariot drawn by two horses.

bireme A galley constructed for use in naval warfare and meant to be rowed rather than sailed, though like all war galleys it was equipped with a mast and sail (left ashore if battle seemed likely). Some biremes were decked or partially decked, but most were open.

It seems that the oarsmen did sit on two levels at separate banks of oars, the upper bank accommodated in an outrigger, and the lower bank poking through leather-valved ports in the hull. One man powered one oar; there were upward of 100 rowers. It was much longer than it was wide in the beam (the ratio was about 7:1), and probably measured about 100 feet (30 meters) in length. A beak (q.v.) was mandatory. The bireme was not designed to carry marines or artillery, or grapple to engage other vessels in land-style combat.

Built of fir or some other lightweight pine, the bireme could be manned only in fair weather, and fight only in calm seas. Like all warships, it was not left in the water even overnight, but stored ashore in ship sheds or pushed up on a beach. Throughout Greek and Romanly Roman times all warships were rowed by professional oarsmen, never by slaves. Slaves sent to the galleys were a feature of Christianized times.

boni   Literally, "the good men." First mentioned in a play by Plautus called *The Captives*, the term came into political use during the time of Gaius Gracchus (q.v.). In the time of Cicero and Caesar, the *boni* were men of ultra-conservative leanings.

Bononia   Modern Bologna, in northern Italy.

Brundisium   Modern Brindisi, on the Adriatic coast of Italy.

Bruttium   In ancient times, the toe of the Italian boot.

Burdigala   Modern Bordeaux, in France.

Buthrotum   In modern Albania, it is now an uninhabited site called Butrinto.

cacat!   Shit!

Calabria   In ancient times, the heel of the Italian boot.

caligae   Legionary footwear, open to the air but more supportive than a sandal. The very thick leather sole was studded with metal hobnails, thus raising the marching foot too high off the ground to pick up painful grit or gravel, while the shoe's open nature kept the foot healthy. In icy or snowy weather, the legionary wore thick socks, rabbit skins or similar inside it.

Campania   The fabulously rich and fertile volcanic basin that lay between the mountains of Samnium and Apulia and the Tuscan (Tyrrhenian) Sea, and extended from Tarracina in the north to a point just south of the Bay of Naples. Very well watered, it grew bigger, better, and more of everything than anywhere else in Italy. Early colonized by the Greeks, it fell under Etruscan domination, then belonged to the Samnites, and finally was subject to Rome. The strong Greek and Samnite elements in its population made it a grudging subject, and it was an area always prone to insurrection.

campus   A plain or flat piece of ground.

Capua The largest inland city of Campania. It had a long history of broken pledges to Rome which led to Roman reprisals stripping it of its extensive and immensely valuable public lands; these included the *ager Falernus,* source of Italy's best wines. By Caesar's time, Capua had become the center of a huge martial industry, catering for the needs of the army camps and gladiator schools all around it.

Carrhae Today, a tiny village named Harran in the extreme south of Turkey near the Syrian border. It was the site of a severe Roman defeat when the Parthians attacked the army of Marcus Crassus.

carpentum A four-wheeled, closed carriage drawn by four to eight mules. Its driver was the *carpentarius.*

Carthage A Phoenician civilization centered upon modern Tunisia, in north Africa. At the height of its power, chiefly maritime, Carthage had an empire including Sicily, Sardinia and all Spain. During the course of three wars with Rome lasting 150 years, its power ebbed and vanished. Its most famous citizen was Hannibal. The adjective pertaining to Carthage is "Punic" (Phoenician).

casus belli A reason for war.

Catabathmos The uninhabited coast between Egypt and Cyrenaica.

catapult In Republican times, a piece of artillery designed to shoot wooden bolts or sharpened logs. The principle was the same as a crossbow. Small catapults were called *scorpions.*

cella A room without a special function. The word is usually applied to the room inside a temple.

Cenabum Modern Orleans, in France.

censor The most senior of all Roman magistrates, though he did not own imperium, therefore was not escorted by lictors. To run for censor, a man had to have been consul, and only famous ones bothered to stand. Two censors were elected by the Centuriate Assembly to serve for a period of five years, called a *lustrum.* Censors inspected and regulated membership in the Senate, and in the Classes and tribes of Roman citizens. They also held a full census of all Roman citizens everywhere in the world. They let the State contracts, and undertook various public works. Usually they could not get on together, and were prone to resign long before the *lustrum* was completed.

Centuries Actually, any body of 100 men. Here, the groups of men in the Classes. Except for the senior eighteen centuries, these groups came to hold many more than 100 men.

centurion A regular professional officer in a legion. He cannot be likened to a modern non-commissioned officer, for he enjoyed an exalted status unaffected by social distinctions. Promotion was up from the ranks; all centurions started off as ranker soldiers. Centurion seniority was graduated in a manner so tortuous that no modern scholar has worked out how many grades there were, or how they progressed. The ordinary centurion commanded the *century* of 80 soldiers and 20 noncombatant servants who were also citizens. The names of the two most senior grades have survived: the *pilus prior* was the senior centurion of his cohort, and the *primus pilus* (shortened by Caesar to *primipilus*) was the senior of the entire legion.

The centurion's badges of office were unmistakable: a shirt of metal scales rather than chain mail; shin guards or greaves; a helmet crest of stiff horsehair that fanned sideways instead of back-to-front; and a stout knobkerrie of vine wood. He was usually festooned with decorations for valor.

Cephallenia   An island in the Ionian Sea to the west of Greece.

Cercina   Modern Kerkenna, an island off the coast of Tunisia.

chersonnese   The Greek word for a peninsula.

Cimbric Chersonnese   The Jutland peninsula (Denmark).

Cimmeria   Situated at the top of the Black Sea, in ancient times it incorporated not only the Crimean peninsula, but much of the territory around it.

circumvallation   A siege wall entirely surrounding the enemy.

circus   An open air arena designed for chariot racing, therefore much longer than wide, and equipped with wooden bleachers for the spectators. A narrow island called the *spina* divided the arena itself down the middle; accidents happened when the chariots tried to drive around the *metae* (spina ends) at a sharp angle.

Classes   There were five Classes of Roman citizens, numbered from First to Fifth, each comprised of Centuries. A means test was imposed by the censors, based on a man's income. Many Roman citizens were too poor to qualify for a Class (see **Head Count**). Electorally the Classes were heavily weighted in favor of the most affluent, the First Class, to which members of the Senate belonged. See also **Eighteen.**

client, clientele   A man of free or freed status (he did not have to be a Roman citizen) who pledged himself to a man he called his patron was a client in the patron's clientele. The client undertook in the most solemn and binding way to obey the wishes and serve the interests of his patron, in return for various favors (usually gifts of money, or jobs, or legal assistance). The freed slave was automatically the client of his former master. So important was the client-patron relationship that there were formal laws governing it. Whole towns, cities and even kingdoms could be clients, and not necessarily of Rome herself. Romans like Pompey the Great numbered kings and satraps among his clients.

client-king   A king who pledged himself to Rome or a Roman.

cognomen   The last name of a Roman male anxious to distinguish himself from all his fellows having the same first and family name as he. In some cases a man might have several *cognomina*, as Gaius Julius Caesar Strabo Vopiscus Sesquiculus. Caesar: "a fine head of hair." Strabo: "cross-eyes." Vopiscus: "the survivor of twins." Sesquiculus: "an arsehole and a half." Which indicates that the *cognomen* was a nickname, often either sarcastic or describing some physical imperfection.

cohort   The tactical unit of the legion, comprising six centuries of troops; in normal circumstances, a legion contained ten cohorts. Roman armies were sometimes enumerated in cohorts rather than in legions, indicating that the troops had not served together as legions.

comitium, comitia   See **Assembly.**

CONDEMNO   The word employed by a court jury delivering a verdict of "guilty."

confarreatio   The oldest and strictest of the three Roman marriage forms. Usually only patricians practiced it, but it was not compulsory. *Confarreatio* was unpopular, for two reasons: it gave a woman absolutely no freedom or independence; it virtually negated divorce, which, if *diffareatio,* was so awful that few could face it.

conscript fathers   By Caesar's day, a courtesy title for senators. It originated under the Kings of Rome, who called their council members "fathers." After they were adlected by the censors, they became "conscript fathers." Once election to the Senate came in, the term held no significance.

consul   The consul was the most senior Roman magistrate owning imperium (q.v.). Modern scholars refer to the consul*ship*, as a consul*ate* is a diplomatic institution nowadays.

Two consuls were elected by the Centuriate Assembly each year to serve for one year. The senior of the two was the one who polled the required number of Centuries first. Each was preceded by twelve lictors. They entered office on January 1, New Year's Day. The senior consul held the *fasces* (q.v.) for the month of January, which meant his junior colleague just looked on. They then alternated holding the *fasces* month by month.

Consuls could be either patrician or plebeian; two plebeians could hold office together, but not two patricians. The proper age was forty-two, twelve years after entering the Senate at thirty. A consul's imperium knew no bounds; it operated not only in Rome, but everywhere Roman, and overrode the imperium of a governor in his province. If armies went into the field, the consul(s) had first choice of commanding them.

consular The title given to a man who had been consul.

consultum, consulta The proper name for a senatorial decree. These decrees did not have the force of law. In order to become law, a senatorial decree had to be passed by an Assembly, and sometimes it was rejected. However, many decrees were not sent to an Assembly, yet were accepted in the spirit of law: decisions about who governed a province, declaration and pursuit of a war, and foreign affairs were in the purlieu of the Senate.

contio, contiones The *contio* was a preliminary meeting of an Assembly, and saw debate about promulgated laws.

contubernalis A subaltern of lowest rank in the military command chain, but excluding the centurions. *Contubernales* were noble youths serving an obligatory year of military experience as part of a future public career rather than an army career.

Corcyra Modern Kérkyra or Corfu Island, in the Adriatic.

Corduba Modern Cordoba, in Spain.

Cornelia the Mother of the Gracchi Daughter of Scipio Africanus and Aemilia Paulla, she married the much older eminent consular Tiberius Sempronius Gracchus and bore him a total of twelve babies. Only three did she manage to rear to maturity: the famous Gracchi (q.v.) and a daughter, Sempronia, who married Scipio Aemilianus (q.v.). When her husband died she declared remarriage unbefitting a Roman noblewoman, and refused, among other suitors, Ptolemy Euengetes Gross-belly of Egypt. One son was murdered, the other suicided, and her daughter was believed to have poisoned her husband, but Cornelia was unbowed, and lived to be very old.

She became the beau ideal of Roman womanhood to later Roman noblewomen, for her heroism in the face of tragedy and her quite unconquerable spirit. Her letters and essays were highly esteemed. After she died her tomb was never without flowers; though the cult was never accorded official sanction, ordinary Roman women worshiped her as a goddess.

corona civica The crown made of oak leaves awarded to a soldier who saved the lives of fellow soldiers, captured enemy ground in a battle and held it until after the battle ended.

corona vallaris A gold crown awarded to the man who was first over the walls of an enemy camp. Gold crowns, oddly, were given for lesser feats of valor. The major crowns were of plant matter.

Cularo   Modern Grenoble, in alpine France.

cunnus, cunni   A choice Latin obscenity for the female genitalia.

cursus honorum   The "way of honor" denoting the path from new senator to consul. It incorporated quaestor and praetor, but not aedile or tribune of the plebs.

curule chair   Curule magistrates were those entitled to sit on a curule chair. This was carved out of ivory, had curved legs crossing in a broad X, was equipped with low arms, but had no back. It seems to have folded up for easy carrying.

Dagda and Dann   The principal god and goddess of the Druidic pantheon. Dagda's elemental nature was water, Dann's earth.

Danubius River   The modern Danube, Donau, or Dunarea.

demagogue   Originally a Greek concept, meaning a politician who aimed to appeal to the crowds. The Roman demagogue was almost inevitably a tribune of the plebs (q.v.), but it was no part of his platform to "liberate the masses"—nor were the men who listened to him from the ranks of the lowly. The term was used in a derogatory sense by ultra-conservative politicians.

denarius, denarii   The largest denomination of Roman coin. Of silver (save for a rare issue of gold), it was worth 4 sesterces and was about the size of a dime. There were 6,250 denarii to the talent.

Dertona   Modern Tortona, in northwestern Italy.

diadem   The Hellenistic symbol of sovereignty; something more costly was felt too ostentatious. It was a white ribbon about an inch wide, worn around the head and tied beneath the occiput. The two ends, sometimes fringed, strayed on to the shoulders.

dictator   An unelected Roman magistrate appointed by the consul on instruction from the Senate to deal with an extraordinary crisis in government, originally a war involving threatened invasion of the home territory. His duties were therefore supposed to be military; his other title was *magister populi*, Master of the Infantry, and his first act was to appoint his subordinate, the *magister equitum*, or Master of the Horse. As seen during the early Republic, his function was to undertake the war and leave at least one consul free to carry on with civilian government. The post was for six months only, the duration of the campaigning season. Appointment was by *lex curiata* (q.v.). The dictator was preceded by twenty-four lictors whose *fasces* held the axes, even within the *pomerium* (q.v.).

Alone among the magistrates, the dictator was indemnified against his actions while in office, could not be brought to trial for them after he stepped down. But gradually, as Rome's early foes were subjugated, the need for a dictator subsided. This, combined with the

Senate's mistrust of the office, resulted in attempts to deal with crises in a less individually authoritarian way, by using the Senatus Consultum Ultimum (q.v.) instead.

When Sulla was appointed Dictator in 81 B.C., after marching on Rome, he deliberately arrogated powers that were real enough at law, but not traditional. Inviolate and indemnified, he used the office to enact laws and frame a new constitution, to fill the empty Treasury, and rid himself of his enemies by executing them. When he did not step down after six months, many assumed he never would, but in 79 B.C. he resigned from all public life. Thus when Caesar became dictator (also after marching on Rome), he found his way paved by Sulla's example, and carried dictatorial powers even further.

dignitas An almost untranslatable concept. It was a man's personal share of public standing in Rome, and involved his moral and ethical worth, his reputation, his entitlement to respect and proper treatment by his peers and by the history books. It was an accumulation of personal clout stemming from his own unique qualities and deeds.

Dionysus A Greek rather than a Roman god, his worship seems to have originated in Thrace, where it was bloodily orgiastic. In later times his worship was a gentler affair, involving wine.

diverticulum A road interlinking the main arterial roads that radiated outward from the gates of Rome. A "ring road."

domine, domina My lord, or my lady (vocative case).

Druidism The major Celtic religion, mystical and animist. It did not appeal to Mediterranean peoples, who deplored its bizarre qualities, particularly human sacrifice.

duumvir One of two men who headed the local government of a town or municipality in a Latin-speaking region.

Dyrrachium Modern Durrës, in Albania.

Eagle The silver standard displaying a spread-winged eagle that Gaius Marius (q.v.) gave each legion to furnish his propertyless soldiers with a patriotic symbol. It was virtually worshiped.

Ecastor! The socially acceptable exclamation women used. It referred to the god Castor.

Ecbatana Modern Hamadan, in Iran.

Edepol! The socially acceptable exclamation used by men. It referred to the god Pollux, Castor's less esteemed twin.

edicta The tenets of procedure issued by a magistrate when he took office; they were guidelines to help those applying to him for legal or administrative decisions.

Eighteen The eighteen most senior Centuries of the First Class, wherein were contained those men who expected by right of family and birth to enter upon a public career, or adorn the top ranks of the business world. The Eighteen were limited to 100 men in each.

Elysian Fields   Republican Romans had no real belief in the intact survival of the individual after death, though they did believe in an underworld peopled by "shades," characterless and mindless effigies of the dead. The Elysian Fields contained the most virtuous shades, it seems because in them, a shade could relive human emotions and appetites after a meal of blood.

Epicure, Epicurean   An adherent of the school of philosophy founded by the Greek Epicurus. He advocated a brand of hedonism so exquisitely refined that it approached asceticism on its left hand, so to speak. A man's pleasures had to be relished, strung out; any excess defeated the purpose.

Epirus   That area of western Greece isolated from the mainstream of Greek culture by the Gulf of Corinth and the high mountains of central Greece. In Caesar's time it was largely depopulated, and had become the fief of absentee Roman landlords who grazed cattle herds for hides, tallow and blood-and-bone fertilizer. It was a notoriously wet land, hence unsuitable for sheep.

epitome   A synopsis or drastic abridgment of a long work that concentrated upon packing a maximum of information into a minimum number of words. Its purpose was to enable readers to gain encyclopedic knowledge without needing to plough through a full work. Brutus was well known as an epitomizer.

ethnarch   A general term to indicate a magistrate of a Greek town or district.

Etruria   The Latin name for what had once been the realm of the Etruscans. It incorporated the wide plains and hills of northwestern peninsular Italy from the course of the Tiber River to the course of the Arnus River. Modern Tuscany.

Euxine Sea   The modern Black Sea.

Fannian paper   Somewhere between 150 and 130 B.C., one Fannius, a Roman, took the worst grade of papyrus paper and subjected it to a treatment that turned it into paper as good as the best hieratical grade. Its cheapness put good paper within the economic reach of all literate persons.

fasces   An inheritance from the Etruscans. The *fasces* were cylindrical bundles of red-dyed birch rods tightly bound together in a crisscross pattern by red leather thongs. Carried by men called lictors, they preceded a curule magistrate as indication of his imperium. Within the *pomerium* of Rome, only the rods (there were probably thirty per bundle, for the thirty *curiae*) were put into the bundle, but outside the *pomerium* a single-headed axe was inserted into the bundle to indicate that the magistrate not only had the power to chastise, but also to execute.

fellatio (and allied terms) Sucking the penis. He who was having his penis sucked was the *irrumator*. A *fellator* was male, a *fellatrix* female.

femina mentula A woman with a penis. A mortal insult.

feriae Holidays. Depending upon the actual gradation of holiday, public business tended to be suspended.

fiscus A purse or money bag. It referred to State moneys.

flamen A priest, but not a pontifex. There were three major flaminates: Dialis (Jupiter Optimus Maximus), Martialis (Mars), and Quirinalis (Quirinus). Martialis and Quirinalis were part-time positions, but the *flamen Dialis* was a full-time priest who was surrounded by taboos: he couldn't wear knots, touch iron or other metal, eat leavened bread, witness death, encounter a dog, mount a horse, and many more. Not the right priesthood for Caesar, who held it from age thirteen until, at nineteen, Sulla assisted him in escaping it. The major *flamines* had to be patricians.

forum A Roman public meeting place.

Forum Boarium The meat markets.

Forum Holitorium The vegetable markets, located half inside the Servian Walls and half outside, on the banks of the Tiber near the Circus Flaminius.

Forum Julii Modern Fréjus, on the French Cote d'Azur.

Forum Julium Caesar's new forum in Rome.

Forum Romanum The old, original forum of Rome, located just below the Capitol. It contained Rome's most important public buildings, and was the political heart of the Republic.

freedman A manumitted slave. He was obligated to wear the cap of liberty, a skullcap. Though technically free (and, if his former master was a Roman, himself a Roman citizen), he remained in the patronage of his former master, and had little chance under the Republic's timocratic electoral structure to exercise his vote in a tribal assembly, as he was automatically put into Esquilina or Suburana, two of the four urban tribes. However, if he qualified economically, as some freedmen did, he might rise high in the Classes.

Further Spain *Hispania Ulterior.* The southwestern part of the Iberian peninsula, more fertile and prosperous than its Nearer neighbor. It was enormously rich in gold, silver, lead and iron.

Gades Modern Cádiz, in Spain.

GLOSSARY

Galatia An enclave of Gauls who settled in Anatolia in the grassy regions between Bithynia and the Halys River. Its ancient city, Ancyra, is now the Turkish capital, Ankara.

galbanum A resin obtained from the sap of Bubon *galbanum*, a Syrian plant. It was used in ancient medicine.

games In Latin, *ludi*. They began modestly under the Kings, but, by the time of the late Republic, had mushroomed into days-long celebrations. At first they consisted of chariot races, but came to include wild-beast hunts, athletic competitions, plays and mimes, pageants and parades. The most popular were the *ludi Romani*, held in September. They did not include gladiatorial combat. Free Roman citizen men and women were admitted, freedmen and non-citizens were disbarred. Women were allowed to sit with men in the circus, but not in the theaters.

garum A highly esteemed flavoring essence made from fish by a process guaranteed to make a modern man or woman ill. It stank!

Garumna River The Garonne, in France.

Gaul, Gauls Any region inhabited by Celtic peoples was a Gaul. The adjective was Gallic.

gens A family. A man's gentilicial name was his family's name: in Caesar's case, for instance, his *gens* was the *gens Julia*, hence his being described as a Julian.

gens humana The human family of all the world's peoples.

Genua Modern Genoa, in Italy.

Gerrae! Utter rubbish, complete nonsense!

gig A two-wheeled vehicle drawn by between one and four mules, and usually not fully enclosed. It more likely had a leather top.

gladiator A soldier of the sawdust, a professional warrior who performed his trade for an audience as an entertainment. Inherited from the Etruscans, he always flourished throughout Italy, hired to perform at funeral games held in a town's marketplace or forum, not in an amphitheater. His origins might be several: a deserter from the legions, a condemned criminal, a slave, or even a free man of a mind to fight as a gladiator. He lived in a school and was not locked up or locked in, or ill treated; expecting to make money from him, his owner was more likely to pamper him. Gladiators were not expected to fight to the death, and the Empire's "thumbs down" verdict had not come into being. The Republican gladiator was a very profitable and attractive investment. Usually he fought for six years or thirty bouts, whichever came first; some became adulated stars. Once retired, he tended to hire himself out as a bully-boy or bouncer. Caesar owned thousands of these soldiers of the sawdust, basing them in schools around Capua or Ravenna, and hiring them out all over Italy.

Gracchi, the Tiberius and Gaius Sempronius Gracchus were high Roman nobles of eminent family; their mother was Scipio Africanus's daughter, their father a censor as well as a consular. Both of them served under Scipio Aemilianus (q.v.), Tiberius in the Third Punic War, Gaius at Numantia; they were conspicuously brave.

Almost ten years older than Gaius, Tiberius was elected a tribune of the plebs in 133 B.C., and set out to right the wrongs the Senate was perpetrating against the poorer elements in the Roman citizen populace. Opposition was rife, and Tiberius committed the unpardonable sin of attempting to run for the tribunate of the plebs a second time. In a fracas on the Capitol, he was murdered.

Turmoil died down until his younger brother Gaius was elected a tribune of the plebs in 123 B.C. Gaius's reforms were wider and of more significance for the poor, and met with even greater opposition from the conservative elements in the Senate. When he had not finished his reforms at the end of his term, he ran a second time, and got in. Then, in 121 B.C., he stood a third time.

When he was defeated, he and his friend Marcus Fulvius Flaccus resorted to violence. The Senate's response was to eschew the traditional resort to a dictator, and pass its first-ever Senatus Consultum Ultimum, or Ultimate Decree. Fulvius Flaccus and two of his sons were murdered, and Gaius Gracchus is said to have committed suicide.

The conservative elements in the Senate may have won, but the Romans themselves held that the Brothers Gracchi commenced the rot which eventuated in the death of the Republic.

The only direct descendant of the Gracchi was Fulvia, daughter of Gaius Gracchus's only child, Sempronia. Significantly, she was the wife of three demagogues: Publius Clodius, Curio, Mark Antony.

grain dole It had long been the custom for famous Roman political men to win favor with the lower classes by subsidizing grain (wheat). In terms of votes they got little out of it except a reputation for philanthropy that stood them in good stead with the electors when it came to high office. (See **tribe** entry.) Philanthropy was thought admirable.

Then in 58 B.C. the tribune of the plebs Publius Clodius legislated a free grain dole providing 5 *modii* of free wheat per month to all Roman citizen men (a ration that enabled a family to bake one large loaf of bread per day). Clodius funded his program by annexing the island of Cyprus, hitherto a possession of the Ptolemies of Egypt. No means test was applied. However, when Caesar was Dictator he cut the free grain dole from 300,000 to 150,000 by introducing a means test.

Hades   The name of the ruler of the underworld, and of his realm. It is not to be confused with Christian concepts of Hell.

Halys River   The modern Kizil Irmak River of central Turkey.

Head Count   In Latin, *capite censi*. These were the *proletarii*, the impoverished lowest stratum of Roman citizens; during a census they were simply counted off as heads, hence the name. They belonged to a tribe (usually one of the four urban tribes), but did not qualify for the Classes. Gaius Marius (q.v.) opened the army to them as a career.

Hector   The son of Priam, King of Troy (Ilium), who led the Trojans against Agamemnon and the Greeks until he fell in battle to Achilles. His wife was Andromache, his son Astyanax.

Hellenization   A term used to describe the Greek cultural influences at work on the ancient world of the Mediterranean and Asia Minor after the conquests of Alexander the Great.

Hellespont   The modern Dardanelles, the straits between the Aegean Sea and the Sea of Marmara, gateway to the Black Sea.

hermed   A pedestal adorned with male genitalia was "hermed."

Homer   By tradition, a blind Greek poet from the Aegean coast of Asia Minor who wrote the *Iliad* and the *Odyssey*, the two most admired, famed and loved epic poems of all antiquity.

hostis   Enemy. The term levied upon a man declared an enemy of the Roman State. It stripped him of his citizenship and property, and usually also of his life, rendering him *nefas*, sacrilegious.

hydromel   A solution of honey and water.

Iberus River   The Ebro, in Spain.

Ichor   The fluid which coursed through the veins of a god or goddess. It was not blood.

Ides   One of the three enumerated dates in the Roman month. It fell on the thirteenth of January, February, April, June, Sextilis (August), September, November and December. In March, May, Quinctilis (July) and October, it fell on the fifteenth.

Ilium   The Roman name for Troy.

Illyricum   The wild and mountainous lands on the eastern side of the upper Adriatic Sea. They included Istria and Dalmatia.

imperator   Properly, the commander or general of a Roman army. Gradually the term came to be given only to a general who won a great victory; in order to be awarded a triumph by the Senate, he had to have been hailed "imperator on the field" by his army. It is, of course, the origin of the word "emperor."

imperium   This was the degree of authority vested in a curule magistrate or promagistrate. Having imperium meant that a man had the authority of his office, and could not be gainsaid within the parameters of his office. It was conferred by a *lex curiata* (q.v.), and lasted for one year unless specifically legislated for longer. The number of lictors indicated the degree of imperium.

imperium maius Unlimited imperium. Its holder's level of imperium was so high that he outranked even the consuls of the year. Until the time of Pompey the Great, it was relatively rare. After him, everyone tried to get in on the act.

in absentia In absence. As used in this book, a candidate for electoral office who stood (or tried to stand) for that office without crossing the *pomerium* into Rome to declare his candidacy.

ineptes Fools, idiots, incompetents.

infra dignitatem Beneath one's notice.

in loco parentis Having the authority of a parent at law.

inimicus Unfriendly, an opponent.

insula An island. It was also the name given to tall apartment buildings, as they were surrounded by lanes or alleys on all sides.

in suo anno "In his year." Used to describe the man who had been elected to magisterial office at the correct age.

Isis The Egyptian goddess. But also, a Hellenized deity. In Rome she was worshiped principally by Greek freedmen, of whom there were many, many thousands. As her rites were flagellatory, most Romans found Isis and her worship highly offensive.

Italian Gaul Italy north of the Arnus and Rubicon Rivers, bounded on its north, east and west by the Alps. Its proper Latin name was Gallia Cisalpina—"Gaul on this side of the Alps"—and its peoples were considered by the Romans as inferiors, Gauls.

Italy, Italia The peninsula south of the Arnus and Rubicon Rivers.

iugerum, iugera The Roman unit of land measurement. In modern terms, one *iugerum* was 0.623 (or five-eighths) of an acre, or 0.252 (one-quarter) of a hectare.

Kalends One of the three enumerated dates in a Roman month. It was always the first day of the month.

knights The Ordo Equester, or First Class of Roman citizens. In the days of the Kings of Rome and the early Republic, these men had formed the cavalry in a Roman army. By late Republican times, the word "knight" indicated his economic, therefore social, status.

Lares Permarini Lares were numinous gods of purely Roman origin who peopled all spheres of Roman existence, from household safety and crossroads to boundary stones. The Lares Permarini were the forces, indefinite in number, which protected the Roman voyager from the perils of the high seas and the deeps.

laserpicium A substance obtained from a north African plant, silphium; it was used as a digestive to relieve over-indulgence.

latifundium, latifundia A *latifundium* was a large tract of public land leased by one person and run in the manner of a modern ranch. The activity was pastoral rather than agricultural.

Latium The Roman homeland. Its northern boundary was the river Tiber, its southern a line running inland from Tarracina; on the east it merged into the mountains of Samnium.

lectus A couch. A dining room usually had three couches, the *lectus summus*, *lectus medius* and *lectus imus*, forming a U.

legate *Legatus.* The most senior members of a general's staff. In order to qualify as a legate, a man had to be of full senatorial rank. Legates answered only to the general, and often held imperium.

legion The smallest unit in a Roman army capable of fighting a war on its own; that is, it was complete within itself in terms of manpower, equipment and function. A legion at full strength contained 4,800 soldiers divided into ten cohorts of six centuries each; it also contained 1,200 noncombatant citizens, as well as artificers and a unit of artillery.

lemur, lemures Creatures from the underworld, shades.

lex, leges A law, laws.

leges Clodiae There were many, but the ones relevant to this book were passed by Publius Clodius in 58 B.C. to regulate the religious activities of consuls, other magistrates, and the Assemblies.

lex curiata A law passed in the special Assembly of the thirty *curiae* that endowed a curule magistrate with his imperium. It was also a law making adoption legal.

lex Genucia A law passed in 342 B.C. that stipulated that a period of ten years must elapse between a man's first and second tenure of the same office.

lex Voconia de mulierum hereditatibus Passed in 169 B.C., it severely curtailed the right of a woman to inherit from a will.

Liguria The mountainous region lying between Genua and Roman Gaul across the Alps, and extending inland as far as the crest of the Maritime Alps. A poor area, it was chiefly famous for its greasy wool, which made splendid waterproof outerwear, and felt.

lingua mundi A language common to all the peoples of the world. In this era, Greek. Later, Latin.

litter A covered cubicle that had poles projecting forward and backward from it on either side, enabling it to be carried by a team of men, usually six or eight in number; some litters were suspended between docile mules. It was a very slow form of transport, but the most comfortable known to the ancient world, as carriages possessed no springs.

locus consularis The place of honor at dinner. It was the right-hand end of the host's middle couch, to the host's right.

Long-haired Gaul In Latin, Gallia Comata. Rome had held Gaul across the Alps around the lower course of the Rhodanus River (the Rhone) for many years, and called it The Province. Gaul beyond the limits of The Province was Long-haired Gaul, a vast region inhabited by "uncivilized" tribes which were divided into Celtae and Belgae. They wore their hair long, and stiffened it with limey clay, hence the name. These peoples possessed no uniting national spirit, were Druidic in worship, and wanted no truck with any people from around Our Sea. Then Caesar, in an eight-year war, forced the Long-haired Gauls to submit to Rome and accept its ongoing presence. Long-haired Gaul extended from the Rhenus (Rhine) to the Pyrenees, and from the Atlantic to the Rhodanus.

ludi The games (see that entry).

Lugdunum Modern Lyons, in France.

Lusitani The Celtiberian peoples of western Spain.

Macedonia In Caesar's day, much larger than at present. On the Adriatic, it went from the town of Lissus south to Epirus; here its two main settlements were the ports of Dyrrachium and Apollonia. It then continued east across the mountains of Candavia, in which arose the Morava, the Axius, the Strymon and the Nestus Rivers. It ended at the Strymon. On its north lay Illyricum and Moesia. On its south lay Greece. Its indigenes were probably Germano-Celtic; successive invasions mixed this original people with others of Dorian Greek, Thracian and Illyrian elements.

A united Macedonia was already in existence at the time of Philip II, but it was he and his son, Alexander the Great, who thrust Macedonia into world prominence. After the death of Alexander, it was first exhausted by struggles for the throne, then defeated by Aemilius Paullus in 167 B.C. Rome didn't want responsibility for Macedonia, so tried to convert it into four self-governing republics. When this failed, it was incorporated into the empire as a province in 146 B.C. Construction of the Via Egnatia (q.v.) commenced not long afterward.

magistrates The elected executives of the Roman republic. They belonged to the Senate by Caesar's time.

Malabar coast At the southwestern tip of the Indian Deccan; it was visited yearly by the Nabataean Arab fleet because of its spices, particularly its peppercorns.

Marius, Gaius The Third Founder of Rome. A New Man from Arpinum, Marius was born about 157 B.C., of a prosperous family. As a young military tribune at Numantia, he attracted the attention of Scipio Aemilianus (q.v.), who encouraged him to pursue a public career in Rome, despite his obscure origins. Backed by the Caecilii Metelli (who were to rue it), Marius entered the Senate as a tribune of the plebs, but his humble birth made higher magistracies unlikely. He scraped in as praetor in 115 B.C. under a bribery cloud, but the consulship eluded him.

Then in 110 B.C. he married Julia, aunt of the great Caesar, whose patrician birth and connections made him acceptable consul material. He went as Metellus Numidicus's legate to fight King Jugurtha in north Africa, and used this to secure the consulship in 107 B.C., much to Metellus's annoyance.

A disastrous series of Roman defeats had drastically reduced the number of propertied men who made up Rome's soldiers, so over the next few years Marius began to enlist the propertyless Head Count as soldiers. Rome was threatened by an enormous Germanic migration; this secured no less than six consulships for Marius, three *in absentia*.

The Germans finally defeated, in 100 B.C. Marius retired from public life for some years. What brought him back was the revolt of Rome's Italian Allies, and another series of Roman defeats. Convinced that a prophecy saying he would be consul seven times was true, he strove to this end, and in 86 B.C. became consul for a seventh time, with Cinna as his colleague.

He died only a few days into office, amid a slaughter of his enemies that horrified all of Rome. His early ally and faithful legate, Sulla (q.v.), had become his enemy.

Marius's story is told in the first two books, *The First Man in Rome*, and *The Grass Crown*.

Massilia Modern Marseilles, in France.

Master of the Horse *Magister equitum.* The title of a dictator's second-in-command.

Mauretania The western end of North Africa, from about the Muluchath River of modern Algeria through to the Atlantic Ocean.

medimnus, medimni A dry measure for grains and other pourable solids. It equaled 5 *modii* (q.v.), and occupied a volume of 10 American gallons (40 liters). It weighed about 65 pounds (29 kilograms).

Memphis Near modern Cairo, in Egypt.

mentula, mentulae A choice Latin obscenity for the penis.

meretrix mascula A mannish female whore.

Messapii The earliest people of southeastern Italy.

mete-en-sa   Ordinary Egyptian priests, not entitled to wear gold.

meum mel   An endearment—"my honey."

miles gloriosus   A vainglorious soldier.

modius, modii   The customary Roman measure of grain. It occupied 2 American gallons (8 liters), and weighed 13 pounds. The grain dole was issued at 5 *modii* of wheat per month per holder of a grain chit. This was enough to provide a large loaf of bread per day.

Mormolyce   A nursery bogey, female and hideous.

mos maiorum   Almost indefinable for us. The established order of things, the customs and traditions of the ancestors. The *mos maiorum* was how things had always been done, and how they should always continue to be done. It was generally used in a public sense, to describe government and its institutions.

municipia   Districts that did not own full autonomy in Roman eyes. They might be in Italy, or in the provinces.

murex   The shellfish that produced purple-dye.

murus Gallicus   A wall of stone blocks reinforced with frequent long wooden beams; the combination gave it the ability to withstand a battering ram. The Gauls originated it.

Mutina   Modern Modena, in northern Italy.

Narbo   Modern Narbonne, in France.

Neapolis   There were many towns named Neapolis, but in this book, it refers to Italian Naples.

Nearer Spain   *Hispania Citerior*. That part of the Iberian peninsula lying between the Pyrenees and modern Cartagena, and extending inland about as far as Segovia.

nefas   Sacrilegious.

Nicomedia   Modern Izmit, in Turkey.

nomarch   The administrator of an Egyptian district, the nome.

nomen   A man's family, or gentilicial, name. Julius, Claudius.

Nones   One of the three enumerated dates in a Roman month. If the Ides (see that entry for the months) fell on the fifteenth, then the Nones fell on the seventh; if the Ides fell on the thirteenth, then the Nones fell on the fifth.

numen, numina   A word used by modern scholars to describe the peculiarly disembodied nature of the original Italian and Roman gods, if god is the right term. Spiritual forces might be better. These numinous old gods were the forces which governed everything from rain and wind to the opening and closing of a door. They were faceless, sexless, and without a mythology. Though it became a mark of culture to subscribe to things Greek, and many numinous gods acquired names, sexes, even sometimes faces, it is incorrect to call Roman religion a bastardized form of Greek worship. Unlike the Greeks, the Romans tied their religion so inextricably to all strata of government that one could not survive without the other. No matter how Greek the outward form, Roman religion was attuned to forces and the pathways of forces, a kind of push-pull, give-and-take relationship between the universe of men and that of the gods.

Numidia That segment of north Africa between modern Tunisia and the Muthul River of Algeria.

nundinae, nundinum The Roman week of eight days (*nundinum*) was counted between market days (*nundinae*).

oppidum A Gallic stronghold.

opus incertum The oldest and most popular kind of Roman wall. A facing of small irregular stones was mortared together on either side of a hollow interior; this hollow was filled with a mortar composed of black pozzolana and lime mixed through an aggregate of rubble and small stones (*caementa*).

Oscan A language of the Italian peninsula spoken by Samnites, Apulians, Calabrians, Lucanians and Bruttians. It differed from Latin sufficiently to permit Romans to sneer at Oscan speakers.

Our Sea *Mare nostrum.* The Mediterranean Sea.

Padus River The modern Po, in northern Italy.

Palus Asphaltites The Dead Sea. At this time, it was the source of the world's asphalt, which rose to its surface and was dredged off; deposits of asphalt around the sea's margins were sulphurated and too hard to be commercially viable. It was highly prized and highly priced, as it was smeared or painted on the stems of grape vines to prevent mildew and pests, and had medicinal uses. The Nabataeans had the asphalt concession, and guarded it jealously.

Palus Ceroliae Despite their engineering genius, the Romans of the Republic never managed to drain this swamp, situated where, later on, the amphitheater of the Colosseum stood.

panem et circenses Bread and circuses. It was Roman policy to feed and entertain the poor to prevent riots and discontent.

Paraetonium Possibly Mersa Matrûh, in modern northwest Egypt.

Parthians The reference was never to Parthia, but to the Kingdom of the Parthians, as Parthia itself was an unknown region to the east of the Caspian Sea. Though "Parthians" might suggest similar blood, they were as polyglot as they were far-flung; the Kingdom of the Parthians, a loose military confederacy, incorporated lands and peoples from the Indus River in Pakistan to the Euphrates River in Syria. It was bounded on the north by the mountains and steppes of central Asia, and on the south by the Indian Ocean and the Persian Gulf. In

Caesar's time, the Arsacid king was a Mazda-worshiping Parni, who ruled from capitals at Ecbatana (Hamadan) and Seleuceia (Bagdad). Though the largely Parni ruling class could speak and write Greek, they had long discarded their Hellenistic pretensions. Neither climate nor terrain made an infantry army viable. Parthian armies were horsed. The noblemen fought as cataphracts (clad in chain mail), the peasants as scantily clad archers. The latter delivered the famous "Parthian shot."

paterfamilias The head of the Roman family unit.

Patrae Modern Patras, on the Gulf of Corinth.

patratio According to Dr. J. N. Adams, the word used to mean a man's achieving orgasm, rather than the act of ejaculation.

patrician, Patriciate The original Roman aristocracy. Patricians were distinguished citizens before Rome had kings, then served the king as an advisory council; during the early Republic they filled the Senate and all the magistracies. Patricians enjoyed a prestige no plebeian could ever own, no matter how noble he claimed to be. However, as the wealth and power of the plebeians grew, the wealth and power of the patricians inexorably declined. By Caesar's day, to be patrician was simply to have more distinguished ancestors. Not all patrician clans were of equal antiquity; the Julians and Fabians, for example, were much older than the Claudians. At the end of the Republic, the following patrician families were still producing senators: Aemilius, Claudius, Cornelius, Fabius (but through adoption only), Julius, Manlius, Papirius, Pinarius, Postumius, Quinctilius, Sergius, Servilius, Sulpicius and Valerius.

patron See the entry on the **client**.

pedarii See the entry on the **Senate**.

People of Rome All Roman citizens of all social strata who were not members of the Senate.

perduellio The most serious form of treason. A man accused of it was tried in the Centuriate Assembly, not in any court.

Peripatetic An adherent of the philosophy founded by Aristotle, but developed by his pupil Theophrastus. The name originated thanks to a covered walkway within the school; the philosophers walked as they talked.

peristyle A garden or courtyard enclosed on all four sides, usually by a colonnade.

persona How a man projected himself. Strictly, a mask, thus how he appeared to others.

phalerae Round, chased, ornamented silver or gold discs about 3 to 4 inches (75–100 millimeters) in diameter. They were decorations for military valor, mounted in three rows of three upon a fancy harness of leather straps worn over the mail shirt or cuirass.

Pharsalus   A small valley on the Enipeus River in Thessaly, not far from the town of Larissa. Where Pompey the Great met Caesar.

Picenum   That part of the Italian peninsula that more or less formed the calf muscle. It bordered the Adriatic, with Umbria to its north and Samnium to its south. Its people were looked down on as Gauls.

pilum, pila   The Roman soldier's throwing missile, different from the *hasta*, or spear. It had a very small, barbed head continuous with a metal shaft for half of its length; this then became a larger, wooden shaft comfortable for the hand. Gaius Marius (q.v.) modified it so that it broke apart at the wood-metal junction as soon as it lodged in an enemy body or shield. Thus it could not be used by the enemy. Artificers recovered them and mended them quickly.

pinnace   A swift, open boat rowed by about eight men.

Placentia   Modern Piacenza, in northern Italy.

plebeian, Plebs   All Roman citizens who were not patricians. It is pronounced with a short "e," as in February. At the start of the Republic, no plebeian could be a senator, a magistrate or a priest. But as the plebeians accumulated wealth and power, they invaded and eroded traditionally patrician entitlements. To endow themselves with some form of aristocracy, the plebeians invented the *nobilis*, a man who ennobled his family by becoming consul.

plebiscite   A law passed in the Plebeian Assembly.

pomerium   The sacred boundary of the city of Rome, said to have been laid down by King Servius Tullius. Marked by stones called *cippi*, it remained unchanged until the time of Sulla (q.v.), who enlarged it because he had added to Roman territory. Religiously Rome herself existed only within the *pomerium;* all outside it was just land belonging to Rome.

pontifex   A major priest, member of the College of Pontifices. In Caesar's time it was an elected office (for life).

Pontifex Maximus   The high priest of Rome. A Republican invention, it was brought into being to curtail the power of the Rex Sacrorum, the old high priest who had also been King of Rome. The Pontifex Maximus was elected (for life), lived in one half of the Domus Publica, and had his religious headquarters in the Regia.

Pontus   A large state in northeastern Anatolia, bordering the Euxine Sea and more or less enclosed by the Halys River.

Portus Itius   A village on the Straits of Dover; it is still not known whether Portus Itius was Calais or Wissant.

praefectus fabrum   Technically he was not a part of the army, but a civilian (quite often, a banker) appointed by the general to equip and supply the army. This went from food to clothing to mules to weapons. Because he let out the contracts, he was in a position to enrich himself; this was not considered inappropriate, provided he remained within budget and the quality of his supplies was satisfactory.

praefectus urbi The urban prefect, appointed by the consuls to man the urban praetor's tribunal on the day of the Latin Festival—in effect, to look after Rome in the absence of the consuls and praetors. It was a great distinction to be chosen.

praetor The second-highest Roman magistrate owning imperium. The number of praetors increased over the course of the Republic, as they headed the courts and there had to be enough praetors to keep all the courts open. They were elected by the Centuriate Assembly for one year, and entered office on January 1.

The *praetor urbanus* or urban praetor was the senior; he dealt with civil lawsuits and decided whether a case should be tried in one of the standing courts established by Sulla.

The *praetor peregrinus* or foreign praetor heard cases that involved non-citizens; unlike the other praetors, who remained in Rome, he traveled throughout Italy hearing cases as well as hearing cases within Rome.

privatus A private citizen. Used in this book to describe a member of the Senate not holding any magistracy.

pro: promagistrate, proconsul, propraetor, proquaestor One who served with the status and imperium of those magistrates, but after his elected term of office was finished. A promagistracy was supposed to last for one year only. If proconsul or propraetor, he probably governed a province, though he might be serving as a senior legate of some general in the field. He lost his imperium the moment he stepped over the *pomerium* into Rome.

proletarii The lowliest of Roman citizens, too poor to give the State anything except *proles*, children (See **Head Count**).

Propontis The modern Sea of Marmara, between the Aegean and the Black Seas.

proscription The Roman name for a practice not confined to Roman times: namely, the entering of a man's name upon a list which stripped him of everything, often including his life. There was no process of law involved, nor did the proscribed man have the right to trial or any kind of hearing in which to protest his innocence. He was *nefas*. Sulla (q.v.) was the first to use proscription widely; after him, the mere mention of proscription sent Romans of the First Class into a panic.

province *Provincia*. The sphere of duty of a magistrate or a promagistrate holding imperium. By extension, the word also came to mean the place wherein its holder wielded his imperium.

publicanus, publicani Tax farmers. These were men organized into companies that contracted to the Treasury to collect taxes in the provinces; implicit in their agreements with the State was the right to extract more money from the provincials than the Treasury demanded, thus creating profits. These could be very large, as the State did not care how much was extracted provided the Treasury got what it had stipulated.

Public Horse A horse belonging to the Senate and People of Rome. During the reign of the Kings of Rome war horses were scarce and expensive, so the State donated each of its knight cavalrymen a horse. The practice survived until the end of the Republic, but was confined to the men of the Eighteen. To own a Public Horse was a mark of distinction.

Puteoli Modern Pozzuoli. A busy, efficiently run port on the Bay of Naples, it was also famous for its glass.

quadriga A chariot drawn by four horses, poled abreast.

quadrireme See **quinquereme.**

quaestor The bottom rung of the *cursus honorum,* the ladder to the consulship. Though adlection by the censors had been a way to enter the Senate, and it was still in use during Caesar's time as dictator to fill the Senate quickly, by his time the usual way to enter the Senate was to be elected quaestor. This happened in a man's twenty-ninth year, so that he entered at thirty. He served for one year, and entered office on December 5. His chief duties were fiscal. He might be seconded to the Treasury within Rome, or to the governor of a province, or to some important Italian port city, or to the grain supply. If serving in a province, his term might be extended as a proquaestorship.

Quinctilis Modern July. Its name was changed during Caesar's dictatorship, as a mark of honor to him.

quinquereme A very common ancient war galley, generally thought too slow and clumsy to be maneuverable, but having the advantage of massive size and weight. It was also known as a "five." Like its smaller sisters, it was much longer than it was broad in the beam, and was designed for no other purpose than war on the sea.

It used to be thought that the quadrireme contained four and the quinquereme five banks of oars, but it is now almost universally agreed that no galley ever had more than three banks of oars, and more commonly only two. The "four" and the "five" most likely got their names from the number of men on each oar, or else this number was divided between the banks of oars on the same level on either side. The top oar bank was always lodged in an outrigger; if the ship was a three-banker, then the middle-bank oars poked through ports well above water level, while the bottom-bank oars poked through ports so close to the water that they were sealed with leather valves.

The quinquereme was always decked, and had room on board for marines and artillery. There were about 270 rowers, 30 sailors, and 120 marines. They were rowed by professional oarsmen, never by slaves, the latter a Christian era practice.

There were bigger galleys, apparently named according to the number of men per oar, including the "sixteener" made famous by Mithridates the Great at his attack on Rhodes.

Quin taces! Shut up!

Quirinus A numinous god of Sabine extraction, he was the spirit of the Roman citizenship, the god of the assemblies of Roman men. His temple was on the Quirinal, the original Sabine settlement.

Quiris, Quirites Citizen, citizens. From the evidence of Caesar in dealing with mutinous troops, it was a term reserved for civilian Romans who had not served in the legions.

redoubt A little fort incorporated into a defensive wall, but outside it. Usually square, it could also be polygonal.

Regia Rome's oldest temple, situated in the Forum Romanum near the Domus Publica. Oddly shaped and oriented toward the north, it contained shrines and altars to some of Rome's oldest and most numinous gods—Vesta, Opsiconsiva, Mars of the sacred shields and spears. The offices of the Pontifex Maximus and the College of Pontifices were attached to it.

Republic The form of government that Rome assumed after the last king, Tarquinius Superbus, was banished in 510 B.C. Ostensibly democratic, in that elections were a large feature of it, it was timocratic in that suffrage was not equal between all voters. Economic restrictions were applied, and the urban lowly were virtually disenfranchised by being lumped into only four of the thirty-five Roman tribes. Thus it was heavily weighted in favor of the First Class and members of the thirty-one rural tribes.

Republicans As used in this book, that group of men who opposed Caesar after he crossed the Rubicon. Led by the ultra-conservative *boni*, they appointed Gnaeus Pompeius Magnus their war leader and embarked upon civil war to crush Caesar. Though decisively beaten at Pharsalus, they continued opposition in Africa Province before going down to final defeat at Munda in Further Spain.

They should not be confused with Caesar's assassins, the Liberators, many of whom had never been Republicans, and some of whom (Brutus, Cassius) had early given up the Republican fight.

res publica   Literally, "the thing public." Rome's government, both legislative and executive.

Rhegium   Modern Reggio, in Calabria.

Rhenus River   The modern Rhine.

Rhodanus River   The modern Rhone.

rostra   The speaker's platform in the lower Forum Romanum. The word means "ships' beaks" and the platform got its name from the two lofty columns upon it, each holding the bronze beaks of enemy ships. Originally incorporated into the wall of the Well of the Comitia, a new, taller and more imposing rostra was built by Caesar after he took the Well as part of the site of his new Senate House.

Rubicon River   The Adriatic boundary between Italy and Italian Gaul had been the Metaurus River, but when Sulla incorporated the *ager Gallicus* into Italy proper, he moved the boundary north to the Rubicon. Most modern scholars argue that it is a small, shallow stream of short length, the modern Rubicone or Pisciatello, whereas I argue that it had to have been a long river with a source very close to the source of the Arnus, Italy's boundary on the western side of the peninsula. Due to extensive medieval drainage schemes around Ravenna, no one knows for sure, but I think it was the modern Ronco, which may have entered the sea lower down then.

saepta   "The sheep fold." An area on the Campus Martius wherein temporary barricades were erected to hold voting meetings of the Centuriate Assembly.

sagum   A circular cape rather like a poncho, with a hole in its middle through which to poke the head. It was waterproof, and was an important item of legionary clothing; it also served as a sleeping blanket. The best were of greasy Ligurian wool.

Salona   Modern Split, in Dalmatia.

saltatrix tonsa   Literally, a barbered dancing-girl. A male homosexual who dressed as a woman and sold his sexual favors.

Salus   Roman god of good health.

Samnium   Rome's most obdurate enemy in the Italian peninsula. An Oscan-speaking region, it comprised mainly mountainous country behind Latium, and extended to the Adriatic adjacent to Apulia.

satrap, satrapy   A Persian title adopted by Alexander the Great, who used it to describe a ruler and region subject to a king.

Scipio Aemilianus   Publius Cornelius Scipio Aemilianus Africanus Numantinus was born in 185 B.C. Adopted into the Scipiones, he was a son of Lucius Aemilius Paullus, equally prestigious. After a distinguished military career during the Third Punic War, he was elected consul in 147 B.C., though not old enough by law, and bitterly opposed by many. Now in command against Carthage, he took the city and razed it to the ground.

An abortive censorship was followed by a second consulship in 134 B.C., during which he destroyed, in eight months, the Spanish town of Numantia, which had defied a whole series of Roman generals over a period of fifty years. His brother-in-law Tiberius Gracchus was interfering with the *mos maiorum* as a tribune of the plebs; though Gracchus was dead before Scipio Aemilianus reached Rome, his death was commonly laid at Scipio's door. In 129 B.C. he died at the age of forty-five, so suddenly that his wife, Gracchus's sister, was rumored to have poisoned him.

A great intellectual with a passion for things Greek, Scipio Aemilianus was the center of a group who patronized men like Polybius, Panaetius and the playwright Terence. As a friend, he was utterly loyal. As an enemy, he was cruel, cold-blooded and utterly ruthless.

Scipio Africanus Publius Cornelius Scipio Africanus was born in 236 B.C. and died around the end of 184 B.C. As a very young man he distinguished himself in battle, and at the age of twenty-six, not even a senator, he was given command of the war against Carthage by the People, and pursued it in Spain. There he did brilliantly, beat the Carthaginians in five years, and took the two Spanish provinces for Rome.

Consul in 205 B.C. at the age of thirty-one, he invaded Africa via Sicily. Both eventually fell to him; Scipio took the name of Africanus. He was elected censor, and became Princeps Senatus.

Brilliant, cultivated and farsighted, he incurred the enmity of Cato the Censor, who hounded him relentlessly for alleged un-Roman corruption. After Cato the Censor ruined his brother Asiagenus, Scipio Africanus is said to have died of a broken heart. But one can see the roots of our Cato's relentless persecution of Caesar; again, the fanatical advocate of virtue concentrated his energies on one of Rome's most brilliant, aristocratic men. Family tradition.

scurra A buffoon.

Senate Originally an advisory council of 100 patricians under the Kings, it expanded to 300 patricians when the Republic began. A few years later, plebeians were also being admitted to it.

Because of the Senate's antiquity, legal definition of its powers, rights and duties was at best only partial. Membership was for life, which predisposed it toward the oligarchy it quickly became; throughout its history, its members fought strenuously to preserve its supremacy and exclusivity. Entry had been adlection by the censors, but by Caesar's day it was through the office of quaestor unless circumstances dictated otherwise.

Senators wore a broad purple stripe on the right shoulder of their tunics, closed shoes of maroon leather, and a ring. Meetings had to be held in properly inaugurated premises. It had its own house, the Curia Hostilia, but also met in certain temples. The speaking order was rigidly hierarchical, though the hierarchy did vary from time to time. The humble backbencher senators, called *pedarii*, were forbidden to speak because they had not held any magistracy. However, they could vote. If the issue was unanimous or unimportant, voting might be by a show of hands, but the formal vote was by a division. The permanent chief of the Senate was its senior patrician, the Princeps Senatus.

The Senate remained an advisory body; it was never empowered to make laws, only recommend them to the Assemblies. A quorum had to be present at a meeting, though how many constituted a quorum, we do not know. Membership went from 300 to 600 in Sulla's time; Caesar raised it to 1,000. In certain areas the Senate reigned supreme. It controlled the *fiscus* and therefore the Treasury, and had been known to refuse to fund a law passed in an Assembly if it disapproved of the law. It had the say in foreign affairs and the conduct of Rome's wars.

Senatus Consultum Ultimum   The Senate's Ultimate Decree, invented to deal with the crisis precipitated by Gaius Gracchus in 121 B.C., thus avoiding the appointment of a dictator. The S.C.U. overruled all legislative bodies and magistrates, and was tantamount to martial law. This name is generally attributed to Cicero, who evidently grew tired of calling it by its proper name: *senatus consultum de republica defendenda.*

Serapis   A peculiarly Macedonian-Egyptian hybrid god, said to have been dreamed up by the first Ptolemy and the then high priest of Ptah, one Manetho. Serapis was a fusion of Zeus with Osiris and the tutelary deity of the Apis bull, and was engineered to appeal to the Hellenized inhabitants of Alexandria and the Delta, who disliked Egypt's traditional "beast gods."

Sertorius   Quintus Sertorius, a relative of Gaius Marius's, was born about 120 B.C. One of Marius's greatest marshals, he fell foul of Sulla after Marius's death in 86 B.C. In 83 B.C. he was given governorship of all Spain, but was driven out by Sulla's dictate, sought refuge in Mauretania, and was invited back by the Lusitani, who loved him. In Spain he seceded from Rome and set up his own "Senate and People" with an emphasis upon the native Spanish, though he also tried to draw rebel Romans into his fold. His military genius was such that he defeated a series of Roman generals up to and including the young Pompey the Great, whom he humiliated on the battlefield between 76 and 72 B.C. In 72 B.C. a desperate Pompey posted a fat reward, and Sertorius was murdered by a fellow Roman, Perperna. Sertorius was said to have possessed animal magic.

Servian Walls   The walls the tourist of today sees did not exist under the Republic, whose walls, now buried, were purportedly built by King Servius Tullius. But as they enclosed more of the city than the *pomerium* did, they were probably not built until after the Gauls sacked the city in 390 B.C. They were massive and kept in good repair, especially when the Germans threatened to invade in Gaius Marius's time. Caesar went to the trouble of rebuilding them around the perimeter of his new forum.

sestertius, sesterces   Though the denarius was more common, the Roman accounting unit was the sestertius, abbreviated on paper as HS. It was a minute silver coin; a talent contained 25,000 of them.

silphium   This small north African shrub, never satisfactorily identified, was almost the sole vegetation along vast coastal tracts between Cyrenaica and Africa Province. It yielded *laserpicium,* a substance that was highly esteemed as a digestive.

Skenite Arabs   A tribe of Arabs who inhabited the area east of the Euphrates River in the vicinity of the Bilechas River. A nomadic desert people, the Skenites received the gift of the Euphrates tolls after King Tigranes of Armenia conquered Syria in 83 B.C. This led to enmity between the Skenites and the local Syrian Hellenes, and culminated in the Skenites' choosing to side with the Parthians. Their king, Abgarus, led Marcus Crassus into the trap at Carrhae.

Smyrna   Modern Izmir, in Turkey.

socii   Persons of non-Roman citizenship but allied to Rome.

Sol Indiges, Tellus and Liber Pater   Three early, numinous gods of Rome whose names invoked a terrible oath, impossible to break. Sol Indiges was a sun-figure, Tellus an earth-figure, and Liber Pater a fertility-figure associated with the vine.

sortition   The process of choosing people by casting lots.

sow   A lump of smelted metal that must have reminded some early Roman smith of a female pig. Iron, copper, silver, gold, tin and metallic alloys were kept as sows of various weight.

Spes   The Roman god of hope.

SPQR   *Senatus Populusque Romanus.* The Senate and People of Rome.

stella critina   A star trailing a mane of hair: a comet.

stibium   A black, antimony-based powder, soluble in water, that was used to tint the eyebrows and lashes, or to draw a line around the eyes. The fact that even the lowliest Egyptian peasant used it to draw a line around the eyes suggests that it discouraged flies from roosting.

Stoic An adherent of the philosophy founded by the Phoenician Cypriot Zeno. The basic tenet concerned virtue and its opposite, weakness of character. Money, pain, death and the other things plaguing Man were not considered important.

Strymon River In Bulgaria, the modern Struma: in Greece, Strimon.

Subura The declivity between the Viminal and Esquiline Mounts of Rome, it was Rome's most famous stew in Republican times, stuffed with the poor and polyglot. It contained Rome's only synagogue. Suetonius says that Caesar lived in the Subura until he was elected Pontifex Maximus and moved into the Domus Publica.

suffect consul If a consul died in office, the Senate could choose a replacement, the suffect, without holding an election.

sui iuris In control of one's own affairs and fate. Used of women who retained control of their own money.

Sulla Lucius Cornelius Sulla Felix was born about 138 B.C. Of an old patrician family, he lived in abject poverty and was unable to enter the Senate due to that poverty. Plutarch says that in order to get the money to qualify, he murdered his mistress and his stepmother. His first wife was a Julia, possibly closely related to Gaius Marius's wife, the aunt of the great Caesar, for Sulla allied himself with Marius for many years. They served together in the war against King Jugurtha of Numidia and Sulla was responsible for the capture of Jugurtha himself, though he deprecated this fact until he wrote his memoirs. He continued to serve Marius through the consulships that Marius held to defeat the Germans, and seems to have performed some kind of undercover work for Marius.

When the Senate swung against Marius, Sulla couldn't get elected as praetor, and so came late to that office, in 97 B.C. As propraetor he governed Cilicia and led an army across the river Euphrates—a first— to conclude a treaty with the Parthians. During the war against the Italian Allies, he served brilliantly in the southern theater.

He became consul in 88 B.C., the year that Mithridates the Great invaded Asia Province, and sought the command in that war—as did the aged Marius. The Senate awarded him command, Sulpicius the tribune of the plebs took command off him and gave it to Marius, and Sulla, in Capua, marched on Rome. Marius fled into exile, Sulla went east to fight Mithridates.

After Marius died and Cinna took control of Rome, Sulla hurried his war and returned home in 83 B.C. Cinna had outlawed him, so he marched on Rome a second time, and had himself appointed dictator. He then proscribed ruthlessly, holding the dictatorship long enough to alter Rome's constitution to something that would muzzle the tribunes of the plebs, whom he regarded as Rome's worst enemies. He laid down the dictatorship in 79 B.C. and retired to a life of vice, dying in 78 B.C.

His life is detailed in the first three books: *The First Man in Rome, The Grass Crown,* and *Fortune's Favorites.*

tacete!   Shut up! in the plural.

talent   The load a man could carry. About 50 pounds (25 kilograms).

Taprobane   Modern Sri Lanka; Ceylon.

Tarpeian Rock   Its precise location is still debated, but it is known to have been quite visible from the lower Forum Romanum, and presumably was an overhang at the top of the Capitoline cliffs. The drop was about 80 feet (25 meters). To be thrown from it was the traditional mode of execution for Roman citizen traitors and murderers.

Tartarus   A different place from Hades. To the Platonic Greeks, a place of eternal torment for wicked souls.

tata   Latin for "daddy."

Taurasia   Modern Turin, in northern Italy.

Thessalonica   Modern Thessaloniki, in Greece.

Thessaly   Northern Greece between the Domokos and Tempe Passes.

Thrace   Loosely, that part of Balkan Europe between the west side of the Dardanelles and the Struma River. In ancient times it had coasts on both the Aegean and the Euxine Seas, and extended north to Sarmatia (Rumania) and Dacia (Hungary). It was populated by Germano-Celtic-Illyrian tribes, including the Bessi and Dardani.

Tibur   Modern Tivoli, in Italy.

Tingis   Modern Tangier, in Morocco.

Tingitanian ape   The Barbary ape, a macaque, terrestrial and tailless.

toga   The garment only a citizen of Rome was allowed to wear. In childhood both sexes wore the purple-bordered toga; once a child came of age, females abandoned it, males wore the plain white toga. Professional female whores wore a flame-colored toga.

Made of lightweight wool, the toga had a most peculiar shape, rather like a central rectangle with stumpy wings. To fit an average man, a toga was over 15 feet (5 meters) wide and almost 8 feet (2.5 meters) in height.

toga praetexta   The purple-bordered toga of childhood and of the curule magistrate.

toga trabea   The toga of a pontifex or augur, striped in purple and crimson.

toga virilis   The plain white toga of manhood. Also *toga alba*.

togate   The correct term to describe a man wearing a toga.

Tolosa   Modern Toulouse, in France.

Transtiberim, Transtiberini   Modern Trastevere, just across the Tiber from Rome. Its inhabitants were Transtiberini.

transport   As used in this book, a ship for transporting troops. These vessels were designed for the purpose and were very large, far broader in the beam than war galleys. They had one or two banks of oars. It is never said whether they were rowed by professional oarsmen or whether the troops were put to rowing, but perhaps, if the troops did row, that was yet another reason why they hated sea voyages. Certainly the practical Romans would have objected to carrying a big number of additional men just to row, though perhaps if the transports were to be returned to a port empty rather than wait for more soldiers, they carried a skeleton crew of oarsmen. Roman soldiers were put to non-military work if there were no battles in the offing.

tribe   By the beginning of the Republic, his tribe to a Roman was not an ethnic grouping, but a political grouping. There were thirty-five Roman tribes, thirty-one of them rural, four of them for urban Romans. Even if born in and permanently resident in the city of Rome, members of the First and Second Classes almost always belonged to a rural tribe; it was the lower classes who were jammed into the urban tribes. Freedmen were put in only two of the four urban tribes, Suburana or Esquilina.

Every member of a tribe cast a vote, but in itself his vote was not significant. The votes in each tribe were counted, then the tribe as a whole cast one single vote, the majority of its members. Which meant that in no tribal Assembly could the massive number of voters in an urban tribe influence the overall outcome. If 5,000 men voted in urban Suburana and only 75 in rural Fabia, the two tribal votes carried exactly the same weight.

tribune, military   Each of the middle officers in the chain of command of a Roman army was classified as a *tribunus militum*. It was a term reserved for unelected tribunes, and went through a number of grades and functions.

tribune of the plebs   This magistrate came into being not long after the Republic, when the plebeians were at complete loggerheads with the patricians. Elected by the tribal Plebeian Assembly, the tribunes of the plebs swore an oath to defend the lives and the property of members of the Plebs. By 450 B.C. there were ten tribunes of the plebs; they served for one year and entered office on December 10.

Because they were not elected by the whole People (patricians were excluded), they had no power under Rome's largely unwritten constitution; their real power lay in the oath the Plebs took to defend the sacrosanctity or inviolability of its elected tribunes, and in their right to exercise a veto against the actions of fellow tribunes of the plebs, or any—or all—other magistrates, or the holding of an election, or the passing of a law or plebiscite, or decrees of the Senate, even in war and foreign affairs. Only a dictator was above the tribunician veto. If his right to proceed about his duties was impeded, a tribune of the plebs could even exercise the death penalty.

The *lex Atinia* of ca. 149 B.C. laid down that a man elected tribune of the plebs was automatically a member of the Senate, so it became a way into the Senate if the censors turned a man down. The office did not have imperium, and ceased to exist beyond the first milestone outside Rome. Tradition held that a man should not stand for re-election, but as it was not law, Gaius Gracchus stood for re-election successfully in 122 B.C. As the real power of the office lay in the veto, tribunician function tended to be more obstructive than innovative. It was an office that held a powerful attraction for men of demagogic inclination, and could be a handy stepping-stone toward the consulship for an ambitious plebeian.

tribune of the soldiers   These were twenty-four men aged between twenty-five and twenty-nine years who were elected each year by the Popular Assembly to serve with the consular legions. Having been elected by the whole People, they were true and legal magistrates, though they held no imperium. If the consuls had no legions, they were rationed out between whatever legions were in the field.

tribunus aerarius   A tribune of the Treasury (*aerarium*). This seems to have been an economic classification of the censors; they were said to have an income of between 300,000 and 400,000 sesterces a year. Presumably civil servants administering the Treasury were tribunes of the Treasury, but that we don't really know.

trireme   With the bireme, the commonest and best liked of the ancient war galleys. Though the word suggests three banks of oars, triremes seem to have had only two, indicating perhaps that the lower bank of oars was staggered in port height.

The average trireme was about 130 feet (40 meters) long, and was no wider in the beam than 13 feet (4 meters) excluding the outrigger. The ratio was therefore about 10:1. The oars were relatively short, each being about 15 feet (5 meters) long. Only one rower manned one oar. The lowest oarsmen worked oars through ports so close to the sea that each was fitted with a leather cuff or valve to keep water out of the hull. Certainly there were 108 oarsmen in this bank or banks; another 62 oarsmen sat in the outriggers, giving a total of 170 rowers per ship. The outrigger oarsmen had to work the hardest, as their oars hit the water at a sharper angle.

Triremes were eminently suitable for ramming, and thus had beaks that became two-pronged, bigger, heavier and better armored as time went on. Most triremes were decked and could carry up to fifty marines as well as artillery. Built from fir or other lightweight pine, triremes were light enough to be portaged on rollers for long distances, and were easily dragged out of the water at night. If they were not hauled out almost daily, they quickly waterlogged. If well looked after and housed in a ship shed, a vessel's seafaring life was about twenty years.

Tyrian purple   Purple was the most prized color in the spectrum of the ancient world, and of all the shades of purple, Tyrian was the most expensive. It had connotations of royalty, therefore was frowned on by Romans. Tyrian purple came only from the city of Tyre, in Phoenicia. It was so dark as to appear almost black, but was shot through with gleams of crimson.

Tullianum   Rome's only dungeon, actually an execution chamber only. It sat at the foot of the Arx of the Capitol.

tumultus   In this book, a state of civil war.

tunic   The ubiquitous article of clothing for all Mediterranean peoples, who despised trousers as barbarian. A Roman tunic was rather loose and shapeless, made without darts, and often had its sleeves cut in one with the bodice. The Greek tunic had darts and fitted the body more snugly, its sleeves usually set in. The ancients knew how to cut, sew and tailor, so they could set sleeves in, and make garments with long sleeves. The customary fabric for a tunic was wool and the customary color oatmealish, but there is ample evidence that tunics came in many colors and patterns.

Twelve Tables   The revered table of Roman laws dating to the middle of the fifth century B.C. The original Twelve Tables were burned when the Gauls sacked Rome, but were reconstituted on bronze, and formed the basis of all subsequent Roman law. Toward the end of the Republic they were memorial rather than legal.

Ultimate Decree   See **Senatus Consultum Ultimum.**

Uxellodunum   A Gallic oppidum, thought to be modern Puy d'Issolu.

vale   Farewell.

veneficae   Witches.

verpa   A Latin obscenity used in verbal abuse. It referred to the penis in the erect state, with the foreskin drawn back, and had a homosexual connotation.

Vesta   A numinous Roman god, of the domestic hearthfire.

Vestal Virgins   The special priestesses of Vesta. Six in number, they were inducted at about seven years of age, and served for thirty years. They were required to be virgins; their chastity was considered Rome's good luck. A Vestal tried for and found guilty of unchastity was buried alive. They lived in the Domus Publica. Once discharged from service, a Vestal was permitted to marry, but few did.

via   A main road or street.

Via Aemilia   Built 187 B.C. It connected the Adriatic coast at Ariminum with Placentia in western Italian Gaul.

Via Aemilia Scauri   Built 103 B.C. It connected Placentia through Dertona with Genua, then followed the Tuscan coast to Pisae on the Arnus.

Via Annia   Built 153 B.C. It connected Florentia on the Arnus with Verona in northern Italian Gaul, and intersected with the Via Aemilia at Bononia.

Via Appia   Built 312–244 B.C. The long road between Rome and its Adriatic ports of Tarentum and Brundisium.

Via Aurelia Nova   Built 118 B.C. It connected Pisae with Populonia on the Tuscan coast of Etruria.

Via Aurelia Vetus   Built 241 B.C. It connected Populonia with Rome along the Tuscan coast of Etruria.

Via Cassia   Built 154 B.C. It ran between Rome and Arretium and Florentia on the Arnus River, traveling through Etruria.

Via Domitia   Built 121 B.C. The long road to Further Spain. It started at Placentia in Italian Gaul, crossed the Alps and the Pyrenees, and terminated at Corduba.

Via Egnatia   Built 130 B.C. It connected Dyrrachium and Apollonia in western Macedonia with the Hellespont and Byzantium.

Via Flaminia   Built 220 B.C. It went from Rome across the Apennines to the Adriatic coast at Fanum Fortunae.

Via Julia   Built 105–103 B.C. The coast road between Genua and Massilia.

Via Minucia   Built 225 B.C. It connected Beneventum with Barium on the Adriatic, then followed the coast to Brundisium.

Via Popillia   Built 131 B.C. It traveled from Capua to Rhegium on the Italian toe opposite Sicilian Messana.

Via Salaria Too old to date, this was Rome's first long road. It crossed the central Apennines from Rome to the Adriatic.

Via Valeria Built 307 B.C. It crossed the Apennines from Rome to the Adriatic.

Vibo A small port on the Tuscan Sea not far north of Rhegium.

vicus A city street.

vir militaris A military man, usually of low birth, who managed to rise to the senior magistracies by virtue of his deeds as a general of troops. Publius Ventidius was an excellent example. So too were Gaius Marius and Quintus Sertorius.